Praise for the *Throne of Amenk*

"I give *The Skewed Throne* four and a half out of five really creepy-ass iconic chairs, and a strong suggestion that it not walk down any dark alleys alone. I highly recommend it."
—Seanan McGuire, *New York Times* bestselling author of the Toby Daye series

"A gritty, edgy, unsettling book. This tough young woman makes her choices in a world where good and evil often look like twins. I was riveted by her story!"
—Tamora Pierce, *New York Times* bestselling author of the Song of the Lioness series

"Joshua Palmatier has written a vivid, passionate story about a tough-minded heroine fighting for survival. What makes her especially compelling is her own struggle to understand right and wrong, and to confront what necessity can force you to do. This promising first novel should lead to equally confident sequels."—Kate Elliott, *New York Times* bestselling author of the Spiritwalker series

"The strength of Palmatier's book lies in Varis. Varis is a bitter girl, hardened by years of living in the Dredge, but she retains a core of humanity. Her ability to slip into what she calls the river, where threats stand out as splashes of red in the currents of the world around her, makes her an intriguing point of view character . . . if you enjoy grittier fantasy, I would recommend picking up *The Skewed Throne*." —Jim C. Hines, author of the Magic ex Libris series

"If you are familiar with Arya Stark in George R.R. Martin's Song of Ice and Fire series, you'll love Varis, who has a similar tenacity and toughness. I highly recommend *The Skewed Throne* and fans of gritty fantasy will love this book."
—Paul Genesse, author of the Iron Dragon series

"This novel grips the reader with a swift-moving tale of political intrigue and economic survival in a world where the most dangerous secrets are never forgotten."
—*Publishers Weekly*

DAW Books proudly presents
the fantasy novels of
Joshua Palmatier:

SHATTERING THE LEY
THREADING THE NEEDLE
REAPING THE AURORA

The Throne of Amenkor:
THE SKEWED THRONE
THE CRACKED THRONE
THE VACANT THRONE

THE THRONE OF AMENKOR

THE SKEWED THRONE
THE CRACKED THRONE
THE VACANT THRONE

JOSHUA PALMATIER

DAW BOOKS, INC.

DONALD A. WOLLHEIM, FOUNDER

375 Hudson Street, New York, NY 10014

ELIZABETH R. WOLLHEIM
SHEILA E. GILBERT
PUBLISHERS
www.dawbooks.com

First Printing, November 2017

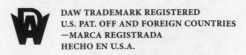

DAW TRADEMARK REGISTERED
U.S. PAT. OFF AND FOREIGN COUNTRIES
—MARCA REGISTRADA
HECHO EN U.S.A.

PRINTED IN THE U.S.A.

THE SKEWED THRONE:
This novel is dedicated to the memory of my father,
Cdr. Philip F. Palmatier, Jr.,
lost at sea in a midair collision of two A-4 Skyhawks December 10, 1990.

THE CRACKED THRONE:
This work is dedicated to my editor,
Sheila Gilbert, and my agent, Amy Stout.
Bold adventurers both. Without them, this book would not be . . .
and would not be half as good.

THE VACANT THRONE:
This work is dedicated to my mom, Beryle Palmatier.
(Pronounced like pearl, but with a B.)
She gave me and my brothers the strength to accomplish anything
we set our minds to, and the ability to dream big.
I hope I've made her proud.

The Skewed Throne

⊹— The Palace —⊹

Over one thousand years ago, a great fire swept through the city of Amenkor. Not a fire like those burning in the bowls of standing oil that lined the promenade to the palace, all red and orange and flapping in the wind that came from the sea. No. This fire was white, pure, and cold. And from the legends, this fire burned from horizon to horizon, reaching from the ground to the clouds. It came from the west, like the wind, and when it fell upon the city it passed through walls and left them untouched, passed through people and left them unburned. It covered the entire city—there was no escape, it touched everyone—and then it swept onward, inland, until it vanished, nothing more than a white glow, and then nothing at all.

It is said the White Fire cast the city into madness. It is said the Fire was an omen, a harbinger of the eleven-year drought and the famine and disease that followed.

It is said the Fire murdered the ruling Mistress of the time, even though her body was found unburned on the wide stone steps that led up to the palace at the end of the promenade. There were bruises around her throat in the shape of hands, and bruises in the shape of boots on her naked back and bared breasts. There were bruises elsewhere, beneath the white robes that lay about her waist in torn rags, the robe held in place only by the angle of her body and the gold sash of her office. There was blood as well. Not gushing blood, but spotted blood.

But the legends say the Fire killed her.

Fire, my ass.

Tucked into the niche set high in a narrow corridor of the palace, I snorted in contempt, then shifted with a grimace to ease a cramped muscle. No part of my body moved out into the light. The niche sat at the end of a long shaft that provided airflow into the depths of the palace.

Any blind-ass bastard could tell what had really happened to the Mistress. And the blind-ass bastard who killed her should have rotted in the deepest hellhole in Amenkor. There were quicker ways to kill someone than strangulation. I knew.

I drew in a slow breath and listened. Nothing but the guttering flames of the standing bowls of burning oil which lit the empty corridor below. The airflow in the palace was strong, gusting through the opening at my back. A storm was coming. But the wind took care of the smoke from the burning oil. And other smells.

After a long, considering moment, I slid forward to the edge of the niche and glanced down the corridor in both directions. Nothing.

With one smooth shift, I slipped over the lip of the opening, dangled by white-knuckled fingers for a moment until steady, then dropped to the floor.

"You, boy! Help me with this."

I spun, hand falling to the knife hidden inside the palace clothing that had been provided the night before: page's clothing that was a little too big for me, a little loose. But apparently it had worked. I was small for my age, and had no breasts to speak of, but I definitely wasn't a boy.

The woman who'd spoken was dressed in the white robe of a personal servant of the Mistress and carried two woven baskets, one in each arm. One of the baskets was threatening to tip out of her grasp. She'd managed to catch it with the other basket before it fell, but both baskets were now balanced awkwardly against her chest, ready to tip at the slightest movement.

"Well, what are you waiting for?" Her face creased in irritation and anger, but her eyes remained focused on the baskets.

I straightened from the instinctual crouch and moved forward to catch the basket before it fell. It was heavier than it looked.

My hand brushed the woman's skin as I took the basket and a long thin slash of pain raced up my arm, as if someone had drawn a dagger's blade across my skin from wrist to elbow. I glanced at the woman sharply, tensed.

The woman heaved a sigh of relief and wiped a trembling hand across her forehead. "Thank you." After a moment to catch her breath, she motioned to the basket again. "Now give it back. Carefully!"

Relief swept through me. She hadn't felt the contact, hadn't felt the slash of pain or anything else out of the ordinary at all.

I set the basket back into the woman's arms, careful not to touch her skin again, the woman grunting at its weight. Then I stepped aside and let her pass. She huffed out of the corridor, vanishing around a corner.

I watched her receding back, then my eyes narrowed. I wasn't supposed to run into anyone, especially not one of the true Servants. No one was supposed to know I was here.

I'd have to be more careful.

I fingered the knife again, considering, then turned away, moving in the other direction, shrugging thoughts of the woman aside. She'd barely glanced up from her baskets, too intent on not dropping them. She wouldn't remember meeting a page boy. Not inside the palace. And there wasn't any time to spare, not if I was to get to the Mistress' chambers before dawn. I was in the outermost portion of the palace, still needed to get to the linen closet with the archer's nook, get past the guards at the inner sanctum. . . .

I shook my head and moved a little faster down the narrow corridor, running through the mental image of the map of the palace in my head, reviewing the timing. The incoming storm prickled through my skin, urging me on. I reached into an inner pocket and fingered the key hidden there.

I had to get to the Mistress' chambers tonight. We'd waited too long already . . . had waited six years hoping that things would get better, looking for alternate solutions. Six long years since the Second Coming of the White Fire, and since that day things had only gotten worse. Legend said that the first Fire had cast the city into madness. The second Fire had done the same. A slow, subtle madness. And now winter bore down on us, the seas already getting rough, unsuitable for trade. With the mountain passes closed, resources low . . .

As I turned into a second corridor, I frowned, with a hard and determined expression. We'd tried everything to end it. Everything but what legend said had worked the first time the Fire came. Now there was no choice.

It was time for the Mistress to die.

Part I: The Dredge

✝— Chapter 1

I focused on the woman with dark eyes and a wide face, on the basket she carried on her hip, a cloth covering its contents. The woman wore a drab dress, had long, flat, black hair. A triangle of cloth covered most of her head, two corners tied beneath her chin, easy to pick out in the crowd of people on the street. She moved without rushing, head lowered as she walked.

An easy mark.

My gaze shifted to the basket and my hand slid down to the dagger hidden inside my tattered shirt. My stomach growled.

I bit my upper lip, turned back to the woman's downturned face, tried to catch her eyes from across the street. The eyes were the most revealing. But she'd moved farther away, paused now at the edge of an alley.

A moment later, she ducked into the narrow.

I hesitated on the edge of the street they called the Dredge, fingers kneading the handle of my dagger. People flowed past, not quite jostling me. I scanned the street, the people, noticed a guardsman, a cartman with brawny shoulders, a gutterscum thug. No one openly dangerous. No one overtly threatening to a fourteen-year-old girl pressed flat against a wall. A mud-streaked girl, clothes more tattered than whole, hair so dirty its color was indistinguishable. A small girl—far, far too small for fourteen; far, far too thin to be alive.

Eyes hardening, I turned back to the mouth of the narrow where the woman had disappeared, watched its darkness.

Then I cut across the Dredge, cut through the crowd so smoothly I touched no one. I slid against the wall of the narrow, crouched low, until my eyes adjusted to the darkness. I listened. The noise of the street faded to a background wind, the world grayed. . . .

And in the new silence I heard the sound of footfalls on damp stone, steady and quick. I heard clothes rustling, heard the creak of wicker as a basket was shifted. The footsteps were receding.

In the cloaked darkness of the alley, I glanced back out toward the street, toward the movement, the sunlight. No one had seen me follow the woman. Not even the guardsman.

I turned back, slid deeper into the darkness, into the stench of refuse and piss and mildew. I moved without sound, with a cold, hungry intent, my stomach clenched and empty, thinking only of the basket, of the food it might represent. The woman's footsteps continued, shuffling ahead on the dirty stone, splashing in unseen puddles. I drew in the stench of the alley, could almost smell the woman's sweat. My hand closed on the handle of my dagger—

And the footsteps ahead slowed, grew wary.

I halted, drew close to the wall, hand pressed against its damp mud-brick.

Ahead, feet shuffled in place. The cold of the alley grew deeper, a coldness I felt echoed in my chest like the harsh burn of hoarfrost.

Then I heard another footstep, a heavier tread, a gasp as the woman cried out, the sound suddenly choked off.

Something heavy hit the cobbles, followed by rolling thuds, by the sound of a struggle: clothes rustling, harsh breaths, a horrifying gasping sound, choked and desperate. Like the gasping sounds of the man I'd killed three years before. Except these gasps were not wet and slick, choking on blood. These were dry and empty.

A sick, feverish shudder of horror rushed through my skin and I pressed against the mud-brick at my back, trying not to breathe. The coldness of hoarfrost prickling in my chest tightened, began to burn white, like the touch of the Fire that had passed through the city three years before. Fresh sweat prickled in my armpits, the center of my chest, making me shudder. My hand clenched on the handle of my dagger.

The gasping quieted, slowed. A strained grunting filtered from the darkness. It escalated, tight and short, then released in a trembling sigh. Almost like sobbing. This faded into soft breathing. Then there was a weighted thud, heavier than the first, and even the breathing faded.

I fidgeted, breath held close, hand gripping the sweaty hilt of the dagger. I'd let the dagger slip completely free without thinking. Had brought it to bear.

But no one emerged from the darkness. Not after twenty shortened breaths. Not after fifty.

And the icy Fire in my chest had died.

I relaxed, drew a steadying breath, then edged forward. A trickle of black water appeared, running through the alley's center. I kept to the left wall, the bricks wet, left hand against the dampness, right hand holding the dagger.

Eleven paces farther on I found the basket turned on its side, potatoes littering the cobbles. The cloth that had covered them was already stained with filth.

Three steps farther, I found the woman's body.

She lay crumpled to the ground, on her back, her feet bent beneath her thighs. One arm lay thrust out, the other close to her side. The kerchief covering her hair had been pushed askew and tangles of her hair lay matted to the stone. Her head lay in the trickle of scummy water, tilted slightly away.

I hunkered against the wall, scanned the darkness ahead, listening. But there was nothing but the sound of dripping water, the taste of damp growth.

I turned back to the woman, edged past her out-flung arm, and knelt.

A dark band of blood encircled her neck, cut into her flesh. Her eyes were open, staring up past me into the darkness of the alley. Her lips were parted.

She looked like she was asleep, except she wasn't breathing and her eyes were open.

I looked at the line of blood across her neck again, leaned forward—

And saw a thin cord loop down in front of my face.

I brought the dagger up instantly, but not before the cord snapped tight across my neck, not before I heard a guttural, masculine grunt as a man crossed the cord behind my neck and jerked it tight. The cord caught the dagger on its flat side and yanked it flat against my neck.

Then the man leaned upward and back, pressed his knee hard into my spine and pushed.

My body arched outward, the cord drawing tighter across my neck. My head fell back against the man's shoulder so that his bearded cheek rested against mine, his breath hot against my chest. It stank of ale and fish and oil.

"A little young and thin for my tastes," he gasped, drawing the cord tighter with a jerk, "but I'll takes what gifts the Mistress gives me, eh?"

The icy pressure flared again in my chest, at the base of my throat, spreading like frost. I tasted the air from the night of the Fire three years before, felt the Fire itself burning cold deep inside me. I sucked in a hard, painful breath of air in shock.

And then my breath was cut off.

I threw myself forward, felt the cord dig deeper, felt a trickle of blood flow as the cord sawed into my skin. The man's gasps ground in my ear and I jerked to the side, felt the cord cut deeper still. And then the grayness of the world focused even more, focused down and down until the only thing I could feel was the cord, the hot fire of not being able to breathe beginning to burn in my chest—

The cold metal of the dagger pressed tight against my neck. I still held its handle in my right hand, held it in a death grip.

As the fire in my chest seethed outward, sending tingling sensations of warmth into my arms, down deep into my gut, I twisted the dagger. Its edge bit into my skin, drew a vertical slice from the back of my jaw downward to my collarbone that stung like a sharp needle prick. I twisted, pushing the dagger outward as the man grunted in my ear, his breath a hissing stench, spit flying from his clamped teeth onto my neck. My focus on the world began to slip, the grayness seeping forward, narrowing to a hollow circle, to a point. Tingling hot fire filled my gut, seeped downward into my legs, into my thighs. A thousand needle pricks coursed toward my knees, through my shoulders and into my arms. The cord cinched tighter. My chest heaved, spasmed—

And then the dagger sliced through the cord.

The man grunted with surprise as his hands jerked wide. The knee pressed into my spine thrust me forward, sent me sprawling onto the dead woman. The man fell backward into the rank alley wall.

My gasp for air was like a warm, shuddering scream.

I lurched over the woman, stepped on her arm, felt it roll beneath me, but the motions felt soft and drawn out. As I fell to my side, I twisted, turned so that I landed facing the man.

He'd already thrust himself away from the wall, was already looming over me, descending, his face a grimace of hatred. His hands reached for me, the cord still twined around his fingers, its cut ends dangling as he reached for my neck.

I brought the dagger up from my side without thinking. The world was still too gray, too narrow for thought.

The dagger caught him in the chest. I felt it punch through skin, felt it grind against bone as it sank deeper, deeper, until it was brought up short by the handle. Then the man's weight drove the handle into my chest.

I had a moment to see a startled look flash through the man's eyes, a moment to feel his hands encircling my throat loosely, and then the pain of the dagger's handle drove the breath from my lungs. I lurched forward, threw the man to the side, and rolled to my hands and knees, coughing like a diseased cat. Pain radiated from the center of my chest. Not the fiery pain of no air, nor the cold pain of the warning Fire, but the dull pain of being punched too hard, too fast.

I coughed a moment more, then vomited.

I was still hunched over, on hands and knees, bile like a sickness in my torn throat, when someone said, "Impressive."

I jerked away from the voice, a tendril of spit and bile that dangled from my mouth plastering itself to my chin as I moved. I came up short against the alley wall with a thud, body tucked in so I was as small a target as possible. A bright flare of pain radiated from my bruised ribs. My hand went reflexively for my dagger, but it was still embedded in the man's chest.

My heart lurched and I cowered lower, head bowed, arms wrapped around my knees. I was trembling too much to do anything more, too weak from the struggle with the man to run. So I cowered, eyes closed, hoping the voice would go away.

After a moment I realized I hadn't heard retreating footsteps. I hadn't heard anything at all.

I opened my eyes, aware of the wetness of tears on my face, and tilted my head, staring out into the alley through the matted tangles of my hair.

A guardsman leaned against the alley wall twenty paces away, the bodies of the man and the woman between us. It was the same guardsman I'd seen on the street before. His arms were crossed over his chest, his posture casual. He wore the standard uniform—breeches, leather boots, brown shirt, leather armor underneath—but no sword belted at his waist. A dagger lay tucked in his belt instead. The Skewed Throne symbol was stitched in red thread on the left side of the shirt.

Red. A Seeker. A guardsman sent to mete out the Mistress' punishments, to pass judgment. Not one of the regular guardsmen; the stitching would have been gold instead.

A new fear crawled into my stomach.

He'd seen me kill a man, had witnessed it.

He watched me with a strange look in his eyes. A confused look that pinched the skin between his brows and tightened the corners of his mouth.

After a moment, his gaze shifted from me to the body of the man.

"Very impressive," he said again, then pushed himself away from the wall.

I flinched back, my shoulders scraping against the moldy dampness of the alley's mud-brick, my breath hitching in my throat. I tasted bile again, felt fresh tears squeeze through pain-clenched eyes.

I heard the guardsman halt.

"I didn't come for you," he said, his voice brusque but soothing. Reassuring.

I opened my eyes to narrow slits, just enough to see him, to watch.

He moved toward the dead man, knelt on his heels near the man's head.

For a long moment, he simply stared at the man's face, at the small trickle of blood that had leaked from the corner of the mouth. Then he spat to one side, his face twisted with contempt. "Vicious bastard. You deserved worse than this."

He jerked my dagger free from the man's chest and in a strangely fluid motion made three quick slashes across the man's forehead. He stared at his handiwork a moment more, then turned on the balls of his feet until he was facing me, elbows on his knees, my dagger dangling loosely from one hand.

I watched the dagger carefully, aware of his intent look. I hadn't realized how important the dagger had become to me over the last three years. I felt exposed without it, helpless.

I wanted my dagger back. Needed it.

The guardsman began swinging the blade back and forth, taunting me, and my gaze shifted back to his eyes. This close, I could see they were a muddy brown, like mine, like most of the people who lived in Amenkor, on the Dredge. There were scars on his face, lots of scars. Scars that ran up into his thinning, gray-brown hair. They made him seem hard, like worn mud-brick bleached by the sun.

"And you," he murmured, the confused look returning. "You don't seem dangerous at all. You're what? Ten?" He leaned slightly forward, eyes narrowing, then shook his head. "Older than that, although you could fool almost anyone. Thirteen at least, maybe more. And you don't talk much."

He paused, waiting. The dagger stilled.

"Maybe you don't talk at all," he said finally, dagger back in motion, the action careless, as if he didn't care.

I narrowed my eyes. "I talk."

The words came out harsh and gravelly, like brick grating against brick, and they hurt—in my chest, in my throat. I wiped the thread of spit and bile from my chin and coughed against the burning sensation. Even the coughs hurt. Hurt worse than anything I'd ever felt before.

The guardsman hesitated, then nodded, the barest hint of a smile playing at the edges of his mouth.

"So I see. You just don't talk much, do you?"

I didn't answer, and his smile grew.

He turned his attention to my dagger, still swinging between the fingers of one hand. With a smooth gesture, he swung it upright in his grip, then stared at me over its tip. All traces of the smile were gone, his eyes flatly serious, expression hard.

"This is your dagger, isn't it?" All hints of the reassuring, casual voice had disappeared. This voice was hurtful, threatening.

I cringed back. "Yes."

He didn't react, eyes still hard, intent. "It's a guardsman's dagger."

My eyes flicked to the dagger tucked in his belt, then back. I felt my stomach clench and tensed, even though it hurt. In my head, I saw the first man I'd killed leaning against the second story of the rooftop, hand outstretched, grasping for me, saw the blood coating his neck, heard the wet rasp of his last short breaths. And I saw the ripped-out gold stitching of the Skewed Throne on the left breast of his shirt.

For the first time since the night of the Fire, the thought of the first man I'd killed didn't frighten me. Instead, defiant anger seethed just beneath the pain.

I glared at the Seeker. "Yes. But now it's mine."

He frowned. He wanted to ask how I'd gotten it, where it came from. I could see it in his eyes.

But he simply shrugged. "What's yours is yours."

He tossed the dagger low across the ground, metal clanging on stone as it struck the wet cobbles and slid to a halt just in front of me.

I reached out slowly and picked it up, unbelieving, the blood on the handle still tacky, my eyes on the guardsman the entire time. He didn't move, just watched. But something had changed. There was a new, considering look in his eyes, as if he were judging me, coming to a decision.

I pulled the dagger in close to my body, kept it ready.

After a long, drawn-out moment, he stood. "I bet you know the warren beyond the Dredge like I know the scars on my own skin," he murmured to himself. And then he tilted his head.

I shifted under his gaze, suddenly aware of the darkness of the alley, of the seclusion and the smooth fluidity of his movements.

"Go away," I said, pulling in tight, ready to flee.

He smiled, a slow, careful smile, as if my wary stance had convinced him of something.

Instead of turning to leave, he crossed his arms again and said, "I could use your help."

"Go away," I repeated with more force, even though the suggestion piqued interest deep inside me.

"You can leave if you want," he said, but he didn't move himself, simply stood, waiting. It was like the dagger again. He was dangling escape in front of me, letting it swing back and forth, taunting me.

I glanced toward the potatoes scattered across the cobbles, barely visible in the light. Hunger twisted in my gut.

The guardsman shifted and I tore my gaze back to where he stood. He hadn't moved forward, only shifted his weight, his eyes on me. "Everyone runs to the slums of the Dredge, you know. Almost everyone. Murderers, thieves, brawlers. Merchants who've lost their businesses, gamblers who've gambled away their lives. A few run to the sea, to the ships in the harbor and the cities they can take them to elsewhere on the coast, but not many. They come here. They think they can hide here. That among all this crowded filth, these warrens of alleys and houses and narrow courtyards, they can somehow disappear."

He paused, still staring at me. Then he frowned, and his voice darkened. "And they're right. Five years ago, before the Fire, they wouldn't have had a chance. The Seekers would have found them, if we were sent after them by the Mistress. The Skewed Throne would have found them. But now. . . ."

His gaze dropped to the dead man in the middle of the alley, his eyes flickering with a black hatred, and I shrank back until my shoulders pressed against the collapsing wall.

"Now the Dredge is more crowded. All the merchants hit hard by the panic after the Fire are drifting here. All of their families. They're desperate. And they have nowhere else to go. You must have noticed how crowded the Dredge has become, little *varis.*" He paused, glanced up, then nodded his head. "Yes. You've noticed. You live off of it, don't you?"

The question struck like a physical blow, harsh enough to make me wince. I narrowed my eyes at him, jaw set, and said, "Yes."

It came out bitter and hopeless.

He nodded again. "You know the Dredge and its underbelly. You live here. You can help me find these men that run."

He paused, still watching me, letting the offer sink in. After a moment he pushed away from the wall and walked toward me, knelt a few steps away, so close I could see his scars clearly, could see his eyes.

I cringed back from him, from the heated danger that bled from him, that set all the warning senses I'd honed on the Dredge on edge except for one, the one I trusted the most: the cold Fire in my chest. That Fire remained dormant, and because of that I stayed instead of fleeing to the street, or in the other direction, deeper into the warren of dark paths beyond the Dredge.

"Do you know where Cobbler's Fountain is?" he asked.

I nodded. I hadn't been to Cobbler's Fountain in years. It was too far up the Dredge, too close to the River and the city, to the real Amenkor. I'd be noticed there, my rags and dirty hair. It wasn't good hunting ground.

"Good," he said, sitting back slightly. "I can help you, and you can help me. Think about it. If you want to help find these men for the Mistress, come to Cobbler's Fountain tomorrow, at dusk. I'll be there."

Then he stood, turned, and strode from the alley, pausing at its edge to adjust to the sunlight before entering the crowd. He didn't look back.

I waited for ten heartbeats, wary, then rose from my crouch, wincing as I drew in a deep breath. I approached the two bodies slowly, every movement sending dull pain across my chest and into my arms, still watching the far entrance to the alley, still uncertain the guardsman had left. A stinging fire burned in a circle around my neck where the dead man's cord had cut into flesh, and a thinner line of fire ran from the back of my jaw down my throat from where I'd pressed my own dagger into my neck to cut the cord, but the pain in my chest . . .

I coughed again, hissed through clenched teeth as I knelt beside the man.

His face was strangely slack, his eyes open. Blood had filled his mouth, had leaked from one corner and matted in his beard. The guardsman had carved the Skewed Throne into his forehead, the cuts raw, with only a trace of blood. A single horizontal slash across the top, two slanted vertical slashes beneath, one shorter than the other. The man had been dead too long for them to bleed much.

I leaned over his face, breathed in his sour smell—piss and blood and sweat and something deeper, something rancid, like rotten butter. I stared into his vacant eyes, frowned as I brought one hand up to the scored line encircling my neck. There was no frigid flare of Fire in my chest now. No reaction at all. The danger had passed.

But as I stared into his eyes I felt again the coarseness of his beard on my cheek, heard his ragged, desperate gasps. I smelled his breath.

Anger grew, deep in my chest, a hard lump beneath the dull pain. An anger I recognized. I'd felt it many times during my life on the Dredge—for the wagon master who'd kicked me, for the nameless gutterscum who'd slid into my niche and stolen my bread. A hatred that was there and then gone. Fleeting.

But this time the anger, the hatred, wasn't fleeting. It was solid. And the longer I looked at the dead man's face, the harder it became. It began to take form, shifting and slithering.

I leaned closer, breathed in the rancid musk of the dead man even deeper.

And then I spat into his face.

I leaned back, startled, my spittle running down the man's skin beneath one dead eye. I was strangely . . . thrilled, arms tingling as if with numbness, with cold. But I wasn't cold. A hot flush covered me instead, lay against my skin like sweat.

I turned to the woman, a pang of regret coursing beneath the heated, sickening exhilaration. Then I crawled to the spilled potatoes, the dropped basket, and collected it all together, as quickly as possible.

I fled toward the back of the alley, away from the Dredge, trying not to think about the dead man, the woman, or the guard.

I focused on the pain in my chest instead. And beneath that, the still lingering anger, coiled now, like a snake.

+— Chapter 2

I woke in my niche deep in the slums beyond the Dredge to vivid sunlight outside, my chest bruised a livid purple-black. I moaned as I rolled into a sitting position, lifted up my ragged shirt, and examined the bruising. Every breath drew a wince, every motion a twinge, yet I prodded the edges of the bruise anyway.

I sat and stared at the basket of potatoes and thought about the round face of the woman the man had killed. The pang of regret returned, but I shoved it aside in annoyance and focused on the guardsman, on the offer to help him.

I frowned and pulled out my dagger, stared at the band of sunlight caught on the flat of its blade.

I didn't need the guardsman. I'd survived without him since I was nine. I'd survived without anyone since Dove and his gutterscum thugs went after that woman and I refused to follow.

I frowned. I hadn't thought of Dove since that night, tried not to feel the ghost of the throbbing bruise on my cheek where he'd punched me after I'd told him I wouldn't help him catch the woman. I'd known he wasn't going to simply rob her. He meant to kill her. I'd seen it in his eyes.

I scowled. I'd decided then that Dove had served his purpose. He'd taught me enough so that I could survive on my own.

I hadn't needed anyone else then and I didn't need anyone else now.

I hesitated. Except, of course, the white-dusty man. I needed him, relied on him occasionally. But that was different.

So I rose with a grimace of pain and crawled out into the sunlight through my niche's narrow opening, the guardsman and his offer pushed aside. The potatoes wouldn't last forever. I needed to hunt.

The Dredge is the only real street in the slums of Amenkor, running straight from its depths, across the River, and into the real city on the other side of the harbor. The Dredge is where those from the city proper mingled with those that lived beyond the Dredge, those that lived deeper, like me—the gutterscum. At fourteen, the Dredge was the edge of my world. I'd never stepped beyond it, never walked down its broken cobbles, past its taverns and shops, across the bridge over the River and into the city of Amenkor itself. The Dredge on this side of the River *was* Amenkor for me. I preyed upon its people, on the crowds of men and women who had somehow fallen on hard times and had been forced to abandon the real city and retreat across the harbor.

And the Seeker had been right. Since the passage of the Fire three years before, the number of people in the slums had increased. Not just people from the city proper either, but others as well, people not from Amenkor at all. People who wore strange clothing, who had different-colored hair or eyes, who carried strange weapons and spoke in accents . . . or didn't speak the common language at all.

But those people were rare.

I peered out from the darkness of the slums now, huddled low, mud-brick pressed into my back. On the street, men and women moved back and forth. I watched each of them as they arrived, caught their faces, scanned their clothing. That man wore tattered rags but carried a dagger at his belt. Yet there was no danger in his eyes. Hard, but not cruel. He carried nothing else, and so he faded from my mind, nothing but a darker blur against the dull gray of the world. Unconsciously, I kept track of him—of all the people—but he'd ceased to be interesting. Not a target; not a threat. Gray.

A flash of fine clothing and my eyes shifted. Not truly fine clothing—frayed edging, a tear down one side of the gray shirt, breeches stained, oily—but better than most. He wore boots, one sole loose at the heel, the nails visible when he walked. He also carried a dagger, hidden, his hand resting over the bulge of its sheath at his side. He walked quickly, tense, and his eyes . . .

But he turned before I could catch his eyes, his torn shirt and loose sole vanishing through a doorway.

He faded.

Gray.

I settled into position next to the wall, wincing once over the bruise on my chest, and let the flow of the street wash around me. When the pain had receded, I focused on the street, squinted in concentration, and felt a familiar sensation deep inside.

With a subtle, internal movement, like relaxing a muscle, the sensation rushed forward.

The world collapsed, slowed, blurred. Buildings and people faded, grayed. Those men and women I'd determined to be possible threats slid into washes of red against the background gray, like smears of blood, moving through the flow of the street. Occasionally, I'd concentrate on one person and they'd emerge from the gray, sharp and clear, so I could watch them, consider them. Casual glances would draw others out of the gray, their actions entering the field momentarily, and then I'd lose interest, determine they carried nothing I could eat, nothing I wanted, and the people would return to gray.

The sound of the street blurred as well, voices and footfalls and rustling clothes all merging into a single sound like a gentle wind rustling in my ears. Threatening noises slid out of the sound, catching my attention, until I'd made certain there was no danger. Then they faded back into the wind.

I submerged myself in the world of gray and red and wind with a sigh, a world that had helped me survive all these years alone, and searched for my next mark.

An hour before dusk, I leaned back against the alley wall, an apple in one hand. The woman hadn't even noticed the apple was missing. She'd set it down on the edge of the cart to pick up the sack she'd dropped. All I had to do was reach out and take it. It wasn't much, not after an entire day's work. But the pain in my chest had kept me from trying for anything more difficult, and I still had the potatoes back at my niche.

I'd just turned away, ready to return to my niche, when I thought I saw the guardsman.

It was a subtle movement, thirty paces farther down the Dredge. As if he had pushed himself away from where he was leaning against the corner of a building, turned, and rounded the corner. All I saw for certain was the vague shape of a man's back vanishing behind the mud-brick, into the darkness of the narrow.

A casual movement, but one that sent a prickle down the backs of my arms.

I hesitated, watched the narrow farther down the Dredge. When no one reappeared around the corner, I finally turned and moved back into the warren beyond the street, letting the world of gray and red and wind slip away, shrugging thoughts of the guardsman aside.

But something had changed.

As I made my way back toward my niche, I stared down at the apple and frowned. It was a good apple. Hardly any scabs, mostly ripe, a small gouge in one side that had browned and begun to spoil, but still a good apple. I should be running back to my niche in triumph, should be huddled against its back wall, body crouched protectively around the apple as I devoured it.

But I didn't feel any triumph. I didn't feel anything at all. My stomach was strangely hollow. Not with hunger either. With just . . . nothing.

I slowed to a halt in the middle of a dark narrow. It was still light out—sun glowed bright ahead—but here there was only a dense darkness, like a smothering cloth. I halted in the darkness and simply stared at the apple. An entire day's work.

The hollowness had started after I'd killed the man, after I'd spoken to the guardsman.

No. The hollowness had always been there. I'd always just ignored it.

But now . . .

I was still staring at the apple when someone said, "Give it to me."

The voice was harsh with violence, a dry, rumbling croak, but I didn't jump. I squinted into the darkness and picked out a figure sagging against one wall. It took me a moment to realize it was a woman, sitting back on her haunches, body piled high with rags. Her hair hung in matted chunks about her face, her skin so wrinkled and ground with dirt it appeared as cracked and dry as mud. Her eyes were tainted a sickly yellow, but were alive and fixed on me.

On the apple.

"Give me the apple, bitch."

I'd seen her before, always huddled in a niche, an alcove, always in darkness. A heaving mound of rags that shuffled from one location to the next. I knew her.

But now, as I looked into the yellowish taint of her eyes, into the blackness at their center, I actually *saw* her. And the hollowness in my stomach took sudden and vivid form.

I recognized those eyes.

They were mine.

I ran, bolted from the narrow into the sunlight with the woman I would become screeching, "Give it to me! Give it to me, you bitch!" behind me. I ran back to my niche and huddled against its back wall and cried. Harsh, bitter tears that only made the hollowness inside me swell larger. I cried until my arms and legs ached and grew numb, until the sobs faded into hitching coughs. I watched the sunlight through the niche's narrow opening and tried to think of nothing at all, ended up thinking of Dove, of the five years since I'd been on my own, of the woman with the potatoes lying dead in the alley, strangled by the man I'd killed. Tremors ran through my arms, shuddered through my shoulders. Every now and then tears burned in my eyes for no reason and I'd squeeze them tight, the dark, hollow, twisted sensation burning in my chest. I'd pull in on myself, hold myself hard, until the burning receded, until my chest loosened.

Until finally the light outside began to fade and I realized what I needed to do.

I avoided the dark alley where the rag woman had been, skirted it by four narrows. The depths beyond the Dredge seemed somehow darker, dirtier. A boy no more than seven pawed his way through a heap of refuse outside a recessed doorway, buried so deep I wouldn't have noticed him if the heap hadn't suddenly heaved upward. He stumbled from it, sludge streaking his face, his legs, his arms. He held a twisted spoon in one hand like a knife, sank to one knee with a snarl like a dog when he saw me, then bolted for the shadows.

The carcass of a rat dangled from one of the boy's hands. It swung wildly as he ran.

That was me, digging through the garbage, snarling.

My chest tightened again, but I shoved the sensation back, began moving faster. The light was beginning to gray into dusk. There wasn't much time.

I slid up the Dredge, keeping to the walls, to the alleys. I watched the people as I moved, suddenly conscious of my clothes . . . no, not clothes. The farther I moved, the more it became obvious I wore nothing but dirt and slime, the Dredge draped over my bones like lichen. I felt myself shrinking and I drew in upon myself, twice halted to turn back—once when a woman stared at me with blatant shock and disgust, and once when a boy spat at my feet, laughing loudly when I jerked back in a cower.

He might not have laughed so loudly if he'd known my hand was on a dagger beneath my rags.

I pushed on, until I crouched in the darkness of a narrow that looked out on the fountain, at the crumbling stone of a woman, one arm raised to hold an urn on her shoulder. Her other arm had once been poised on her hip, but it had been broken off years before so that only a jagged piece jutted out from her shoulder, and only the tips of her fingers remained at her waist. Water had spilled from the urn into the surrounding pool, but now the pool was empty except for dark patches of mold, the mouth of the urn stained with water residue.

I settled back against the narrow's wall. I'd been here before, when I was younger, many times. But the memories were vague, blurred with sunlight. The light glinted off the water in the basin, sparkled with childish laughter. Closing my eyes, I could feel the water from the urn spilling down into my hair, could taste its coolness as it washed down into my mouth. But everything was too bright, too blurred.

I felt a woman's hands touch my shoulders, reach beneath my arms to bring me up out of the water—

"I never expected to see you here."

I opened my eyes and stared up into the Seeker's face, half seen in the dusk. He'd spoken gently, and now frowned as he looked down at me.

"Is anything wrong?"

I wiped at the tears. "No."

His frown deepened, as if he didn't believe me. His stance shifted and the cold, hard danger that edged his eyes softened.

For a moment, I thought he'd reach out and touch me, touch my face. I felt myself cringe back, hand on my dagger, even as something deep inside tried to lean forward. And he did reach out. . . .

A small sack dangled from his outstretched hand.

"Take it," he said when I hesitated.

My dagger clutched hidden against my side, I reached out and took the sack, stifling a surge of disappointment. The sack was heavy, bulged with strange shapes.

I opened it. There were oranges inside. Good oranges—skins firm, unblemished. And a chunk of bread. And cheese.

My eyes teared up, burned so fiercely I had to squeeze them tight. And my stomach seized.

I thought of the rag woman, of the boy with the sharpened spoon and dead rat, and asked hoarsely, "What do you want me to do?"

The guardsman sank down into a crouch before me, the sky dark behind him. "I'm looking for a man, black hair cut down to here, about this tall. His face is thin and sharp, like . . . like a hawk. And his eyes are dark and sharp, too. He carries a knife with a hilt shaped like a bow, sort of bent backward so it curves slightly around the wielder's hand. Just watch for him. If you see him, follow him. See where he goes, where he hides out. Then come find me. I'll be here at dusk every day."

"Every day?" I reached into the sack, grabbed a chunk of bread and crammed it into my mouth.

The guardsman hesitated, as if still uncertain about what he proposed. His eyes were squinted, even in the moonlight. Then he shook himself. "If I'm not here, one of the other Seekers will be here . . . another guardsman like me. Tell him to give a message to Erick. They'll know who I am."

I nodded, mostly focused on the food. The bread was gone, and not much remained of the cheese. I was saving the oranges. They were rare. I'd only seen them once or twice on the Dredge, and even then they'd been half spoiled.

"What's your name?"

I froze, eyes wide, mouth clamped shut. I breathed in raggedly through my nose, and my heart thudded in my chest. The taste of cheese burned against my tongue.

After a moment, I swallowed, the cheese going down like a large stone. I coughed against the pain, then coughed harder against the pain the coughing awoke in my chest.

Erick watched me carefully. "Do you even have a name?"

I had a name, but no one had used it in over eight years, not since my mother had died. No one had cared. Not the woman who'd taken me in at age six; not the street gang led by Dove that I'd eventually fled to after that. No one.

I dropped my head, stared down into the open mouth of the sack, into the darkness where the oranges rested. A stinging sense of shame and something else coursed through me, burned against my skin. The same something that had leaned forward when Erick reached out with the sack of oranges, that had withdrawn in disappointment. Erick couldn't see it. Not in the darkness. Not behind the fall of my hair.

He sat back on his heels. "It doesn't matter, little *varis.*" He paused, and when he spoke again I could hear humor in his voice. "*Varis.* Do you know what that means?"

I shook my head, still not looking up.

"It means hunter." He chuckled softly to himself. "I think that's fitting, don't you, Varis?"

I lifted my head, just enough so that I could see him, then nodded.

He smiled. "Good."

Then he rose and walked down the narrow. Not fast, but steady.

I watched until he slipped into the shadows, then gripped the mouth of the sack of oranges tight.

Varis. Hunter.

I began to sob.

I had a name. Again.

The flow of the street had changed the following day. Not because it was different, but because I was different. I wasn't looking for a loose bundle, a momentarily forgotten basket, a stray piece of bread. Now I watched the people's faces.

Leaning against a narrow's wall, half in shade, moving as the sun rose so that I stayed in the shadows, I scanned everyone, looking at the eyes, at the hair, at the nose. Scars and blemishes, jowls and scabs—they all took on new meanings.

By midday—the sun so high there were no longer shadows—my stomach growled and I realized I'd spent the entire morning looking for the man Erick had asked me to find, the hawk-faced man. The initial excitement had ebbed, and with a strange sense of disappointment, I began to focus on bundles.

I slid into old patterns as smoothly as the sunlight slid into dusk.

The next day was the same. And the next.

By the end of the fourth day, I no longer searched for the hawk-faced man. The oranges were gone, and the potatoes. I hadn't seen the guardsman on the Dredge at all, didn't dare return to the fountain to ask for more food.

I saw the hawk-faced man ten days later.

Clouds drifted across the sky, casting the Dredge into gray shade every now and then as they passed over the sun. I stood at the mouth of an alley, eyes narrowed at the woman across the street. She was haggling with a man pulling a handcart. The cart was loaded with cabbages.

The woman had set her bag on the ground.

I glanced around the Dredge. It was crowded, the weather mild for midsummer. People were moving swiftly. Most were smiling.

I had just pushed away from the wall toward the woman and the cart handler when a strange movement made me pause. It was subtle, like the change in light when a cloud passed, but it didn't fit the rhythm of the street.

I frowned and let the world slip into gray and wind. A moment later, I caught the movement again, closer, and then I saw the wash of red among the gray.

It slid into focus almost immediately. A boy-not-yet-man.

I scowled, growled like a dog sensing another dog on his own territory as I shifted into a better position. My hand touched my dagger briefly. I'd seen this boy-not-yet-man for the first time right after the Fire, had seen him many times since; too many times. Lanky brown hair, wicked eyes, thin mouth. A birthmark shaped like a smear of blood at the corner of one eye marred his smooth, sun-darkened face. Clothes like mine—matted, torn, and stained with the Dredge.

Gutterscum, just like me. Competition.

And he'd targeted the woman yelling at the cart handler. *My* mark.

I felt a surge of resentment, bitter, like ash, felt the hairs at the nape of my neck stiffen.

Without thought, I pushed forward through the crowd, focused on the woman and the cart handler. As I moved, I felt the anger tighten in my chest, tingling in my arms, and I narrowed the focus even further. The woman raised one arm, pointing toward the sky as she yelled. Her other arm clutched the ends of the shawl draped around her head. The cart handler shook his head, both hands still firmly gripping the handles of his cart.

He'd just drawn in a deep breath when my focus suddenly . . . altered.

It was like standing neck-deep in the River that ran through Amenkor to the south, near the palace—sunlight harsh on the water, noise from the shops and streets along the banks strangely heightened as they hit the waves, somehow sharper, clearer. It was like standing there, neck-deep—

And then ducking beneath the surface, into darkness.

I felt myself slide from the world of gray and red and wind I was used to into something else, something deeper. The gray darkened. Eddies of movement I'd barely noticed before smoothed out into nothing but shadowed blackness. The background wind died out completely, only the sounds of the woman and the cart handler and the boy intruding. And these sounds were crisper. Movements grew taut, and slowed subtly.

I glanced toward the boy, toward the woman, toward the bag at her feet, and with the new sense of awareness *knew* what would happen.

I didn't hesitate. I swam through the crush of people on the street, brushing an unseen arm, a shoulder—both sensations transitory, like brushing against unseen weeds beneath the river's surface—and then I was at the back of the wagon full of cabbages.

The cart handler glanced toward me as I mimicked a lurch forward, as if I'd been jostled from behind. My hand slapped onto the edge of his cart to steady myself. He glanced toward it with a suspicious frown. The woman never looked in my direction at all.

Then I was past the cart, the woman's sack clutched loosely in my other hand.

I slid into the nearest narrow, crouched down near its opening, sack resting at my feet, and turned to watch with a half suppressed grin. The anger had passed.

The boy was only ten steps from the woman and the cart when he finally noticed the sack was missing. He froze in the middle of the Dredge, so sharply someone stumbled into him from behind. His gaze jerked from side to side. His eyes narrowed viciously. His mouth tightened to a frown.

Then his eyes latched onto mine.

I grinned. I couldn't help it.

Somehow, his eyes narrowed more, became blacker, and I felt the elation inside me curdle and sour, the strange new focus shuddering away at the same moment, making the sourness worse. The real world rushed forward, the sounds of the street loud. My grin faltered.

I gripped the sack and stood, turning to head deeper into the alley. I didn't know what was in the sack, but I no longer wanted to wait on the Dredge to find out either.

I'd reached the deepness of the alley, the sourness twisting into nausea, when someone grabbed my arm and spun me around.

I reacted on instinct, my dagger out and ready before I realized it was the boy-not-yet-man. Except this close, with his own dagger drawn, he seemed much less boy and more man. We'd never been this close, never spoken except through scowls and heated looks.

He reminded me of Dove.

He stepped back, his breathing hard, anger harsh in his eyes. The red birthmark at his eye appeared black in the light from the mouth of the alley. He said nothing, only glared. After a long moment I drew in a deep breath to steady my shuddering heart and said shortly, "What do you want?"

"I want my sack."

I snorted, felt the strange nausea deepen. I tasted bile at the back of my throat, felt a cramp shudder through my stomach. I grimaced. "It isn't yours," I said through the pain.

"But it will be," he said harshly. He didn't get to continue. I gasped at another cramp, dropped the sack as I hunched over my stomach and sagged convulsively to my knees. The boy jerked back, wary and confused, then lurched forward to retrieve the sack as I collapsed to my side, my knees pulled in tight. The bile was like fire, scorching my throat, and the pain in my stomach radiated through my chest, alternately hot and cold. I sensed the boy leaning over me, felt his breath against my face as he spat in a whisper, "Don't mess with me, bitch," and then he was gone.

I saw a retreating shadow and forced myself to concentrate. "My name is Varis," I murmured to myself as the sunlight at the end of the alley came into view, a white blur interrupted briefly by the boy's form.

I was still focusing hard on the light, the strange pain just beginning to fade, when I saw the hawk-faced man. He walked across the mouth of the alley without glancing inside, there and then gone. I might never have noticed, except I was concentrating so hard on remaining conscious. In case the boy decided to come back. Or in case something worse came along.

I lay stunned for a moment. Long enough for the sunlight at the mouth of the alley to fade as a cloud began to pass.

Then I rolled onto my knees. A wave of reawakened nausea poured through me and I dry-vomited, nothing but a sour taste flooding my mouth. When it passed, I staggered to my feet, using the wall for support, and made my way to the mouth of the alley.

I didn't expect to see him. I'd taken too long getting to the street. But he'd halted about twenty paces away, back toward me. I watched as he scanned the Dredge, as if searching for someone. Then he turned and I saw his face clearly.

He fit the guardsman's description of the hawk-faced man. Black hair, dark eyes, thin face, sharp nose. I couldn't see a knife, but I knew it was him.

He scanned the Dredge one more time, eyes narrowed, then moved into the alley farther up.

I shoved away from the wall to follow, but another spasm of pain hunched me over on the edge of the Dredge, heaving again. The people on the street flowed around me, leaving a wide space, as if I were diseased. I leaned against the near wall until the spasm passed, then stood.

I felt sweaty and chilled at the same time. I wiped my mouth with the back of my hand and began a cautious stagger toward my niche. I didn't feel well enough for any more activity on the Dredge. The hawk-faced man would have to wait.

I spent the rest of the day and most of the night passing in and out of consciousness at the back of my niche. Shudders coursed through me, so violent at times my head cracked against the worn mud-brick, my arms flopping uselessly at my sides, spittle drooling from my mouth. Once, I bit my tongue hard enough to draw blood.

When the spasms passed, I lay back against the stone and cried, so weak I could barely raise my arms. The sobs racked my body as painfully as the spasms, but I couldn't seem to stop. I didn't understand what was happening, didn't know how to stop it.

Eventually, I realized that the spasms were taking longer to come, lasted a shorter time, and weren't so harsh. They decreased, until finally I rolled onto my side, tears running down my face, and stared out at the moonlit darkness beyond my niche, the last tremors tingling down my arms.

There, in the moonlit darkness, I saw the world of gray and red and wind. Whatever had happened on the Dredge that afternoon, whatever had pushed me deeper into the grayness, had caused this. I'd gone too deep. I'd pushed myself so far beneath the gray surface of the river I'd almost drowned.

I closed my eyes and drew myself in tight, even though every muscle hurt. I'd never felt so . . . drained.

I breathed in with slow, careful breaths, slipping toward true sleep. My last, cold thought was that I'd have to be more careful when using the river, the world of gray and red and wind.

I didn't want to drown.

The next day I placed myself near the alley where I'd seen the hawk-faced man. Before settling in, I checked for the cart handler and for the boy-not-yet-man.

I frowned. He wasn't a boy-not-yet-man. Not now. I'd seen that yesterday, seen it in his eyes.

I shook myself, feeling a backwash of weakness slip through me, and refocused on the crowd. Neither the cart handler nor the boy-not- . . . nor Birthmark were in sight.

I frowned again, thinking of how his eyes had narrowed when he'd seen me with the sack, how *black* they'd become.

Not Birthmark. Bloodmark.

"Varis and Bloodmark," I said out loud, then grimaced.

Bloodmark wasn't in sight. And neither was the hawk-faced man.

I sighed and sat back against the wall of the alley to wait.

The hawk-faced man didn't show until almost dusk. I'd snagged two scabrous apples, a potato as hard as a rock, an entire loaf of bread, and was almost ready to give up when I saw his sharp features heading toward me.

I faded back into the narrow, moving casually, watched him as he passed. His gaze followed the people on the Dredge, eyes flickering swiftly from face to face, mouth flat. He clenched his jaw as he moved, the muscle just beneath his ear pulsing. His clothes were well made, but fading now, stained by his stay in the depths. Mud coated his boots.

Tucked into his belt was a dagger, the hilt curved like a bow.

I glanced sharply again toward his face the moment before he stepped beyond the narrow, memorized it—the faint pockmarks on his cheeks, the lines at the corners of the mouth and eyes—then shifted forward to the corner to follow him.

He paused at the mouth of the alley, just as he had the night before, and searched the crowd. After a moment I realized he was waiting—for someone, for dusk, for the right moment, perhaps.

Then he scowled at the crowd, glanced toward the cloudless sky just beginning to darken toward night, and entered the alley.

I waited five breaths, then took a deeper breath to steady myself, and followed.

Daylight fled as the hawk-faced man moved deeper and deeper into the depths beyond the Dredge. I kept close enough I could see his dagger at first, but far enough back I didn't think he'd notice me. The texture of the Dredge changed the farther we moved, worn mud-brick darkening to decayed stone. The faint scent of dampness and mildew and piss that coated each narrow deepened into reeking slime and shit. The water that slicked through the gutters thickened into sludge, and corners and niches rounded with packed, collected refuse.

Twice the man halted, looking back as I slid against a slime-coated wall and grew still. Both times he stood silently, face hidden by the darkness of night, lit only vaguely by the moonlight. I held my breath, aware that now I followed only a silhouette of the man I'd seen on the Dredge, and hoped that he saw nothing behind him but rotting debris from a thousand discarded lives.

Eventually, he'd turn and continue, and after a moment I'd push away from the wall and follow.

Finally, he halted before a bent, iron gate leading into a narrow courtyard black as pitch. The stone wall of the courtyard lay half crumbled in the alley, the curved arch above the gate completely collapsed. He slid through a gap in the twisted bars and vanished in the darkness beyond.

I huddled against a wall twenty paces away and watched the gate, breath barely a whisper. Somewhere, a dog barked, the sound vicious, and a rat scratched its way through the crevices and stone of the wall behind me. I glanced down the alleyway in both directions, saw no one, and frowned at the gate again, at the utter blackness beyond the gaping mouth of the doorway.

I wanted to follow, but when I stood to slip across the alley the hairs on the nape of my neck tingled, shivering across my shoulders. Deep down in my gut I felt the cold, shuddering stirrings of the Fire. Barely a tendril of flame, just a hint of warning.

I hesitated, drew in a deep breath—

And then headed away from the courtyard, back toward the Dredge, back toward my niche.

I knew where he'd gone. The guardsman . . . Erick . . . would have to be satisfied with that.

I ignored the fact that my arms were trembling. And that the tendril of Fire did not die.

At dusk the following day I found my way back to Cobbler's Fountain. Erick was waiting.

"Have you found Jobriah?"

"The hawk-faced man."

Erick laughed. A laugh that sent shivers through my arms. "The hawk-faced man. I like that." Then he seemed to harden, eyes intent, mouth tight. The scars that marked his face stood out in sudden relief. "And can you take me to him?"

I nodded, wary. He didn't seem like the man who'd brought me oranges. This man stirred the tendril of flame that still curled in my gut.

"Good. Take me there."

He made no move to touch me, but when I rose, I veered away from him.

We slid off the Dredge, into the back streets, and headed deep. Worn mud-brick shifted to decayed stone again, piss and filth to sludge and shit. Erick said nothing, just stalked behind me as I shifted from shadow to shadow. He made no attempt to hide, seemed annoyed at my scurrying crouch, but he did nothing to stop me.

By the time we reached the street outside the broken iron gate night had fallen completely and the tendril of flame in my gut had grown to a white Fire. I huddled at the corner of the narrow I'd used the night before. Erick stood at its entrance.

"The gate," I said in a hushed voice and turned to look up at the guardsman's face.

A footfall echoed down the street and without a sound Erick slid back into the narrow. He'd lowered a hand to draw me back as well, but the gesture was unnecessary. I'd already moved.

He cast me a brief, considering look, but then the man on the street caught his attention.

It was the hawk-faced man. Jobriah.

As he had the night before, he paused at the entrance to the gate, then ducked through its bars into the darkness beyond.

Erick shifted forward, body rigid with tension. He surveyed the street, listened to the sounds of the night—a gust of wind, distant clatters of movement, nothing close.

Then, without a word, he walked across the street and ducked into the courtyard, as silent as the night.

The white Fire in my gut flared briefly at the suddenness of his movements, then settled back down. But it didn't die.

I fidgeted at the mouth of the narrow in indecision. Erick hadn't said anything about staying, hadn't said to wait. I'd found the hawk-faced man. My job was done.

I turned to go, and heard another footfall on the street.

Stomach clenching, the Fire twisting its coldness deeper into my chest, I crouched down at the base of the wall and held my breath, waiting.

Another man appeared. In the darkness all I saw was a fat face, large body, sunken eyes. The white Fire surged as he stalked into view, so intense I shivered.

He stepped into the courtyard, pausing only to squeeze his body through the narrow opening.

I straightened from my crouch, placed my hands against the decaying stone of the wall, and bit my lip.

Erick knew about the hawk-faced man, not this other. But he was a guardsman, a Seeker. He could take care of himself.

I turned to leave, the tingling Fire surging through me, and thought suddenly of the woman the man had killed. I'd stood at the entrance to the alley and listened to her struggling as he strangled her. I'd heard her gasps, his grunts, heard her body slide to the ground. I'd done nothing.

In the darkness of the narrow, I saw her body staring blankly up into the night, leg bent beneath her, hair lying in the trickle of filth running down the alley.

She reminded me of the woman Dove had gone after.

And she reminded me of my mother.

I turned, fought down the taste of sourness at the back of my throat, and sprinted across the street for the courtyard. My knife glared dully in the faint light before I slid through the iron bars into the blackness.

My eyes adjusted, but I still couldn't see anything. I crouched down in the dirt just inside the gate, drew in a trembling breath, and let the world slip into gray and wind.

I caught a wash of red sliding through a doorway at the far end of the courtyard—a fat wash of red—and then it vanished behind the walls of the building.

I held my breath, concentrated on the eddies in the gray that I'd barely noticed before—eddies that now showed me the vague forms of rocks, the dead husk of a tree in one corner—and ran across the courtyard to the edge of the door. I glanced inside. Nothing. But a strange lightening of the gray outlined another door. The lightened gray flickered.

I frowned, then let the gray and wind slip.

Candlelight flickered through the doorway from a room deeper in the building.

I picked my way across the small room, careful of the debris of crumbled stone that littered the floor. Boot prints stood out in the dust, many overlapping each other. They all led to the inner doorway. I tucked myself low at the doorway's edge, took in the inner room at a glance.

It was much wider than the outer room. Deeper. The candlelight came from a table set against the wall at its farthest reaches, where the hawk-faced man stood, looking at something on the table, one hand clutching a wineskin that sloshed as he moved. His shadow reached back into the blackness of the rest of the room, long and thin. Blankets lay in a heap next to the table.

I saw no one else in the room.

Before I could frown in concern, Erick stepped out of the shadows. In two long, silent strides he came up behind the hawk-faced man and reached around, knife in hand, ready to slit his throat.

It would have been a quick, decisive stroke, except the hawk-faced man shifted, raised the skin to take a drink.

The cut intended to slit his throat drew a deep gash across the base of the man's chin, so deep it exposed the bone along the man's jaw as he gasped in shock and jerked backward, stumbling into Erick.

The two fell, blood sheeting down the hawk-faced man's chest, a flap of flesh dangling beneath the exposed jaw. Erick cursed, heaved the man off his chest with enough force to crack Jobriah's head into the table. The candlelight jerked. The man screamed again—a low, horrible scream, like a strangling dog—and dropped to his knees before the table. The wineskin thudded to the floor as he clutched at his chin, blood coating his hand, spattering his arm.

He moaned, rocking forward and back, eyes dazed, as Erick rose from the floor and circled around behind him. Erick's eyes were flat with purpose, the spatters of the hawk-faced man's blood on his face black in the shuddering light.

Erick had just knelt on one knee behind the man, had shifted and leaned forward as if to embrace him, knife bared and black with blood, when I caught movement at the edge of the candlelight.

It was the fat man.

He never saw me.

I sprinted across the length of the room, watched as the fat man raised his dagger above Erick's back, ready to drive it down into the base of the guardsman's neck. I saw Erick reach around the hawk-faced man's chest and slide his dagger between the man's ribs. The man stiffened, gagged as blood began to pour from his mouth, his hand falling away from his chin and the dangling flesh there.

Then Erick heard me, turned just as I slammed into the fat man.

We plowed into the stone wall, the fat man grunting in surprise, stumbling over his own feet. Then the grunts turned from surprise to pain and I realized I was stabbing him with my dagger, over and over. I could feel blood against my hand, could hear it pattering against the stone, against the floor as we fell in a wild heap. I opened my mouth and screamed into his startled face, saw the startlement turn to rage, to hatred, saw the shock slide to determination as he shifted to get the arm with his own dagger into a position to gut me.

Before he had a chance, one of my wild thrusts plunged into his neck. I felt it slide in, deep, felt the blade nick the bone of his neck, scrape and slide deeper, felt the thick folds of his skin against my hand for a brief sickening moment before I jerked the blade away.

His eyes widened, and like a suddenly broken spider-web, his arms and body slumped to the ground. Blood seeped from the wound, but not like the hawk-faced man's blood. This blood came slower.

I was still screaming, still stabbing. Then Erick's arms enfolded me and pulled me away from the dead fat man, pulled me away and carried me across the room to the shadows, where he sat and held me, murmuring in my ear until slowly, slowly, my screaming faded down into sobs.

"Shh," he breathed in my ear. "Hush, Varis. Hush."

He held me until even the sobs faded, until I lay in a heap against his body, drained.

Eventually, he set me aside, carefully, and moved back toward the bodies. He rolled the hawk-faced man over, marked the man's forehead with the Skewed Throne, then did the same to the fat man. He collected the blanket by the table, the wineskin, and the candle.

He wrapped me in the blanket, which smelled of old sweat and grease and fire, blew out the candle, and carried me out through the courtyard, through the bent iron gate, and into the night.

┼─ Chapter 3

I woke in my niche, the blanket wrapped tight around me, late day sunlight angling through the entrance. The first thing I thought of was the fat man, the grate of blade against bone.

I closed my eyes tight against the sensation, pulled the blanket close. But it wasn't enough. With a shudder, I felt tears streaking down my face. I fought them. Because they were useless. Because he'd been about to stab Erick and so wasn't worth crying over.

I eventually cried myself back to sleep, my chest aching.

When I woke again, I was instantly hungry and thought of the white-dusty man. But someone had placed a sack just inside the entrance to my niche.

I froze, then fumbled beneath the greasy blanket for my dagger. Fear sliced through my chest that somehow I'd lost the blade, left it behind near the fat man, or that Erick had taken it. But then my fingers closed over its hilt.

I pushed the blanket aside and crawled to the sack. It contained bread and cheese. And oranges.

I only thought of the fat man twice as I crammed the bread in my mouth, then the cheese. I saved the oranges. By then it was dusk, and I thought of the white-dusty man again. I was still hungry. I was always hungry.

I slid from my niche and found the guardsman waiting. He sat on his heels on the far side of the narrow, back against the mud-brick wall. His scars stood out in the half-light. He squinted through the grayness, jaw clenched, thinking.

I sat back against the edge of the entrance to my niche and suddenly wondered how he'd gotten me inside. The opening was too narrow for him to fit. Looking into his eyes, I realized he'd been waiting all day, that he'd heard me wake, heard me sobbing.

New fear lashed through me, close to panic.

He was trying to decide whether I was useful.

He stood. "I think," he said with a careful frown, then paused and seemed to change his mind. "I think, if I'm going to have you hunting for me, I'll need to show you how to use that dagger."

He turned and began to walk away. But he halted just before turning into the nearest alley.

Without looking back, he said, "I'll meet you here at dawn for the first lesson." There was an edge to his voice—regret mixed with something deeper. As if he were about to do something he'd never be proud of, something he'd never forget.

Then he was gone.

I waited, feeling strangely hollow inside, holding my dagger in one hand. It felt . . . heavier. And for a moment—with something close to the panic I'd felt a moment before, icy and trembling—I no longer wanted to touch it.

Erick took me to a courtyard the following dawn. A different one than the one near where I'd killed the fat man, this one wider, more open. He'd brought me clothes, still matted with dirt, still used, but better than the rags I'd been wearing. They still felt scratchy when we stepped through the open space where a gate had once stood into the enclosed courtyard. It was only twenty paces across at most, but I still pulled back, drew tight against the wall.

Erick set down a sack just inside the gateway, walked to the center of the courtyard, then turned. He straightened, instantly wary, eyes searching. It took him a moment to pick me out of the shadows beneath the courtyard's crumbling stone wall.

He grunted and relaxed. "You're never going to learn anything hiding beside that wall. Come here."

I bit my lower lip, forced myself to step out of the darkness into the strengthening sunlight, until I stood two paces away from him. I glared up into his eyes.

He held the gaze, then smiled tightly. "I don't normally train. That's for others in the guard. I'm not exactly certain how to do this," he said. Then he shrugged.

There was no warning. One moment, Erick stood, relaxed, face crimped in perplexed thought, the next his dagger flashed in the sunlight and he lunged.

I reacted instantly, all the years of survival on the Dredge surging forth. I ducked, twisted, and ran. I'd reached the open gateway before Erick's outcry registered.

"Varis! Stop! It was just a feint!"

I slid to a halt in a low crouch, hand against the crumbling stone of the gate's wall, and glanced back. Erick stood where I'd left him, dagger in hand but at his side. He was grinning.

"Gods, you're fast," he said. "Now come back here again. We'll try something simple . . . like holding the dagger."

"I don't want to," I said. My heart was thudding hard in my chest and my arms tingled with fear.

Erick's grin vanished and the hard, dangerous look I'd seen at the fountain rushed forward. Face expressionless, he said, "Do you see that sack?"

I glanced toward the sack he'd placed inside the entrance to the courtyard.

"You get nothing from that sack if you quit now. And you'll get nothing from me again after today unless you stay."

I shot him a defiant glare from where I crouched. The sack was only a few paces away. I could snag it and be gone before he'd barely moved.

But then I'd be back to relying on the Dredge, on the white-dusty man.

My glare hardened, but I stood and moved again to stand before Erick in the center of the courtyard. The dangerous look in his eyes receded.

"Now," he said, calm and relaxed, "let's see how you wield that guardsman's dagger of yours."

He showed me how to hold the dagger—different grips for different thrusts and slashes and jabs—and where to strike. Not just to kill. Sometimes just to maim. Sometimes just to leave a mark, a scar . . . a reminder. And he showed me stances, for balance, for distraction, so the target wouldn't know you held a dagger until it was too late.

Just after midday, Erick called a halt and pulled bread, cheese, and thick chunks of roasted pork out of the sack. My stomach growled at the scent of the meat, my eyes going wide. Meat was rare on the Dredge. Unless you included rat. This was a feast, the meat juicy and tender.

An hour later Erick packed away the remains of the food, glancing toward the sunlight before turning back to me.

"Now let's see if you've learned anything."

We faced each other again, as we had that morning, only this time Erick set his dagger aside. I kept my dagger out, held as he'd told me to hold it, even though it felt strange.

"Attack me," Erick said, his eyes glinting in challenge.

I watched him, saw the muscles already tensed, ready to react. I frowned, gripped the handle of the dagger tightly, then let myself slip beneath the river.

The world grayed, sounds receded, until the only thing in focus was Erick, the only sound his breathing. I felt my own muscles relax, saw Erick register the change with a start of surprise, and then I struck.

Erick blocked the first stab, shunted it aside, and tried to grab my wrist. I slid free, tried to step in close, to use one of the moves we'd practiced that morning. But Erick expected it. I saw his counter on the river a moment too late to react.

His hand latched onto my shoulder as he stepped back. With a quick jerk, he spun me around. I barked a snarl as his other arm snaked around my stomach and drew me in against his body, pinning my dagger arm to my side. I struggled, pushed off with my feet, snarled again as his grip tightened—

Everything he'd taught me fled my mind and instinct came rushing back. I stomped down hard on his foot, and at the same time snapped my head around and bit the hand holding onto my shoulder.

"You little shit!" he spat. He shoved me away as he collapsed to the ground.

I darted to the side, bringing the dagger back up, but halted when I realized he was laughing.

He lay on his back on the ground, hand cradled near his chest, tears streaming down his face, the laughter sharp and loud.

"Oh, gods," he gasped after a long moment, chuckling. "That's enough for today." He rolled to his side, then heaved himself to his feet, favoring one foot. He moved to retrieve his dagger and the sack, shaking his head when he glanced at me.

I followed him slowly. He paused, as if catching his breath, his back to me, then knelt by the sack.

"What about my mark?"

His shoulders stilled for a moment. Then he gathered up the sack and turned. All of the humor had faded from his eyes.

"No marks for now. Not after the last one."

He handed over the sack. I stared down at it, twisted it back and forth, then asked softly, "Who are they?"

Erick hesitated. "They're people the Mistress wants dead."

"Why?"

Erick's brow crinkled, as if he'd never been asked, had never thought about the answer before. "I don't know. Because they've done something wrong, killed someone, hurt someone. Like the man who strangled that woman, the man you killed when I first found you."

"What about the hawk-faced man? What did he do?"

Erick shifted uncomfortably. "I don't know."

Then he pushed the confusion aside, buried it. I saw it in his eyes, in the way he straightened his shoulders. "I'm a Seeker in the guard, Varis. An assassin. I hunt for those that have run to the Dredge. I don't need a reason to hunt them other than that the Mistress wants them dead. I don't need another reason. That's all that matters to me."

"But how do you know they deserve it?"

"Because the Mistress tells me they deserve it. If the Mistress says they deserve it, if the Throne says they deserve it, then they deserve it."

"But what if the Mistress is wrong?"

He stood, reaching down to ruffle my hair. That something deep inside leaped at the touch, yearned for more, but his hand dropped away.

"The Mistress is never wrong," he said, but his voice was flat, as if he were reciting something he'd been taught.

"We'll continue with the training tomorrow," he said, and then he walked away.

* * *

And we did. Every morning I'd leave my niche hoping Erick would be there. Sometimes he was, sometimes not. If not, I'd return to the Dredge. Not always for momentarily forgotten bundles, or the stray potato. No. Erick kept me fed and clothed now, although I still scavenged the Dredge when Erick's food ran low and I hadn't seen him, still went to the white-dusty man if I was desperate. No. After a few weeks of training, Erick started giving me new marks and so I went to the Dredge for the people, to search for the men and women who'd run, who were trying to hide from the Skewed Throne, from the Mistress . . . from Erick.

I trained, but for a long time I didn't have to kill anyone. Erick took care of that. All I did was find them, then lead Erick to wherever they'd hidden in the slums beyond the Dredge.

It worked well.

Until Erick had me find Garrell Cart.

Garrell Cart: about my height, a little older, dirt-blond hair, muddy eyes, and a wide, light-brown birthmark near the base of his jaw that looked as if someone had spilled ale and it had pooled on his neck.

Garrell.

Squatting on the Dredge, back against a sun-baked wall, its warmth seeping through the worn shirt Erick had given me, I searched the passing crowd. I didn't expect to see him. I'd been watching for over twenty days now. I was waiting for Erick to give up and give me someone else to find.

I glanced down the Dredge, not really seeing the people, only the movements of the crowd, and caught sight of Bloodmark.

I frowned, heard again his whispering voice, *Don't mess with me, bitch.*

A brief stab of anger shot through my chest and I stood as I lost sight of him. I found him again, thirty paces down. He'd stopped, was looking at something I couldn't see across the street.

His eyes narrowed, darkened like they'd darkened the day he'd taken the sack from me, then flicked up and down the Dredge. Then they returned to whatever had caught his attention.

His head dipped slightly forward and he bit his upper lip. One hand reached for something beneath his shirt.

I stepped away from the wall and into the crowd, moving across the street. Halfway across I saw his target.

Without thought, I let the world slip into gray and wind, keeping Bloodmark and his target in focus. The crowd became shifting eddies in the gray, eddies I could move through as I continued to cross the street. I settled against the flatter gray of another wall and leaned back to watch.

The man Bloodmark had targeted stood near another man's wagon, hand resting on the back of the seat as he talked to the wagon's owner. Both men were laughing, shaking their heads. Bloodmark's target shifted his weight. As he did so, the small pouch tied to his belt swung into view.

I frowned and glanced toward Bloodmark. He'd moved closer, but not close enough for the strike. He seemed to be waiting.

My frown deepened. I couldn't see what would happen, couldn't *feel* what would happen. Not like before. I thought about the woman with the shawl, about that sensation of slipping deeper into the gray. Everything had been clearer then, crisper, easier to see.

Straightening, I drew in a short breath . . . then hesitated. Because of the nausea, the weakness and convulsions that had followed. I hesitated . . . but only a moment.

I tried to push myself deeper into the river.

Nothing happened except a faint tremor in my chest. I strained against the sensation, jaw tightening.

Then something slipped. With a fluid smoothness, the eddies in the gray-ness washed away, the wind of the crowd died down to the faintest murmur. Bloodmark and the two men near the wagon grew focused, the sunlight around them brighter. Their movements slowed subtly.

And farther down the Dredge, a new eddy emerged from the blackness. A group of five men, heading toward me and the wagon, at least three of the men drunk. They were slapping each other on the back, laughter sharp and biting, like spikes in the heightened sounds of the river.

I relaxed, the tension in my jaw loosening, and settled back against the wall again. The focus remained unchanged. I'd been trying too hard, trying to force it.

When the group of drunken men were almost to the wagon, Bloodmark moved.

He timed it perfectly, motions so subtle, so casual, I almost missed them. As the drunken men drew alongside the wagon, Bloodmark fell into place be-hind them, close, a look of annoyance set on his face, as if he wanted to get around them but there wasn't enough room. When one of the drunks slewed toward the man with the pouch, Bloodmark's hand reached out to push him that extra distance, to make the drunk stagger into the target.

Bloodmark needn't have bothered. One of the other drunks slapped the man on the back instead.

The drunk staggered, a curse spat into the grayness and wind as he reached out and grabbed the man with the pouch to catch his balance.

In the subtle, slow world of the river, I saw Bloodmark shift, saw the blade flash in the sunlight as he neatly sliced the cords of the pouch, the blade and pouch gone in the space of a heartbeat.

Then, the look of annoyance deepening, Bloodmark sidestepped the two stumbling men, the target holding the drunk up automatically.

The others in the group burst out laughing, then rescued their companion from the target. Waving toward the man and the wagon owner, they continued on their way.

Bloodmark skirted across the street, pausing at the entrance to an alley. As the group of drunks passed me, he seemed to sense that he was being watched.

He glanced up and our eyes met.

I nodded, with a slightly turned grin of grudging respect.

He scowled.

I was about to respond with a rude gesture when the cold white warning Fire that had nestled in the pit of my stomach suddenly flared, so strongly a tingle of icy prickles raced down my arms. Simultaneously, a tremor rippled across the dark gray and muted wind and I was struck by the putrid scent of blood and sweat and rotten butter.

I staggered back from the stench, eyes widening, and felt the world of gray and wind begin to slip away under the force of the Fire. Before the grayness completely fled, I reached out and held it. The gray steadied. The rush of wind that had slipped briefly into the roar of a hundred people, a hundred voices, pulled down again to a muted murmur. I'd risen in the river slightly, not as deep as when Bloodmark had lifted the pouch, but I was still deeper than usual.

And I was beginning to feel nauseous.

I glanced quickly toward Bloodmark, still in focus on the far side of the Dredge. His scowl had turned into wary confusion, the pouch in his hand forgotten, probably wondering why I had staggered back. But Bloodmark didn't matter anymore. Only the cold Fire still seething in my gut mattered. And the stench.

I turned toward it, breathing in deeply. The gray shifted sickeningly as I moved, blurring at its edges, but it held.

When I'd spun almost completely around, the stench so thick I thought I'd gag, I saw the tremor rippling in the grayness again. It'd taken on a reddish tint.

I focused with effort and Garrell Cart slid out of the rippling red.

I straightened in mute surprise, hand immediately falling to my dagger. Then the gray and wind trembled and with a gasp I was forced to let it go.

The world rushed back with a roiling twist, the noise of the Dredge almost overwhelming. I drew short, sharp breaths, trying to calm the nausea that came with it, trying to keep Garrell in sight. For a moment I thought I'd lose the battle, felt the bile burning upward in my throat, but I swallowed hard, forced it back with a painful gasp—

And then I was moving. It had taken me this long to spot him, I wasn't going to lose him now.

Instantly, the same trembling weakness that had struck me before coursed through my legs. *I didn't go as deep!* I thought to myself in anger and annoyance, and fought the weakness, pushed it back ferociously as I dodged through the crowd. Without the focus of the river I couldn't move as easily through the people, couldn't see the eddies, the currents. I swore as I stumbled over someone's foot, heard them curse in return, and then I realized that Garrell had stopped.

I halted in the middle of the Dredge, felt someone pull up short behind me, skirt around with a mutter.

Ahead, Garrell had paused near the entrance to an alley, stood leaning against the corner. A woman had spread a stained blanket out on the stone of the Dredge, broken pottery that she had repaired set out on the blanket. Her daughter sat on the corner of the blanket just before Garrell, staring down at a thin, faded green cloth in one hand. She was twisting it in boredom, her blonde hair half-fallen over her rounded face. Unusual blonde hair, the color of straw. She wore a dirty shirt that was too big for her, tied with twine at her waist like a dress. Her mother wore the same. Both were barefoot, feet dirty.

The woman stood in front of the blanket, her own long, straw-blonde hair tied back with a length of rawhide. Her features were more foreign than the girl's, her eyes desperate. A dab of blue had been painted onto her skin near the corner of her left eye, like a teardrop. She cupped a glazed bowl in both hands and held it out to the passing crowd in mute supplication.

I frowned. The two were obviously not from Amenkor. I'd heard of the blue paint mark. The Tear of Taniece, some religious sect from one of the northern cities along the coast.

I snorted. Amenkor didn't need a god; we had the Mistress.

Garrell was staring down at the girl. A slow smile crept across his face.

Something touched against the back of my neck, like a drop of water, then trickled down between my shoulders like sweat. I reached up to brush it away, but there was no sweat, only the sensation, the prickle of water against skin.

My frown deepened and I scanned the crowd behind me. Instinctively, I reached for the river and felt the nausea return, felt my legs weaken, and stopped with a grimace. I scanned the crowd again and saw nothing.

But there *was* something back there. I could feel it.

Then the Fire leaped upward again and I spun back toward Garrell.

He was gone.

So was the girl.

The green cloth lay at the edge of the blanket, twisted in on itself.

For a moment, I felt nothing but the Fire, heard nothing but the grunts of the first man I'd killed as he struggled with his clothing, his hand pressed down hard, so hard, into my chest. I smelled his musty shirt with the Skewed Throne stitching torn out as he crushed my face into his shoulder. I couldn't catch my breath, tasted the mold in the cloth as it pressed into my mouth.

Then the Fire blazed over me and I darted toward the alley where Garrell had been leaning, where the mother of the girl had just noticed that her daughter was missing. I halted at the entrance, leaned against one wall for support as a wave of weakness washed through me. But I didn't have time for the weakness.

I gasped in a few deep breaths, then plunged into the depths of the alley, into the depths beyond the Dredge.

I ran. Into the shadows. Into the familiar stench. The alley angled away after a short stretch and I slowed as my eyes adjusted. Too slow, too slow. There was no one ahead, only mud-brick slicked with mold, a trickle of sludge down the center cobbles, an alcove, a door farther down. I slipped down the alley, keeping close to one wall, my heart thudding in my chest. The Fire had died down, but still sent licks of white flame down my arms. I felt them in my pulse, in my blood, burning.

I reached out to the wall for support as I moved, fighting off another wave of nausea. I wanted to move faster, but didn't dare. Garrell could be anywhere.

The alcove was empty. The doorway had been bricked shut, the brick now beginning to crumble.

I moved on, hesitantly, toward the empty blackness of a window, another alcove.

When I reached the window, the darkness inside so complete I could see nothing, the Fire roiling inside my gut abruptly died down to a single coiled flame.

My stomach clenched and I swallowed against the sudden certainty that I was too late. I lurched toward the alcove, hesitated at its recessed wooden doorway.

Twisting the hilt of the dagger I didn't remember drawing, I pushed the door open with one hand and stepped inside with barely a sound, crouching low and to one side just inside the darkness. I breathed in deep, scented the mildew of the rotting door and something deeper, something metallic. Something I recognized.

I waited, letting the darkness recede into vague forms. Crumbled walls, another window, a second door. A broken table and shattered chair. A body.

I shifted forward.

The girl lay on her back, her too-long shirt rucked up to her armpits, her arms pulled above her head, angled and loose in death, her legs splayed. Her skin was hauntingly pale, except for the black of the blood trailing down from the knife wound in her chest.

I stood over her, stared down at her eyes—mere shimmers against the paleness of her face. The wetness of tears still stained her cheeks.

I thought again of the first man I'd killed, of his hand pressing hard against my chest, and drew in a long, deep, shuddering breath. Tears threatened to blind me.

I'd taken too long, moved too slowly.

The Fire had died, and in its place I felt hot anger. Like the anger I'd felt when I'd knelt over the man's body and spat into his face, flushed and feverish.

I turned to the second door, moved toward it without thought. No thought was needed. I could feel the anger in my jaw, hard and locked and intent. Could feel it in the hand that gripped the dagger.

The door opened onto a wall, a narrow running to the left and right. I couldn't tell which direction Garrell had taken.

I *pushed* myself beneath the river, violently.

Bile instantly rose to my throat, burning, and I collapsed to my hands and knees, hunched over as I vomited. The world of gray and red and wind vanished almost instantly.

But not before I caught the stench of rotten butter and piss and blood. It came from the left narrow.

Spitting out the last of the vomit, I forced myself to my feet, wiped the sourness from my mouth as I stumbled to the left. My legs trembled. One calf cramped.

Twenty steps along the narrow, past a sharp turn, I saw Garrell. He was walking away, his back to me, but moving slowly.

I came up behind him without a sound, touched his shoulder.

He turned with a slight start, that slow grin still on his face. Only now it was deeper, more satisfied. Sated. And now I was close enough, I could see it touching his eyes.

He was still back with the girl. I could see it there, in his eyes. Dark brown eyes.

I slid my dagger up beneath his ribs. The motion felt slow, practiced, but it happened in a heartbeat. I slid it in deep, then pulled it free and stepped back out of range.

I'd missed his heart on purpose.

He staggered back, his eyes widening. He wasn't with the girl anymore. His hands grabbed for both sides of the narrow, but only one made contact. As he stumbled, he tried to gasp. Blood poured out of his mouth with a rough, choked cough. Hand still against the wall, he swung backward, back slamming against the mud-brick. His other hand made contact with a meaty slap.

Then his legs gave out and he crumpled to one side, back skidding down the brick.

I moved forward and knelt over him. He was still breathing, through blood and spit and snot. Blood now stained his shirt where I'd stabbed him. The stain was spreading.

He tried to raise one arm, tried to reach for me. There was anger in his eyes now, and his mouth twisted. His breath was coming in shortened gasps.

"Die, bastard," I muttered.

And he did, his last breath coming in a bubble of blood.

It held for a moment, then burst.

I stared into Garrell's muddy, death-glazed eyes and shivered in belated reaction. Not a shudder of weariness from using the river, nor of nausea. This shiver tickled along my skin and brought hot, sharp tears to my eyes.

I turned away from Garrell's body and looked up into the blue of the sky, into the sunlight that somehow never made it down into the depths of the narrows, into the rooms with the bodies of the dead, or the niches of the living. I looked up at the sky with tears stinging my eyes and thought of the first man I'd killed, the one who'd been a guardsman, the one whose dagger I carried.

After a moment, I let the tears come. Not sobbing, racking tears. Not tears for the ex-guardsman who'd tried to rape me. And not for Garrell. These tears were for the girl whose body rested inside the shattered room, her arms loose above her head. And for the girl I'd been.

I was still staring up at the sky when I heard a rustle behind me, in the narrow.

I turned where I knelt, dagger held before me. At first I saw nothing but the darkness, still blinded by the sky. But then a figure emerged, huddled close to a wall.

The figure was too far away for me to see a face, nothing more than a shape. Before I could move closer, whoever it was turned and faded into the darkness, the sounds of their fleeing footsteps receding into the silence of the narrow.

I thought suddenly of the girl and rose. Leaving Garrell behind, I fled back to the room. I didn't want to think about what I'd done, how easily I'd done it. I didn't want to think about Garrell at all.

So I concentrated on the girl.

I hid the dagger beneath my clothes, then knelt and gently pulled down the girl's makeshift dress, hiding the blood and spatter at the junction of her legs. The length of twine she'd used as a belt was gone, discarded. I scooped her body up in my arms, holding her beneath the neck and knees. Her head rolled back, unnaturally relaxed, and I subdued an urge to sob. I shifted her arms so that they lay against her body, then stood.

She felt weightless, like a bundle with nothing inside, all loose and empty and broken.

It was the most horrible sensation I'd ever felt.

I found the girl's mother where I'd left her. She'd collapsed to her knees in the center of the blanket, her face empty. But her eyes continued to dart toward the faces in the crowd, continued to search. She hadn't seen me. Her shoulders hunched as I approached from behind, hitched with awkwardly silent sobs, her hands covering her face. The green cloth was twisted through the fingers of one hand.

I knelt beside her.

Her hands dropped instantly and she jerked away, face terrified, arms raised defensively. She cried out something in a language I didn't understand. I didn't move.

Then she noticed what I held in my arms.

It only took a heartbeat. And then she screamed. A rough scream of pure anguish that pierced the noise of the Dredge, that caused those passing by to halt in shock, to draw back. But she didn't notice. Her hands returned to her face, trembling inches before her, as if she didn't dare touch herself. Then she reached forward, tentatively, and pulled her daughter to her. She clutched her daughter to her chest, one hand holding the back of the girl's head to her shoulder, the other at the base of her back, crushing the girl to her. She hunched over her as she sobbed, the blue mark of paint near her eye vivid in the sunlight, her face contorted with a pain I didn't understand.

And so I fled. Back into the depths beyond the Dredge, into the narrows and alleys and hidden rooms. I didn't care where I went. I simply moved—away from the dead girl, away from the torn, pleading expression on her mother's face, away from the sensation of weightlessness. I moved, blinded by tears occasionally, but the tears came harder now, hurt more in my chest. I was too exhausted for tears.

Eventually, I realized I was heading toward Cobbler's Fountain.

It was approaching dusk, and I'd found Garrell.

I waited in a recessed doorway in sight of the fountain. I didn't like to come here. Not because of my tattered clothing anymore; Erick had taken care of that. Because of the memories.

I glanced up at the broken fountain, a mere outline in the darkness, and felt sunlight and water against my face, heard laughter. My mother's laughter, soft and deep and throaty as she splashed me. I giggled, splashed back. I could taste the water in my mouth, cool as it ran into my eyes, down the curve of my neck.

Hands lifted me from the fountain. I heard my mother murmur, *Come on. You've had enough fun for today. Time to head home.*

I turned away, shoved the memory aside in anger. It didn't matter. It meant nothing. It was too vague, too bright with sunlight and reflected water, the voice too soft and fluid. I'd been too young.

"Have you found Garrell?"

Erick stood on the edge of the open, cobbled circle around the fountain.

When I glanced up, his expectant face darkened and his stance shifted, became subtly more dangerous.

"What's wrong?"

His eyes shifted behind me, scanned the alley, the recesses, the doors, then back to me. He frowned.

The nausea returned when his gaze fell on me, and I turned away.

"I found him," I said.

I led him back to the narrow, through the night. I didn't look back, but I could feel him following, wary, his hand close to his dagger.

I halted ten paces away from the body and sank down into an uncomfortable crouch against the wall. Erick paused just behind me in the darkness, then edged past, his hand resting briefly on my head. The touch was gentle, reassuring, and I felt my chest clench and harden, my eyes burn again.

I hunched over my knees, pulled them to my chest.

Erick knelt at Garrell's side a long moment, then stood.

"Did you do this?" he asked. His voice was emotionless and he did not turn.

Before I could answer, someone else spat, "She killed him. I saw her."

I jerked upright, hand groping for my dagger.

Erick barely reacted, merely turned toward the voice. "Come here," he said, hard and unforgiving.

Farther down the narrow, a shadow detached itself from the wall and hesitantly moved forward. The figure kept to the deeper darknesses, kept itself hidden, but as it moved closer, it seemed to gain confidence.

When he came close enough to be recognized, he stood straight, face wary but head high.

Erick shifted toward him. "Who are you?"

"Bloodmark," I said sharply, my voice laced with hate.

Both Erick and Bloodmark turned toward me, Erick with a frown, Bloodmark with a contemptuous sneer.

"Is that your name?" Erick asked.

Bloodmark's sneer faded. "It's as good a name as any."

Erick nodded, as if he'd expected the response.

Then he seemed to dismiss Bloodmark entirely and turned toward me.

"Come here," he said.

I hesitated, uncertain what Erick intended. But all of the brittleness had left his voice, and I was used to following his orders now because of the training. I trusted him.

I stepped forward until I stood beside Erick, over Garrell's body.

Bloodmark sank into a crouch less than ten paces away, but I barely noticed him.

I looked into Garrell's face, as I'd done earlier. But now all the hatred and anger had faded. I felt nothing but a trembling, weak shame.

Erick leaned forward, close enough I could feel his breath tickling the back of my neck.

"Go ahead and mark him," he murmured.

I flinched, stepped back in horror, but Erick stopped me, his hand against my back. He pressed me forward.

"No," I breathed, shaking my head.

"Why not? You killed him, didn't you?" Still a murmur, but hardened now, insistent.

"I saw her kill him," Bloodmark interjected. "She touched his shoulder and when he turned she stabbed him!"

Erick jerked his head toward Bloodmark, cutting him off. "If you say one more word, I'll cut out your tongue, gutterscum."

The threat sent a shiver down my back, to where Erick's hand still held me in place. My skin prickled.

Then Erick's breath touched my neck again.

"You killed him, didn't you?"

I nodded, felt the dagger slice up through Garrell's shirt, snagging slightly, then slipping into flesh. With a torn voice, I breathed, "Yes."

"Then you deserve the mark."

His hand left my back and he stepped away. Not far, but enough so that the world seemed to narrow down to just me and Garrell, to his shadowed face and muddy eyes, the ale-stain of the birthmark on his neck a pool of black against his skin.

I knelt, my dagger already in my hand. The stench of death, of blood and piss and shit, filtered through the stench of rot from the narrow.

I hesitated.

"But I killed the man who tried to strangle me. I killed the fat man. You marked them both. Not me."

From what felt like a great distance, Erick said, "You killed the man who tried to strangle you to save yourself. And you killed the fat man to save me. This one is different, Varis. You killed him because it was necessary. Because you wanted to."

I brought the dagger up to Garrell's forehead, placed the blade against his skin, then hesitated again.

I closed my eyes and thought about the man with the garrote, felt the cord as it bit into my neck. I still carried a faint scar, a circle of white, with a vertical line where I'd cut myself with my own dagger to get free. I thought about leaning over him, staring into his face, then spitting on him.

The hot anger of that moment returned with a flush and I opened my eyes, looked down into Garrell's face again. Only this time I didn't see the shadows against his skin, the muddiness of his eyes, the dark blood of the birthmark.

I saw him staring down at the girl with the straw-blonde hair as she toyed with the green cloth. I saw the slow smile as it spread across his face. That slow, casual grin.

The hot anger spread through my chest, down into my arms, and I straightened where I knelt. My jaw clenched, and with firm strokes I sliced the Skewed Throne into Garrell's forehead, then sat back.

There was no blood. And the mark didn't have the smooth lines of the mark Erick had made on the man who'd tried to strangle me. But it was clear it was the Skewed Throne.

Erick moved forward, rested his hand on my shoulder. "Good."

But I barely heard him. Instead I shuddered.

Erick squeezed my shoulder.

Bloodmark snorted. "That's it? She kills him, she marks him, and that's it? You're the fucking guard!"

Erick moved so fast I barely saw him. In three short steps he was at Bloodmark's side. His hand clamped onto the back of Bloodmark's neck where he crouched and with a sharp shove he crushed Bloodmark to the ground, face turned, Bloodmark's ear and cheek pressed into the sludge of the narrow.

"I told you," Erick said, "not another word." He drew his dagger, brought it down to Bloodmark's face.

Bloodmark cried out, began to flail, his eyes wide. But Erick pressed his knee into Bloodmark's back, pinned him hard, hand still on his neck. He leaned close to Bloodmark's ear and the struggles ceased. Bloodmark closed his eyes and whimpered, mouth drawn back in a clenched grin of pain.

"The Mistress wanted him dead," Erick said. "It doesn't matter who killed him. I asked Varis to find him, and she did. It was her mark, her choice. The only question is—" Erick shifted slightly closer, his dagger touching Bloodmark's exposed cheek. Bloodmark gasped. "—what am I going to do with you?"

The narrow grew silent except for Bloodmark's ragged breath, rushing through clenched teeth. I didn't move.

Then Bloodmark grunted, "Use me."

I straightened, panic slicing through me. And something else. Something like what I'd felt when the rag woman had demanded my apple.

The apple was mine. I didn't want to share it. I didn't want to lose it.

Erick paused, drew back, his knee releasing some of its pressure from Bloodmark's back. Bloodmark sucked in a deep breath, coughed hoarsely into the muck. But he didn't move. Erick still knelt over him, hand clutching his neck.

"Use you?"

I shifted forward, started to shake my head in disbelief, in panic, but halted. Erick was considering it. I could hear it in his voice.

Bloodmark coughed again, then said in a choked voice, "Use me. Like you use her." He shot a glare of hatred toward me, one that Erick couldn't see. "Have me hunt for these marks. I can find them as easily as she can."

I drew breath to tell Erick, "No," to tell him about Bloodmark leaning close and breathing, *Don't mess with me, bitch*, to tell him that Bloodmark couldn't be trusted.

But Erick looked at me. He'd already decided. I could see it in his eyes.

"Two pairs of eyes would be better than one," he said.

I let the drawn breath out in a ragged sigh.

It was already too late.

✛— The Palace —✛

Dressed as a page boy, I walked down the center of the hallway, face intent with concentration, as if I were on a crucial errand for someone important and could not be disturbed. I'd worked my way from the outskirts of the main palace to within a few rooms of the edge of the inner sanctum, delineated by the original castle's wall. Those stone ramparts, rather than being torn down, had been subsumed as the original castle grew in size, so that what had once been the castle's main defense now formed the walls of numerous rooms inside the palace itself. What had once been a gate was now the main door into the inner sanctum, where the throne room and the Mistress' chambers lay.

That doorway would be heavily guarded.

I referred to my mental map of the palace, then slowed as the hallway came to an end. The room beyond was lit with oil sconces set into the ceiling's support pillars, but only down its center. To either side, the room was dark and empty of people, but lined with plants—small trees in wide pots; scattered smaller bushes with scented flowers in urns. A complex tracery of vines clung to the wall.

I moved through the room without pausing, intent on the hallway beyond. The main entrance to the inner sanctum should be just ahead.

A moment later, the light in the corridor increased. Then the hallway opened up into a high-ceilinged concourse to the left and right.

I slowed, footsteps echoing as I moved farther out into the open space. Potted trees lined either side of the concourse, separated by huge tapestries taking up entire sections of wall between one arching support and the next. The ceiling rose at least twenty feet overhead, the stone supports curving together and meeting at a sharp peak. Windows appeared black with night high above, darker than the shadows.

Someone coughed, the sound loud in the silence of the concourse. I started and turned to the right, where according to the map, the main entrance lay.

The door was huge, banded with iron and polished to a sheen that almost glowed with its own light. It was recessed almost ten feet, and the original arch of what had been the outer gate of the wall could be seen clearly, the stone gray and stained with the exposure to the elements. Banners of all colors were arrayed around the door to either side, each on its own pole. Standing at attention in filed rank before the door were six palace guardsmen, heavily armored. If it hadn't been for the cough, I would have thought they were statues.

Suddenly aware that I stood in the middle of the concourse staring down its length at six trained men with sharp swords, I turned and hurried to where the hallway I'd used to enter the concourse continued on the far side. I tried to act like a page boy who'd been awed by the spectacle but had suddenly remembered his duty.

Once out of sight of the guardsmen, the look of awe on my face fell into a scowl.

Fool! Gawking before men who'd only want to kill me if they knew who I really was, why I was really here.

I shook my head but kept moving. A few empty rooms, a few more empty, half-lit corridors. After a moment, when there was no sound of pursuit, I allowed myself to breathe again.

There was no way to get through the main doorway, not with all of those guardsmen watching. There were a few other entrances—for cooks, maids, dignitaries that shouldn't be seen entering through the front—but all of those would be guarded as well. The page boy's outfit wouldn't work there either. The guards checked too carefully.

But there was another way.

I entered a waiting room. Pillows were scattered throughout the room amid low tables. A half empty pitcher of water and a tray of picked-over fruit rested on one of the tables. I lifted a clutch of grapes as I passed, but kept moving.

Then I froze, a grape half raised to my mouth, ears pricked. Someone was approaching. Two men, arguing.

As they drew closer, I realized I recognized one of the voices.

I scanned the waiting room, saw a latticework of carved wood screening off a small portion of the room for privacy, and dove for it. Crouched down low in the corner, I plopped the last grape into my mouth as the men entered the room, still out of sight.

"—don't think I can take another one," a man said. His voice shook. "The last one . . . I can still hear her screams. And the way she thrashed in the throne, as if . . . as if it were a bed of hot coals! As if we'd tossed her into a gods-damned bed of hot coals!" He drew in a trembling breath. "I really don't think I can stand to watch another one die. Not if it's like that."

"I agree."

I shifted forward, eyes narrowed. The second man to speak was Avrell, the First of the Mistress . . . the man who had sent me into the palace to kill the Mistress, had provided the map and the clothes and the key. Unlike the other man, his voice was steady and smooth, and soft like warm sunlight.

They were getting closer. But I still couldn't see them, not from this vantage. I pulled myself back against the wall and grew still.

Avrell continued, "You agree that there is no question now, Nathem? That the Mistress is truly insane?"

Silence for a moment, and then, reluctantly, "Yes." A pause. Then with more force. "Yes. Yes, there is no question now. Not after the fire in the merchants' quarter."

I flinched with guilt and shifted uneasily.

"It took the fire to convince you?" Avrell said. "I was convinced when she closed the harbor."

Nathem sighed. "Yes, that, too. How could she order the harbor closed? How can she keep it closed, with resources so tight, winter so close, and now the fire? It makes no sense. We must open the harbor. It's our only chance of surviving the winter."

They stepped into view.

Both wore the dark blue of the priesthood, the robes appearing black in the darkness; they walked without any light. A four-pointed gold star was stitched onto the chest of Nathem's robe, signifying his rank as Second. He was older than Avrell, with dull gray hair and an age-lined face; broader of shoulder as well, but he held his back straighter. And yet Avrell appeared the more poised, his hands hidden inside the wide sleeves of his robes. An eight-pointed star was stitched into Avrell's robe—the four-pointed star that adorned Nathem's robe but with four shorter, daggerlike triangles woven in between.

"But these attempts to replace the Mistress aren't working," Nathem continued as they walked slowly across the room. Neither looked toward the lattice-work. "We've tried . . . what? Seven times now? Something isn't working."

"I don't understand it either," Avrell said thoughtfully. "We're selecting the girls from the Servants as we've always selected them. We've used those with the most talent, those who've shown the most promise and the most skill at using it, but it's as if that isn't enough anymore, as if something *more* is needed." He shook his head, as if confused, but he kept his eyes on Nathem. "This has always been sufficient in the past."

"Yes, but in the past the Mistress wasn't insane!" Nathem interjected. "In the past, we were trying to find a successor because the Mistress was dead!"

Avrell halted. His back straightened, his lips pressed together. He eyed Nathem as the Second continued for another few paces before realizing Avrell had stopped.

When Nathem turned, his brow was furrowed. "What?" he asked.

Avrell said nothing, only gazed hard at Nathem. They'd halted near the table containing the pitcher of water and the remains of the fruit.

Nathem's brow furrowed further, then cleared as realization struck. His head lifted, eyes widened.

"On the Mistress'—" he began. But something seemed to catch in his throat, choked him off.

The room no longer felt open and airy and soft. Now it felt close and tense.

I drew back farther behind the screen separating me from the outer room. Nathem's face was clear through the latticework, even in the darkness.

"You said so yourself," Avrell murmured. "We've tried seven times, used the most powerful Servants, and in all cases the replacement—" Avrell halted, seemed to harden himself even further. "No. Let's be realistic. We can't afford to be anything else. Not now. Winter is too close. In all seven cases, the *women* set to replace the Mistress have died. Good women. Trusting women. Women we've found and raised and trained for this one purpose since they were children. Others have died trying to ascend the throne in the past, but none have died like this." Avrell's voice had risen slightly, but now he paused, collected himself. "Something is wrong. Something is different this time."

Nathem sighed. "The Fire."

Avrell nodded. "The Fire. And as you said yourself, in the past the Mistress has already been dead when a successor was seated on the throne. Even when the Fire first passed through Amenkor. That time, the Mistress was murdered so that another could be placed on the throne. Murdered because the Fire drove the Mistress insane and a successor needed to be named."

"You don't know that for certain," Nathem said sharply. "We only know she was killed. Not why. It was too long ago. There are no records."

Avrell didn't answer. Avrell and Nathem held perfectly still, Avrell rigid and imposing, Nathem indignant and stern, their eyes locked. Nathem's gaze searched Avrell's face, searched hard and quick.

Then Nathem rocked back slightly, as if struck.

A subtle move, but Avrell's shoulders relaxed.

"You can't be suggesting—" Nathem began.

"I'm *suggesting* nothing," Avrell countered, and his voice fell in the room like stone.

Nathem paused. "We're sworn to serve her," he protested, but there was no force behind his words. "We're sworn to protect her."

Avrell reached forward to grasp Nathem's shoulder. "We're sworn to protect the Skewed Throne, Nathem. We're sworn to protect Amenkor. Can you honestly say the throne is safe? That the *city* is safe? Think about the fire, about the closing of the harbor. What will she do next? As it is, we may already have waited too long."

Nathem still seemed unconvinced, his brow furrowed in thought.

"And then there's Captain Baill to consider," Avrell said, stepping back, his hand falling from Nathem's shoulder.

Nathem snorted in contempt. "Baill is a fool."

Avrell shook his head. "Not a fool, Nathem. He has never been a fool. He's following the Mistress' orders to the letter. He's filled the streets with his guardsmen to protect the citizens of Amenkor as she requested, closed the harbor as she ordered—"

"But what are we protecting the people from?" Nathem spat. "It doesn't make any sense! Baill has *seen* the Mistress. He *knows* the orders make no sense!"

"And yet he carries them out without question," Avrell said, voice weighted with meaning. He caught Nathem's eye. "Not even a token protest."

After a long moment, Nathem asked, "What do you suspect?"

Avrell drew in a deep breath, held it a moment before releasing it. "I suspect everything, Nathem, but can prove nothing. In any case, Captain Baill is not an immediate concern. The Mistress is. You've seen her wandering these halls. You've heard her muttering to herself, arguing with herself, sometimes in languages neither of us have ever heard. Are any of us safe?"

Nathem dropped his gaze to the table of fruit. "No," he muttered, his voice so low I could barely hear it. Then, louder, more forceful: "No. None of us is safe. None of us has been safe since the Fire. It did something to her, changed her." He squeezed his eyes shut.

Avrell stood silently, hands again folded inside the sleeves of his robe. He waited.

Nathem finally opened his eyes.

His face clouded as he looked down at the table and paused. "I could have sworn . . ." he began, but trailed off.

Behind the latticework, my neck prickled, the tiny hairs at its base rising. I drew back, even as Avrell tensed.

"What?" Avrell said. Like stone again, all the gentleness he'd shown Nathem gone.

Nathem frowned at the table. "I could have sworn I left a clutch of grapes right there."

Shit!

Avrell turned sharply, his eyes darting around the room, hitting the shadows, the corners, the shield of the latticework.

And there they halted.

I stiffened, could barely breathe. Everything shrank down to Avrell's eyes, to their dark blue intensity, to the narrowed, harsh lines that had formed between his eyebrows.

We held each other's gazes for eternity, for the span of three heartbeats—

Then, in a taut voice, Avrell said, "One of the servants must have eaten them."

Nathem frowned in consternation. "Then why didn't they clean up the table?"

Avrell said nothing, turned toward Nathem.

I drew in a slow breath and shuddered. I tasted fear like blood at the back of my throat.

Avrell held Nathem's gaze a long moment, until the frown faded from Nathem's eyes and he sighed, shook his head.

"Something must be done with the Mistress," he said.

Avrell hesitated a moment, not turning toward me, then said, "Something has already been done."

Nathem stood stunned, back rigid, mouth open, eyes angry. But then his shoulders slumped in resignation.

Avrell led him from the room. Against the realization that they intended to murder the Mistress, that events were already in motion, Nathem's concern over the grapes had been forgotten.

As soon as they drifted from the room, I slid from hiding and moved to the corridor. Avrell had known I'd be in the palace tonight, but he wasn't supposed to know where. And now I'd been held up, when I had to be in the linen closet at the time the guard changed. If I wasn't . . .

I shoved the thought aside, jaw set.

Then I began to run.

✝— Chapter 4

"No. Back off, Varis. Try again."

The river pulsed in my head, sweat running down my face in sheets. I barely heard Erick's order, too intent on Bloodmark's shifting movements before me, too focused on his eyes. His face was sheened with sweat as well, his hair plastered to his forehead in tendrils. Anger had locked his jaw rigid. A muscle twitched above his lip. His breath came in heaves through his teeth. We circled each other in the makeshift training yard, the light overhead beginning to fade. The Fire lay dormant inside me. Somehow it knew this was simply practice.

A surge in the currents warned me a bare instant before Bloodmark attacked. Bloodmark's dagger sliced low across my front, trying to gut me. It wasn't a smooth cut—Bloodmark's moves were never smooth—but it was lightning quick and full of violence. I slid back from the arc, moved forward after it had passed, close enough so Bloodmark couldn't maneuver easily, and made to slice across his face.

He jerked back from the stroke, anger flaring higher in his eyes as Erick barked, "Strike for Varis! Back off and reset. Bloodmark, you're not controlling your slashes! Power means nothing without control."

We began circling again. The anger had settled deeper, so deep Bloodmark was shaking. I'd tagged him five times already; he'd only managed to tag me twice. There'd been three draws. I only needed one more strike to win the bout. In all the weeks of training with him, he'd only won a single bout.

I waited, watching Bloodmark's eyes, sensing his movements. I knew if I waited long enough, he'd attempt a strike.

It didn't take long. It never took long.

He tried to control the lunge; I could see it in his eyes. I stepped to the side, attempted a counterstrike across his torso, under his reach, but he twisted, sidestepped, and cut back. His dagger whipped through empty space and I tried another lunge, but he was being careful now. We feinted and parried and lunged for what seemed an eternity, fatigue beginning to set in, but Bloodmark's anger began to override his caution. His thrusts became more erratic, sharp and loose.

When I thought his anger had built high enough, I exaggerated my fatigue, thrust forward and stumbled, presenting Bloodmark with an opening along my side.

He took it, stepping in close as I'd done before, driving the dagger home sharply. But I wasn't there. Instead, I twisted, fell down hard on my side, and cut upward, tapping his leg lightly with the flat of my dagger. I grinned.

"Strike and match! For Varis." Erick's voice held a note of controlled respect.

Bloodmark snarled, then fell on me with a roar of hatred, hand clutching at my shirt, pulling it up in a bunch as he straddled me. I gasped in surprise. I heard Erick bellow, "Fall back!" and heard his voice approaching, but it came from a distance. Bloodmark's eyes had fixed my attention, his dagger descending toward my chest.

My hand lashed out, caught his wrist and halted it, both our arms trembling. I felt a flicker of rage deep inside, hot and tingling.

"Fall back!" Erick bellowed, voice close now. It sliced through my rage, severed it. The tension in Bloodmark's arm loosened and he made as if to pull back.

I relaxed.

Then Bloodmark hissed, "Bitch," too low for Erick to hear, and the Fire inside me flared up sharply.

Bloodmark's dagger flicked outward, the motion small, and nicked my forearm. I hissed at the pain and my hand snapped out, hitting Bloodmark square in the chest, thrusting him away.

He yelped, landed with a thud, but scrambled up into a crouch in the space of a breath.

"That's enough!" Erick roared, interposing himself between us both. "What the hell happened?"

"The bitch shoved me off her, even though I was moving to get up."

I shot him a dark glare. "He sliced me with his dagger. Drew blood."

Erick's eyes instantly darkened and he turned toward Bloodmark.

"It was an accident," Bloodmark spat. "I didn't mean it."

Erick hesitated, uncertain. "Don't let it happen again," he finally said. "Either of you." Then he glanced toward the sinking sun. "That's enough for today. We'll continue with this tomorrow."

Bloodmark rose, brushed himself off with a sniff, then headed out into the warren of the slums. But not without a sly glance and a sharp grin back at me before he left.

Erick knelt as I shifted into a sitting position and pulled my arm out to inspect the cut. He frowned down at it. The blood had already dried, the pain gone.

"He did it on purpose," I said, even though I knew it was useless. "Why do you believe him?"

A look of annoyed anger crossed Erick's face and he dropped my arm. "Because he's useful."

"He hates me. And he's vicious."

"And you aren't?" Erick countered, standing. He motioned to my dagger. "What about that? A guardsman's dagger. We don't part with them lightly. How did you get it?"

A surge of fear stabbed deep into my gut. For a moment, I was eleven again, felt the ex-guardsman's fingers dig into my arm like spears and wrench me into the alley, crushing me to his chest. I had no time to react, no time to scream.

Got ya, little one, he'd breathed, the words a rumble in his breast. *Got ya.*

And then he'd laughed.

I looked up into Erick's eyes, the fear hardening into anger. "He wasn't a guardsman." I pointed to where the Skewed Throne symbol was stitched into Erick's shirt in red. "The stitching had been torn out."

Erick frowned. "A deserter, then. Did he have a scar along one cheek? From the corner of one eye down to the jaw?"

I nodded, pulled my knees up to my chin, not looking at Erick. I could smell him—the man that had taken me back then—could smell the stench of ale, of dirt, of the Dredge and things deeper. I could taste the mold of his shirt as he cupped one hand on the back of my head and pressed my face into his shoulder.

Don't tremble, he'd breathed, voice as soft as rain. *Don't tremble.*

I shuddered, heard Erick kneel down in the dirt of the old courtyard beside me. I felt him hesitate. Not because he didn't want to hear, but because he wasn't certain I wanted to relive it.

"Tell me what happened."

I squeezed my eyes shut, stifling a sob as I laid my head on my knees, facing away from him. I sat that way a long moment, then felt Erick's hand on my shoulder.

He tried to pull me in closer to him. I resisted at first, then shifted back and leaned into his chest, still turned away.

When I finally spoke, my voice was muffled, distorted with the effort not to cry.

"He caught me in an alley," I said. "Crushed me to his chest so that I couldn't breathe."

And that was all it took. I was eleven again.

And the ex-guardsman had me.

I could not see where he took me. I struggled at one point, but he only crushed me harder, all the time whispering, chest rumbling, breath coming in short, anticipatory wheezes. "Don't tremble, little one. Shhh. Shhh. Not far. Not far now." Then a low laugh, almost inaudible. "Not far."

Grunting, and sudden jolts, as if the man were fighting his way up stairs. Then he turned and crushed me between himself and a wall, one arm—the one holding my head—retreating. I jerked my head back from his shirt, gasped in a deep breath with a small cry of desperation, the air still filled with the stench of the Dredge, but with traces of night air as well. The man cursed, jerked hard on something unyielding that finally gave with a rotted crash, and then the hand was back, pressing even harder, and the flash of night sky vanished and I tasted rot and darkness again. He lurched back from the wall and now his wheezes were gasps, sharp and uncontrolled. His voice had deepened, grown dark and harsh. Now I could hear the death in his voice. No words, no hushes, only guttural needs.

And then the man shoved me away from him, drove me from the crushing darkness of his shoulder into a mud-brick wall. My breath rushed from my body even as I tried to gasp it in. My head cracked into stone.

The world swayed as I crumpled. I could see the stars, the moon, the narrow ledge where we had stopped. The wall I'd hit formed a second floor, smaller than the first, the ledge around its edge only five steps wide. Large enough for the gasping man to crush me where I'd fallen, hand pressed hard against my chest. He hit me, grunting as his fist connected, my head snapping to the side so that I looked along the ledge and over its edge. Dazed, the man moving atop me, scrabbling at my clothes, ripping them, I saw the city of Amenkor across the harbor. Not the Dredge and the slums, but the real city. I could see the waters of the bay, flecked with edges of moonlight. I could see the docks, the masts of ships, the strange angles of the rooftops and buildings as they rose slightly toward me. On the far side of the city, the layers of the palace glowed with firelight, faint and unearthly. I could feel a breeze from the water, clean and pure.

The motions of the man didn't register. Mind foggy, I stared at the water. I knew what was happening, what was going to happen. I'd seen it before, in the slums beyond the Dredge, in narrows and niches and empty holes. I'd heard screams, seen knives drawn, seen blood flow. I'd lived eleven years beyond the Dredge, spent one of those with Dove and his street gang of gutterscum, just long enough to learn how to survive on my own, how to steal without getting caught. I'd become numb to the death, to the disease, to the depravity. I felt nothing. Yet I was crying.

Then, through the haze of pain and numbness, through the night and the tears, I saw the horizon. The moon was high, but in the west, the horizon shimmered with white light, as if the sun were beginning to rise.

Except the sun rose in the east.

I frowned, and for the first time that day, the world began to fade to gray. The man crushing me to the rooftop slipped into a smear of red, his grunts as he struggled with his breeches slipping into the rush of wind. The world collapsed to the brightening line of white on the horizon, spreading north and south, growing in a long arc until it filled the night. It rushed out of the west, faster than the sunrise, a pure, brilliant white. And as it came closer, as the night brightened, I suddenly recognized it.

The White Fire from the legends.

It was exactly as the street-talkers had described it. A wall, filling the horizon, the flames reaching high, higher, reaching into the heavens, swallowing the stars as it came. Relentless, and so terribly swift.

The man atop me froze as the Fire entered the bay and scorched its way across the moon-flecked waters. The shadows of ships on the water and along the docks appeared against its whiteness and then were consumed by it as it swept forward. The docks were swallowed by it, and then it struck land and began sweeping through the city. As it rushed toward us, as it engulfed building after building, street after street, I heard the man atop me draw in a choked, horrified gasp.

Only then did I realize that there was no sound. The Fire was utterly silent.

In the moment before the Fire engulfed us, the instant before it descended onto the roof, I felt the clench of terror. My heart halted, my body tensed—

And then it was upon me, passing through me. I felt it scorch deep down inside me, deeper than the fear, deeper than the terror, deeper than anything I'd ever experienced before. It burned through everything, left everything exposed.

Through its whiteness, I saw the man atop me, saw his frayed clothing, his torn shirt. Something had once been stitched to the breast of his shirt, a symbol, the holes where the stitching had been torn out ragged and unraveling.

The Skewed Throne.

He'd once been a palace guard.

I glanced up into his face, frozen against the whiteness. His eyes were wide in shock, his attention turned inward. His mouth had parted, as if he'd been punched. Grit lined the corners of his eyes, his mouth, and mud streaked his hair.

I felt anger uncoil like a snake. Deep anger, resentful anger.

And then I saw the dagger.

The man's shirt was undone, the dagger exposed. Without thought, with a swiftness I'd learned long ago in the depths beyond the Dredge, a swiftness that had been honed while in the company of Dove and his gang, I snatched the dagger from its sheath.

And then the Fire passed beyond us. Night slammed down, harsh and hurtful.

There was a moment of stillness, filled with the man's tattered gasps, one hand still pressing down hard onto my chest, the other still tangled in the ties of his breeches.

Then the terror in his eyes faded as his attention shifted back to me. Shock twisted back into a snarl. His hand clenched on my chest, fingers digging deeper—

I slashed the dagger across his chest. A black ribbon of blood appeared, slick and smooth, and he lurched back. I didn't give him time to react further. I slashed again, the motion awkward and childish but purposeful. It caught his arm, a gash opening up, blood gushing outward, splattering hot across my face and neck. I slashed again, catching him in the thigh, and this time he screamed. A hideous, wet, animal scream that shattered the night.

My last slash caught him in the throat. Blood flooded down his neck and he lurched farther back, one hand jumping to the wound, the other grasping at air as his back slammed against the wall he'd thrown me against earlier. He hung there, mouth gaping wide, blood slicking his shirt, until he slipped down the mud-brick and sat. His mouth began to work, opening and closing, and still the blood flowed. Guttural, rasping sounds emerged, ragged and torn.

I rolled into a huddled crouch. He grasped at me with his free hand, fingers closing on air. Blood coated the hand at his throat, until it glistened wetly in the moonlight. His grasping hand shuddered, its motions slowing. It began to lower, fingers still clenching, until it rested on the ground. And still the fingers spasmed. The muscles in the arms relaxed and the hand slid from his throat, leaving a second trail of blood down his shirt, a mark on his breeches. Blood dripped from the fingertips.

The guttural, rasping sounds continued, then degenerated into wheezing gasps of air.

Then these ceased as well.

And I fled. Back to the depths. Back to the Dredge.

Back to my niche, the dagger still clutched in my hand.

In the courtyard, Erick wrapped his arms around my shuddering form and drew me in close, rocking me back and forth. The motions were awkward, as if he were unfamiliar with how to hold someone, how to comfort them. But I barely noticed, too absorbed in the memory of the Fire . . . and what had come after. I leaned into him and cried soundlessly.

I hadn't told him everything. I hadn't told him how the Fire had left part of itself behind, inside me, curled and dormant, how it flared up in warning when I was threatened. I didn't tell him that sometimes the Fire still burned.

After a long while, he gripped my shoulders and drew me away so that he could look into my eyes.

"He's dead now, Varis."

I nodded, sniffling, wiping at the tears streaking my face with both arms. "I know."

Erick stroked my hair, squeezed my shoulder once before standing. "Good." He glanced out into the night. The sun had set, the slums now dark except for the starlight. He sighed and turned back to me. "Are you going to be all right?"

I nodded again.

He hesitated, as if he didn't believe me.

I gathered myself and stood before him, looking him in the eye. "It happened almost five years ago. I'll be fine."

He held my gaze, searching, face grim, but finally nodded. "Then I'll see you tomorrow. I may have another mark by then. Someone for you and Blood-mark to search for. Together."

I grimaced but said nothing.

We never searched for the marks together.

* * *

"Have you found him yet, *Varis*?"

I started, Bloodmark's voice emerging from the night shadows at my back. He'd twisted my name, Varis coming out as a vicious hiss, with a tone like that of the wagon owner so many years earlier who'd called me a whore. And somehow, Bloodmark's voice had the same force as that wagon owner's kick, sharp and bruising.

Bloodmark laughed when he saw me start, then settled into a crouch behind me that was uncomfortably close.

I shifted forward. My hand rested on my dagger.

"So have you found him? The 'pug-nosed man'? Is that what you call him?" Even whispered, Bloodmark's tone was mocking.

I frowned in annoyance, then lied. "No. And I call him Tomas."

I'd seen him the day before, but not on the Dredge. In one of the narrows. I'd tried to follow but had lost him almost immediately. He'd had no scent, like Garrell, and there were too many doorways, too many paths he could have taken. If the mark was out of sight, I couldn't find him using the river unless he also had a scent.

And I did call him the pug-nosed man.

I felt Bloodmark staring at my neck, felt my skin prickle, but I did not turn. I kept my attention fixed on the Dredge before me, shifted uncomfortably again.

"Liar," Bloodmark said softly. I could hear the smile in his voice. It sent a shudder down my back, forced me to turn and look at his eyes, cold and empty in the darkness. His birthmark was black in the moonlight.

He held my gaze without flinching. His smile widened slightly.

He *knew*—knew that I'd lied, knew that I'd found the pug-nosed man . . . or at least seen him.

I felt the faint sensation of a hand pressing against my chest, the sensation limned with the frost of the Fire. It closed off the base of my throat, made it harder to breathe, to swallow.

I pulled away from Bloodmark's gaze with an effort, focused on the street ahead.

Bloodmark did the same, shifting far enough forward I could see his face out of the corner of my eye.

"What are we watching?" he asked, and this time he was genuinely curious.

My eyes flicked toward the white-dusty man's door involuntarily, toward the loose stone to the right of the doorway, and I saw Bloodmark's gaze shift, saw him frown as he settled back slightly.

The sensation of the hand against my chest grew. I suddenly didn't want Bloodmark to know about the white-dusty man, didn't want him to know about the bundles of bread the white-dusty man left beneath the stone outside the door if I left a length of linen there . . . and lately I'd needed to leave the linen more and more often. The slums were becoming even more crowded, the food more scarce. People were being less careless, had become more wary. If not for Erick and the white-dusty man . . .

I stood, startling Bloodmark enough he had to catch himself with one hand. His eyes flashed and his frown deepened. I stifled a brief surge of satisfaction at his reaction.

"Nothing," I said down to him. "Nothing at all." I suddenly didn't want Bloodmark anywhere near the white-dusty man's house.

I turned, retreated back into the alley, leaving the white-dusty man's empty doorway and Bloodmark behind. But I paused at the end and looked back.

Bloodmark still crouched near the alley's entrance, his gaze fixed on the white-dusty man's door. Though distant, I could see the frown on his face, the calculating, narrowed look around his eyes.

The hand of frost pressing against my chest flared, then died as Bloodmark shifted toward me. His frown dropped away and in a teasing voice that echoed strangely in the alley, he said, "Shall we hunt 'the pug-nosed man' tomorrow, Varis?"

Then, in a darker voice, "Yes. Yes, I think we shall."

I saw Bloodmark twice the next day. Each time he stood across the Dredge, back against a wall, arms crossed over his chest. His birthmark stood out a startling red in the sunlight. Each time he grinned and nodded, then pushed away from the wall and joined the flow of the crowd, turning into the nearest alley with a backward glance.

The pressure of the cold hand against my chest returned, tightening the base of my throat. But I pushed it down and focused on a loose bundle, a for-gotten sack, a wagon of produce that couldn't afford to miss a single apple or potato. Not now. And I watched for Tomas.

Toward midday, a low rumble rolled through the sky and for a moment people paused, looking up.

The leading edge of a bank of black clouds was just beginning to emerge from the west. As I watched, it began to obscure the sun.

The light shifted, grew gray. When I glanced back down at the Dredge, people were moving swiftly, bundles tucked close, shoulders hunched. Desper-ation fought with weary resignation on their faces.

I sighed. So much for finding more food.

I scanned the thinning crowd as the light darkened further, but didn't see Bloodmark. With a last look at the sky, I turned into an alley and moved deeper into the depths beyond the Dredge, toward the narrow where I'd seen Tomas earlier.

By the time I settled into a crouch beside a heap of crumbled stone, it was raining. Heavy at first, it tapered off as the leading edge of the storm swept past, trailing wisps of whiter clouds beneath it. I let the water wash down my face where I crouched, felt it plaster my hair to my neck, my clothes to my body. The trickle of sludge that traced down the narrow's center grew to a stream.

I scanned the alley, then shifted against the slick mud-brick at my back and relaxed. Time to wait.

A few hours later, I heard a chunk of mud-brick skitter across cobbles. I lifted my head, glanced down the narrow through tendrils of hair dripping water. But the narrow was empty.

I thought about slipping beneath the river. Not far, just beneath the surface. But exhaustion had sunk into my muscles—from lack of sleep the night before, from the wait. So I shifted position instead, dismissed the muted skitter of stone against cobble.

I had just resettled, was about to drop my head forward again, when the prickling frost of the hand returned to my chest. Lightly, like ice rimming the edge of a hand-shaped puddle.

I froze, eyes still on the narrow. When nothing appeared immediately, I let my hand drift to my dagger.

Movement. So close I stiffened in shock, hand still inches from my dagger. But the figure that stepped from a shadowed doorway only paused briefly at the edge of the narrow, then began moving away.

My hand fell onto my dagger and I shifted forward, weight now in my toes. I steadied myself as I watched the figure through the sheets of wind-gusted drizzle. Because of the icy hand against my chest, I thought at first it was Blood-mark. But no. This man was too tall, too broad of shoulder.

He halted suddenly, shoulders stiffening as if he'd heard something, then turned.

It was the pug-nosed man. Tomas. His nose had been broken, crushed and flattened against his face. He scanned the narrow, dark eyes intent, brow furrowed with suspicion.

His gaze had just settled on where I crouched when the hand against my chest flared with ice and a shadow dropped from a window onto the pug-nosed man's back.

The two men went down in a heap, Tomas grunting in surprise. I jerked forward, then forced myself to stop.

Bloodmark had crushed the man to the ground, had him pinned with one knee, as Erick had pinned Bloodmark so many weeks before. Except the pug-nosed man's right arm was trapped beneath his chest.

As I watched, Bloodmark raised one arm, dagger held in one grip, and stabbed the pug-nosed man in the back. Once. Twice. Both strikes were high, in the shoulder muscles.

It happened in a strange, rain-muted silence, the narrow glistening with dampness. The only sounds were a low gasp from Tomas when Bloodmark's dagger struck. Then Tomas seemed to relax, shoulders sagging.

Bloodmark hesitated, dagger raised for another strike. After a moment, he shifted his weight.

The pug-nosed man heaved, pushing up hard with the arm trapped beneath his body. Bloodmark hit the side wall, head thudding against stone, then collapsed.

As smooth as a rat, the pug-nosed man stood and spun. His hand closed around Bloodmark's throat, then lifted the gutterscum's body as if it were made entirely of cloth and shoved him hard into the stone wall.

"You fucking little pissant urchin," the pug-nosed man snarled. "Did you think you could *rob* me? Huh? I have nothing you can gods-damned steal!"

Bloodmark's eyes widened as the man's hand tightened, and an instant later the gutterscum's hands flew to Tomas' arm, grasping at the muscles there.

Bloodmark had lost his dagger.

I saw the pug-nosed man's shoulders flex—even after Bloodmark had stabbed him there—and then he jerked Bloodmark away from the wall, lifted him higher, so his feet were no longer touching the ground, and shoved him back.

Bloodmark gasped again. The pug-nosed man's hand was now shoved up under his jawbone, half hidden in the folds of Bloodmark's flesh. The palm lay against Bloodmark's throat, and as I watched the pug-nosed man began crushing Bloodmark's windpipe.

Bloodmark's eyes flew even wider and his mouth opened, worked hard for breath. His fingers began to tear at the pug-nosed man's arm, gouging at the skin, drawing blood. Tomas snarled again, tightened his grip.

I hesitated. On the edge of the narrow, Tomas and Bloodmark a mere twenty paces away, I hesitated. I felt Bloodmark leaning in close as I lay helpless in the alley racked with nausea, smelled his breath, garlicky and stale, as he breathed, *Don't mess with me, bitch.* I saw him at the end of the alley the night before, his gaze on the white-dusty man's door, eyes dark and intent and unforgiving. I felt the nick of Bloodmark's blade during the bout, saw his self-satisfied grin as he retreated.

I hesitated and thought of Erick, how I'd felt when Erick had glanced up from kneeling on Bloodmark's back and I'd realized he'd meant to use Bloodmark. Erick was mine. I didn't want to share, didn't want to lose him. Erick didn't see how vicious Bloodmark was, didn't see the hatred in Bloodmark's eyes when he looked at me.

Tomas could solve that problem. All I had to do was walk away. I could pick up Tomas' trail again later.

My eyes narrowed as I watched Tomas push even harder, hand flexing as he shifted his grip.

My own hand tightened on my dagger, then relaxed. I began to turn away.

Then Bloodmark's feet began to kick, thudding into the slick stone at his back in a feeble, erratic rhythm.

I'd moved the twenty paces before I realized it, stood at Tomas' back in less than a heartbeat. He never heard me, too intent on Bloodmark's face, now beginning to turn red. My dagger slid up into his back, low, exactly as Erick had taught me. It was the only possible strike. Tomas was too tall for me to reach his throat, his body too close to Bloodmark's for me to get a clear cut in front.

I backed off instantly. In my head, I heard Erick's voice, from the training sessions in the courtyards and darkened rooms beyond the Dredge: *It won't kill instantly, but they're dead just the same. They're walking dead men and they won't even know it. But they're usually pissed.*

Tomas grunted. It shouldn't have hurt that much—if done correctly, he'd never know he'd been stabbed—but I'd purposely tugged it as I removed the dagger so that he'd feel it. His head jerked toward me. Then he snarled and dropped Bloodmark.

Bloodmark gasped, sank forward onto his hands. His arms gave out and he collapsed to his chest, face pressed into the rain-wet sludge as he hacked in deep, harsh breaths.

I shoved Bloodmark from my mind, concentrated on Tomas. He'd turned toward me, reached around with one hand to feel his back.

It came away slick with blood and rain.

"You little fucker," he muttered. He glared at me, eyes so hard with hatred I stepped back. But I didn't hide, didn't cringe. I held my dagger before me and waited, weight balanced.

Tomas grinned. "Courageous little bitch, though."

He stepped forward and his eyes widened in shock as he staggered. He reached out to steady himself with one hand, managed to stumble a few steps farther. He leaned heavily against the rain-slick wall, trembling, breath coming in deep, wet gasps. Water trickled down his face, dripped from his upper lip and chin as his gaze fell on me again.

His eyes were no longer hard. They were surprised, and strangely confused.

"What did you do to me?" he gasped, swallowing with pain.

He stood a moment more, bent slightly forward, wavering as he tried to keep his balance. Then he sagged to his knees, and like Bloodmark, fell forward onto his chest, his arms loose at his sides. He landed in the little stream of sludge near the center of the narrow and water began to fill his mouth, before pooling and escaping around his body.

I relaxed, stood straight.

Bloodmark coughed. "He was my mark," he muttered, voice broken and hoarse.

I frowned at him where he lay on the cobbles, too weak to rise. "Not anymore. Stay here. I'll get Erick."

"Wait!" he barked, but then broke out in ragged, hacking coughs. He tried to rise as I passed, but barely got his chest off the ground before collapsing again.

I ignored him, too pissed to care.

I found Erick at Cobbler's Fountain, standing at the edge of the circle. It was still raining. He wore a cloak—as almost everyone I'd seen outside in the rain this close to the real Amenkor did—the hood pulled over his head.

He straightened as I approached. "What's wrong?"

"Tomas is dead."

He nodded. "And did you mark him?"

"Bloodmark tried to kill him."

Erick tensed. Through the rain dripping from the front of his hood, I saw his expression harden, his jaw set. "Show me," he said.

I led him back to the narrow, the light darkening beneath the clouds even further as night fell. The drizzle slowed, then halted, and overhead the clouds began to tatter, shredding like rotten cloth. The moon appeared. The air smelled crisp and fresh and I breathed it in deeply.

Tomorrow the Dredge would reek.

I noticed Tomas' body had been moved the instant I entered the narrow. I halted, Erick pulling up sharp behind me, his hood down.

"What is it?"

I drew breath to answer, then spotted Bloodmark.

He sat on his heels, back against the wall, a few paces farther down the narrow, almost hidden in the darkness. He turned as he saw us, face hard with anger.

"He was *my mark*," he said.

I lurched forward, knelt beside Tomas' body.

Bloodmark had rolled him onto his back, had beaten Tomas' face to a bloody, fleshy pulp. One ear had been ripped free and dangled loosely against the cobbles. Bruises lightly touched his neck but had not darkened. One side of his head had been crushed in, as if kicked. Or struck with a loose mud-brick.

And carved into his forehead was the Skewed Throne. The cuts were brutal and deep, exposing bone.

I choked on anger. The hot, flushed anger I'd felt staring down into the man's face in the alley off the Dredge. The same anger I'd felt as I sliced the Skewed Throne into Garrell's forehead.

I glanced up at Bloodmark and saw him draw back, eyes widening. I stood, stepped over Tomas' body.

"He was my mark!" Bloodmark barked, jerking upright, back scraping against the mud-brick.

I'd taken a single step forward, hand already on my dagger, when Erick stepped between us, his hand latching onto my shoulder, halting me. He faced Bloodmark, his back to me.

"Did you kill him?"

Bloodmark hesitated, hand going to his throat. The bruising from Tomas' grip had already darkened—a deep, ugly purple that appeared black in the moonlight.

"He was going to kill me," Bloodmark said.

Erick let me go, took a menacing step forward, and Bloodmark skidded farther down the wall.

"But did you kill him?"

Bloodmark shot a hateful glare at me. "No."

"Then he wasn't your mark!" Erick spat, and turned. He studied me for a moment, then stepped up next to me and stared down at Tomas' body.

He frowned. Anger darkened his eyes as well, mixed with something else. A hint of doubt. As if he were beginning to reconsider using Bloodmark. He knew I would never have beaten a mark, knew I would never have slashed the Skewed Throne so deeply into a mark's forehead.

A shiver of icy hope shot through the hot flush of my anger.

"Why did you try to kill him?" Erick asked finally. There was no doubt in his voice now, only anger.

Bloodmark had relaxed slightly, but tensed again. "Because he was the mark—"

Erick turned and with a single glare cut Bloodmark off. "No. You're only supposed to find them, then find me." He began to move forward, reached as if to grab Bloodmark's throat with one hand. But at the last moment he slapped his palm against the stone to the right of Bloodmark's head.

Bloodmark flinched, his hand still raised protectively to his throat.

"You only *find them*," Erick said in a low, angry voice. "Understood?"

Bloodmark snapped a narrowed glance toward me. But then something shifted deep inside his eyes. The glare sharpened, grew sleek and edged, like a honed blade.

Eyes locked on me, he asked, "The Mistress wanted him dead, didn't she?"

Erick pulled away, frowning. "Yes."

Bloodmark turned his gaze directly onto Erick and said with a confident, mocking smile, "Then it doesn't matter who kills him. He was my mark. It was my choice."

Erick's frown deepened, his own words thrown back into his face. He said nothing for a long moment, the air between them heavy with tension.

Then Erick pushed away from the wall. "And it almost got you killed."

I felt an acid surge of disappointment.

Erick turned away, dismissed Bloodmark without a sound. He began moving toward the end of the narrow. I couldn't believe he was leaving.

Bloodmark stepped forward, away from the wall, his hand dropping from his throat. "My choice," he said to himself, under his breath, as he watched Erick retreat.

Erick halted, back stiff. His gaze found mine.

His eyes were confused, uncertain, his face taut with anger. He knew Bloodmark was dangerous—I could see it—but he did nothing.

He must have seen the betrayal in my face for his shoulders sagged. He dropped his gaze and continued on toward the Dredge without a word.

Behind him, Bloodmark looked at me, eyes smug and defiant.

A cold, hard stone of hatred solidified in my chest, just beneath my breastbone.

When Bloodmark turned and left me alone with Tomas' body in the rain-soaked narrow, the stone remained.

I should have let Tomas kill him.

⊢— Chapter 5

I made my way to Cobbler's Fountain purposefully, walking down the Dredge until I was within a few alleys of the fountain, then veering off into the side streets and narrows. I was early—a full hour before dusk—but I wasn't here to meet with Erick.

I was here to stalk him.

I ducked into a narrow and crouched down, slipping from shadow to shadow, until I reached an alcove overlooking the circular fountain. Tucked into the alcove's depths, the wood planking of the door pressed into my back, I could see the statue of the woman holding the urn, her back toward me. Sunlight still touched the top of her head.

I glanced back down the alley, a nervous twinge in my stomach. It was early enough for people to be moving about, early enough someone might notice me. In the slums, no one would do anything but keep their distance. Here, closer to the real Amenkor . . .

There was no one in sight. I settled in to wait.

The sunlight shifted. Overhead, the few clouds in the sky burned a deep orange, like fire. The light began to fade.

Someone entered the area surrounding the fountain, footsteps clicking on the cobbles. I tensed, heart thudding in my chest, but it wasn't Erick. The woman cut across the open area and entered another street, a wooden box clutched to her chest.

I sank back against the door, felt sweat prickle my forehead, between my shoulder blades.

"What am I doing here?" I murmured to myself, my voice barely more than a breath, nerves making me feel sick.

But I knew. I could still taste the betrayal of the night before, like ash in my mouth. Erick should have stood up to Bloodmark, should have threatened him, abandoned him. He should have done *something*.

My brow creased with anger. Instead, he'd walked away. I needed to know why.

Something moved near the fountain, a subtle shift of shadow. I scanned the area but saw nothing.

I was just about to use the river when Erick stepped from the darkness of a narrow.

Bitterness flooded my mouth. I reached for my dagger, but halted, my hand trembling. I tried to ignore it.

Erick moved to the fountain, stared up at the woman's bowed head. In the fading light, I could see his face clearly. His eyes were troubled, the skin around his mouth pinched with worry, with doubt. He searched the woman's features for a long moment, then turned away with a sigh, still troubled. He began pacing the cobbles, circling the fountain slowly, waiting.

For me. Or Bloodmark.

I sat back. The bitterness retreated slightly, still there but not as strong. A queasy uneasiness in my stomach had taken its place beside the anger. Erick's face had been too open, too exposed. My presence suddenly felt wrong, a betrayal of Erick's trust.

But I didn't move.

Dusk fell, deepened into night.

My legs had begun to cramp when Erick's pacing halted. He glanced once up into the night sky, the stars brittle, the moon high, then headed toward the Dredge, not trying to hide, his stride steady.

I waited, felt my heartbeat skip, then cursed my hesitation—cursed the bitterness, Bloodmark, the sense of wrongness—and followed.

I kept far enough back that Erick's figure was just a shadow, seen only in the moonlight that filtered down into the alleys. He moved straight toward the Dredge, but turned before reaching it, paralleling it using the side streets and narrows, heading farther from the slums, toward the bridge where the Dredge crossed over the River into the city proper. The texture of the buildings changed. Crumbling mud-brick no longer littered the alleys, cobbles lay mostly whole underfoot. Candlelight appeared in a few windows, glowing behind chinks in the wood used to cover the openings.

My uneasiness grew. We were moving outside of the slums. The alleys and narrows—the buildings themselves—no longer felt familiar.

Erick only stopped once, half-turned as I slid into hiding behind the remains of a shattered barrel. Breath held tight, I waited—for him to turn back, to pick me out of the shadows and frown down at me in deep disappointment.

My stomach twisted in anticipation. . . .

But after a moment he continued.

A few streets later, he turned. When I edged up to the end of the narrow, glanced around the corner, I could see the arch of the bridge, could see moonlight reflected on the River, could hear the slap of water against the stone channel.

And on the far bank, Amenkor . . . the real Amenkor.

I stared at the buildings, noted with a strange disappointment that they seemed no different than the buildings surrounding me now. But different than those in the slums. These buildings were not half collapsed, stone sagging in on itself under decades of disuse. These buildings had edges and corners.

"Who goes there!"

I tensed, shrank back farther into the shadows, but the rough voice had called out to Erick.

"It's me, you bloody bastard," Erick growled, humor in his voice.

Two guards stood watch at the end of the bridge, pikes held ready. One of them shifted, pulled the pike back into a guard position with a grunt. "It's Erick," he said to the second guard, "the Seeker."

The second guard relaxed, fell back slightly as Erick approached. He appeared younger than the first. Both wore gold-stitched thrones on their shirts and were more heavily armored than any guardsmen I'd seen in the slums.

"Gave me quite a start sneaking out of the shadows like that," the first guardsman grumbled as Erick halted beside him. "You shouldn't scare us regulars."

Erick frowned. "I didn't realize there'd be guardsmen here."

The man grunted. "Captain Baill's orders, straight from the Mistress. 'All entrances to the city proper are to be guarded at all times.' The captain's set patrols throughout the city as well, and increased the night watch near the palace."

"What for?" Erick asked. "What are we guarding against?"

The guardsman shrugged. "Don't know. I don't think Baill knows either, but if the orders came from the Mistress. . . ."

Erick shifted uncomfortably, cast a glance across the river, toward the palace.

"If you ask me," the second guardsman said, "the Mistress has lost it."

"We didn't ask you, did we?" the first guardsman barked. "Now stand up! Hold that pike like you mean to use it, not like some slack-jawed lackwit!"

The second guardsman glared, but straightened, back as rigid as stone, and turned his attention toward the street. The first guardsman grunted, shot a glance toward Erick.

There was fear in his eyes. Hidden behind a thick layer of loyalty, but fear nonetheless.

It sent a shiver through my skin. The Mistress ruled the city. . . . No. The Mistress *was* the city. If something happened to her, it would affect everyone.

Even us gutterscum in the slums.

"Are you headed back to the palace to report?" the first guardsman asked.

Erick nodded, his attention still on the other guardsman, his face creased in thought. "Yes. But I'll be back tomorrow."

"Good hunting?"

All emotion left Erick's face. He turned and caught the first guardsman's eye.

The guardsman stepped back sharply, gaze falling to the stone cobbles of the road. "Forget I asked," he mumbled, voice thin, thready.

Erick didn't answer, simply stepped around him and crossed the bridge.

The guard waited a moment, then turned to the other guardsman and scowled.

Back pressed against the stone of the narrow, I hesitated. I could follow Erick farther if I wanted. The two guardsmen would be easy to distract, and they were watching the street, not the water. . . .

But I was already too far beyond the slums. If I entered the real Amenkor, I'd be stepping onto totally unfamiliar ground.

I wasn't ready to do that.

I hesitated a moment more, then slid back down the narrow, back into the darkness, wrapping it around me like a cloak.

I still didn't have any answers, but I'd seen and heard enough. For now.

I was moving through the depths of the Dredge, moving toward the white-dusty man's door, when I ran across the body. The man had been thrown into a corner of the narrow, where it turned and cut left. His head rested on one shoulder, rolled slightly forward. His hands lay in his lap, his legs stretched out before him, one knee bent outward. He was barefoot, breeches coated with mud, and his muscled chest was bare and streaked with blood. He'd been stabbed four times. Twice in the chest, once in the side, low, and once in the gut.

I halted as soon as I saw him, scanned the narrow in both directions. It was littered with refuse, with broken stone. A rat skittered along the base of the wall, then vanished through a crevice in the mud-brick. But otherwise I was alone.

Stepping close, I knelt, reached forward to push the man's face into view. But I already knew what I'd find, had known the moment I'd seen the body.

It was the mercenary, Bloodmark's and my current mark. Blue eyes, brown hair, sun-weathered skin shaved smooth except for a narrow band of beard on each side of his face, stretching from his ears to the base of his jaw. He reeked of ale, his dried sweat sick with its stench. A trail of vomit touched the corner of his mouth. A pool of vomit had congealed near his side.

Carved into his forehead was the Skewed Throne. Brutal and deep.

Bloodmark.

I lowered the mercenary's head slowly and sat back on my heels. The hot anger had flushed my skin again, but now it felt worn and used. I thought about telling Erick. But Bloodmark always killed the marks now, *our* marks. At least, if he got to them first. And Erick did nothing, said nothing.

Not after Tomas.

The thought sent a pulse of bitterness through the flush of anger, hotter and heavier, aimed at Erick.

I stood, staring down at the mercenary. He was only a shadow in the moonlight now. The sun had set.

I turned away, heading again toward the Dredge. I was hungry.

I crouched down at the entrance to the alley across from the white-dusty man's door and immediately noticed the tuft of cloth peeking out from the stone where the white-dusty man hid the bundles of food. A prickling sensation, like gooseflesh, swept through me and I smiled, my stomach growling. I'd left the linen beneath the stone a few days before, but there'd been no response. I'd thought that perhaps the desperation that haunted everyone's eyes on the Dredge now had finally forced the white-dusty man away, that he'd left, that he'd forgotten me. The thought had hurt. But the white-dusty man hadn't gone, hadn't forgotten.

I almost stepped out onto the Dredge, heading for the bundle without thought, my stomach clenching with hunger. But at the last moment, weight already shifted forward, I remembered Bloodmark, felt his breath against my neck from weeks before.

What are we watching?

I shuddered, pulled back and scanned the nearest alleys, the darknesses. Nothing.

I hesitated at the world of gray and red and wind, then pushed deeper.

I saw nothing, felt nothing, smelled nothing, until I'd pushed myself as deep as I'd ever gone before. There, the ice-rimmed hand began to press against my chest, so faintly it barely touched my skin, as if the hand were hovering a hair-breadth above my breastbone.

I sensed that I could go deeper, but the grayness had solidified so I could see into the shadows, could see oil light flickering a lighter gray in the cracks around the white-dusty man's door and window—oil light I had not seen from the alley. And the ice of the hand seemed distant, removed.

I drew back until only moonlight lit the Dredge, the tuft of cloth.

The hand against my chest faded.

I hesitated a moment more, then scurried across the Dredge, keeping low, keeping to the shadows. I crouched in the thin recess of the white-dusty man's door, removed the loose stone, then dragged out and opened the bundle.

Inside, there was a small loaf of bread and a chunk of cheese the size of my fist.

I smiled, realized I'd been more worried than I'd thought. And hungrier.

I sniffed back the worry, and grabbed the loaf of bread. I was just about to bite into it when the door opened.

Oil light flooded out onto the Dredge. With it came a wash of dense heat—

And the heady, overpowering scent of flour, of yeast and dough.

The scent struck me like a fist and suddenly I was nine again. Nine and cowering in the shadows of an alley, watching a man and woman approach each other, both lost, their eyes vague, in their own gray worlds. The woman had straight black hair, brown eyes like the mud of the buildings after a rain, and a bundle tied too loosely and held too far from her body. The man wore a rough homespun shirt, sleeves rolled to his forearms, old breeches, no shoes. His clothes were coated with white dust . . . with flour. His hands and face were immaculately clean.

They collided, and in the brief moment they were distracted, I stole two of the rolls that fell from the woman's bundle.

I thought I'd escaped as I retreated to a narrow across the Dredge. I thought I hadn't been seen. But when I turned to watch . . .

The man was leaning over the woman in concern. After a moment of wari-ness, she allowed him to help her to her feet. When she reached for her bundle, the man knelt and began gathering the fallen rolls. The woman joined him.

Then the man frowned, brow creasing. He scanned the ground, searching, as the woman slid the last roll into the bundle and cinched it closed.

He turned toward my darkness and stared straight at me.

I don't know what he saw. A girl pressed flat against the wall, mud-streaked, clutching two rolls to her chest. That at least. But he must have seen something more, something else, for the frown softened, relaxed. He settled back onto the balls of his feet, hands dangling between his knees.

What is it? the woman asked.

The man held my gaze a moment more, until the woman began to look in my direction with her own frown.

Nothing, he said, and stood.

And before the woman with the straight black hair and the soft brown eyes turned completely toward me, he touched her arm, distracted her.

I fled. I ran deep, farther than I'd originally intended. Because of the man with the white-dusty clothing. Because of the way his eyes had softened. Because he'd relaxed onto the balls of his feet and dangled his hands, instead of leaping forward to snag my arm, to halt me.

I ate the bread. I cried when I did, and couldn't understand why, but I ate the bread.

I'd followed him the next day, and the next. And eventually he'd begun to leave the bread beneath the stone outside his door when I returned the linen the bread had been wrapped in.

A shadow stepped into the light spilling from the white-dusty man's door. I glanced up. Up into the white-dusty man's eyes—older now, shaded with pain, with weariness. Gray streaked his hair, and wrinkles etched the corners of his eyes and mouth, etched his brow.

But I saw none of that.

Instead, I saw his eyes as they'd been on the Dredge that day, saw them soften as he stared at a girl pressed flat against the mud-brick wall of an alley.

Tears bit at the corners of my eyes. Tears of shame, of need, of hunger. But not hunger for bread or cheese. For something more.

In the depths of the white-dusty man's house, I heard movement. Then the black-haired woman stepped into view.

She held a long wooden paddle before her, charred and streaked with soot. A heap of dough rested on the long end of the paddle, ready to be placed into an oven.

"What is it?" she asked.

I stilled, as I had on the Dredge so long ago. I stilled and caught the white-dusty man's eyes.

He held my gaze a long moment, then smiled.

"Nothing," he said.

Something—a pain, an ache—surged up from deep in my chest and forced itself out in a hitching sob. I tried to hold it in, but it was too much, too large. Tears coursed down my face, and I closed my eyes, the sobs coming hard and deep. Not loud sobs. Wet, throaty sobs that forced deep breaths through my nose, my mouth closed tight, trying to hold it all back, to keep it all in.

The white-dusty man simply waited, not moving.

The ache—the pain—released, like the tension in the bundle when the blade finally cuts through the cloth. It released and the sobs quieted. My breath came smoother, deeper.

Someone touched my face, a gentle touch, and I glanced up into the white-dusty man's eyes again. And this time I saw the gray in his hair, the lines on his face, the age.

His fingers traced down from my forehead to my chin. He tilted my head upward, stared deep into my eyes.

I felt myself trembling, still weak and fluid from the tears. The skin on my face felt tight, my eyes sore.

"You've grown," he said.

Fresh tears burned at the corners of my eyes. It was too much.

And so I pulled away, his fingers sliding down the length of my chin. I stood, back straight, no longer the nine-year-old girl cowering in an alley, no longer a child.

I glanced down at the bread, at the cheese still bundled in the cloth. Then I looked the white-dusty man—the baker—in the eye. I held up the bread a moment, and said in a tight, strained voice, "Thank you."

The baker smiled and nodded, the wrinkles around his mouth and eyes more pronounced. "You're welcome."

I hesitated, felt the wash of heat and the smell of baking bread against my face, then turned and walked away.

I headed back to my niche. I squeezed through the opening, felt the mud-brick scrape my back, my hips, as it always did now. I sat, drew my knees up tight to my chest, the baker's bundle set aside, and dropped my head.

I did not cry. Instead, after a long moment of silence, I simply sighed, raised my head, and reached for the bread.

Erick found me in my niche a few days later.

"Varis?"

I hesitated. I didn't want to speak to him, didn't want to see him.

But I still needed him.

"I have another mark for you and Bloodmark."

My eyes narrowed. He knew about the mercenary.

I moved to the edge of the niche, crawled out into the sunlight, then stood.

Erick stood on the far side of the narrow, back against the wall, arms crossed on his chest. He watched me carefully.

"I've searched for you on the Dredge," he said. When I didn't answer, he added, "Bloodmark hasn't seen you there either."

At Bloodmark's name, I tensed. "I haven't been to the Dredge." I couldn't keep the anger from my voice.

Erick hesitated, asked carefully, "Why not?"

I caught Erick's gaze. "Does it matter?"

Erick stiffened, and his eyes hardened. His hands dropped to his sides. "No. It doesn't matter to me at all."

I flinched inside.

"I have a new mark—two, actually," Erick said shortly, angry now, too. "A man and a woman, Rec Terrell and Mari Locke. The man is thick-shouldered, husky, bald. He had a pierced ear, but the stud he wore was torn out on the left side. All that's left is a mangled lobe. The woman, Mari, has short black hair, a rounded face, broad hips. There's a scar on her forearm, almost healed, very faint. Someone sliced her up. The Mistress wants them both."

Erick turned, began walking away.

"Wait."

Erick paused but did not look back.

I bit my lower lip, thought of the white-dusty man, thought of telling Erick about him. But then I thought of Bloodmark, of the mercenary, of Erick saying nothing, doing nothing, and the anger returned.

Instead, I asked, "Why?"

Erick turned, enough so I could see the confusion in his eyes. "What do you mean?"

I didn't know. Why are you still using Bloodmark? Why did you walk away the night I killed Tomas? Why did you let Bloodmark win?

"Why do you do this? Why are you a Seeker?"

His forehead creased as he frowned. "It's . . . what I know how to do, what I was trained to do. It's what I've always done."

He hesitated, as if uncertain he'd answered my question, or uncertain of his own answer. Then he turned and left.

I should have asked him something else.

I never would have spotted Mari if she hadn't reached for the cabbage.

I was standing near the wagon, the ebb and flow of the Dredge washing unnoticed around me. I'd come out of habit, having nowhere else to go. I didn't need food. I had enough in my niche for a few days. And I wasn't looking for Rec or Mari. Let Bloodmark have them. Erick didn't seem to mind.

And so, when a woman reached for the cabbage and I saw the faint scar tracing down the length of her forearm, it didn't register. Not at first.

I glanced up at her. Rounded face. Short black hair. Brown eyes. A lighter brown than I'd seen on the Dredge before, streaked with yellow.

She met my gaze, smiled tightly, nodded, then turned. I nodded back, belatedly. I thought, vaguely, that she reminded me of someone. Of the woman the man had strangled, the one with the basket of potatoes?

I frowned.

Then it struck. Mari. My mark.

I jerked away from the wall, glanced sharply in the direction Mari had moved. The world slid to gray and wind and red, and I began searching the washes of red to find her.

She wasn't there.

I frowned, let the world return to normal. I stared down the Dredge—

And saw her. She'd halted before another wagon, this one loaded with carrots. She was talking to the wagon's owner, a bunch of carrots gripped in one hand.

My frown deepened. Keeping her in sight, I slid beneath the river again, slowly. Everything slid to gray except Mari.

I let my focus on Mari relax . . . and she slid to gray as well.

I bit my lower lip.

All of my marks had been red before, dangerous and deadly. Some had had smells, but all had been red in the end.

Mari was gray, and smelled of nothing but sweat and the Dredge.

She finished with the carrot monger and began moving away.

I hesitated, chewed on my lower lip a moment more, then followed.

The depths beyond the Dredge began to shift, as they'd done when I'd followed the hawk-faced man. Except now, five years after the Fire, the decay had crept closer to the Dredge itself, like a blight on the city and its streets. Mudbrick slipped to crumbling granite. Streets narrowed to alleys, then narrows, shortened and filled with heaps of decaying filth. Mildew thickened to slime, streams to sludge. The reek of the Dredge deepened, stank of piss and shit and rot. The light darkened, as if the depths of the Dredge were sucking it away, swallowing it as it swallowed everything that lingered too long, that hesitated. Soon, everything north of the River would be subsumed. I could see it happening, could feel the blight of the city on my skin.

Mari began to slow, and the sun began to set, the gray of dusk seeping between the stone. I fell back, crouched behind mounds of filth, behind heaps of fallen stone.

Then Mari turned into an empty doorway.

I glanced up at the sky. The light was fading swiftly, darkness descending like cloth, smothering and complete. In moments, the depths swallowed the last of the sunlight and stars pricked the sky.

I moved forward, edged up to the doorway where Mari had vanished. I stared into the blackness, focused.

An empty room, small, with three doors opening onto their own darknesses.

I stepped inside. Dust covered the floor, disturbed by tracks leading toward the central door straight ahead. Beneath the dust, a mosaic of colored clay tiles could be seen, most cracked, a few missing altogether.

I moved to the central doorway, noticed the flicker of firelight off to one side, through another doorway.

I halted at the edge of the second door.

Mari stood near the fire in the center of the room, the cabbage and carrots laid out on the floor beside her. She shifted a pot over the flames, face already sweating from the heat, then squatted down and began chopping the carrots.

Someone grunted.

Mari froze, the knife in her hand trembling. Her eyes were wide in the firelight.

In the corner, a heap of blankets moved, were thrown aside. A man propped himself onto one elbow. His ear was mangled, like a piece of gristle someone had chewed on and spat out.

His gaze wandered, bleary with sleep, then settled on Mari.

He stilled, grew suddenly focused. The bleariness faded, hardened into something terrible, something cruel.

"Where have you been?"

I drew back from the doorway, sweat prickling the back of my neck. His voice was dark—soft and fluid and dark.

Like Bloodmark's voice.

I no longer wanted to be here.

I heard a rustle of movement, then drew in a deep breath to steady myself and glanced back through the door.

Mari had turned back to the carrots. But her knife was no longer steady as she cut. "The Dredge," she said. Her voice shook.

Rec shifted, stood.

"And what were you doing on the Dredge?"

She didn't answer.

He moved behind her. His hands fell onto her shoulders and she drew in a sharp breath, her shoulders tightening, her body going rigid. She held the knife before her, pointed down, the blade halfway through a slicing of the carrot.

But the carrot was forgotten. Her eyes were locked straight ahead, strangely terrified and blank at the same time. Her lips were pressed tight together, trembling.

Rec leaned forward, one hand moving to her neck, to her shortened hair. His fingers closed into a fist in the tresses, pulled back sharply.

Mari gasped, sobbed, her chest heaving. Tears formed at the corners of her eyes.

"What were you doing on the Dredge?" Rec whispered into her ear.

Mari choked on her own words, her head pulled back, her neck exposed. "Food." Rec jerked her hair hard. "I got us food!"

Rec leaned back, but didn't release her hair. He knelt. His free hand shifted from her shoulder, reached down the length of her arm for the knife.

Her body jerked. "No," she gasped. So low I could barely hear it. "No. You said *never again*," she sobbed, eyes closing. "Never again." Tears coursed down her face.

"Shhh," Rec said. His hand closed about hers.

"No," she breathed, shaking her head.

"Shhh. Give me the knife."

I gripped the dagger in my hand hard, hunched forward, my free hand holding the edge of the doorway. But Rec was too far away, was faced toward me.

He'd see me the moment I moved into the light.

I clenched my jaw as the muscles in Mari's arm—muscles so tensed they seemed like cords beneath her skin—relaxed.

The knife began to slip, but Rec caught it.

Mari let out a sob—of pain, of despair, of weakness—and her arms dropped to her sides.

Rec drew the knife up to her face, let the blade touch the skin of her cheek.

Mari drew in another hitching sob, but her arms stayed lax at her sides. All of the tension had left her body. She lay slumped, head back, neck exposed, supported by Rec's body.

"Next time," Rec began, then casually stroked the knife down Mari's cheek, drawing a thin line of blood, "tell me where you're going before you leave."

Mari sucked in breath through her teeth as the knife cut.

Rec stood, let her hair free with a sudden shove forward. He dropped the knife to the ground beside her, the blade clattering on the stone floor. "What's for dinner?" he asked as he moved away.

Mari stayed hunched over, her shoulders shuddering, her face hidden.

After a long moment, her shoulders stilled. She sat back up, cheeks wet with tears but drying, and reached for the knife. She cleaned it, her eyes vacant and empty, drawn inward, the muscles of her face set. "Stew," she said.

Her voice had changed, had hardened.

Rec grunted. "Best get at it, then," he added, crawling beneath the blankets again. "Wake me when it's done."

My grip on my blade tightened, relaxed, then tightened again. But I shifted back away from the doorway.

I couldn't take them both.

And Mari was gray.

I sat back on my heels a long moment.

I needed Erick. Needed to *talk* to Erick.

I glanced into the room once more before heading toward Cobbler's Fountain. Rec was still wrapped in the blankets in the far corner. Mari knelt near the fire, staring down at the knife, blood and sweat dripping from her jaw.

Erick was not there.

I glanced at the night sky, at the stars. It was past dusk. I'd moved fast, but apparently not fast enough. Erick had already gone.

I sat back against the alley wall, stared out at the fountain.

The woman with the broken-off arm stared down at me, one arm still clutching the urn. I stared at her face as Erick had done weeks before, looked into its time-worn features.

I heard water, heard laughter, felt the warmth of sunlight against my face.

At the mouth of the alley, I stood, began slowly moving forward. Until I stood at the edge of the empty pool, looking down at its cracked bottom.

Except the pool was no longer empty. Not in my memory. It was full. Sunlight on water glared into my eyes and I blinked, felt warm hands catch me up under my armpits, lift me high and naked over the pool's edge. Cool water shocked through my feet, up through my legs, as I was dipped into the fountain. I screamed. A childish scream of delight. A six-year-old's scream. I kicked before my feet touched bottom, splashed water into my mother's face.

She had soft features, blurred somehow with the sunlight off the water, with the haze of memory. But I could see her eyes. Dark eyes, brown, almost black, with tiny flecks of green. They reminded me of the strangled woman's eyes, the one with the potatoes.

She jerked back from the spray, laughed with a slightly scolding tone, then set me firmly on my feet on the pool's stone bottom and released me.

I immediately knelt and began splashing with my hands, shrieking as she splashed back. I slogged away, stumbled on the uneven bottom, fell—

And submerged beneath the water. It closed over my head, enveloped me, cool and fluid, filling up my ears, my nose. The noises of the fountain's circle, of people talking, of children shrieking, of my mother's laughter, dropped away to a dull roar, like wind. The bright glare of the sunlight grayed. I'd clamped my mouth shut instinctively, but I'd kept my eyes wide.

The whole world grayed, grew muted.

Something inside me slipped. In the terror of the moment—a child's terror, riddled with exhilaration as well as fear—something deep inside . . . tore.

And something was released, surged forward. . . .

And then my mother's hands grabbed me, lifted me free of the water. I spluttered, felt water draining from my ears, from my nose. I blew out a rushed breath, water sheeting down my face, my hair plastered to my scalp, to my neck. I gasped in a breath too quickly, coughed hoarsely.

My mother pounded my back. *Are you all right? Breathe, baby, breathe. Come on. Breathe.*

Her voice sounded muted, unnaturally calm, yet edged with suppressed hysteria.

I gasped again, drew in another breath, then another. The spasms in my chest eased.

My mother lifted me from the pool, tucked me to her side so that my head rested against her shoulder, so I could see behind her.

The world was still gray, the sounds of the fountain still muted, as if I were still underwater, submerged.

Come on, my mother said. The edge of hysteria had left her voice, but now it sounded exhausted. *You've had enough fun for today. Time to head home.*

I clutched at her shoulder as she began moving away, trembling slightly, face pressed tight against her shoulder. But something in the gray of the world caught my eye, held my attention.

I lifted my head, and into her shoulder murmured, *Look, Mommy. Look at the red men.*

At the edge of the empty fountain, someone grabbed my shoulder and I spun with a snarl, the harshness of the sunlight, of the water, of the gray and wind and red men, jerking back to darkness and stars and damp, night air.

"It's me!" Erick barked, stepping back out of my dagger's range swiftly, one hand held out before him to stop me.

I halted, breathing hard, heart thudding. Then I blinked.

I'd dragged the grayness of the memory back with me. And beneath the river, Erick was a swirl of gray and red mixed together.

The sight was shocking. I'd never seen someone with mixed colors before, didn't know what it meant.

"I thought you heard me coming up behind you," he said, relaxing his stance. His hand dropped to his side.

Our eyes met, and something he saw in mine made him take another step back. "No," I said, then drew in a deep breath and pulled myself together. "No, I didn't hear you."

He hesitated at the anger in my voice, at its harshness. After a long considered moment, he said, "So you've found them."

"Yes."

He nodded. "Take me to them."

He turned, began heading toward the depths.

I straightened. "No."

Erick halted.

When he turned back, his eyes had gone blank, expressionless. "What do you mean?"

I narrowed my eyes, shifted uncertainly. "Not until we talk."

A flicker of surprise crossed his face. But then it blanked again. "Why now?"

"Because things have changed," I said without thought, and then realized what I'd said was true. Not because of the sense of betrayal that still burned inside me; and not because of the mixed gray and red of the river.

I drew in a steadying breath. "I'm not the girl you found vomiting over the dead body of that man."

Erick smiled tightly. Then the smile faded and shifted, and he seemed to really look at me, to see me standing there at the edge of Cobbler's Fountain in clothes he had given me—still worn, still tattered here and there, but not rags. I no longer crouched, no longer flinched away when someone reached toward me, no longer stayed in the alleys and narrows as much as possible when hunting. My head reached up to his shoulders, not his chest. And I walked the middle of the alleys and narrows now, walked the middle of the Dredge.

"No," he said, "you're not that little girl anymore."

We stared at each other a long moment, and somehow in the silence the heat of my anger faded away.

"So," Erick said, turning fully toward me, "what do you want to talk about?"

"The Mistress."

Erick frowned. "What about her?"

"You said that she picks the marks, that you only find them and kill them. That's what you do, what you were trained to do."

Erick's frown deepened. "Yes."

"You never ask yourself what the marks have done? Why the Mistress wants them dead?"

"No. I told you before. I don't need to know. The Mistress wants them dead, that's all that matters."

"What if she's wrong?"

Erick shook his head. The frown was gone. "She can't be wrong. She sits on the Skewed Throne."

"But—"

"No," Erick said with force. But there was strain in his eyes, doubt. "She can't be wrong. Saying she's wrong is the same as saying the Skewed Throne is wrong. They're the same. If she's wrong, then—"

But he halted, a flash of fear crossing his face—a fear that he quickly suppressed. A fear I didn't think was new, just as the doubt wasn't new. I'd seen both before, in his eyes after he'd backed down from Bloodmark, and again at the bridge leading to Amenkor.

"No," he said again. "The Mistress is never wrong. The marks deserve to die."

"Why?"

"I don't know," Erick said impatiently, not looking at me. "I don't think about it beyond that. I believe in the Mistress. I have faith in the Skewed Throne. There's a reason the marks need to die, one that only she needs to know. I don't. I'm not that important."

The doubt I'd seen in his eyes a moment before had crept into his voice. And I heard the lie. He did think about it, had been thinking about it, at least recently.

His faith in the Mistress, in the Skewed Throne, was wavering.

I hesitated, then said quietly, "Mari isn't a mark."

He looked at me sharply. "Why not? How do you know?"

I almost said, *She's gray*, but caught myself. "I've watched her." I saw Rec drawing the knife down her cheek, saw her eyes, the defeated slump of her body, her lax arms.

Erick's eyes narrowed. "The Mistress . . ." he began, but trailed off. He stared at me hard, considering, then drew himself straight. "Show me."

We didn't speak on the way into the depths. I led, moving fast, not hiding, not lurking, moving with purpose. Erick followed behind me, hissing once for me to slow. But after that he seemed to catch my urgency, sped up, enough that I could feel him at my back, so close he could reach out and touch me, push me.

But I felt as if I were already being pushed. I'd felt it as soon as we'd left Cobbler's Fountain. A pressure against my back, tightening my shoulders, prickling the skin.

So I moved faster. Until the night air burned in my lungs, harsh and loud and cold. As cold as it had been the night of the White Fire. Sharp and piercing. I heard Erick breathing hard behind me, heard him gasping at the pace.

But the pressure didn't relax.

Instead, it grew.

We were close—so close—when I felt the ice-rimmed hand press hard into my chest and heard the first scream. A woman's scream. High-pitched, desperate, and filled with shuddering, as if she were struggling, as if she were fighting.

I stopped cold, Erick staggering to a halt behind me, one hand on my shoulder to steady himself.

It felt eerily real against the icy pressure of the hand on my chest.

"Gods," he gasped, dragging in a deep breath. "Where is it coming from?"

I didn't answer. I knew.

I bolted forward, barely aware that Erick stayed right behind me. The scream filled the air, escalated, then dropped in pitch, fading, although still strong, still desperate. It was falling down into sobs, struggling down, trying not to give up hope.

I was at the doorway, colored tiles beneath my feet. I was at the inner room.

I halted at the door, caught myself at its edge. Rec's body lay half off the blood-soaked bed, his torso twisted, one hand stretched out before him, reaching. The spilled contents of the stewpot created a glistening sheet of wetness in the center of the room. Two figures struggled on the far side of the fire—Bloodmark and Mari. I saw all of it in a heartbeat.

But Erick moved faster.

Bloodmark had hold of Mari's wrists, one in each hand, one grip loose and cumbersome because he still held his dagger. Mari struggled, but there was already blood on her chest, seeping from a deep gash in her side, and another higher up, near her neck, above her breast. Her arms had grown weak, and she was sobbing, her head shaking back and forth.

Bloodmark snarled, let go of Mari's wrist with the hand that held his dagger, and plunged the blade twice more into Mari's chest. Deep strokes. Penetrating strokes. Each followed by a visceral grunt. Spittle flew from his mouth, his teeth clenched.

And then Erick hit him, body to body. Hit him so hard they flew across Mari, struck the granite floor and rolled. Bloodmark's eyes opened wide in terror. His arm flailed, scored Erick hard along his back with the dagger. Erick hissed, lurched back, away, and Bloodmark jerked into a crouch, coming around fast, like an adder.

All of us froze. Erick on the floor, on his side, ready to move, his glare focused on Bloodmark. Bloodmark in a crouch three paces away, breathing hard, dark eyes fixed on Erick. The terror in his face was gone.

Mari gasped, a sickeningly wet gasp. Her arms had fallen to her sides.

As I watched, she tried to roll over, pushing herself weakly up onto her side so that she faced me, her back to Erick and Bloodmark. Her eyes met mine and she sobbed, the sound shuddering in her chest.

She hunched forward, drew her hand up close to her face. It dragged on the floor, trailed through blood, flopped weakly beside her mouth.

She paused, gathered herself with a single breath—

And tried to lift herself up.

I watched her eyes close with the effort, watched the muscles strain, her arm tight, her chest tight, her teeth clenched. I watched sweat break out on her face, watched her eyes squeeze tighter, her neck muscles taut. Her shoulder lifted an inch. Her arm began to tremble. . . .

And then she collapsed, breath expelled in a ragged, hopeless sob. She cried into the floor, shaking, mouth flecked with spit and blood.

She drew in another breath and opened her eyes. She stared straight at me, seemed to be gathering herself for another try, her eyes intent, her palm flat against the stone before her.

And then she died.

✝— Chapter 6

The room held silent for a moment, stilled, expectant. . . .

"She wasn't a mark."

I said it with force, looking at Erick. The fist-sized solidness of stone began to form in my chest, right beneath my breastbone. Familiar stone. Hatred and anger made real. I tasted it, thick and fluid and acidic.

I straightened at the doorway, stepped into the room.

"She *wasn't* a *mark*," I repeated, louder, and knelt down at her side, placed a hand on her shoulder. But I kept my eyes on Erick. "She didn't deserve this!"

"What do you mean she wasn't a mark?" Bloodmark spat. His breath came in ragged gasps, deep and forceful.

"I mean that she didn't deserve this! That there was a mistake!"

Bloodmark snorted, turned to Erick. "That's the woman you sent us after, isn't it?"

Erick pulled his gaze away from mine, glanced down at the woman. He stared at her a long time, then said, "Yes."

"Then she deserved it," Bloodmark said. His breath had calmed, was no longer intense, no longer . . . excited. He shifted, wiped the blood from his blade. "Besides," he added, "she's the one that killed the man. She beat me to it, the bitch."

I shot a glance at Bloodmark.

"Shut up," I said, voice hard, vicious.

He glared at me, shifted his stance again. His eyes bled hatred.

"What? Don't you believe me?" He laughed, without humor. His eyes were dark.

I shifted uncomfortably.

"Oh, yes, she killed him," he said, voice softening. "I watched her do it. She moved from the fire and stood over him while he slept. If I'd known what she was going to do, maybe I would have stopped her, saved the mark for myself." He smiled, a slow smile, like Garrell's smile as he stared down at the girl playing with the green cloth. "She stood over him for a long time. A long, long time. She had the knife in her hand, turned it as she clutched it at her side. Then she knelt down and stabbed him in the throat."

"Shut up," I said again, but this time it didn't have as much force. I saw Mari in that last moment before I'd left, saw her squatting before the fire, staring at the knife.

Her voice had changed after Rec had used the knife to cut her cheek. It had hardened. Her eyes as well.

"I saw it," Bloodmark said, and his smile deepened. "I watched her do it."

"Shut up," Erick said flatly.

Bloodmark flinched, cast a glare in his direction.

Erick had moved while we spoke, so quietly I hadn't noticed. He now squatted, facing Bloodmark, his eyes intent.

"You watched," he said quietly, his voice deadly. It wasn't a question. "Why?"

Bloodmark's brow creased. "What do you mean?"

"Why *didn't* you stop her? Why *didn't* you act?"

"Because I didn't know she was going to stab the bastard. Besides, he was a mark. He deserved it."

"How do you know?"

Bloodmark grinned. "Because you sent us after him."

A stricken expression crossed Erick's face, a grimace of regret, as if he'd tasted something sour. But it cleared, there and then gone in a breath.

"No," he said, and shook his head. "I think you watched because you enjoyed it. I think you enjoy it far too much."

I straightened where I knelt at Mari's side. Hope flared up inside me, like fire.

Erick's gaze narrowed as he watched Bloodmark. I could see him thinking, could see it in his eyes, in the muscle that twitched at the back of his jaw as he clenched his teeth.

Then he shook his head once. "No. It's over. It's gone on long enough."

I almost barked a laugh, caught myself, held it tight.

Bloodmark stilled, and when he spoke, his voice was as low and dangerous as Erick's. "What do you mean?"

"I mean," Erick said slowly and with purpose, "that I'll give you no more marks."

Bloodmark's eyes narrowed. "You can't do that."

"Go back to the Dredge," Erick growled. "I should have sent you back long ago. Should never have brought you in on this in the first place, should have listened to Varis. You're too dangerous."

"They were marks! They deserved—"

Erick took one step, but Bloodmark was expecting it. He launched himself away so fast he seemed a blur. But he halted at the door, shot Erick a dark glare, me one filled with hatred and venom. And something more, something I didn't understand.

"Bitch," he spat.

And then he was gone.

Erick remained motionless, stared at me in mute apology. The flare of hope that had suffused me a moment earlier died, the stone of hatred and anger still burning beneath my breastbone.

I knelt over Mari, trembling, hand on her shoulder, looked into his eyes.

"You shouldn't have let him go," I said. "After what you saw him do. . . ."

"They were marks—"

"No!" I spat. "Don't tell me that! Don't—"

"They were marks!" And now his voice was hard, unforgiving. "No matter what you think, the Mistress said they were marks!"

I drew in a deep breath. "Mari was gray," I said. I ignored the look of confusion that crossed Erick's face, confusion that after a moment transformed into sudden understanding, as if he'd seen something for the first time, something that had been dangling in front of his face, that should have been obvious. I thought of what Bloodmark had said instead, that Mari had killed Rec. I knew what he'd said was true. I'd seen the intent before I left, in Mari's eyes, in her stance. But I hadn't recognized it, had refused to recognize it. "She was *gray*," I repeated. "She wasn't a mark."

"She killed him," Erick said, his voice grudging. "You heard Bloodmark. That makes her a mark."

"Does it?" I spat. "If that's all it takes, then I'm a mark as well."

Erick frowned. "What do you mean?"

"She killed Rec to save herself," I said harshly. "He's the one who sliced her up. He cut her while I was here, before I came to get you. He cut her because he enjoyed it." I shook my head. "Mari killed him to save herself, just as I killed the ex-guardsman to save myself, and the man with the garrote. Just as I killed the fat man to save you."

Erick drew in a sharp breath. Fear flashed across his eyes, and doubt.

But again he pushed the doubt back, forced down the fear. He shook his head, said in a tight voice, "It was Bloodmark's decision, just as previous marks have been your decision. He killed her, just as you killed Garrell."

I flinched, felt the dagger slide into Garrell's chest, felt myself step away. "No," I said, hardening my voice. "No. It's not the same. I *killed* Garrell. Bloodmark *murdered* Mari."

Erick glanced down at Mari's body, but said nothing. The fear shimmered in the back of his eyes, pushed back but not gone.

He knew what I said was true. But if he admitted it . . .

If he admitted it, then the Mistress was wrong, the Skewed Throne was wrong. And then everything that he'd believed in and trusted would be in doubt. No matter that the city had been slowly dying since the Fire, that the Mistress seemed incapable of doing anything to save it. No matter that what the Mistress *did* do only seemed to make matters worse. I knew the Dredge was dying. I saw it every day. I lived it. I saw what it had done to people like Mari, saw what it was still doing to people like her, and to me.

"You shouldn't have let Bloodmark go," I repeated, and then I turned to Mari, shut Erick out. It didn't matter now. It was done. Mari was already dead.

Erick held still a long moment, began to shift closer, but stopped himself.

In a strained voice, he said, "We need to mark her."

I felt the stone of hatred harden further. "No. Mark him, but not her."

Erick hesitated, then shifted away, toward Rec's body. He lifted the man's head, made three clean strokes, and then set Rec's head back down in the pool of blood that was already tacky, already darkening to rust.

I sat next to Mari as he worked. I heard her screaming, saw her in my mind, her body lax against Rec's body, shuddering as he drew the blade down her cheek. I saw her eyes—a light brown, lighter than I'd ever seen on the Dredge, with streaks of yellow—saw them flinch shut as Rec began to cut her. I heard her breath hiss between clenched teeth.

She had been gray.

I should have run faster.

I never should have left to find Erick in the first place.

Erick had finished, had come to stand beside me. He reached for my shoulder, but hesitated, not quite touching me. As if he were afraid to touch me.

His hand dropped.

And then the ice-rimmed hand slammed into my chest, so frigid I gasped. Its ice burned across my shoulders, burned up into my arms. It slammed into my chest with so much force I jerked backward in shock, stumbled where I knelt—

In the next breath, I choked on the smell of yeast, of dough and flour, the scent so strong it overpowered everything, overpowered the stench of fresh blood, of sickening sweat, of oily smoke.

"Oh gods," I choked, and tasted vomit. "Oh gods, oh gods, oh gods."

I suddenly understood the look on Bloodmark's face as he'd left. Hatred and anger, but mixed with self-satisfied content.

He knew how to hurt me.

"What is it?" Erick barked, stepping forward. His eyes were wide with fear. But he was moving too slow.

I turned from him, lurched up into a crouch and launched toward the door, stumbling with the weight of the smell of yeast, with the weight of the ice-rimmed hand burning through my chest. I gasped as I hit the edge of the doorway with my shoulder, then caught myself and ran.

Ran through the outer room, through the room with the shattered clay tiles, out into the narrows, into the depths beyond the Dredge, the depths that had swallowed me as easily as they had swallowed Mari. I ran through the niches, through the abandoned courtyards, through the alcoves and doorways and gaping windows and half collapsed walls, so fast Erick could not possibly follow. I ran through my home, catching glimpses of the other animals of the Dredge. The startled face of a man, no more than skin laid over bones, huddled over a heap of rotten garbage. The rag woman, who cackled as I veered past, her heated laughter echoing down the alley. The boy, no more than seven, who held a broken spoon like a weapon, who clutched a pitted apple in one hand, one side already rotten, already brown and writhing with maggots. I ran, gasping in the frigid night air, muscles burning in my legs. I ran for the white-dusty man's door.

The ice-rimmed hand blazed deeper, tingling now in my hands. The stone of hatred grew harder beneath my breast, grew larger, until it choked me, lodged at the base of my throat. The scent of yeast, of dough, of heat and flour, burned in my nostrils, burned on my tongue, tasting of bread, of rolls, of cheese—

And then the scent flared, so strong I gasped at the intensity, so real saliva filled my mouth, coated my tongue—

And then it died.

I staggered to a halt, cried out to the sky. A raw, unintelligible wail that drew from deep inside. A wail of pure anguish, that sucked everything from me, that sucked the strength from my legs, from my arms, from my chest.

I gasped, collapsed into the nearest wall, hit it hard with my shoulder, scraped down its mud-brick side until I lay huddled in a ball at its base, arms wrapped around my legs, face drawn tight to my knees. I cried—harsh racking sobs that tore in my chest, that filled my mouth with the taste of phlegm, that sent my blood pounding through my forehead, pulsing in my ears. I choked, not able to draw in enough breath, not *wanting* to draw in another breath. I felt a gaping hollowness fill me, a horrible emptiness that claimed everything inside me, everything in my chest, in my arms, in my legs. A hollowness that left me fragile, vulnerable, and utterly alone, that left me abandoned.

A hollowness that crushed me.

And I suddenly understood the look on the woman's face when I had handed her the dead girl. I suddenly understood that pain.

The thought brought my head up, stilled the sobs.

I'd killed Garrell. A sharp thrust to his chest, near the heart.

My eyes narrowed. The stone of hatred beneath my breastbone pulsed, its hardness seeping outward, stilling the tremors of weakness, stilling the liquid sensation in my lungs from the tears, filling the hollowness.

But it didn't touch the frigid burn of the hand pressing against my chest.

I stood, uncoiled from the tight crouch. My dagger was already drawn, already held loosely in one hand.

I had a new mark.

I slid forward, moving swiftly, but no longer at a dead run. Every muscle was tense, every sense alert. I bled from shadow to shadow, everything I'd learned of stealth and silence on the Dredge, everything I'd learned from Dove and his street gang of thugs, everything I'd learned from Erick coming forth.

Ten minutes later I slipped into a crouch opposite the white-dusty man's door. It was cracked open, oil light seeping out.

The ice-rimmed hand still burned on my chest, still tingled in my arms. But it had faded, the edge of intensity dulled.

I glanced down the Dredge in both directions, saw no one.

I moved across the street, slow and quiet, and settled next to the white-dusty man's door. Reaching out, I pushed it open farther. It creaked as it slowed to a halt.

A wash of heat pushed outward, with a scent of yeast, of dough, and of blood.

Something clawed at my throat, acidic and vicious, but I pushed it down, crushed it with the stone in my chest.

Through the door, I could see the opening of an oven, the flames licking upward inside. An oil lamp hung from the ceiling, over a long table, a few chairs. On the table I could see lumps of rising dough, a pitcher of milk, a bag of flour. Another bag of flour lay split on the floor, a white fan against the field-stone. Tracks marred the whiteness. Farther into the room, beyond the table, the long paddle I'd seen the black-haired woman holding when I'd been here last lay on the stone as well, the loaf of freshly baked bread it had once held lying on its side nearby.

And at the edge of the door, just within sight, I could see a hand, palm up, fingers slightly curled. A woman's hand.

I swallowed, felt tears burning the edges of my eyes. I moved through the door in one quick step, crouched low. I ignored the two bodies—forced myself to ignore them—scanned the room, found it empty. I slid to the only doorway, moved into the darknesses beyond, checked the inner rooms.

Bloodmark wasn't here.

I returned to the outer room and knelt down beside the white-dusty man. I brushed at the hair on his forehead, hair lightly dusted with gray, with flour. I let my fingers trail down his cheek, stopped at his jaw. I looked into his eyes, saw them soften there on the Dredge, saw them soften here in the alcove of his door, heard him say, *You've grown.*

I cupped his face with my hands, leaned forward over him, till my forehead touched his.

Then I sat back.

Bloodmark had stabbed him in the chest, had stabbed the black-haired woman as well. But on the white-dusty man's chest he had carved a parody of the Skewed Throne—three long, deep slashes.

I stared at the bloody gashes, felt myself harden further.

I stood, moved into the back rooms, returned with two blankets. I covered the black-haired woman first, then the white-dusty man.

Then I slid back out into the night, closing the door behind me. Standing in the alcove of the white-dusty man's doorway, I looked up into the sky, gazed at the stars and moon a long moment, saw them as I'd seen them the night of the White Fire—clear and vibrant and pure. And I felt the Fire inside me, burning with its cold flame beneath the frigid imprint of the hand on my chest. I felt it seeping through me, not fiery and seething, but slow and gentle.

It filled me with a preternatural calm, as it had that night so many years before.

I glanced back down to the darkness of the Dredge. I straightened, narrowed my eyes at the depths.

And then I slid beneath the river. Deep. Deeper. Until I could feel the pull of the ice-rimmed hand, until I could scent it—like hoarfrost, burning in my nostrils, metallic against my tongue.

I drew away from the white-dusty man's door, slid into an alley—

And submerged myself in the depths.

I followed the scent, the river smooth around me. I flowed from alley to alley, from courtyard to courtyard, through twisted iron gates, past crumbling statues. I moved through abandoned buildings, their insides gutted, their walls collapsed. I saw the gray shadows of people huddled in corners, so many more people now than before the Fire. As I crossed one narrow, I heard a low growl, glanced down its short length and saw a dog, its teeth bared, lips peeled back, saliva dripping from its mouth. Its eyes were feral beneath the river, black and haunted. Drool coated its muzzle, and blood bled from its eyes. Its hindquarters had collapsed, gone numb with disease, and it lay in its own shit and piss, unable to move.

I paused, stared into the low, ominous rumble of its growl.

Then I moved on.

The scent grew, and with it the frost of the hand against my chest. And as I closed in, moving slowly, cautiously, I realized where I'd find Bloodmark. The realization came with a hard twist in my stomach. But at the same time I think I'd known. Part of me had hoped, had thought there would be a refuge, a safe place, a home—

But he'd taken everything else.

A tension fell away from me, a tightness in my shoulders. I moved forward purposefully now, without seeing the depths of the Dredge.

Until I came to my niche.

I paused outside the entrance, knelt down a few paces away to stare into the narrow darkness.

The scent of hoarfrost was strong, overpowering. It rolled from the entrance to the niche like the heat had rolled from the white-dusty man's door, but cold instead. The ice-rimmed hand against my chest burned so harshly it felt as if my skin would freeze, would peel away in chunks.

The sensations were so intense, I never felt Bloodmark approach.

I sensed the kick a moment before it struck, tensed for the blow as I'd done a thousand times on the Dredge, ready to absorb it and flee to a safer darkness.

But this time I wouldn't run.

Bloodmark's foot dug in just beneath my ribs, forced itself up into my stomach with enough strength that it lifted me, flung me to the side, twisted me onto my back. The air was thrust from my lungs, but before I could suck in another breath, Bloodmark stomped onto my chest, his heel landing squarely on the ice-rimmed hand.

I doubled over, curled up tight over the sudden, vicious pain, rolled onto my side, coughed against the burning in my lungs.

I lost my hold on the river.

The instant the darkness of true night closed around me, I felt the backlash of nausea begin in the pit of my stomach, felt the tremors of weakness begin to course down the muscles of my arms.

My eyes flew wide in fear.

"Bitch," Bloodmark said.

I struggled to rise, heard Bloodmark's footsteps as he moved around behind me. The tremors shuddered through my shoulders now, through my legs.

I focused on Bloodmark, on the sounds of his movements, on the pain in my gut, in my chest. I focused on breathing, each intake painful.

"You ruined everything!" Bloodmark spat, punctuating it with another kick, this time to my lower back.

Fresh pain sheeted up my side and I jerked out of the protective curl, rolled onto my back again, then over onto the other side with a barked cry, my arms tucked close to my chest.

But the pain pushed the tremors back.

Bloodmark moved in close, squatted down beside me.

"Did you find them?" he asked quietly, then laughed. "I left them for you. And for Erick." His voice turned bitter. "He was my ticket into the Guard."

"They would never have taken you," I gasped, the words broken, breathless.

"Why not?"

I shifted, enough so I could look up into Bloodmark's eyes, so dark and vicious, enough to free the arm tucked closest to the ground.

"Because," I muttered, so softly Bloodmark leaned down closer to hear, leaned close enough I could see the black smear of the birthmark next to his eye. I smiled—a slow, satisfied smile. "Because you're gutterscum. Just like me."

I shoved my dagger up along his neck, drawing a thin line beneath his chin before the blade punched up under his jawbone. Blood splashed my hand, hot and slick, and then Bloodmark jerked back, a strange, gurgling croak coming from his open mouth. The dagger slid free, followed by another wash of blood, and Bloodmark's hand clamped to his throat, to his jaw. He staggered backward, struck the mud-brick of the collapsing wall beside my niche, and skidded down it until he sat against the heels of his feet.

My hand, the one that held the dagger, slumped to the ground. Tremors were rippling through me now and I could no longer hold it up. I let my head rest against the dirt-smeared cobblestones of the narrow, let the tension in my shoulders release, but I didn't take my eyes off Bloodmark.

He stared at me with horrified, hate-filled eyes. His jaw worked as he tried to speak, but nothing came out except a sickening wheeze of air and a speckle of blood. Blood coated the hand clutched to his throat as well.

I thought of the first man I'd killed, of his hand clutching the cut across his own throat. I thought of the White Fire.

Bloodmark's eyes widened and his body began to slip. The hand at his throat fell away. As it did he lost his balance.

He slumped to one side, falling across the opening to my niche, his body landing with a low, rustling thud.

His blood-soaked hand flopped out toward me, as if he were reaching for me.

I stared into his dead eyes and then the tremors took me.

The world faded, and I closed my eyes. I felt the spasms shudder through my body, felt the pain from Bloodmark's kicks pierce through my chest, but it was all distant, removed. I drew myself away, too exhausted for anything to matter, too beaten down to care. I thought of nothing, simply stared into the darkness behind my eyes and waited.

It took longer than I expected. I'd stayed beneath the river far longer than I ever had before, had pushed myself harder than I ever had before.

When the worst of the spasms finally passed, I rolled onto my stomach and pushed myself up onto my hands and knees, thinking of Mari, of Erick. *You heard Bloodmark. She killed him. That makes her a mark.* Nausea rippled through me and I vomited onto the cobbles. Hanging my head, I waited for this to pass as well, then climbed weakly to my feet.

It was still night, still dark. But dawn had begun to touch the eastern sky.

I stood over Bloodmark, wavering slightly, still weak.

He'd stolen everything from me.

Erick.

The white-dusty man.

My niche.

He'd taken it all.

And I'd killed him for it. Murdered him.

I turned and stared up into the night sky, thought of the Mistress, of the Skewed Throne . . . of Erick.

A searing pain slid through me, as thin as a dagger's slice, but deeper. Tears stung the corners of my eyes and I pressed my lips together hard, felt them tremble.

I could never go back to Erick now, could never look him in the eye, could never face his disappointment. Not after Bloodmark. I hadn't killed him to save myself, or Erick, or anyone else. I'd killed him because I'd wanted to. Because he'd deserved it, whether the Mistress knew that or not.

Erick would never understand that. Not if he thought Mari was a mark. Not if he couldn't see that she wasn't, even after she'd killed Rec.

There was nothing left for me here. Nothing at all.

So I turned and left the Dredge, moved toward the only other place I knew. To the bridge leading across the River.

To Amenkor.

The real Amenkor.

Part II: Amenkor

✚ Chapter 7

Amenkor.

   The real Amenkor.

I stumbled to my knees in the half-light of dawn and vomited into the corner at the base of a stone-brick wall. My stomach cramped and I heaved again, muscles tightening in pain, but nothing came. There was nothing left in my stomach. Nothing but a horrible sickness.

When the spasms ended, I spat and crawled along the length of the alley to a barrel set near its end. I hunched back against the barrel, arms tight across my chest, as shudders ran through me. Reaction to the use of the river had never been this bad. But then, I'd never used it so heavily before, never kept myself submerged for so long. I'd never needed to use it so heavily.

I shuddered again, this time because of the image of Bloodmark choking on his own blood, and the sight of the Skewed Throne carved into the white-dusty man's chest.

I pulled myself hard against the barrel, eyes squeezed tight. I had no defense against the pain. The river, the run to Amenkor along the Dredge, the tension of waiting for the right moment to slip past the guards and cross the bridge and the real River, they'd all taken their toll. There was only weariness, an exhaustion that had settled into my muscles, into my bones. A weariness that dragged at me like a relentless tide.

I leaned my head against the stone-brick wall deep inside Amenkor and let the tide claim me.

A whip cracked, the snap startling me awake with a lurch.

"Hee-ah!" someone cried, and the clatter of hooves and wheels on cobbles receded.

I blinked into raw sunlight, eyes blurred, then shifted.

A boy stood before me.

I froze, muscles tensing.

The boy—no more than six years old, dressed in hand-stitched, fitted breeches, a vest, a white shirt; clothing far too fine for the slums or the Dredge—watched me with intent brown eyes. His hands were clutched behind his back, and he rocked back and forth, onto his heels and then his toes. A strange flattened hat covered shiny blond hair.

"Who are you?" he asked in a clear, precise voice. There was no malice, no fear in his round face. Nothing but curiosity.

I drew breath, my chest, my *lungs*, burning with the effort. But before I could answer—not even knowing what I would say—a woman stepped into view.

"Perci, what in the White Heavens are you—Oh!" The woman gasped, stepped back unconsciously, one hand reaching for Perci, the other reaching for the clasp on the dress near her throat. Her shocked face quickly hardened into something I knew, something I recognized:

Disdain tainted with fear. Mostly disdain.

My eyes narrowed, jaw clenching. My hand slid to the dagger tucked at my side. She wore a blue-dyed dress, fitted at the waist, with sleeves reaching to her wrists. Sandals with many straps covered washed feet. Simple clothes, not as fancy as Perci's. But there were no stains, no ragged edges, no wear marks. The clothes looked fresh, like puddles of water immediately after a storm, before scum slicked the surface.

My gaze returned to her eyes.

Some of the disdain slipped away, the fear edging forward.

"Come, Perci." The hand on Perci's shoulder tightened and she began to draw him toward the mouth of the alley, toward the bright sunlight.

Perci resisted, his face squeezing into a frown of defiance, but when the woman's hand tightened further, he let himself be dragged away. I slid into a crouch behind the barrel as they moved, relaxing only when they'd vanished into the flow of people at the edge of the alley.

The people.

My hand tightened on the dagger and I drew farther back behind the barrel. A fresh wave of nausea swept through me, more fear and dread than sickness from the use of the river.

On the street, men and women moved among carts pulled by horses. Most carried satchels and small bundles tied with twine. A few carried baskets, bread sticking out of raised lids. All wore unstained clothing in strange, bright colors— blues, dark reds, a width of bright yellow. The men wore breeches, boots, white shirts, vests, wide belts with pouches openly displayed. The women wore dresses with long sleeves and sandals, long hair tied back with thin leather straps, some with hats or folded scarves over their hair. They moved without rushing, with heads high, eyes forward. Tall.

They moved without fear.

A pair of black horses clattered into view, tied to . . . a cart. Except it wasn't a cart. It was a little enclosed room, a small door in its side. Through the window cut into the door, I could see a man with a thin, angular face.

When he turned toward me, I ducked behind the barrel.

The sight of the horse-drawn room, of the clothes, of the *colors*, felt like a kick to the gut. What had I done? This was not the Dredge. This was Amenkor. The real Amenkor. I didn't belong here, didn't know the streets, the alleys, or narrows. I didn't know the people, their patterns and reactions. They didn't dress the same, didn't even seem to move the same, the ebb and flow of the street subtly different, more sedate, less frantic.

A strong urge to retreat seized me, clamped onto my throat and held on tight. Run, flee, cower in the nether regions of the Dredge.

But as soon as the urge took hold, it was crushed by despair.

I couldn't go back to the slums. Not now. Not ever. Erick would be looking for me. The first place he'd look would be my niche.

Where he'd find Bloodmark. Erick would know that I'd killed him.

Guilt stabbed hard into my stomach. And shame as I imagined Erick kneeling over Bloodmark's body, checking out the wound, scanning the body for marks. But he wouldn't need confirmation of who had driven the dagger into Bloodmark's neck. He'd know as soon as he saw the body.

No, I couldn't go back to the slums. I'd killed so many for Erick, for the

Mistress, but Bloodmark had been different. I'd killed him for myself. For the white-dusty man and his wife.

But mostly for myself.

I drew in two long, deep breaths to steady myself, felt the shame fade, replaced with regret. Not regret that I'd killed Bloodmark, but that somehow in the process I'd lost Erick as well.

I suddenly thought of that last vision of Erick at Cobbler's Fountain, of seeing him for the first time beneath the river, his essence a strange mixture of gray and red. No one had ever appeared both colors before. Those that were harmless or presented no immediate danger were always gray; those that weren't were red.

So what did the mixture mean? Could Erick somehow be both? Harmless and dangerous at the same time?

Or was it not that simple?

I thought about Erick outside the iron gate, stalking Jobriah, the first mark I'd led him to. He'd been dangerous that day, enough that I'd shied away from him. I'd seen that same black look in his eyes many times since then. And every time I'd shuddered, pulled back and away.

But I could still feel his arms around me as he held me and I told him about the ex-guardsman trying to rape me, of how I'd stolen the dagger and killed the bastard as the White Fire swept through the city. I'd settled closer to Erick then, had been comforted by him.

Was it possible for someone to be both?

I shook myself, thrust the unanswered questions away. Harmless or dangerous, red or gray, it didn't matter anymore. Erick was gone, lost, stolen from me. Just like the Dredge.

I shifted forward, stared down the length of the alley to the bustle of the street, to the ebb and flow of strangers in fine clothing and clean skin.

Who are you? Perci had asked.

I glanced down at my hands. Bloodmark's blood had dried into the creases of the palm, had caked between my fingers. I closed my hands into fists and felt flakes fall away, felt the dried blood like grit between my skin.

"I'm gutterscum," I murmured to myself.

The sensation of having been kicked hard remained, deep inside, the ache like a stone in my gut. I drew in a deep breath through my nose, snorted back snot and phlegm and swallowed it, coughing slightly.

I couldn't return to the slums, but I couldn't remain here either. I was too different. I'd be noticed the instant I entered the street. I needed to get cleaned up, wash the slums from my face, from my clothes.

I stood, slowly, with effort, feeling aches throughout my body, but mostly in my chest and stomach from where Bloodmark had kicked me. Back pressed against the stone-brick wall for support, I lifted my dirt-, blood-, and vomit-smeared shirt. A livid bruise in the shape of a foot lay in the center of my chest, black and purplish-blue, edged in a horrid yellow. Another bruise rose along my side.

I saw Bloodmark's foot stomping down out of the night, winced as I dropped the shirt back into place. I glanced down the alley again in both directions, frowned.

Something else was different here. Something I'd noticed the night I'd followed Erick to the bridge. Something that reinforced the fact that I was no longer on the Dredge with more power than the people on the street, or their clothes, or the strange room on wheels.

The alley had *edges,* seemed somehow more defined, more *there.* There were sharp corners at its mouth, clear recesses for windows, for doors, and none of the windows were boarded up. The cobbles that covered the ground were mostly intact; the path for the runnel of water down its center mostly straight.

Beyond the Dredge, the alleys and narrows were worn, rounded, *used.* The shit and piss and lichen that stained the stone and mud-brick were permanent. The slush of rotten garbage that slicked the niches, collected in the crevices and corners, only shifted. It was never removed.

And on the Dredge, there were no barrels. None completely intact anyway.

I turned to the barrel, leaned down over its opening. It was just over half full of rainwater. I stared down at the ripples on the water, at the face reflected there.

The hair was flat, slicked with mud, matted with splatters of blood. It hung in thin tendrils, like rat tails, shorn short and uneven, nothing reaching farther than the chin. It framed a thin face, mouth pressed tight into a thin line, most of the skin smudged with more dirt, more blood, all dried and flaked like the blood on my hands. What skin wasn't covered with grit—with the Dredge—was sallow, almost gray. And the eyes . . .

I flinched.

The eyes were hollow, wasted, crusted with dried tears. And in the muddy depths—

I stood a long moment, looked deep into the water, into those eyes.

Then I plunged my hands down into the water and scrubbed the blood away, scrubbed until my skin felt raw, until my ragged fingernails left marks. Then, before the water could settle and the reflection could return, I dipped my head into the barrel.

Water closed over my face and I shut my eyes, remembering Cobbler's Fountain, feeling again the terror of that six-year-old girl as she tripped, as the water enveloped her, closed up and over her head. . . .

I jerked out of the rain barrel, water streaming from my hair, down my face. I gasped, sputtered, but scrubbed at my skin and pulled at my hair before dipping back down into the barrel again to wash away the grime, resurfacing with another choked gasp.

"Where did you see this woman?"

The voice filtered out of the general noise of the street. I turned, hair still dripping water. I scanned the alley and realized one more thing that made the real Amenkor different from the Dredge.

The alleys had fewer darknesses, fewer hiding places. Windows and doors actually existed, were not simply empty openings leading to deeper darknesses. I had few places to escape to here.

"Down that alley," a woman said. I glanced back to the street and saw her—the woman who'd dragged Perci away. She stood with Perci, nodding toward the alley. A guardsman, dressed like Erick, but with finer clothing, more armor, and a sword instead of a dagger, followed the direction of her nod.

"And you say she had blood on her hands?" the guard asked. His voice sounded dubious.

"Yes. And on her face and clothes. And I think she had a knife."

The guard grunted and began moving toward the alley.

I turned and moved into its depths, moved without conscious thought. I didn't know where I was going, but I knew I couldn't stay here any longer. I'd have to finish cleaning up somewhere else.

The first time I tried to use the river after killing Bloodmark, a spike of pain slashed into my head behind my eyes and my stomach clenched so hard I collapsed to the ground at the mouth of the alley where I stood. I lay curled where I'd fallen, drawing in breaths in huge gasps. Panic smothered me as the pain escalated, the spike driving deeper, harder, turning white-hot.

I'd never had pain like this. Not *days* after my last use of the river. Especially not after the nausea and weakness had receded.

And then a horrifying thought surfaced, stilled my gasping breath with a twinge of pain in my lungs.

What if I couldn't use the river anymore at all? What if somehow in my push to find Bloodmark I'd overextended myself, burned myself out?

The thought shoved everything away, crushed everything but the spike of pain behind my eyes and a hollow sound in my ears. It left me stunned.

I couldn't survive without the river.

Someone touched me, a gentle hand on my shoulder.

I jerked back with a gasp, struck the wall of the alley.

"Are you all right?"

I could barely see the woman who knelt beside me, her hands lying cupped on her knees. A strange field of yellow, like a film of scum over water, covered my vision, pulsing with the pulse of the spike. Jagged little streaks, like flares of lightning, ran through the field of yellow.

"I'm . . . fine," I gasped, too frightened of what was happening in my head to really respond, to think.

The woman sat back slightly, her dress rustling, the sound unnaturally loud. "You don't look fine." Her voice seemed dull, faded, and seemed to come from much farther away.

I tried to focus through the field of yellow, pushed myself up onto my hands. The pulsing lightning began to recede. "I'm fine," I said with more force.

The woman frowned doubtfully and glanced back toward the street. Her dress was a plain brown, but still clean. Her long, light-brown hair was tied back with a simple green ribbon, pulled away from her round face. And she wore an earring in one ear—gold with a bluish-green iridescent bead.

It reminded me strangely of water.

Across the street, a man and two older boys were unloading sacks of potatoes from a wagon, tossing a heavy bag over each shoulder before toting them through a wide door into the building beyond. One sack had split while being hefted, spilling a few potatoes to the ground. The sack itself had been set to one side at the back of the wagon.

When she turned back, the woman with the iridescent earring scrutinized me through narrowed eyes. Her frown had deepened. Her gaze flicked to my clothes, to my hair.

Neither was splattered with blood now. After eluding the guardsman in the backstreets, I'd gone down to Amenkor's River, washed everything as clean as I could make it. On the Dredge, the clothes Erick had given me had seemed clean, almost too nice to be worn. But at the edge of the River, at the bottom of the stone steps that led down to its walled-in banks, I'd seen the stains, the tattered edges, the small tears.

I felt those tears, those stains, now, under the scrutiny of the woman. Tight anger burned in my chest and I pushed myself back onto my heels.

"I said I'm fine," I repeated, harshly.

Her brow creased. Then she stood and said, "Very well."

I flinched at the slight coldness in her voice, the remoteness.

She moved away, stepped back into the street, but paused when she saw the wagon again, the potatoes. The last of the sacks had been toted into the building and the older of the two boys was holding the split sack while the younger collected the dropped potatoes from the street. They cinched the sack closed as best they could and hauled it inside the building as well.

The woman turned back. "Perhaps . . ." She hesitated, seemed to reconsider, then added in a rush, "Perhaps you should try the marketplace. Or the wharf. You might have better luck there, on the docks."

Then she cut across the street, pausing only long enough to let a man on a horse pass.

I watched where she had vanished for a long moment, feeling a dull ache in my chest, for a brief moment smelling yeast, feeling a brush of oven heat against my face.

But I pushed the ache down, smothered the scents. The spiking pain had dropped down to a throbbing stab and my vision had begun to clear. I still felt weak, but even that was fading.

I stood carefully, then scanned the street.

People moved from shop to shop, building to building. They paused to talk, to laugh. Bells jangled as someone entered a narrow door in the building beside me. The smell of tallow drifted out. But not the harsh, oily tallow of the Dredge. This tallow was mixed with strange scents, wild foreign scents that prickled the inside of my nose. Across the street, another door opened and a roar of laughter escaped into the street, the man who had left waving to the others inside.

I'd have no luck hunting here. The closest I'd come in the last two days had been the split sack of potatoes, and even that would have been risky. That's why I'd tried to use the river. But this wasn't the Dredge. The people might not be wary, but they had nothing to fear. There were too few of them, nothing like the crowds on the Dredge. There were no places for me to blend into, no niches to hide in.

And then there were the guards.

I stepped deeper into the alley as two appeared on horseback. Like the guard the other day, these two were dressed like Erick, but cleaner. Edged, like the alleys. They held themselves stiff and straight, and their eyes . . .

As they passed, the closest guard's gaze fell on me. His eyes were like Erick's as well, but the danger, the darkness that I'd seen hidden in Erick's gaze was blunt and blatant. And arrogant.

The guard's eyes narrowed, as if it had finally registered that he'd seen something out of place, something wrong.

The two passed beyond the entrance to the alley.

I didn't wait for them to return. I moved back into the depths and began to work my way toward Amenkor's River. I'd stayed near the water the last few nights. Because the riverbank wasn't as active as the inner streets, it provided a few more places to hide. And because I could see the slums on the far side, the familiar sight was comforting. But the woman was right. I couldn't continue hunting in this area, especially if I couldn't use the river.

I halted, bit my lower lip, then tentatively tried to push myself beneath the surface. For a moment, the world grayed, noises receded to wind. But the sense was distorted, watery and indistinct.

And then the spike of pain returned, slicing down through my temple. Weakness shot through my legs.

I shoved the river away before the pain increased, sighed in relief as the searing spike began to recede.

When my legs felt stable again, I continued. I didn't know where the marketplace was, but the wharf. . . .

I'd seen it from the rooftops, seen it the night the ex-guardsman had caught me and dragged me there to rape me. I remembered the White Fire as it sped through the harbor, so cold and silent, remembered how it had engulfed the ships, the docks, before surging up onto the land. All I had to do was follow the River down to the sea.

I shivered, felt the Fire stir inside me.

I tensed, half expected the spiked headache to return and the nausea, but the cold flame of the Fire drifted away. Apparently, it wasn't affected by the use of the river.

My stomach growled.

I picked up my pace. I'd have better luck at the docks.

I knelt between two crates behind a pile of tangled netting on the wharf and watched a ship with three masts bump hard into the long wooden dock. A man shouted, voice hard and vicious against the slap of the waves, and men scurried as ties were thrown over the edge of the boat. The dock groaned as the ship drifted away, and then a plank slapped down and more men began unloading cargo, crate after crate hauled down to the dock. Some of the men unloading crates had dark skin—darker than could be attributed to exposure to the sun— their faces flatter and wider, bodies shorter, more compact. All of the darker-skinned men had straight black hair, cut to the nape of the neck. Most had tattoos on their faces and down their necks.

Zorelli. Men from the far south.

I eased forward, hoping for a better look.

It was chaos, men on the ship, men on the dock, the man barking orders left and right, motioning with an arm toward the wharf, toward the ship, arguing with another man who came down the plank as if he owned it. The man coming down the plank glared at the one shouting orders, then gave a curt command. The other man turned back to the boat, bellowing more fiercely than before, cursing, pissed off, taking it out on the crew.

The captain stepped off the plank, dipped his head toward another man waiting on the pier. Both wore fine breeches, heavy boots, shirts with unnecessary ruffles near the throat, and long jackets that came down to their knees. The man on the dock had a dark-red jacket, like blood, with gold threading in strange patterns down the arms and near the cuffs. He was mostly bald, a fringe of dark hair with shots of gray surrounding his head like brown stone around a fountain. He wore rounded wire on his face, with hooks that went around his ears. Every now and then, when he turned, sunlight would glint off his eyes, as if it were reflecting off water, only this reflection appeared flat and rounded.

The captain of the ship wore dark green, with less gold threading, but with more hair and no wires on his face.

As I watched, the captain and the man in the red jacket began arguing. When the argument ended, the captain of the ship stormed back up the plank, the man with the wires on his face watching him go.

Then the man with the wires on his face began moving down the dock toward me, his eyes narrowed in anger. Another man—younger, paler—fell in beside him, dressed similarly but without the horrible jacket.

"What's the matter, Master Borund? What did the captain say?"

The bald man growled. "He said he didn't have the entire shipment. Said the cloth from Verano is missing and the Marland spice couldn't be found. Someone in the city bought it all up before he could get any." He cursed, then drew in a deep breath to steady himself as the two passed by the crates. I'd sprawled back, head down as if asleep, but I needn't have bothered. They were too intent on their conversation to notice me. "This city is going to pieces, William. And neither Avrell nor the Mistress is doing anything about it. . . ."

Their voices receded.

I lifted my head to see if they were far enough away, then shifted forward and watched them merge with the crowd on the wharf, vanishing among the hawkers and dockworkers, the stench of seawater and fish. Then I turned back to the ship.

There was nothing on the ship for me, nothing I could steal. I'd already determined that. But I didn't leave. The ships in the harbor intrigued me. I watched the men unload the crates, watched the ropes and pulleys on the masts sag and dip in the wind. Waves slapped against the ship's sides, and now and then it bumped up against the dock where it was secured. Men shouted and cursed and spat and laughed. White-gray birds shrieked, dove for the water, for the men, before settling on the dock supports and flapping their wings. Someone dropped a crate and with a wrench and a crack of wood it split, sending some type of brown, hairy, rounded fruit rolling along the dock.

I leaned forward, possibilities leaping upward in my chest, but forced myself to settle back.

I couldn't risk it. Not without the river. I'd learned that the first few days on the wharf. I could still feel the hawker's hand latching onto my wrist and jerking me around the first time I'd tried.

Where do you think you're going with that? he'd spat, his voice somehow greasy.

I leaned back against the crates, brought up a hand to wipe at where I could still feel the spit on my face. I'd said nothing, too shocked that I'd been caught to speak.

I'd never been caught on the Dredge. Not since I'd figured out how to combine the river with what Dove and his street gang had taught me. And especially not after the Fire.

But here I had to be more careful, had to take fewer risks. All because every time I tried to use the river that spike of pain returned. I couldn't tell if it was lessening as the days passed; it was still too sharp. So sharp that I hadn't tried to use the river at all in the last two days.

I pushed the nagging worry back, continued to watch the last of the crates being unloaded. The strange hairy fruit was being repacked.

I sighed and turned back to the wharf. I couldn't risk taking anything directly from the docks, where escape routes were restricted, but the wharf. . . .

I slid from my place among the crates and netting and merged with the crowd.

I spent the rest of the day on the wharf, shifting from place to place, watching the hawkers, watching the dockworkers, eyes sharp for the misplaced fishhead, the unwatched crust of bread. The crowds were slightly different here than on the Dredge. The majority of the people were the same—pale skin, darker hair in shades of brown and black, darker eyes as well—but there were more strangers on the wharf. Men with beads braided in their beards; women with feathers in their hair. Others wore cloth draped over them, secured with intricate folds and tucks, rather than being tailored. I saw a few with the blue paint smudge of the Tear of Taniece near the corner of their eye.

The streets and alleys just beyond the wharf were almost like the Dredge as well. The alleys were lined with bundles of netting and meshed crab traps with dried seaweed stuck to them, rather than heaps of broken stone and crumbling mud-brick. The stench: salt and dead fish, rather than shit and stagnant water. I'd even managed to find a new niche—the end of an alley, where crab traps had been piled high, covered over with a stretch of tanned hide against the rain. I'd forced a hole in the center, pulled traps out from inside, until I could squeeze into the narrow opening and move around beneath the tanned hide. It was much closer to the Dredge than the upper city, where I'd been before, where I'd woken to find Perci staring down at me.

I glanced away from the wharf, up past the buildings immediately next to the water to the slope of the hill behind. The roofs thinned as my gaze swept higher, the buildings larger, more ornate and isolated. At the top of the hill I could see three circular walls, the white stone of the palace gleaming in the sun in their center.

In the upper city, there were almost no foreigners, and almost no smells at all. At least nothing that stung the nose or made my eyes water.

My gaze dropped back to the wharf and I breathed in the stench of fish again.

A man cursed and the thud of a dropped bundle hitting the wood of the wharf drew me out of my daze. Night was beginning to settle, and clouds had begun to drift in from the sea.

It would rain tonight.

The man squatted down, began gathering up what had spilled from his bundle, the flow of the crowd parting around him. A few items had rolled. A flat package tied with twine slid against a dock support jutting up from the planking and the undulating water below.

For a moment, I tensed, ready to slip beneath the river, but stopped myself with a shudder, remembering the spiked headache.

I settled back against the alley wall and watched as the man grunted, reaching for a cylindrical package that had rolled farther away than the rest. Only the flat item that had slid to the support remained.

But the man stood abruptly, tossed the cylindrical package into the bundle, then swung it up over his shoulder and joined the crowd.

I stared in shock at the rectangular package he'd left behind.

Then, with a swift glance left and right, I shoved through the people to the dock support and snatched the package up.

Without opening it, I headed back to my niche, pushing through the crowd. Once in the back alleys, I slowed, relaxed, my arms tingling.

All I wanted was my niche.

I slipped down an empty street, toward an alley. Night had fallen completely now, and the first drizzle of rain began to fall. I'd almost reached the end of the alley, my hands still clutching the package, when someone stepped into my path.

I froze, water beginning to drip from the hair hanging before my face. Through the tangles, I could see the man's grin, could see he wore finer clothes than the dockworkers, than the hawkers. Breeches without stains, a leather belt with a dagger tucked into it, a dark shirt, a cloak against the rain.

"What have we here?" he murmured, and like the hawker that had grabbed my arm days before, his voice sounded greasy.

I took a step back, one hand dropping from the package to the dagger hidden beneath my shirt.

The man's grin widened, and even before I saw his eyes focus on something behind me, I heard a sound.

A footfall.

I spun, dagger half drawn—

And a fist crashed down against my face, striking hard along my jaw, so hard I stumbled backward, fell into a clutter of netting resting against a crate. My free hand groped at empty air, my head resting against the crate, a sudden dull roar filling my ears. I'd lost the package, but not my dagger. It was caught in my shirt, still hidden.

My hand found the edge of the crate and the disorientation vanished. Blinking against the rain, against the darkness, I shifted forward, dragged myself into a crouch.

Through the roar in my ears, I heard someone laugh, the sound dull and empty.

Anger flared, frigid and tinged with Fire.

I lowered my head, spat blood onto the rain-slicked cobbles of the alley—

And felt myself slip into the river. Smoothly, cleanly. Like a knife into flesh.

And without any pain. No spiked headache. No nausea.

I almost cried out in joy, hope and relief surging upward into my throat, but I choked it down.

"Come on, Cristoph," someone said. The second man. The one who'd struck me. "Take whatever she's got. It's not safe here."

"Shut up. It's perfectly safe here. No one will see a thing. Besides, this won't take long."

I lifted my head. The alley was no longer dark. I could see the wash of red that was Cristoph, another wash of red that was the second man. The rest of the alley was gray, but with a push I slid deeper, the gray taking on edges, and deeper still, until I could see the crates, the cobbles, the slashes of rain as it fell. The blurs of red deepened as well, until I could see the cloaks, the belts, the knives that had been drawn. I could see their rain-drenched hair, their faces.

Cristoph was moving forward, knife held ready.

The second man's face pinched into a frown. "What are you doing? Just take whatever she dropped!"

"I want more than just the packages this time."

The second man grabbed Cristoph's shoulder, brought him to a halt. "What do you mean?"

Cristoph jerked out of the second man's grip. "Don't touch me."

I slid my dagger out from under my shirt.

Cristoph turned back toward me and I could see what he intended, with a sickened heart could see how it would end.

Amenkor—the real Amenkor—was just like the Dredge. The streets might be cleaner, but the people were the same.

"Don't," I said, and I could hear beneath the warning in my voice an edge of pleading. "Don't," I said again, shaking my head. Softer this time, but more steeled.

Cristoph grinned and I shifted my weight.

He came at me in a rush, his knife forward but not ready to strike. He wanted me docile, immobile, not dead. At least not at first.

I stepped to the side, just out of his path, and brought my dagger around in a hard, vicious slash, all of the training Erick had given me in the depths of the Dredge sliding smoothly into place.

My dagger cut across his arm, high, near the shoulder. I heard him gasp, saw him stumble into the crate.

"Shit!" the second man cried out, then stepped to Cristoph's side, pulling him up roughly. "Stop this!"

"No!" Cristoph hissed as he lurched out of the second man's grasp, glanced at his torn shirt, at the stain of blood there.

Then his gaze leveled on me. "So the bitch knows some knife-play." With a wince of pain, he reached up and tore off the clasp of his cloak, freeing both arms.

"Oh, gods, Cristoph," the second man muttered, still leaning against the crate behind him.

Cristoph ignored him. He edged toward me, eyes intent, breath coming in short little gasps through his nose.

He lunged.

I stepped aside again, slashed, connected with his upper back, slicing along the shoulder muscles, but not deep. Cristoph grunted, spun, slashed low, across my stomach, but I'd already stepped back, out of reach. He changed tactics, tried to slash upward. I leaned back, felt his blade slick past my neck, nick a tangle of my hair, but my own blade had already risen, had slashed across his face, along one cheek. But without pause, without even a gasp, Cristoph pressed forward, forced me to step back, to one side, pushing me—

And suddenly I felt the second man's presence at my back, felt it like an undertow, felt his knife, *tasted* his knife—

I turned, ducking beneath one of Cristoph's slashes, and drove my dagger up into the second man's gut, up under the ribs, in and out with a single hard thrust, and then I stepped back, still half crouched.

The second man tried to gasp, choked instead. The arm that had been raised to slit my throat from behind dropped to his side. He stared down at the gush of blood that had begun to seep into his shirt, that had already spread down to his breeches.

He glanced back up and in a soft, confused, wet voice, said, "Cristoph?"

Then he dropped to his knees, hard, and fell back, knife hitting the cobbles with a thin clatter, body with a solid thump.

I turned to Cristoph. He'd stepped back, almost to the alley wall, and now stared down at the second man's body in cold shock. His knife arm hung at his side, and blood seeped from the slash across his face.

I straightened, and his gaze shifted to me, his eyes sharp and wide. He blew air out through his mouth, rainwater spluttering outward.

"Gods," he whispered.

And then he ran, heading toward the alley's entrance, leaving his cloak and the second man behind.

I watched him go, watched the empty entrance to the alley for a long moment, then realized that someone was watching me.

I turned.

At the far end of the alley, at the other entrance, two figures stood, one slightly behind the other. The second man held a lantern, the light almost white in the gray.

I let the river slip away.

The man at the end of the alley was dressed in a blood-red jacket with gold threading. When he turned, lantern light reflected off the wire he wore on his face.

I tensed, but the two men walked away, leaving me alone.

I stared down at the body.

I felt nothing inside except a cold, flat hollowness.

I thought of the boy, of Perci.

Looking down at the body, rain pattering against the fine clothing, a darker stain beginning to seep out from underneath along the cobbles, I said in a dull voice, "This is who I am."

I turned, picked up the package I'd taken. I ripped away the paper, felt the twine cut into my fingers. But I didn't care.

It was a book.

I flipped through the pages, stared blankly at the black markings.

I couldn't read.

I turned back to the dead body. "You died for a fucking book," I said.

I dropped the book onto his chest.

Then I walked away.

╼ The Palace ╾

"Too late, too late, too late," I mumbled under my breath as I rounded a corner at almost a dead run. The linen closet should be inside the room just ahead. But I could feel the night sky pressing down on me even inside the palace, could feel time slipping away. I should never have been held up by Avrell and Nathem, shouldn't have paused in the concourse, staring at the immense hall, at the guards. I was going to miss the changing of the guard.

"Stupid, stupid."

I rounded the corner and almost slammed into the back of another servant.

Pulling up short, I slid back around the corner and pressed flat against the wall, listening. My breath came in barely controlled gasps. I'd sprinted from the waiting room where I'd overheard Avrell and Nathem talking.

In the adjacent hall, I heard the servant's footsteps pause and I held my breath. After an agonizing moment, the footsteps resumed, receding down the hallway.

I let out a long breath, stole a quick glance around the corner to make certain the corridor was empty, then ducked to the only doorway off of the hall.

It was open.

I slid through it, then closed it behind me and locked it. I scanned the darkened room after my eyes had adjusted. Some kind of library, shelves of books lining three walls. A large table surrounded by chairs filled the center of the room, books stacked haphazardly on the table among numerous candlesticks and half-burned, unlit candles. Parchment and quills and ink were placed before some of the chairs.

Against the back wall, inconspicuous among a few scattered plants and more comfortable reading chairs, sat a door with wooden slats and inset panels. The linen closet.

I bolted across the room. The door was locked.

Reaching into the inner pocket, I drew out the key Avrell had provided, thinking once again it was odd to lock a linen closet, then inserted the key and turned. The catch sprang and the door snicked open.

I stepped inside, closed the door behind me and took a moment to peer through the wooden slats into the library.

No one had followed.

Then I turned and my heart froze.

The closet was full of . . . of linens. Stacked floor to ceiling. No wall was bare. There was no entrance to the inner sanctum.

Horror set in—that I'd made a mistake, that someone had betrayed me. Taking a quick step forward, I grabbed a stack of linen and yanked. The stack gave way, collapsing with a low, rustling *whmmp* into the small space behind the door, revealing a rough stone wall. In the center of the wall, but low to the floor, a narrow aperture glowed with torchlight coming from the opposite side.

I drew in a steadying breath of relief, then crouched down next to the opening.

It was three hands high, almost two hands wide, and had originally been a slot for archers on the outer wall of the castle, a window so that they could fire down onto an invading force. For some unknown reason, during the construction of the newest parts of the palace, the archer's niche had not been filled in and sealed up. I knelt and placed a hand against the outside of the opening, felt the grit of the granite that had made up that original wall. Not the smooth white stone of the more recent palace. This stone was rough, flecked with impurities, colored a blackened and sooty gray by exposure to the elements, even though now it never saw daylight.

Through the archer's window I could see the small niche where the archer would have sat, ready to defend the wall, and beyond that a hallway. Shifting slightly, so that the torchlight from the hallway lit my face in a long thin bar, I could see a doorway guarded by two guardsmen. They wore the edged clothing of the guards of the real Amenkor, carried themselves with the same blatant sense of danger and arrogance, but they wore more armor. The Skewed Throne symbol stitched to their clothing was gold. Firelight from the palace's wide bowls of burning oil glinted off the metal of wrist guards, of the pommels of sheathed swords, and of shoulder guards.

Perhaps I hadn't been slowed down as much as I thought.

I'd just turned to settle in and wait when one of the guardsmen looked toward the other and sighed. "We've only just started and already I'm tired. It's going to be a long watch."

I fell back against the granite wall and said, "Shit," even as the other guard grunted in agreement.

I'd missed the changing of the guard after all.

Drawing in a deep breath, fingering the handle of my dagger, I grunted and bit my lower lip.

Shit, shit, shit. Now what?

┼─ Chapter 8

I was working the wharf, had been working the wharf for the past week, ever since killing the man in the alley. I was leaning on a support, the sounds of the docks a muted rush of wind in the background. Beneath me, I could feel the support quiver as waves slapped up against it below. The world was a wash of blurred gray, except for a narrow window of focus, where sunlight glared on a mostly-white cloth spread out over the back end of a cart. Stacked on the cloth were piles of vegetables and fruit.

In the sunlight, the colors of the fruit stood out vibrant and harsh. Everything looked perfect, the flesh smooth, unblemished. There were no scabs, no bruises, no softened spots of decay.

Since coming to the wharf, I hadn't seen anyone selling fruit. I'd seen noth-

ing but fish—fish heads, fish bones, fish guts—and crabs, which smelled like
fish but tasted sweet.

I glanced up from the apples, from *the* apple that had rolled slightly to one
side, near the edge of the cart, and watched the man who knelt in the back of
the cart behind his wares. He was arguing with a woman over the price of
some carrots, but his eyes flicked toward everyone that came within two paces
of his cart.

I frowned . . . and my stomach growled. I looked at the apple again, thought
for a moment I could actually *taste* it.

The sunlight brightened, the narrow field of focus widening. More people
slid out of the gray, and everything took on a sharper edge.

I pushed deeper, until the world in focus had sharpened so far it felt brittle.
Then I relaxed . . . and waited.

The crowds of dockworkers and fishermen, of fishwives and seamen, ebbed
and flowed around the cart. The fruit seller eventually threw up his heavyset
arms in disgust with the woman, tossing the carrots back onto the cart. The
woman spat on the wharf, flung a rude gesture at him with one hand, and
huffed off.

More customers came, and still the fruit seller eyed everyone who approached.

And then a woman towing three young children bled out of the gray.

I straightened, and with single-minded intent *pushed* at the river, forced it
forward . . . and saw what would happen, saw how I could get the apple . . . how
I could get more than just the apple.

I licked my lips as my eyes darted to the fruit seller, to the sour-faced man
he was currently haggling with, to the woman who had just seen the cart, to the
three children. The oldest boy reached out for no apparent reason and shoved
the middle girl to the ground. Without turning, the mother cuffed him on the
back of the head and said, "Leave your sister alone." Her voice sounded tired
and bitter. The youngest boy hung back, out of the reach of both mother and
older brother.

The mother swerved toward the cart and the three followed.

I pushed away from the support and began moving forward.

The fruit seller glanced from the man to the mother, then down toward the
three trailing children, and frowned.

"How much for the turnips?" the mother asked. The daughter squeezed in
front of her, her chin coming up to the lip of the cart. She reached for a turnip,
but couldn't quite make it.

The fruit seller opened his mouth to answer. At the same time, the older boy
reached around his mother and hit his sister. Her arm, straining for the turnips,
jerked and sent the entire pile tumbling.

I heard the fruit seller shout, heard the mother spit out a curse, heard the daughter scream and begin to wail. The fruit seller lurched to save the turnips, the daughter spun, eyes flaring with anger. Everyone was turning toward the boy, toward the rolling turnips, toward the noise.

I was two steps away from the apple—from an armful of apples—with no one watching, when a hand closed about my upper arm.

I jerked and spun, dagger out before I thought. I would have killed him, thinking *This is who I am,* but just before the dagger drove forward, toward the midsection just beneath the armpit, I smelled oranges. Not from the fruit seller's cart. He had no oranges. I smelled oranges in the gray world of the river.

I pulled my thrust. The dagger sliced through the man's shirt, beneath his arm and across his chest.

The man gasped and lurched back, releasing my arm. He stared at me in shock, the hand he had used to grip me held out to stop me from a second attack. The other hand clutched his chest over the rent in his shirt.

I glared at him, saw that he was gray, harmless, and turned to leave.

"Don't!" he choked, stepping forward. "Just wait!"

I hesitated. Because even after I'd almost killed him, he'd stepped forward to halt me, not away. And because of the smell of oranges.

Behind me, I heard the mother bark at her oldest son, heard them drawing away. My chance for an apple was gone.

"What do you want?" I asked, shifting my focus completely toward the man. I suddenly realized I recognized him, recognized the finely-made breeches, the white shirt with ruffles at the throat.

It was the man who had accompanied the red-coated merchant I'd seen on the dock.

"I—or rather, someone else—wishes to speak to you." He straightened, his outstretched hand dropping, then winced. When he drew his other hand away from his chest, I could see a few rounded stains of blood against the white of his shirt.

I crushed a pang of guilt. "What for?"

The man hesitated, then said stiffly, "I don't know. You'd have to ask him yourself."

I frowned.

He had black hair, shorn short, wild and untamed, but not dirty or matted. His face was rounded, the skin a little pale. His eyes were green, shadowed with fear, still a little too wide from shock. They kept darting toward the dagger. But there was nothing else beneath the fear: no hatred, no contempt, no danger. And no pity.

I slid the dagger back beneath my shirt. "Where?"

He heaved a sigh of relief, tension draining from his shoulders. "Not far. My name is William." He held out a hand, as if expecting something, like a beggar on the Dredge.

I stared at it in confusion and said, "Varis."

After a moment, he withdrew the hand, coughed slightly into it. "Ah, yes. Varis. If you'd follow me?"

He began to move away, off the docks, along the wharf toward the real Amenkor.

I waited a moment, thinking I should slip away.

But in the end I followed him. Because of the smell of oranges.

We moved through the back streets of the wharf, William ten paces ahead of me. I followed warily, my eyes darting toward every blur of red. I felt unsettled, and moved slowly. William turned back once, his eyes catching mine, and he smiled encouragingly. The scent of oranges drifted over the sharper smells of sea and salt, like a breath of wind.

I halted uncertainly, struggling with a new sensation, something deep in my gut that trembled.

William's smile faded and he moved back toward me. "It's not much farther," he said.

He reached out as if to take my arm again, but I drew back, my eyes hardening.

"Go on," I said, and nodded down the street.

He continued, but not before giving me a confused frown.

He halted a few streets farther on at a door beneath a sign with a ship carved into the wood, its sails torn and ragged, the central mast broken. When he opened the door and gestured me inside, laughter and the sounds of a dozen voices rolled out into the street.

I stepped back, glanced toward William. I knew it was a tavern, had heard the raucous noises through opened doors before, knew the smells. But always from the street, from the Dredge. I'd never actually been inside one.

William's brow furrowed as he waited. He didn't understand my hesitation.

Before he could say anything, before the frown began to touch his eyes with real concern, I straightened and stepped past him into the inner room.

The sudden influx of sensation was overwhelming, the sound and motion and scents too intense. A dozen conversations, twenty voices or more, rushed out of the background noise, roaring forward like a gale, somehow trapped inside the little room, confined. A thousand scents struck like a blow—fire, ale, sweat, tallow, rot, cooked meat, bread, heat—all mixed and compacted, enough to gag. And through the sound, through the smells, in the dulled transition from sunlight to candlelight, people were moving: clapping each other on the back, stumbling up from tables, wandering toward the fire, reaching for food, coughing, carrying mugs of ale, drinking, eating, choking.

It was too much. The river began to close in, the water closing up and over my head, smothering me. My breath caught in my chest with a sharp pain and held there. My shoulders tensed. My hand closed in a death grip on my dagger. The room rushed in to crush me.

Then, with effort, I forced the darkening gray of the world to focus. I felt the river push back, resist, struggle—

Then the noise bled into the background. The scents slid away. And the giddy rush of motion pulled back, stabilized.

I gasped as the river gave way and began to balance, coughed as if water were caught in my throat, in my lungs—like when I'd surfaced from the water of Cobbler's Fountain at age six.

William stepped up behind me and I felt the light fade as the door closed. His hand moved as if to touch me, his eyes concerned, but he stopped himself at something he saw in my face.

"Over here," he said, and led me through the mass of people toward a table in the corner, where the man in the red coat sat. I felt confined by the low roof, the people, but when I saw the red-coated man, all of that sensation fled.

The scent of oranges grew so strong it dampened out everything in the room, so sharp my eyes began to water.

I slid from the river, and the noise of the tavern rushed back, the scents. But in the real world they were not as overwhelming. In the real world, they were no worse than the crowds on the Dredge.

William moved behind the table, to where the red-coated man sat. He leaned down to murmur something in the red-coated man's ear, but the red-coated man's eyes never left mine. He watched me intently from behind the wires on his face. When William finished, he only nodded, and William stepped back to stand behind his shoulder, arms behind his back.

The red-coated man motioned to the only other chair at the table. "Would you like to sit?" he asked. His voice was soft and hard at the same time, careful and wary.

I glanced toward the chair, felt the motion of the room at my back, the steady stream of people, and shook my head.

He nodded, as if he'd expected that response. Then, in a deeper voice, one much more dangerous than before, he asked, "And do you know who I am?"

I shook my head again.

He watched me for the space of two breaths . . . and then his gaze shifted out into the crowd behind me. "Moll, could you bring a plate of the pork and some ale. And bread with butter, of course. Enough for three."

I turned and watched a woman nod in our direction and hustle off toward a door.

When I turned back, the red-coated man was watching me again, this time with a frown.

"We saw you kill that boy the other night."

It was a statement, and when he reached beneath the table I tensed, a cold sensation rushing up from my stomach. But not the warning Fire. This was simple panic. My hand went for my dagger—

But then the red-coated man drew forth a section of black cloth, finely made—too fine for what I'd seen on the common people of the wharf. It was stained with mud, with blood.

It was the cloak Cristoph had dropped, the one he'd left behind.

The red-coated man pushed the cloak back down beneath the table.

"I sent William back for the body. He tossed it into the harbor, but he brought the cloak and the book to me. If the body is found, the boy's family will think he was roughing it in the wharf region for fun, that he got involved in something he shouldn't have—dice, too much drink, the wrong crowd—and that he was killed for his money."

"What about the other one, the one who ran away?" I asked.

Borund grimaced. "I don't think he'll cause a problem. He'd have to admit he was on the wharf in the first place, attempting . . . whatever he was attempting. I find that unlikely."

I shifted uneasily. "Who were they?"

"Does it matter?" When I didn't answer, he shook his head. "Merchants' sons. They shouldn't have been messing around on the wharf. They certainly shouldn't have been down here preying on the likes of you. Don't you agree?"

William snorted. The red-coated man frowned but didn't turn around.

"In any case," the red-coated man continued, "William has convinced me that you could be . . . useful."

I glanced toward William, but his face was blank, his eyes focused inward. "How?"

The red-coated man drew breath, but suddenly Moll appeared with a tray heavy with shredded pork smothered in some kind of sauce. The meat steamed, the scent of heat and smoke and juice powerful, drawing a rumble from my stomach. She set the tray down with a grunt as a second, younger woman arrived with a huge pitcher of ale and three wooden cups—except they were larger than any cups I'd ever seen; deeper and with large handles. Yet another woman arrived with a flat board with bread already sliced and a bowl with butter in it. A small knife, as long as my finger and strangely flattened, was half-buried in the butter.

My stomach clenched.

"Will that be all, Merchant Borund?"

"For now, yes, Moll."

The three women nodded and wove back into the crowd behind me, but not before considering me with curious frowns. Moll nodded to me as she passed, with a tentative smile.

After they left, Borund sighed and relaxed back into his chair. Motioning toward the food, he said, "Please, have something to eat. You as well, William."

I hesitated, too shocked to move. There was more meat on the tray than I'd eat in a week, and the bread. . . .

William shifted forward, used the small knife to spread the butter over a slice of bread, then used something else with three small prongs to stab a chunk of the meat. He placed the meat on the bread and then stepped back to eat.

I watched a moment, still stunned, then stepped forward. I resisted the urge to grab the entire loaf of bread and run. Instead, I picked up a single slice and when no one reacted, stepped back. I half expected Borund or William to shout, or reach out and grab my arm as the hawker had done when he'd caught me trying to steal from his stall.

Instead, Borund leaned forward and said, "Here. Try some butter on that."

I held out the slice of bread I'd taken. Borund took it and slathered it liberally, then handed it back.

The bread was warm, and the butter had already begun to soak into the slice. It smelled sweet, tasted sweeter, soft and warm and smooth against my tongue. The flavor flooded my mouth, and a trail of it trickled down my chin like drool.

It was the best thing I'd ever tasted, sent tremors through my arms.

I stuffed the rest of the bread in my mouth, wiped the trail of butter away with the back of my hand while still chewing the last of it.

Borund leaned forward with a smile. "Now have some with the meat."

He waited until I'd gotten another slice, with plenty of butter, more than Borund had used, and some meat, then sat back while William poured three cups of ale.

"Amenkor is dangerous, Varis," he began, then hesitated. "May I call you Varis?"

I nodded around my third helping of butter, bread, and meat.

"Not just here on the wharf. It's dangerous in the upper city as well. Perhaps more so. Especially since the White Fire." He paused, grimaced to himself, then focused again on me. "I did not think it was that serious—not as serious as William claimed—until . . . until we saw you being attacked in that alley by those boys. I was willing to dismiss how bad things had become in Amenkor until then. But now. . . ." He shook his head, shifted uncomfortably in his seat, his gaze moving toward the crowd behind me.

I stopped for a moment, suddenly uneasy. Inside, I felt a tendril of the Fire flicker upward, there and then gone. But the motions of the room behind me began to filter into my awareness, no longer part of the background.

Borund's gaze moved from person to person.

"Now," he said, "I no longer feel safe. Even here, where I've come since my father first brought me to the wharf." He smiled, the gesture bittersweet and brief, and returned his attention to me. "And that's where you come in, Varis. I need someone to guard over me, protect me."

I stopped chewing. Through a mouthful of bread and gravy, I sputtered, "What?"

Borund leaned forward. "I want you to accompany me to the wharf, to the city or palace, wherever I go, and make certain no one harms me. I know you can handle a weapon. I've seen it. I know you can defend yourself. That boy you killed . . . he was *trained,* Varis. He knew how to use a knife. And yet you bested him without any effort at all."

I swallowed painfully, the lump of bread too large and tasteless. "He was stupid."

"Perhaps. But in the end you walked away, not him. I'm willing to bet you can best almost anyone. Especially anyone that may be hired to kill me."

"Who would want you dead?"

William snorted again and took a long pull on his ale. William had drunk plenty of ale. I hadn't touched mine. Neither had Borund.

"Other merchants. Perhaps others from the upper city with power. People here on the wharf who have become . . . desperate." Now Borund reached for his ale. "There are plenty who might try." He drank, watching me carefully over the top of the cup, then set the cup aside. "See this jacket? The red signifies my merchant house, the color chosen typically as an indicator of the product I traded in when my house was first certified as a member of the guild. Mine is red because at the time I dealt mainly in imported wines.

"But my house has grown since then," he said. "I deal in many commodities now—spices, grain, cloth. The gold embroidery on the sleeves of the jacket and around the neck indicate all of the wares that my house has dealt in before." He pointed to his cuff. "These three lines cinched tight in the middle mean that I've traded in flax, that perhaps I have a source if someone is interested. This elongated circle indicates I've dealt in silks from the eastern city of Korvallo, across the mountains. The more embroidery, the more powerful the house. The jacket and the embroidery are a necessary part of the work of the guild, are in fact essential if my house is to remain influential in the guild and in the palace. But it has a drawback. It announces to the world exactly how powerful I am. And it attracts . . . undue attention."

"It makes you a target," I said.

Borund did not respond, turned his attention toward the ring of spilled ale the cup had left on the table instead, began spreading the ale around with one finger in small circular motions.

"You would no longer live on the wharf, of course, in your little pile of traps. If you came to work for me."

My eyes narrowed, a pulse of anger uncoiling deep within.

He glanced up briefly, then continued playing with the ring of ale. "Yes. I had you watched. I had to make certain you were trustworthy. That you weren't sent by one of the other merchants, as a spy perhaps." He sighed. "If you are interested, you would have to live in my house in the inner city. Sleep there, eat there. My schedule is not fixed, so I'd need you close, in case I had to leave quickly. I would provide everything you needed, within reason." The small circular motions stopped and he lifted his finger from the ale, lifted his eyes to me. "It would be a much better life than stealing what you can from the wharf."

I hesitated. The anger that he had followed me, had watched me—that he had done so without me noticing—felt raw and hot inside me. I should have seen them, should have noticed whoever had been sent to stalk me.

And that's exactly how I felt. As if I'd been stalked.

Suddenly, the bread and meat and butter felt heavy and sour in my stomach. I felt sick, the air inside the tavern too close, stifling. The noise and motion of the people began to push forward again, overpowering, like when I'd first stepped into the room.

Feeling feverish, I stepped away from the table. "I don't know." I took another step, the urge to run creeping up slowly from inside, tingling through my arms, even though there was no warning from the Fire inside me, no hint of danger.

Borund stood as well, sharply, frowning, one hand slightly outstretched as if to catch me before I fled. He seemed about to protest, but then he stopped, let his hand fall back to the table.

"Perhaps this was a mistake," he said.

And then the pressure of the room became too great, the noise and scents too harsh.

I turned, hesitated. . . . But in the end I slid through the crowd to the door and out into the new-fallen night.

Once outside the stifling tavern in the night air, I moved swiftly toward my niche, past people I barely saw before swerving around them. My mind was blank, empty. There was nothing to feel except the heavy weight of food in my stomach, nothing to taste but a strange fear tinged with a sickening excitement, all flavored like butter, smooth and slick inside my mouth. . . .

I stumbled over a trailing length of rope attached to a crab trap, caught myself against a wall. My heart thundered in my chest, so hard it hurt just beneath my breastbone. I coughed roughly, then straightened.

Drawing in another deep breath, I leaned my head back against the stone of the wall behind me.

I could still smell oranges.

I drew in a few more deep breaths, coughed half-heartedly, and sank down into a crouch, weight on my heels. On the street before me, a few people moved. Some slowed, watched me warily. No one came close.

I closed my eyes. Against the darkness, I thought about William grabbing my arm, felt the instant surge of fear, of desperation, of dread that this was another rapist like the first man I'd killed . . . or another Bloodmark.

But William wasn't one of those men. I could see it in his eyes, in his confused expression, in his mussed, clean hair. I could see it in the way he'd held out his hand to stop me from attacking a second time. And it was in his smile.

I shifted uneasily, feeling again that trembling sensation deep inside, somehow warm and tense at the same time, and strangely guilty.

I turned away from the sensation, thought about Borund instead, about how he'd offered the food, about his eyes. He'd been wary, reluctant at first, the wrinkles near his eyes tight. But then he'd relaxed, smiled, put the butter on that first slice of bread. Not the slow smile of Garrell Cart before he'd taken the girl on the Dredge, before he'd killed her. No. Borund's smile had been amused as he watched me take that first uncertain bite, as he watched me slather the butter onto the second slice myself.

But he'd also had me followed, watched, stalked. Like I imagined that ex-guardsman I'd killed had stalked me, or like Garrell Cart had watched the girl with the green cloth. Predatory.

Wariness twisted my stomach, made worse by William's confused eyes, by Borund's smile.

And by the oranges.

Erick had given me oranges. I'd trusted him. I trusted him still, even though I felt that I'd betrayed him in some way by killing Bloodmark. Even though that last image of him, at the edge of Cobbler's Fountain, before we'd found Mari, had been gray mixed with red. I didn't know what the red mixed with gray meant exactly, but I still trusted him.

I squeezed my eyes tighter, felt tears near the edges, felt them burn.

I suddenly wanted Erick back, wanted him there, at the edge of Cobbler's Fountain, waiting. I wanted to see his hard expression, his dark eyes, his scars. Even if it meant that the moment he saw me, the moment he laid eyes on me, he denounced me. Even if all he did was cast me out.

But I couldn't get Erick back. Not now. I'd made my choice.

I opened my eyes, wiped at them forcefully, then glared at a man who'd paused on the far side of the street.

He turned quickly and moved on.

I glanced around, dipped beneath the river briefly but saw no red, then stood and began moving toward my niche.

Sunlight glared off the rolling waves of the harbor in flashes, forcing me to squint and raise a hand to shade my eyes. At the end of the dock, a ship with three masts creaked against its lines as workers—Zorelli and Amenkor natives alike—hauled boxes and barrels down the ramp to the dock itself. It was the usual chaos that normally kept me enthralled with a strange tingling excitement deep down inside my stomach, but today I wasn't interested. Today, only William and Borund held my attention.

Both stood at the end of the plank that led to the deck of the ship, Borund dressed again in the red coat. William stood back and to one side, in a white shirt with ruffles down the front and brown breeches tucked into boots. Both were frowning in thought as the captain of the ship talked. I could only catch a few phrases of the conversation at this distance, and none of those phrases made sense. But I couldn't get any closer without revealing myself. I wasn't well hidden as it was.

Borund's frown turned grim and he shifted so that he was looking out toward the sea, toward where the two promontories of land to the west of the city jutted out and curved toward each other, forming a narrow inlet into the bay.

The captain of the ship finished his report and even through the chaos of the unloading around them, I could sense the silence between the three men growing. The shipmaster's fingers nervously kneaded the edge of the hat tucked under one arm as he watched Borund's face.

Finally Borund sighed and turned away from the sea. Forcing a smile, he gripped the shipmaster's arm at the elbow, squeezed once as he said a few words, and then the two nodded to each other, the captain donning his hat as Borund and William turned away.

I pulled back behind the stack of crates and waited, breathing in the salt air and looking up at the blue of the sky, the bustle of the wharf a few paces away.

When William and Borund passed by, I waited until they'd moved twenty paces farther on, then slipped into the flow of the wharf traffic behind them, close enough to hear what they said, but far enough back they wouldn't notice me. I'd been following them for the last week, whenever I managed to catch them on the wharf.

". . . getting worse," Borund was saying. The grim expression I'd seen on the docks had returned. "Mathew says that all the ports are as bad off as we are.

He's barely finding enough to trade and still keep his ship. If it doesn't pick up soon, he'll have to ground her or sell her."

"Perhaps you could buy it from him," William said. "Keep him on as captain."

Borund grunted. "Not if we can't get more trade going through the city. We've had to start cutting into the reserves as it is. There's just nothing out there. Too dry to the north, too wet to the south. And I don't know what the hell happened to the spice and silk routes through Kandish. The entire nation seems to have vanished. Avrell announced to the guild that nothing's come through the mountains in the last three months—no emissaries from Kandish, no caravans. He hasn't even heard from his own diplomats, and you know how widespread his network is."

He glanced toward William. "Something is happening, here along the Frigean coast and on the other side of the mountains. We have to find another source for our staples. Mathew says that he grabbed the last of the wheat in Merrell, and nearly all of the barley—as much as he could load into the ship without foundering. He paid a hefty price, but I think it was a wise choice."

"Should I send it on to Richar in Kent? Raise the asking price to compensate?"

Borund hesitated, then halted, his gaze once again turning toward the harbor. The flow of people on the wharf parted around him, like water around a dock support.

Twenty paces back, I slid into place beside a cart loaded with dead fish, their mouths open, eyes filmed with white. The hawker glared at me a moment, then turned back to the passersby, shouting with a startlingly loud voice, "Fresh fish! Just from the ocean! Fresh fish!"

At the center of the flow of people, Borund turned from the sea, his gaze traveling over the city of Amenkor itself, taking in the far side of the bay, where the buildings at the edge of the bluff rose to the mismatched angles of the roofs behind. It created a strange pattern above the slate of the water, and as I followed his gaze I suddenly realized with a sickening twist in my gut that there, among those roofs, across the bay on the other side of the River, lay the Dredge. And that on one of those roofs, almost six years ago, I'd watched the Fire emerge from the west and cut across the harbor, consuming everything.

And then I'd killed a man.

"No," Borund said, and I tore my gaze away from the buildings and from memory to see that Borund was now staring at the people moving about him, watching them as they haggled and cursed and rushed along the wharf. His voice had sharpened somehow, and his gaze flickered from face to face. But he didn't turn toward me. "No. Don't send the grain on. Tell Richar we have none to spare. And tell Mathew to purchase whatever he can find, no matter the cost."

Borund caught William's eyes and something passed between them, William's back straightening.

"Very well," he said.

Borund sighed and glanced up at the sun, the skin around his eyes wrinkling as he squinted. "I feel the need to check the warehouses suddenly. Take inventory. See exactly what and how much we have in stock, ready for use."

William stepped forward and they began walking away. I stayed behind. I'd followed them to the warehouses once before. There were no people around, no places to hide. And both William and Borund had disappeared into a single building for four hours while I waited in the rain.

I glanced down as they vanished into the crowd and caught sight of a small fish at the edge of the cart, its one eye slightly sunken into its head. Its scales had dried in the sun.

I cast a quick look toward the hawker.

Five minutes later, I was deep in the back streets, headed toward my niche, the dry fish held loosely in one hand.

Two days later, I settled into the edge of an alley across the street from the inn where William had first taken me to see Borund. It was early yet, the sky still blue, with thin bands of clouds, but within the hour it would be dark. I stared at the door to the inn, listened to the noise from inside spill out when someone entered, and tasted butter. Tasted it so badly I had to swallow.

I couldn't see far inside the inn, but Borund and William never showed up this early when they came. After a moment, I sat back on my haunches, leaned against the alley wall, and waited, closing my eyes.

William instantly rose to mind. His black hair, tugged by the wind coming in off the sea. His green eyes.

The liquid guilty sensation returned in the pit of my stomach, but this time I didn't force it away. It was strangely exciting. Different.

I found myself smiling for no reason.

And then the scent of oranges intruded.

I opened my eyes and sat forward. Twilight had settled onto the street, the sky gray now, the clouds tinged with the last of the sunset. Even as I inched forward, catching sight of Borund and William moving toward the door to the inn, the deep sunlight faded and died.

Borund halted at the door to the inn to talk to someone—another merchant by the man's dark green jacket, the amount of gold embroidery on his sleeves roughly equivalent to Borund's. But this merchant was accompanied by two other men. The merchants clasped arms, hands gripping forearms, and nodded to each other. William kept back a pace as they talked, but his attention was on the conversation. I watched him as he scanned the street around them, keeping a careful eye on the two men with the other merchant.

Perhaps I'd refused Borund's offer too quickly, I suddenly thought. I'd followed them for days, watched carefully to see if I was being followed still, tracked. But there'd been nothing. Neither Borund nor William had done anything aside from checking the docks, checking their warehouses, meeting with other merchants and with shipmasters on the pier.

I almost stood and moved across the street, moved to catch William's attention, but Borund ended the conversation with the merchant. He turned and motioned William inside, rough laughter breaking out from inside the inn as William opened the door. Borund nodded once toward the merchant with the green coat, who smiled and nodded back, and then the door closed and the laughter cut off.

I was just about to settle in and wait for Borund and William to leave, when the green-coated merchant turned.

The smile had vanished. In the last of the fading light, I saw the merchant's eyes narrow, his face harden with hatred.

A shudder slid through me and without thought I dipped beneath the river. In the rushing noise of the street, the merchant was mostly gray, but with faint traces of red at the edges.

Like Erick had been the last time I'd seen him.

I pulled back sharply, stared wide-eyed at the merchant across the street. For the first time since I'd killed Bloodmark and fled to the docks, I wondered what it meant. There'd been no need to wonder; I never expected to see Erick again, and I'd met no one else with the strange mix of red and gray.

But now . . .

I shifted forward, watched the merchant intently. He had a thin face, but soft somehow, not gaunt. His eyes were dark, but in the light I couldn't tell what color they were. His hair was dark as well.

For a moment, he searched the street, his eyes halting as he caught sight of a thin man leaning against a wall close to where I crouched. He pressed his lips together as if considering, then nodded once toward the thin man before turning away.

With a sharp gesture, the green-coated merchant called the other two men to his side. They left, moving swiftly.

I turned my attention toward the thin man leaning against the wall.

For a long moment, he did nothing but stare down at the cobbles of the street. Then he smiled and pushed himself away from the wall, moving sedately toward the inn. As he moved, he pulled a slim knife from his belt and tucked it up one sleeve of his shirt.

A shiver sliced through my gut, but before I could react, the man had opened the door to the inn, some type of music now mingling with the sound of voices spilling out. Then the door shut and the man was inside.

With Borund. And William.

I hesitated at the door to the inn, barely conscious of the fact that I'd crossed the street at a dead run, or that I'd slid beneath the river, deep. I shuddered at the memory of the last time I'd entered the inn, of how the people and voices and scents had overwhelmed me. But the memory lasted barely a breath before I pulled open the door.

It was as bad as the last time. Music, laughter, voices, belches, clattering pottery, creaking benches, all of it crashed into me, surged forward like a rolling wave on the bay, slapping into one of the dock's supports. And with it came the instant disorientation of the crowd, movement without purpose, without order, and the strong blanketing stench of sweat and smoke and ale.

But this time I forced everything into the background with a mental shove and focused, sifting through the noise and chaos.

The entire room . . . solidified. The blur of motion became bodies, servers weaving through the patrons with trays aloft, patrons clapping each other on the back or tossing back drinks. A man with garish clothing belted out a song while playing a strange instrument, and two women dressed like prostitutes but who weren't wove through the edges of the crowd, trailing filmy cloth, dancing. All noise bled into the background wind, making the foreground eerily silent. And the stench was damped, as if it had been shoved close to the floor—still there, lingering, but not strong.

A man staggered toward me and I stepped out of the way a second before he would have jostled into me. A look of annoyance crossed his face for a brief second, but he bumped into the next man through the door and stole that man's purse before leaving. My movement placed me in the midst of the crowd.

I spat a curse. I could no longer see, the people too close, blocking my view.

But I caught the scent of oranges.

Focusing on that, I sifted through the crowd, barely touching anyone. But the deeper I moved into the room, the greater the cold sense of urgency in my gut grew. I remembered the man's knife as he slipped through the door of the inn, could see his slow smile as he pushed away from the wall.

I gave up trying to go unnoticed and began shoving my way forward. The cold sensation flickered, then curled into a wisp of the Fire.

I staggered out of the press of bodies into an open area of tables. Gasping, I grabbed the back of a chair and scanned desperately for the thin man, for Borund and William.

I found Borund almost instantly, sitting at a back table. Moll, the woman who had served him before, was just setting down a platter of roasted meat and vegetables. I couldn't see William. Or the thin man.

I dove deeper into the river, going as deeply as possible, thinking of Garrell and the girl with the green ribbon. I hadn't been able to help the girl. I'd been too late. But I could help Borund.

I searched the crowd for splashes of red, realizing suddenly that I hadn't used the river outside when I'd seen the thin man. I'd been too shocked. Now I had no marker, no scent for him.

I latched onto a blur of red, almost lurched forward, hand already on my dagger, but realized it wasn't the thin man. Someone else, someone watching me closely, but too far away to worry about now. Another blur of red, and another, neither the thin man.

The Fire curled higher, grew, began to move up into my chest, toward my throat. The taste of oranges flooded my mouth.

There were no other splashes of red in the inn. The thin man wasn't here. Unless . . .

I paused, realized that all of the men who appeared red were watching me, were focused on me.

The thin man wasn't interested in me. He was interested in Borund.

I hesitated a moment, then closed my eyes and drew in a deep breath, frowning as I concentrated. I could feel the Fire growing in my chest, tingling in my shoulders, but I ignored it, focused on the separate sensation of the river instead, on its flow as it pushed around me. I reached out and touched it, pushed it, tried to alter its focus, turning it away from me . . . and toward Borund.

When I opened my eyes again, the texture of the room had changed. Everything was still gray tinged with other colors, but now there were more of them. The three men who had appeared red before were still red, but now they were somehow removed and unclear, faded. Now, there was a new set of red, a darker red than the others.

The men dangerous to Borund.

I unconsciously stepped forward, scanning the new faces.

The Fire began moving along my arms.

At the table, Borund took a swig from his ale, his meat already half eaten. He reached for a chunk of bread.

And then I saw the thin man.

He stood just behind Borund, within five paces. As I watched, the Fire sliding down to tingle in my fingers, the thin man's knife dropped from its hiding place in his sleeve into the palm of his hand and he began to move forward.

At the same time, someone halted just beside me and in a startled voice asked, "Varis?"

I turned, saw William's surprised eyes, his brow wrinkled in confusion—

And then he saw the dagger in my hand. I didn't remember drawing it.

His eyes went wide, and one hand rose as if to grab me . . . or maybe to ward me away as he'd done on the wharf when he first grabbed my arm and I attacked him. But before I could find out what he intended, I bolted toward Borund.

I think William shouted in alarm, but it was too hard to tell, his voice drowning in the background wind. The thin man now stood a pace behind Borund, had brought his thin dagger up toward Borund's back where he sat. I could see what he intended: a quick thrust up between Borund's ribs, like the thrust I'd used to kill Tomas, the man who'd attacked Bloodmark. If done right, Borund would barely feel it, might think it was someone bumping into him from behind, but it would kill him nonetheless.

Borund saw me at the last moment, a forkful of shredded meat raised half to his mouth. He jerked back, shock and fear registering in the breath before I crashed into him, his chair, and the thin man.

All I could think of as the three of us tilted, Borund grunting at the impact, was the dead girl's body—the girl with the green cloth.

Then we hit the floor. The edge of Borund's chair ground into my hip and with the sudden sharp pain I lost the river. Sounds crashed down—the splinter of wood, gasps, a scream, clattering pottery, and close, the rustling of clothes and bodies. My face was crushed into the thin man's shirt, into his chest, and the stench of salt and dead fish blotted out even the scent of oranges. I gagged on the cloth—

Then felt the shivering touch of metal as a knife sliced into my side, not deep, but enough to draw blood.

I hissed and jerked back, one hand finding purchase on the floor, catching the thin man's face as he struggled to pull away from me, from Borund. His arm was trapped beneath Borund's chair, held in place by Borund's weight, but his knife arm was still free.

Without thought, barely on my knees and with only my own dagger hand free, I sank my dagger into the thin man's stomach and pulled up, cutting hard and deep. Blood instantly stained his shirt and he gasped, eyes flying wide open. He flailed for a moment, and then all of the strength left his arms and shoulders and his free arm sank to the floor.

"What the bloody hell!" Borund shouted, still tangled up in the remains of his chair.

I pushed back and sat up on my knees over the thin man's body. He was still alive, gasping harshly, head and eyes moving back and forth as if he were searching for something. His hand spasmed and he dropped his dagger.

His eyes caught mine, held there for two short gasps, and then he died.

Inside, the Fire pulled back from my arms, from my chest, and settled quietly in my stomach.

Then someone grabbed me from behind, jerked me to my feet. Others grabbed my arms. I let them, only struggling when someone attempted to take my dagger. They backed off under my glare without touching the blade.

William emerged from the crowd into the space around Borund's table and instantly dropped to Borund's side, helping him untangle himself from his coat and the chair. Meat sauce stained the front of his coat, blood stained the back.

As he helped Borund up, William's gaze fell on the bloodied body of the thin man and he jerked back in distaste, cast a startled glance toward me.

The look in his eyes—fear, loathing, disgust—sent ice through my gut, as if someone had dashed frigid water up against my spine.

"What in hell is going on here?" Borund snapped the moment he was standing. He glared at me, until William leaned in close and whispered something in his ear.

Then his gaze fell on the body as well and the glare died in his eyes. He became suddenly very calm, no emotion showing at all, his back stiffening.

A man shoved through the crowd, his eyes angry. "What's the meaning of this?" he asked, but then he saw the body, saw me and the dagger. "Call the Guard."

"They're already here," someone said roughly, and two guardsmen pushed into the open. "What happened?"

"She killed him," someone said, and only then did I realize that the inn was silent. No music, no laughter, no voices. Only the rustle of bodies and a few taut whispers.

"Is this true?" one of the guardsmen asked Borund.

I watched Borund. I hadn't taken my eyes off him since William had helped him up. He stared at me intently, his face unreadable.

"Yes," he said. But before anyone could move, he added, "But she's my personal bodyguard, and this man was trying to kill me."

⊢ Chapter 9

"He tried to kill me!" Borund spat. I stepped back from the violence in his voice, almost slid into the darkness of the alley at the side of the tavern and vanished, an instinctive response from the Dredge. But Borund's violence was without a mark, and tinged with shock. "He tried to kill me, openly, in the middle of a tavern!"

We'd moved out of the tavern, stood now outside the door. Borund had removed his blood- and sauce-encrusted jacket, had folded it and handed it to William. William kept back a few paces from Borund, his face white and shaken, eyes wide. Like when I'd spun on the wharf and almost sliced open his chest. The horror of what I'd done, that I'd seen in his eyes earlier inside the tavern, had died. This was delayed reaction.

He glanced toward me. I held his gaze, didn't waver, even though I felt sick to my stomach.

"You're hurt," he said, but his voice was distant.

I looked down, grimaced at my sliced shirt, at the cut that had already stopped bleeding. "I'm fine. It's nothing. Barely a scratch."

Borund didn't notice.

On the street, a group of raucous men passed, pausing at the door, and Borund moved farther down the street, watching the group warily. Some of the shock was beginning to fade, replaced by a heated calm. I could see it in his eyes, even in the darkness.

He remained silent until the roar and music of the tavern was cut off behind the group of men. "He wasn't acting on his own. I've never seen the man before. He must have been hired."

"I wonder who sent him," William muttered.

Borund turned toward William. "That is the question, isn't it?"

"It was the green-coated merchant," I said.

Borund turned toward me. "Charls?" he asked incredulously.

"The one you spoke to before entering the tavern." I could see him clearly, the thin face, dark eyes filled with hatred. Gray mixed with red.

Borund stood still, as if unable to move, his mouth slightly parted.

Then the tavern door banged open and the guardsmen stalked out. I pulled back unconsciously, but Borund straightened as they turned and nodded.

They glanced once toward me, eyes suspicious, mouths tight. A new fear clawed through me. I wondered if Erick had told them about me, had told them to watch for me, that I'd murdered someone and then fled.

But there was no recognition in these guardsmen's eyes, only a generalized distrust, as if they still didn't believe Borund's story, knew that something about it was wrong. But they couldn't figure out what. Not with William supporting the statement. No one else in the tavern had seen anything, or was willing to come forward.

The guardsmen nodded again and stalked off, heading toward the palace, its walls on the hill overlooking the city lit with oil light. I felt tensed muscles relax, in my shoulders, in my gut.

When the guards faded into the darkened streets, Borund turned toward William. "You tried to warn me before. Did you know it was Charls?"

William shook his head. "No. I only knew that it no longer felt safe to move around in Amenkor, especially at night. I didn't realize there was such a . . . personal threat."

Borund grunted. "Then it was good you brought up your concerns when you did, otherwise I'd be dead."

He turned toward me, his eyes intent, as hard and unreadable as stone. "And you," he said softly. "It was a gift of the Mistress that you were here. A very fortuitous gift."

I straightened under his stare and said, "I've been watching you, following you." The words were harsh, defensive, defiant.

"I see. Is that how you know it was Charls?"

"After he spoke with you, he motioned to the man who tried to kill you. Then left."

"And you followed that man into the tavern? To stop him from killing me?"

I drew breath to answer, then glanced toward William. He still seemed shocked, his hair appearing even wilder. But he was more focused now, paying closer attention.

Instead of answering out loud, I simply nodded.

Borund considered this, his gaze so intense I was forced to look away.

Finally, he murmured, "Fortuitous gift indeed." As if he'd reached a decision, he stirred, glanced once toward William and back. "Have you reconsidered my offer? I'm forced to agree with William now. A bodyguard is necessary."

I stood straight, hesitated only a moment, and said, "What do you want me to do?"

They led me through the streets of the wharf, beyond the warehouses, and up into the streets below the palace, into the upper city. Borund offered to return to my niche, to gather up whatever I wanted, but I had my dagger, my clothes. There was nothing in the space I'd formed out of crab traps and tarps. Nothing worth returning for.

We moved swiftly through the streets, William ahead while I trailed behind, both of the men tense, wary.

At one point, we passed the end of the bridge where I'd crossed the River from the Dredge into Amenkor. I paused, stared out over the expanse, over the river water, and thought of Erick, of the white-dusty man, of Cobbler's Fountain.

Then I turned away. Both Borund and William had stopped farther on up the road, were looking back at me, but neither said anything when I moved to follow them.

Carriages appeared, and men on horseback, and once two guardsmen. Each time Borund slowed until the men and horses had passed. The buildings— crowded and close at first, with narrow alleys—changed. Courtyards appeared, not ruined and decayed like on the Dredge, but with closed iron gates and trees. Alleys widened. Surrounding walls appeared, the buildings set back from the streets, enclosed and protected. And the stench of fish and salt and sea faded.

Then William paused on a corner, scanned in all directions, and moved purposefully across the street to a small gate set back inside an alcove in a wall. A moment later, Borund and I joined him.

As William unlocked the wrought-iron gate, Borund turned and muttered, "This is your new home, Varis."

We stepped inside a garden, pathways curling away in all directions, clear in the darkness because they were made of white stone and glowed in the moonlight. Trees, branches hanging down limply, sighed in a sudden breeze from the harbor, smelling of the ocean. Everything was shadowed, details hard to make out in the darkness.

Borund strode quickly into the garden, toward a building I could barely see, leaving William and me behind.

"What's wrong?" William asked.

I looked up into William's eyes, saw the stars behind him, and said, "There should be buildings here. It shouldn't be so . . . empty. It's unnatural."

William smiled. "It's a garden. It's supposed to be empty, without buildings." He shook his head, then moved out into the garden.

A twinge of guilt slid through me, as if I'd done something wrong. I watched him a moment before following.

We passed into the shadow of the building, to another door. Borund was waiting for us inside, at the beginning of a long hallway, along with an elderly man and a woman who carried a lantern. More light could be seen farther down the hall.

"Lizbeth," Borund said, and the woman dipped her head anxiously. "This is Varis. She's going to be staying here for the immediate future. Have a room made up, with whatever she requires."

Lizbeth turned her gaze on me, frowning. Her eyes were sharp, like Bloodmark's, catching every detail, noting every mark, every tear, every smudge and bruise. "Will she be needing new clothes?"

Borund turned to look at me, then smiled tightly. "Yes. New clothes. But nothing too removed from what she's wearing right now. No dresses. Nothing . . . ruffled or anything. Bring her a variety and let her choose."

Lizbeth nodded. "And water for a bath, I expect. Soap, too. Lots of soap."

"Whatever Varis wants, nothing more." There was a hint of warning in Borund's voice, and Lizbeth shot him a questioning look. "Varis is part of the household now."

"As what? We can't afford any more help."

A wave of annoyance passed over Borund's face and he frowned heavily. "Varis is my new bodyguard. She'll be with us whenever we leave the manse."

Lizbeth backed away slightly, her sharp gaze returning to me with renewed interest. "I see. I'll go get the water started in the bathing room. Is the east room acceptable?"

Borund glanced toward me. "No. The east room is too big. Give her Joclyn's old room for now."

"Joclyn's room? But that's just a serv—" Lizbeth cut off abruptly, going still as Borund placed a hand on her arm.

"Joclyn's room, Lizbeth. I know what I'm doing." There seemed to be something else in Borund's voice—caution or warning.

Lizbeth nodded, although her brow remained creased with a frown. Borund let his hand drop, and Lizbeth handed the lantern over to the other man, took Borund's stained jacket from William, then hefted up the edges of her skirts with her free hand and dashed down the hall, vanishing through a side door.

The rest of the group turned to follow. I trailed behind.

"Gerrold."

"Yes, sir," the older man answered.

"Have some food brought to Varis' room. Whatever you have to spare in the kitchen at this late hour. Bread, wine . . . no, make that water, and . . . and butter." Borund grinned and glanced back briefly. "Lots of butter. Once that's done, meet William and me in the office." And here, Borund's voice grew dark. "We have much to discuss."

"Yes, sir."

I was awake when someone knocked on the door of the room Lizbeth had led me to the night before. The room was too large, containing a bed, a desk, a chair, a lantern, and a tall piece of furniture with many drawers against one wall. A large bowl rested on top of this last piece of furniture, with a pitcher full of water.

"Varis?" Lizbeth called, her voice muffled by the door. "Varis, are you awake? Borund would like to talk to you and he asked me to get you ready."

There came another light tapping at the door, and then Lizbeth opened it, tentatively, and peeked in. When she saw the bed hadn't been slept in, she opened the door wide in alarm, then caught sight of me.

The panic on her face vanished and she raised the hand not holding a stack of clothes to her breast and sighed heavily. "Thank the Mistress! Is everything all right? Where in heavens did you sleep?"

My gaze flicked unconsciously toward the darkness beneath the bed, then back toward her as the muscles in my shoulders stiffened defiantly.

Lizbeth frowned in incomprehension, head turning, and then nodded. "Ah."

Her expression softened. "Not used to beds? Nor baths either, I expect." Her eyes narrowed as she took in my hair, my face. She'd left me standing over a large tub of water the night before. I'd stared at the water a long time, thinking of the barrel of rainwater I'd used after fleeing the Dredge, wondering why this tub was so large. I'd dipped my arms into the water, shocked at how cold it was. After scrubbing at my arms, I'd discovered the steps on one side and realized I was supposed to climb into the water, like when I was six at Cobbler's Fountain.

"Looks like we'll be needing another bath," Lizbeth said at the door, more to herself than to me. "Apparently, all that murky water I drained away last night was only the surface dirt. At least today we've had time to haul in and heat the water." She came farther into the room and set the clothes down on the bed, moving carefully. "William explained the situation last night, after I left you at the bath. He said I was to help you . . . adjust."

She turned toward me, the harshness I'd seen in her eyes the night before gone. Then she stepped forward, stopping a few paces away with an uncertain smile. "He said to be careful with you. That you might not understand how things are done around the manse, and that anything you wanted was to be provided. Is there anything you'd like this morning?"

I didn't answer. She held my gaze a moment, but then her eyes drifted to my clothes.

"Nothing this morning? Well then, I brought you some new clothes, something better than those rags." Her eyes returned to mine, narrowed shrewdly. "And I expect you'd like something to eat? Eggs perhaps? Maybe some bacon?"

I shifted forward and my stomach growled, loudly enough for Lizbeth to hear. I frowned in annoyance, and Lizbeth smiled tightly, trying to control a grin.

"I thought so. Let's get you into a bath first, then try out these new clothes, and after *that* we'll see what they have in the kitchen. How does that sound?"

Lizbeth led me to a hallway outside a large wooden door three hours later, my skin feeling raw from the bath Lizbeth had presided over, my new clothes scratchy, loose, and smelling of soap. I wore a brown shirt, brown breeches with a thin leather belt, and sandals. My hair hung damply around my face in tendrils, my head aching from how often my hair had been pulled by Lizbeth. She'd finally given up trying to untangle it and had cut most of the length away with a pair of scissors. It now hung down to my chin, rather than past my shoulders.

I'd glared at her the entire time, but she'd ignored me. She'd ignored my grunting protests when she'd tried to dip my head underwater as well, simply placing her hand on the top of my head and pushing me under with surprising strength. She'd soaped up my hair before I'd stopped spluttering, talking the entire time about the manse and how it was run.

Now, she rapped on the large wooden door and cast one last critical glance over me as I stuffed the last of the buttered bread into my mouth.

"You'll do," she mumbled, then caught my gaze and added sternly, "for now. I'll show you around the manse once Borund is done with you." She eyed me carefully for a long moment, and then her eyes softened and she relaxed. Like the white-dusty man had relaxed when he'd seen me take the rolls.

Something tightened at the base of my throat, hard and hot, making it difficult to swallow the last of the bread. I choked a little, turned away to cough as my eyes blurred with tears.

When I turned back, she was already halfway down the hall.

Then the door opened and instinctively I reached for the dagger and backed against the wall.

I caught myself just as my hand touched steel, recognizing William.

"Borund's waiting," he said, ignoring my sudden movement.

I straightened and followed him as he turned away, moving into a huge room. I'd thought the bedroom had been large until Lizbeth had led me to the kitchen. But this room was twice the size of the kitchen. The walls were lined with shelf upon shelf of small statues, wooden boxes polished to a high sheen, cut stone, glass vases, candleholders, and plants. A large rug covered most of one wall, above a stone fireplace with no fire, but stained with soot. A large sword, three times the length of my dagger, rested in a sheath on a shelf above the fireplace. The wooden floor of the room was scattered with chairs and rugs and small tables. Most of the objects were obviously from Amenkor, but a few were too exotic, the patterns too strange. An intricately carved staff leaned against one corner, the dancing figures clearly Zorelli.

Borund sat behind a large desk in the center of the room, papers spread out before him in every direction. William took a seat to Borund's left behind the desk and pulled a set of neater pages toward himself. He dipped what looked like a stick into a small black bottle and scratched at the pages.

I halted at the door, wary of the size of the room, then forced myself to move toward the desk.

Borund sighed in disgust as I approached. "Put half in the warehouse and send the rest on. Send all of the spice to Marlett."

"They don't want the spice," William said as he made more scratches. "They want the wheat."

"Well, they can't have it. Not at that price. And they won't be willing to accept the price I *would* take for it, so they'll have to choke on the spice."

"What if they won't take it?"

"Then it will have to rot in our warehouse in Marlett rather than here. We don't have enough room here."

"We don't have enough room in Marlett either. Not for spice."

"Then let it rot on the ship!"

William stared at Borund with a frown and said distinctly, "Very well."

Borund drew in a deep breath, face darkening, then blew out the air in a rush, raising a hand to his forehead. He massaged his temple, then removed the curved wire from his face. This close, in the light streaming in through the windows to one side, I could see glass inside the wires and suddenly realized why they had flashed in the sunlight on the docks. I hadn't seen the glass in the tavern, nor on the streets outside. It had always been too dark, or I'd been too far away.

"Apologies, William. I think the attack yesterday has affected me more than I want to admit."

"You've been working all morning. You should take a rest."

Borund grunted. "If only I could. But it's become so much harder. It's already midsummer. Winter is approaching fast and we haven't half of what we need in the warehouses." He shifted all the papers to one side in a disorderly stack and turned his attention to me.

His eyes widened in slight surprise. "I see that Lizbeth has been at work. You look . . . like an entirely different person." He paused and I shifted my stance, weight settling slightly forward, arms spread farther away from my body. My eyes narrowed, face hardened.

"Ah," he mumbled. "There's the Varis I know."

My shoulder muscles tensed. "You never told me what you wanted me to do."

He smiled, leaned back in his chair. William had set his papers aside and was now organizing Borund's stack.

"I want you to protect me. It's as simple as that. Just as you did last night at the tavern. I want you to accompany me whenever I leave the manse, follow me, like a shadow. Warn me of any dangers, protect me if you need to. But I expect you to warn me first. Is that acceptable?"

I thought suddenly of Mari, saw Bloodmark kneeling over her, his knife cutting down sharply and deeply, heard her screaming. I saw her trying to push herself upward after Erick had knocked Bloodmark aside, saw her watching me.

And then, abruptly, I saw the white-dusty man's face, saw the blood splattered on his forehead and cheeks from the Skewed Throne symbol that had been carved into his chest.

I hadn't been able to protect them. But I hadn't realized they needed protection, especially by someone like me. I'd always assumed they could protect themselves.

I stared into Borund's eyes—a dark brown, like mud—then drew myself upward and said, "I can protect you."

For a moment, I felt a faint curl of the Fire deep inside me rise up, sending a cold shiver through my gut. But then it died.

"Good," Borund said, then rose from his seat. William rose as well, putting the neat sheaf of papers to one side. Borund reached for a small pouch on the corner of the desk, lifted it, and held it out for me.

I frowned, hesitated, then took a step forward to take the pouch.

It held coins. More coins than I'd seen my entire time on the Dredge.

Gutterscum didn't deal in coins.

I turned a confused glance toward Borund, then William.

"Those are your wages," Borund said quietly, his voice gruff, but undercut with a note of pleasure. "It's what you'll earn every month you're in my service. I'll provide room and board as well of course." He smiled. "And as much butter as you want."

I held the pouch, not knowing what to do with it, until Borund cleared his throat.

"I'll have Lizbeth put that in your room for you," he said, leaning across the desk to take the pouch back. "For now, let's begin with a courteous visit to our dear friend Charls."

His voice was light and carefree, but tinged with darkness.

We stepped out into sunlight through a polished wooden door twice my width, banded with iron. Three wide, curved, tiered steps led down to a white-cobbled path wider than the Dredge. It led straight through the garden I'd seen in the darkness last night to an open front gate. Trees rustled in the sunlight. Gerrold waited at the bottom of the steps with three horses and a young boy I didn't know holding the three sets of reins. One of the horses stamped its foot and shook its head.

My eyes narrowed as Borund and William moved toward the horses. I stayed on the rounded top of the stairs, by the door. On the Dredge, horses were to be avoided, unless they could be ducked under for a quick but dangerous escape. Most were larger than me, and definitely heavier.

Borund was already seated before he realized I hadn't moved. "I assume you haven't ridden," he said dryly.

"No."

He frowned. "That will have to change. But not today. We'll move slow enough you can follow." He turned toward Gerrold. "Gerrold, you should have known she couldn't ride."

The man ducked his head briefly. "My apologies. I didn't think, sir."

Borund nudged the horse toward the gate.

William mounted with smooth skill, then motioned the boy and the remaining horse along another path toward the back of the manse. He turned toward me. "The horse won't bite," he said. "Come and touch him."

Ahead, Borund had paused, had turned back in his saddle to watch, annoyed.

I came down the steps reluctantly, halted just out of reach of the horse. He snorted, nosed forward as if trying to smell me, but William kept him in check with the reins and a soft clicking sound. The horse's ears swiveled back at the noise, then forward as he lowered his head.

I had to look up into his eyes, but I reached out tentatively with one hand, glancing toward William. William smiled and nodded his head, so I touched the horse on its neck.

The horse remained still, not moving, a shudder running down the muscles in his neck. The short brown hair felt smooth and warm in the sunlight, taut with energy, ready for motion. I stroked the horse's neck and the creature snorted again.

I smiled and laughed, the sound strange and startling in the late morning stillness.

When I looked up toward William, he was grinning, his face open, easy to read, his eyes bright. "I never would have thought to hear you laugh," he said, and then *he* laughed himself, as if the statement were somehow absurd.

He turned the horse, slowly, so the movement wouldn't startle me. Farther down the path, Borund turned back to the gate. His annoyance had vanished, replaced by amused tolerance. I fell into step a few paces away from William and his horse, far enough to run if necessary, but close enough I could still smell the horse's dark humid sweat.

"The horse's name is Fetlock," William said as we caught up to Borund and entered the street, "and Borund's mount is called Brindle, because Gart—the stableboy—thought the horse's color was shit-brindle brown when we bought him. The name stuck."

Borund snorted and mumbled, "Bloody stupid name," under his breath, shaking his head. But he was smiling. He reached forward and patted Brindle's neck roughly, the horse nodding his head as if in agreement.

The streets of Amenkor this close to the palace were practically empty and I gazed up at the sky as I had done on the Dredge, raising one hand to shade away the sun. There were no clouds today, the sky a pure blue. A steady breeze blew in from the harbor.

I let my gaze drop to the water of the harbor. Borund's manse was situated high enough up the slope that I could see down over the rooftops to the wharf, could see the masts of the ships tied at the docks. More ships sat in the harbor itself, appearing calm amid the slate gray of the waves.

I ignored the far side of the bay to my left, across the River, where the Dredge ran. Instead, I turned my gaze in the other direction, upward, toward the palace.

In the sunlight, the walls seemed smooth, colored like brown eggshell, with only a few windows at the lower levels. There were three layers of walls, the palace offset from the center inside the third wall, a few towers rising into the empty sky. Flags and banners flapped in the wind, too far away to be heard, their colors bright against the light brown of the palace and the sky.

"That's where we're headed," William said beside me, nodding toward the palace and the walls. "The old city. It's where we're most likely to find Charls this time of day."

I stared at what I could see of the palace between the buildings and above the walls a long moment, then turned my attention to the street. We were moving from the mostly empty streets where Borund's manse lay into more crowded areas, and almost without thought I slid beneath the river.

It was just like the Dredge. Or the wharf. A world of gray and red, a wash of sound in the background.

The tension in my shoulders and back shifted, from nervousness about the horses and William and Borund, to apprehension about protecting them from Charls. I could still feel the tavern, the desperation as I'd fought through the crowded tables, searching. I glanced up to William to see if he'd noticed, but he was watching the street intently, frowning, as focused as I was. He could still feel the tavern as well. I could see it in his eyes.

So I turned back to the street and with a subtle push on the river felt it shift, new people emerging to the fore, those that were possible threats to Borund. Those that were threats to me—the guardsmen, men with visible weapons—mostly slid into the background, a bleached red.

I settled in to watch.

We emerged onto a wide, crowded street and turned into the general flow heading up toward the palace. The noise increased, people shouting, hawkers bellowing, men cursing. The crush of horses and men—many more horses than I was used to—forced me to walk closer to William and Fetlock, almost touching the horse's side. Up ahead, I could see the first wall, an arched gateway standing open to the street. As we approached, the crush of bodies grew worse, as bad as the press of the tavern, tight and restrictive. The background noise beneath the river tripled and I felt my control beginning to slip, felt sweat break out on my back, in my armpits, felt my breathing increase.

Then we were through the gate, past the wall, and the crowd fell back, loosened.

I blew out a held breath, then steadied. Neither Borund nor William seemed to notice me or the crowds, continuing on up toward the second wall.

I tried to calm myself, my heart still shuddering in my chest.

"This is the outer circle," William suddenly said, motioning toward the surrounding buildings, "or rather, outer oval. This is where most of the merchants live, along with a few of the highest-ranking Guard and sea captains. Those with some influence. Essentially it's a residential area, close to the palace for when there's a need for the merchants to speak with Avrell, the First of the Mistress—or, more rarely, the Mistress herself—about trade negotiations and how they might affect the city or our relations to the surrounding cities of the coast. It's also close to the guild halls in the middle circle, and the wharf and the warehouse district below, on the harbor. Borund could live here if he wanted, but chose to live below, in the city. He always felt that living here would distance him from the everyday man. He was raised near the wharf, built his merchant house out of nothing but spit and hard work." William had straightened in his saddle, watched the passing buildings with a strange hope in his eyes. Almost under his breath, he added, "I want to live here someday, though."

I glanced around and frowned. This close to the main street, the buildings were tight together, almost as tight as the Dredge, and each doorway had a painted sign over it, all with designs that had no meaning to me. Two crossed swords on one, a three-masted ship on another. One seemed to be three squiggled lines, like waves. Through the paned windows, I could see mostly empty rooms, the only furnishings desks and chairs and high countertops. Shelves lined the walls, packed with statues and plants like Borund's room. A few had large sacks and barrels instead. Most had sheaves of papers scattered over the desks and on the walls. And then I noticed that here and there, almost lost among the rest of the shops, were a few empty buildings, doors closed, windows boarded up. The empty buildings sent a cold shudder across my shoulders, as if someone had just breathed against the nape of my neck.

The empty buildings reminded me of the Dredge. This is what the Dredge must have once looked like—its buildings intact, its streets full of merchants and shoppers. But now this street was beginning to decay, beginning to fade. The empty stores were simply the first outward sign. My frown deepened.

"There's nothing for sale in those shops," I said.

I meant the empty buildings, but William didn't seem to notice them, didn't even seem to see them. He smiled without looking down at me. "Ah, but that's the thing. Amenkor is the crossroads of the Frigean coast, the gateway to the nations in the east, on the far side of the mountains. *Everything's* for sale in these shops. You just have to know the right person."

I didn't answer, uneasiness settling into my stomach.

Up ahead, we were approaching another gate and the second wall. William turned away from the shops toward the wall. "And this is the middle circle. All the guild halls are in here. We'll find Charls at the merchants' guild, no doubt." His voice darkened when he mentioned Charls. "That's where most of the actual business of trading and selling takes place."

We passed through the second gate into a large, open, square marketplace with huge stone buildings on all sides, broken up by various streets. The marketplace was crowded, but there were fewer hawkers than on the wharf. They stuck mainly near the center of the square, around the towering fountain. I paused to stare at the three stone horses that reared toward the sky, a spit of water pouring out of the top, three more spouts of water emerging from the horses' mouths. The water collected in a giant pool at the base.

Cobbler's Fountain seemed suddenly small and insignificant, almost childish.

William and Borund continued across the square, toward the largest of the stone buildings, its front riddled with carved statues of men and women, lying down on stone benches, standing and reaching for the sky, most wearing nothing at all. Some appeared to move until we got closer and I realized there were birds in the crevices of the carvings. There were birds everywhere, on the cobbled square itself, lining the stone steps leading up to the doorway that seemed small in comparison to the rest of the building. They fluttered out of the way of passersby, muttering soft, throaty coos of protest.

I followed Borund and William numbly, but we didn't approach the steps. Instead, we moved toward a side street, passing beneath an arch and along a narrow until it opened up into a courtyard where men practiced with swords and boys rushed, running errands. As soon as Borund and William appeared and dismounted, two boys stepped forward and led the horses away.

Borund motioned to William as we entered the merchants' guild through a side door and began climbing stairs. "He'll be in the Great Hall now," he said, glancing back quickly toward me. His mud-brown eyes were hooded and dangerous, but not like Erick's had been. Erick's eyes had been cold, purposeful, casual. Borund's were heated and intense, angry.

We passed through a low-arched doorway and into the Great Hall and I tensed, the hackles on the back of my neck rising. I resisted the urge to crouch, to draw my dagger and slip back through the doorway. I couldn't stop a harsh hiss of warning, like a pissed-off cat.

In the swirling gray world of the river, almost everyone in the room was red. A shroud fell over me, covered me like a blanket, pushed me down with its weight. All of the awe over the size of the room—over the fountain and the buildings and the walls outside as well—died, replaced by the instincts of the Dredge.

"What is it?" someone murmured, the voice muffled by the pressure I felt from the river. Then someone touched my arm.

William. I could *feel* him, smell him. Borund, as well. But I didn't turn to look at them. Instead, I kept my gaze focused on the room, on the people milling about, on the soft background noise of their conversations.

"What is it, Varis?" Borund asked, his voice a little more commanding than William's.

"Everyone here is dangerous," I said.

He grunted. "How can you tell?"

"I can see it," I answered without thought. "They're all red."

A long, heavy silence followed, but I was too distracted by the pressure to notice until Borund spoke again, his voice tight. "I'm only interested in one of them today, and I don't see him. Do you?"

I drew a deep breath and tried to concentrate more. As I submerged myself deeper, the reds shifted into various shades, some darker, like blood, others more vibrant.

I focused on those like blood, pushed the others into the background. There were fewer of them, and one of them was Charls.

He wasn't a mix of red and gray now, but a deep red. Even when I shifted the focus of the river back to myself briefly.

"There," I said, and pointed.

Borund laid a hand gently on mine and lowered it slowly. "Don't draw attention. Just nod in the right direction. We don't want anyone here to know the real reason we came."

I frowned, then realized it was like the Dredge, like standing at the edge of a narrow, looking for a mark.

Borund wanted us to be gray.

I nodded in the direction of Charls, and with a swift look at William, Borund began to move through the room. I kept my attention fixed on Charls and the few other washes of blood red. Borund paused occasionally to speak with other merchants, some dressed like Borund in long coats of differing colors with gold embroidery. Most had less gold than Borund, and after a quick scan of each, I dismissed them as harmless.

We edged closer to Charls, moving in a wide arc.

"Borund!"

I turned to see a dark blue-coated merchant approaching, arms held wide. He had a plain face, a wide grin, hazel eyes, dimples. His hair hung down to his shoulders and had been tied back into a ponytail. He had no trace of red to him at all.

Borund smiled as they grasped arms at the elbows and clapped each other on the back. "Marcus, it's good to see you! How's Marlett?"

A bitter expression crossed Marcus' face and he scowled. "The city's hurting. Not enough wares to be found. And what we can find is becoming too expensive to buy."

"Not much better here in Amenkor, I'm afraid."

Marcus turned serious. "I heard about the tavern."

"Word travels fast."

"Good you had a bodyguard, eh?"

There was a hint of something more behind Marcus' voice and Borund fell silent. I gave Marcus a dark stare. Unconsciously, he shifted away.

"Yes. My bodyguard."

After a moment, Marcus cleared his throat. "I also hear you have some grain in storage?"

"You shouldn't always listen to rumor, Marcus. Now spice! I have plenty of spice!"

"I don't need spice," Marcus protested darkly, and the two began bargaining, just like any hawker and his victim on the Dredge or wharf. I let the conversation fall into the background and turned back to Charls.

He'd shifted, moved to the edge of the room, toward one of the walls covered in tapestries. Most of the room was empty of furniture, the polished stone floor bare, but near some of the walls sat a few chairs. Light streamed through tall, thin windows, slanting across the floor at an angle, but Charls stood in the most shadowed corner of the room now.

He spoke with someone I could barely see. Someone as blood red as himself. Another merchant.

I stepped back from Borund, Marcus, and William and focused.

He wore a dark yellow coat, like mustard, covered with gold thread. Ruffles filled the neck, puffed out of the sleeves. His face was narrow, but not thin, his nose long. He had a mustache, neatly trimmed. His brown hair was streaked heavily with gray and hung down his back in a ponytail longer than Marcus'.

He seemed somehow vaguely familiar.

I felt William step up beside me and realized that Borund had broken away from Marcus and moved on. I turned back to Charls, drew breath to ask William who Charls was speaking to, but the mustard-coated merchant had vanished.

Charls had moved back out into the light when Borund finally approached him. He smiled graciously.

"Master Borund," he said, his voice deep and somehow slick, like the dead fish on the wharf.

"Master Charls," Borund murmured. None of the danger I'd seen in his eyes touched him as he reached out and grasped Charls' arm at the elbow, as he'd done with Marcus, the contact brief.

Deep inside, I felt the Fire stir, a shiver running down the backs of my arms. I shifted slightly forward.

"Rough crowd down at the Broken Mast Tavern, so I hear," Charls said.

"Nothing I couldn't handle." Borund grinned. "That's why I like the docks. Always something . . . unexpected."

Charls' eyes flicked toward me, absorbed me with one quick, careful, considering glance, then stole away, back to Borund. "Yes. Something 'unexpected' always seems to intervene when you least expect it." There was a tinge of sourness to the words. But then Charls shifted. "But Amenkor has become desperate. Roughness is to be expected, just to survive. Wouldn't you agree, Master Borund?"

"No," Borund said shortly. And now he let the anger inside darken his eyes, blatant and targeted. "No. And it won't be tolerated either. The Mistress will see to that."

Charls seemed surprised, but then his smile widened.

The tendril of Fire inside surged higher and my hand stole toward my dagger. William sensed the movement and shifted farther away.

"Ah, Borund," Charls murmured, his voice soft. "I think you place too much faith in the Mistress. I don't think she rules the city anymore. Haven't you heard? The Mistress has gone insane."

Borund snorted. "And now you deal in rumor?" An edge entered Borund's voice. "Beware of what you play at, Charls. There is more at stake here than just business. You're dealing with the life of the city. The Mistress will hear about the attack last night."

Charls chuckled. "Yes, yes. Tell the Mistress, if you can reach her. She doesn't grant audience to anyone anymore. To even get into the palace you have to get through Captain Baill and his guards. And then your chances of seeing Avrell, let alone the Mistress, are slim. The Mistress has never been this hard to reach in the past. I wonder why? And as for the city . . ." Charls leaned forward, his eyes going dark and tight. The Fire inside flared and I stepped forward, stepped between the two, near Borund's shoulder, my hand on the dagger hidden at my side.

Charls didn't flinch, his eyes fixed firmly on Borund.

"You would be wise to leave the city alone, Master Borund. Powers are shifting, have been shifting since the Fire scoured its way across Amenkor. You slipped through the net once; I wouldn't wait around to see if it happens again."

Charls backed off, smiled thinly and reached to brush nonexistent lint off of Borund's shoulder. I halted him with a look and a slight shift in weight.

His smile faltered.

Then he moved away, engaged another merchant in conversation, his laugh echoing loudly over the conversations in the hall at something the merchant said. The merchant looked confused, but Charls put his hand on the merchant's back and guided him away, head bent close.

He glanced back once, smile tight and self-satisfied.

Then he was lost among the crowd.

At my back, Borund trembled with suppressed rage.

⊦— The Palace —⊦

My heart had barely begun to calm, back still pressed against what had once been a granite wall outside the archer's niche, when there were sudden hurried footsteps from the corridor on the other side of the little window.

I slid down close to the opening and peered into the hallway just in time to see the two guardsmen I'd noted before jerk to rigid attention on either side of the doorway they guarded. They'd barely managed to compose themselves when another guard appeared, approaching fast, almost at a run.

I saw him just before he reached the two guards and shuddered, drawing back from the old window.

Captain Baill.

Beside the archer's window, I cursed, then slid back to watch, eyes narrowed in anger and suspicion. What was Baill doing here now? He should be safely occupied elsewhere. In the city, on the walls, at home in bed—anywhere but in the inner sanctum of the palace.

Unless someone had warned him, had alerted him to my presence. But who?

Captain Baill wore all the armor of his rank, was moving swiftly, his eyes darkened with intense irritation and something close to hatred. His bald head gleamed in the torchlight, his face covered in scars. Old scars. *Earned* scars. They surrounded dark eyes that shifted restlessly even as he walked— calculating eyes that saw everything, and *remembered*.

He moved toward the two guardsmen with purpose, barked, "Has anyone passed by here in the last hour?"

"No one, Captain."

"Fuck!"

The two guards glanced at each other, startled. Baill stared at the stone floor a moment, one hand rising to rub across his bald head.

Then he glanced up, scarred face hard.

"Come with me," he said.

One of the guards began to protest, motioning toward the door they guarded.

"It's a fucking audience chamber!" Baill roared. "There's nothing in there! We've got bigger problems."

And he began moving away, fast. Toward the main entrance to the inner sanctum, the doorway that had once been an outer gate.

The two guards hesitated a moment, then followed.

Then they were gone.

*   *   *

I dropped back from the archer's window, heart suddenly pounding. *Did* Baill know I was here? *Had* he been warned?

The fear twisted into anger, the taste of sickness on my tongue now bitter, like ash.

Had Avrell had a change of heart and warned them? Had *he* betrayed me?

It seemed unlikely. He was the one who'd hired me. He'd been the one arguing so fervently with Nathem to convince him that the Mistress' death was essential.

But who else could it have been? No one else knew I was here tonight except Avrell. He'd seen me in the meeting room, knew exactly where I was. . . .

A sudden flood of relief washed over me. It *had* been Avrell. But he hadn't warned Baill to betray me. He'd done it to help. Avrell knew the plan, knew I'd been in the meeting room, *knew that I was behind schedule*. He must have assumed I'd miss the changing of the guard.

So he'd provided the guardsmen with a distraction.

My hand tightened on my dagger in determination and I spun back to the archer's window, gauged the narrow opening. It didn't matter if Avrell had warned Baill to help me, or if someone else had warned Baill to stop me. Whatever the case, this might be my only chance to get past the outer perimeter of palace guardsmen. And I *had* to reach the Mistress tonight. There was no more time left, not if the city was to survive the winter.

Placing one hand at the top of the opening, reaching through with the other, I shoved my head and shoulders through. If I'd had anything in the way of breasts, I'd have been fucked. It was the only reason I'd been passable as a page boy, and one of the only reasons the plan to get me into the inner sanctum of the palace would work.

I exhaled sharply, pushing all the air out of my lungs in one hard gasp, and wedged my chest through next. Pausing to get a better grip on the granite, I drew in a gulp of air, the window crushing me. Too tight. I couldn't draw in a full breath. Pain shot up through my lungs. I gasped, began breathing in short huffs, exhaled all the air again and shoved, the window's edge scraping down to my hips.

For a heartrending moment, I thought the opening was too small, my frame too big. I panicked. Sweat broke out in the pits of my arms, slicked my palms. I shoved again, strained against the granite, felt it grinding into my pelvic bones—

And then, with a sharp, stinging pain, my hips scraped through and I collapsed into the archer's niche on the far side with a hiss, legs still dangling out the other side, into the linen closet. I pulled them through, lances of pain shooting up my sides, but I shoved that pain away and crouched in the niche.

In both directions, the corridor was empty. But I could hear voices now, shouts, heavy boots running in my direction.

I darted across the corridor to the door of the audience chamber. The unguarded door opened without a sound, but slowly, the solid wood heavy. I ducked inside, pulled it closed behind me and turned.

I was inside the palace's inner sanctum.

And all hell had apparently broken loose.

✝— Chapter 10

William thrust open the door to Borund's office with such force it cracked against the wall and almost rebounded back into his face. I'd moved halfway across the room without making a sound, dagger drawn, before I recognized him. Even after two months guarding Borund, I still hadn't relaxed when in his manse. Some habits from the Dredge were hard to break.

William stood in the doorway, mouth opening and closing, staring at Borund.

"What is it?" Borund said, rising from his seat behind his desk. His voice was steady, but since I'd been guarding him, I'd learned to read the undertones. They were touched with dread, as if he already knew the news, or already suspected.

William must have noticed as well, for he sagged slightly and drew in a breath. "Marcus is dead."

I frowned down at the floor, raced through all of the merchants I'd met. I'd accompanied Borund everywhere for the last two months—on excursions to the warehouses, to the docks to meet the ships, to the local taverns and the guild hall for meetings with merchants and captains and sources of information. I'd met dozens of merchants, some from the cities along the Frigean coast, others from more distant places, like Warawi, a city in the southern islands.

At first the outings had been tense, Borund expecting another attack. He'd gone to the palace to complain to Avrell but had been met by the palace guard instead. They'd sent for Baill, refused to send a message to Avrell or even the Second, Nathem, until we'd spoken to the captain.

I'd been on edge the entire time, eyes furtively scanning the guardsmen as they passed through the gates of the inner wall, expecting to see Erick, expecting one of the guards to gasp and point, then drag me away.

Instead, Baill had arrived, his bald head shiny in the sunlight, his eyes flat and impregnable. The moment I saw him, I knew we weren't going to see Avrell or Nathem. We weren't going to see anyone. Baill was a wall—dressed in armor, body solid, face scarred, but a wall nonetheless.

Borund sensed it as well. He straightened outside the gates, jaw tightening.

He told Baill of the attack at the tavern, told him of the attempt on his life, even implicated Charls.

"Can you prove it?" Baill had asked. His eyes were intent, attention completely on Borund and his story, noting everything—every frown, every glance, every nervous shift in position.

Borund motioned toward me. "Varis, my bodyguard, saw Charls outside the tavern, saw him give the order."

Baill turned his gaze on me and inside I felt myself cringe. Baill was the man Erick would report to. If Erick had told anyone about me, about how I'd killed Bloodmark, it would be his captain.

But there was no recognition in Baill's eyes. Nothing but the same harsh glare he'd given Borund. As if he were assessing me, deciding whether I was a threat or merely an inconvenience.

We were a distraction, one that he did not want to deal with right now. There was something else weighing on his mind.

"What exactly did you see?" he asked. His voice was low, rolled like thunder.

I told him—of the hatred in Charls' eyes, of the nod.

Baill grunted, turned back to Borund. "I can't arrest anyone based on a look and a nod."

Then he headed back inside the gates, the matter already dismissed from his mind. In that single unguarded moment, when he was turned away, I saw something in his eyes. Fear, concern, uncertainty. Nothing but a flicker, there and then gone.

Borund watched Baill's retreating back in shock.

Borund protested again, but there was no proof that the attack at the tavern had been anything but a simple theft gone bad, a consequence of the rich roughing it where they shouldn't be. And when no more attacks occurred against Borund, the matter was shrugged aside by the guard.

The Mistress wasn't informed. Any attempts to see her, or Avrell, or any of the rest of Avrell's staff concerning the attack, were blocked by Baill and the guardsmen. Access to the palace had been restricted. On the Mistress' orders.

Two weeks passed without anything suspicious occurring as Borund went about his business. No subtle threats except through words on the floor of the guild hall. No one following Borund or William on the streets between his manse, the wharf, and the warehouse district.

After a while, Borund began to relax, began to think that perhaps Baill was right, that perhaps having a bodyguard was unnecessary.

My stomach had tightened at the muttered thought, but he never approached me about leaving. He looked at me with a troubled glance, as if he didn't know what to do with me, as if he wanted to let me go but found that he couldn't.

Then the attacks had begun on other merchants. All of them had been described as accidents, or muggings. And all of them reeked of something else.

Borund stopped mumbling about letting me go.

He discussed the situation—Baill, the attacks, the threat—with William. We all knew who was behind it. But nothing could be proved.

Borund went back to the palace anyway, met with Baill again. But the answer was the same. There wasn't enough to convince Baill that these weren't simply random attacks. That had been four weeks ago, after the second death. Captain Baill had been so abrupt and condescending that Borund hadn't bothered when the third merchant died. The palace guard wasn't going to help.

Marcus. I suddenly remembered the dark blue-coated man at the merchant's guild. The one with dimples. The one who didn't want spice. From Marlett.

The attacks were no longer restricted to the merchants of Amenkor. They'd expanded to include merchants from other cities along the coast.

I heard something fall heavily, like deadweight, and glanced up. Borund had collapsed back into his chair.

"Marcus?" He stared down at the papers before him blankly, then said again, "Marcus?"

William moved into the room, shut the door behind himself.

At the small noise, Borund looked up and he slapped his palm flat against his desk, sat up straight. "That's the fourth one since the attack in the tavern. And he wasn't even from Amenkor. This merchants' war has gone too far. It has to end."

"It's not going to stop," I said.

Both William and Borund looked toward me. I rarely spoke, kept myself in the background, uninvolved unless one of them addressed me with a specific question, especially when it dealt with Borund's business.

But this wasn't business. At least, not normal business.

Borund's eyes held mine, mouth pulled down into a frown. He didn't want to believe what I said, didn't want to think that Amenkor had degenerated that far.

"No," he said, turning away from my blunt stance. "No, it *must* stop. It's gone on long enough. I don't care how 'accidental' some of the previous deaths looked, they weren't accidents. And I don't care that we can't prove anything, that it's all hearsay and circumstance. Baill can just . . ." He paused, steadied himself with an effort, then asked in a harsh voice, "How did Marcus die?"

"Knife to the throat, on the docks. It happened a few days ago, or at least

that's when he was last seen. They found him floating in the harbor this morning. It *looks* like another random mugging."

Borund snorted. "This was no mugging. We all know that. I'm beginning
to think even Baill knows it, and he's simply choosing to do nothing about it,
for whatever reason." The longer he sat behind his desk, the angrier he became.
His fingers were tapping at the papers, his eyes flicking blindly from sheet to
sheet.

Finally, he slapped his palm down on the desk again and stood. "No. It has
to stop. Get Gerrold to ready the horses. We're going to the old city."

"The guild?" William asked, moving to the door.

"No. To the palace. I want to speak to the Mistress herself this time. Or at
the very least Avrell. If I have to, I'll tell Baill it's guild related. He'll have to let
me in then. It's my right as a member of the merchants' guild, damn it!"

William paused at the door, back rigid in shock, but nodded and left without a word.

"My apologies, Master Borund," Avrell, the First of the Mistress, said as he
emerged from an open arch into the sitting room, "but the Mistress is not seeing anyone today."

Borund rose from his seat among the pillows, stiff with angry irritation.
William rose as well. I was already standing, back to a wall so I could see the
entire room. It was small, scattered with low seats, piles of cushions, and tables
holding pitchers of water and plates of fruit. A few lattice-worked screens
placed near the corners of the room sectioned off areas where people could
meet more discreetly.

"I don't understand why it's taken so long for someone to see us," Borund
said. "We've been waiting for an audience all afternoon!"

"I know. I was informed just now by the Second and came immediately."
The First bowed his head and cast a measured glance toward me.

For a moment, he stiffened, his eyes widening slightly in surprise. Then he
seemed to catch himself, his expression going blank, revealing nothing.

I frowned, felt a tingle of worry across my skin. I concentrated, pushed
beneath the river.

The First swirled both gray and red. When I shifted the focus to Borund,
the First was simply gray.

Avrell had raised his head and was now regarding Borund, but his attention
seemed fixed on me, as if he were still watching, still . . . assessing.

I shifted uncomfortably. The First wore dark blue robes, an eight-pointed
star symbol stitched on the chest in gold. His hands were clasped inside the
wide sleeves, hidden. But he wasn't a threat to Borund, and wasn't an immedi-

ate or direct threat to me, if the red-gray coloration was any indication, so I forced myself to relax.

Instead, I took in his dark blue eyes, the lines of his face, his dark features, eyebrows and hair black. I listened to his voice, steady and soft, and watched his movements, every motion precise, considered. Occasionally, he would look in my direction. Nothing direct, but enough to make me stir. After a moment I realized why.

I never faded into the background for him as I did with almost everyone Borund dealt with. I never became gray.

Avrell was far too interested in me.

"I've tried to see you or the Mistress repeatedly over the last few months," Borund said, "and I've been turned aside by Captain Baill at every attempt. I'm beginning to think the rumors about the Mistress are true!"

Avrell froze, every muscle stilling with sudden interest. For the first time, his attention seemed to focus completely on Borund. "The Mistress is simply unavailable today," he said, voice hard as stone. "And, in general, I have been extremely busy. As you know, the coastal cities are in a stage of flux, everyone uncertain about the meaning of the passage of the White Fire six years ago. Now we've lost contact with Kandish and the other nations on the far side of the mountains, and winter is bearing down on us. . . . It is a difficult time. Surely, as a merchant of the guild, you see that?"

Borund sighed. "Of course. Business has been rough lately. That is precisely why I wanted to speak to you. Forgive my irritation, but Captain Baill. . . ." Borund clenched his jaw, shook his head slightly.

Avrell's stance relaxed, so subtly that Borund didn't seem to notice. The First seemed relieved.

In much too casual a tone, he asked, "Baill?"

"Yes, Captain Baill," Borund said shortly.

"He did not inform me that you had come to the palace to see me regarding guild matters before this."

Borund winced. "This does not pertain directly to the guild. I used the guild to gain access to the palace. To you."

Avrell did not react at first. "I see," he said finally. His brow creased in confusion. "So what did you need to see me or the Mistress about then, if not for guild matters?"

Borund hesitated, shot a quick glance toward William and me, then straightened. "I trust you will bring this to the Mistress' attention?"

"Of course."

Borund nodded in relief. "Another merchant has died. Master Marcus, a representative of Marlett."

I felt the air in the room grow tense.

" 'Another' merchant?"

Borund stared at Avrell in shock. "Yes. I would have thought you would have been informed."

"I *should* have been informed," the First said, his tone harsh. He stared for a moment at a blank wall, gaze abstracted and annoyed, as if he were looking at something deeper inside the palace. Unnoticed by Borund or William, he mouthed "Baill" as if it were a curse under his breath. Then his attention snapped back to Borund. "Captain Baill has not kept me informed of your . . . complaints," the First said. "Nor of the deaths of any merchants. When did this happen? How?"

Borund sighed, the sound short and sharp. "Marcus' body was found this morning in the harbor, a knife wound in the throat."

"And there are more deaths? How many have there been?"

"Four."

The First's eyes narrowed. "Four? Amenkor has become extremely dangerous for merchants lately."

Borund barked a short laugh that held no humor, then caught the intent look in the First's eyes and went still. They watched each other a long moment, something passing between them wordlessly. Borund's expression grew grim.

Eventually, the First stirred. "Thank you, Master Borund. I'll see what can be done. I'm sorry to say that I've been extremely distracted lately with other matters pertaining to the Throne and outside the guild. But perhaps I can pay you a visit sometime, so that we can discuss this problem," he cast a quick glance toward me, "and perhaps other issues, in more detail?"

Borund hesitated, then nodded. "Very well." He wasn't totally placated, that was clear in his voice, but he motioned William to his side. William nodded as well.

The First acknowledged them, then turned to leave, but not before glancing once more toward me.

I didn't move, kept my eyes hooded, unreadable, stance rigid.

A slight smile tugged at the corner of the First's mouth a moment before he passed through the arched opening into the next room. He seemed somehow satisfied, as if a nagging problem he'd been fretting over for days had just been solved.

"Do you think anything will change?" William asked Borund as we passed through the gates of the inner ward of the palace into the middle ward containing the guild halls. William and Borund were both mounted. I stood between the two horses and slightly forward, on foot.

"Perhaps," Borund answered distractedly. He'd been deep in thought since the meeting with the First. "There's more going on here than a shifting of power in the guild of merchants. Much more."

"But what?"

Borund shook his head. "I don't know. Something in the palace? Something to do with the Mistress? I don't know. If Avrell and Baill are involved, then it must have something to do with the throne." Borund's voice was lowered, as if speaking to himself.

I was more concerned about Avrell himself. He'd watched me too closely, had been far too interested in me for comfort.

They fell silent and I scanned ahead. We were on one of the narrow streets behind the guild halls, headed toward the large market square with the horse fountain. The last of the sunlight was fading from the sky, and the shadows were collecting beneath the buildings, dark and thick like on the Dredge.

The thought sent a shiver through me, and with a cold start I realized the Fire inside my gut had shuddered to life. Low, almost nonexistent, but there, trembling.

I straightened. But there were few people out this late, not in the middle ward of the old city. The old city was dead.

I shifted back, moved in closer to Borund, William, and the horses. None of them seemed to notice.

"What *can* they do to stop the killings?" William asked again a short while later.

Borund didn't reply. Not even with a grunt.

William sighed and gave up, staring forward into the darkened street.

The Fire was burning higher now, curling up into my chest. We passed a cross street and I tensed, glancing down the new street in both directions, but it was empty. Most of the windows in the surrounding buildings were dark as well, only a few glowing with internal candlelight. Torchlight flickered on the old city's surrounding walls, but it was distant, out of reach.

The cross street fell behind. I glanced back once, but saw nothing.

The cold Fire began to travel through my shoulders, prickled the base of my neck.

We passed into the shadows of the next building and I looked up, toward the thin band of the night sky, toward the stars. The stone of the buildings seemed suddenly too close, too confining, pressing down, cold and immobile.

And then I caught movement out of the corner of my eye.

My gaze snapped down to the street, to the sides of the buildings, and in the patterned gray I saw the darknesses: the arch on the left side that led to an inner courtyard, the niches on the right that led to small doors. The movement had come from one of the niches twelve paces ahead, but we'd already drawn abreast of the first niche, were pulling up alongside the arch to the courtyard.

The Fire inside suddenly flared, but it was too late.

I drew my dagger, yelled out, "Borund!" in warning, but the figures hidden in the niches and in the arch dove out of the darkness.

Borund's horse reared as he pulled on the reins, then it screamed, hooves kicking the air, and came down hard, caught one of the men with a crushing blow, trampling him underfoot. The sharp scent of blood flooded my senses, staggering in its intensity. I turned and surged forward, but Borund's horse foundered, fell to one side, knocked William's horse away. Startled, William lost his seat, slipped sideways in his saddle as it danced for footing, but the motion forced me back.

And then I felt the man behind me.

I stilled, plunged deeper, beneath the scent of blood, beneath the chaos of the men and the huff and stamp of the horses. Like that first fight on the wharf, with the merchant's sons, I sank deep enough I could taste the metal of the knives the men held, could feel their sweat, their desperation. Deep enough that I could sense their movements before they made them.

The man behind me swung, the blade silent as it slashed through air. With the cold grace and brutal quickness Erick had trained into me, I ducked to one side, beneath the man's too wide slash, and thrust backward, hard, felt my dagger slip in and out of flesh, scrape against bone, and then I shifted forward, before the man had even gasped. I felt his knees hit the cobbles at the same time as William's body struck the wall of the building to the right. For a moment, a horrible pain swept through my stomach as I thought he'd been crushed between the building and his horse, but Fetlock gained his balance at the last moment, William slipping gracelessly between the horse and the wall to the road, foot still caught in one stirrup.

One of the horses screamed again. The other snorted in terror.

My attention flicked to Borund. His horse had separated from William's. Borund and the horse stood in the center of the street, one of the attackers crumpled at the horse's dancing feet, three others closing in tight, hemming in the terrified horse. Of the three, two were too close, a danger to Borund. The third wouldn't get to Borund in time. I could finish him off later.

One of the attackers reached up to pull Borund from his mount, and I moved.

The first never saw me, never heard me. My blade slid across his throat even as he took a step toward Borund. The man gripping Borund saw the movement, released Borund and jerked back, his face startled, but he was too slow. I felt warm blood on my hand as my dagger darted upward and across into his exposed armpit, sinking deep. It slid out, slick and smooth and silent.

I turned toward the last man, on the other side of Borund and his horse, but he wasn't there, wasn't where I expected—

And then I *felt* William, felt the cold Fire surging along my arms, tingling in my fingers.

No.

I halted, searching, feeling too slow, the same terror I'd felt when racing across the Dredge toward the white-dusty man's house now mingling with the Fire.

William had regained his feet. His horse had moved a few paces farther down the street. William was still leaning over, gasping for breath, when the last man's knife sank into his side from behind.

I felt the pain, tasted it, like stinging, bitter sap. It seared through me, through the Fire, through the terror, slashed into my side like molten metal, and I gasped.

William arched back, the shock on his face clear, so close, almost tangible. Neck muscles pulled taut with pain, jaw clenched, he stared toward me, toward Borund, then sank to his knees, arms lax.

The man jerked the knife from his side, shoved him forward to the cobbles, then ran.

For a moment, the narrow street was silent, still, nothing but the nervous snort of the horses at the scent of blood. Then Borund shouted, "William!" and stumbled down from his mount. He tripped on the cobbles, but lurched to William's side.

Blood was already pooling on the street, dark and black and cold in the starlight.

The serpent of rage around my heart that I hadn't felt since the Dredge uncoiled and slid free. I tasted the blood—William's blood—tasted the scent of the man who had stabbed him.

The scent led into the night, down the street to another arch. I could almost touch it.

My nostrils flared. The same calm anger that had consumed me on the Dredge after finding the white-dusty man's body enveloped me. I could hunt this man down, could find him no matter where he hid. . . .

I'd made it to the arch, not even conscious of moving, when Borund snapped, "Varis!"

I glared back at him, saw him recoil at whatever he saw in my eyes, on my face. I didn't care. This was my hunt. This was what I was.

But then Borund gasped, "He's still alive! We need to get him out of here and I can't move him myself!"

The naked desperation in his voice, the pure pain and the force behind it, cut through the white-cold anger. My gaze flicked down to William's face, held in Borund's hands. Beneath the river, I could see William breathing, his breath like steam in the air.

"Please," Borund whispered.

With effort, I let the scent of the man slip away, shoved the anger aside, and ran to William's side.

"We have to stop the bleeding," Borund muttered, shrugging out of his jacket with the gold embroidery. The white ruffled undershirt beneath was already flecked black with William's blood. "Get his horse. I'll have to hold him in the saddle as best I can while you run ahead to the house and tell Gerrold and Lizbeth to find a healer and prepare a bed."

"I can get the guards," I said, rising, but Borund's hand clamped down hard on my wrist, halting me.

"Tell no one else!" he hissed, eyes black with anger. "Especially the guards. After what Avrell told us, and especially after dealing with Baill, I don't trust the guards. Only Gerrold, Lizbeth, and the healer."

I hesitated, ready to protest that there was still one man out there, that leaving him alone with William was dangerous, that the manse was too far away, but the desperation in his eyes halted me.

He'd never listen, and I already knew that the last man had fled.

We hefted William up into the saddle of his horse, Borund grunting with effort, Fetlock snorting and shying, eyes white at the smell of blood. I suddenly recalled carrying the dead girl back to her mother, remembered how weightless the girl had felt in my arms, as if she were nothing but an empty grain sack, loose and useless.

William didn't feel empty, nor weightless.

Hope surged through me, like warm water.

Then William was seated as best we could manage and Borund snapped, "Go! Tell Gerrold to fetch Isaiah. Quick!"

And I ran, faster than I'd ever fled on the Dredge.

I stood inside one of the empty bedrooms at Borund's manse, tight against one corner, and watched the healer lean over William's body. He moved frantically, sweat dripping from his face, even though he wiped at it continuously with a cloth. His eyes were wide but intent, trained on his swiftly moving hands as they ripped clothes, pressed clean rags against the flow of blood, held them until they were soaked through, then tossed them aside. He whispered as he worked, short, terse statements that sounded almost like prayer.

Already, the floor was covered with blood-soaked rags. A black-red fan of blood stained the sheets of the bed, dripped with slow, viscous droplets to the hardwood floor. I stood still in the corner and watched the blood gather at the edge of the bedsheet, form into a pregnant drop, then stretch.

"Blessed Mistress, help us! Why won't the bleeding stop?" Isaiah hissed to himself.

And suddenly it was too much.

I fled the room, startled Lizbeth in the hall outside as she rushed to the room with more linen. She called out, "Varis!" but I was already past.

I flung myself into my room, so small in comparison to the one that held William, but I wrapped the closeness about me as I crouched into the corner, pulled myself into a tight ball. Tears threatened, but I thrust them back, cloaked myself in the coiled anger that still simmered, hot and deep. As deep as the Fire.

In the harshness of the anger I saw the street again, saw the fight, saw the three men surrounding Borund's horse. I felt my dagger slit the first man's throat, shudder into the second man's armpit. And the third man. . . .

I heard someone open the door to my room, slowly, hesitantly, and I pulled deeper into myself, the skin around my eyes tightening. Footsteps crossed the room, light and careful, and then Lizbeth murmured, "Oh, Varis."

She hesitated a long moment, her uncertainty like a stench on the air, then touched my shoulder.

At Lizbeth's touch I gasped, choked on the taste of thick phlegm in my throat, and crushed my knees in close.

Lizbeth sat awkwardly on the floor in the corner, hesitated again, then pulled me close to her chest, brushed my hair with one hand.

"I thought the last man was going for Borund," I hitched between gasps, voice so thick the words were almost unintelligible. But I would not cry. "I thought. . . ."

"I know," Lizbeth said. "Hush now. I know." And she began rocking back and forth, holding me tight, like the woman on the Dredge had rocked as she held the dead girl with the green ribbon in her arms.

Slowly, reluctantly, I let the tension drain out of my body, curled tighter to Lizbeth's chest.

A long time later, when the anger had finally settled, when my chest ached and I felt empty and weak, Lizbeth still stroking my hair, I glared out at the floor of my room, unseeing, and said quietly to myself, "I thought he was going for Borund."

Borund sat at his desk in his office, the papers that littered his desktop forgotten. A large decanter of wine sat squarely on top of them, a glass to one side, mostly empty. Some wine had spilled, but Borund didn't seem to notice.

I stood against one wall, a few paces distant, where I always stood. The large room, with the chairs, the tables, the scattering of statues and vases and shaped stones, felt hollow and empty.

Borund reached for the glass without looking, tipped it back with a violent gesture, and swallowed the remaining wine, placing the glass back on the table gently. His eyes never left the blank spot on the wall in front of him.

I shifted uncomfortably.

"He began his apprenticeship with me when he was nine, you know," Borund said suddenly, his voice too loud in the silence.

I didn't respond, watching him warily. It had been two days since we'd brought William back to the manse and Borund hadn't left the grounds once. He'd barely left his office, Gerrold bringing him food and wine. Lots of wine. Borund had sent Gerrold and Gart back to the street where we'd been attacked with a cart to take care of the bodies, but when Gerrold and the stableboy returned, they'd reported they'd found only blood on the cobbles. No bodies. Someone had already carted them away. Charls wouldn't have wanted Borund's body to be found in the middle ward. Not when he needed everyone to believe that the deaths were accidents. He must have had a cart waiting, ready to transport the corpses.

He just didn't get the corpses he expected.

A few doors away, William slept fitfully and deeply. Isaiah had stopped the bleeding eventually, had cleansed and sewn shut the wound, but he'd said it was up to the Mistress whether William would live. The knife had gone deep, and William had lost more blood than he'd ever seen a man lose before and still live. There was nothing any of us could do now except wait.

Borund smiled. "I remember him standing at the edge of the desk, barely able to contain himself, his hands twitching as he clutched them behind his back. He'd glare at me when I ordered him to stand still. Oh, not openly. When he thought I wasn't looking. And he hated keeping the records, writing down all those numbers in the logbooks, keeping track of the price of acquisition, the price the goods were sold for, the amount of the sale and to whom." Borund's smile widened. "But he got over that with time." His voice was slightly slurred, the imperfections caused by the wine barely noticeable.

He looked up at me. "You don't read or write, do you?" He didn't wait for an answer, merely grunted, as if he were disgusted with himself for not thinking about it in the first place. "We'll have to fix that. But not today."

It's what he'd said about the horses. I hadn't ridden one yet.

His attention faded for a moment, then focused on the empty glass. He shifted forward enough so that he could reach the decanter and poured himself another glass, taking a good swallow before dropping back into his chair with a heavy sigh.

"Nine," he muttered, and his eyes darkened. "The bastard."

I knew he wasn't talking about William anymore. Over the last two days, he'd only talked of two things: memories of William. . . .

And Charls.

I shifted again, straightened slightly, suddenly attentive. The last few days I'd moved around the manse in a state of shock much like Borund's. This morning, something had changed. I'd had an idea. But I didn't know if Borund would agree to it.

"The bloody bastard," Borund hissed. "Vincentt, Sedwick, Terell, Marcus . . . all dead. Accidents, my ass." He took another swallow. "Charls has to be stopped."

I shifted forward, hesitated barely a breath, then said coldly, "I can do it."

He didn't seem to hear at first, his gaze fixed again on the blank wall. Then he looked up, almost startled. But the expression faded fast, smoothed out into cold consideration, the expression of a merchant, weighing options, gains, risks.

This didn't last long either. The cold consideration of the merchant slowly shifted into dark anger. An anger I recognized. It was the anger that had seized me on the Dredge, when I'd gone in search of Bloodmark that final time, the same anger I'd felt on the street in the middle circle, when Borund had called me back from the hunt for the man who'd stabbed William.

"You can kill him? Without being seen?" he asked.

"It will take a little time. I'll have to follow him, figure out his patterns. But I can do it."

Something between us shifted. For the last few months, he'd wavered between ordering me to do things, and asking me, one moment laughing and joking with me, the next wondering whether a bodyguard was necessary, worth the expense. It had been awkward and unsettling. He didn't know whether to treat me as family, like William, or as a servant.

But now, as he watched me, I saw his uncertainty over how to treat me, how to think of me, solidify.

He'd seen me kill before, had seen me stand over the bodies. And this was the image that settled into his eyes there, in his office, as he leaned slightly forward, one hand resting on the desk. He saw me as I was: a dagger, a weapon, a tool.

I'd never be family.

Some part of me twisted inside, tightened with regret. But it was small and was smothered by anger. At that moment, I wanted Charls dead as well.

"Then do it," Borund said, and there was no longer a slur in his voice.

I straightened, hand resting on my dagger.

I would have done it anyway, no matter what Borund said.

But it felt good to have his approval.

I followed Charls and his men for the next two weeks, noted the taverns he liked to visit, the streets he traveled to get to his warehouses and the wharf, his manse behind the first set of walls in the residential district. At first, I stayed back, over fifty paces, just close enough I could keep him in sight. It wasn't hard to track him; he always kept at least two men at his side, like that first night I'd seen him, outside Borund's tavern. Bodyguards, like me. Gutterscum. But after a while I realized his bodyguards weren't as wary as someone from the Dredge would be, and so I shifted closer. Not enough to catch their attention, but enough to note that I wouldn't be able to kill Charls on the street, or at the warehouses or wharf. Not without being seen.

That left only one option: his manse.

At the end of one of these excursions, coming up onto the gates of Borund's manse, I saw Avrell leaving through the side entrance to the gardens. He checked the night-darkened street, but didn't see me. Then he drew a hood up over his head and moved away, toward the old city, his pace quick.

I frowned, wondered what he had come to Borund to discuss. But I said nothing.

That was Borund's business. My business was Charls.

And I was ready.

I stood at the side of the bed and stared down at William, at his rounded face, his wild hair, his eyes closed in sleep. His breathing came in soft sighs, barely audible. Even in the moonlight that came in through the open window, I could see that the grayness of his skin had faded in the two weeks since the attack. He was still weak, could move about his room with the aid of the wall and the furniture, but it caused him extreme pain.

The anger inside me writhed as I remembered how his face had contorted the first time he collapsed. Sweat had drenched his skin just from sitting upright. His face had blanched. When he'd tried to shift his weight to his legs, his feet hanging over the side of the bed, they'd given out, folded like cloth.

He'd gasped as he was falling, but when he hit the floor, Borund not swift enough to catch him—

I flinched back, heard the scream again, heard the agony. And as I drew in a deep breath I smelled the stench of his pain—old sweat and rotten meat.

I shook myself. The anger held a moment more, then calmed. The remembered stench faded into the salt of the sea as a breeze pushed past the curtains at the window.

William.

His brow creased, face tightened. Sweat sheened his skin, and one arm twitched.

"No," he murmured. "No!"

I reached forward, almost touched his cheek, but halted at the last moment. Something twisted in my stomach and I snatched my hand back.

I'd seen the way he looked at me at the tavern, after I'd killed that first man. Not fear. I'd seen fear plenty of times on the Dredge. No. William was more than afraid, he was terrified. Of me. Of what I could do, what I held inside. He was afraid of who I was.

I crouched down beside the bed, shifted closer so that I could see William's face better in the darkness. I could smell his sweat, his scent. On the sheets, in the air.

His face was still contorted, and this close I could hear him whimpering.

I'd come into his room every night since I'd offered to kill Charls, and every night William fell into nightmare. Borund didn't know, but Lizbeth did. I wasn't certain how, since I made certain no one was near before I came, but somehow she knew.

Leaning even closer, I said softly, "Tonight."

William shook his head, mumbled "No" again, but the tension around his eyes relaxed. His brow smoothed and his breath calmed.

I watched him a moment more, then looked up toward the window, out into the night.

Tonight.

Gerrold let me out of the side entrance, the one Borund and William had used to bring me to the manse. I stood in the shadow of its alcove and stared out at the side street. I wouldn't move until the patrol had passed by.

A few days after the attempt on Borund in the middle ward, palace guardsmen began to appear in the city. Patrols had wandered the city at random before; that had started even before I killed Bloodmark and fled along the Dredge. I remembered the woman who'd halted one that first day in the real Amenkor, remembered watching them move on the streets after that, some on horseback, others walking. But after the attack on Borund. . . .

Now the guardsmen were everywhere, their patrols passing through the streets of the upper city at regular intervals, a few patrols scouring the wharf and docks below. Neither Borund nor I knew who had ordered them, Avrell or Baill. Perhaps it had been the Mistress. The guardsmen did nothing except ride by, watching, their eyes hard and dangerous, cold, their horses' hooves clopping on the cobbles. No words were spoken, unless they were interrupting a fight. But they were *felt*.

Instead of making Amenkor feel safer, the streets now felt closed, somehow restrictive. As if the hand resting at the back of your neck, meant to be reassuring, had suddenly grown more viselike.

The first time Borund and I had seen them in the street, he'd watched them canter by with surprised approval. But when we'd passed the third patrol an hour later, he'd sent me a grim look, mouth pressed tight. "Heavy-handed," he'd muttered.

The rest of Amenkor agreed. I could see it in the people's eyes, in the way they kept their heads down, shoulders lowered. Hooded capes had become common almost overnight.

And it had made following Charls harder.

I pulled back deeper into the alcove as I heard clipped hooves on stone. A moment later, two guardsmen appeared on horseback, moving sedately down the street. One of the horses snuffled and nodded its head as it passed, scenting me, but the guards didn't pause.

As soon as they vanished around the corner of the main thoroughfare, I slid from the alcove and into the lesser shadows of the street. I knew where I was headed: the outer circle of the old city, where most of the merchants had their own estates, including Charls.

The streets of Amenkor were empty. Completely empty. It sent shivers down my back as I moved. On the Dredge and the wharf there were always movements, a sense of motion, even if the alley or street seemed clear. Things moved behind the walls, sometimes in the walls—dogs and rats and gutter-scum.

Here, there was no life. Nothing but stone.

I moved swiftly, but slowed when I neared the gates to the outer circle.

They were open. Occasional patrols passed through them, the guards saluting each other or pausing to talk in low, mumbled voices to the two sentries posted there. The sentries stood to one side of the open arch, but they were relaxed, occasionally speaking to each other. Laughter broke out across the street as I settled into shadow twenty paces away from their position.

I glanced up to the night sky, toward the slice of the moon and the stars. There were no clouds tonight, nothing to obscure the light.

I suppressed a sigh and crouched low, grew still.

I submerged myself, deeper and deeper, until the balance felt right, until I could see into every shadow, see every guardsman's face as they passed by and the lines of exhaustion and boredom on the sentries' faces.

Then I focused, felt the currents alter around me, bend and twist, tighten, so I could see what *would* happen—

There.

I relaxed, shifted where I crouched, and waited. Guards moved, chuckled quietly, slapped their horses' necks, a steady flow. A few breaks occurred, where no one passed through the gate, but none long enough for me to move, and none where the two sentries were distracted.

A hundred measured breaths later, a pair of guardsmen disappeared down the street. As the last hoofbeat faded into silence, one of the sentries turned to the other, motioned out toward the city below, away from my position.

I moved.

As I slipped into the shadows of the outer ward, the gates behind me, I heard one of the sentries grunt and chuckle, slapping the other on his back. I paused a moment to make certain they hadn't seen me, then continued on.

The streets of the outer circle were subtly different. Closer, near the main thoroughfare leading up through the old city's walls, but then they widened out. As I moved, I found myself settling down into a familiar pattern, one I didn't recognize at first. But, pausing at a corner, I realized that the tension in my shoulders, in my legs as I balanced on the balls of my feet, came from the Dredge, from Erick.

I smiled slowly. I was hunting.

Sliding from darkness to darkness, I came up on Charls' manse, stared up at the top of the wall above my head. Reaching for familiar handholds, I hefted myself up to the top. I watched the building closely, my heart beating faster in my chest. As soon as I slid down into the garden I'd be in unfamiliar territory. I'd only come to the top of the wall in my previous excursions, watched the house from a distance to get an idea of where Charls' rooms were, to get a feel for the movements of his servants.

The manse should have been quiet, but candlelight glowed in a few of the lower windows.

I hesitated, considered leaving.

I saw William's face, eyes closed in sleep, brows furrowed and sweaty.

I dropped into the garden. The moment my feet hit the ground, the Fire awoke, spreading cold across my chest. I ran across the garden to the house, toward a side door used by the servants to get to the carriage house and stables. I sensed nothing, heard nothing.

The door opened easily.

Charls' manse was similar in layout to Borund's. I stood in a servants' entranceway, a narrow door before me. Stairs to my left ascended to the servants' rooms above. The kitchen stood on the other side of the manse, with another set of servants' stairs there. The door before me should open onto a long hallway running the length of the house, intercepted only by the large open foyer with the main stairs leading up to the second floor. Rooms opened up on either side.

I stepped to the inner door, past the stairs, listened, then stepped into the long inner hallway. Two doors down, candlelight spilled out into the hall. I stilled, heart halting, but the hallway remained empty.

Silently, I edged up to the open doorway, heard voices as I approached.

"Tarrence has seized all of the available resources in Marlett. It took him longer than expected though, even with Marcus gone. Some of what we expected to find in Marcus' warehouses had already been purchased by others."

"By whom?"

At the door, I settled down on my heels, one hand on the floor for support.

I recognized the first voice as Charls, but didn't recognize the second. Sliding deeper beneath the river, I stole a glance into the room.

Four men, seated at a round table in a room like Borund's office, but more sparse.

"Regin, Yvan. And Borund." Contempt filled Charls' voice.

"Borund," the second man said flatly. He watched Charls carefully as he spoke. He had a long nose, mustache, gray-streaked hair pulled back in a pony-tail, vaguely familiar.

I frowned, then remembered: the merchant with the mustard-colored coat from the guild hall. The one Charls had spoken to at the edge of the room, before Borund had approached him.

The other two merchants were familiar as well, people Borund spoke to in the hall on a regular basis. Both shared a glance and shifted in their seats, but said nothing.

I pulled back, contemplated moving back to the servants' entrance.

"Yes, Borund," Charls spat. "He's become increasingly annoying. If he'd only died that night in the tavern. Or at least during the ambush in the middle ward."

"But he didn't," the other merchant continued. "In fact, since that night, the other merchants have begun hiring their own bodyguards. And Borund has increased his purchases of essentials like grain and salt and fish, storing them in the warehouses here in Amenkor rather than shipping them out to the other cities. This is why he was to be eliminated in the first place."

"He's proving harder to get rid of than expected."

"Obviously."

I heard someone shift forward, his chair creaking.

In a much softer voice, the unknown merchant said, "In order for this to work, in order for us to gain and keep control of the city, our little group must be the only ones in the city with vital goods to sell. If we cannot get our hands on what Borund has stored away . . ."

He let the sentence trail off and I heard him shift again.

After a long silence, Charls said, "I'll take care of Borund . . . and his body-guard."

A cold shiver of fear coursed through me, tinged with anger. Charls wasn't going to let it go.

Then, farther down the hallway, I heard footsteps.

I spun and headed back to the servants' entrance, closing the door softly behind me. But not before I saw a servant carrying a tray with a decanter of wine and four glasses into the room.

I paused in the small entryway, wondering if I should return to warn Bor-und that there were more merchants involved than just Charls. But I'd come for

Charls, and now that I'd actually heard him threaten Borund, I found I couldn't leave.

Warning Borund of the others could wait.

I took the stairs two at a time, easing out into the hallway at the top. It was a servants' corridor, narrower than the one below, running the full length of the manse. The main hallway on the second floor paralleled this one, the two separated only by a wall. A single door on the left opened onto the main corridor at this end of the servants' hallway, other doors on the right leading to the servants' rooms.

Charls' bedroom was the closest on this side of the house, off the main corridor.

I pulled open the door into the main hallway and peered out.

Nothing. But the tendrils of Fire inside my gut increased slightly.

I slid out into the upper hall, stepped to Charls' bedroom door, and entered.

The room held a bed, a large chest at its foot, a desk, two chests of drawers, and a stone fireplace against the right wall. No candles were lit, but everything was clear. Papers and a small knife used to break wax seals sat out on the desk, everything organized and neat. Clothes were tossed onto the chest at the end of the bed. The curtains over the windows were drawn, letting in no moonlight.

There were no places to hide, no real darknesses except the room itself.

Frowning, I stepped to the side of the door and readied myself for the wait.

I'd shifted into a casual crouch by the time Charls finally retired for the night, my legs beginning to cramp from standing. I didn't hear him approach. The door suddenly opened, swinging wide at my side, almost striking my knees.

I stood in one fluid motion, feeling the door before me, concealing me. On the other side, Charls sighed with exhaustion, stepped into his bedroom, and brushed the door closed behind him. No one else entered, and I heard no one else in the hall.

As the door swung away, revealing Charls, his back to me, I stepped forward, brought the dagger up, and sliced cleanly across his neck.

Charls hunched forward, a sickening gurgling sound filling the room as blood fountained, spraying his upraised hand, the edge of the bed, the clothes on the chest, the rug over the hardwood flooring. He staggered a step forward, stumbled to one knee, then twisted as he fell, a hand reaching toward the chest for support.

I stepped forward as he collapsed, his body turned toward me now, his eyes opened in shock, in terror, his face a cold white in the moonlight, the blood black in a sheet across his chest. I wanted him to see me, to recognize me. I wanted him to *know*.

And he did see. He jerked, shoulders pressing back, eyebrows rising.

Warmth spread through my chest, deep and satisfying.

I knelt a pace from him, a hard frown tightening my mouth, the corners of my eyes. "You should have left Borund alone," I said. But I wasn't thinking of Borund at all.

He sagged against the arm holding the chest, the other hand clutched against his throat. But the strength was leaving his body. He shuddered, lost his grip on the chest and fell to the rug. The blood began to pool, spreading.

The hand at his throat reached for me, trembling, grasping. His eyes caught mine, held me, pleading, and in their shimmering depths I saw—

I saw Charls. Not the businessman at the tavern, turning and nodding to the killer waiting for his instructions. Not the merchant on the guild hall floor, speaking quietly of threats and death. I saw none of these.

Instead, I saw Charls as he saw himself. A man who had clawed his way up into the highest ranks of the merchant guild. A man who had allied himself with someone too powerful for him to control and had found himself lost. A man who was even now trying to find some way to survive.

He'd let the face he presented to the world slip when he entered his own bedroom, had let it fall away when he knew he was a dead man but was unwilling to accept it.

I saw it all there, in his eyes. His dreams, his hopes, his desperation. He wanted to live, fought hard even as the strength drained from his arms and he sagged back against the chest. I saw the man beneath the merchant. The man I'd just killed.

The realization sent a shiver of shock through me, down to my core, and I jerked back. All of the satisfied warmth fled, gone in one gasp.

I stood abruptly, and Charls' outstretched hand dropped to the floor, all of the life, all of the straining tension leaving his body. I backed away from the corpse. Panic tingled through my arms, through my skin, prickled the hair on my arms, at the base of my neck.

When my back hit the wall, I gasped and grew still.

And then I ran, out into the hall, to the servants' passage, down the stairs, and out into the garden. I met no one, saw no one, not even as I dropped down from the wall surrounding Charls' manse. I fled through the streets of the outer ward, barely seeing where I ran, moving without thought, hearing nothing, smelling only the dark, viscous scent of blood. I saw only the bodies, all of the bodies, but mostly Charls, his eyes, the thick spatter of blood on his sheets, on his clothes, saw his mouth working to say something, to draw in breath when there was nothing left to do but choke.

I rounded a corner, entered the main thoroughfare near the gates, and slammed into a guardsman. The shock of the collision sent both of us sprawling, my body hitting the ground hard, head cracking into the stone cobbles of the street. My teeth rattled, bit the edge of my tongue, and I tasted blood, like bitter copper. Back against the ground, I swallowed the blood, heaved in deep ragged breaths and stared up at the moon and stars, stunned.

I heard the guardsman curse, heard shifting cloth as he climbed to his feet.

Then he leaned over me, blocked out the night sky, and I froze with a sharp, drawn breath.

He stared down at me in shock, one hand reaching tentatively for my face, reaching to brush away my hair. "Varis?"

Erick.

The panic returned, sharper than before, seizing my heart, my throat. I couldn't speak, and the breath I held escaped in a harsh rush that tore at my throat.

I had to get away. Guilt rose up, like acid, and I felt sick. I'd killed Bloodmark without Erick's permission, without the Mistress' blessing. Somehow, since meeting Borund, I'd managed to shove that fact deep down inside me, managed to forget it. I'd allowed myself to relax.

But now Erick had found me.

And I suddenly realized it was infinitely worse than just Bloodmark.

I'd just killed again. Not to save myself, not to save Borund. I'd killed Charls because I'd wanted to, because he'd hurt William.

I had to get away. The impulse was like a scream. I couldn't face Erick now, not with blood on my hands, on my shirt and dagger.

But I couldn't move. Erick held me with his eyes, softening from shock and irritation to something else . . . concern and wonder.

And then he touched my face, his fingers trailing down my forehead to my ear, and I broke, the tears coming harsh and hot and wet. My breath hitched in my chest.

"Varis," he said again, without question.

"I killed him," I sobbed, the words thick with phlegm, almost incoherent. "I killed him, I killed him, I killed him."

"Who?" He was cupping the back of my neck now, had lifted me to his shoulder, my eyes closed. I held him tight, feeling as if I were fourteen again.

"Bloodmark," I gasped into his shoulder. "Charls." He grew still, but his hold didn't lessen.

On the street, someone gasped, and I drew back from Erick's shoulder sharply, the tears choked back, abruptly realizing I no longer held my dagger. It had clattered to the street when we collided, lay just out of reach.

Vulnerability hit me, even as Erick rose.

Twenty paces away, a man stood at the edge of a cross street, wearing a cloak with the hood pulled back. I could see his face clearly in the moonlight, recognized the arrogant stance, the shocked look on his face.

The merchant's son, Cristoph. The man I'd fought in the alley on the wharf after first coming down to the docks.

I'd killed his friend.

And he'd heard me tell Erick I'd killed Bloodmark and Charls. I knew it as clearly as if I'd been beneath the river, had smelled it there. And there was something else, something that took me a moment to recognize.

Cristoph reminded me of the merchant with the mustard-colored coat, a younger version. That's why the merchant had seemed familiar at the guild hall talking to Charls, why he'd seemed familiar tonight.

Cristoph must be that merchant's son.

Erick took a single step forward and Cristoph turned and fled, his footsteps echoing off the outer walls before fading completely.

Panic seized me. I lurched toward my knife, grabbed the bloody blade in one hand and turned to face Erick in one smooth move. The urge to cry was gone now, the tears dried. Only a raw hollow near my heart remained, and I could feel myself pushing that away, discarding it, hardening myself against the pain. The emotion was useless.

I was no longer on the Dredge, no longer fourteen. I didn't need Erick.

We stared at each other a long moment, and then I said, "You can't protect me anymore."

And I ran.

I dodged into the street where Cristoph had vanished, eyes hard and intent, Erick shoved into the back of my mind. I'd deal with his reappearance later. For now, Cristoph was a threat. He'd seen me, had heard me say I'd killed Charls. I wasn't supposed to be associated with Charls' death at all.

I saw a flash of movement farther down the street as someone dodged into an alley, nothing more than a flicker of a cloak. I focused, drew the river up around me, but saw no one on the street. Nostrils flaring, I dashed down to the alley, ducked around the corner and searched the darkness.

Nothing.

I drew a deep breath, sorted through the scents on the river. But there was nothing I could attribute to Cristoph. I didn't remember him having a scent down on the wharf, when I'd killed his friend. But not everyone had scents.

Not willing to give up, I searched the alley, the recessed doorways, the alcoves. All of the doors were locked, and the alley ended at the edge of an empty street.

Shit!

The pressure of running into other guardsmen began to assert itself. And then there was Erick.

Would he send the guard to find me? Would he warn the sentries at the gate? He knew I'd killed someone. He'd seen the blood, heard me confess.

The guilt stabbed again into my gut, sliced through the last of my hesitation. Cristoph had escaped. I'd have to deal with him later.

I headed back toward the gates, approaching warily.

The two sentries remained on duty. They didn't appear to be any more alert than when I'd passed through earlier that night.

I breathed a heavy sigh of relief, wondered why Erick had not warned them, but pushed the thought aside and concentrated on getting through the gates without being seen by the sentries.

I had to wait an hour, but eventually they were distracted long enough so I could sneak through. I headed into the outer city, back toward Borund's manse to report.

I did not see Erick or any other guardsmen along the way.

✛— The Palace —✛

I didn't wait at the audience room's door. Instead, I moved immediately across the dark room, slipping between chairs and tables in the darkness, between vases of flowers, sculptures, and plants. On the far side of the room was another door, smaller, heading deeper into the inner sanctum, leading toward the throne room and the Mistress' chambers.

I padded toward the door, hesitated before opening it in order to listen. I couldn't use the river to see if anyone was on the far side since the door was blocking my view, but it was possible to pick up noises, scents. . . .

Nothing.

I was just about to open the door when something whispered at the edge of hearing. Stilling, I concentrated, let my breath out slowly and held it—

And heard a soft rustling, like dry leaves scraping across cobbles. I frowned, brow creasing. I'd heard this once before when inside the palace, during one of Avrell and Borund's meetings. But then it had only been a whisper, there and then gone. This was much louder.

Hesitating a moment, I focused.

The sound of leaves intensified, seemed to reach out toward me from a distance, and as it grew louder, the rustling sound began to resolve into voices . . . hundreds of voices all speaking at the same time, all clamoring for attention.

I jerked back from the door, but the voices vanished as soon as I quit concentrating, as soon as I let the river slip away. The room was silent. Dead.

Something clattered against the door on the other side of the room, where the guards had been posted. Without thought, heart thudding sharply in my

chest, I pulled the door in front of me open and slid through, ignoring the
strange voices for now. They would have to wait.

The door led to a narrow corridor, a hall for the servants that curved slightly
away out of sight. I scanned in both directions. No one was in sight.

I bit my lower lip, took a moment to consult the mental map Avrell had
given me. It wasn't as complete as the one for the outer portion of the palace,
did not include all of the servants' passages.

I grunted in annoyance and turned right, slipping forward without a sound,
one hand brushing along the rough granite wall to my left for reference. Ten
steps farther on, my outstretched hand found the edge of a door.

I placed an ear to the wood, heard nothing on the far side.

I moved on.

Two doors later, the flickering light of a torch appeared at the end of the
hall, around the edge of the curved corridor, followed by voices and the soft
thud of a closing door.

I crouched down immediately, felt for the latch on the door at my back.

"What's going on?" someone demanded, his voice tired.

"Baill's got the entire guard out looking," someone else growled, "but he
decided that wasn't enough so he called out all the servants as well." For a moment the torchlight flared, and in the brighter light I could see small bowls of
oil lining the wall on either side.

They were lighting the sconces. The entire palace would be lit within the
next fifteen minutes.

"And what in hell does he expect us to do!"

"Help him."

"And then what?"

I drew in a tight breath, then opened the door at my back and slid through
it as the light of the torches and oil sconces grew, the voices getting closer. The
door shut with a faint click, the wood muffling the conversation in the hall on
the other side.

I waited until I heard their voices receding down the corridor, then turned
to see where I was.

My stomach tightened.

"Shit," I muttered.

I'd backed myself into a storage closet with no other exit.

"Shit, shit, shit," I muttered under my breath, then turned back to the door.
Pressing my ear to the wood, I listened intently for sounds in the corridor
outside, but heard nothing. The men lighting the oil sconces in the hallway
had passed by, but anyone could be out there now. The entire palace had been
awakened.

I sighed heavily, cast an angry look at the door, then slid beneath the river.

The instant I submerged, I felt the strange whispering of leaves I'd heard in the outer room rushing forward. Only this time it was much louder, the hundreds of voices streaming out of the silence like a gale-force wind, reaching for me. I gasped, jerked back away from them, and at the same time shoved myself up and out of the river, hard, fast.

The real world returned with a lurch. I sat back on my heels, still gasping, felt sweat prickle my chest. Reaching forward, I hugged my knees to my chest until my heart stopped racing.

I had no idea what the leaf voices were, had no idea where they were coming from. But whatever they were, they wanted me. I'd felt them reaching for me, straining. And I'd felt the force behind them, a weight that could crush me.

I shuddered, pushed myself back up into a kneeling position before the door. I listened, using only my ears.

Nothing.

I nudged the river, as if I were at its edge and had dipped my toe into its waters.

A whisper of dead leaves, calling me.

I shivered, then leaned my forehead against the wood of the door. Until I knew what the leaf voices were, I didn't dare use the river.

Which made killing the Mistress that much harder.

I pulled myself upright, jaw clenched, then opened the door and stepped out into the hall.

No yell of alarm. No shrieks. The hall was empty.

But completely lit. The only places left to hide were the doorways.

I bit off another curse at Avrell, at Baill, at life in general, and continued down the hall at a brisk but quiet trot. No use skulking now.

I paused at the next door, heard muffled voices, and moved on quickly. The hall continued to curve, most of the doors on the left side. But, according to Avrell, they wouldn't lead me to the Mistress' chambers. Her rooms lay on the other side of the palace, to the right.

I came to another door on the right and paused again. Nothing. Opening it a crack, I peered into another antechamber like the first. Only someone had been here recently. All the candles were lit.

I closed the door quietly and proceeded down the hall.

Twenty steps farther on, I heard someone enter the hall behind me, heard the distinct sound of metal armor.

Guardsmen.

Without hesitation, I sprinted forward, eyes wide, heart pounding. The hall curved away, the right wall maddeningly empty, two doors, no three, passing on the left. The sounds of the guards grew louder, but I hadn't heard a shout. They were getting closer, though. I could hear their voices.

I'd almost decided to duck into one of the doors on the left, risk another closet, or something worse, when a door on the right appeared. The hall ended shortly after that, with one last door on the left. I darted toward the door on the right, grabbed its handle and eased it open smoothly. No time to listen for someone on the far side. The guards were too close.

I slid through, pulled the door closed behind me as quietly as possible, and then turned and halted, heart wrenching in my chest. I let out an involuntary gasp.

I'd entered a long, wide hall from a side entrance. To my right, four huge pillars stretched from the marbled floor to the ceiling. Another four pillars stood on the far side of the room. Shadows filled the recesses behind the pillars where I stood, and behind the pillars on the opposite side of the hall. Down the center, between the two rows of pillars, stretched a wide walkway, leading to two large wooden doors banded with metal.

Directly ahead, at the height of a dais, I could see the side of a throne lit by torchlight, the throne facing the walkway and the double doors.

The Skewed Throne.

My body shuddered and I blinked in the half-light, tried to focus on the throne, my eyes refusing to settle, the air distorted somehow. After a moment, I realized that the problem wasn't with my eyes at all, but with the throne itself.

It was a simple stone slab with no back and four supports, one on each corner. But even as my eyes held onto this image, it seemed to waver, twisting, one leg suddenly shorter but supporting a corner that appeared higher than all the others. The throne warped, turned in upon itself, the stone slab that formed the seat was no longer flat, the edges that had appeared sharp and well defined before were now smooth and rounded. Then it shifted again, now chipped and chiseled, rough-hewn.

The motion turned my stomach, sent a feverish heat tingling through my skin. I shuddered again and turned away from the throne, away from the dais and the three wide stone steps that led from the main walkway between the pillars up to the throne itself.

With a deep breath, I steadied myself.

And felt the throne at my back reach out toward me, felt it pushing against my shoulders, almost like a physical presence. The rustling of dead leaves returned, shivering through the air, growing even as the skin at the nape of my neck began to prickle. The voices emerged from the rustling sound, called to me, echoed in my ears.

I tensed in horror. The voices came from the throne. The throne knew me, had tried to call to me earlier, was calling to me now.

And I hadn't touched the river since the voices had rushed me in the closet.

I stepped back, tried to block the voices out—

Then I heard the clatter of the guards on the other side of the door, in the hallway behind me.

Not looking toward the throne, I darted to the right, down the long walkway, between the rows of pillars, across the half-dark room to the main entrance. I felt the throne behind me, a hot, scrabbling pressure against my back, felt it flowing from shape to shape, twisted and tormented, calling to me, the voices more urgent now, more desperate.

I gasped as I neared the doorway, passed through and out into the empty hallway beyond with a low, moaning cry. The gasp turned into a shudder of relief as I felt the ornate oaken door thud home behind me, cutting off the voices and the sensation of hands scrabbling across my back.

I leaned against the door a long moment, shudders running through my body. Sweat dripped down my face and I wiped it away with the back of my arm, heart thundering in my chest. I drew in deep, ragged breaths, steadied myself.

It took longer than I expected.

Then I straightened. I set the eerie sensation of the Throne, of the haunting voices and their immense power, aside.

I'd reached the edge of the Mistress' private rooms. Time to shed the page boy disguise. It was almost finished.

My gaze hardened, face grim as I stepped down the unguarded hall to a new set of double doors, the *last* set of double doors, drawing my dagger as I went.

✝— Chapter 11

"The mustard-coated merchant's name is Alendor," Borund said, and sank back into the chair he'd had moved into William's bedroom. "Cristoph is one of his sons, the youngest. And if Alendor's involved. . . ."

He trailed off into silence. It was late morning, the day after I'd killed Charls, and I'd just told him what I'd heard at Charls' manse, and that Cristoph knew what I'd done. But I hadn't told them everything. I'd only said Cristoph had seen me leaving Charls' manse, blood on my clothes. I hadn't mentioned Erick at all.

On the bed, William struggled into a sitting position, using the pillows and the headboard for support. He grimaced in pain as he moved, a sheen of sweat breaking out on his forehead, but neither Borund nor I moved to help him, careful of his pride.

When he'd made himself comfortable and caught his breath, he asked, "So what does he intend to do? He's buying up all available resources, gaining others from those who have it and aren't willing to sell by intimidating them or killing them, but for what purpose? A monopoly?"

"Yes." Borund nodded thoughtfully. "But a monopoly not just on a single commodity. He wants to control everything. He's forming a consortium, a small group of people that will control all of the trade in the city, perhaps in the surrounding cities as well if he already has Tarrence working for him in Marlett."

William snorted, then winced, one hand moving to his side. "That's not possible, not in Amenkor. And not anywhere else either."

Borund shifted forward again. "Isn't it? Look at what he's done so far. Besides Alendor, Charls, and the two other merchants Varis saw at Charls' manse, who else in the city has—or had—any stock of fish? Or wheat?"

William frowned in thought. "We do, in the warehouses on the docks. I think Darryn has some in storage as well. . . ." His voice trailed off, and then he looked toward Borund, eyes wide. "And that's it. Alendor controls almost all of the wheat and fish."

Borund nodded, his voice grim. "And what about other resources, such as fruits and vegetables? Or wine? What about cattle or pigs? There haven't been any drovers from the north since Regin purchased that herd in the spring. Since it's now almost winter, we can't expect to see any more herds like that for at least five months. Even non-food stocks, like cloth. We haven't had a shipment of wool or flax from Venitte in over four months, maybe even six."

"Six," William said distractedly. He'd sunk back into his pillows as Borund spoke. "And since it *is* almost winter, there won't be many ships in the coming months. We've only got a few weeks left of decent enough weather to risk sending out more ships, maybe a month at most. What resources we're going to have are already in the city."

They both fell silent.

In one corner of the room, I shifted my stance, uncomfortable. But not from the weighted silence. In my mind, I could see Charls reaching for me, his hand grasping at air. I could see his blood, black against his skin. Then there was Erick and—

"What about Cristoph?" I asked.

Borund frowned. "What do you mean?"

I straightened. "He knows that I killed Charls, knows that I killed his friend down at the wharf. He could go to the Guard."

Borund shook his head. "He won't. Alendor won't let him. It would attract too much attention to his house. Right now Alendor must be wondering whether you saw him at Charls' manse, whether we even know about the consortium. He'll want to stay out of sight until he knows for certain. Alendor will handle Cristoph for us."

I nodded, relaxed back against the wall.

That still didn't solve the problem of Erick. But he hadn't reported me to the guard after Bloodmark's death, hadn't warned the sentries at the gates last night. . . .

I sighed and closed my eyes, intent on pushing Charls' pleading gaze out of my head.

When I opened my eyes, I caught William watching me.

He flinched away, turning to look down at his feet.

My stomach clenched and I stared down at the floor, mouth pressed tight.

Into the awkward silence, a horn blew, long and hollow and forlorn.

Both Borund and William looked up toward the open window. It looked out onto the harbor.

With a frown, Borund rose and moved to pull back the curtains. I followed, stood at his side. The first horn was followed by others, the sounds filling the room in a strange cacophony of noise.

"What's happening?" William said. I could hear the impatience in his voice. He wasn't used to being restricted to a bed, unable to move about.

"Something in the harbor," Borund said.

"But what?"

"Wait," Borund said, his voice lowering, his forehead creasing in confusion.

On the slate-gray water of the harbor, ships flying the Mistress' colors of gold and white were preparing to make way on the docks. But these weren't the usual ships I'd seen off-loading crates and barrels. These were smaller, leaner, and somehow more dangerous, more purposeful, their sails crisp beneath the white-scudded sky.

And more maneuverable. As we watched, they pulled away from the docks and headed straight out toward where the spits of land on either side of the bay curved in toward each other, creating an opening to the ocean beyond. They passed a large merchant ship headed toward open water without pausing.

Gerrold appeared at the door to the room. "Something's going on in the harbor, Master Borund."

Borund grunted. "Yes, I see. Send Gart to see if he can find out what's happening. Quickly."

"Yes, sir."

Gerrold left, and Borund shifted forward, his stance going rigid, a dark frown touching his eyes, his mouth. "What . . . ?" he began, but didn't continue.

The Mistress' sleek ships began to slow, drawing up alongside the mouth of the bay. They began a slow pattern, weaving back and forth across the opening of the harbor. The merchant ship made slow progress forward, but when it got close to the line, one of the sleek ships broke from the formation and approached. The ships were too distant to see anything more than blurred movement on the decks. But there was movement, even as the merchant ship slowed to a halt, sails going slack.

Borund sucked in a breath, held it.

"What is it?" William barked.

Borund didn't respond, simply shook his head.

On the water, the sleek ship backed away and the merchant ship began to move again. But the sails didn't go back up in the same configuration.

The merchant ship began to turn, and Borund let his held breath out forcefully, as if someone had punched him in the gut.

Behind, I heard someone tearing up the stairs and down the hallway. The door burst open and Gart skidded to a halt just inside.

"The Mistress . . . has closed . . . the harbor," he gasped, eyes wide in shock, fear, and a child's uncontrolled excitement.

The gates to the palace were thronged by the time Borund and I made it up through the two outer wards. Most of the men yelling at the palace guardsmen lined up in front of the closed and barricaded doors were lesser merchants and representatives from the ships—both local and foreign—that were now locked inside the harbor, all with a sick desperation on their faces. Beneath the river, the mob was a nauseating churn of anger moving in strange, unpredictable eddies that tasted of salt and smelled of sweat. Tensions were so high I had edged in as close to Borund as I could get without touching him, leaving myself barely enough room to wield my dagger if necessary. He stayed back from the main crush of bodies, but even so I was jostled into his back once or twice.

Borund swore under his breath after scanning the mob, then thankfully turned and edged away from the gates. "We'll never get into the palace. Captain Baill must have shut the gates before he issued the orders to close the harbor, and this crowd isn't likely to disperse any time soon. Damn! I need to know what's going on!"

I continued to scan the crowd, shoulders tense, uncertain whether I should make any suggestions. That was William's job.

I caught Borund's eye, saw the stress around the edges of his face, the darkness from lack of sleep. The exhaustion was clear. I suddenly wondered how often he had gone in to watch William sleep late at night, as I had.

I drew breath to suggest we go to the guild hall, but someone stepped up to Borund's side, someone gray.

"Master Borund?"

The boy was short, dressed in ordinary clothes from the docks, with dirty hair and a round, grime-smudged face. His eyes were large and intent and flicked continuously over the crowd.

Borund frowned as he tried to place the boy. "Yes?"

"Avrell, the First of the Mistress, would like to see you," the boy said. "He said to give you this." He handed over a small chunk of stone, the outlines of an ancient snail embedded in one side, then darted back into the press of bodies near the gates.

Borund grunted. I recognized the piece of stone from Borund's office.

And I suddenly recalled seeing Avrell leaving through the side entrance to Borund's manse.

Borund motioned for me to follow.

The dock boy led us through the edge of the mob, at first heading toward the gates. But before the press became too close, the boy angled away and we passed into a side street of the middle ward running parallel to the wall enclosing the palace. Once we were free of the area in front of the gates, we moved swiftly, the boy motioning us forward while checking to see if we were followed.

I scanned behind as well but saw no one.

The boy ducked into a small building set back from the wall that was once a stable. The reek of manure still clung to the musty air inside, but there were no horses. Instead, the building was packed with marked crates, straw poking out through the cracks between the wood.

Borund gasped as the dock boy led us into a narrow space between the stacked crates. "Capthian red! Crates of it! I haven't been able to get this since last winter, not a single crate!"

The narrow path turned, branched once, then opened up into a small niche that barely fit the three of us hunched over. The dock boy motioned us out of the way, then pulled at a chunk of the plank flooring. A section lifted away, cut with a ragged edge so that it couldn't be seen when set in place.

The boy motioned us down into the rounded opening below. I could see that it dropped down into a thin tunnel, even though there was no light.

Borund hesitated, glancing at me for confirmation.

"It's safe," I said. "It drops down to a tunnel. There's no one down there, and I can see a lantern ready to be lit."

Borund nodded and, with a bit of maneuvering, managed to lower himself down into the hole. The dock boy stared at me the entire time.

"How did you know there was a lantern?" he finally asked. "It's too dark to see it."

I didn't answer, simply dropped down smoothly after Borund once he moved out of the way. The dock boy followed, handing the lantern to Borund along with an ember box to light it. The ember inside was still glowing hotly.

The lantern flared just as the dock boy fit the cover to the tunnel back into place. Squeezing past both me and Borund, he took the lantern and said, "Follow me."

The tunnel grew narrower at first, until we had to proceed sideways, backs scraping the rough-chiseled wall, then branched to the left and right. We'd followed the left path for twenty paces before I realized the wall to the right was the same eggshell color as the wall of the palace, but darker, not as sun-bleached as the walls above. More tunnels branched off to the left, but we continued forward for another hundred paces before turning away from the palace wall. After two quick rights, we hit stairs leading sharply downward. The twists and turns, darkness and narrow niches, reminded me forcibly of the Dredge.

When we reached the bottom of the stairs, Borund turned back and murmured in a subdued voice, "We're passing under the palace walls."

After twenty paces, a new set of stairs led up to a door set in the ceiling. The dock boy set the lantern carefully on a shelf, then rapped lightly on the door.

It lifted open, light pouring down into the mostly darkened tunnel. Blinking away the sudden brightness, I saw a palace guardsman kneeling, holding the door, and standing above him was the First of the Mistress.

"Welcome to the palace," he said.

Then another guard leaned down into the tunnel with an outstretched hand to help pull us up.

"We haven't needed those passages in years," the First said, almost to himself.

We'd moved from the small room where we'd emerged, through a few short corridors lit with wide oil sconces, to a bare room containing wooden chairs and a table with wine and a platter of breads and cheeses. The room was dusty, the walls stained with old soot from torches.

I sat on my heels in one corner, quietly watching Borund and the First where they stood. The guards had been positioned outside, and the dock boy had split from the group on the way to the room. The only other person I'd seen was a woman robed in white who had brought the food and wine. One of the Mistress' servants. She'd smiled as she set the platter on the table, but the smile had faded when she turned back to Avrell and gave him a solemn nod before leaving.

Avrell's mouth had tightened . . . and then he'd pointedly ignored me.

"Why is the harbor closed?" Borund asked tersely. "Who ordered it?"

The First sighed and motioned to a chair. "The Mistress herself ordered it."

"What! But why?" Borund shook his head in confusion. "It doesn't make any sense."

"No, it doesn't," the First said flatly.

It took Borund a moment to catch all the implications the First had put into his voice, but when he did, he leaned back into his chair, the wood creaking in the heavy silence.

"So the rumors are true," he finally murmured. It wasn't a question.

The First nodded. "I wasn't certain, *can't* be certain, even now. The Mistress has been acting erratically since the Fire, but nothing alarming, nothing that couldn't be explained at the time as rational, if a little odd. But recently . . ." He sighed, his rigid stance sagging slightly. He moved to a chair. "Maintaining the Skewed Throne is not as simple as it would seem. The Mistress has always acted strangely in the past, given orders that made no sense at the time. But later you could always look back and see why the order was given. And none of the previous Mistresses . . . *changed* while seated on the throne. Not in any significant way.

"But since the Fire, this Mistress has. Her orders no longer make sense. There is no reason to close the harbor, and no real reason to saturate the city with the palace guard."

"So that wasn't you," Borund interjected. "Or Baill."

Avrell shook his head. "No, that came directly from the Mistress."

He paused, as if undecided whether he should say anything more. He watched Borund carefully, and Borund stirred in his seat under his gaze. Then he turned to me.

I held perfectly still, tried to remain expressionless.

Avrell considered me a moment more, then straightened and turned back to Borund, as if coming to a decision. "In the past few months, the Mistress' actions have shifted from simply eccentric to truly bizarre. She ascends to the tower and stares out at the sea at odd hours, even in the dead of night, in the rain, remaining there until one of the servants or the guards is forced to drag her back inside. She roams the halls of the palace, mumbling to herself, laughing, sometimes singing, sometimes growling, often in languages that no one understands. I've placed guards at the door to her chambers, to follow her, to make certain she does not harm herself, but somehow she manages to elude them. I ran across her in one of the gardens not two days ago, staring down at the roots of a tree when she was supposed to have been sleeping. She told me the sea was red with blood, the throne was cracked, and that the garden had once been a plaza. I took her back to her rooms, and the guards assured me they had not seen her leave. Nothing like that happened before the Fire passed through the city."

Borund had grown increasingly uncomfortable as the First spoke. "Why are you telling me this?"

The First kept quiet for a moment, then smiled grimly. "Because more is going on than it would seem. If it was the Mistress, and only the Mistress, I believe I could handle the situation myself. But no. There's too much going on in the city. You told me yourself about the attack in the Broken Mast, and the deaths of the merchants."

"Yes."

The First nodded. "I heard nothing of it until our meeting a few weeks ago, the night you were attacked in the middle ward and your assistant—William, I believe?—was wounded."

Silence, as both Borund and the First watched each other.

The First stirred. "There is a conspiracy among the merchants, an attempt to seize control of trade within the city at a time when trade, not only here in Amenkor but everywhere on the Frigean coast, is in peril. At first I thought it was something that should be left to the guild to be sorted out. Guild politics in play, if you will. But after speaking to you a few weeks ago at your manse . . ."

He let the thought fade, but Borund picked up the thread.

"You think that this conspiracy—I've been calling it a consortium—extends into the palace itself."

"Consortium," the First muttered, as if trying out the word for the first time. He smiled. "I like that. But, yes, I think this . . . consortium is much larger than a few merchants, and has connections in the palace. In particular, I think it includes the good captain of the palace guard, Baill." Avrell's voice twisted with distaste at the captain's name.

Borund's face darkened as well. Reaching for the glass of wine that had so far gone untouched, he drank, brow creased in thought. The First eased back in his seat and waited.

After a long moment, Borund glanced in my direction.

I dove deep beneath the river, shifting the currents toward Borund as I went, then turned toward the First.

In the swirling gray currents, the First appeared gray.

As I let the river go, I felt something tug at the currents, heard a vague noise, like the dry rasp of dead leaves blown across stone, like a voice . . . or many voices. But it faded.

I nodded to Borund, Avrell watching the exchange with interest. He said nothing, but his gaze was intent, much more focused than before.

I sat back and dipped beneath the river again, but the sound of dead leaves was gone. I shrugged it aside.

"Charls is dead," Borund began.

The First straightened slightly. "So I heard."

Borund grunted. "I thought he was the man behind the deaths of the other merchants, and in one respect I was right. He was the one organizing and ordering the deaths. He tried to kill me at the tavern on the wharf, but failed due to Varis' intervention. I suspected he was behind the deaths of the other merchants after that."

Borund paused, and the First glanced toward me. I didn't react.

"I see," he said. And he did see. I could hear it in his voice.

"Only after the fact did I learn that it wasn't really Charls giving the orders, that more merchants were involved."

"And do you know these merchants?"

"Yes. But the only one of consequence is Alendor. He controls almost half of the trade in Amenkor himself. If you factor in all of the other merchants I believe he has sway over . . ."

"He can control the entire city, especially if he feels he has power over the guard."

Borund nodded in agreement. "There are only three significant merchants left in the city *not* under his control: myself, Regin, and Yvan. I had thought that if the three of us allied ourselves together, we could send out what ships remained under our control still in the harbor before the weather changes. Perhaps we could find enough resources, buy enough staples, that the city could survive the winter months. William and I were just beginning to discuss this option when we heard the noise in the harbor."

The First grimaced. "By order of the Mistress, the harbor has been closed. Not even Baill expected this. He protested more than I did."

Borund leaned forward, placed his hands flat on the table. His face was drawn, his voice so intent it almost shook. "I've calculated what stores Regin, Yvan, and I already have here in the city."

"And?"

Borund shook his head. "The city will never survive the winter. There will be famine. At least half the city will starve, and that's assuming the winter is mild."

"And where there is famine, there will also be plague." The First frowned, looking down at the floor. "What of Alendor's stores? Would the city survive if we could seize control of what this consortium holds?"

"I cannot say. Based on what we know they hold, perhaps. But I don't have access to Alendor's books. Nor Charls'."

Avrell's frown deepened, his shoulders tensing as he thought. Anger and desperation flowed off him in waves, tightly controlled.

Borund stood. "We *have* to get our ships out of the harbor," he said, voice tight, "or the city will starve."

When Avrell glanced up, his eyes were dark. "I believe that Nathem, my Second, and I can deal with the Mistress. Somehow, we will get her to open up the harbor again. But even if we succeed with the Mistress, there is still the consortium. We need their stocks, and if Baill is in league with them, we cannot take them by force. We have to break the consortium itself. Now."

Borund nodded grimly. "In my opinion, the best way to do that is to eliminate Alendor."

The First's lips thinned.

And then they both turned toward me.

*   *   *

On the walk back to the manse, Borund muttered to himself continuously about what would need to be done once Alendor was dead, but I ignored him. I watched the street for threats, but did not see it. Not really.

I had agreed to kill Alendor. Another hunt, like Charls. Only this one would be worse. Because now I wouldn't see the man threatening Borund and William and the other merchants of the city. I wouldn't see the man attempting to gain control of all of the trade, the man willing to starve all of Amenkor to do it. No. I'd see the man underneath as well, the man that would plead for his life at the end if he had the chance.

We reached the manse, Gerrold opening the iron gate outside to let us in. Borund had ordered it kept locked since the first attack.

As we passed inside, something drifted through the river, a scent I felt I should recognize but couldn't, like lantern oil and straw.

I straightened, halted just inside the gate and stared out at the street, gaze flickering swiftly over the few people, scanning the few alcoves where someone could hide. But I saw no one, and the scent—so vague—was already fading.

"Varis?" Borund asked behind me. "Is something wrong?"

Frowning, I turned and said curtly, "No. Nothing's wrong."

He pulled back, hearing the lie in my voice. But he said nothing, confused, as I moved past him to the house, Gerrold shutting the gates behind us.

I went to my room, that had once been Joclyn's—a servant's—room, and stood inside the doorway. Nothing in the room had changed in the past few months except that now there were a few clothes folded in the chest of drawers. I moved to the chest and opened up one of the drawers, stared down at the pouches inside, pouches full of coins. Lizbeth placed them there on a regular basis, but I hadn't used any of them. Borund provided everything I needed: clothes, food. I'd never needed anything else.

Looking down at the pouches, I suddenly realized I didn't like Borund.

I closed the drawer, glanced once swiftly over the room, and then wandered out into the hall, turning toward William's room without thought.

William was sitting upright on the bed, sheets of paper scattered all around him. He smiled when I knocked and stepped inside the room.

"Varis," he said, his voice weary but light. Something had changed around his eyes though, something subtle. They were no longer wide and bright and open. Instead, they appeared pinched and dark.

It could have been simple exhaustion, but I didn't think so.

His smile faltered slightly, troubled, but remained. He motioned me inside. "Come in. I need a break."

I moved a few steps closer, but didn't approach the bed.

"Borund wants me to kill Alendor," I said.

His smile froze, then faded. His shoulders slumped and he turned to stare out the window. He'd had the bed moved since that morning, so that he could see the harbor and the Mistress' ships guarding the entrance to the bay.

"And what did you say?" he asked. His voice was flat, without inflection, without judgment.

I swallowed, standing rigid. "I'll need to know where I'll most likely find Alendor this evening. Borund said that you would know, that you know what inns and taverns most of the merchants frequent."

Silence. William didn't turn, but after a long moment nodded, as if to himself, as if he were finally accepting something that he had not wanted to believe. In a voice a little rougher and softer than the first, he said, "Alendor will be near the warehouses tonight. He usually checks on his own stocks, then finds his way to the Splintered Bow for dinner."

I nodded, then hesitated, waiting for more, but William stared stoically out at the harbor, what I could see of his face hard and harsh, closed off. All traces of the smile were gone.

I turned to leave, feeling a warm pain deep inside my stomach, as if I'd been stabbed and was bleeding on the inside. And the blood flow wouldn't stop.

I'd almost reached the door when William said, loudly, "Varis?"

I stood still, looking out into the corridor through the open door. I could tell by William's voice that he'd turned toward me, was staring at my back, but I didn't turn around. "What?" I was surprised at how thick my voice sounded.

"How . . . ?" he began, but he didn't continue, struggling.

I looked down at the floor and closed my eyes, then turned toward him purposefully. "When I was six, my mother was killed by two men when we were returning from a trip to Cobbler's Fountain. We lived on the outskirts of the slums, near the Dredge. Or at least I assume so, since that's where Cobbler's Fountain is. I don't remember much from before." I paused, seeing again in my head the two red men, heard myself say in a child's innocent voice, *Look, Mommy. Look at the red men.*

Then I focused on William's face again, on his steady, green eyes. "They killed her for what little she'd carried with her . . . some coin perhaps. They did nothing to me, left me with her body in an alley on a backstreet I didn't recognize. I didn't know what to do, didn't know where to go, where to run to, so I stayed there, next to my mother's body, until the guardsmen came.

"They didn't know what to do with me either. They were arguing about it, trying to decide, when a woman that my mother knew showed up and offered to take me in." I shuddered. "The guards handed me over without much hesitation— what else were they going to do with me?—and for a while I lived with this woman. She wasn't bad I guess, but she had five kids of her own already."

"But what about your father?"

I thought immediately of Erick, of the white-dusty man, but grimaced. "I don't remember my father. I don't remember much of anything from before Cobbler's Fountain and the night my mother was killed, mainly flashes of scenes, nothing significant. So I went with the woman."

I clenched my jaw at the memories—resentment and pain held tight but still leaking out into my voice. "After about a year—a year of defending myself from the other kids when she wasn't looking and fighting to get enough food to eat—I decided I'd be better off on my own. So I left. I ran away, moved deeper into the slums beyond the Dredge. I lived like an animal there, scrounging in garbage heaps, eating anything I could find, scraps you and Borund wouldn't even feed to a dog. I was dying and I didn't even know it. Then I ran into a street thug named Dove and his gang. They showed me that I could do much better if I was a little more daring. They taught me how to survive, how to steal, how to pick pockets, how to be quick and subtle, and how to distract. I was especially helpful to them for that. All I had to do was sit in the shadows of an alley and cry and someone would come in to investigate."

Some of the hardness had seeped out of William's eyes, but for some reason that didn't make me feel any better.

"So what happened?" he asked after a moment of silence.

I looked away from him. "Dove took one of the setups too far. One of the takes decided to run and it awoke something inside Dove that I didn't like. I told him I wouldn't help him hunt the woman down and so he abandoned me." I winced, feeling again Dove's fist as he struck me after I'd said no. "But it didn't matter by then. I was almost eleven and I'd learned everything I needed to know to survive in the slums."

The room fell completely silent. I could feel William's eyes on me, but did not look up. Strangely, the anger I'd felt had died, along with the tension in my shoulders, in my jaw. As if telling William had released me somehow.

"So why did you leave the slums? How did you end up on the wharf, where we found you?"

I did look up at this. I didn't want to tell him about Bloodmark, about Erick. So instead, I said, "Someone pushed me too far. And I finally realized that I didn't want to just 'survive' anymore. I wanted something else."

And now I found myself in the same situation, I thought wryly. I didn't want to go on killing. I wanted something else.

William said nothing, trying to understand, the intent clear on his face. "So you . . . grew up in the slums?"

I laughed, the sound without humor. "I *survived* the slums," I said with force. "Any way I could."

"But . . . how can you do it? How can you—"

"Because it's what I am. It's all that I know."

A pause, and I turned to go. Then, in a voice much less harsh, he said, "But you have a choice now."

I tried not to sigh. "No. I don't."

And I left.

I waited outside the Splintered Bow in a darkened side street, leaning against a wall. Outside the tavern, torches flared and spat in the breeze coming off of the water, and clouds roiled overhead, blocking out the stars and the moon. Winter clouds. The air tasted of rain, a cold rain, but it was still distant. Alendor had entered the tavern an hour before, with three others—another merchant, one I'd seen at Charls' manse, and two men I didn't know—and so I waited, trying not to think of William or Borund, Erick or the white-dusty man. I tried not to think of anything at all, submerging myself beneath the river, floating there.

On the side street, no one tried to approach me. A patrol of palace guards on horseback sauntered by, but they said nothing, only watched me with contempt before turning and vanishing up the main thoroughfare, heading toward the palace.

The tavern door banged open and I shifted away from the wall as Alendor moved out onto the street. He stood straight, a cloak draped over his merchant's coat. The other merchant followed a few steps behind him, like a mongrel. The remaining two men moved like guardsmen, casual and deadly, eyes always watching.

I frowned, suddenly glad there were clouds. I'd need the darkness. In the warehouse district, there were few places to hide. I'd discovered that when trying to follow Borund.

Alendor turned and said something to his bodyguards, then motioned back toward the warehouses near the docks. When they headed away from the tavern, I fell in behind them, far enough back that the guardsmen wouldn't see me.

At the same time, the Fire inside stirred. I'd been expecting it.

They moved slowly, warily, deeper into the warehouses, taking side streets, doubling back once. I pulled back even more, allowed them to get farther ahead. I knew the main thoroughfares here from accompanying Borund and William, but Alendor wasn't using the main streets. He used the narrows, the alleys between the large buildings.

As I followed, the Fire continued to grow, tingling down along my arms.

Ahead, Alendor and his group turned into another alley, this one half the width of the street we were already on. I waited to see if they would double back, one hand resting on the wooden wall of the warehouse to my left.

After twenty slow breaths, I sidled forward in a crouch, shifted around a rain barrel and glanced down into the alley.

Nothing but a stack of broken crates. They'd already moved out the far side. Or entered the building through a door I couldn't see.

I ran into the alley, already searching for Alendor's scent.

The Fire surged, burned down my arms to my fingers. I kept moving, thinking the sudden blaze was a reaction to Alendor's disappearance. I didn't realize it was something else until someone stepped out from behind the stack of crates into my path.

I slowed to a halt, the figure five paces away. I didn't recognize him, his face shadowed, dark with a trimmed beard and mustache, shaved head. A few scars marred his cheeks.

The Fire flared even higher as I plunged myself deeper, drawing my dagger, and I suddenly felt more men.

I spun, slipping into a crouch, as three more stepped out of the darkness into the end of the alley. Without turning, I felt more behind me, stepping up to join the man with the beard.

The Fire churned in my chest, and my stomach tightened, a different sour taste flooding my mouth: fear and despair, dark and wet and acidic.

It tasted of the Dredge.

My gaze flicked to the alley walls, looking for an alcove, a niche, a hole, a darkness. But this wasn't the Dredge. The buildings weren't crumbling to ruin, full of empty doorways and shattered walls.

The desperation clawed at my throat and I shifted my attention back to the three men before me, face hardening. My nostrils flared.

Then someone behind me laughed.

My head snapped back to the bearded man, to the two men who'd joined him. I thought it was the bearded man laughing, but it wasn't. Someone else stepped into the alley, wearing a cloak.

Cristoph.

I felt a sliver of surprise course through me. I'd expected it to be Alendor.

"It's not just me and a friend this time," Cristoph said. His voice shivered through me. I remembered it from the alley on the wharf so long ago, from that first kill in the real Amenkor.

The men began to shift forward, and Cristoph removed his cloak as he said, "Careful. She knows how to use that dagger."

I blew out a harsh breath through my nose and then dove deeper.

They came all at once, crowding into the narrow alley, laughing, bodies rushing. I felt them surge around me, felt their movements, tasted their blades, but there were too many of them. It became a mad rush and I spun, slicing out with short arcs, dagger gripped loosely because I had no real target, only a shifting, startling world of reds.

The dagger cut deep as hands grappled me and I cried out. The river was

suddenly flooded with the stench of blood. And then even that was overwhelmed with sweat, with raw grunts and curses and shouts. I flailed, felt my
dagger connect again, a shallow cut, heard someone bellow and felt emptiness
as they pulled back, but then someone shifted and closed in and the river broke,
became nothing but a wild current of sound and scent and rough skin.

The first punch caught me on the cheek and I gasped, growled low like an
animal, and dug my dagger down and into someone's side. A scream and more
copper-tasting blood, hot and fluid, and then a fist connected with my side, my
shoulder, another to my back, low, and pain shot up through my spine. I cried
out again, felt hands grappling with my arms, felt wetness against my side—
someone else's blood—and then there was only weight, pressing me down, hard.

I hit the cobbles of the alley with a grunt, on my stomach, my face to one
side, bodies crushing my legs, my chest, a hand splayed over my head. It
gripped and lifted and thrust my face into stone, pain shooting down into my
neck as my lip cracked and split, blood flooding down into my throat, coating
my tongue. Someone laughed and then the weight shifted off my body.

I bucked, but there were too many on my legs, too many holding my arms,
and then any thought of movement halted as a foot connected with my stomach from the side.

I gasped, sprayed blood and spit onto the cobbles from my lip, and couldn't
catch my breath, my chest seizing. A sheet of white pain spiked into my skull,
blinded me, and after a horrifying moment something in my lungs tore and I
heaved in air.

A foot stomped down onto my back, flattened me to the cobbles, and I lost
my breath again, coughed it out with a hacking wheeze.

A pause, but the hands on my arms tightened and the weight on my legs
didn't move. I heard footsteps approach, realized I still held my dagger in one
hand in a death grip.

Someone leaned down close, breath against my neck.

I strained, struggled to move, neck straining with effort. Someone chuckled
and I spat out blood in frustration.

"This is for Bellin," Cristoph whispered into my ear. "And for Charls."

He shifted away, but not far.

A hand closed around my neck, tightened as I gasped and tried to pull
away, then held me still.

Cold metal touched my throat.

In the chaotic roil of the river I tasted the blade, gasped in the sharp scent
of lantern oil and straw: Cristoph's scent.

He hadn't had one before, but he did now.

I sobbed, the sound thick and distorted.

The blade began to press down, and then I scented something else.

Oranges.

"Let her go," someone said, voice calm and cold and dangerous, like the Dredge. And I felt a blade slip through the currents, swift and smooth, another dagger, distant—

And someone screamed, a gargled, bloody sound.

The knife at my throat jerked back suddenly, and Cristoph roared, "Kill him!"

And suddenly the weight holding me down released, pulled back sharply with the sounds of scuffling feet and grunts and the focused intensity shifted away from me, one step, two, down the alley.

I tried to roll onto one arm, felt pain sear through my chest from where the men had kicked me, and choked on my own blood. Pushing the pain away, I drew the river close, pulled it in tight, and concentrated on the struggle only three paces away.

Cristoph and his men had surrounded Erick. One man lay slumped to one side, his throat cut, but there were still six men left.

Too many for Erick to handle. Too many.

I rolled onto my side and gasped at the renewed pain but dragged myself up onto one arm, to one knee.

I still held my dagger.

I pulled myself into a crouch, turned toward the fight. The men were closing in.

And then Erick saw me. "Run!" he barked. His voice cracked with command, the voice he'd used to train me, to drill me, more a growl than a shout. His eyes flashed and he shouted again, "Run!"

One of the men turned—Cristoph—and I spun, stumbled, caught myself, and ran. I obeyed without thought. It had been drilled into me.

Behind, I heard a clatter of blades, heard Erick cry out in pain, heard someone roar in triumph.

And then I was in the street, fleeing down narrows and alleys I didn't recognize, running without a place to run to. Pain flared at every step, in my stomach, in my chest, across one shoulder. My face throbbed, and blood trailed down from my lip, down my neck.

I stumbled to a halt, gasping, in a narrow a hundred paces out when I realized no one was following me, leaned over near a wall, one arm out for support, and coughed. My eyes burned and my hair was tangled and matted. My lip throbbed with a pain unlike anything I'd ever felt before, and there was a thin sliver of cold pain up along my neck from Cristoph's blade, but the pain in my chest receded as my coughing fit ended, each breath no longer so piercing. I didn't think anything was broken inside, just bruised.

I drew myself upright, suddenly fourteen, back on the Dredge all over again.

And then I heard William's voice: *You have a choice now.*

My breath caught and I stared out into the black street. I choked, coughed hoarsely, and spat more blood, winced at the bruising in my chest, and thought about Erick, about Alendor, about Cristoph.

Suddenly, the pain in my chest didn't seem so harsh. Because I wasn't fourteen anymore, waiting for the next kick, the next shouted "whore!" Because I didn't have to listen to Borund . . . or Erick.

I shoved myself away from the wall, staggered back toward the alley. By the time I'd reached its entrance, I'd let the writhing snake of anger inside me uncoil and drawn the river and the Fire up around me like a cloak. It subdued the pain, pushed it into the background. But it was going to cost me. I could feel the nausea rising even now, a nausea I hadn't felt in over a year, since Bloodmark. But I'd never pushed myself this deep for this long into the river's depths since then.

And it didn't matter. All that mattered was Erick.

I rounded the corner, moving with the quick, quiet stealth I'd learned from the Dredge, as fluid as a cat. At the far end of the alley, I could see the men that surrounded Erick's body where it lay, laughing as they kicked him, muttering to each other, goading each other on. Cristoph stood back from the group. Only four men left, besides Cristoph. Two other bodies lay scattered through the alley.

Erick had little time. He'd be dead in the next twenty breaths if I didn't act. Cristoph would kill him. Even as I watched, Cristoph smiled. The same slow, cruel smile I'd seen on Garrell Cart as he gazed down at the little girl with the green ribbon.

I pushed away from the wall, the last vestiges of the pain smothered. Everything became focused, became clear.

Twenty breaths.

The first man died two breaths later, my dagger slipping up and in and out. He jerked forward, arched back, began to fall, but I was already moving. I felt Cristoph see me, heard his drawn breath like a gasp in my ear. But he was the farthest away, and not close enough to harm Erick.

The others first.

The second man heard the first one's startled gasp, but he wasn't fast enough. My dagger punched into his neck even as the muscles there contracted and his head began to turn. He staggered back, hands shooting to the spray of blood, struck the wall to the left of Erick's crumpled body, slid down its side. His pulse thrummed through my head, a dark ripple, and I tasted the heat in the air, the sweat.

Eight breaths.

"'Ware!" Cristoph shouted, sharp and brittle with tension, anger, and terror.

I spun, caught his eyes.

He saw something there, deep inside me. The harshness tinged with annoyance in his gaze vanished like a burst bubble, replaced solely with fear.

He stepped back.

At the same moment, the third man snarled and lunged for me.

Almost without thought my blade sliced up and into his side. I caught his weight as he fell into me, felt his last gasp of breath against my shoulder and neck. It smelled of garlic and potatoes.

He was heavier than I'd thought and I staggered, sliding to one side, out from underneath him as he fell. His blood coated my hand, slick and coppery.

Twelve breaths.

And then the river echoed with running feet. Slipping my blade free of the man's side, I rolled his body away from me, turned to see Cristoph and the last man dodging around the corner of the alley.

My nostrils flared and I drew in the deep scent of lantern oil and straw.

I smiled and turned away from the fleeing men, kneeling down at Erick's side.

His face was a bloody mess, cuts and gashes and dirt and pebbles mired across the scars he already had. The whites of his eyes were startling, his breath coming in short gasps. Blood dripped from his nose to the cobblestones, and his arms were hunched protectively about his body. Every breath he drew sent a shudder through his chest, his legs twitching.

"I told you to run," he wheezed.

I leaned in close and smiled. "And I told you you couldn't protect me anymore."

He stilled for a moment, regarding me, and then he chuckled, the sound wet and thick. The chuckle edged into a moan and he rolled onto his back, straightening slightly. "The Mistress' tits, it hurts," he gasped, then winced as he moved his arm.

I dove deeper, focused as I laid a hand on his chest to keep him from moving. Nausea bubbled up, but I thrust it aside. I still had work to do tonight. The scent of oil and straw pulled me.

I could see that Erick wasn't as hurt as he looked, beaten but not broken. Cristoph had been the real threat. Erick would survive if he'd stay in the alley and wait for me. No one would disturb him here.

I relaxed and leaned in toward him. "Don't move. Stay here and wait for me. I'll be back to get you."

He looked at me a long moment, surprised, but then nodded. "I'll stay," he muttered.

I pushed away, but he halted me before I'd moved two steps with a barked, "Varis!"

I turned back, face creased with annoyance. The scent of oil and straw was strong, almost overwhelming.

"He's a mark now," Erick gasped, so intent on what he said that he'd risen slightly, his upper torso wavering a few inches off the ground.

I smiled and nodded. "I know."

He collapsed back to the cobbles with a groan.

I'd reached the end of the alley and turned before I realized that I'd spoken to him with the same harsh crack of command he'd used to train me.

Lantern oil and straw.

I drew in a deep breath, glanced upward toward the roiling clouds. The pressure of rain weighed down on me, heavy and cold. I was barely keeping the nausea at bay now, drawing more and more on the protective Fire to keep it back.

I had to find Cristoph. I wouldn't be able to hold on much longer.

I dodged across a main thoroughfare, ducked through an alley and sped down the street on the far side. Cristoph was moving deeper into the warehouse district, traveling fast. The other man was still with him, his scent warm, like stagnant water, and not as strong. But Cristoph's scent intensified as I ran, seemed to be gathering like a pool of water not far away.

Another street, down the edge of a long warehouse, through another alley—

A warning pulse in the Fire and I slowed, felt a shudder as the scent of stagnant water suddenly sharpened. I tasted metal.

The man that had fled with Cristoph was quick. His blade flashed out from behind a stack of empty crates and caught me in the arm before I could jerk back. I felt the tug as it sliced through my shirt, through skin, tasted my own blood, but the silvery jolt of pain was smothered almost instantly by the Fire.

I stepped back from the crates as the man moved out of hiding. He growled, a low, dark sound, and his eyes flared with hate. But I could smell his fear in his sweat, thick and putrid. It was the bearded man, the one who had first stepped from hiding in the alley where I'd been caught.

He circled me and I turned slowly, followed him. In the darkness, he could barely see me, was listening more than he was seeing. I could see it in the turn of his head. His breathing was harsh, drowning out most sound.

"Where are you, little bitch?" he hissed, almost too low to hear.

I grinned.

He lunged forward, knife striking. I parried, ducked to one side, sliced up and out toward his chest, but he was already moving, grunting with the effort, pulling back.

My blade caught his shirt but nothing else and then we were circling again. My grin was gone. He was breathing harder, but there was a change in his stance. He wasn't trying to see me anymore. He'd given up, was relying on his other senses.

His nostrils flared and I suddenly wondered what I smelled like, but then he dove, moving in tight and close.

My blade grated across his and I felt his breath on my face, the stench of stagnant water overpowering. His free arm snaked around my back, jerked me in tight, our blade arms caught between us. Just as I began to twist out of the hold, his foot caught the back of mine. He turned, spun me in the direction I'd been about to twist, and I tripped over his foot.

I landed hard on my shoulder, gasped as numbness sank into my flesh, my arm going dead for a moment, then tingling along its entire length. I felt my dagger slipping from my numbed fingers, heard it clatter to the cobbles of the street, but I didn't hesitate. I rolled onto my back, reached up with my other arm and caught his wrist as he struck downward, dug my fingers into tendon and muscle. He hissed and dropped down onto my chest, knees to either side, but he didn't lose the knife. My grip was too tenuous, my fingers in the wrong place.

He leaned forward, arm trembling, and forced his knife closer. His other hand clamped onto my arm, tried to wrench it free, but I held tight. He snarled in frustration, his knees tightening about my sides. Sensation began returning to my useless arm, a horrible burning fire, but I fought it back and began scrabbling for my lost dagger. Giving up on wresting my hand free, he pulled back and punched me.

The sheeting white pain from my already split lip almost wrenched me from the river. The Fire wavered and I spasmed, bile rising to the back of my throat. I choked it down, seized the river again, the protective Fire returning just in time for me to halt his knife a few inches from my chest.

He shifted, laid his hand on my chest, and put his entire weight behind his knife.

It was too much. I couldn't hold it. My arm was trembling already, weakening. I could see the strength flowing out of it in tendrils. I could smell my own sweat, tainted with terror.

The knife lowered, touched my shirt, pricked my skin. Blood began to stain the cloth, and the man smiled, a wicked, vicious smile. I strained harder, the muscles in my arm burning, but the knife sank lower, digging in. The tip of the knife scraped bone.

The scent of blood intensified. White-hot pain began to flare through my chest, so hot the Fire couldn't hold it back. I gasped, my eyes going wide—

And I pulled the river close, formed it into a hard, solid ball between me and the grinning face of the bearded man, and punched it forward.

The man jerked back with a gasp, the knife tip sliding free of my chest as his arm went weak and I thrust him away. My other hand found my dagger and with a heave I pulled myself up off the ground and into a crouch, weight in my heels.

The bearded man never had time to recover. He was still gasping, arms cradling his chest where I'd punched him with the river, when I slit his throat.

I stepped back, staggered under a sudden weight of weariness, but forced that back as well as I caught myself against a wall. The scent of stagnant water was fading, the lantern oil and straw now so strong it overwhelmed everything else, even blood. Using the wall for support, I stumbled down the street, turned, and saw the door.

I halted. The warehouse took up the entire block and had two floors. Lantern light glowed through the few windows surrounding the doorway. The entire building reeked of oil and straw.

I pushed away from the wall and moved across the street. I was no longer moving fluidly. My arm still tingled with the last traces of numbness and my chest throbbed with a dull, hideous pain that the Fire could not suppress. My face had begun to throb as well. But the writhing coil of anger urged me forward.

I didn't hesitate at the door. Instead, I kicked it open.

At the far side of the little room beyond, Cristoph jerked around. He held a lantern and was just about to step through a second, open doorway into the warehouse itself. The room we were in held two desks and numerous ledgers on shelves.

When he saw me, Cristoph bolted through the door, taking the lantern with him.

I staggered past the desks to the door, stared out into the warehouse beyond. Crates filled the immense room, stacked high, so that the warehouse was nothing but a warren of narrow walkways and niches. But Cristoph's scent was strong, and I could see the flicker of lantern light clearly.

I slid forward.

Cristoph turned and twisted through the passages, ducked and doubled back. But he couldn't hide. Not with his scent so strong. As I got closer, I could hear his breathing. It was panicked, punctuated with gasps and moans.

I moved faster, my nostrils flaring. I was close. I could almost taste him.

Then the sounds of panic quieted. I paused, edged around a corner.

He stood in the short passage on the far side, and the moment he saw me he heaved the lantern at me.

I ducked under it, sped forward, heard it shatter as it struck the crates behind me. The scent of lantern oil was suddenly stronger, as intense as the blood earlier—

And then there was a faint whoosh of sound. A wave of heat washed forward and I paused.

Ahead of me, a look of horror passed over Cristoph's face as the sheen of light intensified. He held still in the flicker of flames, then dropped his gaze to me and fled to the left, down another passage.

I turned back, smoke suddenly choking me. The entire passage behind me was consumed in flame. And it was spreading. Fast.

The entire warehouse would burn. And it wouldn't end there.

I spun and rushed after Cristoph. He was too close to let go now. And he knew the quickest way out.

I caught up to him twenty steps farther on. He was trapped at a dead end, backed up against a wall of crates.

"Please," he gasped.

The wall of heat from the fire pulsed behind us and now the river was saturated with the sounds of wood crackling, splintering.

Cristoph glanced toward the fire, then seemed to sag, the panic pulling back. "We're trapped. The only way out was back through the fire."

I frowned, then stepped forward. He only had time to tense, to draw in a sharp breath, before I struck.

I made it as painless and quick as possible. He was a mark, nothing more.

When his body slumped to the floor, I stood over it a moment. But I felt nothing. No satisfaction. No anger. No remorse.

Then I turned to look at the fire. I could see its light at the end of the passage, could see the light flickering on the wood of the ceiling high above. I could feel it pushing toward where I stood, a ripple of heat and smoke and light.

I glanced up to the top of the crates. They were stacked high, but not all the way to the ceiling.

I was small, thin. I could fit through narrow spaces.

I stepped over Cristoph's body and began pulling myself up.

I stumbled out of the warehouse through a back entrance, where goods were loaded and unloaded. The smoke on the air was heavy and thick, cloying beneath the river, but I didn't dare let it go. I still had to reach Erick, and the fire inside was raging, had already spread to the warehouse on one side.

The entire warehouse district might go up in flames.

I shoved the thought from my mind, gathered the Fire and the river about me as tightly as I could, and set out at a half run toward Erick. Halfway there, shouts began to rise in warning. Someone ran past with a bucket and I snorted, feeling a shiver of guilt. But there was nothing I could do. And the bucket wouldn't help.

I stumbled into the alley where I'd left Erick, half expecting him to be gone, but he wasn't. He was sitting up instead, back against the alley wall. I knelt beside him and he chuckled when he saw me.

"You look like hell," he said, and I grinned. But it was weak. I was barely holding on, the nausea and pain steadily overtaking the Fire.

"Come on," I said, pulling him upright. He groaned, rolled to his knees, and then with help managed to climb to his feet.

"What in the Mistress' name did you do?" he wheezed as we staggered out onto the street. He was supporting me more than I was supporting him. The fire could be seen clearly beneath the lowering clouds.

"Cristoph started a small fire."

He laughed, winced, then shook his head.

We made it to the edge of the warehouse district before I lost the river completely. It slid away without a sound, even as I reached for it, and the sudden pain and nausea was instantaneous. I vomited in a corner, Erick leaning over me, while people on the street panicked. The fire lit up the clouds behind us, thick smoke roiling skyward, reflecting the flames.

"What did you do?" Erick said again in awe as he watched.

From where I knelt, hunched over my own puke, I glanced up at him. I wasn't going to hold out much longer. "Get me to Merchant Borund's manse," I croaked.

He nodded.

I felt the first fat drops of rain strike my face and then I let the nausea and pain overtake me.

I never felt myself hit the ground.

I woke when the first tremors hit.

Erick was carrying me. He clutched me tight at the beginning, but then the spasms became too violent, my arms twitching, my back arching, and he was forced to set me on the ground.

"Gods," he muttered. His voice was muted, as if coming from a distance. In the background, I could dimly hear screams, running feet, the roaring crackle of fire. Rain poured down, sluicing my face, dripped from Erick's hair as he knelt over me, his hands pressing me down, trying to hold me still. Fear was stamped across his face, stark and surreal.

Eventually, the tremors passed. The last thing I saw before weariness claimed me again was Erick, staring down into my half-lidded eyes, his face grim.

The second time, the tremors were worse. I never opened my eyes, *couldn't* open my eyes. My body was so taut I could feel the cords of muscle in my neck. My teeth were clenched so tight my jaw ached and tears squeezed from between my eyelids. Erick didn't set me down this time, and there was shouting.

"Open the damn gate!" Erick bellowed, but again everything was distant, removed.

A clatter of metal, a screech as I was jostled in Erick's grip, his balance shifting. He must have kicked the gate the moment it was unlocked. And the next instant he was running.

"What is this?" someone demanded, a voice I recognized, but it took a moment. Gerrold.

"Varis," Erick barked. "Are you Borund?"

"No."

"Get me Borund!" The training voice.

"What's this?" Lizbeth now, her voice harsh but shrill.

I felt the tension in my neck relaxing. The sensation of rain had stopped. We were inside.

Someone else approached. "What is the meaning of this?" Borund demanded.

"Varis is hurt."

"What?" Borund's voice moved closer. I felt a hand press against my face. "By the Mistress . . . Gerrold, go fetch Isaiah."

"But the fire—"

"Now!" I couldn't be certain, but I thought I heard true agony in his voice. Perhaps I was something more to him than a tool, a weapon.

Receding footsteps. My neck muscles had almost completely relaxed.

"Lizbeth—" Worry now.

"Towels, hot water, I know." Not as shrill as before. Determined and grim. Even with my eyes closed I could see her hitching up skirts, darting off toward the kitchen.

"Right. Now. You, Guardsman—"

"Erick."

"Whatever. Follow me. We'll take her up to her room."

More jostling. We'd almost reached my room when I began to thrash.

"Gods!" Borund gasped.

Erick shoved someone out of the way and tossed me onto the bed. "Hold her, damn it! She'll hurt herself!"

Hands clamped down onto my shoulders, a body pressed down over my chest. More hands gripped my legs.

"Gods, she's strong," Borund muttered. One leg tore free. My knee connected with something soft and fleshy and I heard Borund bark, "Shit!" before he recaptured the leg.

I heard Lizbeth gasp as she returned, and then there was a flutter of quick movements and a moment later, still thrashing madly, someone pressed a hot cloth against my forehead, water drenching down into my hair.

"She's sweating up a storm," Lizbeth said.

Erick only grunted.

I felt the tremors easing again, felt the strength draining away, leaving me empty.

"I think it's stopping for now," Erick muttered, and he drew his body weight off me, carefully.

I began to sob, the tears hot and salty, my chest hitching painfully. I tried to speak, but the strength was draining away too fast.

"Shh," Lizbeth murmured, her voice close, her breath tickling my ear. "Hush, you're safe now."

Exhaustion dragged her away. Just before it claimed me again, I heard Erick say faintly, "That's not the end of it."

And it wasn't. I rode the waves of tremors and exhaustion as I'd done before on the Dredge, waking enough that I could hear things faintly. But the pain was too intense. I never opened my eyes, only listened.

". . . in bloody hells happened!" Borund, voice vehement.

"It was an ambush," Erick spat back. "They were waiting for her!"

"Who?"

"She called the one Cristoph."

"Cristoph? But she was supposed to be following Alendor!"

Erick grunted. "He knew. He must have led her to the alley where Cristoph was waiting."

Silence. Then Borund said, "Cristoph *is* Alendor's youngest son. Perhaps Alendor is more daring than I thought. Or more desperate."

Another silence. "She'd be dead if I hadn't intervened."

Someone else entered the room. "Master Borund. The fire has spread through the warehouse district and entered the wharf. All ships have taken to the harbor, but, of course, with the blockade none can leave."

Borund swore. "Damn Avrell! Why can't he get the harbor opened? All our ships are safe?"

"Yes."

Borund sighed, began pacing. "What about the rain? Is it helping? Are we safe here?"

"The wind is blowing the fire toward the wharf. There's a chance it will jump the river to the other side of the harbor, but the rain seems to be keeping the fire damped. It's hard to tell. . . ."

I felt Borund approach, stand over me. But I could feel myself fading. "We'll stay here as long as possible. I don't want to move her."

A breath against my face as someone leaned close. Then I heard Borund whisper, "You damn well better come back, Varis. I can't lose you. Not after almost losing William."

His voice was choked.

Darkness. Soft darkness, like cloth.

Then a patch of light.

"How long will she be like this?" Borund asked.

Someone's hand pulled away from my chest. The trembling fit had abated and I could already feel the exhaustion pulling me down, the cloth moving back over my head.

"Hard to say." Isaiah, the healer. "But the seizures aren't as strong now as before. She's recovering. . . ."

More darkness. I pulled its cloth close, smothered myself in it. But another patch of light intervened.

"And what about Alendor?" A new voice, smooth and careful. I struggled with the cloth of darkness, pushed it back. It was Avrell, the First of the Mistress.

"No one's seen him since the fire," Borund answered.

Avrell sighed. "Parts of the warehouse district are still smoldering."

"Thank the Mistress for the rain. All of Amenkor might have burned." Borund had moved closer. "But it doesn't matter," he added. "With the warehouse district gone, we've lost most of our food stocks. The consortium is dead whether Alendor survived the fire or not. There's nothing left in Amenkor for the consortium to control."

"He's still a danger."

"I won't kill him," I tried to say, but the darkness was returning. I couldn't tell whether anyone had heard me, whether I'd even spoken out loud.

Borund leaned in closer. "Not anymore."

I fought the darkness, screamed at its resilience. "I won't kill him!"

Avrell moved closer as well. "In any case, we still have the problem of the Mistress. Nathem and I have tried to replace her, to seat someone else on the throne, but it isn't working. And the current Mistress still refuses to release the blockade."

Silence. "And what do you expect me to do about it?" Borund sounded tired and distracted.

I felt Avrell leaning over me, felt his presence like a weight. "Remember our discussion when I came to your manse a few weeks back? You told me that Varis once said she sees people as 'red,' and that is how she knows who to protect you from."

Borund grunted.

"I questioned that Seeker who brought her to you. He told me a similar story, that Varis claimed one of the Mistress' marks that she helped him to hunt down was 'gray,' that Varis told him that meant the mark was innocent. I'd heard of this before, so when you and Varis came to the palace, I had one of the Servants check to confirm my suspicions."

I stilled, felt the darkness drawing in close and tight and struggled against it. But I was still too weak.

Avrell leaned back, his clothes rustling. "I know what needs to be done now."

Before Borund could respond, or Avrell could continue, the darkness claimed me. One last time.

When I woke again, it was from true sleep. No feeling of cloth darkness shoved aside for a brief moment. No patch of light. No uncontrollable trembling. Instead, there was weariness, sunk so deep into my bones I could barely move. But I opened my eyes.

Sunlight. It flooded the room . . . my room.

I blinked up at the ceiling, let the throbbing of my face, my chest, my entire body flood through me. The pain in my chest was edged and concentrated. The pain in the vicinity of my lip was dull and spread out. The rest of my body was simply bruised, muscles and flesh worn and tired and completely drained of strength.

I lay a long moment and simply breathed. The air was tainted with smoke.

"Welcome back."

I turned my head, ignored the warning pangs from my neck.

William sat in a chair on the opposite side of the room, watching me. He smiled, and I felt something inside the empty hollowness of my gut warm. "Aren't we the pair," he added, then laughed.

I smiled, or tried to. There was more wrong with my face than the split lip. I remembered the bearded man punching me and lifted one arm tentatively to my cheek. It felt swollen and hot to the touch.

I let my hand drop back, more for lack of strength than anything else.

"How long?" I asked.

William leaned forward. "Five days. The first two days we were afraid we'd have to move you because of the fire, but the rain halted that, or at least held it at bay. By then we realized that the seizures weren't as bad each time and were spaced farther apart. We figured it was only a matter of time." He hesitated, then asked, "What happened to you?"

I turned away, stared up at the ceiling again. A surge of fear rippled through me, but not as strong as I expected. I'd never told anyone about the river, about what I saw. Not directly.

But Avrell knew now, and I assumed Borund. I found it strange that they had not told William.

"I don't see things the same way you do," I said. I paused, but the ripple of fear was smothered by the warmth. "When I want to, I can make everything a blur, as if I'm staring through water. Only the things of importance are clear. But it isn't easy. Sometimes, when I push things too hard, or when I do something unexpected, something I didn't realize I could do before, I get sick."

I waited, not certain what to expect.

After a long moment of silence, I turned back to see William still sitting forward watching me. He smiled again, then stood.

Moving carefully, one hand holding his side, he came up to the edge of the bed.

"I'd better go tell Borund you're awake. He and Avrell want to talk to you."

My stomach clenched and I thought, *I won't kill him,* but then William reached forward and gently brushed my hair away from my face, distracting me. A light touch that sent shivers down my neck and shoulders and into my back.

I held myself perfectly still and watched as he left the room.

I stood at a window in the palace and stared down at the city and harbor below. It had taken three days to recover enough so that I could get out of bed, and another two days before I felt well enough to come to the palace with Borund in order to see Avrell.

Borund had tried to push me. But I didn't listen to Borund anymore. I made my own decisions.

On the harbor below, patrols still blockaded the inlet, the sleek ships flying the Mistress' colors weaving back and forth beneath the sun. On land, a large chunk of the city close to the water was blackened, a few charred walls and half buildings still standing. Some warehouses had survived, and most of the docks, but close to a quarter of the city had burned.

I thought of Cristoph heaving the lantern at me and frowned.

I thought of Erick and bit my lip. I hadn't seen him since that night, had only heard him in the days that followed. And he hadn't been there at the end, when the tremors weren't as bad. I'd only heard Borund and Avrell.

Behind me, Borund suddenly blurted, "Where in bloody hell is he?" and stopped his pacing.

As if he'd heard, the door to the little room opened and Avrell stepped in. He was followed by Erick.

I shifted away from the window unconsciously, but halted. Erick's face was set, grim and determined and dangerous. The same face he wore on the Dredge, when he was about to kill a mark. As if he were about to do something he regretted, but that he felt was necessary.

His eyes caught mine but revealed nothing. He didn't even nod in acknowledgment.

I settled back as Avrell moved forward, suddenly uneasy.

Avrell approached Borund first, caught his gaze, and said simply, "It didn't work. We'll have to do what we discussed earlier."

Borund tensed. "Are you certain? There's no other option?" He did not look toward me as he spoke.

"I see no other way," Avrell said.

Borund sighed, shoulders sagging, and nodded. Then they both turned toward me.

I straightened at the looks on their faces, felt my bruised shoulders tense, felt my face set into a guarded expression. I watched Avrell, but it was Borund who moved forward.

"Varis, we need your help."

My stomach tightened and I drew in a deep breath, anger flaring, but before I could say anything, Borund continued.

"The fire that was started in the warehouse district . . . it burned up a significant portion of our reserves. The food we'd put aside, the food that had become scarce even before the fire, all of that . . . is gone. If we gather together everything that's left, from all the merchants in the city, and if we buy and ship as much as we can from the nearest cities, we might be able to survive until the spring harvest. But in order to do that the ships *have* to leave within the next five days. They have to leave *now* or they won't make it back before winter makes the seas too rough. Do you understand?"

I shook my head, the tightness in my stomach beginning to sour. Because a part of me *did* see, already knew what was coming. "No, I don't understand."

He sighed heavily. "We can't buy and ship what we need when the harbor is blockaded."

I glanced toward Avrell. "Then unblock the harbor. Let the ships out."

Avrell didn't move. "We can't. The Mistress ordered the harbor closed. The Mistress has to order the harbor opened again. Baill won't listen to anyone else, including me. He doesn't *have* to listen to anyone else, not when given a direct order from the Mistress."

My gaze darted back to Borund. "Then get her to change her mind."

"She won't," Borund said. "We've tried."

The room fell silent. I knew what they wanted, but I wanted to hear them say it.

"What do you want me to do?"

And now no one wanted to speak. Borund drew back, breath held. Avrell stilled. Erick stood by the closed door and watched me, his expression still hard, closed.

"She's insane, Varis," Borund finally managed. I was surprised. I'd expected Avrell to speak first. "We want you to kill her."

"No." I said it almost before he finished, and he stepped back at the vehemence in my voice. "No, I don't want to kill for you anymore. Find some other way."

"There is no other way!" Borund said. His voice became hard, commanding, desperate. "We've tried reasoning with her, we've tried countermanding her orders. We've even tried replacing her—"

"Enough."

Avrell's voice cut Borund short and he turned, angry and belligerent, but Avrell ignored him. Instead, he watched me.

"You heard us discussing this before. The Mistress is insane. Something in the White Fire six years ago drove her insane. She ordered the palace guard into the city, infiltrating the streets when there was no serious threat. She ordered the blockade of the harbor, for no reason whatsoever. But that isn't the worst." He stood, moving forward, taking the place of Borund, who fell back.

Behind them both, Erick perked up, suddenly attentive.

Avrell stopped in front of me, held my gaze. "When the fire started in the city below, the Guard instantly responded. We moved to form brigades to the harbor, lines of men to pass buckets of water to help put it out, or at least try to contain it. But the Mistress ordered the guardsmen not to help. And so they didn't. I stood on the tower beside the Mistress, stood there in the rain, and watched the city burn, *let it burn*. Because that's what the Mistress had ordered. And do you know what she did as it spread toward the docks? She smiled." He paused, and I saw rage in his eyes. "She let the city burn, Varis. If I had any doubts about her sanity before, they're gone now."

"Then replace her," I said.

He shook his head. "I tried. Everyone I seat upon the throne dies. Horribly. The throne twists them somehow, tortures them without leaving a mark upon their bodies. Looking at the histories, no one has ever tried to replace a current living Mistress. The Mistress has always been dead before a new Mistress was named. No." He shook his head again. "No. The current Mistress has to die before I can replace her."

"I'm sworn to protect the throne, not the Mistress."

I looked into his eyes and saw how much it had torn him inside to admit it. A deep tear, as deep as anything I'd learned on the Dredge . . . or in Amenkor. Because in the end both the Dredge and Amenkor were the same. The *people* were the same.

My gaze shifted toward Erick, took in his rigid stance. "Find someone else to kill her. Like Erick. Make her one of the guardsmen's marks."

Avrell shook his head. "No. It has to be you, Varis." He shot a quick glance toward Borund, who shifted uncomfortably. "Borund told me that you see the world differently, that you say those that are dangerous to you and to him are 'red'. Erick says you told him something similar when you hunted for him on the Dredge."

I felt a hot shudder of betrayal snap through me, shot a glare at Borund, then Erick, but Avrell had already continued.

"The Mistress knows when someone is approaching, so someone like Erick won't be able to get close enough to kill her. No. The only one who might have a chance is someone like you, someone who uses senses other than the normal senses." Avrell had shifted close to me, stood directly in front of me so that I was forced to focus on him, not Erick or Borund. "I don't know how this . . . talent of yours works, but it's our only chance to kill her. You are the only one capable of getting close enough to try. It has to be you, Varis."

He felt me hesitate, and so added, "You wouldn't be killing her for us, Varis. You'd be killing her for Amenkor." Then he backed away.

I sagged slightly, turned toward Erick, appealing to him for help, for support.

His expression was set, hard and unforgiving. "I've seen her, Varis. She truly is insane. But you already know that. You saw it first, there on the Dredge. Remember Mari?" He drew in a breath, let it out slowly. "You told me she wasn't a mark. I didn't believe you then, but I do now. The Mistress was wrong. Mari shouldn't have died. Someone who can't see the difference shouldn't be sitting on the throne."

I frowned at Erick, feeling cheated somehow, the sense of betrayal deepening, and turned back to Avrell.

Something else flickered behind his eyes, something deeper, as if he hadn't told me everything, as if he were still holding something back, some hidden purpose.

"Find someone else like me," I said, but my voice was defeated. I'd already decided.

"No." He shook his head, a smile touching his lips, and I saw again that flicker in his eyes, as if he were leaving something out, as if he'd lied in some way. But he'd heard the defeat in my voice as well. "There is no one else. It has to be you."

I stared at them all, one by one—Borund, Avrell, and Erick. Something wasn't right, something that I couldn't see.

This is what I am, a small part of me murmured.

But this time it was my decision, my choice.

I sighed, the sound heavy, and asked, "How do you intend to get me into the palace?"

✛ The Palace ✛

Two days later, I found myself tucked into a niche in the palace, squeezed into shadow, knees to my chest, looking down on a corridor lit by oil sconces. I'd come in through the passage beneath the wall. Avrell had given me a rough sketch of the palace, page boy clothing, and the key to a linen closet. I wasn't to be seen. No one was to know I was there, especially not Baill. And I had to kill the Mistress tonight. The ships had to be released in the next three days. There was no time left.

Almost the moment I started the hunt, a passing Servant saw me, asked for my help. But the marks were my choice now, and so after helping her with the baskets I let her go. I waited until she was gone, then headed for the linen closet.

I passed through rooms, gardens, halls. I slid into a familiar waiting room, ducked into shadow, listened to Avrell tell Nathem he had ordered the Mistress' death. After they'd passed, I slid from room to room with less stealth and more speed, until I'd found the linen closet Avrell had told me about, the one with the arrow slot I could squeeze through to enter the inner sanctum, the true palace.

I'd entered the throne room, seen the Skewed Throne itself, listened to it.

And now I stood before the Mistress' own chambers, dressed in a page boy's shirt and breeches. The hallway blazed with light, every sconce flaring high, flames flapping and hissing. The entire palace was lit, every hall, every corridor, every room. I could feel the energy in the building, people searching, scouring the halls, the audience chambers, the storage areas. I could feel them, guards and servants, everyone Baill could call to hand, even though I held the river at bay, the voices of the throne there too strong, too demanding for me to trust myself beneath its surface. I hadn't used the river since entering the palace.

No one stood guard over the Mistress' chambers.

I didn't hesitate, even when a shiver of doubt coursed through me. Someone should be here, watching. Avrell had said he'd placed guards here, to watch over her. But it didn't matter. Part of me already knew what I would find.

I plunged into the rooms, into the antechamber with trailing curtains, soft scattered pillows, tables of fruit and drink and platters of cheese. Empty. I slid without sound to the bedchamber, drew close to the veiled bed itself, drew back the curtains.

Empty.

And then I knew.

Baill wasn't hunting me, he was hunting the Mistress. She'd slipped past the guards at the door again, just as before, had hidden herself somewhere in the palace.

And I knew where she would be.

She'd been calling me all night. I'd just refused to listen.

⊬— The Throne Room —⊬

The corridor to the throne room was still empty and I stepped up to the wide double doors without skulking, standing straight, back rigid, blade drawn but held loose at my side. I stood in front of the wooden doors banded with delicate ironwork for a long moment, staring at the subtle curves of the iron, the gleam of the rounded metal studs that held it in place, the polish of the wood beneath. Old wood, the age obvious. But the grain still glowed with an inner warmth.

The Mistress waited for me inside, with the throne. I hadn't seen her before, but I knew she was there. She'd been calling me with the voices—that dry rustling of leaves—since I'd entered the inner sanctum of the palace. Avrell had said she knew when someone was approaching, and she knew about me, knew I was here. The river hadn't masked me from her at all. Nor the Fire.

Fear crawled across my shoulders, making the muscles tense and twitch. My hand clenched the handle of my dagger, then released.

But then why were there no guards to protect her? Why hadn't Baill and a retinue of twenty guardsmen been waiting for me outside of the Mistress' chambers if she knew I was coming?

I glanced down the empty hall, suddenly wary. Someone should have been here. Unless . . .

I turned back to the iron-banded door with a frown.

Unless the Mistress *wanted* me to come.

I suddenly thought about the ease with which I'd moved through the palace, the lack of guards, the way Baill had drawn them away from the entrance to the audience chamber. At the time I had thought the lack of guards was fortuitous, or something arranged by Avrell himself, but now. . . .

What if the Mistress had arranged it all, instead of Avrell? What if she'd somehow led Baill astray?

I shivered, steeled myself, shoulders tightening. It didn't matter. I had agreed to kill her, to save Amenkor. If I could get close to her, I still might have a chance, whether she knew I was coming or not.

I reached for the ornate wrought-iron handle of one of the doors and pulled it toward me. The wood groaned, the sound loud in the empty corridor, but I didn't cringe, didn't duck into the nearest shadow. I stepped into the throne room instead, pulling the Fire that still curled deep inside me around myself in a protective wall.

The force that was the throne, that writhed and warped within the throne room and pricked the back of my neck, came suddenly, but I was expecting it this time. With a horrifying weight, it pushed me down, tried to force me beneath the river. For a moment, it almost succeeded, the Fire I'd raised to shield myself flickering as if doused with water. I grunted under the onslaught, brought my hands up to ward the intense pressure away, even though there was nothing physical for me to fight against, but the Fire held, drawing strength as the pressure relented, backing off.

But it didn't leave. I could feel it, filling the room, saturating it. I tasted it with every breath, felt it prickling against my skin, alive and predatory. It sent sparks of static through my skin, like lightning. I shivered at the sensation, tried to brush it aside.

I suddenly remembered that I'd felt the presence once before, weeks ago, when I'd come with Borund through the passage beneath the palace wall to meet with Avrell that first time. It had tasted me then, when I'd used the river to make certain Avrell was sincere. I remembered hearing the brush of dead leaves on stone.

It hadn't been certain then, had withdrawn, but it wanted me now.

The thought raised the hackles on the back of my neck, set every instinct for danger I'd learned on the Dredge on edge.

I could feel it pacing the room, felt its presence like the growl of a feral dog, but I forced myself to breathe, to scan the room.

Eight thick granite pillars rose to the vaulted ceiling, four on each side, resting at the top of three tiered granite steps, surrounding the wide flagstone walkway from the doors to the throne, just as before. But now every sconce along the hall had been lit, the throne surrounded by bright candelabra; only a few of the candles had been lit when I passed through the room before. The white-and-gold emblem of the Skewed Throne hung above the throne, the folds of the banner sharply defined in the light—a banner I had not seen before, in the darkness. I refused to look at the throne itself, at its shifting shape. I could already feel the feverish heat against my skin, the same heat I'd felt when I'd entered the room before.

The hall was empty, the two doors on the other side of the room—one of which I'd used to enter the throne room earlier—both closed.

A wave of uncertainty passed through me. I suddenly felt as if I were being hunted, as if someone were watching me from the shadows.

I hated being stalked.

I took one step forward, searching the darknesses behind the pillars to either side. The weight in the air surged forward like a tide, restless, the growl vibrating in my skin, but abated when I winced but did not waver.

My grip shifted on my dagger, slick with sweat.

I moved forward, not pausing now, searching the shadows behind the pillars, searching the niches. But the room was truly empty.

I halted in the center of the throne room, confused. I knew the Mistress was here, could feel her eyes on me. I could feel the throne as well, somehow heavy and solid, even though I could see it shift at the corner of my eye, could feel it gnawing at my stomach. It felt more real than the room itself.

I swallowed, turned away from the throne, back toward the door I'd entered through—

And a laugh echoed through the room, soft and cold. The laugh of a child. Behind me, the door groaned and pulled itself shut with a hollow thud.

My mouth went dry, my tongue parched. My breath quickened and something hard and hot lodged itself at the base of my throat.

The laugh came again, closer, and I spun, settling into a light crouch instinctively. I reached for the river, out of habit, out of necessity, and the pressure stalking on the air surged forward again greedily, rising high, the world shifting into gray and a roar of wind before I jerked myself back with a shudder. Pulling the Fire closer, I shot a glare of anger out into the room, drew myself up straight, and searched the room again.

The laughter had come from inside the room. Someone *was* here.

I stilled when a new voice filled the room, singing quietly to itself.

"... o-ver the water, o-ver the sea,
Comes a Fire to burn thee.
White as whitecaps, harsh as the scree,
Here it comes to judge thee."

The woman's voice finished with a chuckle. The sound filled the room, throaty and deep. Totally unlike the child's laughter a moment before.

"It came for me, Varis," the throaty voice said. My flesh prickled, my hackles standing on end at the sound of my name. I tasted my fear, like old musty cloth. "Oh, yes, it came. And it destroyed me." Another laugh, this one bitter and choked, dying off harshly into nothing.

Calming myself, I grew still and listened instead. For a breath. For a rustle of clothing. For the tread of a foot. But there was nothing, the voice echoing strangely, seeming to come from everywhere and nowhere at the same time.

I turned. Someone watched me, was judging me, and I struggled not to slip beneath the river as I would have done on the Dredge, because I could feel the throne watching as well, circling patiently.

"What's the matter, Varis?" the woman's voice said smoothly, mockingly. "Can't you see me? Can't you find me?"

I clenched my jaw in anger, tightened my grip on my dagger.

Another chuckle, again soft and throaty, cut off sharply as the woman barked, "Perhaps you aren't using the right Sight!"

I halted my slow, careful spin and the voice laughed again, this time the sound draining down into choked sobs.

Enough, I thought.

Standing straight, I chose a random spot between two pillars on one side of the room and stared at it resolutely, my breath tight and angry.

The sobbing ended and the air in the room shifted from confrontational to curious. I felt the shift like a wind across my back and shivered.

"Not going to play, are we?" A different voice, aged but still strong. The voice harrumphed, like an old woman. "We'll see about that!"

I jumped, startled, my hand raising the dagger defensively. The last statement had come sharp and close, as if the old woman were standing right beside me. But before I could even catch my breath I saw movement at the base of one of the pillars, heard the rustle of cloth.

A woman uncurled from a hunched-over posture, the folds of her dress falling to her sides. She was clothed in white, with long hair as black as pitch, the simple dress stitched with smooth, curved lines of gold at the throat and at the hem, the lines curling upward like fire, as if she were surrounded in the vague outlines of flames. Her skin was smooth, not aged with wrinkles as the voice suggested, and her cheekbones were high.

But it was her eyes that held me. A depthless brown. The darkest features of her narrow face somehow, even against the ebony hair. They captured me, didn't allow me to look away. They commanded me, ordered me to obey even before she spoke.

"You've come to kill me," she said, her voice neither the child's voice, nor the singer's, nor the old woman's, but a strange mixture of all three, resonating with even more voices underneath. "So do it."

The muscles on my shoulders crawled, an unsettled feeling trailing down my back. I'd walked right past her when I'd searched the room, close enough she could have reached out and touched me . . . killed me. I hadn't seen her, hadn't even felt her. My back stiffened and I suddenly felt vulnerable, exposed.

And angry. She was toying with me, batting me about like a cat with a rat.

"Why couldn't I see you?" I asked, voice harsh. But inside I was reeling, trying to figure out what she wanted, what she needed. Was she insane? Or was she simply having a little fun?

Her brow creased a moment, but then she smiled. "Because you chose not to see me. You've come to kill me, but you don't want to. So much easier not to kill when you can't find the mark, isn't it, Varis?" Her head lowered, her eyes narrowed. "But you see me now. And you haven't got much time, Varis. I can occupy the guards only so long. They can't be held at bay forever. Even Baill."

As if she'd called them into existence, guards pounded on one of the side entrances to the throne room, voices muffled by the door. The door began to rattle as they tried to force it. The sounds echoed loudly in the room.

The Mistress didn't move. "Kill me now, Varis. They'll find their way in eventually."

But I didn't move. I didn't trust her. The image of the cat and the rat was too vivid in my mind.

The rattle at the side door stopped. Shouts rang out. Someone called for Baill, someone else for Avrell.

"You have to kill me," the Mistress said, her tone soft and reasonable. "You have to kill me or the city will crumble. It's already started. You've seen it. On the Dredge, on the wharf, even here at the palace." She raised her head, held herself imperious and still. "And I want to die, Varis," her voice still calm. "I *want* you to kill me."

Cold shock ran through me, from my neck down to my toes. The dagger felt suddenly heavy in my hand, weighted, my body somehow light.

"Why?" I asked, my voice sounding distant, removed.

She smiled, and at the edges of her eyes I saw the insanity I'd heard in the laughing child's voice, in the song, in the old woman's voice. I'd seen it enough on the Dredge, recognized it as easily as I recognized the feel and weight of my dagger, cold and deadly and familiar. I recognized it now, staring up into her face, and realized that she held the insanity at bay. Somehow the real Mistress had found herself amid the madness, and she was clinging to herself with a cold, granite desperation that was steadily slipping away from her. If I didn't act soon, she would lose control completely.

"I'm destroying Amenkor, Varis," she said, her voice strong but wavering. "The Fire did something to me and I can no longer control the throne. It's begun to take over, to consume me. You need to kill me before it takes over completely."

I hesitated, still uncertain, and her face suddenly hardened into a frown.

"Do it," she barked, her voice filling the room, the command clear in her voice, in her stance. "Please."

It was the tremble in the last word that convinced me, the way her lips pursed at the end, her muscles rigid with effort. I still didn't trust her, the cat and the rat image still too real, but I had to try. It was an opportunity.

I gripped my dagger firmly, stepped forward, up the tiered stairs, watched her warily as I moved to her side. She drew in a deep breath and as I shifted in behind her, I realized sweat lined her forehead, stained her dress with fear and the effort to control herself. She lifted her head, exposed her pale neck, her stance taut, breath coming in gasps through her nose, and closed her eyes.

I drew up close behind her, but halted.

She was too tall, at least a foot taller than me. I couldn't reach her neck.

I shifted my stance, changed tactics, adjusted so I could slide the dagger into her back, low and quick, but she must have realized my problem. She sighed and grabbed her dress in two fists, kneeling in front of me. Tossing her head back to clear her hair, back straight, she exposed her neck again.

"Do it now," she said, and the strain in her voice was clear, made worse when the main entrance doors began to thud.

The guards were at two of the entrances now, were trying to break through with what sounded like a battering ram.

"Quickly!" the Mistress spat.

I reached forward, around her head, one hand on her shoulder to steady her, the edge of the dagger against her throat. I felt her heat through the cloth of the dress, felt the embroidery. Her pulse shivered up the blade of the dagger into my hand.

I drew a short breath, tensed the muscles in my arm, but hesitated.

It felt wrong. Too deliberate. Too manipulated.

It felt like the eyes of a cat, watching coldly, body perfectly still, as the rat began to twitch, to gather its muscles for a darting escape.

It felt like entering the alley while following Alendor. An ambush.

Fear suddenly spiked through me and I tensed, muscles contracting, ready to slip the dagger across her throat in one smooth motion—

But I was too late, too slow. The cat pounced.

A hand clamped down hard on my wrist, locked so strongly I felt my forearm go numb. At the same moment, the Mistress shuddered beneath my other hand, her muscles pulling taut.

I had a fleeting moment to think, *Trap!*, a fleeting moment to feel terror cascading down through my muscles like ice—

And then the Mistress wrenched the arm holding the dagger out and away, snapped it around with enough force to pull me off-balance. I lurched forward into her back with a gasp, lost my hold on my dagger. It clattered to the floor, down the three tiers of steps to the walkway.

Terror slid into panic. I froze.

The Mistress reached around her own shoulder with her free hand and grabbed my shoulder. The shuddering thud of the battering ram echoed through the room. Wood splintered, groaned. Metal shrieked. The Mistress jerked me around in front of her, my arm twisting. She shifted her grip on my wrist, pulled it up sharply behind my back, and drew me in close, our foreheads touching. Her sweat dripped onto my cheek, her wavy black hair tickling my neck. She smelled of wine and cheese.

"Not quite yet, little hunter," she gasped in the throaty voice. "Not unless we have to. There's another way now that we've gotten rid of your dagger."

And I looked into her eyes, body still in shock, muscles still frozen in panic.

She hadn't lost control. The real Mistress still held the insanity at bay.

A sharp grinding pop filled the hall and the Mistress pulled back as something heavy and metallic hit the floor. The noise from outside in the corridor grew suddenly louder: shouts of triumph, a bark of command.

I recognized the voice. It was Baill's.

"Not much time at all," the Mistress murmured to herself, then turned back to me. With a thin smile she flung me down the tiered steps to the walkway, in the direction of the throne, away from my dagger.

I landed hard, unable to control the fall. But as I hit the flagstone, the panic that had seized my muscles released, replaced with anger.

She'd tricked me. And now I had no weapon.

I snarled, twisted out of the sprawl into a crouch, and caught the Mistress descending the tiered steps slowly, almost languidly. Behind her, my dagger lay on the floor, and farther down the hall a glittering hinge from the large doors. The base of one of the doors was skewed into the hall, wood splintered.

The door shuddered again, bucking inward. The men outside bellowed.

I focused on the Mistress. Her face had turned solemn, grim. "It's time, Varis."

My gaze flicked to my dagger, so far out of reach, then back to her face. Desperation clawed at my arms, at my chest. My breath came ragged and torn through my nose, my jaw clenched, anger a hot lump in my throat.

The Mistress halted between me and the door. The Skewed Throne stood behind me.

"It's time," she said again, with a hint of sorrow, and then she raised her hand.

I reacted without thought, not certain what she intended, what she could do, only knowing that without the dagger I had only one defense: the river.

I dove beneath its surface, pulled the Fire around me as closely as possible as I felt the currents envelop me, smother me, the world graying, drowning. I dove deeper, and deeper still, using the force of my anger, my fear, noting the details in the stone, in the door, in the floor, in the light, as they shifted and clarified. The sounds of the battering ram, of the men in the hall outside the two doors, of the guttering flames in the sconces and on the candelabra, collapsed into the vibrant background wind I'd known since I'd almost drowned in Cobbler's Fountain.

For a moment, the river held me as it had always held me, warm and comforting, like my mother's embrace.

But then the other pressure—the throne—pounced down upon me, a surging, growling ocean of sound and sensation. I screamed, the sound reverberating around the room, and drew the White Fire up as a shield against the onslaught. But the pressure, so vast, so dark, so like the ocean, smothered me, crushed me flat against the flagstone of the hall. Granite cut into my back, each minute crack in the time-worn flagstone like a chasm, each grain of dirt and grit like a boulder. I screamed again as the pressure built, but the scream faltered as the breath was pressed from my chest.

And then I realized that the Fire still held, that it formed a thin shield between me and the howling pressure of this other presence on the river. Trying to draw breath, strange spots already forming on my vision, I pushed the shield of Fire upward with all my strength, pushed it away a hair's breadth, another, then an inch. I gasped through clenched teeth, desperately sucked in air, and pushed harder, straining at the forces, at the eddies and currents that wove around me in a mad frenzy. I shoved the Fire upward until I could finally draw myself up and settle back onto my heels.

Breathing hard, I glanced up at the Mistress, my anger unleashed, coiling and spitting inside me. I intended to kill her now, no hesitations, no doubts.

She'd halted a few steps in front of me. Behind her, the door shuddered again, but the noise was relegated to the background, so muffled by the raging voices I held outside the Fire it almost couldn't be heard.

The Mistress frowned, her hands at her sides.

I didn't give her a chance to think, to respond. As I'd done with the bearded man on the street, I pulled as much of the river as I could as tightly to my chest as possible, compacted it down, and punched it toward the Mistress' chest, my eyes dark with intent.

She raised one hand casually, palm flat, facing toward me.

The hard ball I'd thrown at her hit an unseen wall a foot from her hand and stopped. A backlash of force surged toward me, hit me hard in the chest. I gasped, in surprise and in pain, landed hard on my ass, coming up sharp against the first step in the dais to the throne.

A cold wave of real fear coursed through me, cutting through the anger like a scythe.

The Mistress knew of the river, could use it as I could.

I licked at something warm at the edge of my mouth, tasted blood. Ignoring it, I narrowed my gaze, concentrated through the pain in my chest and the taste of blood, and focused on the area in front of the Mistress' hand.

Faintly, I could see lines of force, almost nonexistent, woven so elegantly and so tightly they seemed to merge with the raw energies of the river around her. The energies formed a solid wall.

The gathered ball of energy I'd flung at her seemed suddenly childish and frayed.

"What is that?" the Mistress asked quietly, advancing forward. Her tone was hard, demanding. "What is that around you? It tastes familiar. . . ."

I scuttled up the steps of the tier, to the base of the last step, but the Mistress continued her advance, the subtle wall protecting her moving with her. I could feel the Skewed Throne at my back. It was a vortex of energies, white and blazing, the focus of the prowling pressure that had tried to overwhelm me and still beat at the shield of White Fire that protected me.

The Mistress halted, the wall of force she held before her inches in front of me. I couldn't back up any more. The throne blocked my way.

The Mistress' frown grew deeper and then she locked eyes with me. "What is it?" she demanded again, voice as hard as stone.

I didn't answer. My eyes were hooded, the anger back. My gaze flicked toward my dagger, so clear beneath the river, too distant to retrieve, then returned to hers.

Neither one of us moved for a long moment, our breath the only real sound. Somewhere in the background, another grinding pop reverberated through the room, followed by a much heavier clatter. Ripples of force shuddered through the flagstone up the hall to the dais and the throne as one of the main doors pulled free of its last hinge and struck the floor. Men shouted, surged into the room. I could taste the steel of their blades, the tincture of their armor. I breathed in their sweat and fear and confusion as they halted, taking in the Mistress and me on the dais. I felt the air shift as they moved aside, letting Baill and Avrell move to the front of the room. But it was all muted, flattened somehow.

The only thing that mattered was the Mistress. Her eyes, her will, her intent. She watched me silently.

Then her mouth tightened. "Never mind. It doesn't matter."

And she reached forward, her flat palm changing into a clawed grip. The wall she'd used to protect herself released and she grasped the front of my shirt, lifted me up, and thrust me back onto the throne.

For a moment, the room held, the Mistress taking one step back. No one else moved. The throne beneath me twisted and shifted, the sensation sending a feverish heat through my skin, making it crawl and shudder, prickle with sweat. The river held unchanged as well, the energies roiling.

Then the river exploded.

The Fire flared, rising to consume everything in sight as the swirl of gray energy that had once been the river blackened, charred, became a frenzy of pure motion that refused to resolve into images, into sight. The throne room fell away, and the voices that had plagued me since I'd entered the palace surged forward. As I cowered behind the Fire, I realized that was exactly what they were: voices. A thousand voices, more, all screaming to be heard, all hammering at the shield of Fire, demanding my attention, howling for it. It created a maelstrom of vicious wind, a hurricane force that threatened to overwhelm the Fire, to overwhelm me. And I knew with sudden certainty that it would have crushed me if not for the Fire.

I strained against its force, held the Fire rigid and impenetrable, and after a while realized the Fire would hold.

I relaxed, eased back within the confines of the shield. It still took effort, but not as much as I'd thought. I couldn't hold it forever, but for now. . . .

I drew a deep breath, let it out in a slow sigh.

Varis.

In the white of the shield, the voice was barely a whisper, a rasp of dead leaves blown against cobbles.

Varis.

I shifted toward the voice. The throne raged around me, the voices angry. Some spat curses, others howled, others whined. A group joined forces and surged against the Fire and I was forced to fight them back, tasting sweat against my lips, tasting blood. They retreated.

Varis.

I found the voice. A woman's voice, deep and throaty. A voice I recognized. It was the woman who had sung earlier. Not the child, nor the old woman. And not an amalgamation of many voices. A distinct voice, soft and calm, but tinged with fear.

Varis, there isn't much time.

I'm here, I thought, pausing at the edge of the Fire. The woman's voice came from the far side, among the whorl of the other voices.

A sigh, a hint of wine and cheese, of desperation. *You have to take control. I can't hold it any longer.*

I shuddered. *Control of what?*

The Skewed Throne.

I don't understand. The Fire wavered. I flung it back up, tasted more sweat at the effort, salty and sick.

The throne. That's what this is, Varis. All of these voices, all of these people. They are the men and women who created the throne, the women who have sat upon it since that creation. All of them—all of their thoughts, their hopes, their dreams. They are the throne. But they need someone to control them, someone to order them, keep them in check.

You control them.

A snort, a sigh. That scent of wine and cheese again. *I did control them. But not anymore. Something happened. Something happened to the throne when the Fire passed through it. But it was too subtle a change. I didn't notice it, not until later, when it was much too late. By then, there was nothing I could do. And the other voices—oh, gods. . . .*

Dread bled through the Fire, pooling like oil, thick and viscous. I heard sobbing.

You have to take control, Varis. I can't hold them together any longer. There are too many. Far, far too many! I barely managed to keep control in the throne room tonight.

I was already shaking my head. *No.*

You have to. And now the voice was harsh again, cold. The voice of a woman used to being obeyed. *You have to take my place, become the Mistress, or Amenkor will fall. I'll destroy it, without knowing what it is I'm doing. I'll destroy it, Varis, without meaning to. It's already started. You have to stop it.*

No.

Silence. *Then you'll have to kill me.*

I winced, felt sweat prick the corners of my eyes. I blinked back tears. *And if I kill you, what happens to the city?*

A pause. Something beyond the Fire shifted, a shuddering, gathering of forces that was vaguely familiar, something I'd done on the river many times, only this was much more powerful.

The Mistress pushed herself forward, to see what would happen. For a moment, the voices surging all around the Fire quieted, expectant.

The city will survive, the Mistress said with a heavy sigh, the energies shifting back. *But barely, and not as it is now, not as Amenkor. It will be changed, completely. And many will die.*

The voices hesitated, as if stunned, but then roared back to life.

Why?

Because the city needs a ruler. I've done so much damage—

No, I broke in. *Why me?*

Silence. *Because you have the Sight, what you call the river. Because you know how to survive.* The woman paused. *And because the Fire changed you as well. I felt it before I pushed you onto the throne, but I didn't recognize it. The Fire is protecting you. I can sense it clearly now. It has to be you, Varis. I don't think anyone else can handle the throne anymore. It's too powerful. It will kill anyone else. It has killed everyone else. Avrell tried with others that had the Sight, many times, but the throne overwhelmed them all. It crushed them. Killed them. But you have the Fire to protect you. They didn't.*

Her voice, so soft and clear at the beginning, had become strained.

I'm not going to be able to hold them off much longer, Varis. I felt a surge on the other side of the Fire, like a punch. The voice gasped. *Oh, gods! I can't—*

Then the voice was lost, torn away violently. I reached out, tried to hold on to her, my breath caught up short.

At the same time, a shudder ran through the Fire again and I was forced to hold the Fire steady instead. I stood behind it, frozen, feeling suddenly empty, drained, and lost. Abandoned.

Despair washed over me. I was trapped in my own little niche.

And then I thought about the Mistress.

She'd given me a choice.

I listened through the Fire to the voices. Thousands of them, howling and jabbering. Their noise increased, roaring even higher as they assailed the Fire. I felt it beginning to give. They wanted me, needed me. I could feel them pulling, trying to draw me in and consume me.

I shuddered.

Kill the Mistress, or take the throne.

There was no choice. Not in the end. Not if I could save the voice, the woman whose throat had already felt the touch of my dagger. Not if I could save Amenkor at the same time.

I rested my head forward, sighed heavily, then looked out into the black maelstrom that was the Skewed Throne, the thousands of voices that had sat upon it, that had become it. The thousands of voices that could consume me utterly, as they'd consumed the women Avrell and Nathem had tried to place on the throne before me.

For a moment, I heard those women screaming, so hard their own voices tore their throats. I felt them convulsing, muscles spasming, twisting them, contorting them. I tasted their blood as they bit out their own tongues, gouged out their own eyes, clawed their own faces.

Then I drew in a deep breath, steadied myself, and dropped the shield of Fire, exposed myself completely to the river, to the throne.

I didn't even have time to gasp. The throne pounced and sucked me in.

It was like the time I entered the tavern behind William. The sensations—the sounds and sights and smells—overwhelming. I thought I would be crushed, but it was infinitely worse. Instead, I was picked up by the maelstrom of voices, tossed about on the wind of their noise, turned and twisted until I was completely disoriented. My breath came in short little gasps and I felt my chest constrict, my throat tighten.

And then the images began. Only they were more than images. They were parts of the voices, parts of their lives.

And I didn't simply witness them, I was forced to *live* them.

A scream and I stared across a wide round room made of black stone toward Silicia a moment before she collapsed to the floor, a trickle of blood snaking from her mouth where she lay. But there was no time for concern. The power in the room was too great, shuddering beneath our control. I winced as it stabbed a dagger of raw hate down my left side, the pain visceral, enough to make me stagger, but I held firm. My gaze flicked around the room, toward the five others that still stood with me, encircling the two thrones that stood in the center of the room.

The power grew, surged higher, oppressive and dark, and as one, those of us that remained focused the power on the thrones, concentrated it, wielding it like a sword or hammer.

Sweat broke out on my brow, and another sheeting dagger of pain coursed down my side. I gasped, felt my hands clench into fists, felt my back arch as every muscle in my body pulled taut. But still I forced the power down, compacted it, squeezed it into the granite of the two thrones.

Thunder rolled through the room, vibrated in the obsidian floor. Someone else cried out, the shout cut short. *Garus,* I thought, *my love.* A different pain shot through my heart, but I couldn't turn to see him. Not now. The power was too intense, the construction of the two thrones almost complete. A moment more, just a moment, and we would be finished. . . .

Something slipped, a barrier dropping away as the power culminated, crested, and suddenly it began to funnel into the thrones, fast, faster than we had calculated. Those remaining in the group gasped as one, and through the sudden funneling roar of energy I felt one of the others—Atreus?—struggling, trying to pull herself out of the construct. But it was too late, far, far too late.

The funneling of power increased, surging forward, sweeping down and down until it split into two distinct vortices, one for each throne, the power seeping into the simple stone of the two thrones, saturating them, and still the thrones wanted more.

I began to feel it pulling at me, felt myself caught at its very lip. With a gut-wrenching churn of despair, I knew none of us would escape. The thrones needed too much. But I began to struggle anyway, like Atreus, tried to draw myself up over the edge of the funnel, the whirlpool of energy. New pain shot into my side, paralyzed my left arm with a burning tingle. I collapsed to the floor, juddered there, seizures racking my body. My head pounded into the black stone. I felt blood seep, felt my hair grow matted, felt warm coppery wetness slip down my back.

Then the funnel took me.

I screamed, my roar echoing in the cavernous room, and for an instant I saw my lifeless body crumbled to the stone, saw my empty eyes, saw my face stained with blood, my silk shirt soaked, the fine yellow stained a deep red.

I had a moment to think, *We are the last. What have we done?*

And then I gasped, the vision tattering away as I wrenched myself from the maelstrom.

I had time for a single desperate breath, a single desperate thought—*Two thrones?*—and then

Someone wrapped their thick-fingered hands around my throat from behind and squeezed.

I gagged, hands flying up to scrabble at the heavily-muscled forearms, managed to suck in a strangled, weak sliver of air—

And then the muscles in the arms bunched and the man flung me into the wall to the right. I struck the rough eggshell-colored stone hard, my head cracking against an edge, and then I was falling, slumping downward, my vision spinning.

It's dark, I thought, staring up into the night sky. Through blurred vision, disoriented, I noticed stars, saw the edge of the palace. I recognized the architecture: one of the balustrades before the palace, on the promenade. Flames from the oil sconce flapped raggedly in the wind, like a banner.

Then someone kicked me, the pain sharp, drawing me up out of the daze, and I screamed, the terror I'd felt an hour before as the strange White Fire swept over the city returning. I could feel the city surging in my blood, could feel its terror, and I screamed again as the foot dug deep into my side, rolling me over onto my stomach.

The blood-pulse of the city thrummed in my ears, and beneath that the thousand voices of the throne, all screaming, all horrified. But I still held them under control, still contained them.

Then the hands returned to my throat, crushed it closed. I gagged again, felt the hands shift until only one held me by the neck, fingers large enough to squeeze out all but the barest of breaths. The other hand began tearing at my robes, ripped them back from my shoulders, the man behind me, pressing his weight down hard into my back, grunting with the effort.

The hand at my throat lifted me roughly, my back arching. The other hand reached around and cupped my exposed breast, then squeezed it with bruising force.

"This," a ragged voice hissed in my ear, spittle flecking my cheek, "is for refusing me."

My eyes widened in shock as I recognized the voice.

Neville.

Neville twisted my captured breast viciously, then thrust me hard to the stone of the portico above the promenade, hand still tight across my throat.

A fumbling of clothes, a shifting, and I felt night air against my exposed legs. Blind spots began to appear in my vision and I sucked in a hard breath under the grip of Neville's hand.

And then he thrust, penetrated with a guttural, visceral grunt of pure pleasure, and I screamed, screamed so hard my throat tore, his hand jerking my head so far back I could no longer breathe.

The scream cut short. The blind spots wavered and grew as he thrust again, crying out. Something tore, deep inside, and I felt blood, but the blind spots were widening, reaching out to engulf me. Another thrust, another tearing, and the voices of the throne inside me screamed.

I spun away, caught and pulled and throttled by the maelstrom.

Panic began to set in. I felt myself fraying, felt everything I knew—the Dredge, the wharf, Amenkor—losing cohesion, tattering and ripping under the force of the voices.

I was losing myself to the throne. I couldn't control it.

It was going to win.

I stood on a tower overlooking the night harbor. Light reflected on the water from lanterns on ships. Lights glowed in the windows of the houses below the palace.

A breeze touched my face and I lifted my head to meet it, closed my eyes.

In the darkness of my mind I could hear the throne, could feel the entire city resting below me. It throbbed and flowed, beat with its own pulse. A living thing that I could feel in my blood. Amenkor.

I smiled, drew in a deep satisfied breath of clear, salty sea air.

And then, far out over the sea, there was a pulse of power.

I opened my eyes, the smile fading away. I watched the horizon.

An invisible wave, like a ripple on a pool of water, rushed out from the ocean, brushed past me with a gust that pushed me back a step. I blinked at it, frowned at its taste. Something powerful, something immense. Something greater than the throne itself. Older. Ancient.

I waited. Dread stirred in my stomach, thickened in my throat.

In the back of my mind, the voices of the throne paused.

Some of them recognized the taste of the power, but not what it was for. One of them knew it personally, had seen it before.

It had spelled her doom.

I leaned forward, hands resting on the top of the tower. I waited.

There.

The western horizon was tinged with white, as if the sun were beginning to rise.

But the sun rose in the east.

My hands tightened against the grit of the stone wall.

The white light grew, spread across the sky, a wall of pure white Fire. It swept in from the sea, swift, stretching from the ocean to the clouds, immense and horrifying.

The voice in my head that had seen it once before cowered before it in gibbering fear.

The Fire struck the bay, surged through the harbor, seared its way forward, utterly silent. It swallowed up the ships, swallowed the docks, scorched onto land, up toward the palace, sweeping forward with swift, cold intent.

I gasped the moment before it consumed me, stepped back—

And then it filled me, burned down to my core, wrenched me open and exposed me, exposed all of the voices of the throne. For a moment, everything was silent, the voices stilled for the first time since they'd tossed me on the throne to see if I'd survive. I tasted the Fire, felt it burn deep, deeper, felt it judge me.

I felt its purpose. Nothing to do with Amenkor, nothing to do with me. It was residual energy, the remains of an event so powerful it had stretched across the ocean, burned across the sea from a distant land. The consequence of a magic that no one in the throne knew the intent of, that was totally unfamiliar. It was nothing to us.

I felt it beginning to fade, felt the voices of the throne returning to normal.

Then something inside the throne twisted and tore. Pain lanced up from my stomach into my throat and head and the Fire left me, passed on, sweeping across the city behind and onward, toward the mountains. I staggered into the stone wall, felt its rough surface bite into my arms, and almost vomited over the side. Breathing shallowly, I pulled myself upright.

The pain receded, drew away almost as swiftly as it had come.

I frowned, tested the throne, tested the voices. They were quieter than usual, but that wasn't unexpected. The one that had recognized the Fire was utterly silent.

When I freed her, I found her lying on the steps of the promenade leading up to the palace, her robe torn and ragged about her waist. There were bruises on her neck, on her breasts. And there was blood.

I pushed her back, shuddered at her pain.

The Fire had destroyed her. The guard Neville had raped and killed her over a thousand years before.

I turned and stared in the direction of the mountains. The Fire was a white light beyond their rim, fading even as I watched.

I reached for the city, felt its pulse. I could hear screams already, could see lights appearing in all quarters. The people were panicked, some driven mad. I could feel the disturbance, the throb of the city swift and erratic. It would take time to settle.

But at least the Fire, wherever it came from, whatever it had done, had done no harm here.

I cried out, wrenched myself away from the maelstrom and the memory of the Mistress. My breath came in ragged gasps. More memories surged forward. I saw a thousand deaths, saw the city burn, the palace gates collapse, walls crumble, the palace rebuilt, the palace expanded, another tier of walls go up, all in a blinding flash. Sunsets roared across my vision, starscapes, gardens, streams, grottoes, storms, lightning flaring sharp and smelling of seared air. I was slapped, choked, knifed, spat upon. I was kissed, hefted up into an embrace, dropped down to a bed, to a rug, thrust to a stone wall, onto the seat of a rattling carriage, onto cool grass. I was held to a wall and lashed, held to the ground and raped as I screamed, moaned and bucked, gibbering in fear. I was tortured, hot iron pressed into flesh, charred and blinded, my toenails ripped out, wood shoved under my fingernails. I was kicked, feet driving into my stomach. I was drowned, water closing up over my head, cold and terrifying and inviting. I heard my mother's laugh.

I latched onto the memory, onto Cobbler's Fountain. I latched onto the sensation of water, filling my nose, my ears, muting out the sound of the world, everything collapsing down into a blur of wind, a wash of gray filled with ripples from the surface of the water above. I saw shadowy shapes there, saw sunlight reflected, refracted, dazzling and bright. But that was above the water, removed.

Beneath the water, it was just me. Not the man being sucked into the two thrones at their creation. Not the woman being raped above the steps of the promenade. Not the woman who'd witnessed the Fire from the tower of the palace.

Just Varis.

I felt something else struggling deep inside me, pushing forward. Someone young, no more than six. Someone who had died that day at the fountain, when she had witnessed her mother's death in the alley at the hands of the red men.

Ash.

The name was no more than a whisper, spoken with my mother's voice. The name I had been given, that I could not reveal to Erick when he asked. But the little six-year-old girl who had tripped and fallen in Cobbler's Fountain eleven years before stood beside me now. I could feel her.

We were both drowning. Varis and Ash. We were dying inside the throne, together, as one.

I could let the throne consume me. There would be no more deaths then, no more marks. There would be nothing.

But then the Mistress would not be released.

No, not the Mistress. Her name was Eryn. Eryn would not be released.

And then what of Amenkor? The Mistress had said it would survive, but barely. It would survive but would not be the same.

I stared up at the shapes moving above the water, blurred beyond recognition. The shapes of the people inside the throne, those that had created it, those that had sat upon it or touched it since its creation.

If I stayed, I needed to find a way to control them, and I suddenly realized I knew how. It was just like the crowd at the tavern. It was a choice. I could be Ash, sit back and watch, hover around the dead body of Amenkor and do nothing, let the throne overwhelm me, let the guards send me where they willed.

Or I could be Varis. Ruthless. Hard. Forceful. I could seize control.

This is who I am.

I drew a deep breath and pulled everything that I thought of as myself, all of my memories of the Dredge, all of my emotions, everything that was *me* together, wove it tight.

And then I pushed myself up through the water. I left my mother behind. Left the six-year-old girl named Ash behind. That wasn't me anymore. I'd changed.

At the last moment, just before I breached the surface of the water, I felt the Mistress' hands—Eryn's hands—reach down to grab me beneath my arms and help pull me up into the sunlight.

Welcome to the throne, Varis.

And it *was* just like the tavern.

I opened my eyes to the throne room in Amenkor. Baill and Avrell stood a few steps down from the dais, watching me carefully. Baill's sword was drawn, but he was a step behind Avrell, the First of the Mistress holding him back with one hand. The rest of the guards were farther back, clustered around the broken throne room door and the pillars to the right and left.

I glanced down. The Mistress had collapsed to the floor, her figure crumpled. Her face was worn, sheened with sweat and tears.

Beneath me, the throne no longer twisted and turned, warping itself into different shapes. It had solidified into a stone curve with armrests and no back, the edges of the armrests curled under. My arms rested lightly on its edges, hands gripping the ends. My back was rigid.

I felt a heavy throb beating all around me, recognized it from Eryn's memory of the tower.

It was the city. Amenkor. From the Dredge to the palace. A steady pulse of teeming life. I could reach out and touch each one of those lives if I wanted, could watch them live, could help them. Those in the slums, rooting through garbage. Those on the wharfs and in the ships blockaded inside the harbor. Even those sorting through the burned-out rubble of the warehouse district.

I drew in a deep breath, felt the city warm and vibrant inside of me.

I let the breath out with a sigh. The city could wait.

I turned toward the Mistress, who began to stir. On the river, lines of energy entrapped her, bound her to the throne. I began to pull the threads apart, carefully. The voices fought me, but I knew myself and ignored them, thrust them into the background as I'd done my entire life with all the noises of the Dredge that were unimportant. Just like the tavern.

By the time the Mistress roused completely, sitting upright with a groan, she was no longer the Mistress. She was Eryn again, wholly her own.

She raised a trembling hand to her head and gasped, shooting a glance toward me. Avrell stepped toward her, one hand outstretched.

"Mistress?"

She turned toward him, then shook her head. "No," she said, then sobbed, hiding her hands in her face.

Avrell's hand dropped and he stood up straight, turning toward me. His face became a solemn mask and he folded his hands formally before him. He bowed his head slightly.

"Mistress."

I turned to Baill, eyes hard and intent.

He glanced toward Avrell with a frown, then lowered his sword and sheathed it. He bowed down, the motion quick and barely deferential. "Mistress."

Behind him, the guards that had gathered, mixed with a few white-robed servants, bowed down as well, a clatter of sound and shuffling cloth.

I wondered briefly how many of those servants were true Servants, young girls and women who had a touch of the power like me, who had been brought here to be trained with the hopes that one day they could control the throne.

I wondered how many of those Servants had died on the throne when Avrell and Nathem had tried to replace Eryn.

Avrell stepped forward to catch my attention.

"What of the city?"

I felt the city rushing inside me, hurt but vital, beaten but not destroyed.

I smiled and thought of the Dredge, of the wharf, of the palace itself. I felt the scar of the fire in the warehouse district, felt the ships gliding on the waters of the bay, felt the River surging through the center of the city. I heard the steady pulse of its blood in my ears, full of heat and strength.

"It will survive," I said, and behind my voice I heard other voices, all of the women who had sat on the throne after its forging, all of their strengths, all of their memories.

It would not be easy.

But it would survive.

The Cracked Throne

⊣— Chapter 1

I crouched down behind a pile of broken stone to catch my breath and gazed down the darkened narrow in the warren of buildings of the Dredge. In the moonlight, the alley was mainly shadow, with edges of dull light. Water gleamed in a thin stream in the alley's center. No doorways, no windows here. At least none that I could see.

A sound came from behind, a rattle of stone against stone.

I spun, breath catching, heard my heart thudding in my ears, poised on the verge of bolting. My feet skidded in the wet dirt on the cobbles—

But there was nothing behind me. The alley was as dark as it was ahead. There were many places to hide, but nowhere to escape to. He could be waiting for me, hidden in any of the shadows, ready to pounce if I turned back.

A sob tightened my chest and I fought it back, closed my eyes against the sensation. I breathed in slowly, tried to calm myself.

Use the river.

The thought slid across the darkness behind my eyes and I frowned. But then there was the unmistakable tread of a foot, moving cautiously, and far, far too close.

My eyes flew open, my heart shuddered, and I lurched out from the shelter of the broken stone into the alley, moving almost blindly, eyes catching glimpses of heaped stone, piles of shattered crates, and rotting refuse. My bare feet pounded against the slick cobbles, splashed in the trickling stream. I heard a curse, and a hail of loose dirt and stone as someone pushed away from a crumbling wall, then heavy footfalls. A cold sliver of fear lanced down my side, sharp with pain. I slapped a hand against it, tried to force it away, and then the alley turned.

I swerved too late, felt my feet skid in the muck, slip, begin to pull out from under me, and then I slammed into the mud-brick wall in the corner. My breath whooshed from my lungs, but I didn't pause. I used the wall to catch my balance, shoved away from it before I'd truly gained purchase, and stumbled down the left turn.

A door. I needed a door, a window, an escape.

Behind, the footfalls burst into a run. Someone shouted, cursed as he stumbled into a stack of garbage, tripped, and fell.

I darted along the new alley. Still nothing. No door, no window. I sobbed, breath hitching in my throat. The dagger of pain in my side dug deeper. I was no longer running smoothly, the pain too harsh, making me stumble. I'd been running too long.

A cloud moved across the moon. The alley plunged itself into total darkness. I stumbled to a halt, leaned heavily against one wall, one hand still clutching my side. My breath came in ragged gasps. Too loud, too filled with desolation. My eyes widened as I tried to catch even the faintest light, but there was nothing. Only the reek of shit and stone, rot and death.

The footsteps behind stopped.

I drew a deep breath, held it to listen.

Breathing. He was still there. But he'd learned caution. I'd hurt him when I'd first escaped, bitten into the fleshy part of his hand hard enough to break the skin, then shook it like a dog with a rat carcass while he screamed. I could still taste the blood in my mouth and smiled with grim satisfaction. He'd let his guard down, but that wouldn't happen again.

Use the river!

I tried to slip into that other world, tried to force everything to blur and gray, tried to suppress all sound into a dull wind—something I'd been able to do without thought since I was six; something I'd relied on to survive on my own since then—but nothing happened.

The river was gone.

Choking down a sob, smile fading, I turned to the wall I could no longer see, pressed my shoulder against it a moment, then, with effort, forced my weight away and began edging down its length. With my shoulder scraping the stone for support, I ran with one hand ahead of me, felt for a corner, an edge, an opening. I'd only get one chance at escape.

Behind, the man heard my movements and edged forward. But he came too fast in the total darkness. His foot splashed in the stream, and then he stumbled over loose stone. I heard a bark of pain, followed by a bitten-off curse. But he got back up. I heard clothing rustling against stone, more cautious this time.

My fingers slid off the stone wall in front of me into open space. I halted, explored with my hand.

Another corner. The alley turned again.

I edged around the side. The sounds of pursuit quieted, but I pushed on. He wasn't going to give up, even in the dark. I'd hurt him too much for that, dared to defy him in front of all the others, dared to run.

A sense of uselessness, of total despair, washed over me. I tasted it, like grit in the back of my throat, and forced it back with a hard swallow. For a moment, I leaned more weight against the wall, heard my tattered clothes scraping harshly against the mudbrick. But I kept moving. Why couldn't he just leave me alone? Why couldn't he just let me go? He had other workers. He didn't need me.

But I knew. It was because I'd bitten him. I could still hear his howl of shock and rage.

"I won't go back," I mumbled, too softly for anyone to hear, voice choked with tears and anger.

My fingers found another opening: a window, its edges ragged and broken with decayed stone.

With a surge of hope, I stepped back from the wall, placed both hands on the crumbling ledge, and pushed my small form upward. Stone ground into my stomach and the sharp pain in my side lanced down into my leg. I began to flail, tilting forward. I couldn't see where the window led, but it didn't matter. Anywhere was better than here.

I began to fall forward into the darkness, gasping with effort and triumph.

A hand latched onto my ankle.

"No!" I screamed, hope flailing desperately in my chest. "I won't go back! I won't!"

"You bloody well will," the man grunted.

Another hand grabbed the waist of my breeches, gripped the cloth tight, and as the man heaved, I felt myself lifted up off the window's ledge by the pants and ankle and thrown backward, out into the alley.

I hit the opposite wall hard. As I collapsed to the ground, no longer able to breathe, the moon reappeared from behind the clouds, startlingly bright. I tried to catch myself with my hands, but I had no strength left. My arms crumpled and the side of my face struck the mud-slicked cobbles. Pain jolted through my jaw, and I tasted fresh blood. My own blood. I moaned.

The man didn't give me time to recuperate. My arms still useless, my hands grasping feebly at nothing, the man kicked me hard in the stomach, the force of the blow throwing me onto my back. I coughed as blood trickled down into my throat, tried to curl into a protective ball, but a hand latched onto the front of my shirt and hauled me upright. The man loomed over me, then jerked me in close, my feet no longer touching the ground.

"Thought you could run, eh?" Putrid breath blew across my face. "No one runs from Corum."

My head rolled sideways, no longer under my own control. I had no more strength left. And for the first time I saw my attacker.

His face was screwed up into a snarl of hatred, eyes sharp and black in the moonlight, teeth yellowed and crooked. Brown hair lay in tangles on fatty, bulging skin, a few locks twisted and tied together with thin, colored string.

"No one," he said again when he saw he'd caught my attention.

I spat into his face.

He hesitated a single moment, trembling in shock. Then he growled and threw me again.

I hit the mud-brick wall, bounced off it into something wooden resting in another corner, where the alley turned yet again. I caught myself on its edge, one hand holding, the other slipping off and splashing into collected water.

A rain barrel. Or what was left of one.

I steadied myself, pulled myself upright so that I was kneeling over the water.

And then I froze.

Confusion stabbed deep into my gut as I stared down into the reflection on the rippled surface of the water.

It wasn't me. It was a boy, not yet ten. Round face with smooth skin encrusted with the Dredge, with dirt and blood and tears. Light brown eyes wide and desperate. Hair short and crawling with lice.

Then the reflection of the moon in the water was eclipsed by Corum's shadow.

I jerked back, but Corum was too quick. His hand fell onto the back of my head, fingers curling tight in my hair. I screamed as Corum, nearly three times my height and weight, dropped to one knee beside me and in a rough voice spat, "No one!"

He placed his other hand over the one wrapped in my hair, then thrust my head downward. Stagnant water closed up and over my ears, drowning out my screams, drowning out Corum's harsh breathing as he held me down with his full weight. I struggled, pushed back from the barrel, kicked my legs, writhed and squirmed and fought. Water splashed out of the barrel, soaked into my clothing. But there was no purchase, no strength left in me, and then water filled my mouth and I drew it in, pulled its coldness down into my lungs and I felt it filling me, seeping into every part of my body. And as it touched my arms, I felt my struggling relax, felt my arms go numb and slack. Strength ebbed from my legs. And then I felt myself sinking, down and down into the depths of the barrel, down and down forever.

As I sank, I suddenly realized why I couldn't use the river.

Because this wasn't me dying. It was someone else. Someone who lived in the slums beyond the Dredge.

And then I woke.

I lurched out of the dream with a sharp cry, choking on the slick coolness of rainwater even though my mouth was dry. Sick, I crawled to the edge of the immense bed, arms tangled in sweaty sheets, and coughed into the darkness of the room. Harsh, racking coughs, as if I were trying to purge my lungs of nonexistent water.

When the coughing faded, I fell back onto the bed, my entire body trembling with weakness. I swallowed, throat raw, then felt the strangeness of the room around me and sat up slowly.

The Mistress' chambers.

Because I was the new Mistress.

I shuddered, drew my knees up to my chest and hugged them close, the unfamiliar cloth of the shift I wore rustling in the darkness.

As the last of the dream faded, reality returned. Except that the dream felt more real. I knew the Dredge, knew the warren of alleys and niches filled with filth and refuse. From the age of six until I'd fled to the upper city at fifteen, I'd spent my life living in its decaying buildings, surviving off of the streets any way I could, stealing my food, rooting through the garbage for that discarded chunk of moldy cheese, that weevil-ridden crust of bread. I was a thief, gutterscum, spat upon and kicked out of the way. The only reason I'd survived as long as I had was because of the Seeker assassin, Erick . . . and because of the river.

For a moment, I let the darkened room around me shift, let myself sink into the special sight that I called the river. The blackness shifted to a lighter gray, took on edges and forms as I picked up the faint moonlight seeping around the drawn curtains leading to the balcony. It was like sliding beneath the surface of water, and as I pushed myself deeper, the details of the room clarified. Still gray, but now they were visible when before there hadn't been enough light.

But it was more than that now, different than what it had been even on the Dredge. Because now I had the power of the Skewed Throne augmenting the river. I could feel the throne pulsing around me, heightening my awareness, taking it beyond what I was used to. The new power felt raw, almost unwieldy, barely under control.

I shifted my focus, turned back to the bedroom.

It was large, the largest room I'd ever slept in, even after I'd escaped the Dredge and taken up residence in the merchant Borund's manse as his bodyguard. The bed stood against one wall, four posts rising from its corners, the canopy tied high above bowing down toward me. Tables stood at various points about the room, mixed in with potted trees and plants, a settee, chairs. Large wardrobes stood off to my left, and chests with linens and clothes, none of the contents mine. One of the tables held a large pitcher filled with water set in a basin so that I could wash my face in the morning; another held the dagger I'd taken from an ex-guardsman after he'd tried to rape me and I'd killed him. I'd only been eleven then.

Across the room, opposite the bed, were a set of double doors leading to the antechamber and the rest of the palace. In the grayness of the river, I could sense the two guardsmen who waited on the other side of the doors, in the antechamber itself. They were arguing, their voices too low for me to catch. But their emotions coursed through the river like a current. Fear and uncertainty; mostly uncertainty. They must have heard me thrashing around in my sleep, couldn't decide whether to enter the room.

Before I'd taken control of the throne, I wouldn't have been able to sense their emotions in such detail. I wouldn't have been able to sense them at all, since they were behind a closed door. On the Dredge and then later in the upper city as a bodyguard for Borund, I needed to be able to see my targets before I could use the river against them. But now, with the power of the throne behind me . . .

The guardsmen didn't know what to think of their new Mistress, of the seventeen-year-old girl who had somehow entered the palace two nights ago dressed as a page boy, had slipped through all of the patrols, had bypassed every guardsman, and somehow made it to the throne room and taken control of the Skewed Throne.

I pushed the river away, let the darkness of the room return, the emotions of the two guardsmen fade. I'd done more than taken control of the throne, though. Because whoever controlled the throne controlled the entire city of Amenkor.

I pulled my knees in tighter, tried to suppress a sudden flare of anger but failed.

I'd never intended to seize the throne. I'd been sent by the administrator Avrell, the First of the Mistress, and Borund after I'd escaped the Dredge. Sent to kill the previous Mistress so that someone else could take her place. They'd claimed it was the only way to get the insane Mistress off the throne, that they'd tried everything else and failed; that if it wasn't done soon, the city would never survive the winter. In her insanity, the previous Mistress had blockaded the harbor and cut off trade when food was desperately needed, had allowed a quarter of the city and a significant portion of the stored food to burn, had ordered the city and palace guardsmen not to help in putting out the fire. She had to be removed, and I was the only one who could do it. Because I'd been trained by the Seeker Erick to be an assassin . . . and because of the river. I was the only one who could get close enough to kill her.

So I'd agreed. Because I'd believed the Mistress *had* gone insane, and because Erick, my mentor, convinced me that I was the only one who could succeed.

But it had been a trap. The Mistress had been waiting for me, had manipulated the guardsmen and servants of the palace so that I would make it to the throne room unimpeded.

Instead of killing her, I'd been forced to touch the Skewed Throne.

My anger flared higher—at Avrell, at Borund, and especially at Erick's betrayal—but it paled at the sudden surge of horror at the memory of the throne.

I shuddered, stifled a moan, laid my head down on my knees and closed my eyes, felt the exhaustion that had plagued me since that night washing over me.

I let myself sink back into the river, dove deep, heading straight for the edge of the spherical White Fire that burned continuously now at my core. A power separate from the river, the Fire had saved me more than once on the Dredge, flaring up to forewarn me of danger, of threats that I had not yet seen. And now it protected me from the voices within the throne and their immense force. I would never have survived the Skewed Throne without it. The voices would have crushed me, smothered me beneath their weight.

I winced as I grew closer to the boundary, drew a slow steadying breath as I felt the throbbing pulse of the throne's power, and halted just outside the seething barrier of white flame.

On the far side, a maelstrom of voices roared, almost deafening. Hundreds upon hundreds of voices clamoring for my attention, screaming defiance and hatred, pleading for release, for pity, all of them trying to take over at once. They were the voices of all of the previous Mistresses, all who had sat upon the throne and ruled Amenkor since the throne was created, as well as the voices of any who had dared to touch it since then. Hundreds of Mistresses; even more of those who had touched the throne and not had the power to survive. I felt the pressure of their personalities, of their emotions, against my face like heat, white-hot and hissing. Anger and hatred and raw desperation—all trapped by the throne.

And now trapped by the Fire as well. After being thrust onto the throne, forced to face its power, I'd used the White Fire to capture those voices. I'd surrounded them in its protective flame and now held them deep inside myself with the power of the river.

The voices had driven the previous Mistress to the edge of madness. But she'd managed to lure me to the throne room by distracting the guards, had managed to use the throne to overpower me and shove me forcibly onto its seat.

And then she'd given me a choice: die and let the city of Amenkor die with me during the coming winter, or claim the power of the throne myself and release her, giving the city a chance to survive.

My anger returned, hot and fluid and bitter. It hadn't been much of a choice at all.

I let the river go again with a hard thrust, sat up straight in the Mistress' bed—my bed now—legs folded so I could rest my elbows on my knees. If they wanted a new Mistress, then I'd be Mistress. But I was tired of being manipulated, of being given choices that were not choices at all.

One of the guards knocked on the door to the antechamber, followed by a muffled argument, pitched high with concern.

I scowled. When the knocking resumed, more urgent, I slid off the bed and moved to the door, walking carefully through the unfamiliar room in the darkness.

I jerked the door open, the two guards outside stepping back sharply. They regained their composure quickly, standing stiffly at attention, but still a little uncertain. One of them was one of the previous Mistress' palace guardsmen, the other was one of the assassin Seekers.

"What?" I spat.

The regular guardsman, the one who had knocked on the door, licked his lips, glanced toward the Seeker for reassurance, then answered. "We heard a cry—"

"If there'd been an assassin," I said, "I'd have been dead by the time you decided to open the door."

The guardsman stood, mouth open, with no idea what to say.

I moved to close the door, but the Seeker stepped forward.

"Is everything all right, Mistress?"

My stomach clenched, a sudden wave of loneliness, of desolation and instability and doubt washing over me.

Two days ago, I'd been a bodyguard for a somewhat powerful merchant. Today, I ruled the entire city—a city on the verge of winter starvation.

A chill shivered through my skin, tingling, raising the hairs on my arms.

I swallowed, met the Seeker's eyes. Dark eyes, with a dangerous glint that I recognized. I'd seen it in Erick's eyes when I was fourteen and he'd found me in an alley off the Dredge, vomiting over the corpse of the second man I'd killed. Erick, the man who had trained me, had given me the chance to escape the Dredge when I was fifteen and become a bodyguard for Borund.

This man had the same stance as Erick, totally relaxed, fluid, with an edge of death. But unlike Erick, this man had few scars lining his face, had less gray in his dark hair, his nose more pointed and straight because it had never been broken.

Unlike the regular guardsman, the Seeker carried a dagger instead of a sword, wore leathers instead of armor. Of the two, he was the more dangerous, and yet I felt more comfortable speaking to him than to the palace guardsman.

"I'm fine," I said, then hesitated.

I could feel myself trembling, alternately hot with rage and cold with terror at the thought of what I would be expected to do as Mistress.

The room behind me suddenly felt both too large and too confining.

I drew in a ragged breath and let it out slowly. "No," I said. "No, I think I need some air. Take me to the roof of the palace."

The Seeker nodded, then said in a carefully neutral voice, "You should probably change."

I glanced down at my sweat-matted shift, rumpled and wrinkled, then glared at both of the guards before closing the door without a word.

The Seeker guarding the door to my chambers led me to the roof of the palace, halting at the opening to the stairwell with a nod. Dressed in Eryn's white robes, the predawn air felt chill and close, still damp with the autumn rains and with a bite of winter. As I moved to the low wall at the edge of the roof overlooking the port of Amenkor, I repressed a shudder at the robe's unfamiliar weight and movement. I was used to close-fitting clothes, shirts and breeches, nothing loose that would interfere with my dagger, with my movements. But the previous Mistress did not have breeches, did not carry a dagger. And someone had removed the page boy's clothes I'd worn to infiltrate the palace. Her white robes, with bands of gold embroidery around the neck and hem, were the only clothes I could find.

I glared out over the city of Amenkor in irritation, trying not to scratch myself. Things would have to change, starting with the clothes.

On the harbor, ships rocked in the waves, silhouetted against the water by the reflected moonlight. All but those guarding the harbor's entrance were at the docks, where they'd been since the previous Mistress had blockaded the harbor. A few were loading cargo, by the light of torches lining the wharf, but I couldn't see which ships in the darkness, could only see vague forms moving in the glow of the lanterns along the docks. Closer in, there was a patch of darkness where the warehouses had burned, the buildings nothing but charred husks.

I felt a weight of guilt settle onto my shoulders, a clench of nausea tug at my stomach. I may not have started the fire that destroyed the warehouse district, but the lantern that *had* started it had been thrown at me by a boy attempting to save himself from my blade.

I turned away from the black scar, toward the barely discernible streets, the River, and the outer walls of the city.

At the same time, I heard footsteps behind me.

I slid beneath the river, felt the world shift to gray, the sounds of the night muting to a soft wind, and targeted the woman who approached.

Eryn, the previous Mistress.

I tensed, back rigid, comforted by the presence of my dagger at my side, tucked into a makeshift belt. I'd seen little of the previous Mistress since I'd released her from the throne and assumed power. There'd been little time. I'd spent a full day seated on the throne, afraid to let my guard down, afraid the voices would overtake me the moment I turned my back. Eventually, I'd isolated them behind the Fire, stabilized it so that it burned without conscious thought. Only then had I stepped away from the throne.

But the effort had drained me. I'd collapsed in exhaustion almost immediately, been taken to the Mistress' chambers to rest. When I'd woken, after only a few hours of sleep, the palace had been in turmoil, the guardsmen seething with anger, the servants confused. Nothing had been accomplished, all of Avrell's time spent calming everyone down.

There'd been nothing I could do at the time, so I'd retired early, still exhausted . . . and dreamed.

Eryn moved up beside me, placed her hands on the stone parapet of the tower, and gazed out over the city. In the moonlight, her hair was blue-black, her skin washed a pale white, as white as the simple dress she wore. She held herself formally, head high, chin lifted. Not arrogant, but assured. The stance of a ruler.

I felt small beside her. And not only because I was two hands shorter and probably less than half her age.

"Couldn't sleep?" she asked a moment later, after a heavy sigh.

I shifted, slipped into a stance the Seeker watching us would have recognized, and answered, "No." It came out harsher than I'd intended. I suddenly wondered where she had slept last night, what she had done while the palace was in chaos.

She turned toward me, eyes narrowed, lips pursed. She looked exhausted as well, dark smudges beneath her eyes, her skin tight, as if she'd been sobbing for hours. It had aged her. Instead of the nearly forty-year-old woman who'd so confidently bested me a few nights before, she appeared fifty . . . and totally defeated.

I found my anger and wariness faltering, forced myself to remember that this was the woman who had almost killed me days before.

"It's hard," she said, tight and controlled. "I've lived so long with the voices of the throne that now that they're gone . . ." She grimaced, shrugged, then laughed bitterly, no humor touching her eyes. "I know I'd be dead by now, if you hadn't come to kill me. I could never have withstood the throne. It was too powerful, and the voices . . . they were wearing me down. They would have driven me insane eventually. But still . . ."

I said nothing. I'd seen the insanity in her eyes in the throne room, seen how much she'd fought to hold herself together at the end.

Eryn straightened. "I think . . ." Her voice had changed, some of the bitterness seeping away. "I think, if you hadn't come, I would have thrown myself from this very wall."

I stilled, startled, then shifted forward so I could see down the height of the wall, down past the gaps of the inset windows, past the banners, to the stairs at the wall's base.

The stone of the steps gleamed white in the moonlight.

Something tightened in my chest, and I pulled back from the edge with a sharp gasp. For a brief moment, the world tilted around me, and I felt off-balance, dizzy with the height. I placed my hands carefully on the stone wall to steady myself and felt the last of my wariness vanish, lost in the thudding of my heart.

"You used to come here often," I said. "Avrell said that on the night the warehouses burned, you came up here to watch the fire. He said that you smiled."

Eryn didn't answer at first. She simply stood, staring down at the stone steps below, her eyes distant. Almost contemplative.

"That wasn't me standing here that night," she said, her eyes haunted and lost. "It was the throne."

For a horrible moment, I thought she was on the verge of jumping as she'd planned earlier. I could see it in her eyes, almost like the madness I'd seen in the throne room before, but somehow more terrifying because she was so calm.

But then the moment passed. Her eyes narrowed and she turned away from the wall, from the steps far below, and looked at me.

"You dreamed," she said. There was no doubt in her voice. The assured woman who'd first stood beside me had returned.

I thought about lying, but saw no point. She'd been the Mistress for longer than I'd been alive. "Yes."

She frowned. "That's unusual. It took at least three months after I assumed the throne before I dreamed. Tell me, what happened in this dream?"

"I drowned," I said curtly. "A man shoved my head into a rain barrel and I drowned. Except it wasn't me, it was a boy I didn't know."

Eryn nodded, turning back toward the city. "And do you know where this happened?"

"The slums beyond the Dredge."

"And did you see the man who killed you—or rather, did this boy you don't know see him?"

"Yes. His name was Corum."

"Then you must send the Seekers after this Corum. He is a mark. He deserves to die."

I felt a warm surge of satisfaction course through my blood at the thought. My hand closed into a fist about the hilt of my dagger. Corum's face rose sharp and clear in my mind and my jaw clenched with hatred. "I can look for him myself. I can kill him."

Eryn turned sharply at the harshness in my voice, her eyes going wide in alarm. "Varis," she said, taking a tentative step forward.

Beneath the river, her movement was slow, almost languid. I'd sunk deeper than I'd intended, had let the world gray almost to black, the city spread out below me—once half lost in the darkness before dawn—now sharp with edges and clearly defined. And there was a tug on the currents, a pull. Nothing focused or clear, but a scent. I doubt I would have sensed it without the added power of the throne behind me. I faced it, reached out for it, and found myself focusing across the buildings of the merchants' quarter, across the wharf and the harbor, across the real River that emptied into the bay, to where the cobbled street called the Dredge ran into the slums of the city. The scent grew clearer, more intense. As sharp and fresh as new-fallen rain—

And suddenly I knew I *could* find him, could find Corum wherever he hid on the Dredge, using the river, using the throne. I could already smell his putrid breath, could feel my dagger sliding up beneath his ribs. I could taste his death.

"Varis, no!"

Eryn's voice was hollow, distant. But then she slapped me, hard, the stinging sensation piercing through the eddies of the river like a blade. I pulled back from the edge of the city with a jerk, snapped back into myself at the edge of the palace wall hard enough I stumbled back. Eryn was already there, holding me up, steadying me. Her face was a steel mask of terrified anger, cold and stark in the moonlight.

"Never do that again!" she spat. "Never reach out like that using the Sight or the throne!"

"But I can find him," I gasped, still disoriented. I felt an urge to vomit, but fought the sensation down, swallowed hard as I caught my balance. "I can scent him—"

"No!" she growled. "It's too dangerous. Reaching like that, extending yourself out so far. . . ." She shook her head. "You could lose yourself, never find your way back. Previous Mistresses have been lost in such attempts before. No. It's better to send the Seekers. That's what they've been trained for." She squeezed my shoulder, locked gazes with me, her voice brittle. "Tell me you will not try that again. Tell me!"

I nodded, still feeling sick. "I won't."

"You'll send the Seekers?"

I nodded again.

The terror began to fade from Eryn's eyes. "Good." She loosened her grip and stepped back, eyeing me carefully. Then she sighed. "Good. Now you should get some rest. Avrell and the others will want to talk to you tomorrow. There are things you must decide on, and decide on quickly, if Amenkor is to survive."

"If it's to survive what?"

Eryn hesitated, her eyes searching. But I was still shaking from the . . . the Reaching into the Dredge.

Eryn's mouth turned in a sudden frown. "Winter," she said. "If we're to survive winter, of course."

Then she turned and walked steadily to the stairs, without looking back.

I stayed on the tower to watch the dawn. To the east, over the hazy shadow of mountains, the sky lightened. I'd never seen what lay beyond the city of Amenkor, had always been hidden inside the streets, unable to see what was outside of the walls and buildings. From the tower of the palace, though, as the sun rose, I could see how the city crowded around the enclosed bay and the River. To the north, the Dredge ran up into the decaying buildings of the slums, which clung to the rocky cliffs of the northern portion of the harbor before reaching the top of a ridge and spilling over beyond view. To the south, the land fell away steeply from the edge of the outer wall of the palace toward a coastline dotted with windswept trees. A road cut through the landscape in both directions—north and south—intersecting another road heading from Amenkor to the east, toward the mountains.

I stared at the road and the River snaking out into the foothills of the mountains, eyes wide. The entire landscape was covered with trees, more trees than I'd ever seen, could ever have imagined. I followed the dense forest as it faded into the haze at the base of the mountains, noted a cleft in the peaks in the far distance: the pass that led to the lands beyond.

As the sun rose higher, dawn slipping away, I turned back to the city below. Amenkor. The real Amenkor.

My Amenkor.

I leaned forward, stone gritty beneath my palms, and stared out over the streets, over the water of the river and the harbor, over the two juts of land that reached out to enclose the bay, protecting it. Barely discernible in the distance, at the ends of each jut of land, I could see two towers, like sentinels at the harbor's entrance. And before that entrance I could see the Mistress' ships blocking the water-course, preventing all ships from entering.

And leaving.

I frowned. But I shrugged aside the sudden uneasiness and turned back to the city. Lights had been doused and people had begun to emerge into the streets. As the cries of the dockworkers and hawkers on the wharf began to filter up to the tower, I turned to where the Seeker waited patiently. With a nod, we descended.

Erick was waiting outside the Mistress' chambers. He was alone, aside from the palace guardsman I'd left outside the door earlier, and he smiled when he saw me, the skin crinkling around his eyes.

I halted, the Seeker who accompanied me stepping to one side behind me. My eyes narrowed in anger, my hands tightening in the folds of my white robes. I hadn't seen him since he, Borund, and Avrell had convinced me to kill the Mistress. Like Eryn, he appeared haggard, older than he was.

"Varis," he began.

"Don't," I said, cutting him off, moving forward and past him to the door. "I don't want to talk to you."

"Varis, wait."

I stormed through the antechamber into the Mistress' rooms, paused when I saw the neatly folded page boy's clothes stacked on the chest at the bed's base, then turned and strode to where the curtains were drawn across the glass doorway that led to the balcony. I halted before them, but did not pull them back.

I heard Erick enter behind me, heard the door close.

"Varis." His voice was hard, commanding. The same voice he'd used to train me to be an assassin in the slums of Amenkor. But things had changed in the last few weeks. He was no longer my mentor, had not been my mentor for two years, since I'd left the Dredge. Neither he, nor Borund, nor Avrell, could command me now.

I spun. "What?"

Erick stood just inside the door, back straight, eyes dark, jaw tight, clearly angry. He crossed his hands over his chest, spaced his feet a shoulder's width apart, and said nothing. The scars that lined his face, that marked him as dangerous even when he was relaxed, stood out in the light.

For a moment, I saw him as he had appeared on the Dredge almost four years before, when he'd found me: cold, arrogant, and unreadable. A guardsman. A Seeker. I was nothing then. A wisp of a girl barely surviving off the dregs of Amenkor. Gutterscum. I'd looked no further than the next rotted apple or scabbed potato.

But he'd changed all that. I'd discovered he wasn't as cold and arrogant and distant as he had seemed.

The anger I felt began to ebb, to drain away as the silence between us deepened. But it didn't vanish completely.

"Did you know?"

His forehead creased in confusion. "Know about what?"

"Did you know it was a trap! That they sent me to kill the Mistress simply to get me into the palace, to get me to the throne room?"

He shook his head. "No." A flat denial. No hesitation.

I looked hard into his eyes, wanting to believe him, and found them completely open, nothing hidden. The tension in my shoulders released and I turned away. "Good," I said, my voice still sharp, even though I felt a wave of relief. I hadn't realized how betrayed I'd felt, how horribly deep it had cut me, until I'd seen him.

Behind, I heard Erick move a few steps farther into the room.

"I don't think Borund knew either," he said. "He and Avrell only wanted me to convince you to kill the Mistress. They thought I'd have a better chance at it than they would by themselves. They thought you trusted me. Neither one of them mentioned anything about you becoming the Mistress."

I grunted without comment.

Erick was quiet for a long moment, then added, "It took them a long time to convince me that killing her was necessary. And in the end they didn't convince me that she was insane. You did."

Startled, I turned to see his face. "What do you mean?"

He moved forward, until he stood only a few paces away. "You knew that something was wrong with the Mistress when she sent me to kill Mari. You knew Mari wasn't a mark just by looking at her. After that I began to question every mark the Mistress sent me after. By the time Avrell and Borund approached me, I already knew that the Mistress was insane and that something needed to be done. But I didn't know what. All they had to do was convince me that killing her was the only option."

"But you don't think Borund intended for me to become the Mistress? Or Avrell?"

"Borund, no. I don't know about Avrell."

I thought back to that meeting only four days before. I'd thought then that Avrell was hiding something, that there was something he wasn't telling me, something he'd kept back. I hadn't gotten the same sense from Borund or Erick. Was it possible Avrell hadn't known the Mistress' plans? Had he been manipulated by her as well?

I shook my head in annoyance and moved to the chest where the page boy's clothes rested. On top of the neatly folded linen shirt lay a key.

I reached down and picked it up. It was the key to the room that held the archer's niche I'd used to bypass Baill's guards during their watch. Avrell had given it to me, along with the page boy's clothes.

"I don't think Borund knew either," I said, distracted. Then I sighed and set the key back onto the clothes, turning away.

"I don't want to be the Mistress, Erick."

Erick snorted. "But you are. Nothing can change that now."

I felt a surge of rebellion. Erick must have seen me tense.

"Where would you go, Varis? You can't go back to the Dredge. You spent too much time as Borund's bodyguard to return to living off the slums. And could you be a bodyguard now? After what's happened here?"

I thought about the Dredge. But Erick was right. There was nothing for me there. I'd left that long ago, had abandoned it after killing Bloodmark. But I could become a bodyguard again. Not with Borund, no. Not now. But still . . .

I ran my hand over the page boy's clothes and felt for the voices of the throne in the recesses of my mind, still kept at bay by the Fire. If I let the Fire relax just a little, let it dampen . . .

I felt a flush of heat flow through me, tingling in my skin, coursing along my arms, across my shoulders, down my legs. And then the heat flowed outward, suffused and surrounded me completely, extending out through the room, through the palace, and then out farther . . . until it reached the edges of the city itself, pulsing in sync with my blood.

I could feel the city, from the palace to the Dredge, from the River to the two towers that guarded the harbor. Its heartbeat matched mine. Its life flowed through my veins.

I drew in a deep steadying breath, then pushed back the sensation of the city, forced the power behind the protective curtain of Fire again. My hand slid from the page boy's clothing to my side. Erick was right about being a bodyguard as well. How could I return to that now? I was bound to the throne, and through it to the city. Bound by my own choice. Eryn may have lured me into the throne room and forced me to touch the throne, but in the end she hadn't forced me to assume its powers, hadn't forced me to take control. It had been my decision. I could have said no.

"These aren't even my clothes," I said and turned away from the page boy's clothing toward Erick. "I want my own clothes."

Erick grinned. "Let's see what we can find. Then we need to find Avrell. He has a meeting set up with the rest of the people in control of the palace staff. They're all anxious to meet the new Mistress of Amenkor."

I shot him a hard glare but his grin only widened.

". . . no idea what she's going to want, Matron Ireen. You'll have to ask her when she arrives."

I heard Avrell's voice the moment Erick opened the door to the meeting room, his tone calm and casual but tinged with irritation. He drew breath to continue, but someone else coughed discreetly and there was a loud rustle of cloth and the scraping of chairs.

A small group of men and women rose from their seats as the door opened fully, Erick stepping into the room in front of me and then to one side. The moment I caught their collective gaze, I reached for my dagger and slid beneath the river, but managed to keep from drawing the blade. Instead, I gripped its hilt, hard enough that my knuckles turned white. Then I scanned the room.

A simple table with seven chairs sat in the middle of the room. A few potted trees rested in two of the corners, the other two taken up by small tables with trays of cheeses and fruit and a pitcher with glasses for drinks. The wall behind the tall chair at the head of the table was covered with a white banner with the gold insignia of the Mistress: the stylized marking of the Skewed Throne—three slashes; one horizontal, the two others angled down and out from that, one shorter than the other. All of the remaining walls were bare.

There were six people waiting at the table. Avrell and Nathem I already knew, both administrators of the Mistress, the First and Second respectively. Next to Nathem stood a woman I had never met before, broad shouldered and older, dressed in the Mistress' whites, her face squinched up into a penetrating frown. With one quick glance, she took in my brown breeches, soft-skin shoes, and the loose linen shirt Erick had borrowed from one of the guardsmen. Then she harrumphed and shook her head in disapproval. The shirt was too large and the breeches itched, but the shoes were well worn and comfortable. I shifted beneath her hostile glare, even though beneath the river she was completely gray and so not a real threat. Both Avrell and Nathem, dressed in the blue-and-gold robes of the Mistress' order, appeared gray as well.

But the three men on the other side of the table were not gray. Baill, captain of the palace guard, stood rigid, face set, hands folded comfortably over his sword belt. His eyes held mine with a reserved look, but they noticed everything: my clothes, my dagger, my hair hanging loose and uncombed about my face. His reaction was impossible to read. Beside him, also dressed in the burgundy silk shirts and brown breeches of guardsmen, were two men I did not know. The first was tall and thin, with the same cold, casual, dangerous look that surrounded Erick. A Seeker. He wore no visible weapons and nodded to Erick before turning his attention to me. When he saw my clothes, a small smile lit in his eyes and his lips twitched. The second man was shorter than the Seeker and wore a sword. He barely glanced in my direction. All three appeared red.

After a long, uncomfortable moment, Avrell cleared his throat and said to the room in general, "May I present Varis, the Mistress of Amenkor."

Another awkward pause, and then everyone gave a short bow, Avrell and Nathem first, with Baill giving a belated brief nod at the end.

Erick moved to the far side of the room and stood behind a high-backed chair, resting his hand on one corner of its back.

"If the Mistress would care to sit," Avrell said, motioning to the chair.

I shot him a glare, but he was too much the diplomat to react. Nothing touched his dark brown eyes as he gave me a casual smile. He was too practiced, had spent too much time around Mistresses and the throne. To all appearances, my seizing of the throne had come as a pleasant surprise.

But I didn't trust him. If he'd helped Eryn to lure me to the throne room, then he'd manipulated me without remorse. And if not, then he'd hired me to kill her, betraying the woman he was supposed to protect. I couldn't afford to trust him.

Captain Baill was no better. Numerous merchants within the city had been murdered during the last year by a consortium of men led by the merchant Alendor in an attempt to take over all of the city's trade. Baill had been suspected of helping the consortium, although he'd done nothing but what the previous Mistress had commanded, so nothing could be proved.

Uneasy, I glanced around the room once more, then stepped around Avrell's side of the room to the chair. As I moved, the guards posted outside the room closed the door behind me and all but Avrell and Erick took seats.

"Let's begin by introducing everyone," Avrell said. "Avrell Tremain, the First of the Mistress." He bowed his head again, then motioned to his left. "This is Nathem Ordaven, the Second of the Mistress—"

"I know."

Nathem seemed startled and somewhat nervous, his brow creasing in thought as he tried to figure out how I knew him. But we'd never met officially. I only knew him because I'd overheard Avrell speaking with him about the Mistress while I was inside the palace, on my way to the throne room.

"I see," Avrell said smoothly. But he shared a troubled glance with Erick that made me smile with satisfaction. He moved on, motioning to the woman. "Matron Ireen is the head of the Mistress' servants. She'll handle all of your needs—clothing, food, whatever you want. She'll want to speak with you at length *after* the meeting."

Ireen had shifted forward, ready to speak, but under Avrell's glare she sank back in her seat and crossed her arms on her ample chest with a grunt.

Avrell turned toward Baill. "And this is Captain Baill Gorret of the palace guard. I'll leave it to you to introduce the others, Captain Baill."

Baill gave Avrell a dark look, then stood and motioned to his right. "Karl Westen, Captain of the Seekers, and Arthur Catrell, Captain of the city guard."

He sat as the other two guardsmen nodded.

An unsettled silence followed, as if everyone were waiting for something. Captain Catrell sighed and shifted with nervous agitation, his gaze darting around the spare room as if distracted. Nathem still seemed deep in thought. Baill simply stared at me, his expression unreadable, neither curious like most of the others, nor contemptuous.

For a long moment, I stared back, but then I shifted my gaze to Avrell. "What have you done with the previous Mistress, Eryn?"

Caught off guard, Avrell sat forward and in an uncertain voice said, "I didn't know what to do with her. We've never had an . . . ex-Mistress, so to speak. So I assigned her rooms in the palace and allowed her to keep her usual servants." He recovered his poise as he spoke. "She's been part of the palace since she was eight, and she doesn't really have any other place to go. Were there . . . other arrangements you wished to make?"

I frowned. With a simple inflection, he'd made it sound as if any other arrangements would be unreasonable.

"No," I said grudgingly. I didn't know if keeping her in the palace was a mistake or not, but for now I was willing to wait.

But I felt as if I'd been manipulated again, the decision taken away from me.

With irritation I didn't bother to suppress, I asked, "What did you want to talk about?"

"There are many things to discuss," Avrell said, nodding as if the meeting were back on track. "The blockade of the harbor, the work to be done in the warehouse district after the recent fire, the food shortage and the advent of winter, the sudden cessation of communication with the Boreaite Isles, but I think the first thing that needs to be discussed is the—"

"I think," Baill interrupted, voice loud to override Avrell. Avrell's gaze narrowed as he looked across the table at Baill; Baill's gaze never shifted away from me. "I think the first thing that needs to be discussed is how Varis managed to get into the throne room of the palace without being discovered by the guard."

Nathem drew in a sharp breath, and Captain Catrell's attention suddenly focused as he shifted forward in his chair.

With a casual movement, Baill turned to Avrell. "She couldn't have done it without help," Baill continued. His voice was as calm and collected as Avrell's, but there was a deadlier undercurrent to it, a threat of violent death.

Avrell did not flinch. "I helped her. I let her in through the tunnels beneath the outer walls, gave her maps of the palace, and told her the movements of the guards."

The captain of the city guard grunted as if punched. "You compromised the Mistress' security? What for?"

Avrell glanced toward Captain Catrell, but only briefly, his eyes dropping to the table before turning back to Baill with a challenge. "I wanted Varis to kill the Mistress."

There was a brief moment of silence. Then Captain Catrell stood and in a surprisingly smooth movement brought his sword to bear, the blade reaching across the table toward Avrell's throat without wavering.

"Then you are a traitor," he said simply.

No one in the room moved. Avrell held the gaze of the captain of the city guard, not even glancing down at the sword.

"I made a vow to protect the throne and the city of Amenkor," Avrell said with a tinge of disdain. "Not the Mistress herself."

To one side, I saw Baill frown and shift in his seat as if uncomfortable. He no longer seemed as certain as he had a moment before.

"Besides," Avrell continued, turning his attention to me, still refusing to acknowledge the presence of the sword, "I could only get Varis into the palace. There was nothing I could do about the guardsmen after that. It was the Mistress' own luck that Varis made it to the throne room without being seen."

Avrell's gaze locked onto mine, but it was completely unreadable. I thought about the key he'd given me to get into the inner sanctum of the palace, the key to the archer's niche. But then I realized that Avrell was right. The key could only get me so far. It was the Mistress herself who had distracted the guards beyond that point.

Grudgingly, feeling as if I'd been cornered again, forced into speaking against my will, I said, "It wasn't luck."

With a glare at Avrell, I turned to Baill. "The Mistress—the previous Mistress—lured me to the throne room herself. She wanted me to ascend to the throne. She's the one that diverted the guardsmen from the outer corridor so that I could enter the inner sanctum."

Baill considered for a long moment, his gaze never wavering from mine. Something flickered behind his eyes, there and then gone, too quickly for me to read. Then he nodded. "Lower your sword, Arthur. I believe her."

Captain Catrell hesitated, then resheathed his sword and sat down.

"Now," Avrell said. "About the food shortage—"

"No."

A look of annoyance passed over Avrell's face and he turned toward me with a frown. "No?"

I drew in a deep breath and leaned forward, letting my anger touch my voice. I was tired of being manipulated. "If we're going to discuss the food shortage, I want all the remaining merchants here. Borund in particular."

"But if we're going to be able to find more resources to replace those lost in the fire in the warehouse district, we need to act quickly. Winter is approaching fast. We have only a few more days left to send out ships. After that, there won't be enough time for the ships to travel to the other cities, trade and load cargo, and return before the seas become too rough for safe passage. We can't wait for the merchants. We need to act now!"

I glared at Avrell, and then felt something shift. A strange warmth enfolded me, and suddenly the room grew distant, as if somehow I'd taken a step back from the table, even though I was still seated.

In a cold voice, I said, "The ships belong to the merchants, or are owned outright by their captains. I will not order them to sea without the merchant's or the captain's consent."

Without waiting for a response, I shifted my attention to Captain Catrell. "Can you send guardsmen to Merchant Borund's manse?"

"Of course."

"Then send them. Tell him the blockade on the harbor is lifted, that he may send ships out at once if he wishes, and that they are to find and buy whatever food they can and return. They will be compensated by the palace. Also tell him to gather together the resources he has left in the city, those that weren't destroyed by the fire in the warehouse district. He is to bring a report to the palace tomorrow morning, early. Get from him the names of all of the remaining merchants in Amenkor and give the same message to them. I want the entire merchants' guild to be represented at this meeting."

Captain Catrell stared, stunned, then nodded and said, "Very well." He sat a little straighter in his seat and no longer seemed as distracted as before.

Baill leaned forward. "So the blockade is to be lifted?"

"Yes."

Baill nodded with approval and leaned back in his seat. Avrell had told Borund and me that Baill refused to lift the blockade, had made it seem as if Baill was at fault, that Baill's claim that the Mistress had ordered the blockade kept even after the merchants protested was a lie. Now I began to wonder.

What if Captain Baill *had* simply been following the Mistress' orders? We had no evidence he'd been working for the consortium at all.

"Was there anything else?" I asked, in a tone that suggested there shouldn't be.

Everyone in the room stilled, as if they'd all drawn a sharp breath and were holding it. No one said anything.

I suddenly wanted to leave, the urge like a prickling sensation across my back. The room felt too hot, too closed in and dense. And still distant.

I stood. "Good."

"But what of the guard patrols in the city?" Avrell said abruptly, standing as well. "And the arrangements for your servants?" He motioned toward Ireen.

The prickling sensation across my back increased. "Keep the patrols. As for the servants. . . ." My gaze fell on Ireen, who sat forward expectantly, face set into a stern frown. "Do whatever you want."

The frown vanished, replaced by confused shock, followed by stern elation.

I suddenly pitied the servants of the palace. Ireen seemed a harsh mistress.

I stalked from the room, Erick following with a slight frown. I ignored

Avrell's attempt to catch my attention, but he raised his voice to shout after me, "We need to discuss the political situation with the rest of the coast! We'll have to discuss it at some point!" The others stood awkwardly, nodding as I passed.

Once out into the hall, I turned toward the Mistress' chambers, four palace guardsmen falling into step behind Erick. As we moved through the corridors, passing servants in the hallways and rooms who paused in their work to gaze after the new Mistress with blatant curiosity, the sense of distance dissipated and the tension in my shoulders loosened. But I still felt agitated. The river roiled around me, but I didn't want to let it go. All I could think about was Avrell. And Baill.

Back in the Mistress' chambers, I began pacing the room, Erick closing the doors behind us, the four guardsmen remaining outside, two in the corridor and two in the antechamber.

"You *will* have to speak to Avrell at length," Erick said. "He can tell you everything you need to know about being the Mistress. At least regarding the everyday workings of the palace."

I frowned but didn't answer, circled the room, to the bed, the low table with the basin and pitcher of water, the doors looking out onto the balcony. Someone had entered while I was gone, had drawn back the curtains and opened the doors so that the breeze could enter the room. I could see the entrance to the harbor, the view slightly different from what I'd seen from the rooftop. This looked out along the southern jut of land, rather than the main part of the city and the river. But the view didn't hold me, and I returned to the bed.

My hands itched.

I halted, staring at them a moment before sinking down into a seat on the bed.

Then I looked up at Erick.

"What is it?" he asked.

"I don't know."

Except I did.

Erick nodded as if he understood, then moved to a second table I hadn't noticed before. A platter of fruit had been set out, and a pitcher of some type of dark red drink.

He picked up a few grapes.

I glowered at his back, then said, "It's not simple anymore."

"What do you mean?"

I sighed, looked back down at my hands. "On the Dredge, it was only about survival. I hunted—for food, for the easiest target, and then later for marks you sent me after. Whatever it took to survive. Then, for Borund, I hunted again—for those targeting Borund."

Erick turned. "And now you don't know what to hunt for?"

"Yes. No." I shook my head in annoyance. "It's more than that."

Erick hesitated, then came forward. "No, it's not. You're still hunting, just as you hunted for Borund. Except this time you're hunting those that are targeting the city."

My hand still itched and with a casual move I drew my dagger, held it before me. The blade was worn, the handle nicked. A guardsman's dagger. I could still feel the blade slashing across the ex-guardsman's throat, the motion awkward and fumbling, inexperienced, but it had been enough. He'd been the first man I'd killed. My first mark. After that, the process had been easy: identify the mark and kill.

Identify and kill.

Simple.

"Except now the marks are winter and starvation," I said, and looked at Erick. "I can't hunt starvation. I can't kill winter."

A troubled look crossed his face, but at the same time the sound of bells came through the window to the balcony, followed by the low bellow of a horn, sounding close, as if originating from the palace itself.

Erick moved to the balcony. I trailed behind, putting away my dagger.

The balcony was long and narrow, with a few flowering vines on trellises in the corners and a black wrought-iron railing encircling all three sides. As I moved up to its edge, I let the Fire relax and felt the pulse of the city course through me.

In the harbor, the Mistress' ships were pulling back from the entrance, moving swiftly and silently. On the docks, there was a sudden frenzy of activity as men began to load cargo that had rested idle on the wharf for days. A few of the merchant ships that had remained loaded even after the blockade were already tossing their lines and pushing away from the docks.

Erick grunted. "The tide is good. They should be able to leave quickly." Then he turned to me, motioning to the ships below. "You are hunting, Varis," he said. "But you're using ships instead of a dagger."

I glanced toward him, uncertain what to say. But the tension in my shoulders had completely faded. And there was no prickling sensation along my shoulders, no itching in my hands.

I leaned my weight forward onto the railing and watched the ships, *felt* them as they glided through the water. Fixing my attention on the lead merchant ship, I followed it, feeling a sense of elation as it surged forward under the wind. Sails whuffled, snapping taut as they belled out, men scrambling on the deck and through the rigging. I felt the tension of the men's muscles, felt their sweat. Then I noticed the flag flying on its highest mast: gold on a red field. Borund's flag.

Of course. He would have known the blockade would be lifted soon after he'd learned I'd seized the throne. He'd been waiting for it. It must have been his ships loading up at the docks before dawn.

Borund's ship neared the entrance to the harbor, then slid through the ends of the two juts of land and the watchtowers, passing out into the darker blue ocean. As it passed the towers, my connection to the ship began to fade. I felt a painful sense of loss as the sensation of wood and rope and water, of the men's sweat and blood, slipped away, then ended.

Apparently, the power of the throne and its connection to the city ended at the entrance to the harbor.

I sighed, watched the remaining ships for a long moment, then felt a familiar tug on the currents of the city.

I turned, straightened where I stood.

The Dredge.

My eyes narrowed.

"I have a mark for you," I said, then turned toward Erick.

He stood, back rigid, eyes dark and serious, as deadly as he'd appeared to me at first on the Dredge. "I live to serve, my Mistress."

I shivered, uneasy at the words, but nodded in response. "His name is Corum."

✥— Chapter 2

I woke to bright sunlight, the sound of midmorning bells from the city below, and a hollow sense of fear.

I couldn't do this. I was a hunter, an assassin, a thief. I didn't know the first thing about ruling a city.

Something clattered and I turned my head sharply, the fear quashed, my hand sliding up under my pillow to the hilt of my dagger. Three servants dressed in white, all young girls around fifteen years old, moved about the room, setting down trays of cheese, opening the curtains and balcony doors, and laying out clothes for the day. I watched them cautiously, but none of them approached and finally the tension bled away.

I dragged myself into a seated position on the edge of the bed, moving slowly, one hand raised to my head. I'd slept later than I'd wanted, but the lack of sleep over the last few nights had finally caught up to me. I moaned, yawned, then scrubbed at my gritty eyes. I felt as if someone had beat me senseless and left me for dead in a back alley.

Someone coughed and I glanced up to see one of the servants—a girl close to my age, with blonde hair, a roundish face, and soft gray eyes—standing before me holding out a cup of something brown and steaming. It smelled of dead, dried leaves.

The girl ducked her head and muttered, "Mistress." She watched me closely behind lowered lashes. A quick touch on the river revealed she was gray. All three servants were gray.

I frowned but took the warm cup. Bringing it close, I breathed in the steam, wrinkled my nose at the smell. This close it smelled more like muddy water. But I could actually see small pieces of crumbled leaves floating in it.

"What is it?"

The girl seemed surprised. "It's tea, Mistress. From Marland."

I took a tentative sip, expecting it to taste as if I'd licked a mud-brick on the Dredge. Instead, its warmth seeped into my chest, the bitterness making my tongue tingle. It did taste like dirt, but not like the stagnant rot on the Dredge. More like the gardens surrounding Borund's manse. Earthy, like loam.

I unconsciously straightened as I took another sip, no longer feeling so exhausted.

After I'd drunk half the cup, the gray-eyed girl nodded to one of the other servants, who brought forward a stack of clothes. "Some of the merchants have already arrived and are waiting to see you, Mistress."

Borund.

I stood, setting the cup aside on the bed. "Where are my clothes?"

The gray-eyed girl frowned and picked up the cup before it could spill. "Right here," she said, motioning to the second servant, who unfolded a white-and-gold dress.

I grimaced. "No, where are *my* clothes? The breeches and shirt I wore yesterday?"

"Oh! The Matron said we should remove them."

My eyes narrowed, and the gray-eyed girl took a tentative step back. "The Matron?"

"I-Ireen," she stammered.

I recalled Ireen's elation yesterday and suddenly regretted telling her she could do whatever she wanted.

"Find them."

The gray-eyed girl cast a terrified glance toward the girl holding the clothing. "We—we can't."

My eyes narrowed further. "Why not?"

The girl swallowed and seemed on the verge of bolting from the room. "Matron Ireen—" she began, voice tight, eyes wide, then finished in a low rush, head bowed, "Matron Ireen had them burned."

I drew in a breath to respond, then halted, too stunned to know what to say. "Burned?"

The girl nodded.

Anger flooded me. My hands itched for my dagger, but I managed to keep myself in check.

"Find me some breeches and a shirt," I said with suppressed rage. "And get rid of all these . . . dresses. Breeches and tunics, that's all I want to wear. Go to Master Borund's manse and get all my clothes from there if you have to."

"Yes, Mistress. Right away."

The girl backed off, dragging the servant holding the offending dress with her. They held a hissed conversation, punctuated by hand gestures, and then both girls nodded formally in my direction and fled the room.

I wondered how many of them were true Servants—girls who could sense and use the river like me, girls that could one day be the Mistress if they could learn to control the throne well enough. They were here because someone had noticed they had the talent and had brought them here to learn to use it. But because of that, they were as dangerous to me as Avrell and Baill.

A soft footfall sounded and I spun, eyes catching the last girl on the far side of the room. She stilled, tried a tentative smile and a small bow, then began a frantic and unnecessary rearrangement of the curtains.

I sighed and thought of Erick, suddenly wishing I hadn't sent him after Corum after all, that I'd sent one of the other Seekers instead. I was surrounded by people I couldn't trust; having him here would have given me someone I could rely on.

I scanned the room, the hollow feeling in my gut returning. With a small push, I let the Fire relax and felt the sensation of the city flow through me, let the voices of the throne rush forward. Not far enough to overwhelm me, but enough so I could hear distinct voices clamoring for attention.

I ignored them, focusing instead on the city. Closing my eyes, I reached out, wary of Eryn's warning about pushing myself too far. I thought of Erick, of how he felt when I saw him beneath the river, about his scent—sweat mixed with a tang of oranges.

After a moment, I sensed him in the city, somewhere on the Dredge, lost in the darker turmoil of the emotions of the people that lived there, that *survived* there. I smiled, the tension in my shoulders relaxing as I felt him moving, as I drew in the tang of orange that surrounded me.

Erick was hunting.

I felt a momentary urge to take my dagger and join him, escape from this palace with all its meetings and servants and guardsmen. For a moment, I gave in, let myself drift forward, heading toward the Dredge on the flows of the river, following Erick's scent, Eryn's warning forgotten.

But when the sensation began to stretch, when I could no longer feel a tenuous connection to my body, before the last threads broke, I pulled back.

The feeling had been glorious . . . and frightening at the same time.

I breathed in one last calming breath, then shifted my attention to the Dredge itself, to the seething roil of desperation. I couldn't pick out individuals, couldn't even narrow my focus down to a street, but I sensed that it was possible. It wasn't the same as stretching toward Erick, or even Reaching to find Corum as I'd done on the tower. I'd had a known scent to follow then, something concrete to focus on. Without that scent, the eddies and currents were a jumbled mess, too complex to separate. For now.

But I could sense the fear. The people of the Dredge were terrified. The tension on the river was palpable, a tension I recognized because I'd survived on the Dredge for so long on my own. Winter was approaching, and the Dredge would be the hardest hit. The people in the slums were worried about where their next chunk of bread or gobbet of meat would come from.

There had to be a way to help them, to feed them this winter and beyond.

I pushed the voices and the city back, let the river slide away with a sigh, and turned my attention to Borund and the merchants.

An hour later Marielle, the gray-eyed servant, led me through the palace to one of the sitting rooms, where Avrell, Borund, and two other merchants were waiting, talking animatedly. I heard their voices from two corridors away.

"—but look at what happened in the warehouse fires!" Borund spat, his voice easy to recognize.

"I realize that," Avrell countered, voice as slick and fluid as it had been during the meeting the day before. "But in the interest of organization and control—"

"It won't matter how well organized or controlled it is if some other disaster wipes out the remaining supplies. We cannot take the risk!"

All voices ceased as Marielle and I entered, all four men turning toward me with dissatisfied, angry frowns. With a faint twinge of surprise, I realized I'd already been in this room. Low tables and pillows were scattered among plants and a few latticework screens designed to provide small alcoves for private conversations. I'd hidden in one of those screened-off alcoves when I'd infiltrated the palace, had overheard Avrell and Nathem discussing the decision to kill the Mistress.

Once the merchants realized who had interrupted, their anger faded, replaced by cautious but curious frowns from the two merchants I didn't know, and a genuine smile from Borund. Warmth flooded through me at the smile, and I grinned in return. Borund was dressed in his formal red-and-gold merchant's coat and ruffled white shirt, the wire rims of his spectacles catching the light. He was mostly bald, skin shiny on the top of his head, but with gray-brown, wispy hair above his ears and circling around to the back.

"Varis," he said, rising to give a low bow at the waist. The others rose as well. "I mean . . . Mistress. May I introduce Merchants Regin and Yvan."

Both merchants gave stiff bows. They were dressed much like Borund, but with different colors: Regin wore a dark blue-and-gold coat, while Yvan's was cream-colored, with black embroidery. Yvan was fat, with cold, hard, intelligent eyes and a shiny, completely bald head. Regin was thin, poised, and had long, wavy, dark hair.

"Forgive me," Regin said, surveying my clothes. Marielle had found boots, breeches, and a white shirt that actually fit. My dagger was tucked into one of the soft-sided boots. "I did not recognize you, Mistress."

My eyes narrowed, but I couldn't decide whether he'd meant it as an insult or not. "What were you arguing about? And where are the rest of the merchants?"

"This is all that's left," Borund answered, then glanced angrily at Avrell. "And we've been arguing over where the supplies we have should be kept. I think they should be moved to various locations throughout the city, to protect them and to make it easier to distribute them once winter sets in. Avrell wants to store them in a central location."

"We can keep better control over the supplies and their distribution if they are in one location," Avrell countered. "The palace, for instance. It would be easier for the city and palace guards to protect them if they were not scattered throughout the city."

Borund snorted. "But look at the fire in the warehouse district. With one mishap, we lost close to half of our winter storage. Granted, most of it was Alendor's, but . . ."

"Alendor," I interrupted, moving forward to take a seat on one of the pillows, legs crossed so I could rest my elbows on my knees. "What happened to him?"

The merchants shifted uncomfortably where they stood, then slowly took their seats around me, along with Avrell. Marielle was nowhere to be seen.

"No one has seen him since the night of the warehouse fires," Avrell said. He cast me a warning glance to keep quiet, motioning slightly toward Regin and Yvan. Neither of them knew I'd followed Alendor into the warehouse district that night in order to kill him, to break the consortium of merchants he'd built up. The consortium had been buying up and hoarding the resources of the city to form a monopoly, killing off any competing merchants. Instead of killing Alendor, I'd ended up killing his son, Cristoph, and in the process the warehouse district had caught fire.

"Tarrence—and the merchants in the city that we know were part of Alendor's consortium—all scrambled to leave the day after the fire," Avrell continued.

"How do you know?" Borund asked.

"Once I knew who was part of the consortium, I had them watched by the city guard. I also have sources scattered both inside and outside the city. Tarrence, for example, was sighted yesterday south of here, in the port city of Kent."

Borund grunted with grudging respect.

"Is that all?" I asked.

Everyone stilled.

"What do you mean?" Regin asked, his voice tinged with condescension.

I bristled where I sat, turning my full attention on Regin. I noted his merchant's jacket had more gold embroidery than Borund's. Borund had told me once that the color of the jackets indicated what commodity the merchants had dealt in when they applied for membership in the guild—red for wine, blue for fish, cream for dairy—and that symbols in the embroidery indicated what they currently dealt in. More embroidery indicated a more powerful merchant.

Judging by his embroidery, Regin outranked Borund in the guild.

"Alendor tried to seize control of *all* trade within the city," I said, "tried to seize control of the merchants' guild, of all resources within Amenkor, including your own. He ordered the deaths of members of the guild itself, as well as merchants from other cities along the coast. Are you saying the guild isn't even searching for him?"

Yvan snorted, but it was Regin who answered, his voice laced with anger.

"Of course we're searching for him. The guild itself has condemned him and all of those that were part of the consortium. Their licenses to the guild hall have been revoked and all of their rights rescinded. In effect, they can no longer legally act as merchants, either within the city of Amenkor or any of the ports that recognize the merchants' guild as a power. Alendor's name means nothing. All connections to any trading houses along the Frigean coast are gone. He has been destroyed as a merchant. He's not in the city, and he has nowhere else to run to, nowhere he can expect safe haven, at least from the merchants' guild. What more do you expect us to do?"

Regin halted, his jaw clenched. Raw hatred blazed in his eyes, but it was not directed at me. Alendor's betrayal had cut Regin deeply. He wanted more than just Alendor's downfall. He wanted Alendor dead.

I drew back from Regin's gaze, glanced quickly at Borund and Yvan, saw the same rage in their eyes, then turned to Avrell.

"Is there anything else that can be done?"

"Outside of the city?" He thought for a moment, then nodded. "You, as Mistress of Amenkor, can contact the rulers of the surrounding cities and warn them of Alendor and his cohorts, ask them to use their own guard to watch for him and—if he is found—send him back to Amenkor for punishment. Those that we have good relations with at the moment—Venitte, Merrell, some others—will agree, and if they find him, return him to us." He hesitated a moment, then added, "You can also send the Seekers."

I straightened where I sat, but before I could say anything, he halted me with a frown.

"There is a risk in sending the Seekers after targets beyond the city of Amenkor. The rulers of the surrounding cities do not take kindly to having Amenkor assassins roaming their streets in search of citizens."

"Even for known criminals?"

"Even for known criminals. Sending the Seekers beyond Amenkor should only be done in an extreme situation. Since we don't even know in which direction Alendor may have run . . ."

He let the thought trail off and I grimaced.

"I want him found," I said, and heard more emotion in my own voice than I had intended. I could still hear Alendor's voice ordering Borund's death, could hear the cold, businesslike finality in it.

"He will be found," Avrell answered. "My contacts in all of the ports will keep their eyes open. He cannot hide forever."

Not completely satisfied, I turned to Regin. "What about the other ports? Have you sent word to them, warned them?"

Borund cleared his throat. "Our main form of communication with the guilds in other cities is through our ships. Since the harbor has been closed to trade . . ." He shrugged.

Regin picked up the thread. "We sent word overland, but that takes time. Now that the harbor is open again, the word will spread more quickly. The merchants' guild will keep its eyes open for Alendor as well."

I nodded. "And what of Alendor's—and the other merchants'—resources?"

"They couldn't have loaded everything up and left, at least not by ship," Avrell said. "The harbor had been blockaded by then. And taking everything by wagon or cart would have attracted too much notice. They must have left something behind. But I have no idea where they may have stored goods besides the warehouse district. That's a guild matter."

Regin stirred. "I believe we can search the guild records to see what property each of the members of the consortium owned. Then, perhaps, with the city guard's help, any stores left behind could be seized by the guild and allocated to the remaining guild members—"

"How?" Yvan interrupted. His voice was like stone grating against stone, rumbling from his chest as if from the bottom of an empty barrel.

"I don't understand—" Regin began, but Yvan cut him off.

"How are you going to allocate it to the remaining guild members? Evenly? By percentage of the share in the guild? By status? Does Borund gain more from the seizure simply because he owns more property than I do?"

"I'm certain that the guild can come up with a fair method of distributing what we seize." Regin's voice was laced with heat and an undertone of warning.

Unconsciously I slid beneath the river and almost recoiled at the blatant hostility I found seething on the currents. Hostility toward each other that had not shown in the merchants' faces a few moments before.

Yvan shifted forward, the motion requiring some effort. His voice was laced with suspicion. "Perhaps we should discuss that among the guild members before we attempt to seize any abandoned property."

"That," Regin declared, going rigid, "would be a waste of time."

The two locked gazes, both bristling, like two mongrel dogs on the Dredge preparing to fight over a rotting fish head. Yvan leaned farther forward, ready to respond. . . .

And another voice intervened, sliding smoothly along the currents of the river.

Take it. Take it all.

I tensed, my forehead creasing as I frowned. The soft, sibilant voice was barely more than a whisper, and with it came the heady scent of oak and wine. I breathed in the scent deeply, then halted.

The voice had come from the river, had come from the throne.

Pushing the argument between Regin and Yvan into the background rush of the wind, I dove deep, caught the scent again and followed it, down and down, until I came up to the edge of the spherical Fire at my core that kept the voices of the Skewed Throne in check. Through the white blaze I could sense a woman, the smell of oak and wine strong, constant. An older woman, her essence solid and consistent, removed from the rest of the maelstrom of the other voices. I could feel her holding herself together, resisting the pull of the rest of the throne.

Who are you? I demanded, but she ignored me.

Look at them. Her voice shook with contempt, with the effort to hold herself together against the chaos. *Look at them bickering. How petty.*

I turned back, saw Regin and Yvan arguing, Borund breaking in now and then, trying to calm them down. Both men seethed with aggression, both trying to gain the upper hand.

I felt a bubble of contempt well up inside me, acid with anger.

They're fighting over food, Varis. Over food that belongs to the city. Food that the city needs to survive. We won't last through the winter if they control everything. They'll hoard it, ration it, give themselves more and give the people of the Dredge less. They don't care about the gutterscum. They'd rather the gutterscum die.

The bubble of contempt rose higher. I could taste it now, the anger like ash in the back of my throat.

Behind the Fire, I felt the presence of the woman ease forward, closer to the white flames. They reacted, the wall of the sphere thickening, pulsing, but the woman didn't waver, didn't back off.

You're the Mistress, Varis, she whispered softly. *The city and everything in it is yours.*

The Fire thickened even more. Regin and Yvan were close together now, faces barely inches apart, eyes locked, both hard and unrelenting. Avrell sat back silently, watching, his eyes intent, calculating. Borund sat nervously, uncertain whether he should interfere more than he already had.

You can simply take everything, the woman said, voice low and reasonable, and so close now I could almost feel it, like a breath against my neck, cold and vibrant. *Let me help you, Varis. Let me out . . . so I can help.*

I snapped around.

"No!"

I forced the Fire toward her, eyes blazing, and the woman jerked back with a cry of fear and hatred. I'd startled her out of her carefully held control, and with a shriek of triumph the maelstrom of the throne took her, dragging her down as she cursed and screamed.

Within moments she was lost, trapped again by the throne, her scent mingling with all the others.

I turned back, a sheen of sweat touching my forehead, the palms of my hands. Avrell, Borund, and the two merchants were watching me, startled, and I suddenly realized I'd shouted out loud. And that the bubble of contempt and anger remained.

I glared at both Regin and Yvan. Regin drew breath to speak, but he never got the chance.

"Enough," I spat. The raw edge in my voice silenced everyone, forced Yvan to lean back in shock. I was breathing hard, almost shaking. But the woman, whoever she had been, was right. I *was* the Mistress.

"The guild will get none of the resources left behind by the consortium." Regin and Yvan instantly shifted forward to protest, but I cut them off. "Everything will be seized by the Skewed Throne, stored by the palace wherever I see fit, and protected by the city guard. That can be done?"

I glanced at Avrell for confirmation, suddenly uncertain, and he nodded once, abruptly, as shocked as the merchants. But Avrell was recovering already. I could see it in his eyes, along with approval.

"You," I said, turning back to Regin, "will provide the guard with a list of all of the properties owned by Alendor and the consortium, as well as lists of all the food you and the remaining merchants have stored in the city."

"But," Regin interposed, "the trade of the city has always been carried out by the merchants' guild."

"Not this winter."

"Mistress," Yvan began, voice as slick and reasonable as the woman from the Fire's had been, and just as false.

"No," I growled. "This winter the merchants will work with me so that everyone gets fed and survives to the spring harvest. Everyone." I switched my attention back to Regin. "Don't force me to seize more than just the consortium's property, Master Regin."

Regin halted, his eyes hooded with anger at the threat, but he backed off. Yvan did the same, reluctantly, with a low, dangerous grumble.

There was a moment of tense silence, then everyone turned at a clink of glass, movements sharp. Marielle stood uncertainly in the entryway, holding a large platter of food and drink. She bowed slightly, balancing the weight of the platter.

"I thought some food and wine would be appreciated," she said, glancing in my direction, eyes questioning.

I nodded.

As she went about setting up the food at the various tables, the tension in the room eased. No one spoke, Regin and Yvan watching me carefully, Borund glancing back and forth between them and Avrell. Avrell was subdued, hands folded neatly in his lap, his eyes hooded, deep in thought.

When Marielle came forward offering drinks, Borund coughed. "Mistress, I've brought the lists of my own resources within the city, as well as those I have stored in other cities that there is still time to reach before winter. As you requested."

He passed the papers to me, script neat and orderly on every page. But it was completely meaningless because I couldn't read.

I hesitated, staring down at the pages in my hand blankly. All of the confidence I'd felt a moment before fled, replaced by a sudden sense of inadequacy. A shudder ran through me, and I became aware of how Regin and Yvan must see me: a fraud. Gutterscum risen above her station. A street player, mimicking the Mistress.

The awkward silence in the room shifted. Both Regin and Yvan sat back uncomfortably. Borund suddenly realized his mistake and began to color.

Before the full horror could set in, I felt a hand against my arm. I jumped.

Avrell had leaned forward to take the papers. "Allow me, Mistress?"

I nodded and he took the papers, sat back, and glanced through each page, lips thinning.

After a long moment, he looked toward Regin and Yvan. "And your own reports?"

Both Regin and Yvan straightened where they sat, but said nothing.

"The Mistress did request that you bring a report with you today, did she not?"

"Yes, but—"

"I see."

Regin bristled. "It was not possible to get a full accounting in such a short amount of time."

Avrell blinked. "Are you telling me that one of the most powerful merchants—no, now that Alendor is gone, you are *the* most powerful merchant in Amenkor, are you not?"

Regin nodded.

"Are you telling me, then, that the most powerful merchant in Amenkor does not know what his own assets are on a day's notice? I find that impossible to believe, Master Regin. Most impossible." Avrell's eyes darkened, his voice tinged with anger.

Regin fidgeted where he sat, then exhaled. "A report will be sent immediately."

Avrell turned his stare on Yvan, who grumbled, "From my house as well."

"Good." Avrell shot a questioning glance toward me, but I had not quite recovered and motioned for him to continue. "Then we can turn to the real question: do we have enough to survive the winter? Taking into account all of the combined merchant houses and their resources, sparing nothing."

"And the fact that we must feed the entire city," I interjected, shooting a hard look at Regin. "*All* of it. Those on the Dredge included."

Regin frowned, glancing toward Borund and Yvan before turning back to me. I read the answer in his eyes before he spoke.

"No."

There was a collective, drawn-out silence. No one reached for their drinks, or the small plates of food Marielle had set beside each one of us as we spoke. Marielle herself stood silently beside the tray of food, her fingers drumming lightly against the side of the bottle of wine. Her eyes caught mine, wide and fearful. She bit her lip before turning away.

"How bad is it?" Avrell finally asked.

Borund stirred. "Right now, there's enough that the entire city won't starve, but not enough to feed everyone. I'd say we can feed half the population for the winter with what we have already stored in the city, making certain assumptions about what portion of Alendor's supplies remain. Some of what was lost can be replaced if we bring in whatever the fishing boats can catch over the next month, before the water becomes too hazardous to fish."

"What about the ships that have already left?" I asked.

Regin shook his head. "They're trading mainly for land goods—fruits, vegetables, salted meats, and grains. If all of them find trade goods it's possible that they will return with enough food to supplement what we have and last through to the early spring harvest, but we aren't the only city facing starvation this season. The autumn harvest was not good anywhere on the Frigean coast—too much rain in some parts, not enough in others—and the trade routes to Kandish across the mountains and to the other eastern countries were cut off."

"Why?"

"Heavy snowfall in the passes would account for some of it, but not all," Avrell said. He seemed as troubled as the merchants. "Something more serious has happened to the east, but we have had no word yet on what that might have been. None of our envoys have returned, and I've received no messages from any of my diplomatic sources. There was a certain amount of political unrest in the area in the last few years, especially regarding the aging emperor and his succession. It's possible that he has died and there is a succession war going on that has closed down the communication lines. But this is purely speculation."

Avrell's report was followed by silence. I knew nothing of the eastern cities.

Regin cleared his throat. "The ships we sent should return with some food, since each of us had some stored in other cities—"

"If the rulers of those cities haven't seized it yet," Yvan rumbled.

Regin frowned but continued as if he hadn't been interrupted. "However, I'm not certain how many new resources they will be able to find and purchase."

"Hopefully, it will be enough," Borund said, his voice low.

"When will we know?" I asked.

"I don't know," Regin answered. "The earliest the ships will return is sometime next week. We can expect them to arrive any time after that for about two weeks, but a month from now we can't expect any more to return. The seas will be too rough for safe passage. That's why it was imperative that the harbor be reopened now. It will take a month for some of the ships to reach their intended ports and then return."

Another moment of silence.

"Then send out the fishing fleets," I said abruptly. "Bring in as much fish and crab as you can. We'll determine how to distribute what we have later, once we have a full accounting from everyone, and once the ships have returned. In the meantime, I suggest we start rationing now."

Regin and Yvan took this as a dismissal, downing their glasses of wine quickly before exiting with perfunctory bows. Borund followed more slowly.

As he stepped to the outer corridor, he paused to give a respectful bow. "It is good to see you well, Va—" He caught himself with a self-deprecating smile. "Mistress."

Then he left. I watched his departing back and realized that things had changed irrevocably between us. I was no longer his bodyguard, no longer took his orders. But there was still an intangible connection between us. We'd always been uncertain of how to treat each other.

But his absence didn't hurt as much as Erick's.

Avrell sipped at his wine, set it aside slowly before turning to me. "You cannot read, can you?"

I felt myself harden defensively. "There's no need to read on the Dredge, and Borund never found the time to teach me."

"I see." Avrell reached down to collect the loose pages of Borund's report, not reacting to my anger. "We shall have to find someone to teach you. Perhaps Marielle?"

Marielle stilled at the mention of her name, a thread of fear coursing through the river. A fear associated with Avrell. But it was fleeting. Without a word, she turned back to picking up the plates and glasses the merchants had left behind.

"In the meantime," Avrell continued, "I can keep track of all of the reports and papers that you need."

I frowned. I didn't know how much I trusted Avrell—didn't know how much I trusted *anyone* yet, besides Erick and Borund. But there was no one else.

Avrell stood when I said nothing, gave a short bow, and then left, moving slowly. I watched his retreating back, then said softly to myself, "One month."

Westen, captain of the Seekers, was waiting for me outside the meeting room where I'd met with Avrell and the merchants. He stood leaning casually against one wall, body relaxed, arms crossed in front of his chest. The stance sent a shiver of recognition through me, rewoke the ache I'd felt since rising that morning.

Erick had stood that way while waiting outside my niche to give me a new mark.

When I hesitated, Westen pushed himself away from the wall and smiled. "I'd like to speak to you, if you have the time."

I was suddenly aware of the four guardsmen who'd fallen in around me. Without looking, I sensed that they were all Seekers, their presence too still, the tension on the river sharp and ready.

The hairs on the nape of my neck stirred. The palace guardsmen who had accompanied me to the meeting had been replaced.

"Do I have a choice?"

The corner of his mouth twitched, and he motioned me forward, falling into step beside me. "You are the Mistress. You always have a choice."

I snorted, felt the other four Seekers reposition themselves behind us. We moved deeper into the palace, passing open windows looking out onto gardens and through wide rooms decorated with trees and tables. We passed a few servants, all of whom paused and nodded or bowed their heads as I passed. Westen said nothing for a long while, content to simply walk beside me. But he never relaxed, the tension that all Seekers radiated never faltering.

When he finally did speak, his soft voice startled me. He'd said nothing at all during the meeting the day before, but for some reason, I'd expected his voice to be harsh, like the Dredge.

"Erick's told me much about you," he said.

Wary, I glanced at his face, at the dark brown hair, the dark eyes, the nose that had been broken at least twice. There was none of the deadly danger I associated with the Seekers in those eyes now. I felt myself relaxing. "Such as?"

He grinned. "He told me how you killed that man the first time he saw you, how you used the dagger to slice the cord wrapped around your neck, how you punched the dagger into his chest."

I snorted. "I didn't punch the dagger into his chest. The man fell on top of me. I was lucky the dagger was pointing up. And I puked after the man died."

Westen chuckled. "Everyone reacts differently after their first kill. Puking is not uncommon."

I frowned. That man hadn't been my first kill—and Erick knew that. He hadn't told Westen everything, then.

"He also told me how you helped him hunt for his marks in the slums beyond the Dredge," Westen continued. "How you eventually helped him kill them as well."

"Yes."

"And he told me of Bloodmark."

I halted at the tone in his voice and he turned to face me.

"What about Bloodmark?"

Westen was no longer smiling. "Bloodmark wasn't one of your marks, was he? He wasn't someone the Mistress had sent Erick to find, to judge?"

"No."

"And yet you hunted him down and killed him."

I felt a flush of shame course through me, old shame that I thought had faded. But this tasted fresh and bitter against my tongue. "He killed the baker and his wife—people who helped me survive the slums, who cared for me—for no other reason than to hurt me. He deserved to die."

Westen watched me closely, his eyes searching my face, then he grunted. "Perhaps. But back then it wasn't your decision to make, was it?"

He turned away, continued walking down the length of the corridor. We'd descended to the level of the courtyard and the main gates, but were on the opposite side of the palace. I didn't recognize any of the rooms. None of this had been on the maps Avrell had given me when I infiltrated the palace and was making my way to the throne room.

Reluctantly, I followed Westen as he emerged into an open room with darkened alcoves on either side, a door on the far side, and nothing else. The floor and walls were bare stone—no tapestries or banners, no furniture or potted plants. Tall metal sconces with bowls of burning oil at the top lined the walls, three on each side of the room.

Westen halted halfway to the far side, turning to face me. "But none of that

matters now. You are the Mistress, and I agree that Bloodmark needed to die."
Belatedly, I realized that the four Seekers that had accompanied us were gone.
We were the only two in the room. "What's more interesting is that Erick told
me he trained you. I'd like to see how much you've learned."

And with that, he drew his dagger.

I stopped, ten paces from the door, only five paces away from Westen. His
voice had grown even softer, and the dark dangerous glint that I recognized in
all the Seekers had returned to his eyes. I kicked myself for having followed
him, for allowing myself to be drawn into an unknown part of the palace, into
a room I didn't know how to escape. On the Dredge, such a mistake would have
meant rape at the very least. More likely death.

Or both.

"Go ahead," Westen said. "Draw your dagger. You are the Mistress, and
unlike Avrell or Baill or any of the other guardsmen, the Seekers are sworn to
the Mistress, sworn to *protect* the Mistress, not the city and the throne."

Angry at myself, I reached for my dagger, slid into a stance that made Westen
nod in approval, still uncertain what the Seeker intended. At the same time I slid
beneath the river, wrapped the currents around me, and reached toward the
Seeker captain. He held no malice, no hatred; he didn't intend to hurt me.

"You don't report to Baill?" I asked, and even before Westen answered, I felt
myself slipping into old rhythms, into old patterns that I'd learned while sparring with Erick in the back alleys and decaying courtyards of the slums of
Amenkor. I hadn't trained with Erick in over two years, hadn't faced a true
Seeker since then.

"No. The Seekers report only to the Mistress." He grinned slightly. "To you.
We consult with Baill as a courtesy. And even then . . ." He shrugged.

And then he attacked.

He cleared the five paces between us with a speed I never expected, faster
than Erick, faster than anyone I'd ever seen before, his blade flashing out and to
the side. I barked in surprise, lunged hard to the left, his dagger slashing through
the space where I'd just stood, and in the same movement I twisted, dropping
my weight down onto one hand and sweeping out with my foot in an attempt to
trip him, momentum and a push with my supporting arm thrusting me back up
into a crouch when my foot connected with empty air. Heart pounding in my
throat, breath coming harder, I pushed myself deeper into the river, felt the
textures of the room darken, tasted the burning oil on the air, the smoke and the
sweat and the blood. New sweat, but also old. The blood old as well.

"This is a training room," I murmured, my attention shifting back to
Westen, who crouched as I did a few paces away.

"Yes," he said, but he spoke in a distracted voice, his attention on me, his
eyes hard, measuring, judging. "For the Seekers."

Then he spun forward, his motions fluid, graceful, his weight perfectly balanced. As I parried, raising a hand to block his forearm, thrusting him away even as I sliced in tight with my own dagger, I found myself sinking deeper, found the room itself fading, until there was only Westen, only the subtle shift in stance, the liquid and deadly flick of his dagger, the movements of his arms, his feet, his body. He *flowed*, a slow and dangerous dance, closing in for a wicked cut, a sharp block, a vicious slash, and then away to circle, to watch, and then back again, smoother than Erick had ever been.

There was no sound except the rustle of cloth, a grunt, a gasp as a hand connected with chest or an elbow with a thigh. Sweat broke out in my armpits, slicked my arms and chest beneath my breasts, the white shirt Marielle had found for me stuck to my skin. My hair grew matted and clung to my neck in wet tendrils. And still Westen attacked, sweat sheening his own face, his eyes narrowing as he moved faster, his tactics changing, his thrusts aimed toward my chest at first, then shifting to my legs, then my back, testing me and withdrawing before striking again.

Then Westen closed in hard and quick, changing tactics yet again, one hand clamping around my free wrist and twisting me around, catching me across my chest with my own arm, pulling me in tight to his body, so that I couldn't move, my dagger arm caught in the strange embrace.

I spat a curse, breath heaving in and out through clenched teeth.

I felt Westen shift, but not enough for me to break free. His breath cooled the sweat of my neck as he leaned in close. He wasn't even breathing hard.

"You're only defending yourself," he whispered. "I want you to attack."

Before I could respond, his dagger snicked across my arm, slicing through cloth and scoring along flesh as he released me and he thrust me away. I hissed, in both shock and pain, stumbled to a halt and stared down dumbfounded at the beads of blood welling in the rent of cloth, staining the fabric in bright little circles.

A scratch, nothing more, the blood already congealing. But during all of the sparring with Erick, he had never intentionally drawn blood.

"But . . . I'm the Mistress," I hissed, shooting Westen an angry glare.

He shook his head, face deadly serious. "Not here. Here you're only a Seeker. Now attack!"

Anger flaring, I slid into a new crouch. Westen responded, circling. Vaguely, I sensed others in the room now, hidden in the darkness behind the alcoves, watching. But I ignored them, focused exclusively on Westen, watched his muscles as they tensed and relaxed, watched his eyes as they watched me.

I lunged forward, not as graceful as Westen, not as smooth, but I had the river and I used it. Pushing along its flows, I saw where Westen intended to shift, saw his movements before he made them, before his muscles even flexed, tasted his blade as it arced through the air, every motion distinct and brittle under the gray glare of the river. My blade flicked in hard and sharp, caught nothing but air as Westen twisted, but I brought it back in tight again, shifting my grip, and felt it catch cloth. Westen barked out in surprise, even though I knew I hadn't touched skin with the blade, couldn't taste the blood on the river, and in the moment of his distraction the palm of my empty hand slammed into the joint of his shoulder.

He staggered back, his arm hanging momentarily limp, his dagger falling from his hand and clattering to the floor. Even as he recovered, slipping into a new stance, his empty dagger hand flexed, fingers clenching. The numbness was already wearing off, so I pressed my attack, hoping to take him down now and end this while he was defenseless.

But even as I closed in, he grinned, as if he knew what I was going to do, and the next thing I knew his other hand punched forward and struck me in the gut. All strength fled from my legs, and I dropped to my knees with a sharp cry, my dagger forgotten as pain flashed upward from my stomach, hot and visceral. One arm still twitching back to life, he twisted my dagger hand up behind my back with the other, my own hand going numb, and I heard my dagger clatter to the stone floor.

Both of us gasping, Westen once again behind me, my hand throbbing with pain in his grip, he chuckled.

"Erick taught you many things, but you still have much to learn."

He waited, the heat and intensity of the fight bleeding out of the room, out of our bodies. Then he let my hand go.

I sagged forward, coughed as I relaxed enough to taste the acrid smoke in the air, my throat dry.

Then Westen stood before me, one hand extended to help me up. His eyes were bright.

"I look forward to training you in the ways of the Seeker, my Mistress," he said, and then he grasped my hand and pulled me to my feet.

I followed Borund as we approached the throng of angry people outside the closed doors of the gates to the inner ward, eyes scanning the crowd as he pressed ahead, shoulders tensed as I tried to stay close, my hand on my dagger, the river pulsing around me. But no one seemed interested in Borund, and no one seemed interested in me. I was just his bodyguard. Everyone was focused on the guardsmen at the gates, demanding answers, demanding to know why the harbor had been shut, why their ships and cargo were being kept in the city.

Someone shoved me into Borund's back and I hissed, apprehension rising as the angry crowd pushed closer. I barely had enough room to wield my dagger to protect Borund if necessary and felt sweat break out between my shoulders.

I was about to grab Borund's shoulder and pull him back when he turned and swore, eyes blazing.

"We'll never get into the palace. They've closed the gates, and this crowd isn't likely to disperse any time soon. Damn! I need to know what's going on!"

I drew breath to suggest retreating to the guild hall, feeling as if I'd done this all before, the sensation prickling along the nape of my neck, but a boy with a round face and dressed as a dockworker stepped from the crowd. When I saw him, my uneasiness grew, my hand falling to my dagger. But the boy was gray. Harmless.

Yet I felt I knew him, even though I'd never seen him before.

"Master Borund?" the boy asked.

Borund frowned. "Yes?"

"Avrell, the First of the Mistress, would like to see you," the boy said. "He said to give you this."

The boy held out a chunk of stone, the outline of a snail embedded in one side.

Borund drew in a breath sharply.

We followed the dock boy through the edge of the mob, at first heading toward the gates, then angling away, passing into a side street running parallel to the palace wall. We passed no one, the buildings mostly vacant.

A cloud drifted overhead, the bright sunlight fading to a dull gray. I shivered.

The boy ducked into a small building that had once been a stable. The reek of manure still clung to the musty air inside, but there were no horses. Instead, the building was packed tight with marked crates, straw poking out through the cracks between the wood.

Borund gasped as the dock boy led us into a narrow space between the stacked crates. "Capthian red! Crates of it! I haven't been able to get this since last winter, not a single crate!"

Irritated, the boy motioned for us to hurry, and I felt tension crawl across my shoulder blades again. As if I were missing something. Something important. I shrugged it aside as the narrow path between the crates turned, branched once, then opened up into a small niche that barely fit the three of us hunched over. The dock boy shoved us out of the way, then pulled at a chunk of the plank flooring. A section lifted upward, cut with a ragged edge so that it couldn't be seen when set in place. I stared down into the rounded opening below. I could see that it dropped down into a thin tunnel, even though there was no light.

Borund hesitated, glancing toward me for confirmation.

"It's safe," I said. "It drops down to a tunnel. There's no one down there, and I can see a lantern ready to be lit."

Borund nodded and managed to lower himself down into the hole.

The dock boy stared at me the entire time.

"How did you know there was a lantern?" he finally asked. "It's too dark to see it."

I didn't answer, simply dropped down smoothly after Borund as he moved to light the waiting lantern. Then I turned, expecting to see the dock boy staring down at me through the circular opening.

But it wasn't the dock boy anymore. It was Eryn.

I shouted, lunged in front of Borund to protect him, drew my dagger without thought, the weight of the blade heavier than usual.

At the edge of the tunnel's entrance, Eryn's face darkened into stern concern, eyes tight, lips thin. She knelt at the edge of the hole, hands gripping the edge of the entrance tightly, the motion sharp and urgent.

"Do you see, Varis? Do you see?"

Then the lantern flared to life behind me, yellow light pulsing outward in a blinding flash, and I jerked awake.

I gasped and flailed in the bedsheets, heart pounding. But then I recognized the room, realized I'd been dreaming, and collapsed back onto the tangled sheets, breathing shallow and fast.

Slowly, my heart rate slackened, and my breathing eased. When I felt calm, I slid out of bed and padded to the dressing table to pour myself some water, moving through the now familiar room without pausing, wincing only slightly from the bruises I'd received the last few weeks while training with Westen. Washing the sour taste of sleep from my mouth, I drifted to the balcony, letting the doors swing shut behind me.

Staring out over the darkness, I frowned. This was the third time in the last three weeks that I'd had the same dream. Except that it wasn't truly a dream. It was a memory, from when I'd been a bodyguard for Borund. I remembered it clearly, heard the bells tolling in the harbor as word was spread that no ships were to leave the city, felt Borund's rage that the Mistress would dare do such a thing. We'd tried to go to the palace to find out why, but the gates had been sealed. Then the dock boy had shown up and taken us to Avrell.

The first two times I'd relived the memory as I slept, nothing had changed. We'd entered the tunnel, crawled through the passages to the palace. And then the dream had ended.

But this time, Eryn had appeared.

I hadn't thought much about the dreams before. But now . . .

I shivered and stood straighter, rubbing my upper arms for warmth. The night air was sharp. In the three weeks since the meeting with Avrell and the merchants, the signs of winter had become more obvious. The air had gotten colder, the daylight thinner. The vines of the plants on the balcony had begun to turn brown, some of the leaves dropping to the floor.

And the day before, Marielle had pointed out across the harbor to the barely discernible waves of the ocean. "See?" she'd said. "There are more white-caps now, no matter how the wind blows. And the spray of the waves pounding against the rocks is higher."

I glanced down at the wharf in the moonlight, counted the masts of the ships at dock, and frowned in thought.

Since becoming Mistress, I'd settled into the steady pattern of the palace, become familiar with the eddies and flows of the guardsmen, of the servants and the supplicants from the city, with an occasional break—never announced, always at random—when Westen would appear and escort me down to the training room. Avrell had guided me through the first few rough days, when I'd been forced to see and hear grievances from the people of the city and the guilds and then asked to make a decision. At first, such grievances had occurred every day, but as the days edged toward winter, they slowed to a trickle.

At one point, Avrell had muttered that we were fortunate I'd taken control of the throne at the beginning of winter. When I'd asked him why, he'd said that there were few envoys and delegations from the surrounding cities during winter. Everything of major political importance had already been settled, and he'd have time to familiarize me with the coast and all of its cities during the winter months.

I'd scowled at him in annoyance. I already disliked dealing with the squabbles of those in the city. I didn't want to think about dealing with the entire coast. He'd already started tutoring me, though, a few hours a day spent discussing the other city-states along the coast—Venitte, Marland, Temall, and Merrell—as well as the Kandish cultures to the east and the Zorelli to the south.

And then there were the dreams—of murders, of rapes and killings and mutilations—most of which occurred in the slums beyond the Dredge. I sent out the Seekers when I could, just as I'd sent out Erick to find Corum. But a few of the dreams hadn't provided me with enough details—a face, a place, a name—to send someone searching. In those cases, there was nothing I could do except remember.

But this dream was different. I wasn't living someone else's life as it was ended or as they were hurt. This was a memory.

Except this last time, at the end, it hadn't even been that.

A few hours later, dawn's light just beginning to break the horizon behind me, I heard a cautious step on the balcony and turned to find Marielle holding out a cup of hot tea.

"Mistress."

I took the cup, shivering in my shift. Below, beyond the three stone walls that surrounded the palace, the streets of Amenkor were coming alive. I watched the movements of the people as I drank deeply, then sighed, turning away.

"I want to speak to Avrell."

"Shall I have him summoned?" Marielle asked as we stepped inside, motioning sharply to the other girls in the room. They began arranging my usual clothes, one moving to pull back the sheets on the bed. I watched intently as the sheets were stripped off, wadded up, and new sheets laid down. I suddenly realized I'd never made a bed before, never even seen it being made by someone else, not even here at the palace since I'd taken the throne. At Borund's manse, it had always been made when I'd returned, and on the Dredge I'd never had a bed.

"No," I said, distracted, watching the servant work. "I'll go to him."

"Very well, Mistress."

When I turned around, Marielle and the girl presenting my clothes were trying to suppress smiles.

I growled and grabbed for my shirt.

I found Avrell in a section of the palace I'd never seen, hunched over a table with a slanted top covered with parchment, Nathem at his side. His hands were stained with ink, and his brow was furrowed in concentration. One hand trailed down a column of numbers, and he mumbled something to Nathem under his breath, the creases in his brow deepening.

I hesitated a moment, then asked, "Where are the ships?"

Both Nathem and Avrell glanced up, Avrell's eyes darkening briefly at the interruption before he recognized me. Leaning back, he stood and stepped out from behind the desk with a small smile.

"Mistress, you did not need to come down here. If you needed me, I could have come to you." He noticed the ink on his hands and folded them together, hiding them in the sleeves of his robes.

But then you would have had time to prepare, I thought.

Behind him, Nathem began shuffling the papers, discreetly continuing whatever they'd been working on.

"I needed to get out of my rooms," I said, and began pacing restlessly. "Regin said that most of the ships should return within the month. We're already at the end of the third week and there are only three ships at the docks. Where are the others?"

"I don't know."

I paused, hearing the undertone of concern in Avrell's voice. Concern that he was trying to hide.

He shifted back to the table, impatiently waving Nathem to the side, tapping the papers he'd been reading. I glanced down at them, but could only pick out a few letters and numbers. Marielle had been working with me on a daily basis, but

I had no patience for such things. I fought back a surge of frustration. I didn't like having to rely on Avrell, didn't like having to rely on anyone for anything.

"These are the reports from the captains of the ships that have returned," Avrell said. "The first two are from Marlett and Dangren, both towns within a few days' sail north of here. The ship that returned yesterday came from Merrell, much farther up the coast, also north of Amenkor. All of the captains report rough water, and all three of the cities are in the same condition we are: short on food and supplies for the winter. However, none are worse off than we are. Most have sufficient grain and other essentials for the winter, and a few have some to spare. After some heavy bartering and with quite a few favors called in, all three ships managed to return with at least three quarters of their holds full."

"What of the other ships?"

Avrell shook his head. "Nothing, not even a message returned by land." He caught my gaze. "We should have heard back from them by now, even if it was to say they were caught in port by the seas or storms. But we aren't the only ones who've lost contact with their ships. Both of the captains from Merrell and Dangren said that ships have vanished from those cities. The most common explanation is piracy and early winter storms." His voice was tinged with doubt.

I began pacing the room again, Nathem shifting out of my way. "But you don't believe that."

"No."

"Why not?"

Avrell's eyes darkened. "Piracy rises when food is short, but not to this extent. And ships and their crews don't vanish completely without sign, by storm or by piracy. Wreckage or bodies would wash ashore somewhere. We've heard nothing from any of the small villages and towns along the coast concerning raiders or unexplained debris from destroyed ships."

I paced silently for a moment, Avrell watching.

"So where do we stand on resources for the winter with what Alendor and the consortium left behind and what these three ships have brought back? Along with what the fishing boats have harvested."

"With strict rationing, we can feed perhaps three quarters of the city now. No more."

I swore, Avrell raising an eyebrow at my vehemence. Even Nathem seemed surprised, coughing as he pulled out a second sheaf of papers and began working at another table.

"There is some good news," Avrell said. "Merrell has promised to send a shipment overland, but there's no telling when it might arrive. Perhaps not till spring. The roads between Amenkor and Merrell are not good even in the summer. But the grain they've already sent will be helpful."

"So," I said, halting. "What can we do?"

"Hope more ships arrive," Nathem deadpanned, without looking up from his own papers.

I frowned at him in annoyance, then bit my lip in thought.

Avrell straightened almost imperceptibly under my steady gaze. "What is it?" he said, voice guarded.

For a moment, I considered telling him about the dream. But then I recalled his face the night he and Borund and Erick had convinced me to attempt to kill the Mistress, saw his eyes.

I wondered if he was lying to me now, holding back supplies. But why? He had more invested in Amenkor then I did. He'd only be hurting himself. And I knew he wouldn't hesitate to replace me if he didn't like my decisions. He'd already attempted to assassinate Eryn, a woman he'd aided for years. He barely knew me.

Except that we both knew he would never succeed. He'd tried to place other Servants on the throne before resorting to me, and they'd all died. No one else could control the throne and survive.

And besides, I'd been trained as an assassin. He'd never get anyone close enough to kill me. The throne would warn me that they were coming, and I had my own skills, learned on the Dredge and now being expanded by Westen, to keep me alive after that.

I growled, shoved away the useless doubts and mistrust. "I need to get out of the palace."

The words came out more heartfelt than I'd intended.

Avrell hesitated, then said, "Of course. You've been inside the inner ward since you seized the throne. You're used to having the run of the city." He paused. He knew I was holding back something, but he couldn't determine what it was. "I'll arrange an escort."

He moved to the door, where my usual escort of four guardsmen waited outside. His hand had just fallen on the handle when I said, "I'd like you to come with me."

He stilled.

"Of course," he said in a neutral voice. Then he opened the door and said something to the guards outside.

An hour later, I stepped out of the main doors to the palace onto the wide stone steps of the promenade. They descended down to a circular courtyard where an escort of ten guardsmen and two Seekers waited on horseback, two other riderless horses saddled and ready near the front. The two Seekers nodded in my direction with cool smiles—I'd sparred against both of them under Westen's watchful eye—and the other guardsmen nodded as well, with obvious respect.

I frowned. Westen had said word that I'd disarmed him during our first match was spreading among the guard.

Avrell came up behind me, his blue-and-gold robes replaced with a fine blue shirt, leather breeches, and boots. He looked strange in the new clothes; I'd only ever seen him in the First's robes.

"Are we ready?" he asked.

"I don't know how to ride a horse," I said.

Avrell paused. "I see. Then I suppose we'll have to go on foot."

He motioned to the lead guardsman, who issued a curt order. All of the guardsmen hesitated, glancing at each other in confusion, then slowly began to dismount. When Avrell and I descended the last few steps of the promenade and headed for the gate, they formed up around us.

The first thing I noticed was that I was at least two hands shorter than any of the guardsmen or Avrell. The second was that they formed a tight group. I suddenly understood why Eryn had slipped away unnoticed on occasion, causing Avrell, Baill, and the guardsmen so much grief. They'd thought it was her madness, but I began to wonder. Having an armed escort all the time, even in the halls of the palace, became tiring.

We passed out through the inner gates into the middle ward, the entire group pausing just outside the gates.

I drew in a deep breath, smelled the sea salt on the air, a weight lifting away from my shoulders. I hadn't realized how confined I'd felt inside the palace. The sensation of openness enveloped me and I grinned. This was the Amenkor I knew: the streets, the alleys, the narrows.

The people.

A small crowd huddled around the gates waiting to get in, mainly servants and guardsmen, a few men and women that my gutterscum eye marked as easy, rich targets. They turned to look, curiosity mingled with suspicion lining their faces.

After a long moment, a few heads bent together and the suspicion faded, replaced with awe. A few pointed toward me, and I suddenly felt uncomfortable.

On the Dredge, and working as Borund's bodyguard, I'd always faded into the background, become gray. I'd depended on not being noticed, never being seen. But now . . .

I turned away from the gawking faces, from the sudden flurry of noise as word was passed down through the crowd, like a ripple on water.

Avrell grunted.

"What?" I asked, not looking toward the group.

Avrell glanced at me, then turned to survey the crowd, back straight, head held high. In the shirt and breeches he seemed somehow more . . . regal, more arrogant and severe. "News that there was a new Mistress flew quickly through the city," he said, turning back to me, "especially after you lifted the blockade. But no one knew who you were. It took them a moment to realize *you* were the new Mistress because the Mistress almost never leaves the palace. And when she does, she's always either ridden a horse or left by carriage. You'll have to learn to ride eventually." He glanced at me, scanning my clothes. "I'm certain they expected something . . . different."

I glowered at him, then turned back to look at the crowd. "Why are a few of them bowing?"

Avrell's eyebrows rose. "Because you are the Mistress, and most of the people of the city revere the Mistress. You are their liege, their protector . . . their god."

I shuddered, an emptiness opening up inside me. Uncomfortable, I turned away from the bowed heads.

"Let's go," I said, heading off to the right. The guard fell in smoothly around us.

"Where are we headed?" Avrell asked after a moment, his eyes darting down each street we passed, his brow furrowed in consternation.

"Wait." I didn't want to tell him, wanted to watch his reaction.

He sighed, but continued to scan the streets, perplexed.

I walked swiftly, turning down a few streets and alleys, but keeping the palace wall in sight. People moved out of our way, staring after us in confusion or awe once we'd passed, but I ignored them all, attention on where we were headed. I paused once, uncertain, but chose a street at random and reoriented myself once we'd reached the next cross street.

Twenty minutes later, the number of people on the streets dropped off. The buildings took on an empty air, windows blank, doors shut, some boarded up with signs in the window. The middle ward held all of the guild halls, housed some of the more influential merchants and their offices. But since the coming of the Second Fire six years ago—when the huge wall of White Fire had swept in from the ocean and burned its way through the city, leaving a small part of itself embedded inside me—the economy had slackened. Many of the buildings that had once held thriving businesses were vacant, the store owners and their employees now residing in the lower city.

Or the Dredge.

We rounded a corner and came upon the stable, the entire entourage halting.

"Do you recognize it?" I asked, watching Avrell's face closely.

Avrell nodded. "Yes. It's the building that houses the entrance to the tunnel beneath the palace wall. But why did you want to bring me here?"

"Who owns the building?" I thought I knew the answer already, but I had to be certain.

"The palace, of course."

I nodded. Avrell seemed as perplexed as when we'd left the gates behind. "Let's go inside."

I'd taken a few steps before I realized Avrell hadn't moved. "I don't understand what we're doing here," he said.

I sighed. "I have something to show you."

Avrell shook his head but followed.

The guardsmen pulled back the stable door and we stepped inside, the
smell of old manure and fresh straw sharp on the musty air. Avrell covered his
mouth with his hand and grimaced as he glanced around at the stacked crates
that filled the building. A narrow path led down the center to the trapdoor and
the tunnel.

"What did you want to show me?" Avrell asked, voice strained. He was
trying to breathe through his mouth.

"Look," I said, moving up to the crates.

Avrell squinted at the markings on the sides. "Capthian red," he muttered,
straightening abruptly. His eyes flashed. "We haven't had Capthian red in the
palace in six months. It's been almost impossible to find."

I eyed him carefully, but he was scanning the crates in confusion, shoulders
tight. I felt my suspicions begin to shift, turning away from Avrell, focusing on
someone else. "Then who does all this belong to?"

Images of the lists provided by the merchants' guild flashed through Avrell's
mind, I could see it in his eyes. Though his hand still clutched his nose and
mouth, he no longer seemed annoyed about the forced outing, or the smell.
Instead, his body was tense with concentration.

After a long moment, his gaze caught mine. "No one. None of the merchants reported owning any Capthian red." He glanced around at the number
of crates, stacked to the ceiling. "Not in such quantities at any rate."

He thought for a moment, then stepped closer, inspected the markings on
one of the crates. "There are no ownership markings on the crates either."

"Which means what?"

He stood, brow furrowed in confusion. "It means that this was smuggled
into the city. But who would smuggle in this much wine? Alendor? One of the
other merchants?"

I shook my head, a spark of anger igniting deep inside me, coloring my
voice. "The building belongs to the palace. Alendor would never have hidden
it here."

"Then who?"

I walked up to the nearest crate, glared at the markings on the side that were
still gibberish to me, and said with utter certainty, "It was the Mistress."

I turned at Avrell's shocked silence, my face hard.

"It was Eryn."

⊢ **Chapter 3**

"How?" Avrell spat.

"What do you mean?" I asked. We were moving down the corridor leading toward Eryn's chambers, the guard escorting us—reduced to the usual four now that we were inside the palace—scrambling to keep up.

"How did she smuggle it into the city? How did she find the contacts? How did she get the wine into the defunct stablehouse without me knowing? She's barely left the palace for the last three years. She *can't* leave the city."

I pulled up short. I couldn't tell what bothered Avrell more: that Eryn had managed to smuggle the wine into the city, or that she'd done it without his knowledge. But that wasn't what had brought me to a halt.

"What do you mean she can't leave the city?"

For a moment, Avrell looked puzzled, too intent on Eryn's betrayal, but then he realized what he'd said and his eyes widened. "Nothing. It's not important now."

Some of the anger I felt toward Eryn shifted to Avrell. I took a small step forward, my hand dropping to my dagger.

Avrell flinched, then, with a small shudder, took control of himself. His back straightened and the poise he usually showed erased most of the rage from his face. He became the diplomat I'd seen when guarding Borund, except now that I knew him better I could see flickers of the rage he'd suppressed in his eyes.

"The Mistress is tied to the throne," he said stiffly, "and the throne is tied to the city. Because of this, the Mistress can never leave the city."

"What happens if I try?"

"You'll die."

I clenched my jaw, nostrils flaring. "Of course."

I didn't understand why being trapped in the city turned my stomach. I'd never been outside the city streets, had lived on or near the Dredge until I was fifteen, and after that I'd lived in the lower city, guarding Borund. I'd never even been close to the city's outskirts, had never considered what lay beyond except in a vague way. What lay outside the city couldn't help me on the Dredge. Even Avrell's discussions of other cities, other places, seemed unreal—nothing more than words or stories.

But now I couldn't escape, even if I wanted to.

I shoved the thought aside and spun, continuing down the corridor to

Eryn's chambers. After a moment, I heard Avrell trying to catch up. At least now he was quiet.

Eryn had kept to the rooms Avrell had given her after I'd taken control of the throne, and I'd had no urge to seek her out. I still felt too unsettled around her, too off-balance. I didn't know if I could trust her after she'd manipulated me onto the throne, and so I'd ignored her, shoved her to the back of my mind, where she was a constant nagging threat. The only other time I'd seen her had been on the rooftop after I'd dreamed of Corum, and that confrontation had been strained.

I didn't slow as I came up to the outer doors to her chambers. I jerked them open before the guards could reach them, stalked into the waiting room, scanning it with one swift glance. A forest of potted trees, a few scattered chairs and tables, a settee, a door to the inner chambers.

With barely a pause, I headed toward the door. At some point, I'd slid beneath the river.

"Varis, wait—" Avrell began, but with a surge of power I shoved him back without turning, heard him grunt as the eddy struck, and then I was through, into the inner bedroom, the door cracking sharply into the wall.

A servant shrieked, dropped the linens she was holding with a soft *fwump*. "Where is she?" I asked.

With a trembling voice, the girl said, "The garden."

I frowned, but she pointed toward a curtained doorway, the door open, a slight breeze pushing the curtain out into the room.

I shoved aside the curtain and stepped out onto an open veranda of white stone, a little larger than my own balcony, with a small table and chairs. A wide stone balustrade lined with fat pots separated the veranda from the small private garden beyond. In the evening sunlight, the trees and trellised vines of the garden were vibrant, the white stone of the curving paths harsh to look at. I hesitated, let my eyes adjust, then stepped to the three stone steps leading down to the garden.

I didn't feel the wall of force at the top of the steps until I ran into it, too blinded by rage. I hit it hard, staggered back with a barked curse, tasted blood on my lip.

"What is it?" Avrell asked, catching my elbow to steady me. The guards fanned out behind us, eyes sharp, hands on swords.

I ran a hand across my mouth, grimaced at the smear of blood. "Eryn."

"I felt you coming."

Everyone turned, the guards closing in tighter as Eryn stepped away from a trellis full of wide white flowers I'd scanned a moment before. I suddenly recalled the throne room, how she had hidden right in front of me, emerging only after I'd refused to play her games. Or rather, the throne's games. A trick of the river that I didn't know how to use . . . or see through.

Eryn stepped into direct sunlight, turned a hard gaze on the guardsmen. "You can leave now."

The guards turned, then hesitated, uncertain, confused. They'd taken orders from Eryn for years. The instinct to obey was automatic.

After a moment, Avrell gave them a short nod and they retreated to the inner rooms.

I frowned in annoyance. They should have waited for a signal from me, not Avrell.

As soon as they were gone, Eryn turned to me. "Why have you come here? This is my retreat, my private garden. I want nothing to do with the throne now. I don't want to be disturbed."

I stepped forward, halting at the edge of the wall of force. "Why didn't you tell me about the wine?"

Eryn frowned. "What wine?"

"The Capthian red you had smuggled into the city without my knowledge," Avrell said, his voice acidic. "The wine stored in the stablehouse in the middle ward."

Eryn didn't answer at first. "Are you certain it was me?"

"Who else could it have been?" Avrell countered. "None of the merchants would have dared hide illegally obtained wine in a building owned by the palace, let alone a building containing a passage beneath the palace walls!"

"Some would argue such a building would be the perfect place to hide goods," Eryn said. "Why would we search our own buildings?"

"But they wouldn't have known of the passage," I spat, "wouldn't have stacked the wine so that the entrance to the tunnel would remain open. And if they had known of the passage, they wouldn't have risked the wine being found if the tunnel *were* used."

A troubled look passed through Eryn's eyes and her poise wavered, her gaze dropping to the stone of the garden's path. "I see."

Before me, the wall of force on the steps shuddered, then unraveled, rigid currents sliding back into their regular flows.

I relaxed, felt my pulse begin to throb in my cut lip now that my rage had been blunted. It hurt like all hells. "Why didn't you tell us about the wine?" I asked again, my voice calm but still laced with anger.

Eryn sighed and glanced back up, her eyes worried, watery and red, as if she were on the verge of tears. "Because," she said in a stern voice, "I don't remember smuggling in any wine."

Neither Avrell nor I moved.

"But you told me about the wine," I said, incredulous. "You showed it to me!"

"How?" Eryn said, stepping forward to the edge of the steps, so that Avrell and I were looking down at her. "How did I show you?"

"I dreamed I was coming to the palace with Borund, to meet with Avrell. We were following a dock boy, who led us to the stables and the tunnel. The first few times that was all it was, as if I were reliving the memory. But this last time, after we'd seen the crates of wine, the dock boy changed into you."

Both Avrell and Eryn seemed confused, staring at each other with furrowed brows.

"Could you have influenced her dream somehow?" Avrell asked, voice tinged with doubt. "Perhaps without knowing? We've never had two Mistresses alive at the same time before. Is that possible?"

But Eryn was already shaking her head. "No, I don't think so. The Sight doesn't work that way, and none of the previous Mistresses trapped in the throne had any knowledge of such a thing that I remember." She turned to me, frowning. "However . . ."

I shifted beneath her gaze. "What?"

Eryn sighed, her shoulders sagging in uncertainty. "It could be the throne itself. Or at least one of the personalities in the throne."

"What do you mean?" I asked, but I thought I already knew. The older woman who had smelled of oak and wine.

Eryn hesitated, glanced at Avrell, then moved up onto the veranda to the table and chairs, taking a seat. After a studied pause, Avrell moved to join her. I shifted to a place near the table, sitting back against the stone balustrade, arms crossed over my chest.

"The throne is a malevolent thing," Eryn said, her voice tired. She made a small motion toward the door and in the darkness behind the curtain I sensed the servant I'd startled before moving away. "All of those women—and a few men—all of whom at some point touched the throne and thus became a part of it, they all want the same thing: control. They know that they're dead—some of them have been dead since the throne's creation almost fifteen hundred years ago—but there is always the temptation to gain control, to seize it if necessary. If they can overpower whoever sits on the throne, then they can live again through that body. It's happened before. Someone ascends the throne, someone weak. Then the throne takes control, claims the power. In most cases, the person doesn't survive long after that. The throne itself overwhelms the inhabited person's body, destroys it."

I glanced toward Avrell, his mouth pressed into a tight, thin line. I had heard him talking to Nathem in the waiting room, had heard him describing how the women he'd tried to seat on the throne before me had died. I'd lived their deaths, in the moments when the throne threatened to overwhelm me, and I shuddered at the screams, at the memory of clawing my eyes out, of biting off my own tongue, of having my heart beat so hard and fast that it finally burst in a white-hot, searing explosion of pain.

And I remembered the meeting with the merchants, heard again the voice of the woman sliding through the currents of the river. She'd removed herself from the rest of the throne, fought her way free. And she'd wanted control, wanted me to give her control.

"But not all of those the throne took control of died," I said.

Eryn shook her head. "No. A few of them survived, overpowered by one or all of the personalities. In those cases, the new personality is subsumed, lost in the storm, and someone else takes over."

I thought of the throne room, recalled the voices echoing in its chambers the night I attempted to kill Eryn. A girl's voice, perhaps twelve, and an elder's voice, rough with spite and anger.

But in the end, Eryn had regained command. It was Eryn who had pushed me onto the seat of the throne. It was Eryn who gave me the choice to take control . . . or let the city die.

Eryn continued, "All of the women who have sat upon the throne before— and there have been at least two hundred—have had the Sight . . . what you call the river, Varis. And when the throne was first established, the Sight was enough. The Mistress could use it to build a barrier between her own person- ality and those within the throne. But as more and more people became part of the throne, that barrier had to be stronger and stronger, each new Mistress more powerful than the last. Not everyone who was seated on the throne had the power to master it, and those that didn't died. Close to a hundred have died in this way, most of them within the last few centuries. But we've reached an impasse. The throne has become too powerful for even the strongest of us with the Sight."

Eryn leaned forward, her eyes intent. "But there's something different about you, Varis."

I shifted uncomfortably.

"I sensed it in the throne room," Eryn went on, voice soft. "A Fire. A White Fire, like a small ember of the Fire that burned through the city six years ago. It burns inside you, protects you from the voices when the Sight cannot."

Avrell stirred. "Is that why you chose her to be the Mistress?"

Eryn shook her head, never taking her eyes off me. "No. I didn't know about the Fire until the throne room. I only knew that Varis was the only one with the Sight in the city strong enough to have a hope of controlling the throne. None of the Servants here would have survived, not even Marielle. You know. You tried the strongest—Beth, Arrielle, Cecille—" Her voice grew rough and she halted, swallowed hard. "You watched them die."

I suddenly understood the fear I'd sensed in Marielle weeks earlier. She was a true Servant. If Avrell had not shifted his attention to me, she might have been thrust on the throne herself . . . and killed.

No wonder Marielle feared him.

My gaze fell on Avrell. "So you knew," I said.

He looked at me blankly. "Knew what?"

My back straightened. "You knew that I was never supposed to kill Eryn, that it was a trap, the assassination just a ploy to get me into the throne room."

"Yes."

I snorted in contempt, even though part of me was relieved. At least now I knew he'd wanted me to be the Mistress, that my ascension to the throne wasn't a complete surprise.

"It wasn't his idea," Eryn said. "But he did bring your presence to my attention. He noticed you when he first met with you and Borund, told me of his suspicions that you used the Sight. It was my idea to have you attempt to kill me."

"Why not just have me brought to the throne room? Order me there?"

"Because of Captain Baill," Avrell answered, voice thick with derision. "He would never have allowed it. His position was too strong with Eryn on the edge of madness. He would never have given that up."

"And because you would never have accepted the throne unless you were forced to," Eryn added. "No one willingly takes the throne. Not now."

I thought about entering the throne room that night, of feeling the presence of the throne stalking me, hunting me as if I were prey, and shuddered. No. No one would willingly take the throne. Not once they came into the throne room and felt its presence anyway. Even those trained for it, like the Servants.

Silence settled, interrupted by Eryn's servant bringing a pitcher of chilled water and a set of glasses. As the girl poured three glasses from the pitcher, she glanced toward me and I sensed her relief.

Relief that someone else had assumed the throne.

I frowned as the girl bowed her head and left, slipping silently through the curtain to the darkness of the inner room. I wondered if she would have been next.

Avrell took a sip of water. "How does that explain your appearance in Varis' dream?"

Eryn sat back with a small sigh. "Everyone is vulnerable when they sleep. Our defenses are weakest, our protective barriers thin. I think that one of the personalities in the throne penetrated Varis' defenses, enough to influence her dreams. At first, whoever it was probably triggered her memory, hoping that would be enough for Varis to realize that the wine was in the stable. But when that didn't work, they used something more direct." She paused. "They put my image in the dream."

"But why your image?" Avrell asked. "Why use you?"

Eryn grimaced. "I don't know." She gave me a long, considering look. "But maybe we can find out."

I straightened, a thin coil of unease uncurling inside me. "How?"

Eryn look a thoughtful sip of her water, set the glass down carefully.

"You have an advantage that none of the previous Mistresses have had, Varis: me. I know how to use the throne, know how to manipulate *its* powers as well as the Sight. I could show you how to search for whomever is influencing your dreams, perhaps even show you how to protect yourself from them using the Sight. None of the previous Mistresses had a living Mistress to aid them, to guide them after they took the throne. We all had to rely on the voices, had to determine which voices we could trust to help us and which to ignore. All on our own. And there *are* voices within the throne that you can trust, Varis.

"Let me help you," Eryn said, her eyes imploring, a tinge of desperation entering her voice. All signs of the regal, imperious woman I'd seen on the roof had vanished. "I could help you with the Sight, as well as the throne. Please."

Beside her, Avrell nodded to himself, his face intent, as if a problem he'd been wrestling with had been solved.

I hesitated, the coil of unease sliding deeper into my chest. If I allowed Eryn to get that close . . .

But I already knew my answer. I didn't want anyone influencing my dreams. The thought itself sent shudders down my back. It made me vulnerable, weak. And I did need help protecting myself from the voices in the throne. The Fire wasn't enough. The woman who had smelled of oak and wine proved that.

"We can try," I said, and I saw relief flash in Eryn's eyes. She smiled. The first real smile I'd seen from her.

"Good," she said, relaxing back into her chair as she took a sip of water.

"But first," Avrell said, suddenly all business, "the wine. You said you don't remember smuggling in any wine, but obviously you did. Did you smuggle in anything else? And how did you do it without anyone knowing?"

Eryn glanced toward me, her smile widening. "Now, Avrell, you don't expect me to reveal all of the Mistress' secrets, do you?"

He grunted, not finding it humorous. "Of course not. However—"

"No." A trace of steel entered Eryn's voice. "I won't tell you everything, Avrell. You've learned enough about the Mistress' powers today."

Avrell drew breath to protest but caught himself, stiffening beneath Eryn's gaze. "Very well."

Eryn turned back to me, her face serious now, the smile gone. "I smuggled in some food and had it stored in various places throughout the city."

"What and where?" Avrell asked, leaning forward.

Obviously irritated, Eryn replied, "Some cured meats—pork and beef mainly—grain, potatoes . . . all staples. But not enough to feed the city for the entire winter."

"But it's more than we have now," I said.

Eryn frowned. "What of the ships you sent out?"

I shook my head, and Eryn sat back heavily and bit her lower lip.

"But if you don't remember smuggling in the wine," I said, "then maybe there are other goods you smuggled in that you don't remember."

She nodded. "Or worse. We may find that what I do remember is not, in fact, true. At the end, the throne was too powerful. What I think I remember may have been delusions, thoughts brought on by the other voices in the throne, or perhaps even their own memories that I've absorbed as my own. That's why I didn't come to you earlier. I don't know what I actually *did*, and what I only *wanted* to do, or attempted to do and failed." A forlorn look passed across Eryn's face, harsh with pain and loss. "For a time, I believe I actually was insane."

No one spoke for a long moment. Then Avrell turned to me, concern for Eryn clear in his eyes. "Perhaps whoever touched your dream to show you the wine knows where the other stores are hidden."

I nodded in agreement, but my mind had taken a different path.

I looked up at Eryn sharply. "Why did you blockade the harbor?"

When Eryn didn't answer, I continued. "You smuggled goods into the city, were preparing for a harsh winter . . . so why did you block the harbor and interrupt trade, keep ships with supplies from entering, and force our own ships to stay here, unable to get more?"

Eryn shook her head. "I don't know. Ever since that cursed Fire passed through the city, I've steadily lost control . . . of the throne, of my power, of my mind. I don't understand much of anything I did in the last few years. It's all mixed up, with large sections of it just . . . gone. As if I'd lost part of myself somehow. Just . . . gone."

Avrell shifted uncomfortably at the desolation in her voice, caught my attention meaningfully, then stood. "We should attempt to find some of these hidden stores," he said quietly. I pushed away from the balustrade I was leaning against. "Perhaps if you could tell us a place to begin searching?"

Eryn rose suddenly as well, suffused with new energy. The conversation had changed her. Instead of the morose woman I'd encountered on the tower or found wandering her garden moments before, she was now vibrant with purpose. "I can do better than that," she said with a grin and a lifted eyebrow. "I can show you."

Eryn burst out laughing at something Avrell said as we were escorted by the palace guardsmen through the market square in the lower city. We'd come from the outer ward, where Eryn had led us to an old building on Lirion Street stacked with barrels of salted fish. Avrell had been shocked, had sent one of the guardsmen back to the palace to retrieve paper, a quill and ink, and a small foldable table so that he could record what we'd found. Immediately after the guardsmen had left, he set the remaining escort to counting the stores.

Now we were heading down to some warehouses along the River, near the meat market and stockyards. Eryn and Avrell had been talking animatedly since we'd left the palace.

I watched them from behind as we moved through the crowds at the edge of the market and passed into the streets beyond. They were talking about the city, about things that had happened years ago, problems they had resolved together while Eryn was Mistress, people they had met. People I'd never heard of, and events that had only affected the upper city, the real Amenkor, that had never reached the slums beyond the Dredge.

I felt a pang of . . . jealousy? Loneliness? Something deep in my chest, vaguely familiar. Like the yearning I'd felt whenever the baker—the white-dusty man, I thought, and smiled tightly—had reached out to touch me.

I wanted to be part of the conversation, wanted to share in the laughter, in the memories. But I couldn't. I'd been gutterscum back then, nothing more than a girl dressed in tattered rags hunched protectively over a half-rotted apple.

My mouth twisted into a scowl.

Ahead, Eryn gasped and said, "Do you remember when Alden came to the fete with that frilly lace thing around his throat?"

Avrell grinned. "He claimed it was the highest fashion in Venitte at the time."

"That's right! I'd forgotten!" Eryn's hand gripped Avrell's upper arm, a casual gesture. Avrell didn't react. "It turned out he'd gotten the thing from some 'captain' at the wharf." She snorted, shaking her head. "Just punishment, I say."

We reached the edge of the River and Eryn's hand fell away from Avrell's arm.

"Here we are," she said, turning back to look at me. A smile still touched her lips, but she'd straightened, back to the business at hand. "There should be cured meats in here."

Avrell nodded, the guardsmen already at the wide doorway. When the leader of the escort motioned them forward, we stepped into the shadowed interior.

The place was smaller than the ones I'd visited in the warehouse district while acting as Borund's bodyguard, support pillars reaching to the ceiling, the rafters dusty and filled with cobwebs. A dry mustiness assaulted my nose, and one of the guardsmen sneezed. Avrell raised one hand to cover his mouth, as he'd done at the stablehouse.

Other than the cobwebs and a few traces of straw, the warehouse was empty.

"I don't understand," Eryn said, her voice tight, her brow creased in confusion. "I remember having cured meats shipped here. Unless . . ."

She halted, all of the confidence she'd shown since we'd left the garden trickling away.

Avrell motioned to the guardsmen, who scattered through the warehouse, checking the far corners, a few ascending the stairs against the back wall to see if there was anything in the rooms above. The floor creaked as they moved around, dust sifting down through cracks between the boards.

Stepping forward as we waited, I circled the bottom floor of the warehouse. In the far corner, the dust had been disturbed, as if something had been stored in the warehouse recently, but had been moved.

I frowned, began wandering back to where Avrell and Eryn stood.

Both Avrell and I knew what the guardsmen had found before they returned. We shared a look, Avrell's lips pressed thin with concern.

"I know I had cured meat stored here," Eryn said, back stiff, voice adamant.

"But you said yourself you weren't certain whether the memories were yours or not," Avrell said soothingly. "It could have been someone else's memory, one of the previous Mistresses."

"No! I stored meat here. I *remember!*"

The guardsmen had all returned. The leader of the escort shifted uneasily as we turned. "There's nothing here now, Mistress," he said to Eryn. He winced as he realized his mistake, shot a horrified glance at me. "I mean, Eryn."

An awkward silence fell. Then Avrell stirred. "Were there any other places where you thought you'd stored supplies?"

Still troubled, Eryn shook herself and frowned in thought. "Yes, a few other places. The closest would be on the other side of the River, on the Dredge."

A sharp pain lanced down into my stomach and I stilled, my mouth suddenly dry.

I hadn't been to the Dredge since I'd killed Bloodmark and fled the slums. I hadn't even been to the far side of the River since then.

All eyes were turned on me, Avrell's filled with an unspoken question.

I shrugged aside the queasy terror in my gut, met Avrell's gaze, and said, "Let's go."

We left the empty warehouse behind, Avrell and I falling into step behind Eryn, the guardsmen fanning out around us. Curt orders were passed as we neared the Dredge and the stone bridge that arched across the River and the guardsmen closed in tighter around us, but no one else spoke. Eryn was intent, focused on where we were headed; Avrell seemed on the verge of speaking, but I shot him a glare and he subsided.

As we crossed over the bridge, my stomach knotted and my hand fell to my dagger. Without thought, I slid beneath the river, slid into old, familiar patterns with an ease that was sickening.

The Dredge had changed in the two years since I'd last been here.

We moved through streets filled with people—more people than when I'd last been here—their clothes worn, spattered with dirt and grime, some with tattered shoes or bundled rags covering their feet, but most barefoot. They moved slowly, shoulders hunched, heads down, arms held listlessly at their sides or clutched tight to their chests. A few carried bundles. A significant portion of them were foreigners—dark-skinned Zorelli from the south, Kandish with scraggly feathers entwined in their hair, Taniecians from the north with the blue marking of the Tear of Taniece smudged on their right cheek.

But it wasn't their clothes or their postures that tightened the knot in my stomach, that pressed something hard into the base of my throat. It was their eyes. They were empty, without hope, desolate and beaten. A few were harsh with anger, or hard with desperation, but mostly they were like walking dead, already lost and forgotten. And everywhere there was a sense of darkness, of decay, of buildings crumbling and streets narrowing—a crushing sense of oppression, as if the very sky were closing in.

I felt the pressure creeping in on me, closing off my throat so that I couldn't breathe, settling over me like a smothering blanket. My pulse quickened, throbbing in my temple, thudding in my chest. I tasted the Dredge, the grit and refuse harsh against my tongue, the scents of dampness—of rot and shit and malignant growth—cloying, stronger than it should be. All of the memories of my life beyond the Dredge crashed down on me at once, heightening the sensations, making them more real, more vivid, and infinitely worse.

I turned toward Avrell in horror. His eyes widened, and he reached toward Eryn to stop her, to turn us back, but before he could say anything, Eryn halted and said, "Here."

I choked back the overwhelming sense of the Dredge, forced myself to focus on where Eryn had pointed, to ignore the prickling sensation crawling across my shoulders and up my neck.

It was a building like all the rest on the Dredge, edges worn, windows bricked shut, so that the only entrance was through a doorway half filled with shattered stone and debris.

"Are you certain?" Avrell said, doubt clear in his voice.

"Yes," Eryn said, more confidently. "I can see the ward I placed on the door. There's something here."

And as she spoke, I saw the ward as well, saw the subtle currents of the river where they twisted into a pattern I didn't recognize near the heap of stone around the door and around the base of the building and windows.

But the pattern's intent was obvious. As I moved closer to the building, I felt the river pushing me away. I resisted it, came to a stop before the door beside Eryn.

"Let's see what's here," I said.

Eryn reached forward with one hand and the ward fell away.

I scrambled up over the debris, stone and dirt shifting beneath my weight, and heard Avrell and the guardsmen protest behind me. Three guardsmen followed me instantly, but I knew there was nothing dangerous inside the building. I'd already checked using the river.

"Is it empty?" Avrell asked, coming up to the opening.

"No," I said, and heard Eryn sigh with relief. "It's filled with crates. I can't tell what's in them."

Avrell climbed through the entrance, balancing carefully, grimacing in distaste. He brushed off his hands and eyed me carefully. "Are you all right?"

I nodded sharply. "I'm fine."

He shook his head at the obvious lie, then motioned toward the guardsmen, who began assessing the crates, one of them setting up the foldable table in the diffuse light coming through the doorway. "We don't need to stay here long."

I didn't respond, watched the guardsmen at work for a moment instead, then turned and crawled back out into the sunlight.

Eryn stood at the edge of the Dredge, a few of the guardsmen to either side. As I moved up beside her, she said, "We're attracting attention," and nodded toward the people on the street who were eyeing Eryn and the guardsmen warily. Most dropped their gazes and moved on quickly; others glared openly. One man with a clouded white eye hawked a ball of phlegm to the cracked stone cobbles before skirting those around us and disappearing down a darkened narrow.

"Guardsmen always attract attention on the Dredge," I said.

Eryn pressed her lips together tightly, and I felt the guardsmen to either side tense. Their hands fell to the pommels of their swords.

"Is this what it's like all the time?" Eryn asked.

I shrugged uncomfortably. "It's worse now than it was. It never used to be so . . . crowded. Or dirty this close to the River. The slums—the true slums—hadn't crept so far in this direction. I would never have come this far up the Dredge back then. There wouldn't have been any reason to." Glancing down the street, I realized that we were close to Cobbler's Fountain, where I'd meet with Erick when I'd found one of his marks, where my mother had brought me to play when I was six, before the Dredge had taken her.

I frowned, focusing on the people before us again.

We *were* drawing a crowd. A restless crowd.

The back of my neck prickled with unease and my hand gripped my dagger.

Murmurs began to run through the group, low at first, people muttering under their breath, but nothing more. I suddenly recalled the man with the milky eye, saw the derision on his face as he spat, saw his hatred.

I shifted my weight, settled into a defensive stance. "Get the others."

"But the First is not done," one of the guardsmen protested.

Before us, the crowd seemed to ripple, the murmur rising.

Far down the Dredge, something on the river shuddered. Someone shouted. The tension in the air spiked.

"Get them now!" I spat, and stepped forward, in front of Eryn, two guardsmen following my lead, shoving Eryn behind them, the other scrambling up over the debris and vanishing into the building.

"What is it?" Eryn asked.

I didn't answer.

Down the street, the shouting intensified and the river recoiled, fear and anger and retribution mingling sharply with the scent of sweat. The crowd—no, it wasn't a crowd anymore—the *mob* before us shuddered again, the angry faces at the forefront surging forward as if pushed from behind, then receding like a tide.

And then Avrell was there, the rest of the guardsmen closing in protectively on either side. At the same time the tidal surge of the mob pushed forward again, threatened to overcome the guardsmen at its edge, before pulling back and parting.

Into the opening left by the crowd strode a group of armed men.

The palace guardsmen stiffened. The leader barked out an order, and swords snicked from sheaths.

On the river I could taste the advent of blood, like copper. I breathed it in through my nostrils, my hand kneading the hilt of my dagger, and thought, *This is the Dredge. This is where I come from.*

But not where I belonged.

The group of men advanced, their makeshift weapons—half-rotted boards, a few knives, stones—at the ready. Only the leader of the mob carried a sword, his face twisted into a scowl of hatred, but the blade wasn't drawn. Not yet. His hair hung in lanky brown chunks below the shoulders, and his breeches and tunic were stained but not crusted with dirt like the others. A scar marred the sharp line of his jaw and his brown eyes blazed.

"What are you doing here?" he spat as he approached, halting a few paces away. His voice was low and rough with rage. The crowd's grumbling increased, a few men openly cursing. The old man with the milky eyes spat on the ground again a few paces behind him. "Get out! You don't belong here!"

The guards bristled, stepped forward with swords raised, but Avrell halted them with a barked order.

I drew in the copper taste of blood with flared nostrils, then shifted forward, stepped clear of the guardsmen to face the leader, my hand still on my dagger, the river tight around me.

"We're here," I said slowly, "to figure out how to feed you."

The man hesitated, the tension on the river wavering—

Then he burst into laughter. "Here to feed us!" he roared. He turned to the crowd. "Did you hear that! They're here to feed us!" The crowd responded with a roar of its own, half laughter, half angry derision. A roar that sent shudders through my spine.

Then the man with the lanky hair spun back. "And how do you intend to do that?" he hissed. All humor had left his eyes. There was nothing left but a deadly glint, cold and heated at the same time.

When I didn't respond, he snorted with contempt. "That's what I thought."

He'd already started to turn away when I asked, "What's your name?"

He halted. "Why?"

"Because I want to know."

He sneered, then hesitated, his eyes catching mine. The sneer faltered, became a frown.

Then he gave a mock bow and growled, "*Lord* Darryn, at your service," twisting the title with contempt.

My lips twitched and a few of those in the crowd chuckled, but when Darryn had straightened, I became deadly serious. I saw him jerk back as he caught my gaze again and I stepped into the opening, moving close enough to keep him off-balance.

"I am the Mistress of Amenkor," I said, loud enough so everyone could hear, and felt a surge of satisfaction as some of those gathered gasped, as Darryn himself blinked in surprise, "originally from the Dredge. And I *will* find a way to feed you."

Then I stepped back, turned to catch Eryn's eye, saw Avrell motion quickly to the guards, who began to force a way out through the crowd. The people of the Dredge refused to part at first, hesitant, their eyes on Darryn, but when he said nothing, did nothing, they grudgingly gave way.

When we'd worked most of the way free of the press of the bodies, Eryn moved up beside me.

"I replaced the warding on the building."

I nodded, afraid to speak. Tremors had begun to run through my arms and my hand trembled. I gripped the handle of my dagger to make it stop, turned my attention to Avrell.

"Did you get what you needed?"

He swallowed once, his face pale, his eyes wider than usual. "Yes. I think so."

"Good. Let's head back to the palace. I've had enough of the city for one day."

Eryn snorted, the sound weak.

I didn't stop trembling until we passed through the inner gates.

When Erick returned from his hunt on the Dredge, I was working with Marielle, huddled over a padded board, a piece of chalk clutched tight in one hand.

"You're pressing too hard," Marielle said. "You don't need to force the chalk into the slate. And you're holding it too tightly. No wonder your hand hurts after each session. Just relax."

I growled with frustration, shot Marielle a hateful glare which she ignored, then focused again on the black stone.

Marielle had drawn a few lines at the top and written letters between them, the writing smooth and fluid. Beneath, she'd drawn more lines, with the same spacing.

I'd copied the first two letters onto the second set of lines, my script shaky and jagged. I frowned at the attempts. "I hate this."

"You're doing fine," Marielle said, but I could hear the strain in her voice. "Try the next one. And this time don't press so hard."

I sighed, took the chalk in a death grip, and scanned the next letter. I bit my lower lip and concentrated, the room fading away behind me as I touched the chalk to the slate. I began a slow, careful curve, but it began to waver almost immediately. I gripped the chalk harder, but that didn't help. I felt sweat beading on my forehead.

When the chalk broke halfway through forming the letter, I barked in a half yell, half growl, "I can't do this!"

"Can't do what?"

Both Marielle and I shot a glance toward the door—Marielle's in relief, mine in irritation. Erick stood there, his Seeker's clothes stained with the Dredge, his eyes bright with laughter.

I grinned, then stood abruptly, shoving the slate behind me. "Nothing," I said.

Erick's brow furrowed and he stepped through the doorway. Eryn moved into the room behind him.

"I ran into her in the corridor and escorted her here," Erick said as he approached, voice low. He paused, caught my shoulders and held my gaze, expression suddenly serious. "It's done. Corum's dead."

I straightened, regret leaving a bitter taste in my mouth. Regret that I hadn't killed Corum myself, not regret that he was dead. But even that regret faded, washed away by the metallic taste of rainwater, leaving only a sense of rightness, of balance and satisfaction.

Erick watched me closely, then nodded in approval, letting his hands drop from my shoulders.

"What about those he had working for him?" I asked. "The other gutter-scum he was using as slaves?"

Erick's face turned grim. "Most of them scattered when the guardsmen raided the building where he had them working. They're back in the slums beyond the Dredge. A few didn't have anywhere to go or were too weak to run. The guardsmen have them right now, down in the barracks. A healer is check-ing them for disease and wounds."

"And what happens to them after that?"

Erick shrugged. "We let them go."

"Back to the slums," I said bitterly, "where they end up with someone else like Corum."

Erick shifted uncomfortably. "What else can we do with them?"

What could we do with them? I didn't know. But there must be something. I couldn't get Darryn's face—his contempt, his hatred—out of my mind.

But he'd let us go without harming us.

"So . . ." Erick said, his voice too casual, "I hear that you disarmed Westen in your first match."

I snorted. "And then he brought me to my knees, my arm twisted up behind my back. With one hand."

Erick didn't laugh. "No one's ever disarmed Westen in a bout before, not since he became captain of the Seekers."

I hesitated, hearing the serious note in Erick's voice. "I cheated," I said fi-nally. "I used the river."

His eyebrows rose. "That's not cheating. And the Seekers have let the palace and city guardsmen know. You shouldn't have any problems with the guard after this. If they doubted your ascension as Mistress before, they don't now."

I didn't know what to say, a strange sense of exhilaration filling me at the pride I heard in Erick's voice.

"You're also the talk of the Dredge," Erick added. "I don't know what you did yesterday, but it certainly caused a stir."

There was a hint of disapproval in his voice—probably over the fact that I'd confronted Darryn personally—but before I could answer it, someone coughed lightly and Erick stepped aside, revealing Eryn, the moment broken. She had halted three steps into the room, her hands folded before her, her black hair loose, spilling down her shoulders, stark against her dress.

"If you're ready," she said. "I thought we could try to determine who is in-fluencing your dreams today."

I frowned, stomach tightening into a knot. Setting aside the slate, facedown so that Erick wouldn't see it, I nodded to Eryn. "What do you need me to do?"

Eryn hesitated, then seemed to steel herself. "I think it would be best if we tried this in the throne room."

I froze, eyes going slightly wide. The tension in my stomach doubled and I swallowed, hard.

I hadn't been to the throne room since the night I'd taken control, had been avoiding it completely. My only concession had been to issue an order to have the damage done to the doors by Baill and his guardsmen that night repaired.

"Very well," I said weakly.

Eryn turned to lead the way into the hall.

I shifted, caught Erick's eye.

"I'll come with you," he said.

I felt better instantly.

The entrance to the throne room wasn't far from my chambers. The three of us halted before the iron-bound, wooden doors, the wood gleaming with an inner warmth. The soft curves of the ironwork were delicate yet formidable, newly wrought after Baill and the guardsmen had ripped the doors from the walls trying to gain entrance to the throne room almost a month before. I could still hear the iron hinges clanging to the marble floor inside, could hear the crack of the wood as it split under the battering ram. I remembered standing outside these doors that night, knowing that the Mistress waited for me inside, that the throne waited for me, and that it was a trap.

I felt sweat break out on my palms, felt nausea rising as Eryn hesitated. For a moment, we shared a look, and I saw in her eyes the same apprehension I felt.

Then Eryn nodded to the guardsmen who opened the doors with a ponderous creak of new wood and the faint squeal of new hinges.

Eryn and I stepped into the room together, Erick a pace behind. A long walkway led up to a tiered dais, thick columns rising to either side. Every torch and sconce of oil in the room had been lit. There were no darknesses, no places to hide. And at the end of the walkway, on the dais, sat the Skewed Throne, a white-and-gold banner covering the wall behind it.

It was just as I remembered. A twisted thing, its shape shifting before my eyes, at one moment a high-backed seat of stone with flat square arms, the next the stone warping, the seat molding itself to a new form: a simple chair, but with one leg shorter than the others. And then it would twist again, shifting fluidly, the motions sickening and silent, straining the eyes. A long divan; another square throne but with etched scrollwork and no arms; a river-worn rock.

But it was always stone. Cold, hard granite.

I shuddered, turned away. Before, I'd felt the power of the throne throughout the room, stalking me, a predator circling me, hunting me as I hunted for Eryn, my only protection the Fire inside me, and the river, holding it at bay. But now the voices were a part of me, and I felt them respond to the presence of the throne. Their shrieking increased, harsh with anticipation, with expectation.

With a conscious effort, I strengthened the Fire holding them back, felt a surge of hatred in return.

"You must sit on the throne," Eryn said, her voice steady but weak. We'd moved to the bottom of the dais, and I could see that she would not move closer, would not risk touching the throne again. Any qualms I'd had about having her there, so close to the throne, so close to seizing power again, faded. She feared the throne as much as I did; perhaps more, since she knew what it was capable of, knew what it could do.

I suddenly wondered what she'd felt when Avrell had tried to replace her with one of the other Servants. Had she felt them die? Had she died along with them?

Or had she helped kill them, however inadvertently?

I left her at the bottom of the dais, moved up the steps slowly, and stood before the twisting shape.

Then I turned, braced myself, and without further thought sat down.

I felt the throne move beneath me, revulsion prickling along my skin, shuddering up through my body as my breath caught, as my heart quickened. The voices surged higher, melding as one into a roar—

And then they relaxed, suddenly calm.

The throne stabilized, solidifying into a smooth curve of stone with two arms and no back. My hands curled around the edges of the arms and my back straightened, the pose completely natural. I felt suddenly heavier, the room before me more solid, more real. And through my pulse I could feel the city, could feel its heartbeat, could feel the people moving through the streets, the ships floating at the dock, the water of the harbor and the river slapping against the wharf and the riverbed. I throbbed with life, with emotion, an immense rush of sound and movement I could feel tingling in my skin.

I drew in a deep, steadying breath, let it out slowly as I submerged myself in the sensations of the city, and then I turned to gaze down on Eryn at the bottom of the dais, at Erick shifting uncomfortably a few paces beyond. Erick smelled of sweat and oranges, the scents more intense now. Eryn smelled of loam and leaves, like tea.

I focused on Eryn, felt the currents of the city shift around me. "What do I do?" I asked. My voice sounded thicker, more dense, as if it had the weight of all of the voices of the throne behind it, but neither Eryn nor Erick reacted.

Eryn licked her lips. "Focus on the voices, but don't try to pick out any words. Just listen to them as a whole. Think of them as . . ." her brow creased in thought, ". . . as people in a marketplace, all yelling and talking at once. You're just standing at the marketplace's edge, letting the roar wash over you, not really paying attention."

I frowned, closed my eyes on the throne room and focused on the pulse of the city around me, moving deeper into its life until I came to the edge of the White Fire that protected me. The voices reacted as I drew nearer, the stronger ones pushing forward, but I pushed them back, never let the Fire waver. I tried to imagine the marketplace in the middle ward outside the merchants' guild hall, tried to picture myself at the corner of a street, staring out over the white stone plaza at the rearing bronze statues of the horses at the fountain in its center, the voices of the throne individual people in the square. But the image wavered, grew ragged and torn at its edges, until I couldn't hold it anymore.

I grunted as it slipped away, clenched my hands tighter on the edges of the throne as I gathered my strength to try again.

Below, I could feel Eryn's expectant tension, could taste Erick's concern, like musty clothes.

I re-formed the image of the marketplace—the four horses, the gurgle of the fountain—tried to place the voices there . . . but the image began to slip again. I grasped at it in desperation—

And felt something pull.

The marketplace darkened, white stone growing grimy and gray, regular flagstone shifting to odd cobbles. The roar of the hawkers on the square became the raucous noise of a street.

Then, there was a gut-wrenching lurch.

Instead of standing at the corner of the guild hall's plaza, I found myself crouched at the mouth of an alley on the Dredge, the sound of the hundred voices of the throne now the familiar rushing background wind of the river.

My hands unclenched from the arms of the throne, and my breathing slowed.

After a long steadying moment, I said softly, "I've got it."

"Good." Eryn's voice seemed distant, as if coming from a far corridor, but I could still smell the scent of tea close by. "Now, think about the dream. But not what happened in the dream. Think about what the dream *felt* like. If someone was influencing the dream, changing it in some way, you should be able to feel them, like . . . like a shadow in the background."

Like gutterscum on the Dredge.

I began to replay the dream in my head, starting at the gates, moving swiftly through the streets to the stable, to the trapdoor and the tunnel. I let the dock boy's conversation seep past me, tried to focus on the movements, the tread of feet, the brush of clothes against the crates as we squeezed through the narrow opening to the tunnel's entrance. But there was nothing.

I tried again, slower, heard the rasp of our boots on the cobbles, felt the light from the oil lamp as Borund lit it from behind.

Nothing.

On the third try, as I lost track of the dock boy and Borund, as they melded into the smooth flow of motion, I caught the shadow. But it wasn't a feeling, it was a scent: loam and leaves. Like tea.

I jerked back, stumbled deeper into the alley, away from the Dredge, then caught myself.

In the depths of the throne room, I heard myself say, "It's you."

"What?" Eryn asked, voice still remote, but tinged with confusion.

"The shadow I sense behind the dream is you," I said more forcefully.

A pause, the noise of the Dredge still surrounding me.

"But that's not possible," Eryn said. "The Sight can't be used that way. And besides, I didn't know about the wine! I don't remember hiding it in the stable!"

Ignoring Eryn's growing agitation, I edged back up to the alley's mouth, crouched down behind a wagon half full of scabrous apples. "Wait," I said.

On the eddies of the Dredge, where all of the voices of the throne lay, I'd caught a scent. Faint, but there.

I drew in a breath, let the instincts I'd honed on the Dredge take over . . . and caught the scent again.

I pushed forward, past the wagon and into the crowd, moving swiftly. But unlike the real Dredge, the people on this Dredge didn't ignore me. Instead, they turned, shouted in my face, grasped at my tattered clothes, at my arms, thrust themselves in my path to catch my attention. I struggled through them, noticed that they were almost all women, old and young, pockmarked and fair, with blonde hair, black, a muddy brown with green eyes, in all manner of clothes. All of the past Mistresses, and anyone else who had somehow touched the throne, all trying to gain my attention, hundreds of them. I fought them, fought through their scents: tallow, ripened melon, sea salt, and dead fish. I followed the scent of tea.

Until I rounded a corner at the edge of a narrow, where I halted.

Just inside the narrow, huddled in the darkness, was Eryn. But unlike the voices of the throne behind me, this Eryn was somehow less real, a shadow compared to the rest. A ghost.

The shade of the Eryn I knew raised her head, her eyes haunted, darkened around the edges with fear and strain.

"Look," she murmured, then pointed down the narrow, away from the Dredge, into the darkness.

I turned, brow creased, mouth set.

But instead of the narrow I expected, the darkness looked out over the city of Amenkor.

With a start, I realized I was standing on the roof of the palace tower at night, Eryn's shade beside me. The city lay spread out before me: the inner ward, the middle ward, the outer ward; the wharf, the warehouse district, the lower city; and across the River, the slums beyond the Dredge.

And the city was burning. All of it. Huge pillars of smoke boiled into the air, tinged red from the fires beneath. On street after street, husks of buildings stood out as fire ate at their foundations. Ships burned at the docks, a few blazing cold and harsh in the water, flames reflected on the waves. Even as the full extent of the scene began to register, to penetrate through the shock, I felt a surge of power—a pulsing wave on the river—and one of the guard towers at the entrance to the harbor exploded, stone and wood debris flying up and out, arching over the water of the bay, trailing flame and smoke and embers. The fire was a living thing, hissing, spitting. A sizzling *fwump* rose up from the middle ward as a guild hall collapsed, stone cracking, more embers rising high into the night.

As I stepped to the edge of the rooftop, horror welling up inside me, choking me, closing off my throat, the water of the harbor caught my attention, rising on slow swells, dark and viscous.

The harbor water was red. Not with reflected firelight, but with blood. And the waves were choked with bodies.

Eryn's shade drew up close behind me. "Do you see!" she shrieked, her voice cracking with insanity. "Do you see!"

Then the winds shifted, blew smoke into my face so that I squinted, blew Eryn's black hair back in streaming tangles. And the smell from the city below hit, a noisome wave of smoke and ash and blood, of salt and sea and death.

I turned away from the stench, doubled over as my gorge rose, and in a panic I let the river go, shoved it aside with a wrench. I felt the Fire inside me flare as if to protect me, felt part of it get caught and tear free as I shoved the vision of the city away in desperation. I heard Eryn scream in pain as the wave of power spread out on the river, as it tore through the vision of blood and water and fire.

Then I fell off the throne, collapsed to my hands and knees, trembling with weakness, and vomited onto the top step of the dais of the throne room.

⊹— Chapter 4

"But she's been like this for two days!" The voice filtered through the darkness, followed swiftly by tremors throughout my body. But all of it was distant, coming from a farther shore, removed from me here, where I floated on the river. So I kept my eyes closed, let myself drift on the surface of the water, half submerged, and listened.

"I know, Borund." A familiar voice, hard and soothing, weary and comforting. Erick's voice. It made me want to open my eyes, to struggle from the river, but I felt too tired, the river currents too strong. "Remember what happened to her after the warehouse fire. You know it can take a while for her to recover."

Borund grunted. "I can still feel where she kicked me during one of the seizures then. But I'm not sure how much longer we can wait. Decisions have to be made about how to distribute the food. We can't just hand it out to whoever comes to the warehouses. And I have no idea how we're going to include the people of the Dredge."

Movement. Someone shifting closer.

"Are you certain this is the same as after the fire?" Borund asked, his voice concerned.

More movement. Then someone touched my forehead, brushed away a lock of my hair, the sensation faint and tingling, sending a shiver through me.

"Yes. She'll be fine."

Borund muttered a wordless agreement. "What about Eryn?"

The voices moved away.

"She's fine as well. She woke yesterday, according to Avrell."

"Did he say what happened? Did Eryn say?"

"No. Eryn refuses to discuss it. She's waiting for Varis to recover."

A pause. Then, in a softer voice, "You should get some sleep, Erick. How long have you been here?"

"Since it happened."

A subtle shift on the river. When Borund spoke, I could hear a more significant question hidden behind the simple words. "Watching over her?"

"Guarding her." Stiff and formal. Stubborn.

I smiled.

"If you insist," Borund said. I heard humor in his voice, a shared understanding. And also an acceptance, tinged with regret. Their attention returned to me. I could feel it, like sunlight against my skin. "You'll be a better . . . mentor to her than I will. You already have been."

Silence from Erick. I stilled, caught my breath, part of me confused, but part of me shivering with an unexpected need, hard and tight inside my gut. I'd never known my father, my mother nothing more than a wisp of memory, killed when I was six years old. I'd survived alone on the Dredge since then, after learning what I needed from a gutterscum street gang led by a boy called Dove. I'd had no one since then. At one point, I'd thought that the baker who'd taken pity on me and fed me on a regular basis would be something more than just a face I needn't fear. But no. He was dead now.

Which left Erick and Borund.

I'd never thought of either as being more than a trainer, or an employer.

Except that wasn't true, was it? I'd always wanted something more, but had never realized what it was. Not until now, when Borund put it into words.

Breath held, I reached out toward Erick, felt a bitterness inside him, felt his self-hatred. "I trained her to kill," he finally said, the words soft yet harsh.

"No," Borund said, his words just as harsh, refuting Erick as strongly as he could. "You taught her how to survive. You never wanted her to kill, like me. You always gave her the choice, killed for her if she said no. You trained her so she could protect herself from all of the dangers of the Dredge. No." Borund's voice was emphatic. "I ordered her to kill, to make my life easier. I *used* her, like a tool." He paused, a tremor of pain entering his voice. "She deserves more than that," he added, the words thick with suppressed emotion.

Erick didn't respond, but I could sense that the self-hatred he felt had been blunted, that he was watching me with a considering frown. The hard core of need inside me shuddered, and I relaxed, the held breath releasing in a slow sigh.

It was enough for now.

Borund stirred, his roiling emotions settled somewhat. I felt a surge of pity for him. He'd tried to think of me as more than a tool, especially at the end, when I'd returned from the fire in the warehouse district with seizures. But my usefulness as a weapon kept getting in the way, first with the merchant Charls, then Alendor, and finally with the Mistress. He'd never had the chance to think of me as anything else.

"I'll have the servants send in something to eat," he said.

"What are you going to do?"

A pause. "I'm not certain. We need her, Erick. Somehow, she keeps everything balanced: Avrell, Baill, the merchants."

"Eryn can help."

A sigh. "Perhaps. But not for long. She doesn't have the power of the throne behind her anymore. The merchants might listen to her for a time, out of remembered respect, but it won't last. We need Varis. She's more forceful than Eryn, more direct. And I think the merchants fear her."

"Because of the throne?"

Borund snorted. "No. They fear her for who she is, for what they know she can do with that dagger of hers. They've seen her in action, protecting me from Alendor and the consortium. And they've heard the rumors of what she did on the Dredge."

"Some of those rumors aren't true."

"But some of them are?"

A long, considering pause. A little of the self-hatred returned, but it was balanced by a shouldered responsibility. "Yes," Erick finally said, his voice somewhat defiant.

"Then the merchants have reason to fear her."

Silence, and then Borund heaved a heavy sigh. "I should return to my manse." Shuffling movement, growing more and more distant. "I left William in charge of organizing the storage—"

The voices faded. Where I floated on the river, eyes closed, I felt a pang deep inside, followed by sudden heat.

William. Borund's apprentice. I saw his tousled black hair, his eyes, green like the waters at the edge of the wharf, his smile, soft and tentative.

The heat in my gut turned fluid, spread to my chest. I smiled, stretched out in the sensation, arched my back.

Distantly, I heard the rustle of sheets as I moved, heard Erick returning alone to stand over me. I could feel him willing me to wake with a simple, direct stare. And I wanted to wake now, wanted to see him, wanted to see William. William must have recovered from the knife wound in his side if he was helping Borund at the warehouses.

But then I felt my own twinge of doubt, of regret and responsibility. William had been hurt because I'd failed to protect him, failed to anticipate the intent of the men who had ambushed us.

In my mind, William's smile faded. His eyes darkened with accusation, then shifted again, grew troubled. Fear bled into his features. His eyes flew wide open. Muscles tensed around his mouth and jaw.

This was how he had looked in the tavern when I'd gutted the assassin attempting to kill Borund. This was how he'd looked when I'd almost stabbed him on the wharf. Afraid. Terrified of me, of what I could do, of what I had already done. I could kill, without remorse, viciously and bloodily.

It was who I was. It was what made the other merchants fear me.

The heat in my center curdled and I curled in upon myself, drew away from Erick's presence hovering over me, away from the Mistress' bedchamber where I lay.

I didn't want to wake. Not yet. Not for Erick, nor for William. I was too tired.

Let Eryn deal with everything for now. All I wanted to do was sleep.

So I let the river pull me down into darkness.

I opened my eyes to bright sunlight filtered through drawn curtains and saw the simple white canopy above my bed. The folds of cloth rippled in a breeze.

I blinked, felt the grit around my eyes, the tightness of my skin caused by too much sleep, and heard a low murmur of voices.

I turned my head, wincing at the twinge of fading bruises and strained muscles, and saw Erick and Marielle sitting on the settee that I used to work on my writing, their heads bowed down over my slate.

The initial surge of contentment that slid through me on seeing Erick was cut short by a thread of anger and embarrassment. I didn't want Erick to see my work, my scratchings that were nothing like the smooth lines of Marielle's writing.

"I don't know what to do," Marielle said, her voice hushed but carrying easily. "She's trying so hard, but the letters don't come naturally to her. It's not a matter of her learning to read—she'll master that with little effort; she remembers everything—but the writing . . ." She shook her head.

Erick frowned down at the slate. "She's thinking about it too much," he said. Then he pointed to the board. "You can see the strain of it in the lines of each letter. Here. And here. She's trying too hard to do exactly what you do, to make the letters as smooth and flowing as yours are. But Varis isn't elegant and meticulous like you. She's blunt and direct. Forceful. You have to find a way to make the writing as blunt and forceful as she is."

Marielle's brow furrowed in thought. "How do I do that?"

I struggled up onto one elbow, tried to speak, the anger overtaking my exhaustion, but the words came out in a raspy cough instead. Both Erick and Marielle glanced up, then stood.

"Water," Erick said sharply, and as Marielle darted to the side table where she'd left the pitcher and glasses, he moved to the edge of the bed. The slate was left forgotten on the settee.

I glared at him as he helped me into a sitting position, then took the glass of water Marielle offered. I swallowed carefully, my throat raw, but the water washed the sour taste away and made my stomach rumble.

"I didn't want you to see," I said hoarsely, motioning toward the slate.

Marielle harrumphed. "He's been here for the last three days," she said, taking the glass of water away before I drank too much and made myself sick. "He was bound to see it eventually." She passed over a chunk of bread.

"You didn't have to show it to him." I switched my glare to Marielle, but she didn't flinch.

"I'll go tell the others you're awake," she said. "And get some soup from the kitchen. That's probably the best thing for you right now."

Erick waited until she was gone, then pulled a chair sitting next to the bed closer. He leaned back, made himself comfortable, then said, "She's trying to help."

I scowled and plucked at the sheets, ignoring the smile playing about Erick's lips.

But the smile faded and his attention shifted. "What happened?" he asked, voice serious.

My nervous hands stilled. I thought about the vision of the city on fire, of the blood and bodies in the harbor. I shuddered, felt a twist of nausea in my stomach that echoed what I'd felt while touching the throne, but fought it back. The image was too real, too . . . visceral. I couldn't keep it to myself.

I turned to Erick, frowned intently . . . and suddenly realized I wouldn't be sending him out in search of any more marks. The last few weeks without him had been too lonely, and I hadn't realized why until he'd returned, until I'd overheard Borund and Erick earlier. But now I knew what I wanted, without any doubt.

"I saw Amenkor," I said. "The city was on fire, everything burning: the palace, the docks, the Dredge. Even the ships in the harbor. And there were bodies in the water." My voice grew rough, cracked, but with effort I managed to control it. I swallowed down the horror, tasted its bitterness. "The harbor was filled with blood, a whole sea of it. And in the end it was too much to take, and so I shoved it all away. Hard.

"That's when I fell off the throne."

Erick nodded, his eyes thoughtful. "That's when Eryn screamed and collapsed as well."

I sat forward. I remembered the scream at the end, when the power I'd used to push the image away had rippled outward, a second before I'd fallen. I'd thought it had come from the shade of Eryn, since she'd been on the tower with me, witnessing the fire. But if it had truly been Eryn, not her shadow . . .

"Is she all right?"

Erick grunted. "She's fine. She was a little shaken, but she says there was no harm done. None that she can see." He stilled. "What do you think the vision means? Was it just an image, like in a dream, or was it something more?"

I thought back, tried to ignore the scent of smoke and ash, still sharp, making my nose itch and wrinkle in distaste. "I don't know." I thought about how I'd always used the river to see what *could* happen, to find the best time to snatch away the apple, or the easiest way to elude the guards. The vision had the same feel, viscerally real but also stretched somehow, not fully there.

I shook my head. "I need to ask Eryn. She has more experience with the throne. But I think I understand why she closed the harbor."

"Why?"

"Whatever destroyed the city in the vision . . . it came from the ocean. I could sense it."

We stared at each other for a long moment without speaking. Then Erick said in a tight voice, "So perhaps Eryn wasn't as insane as she seemed."

A hard lump closed off my throat as I realized that he was right. She'd had reason to close the harbor, reason perhaps to increase the guard in the city. I'd been sent to kill her—had agreed to kill her—on the assumption that she had gone mad. But what if that wasn't true? What if there *were* reasons for all her actions? Avrell himself had said that sometimes the Mistress' orders made no sense at the time, but were obvious in retrospect.

Then I shook my head, the lump in my throat easing. No. The vision still didn't explain her order to let the warehouse district burn, or her wandering the palace talking to herself, speaking in unknown languages, as the guards claimed. And I *knew* she had gone insane. I'd seen it in the throne room when I tried to kill her.

No. Eryn had been on the verge of total madness when I'd seized control. There was no doubting that. She'd admitted it herself.

But I didn't get a chance to explain to Erick. Someone knocked and a moment later opened the outer door. One of the guards outside leaned in.

"The First of the Mistress and a Master Borund are here to see you," he said when he saw I was sitting up in bed.

I sighed and leaned back into the pillows. Erick stood.

"I could send them away," he offered quietly.

I shook my head. "No, send them in."

Erick nodded to the guardsman, who stepped in to allow Avrell and Borund entry, then closed the door behind himself as he left. Both Avrell and Borund moved up to the bed, opposite Erick.

"Mistress," Avrell said with a formal bow of his head. "It is good to see you recovering."

"Yes, it is, Mistress," Borund said. "What happened?"

I glanced toward Erick, giving him a warning frown before turning back. "The throne was more powerful than I thought. I was too . . . *forceful* in my efforts to control it."

Erick shifted uncomfortably.

"What have you done while I was recovering?" I asked.

Avrell cleared his throat, catching everyone's attention. "We've managed to locate and secure the stockpiles of food that Eryn smuggled into the city, ten in all, by searching all of the buildings owned by the palace. There may be more, but Eryn couldn't have hidden anything outside the city by herself and we can't search every building in the city without rousing protests, so for now we've stopped looking."

"Now we need to decide how to store the goods we do have," Borund broke in, "and figure out how to distribute them among the populace over the coming months."

"I still argue for a single location that can be easily guarded," Avrell said.

Borund frowned. "And I still say it should be at a few separate locations in case something happens, like a fire."

As Avrell and Borund traded glares, I thought of the fires burning in the vision and sighed wearily.

"I've already decided," I said, cutting the two off before they could launch into a repeat of the argument they'd had a few weeks ago. "We'll put the food in separate locations." Borund smiled and nodded in triumph. "Avrell, choose

the locations and let Baill and Captain Catrell know so they can assign guardsmen. There should be one in the middle ward, another in the outer, and at least
one somewhere in the slums. Find an empty building in each area, something
that Baill thinks will be easy to defend and control, and use that. There are
plenty of empty buildings. The buildings that remain in the warehouse district
can be used to cover the wharf and the upper city."

Avrell sighed disapprovingly. "Very well."

I caught him with a hard stare. "I have my reasons," I said sharply.

He frowned and straightened, looking questioningly at Erick, who didn't
respond, his face blank.

I turned to Borund. "Once you have the locations, distribute them among
the merchants and let them know where they're to store their goods. Some of
it can stay in their own warehouses, of course, but any excess and anything
from Alendor's or the consortium's supplies should be divided among the other
locations. I expect the merchants to keep track of all of the supplies under their
control, and to distribute them fairly when the time comes. Don't store all of
the grain in one spot. We don't want to lose our entire supply of any one staple
because of some accident."

Borund simply nodded.

"And how *are* we going to distribute this food as the winter progresses?"
Avrell asked, his brow creased with honest concern.

I sighed and leaned back, feeling tired already. "I don't know yet. Just move
the supplies for now."

Erick shifted forward, eyes worried. He searched my face and must have
seen the exhaustion there. "I think that's enough for now," he said meaningfully.

Avrell seemed about to protest, but he subsided under Erick's flat stare and
a quick look at me. "Of course. We'll continue this tomorrow, after you've had
more time to rest."

I said nothing as they departed. Almost immediately after they'd left, Marielle returned with a tray containing a steaming bowl of soup and a small dish
of fruit. She began to set it up next to the bed. I was already beginning to feel
sleepy, but the thought of food kept me upright and awake. The smell from the
soup made my stomach clench and growl.

Erick began to turn away, but I stopped him with a touch on his hand. He
gave me a grave look, eyes intent.

"Thank you," I said.

I wasn't certain what I was thanking him for—wasn't certain he knew
either—but his expression softened and he smiled, then reached up and flicked
away a sweaty lock of hair from my forehead before settling into the chair to
watch me eat.

*   *   *

"So tell me," Eryn said, taking a slow sip of her tea, "what did you find when you were on the throne?"

We were sitting in chairs in the doorway of the balcony in my rooms, a small table with our cups and the pitcher of tea between us. Erick had dozed off in the chair next to my bed. Eryn had arrived almost an hour before, our initial conversation tense and meaningless, lapsing into thoughtful silence interrupted by Erick's snores as we stared up at the pale winter sky hazed with thin clouds. The afternoon light had just begun to fade toward evening.

I shifted uncomfortably. I'd been dreading this meeting since I'd seen Eryn's shade on the mock Dredge, since her shade had shown me the city burning. But Eryn hadn't come to see me, and I'd been too weak to go to her . . . and too angry.

But I hadn't hidden in my room doing nothing. I'd experimented with the throne's powers, searched the city for more of the wardings like the one she placed on the building in the Dredge. I hadn't found anything. I didn't think any of the other buildings hiding stored foods had wardings. Once I knew what to look for, the warding in the Dredge had been easy to spot.

I'd also tried other things, tested the throne's reach, tested my own reach. But I'd been careful, never letting the tenuous connection to my body break.

I just didn't want all of my knowledge about the throne to come from Eryn. I didn't trust her yet.

Eryn's gaze dropped to her cup. "You said that it was me."

I nodded, thinking back to the dream. I felt a surge of that anger now, but it was smothered by the sudden need to understand what had happened. "It was you behind the dreams. You were there, in the shadow as you said, nudging me to remember, and finally appearing yourself."

Eryn frowned. "That would explain why it was my image that appeared at the end of the dream," she said. "But it couldn't have been me. The Sight can't be used in that fashion. I know it! I've tried since then to influence Laurren's dreams, but it doesn't *work*!"

She set her cup down with a sharp clatter, tea spilling over one side, then stood and crossed her arms, moving stiffly toward the edge of the balcony.

My lips thinned, but my anger faltered. Her emotion was too raw to be faked, her distress too sincere. "Who's Laurren?"

Eryn huffed, then tensed in an effort to control herself. In a much calmer tone, she said, "Laurren is my principal servant, also one of the true Servants, one of the more powerful ones here. I've known her for years. If I could influence anyone's dreams with the Sight, it would be hers."

I hesitated, then stood and moved to Eryn's side, leaned against the iron railing as I stared down at the palace and city beneath us. "I don't think you used the Sight to influence my dreams."

Eryn flicked a glance toward me, confused and irritated. "How else could I have touched your dreams?"

I grimaced. "I think you used the throne."

Eryn straightened. "But that's impossible," she scoffed. "I'm not connected to the throne anymore. I can't feel it, can't hear it. When I reach for it, even out of habit, there's nothing there!" There was a tremor of loss beneath her voice.

"I know. I don't think you're connected to the throne anymore either. I can't sense any of the threads that bound you to it, the threads that I removed when I seized control."

"Then how could I have used the throne to touch your dreams!" Eryn said sharply.

I felt my shoulders tense. "I think part of you is still inside the throne," I said bluntly.

Eryn stilled, anger building tight and fast, like a storm cloud. "What—?" she began. But then she stopped herself, forced herself to think instead of react.

I seized the opening. "There's a piece of you still inside the throne. I sensed it, found it hidden among the rest of the voices. A shadow of yourself, almost an echo, as if somehow, when I took control, when I cut the bonds between you and the throne, a memory of you got left behind. And I think that piece of you holds the memories that you've lost."

I halted, waited. I'd tried to connect with the shadow of Eryn in the throne itself, the one that had shown me the vision of the city burning. Tried to find out from her where some of the stores might have been hidden. But she refused to speak to me, didn't even appear to be sane.

The thought of a piece of myself being torn away, imprisoned outside of myself, sent a queasy shudder through my gut, made my mouth dry and tasteless. I expected Eryn to react the same way.

Instead, Eryn stared out across the harbor, her face unreadable, eyes pinched, skin taut.

"That's why I don't remember the wine," she said to herself, anger still evident in the curt words.

I felt the tension in my shoulders release. "And why the shadow of you does."

Eryn remained quiet, then said in a trembling, vulnerable voice, "I thought I'd escaped the throne."

I didn't know what to say, so I said nothing. The statement was at odds with the loss I'd heard in her words before. I wondered which emotion would eventually win out: yearning for the throne, or acceptance that it was lost.

Before us, the thin clouds became tinged with dark orange as the sun set.

In the courtyard of the palace, a troop of guardsmen tramped in from the city and after a pause broke up, each guardsman going his separate way. On the wall of the inner ward, I saw the palace guardsmen changing shifts as well.

Eventually, the turmoil I felt from Eryn subsided. She turned to me. "But that doesn't explain your reaction at the end. Something else happened, something that startled you, frightened you." When I didn't respond immediately, she shifted closer, her voice hardening. "If you were better trained, you would have killed me with that blast of power."

I flinched, but straightened, my hand dropping to my dagger at the threat in her tone. "But I didn't kill you."

Eryn's face darkened, her head lifting. "No, you didn't. Instead, you knocked me unconscious and seriously overextended yourself."

"I've done it before and survived," I said, annoyance rising at the rebuke.

Eryn snorted. "Then you were lucky. You could have killed yourself as well, pushed yourself too far. All it takes is one careless mistake, and you could end up lost, your body nothing but a husk, your focus too scattered to bring you back. You need to be better trained in the use of the Sight."

I bristled, but Eryn halted, her lips pursed. She shook her head and let it drop, turning away as she asked, "So what happened?"

I felt an urge to confront her, my skin prickling, hand gripping tight on my dagger, but I forced my breathing to slow, forced the anger back. It didn't feel right, too sharp and quick and uncontrolled. Too impulsive.

Once I'd calmed, I said, "The memory of you still inside the throne showed me a vision of the city burning, all of the people slaughtered. It was horrible, so I used the river to shove it away without thinking."

Eryn frowned. "I don't remember any such vision. But if the Eryn inside the throne, my shadow, knew of it . . ." She trailed off, thinking. "Do you think it was a scrying, a vision of the future?"

I shuddered. "Yes."

Eryn's expression grew grim. "Then you must prepare."

I laughed, the sound short and humorless. "For what? There was nothing in the vision except fire and death, nothing but smoke and ruin."

"But it is still a warning. My shadow was trying to help you, with the wine and now with this. Think back to the image, look for details. What season was it? Winter? Spring? Summer?"

I thought about refusing, but under Eryn's harsh glare, I closed my eyes and concentrated. At first, I held the image still, just a memory of what I'd seen before, static and senseless.

But then I felt the vision twist, felt the power of the river surge through it.

The image enfolded me again, as real as it had been on the throne, full of sound and sensation, and I found myself back on the roof of the tower staring out over the city. My breath came in shorter gasps as I tried not to breathe the smoke, as I tried not to choke on the stench, even though I knew it didn't exist. Heat touched my skin, turned it waxy and slick, and from the city below I heard screams.

I pushed the horrible sound away, looked up at the sky clouded with plumes of smoke and ash. "I can't tell what season it is," I said, voice raised over the crackle of flame, the sucking roar of fire. "It's dark. Nighttime. I can only see smoke and flames in the streets. I can't even see the stars, or the moon."

Distantly, I heard the rustle of cloth as Eryn shifted closer, smelled the perfume she was wearing, the scent of the large white flowers from her garden warring with the reek of the smoke. "Look at the banners on the palace walls. What color are they?"

On the tower, stone cracked with a sharp retort and part of the palace wall fell away, slowly, but I ignored it and leaned out over the edge of the rooftop, hands pressed to the gritty stone. For a moment, the same dizziness that had overwhelmed me before sent the world spinning. A blast of heat hit my face, but I squinted, fought the vertigo long enough to see the banners, then lurched back with a gasp.

"They're yellow! A bright yellow!"

"Summer, then," Eryn said.

I continued to gasp, the raw stench becoming overpowering, then broke out in ragged coughing, the smoke invading my lungs. I doubled over, felt Eryn's hands on my shoulders, attempting to steady me.

"Look to the harbor," she commanded. "Look at the ships. What flags are flying on the masts?"

Still doubled over, coughing harshly, I forced myself to straighten and move to the edge of the tower, Eryn helping me to stand upright. I gagged, swallowed the sickening taste back, and scanned the ships burning in the water, trying not to see the bodies rolling in the movement of the waves.

"I can't see," I said. "I can't—"

The river suddenly gathered, and I drew in a harsh breath, felt the weight of the river coalesce into a focused thrust and release.

Far out on the edge of the harbor one of the watchtowers that guarded the bay exploded.

"They can use the river," I gasped, as the debris from the watchtower began to rain down into the bay, the realization sharp and horrifying, like a hand at my throat.

Then something else caught my eye. The warehouse district.

A plume of smoke drifted directly over the tower and I drew in a lungful of char and ash. Doubling over again, I lost my grip on the vision, felt it tatter and shred as I fell back into Eryn's arms. She guided me to my chair as tears streamed down my sweat-drenched face; reaction from the smoke. But of course there was no smoke, no fire.

Not yet.

"They can use the Sight," I managed between wheezing breaths, the sensation of heat and flame fading.

"Who?" Eryn snapped.

"The ones attacking Amenkor. The ones burning the city. They used the river to destroy one of the watchtowers."

Eryn's eyes flashed, then handed me my cup filled with tea. "Drink this."

I sipped as I shook my head, scrubbed the tears away from my face with the back of a trembling hand. My throat felt raw, my lungs dirty with soot. "Who else along the coast has Servants—true Servants?"

Eryn hesitated. "Everyone. There are men and women all along the coast that have and can use the Sight. Most don't realize what they are doing, using it in only mundane ways—to coax the fish into the net, to calm the deer's heart during a hunt, to smooth the escalating tensions in the tavern to avoid a fight." Her frown deepened and she turned away, moved toward the edge of the balcony. "There's only one other city that actually trains Servants as we do."

"Which city?"

"Venitte." Short and terse. "They have a school, almost exclusively male students. In fact, we have an agreement with them: they send any women proficient in the Sight here to be trained, we send the men down there. Anyone with sufficient power on the coast ends up here or there eventually."

"Why?"

Eryn shrugged. "It's always been that way. Venitte and Amenkor are sister cities, the ties between us old and strong. And we've always been the greatest powers on the Frigean coast."

"But if the people in the vision are using the Sight, then it must be Venitte that is attacking."

"I don't believe that." Eryn caught my gaze briefly, her eyes flaring, before returning to her scrutiny of the harbor, back stiff. "We've had good relations with Venitte for decades. There's no reason for Venitte to attack. It makes no sense."

I shifted in my seat, trying to recall everything that Avrell had told me regarding Venitte during the last month. But there was nothing. Nothing important anyway. Venitte had always aided Amenkor whenever possible, the Mistress and the Lord of Venitte always on good terms. There were occasional trade disputes, but Venitte was far enough south that these were rarely so serious that the merchants' guild couldn't handle it themselves. The rulers of the two cities almost never got involved.

Eryn suddenly sighed. "It doesn't matter," she said, turning away from the city to face me. "Whoever is attacking—Venitte or someone else—they are using the Sight. Which means we need to prepare."

"How?"

Eryn grimaced. "We need to begin training the remaining Servants. Marielle and Laurren have already had the minimal training required, so they can help. But if what you have Seen is true, then those that are attacking are extremely powerful. It takes effort to destroy a building as large as the watchtowers with one strike. It takes brute force. We'll have to start building on Marielle's and Laurren's abilities as well, and anyone else who shows early promise."

"When should we start?"

"As soon as possible. If the attack is coming this summer, that doesn't leave us much time."

I was already working with Avrell, learning about the political situation along the coast and the daily activities of the Mistress. Then there was Marielle with the reading and writing and now numbers, Westen for dagger play and defense. . . .

I sighed.

Eryn placed a reassuring hand on my shoulder, misinterpreting my sigh. "Scrying, especially that far into the future, is always unreliable and difficult to control. There may not be an attack coming at all. And if it is coming, it may not be this summer. Right now, we have more pressing matters."

"Such as?"

Eryn didn't hear the sarcasm in my voice, or did and chose to ignore it. She settled herself into her seat. "Such as figuring out how to distribute all the food we have stored for the winter."

I scowled. "I don't see why we can't just hand it out."

Eryn laughed and shook her head. "And how would you go about doing that? Look at all the people in the city, Varis. Think of how many of them there are. How are you going to make certain everyone gets what they deserve? And what about the people that already have supplies of their own? We don't want to be giving food out to people who don't need it, and there are plenty of people in the city who would take advantage of something like that. Even if they don't have their own foodstocks, what's to stop them from going back twice? Or going to two different warehouses? Or three? No. Hoarding is going to be a serious problem, no matter how we distribute the food."

I thought about what she'd said, thought about how I'd lived on the Dredge, taking whatever I could, storing it for leaner times when necessary, especially during winter. On the Dredge I would have killed for food if I'd needed to. Most of those who lived in the warrens beyond the Dredge would. None of them would think twice about it.

I grunted in agreement, suddenly thankful the baker—the white-dusty man—had been there to keep me from such desperation. "I didn't think it would be this difficult."

Eryn smiled in understanding but didn't say anything, sitting back thoughtfully.

I tried to take another sip of the tea but found the cup empty. "So, how are we going to distribute the food?"

Eryn glanced toward me. "I have a few ideas. Avrell seems to think they'll work as well."

I frowned. I hadn't realized Eryn and Avrell had been discussing it, and didn't understand why the thought bothered me so much. "What ideas?"

Eryn hesitated. "I think we should make them work for it. Have the women make bread from the grains at common ovens, or curdle milk for cheese and butter. Have the men help to rebuild the warehouse district, fish when they can, butcher the cattle. Children can help with the hauling of wood and rock, or water for the workers. Find something to do for everyone willing, something constructive. For every day's work, they get an allowance of food."

Rebuild the warehouse district.

I felt my stomach clench. But not from regret over causing the fire that had destroyed it. No. Not this time.

My stomach clenched because in the vision the warehouse district had been burning, just like the rest of the city. Because it had been rebuilt.

Before I could respond to Eryn's suggestion, or tell her about the warehouses burning in the vision, a horn began to sound from the city below, followed closely by the sudden clamor of bells. The noise grew as more and more bells were added, until it seemed every bell in Amenkor was tolling.

Eryn and I shared a look, then rose and moved to the balcony's edge.

At the docks below, men were scrambling to clear a mooring, others lining up along the wharf, crowding its edges in the last of the sun's light.

"Look," Eryn said.

I turned to where she pointed and saw, coming through the entrance to the harbor, a ship. One of its masts had been snapped off, and its sails were torn and ragged.

I felt Erick move up behind me. I hadn't even heard his snoring halt.

"What is it?" he asked, without a trace of sleepiness.

"It's one of the ships we sent out to search for supplies," I said, as it began a slow crawl toward the dock.

The wharf was thronged with people, all trying to see the ship as it pulled in to dock, their faces tense with worry in the torchlight. The entire wharf was ablaze with light, every torch, lantern, and wide bowl of oil lit.

I frowned as my escort of guardsmen began forcing a way through the crowd. The escort was led by Baill, who'd been waiting at the bottom of the steps of the promenade with twenty guardsmen behind him when I'd emerged from the palace. Without a word, Avrell had joined up with Eryn, Erick, and me inside the palace. It had taken us only thirty minutes to reach the wharf, the streets nearly empty.

"I can't see the captain of the ship," Avrell said, frustration clear as we ground to a halt.

"It's Mathew," I said. At his questioning look, I added, "It's Borund's ship, the first one to leave once the blockade was lifted. I can tell by the flags on the main mast."

He nodded. Ahead, Baill suddenly bellowed wordlessly and the crowd parted, startled.

We began moving forward again, tension rising as the crowd closed in behind us and crushed us together. I gasped as the escort was pressed up on all sides, started to panic when I realized I was too short to be noticed and could get trampled. Then a reassuring hand grabbed my shoulder, and I twisted to see Erick behind me. He smiled tightly, eyes darting to either side. Eryn and Avrell were close behind him.

"I wonder what happened," Erick said, shouting above the noise. "Did you see the mast had been broken?"

I shrugged, didn't try to answer as I was jostled sharply to the left, a piece of guardsman's armor digging into my side. I hissed in pain and irritation, fought the urge to shove back, to draw my own dagger in response.

Just when I felt the crowd becoming too much for me, even with Erick at my back, we broke through to the dock, spilling out into cleared space. A line of guardsmen held back the throng of people, the noise on this side almost deafening. People lined the wharf in both directions, those on the edge threatening to drop over into the dark water. A few hapless fools already had, bobbing in the swells as they fought their way back to shore cursing and spluttering. Others had mounted the wharf's supports, or were dangling out over the water, one foot on solid dock, held up by a grip on a rope. Those lucky enough to be on a ship moored close were packed at the railing or swung from the rigging. Almost everyone was shouting or whistling.

"They all know we're low on food for the winter," Avrell said grimly, scanning the mob. "And they know the ships were sent out to find more. It's going to be all kinds of hells getting this to a safe warehouse without the mob running off with it."

Baill turned from scowling at the crowd to look toward the end of the dock, where the battered ship was already moored. "Looks like the ship's already docked," he muttered.

"And Borund has already beaten us here," Avrell added.

Baill grunted.

I looked toward the end of the dock, saw Borund's red-and-gold coat, easy to pick out among the scrambling dockworker's drab grays and browns and bare skin. William stood at his side, and I felt myself straighten. They were both talking to Mathew, the ship's captain dressed in the same dark green coat he'd worn the first time I'd seen him, years before. But his face looked haggard, eyes dark with lack of sleep and shadowed in the flickering light.

"Let's find out what happened," I said grimly, thinking of the vision.

We headed down the dock, stepping over coils of ropes and around stacked crates, the wood creaking beneath us as the waves slapped against its supports. The closer we got to the ship, the more damaged it appeared. The sails were shredded, held together by hasty stitching and prayers. The foremast had been torn completely away, the splintered stump at the prow the only piece remaining. Rigging hung limp and useless, what was left working obviously repaired. The workers hastily unloading casks and cargo seemed shaken, eyes wide, movements sharp, even the few darker-skinned Zorelli workers from the far southern islands. And there weren't as many crew as there should have been.

My frown deepened.

"—found a good supply of dried fruits in Temall nonetheless," Mathew was saying as we approached. His voice was hollow, sounding aged and empty.

"Good, good," Borund muttered, motioning to William, who was keeping a running tally, marking papers beneath the lamps scattered along the end of the dock. "What else?"

Mathew drew breath, but then held it as he saw us approaching, his brow creasing.

Borund caught the look and turned, straightening. William scribbled down a last item, then glanced up, stilling when he saw me, eyes going wide before darting sharply away.

Something stabbed deep into my chest, thin and cold, like a dagger's blade. I winced, found I didn't want to be here anymore, but bit back the feeling and concentrated on Borund and Mathew.

"Mistress," Borund said, his voice happy, relieved, and pained at the same time. He bowed, Mathew and William doing the same a moment later. As he rose, he said, "Mathew has brought us back a full load of food for the winter."

"But at a cost," Mathew said. "We lost twenty crew to the storm."

"So this was done by a storm," Eryn said, voice sharp and commanding. The Mistress' voice.

"Yes," Mathew said, uncertain where to look, at Eryn or me. "We picked up our last cargo a week ago in Temall. We knew we were cutting it close—the sea was already rough—but thought the need for the food was worth the risk. We headed out to sea immediately." He drew in a steadying breath, wincing. I suddenly noticed his hands were bandaged and raw from working the ropes and wondered how many bruises were hidden by the clothes he wore. "The storm hit us only half a day out. We thought to skirt it, but got caught in the squall and were dragged out to deep ocean. By the time it ended, we were two days off course, our mast was broken, and we'd lost good men. We managed to limp back, but it wasn't certain we'd make it. The seas are the worst I've seen in years."

"But the cargo is intact?" Avrell demanded.

I glared at him, and he stiffened.

"I'm sorry, Mistress, but if he's brought back a full cargo, without spoilage, then we may have enough supplies for the city to survive the winter with tight rationing."

I wasn't about to let it go, but Mathew interceded by saying, "Then perhaps the loss of men was worth it."

I let the awkward silence hold for a moment, then turned to Mathew. "So a storm caused all this damage?"

"Yes," Mathew said again, and I traded a relieved glance with Eryn and Erick. "Why is that important?"

Before I could answer, Borund spoke, his tone serious. "Because most of the ships we sent out along with yours haven't returned. We've had no word of them. In fact, we'd assumed your ship was lost as well. We'd hoped you'd have word of the others' fate."

Mathew shook his head. "I heard nothing of the other ships at any port we stopped at, even on the return trip."

I swore silently to myself. What had happened to all of the ships? Where had they gone? And did it have anything to do with the city burning to the ground?

No one said anything for a long moment, faces taut with worry.

Finally, Borund said succinctly, "We should get these supplies off-loaded and to the warehouses."

"Of course," I said. I glanced toward William, but he refused to look at me, head lowered to the papers he clutched, white-knuckled, in one hand.

The dagger of pain I'd felt earlier inside me twisted, dug deeper.

I nodded to Mathew, not trusting myself to speak, then turned away, my escort enfolding me.

"So," Avrell said as we moved, "we know nothing new."

Trying to keep the bitterness over William's reaction out of my voice, I said, "But we have food."

Behind, I felt Erick's attention fix on me, concerned and troubled, but he said nothing.

"I'll have to bring down another brace of guardsmen from the palace in order to control this mob and help get the food safely to the warehouses," Baill said, voice all business. He turned to me for permission, his face harsh with scars in the firelight on the docks.

I wondered again if he'd had any dealings with Alendor and the consortium or whether he'd simply been following the Mistress' orders, but nodded. "Do it."

I sighed, pushed thoughts of William and Baill and the consortium into the background, and looked over the horde of people on the docks. I saw a riot of faces, mostly those from the coast, with dark hair and light skin. But there were others as well: the small, dark-skinned Zorelli from the south, of course; a few of the followers of the Tear of Taniece, their straw-colored hair vibrant in the torchlight, the blue mark of the Tear beneath the right eye appearing black in the night; even a few of the Kandish from the east, their hair braided and feathered, their clothes merely lengths of cloth wrapped and tied around them in intricate folds. All people we had to keep alive. There wouldn't be any more ships, any more food. Not until spring. I could feel it, an emptiness deep inside. Like hunger.

"Now all we have to do is survive."

⊹— Chapter 5

"Now hold on to the threads, and I'll attempt to break through the barrier," Eryn said.

We were standing at opposite ends of a rectangular plot of winter-dead flowers in one of the palace's enclosed gardens. Ten Servants including Marielle and Laurren—a third of the total Servants in the palace—were arrayed around the edges of the garden, watching, their eyes intent, focused beneath the river on the eddies and currents. In a few moments, they'd be asked to do the same thing. Most of them were nervous, the river rippling around them, disturbed. Only Laurren appeared calm, her mouth turned down in a frown.

The stone of the path crunched under my feet as I shifted, but the noise was lost in the background sound of wind, the currents of the river flowing around me smoothly. I concentrated on the threads of the river I'd woven into a wall of force before me. Not as solid as the barrier that Eryn had constructed in her private garden, when I'd stormed in to confront her about the wine hidden in the stablehouse, it was still stronger than anything I'd constructed before. I'd improved steadily during each daily practice session, after Eryn had tested my strength the first week, determining what I had already learned by necessity on the Dredge and as Borund's bodyguard. In the weeks since, she'd pushed me harder and harder, focusing on the techniques I already knew, refining them, using me as an example to hone the Servants' skills. And I'd continued to experiment on my own.

"Are you ready?" Eryn asked, voice deceptively calm.

Tying the last threads of the wall together, I scanned the close-knit mesh of power for flaws, then glanced across the plot of dried leaves and spent flower stalks at Eryn. Her hair gleamed a shiny black in the winter sunlight, her face calm and expectant, hands folded before her.

My eyes narrowed. She expected me to fail. I could see it in her eyes. We'd worked on the barrier for the last two weeks, and each time I'd broken under her assault, the threads fraying as she beat at them relentlessly. And when the barrier failed, Eryn would send out a final punch that would knock me onto my ass.

But not this time. I was tired of picking myself up out of the dirt. Especially in front of all of the others.

"I'm ready," I said, and settled into a relaxed stance.

Eryn struck before I'd finished answering, a hard thrust hitting low, where she'd caught me unprepared once before. But I'd reinforced the barrier there, and the thrust slid to one side, its power dispersing into the natural flow of the currents around me. Another lesson it had taken a week of bruising to master. I didn't need to stop the blows; that used up too much energy. All I had to do was turn them to one side, let the river itself take care of it once the danger was past.

Eryn nodded in approval, then followed the initial thrust with three hard punches directly at the center of the barrier. Unlike the first thrust, which had been edged like a sword thrust, these punches were blunt, with all the weight of Eryn's power behind them, like fists.

I grunted as they struck, twisted slightly as I let the threads bend and absorb some of the power before turning them aside. Immediately, I reset the barrier, slid back into the balanced stance I'd learned from Erick.

"Good," Eryn said. "Very good."

To either side, I heard the other Servants murmur, but I didn't relax, never let my gaze waver from Eryn, my jaw set.

Eryn's eyes hardened. "Now let's see how long you can hold it."

I barely had time to draw a breath to brace myself.

She struck high, a single thrust as thin and deadly as a rapier, followed almost simultaneously with two blunt punches near my midsection. Blows began to rain down on my left flank, hard, vicious cuts that made me gasp with the effort to turn them, while at the same time, macelike thuds landed to my right. I deflected them all, breath coming sharper as the attacks continued, slicing from the left, from above, dagger blades of power cutting in from below, scoring hard against the barrier. The wall flexed, allowed the heaviest thrusts to slip off to the sides, then firmed to allow the blade cuts to glance away. The attacks didn't cease, coming harder, faster, from all sides. I heaved short breaths through my nose, my stance shifting from the relaxed pose of a Seeker to the more familiar defensive half crouch of gutterscum on the Dredge. My breathing altered, coming in gasps now, and sweat broke out on my forehead, between my shoulder blades and breasts, in my armpits.

But the barrier held.

On the far side of the flower bed, Eryn's expression changed. Her mouth pressed into a thin line, lips whitening. Creases appeared in her forehead as she focused. The hands clasped so casually before her tightened.

I felt a surge of triumph. She'd broken through my barriers before without blinking, had barely even moved. I used the sudden elation to shore up the barrier's edge, only to feel Eryn suddenly retreat, her energy pulling back, swirling around her as she regrouped.

I hesitated, uncertain whether the match had ended, began to let the barrier go as I straightened, a tentative grin touching my lips.

When my threads started to unravel, Eryn struck again.

The initial impact was stunning, and I cried out and fell back, felt my barrier shudder beneath the assault, felt its edges fray before I could regroup. Stone bit into my hand as I stumbled and caught my balance. Then I lurched forward with a sharp curse, knelt down painfully on one knee, and poured energy into the wall. A cruel smirk twisted Eryn's mouth, and I growled, thrusting the barrier higher to match the intensity of her blows. Without pause, she hammered at the wall on all sides, each blow shuddering with force, beating at me mercilessly.

I found myself using every last bit of strength just to keep the barrier erect, coherent and solid. I had nothing left to put into deflecting the thrusts, into shunting their power aside. I raised my hands before me, fingers splayed, and braced myself against each crashing blow, wincing at the sheer force Eryn put behind each one.

I wasn't certain how long I could hold out, but I gritted my teeth and dug in. This was the longest I'd lasted against her since the training had started. I wasn't about to yield.

It's a trick.

I hissed as the voice bled through the currents. A man's voice, scented with a pungent incense I didn't recognize. Someone from the throne.

Fear lanced through me. The Fire was weakening. But I couldn't shore it up. All of my energy was pouring into the shield.

It's a trick, the man's voice repeated, more sharply this time, stronger, full of authority, the accent strange, almost indecipherable. *She's distracting you with the heavy bludgeoning. She's undermining you somewhere else while you try to hold steady.*

A cold presence slid around me, ephemeral and heavily scented, like smoke. I could feel him as he paused before my barrier, could see a vague shape, a hint of clothes, of a wide face with a short, angled beard and shoulder-length hair. He scanned the shield, dark eyes darting left and right, examining the ripples on the barrier's surface as I repulsed each blow.

The shield was weakening. My strength was ebbing, draining away faster than I thought possible.

There! the man suddenly spat, turning toward me, the vague essence of an arm pointing to the left corner of the barrier. *Look! She's penetrated the shield there!*

I hissed and frowned, but scanned the area he'd indicated, crying out as Eryn struck again, the energy from the thrust seeping through the wall and hitting my shoulder with bruising force.

And then I saw it: a thin hole in the shield. As if someone had poked through with the tip of their knife. A thin ribbon curled out from the hole back to Eryn.

The cold presence of the man stepped closer, close enough so I could see the color of his eyes. Tawny brown, flecked with yellow. *She's stealing your strength, Varis,* he hissed. *Stop her.*

I shot the man a hateful glare, spat through clenched teeth, "How?"

His eyes narrowed in confusion, then cleared with sudden understanding. Shoulders straightening, he turned abruptly and said, *Like this.*

Something slid through me, shivering up through my body—

And then part of the shield let go, the threads parting like wisps.

On the river, Eryn's shoulders straightened with pure satisfaction and the eddies around her gathered for another blow. She released the hammer blow. It contained enough force to shatter the rest of the shield, to knock me flat, and it descended with horrible, hideous grace.

A moment before it struck, the threads of the unraveled section of the shield coalesced into a small ball of dense force and shot through the needlelike hole, down the ribbon, and hit Eryn.

At the same time, the shivering presence inside me vanished.

Crying out, hearing an echoing cry of pain and surprise from Eryn on the far side of the garden, I seized control of the fraying barrier and threw it up in front of Eryn's final blow.

It landed. The barrier held for an instant, for a single in-drawn gasp, shunted part of the force aside . . . and then it shattered.

I was crushed to the ground with bruising force, stone cutting into my hands, into my side and my face. I lay gasping, stunned, vaguely aware of cries from the other Servants, of shouts from the ever present guardsmen who'd been watching and waiting outside the garden, unable to believe that Eryn would put that much energy into destroying my shield. Anger punched through the daze, and I shoved myself up into a seated position before suddenly remembering the voice from the throne.

I thrust myself deep, heading for the barrier of Fire. I built up a new barrier as I went, weaving the threads in a slightly different pattern, one that Eryn had taught me for use against the personalities in the throne. I held it before me like a net as I came upon the Fire, the mesh tight and not as flexible as for defense. I couldn't believe that the Fire had weakened so much that one of the personalities had escaped, had been freed enough that he could create a semi-tangible form on the river, enough that he could seize control of the river itself through me. Whoever the man was, he'd *used* me, taken control of the shield I'd held long enough to rip a hole in it, to shape that power into a stone to strike out at Eryn.

A frisson of fear for Eryn flashed through me, but I thrust it aside as I scanned the blazing white flames that contained the voices, listening to the raging cacophony on the far side. They seemed to be shrieking with laughter, the strongest close to the edge of the firewall, taunting me, belittling me. I stoked the Fire enough to send flames reaching toward them, scattered them like leaves before a wind, but they returned, the mocking laughter increasing.

I growled in frustration, keeping the net ready, and began a methodical scrutiny of the Fire, circling it, searching for weaknesses, for areas where the wall of the Fire had thinned.

But there was nothing. Nothing I could see anyway.

Something Erick had said while training me on the Dredge echoed up from memory: *No defense is perfect. There is always a flaw. You just have to be patient enough to find it.*

I'd used the advice on the Dredge and while guarding Borund in order to survive. But I'd always been the one searching for the flaw in someone else's defenses.

Now the blade was reversed.

I found I didn't like the feeling.

Frowning, I concentrated and traced the scent of pungent incense on the eddies, found it residing inside the sphere of Fire, as expected. Inside, even though somehow the man had penetrated the barrier enough to take control. I could feel him watching me, could sense that there were others around him, also watching, not taunting me or screaming or howling like those voices beating against the edge of the Fire. One of those with him was the woman who smelled of oak and wine.

Who are you? I asked, curt and demanding.

My name is Cerrin, he said, not reacting to my anger. Then he added, *Not all of the voices in the throne are your enemies, Varis.*

I glared at the seething wall in consternation, let the chaos of the voices inside roll over me, then spun and retreated. The net I'd formed unraveled around me as I went.

"Mistress!"

I surfaced from the river with a shudder, blinked up into the winter sunlight and the blurry faces of Marielle, another Servant, and a concerned guardsman until my eyes adjusted, then dragged myself to my knees and stood, glancing around, a pair of guardsmen reaching out to help steady me.

"Mistress," Marielle gasped again, eyes white with concern. "Are you all right?"

"I'm fine," I spat, fuming. "Where's Eryn?"

Marielle, the Servants, and the guardsmen stepped back.

Any anger I'd felt for Eryn evaporated when I saw her crumpled form on the far side of the dead garden, two other guardsmen leaning over her, Laurren and another Servant kneeling at her side. Laurren rolled her onto her back as I watched and Eryn moaned.

"What did he do to you?" I murmured to myself and I pushed through the concerned Servants and guardsmen and knelt down beside Laurren. I couldn't see any marks on Eryn, couldn't see any damage.

"What did you do to her?" Laurren spat, both fear and awe in her voice.

"I don't know," I said.

Eryn moaned again, and her eyelids fluttered open, wincing at the sunlight. She brought one arm up to shade her eyes. "What happened?" she asked, but then she seemed to remember, her eyes focusing sharply on me. "Where did you learn to do that?"

My stomach knotted. I didn't want to admit to her that it had been one of the voices. Didn't want to admit to myself what that might mean.

So I let the anger surface, let it color my voice. "I didn't *learn* to do *anything*. I did what I had to in order to survive, as I've always done." I sat back, giving her room to sit up, waving the uncertain Servants and guardsmen back. She reached out one arm for support. I caught it before Laurren could, helped her steady herself. "I was winning," I said, "but then you cheated."

"Cheated!"

"You started draining away my strength!"

"That's not cheating," Eryn huffed. She struggled up from where she sat on the stones, brushed the dust and dirt off her white dress. "In a true battle, do you think your opponents are going to show you all their tricks before they attack? Of course not! They're going to do whatever it takes to win."

I scowled, but there wasn't much force behind it. There had never been any rules on the Dredge, I didn't know why I expected rules here in the palace. "You almost killed me with that last blast."

Eryn's face suddenly paled. "Oh, gods! I never meant for the blow to fall, at least not with that much force behind it. I meant for it to frighten you, but at the last moment I was going to pull it back, hit you with enough to knock you off-balance. But then that . . . that dart of power punched me in the gut along my own conduit and I lost control." She paused, the corners of her eyes tightening in what I'd come to recognize as a sign she was using her Sight.

After scanning me thoroughly, she relaxed.

"I don't see any permanent damage. But I'm surprised you survived it so unscathed." She frowned, then added in a considering voice, "You must be much stronger than I initially suspected."

I grunted, trying to hide the satisfied grin that tugged at the corners of my mouth. "What *did* I do?" I asked.

Eryn didn't answer, seemed suddenly to become aware of the Servants and guardsmen watching and listening closely. She scowled. "Break up into pairs as usual," she barked, motioning toward the Servants. "Marielle and Laurren, walk among them and help out where necessary."

After a pause, the Servants began to drift away, animated conversations instantly breaking out in lowered voices, glances shooting toward me. Marielle gave me a tentative smile, then caught Laurren's arm. But Laurren refused to budge.

"I'm fine, Laurren," Eryn said. "Go help the others."

Grudgingly, Laurren allowed Marielle to pull her away.

I nodded to the attending guardsmen, who drifted back to their posts on the outskirts of the garden.

Eryn moved toward a stone bench in one corner, wincing as she went, one hand going to her side. I followed, sitting down heavily. I was hot and sweaty and covered with dirt. And I felt bruised from head to toe.

We watched the Servants as they practiced for a moment, Laurren barking out orders to strengthen an edge, to tighten those flows, Marielle pointing out weaknesses in a soft voice, smiling and nodding encouragement.

"So was it Cerrin? Or Atreus?"

Eryn turned when I stiffened in shock.

"I don't believe you just 'happened' to suddenly discover how to send that dart through my conduit. I'm surprised you found the conduit at all. Someone from the throne must have helped you. So who was it?"

My eyes narrowed defiantly, but Eryn's gaze never faltered. I could see her exhaustion in her face, her weariness, but she still had a core of stubborn strength remaining.

I forced myself to back down, took a deep, steadying breath. "It was Cerrin." When Eryn only nodded, I asked, "Who is he?"

"One of the Seven. They are the ones that created the Skewed Throne nearly fifteen hundred years ago. They are the heart of the throne, the force that binds it and holds it together. To some extent, they can control the other voices of the throne as well."

I thought about the group of voices I'd sensed surrounding Cerrin in the throne. The calm voices in the maelstrom. And I suddenly recalled, with horrid clarity, the creation of the throne. I'd been forced to relive it when Eryn had thrust me onto the throne months before, had felt one of the Seven's pain as they watched the others die as the two thrones consumed them.

I shuddered.

"Have you felt them before today? Have they . . . influenced you in any way?"

When I opened my eyes, I found Eryn watching me closely.

"No," I said, but then caught myself, thought back to that first meeting with Avrell, Nathem, Ireen, and the captains of the guards. I'd felt something then, as if I'd stepped back . . . or been pushed aside. And then there was the woman who smelled of oak and wine. "Yes. It's happened before. But not like today. A woman tried to seize control while I was meeting with the merchants. But she simply tried to convince me to let her have control. Cerrin slipped free even while I was trying to hold him back. He's the one who manipulated the river and sent the stone through the conduit."

Eryn's eyes grew grim. "The woman was most likely Liviann, another of the Seven. As long as the other Seven are with her, she's not a threat. But if she's alone . . ." She shook her head. "I'm more concerned about Cerrin being able to slip past the Fire enough to seize that much control of the river. Not to mention the protective net I showed you."

"Can I alter the net somehow to keep him contained?" I thought back to the transparent image of the man who'd taken control, recalled the faint outlines of the clothes he wore. A long, tapered coat, the cut archaic; a yellow silk shirt with a strange neckline; breeches of the same material as the coat. And boots, the leather sides high and flared wide, folded down in a style I'd never seen before. His voice had been accented as well, the words somehow clipped, the flow of the sentences not quite right.

"I don't know. I've shown you the strongest net I know of for containing the voices." A note of weariness had crept into her voice. She stood, began to make her way toward the open double doors to the garden, pausing only to allow the still practicing Servants to pass. "We'll have to experiment," Eryn continued. "Try to strengthen it somehow. Perhaps tomorrow."

"No," I said, too sharply.

Eryn glanced toward me, eyebrow raised.

I sighed, then grimaced. My muscles were already beginning to protest. "Avrell wants to show me the construction on the new warehouse district, and the setup of the kitchen and warehouse on the Dredge."

Eryn nodded, forced a smile through her exhaustion, her shoulders sagging slightly. "That's just as well," she said. "I think I'm going to be bruised after today. A day to recover would be welcome."

She halted as we entered the shaded interior of the palace, then grinned. "It appears that you're going to need the rest more than me, however."

Frowning, my eyes still adjusting to the shadows, I turned—

And groaned aloud when I saw Westen leaning patiently against the far wall.

"Ready to play?" he asked with a grin.

I leaned down to pick up a stray mud-brick but halted halfway, jerking upright with a gasp and a blistering curse.

"Mistress?" Avrell asked, real concern in his voice. He'd halted a few steps ahead of me in his careful progress down the street on the edge of what used to be the warehouse district. The street was littered with stacked stone, lumber, loose rope, and mud-brick, and was coated with thick dust.

"I'm fine," I said through gritted teeth, silently sending Eryn and Westen to the deepest of hells while massaging the muscle screaming in protest in my lower back. But it wasn't just them. Avrell had gotten tired of walking every-where within the city and forced Marielle to start giving me riding lessons. The first lesson had been excruciating, worse than one of Westen's training sessions. I'd hurt in places I hadn't even known existed.

And all of it was beginning to wear on my body.

Avrell hesitated, but moved on. Beside me, Erick scooped up the mud-brick I'd reached for and replaced it on the nearest heap.

"*Are* you all right?" he asked, pitched low so that none of the accompanying guards could hear.

I bit off another curse and nodded. "Fine. Just a little . . . weary."

Erick nodded as if that explained everything, face serious. But I could feel him silently laughing underneath.

Ahead, Avrell halted on the edge of a wide break in the buildings and streets. As we pulled up even with him, both Erick and I raised a hand to shade our eyes from the sunlight.

"Impressive," Erick said after a moment.

I had to agree.

Where the warehouse district had been reduced to charred support beams and soot-stained, crumbled stone in the fire two months before, Avrell and his labor crews had cleared a wide swath of flat land. Men, skin drenched with sweat, clothed only in breeches, were loading up carts with debris on all sides, keeping only what stone could still be used in the new construction. Every-thing else was being carted away, to the edges of the city, near the uninhabited northern jut of land that enclosed the harbor. I'd seen the work from my balcony and the roof of the tower over the last few weeks, but that had been from a distance, the sheer scope of the work being done somehow reduced. But here, where I could see the workers coated with char and dust from shifting the stones, hear the group leaders barking orders . . .

"We're just about finished sorting and clearing out the old stone, salvaging what we can from the lost buildings themselves," Avrell said. "Once we're done with that, we'll shift the workers to laying down new foundations, or shoring up the old ones where possible."

"How long do you think it will take to rebuild everything completely?" I asked.

Avrell scowled. "At this rate, all winter and most of the summer besides. But I expect that things will pick up shortly."

"Why's that?"

The First motioned toward the work crews loading up the carts. "Because we don't have many workers right now. It's early in the winter yet. Most people have put their own stores back and are using them now."

"So there's no need to send anyone to the work lines to get the credit chips for food," Erick said.

"Correct. But once people's personal stores begin to run dry . . ."

I grunted.

Captain Catrell had sent the city guardsmen out to warn people to ration, and that theft and hoarding of goods would be punished severely. Two houses had been raided in the first week after the announcement, the families arrested and confined, their food portioned and distributed among the warehouses being run by the merchants. At the same time, the guardsmen had announced the work policy. Men, women, and children could report to the warehouses for work details. In exchange for a day's labor, they'd receive enough rations for a meal, which they could get in one of the kitchens the servants from the palace had established near each of the warehouses. Most women were sent to grind grist into flour, or to the communal ovens to bake the bread that would be distributed at the end of the day to the kitchens, or to repair the fishing nets for the fishing fleets, or any of a hundred other similar tasks. Some worked in the kitchens themselves, along with the children, under the supervision of the palace servants. Most of the men were sent to the warehouse district or the fishing boats, or into the forests east of the city to hunt for game or cut down timber for the reconstruction. Some joined the city guard, if they could show some skill with a sword, then were used to police the makeshift warehouses, the kitchens, and the supplies.

Things had changed in the palace as well. A small stock of food had been kept inside the palace walls for use in the palace itself. The rest had been sent into the city. I'd insisted, despite protests from Avrell and Erick, who argued that the palace had to remain visibly stable and that the guards needed to be well fed to be effective. I'd relented somewhat regarding the guardsmen, but if the city was going to starve, then so would everyone in the palace.

I'd lived on the Dredge. I knew what it was to be hungry, knew that I would survive. Avrell and the others would learn they could survive on very little as well.

"Would you like to take a closer look?" Avrell asked, breaking into my thoughts. I glanced toward him, saw the look of appeal in his eyes, hidden behind his administrator's blank mask.

"Of course," I said.

Avrell grinned, then led us into the open space, pointing out piles of stone and stacked lumber as we moved. "This is the largest building that was lost. You can see the outline of the original foundation here and here. Nathem and I decided to start with that building first, then move on to the others later, since we can use this one's walls for supports for the others if necessary. We salvaged enough stone to get the entire building built, and I've got carpenters and masons from the guilds planning how to repair and relay the foundation, starting within the week."

Avrell's voice fell into the background as we continued, relating all the plans. The farther afield we moved, the more I began to orient myself, using the surrounding streets and the outlines of the lost buildings as reference points. A warm hand of dread began to close over my heart as I realized we were approaching the alley where I'd been ambushed by Alendor's son, Cristoph.

I halted in the spot where the alley had stood, kicked at the blackened dirt and the stone of the cobbles. All trace of the walls that had trapped me—of the crates that had hemmed me in and hampered my movements as Cristoph and his men surrounded me and beat me—were gone, cleared away by the fire and the workers.

Alendor had led me here, let me follow him and his own bodyguards from the tavern called the Splintered Bow so that his son and henchmen could trap me in the alley. All because Cristoph had tried to kill me earlier on the wharf and I'd managed to turn the blade against him and his friend instead. Cristoph had survived the encounter. His friend hadn't.

I glanced toward Erick, saw the grim expression on his face. He recognized the alley as well. I'd only survived the ambush because Erick had arrived and intervened. He'd almost died here, trying to save me.

I could see the same thought echoed in his eyes.

"Is there something wrong?" Avrell asked.

I suddenly realized his constant stream of information about the reconstruction had halted minutes before, and I turned toward him with a tight smile. "No. I was here once before. Before the fire. This is where Alendor's son ambushed me."

Avrell glanced down solemnly at the scuffed and fire-cracked cobbles. "I see."

We lapsed into an awkward silence, broken by a sharp yelp of pain and the sounds of a scuffle from the nearest line of men loading up the carts.

All three of us turned. The escort of guardsmen closed in around me, but I pushed forward, Erick and Avrell falling into step as we came up on the group of men. The gathering parted as soon as they saw us coming, revealing two men grappling with each other on the ground, cursing, dirt and dust flying. One of them was younger, leaner, only a boy, body writhing like a snake as the other, heavier man tried to force him to the ground.

"Bloody cursed gutterscum," the older man growled. Then he landed a sharp punch to the other's gut, the boy doubling over with a whoof of pain followed by a hiss of pure fury.

The heavier man thrust the boy to the ground, then staggered upright, panting heavily, eyes dark. He wiped a hand across his mouth, spat blood, lip curling up in a snarl. "This will teach ya."

He drew his foot back to kick the boy in the gut while he was down.

Rage flared inside me, hard and sharp, and without thought I lashed out, punching the heavyset man in the chest with the river.

The man staggered backward, eyes going wide in surprise, breath gushing from his lungs. The punch had come from nowhere, been landed by nothing that he could see. The ring of spectators caught him before he fell, as surprised as he was, then set him roughly on the ground as he tried to catch his breath.

The boy had dragged himself into a defensive crouch, watched me now with a feral, hateful gaze as I stepped forward between the two men. I could see the Dredge on the boy, like a dark cloak hanging over his shoulders. He was maybe fourteen years old, with sharp dark brown eyes and blond hair made muddy by layers of dirt and soot and sweat.

"What's going on here?" I asked, voice hard as stone. I glared at the heavyset man where he sat, legs still weak from my punch, breath still short. When he didn't answer, I turned my gaze on the rest of those gathered.

They shuffled where they stood, eyes not rising to meet mine. They'd recognized me, knew me as the Mistress.

I grunted with contempt, then turned to the boy.

He shifted backward, the movement hauntingly familiar. He was gutterscum, just like me. I could guess which way he'd bolt, could see the careful balance of options in his eyes.

The fact that he hadn't bolted already told me how desperate he was.

"What happened?" I asked, voice still hard. He wouldn't respond to anything else.

His gaze darted to the heavyset man, then returned. "He kicked me."

"Lying, filthy, fucking shit!" the man spat, face turning red as he tried to regain his feet. But I could read the truth in the men around him, the way they shifted away from the man, the way their eyes couldn't meet mine.

The boy scowled, and I could see him on the edge of fleeing. Back to the Dredge, back to the life he knew. His despair was clear: he'd taken a chance on the rumors of food for work, had risked coming out of the Dredge to find out if it were true, and this is what he'd found, what he'd expected to find.

It was more than I had risked at his age.

I shifted and the heavyset man halted where he'd struggled to his feet, eyes fearful.

I turned back to the boy. "Why did he kick you?"

Disbelief clouded the boy's eyes briefly as he realized I believed him, then he shot the man a deadly glare. "Because I'm gutterscum."

Another man stepped forward, and the guardsmen behind me tensed. Erick motioned for them to wait as the man ducked his head.

"The boy's right. Hant's been after him all day, makin comments, flickin him with stones when he wasna lookin. I wouldna taken it as long as the boy did."

Behind, Avrell shifted closer and murmured, "The boy's one of the few we've had come to work for us from the Dredge."

Avrell's words were bland, but the meaning was clear. He expected this type of condescension for those that came from the Dredge to continue.

Unless something were done now. Something significant.

I turned to Hant. The heavyset man was now uncertain. He could feel the shift in attitude among the men around him, could feel the blade now balanced against him.

"Erick," I said, and felt Erick step up beside me, motions precise and formal. "Yes, Mistress."

The boy gasped as he realized who I was. A low murmur ran through the gathered men as well. What they'd suspected had been confirmed.

"This kind of attitude can't continue. It *will not* continue." I pitched my voice loud enough so that all of those around us could hear. "No one in this city is better than any of the others. If those on the Dredge want to help us rebuild the warehouses, then they are welcome, and they will be treated exactly as everyone else is treated. There is only one city here: Amenkor." I turned back to Hant with pure contempt. "I want him punished. Do whatever you feel is necessary."

Avrell stepped forward, as if he'd been waiting for the opening. "I would suggest a public whipping."

I frowned, glanced toward Erick, who nodded minutely. "Do it," I said.

With a simple motion of his hand, Erick had the escorting guardsmen seize Hant and drag him, kicking, to one side. The rest of the workers stood silently, some with open shock, others with satisfaction or sympathy. I ignored them, turning to the man who'd stepped forward to defend the boy. "What's your name?"

The man seemed distracted by the scuffle Hant was raising behind me, but managed to say, "Danel, Mistress."

"And what do you do?"

Danel's attention began to focus more on me. "I'm a cobbler, Mistress."

I nodded, shot a questioning look toward Avrell.

The First must have read my intent on my face, for he said, "I believe we've been wasting your talents here hauling stone, Danel. We are always in need of people who can organize and lead the workers. Would you be interested?"

Danel nodded, too stunned to speak.

"Good," Avrell said. "Report to Nathem, the Second of the Mistress, to-morrow at the Priem warehouse in the upper city. He'll inform you as to what to do."

Danel nodded again, then stepped hesitantly back, where a few friends pat-ted him on the back, eyes alight and excited.

I turned to the boy with a heavy frown, took in his relaxed stance—or as relaxed as anyone who lived on the Dredge ever got. "And your name?"

The boy frowned, the reaction automatic, then caught himself. Straighten-ing slightly, burying his fear deep, so that most people wouldn't see it, he said defiantly, "Evander."

I waited until his defiance faltered slightly. "Tell those on the Dredge that if they're willing to work, we can feed them. Not much, but more than they're likely to find on the Dredge this winter."

Then I turned away, retreating with Avrell, Erick, and the two remaining guardsmen who weren't dealing with Hant.

"You handled that well," Erick said, voice low enough only Avrell and I could hear.

I grunted. I wasn't so certain.

But Evander had done one thing: he'd reminded me of myself, of what the Dredge had been like.

"Do you think he'll spread the word on the Dredge?" Avrell asked. "Do you think he'll be believed?"

Memories churning up from the depths, I said with utter certainty, "He'll be believed. And he'll be more effective than the guardsmen."

"Why?"

I cast Avrell a knowing look. "Because gutterscum always recognizes gut-terscum. Evander didn't see me as the Mistress. He saw me as Varis, from the Dredge."

I let Avrell think about that for a moment, then asked, "What about the kitchen and warehouse on the Dredge?"

"A shipment of food is being taken down there today. We're to meet up with Baill and the guards escorting the shipment near the bridge over the River."

Behind us, there was a sharp slap and a barked scream.

Someone had found a whip.

We reached the bridge where the Dredge crossed the River and found Baill and the guardsmen already waiting, restless. Each of the three wagonloads of food was surrounded by twenty guardsmen, all with their hands on the hilts of their swords, all sweating nervously. They knew what had happened the last time we'd come to the Dredge. Only Baill seemed unconcerned, his bald head shining in the sunlight, his face fixed into a permanent frown.

"They know we're coming," the captain of the guard said as I approached. "We've seen at least three watching from the alleys and windows."

Which meant that there had probably been twenty. The entire slum would know by now.

"Are your men ready?" I asked. Baill grunted and nodded. "Then let's go."

He barked out an order and the first wagon lurched forward, two guardsmen in the seat. Avrell and Erick fell in beside me behind the first wagon, my escort staying close, drawing in tight, the other two wagons behind us. Baill remained in the lead.

As we passed over the arch of the bridge, the River flowing dark and smooth beneath us, I felt a niggling touch of the overwhelming dread I'd felt when we'd come the first time. But when the buildings closed in around us, the clean stone of the real Amenkor falling away to the decayed grit of the slums, that niggling sensation faded. Evander had helped me remember what I had been, and that I'd taken a chance and escaped.

Perhaps this winter, some of the others willing to take a chance could escape as well.

We were almost to the warehouse where Eryn had hidden the stores she'd smuggled into the city when Erick said suddenly, "Something's wrong."

"What?" Avrell asked.

I jerked out of my thoughts of Evander, of my old life, my hand settling onto my dagger. I glanced around in consternation, trying to pick up on what Erick had felt, then dove beneath the river. . . .

And felt it, too.

The Dredge was quiet.

But it wasn't empty.

I spun, tasting terror in the back of my throat as I darted forward past startled palace guardsmen, past the wagon, knowing even as I picked up speed that I was too late.

Behind, I heard Erick shout in warning, then curse under his breath as he started to follow. Ahead—

"What's the meaning of this?" Baill demanded, his voice loud, ringing out in the silence.

Too late, too late.

I rounded the front of the wagon, saw the street ahead blocked by a throng of men. No, not men. These were the dregs of the slums, the animals that hid in the deepest depths, that preyed on the gutterscum that were only trying to survive. Their grizzled faces, marked by scars and pockmarks and disease, were harsh in the sunlight, their mouths twisted into feral grins, their eyes insane with rage and death.

No wonder the Dredge was empty.

"We've come to take what's ours," the leader said.

And then a stone shot out of the crowd and found its mark, slamming into Baill's forehead with a sickening thud, and as he fell, as the scent of blood flooded the river, bitter and warm, the mob broke into a scream and roared forward.

The palace guardsmen surged forward to meet them. At my side, the horse pulling the first wagon screamed and reared up onto its hind legs, its eyes white with terror.

And then the mob collided with the guardsmen, and the world broke into a crush of bodies and sweat, of flickering blades and a hail of stone. I felt the initial impact of the two forces on the river, a pulsing wave rippling outward.

And then I was overwhelmed, men suddenly on all sides, the rearing horse thudding down into the mass of bodies with a sickening crunch. The scent of blood on the river became so thick I almost gagged.

"Varis!"

I spun, Erick's shout was almost lost in the tumult. Men crowded close on all sides, and my dagger was out, already blooded, although I didn't remember using it. A few palace guardsmen held my back for a moment, desperately trying to protect the wagonloads of food, before the thrust of the mob shoved them away and they were lost. The denizens of the slums closed in from all sides, coming from the alleys, from the narrows, crawling through the vacant windows of the buildings, through the darknesses that I'd always thought of as escapes. Through the press of bodies, I saw Erick lash out with his own dagger, saw a man scream in pain, blood flying, saw another lurch back before Erick's dagger took him in the throat. Thrusting the body aside, Erick stepped forward. But there were still too many men between us, all screaming, all intent on overwhelming the guards, on the food. Some had already reached the wagon, were smashing into the crates and barrels, clutching potatoes and squash and sacks of grain to their chests before leaping back into the mob. A sack of rice split and grains of white rained down, a few flicking my face, catching in my hair.

Rage enveloped me, sudden and intense, and pushing deep beneath the river, breath rushing out through flaring nostrils, I *pushed*, grunting with the effort.

Before me, men went flying, lifted forcibly up into the air and thrust away, and suddenly there was a clear path between Erick and me. Startled, he hesitated, then leaped into the opening, grabbing my arm.

"We have to get out of here!" he shouted.

I gave him a scathing, sarcastic glare and shot back, "Avrell! We have to find Avrell!"

He swore under his breath, scanned the mob, ducked as a piece of mud-brick shot past his head, then used his grip on my arm to shove me in a new direction. "This way!"

I stumbled forward, using my dagger and the river to force a path through the mob, Erick a steady presence at my back. As we angled away from the wagons, the press of bodies slackened.

And then suddenly we broke free, into the depths of an alley. Gasping, Erick drew up close to the wall, back brushing against the slick mud-brick. I settled into a crouch, breath harsh in my throat, heart thudding in my chest so hard it hurt, then jerked as someone else broke through the mob, streaking past us without a glance, a loaf of bread crushed to his chest, his expression ravenous.

I sucked in a haggard breath, then asked hoarsely, "Do you see Avrell?"

Erick shook his head. "No. Nor Baill. The mob's taken over all of the wagons now. The guardsmen have retreated to the kitchen. I don't think they can get into the warehouse. It's still warded. But I think they have Baill."

The roar of the mob was suddenly broken by a piercing animalistic scream.

Erick's face turned grim. "They must be running out of food on the wagons. They're after the horses now."

I stood up from my crouch, glanced over the seething morass of people, felt the wave of darkness it generated on the river and felt sick. "We have to find Avrell."

"I have him."

Both Erick and I spun, daggers raised, our movements almost exactly the same.

In the darkness of the alley behind us, Darryn stood, flanked by two other men and the elder with the milky eye. Darryn's face was blank, eyes centered on me. After a considering moment, he glanced toward the mob, then scowled before turning back to me.

"I can take you to him. You can stay with him under our protection until this dies down."

I almost spat in contempt, as the milky-eyed elder had done to me, but stopped myself.

Straightening, I nodded.

He led us deeper into the alley, back into the warrens that three years ago I had called home, the others falling in behind us, guarding our backs. As we slipped from narrow to narrow, passing through crumbled alleys and dead courtyards, the roar of the mob falling behind, I found the dread returning, not as powerful as before, but still there.

I shivered.

Then Darryn ducked through a low opening, nothing more than a hole in a wall.

I glanced back at Erick, saw him nod, and followed.

It opened up into a wide room, half sunk below ground, filled with tables, a few chairs, pallets against one wall. In the center of the room was a circular basin which must have once been a pool or fountain. A few chipped tiles remained at its edge, dirt ground so deep into them that there was nothing left of the pattern they must once have held.

Sitting on one of the chairs was Avrell, one hand clutching the opposite arm. Blood stained his shoulder, his dark blue shirt ripped aside. A man leaned over the wound.

"Mistress!" he said as I entered, then gasped as the man prodded the wound. "It was only a stray mud-brick," he finished weakly.

Darryn moved up to the man's side. "Well?"

The man grunted. "It needs a good cleaning and some stitches, but he'll live."

The rest of the men scattered throughout the room, one collapsing onto a pallet. The elder with the milky eye stayed behind at the rough opening, keeping watch.

Darryn turned back to me, ignoring Avrell's yelp of pain as the man I assumed was a healer began washing his wound. "And is this how you intend to feed the Dredge?" he asked acidly.

Erick's hand fell heavily onto my shoulder, restraining me. His grip was tight, the fingers flexing in warning as I tensed, trembling with rage.

I forced myself to relax, forced the hand that held my dagger to drop to my side. "You know how I intend to feed the Dredge," I said.

"Ah, yes. A day's work for a day's worth of food." He smirked. "How's that going to work if you can't even get the food to the kitchen?"

I gritted my teeth, jaw flexing, my hand kneading the handle of my dagger.

And then all the tension drained out of my body, and I smiled. "You're going to help me."

One of the other men barked out a short burst of laughter, but Darryn's face had gone completely blank. "What do you mean?"

I stepped forward, slipping out of Erick's grip. No one in the room moved, not even the healer. He held a needle in the air with a thin thread of gut running from its end down to Avrell's half-stitched wound, his face openly shocked.

"The crowd we drew on the Dredge when we first visited the warehouse didn't attack because you didn't want them to. They looked to you for permission. They obey you."

Darryn snorted. "Have you seen the Dredge today, Mistress? I don't control anyone."

I shook my head. "You don't control everyone. The ones ripping the wagons to pieces right now aren't the real people of the Dredge. The real people—the people I want to help survive this winter—are all cowering in their own niches right now, waiting for the animals to finish feeding so they can pick up the pieces. Just like you. Those are the people you control. And if you can get them organized, get them to cooperate . . ."

The man who'd laughed before began to chuckle.

"Shut up, Greag."

The room fell silent. I stared into Darryn's eyes, saw his age in the wrinkles around his eyes, saw the gray beginning in his hair. He watched me in turn, considering.

Then his gaze flicked to Erick. "Is she serious?"

"She's always serious."

Darryn frowned. "How do you expect to protect the food once it's here?"

"The warehouses will be warded by the Servants, who will also be present in the kitchen. And there will always be palace guardsmen—" I halted. Darryn was shaking his head.

"That won't work. The Servants maybe, but not the guardsmen. If you're truly from the Dredge, you'll know that."

And I did. The guardsmen wouldn't survive as a permanent presence on the Dredge. They were too feared, too hated.

"What do you suggest?"

Before Darryn could answer, Erick stepped to my side, motioned toward the sword that hung at Darryn's waist. "Can you use that?"

Darryn stiffened. "Yes."

"What about these others?" Erick said, nodding toward the rest of the men hidden in the niche along with us.

Darryn shifted uncomfortably. "To varying degrees." Behind him, the healer grunted and returned to his stitching.

Erick turned to me. "Then have them protect their own warehouse and kitchen. Form a militia, made up of people from the Dredge, under Darryn's command."

I frowned, saw Avrell frowning as well but ignored him. "What do you think?"

He glanced around at the men in the room, asking a silent question and receiving silent answers—a nod, a shrug.

Then he turned back to me. "I think it might work."

"Mistress," Marielle said, her voice soft but strained. She winced as lightning flared through the open doorway leading out to the balcony, silver light flooding the room, followed a few seconds later by a harsh crack of thunder that shuddered through the air. "Come back to the settee, please! The storm is too close!"

I turned away from the balcony with a smile, felt the cold wind sweep into the room around me, tugging at my hair. Rain hissed onto the stone of the palace, harsh and relentless, a fine mist touching my face. The storm raged around me, prickled my skin, and with each flash of lightning I felt my heart respond with a quickened beat. Each roll of thunder shivered through my body, raised the little hairs on my arms, at the nape of my neck. I reveled in the sensation.

"Can't you feel it?" I said.

Marielle shuddered with terror. "Please! Come to the settee!"

Deeper inside the room, Erick shrugged, his expression as unconcerned as my own. We'd both been hardened to the weather. On the Dredge, there was little protection if you were caught in a storm.

Thinking of the Dredge brought a small surge of satisfaction. The kitchen and warehouse had finally been stocked with Darryn's and the Dredge militia's help. The militia only consisted of twenty men so far, and Baill was furious that the unit had been formed in the first place, but even now he and Captain Catrell were training more Dredge denizens who, when their training was complete, would be added to the force.

And more laborers were reporting to the warehouse district for work as well, a significant portion of them coming from the Dredge.

Lightning flared, the resultant thunder almost instantaneous. Marielle let out a small shriek. "Mistress, please!"

I sighed, closed the balcony door, but refused to draw the curtains, leaving the windows open. I moved to the settee, took the slate from Marielle's relieved hands. She stood and moved to pour me some tea to ease her own nerves.

I glanced down at the slate, picked up the chalk loosely in one hand. After her discussion with Erick, Marielle had given up trying to get me to draw elegant, curved letters. Instead, she'd had me think of the shapes as slashes, as if from a dagger—sharp and linear, with cutting, blunt edges. Forceful.

My letters had improved dramatically. We were working on words now, and simple sentences.

I stared down at the three-word sentence Marielle had scrawled on the top line, but as thunder shook the building again, Marielle casting a frightened glance toward the ceiling, I set the slate aside and stood.

"How long is the storm going to last, do you think?"

Erick cocked his head, listening to the wind, to the rain lashing against the stone. "It moved in swiftly from the ocean about midafternoon," he murmured, "but it doesn't sound like it's letting up any. I'd say not for another few hours."

I began pacing the room, too energized by the storm to remain still. "Then let's go see Avrell."

Erick nodded.

I stepped toward Marielle, who'd set my tea down. "Are you coming, Marielle?"

She turned. "If it's all right, I'll stay. I have . . . things I need to finish here." She cowered as more lightning flickered through the room.

I frowned, but nodded, turning toward Erick who held the door to the rest of the palace open for me.

We found Avrell in his office, poring over sheets of parchment with Nathem, Baill, and two masons I'd noticed leading labor crews at the warehouses.

"Avrell," I said.

All five men looked up, startled, their muttered argument cut short.

Avrell frowned, then stepped forward. "Yes, Mistress?"

Wondering what Baill was doing here, I asked, "What's happening with the warehouses?"

Avrell relaxed slightly. "We're progressing nicely, mainly due to the sudden influx of labor. The foundation to the main warehouse I showed you has now been finished and we've started on the walls, but of course we can't work on those today."

As if in answer, a rumble of thunder sounded, muffled by the stone of the palace this deep inside, but still audible.

Behind Avrell, one of the masons coughed meaningfully. Avrell's brow creased with annoyance.

I sighed. "What is it?"

Flashing his own glare of irritation at the mason, he said, "Two things actually. And at this point, neither of them have been investigated in any great detail."

I let my gaze narrow and Avrell stepped back behind his desk, pulling out a few sheets of paper. He still favored the shoulder that Darryn's healer had stitched up, moving the arm carefully as he shuffled through the pages. "The first is regarding the stone we need to rebuild the warehouses. As I said before, we have enough to rebuild the main warehouse, which is what we're working on now, but quite a bit of the stone used in the original buildings has been cracked by the heat of the fire and can't be reused in the new buildings."

Nathem spoke up. "We've been trying to figure out where to get stone from. We do have a quarry, but that is some distance away. Transporting the stone into the city during winter would be extremely difficult. Plus it would take time to cut the stone even before we begin to transport it."

"What about mud-brick?" I asked.

Glances were passed among everyone except Baill, who stood silently in the background, arms crossed, watching intently, his face the usual unreadable mask. Except that recently—since I'd forced him to initiate the militia on the Dredge—it had taken on an edge of bitterness.

"Mud-brick is possible," Avrell finally answered, "but it is somewhat unreliable, especially for the size of these buildings. And it is also labor-intensive. We'd still need to transport in the material used in the bricks, and then it would have to be mixed and fired. . . ." He shook his head.

"Why do you need to make it? There's tons of mud-brick from old buildings sitting unused in the Dredge."

Avrell and the masons looked momentarily stunned. Then Avrell turned to the masons. "Is that possible?"

The masons stared at each other a moment. "I don't see why not," one of them finally said. "We'd have to pick through it carefully, make certain it was sound. And we'd still need good stone from the quarry for the foundations and a significant portion of the walls. But . . ."

"Good," Avrell said. "Send some work crews down to the Dredge as soon as you can and check it out."

"Make certain they get in touch with Darryn," I said. "He'll want to warn the residents of the Dredge that you'll be there and what you'll be doing. And he'll want to escort the work crews while they're there, for their own protection."

I shifted my gaze toward Baill. An ugly red-and-purple scab marked where the stone had struck his head during the riot. He still hadn't spoken, and I couldn't see why he'd be involved in an argument over where to find usable stone for the warehouse construction. "What's the other problem?"

In an almost concerted move, the stonemasons and Nathem stepped back, eyes looking anywhere but at me. Avrell remained at the desk, but deferred to Baill.

A smile tugged at Baill's mouth, but it was fleeting.

Without moving, he said flatly, "We may have some stores missing from one of the warehouses."

I stilled. Missing supplies was a far more serious problem than where to find stone. "Is it missing from the Dredge?"

"No."

I almost heaved a sigh of relief. I wanted to believe Darryn could be trusted, *knew* he could be trusted if the river was any indication, but having supplies go missing almost immediately after I'd given him control . . .

I focused again on Baill. "Then how is that possible? I thought the city guard was watching over each warehouse on this side of the River, that the merchants were keeping track of the supplies under their care."

Baill nodded. "They are."

"Then how could some of the food have been taken?" Anger had begun to tighten my voice, and Baill reacted by straightening subtly, an answering flare of anger passing swiftly through his eyes.

"We don't know. As Avrell said, we don't even know for certain that the food is missing."

Avrell stepped forward cautiously. "According to our records, and the merchants' records, the Priem warehouse was supposed to have eighteen barrels of packed, salted fish. However, upon inspection, we couldn't find those barrels. It may just be a clerical error, or the barrels could have been taken to a different warehouse by mistake. It's too early to tell. I summoned Baill immediately and we were just beginning to discuss a course of action."

Baill nodded. "I think we should start with an inventory of the warehouses done by the guard, to verify that all of the supplies supposedly stored in each warehouse are actually present. If anything else is missing, we should find out now."

I considered for a moment, then said, "Do it."

Baill moved to the door. As he stepped outside and began to issue orders, I turned to Avrell.

"Which merchant has control of the Priem warehouse?"

Avrell's eyes never wavered. He'd been expecting the question. "Regin."

I bit off a curse, then forced myself to stop leaping to conclusions. Avrell admitted that perhaps the fish wasn't missing. Maybe it had simply been misplaced.

But somehow I didn't believe that.

In the corridor outside there was a sudden commotion, brief but loud enough to hear over the continuing thunder. I turned as the doors to Avrell's study opened and Baill stepped back through. His brow was creased with a frown, and his clothes were disheveled and damp in patches.

"There's someone here to see the Mistress," he said formally. "He wouldn't say what it concerned." Then he shifted to one side.

A boy stood behind him, surrounded by guardsmen, wide-eyed and breathing hard, splattered with mud and soaked to the bone, a puddle forming on the floor beneath him. He was dressed in a rough homespun tunic and breeches with no boots, his face pale, lips almost blue.

As I stepped forward, he shuddered with cold. "What is it?" I asked.

Teeth beginning to chatter, the boy sputtered, "There's been a shipwreck down in Colby."

✠ Chapter 6

"From what I can gather from the boy," Avrell said, leaning back in his seat, wincing as he adjusted his shoulder, "the villagers didn't find an actual shipwreck. What they found was debris on the beach, large sections of a ship, just before the storm struck. They managed to haul the largest pieces of the debris up above the storm waters so that it wouldn't wash away, and then they sent the boy here."

After the boy's bald statement in Avrell's office, Avrell had taken him aside and questioned him, with my repeated assurances to the boy that it was safe to talk to the First. Servants were sent for dry clothes and food, while others were sent to inform the other captains, Eryn, and Borund. We'd convened in the same meeting room Avrell had used to introduce me to the captains of the guard.

"Were there any survivors?" I asked.

Avrell shook his head, mouth turned down with regret. "According to the boy, there weren't even any bodies washed ashore. Just wood and rigging, a large portion of the mast. . . ." He shrugged.

"But enough to identify the ship as coming from Amenkor?" Borund asked. He was still damp from his brisk ride up to the palace in the rain after being summoned.

Avrell nodded.

At the far end of the table, Captain Catrell of the city guard leaned forward. "The question is, how did the ship founder?"

At his side, Westen nodded in agreement. "Was it by storm? But if so, what storm? The villagers found the wreckage *before* this hit." He glanced at the ceiling. The storm was moving off now, but the occasional rumble of thunder could still be heard through the thick stone walls. He leaned forward, eyeing Avrell. "How old was the wreckage?"

"The boy didn't know. The villagers sent him almost immediately after finding the debris. Aside from what I've told you already, he knew nothing."

Silence fell. Glances were exchanged between Eryn, Erick, and myself. We were the only ones in the room that knew of the vision of the city burning, and I could see in both Erick's and Eryn's eyes that I wasn't the only one thinking the wreckage could be from something other than a storm.

Straightening in my seat, the motion enough to draw everyone's attention, I said flatly, "I need to see the debris."

There was an awkward pause, and then Baill said tactfully, "Colby, the village where the wreckage was found, is outside of the city."

I frowned, confused, and then suddenly remembered.

I was trapped inside the city by the throne. I *couldn't* go see the wreckage.

I swore vehemently, startling both Captain Catrell and Baill. Catrell seemed shocked; Baill simply seemed intrigued.

"Someone has to go look at the wreckage," I said. "I need to know what ship the debris came from, how long it has been since it foundered, if possible, and how it was lost in the first place."

A few of those present seemed surprised at the force behind my voice. But then I realized: To them it was simply an unfortunate accident, a ship lost at sea, most likely by storm or from running onto a hidden shoal or perhaps piracy. They didn't have the vision haunting them. They couldn't see the bodies floating in the harbor, hadn't choked on the smoke of the fires.

Reacting to the intensity of my voice, Captain Catrell stood. "I'll send a contingent of the city guard immediately. We can leave tomorrow morning and be in Colby by late afternoon, with enough light left to investigate the wreckage so that we can return the following day."

Baill shifted forward. "I'll send a few palace guards along as well."

I shook my head, and Baill frowned, a flash of annoyance crossing his face. "No, Captain Baill. I want the palace guards to devote their energy to the food missing from the warehouse."

"Very well," Baill said.

It was clear he was unhappy I'd countermanded his suggestion.

But that still didn't solve the real problem. Captain Catrell didn't know about the vision. He and his men wouldn't look at the wreckage with alternative possibilities in mind. He'd probably already assumed it was from a storm, and that the debris had been lying on the beach for weeks. I needed someone who could factor in the warning given by the vision.

I glanced toward Erick, but hesitated.

Since he'd first returned from tracking down and killing Corum, he'd been a constant presence, my personal bodyguard, always near at hand, even if he wasn't always in the same room. I'd grown accustomed to having him there, for advice and for support.

He caught my gaze, gave me a slightly questioning look, as if to ask why I was waiting. He'd already assumed he would go.

But the thought of sending him filled me with sick dread. He was my only true ally in the palace. Marielle was beholden to Avrell; all the Servants were. And the guardsmen were under the control of Baill, even Captain Catrell. That left only Erick and the Seekers, and I'd discovered there weren't as many Seekers as I'd first thought. Westen had revealed that there were only about thirty Seekers in the palace—one Seeker for every ten guardsmen under Baill's and Catrell's control. So even though the Seekers swore their loyalty to the Mistress, and even though the Seekers were more deadly and skilled than the guardsmen, they were seriously outnumbered.

I didn't want to send Erick or Westen, not when there were so few I trusted.

Before either Erick or I could speak, there was a silken rustle of clothes and Eryn said, "Send me." She sat on the edge of her seat, her eyes wide in mute appeal.

I frowned, uncertain. Eryn was still an unknown, even after the hours we'd spent in training in the garden with the other Servants. Yet she'd done nothing but help me since I released her from the throne.

"Why?" I asked.

Eryn shifted slightly, and suddenly she was the woman who'd once sat on the throne, regal and composed. "Because until I was eight, I was raised on the rocky coastline, in a village much like Colby. I've seen debris from all kinds of shipwrecks. I know what to look for." She hesitated, then added in a much more emotional voice, "And also because I haven't been outside of the city for over twenty years."

My gaze narrowed. I'd heard what she'd not said, what she had really meant. She'd not been outside of the city because of the throne. This would be a good way to test whether she was truly free of its power. She was willing to risk death to make certain she was free, and this gave her an excuse to try.

And she did know what to look for. Like Erick, she knew of the vision, of what it foretold.

"Very well," I said, "but I'd like Borund to go, too." I turned toward him and saw his eyes widen slightly in surprise. "You know most of the ships we sent for supplies," I explained. "You'll have better luck identifying the ship."

Comprehension dawned, and he relaxed. "I believe William can manage for a few days while I'm away."

I suppressed a grimace at the mention of William's name, then stood. "Good. Then I'll leave you to your preparations."

Everyone stood, made short bows, and departed, Captain Catrell and Baill moving swiftly since they had orders to give, the rest at a more leisurely pace.

Once the others had left, Erick said quietly, "You could have sent me as well."

"I know," I said. I hesitated, almost added an explanation, but in the end said nothing. I didn't even turn to look at him, afraid he'd see the relief in my eyes that he was staying.

The party left an hour after dawn the next day. Along with Erick and my own escort, I accompanied Eryn, Borund, Captain Catrell, and a group of five other guardsmen to the edge of the city, all of us on horseback. One of the guardsmen carried the village's messenger boy behind him, the youth clutching tightly to his waist. Since it was the first time I'd been outside of the paddock on a horse, we took it slow, winding down from the palace and out the outer walls, then cutting east, passing through streets I wasn't familiar with. Following the River, we passed near the stockyards, the reek of slaughter washing over us on a faint breeze, even though fresh meat was scarce. The horses shied away from the smell, but we turned south before it became pervasive, moving parallel to the outer walls, the land dropping away from the palace and the hill that it sat upon. The buildings and streets thinned, until there was nothing but the southern road, rocky land, a few small bent trees, and scrub brush.

I glanced up at Eryn as the group paused on the rough road leading south from the city, the protective walls of the city above us, far up the steep slope of the southern part of the hill. Most of Amenkor lay north of the palace—on the edge of the harbor and along the northern jut of land that enclosed it—and east along the River. The openness here felt strange. I was used to buildings on all sides, or the waters of the River and harbor. I'd never ventured outside the Dredge or the lower city, wharf, and palace before becoming the Mistress. Here, where I could see the land to the east rising up to distant forested mountains and south along the dark rock of the jagged coastline, I felt exposed and vulnerable. But I quashed the sensation and turned to Eryn.

"Do you feel anything?" I asked, pitching my voice low so that only Eryn, Erick, and Borund could hear, brushing my hand along my mount's neck to keep it calm. I still hadn't grown comfortable astride the animal.

"No," Eryn said. "You?"

I shivered. "Yes." Deep in my gut, a gnawing sensation clawed at my stomach, like hunger but far worse. And it was steadily increasing the longer I stayed. I knew I was on the edge of the throne's reach. If I went much farther . . .

A look of pure wonder passed across Eryn's face. "Then it's true," she murmured, not hiding her disbelief. "I'm free of the throne."

She laughed, her joyful grin infectious. For a moment, I saw the young woman she had once been, carefree and mischievous.

Then she caught my eyes, saw my pained answering grin, and the Mistress in her took over, pushed her elation down, replacing it with a look of concern and pity. But not completely; there was still a smile on her lips. "Varis—" she began.

I halted her with a sharp shake of my head. With more force than I intended, I said, "It doesn't matter. I've lived my entire life inside the city. I don't need to go beyond its walls."

Eryn's face clouded with doubt, but she nodded. Perhaps she heard the lie. Now that I'd seen what lay outside the city, I wanted to see more. But that couldn't be helped.

"I'll be back tomorrow," Eryn said.

Then she turned and kneed her horse forward, the guardsmen starting out ahead of her at her signal. She rode gracefully, back straight, Borund falling in a few paces behind.

As she passed completely outside the throne's influence, the blissful smile relit her face.

I sighed, grimacing in pain as I placed a hand over my stomach. It felt as if someone had stabbed me and was now working the blade back and forth, slicing up my guts. "I need to get back to the city," I said, feeling suddenly flushed. And the horse was picking up on my discomfort.

Erick motioned sharply to my escort and we headed back, moving the horses as fast as the pain in my stomach would allow.

A hundred paces from the southern wall, the last of the sickening sensation faded.

I was home, I thought bitterly.

I spent the morning working with Nathem and Avrell on the rebuilding of the warehouse district, answering questions about what I wanted rebuilt where, settling disputes between workers and merchants. At my insistence, we visited one of the warehouses and kitchens so I could see how the merchants were organizing the work details and how they were handling the distribution of the food, then we headed toward the communal ovens, where the women and children were busy baking breads. But the smells of yeast and dough and flour reminded me too forcefully of the white-dusty man who'd helped me to survive on the Dredge before I met Erick—the baker who'd been killed because of me—and so I had Avrell take me back to the palace.

By then, Avrell had been put on edge. I'd never spent so much time with him before, had never asked him so many unimportant questions about how things were run, and my apprehension over the wreckage at Colby had transferred to him. I could see him casting suspicious looks at me, and so at mid-afternoon I released him. I didn't want him to think about Colby and what might be found there. His interest had already been piqued too much.

And perhaps there *was* nothing to find at Colby. Perhaps the debris was simply from the ship running aground on some hidden rocks, or breaking apart after being caught in a storm.

Or so I told myself as I paced my room.

In an effort to distract myself, I summoned Marielle and tried to pay attention to my lessons.

"Try to sound it out," Marielle said. We'd been working for two hours and her voice was frayed, her hair wild from running her hands through it in frustration. "You know all the letters."

"I know," I spat, a twinge of guilt stabbing through me even as I spoke.

Marielle tensed and in a hard voice said, "Just try."

I drew in a deep breath, closed my eyes, tried to gather my scattered wits, then opened my eyes and stared at the book in my lap. I focused on the word beneath my fingers. A long word, but one I knew, because I'd read through this page days ago.

But no matter how hard I tried, the letters wouldn't hold steady. My attention drifted. First to the uneasy fact that Marielle was one of the stronger Servants, that she could use the river if she wanted, that in fact I was training her to take my place. When I'd entered the palace to kill the Mistress, I'd run into one of the true Servants. But the only reason I'd known was that I'd touched her, had felt a thin slice of pain running up my arm, like the cut of a dagger. I'd always thought I'd know someone who could use the river just by looking at them. But no. I hadn't recognized that Eryn could use the river when I'd first met her in the throne room, not even after touching her. She'd actually used the river to block my attack before I'd figured out that she could control it. Was that because of the throne?

Marielle had never used the river in my presence except in the gardens while training. None of the Servants had. Was that because of Avrell? Had he ordered it?

I shoved the useless supposition aside, shook myself, and returned to the book. But I glanced toward the balcony to judge the time by the light.

It seemed the sun had barely moved since the last time I looked.

"Enough," I said, closing the book with a frustrated snap as I stood. "I can't do this now. We'll have to try again tomorrow."

A look of extreme relief passed over Marielle's face before she could suppress it. She stood, hands held carefully before her. "Is there anything else you wish to work on?" she asked.

I tried not to let the dread in her voice irritate me. "No. Just go." I waved her out, pacing to the balcony as she made her escape. Outside, she had a terse conversation with Erick, their voices too low for me to hear, and then Erick stepped into the room.

I glared up at the clouds scudding across the sky, then down at the city. From here, I could see the construction on the warehouses, the outlines of the walls now visible. The small figures of the men moved back and forth, and occasionally the breeze would bring the sounds of hammering and the bellows of the work leaders.

The activity somehow soothed me and the tension in my shoulders began to release.

"You're restless," Erick said.

I grunted. "You don't have to stay. I'm fine."

I heard movement and with a pang of regret thought he would actually leave, but he'd only shifted closer. "You've never been impatient before," he said, then added with a touch of humor, "except possibly when working with Marielle. On the Dredge, you had to wait often—for the mark to arrive, for the right moment to steal the apple. Why is waiting for Eryn to return and report any different?"

I shrugged. "Because then I knew what I was waiting for? I don't know. But it is different."

"You've changed in the last two months, since you became the Mistress," Erick said after a moment.

I didn't answer. Had it only been two months? It seemed like much longer than that.

Erick sighed. "So who do you want to harass now? Nathem? Baill? Westen? What about a little sparring lesson with me? I'm certain there's something I forgot to teach you on the Dredge that Westen hasn't already covered. He doesn't know everything you know."

I laughed and turned from the window, the offer to spar tempting. We hadn't fought each other since the Dredge, more than two years ago, and the thought that I might have learned something new on my own or from Westen, might have improved enough to actually beat him in a fair match, was almost too difficult to resist. But it was late, and if watching those working in the warehouse district could calm me, then maybe I could do something similar to calm my nerves even further. "No, I think I'll go to the throne room instead."

Erick's face grew somber, his stance tightening with disapproval. "Very well."

I shook my head, irritated again. "I just want to check on the city. Besides, I've been working with Eryn on controlling myself, and on protecting myself from the throne. I'll be fine." I knew from testing the throne on my own that I didn't need the throne to check on the city, that touching it wasn't required—I could sense the city even now—but touching it made sensing the emotions of the city as a whole easier. And right now all I wanted to do was relax.

Erick didn't look convinced.

In the throne room, at the sight of the amorphous throne shifting at the far end of the hall, my confidence faltered. But I straightened resolutely and walked down the central walkway, Erick at my back. He'd insisted on coming and, since the last time I'd used the throne I'd ended up unconscious on the dais steps in my own vomit, I couldn't argue with him.

At the base of the dais, I paused. Inside, I could feel the voices of the throne waiting, strangely quiet. I thought about Cerrin, who'd somehow escaped the Fire, and with careful deliberation I slid beneath the river and began to weave the protective net Eryn had drilled into me, trying a few of the alterations she'd proposed to help keep Cerrin and the rest of the Seven under control. Slipping deeper, I threw the net around the blazing sphere of White Fire that contained the voices at my core. The mostly quiet voices grew suddenly grim and disgusted and drew back from the wall of flame.

The net secured, I did another circuit around the sphere, searching for signs of the flaw that I knew must exist, but again I found nothing.

I turned to Erick. "I'm ready." I was surprised my voice was so steady.

He nodded, his stance alert.

Drawing a short breath, I moved up the steps and sat on the twisting stone.

Involuntarily, I winced, expecting the voices to come crashing down around me, smothering me as they had done before, now that they were close to their source of power. But while the same weighted blanket settled over, making the room feel more real, more dense, the voices barely stirred, only the intensity of their movements behind the Fire increasing.

I let my breath out slowly, let the pulse of the throne course through me. Taking another moment to check the security of the protective net, I smiled at Erick in reassurance, then sank myself in the sensations of the city.

For a long moment, I simply hovered, the city spread out before me, as if I stood on the rooftop of the palace's tower staring down over its sprawling streets and tightly packed buildings. The roiling flow of the people's emotions washed over me in rhythmic swells, like waves. The scent of the waves was cool and smooth with tentative contentment. Winter had set in, the ocean was turbulent outside the bay, but here, in the harbor, where the River met the sea, we'd survived. Where before there had been a riot of apprehension, concern over whether there was enough food, uncertainty about the sudden change of power in the palace, and fear about the repercussions of the madness everyone suspected in the old Mistress, now there was hope that everything would turn out all right. There was food. They'd seen it in the warehouses, seen it being offloaded from the ships, knew that if they were willing to work for it, the food could be theirs. Where before I'd sensed anxiety and despair, now I found industrious activity.

Not everywhere, of course. There was still a feeling of discontent near the Dredge. I focused on that part of the city, until I hovered over the Dredge itself, felt the people flowing down its streets and alleys.

Evander had done as I asked, had told those that lived on the Dredge of the work details, of how a man had been punished to protect him, even though he was from the Dredge. And Darryn had spread the word as well, had created the militia using people from the Dredge. Within the following week, Avrell's work force had doubled. Many were men and women who had simply fallen on hard times after the passing of the White Fire through the city six years before. People who had lived and worked in the lower city before the Fire, their only recourse to abandon the lower city for the Dredge after it had passed. In the fear and uncertainty it had left behind, trade had faltered. But a few were like

Evander, like me—gutterscum that had known nothing else but the Dredge, that were willing to take a chance on something better.

I let the Dredge roll over me, then turned away. I'd done what I could for them. For now.

Next, I moved to the wharf, watched the workers packing fish in salt, rolling the barrels into storage. On the waters of the harbor, others were in small boats, hauling up crab traps, searching even though it was out of season. Still others were working in the rigging of the trading ships or on the decks, making repairs to rope and wood, pulleys and sails.

I stayed here the longest. The sailing ships had always intrigued me, even before I'd begun working as Borund's bodyguard. While hunting for easy marks on the wharf, I'd often sit for hours watching the dockworkers unloading cargo, dreaming about what strange foods the crates and barrels could carry, of what I could steal if given the chance.

It had been impossible then to imagine that I could have boarded one of the huge ships and left with it, escaped the city entirely. At that time, all I knew was Amenkor. There was nothing outside the warren of the Dredge, the streets and alleys of the wharf and the lower city. But I suddenly realized that I *could* have escaped on one of the ships back then. Perhaps not easily, but it could have been done. I could have traveled down the coast to the south, to the cities Avrell had told me about—to the cliffs of Venitte and the maze of caves and streets of that ancient sister city; to the rolling hills and vineyards of Marland; or even farther south, across the sea to the islands of the Zorelli.

But not now. I was bound to the throne now.

I drew back from the wharf and the activity on the docks reluctantly, then turned my attention to the warehouse district. But even with the sense of regret I now felt, watching the people of the city had worked. I no longer felt so tense, and for a brief moment I'd forgotten about Eryn and the group that had probably already arrived in Colby.

Unconsciously, I looked out over the city along the southern coastline. Where the influence of the throne ended, the undulating flow of the river became listless. The river still existed beyond the city, but it didn't have the same power without the throne behind it, its scents and tastes weren't as vibrant. It was just the river, the same power I'd used to survive on the Dredge.

Somehow, with the full power of the throne flowing through me, that now seemed paltry. Even with what I'd learned practicing with Eryn, who even without the throne's supporting power could do more with the river—or the Sight as she called it—than I'd managed to learn on my own on the Dredge.

Far down the coastline, outside of the influence of the throne, something flared.

I frowned, turned my full attention south.

And caught the flicker of light again. A white light, far enough away that it could barely be seen.

But now that I had seen it I realized I recognized it.

The White Fire.

Without thought, I reached for it, as I'd reached to find Corum on the Dredge that night on the tower, as I'd reached for Erick as he hunted. But then Eryn's warning brought me up short, like a slap.

Frowning, I withdrew to the palace's tower in my mind, began to pace its length, casting furtive glances out toward the tiny blinking white flame, Eryn's warning echoing through my head.

It's too dangerous, her voice whispered from memory. *Reaching like that, extending yourself out so far. . . . You could lose yourself, never find your way back.*

And that had been when I'd tried to reach out to the Dredge.

This looked much, much farther away.

I drew to a halt at the edge of the palace tower, facing the faint white light. I'd spent a lot of time pushing the boundaries of the throne recently, stretching farther and farther out over its influence without letting the connection to my own body break.

But if I reached for this Fire . . .

Don't.

I jumped, felt a tingle of guilt sweep through me as if I'd blushed, then steadied myself, the guilt hardening into anger and a trace of fear as I drew in the sharp scent of that strange incense, as I recognized Cerrin.

He stood next to me on the edge of the tower, the wind from the ocean flapping in the tails of his coat, his very presence more solid, more real. Here, the yellow of his shirt was vibrant, his coat a deep, rich brown. His short beard was trimmed to a sharp point and his tawny eyes glittered with a hard intelligence . . . and a deep melancholy.

Why not? I asked.

He shook his head. *Because what Eryn said is correct. It is dangerous. It is foolhardy. It is stupid. More than you know have lost themselves by Reaching. But also because even if you can find your way back—which I doubt—you will be drained. And for what?*

I turned away. *How are you escaping the Fire? How are you escaping the net?*

We are the Seven. Almost fifteen hundred years ago we realized that we were the last of our kind, the last that had power—true power. The last that could wield all of the elemental magics. There was no one who would follow us. But we knew that someday there would be someone of true power again, and so we tried to preserve our knowledge. So we created the thrones—to preserve what we knew until it could be used again, and to protect the Frigean coast against those who would destroy it.

He looked out over the southern coastline. *There is more magic than just the Fire. Or the river. Don't Reach for the Fire. It's too dangerous.*

And then he vanished, his form tattering to shreds like a piece of cloth.

My jaw clenched. He hadn't answered my question.

Fuming, I stared out at the faint flicker on the horizon. I paced to the edge of the tower, arms folded across my chest, then paced back and bit my lower lip.

But the presence of another White Fire like the one that burned at my core was too tempting, too intriguing to resist.

And I knew I could find my way back, no matter what Eryn or Cerrin said.

Shoulders set, I reached for the distant flame.

For a fleeting instant, the world stretched out below, the sensation terrifying. Like the moment of total balance at the edge of a rooftop just before you jump, when you realize that what seemed like such a short distance down to the ground is really two stories, not one, but it's too late to turn back. But I could still feel my body, still feel the tenuous connections.

And then I leaped, letting my body go.

The coastline sped by below, too swift to see much more than white spray as ocean waves crashed into rocky cliffs, shooting up huge plumes in the late afternoon sunlight, the thunderclaps that followed muted. I barely spared a glance even for this, my heart thudding at twice normal, my gaze locked on the flickering White Fire ahead. Eryn's warning was sharp in my memory; I didn't dare look away, afraid I'd lose sight of the light. It blazed on the horizon, drew steadily closer. Heart pounding, I watched it pulse, like a beacon—

And then, suddenly, it was there.

I fell down into it, felt its flames envelop me without burning, just as the White Fire had on the night it passed through Amenkor six years before. In the instant before it claimed me, I saw the rocky coastline break into a stretch of beach strewn with pebbles and driftwood, saw a cluster of ramshackle buildings a little farther inland over a crest of scrub grass and dunes, smelled smoke from a real fire, mixed with the scents of stew.

And then there was only the Fire.

"Would you like something to eat?"

The woman's voice, rough and uncertain with nervousness and awe, filtered through the white wall of flame that surrounded me, that held me suspended at its center. For a moment, my heart thudded with panic at the thought that I was trapped, like the voices were trapped inside the Fire at my core. I flailed at the wall before me, shoved at it hard, and felt it give way.

I found myself staring out at a bare cottage and an older man seated at a rickety table, face in a tight scowl that appeared permanent, scarred with the sun and covered with a grizzled, patchy beard. Wisps of thinning white hair drifted above his head, his eyebrows the same ancient, steely gray but heavy and thick. A dark mole the size of my thumbprint marred his forehead over his left eye.

He was watching me intently, his light gray eyes sharp.

Beside him, stooped over the pot steaming above the fire, the woman who had spoken—as thin as the man and just as wizened, her long wiry hair kept back from her face by a kerchief—lifted a ladle of the thin stew. "It's rabbit. Not much, but . . ."

I tried to shake my head, raise a hand to ward away the soup since it was obvious these people had little to eat, but instead I heard myself say, "Thank you, just a cup," and felt my hand reach out to accept the small steaming cup that was proffered.

Except it wasn't my hand that grabbed the hot cup and raised the thin stew to my lips to sip. It was Eryn's hand, Eryn's fingers that got burned, Eryn's tongue that was scalded, and Eryn's voice that spoke. But I felt it all, tasted the salty broth of the stew, smelled the steam.

And suddenly I realized that the Fire I had searched out was inside Eryn, that I was looking through her eyes, feeling what she felt, tasting what she tasted as if I were actually there.

"It's delicious," I heard myself say, but the contradiction of hearing Eryn's voice muttering the words, of feeling Eryn turn her head so that her gaze fell on Borund and Captain Catrell, both huddled inside the small hovel, of Eryn acting without any control by me, was too much. I drew back, isolated myself from Eryn's actions so that there was a clear distinction between her and me, between what I wanted and what she wanted. I sensed that if I didn't remove myself, if I remained, I'd eventually get confused between what was her and what was me. And I also sensed that with a little effort I could actually make myself be felt, that I could actually seize control of Eryn.

This must be what it felt like for the voices inside the throne: always present, able to feel what I felt, see what I saw, smell what I smelled. Except they were all dead.

No wonder they wanted control, fought so hard against the Fire I caged them with. Behind the Fire, they couldn't truly feel me, couldn't taste and smell and touch. Couldn't act, not of their own volition. But the temptation to take control was always there, just out of reach.

And no wonder the Mistress couldn't retain control once the voices were let free. If one of them were let loose, remained loose for too long, the distinction between that personality and the Mistress herself would begin to blur. They'd begin to overlap, until neither remembered where their own personality ended and the other's began.

Or as Eryn had suggested earlier, until one of the personalities dominated the other.

I shuddered, withdrew even further, not certain whether Eryn could sense me, not wanting her to sense me. I didn't think she had, but then there'd been no outward sign that the soup was too hot. She'd hidden the pain behind her smile, not wanting to offend the woman of the house. Perhaps she'd hidden her reaction to my presence as well. She'd been the Mistress for almost twenty years; she was practiced at deception.

But how had this happened? How did the Fire get inside her? I hadn't noticed it in anyone else, had worked with Eryn closely during my training and hadn't seen it then.

And how would I get back?

Cerrin's warning about the risks of Reaching too far afield suddenly assailed me and I shot a glance toward Amenkor, realizing only then that I was still beneath the river. But Eryn was inside the cottage and I couldn't see through the walls of driftwood and lumber. Not without the power of the throne behind me. I'd have to wait until Eryn moved outside.

Uncertain now, wishing I'd listened to Cerrin's advice and not reached for the white flame on the horizon, I settled back to wait.

Borund and Captain Catrell both took steaming cups of the stew at a stern glance from Eryn, Borund sipping politely, Catrell swallowing in gulps. After a brief pause, Eryn lowered her cup to her lap and turned toward the old man, meeting his gaze squarely. "You sent the boy?"

"Ayu," he said, his accent thick. He leaned back and crossed his arms over his chest, the chair creaking beneath his weight.

Eryn nodded. "We'd like to see the wreckage."

"Why?"

Eryn frowned. "I don't understand."

He sat forward abruptly. "We's found parts of wrecked ships afore, and none's come to see it. Always too busy. Why's this un different?"

Eryn shot a startled glance toward Borund, who shrugged, then turned back to the fisherman. "Because we sent out quite a few ships recently, and only a few of them returned. We'd like to know what happened to the other ships. If this is one of them . . ."

"Ayu," the man grunted. He cast a dark eye on Borund, who shifted beneath the glare and took a hasty sip of his stew. He took in Borund's red-and-gold coat, the clean-cut breeches, and white shirt so out of place in this barren cottage, and his scowl deepened.

He turned back to Eryn. "I ken show ya the wreckage," he said, but he made no move to rise from his seat, the woman ladling out a much larger portion of the stew and setting it in front of him. As if the matter were settled, he turned to the stew, completely ignoring everyone else in the room except the woman, who began ladling out a bowl for herself.

Eryn stiffened and said tightly, "We'd like to see it before the sun sets, if that's possible. We want to return to the city early tomorrow."

The man acted as if she hadn't spoken, scooping out a chunk of meat from the stew with two fingers and slurping it up. The old woman sniffed in disapproval, thunked her own stew down on the table with force, and gave him a glare.

The old man caught her gaze and for a moment they warred, his scowl deepening, her hands settling on her hips.

Finally, the man snorted, slammed his stew down to the table, and stood. Without glancing at Eryn, Borund, or Catrell, he stalked from the hovel with a curt, "Folla me."

"Excuse Gellin," the woman said, her eyes casting daggers at his retreating back. "We don't see people from the city often."

Eryn gave her a reassuring smile, then stood, setting the stew to one side. "The stew was wonderful," she said, then bowed her head and followed Gellin. Borund and Catrell followed close behind, Catrell motioning the other guardsmen waiting outside the cottage to their side.

"He doesn't seem too happy to see us," Borund said as they moved past the few ramshackle houses that made up the entire village. All were built of wood and all had a long, thin boat turned upside down outside, traps and thick nets heaped underneath the boats or stored in small hutches next to each house. Through open doorways, faces peered out cautiously. "None of them are very welcoming."

"Can you blame them?" Eryn said, maintaining her smile. "As Gellin's wife said, they don't see people from the city often. I'm certain that when they do see us, they take it as a sign that there's trouble ahead. I know the elders in the village where I was raised did. Men from the cities were an omen, a harbinger of bad times. The last time the guard arrived in my village, they took me away kicking and screaming and brought me to the palace. I was only eight at the time."

The heat in Eryn's voice caused Borund's stride to falter.

"Whatever for?" he asked.

"To become the Mistress, of course," she said, voice blunt and filled with long-held hatred.

Borund backed off, his brow furrowed in consideration.

The old man led them through the village, out across the dune that protected the inland from the waves, toward a rocky rise to the south. They climbed over the granite, using scrub brush and small, twisted trees with long needles and rough bark to help them over the steepest parts. The guardsmen cursed the terrain, their armor clattering against the stone when they stumbled or fell while Gellin smirked, but Eryn climbed the stone smoothly, the stone rough enough to provide plenty of hand- and footholds.

When they crested the rise, they looked down into another stretch of beach, another plinth of rocky outcropping on the far side, the stone biting into the sea. Waves crashed into the rock and hissed onto the stone of the beach. Well above the cove's waterline lay three large pieces of what had once been one of the merchant ships: a section of mast as thick as my waist and twice my height, the wood scarred and pitted; a large section of the prow; and a flat section of deck, part of the square hole that would have led down into the hold cutting into one of its sides.

"There," the old man said. His biting tone had mellowed, as if the sight of the crushed ship had sobered him somewhat.

Captain Catrell and a few of the guardsmen began the climb down the far side. Eryn stood silently for a long moment, searching the wreckage, but from this distance it appeared that the ship had been torn apart, perhaps against the rocks of the shoreline.

Eryn pursed her lips, then turned and began a careful descent to the beach, Gellin watching her closely.

"You fisherfolk," he said, as Eryn jumped the last stretch, landing in the loose rounded rock of the beach.

"Yes," Eryn said. "I grew up in Tallern, on the coast."

Gellin nodded succinctly, his eyes no longer so hostile.

Stones rattled against each other as they began to make their way to the wreckage. The guardsmen scattered out along the beach to search for more debris, some heading farther inland to scout, to where the beach gave way to overhanging needled trees and grassy underbrush. Borund and Catrell headed straight for the wreckage, Borund struggling to maneuver among the drift-wood and dried seaweed at the waterline. He swore as he slid off of a piece of wood into a patch of dried, crusted seaweed, sand fleas and flies hopping and swarming around him as he danced away, yelping.

Eryn grinned, and even Gellin chuckled, but the mood sobered instantly as Eryn came up onto the wreckage.

She knelt down beside the piece of decking. The edges away from the open-ing to the hold were jagged with splinters, the boards ripped forcibly away, as if a giant had grabbed both ends of the deck and simply snapped it in half. But Eryn ignored the obvious signs of breakage and looked more closely at the wood, sitting forward to run her hands over its surface.

"You pulled this off the beach before the storm hit?" Eryn asked.

"Ayu."

"And when was the last storm around here?"

Gellin squinched his face up in thought. "Last howler come two hands before."

"Ten days," Eryn muttered under her breath. Then, louder, "And this wasn't here then?"

"Boy come here ever odd day," Gellin said. "Not here two days back."

"It could have been caught in the last storm, offshore, and just now found its way onto the beach."

Eryn looked up at Captain Catrell's voice. She hadn't heard him approach, too busy examining the deck before her. "This piece is heavily pitted and water-logged," she said, shaking her head. "It's been in the water a long time. And look at these markings." She pointed to where the wood of the deck had been scarred black, a thick line running toward the opening to the hull, then angling sharply off to one side.

Catrell frowned. "Looks like the deck caught fire. I found some gouges in the mast that could have come from swords or axes. Perhaps it was piracy."

"Perhaps." I edged forward, hearing the doubt in Eryn's voice. She didn't believe it was piracy at all.

She ran her hand over the scorch marks in the wood, her frown deepening, then stood, moving across the sand and jumble of driftwood to Borund's side at the piece of the bow of the ship. The merchant was leaning over the jagged end of the bowsprit where it had been snapped off and now jutted out of the sand. Only a section of the bow had survived where the bowsprit joined the hull. But enough of the hull to either side remained intact for Eryn to pick out the roughly carved shape of a naked woman's head and upper body, her back arched at the junction as if supporting the weight of the ship.

As Eryn, Catrell, and Gellin approached, Borund stepped back from the largest section of the hull. "It's definitely from Amenkor," he said, brushing sand off of his hands and coat. "The Amenkor sigil is clear along the hull. And based on what's left of the bowsprit and the coloration of the hull, I'd say this was the *Tempest*." He turned to look at Eryn, his face mournful. "One of my ships. It was headed south, to Verano."

"South again," Catrell said.

Eryn nodded. "Only one of the ships that returned was from the south, and from what I could gather, that ship never strayed far from the coast. It hopped between towns on the way back, trying to trade for as much as possible in the smaller ports."

Borund nodded. "Captain Mathew has always understood what needed to be done. And been willing to do it."

"But he also didn't travel that far south. Since he was entering more ports, he had to sacrifice distance. The rest of the ships were traveling farther. They had to catch the currents farther offshore."

Borund grunted agreement.

"Then we *are* dealing with pirates," Catrell surmised. "They're hitting the trade routes off the southern coastline."

Eryn said nothing. I could feel her disagreement though and thought of the scorch marks. The ship had clearly been attacked. The marks of a fight that Catrell had found on the remains of the mast confirmed that. Then the ship had most likely been set adrift, left to be torn apart by the storm. Or it had foundered during the attack itself.

But something wasn't right. Eryn felt it. For now though, she seemed willing to let Borund and Catrell think it was piracy.

She turned toward the fading sunlight, shadows beginning to edge along the beach. "It's getting dark. We should head back to the village."

Catrell nodded, then whistled sharply, the guardsmen congregating around them as they headed back to the rocky rise and began to climb. The few clouds above were just beginning to burn a deep gold when Eryn reached the top of the rise and looked north, one hand raised to shade her eyes.

Seizing the opportunity, I edged forward, scanned the horizon and saw a blazing white light to the north, like another setting sun, much larger than the flickering flame I'd focused in on to find Eryn. Without hesitation, I gathered myself tight and as I did so I realized the Fire that lay within Eryn had a scent: old blood and freshly turned earth. An undertone, like the shadow scent Eryn had left behind after manipulating my dream.

But old blood and freshly turned earth was my scent.

The Fire in Eryn had come from me.

Startled, I paused. But Eryn dropped her hand, began to turn away. And so, without thought, I leaped for the white light on the horizon, leaving Eryn and the mystery of the White Flame inside her behind. The darkening landscape rushed past, waves edged in brittle sunlight like the clouds above, dense trees softening the edges of the rocky defiles and hidden coves below.

Then I saw the edge of the city of Amenkor, felt the presence of the throne grip me as I entered its influence, saw the throne room crowded now with guardsmen and a few Seekers at the doors, at the side entrances, Avrell and Erick on the dais talking animatedly, shouting at each other—

And I fell into my body, drew in a halting, rough gasp that hurt my chest, my heart stuttering before finding its beat.

"—don't know what's happening," Avrell said, voice tightly restrained but loud.

"Bloody hells you don't," Erick growled. "You're the First of the Mistress! You—"

He cut off sharply at my gasp, almost lurched forward to touch me, but Avrell clamped a hand roughly onto his arm and held him back, his knuckles white with the effort.

"Don't touch her," the First ordered, voice like stone. "Let her recover. I don't know what the throne will do." Real fear pinched his face, and I suddenly realized what he meant.

He wasn't certain it would be me that returned.

And he was right. For all he knew, one of the voices of the throne had taken over.

Swiftly, I dove to the Fire, checked the net I'd put in place, checked the wall of Fire. The voices were seething with confusion, the maelstrom turbulent and enraged, all of them trying to gain my attention, but I ignored them all. The barriers—both the net I'd woven and the Fire itself—were intact as far as I could tell.

Not that it mattered against the Seven it seemed.

I turned my attention to Erick and Avrell, slowed my breathing, calmed my heart.

"It's me, Varis," I said, and then demanded, "What happened?"

Erick broke in first, voice rough and heated with emotion. "You went rigid, stopped breathing. I didn't dare touch you, so I summoned Avrell."

Avrell scoffed. "She was still breathing, just very slowly."

"You weren't so certain an hour ago," Erick spat.

Avrell seemed ready to rise to the bait, so I cut in. "Enough. Why are there so many guardsmen?"

Avrell answered. "When the trance lasted more than an hour, I decided it was prudent to secure the throne room. I summoned the guardsmen, to make certain you were safe. With only Erick here, and your escort outside, you were completely vulnerable in that state."

Meaning Avrell didn't trust Erick, knew he wasn't under anyone's control like the other guardsmen. And I didn't quite believe Avrell's explanation that they'd been summoned for my safety. He'd called them in case one of the other voices had returned, rather than me.

Even as the thought crossed my mind, I noticed the two guardsmen to either side of the dais, hands resting casually on the pommels of their swords. Behind each, standing too close and too tense for comfort, were two Seekers, their eyes intent on me, on Erick, waiting for a sign from either of us to attack the guardsmen to protect their Mistress.

The guardsmen and the Seekers were on the verge of an all-out fight in the middle of the throne room. The tension on the river tasted slick and metallic.

I shot a hard glance at Avrell. "Call them off."

Avrell's gaze hardened.

"Call them off!"

With a subtle hand gesture, the two guardsmen shuddered and fell back. But they didn't go far. The two Seekers who'd been threatening them shifted casually, placing themselves near the first set of columns, still within a few deadly steps of either guard.

Taking a small step forward, Avrell demanded, "What happened?"

I tensed. A day before I would have answered him, told him the truth, or at least most of the truth. But I could still feel the presence of the guardsmen at my back, could still taste the edge of the blades, could feel Erick enraged at Avrell's side now that he realized Avrell's true intent behind summoning them to the throne room.

I also realized that Avrell had spoken the truth earlier. He really didn't know what had happened.

Drawing in a steadying breath, I said, "I was keeping an eye on Eryn. They found the wreckage. They should be returning tomorrow, as expected."

Confusion crossed Avrell's face. "How—?" he began, but cut himself off.

I raised a questioning eyebrow in challenge, my displeasure clear.

Avrell backed off, disgruntled.

I glared out at the guardsmen and the few Seekers spread throughout the hall. "The extra guards are no longer necessary," I said.

After a hesitant moment, they began to file out. Outside, I saw my usual escort of palace guardsmen frowning as they passed.

As the last of the summoned guardsmen departed, I turned my glare on Avrell. "You may go as well. I'll send for you tomorrow, after Eryn returns."

He bristled, jaw working, but said nothing, bowing low before stalking down the hall.

Releasing the throne, I stood and stepped down from the dais, watching his retreating back with a frown.

"I didn't realize what he'd summoned them for," Erick said, "or I would never have let them into the throne room. I thought they could be trusted. Then, when nothing changed, when you were still . . . gone, I summoned the Seekers."

"Some of the guardsmen can be trusted," I said. "We'll have to find out which ones."

Erick nodded. "I'll take care of it." He hesitated, then asked, "So what did happen?"

"Exactly what I said. I followed Eryn, saw the debris from the ship."

"And was it lost because of a storm?"

I shook my head. "No. Eryn doesn't think it's piracy either, but I don't know why yet. Someone attacked the ship. Even Catrell agrees with that."

"Who could it be? One of the other cities? Venitte? Verano? But we've had good relations with them all for the last twenty years, since Eryn took the throne, since before that. And as far as we know, none of them has any kind of war fleet. Nothing fit for the open ocean anyway."

"I don't know. But I think Eryn does. It has something to do with the marks of the fire they found on the debris." I turned to Erick. "We'll just have to wait and ask her."

┼— Chapter 7

"We have to blockade the harbor," Eryn said as soon as she swung herself down off of her horse and handed the reins to the waiting stableboy. She was covered with dust from the road, her mount lathered with sweat from the hard ride from Colby, its muscles shuddering from the exertion.

"Where are Captain Catrell and the other guardsmen?" Erick asked. We had been waiting for Eryn at the outer gates to the palace since I'd felt her enter the city and the influence of the throne.

"Still a few hours outside of Amenkor. They couldn't keep up, and I needed to talk to you as soon as possible," Eryn said, shooting me a sharp warning glance. "In private."

"Why?" Erick said. His voice was hard, eyes intent.

"Because of the fire on the deck," I said.

That brought Eryn up short. She drew breath to say something, then noticed the array of palace guardsmen that surrounded us. Grunting, she said sharply, "The gardens."

Eryn led the way, clearly puzzled as to how I knew about the fire on the shipwreck in Colby, but willing to wait until there was no one able to overhear. When we passed through an archway out into open sunlight and the gardens, I motioned the escorting guardsmen back and proceeded with Erick to a small section of the garden flanked by a few trees surrounding two stone benches, Eryn in front of us.

The moment the guardsmen were out of earshot, Eryn straightened, brow creased in a frown, her stance imperious. "How did you know?"

I hesitated. But I had to trust someone. If Eryn had wanted the throne back, she could have taken it by now. She could have killed me "accidentally" during one of our private training sessions here in the gardens, could have touched the throne while I was searching for the presence behind the dream, or at any other time for that matter since she knew how to conceal herself from the guardsmen using the Sight. But all I'd seen whenever she was in the presence of the throne was terror.

No. Eryn didn't want the throne. But she was having a hard time giving up being the Mistress.

I drew in a deep breath. "I saw the wreckage on the beach. I saw the mast, the deck, the broken bowsprit. I saw it all through your eyes."

Eryn's eyes clouded with confusion. "You Reached even after I warned you not to? You Reached all the way to Colby? How is that even possible? How could you even see that far beyond Amenkor, when the throne has no influence there?"

"I had something to focus on, to guide the Reaching," I answered, then continued before Eryn could respond. "It's the White Fire. There's a small flame of it burning inside you, which is what caught my attention in the first place. I used that to Reach out toward you. After that it was like watching everything through your eyes. I saw everything you saw, tasted everything, touched it." I halted, on the verge of telling her that for a moment I had almost seized control, knew that I could if necessary.

But trust only went so far. And there was no way to tell how she'd react to that after fighting the voices within the throne for so long.

Eryn didn't believe me. I could see it in her eyes.

"What were we served by the fisherwoman when we arrived in Colby?" she asked.

I sighed. "Rabbit stew. You didn't want to take it because you knew they had little enough to eat—you know what life is like in a fishing village—but thought it would be polite to accept a small cup. You forced Captain Catrell and Borund to eat some as well. The village's elder, Gellin, was a little rude, but his wife put him in his place before he took you to the wreckage."

Eryn's eyes widened as I spoke. Now she whispered, under her breath, "Mistress' tits! You really were there."

Erick seemed startled by the curse.

"Oh, please," Eryn said, waving a hand dismissively at his raised eyebrows. "I grew up in a fishing village. I knew worse curses than that before I was five." Then she turned to me, her eyes narrowing down to slits. "Is the Fire still there? Can you see it now?"

I slid beneath the river, felt the throne augment my power, felt the guards at the two main entrances to the gardens, felt the stronger eddies of the city waiting outside . . . but drew myself away from those currents reluctantly, turning my attention on Eryn instead. I could sense the voices of the throne watching intently, somehow more focused and calm than usual.

"Yes," I said. "But it's harder to see it now. When I was looking from the top of the tower before, when you were in Colby, it seemed much brighter, like a beacon."

I withdrew from the river. Eryn began pacing, deep in thought. "It must be the throne. The power here in Amenkor is so dense, almost like a weight, a cloak. The currents must be masking the Fire. But that still doesn't explain how the Fire got there in the first place. Could it have been left behind when the Fire passed through the city six years ago, as happened to you? But why didn't I sense it then, as you did? Why can't I sense it now?"

I suddenly remembered that moment in the throne room, after the shadow Eryn, still trapped inside the throne, had shown me the vision of the city burning to the ground. I'd shoved the vision away, felt something tear in the process, heard Eryn scream. . . .

"The Fire came from me," I said. "It has my scent—old blood and fresh earth."

Eryn stopped pacing, a hundred questions in her eyes.

But Erick cleared his throat and said curtly, "The pattern of fire on the wreckage?"

Eryn frowned in annoyance. "Of course. We can discuss the Fire later." She motioned to the stone benches along the garden path. Eryn and I sat; Erick remained standing.

"Tell me what you saw in the wreckage," Eryn said curtly.

I drew in a deep breath, then halted, not certain what to say. I'd been thinking about the remains of the ship since I'd seen it through Eryn's eyes, had scrutinized the damage over and over in my mind, but I couldn't figure out what had made Eryn so certain that the ship hadn't been attacked by pirates.

I looked at Eryn, then sighed. "I don't know. I saw what you saw: the deck had been broken, the wood splintered as if the ship had been snapped in two. Captain Catrell reported that there were signs of a battle. Borund verified that it was a ship from Amenkor, one of his ships actually, the *Tempest*. And I saw the marks made by the fire on the deck. I know that's what concerned you the most, but not why."

Eryn nodded, placed her hands in her lap and leaned forward intently. "The fire *is* the problem. If it hadn't been for those markings, I would have concluded piracy as well, just as Captain Catrell did. But the fire . . . it wasn't made naturally."

I frowned in consternation. Behind me, I felt Erick shift closer, grow more tense. "What do you mean?"

"I mean, the fire that helped to destroy that ship was controlled by the Sight. Think back on the markings. The scorch marks on the deck are too focused, the damage confined to a narrow path. And that path isn't even linear. The markings on the deck ran straight and true, and then veered off sharply in another direction. Fire doesn't behave that way naturally. This fire was guided." Eryn sighed. "My guess is that whoever attacked the ship had the help of someone with the Sight. That person used the fire to target people."

I thought back to the shattered decking Eryn had leaned over on the beach, saw her tracing out the path of the fire with one hand, the way that path angled sharply away from the opening that would have led down to the hold.

In my mind's eye, I saw one of the deckhands on the ship running, terrified, fire scorching along the deck behind him. I saw him turn when he reached the opening in the deck in an attempt to escape, saw the fire turn to follow.

There would be no escape from such an attack.

I shuddered, looked up into Eryn's eyes again with an expression of horror.

Erick stepped forward. "How does that rule out piracy? Couldn't the pirates have someone like Varis with them? Someone who learned to control the Sight on her own?"

Eryn's brow creased in thought. "It's possible, but unlikely. Controlling fire in such a specific way . . . that requires training. It's not something most of the Servants in the palace could do even after training. You have to have power, and you have to have an extreme force of will, a focus that doesn't typically come naturally to anyone with the Sight."

"Could you do it?"

Eryn turned toward me, thought for a moment, then nodded. "Yes. I'm not sure how, precisely. I've never seen it done before, never even really thought about trying it. Fire isn't solid, rigid, like stone. It's too flexible. And because it's so amorphous, it would require much more power to mold, to shape and control it in a precise way. But with enough time I think I could figure out how."

Short, succinct, matter-of-fact. It was a small reminder that Eryn was powerful, even without the throne behind her. And it sent a shudder down into my core.

I shifted uncomfortably on the stone bench.

Erick had begun pacing. "How can we be certain that it isn't pirates? And if it isn't, who else could it be?"

Eryn shifted. "The only other possibility along the coast is Venitte. The men at their school would have the training necessary to direct fire, but I don't think they'd have anyone with enough power to actually do it."

"We keep coming back to Venitte," I murmured.

Eryn frowned. "I know. It's becoming harder and harder for me to convince myself that somehow, in some way, March isn't behind this."

"March?"

"The Lord of Venitte. He rules our sister city, much as the Mistress rules here, except he has no throne—at least nothing like the Skewed Throne. He is . . . a very old friend." She smiled, but it was filled with sadness and regret, tremulous and hurt at the same time.

"Does Lord March have the means to build ships of war?" Erick asked into the silence. "Would he have ordered an attack on Amenkor's trading ships?"

Eryn shot him a glare, back stiffening, then faltered.

Looking down at her hands clasped in her lap, she said, "Yes. He has the means to build ships of war. But," she said, turning blazing eyes on Erick, "there have been no reports of any type of ship construction in the last few years. Nothing of this significance. Ask Avrell. He has agents in all of the key ports along the Frigean coast."

"I don't want Avrell to know," I said.

Eryn seemed startled. "Why not?"

I bit off a sharp retort, realized she didn't know about the incident in the throne room, when I'd Reached toward Eryn and Colby. She hadn't been back in the city long enough to find out.

I straightened. "I'm not so certain I trust him completely yet." At Eryn's confused look, I added, "I'll let Erick explain. For now, let Captain Catrell spread the rumor that it was pirates who destroyed the ship until we know otherwise."

"He's going to be suspicious that it's something else," Eryn warned. "I wouldn't have abandoned the escort on the return from Colby if I thought the ship had been attacked by pirates."

Erick grunted. "That's even better. If the ship was attacked by someone else, having a little doubt spicing the rumor of piracy should make it that much less of a shock when we reveal who it really was."

Eryn didn't respond, but it was obvious she didn't agree. "And what about the harbor? Are you going to reestablish the blockade?"

I considered a moment, then shook my head. "No. I don't see any reason to."

Eryn's expression darkened. "Even after the warning vision of the city burning? Even after seeing the scorch marks on the deck?"

"No. Whoever is attacking the ships hasn't made any attempt at our harbor—"

"Yet," Eryn cut in.

"—yet," I added with a glare. "Until we know who the attackers are, and what they want, I'm not going to risk causing a panic in the city, not when the people are already concerned about starving this winter."

And I didn't want to give Avrell a reason to think I needed replacement either.

I rose from my seat. Eryn followed suit.

"And how are we going to find out who the attackers really are?" she asked as we made our way out of the garden.

"I don't know," I said.

But I had an idea.

"Good," Marielle said as she passed behind me and glanced over my shoulder at the slate. I was working on my sentences on the settee in my chambers, sunlight streaming through the balcony doorway. A breeze blew in through the opening, cold with the edge of winter, but not cold enough to keep the doorway closed. "Now try to construct something more complex. Then I think we'll shift to mathematics."

I growled. I hated mathematics, and Marielle knew it. Out of the corner of my eye, I caught her smile.

I turned my attention back to the slate, wiped off the simple sentence I'd written with a damp cloth, then began a new one. I grinned maliciously as I began to write, the letters coming easily now.

"Let me see," Marielle said when I finished.

I held up the slate.

Marielle gasped, brought a hand up to cover her smile even as her expression grew stern. "Mistress! I didn't teach you such language! Where did you learn that?"

I laughed and set the slate to one side, then paused with a frown.

Where had I learned those words?

Marielle picked up the slate and sat down on the settee beside me, shaking her head. "You did misspell 'horsefucker,' though. We'll have to work on that."

She said it in such a serious tone that I burst out laughing. Marielle joined me a moment later.

When the laughter had died down, Marielle wiping tears from her face, she asked, "Who is Bloodmark anyway?"

I grew quiet instantly, turned away. "Someone I killed on the Dredge."

Marielle stilled. I thought she'd pull away, horrified, as William had always done, realized that I'd already tensed myself in preparation for that reaction and how it would hurt.

But instead, Marielle placed a hand on my forearm. I turned toward her, startled, saw the sympathy in her eyes, an attempt at understanding, even though she couldn't possibly relate. She'd been raised in the palace since she was six.

Before I could respond, someone knocked on the outer door.

"That's probably Erick," I said as Marielle rose to answer it. I stood as well and moved to the entrance to the balcony without stepping out to its edge, my mind shifting from sentences and Bloodmark and death to my idea on how to determine who was attacking the trade ships. From the balcony doorway, I could see one side of the jut of land that enclosed the bay and the stone tower that guarded the entrance.

I didn't want to have to blockade the harbor unless it was absolutely necessary. When Eryn had done it, it had thrown the city into a panic. I could still remember the mob thronging the palace gates within minutes of the bells tolling, issuing the orders.

Behind, I heard Marielle lead Erick into the room, then turn to leave.

"Marielle," I said, heard her halt. I turned. "I think you should stay."

"As you wish," she said, although her brow creased as she frowned. She clasped her hands in front of her and stood, waiting.

"You wanted to see me?" Erick asked formally. He'd come as a guardsman, a Seeker, not as a mentor.

"Yes." I motioned to the settee, but he shook his head, preferring to stand, his gaze intent. "I wanted to talk about how to find out who has been attacking the trading ships."

Erick grunted. "I thought you were going to talk to Avrell about it eventually. As Eryn suggested."

My nose squinched up in annoyance. "Maybe. But by talking to Avrell we'd only be guessing. Avrell has already said he hasn't received word from his contacts in the other cities regarding the missing trade ships. I want to know who's attacking us, without any doubts, even if in the end it is only pirates."

"What did you have in mind?"

I hesitated, biting my lip as I moved away from the balcony window back into the room. "I want to use the Fire."

Erick frowned. "I don't understand."

Behind him, Marielle shifted uncomfortably as well. She'd never been asked to stay behind during any discussions between me and Erick, or any of the others for that matter. It was obvious she felt she shouldn't be overhearing this conversation. But for the moment I ignored her, focused on Erick.

"You know that I saw what Eryn saw in Colby," I said, beginning to pace. Now that it came down to explaining my idea, it didn't seem as solid as it had before. "What you don't know is that I think that during the first use of the throne, when Eryn was trying to explain how I could find out who had been manipulating my dreams, somehow I placed a portion of the White Fire inside her in the process. At the end, when the vision of the city burning became too horrifying, I shoved it away. I think I tore a piece of the Fire inside me off in the process and it attached itself to Eryn."

Erick remained standing, eyes narrowed as he watched me pace. "How is that going to help us find out who's attacking our ships?"

I halted. "I want to send out more ships. I want to try to tag some of the people on those ships with the Fire as I accidentally tagged Eryn, and then I want to use the ships as bait. Hopefully, whoever is attacking the ships will seize the opportunity and attack again. Only this time, I can be watching using the Fire, as I watched what Eryn did in Colby."

"And what about the people on that ship? The one that gets attacked?"

I grimaced. I'd already thought of that. "They'll be prepared. They'll know what to expect."

"No, they won't. Not if what Eryn says is true and they have someone who can use the Sight participating in the attack. They won't be able to defend against that."

My shoulders tightened at the rebuke in his voice, but I said nothing. Erick watched my reaction, then lowered his head as he thought.

I glanced toward Marielle. She'd gone still, was staring at me with a slight look of bewilderment and fear. Then she glanced away, as if ashamed.

I wondered what she was thinking, but then Erick grunted and looked up.

"It has possibilities, but I don't think you've thought everything out yet."

"Like what?"

"Like the fact that you'll be sending out a ship in the middle of winter. Have you seen the waves out beyond the harbor? They're high and strong. The seas won't be kind. It's possible that the ship will founder simply because of the weather. You'll have to find captains and crews willing to take that risk. Because of that, you won't be able to send out more than one or two ships at best. Most won't go, even if it is the Mistress ordering it. The captains and their crews aren't stupid." He began pacing.

"So let's say you get one ship, with a crew crazy enough to try this. There will have to be a contingent of guardsmen on board in case they do actually get attacked. You won't be able to get the crew to go unless they feel they have a fair chance of surviving the attack. That requires even more men agreeing to the plan. But that shouldn't be a problem. You *can* order the guardsmen to go and expect them to obey. As long as we choose the right men. We'd have to pick men familiar with ships and the way they operate.

"Then there's this idea of 'tagging' one of the crew members. From what happened in the throne room when you Reached for Eryn, I'd say you have to be in contact with this person in order to witness the events. But what if the attack comes when you aren't connected? You won't be able to watch them continuously. You *are* the Mistress. Amenkor is relying on you to get every-one through the winter. They have *faith* that you'll get them through. That faith will falter if you vanish for a week or more while you deal with the ship. Even if you aren't actively doing anything, just your presence out in the city—down in the slums, out at the communal ovens, on site at the rebuilding of the warehouses—is enough to keep the people going. I've *seen* the change in the people since you started visiting the construction sites and the warehouses, since you set up the kitchens and the Servants have been seen more outside the palace. You won't be able to continue that if you're tied to the throne watching the ship."

"He's right," Marielle broke in. She swallowed when we both turned toward her. "The people *talk*, Mistress. And for the first time since the Fire swept through the city six years ago, they're speaking with hope. Even though it's winter, even though food is scarce. All of the Servants have noticed it while working in the kitchens, handing out food. The people *need* you."

I shifted uncomfortably at the intensity in Marielle's voice. I hadn't realized people were paying such close attention to me, hadn't realized that what I did mattered. Not to that extent.

"So let's review," Erick said, voice tight. He began ticking off points on his fingers. "You need a ship. You need a captain. You need a crew. You need guardsmen. And you need the gods' own luck to be in contact when the ship gets attacked."

"But we need to know who's attacking the trade routes," I countered, a defensive note creeping into my voice. "If it were simply a matter of a few lost ships, then I'd wait until spring. But it isn't! More than a few ships have been lost, and according to Avrell, it isn't just Amenkor that's lost ships. And then there's the vision."

Erick scowled. "I thought Eryn said that what happened in the vision didn't occur until summer. And she couldn't even guarantee that it was this summer."

"But she also said that the visions weren't always accurate."

"Which means that there may not be an attack on the city coming at all!"

Now it was my turn to scowl. "Can you think of any other way to find out who has been attacking the ships? Besides using Avrell for educated guesses."

Erick, who'd drawn breath to speak, subsided, then shook his head. "No."

I sighed. "All this speculation won't matter much if I can't tag someone with the Fire in the first place."

"True," he said. "Who do you—" He halted in mid-sentence, eyes narrowing suspiciously. "You want to try to tag me, don't you?"

I nodded. "If it doesn't work, then we'll go speak to Avrell, even if I don't completely trust him. If it does work . . ."

Erick seemed about to say no, but then his shoulders sagged. "What do you want me to do?"

I motioned to an empty chair. "Have a seat, get comfortable."

As he moved to the chair, grudgingly and somewhat nervously, I turned to Marielle, who jumped as if goosed by one of the guardsmen.

"Yes, Mistress?"

"I want you to watch us," I said, "that's all. Put a protective shield around us both, as we've done during training, something that will contain . . . whatever it is that might happen. If something goes wrong, I want you to find Eryn." If something did go wrong, there probably wouldn't be anything Eryn could do, but still. . . .

Marielle nodded, tension draining out of her in a rush. "Of course, Mistress. I thought—" but she cut herself off. She seemed extremely relieved. "Never mind. Where do you want me to sit?"

I placed Marielle on the settee and watched her draw a few deep breaths before she relaxed and went still. A moment later, she murmured in a distant voice, "I'm ready."

I moved a chair a few paces in front of Erick and sat down.

Erick looked at me across the short distance between us. His eyes had hardened, as if he'd steeled himself for some horrible task and wasn't expecting to survive. "Are you certain this will work?"

I dove beneath the river, felt Erick's true fear—fear that he was hiding behind a mask of bravado—wash over me, felt Marielle's more exposed fear behind me. Where Marielle sat, the river felt more dense, as if the eddies and currents had gathered there more closely. She hadn't constructed the shield yet, was waiting for me to define the boundaries where I would work.

I smiled at Erick in encouragement, then said, "No."

He frowned in annoyance and darkened his glare, but I felt his amusement.

Shifting my position on the chair, I pushed myself deeper into the river, dove down to the sphere of White Fire at my core, and held there. The voices of the throne behind the Fire were animated, pushing up as close as possible to the flames, but they didn't feel malevolent, weren't screaming and thrashing and trying to break free. Instead, they were thronged together like a crowd of gutterscum children surrounding a street-talker telling stories on the Dredge, shoving each other aside for a better position. And they were talking, arguing with each other, scoffing at and berating each other's ideas. I could smell the unfamiliar spice of Cerrin, could feel his presence at the back of the crowd, standing with five others. Liviann, the older woman who smelled of oak and wine, stood at the forefront, close to the Fire, watching intently but not participating in the conversations of the other voices around her.

These were the Seven I'd witnessed create the thrones when I'd claimed the Skewed Throne. The Seven who had poured their energy—and in the end, their souls—into their creation. I'd felt them die, the demands of the thrones too great to withstand.

The other voices in the throne made way for them, deferred to them. For these other voices, what I was attempting was something new, something the majority of them had never seen before. Some of them wanted me to succeed; others wanted me to fail. I could feel their shifting intents. For now they were mostly curious.

But from the Seven . . .

From the back, I felt Cerrin nod encouragement, felt the same from the rest of the Seven as well.

I shrugged aside their attention, focused on the Fire, on the presence on the river that was Erick. Then I halted.

I wasn't certain how to do this.

I felt the Fire pulse, felt some of the voices chuckling as they sensed my hesitation. Angry, I reached out and forced the Fire higher, forced the voices to retreat slightly. They hissed in irritation.

I focused again. "I'm ready," I said, and the river responded as Marielle drew its currents tight, weaving them into a strong shield that enveloped Erick and me where we sat.

Concentrating, I tried to slice a portion of the flame off of the main barrier, tried to use the river as I would my dagger, a sharp blade that could sever and cut. But the Fire bent away from the blade, as if pushed away by the blade-eddy I'd created. The Fire wasn't rigid enough for the blade to slice into it, too amorphous and flexible for such an attack.

Eryn had been right.

I tried a few more times, using various thrusts and stabs Erick had taught me during my training in the slums, then newer techniques taught by Westen, but none of them worked. The Fire was too resistant.

A few of the voices snorted in contempt and began to wander away, their attention shifting elsewhere. Those that remained began calling out suggestions, some of them trying to help, others jeering and making crude comments.

Cerrin shifted forward as the crowd thinned, coming up to stand behind Liviann, who remained close to the front, still watching intently.

I frowned, let the blade-eddy dissipate back into the general currents of the river.

"What's wrong?" Erick asked, an edge of tension in his voice. I could taste his sweat, salty and pungent. The inactivity was making him more nervous. His cold, calm bravado had begun to fray.

"Nothing," I said. "My first attempt didn't work. I'm going to try again."

I thought about what had happened when I'd tagged Eryn. Then, I'd been terrified. I'd shoved at the river, pushed it hard, with enough violence that I'd torn a piece of the Fire away. It hadn't had time to react, to bend and adjust to the currents. And I'd shoved everything away, in a wide wave, with no focus.

Maybe the blade-eddy was too focused.

I shifted so that both Erick and the Fire were in view, then began gathering the river before me, tightening it so I could punch it outward. I could feel the pressure build as I channeled more and more of the river into the punch, heard Eryn's voice from the training sessions as she explained how to tighten the flows, how to make them more intricate and thus more dense.

"Get ready," I said, and heard the strain in my voice.

Erick heard it too. "Is this going to hurt?" he asked suddenly.

"Perhaps."

I was just about to release the energy, felt it pulsing under my control, when Cerrin barked, *Don't!*

I staggered, barely kept hold of the pent-up energy before me, then snapped, "What!"

Through the river, I sensed Erick's confusion, felt Marielle shift forward on the settee in concern.

That won't accomplish anything. It will only hurt the Seeker.

I pulled back on the energy, allowed some of it to disperse back into the river. "It worked once before."

I could feel Cerrin's contempt radiating from behind the Fire. *You were lucky before. And Eryn had her own defenses from the Sight. This Seeker has nothing.*

His contempt and condescension sparked an anger deep down inside me. Cerrin sounded like Bloodmark, his words harsh and bitter with ridicule.

And yet he'd stopped me from harming Erick. Bloodmark would never have done that.

I let some of my own anger tinge my voice as I asked, "Do you know how to do this?"

I felt his presence pause behind the Fire, felt the oak-and-wine-scented woman's attention focus on him.

You were always more talented with Fire than the rest of us, she said.

The other members of the Seven had shifted forward as well, the other voices in the throne crowding around them.

She does have more Talent than any of the previous Mistresses . . . at least within the last few hundred years. This from a woman, younger than Liviann, her hair long and black and straight. I remembered her from the creation of the throne, remembered her struggling to get free.

Yes, Atreus, another man said, his voice sharp, his eyes like flint, *but she is certainly no Adept.*

She's not an Adept, no, Garus, Cerrin said. *But she does have the Talent.*

Do we trust her? Liviann asked.

The silence stretched. I began to think Cerrin wouldn't answer, began to grow irritated, but then:

Yes.

He shifted forward, ahead of the others, moving to the edge of the Fire.

"How do you know how to do this?" I demanded, my irritation at being excluded from their conversation, at only being given half answers both here and on the tower before I Reached for Eryn, coloring my voice.

Because before the Seven created the two thrones, I worked with Fire. That was my strength. That's why I can escape the net you have placed over the voices, why I could help you earlier when you sparred with Eryn. The net can't hold me because I can slip through the Fire instead, bypass it.

I drew breath to ask him about the Talent, about being an Adept, about how he could use the Fire to bypass the net—

But I let the breath go with a shudder.

"So how do I tag Erick with the Fire?"

Cerrin hesitated, then said, *Like this.*

I felt him reach out across the net Eryn had shown me how to use to contain the voices, slip through the protective barrier of the Fire itself, and heard the other voices within the throne gasp. A few tried to take advantage, tried to stretch the same way the man had, reach out from their prison, but they screamed when their reach touched the Fire. The oak-and-wine-scented woman stepped forward but halted, watched carefully but did nothing.

The man's essence stayed behind the Fire, but as I watched, the river between the Fire and Erick began to change beneath his direction. A whirlpool formed, swirling like a funnel, the mouth at the edge of the Fire, the tail trailing away, snaking back and forth slightly as it elongated, extending out until it reached Erick. I heard Erick gasp as it touched him. But not with pain. In surprise, his body tensing, then relaxing.

Now push the Fire along the conduit, Cerrin said. When I hesitated, he added, *Now! I can't hold the conduit forever.*

I let the ball of energy I'd been holding in reserve release, turned toward the Fire and pushed it outward, not with the sharp edge of a blade but like a shield. It flared higher, and a tendril of it coursed out along the conduit, down the funnel.

As soon as it reached the end, touching Erick, who sucked in another shocked breath, Cerrin closed off the mouth of the funnel, neatly cutting through the tendril of Fire. What had been contained in the conduit surged down along the collapsing length until it settled into a steady flame near Erick's heart.

I felt Cerrin's reach draw back behind the barrier, felt him beginning to withdraw.

"Wait!" I said, no anger or irritation in my voice now. When he paused, I said, "Thank you."

He seemed surprised. Then he nodded, eyes closed, the gesture somehow intensely formal, and turned away. As he retreated, the rest of the Seven closed in around him, the other voices surging forward in animated discussion.

I turned to Erick, verified the Fire still burned inside him, although muted as it had been with Eryn here in the city, then pulled myself up out of the river.

Marielle had moved and now stood behind me uncertainly. She'd let her protective barrier drop. "Is everything all right?" she asked when I looked over my shoulder. "Who were you talking to?"

I shuddered, felt exhaustion settle into my muscles. "I had some help from one of the voices in the throne."

"Something definitely happened," Erick said. "I felt a tingling sensation, and a bitter cold. But I don't feel anything now."

I smiled. "I think it worked. We'll have to test it tomorrow. Send you out of the city, perhaps to check up on the timber operation to the east."

"And then what?"

Erick rose when I stood, touching his chest over his heart as if looking for damage.

"Then we talk to Borund about a ship," I answered.

Trees. I'd never seen so many, so close together.

They closed in around Erick and his escort of guardsmen as they entered the forest east of the city. As he rode beneath the canopy into the forest's shadow, I felt the heat of the sun drop, the shadows closing in, and drew in the spicy scent of pine as Erick breathed in deeply and held it. The air was cool and sharp and dark, laced with greenery, with lush earth and sunlit dust motes.

It was a scent I recognized. Cerrin. The elusive incense that I had not been able to recognize before was the scent of the shade of the forest.

Something stung the back of Erick's neck and he swore, swatting at it. He slowed his horse to a walk, patted its neck as he murmured to it, its ears flicking back in answer. Behind him, I heard the two other guardsmen's mounts slow as well.

Then, reluctantly, I let the protective Fire within Erick go, pushed myself up on the currents of the river—reduced here so far away from the presence of the throne—until I broke through the tops of the pine trees and could look west, toward Amenkor and the white blaze that would guide me back to myself.

I'd experimented as Erick rode east, before he'd reached the confines of the forest. I found that I didn't need to see the Fire itself as long as I was willing to risk Reaching outward into unknown territory, as I'd tried to do on the tower when searching for Corum, before Eryn pulled me back. All I had to do was Reach out until I had the Fire within sight, then I could find my way back.

I streaked toward Amenkor, the world blurring below me, slowed as I entered the city, and felt the power of the throne settling back around me.

As I flew toward the throne room, I spotted another Fire, in the gardens of the palace.

Eryn.

I halted, hovered high over the stone path. Below, Eryn was speaking with Avrell as they moved sedately across the garden, her voice low. Avrell was frowning, his expression dark.

I hesitated a moment. But only a moment.

I dove down and settled into the Fire inside Eryn.

"—she needs to blockade the harbor!" Eryn said. "I don't understand why she's not doing anything."

"Perhaps because she doesn't feel a few burn marks on a shipwrecked deck is enough to warrant such a course of action," Avrell answered.

Inside my cocoon of Fire, I stilled, shocked.

Eryn had gone to Avrell after all, even after I'd asked—no, *ordered*—her not to.

"But it's more than that," Eryn continued. "Look at all the ships that have gone missing from Amenkor and the surrounding cities over the last year. Almost a dozen, if your sources can be believed. That's more than mere piracy and weather. And then there's the vision."

Avrell halted. "What vision?"

I hissed, shock changing over into anger. I pushed to the edge of the Fire, willed Eryn not to speak, almost reached out to seize control, to force her not to speak.

"There's a portion of me still trapped inside the throne," Eryn said. "That shadow of me showed Varis a vision of the city totally destroyed after an attack." Eryn turned to face Avrell. "The attack came from the ocean, Avrell. That, along with the missing ships, the fire on the deck, the fact that she sensed the people attacking in the vision were using the Sight. . . . We need to protect ourselves from whatever is out there. That must be why I blockaded the harbor before, to protect the city from an attack."

Conflicting emotions raced across Avrell's face. Fear, doubt, suspicion.

In the end, he settled on almost no expression at all, his stance reserved.

"Why hasn't Varis come to see me about this?" he asked.

Eryn snorted. "Because she's afraid you're trying to replace her just as you replaced me."

"Why would she think that?"

"You had the guardsmen waiting for her inside the throne room before, didn't you?"

"That was because I didn't know what was happening!" he spat. "If I've learned anything over the last few years it's that when it comes to the throne you can never be too careful. As soon as I realized that Varis was still in control, I called the guardsmen off!"

"Not soon enough for Varis."

I drew back from the Fire as the two halted, Avrell's eyes hard with anger. I felt Eryn force herself to relax, her voice to calm.

Avrell suddenly turned, moving swiftly across the garden, back toward its main entrance.

"Where are you going?" Eryn called after him.

Avrell halted, looked back over his shoulder. "To see the Mistress."

Eryn stilled, her breath held, her heart stuttering. A moment of panic shivered through her.

Then the anger kicked back in, the certainty that she was right, honed by over twenty years of being the Mistress herself.

She moved to follow.

I pulled myself up out of the Fire, catching one last glimpse of Avrell passing through the archway of the garden into the palace before I sped back to the throne room, the White Fire blazing up around me. I gasped as I reentered my body, felt Marielle's presence in the throne room, along with the usual four guardsmen. I'd had them wait inside the throne room this time, since Erick wasn't present.

Marielle took one hesitant step up to the dais where the throne sat, reached a hand out unconsciously before stopping herself. "Mistress? Is everything all right? Did it work?"

"Yes," I said, my voice surprisingly calm, even though it vibrated with underlying anger, with the power of the throne. "Everything worked fine. Erick's inside the forest."

I motioned to the guardsmen, the one in charge stepping forward. Before he'd left, Erick had introduced him, had told me he could be trusted.

"Keven."

"Yes, Mistress?"

"The First of the Mistress will be arriving in a moment, along with the *former* Mistress, Eryn. I want your men to be on either side of the throne."

Keven hesitated at the emphasis on "former," frowned, then said, "Yes, Mistress." He motioned to the other three guardsmen, ordering two to one side of the throne, the third taking his place beside Keven on the other.

I nodded in approval.

"Marielle."

"Yes?"

"Stay where you are."

Marielle turned as the main doors on the far side of the throne room swung open, a guardsman stepping hesitantly inside. He'd been ordered to keep everyone out.

Before he could speak, I said, "Let them in."

He nodded, then pushed the doors open wider to let them pass.

Avrell came in first, followed almost immediately by Eryn. They moved down the central walkway quickly, coming to a halt just before the dais.

"Forgive me, Mistress," Avrell said, nodding his head slightly.

"She told you about the shipwreck," I said without preamble.

Avrell appeared momentarily shocked, but recovered quickly.

I did not watch him. I stared at Eryn, did not try to hide the anger I felt coiling inside me.

"And about the vision of the city burning," Avrell added.

I stood. The moment my fingers left the throne I felt it begin to twist behind me, reshaping itself into another form. But the sensation no longer crawled across my shoulders, no longer prickled against my skin.

The room fell silent. I felt the guards at my back tense, felt Marielle stiffen at my side.

"I told you not to talk to Avrell about this."

"I thought that—"

"No!" I barked, and anger sparked in Eryn's eyes. Her back straightened and her nostrils flared briefly. Beside her, Avrell flinched, then drew himself upright, back stiff, face expressionless—the face of a diplomat, a politician. "There is no excuse," I said. "I told you not to speak to him, and you did."

"You weren't *doing* anything," Eryn protested, her voice cold, hard, strained.

"You aren't the Mistress anymore," I said flatly. "I am."

Eryn drew in a sharp breath, held it, but said nothing. I glared at her from beside the throne, felt it flowing smoothly from one shape to another behind me.

We held each other's gazes for a long moment, then I stepped down from the dais purposefully, motioning to Keven. "Get an escort ready. We're heading into the city."

"All of us?" Avrell's voice was neutral, without any inflection whatsoever.

I glanced toward him. "All of us."

"And where, may I ask, are we going?" Avrell asked as he fell into step beside and slightly behind me. I motioned Marielle to my other side; Eryn followed behind.

"To see Borund about a ship."

We found Borund at the warehouse that had been set up on the Dredge, the kitchen next door bustling with activity, a few members of the Dredge's militia standing at the doors to both the warehouse and the kitchen, their faces hard and serious, their hands on the pommels of their swords.

The escort paused outside the warehouse—blocked by the activity on the street because I'd refused to bring horses down to the slums after the mob attack—and I nodded to the Dredge guardsmen. As I stood there, I glanced down the Dredge, slid beneath the river unconsciously, felt the pulse of the street, the eddies and flows. I stared at the people, at their torn clothing, at the dirt on their faces, and beneath the river I could feel their hope. A living thing, passing through them and around the streets, seeping into the narrows and alleys that made up the deepest part of the slums. I thought of Evander, working stone in the warehouse district, thought of all the men and women he'd brought with him since I'd had the abusive work leader Hant whipped. I thought of Darryn and his militia, of the order he had imposed. And I thought of what Marielle and Erick had said before I'd placed the Fire inside of him, of how the people had hope again.

A few of the gutterscum and denizens of the Dredge paused at the sight of so many non-militia guardsmen, then caught my eye. A couple of the younger boys sneered, made rude gestures. One woman slapped one of the boys on his head, spoke to him harshly, as he glared at her.

Then the woman smiled and bowed toward me, making the sign of the Skewed Throne across her chest before moving on.

I turned back, away from the Dredge, saw Avrell watching me closely, face still expressionless. But he was gray beneath the river. So were Eryn and all of the rest of the escort.

The guardsmen moved forward.

"What can I do for you?" Borund asked as soon as my escort allowed me into the building. Behind him, women were hauling large sacks of bread still warm from the bakeries and ovens along the Dredge into the adjacent kitchen. A few came inside the warehouse and placed some of the bread on long tables before retreating back out into the streets. Behind the tables, crates were stacked almost to the ceiling, straw poking out from between the wooden slats. Dangling from the ceiling were strings of onions and garlic and smoked dried meats that would keep well in the cool, dry air of the building. From where I stood, I could see barrels labeled salted fish and on the far side of the room—

William.

I turned my attention back to Borund. "I need a ship and a crew to man it."

Borund's eyes widened and he turned his full attention on me. "What for?"

My entourage of guardsmen had finally caught William's eye. He moved up behind Borund as I answered.

A day or two ago, William's presence would have flustered me, forced me to back off. But not now, not today.

"I want to send it out as a trap," I said, then I outlined my plan, what Erick and I had discussed. I told him about the shipwreck in Colby, about the fire, about how I could keep in contact with the ship, about the vision. I told him everything.

Through it all, I kept my eyes on Borund. He listened intently, didn't interrupt. His only reaction was to rub his hand across his bald head, smooth down the hair that still grew in a half circle around his ears and in the back. The movement jostled the wire glasses askew on his nose, but he didn't adjust them.

At the end, he grunted. "It's a suicide mission for the ship, even with the guardsmen on board," he said. "You realize that?"

I nodded grimly.

He frowned, then said, "Give me three days. I'll find you a ship, and a captain and crew to man it."

I nodded. "I'll be ready."

Borund turned back to the warehouse. For a moment, William watched me uncertainly, as if he wanted to say something, then he turned to catch up to Borund.

My gaze followed William as he paused to snatch up a sheaf of paper from a desk set against one wall, but then he ducked into the depths of the warehouse.

When I turned around, I met Avrell's gaze.

"An interesting plan," he said. "Let's hope Borund can find a ship."

I didn't answer.

As the escort moved out onto the Dredge, Eryn came up beside me.

"You could have told me," she said, too low for anyone else to hear.

Without looking toward her, I said harshly, "I would have. You didn't give me enough time to figure it all out."

Then I stepped away, leaving Eryn behind.

╋━ Chapter 8

"Borund found a ship," I said. "And a captain and crew to man it." It had taken him five days, not three. I'd called together the captains of the various guardsmen—Baill, Catrell, and Westen—as well as Avrell, Nathem, Eryn, and Erick, to discuss who else should be sent. We were in the same conference room Avrell had used to introduce me to everyone after I'd taken the throne, but this time the room felt different. Before it had been closed in, confined, and crowded. The few potted trees and small tables in the corners, the Skewed Throne banner against the back wall, had all been threatening. And over two months before, in these people's eyes, I'd been nothing but an unknown, a nervous and somehow dangerous girl who'd managed to steal the throne from beneath them.

Today, I'd barely noticed the potted plants, the banner, the tables. And the men who had thought they ruled the city were hesitant, wary, and uncertain around me. Before, I'd been someone they could sidestep if they needed to, a ruler only in name, too young and inexperienced to be truly dealt with.

But almost a week ago, I'd truly claimed the throne. Not just in name, but in action. I'd become the Mistress. They'd heard from their guardsmen what had happened in the throne room. Suddenly, they didn't feel as secure in their positions and it showed. In the way they sat in their seats, in the way a few of them wouldn't meet my gaze.

"And what is it that you need from us?" Baill asked. He looked tired, the skin around his eyes pinched and strained. But his gaze was as penetrating as ever. He sat in his usual place at my right side, Eryn on my left, the rest of them arrayed down the length of the table on either side. Erick stood behind my seat at the head of the table. "We're guardsmen, not sailors."

I frowned at the curtness in his voice. "I need a small force of guardsmen to man the ship, since the intention is for it to be attacked. I asked you here to help me select the number of men on that force, as well as someone to lead them."

"You could have done that without us," Westen said. "You are the Mistress."

"I know," I said, bristling. Then I caught Westen's eye.

He had not meant it as a challenge.

I let some of the tension I felt ease from my shoulders, cursed silently. Baill had put me on the defensive with a single question. "I'm asking you for your advice," I said in a much calmer voice.

Westen's eyes narrowed in consideration. Then he nodded, as if satisfied. "Then I suggest you send at least twenty guardsmen with the crew. That should be sufficient."

Baill snorted. "Twenty? The crew of the ship will be stumbling all over them the entire journey. And what do you expect these men to do if the ship *is* attacked? They're guardsmen. They traipse around the city and stop street fights. What can they do on a ship?"

Captain Catrell's eyes darkened at the condescension in Baill's tone. "With all due respect," he said, not looking in Baill's direction, "the city guardsmen would be better on a ship than the palace guardsmen. They're used to fighting in close quarters and in strange and varied locations. Sir."

Baill shook his head. "But the palace guardsmen have their own ships."

"That they barely take out of the harbor!" Catrell protested. "A trading ship is completely different."

As the argument continued, I glanced toward Avrell, shot him a questioning look. The first time we'd had such a meeting, the guardsmen had been united, a single front in opposition to Avrell and his manipulations to get me onto the throne, Baill in control, backed by Catrell. They'd only relented when it became clear that Eryn herself had wanted me to become the next Mistress, that Avrell was simply doing what she'd intended.

But now it appeared that there was some friction between Catrell and Baill. They were both clearly on edge.

Avrell caught my glance, frowned and shook his head slightly, uncertain.

I slid beneath the river, watched the confrontation through the currents.

Catrell had set himself up in firm opposition to Baill, but I could not tell why. He seemed agitated, the flows around him harsh and swift, more gray than red, as if he were being torn between two opposing forces, being forced to choose. Baill seemed irritated that Catrell was arguing with him, but implacable, the river more focused and intent. He expected Catrell to relent, was getting frustrated that he hadn't yet.

And Baill was completely red.

Westen, gray and harmless, was watching the entire confrontation with interest.

"But ten men isn't going to be sufficient if they do get attacked," Catrell said. "That wouldn't be sufficient against a band of pirates! If this is something more—"

"If this is something more," Baill interrupted, words forced out through gritted teeth, "it's not going to matter if there are ten men or thirty! They're all going to die!"

Catrell drew breath to continue, eyes flaring, but I cut them both short.

"That's enough." They both turned toward me, Catrell still agitated, face slightly red. I frowned at Baill, at the closed expression on his face. "I think it best to send as many guardsmen on the ship as they can handle, to give them the best chance of survival."

Baill's face closed off even more. He leaned back in his chair, crossed his arms over his chest. He became a silent wall of disagreement, of discontent.

I didn't turn away, didn't back down. "And," I continued, "I think the force should be mixed. The palace guardsmen that have experience on the patrol ships in the harbor will make up the majority of the force. Select twelve men from those forces, Captain Baill." I shifted my gaze. "I want another eight from you, Captain Catrell. Try to get men who've worked on the docks before, or worked on ships or come from fishing villages. Guardsmen who may be used to the ocean."

Catrell nodded sharply, satisfied, his shoulders relaxing. He cast Baill a dark look before shifting his gaze to the table.

I turned to Westen. "Would you like to send some of the Seekers as well?"

Westen seemed surprised I'd asked. "Unless you wish to, I don't see how they would be any more effective than the regular guardsmen on a ship."

I nodded, then turned to the room as a whole. "Then who should lead them."

There was a moment of suspended silence, and then Avrell shifted forward. "It should be someone you trust," he said, "and someone who trusts you. After all, this person is going to be your link to the ship."

I frowned, glanced toward Baill and Catrell and Westen. Out of the three of them, I trusted Westen the most, simply because I'd dealt with him and his Seekers more than any of the others, calling on them whenever I'd dreamed of someone that needed to be dealt with, someone like Corum. Catrell I knew from the excursion to Colby and the wrecked ship. Outside of that, I'd only had contact with him on a few excursions to the city, when he'd been part of my escort. No other direct contact was necessary. And Baill . . .

Baill had been busy organizing the patrols that protected the supplies in the various buildings that had been converted into warehouses and kitchens now scattered throughout the city. With Catrell's help, since the city guard made up the majority of the force guarding each warehouse. Baill had barely been in the palace over the last few months.

So which of the three did I trust the most?

Behind me, I heard Erick shift forward, stepping up to my right side. "It has to be me," he announced to the room.

My heart dropped. Cold fear tightened in my chest, coursed through my body like ice, tingling in my arms and fingers. "No," I said without thinking, even as inside the cold fear shifted into an even colder acceptance.

I'd known I would be sending Erick on the ship for days, practically since the moment I'd successfully placed the White Fire next to his heart with Cerrin's help.

I'd known, but I still didn't want to accept it.

I caught Erick's eyes, saw the determination there, the intent. His face was hard, his stance rigid. It was a stance I recognized instantly from the Dredge. He'd already made up his mind, and nothing was going to sway him.

On the Dredge, it would have worked. I would have backed down, as I'd done when he'd decided to recruit Bloodmark as one of his trackers. I'd known that was a mistake, but I'd relented. Because I was young, and I didn't want to lose the only chance I had to escape the slums.

Now I was the Mistress. I didn't have to relent. I *could* deny him, could *order* him to stay—

But I knew I wouldn't.

Feeling the coldness deep inside, a coldness of the heart that left me feeling empty, I drew breath to agree—

But someone touched my arm.

I snapped my head around, letting anger fill my eyes. I expected the person to flinch back, to retreat.

But it was Eryn. The stern expression on her face never faltered. "It's the best choice," she said, her grip on my arm tightening slightly. "Out of everyone here, you trust him the most. Who else can you send?"

"I know," I said, letting the coldness touch my voice. We'd barely spoken over the last week, since I'd confronted her in the throne room; we'd been avoiding each other as much as possible. But I still respected her advice, and so in a softer voice, repeated, "I know."

Suddenly, twenty guardsmen didn't seem like enough. Suddenly, the entire plan seemed flawed.

Eryn's grip on my arm relaxed. A knowing sympathy tightened the corners of her eyes.

I turned back to the table. The coldness inside had grown, now spread to my arms, numbing them. "Does anyone want to argue?"

No one said anything. Of course, I thought bitterly, trying to shove the coldness away. Erick's departure weakened my position, and strengthened theirs. Baill actually shifted forward, his obstinate wall relaxing with a hint of approval.

"Then Erick will lead the expedition," I said, and felt something stab deep down inside me, something more than a political consideration.

Nathem leaned forward, shuffled a few pieces of parchment before him. "Then we need to discuss the allocation of provisions for the ship," he said, and began a litany of supplies that would be needed and which warehouses those supplies could be found in.

I barely listened. His voice faded away into nothing but a dull roar, the sound like wind in my ears. The world faded to gray. But I hadn't slipped beneath the river. This was something different. This had no focus, no intent, no currents. This was simply nothing. No feeling, no emotion. Nothing but a quiet, cold numbness, throbbing with the slow beat of my heart.

I don't know how long the numbness held, how long I hovered in silent shock, listening to my heart. It felt like eternity, but it couldn't have been long. When the world began to fade back in, the numbness retreating, I heard Nathem say, "—although we have enough stores. I just don't understand how we could have misplaced those crates."

"What crates?" Avrell asked.

Beside me, I felt Baill straighten in his seat, suddenly attentive.

Nathem shook his head, face perplexed. "There were supposed to be ten crates of Capthian wine in the warehouse on Havel Street near the wharf. Instead there were only seven when we counted."

"Weren't supplies missing from the Priem warehouse a few weeks ago?" I asked. The words felt distant, the coldness still enveloping me. But even as Avrell answered, the last of the numbness faded.

"Yes." Avrell glared across the table. "Captain Baill was supposed to look into it."

Baill shifted in his seat, the motion careful and considered. "We searched the entire Priem warehouse, using Master Regin's master list. We found that indeed a few barrels of salted fish were missing. However, we have yet to determine if they were simply misplaced or were actually stolen."

"But now more supplies are missing?" I asked. "From a different warehouse?"

"Yes. But I'm not surprised. We're far enough into winter that the people have begun to feel the effects of the rationing. Those that aren't willing to work for their fair share are becoming more desperate. And we all know what people are capable of when they're desperate." His steady gaze fell on me as he spoke. I felt my stomach tighten, felt my hand slide toward my dagger, still always within reach.

"But I thought it was the guardsmen's job to keep the supplies safe from such . . . desperation," Avrell interceded. His glare had darkened at Baill's veiled slight; now Baill's eyes hardened at Avrell's implied insult.

"Enough," I said. "What matters is that we find out what's happened to these missing supplies. What do you suggest?"

Avrell thought for a moment. "We need to do a complete inventory. All of the merchants need to check the supplies in their warehouses against the master lists at the same time. Once we know what's missing, perhaps we can find out how it's being stolen from the warehouses without the guardsmen's knowledge, and where it's being taken afterward."

I nodded. "We'll deal with that later. Right now, I want to get the ship's expedition organized and away." I turned to Catrell and Baill. "Have your guardsmen meet me at the docks by noon. Nathem, work with Borund to get the supplies for the ship loaded by then. The ship's name is *The Maiden*. The captain is Mathew."

Baill and the rest of the captains rose and left, Captain Catrell giving me a short bow before departing. Nathem did the same. Avrell, Erick, and Eryn stayed, Eryn deep in thought.

"Mathew is the one who survived the storm and brought in the last shipment from the south, isn't he?" she asked.

I nodded, recalling his haggard look on the docks as his crew was greeted by the mob of townspeople on the wharf. "Yes."

She caught my gaze. I saw a mute apology in her eyes. It was the closest she'd come to acknowledging that she had overstepped her bounds by talking to Avrell about the shipwreck in Colby and the vision of the city burning.

"Have you given any more thought to the fact that if the ship is attacked there will more than likely be someone using the Sight on the enemy's side?" she asked.

I hadn't, but I didn't see what could be done about it. "They'll have to rely on the guardsmen to protect them."

Eryn hesitated, then nodded, stood, and departed with Avrell.

Which left me and Erick alone.

I didn't look toward him, felt him shift his weight from one foot to the other behind me, his clothes rustling.

The silence between us stretched. Until it became too uncomfortable for me to bear.

I stood.

"It had to be me," he said, his voice rough.

I spun, the coldness I'd felt earlier returning with a bitter taste in the back of my throat, like metallic water. "It *could* have been someone else. It could have been *anyone* else."

He shook his head. "No. You've already tagged me with the Fire. You already trust me. You know how I'll react. And I can't be your personal bodyguard forever."

My stomach constricted. I wanted to tell him he was more than a personal bodyguard. I wanted to tell him that I felt relaxed around him, more confident, more certain. I wanted to tell him I was afraid of losing him, that he was a mentor to me. No. More than that. That he was a father to me.

I wanted to tell him many things, but all I said was, "I don't want you to go," my voice tight and ragged.

He smiled, and in his eyes I saw that he knew why I didn't want him to go, that he understood all of the things that I couldn't bring myself to say. And he knew why I couldn't say them as well.

He reached out, pushed a few loose strands of hair from my forehead.

I took the single step between us and hugged him tight, head against his shoulder, tears I refused to shed burning in my eyes. He stiffened for a moment, then enfolded me in his arms, one hand stroking my hair.

I closed my eyes, drew in a deep breath to remind myself of his scent: the sharp tang of oranges. And something else, something subtle, that I hadn't noticed on the Dredge, that I could only smell with the power of the throne behind me. Lavender.

I sighed.

"I'll be fine," he said, his chest rumbling beneath my face, his voice thick and coarse.

And even though I knew it was a lie, I felt better.

"Where in hells is he?" I growled.

At my side, Erick scanned the raucous crowds on the wharf, men and women going about their usual business, a few of them pausing to stare at the activity surrounding *The Maiden* and the large group of guardsmen and soldiers that surrounded me, Erick, and Avrell on the dock. Captain Catrell was already here with his group of eight city guardsmen, all dressed in armor, the metal glinting dully in the pale winter sunlight. All eight men were bristling with confidence, all in their mid-twenties or early thirties, all with unforgiving eyes and an impressive array of scars in visible places. On the Dredge, I would have given them all a wide berth.

"Your directions were clear," Avrell muttered from my other side. "He's doing this on purpose. I think—"

"Here he comes," Erick cut in. Then his voice darkened with contempt. "With his twelve guardsmen."

I scanned down the wharf, saw the usual eddies of the crowd interrupted near the end of the dock a moment before Captain Baill emerged, twelve palace guardsmen trailing behind him.

Avrell hissed, stiffened in outrage. I felt my body tense as well, my jaw clenching.

I placed a hand on Avrell's arm to restrain him as Baill and his men came to a halt before us all. The loading of the ship continued around us unabated.

"Mistress," Baill said.

"Captain Baill." I scanned the group of men behind him. "And are these the men you've chosen for this venture?"

They were a ragtag group dressed in armor and with swords in sheaths. At least half of the men were my age or younger, inexperienced youths with excitement in their eyes, nervously shifting from foot to foot. The majority of the rest were old, at least in their forties, their hair mostly gray, their eyes tired, grudging but willing. They didn't fidget like the younger men, but it was questionable whether some of them could draw their own swords. Only three of them were of the same strain as the men chosen by Captain Catrell. But these had a shifty look in their eyes, their expressions dark, eyes flicking toward every movement. They reeked of trouble and my nostrils flared.

Gutterscum always recognizes gutterscum.

"Twelve palace guardsmen," Baill said, "as you requested."

I turned my gaze on him.

He met the gaze evenly, a hint of challenge in his eyes.

"Then let's get them on the ship," I said in answer, turning toward Erick.

His eyes blazed with anger, but he said nothing.

Catrell barked out a command and his eight men gathered together their small packs and marched up the lowered plank onto the deck of the ship, where the ship's crew—men from Amenkor mixed with the usual darker-skinned and slighter forms of Zorelli men from the south—scrambled to prepare the sails and rigging for departure. Captain Baill motioned his contingent aboard as well. They sidled up the plank, the younger men chattering, the older ones and the troublemakers looking on in contempt, or with no expression at all.

"Not a very impressive command," Erick murmured, so low that only Avrell and I could hear.

"He meant it as a slight," Avrell spat.

"I meant it as a warning," Baill said behind us. All three of us turned. "This is a fool's errand. There's nothing to be gained here, nothing to be learned. I'll not waste good men on an expedition bound to fail."

With that, he moved down the dock and vanished into the crowds.

"He gave us his least experienced and most feeble fighters," Avrell said.

"And his troublemakers," Erick added.

"Will you be able to handle them?"

Erick nodded. "I shouldn't have any problems. Catrell gave us some of his best men. That should be sufficient."

As he spoke, Captain Catrell approached and nodded. "All of the guardsmen are aboard, Mistress."

"Good."

He nodded again, then retreated toward my usual escort of guardsmen, led by Keven, keeping themselves out of the way of the dockworkers to one side.

Erick watched Catrell silently. Then his stance shifted, became more formal. "I put Keven in charge of your escort while I'm gone. We went through our training together, at least until I was chosen to become a Seeker. He'll guard you with his life. I trust him, and his advice. Listen to him. I've also chosen all of the guardsmen in his contingent, so you should be surrounded by those you can trust implicitly."

I tried to speak, but something hard had lodged in my throat. I stared up into his face instead, saw him start to smile.

Then his gaze shifted to something over my head.

I turned and saw Eryn, her personal Servant Laurren, and an escort of guardsmen making their way down the dock. Laurren was carrying a satchel.

Eryn's movements were stiff with purpose. "Good, the ship hasn't left yet," she said as she came to a halt in front of us.

"You didn't need to come down here," I said.

"Yes, I did." She met my gaze, held it steadily. "I want to go on the expedition."

I stilled, felt my face go slack, devoid of expression. "Why?"

Eryn lifted her head. "Because we know that whoever is attacking these ships is using some form of the Sight, a form we've never seen before if they can truly control fire. If there's to be *any* hope of the ship surviving, it needs some form of protection from that. I'm the best chance they've got."

Hope flared inside my chest. If Eryn were on the ship, if she could protect them from someone else using the Sight. . . .

It might give the men on the ship a fighting chance.

"You can't send her," Erick said flatly.

Both Eryn and I sent him a scathing glare. "Why in hells not?" Eryn spat.

"Because Varis needs you here. For training, for advice on how to rule, for any of a hundred reasons. You can't be spared for a suicide mission."

Eryn frowned, her glare growing heated. Then she growled in exasperation, turned to me and spat, "Then take Laurren. She knows almost as much as I do. She can help."

In Eryn's eyes, I saw the real reason she'd wanted to go. She'd wanted to atone for speaking to Avrell. But Erick was right. I couldn't spare her. There was still too much I needed to learn.

I shifted to Laurren. She straightened as my gaze fell on her. Her short-cropped brown hair caught in a breeze from the harbor and the freckles on her cheeks stood out sharply in the sunlight, somehow in opposition to the hardness in her eyes. She knew the risks of the mission. The knowledge had pulled the skin around her mouth taut. "And do you want to do this?"

Her rounded face tightened, eyes flashing. "Of course," she said with conviction. "I live to serve the throne."

I grunted. "Do you need to get your own clothes?"

"No, Mistress. I'm about the same size as Eryn, I can use hers."

I nodded, was about to motion her toward the ship when Erick said sharply, "You should tag her with the Fire as well. It will give you another advantage . . . in case something happens to me."

I frowned, chose to ignore his last statement. "Are you willing?"

Laurren glanced once toward Eryn, but nodded.

I dove beneath the river, felt the Fire that surrounded the throne, felt the voices, sensed Cerrin, Liviann, Atreus, and the rest of Seven watching.

Do you want help? Cerrin asked.

No, I said, not speaking out loud.

I plied the river, created the funnel as Cerrin had done earlier, conscious of the Seven watching, of all of the voices watching behind them. The eddies only wavered once, but then I steadied myself, let the Fire course down the tendril after it attached to Laurren.

Distantly, I heard her gasp, heard Erick say, "Don't worry. It doesn't hurt . . . much."

Then I sliced the Fire at the mouth of the funnel, felt the funnel collapse, a small flame of the Fire settling near Laurren's heart.

The Seven murmured with approval as I let the river go.

"I can't feel anything," Laurren said, her voice detached.

"It's there," Eryn said. "If I concentrate hard enough, I can feel it. I can't see it, but I can sense that it's there."

I nodded toward the ship. After a momentary hesitation, Laurren stalked up the plank, halted at the top to scan the deck, then strode purposefully toward the foredeck.

"That may make a significant difference if we do run into trouble," Erick said.

Eryn snorted, then bit her lip with worry. "I hope so. It's a huge sacrifice on my part. She's the only Servant who knows how to make a proper cup of tea."

I laughed, a short sharp sound, a horrible nausea twisting my stomach as I lost sight of Laurren in the frenzy of activity on the deck. The realization that I'd most likely sent Laurren to her death along with Erick had just sunk in.

Borund and Mathew appeared at the top of the plank, began to make their way down. On the dock, the last of the crates were being hoisted up into the hold, or hauled up other planks to the deck. Activity was shifting from the dock to the ship itself, men clambering up the rigging, ropes tied off. The sense of excitement began to climb.

"We shouldn't have any troubles outside the harbor," Mathew was saying as he and Borund approached. He glanced up toward the sky. "Weather is holding steady today. But farther south . . ." He shrugged.

"Do the best you can," Borund said. He made a deep bow as they drew near. "Mistress."

"Borund. And Captain Mathew. Is everything ready?"

"Yes, Mistress. All provisions have been loaded, the guardsmen are aboard. We're ready to set sail."

I nodded, the lump returning to the back of my throat. I tried not to look at Erick. "Then good luck."

Mathew grinned. "I have a good crew. We don't need luck."

He turned back to his ship, stepped away with a barked command, the men at the railings darting away, repeating the order all along the ship. Lines tethering the ship to the dock began to be unwound. More men scrambled up into the rigging. Mathew stepped to the plank, began to make his way aboard.

Erick stepped away from the group, back rigid. He followed Mathew up the plank without a word, without glancing back.

I swallowed hard, closed my eyes briefly, then forced myself to draw in a deep breath and steady myself.

When I opened my eyes, Borund was watching me. He smiled, grasped my shoulder, and squeezed once.

The plank was withdrawn. Sails began to unfurl, and the ship pulled away from the dock. Slow at first, then picking up speed as the wind caught, the limp sails filling out with small muffled *whumphs*.

We watched the ship as it made its way across the harbor, smaller fishing craft skimming out of its way. No one spoke.

Then it passed out between the two juts of rocky land that enclosed the harbor, the two small guard towers on either side silhouetted against the skyline. I felt it fade from the throne's senses.

I dove beneath the river, reached up and out to search for the White Fires

I'd used to tag Erick and Laurren. Without the full power of the throne behind me, I could barely sense them, didn't dare Reach for either one.

I sighed, found Eryn, Avrell, Borund, and Catrell watching me with mixed expressions of concern and sympathy. Keven and the escorting guardsmen had moved up behind them.

"Now all we do is wait," I said.

I huddled inside the White Fire within Erick and tried not to let the motion of the ship make me sick.

Through Erick's eyes, I watched the deck roll, saw a wave of water approaching hard and fast from the right and felt Erick grip the handrail of the deck a moment before the wave hit. Wood shuddered beneath the onslaught, spray kicked up high over the bow, pattering down on the deck like rain. It pelted Erick's face, sharp and stinging, and then he dragged himself toward the bow of the ship, using the handrail and a rope for support. Overhead, black clouds boiled, the sea on the horizon a cold slate gray with wind churning the tops of the waves into whitecaps. Far off to the left, sunlight pierced down through the clouds, the rays vibrant against the receding blue sky.

"How long until the storm hits!" Erick shouted as he reached the bow of the ship.

Mathew turned to glare at him, face deadly serious. "Not much longer!"

Another wave crashed into the ship, sending a sheet of water over Mathew and Erick. I tasted the sea salt on my lips, felt the water seep down through my clothes, instantly soaked.

"You should get down below!" Mathew bellowed, his voice almost lost on the wind. He motioned with his hands, then physically shoved Erick back along the deck, following behind.

Erick hunched down, the ship lurching to the right. As he moved, I could see the black ocean now on the left, where the heart of the storm lay.

I shuddered. Even as I watched, a thin bolt of lightning pierced down out of the clouds and struck the water, a frigid crackling blue.

A moment before Erick reached the hatch leading down to the guardsmen's quarters in the hold, a torrential sheet of rain fell from the sky without warning. He gasped as it stung his face, struggled to find the ladder rungs as the ship lurched and creaked beneath another wave, and then Mathew slammed the hatch closed in his face.

I gathered myself together, then withdrew from the Fire, leaving Erick soaked, chilled, and dripping on the lower deck of *The Maiden*. I drew myself up into the roiling forces of the storm over the ship, fought their violent flows, then searched the horizon to the north until I'd found the white beacon of Amenkor. I sped away, leaving the ship to the storm.

There was nothing more to see there. The ship wouldn't be attacked in the middle of the storm. All I could do was hope that Borund's confidence in Mathew as a shipmaster wasn't misplaced.

I sank back into myself and opened my eyes to the throne room with a gasp. A harsh tremor of weakness sank into my arms, my legs, holding me tight for a breath, for two, and then it began to fade.

"How was the weakness this time?" Marielle asked. Marielle was waiting a few paces away with a blanket, Keven and his guardsmen arranged around the throne. He refused to wait outside. He'd become overly protective of me since Erick had left.

"Worse than the last time, but it's passed now." I stepped down from the throne and Marielle enfolded me in the blanket.

"You're shivering," she said in a scolding tone.

"The ship's headed into a storm," I said, teeth chattering. The blanket felt warm and dry. I couldn't shake the feeling that I was soaked to the skin, as Erick had been. "The rain was bitter cold. I don't think we have to worry about them encountering an attack any time soon."

Marielle simply nodded. I'd been checking up on Erick, Laurren, and the ship on a regular basis over the last few days and she'd grown accustomed to odd reactions, such as me feeling bitterly cold or wet . . . or nauseous. I didn't react well to the movements of the deck. Marielle had started bringing blankets and hot tea to the throne room.

And then there was the weakness. The longer I Reached, and the longer I stayed out, the more my body reacted when I returned. At first, it hadn't been anything more than a sense of fatigue, as if I hadn't slept in days. But the farther Erick and Laurren traveled from Amenkor, the more exhausted I'd felt, until now when I returned my limbs trembled, as if my muscles had been abused, as if I'd just spent the last few hours working with Westen instead of sitting on the throne.

Marielle handed me a steaming cup and I sipped, letting the warm, soothing liquid and hot steam take away the chills as I recovered, ignoring the tremors in my hands.

"How far south are they?" Keven asked. He was broader of shoulder than Erick, heftier, and held himself more relaxed than most of the guardsmen of higher ranking in the palace. He didn't exude the same sense of dangerous calm that enveloped Erick, since he hadn't been trained as a Seeker, but like Erick he felt solid, immovable, and always alert.

"Somewhere near Urral."

Keven grunted. "That's a third of the way to Venitte. They're entering the prime target area now. Most of the ships that have vanished have done so there."

Which meant I'd have to keep a closer eye on the ship from now on. I sighed. Using the throne in this manner was exhausting.

No longer feeling so cold and wet, I handed the cup of tea back to Marielle and nodded to Keven and his men.

"Avrell, Nathem, and the rest of the merchants are meeting in the upper city shortly to begin the inventory of the warehouses. Get an escort ready."

Keven bowed, then motioned to one of his men, who immediately headed toward the throne room doors.

Marielle came to retrieve the blanket.

We met another five guardsmen at the gates to the middle ward, effectively doubling my guard, then headed on foot toward the merchants' guild hall. As we passed through the middle ward, the people on the street stepped out of our way, most with a short bow of respect or a quick tracing of the Skewed Throne across their chest. I watched them all closely, saw the signs of the rationing in their faces, a look of haggardness. But most of these people had their own stores put back and were living off of that. They had no need of what was stored in the warehouses or came from the kitchens yet.

When we reached the merchants' guild, Keven led Marielle and me through an arched entryway into the back courtyard, then into the hall itself through a back entrance. I couldn't help thinking that this was how I'd entered the guild hall the first time, as Borund's personal bodyguard. Borund had just discovered that the merchant Charls was the one attempting to kill him. He'd wanted Charls to know he knew, had brought me along for protection . . . and as a warning. It hadn't worked.

We entered the main hall and I almost gasped.

When I came as a bodyguard to Borund, the hall had been crowded with merchants and ship captains chatting, trading, doing business. It had bustled with activity, the roar of conversation loud, almost overwhelming.

Now, the hall was almost empty. The huge support pillars and tall ceilings only made the emptiness more pronounced. Light streamed down through thin windows, revealing a marble floor, scattered rugs, and a few chairs on the edges of the room for more private and relaxed conversations. Tapestries and banners hung from the walls or in between the support pillars, limp and forlorn. The entire room smelled musty with disuse.

On the far side of the room, near a set of stairs leading up to a second level, Avrell and Nathem were gathered together with Borund, Regin, Yvan, and a few lesser merchants. Their conversation echoed in the open hall, the sounds strangely intrusive.

"—rather simple, Yvan," Avrell was saying as we approached, his voice tight. "Some of the stores have gone missing. We want to know why and who's been taking them. In order to do that, we need to know about everything that's missing. So the Mistress has ordered that an inventory be done of all of the warehouses. *All* of the warehouses. To be inventoried *today*. Is that understood?"

Yvan snatched the master list that Avrell was holding out toward him, almost ripping the paper in the process. His eyes shot daggers. "Yes. Perfectly."

"Good. I want a comprehensive list of everything that's missing by this evening."

Grumbling, most of the merchants took their lists and began to filter out, the majority giving orders to apprentices as they left. Yvan passed his list to his apprentice without looking at it, then began a slow, awkward walk to the exit, his heavy form lumbering along. He was breathing hard before he made it halfway across the room.

Regin stayed behind. "Some of us have more than one warehouse under our control," he said, "as well as our personal estates."

"I know." Avrell handed him a list. "Nathem is going to oversee the Priem warehouse while you handle the Duncet warehouse and your own estates. I'll be taking care of Yvan's second warehouse."

"And the warehouse on Lirion Street?"

"Borund is handling that, as well as the warehouse on the Dredge."

Regin nodded. "Very well. I'll have the list ready by this evening." He followed Yvan, moving swiftly.

Avrell sighed heavily as he left, then caught sight of me. He visibly gathered himself together, but his face looked weary. "Mistress. I didn't expect to see you here."

"I thought perhaps I could help," I said, as the escort came to a halt.

Avrell relaxed slightly. "Of course. In fact, I can have you deal with Borund's warehouse on the Dredge, while he handles the one on Lirion Street, if that's all right with him?"

Borund grunted. "Be my guest. I've got enough to do at Lirion."

Avrell handed over the appropriate list, then asked quietly, "The ship?"

"Heading into a storm." I couldn't keep a note of worry from my voice.

Borund nodded. "Mathew knows what he's doing. They'll be fine."

The group broke, Avrell and Nathem setting off for the lower city, Borund turning toward Lirion Street in the middle ward. I headed toward the Dredge, Keven, Marielle, and the escort in tow.

When we reached the warehouse, it was bustling with activity. I paused to watch the flow of workers, then caught the arm of one of them as he passed.

"Who's in charge here now?"

The man looked annoyed until he noticed the escort and realized who I was. He immediately knelt and bowed down, almost reverentially. "William, Mistress." He pointed toward the left side of the warehouse without looking up.

My heart sank, and I suddenly regretted offering to help. I should have stayed up in the palace, working on mathematics or something.

As I hesitated, I caught Marielle's eye. She glared at me, then motioned toward the kneeling man with her head.

"Oh!" I said. Then I frowned, reaching down to touch the man's head awkwardly. "Thank you."

The man ducked his head, then backed away in a half crouch before turning and fleeing back into the warehouse with a stunned look of awe.

I shook my head, glanced down at the sheet of paper in my hand, then sighed. Gathering myself together, I went in search of William.

He was working in the back section of the building, ordering workers around while consulting a list of his own. His hair was as wild as I remembered it from the first time I'd seen him on the dock, but he'd changed. He stood straight, shoulders back, head high, gestured with his arms as he spoke. He seemed taller somehow, more visible. Before, he'd always been a part of Borund's shadow, but here, in the warehouse, without Borund around . . .

"No, no, no!" he said, waving his arms to catch the worker's attention and stop him. "I said put that in the second section, not the third. It should be stacked with the dried peas."

The worker had stopped, but he wasn't paying any attention to William. He was gawking at me and my entourage.

"Well?" William said, frowning in exasperation. "Why aren't you moving?"

The worker nodded in my direction.

William turned, then froze, a look of terrified shock passing across his face before he composed it into a blank expression. He fumbled briefly with his papers, then forced his hands to stop moving, and drew in a deep breath. "Mistress, what can I do for you?"

"I'm here to take inventory."

"Ah," William said, then paused. A look of confusion crossed his face. "I thought Borund was going to do that?"

"He was. I volunteered to help, and they gave me this warehouse."

"Ah," William said again.

Another pause, this one long enough to become awkward.

I glanced around the warehouse, at the stacked crates and barrels. "Shouldn't we get started?"

William jumped as if I'd pinched him, then nervously turned around. "Of course, of course. Let me just . . ." He spotted the worker, who still stood gawking. "Harold! Take that to section two!"

The worker jerked, mumbled something indistinct, then vanished behind a stack of crates.

William turned again. "Let me just . . . get rid of these papers. Yes. And then we can get started." He started to put the papers back into some type of order, but they became even more disorganized. Finally, he gave up, shoved them into a heap, and said, "Follow me."

He led us back to the front of the warehouse where he had a table set up with extra paper, ink, and a chair set up like a desk. He put the loose papers down on the desk, then turned. He seemed to have composed himself on the way to the desk.

"How do you want to proceed?" he asked.

I shrugged. "However you want. You're in charge of the warehouse."

He hesitated again, looked at me as if he thought I was trying to trick him somehow, then he straightened. "First, we'll have to keep everyone not doing inventory out of the warehouse."

"Very well."

William called all of the workers to the front of the building, then sent the majority of them away on other tasks on the Dredge, or transferred them to the communal ovens or the docks. Those that remained were men and women who could count and a few who could read. He broke these up into teams and dispatched them to various places in the building to count crates. Only two of those present could write. These he kept near the front of the warehouse to record the amounts and types of food and supplies each team had counted.

Once the teams were dispatched, he turned to me.

"How long do you expect this to take?" I asked.

William shrugged. "A couple of hours at most. We have quite a few teams."

"I see."

From the back of the warehouse, I could hear the teams beginning to call out numbers and foodstocks.

I frowned at William. "I can count, you know."

He stared at me in incomprehension.

I sighed. "I came down here to help. Why don't we form a team and start counting?"

Light dawned. "Of course! I didn't think. . . ." He trailed off, then shook himself. "Of course. Follow me, we'll start on the second floor."

He headed toward the back of the warehouse again. Before following, I motioned to Keven. "Have the escort watch the warehouse. I don't think I'll need an entourage to help me count boxes."

"I'll stay with you," he said, with a tone that suggested I'd better not argue. I gave him an irritated glare, but he only smiled.

As he sent the other guardsmen to patrol the warehouse, Marielle shifted closer, grinning hugely, her eyes sparkling.

"What?"

She leaned in close and whispered, "He likes you."

"Who, Keven?"

"No," Marielle said, rolling her eyes in disgust. "William."

I shot her a dark frown, but deep inside something surged upward—hope and dread and a queasy excitement that warmed my blood and tightened my chest, making it harder to breathe.

Then I remembered William's look in the tavern after I'd gutted the assassin that had tried to kill Borund. Horror and revulsion had contorted his face, obvious through the shock. He'd had the same look when he realized I was going to kill Alendor.

"No," I said, trying to crush the roiling hope in my chest. "He despises me."

Marielle seemed surprised at the harshness in my voice, taking a small step backward. But then the knowing grin returned, somewhat subdued.

"I don't think so," she said. Then she swept past me, following William.

I glanced toward Keven, who pretended he hadn't heard. But the twitch at the corner of his mouth gave him away.

I snorted, then headed for the stairs.

We began at the southern corner of the floor. I clambered up to the top of the stacked crates, Marielle following, surprising both William and Keven. Then we began working our way northward, Marielle and I counting as we went, calling down numbers to William below. Keven dealt with the crates closer to the floor, William reading the labels. The tops of the stacks were dusty and filled with cobwebs, and both Marielle and I were covered and sneezing in fits by the time we reached the end of the first stack. Crouching and straddling the crates as we moved down the line was also hard work, and soon we were drenched in sweat. But it was the first time that either of us had done anything outside of attend meetings in the palace or train using the Sight in the gardens— or the dagger under Westen's eye for me—in a long while. The sheer novelty of manual labor was exhilarating.

We climbed down from the first stack and burst out laughing as we saw each other in the full light. Both Keven and William were grinning as well. Dusting ourselves off, we moved to the second section.

The hours went by quickly. At one point, Marielle claimed exhaustion, and so William climbed up to the top as she took over recording the results. At first, having William that close, in such a confined area, felt uncomfortable. But as soon as we began counting, that awkwardness faded. For the first time since we'd known each other, I was not a bodyguard or assassin or the Mistress. I was simply Varis.

As we reached the end of the last stack, I shifted to the edge of the crates and sat, legs dangling. I was breathing heavily, my white shirt stained a drab gray, my breeches caked a uniform brown with the combined sweat and dust. William moved to sit down beside me, breathing hard as well. He had cobwebs caught in his hair, his face smeared with dust and grit and sweat. But his eyes were bright.

He turned toward me and the strange exhilaration I thought I had crushed came back, pounding in my chest.

He smiled and I grinned in return.

"You should come up to the palace more often," I said, and instantly cursed myself.

His smile faltered, then steadied. "Perhaps I will from now on."

Down below, Marielle shouted, "We're all done down here. What are you two doing up there?"

We leaned over the edge, peering down at Marielle's and Keven's upturned faces. Marielle was smiling. A little twisted smile. She raised her eyebrows suggestively, and I replied with a heated glare.

Leaning back, I sighed. "I suppose we should climb back down, see how the rest of the teams are doing." But I realized I didn't want to go. Not yet. I wanted to stay there, with William, covered in dust and cobwebs, the taste of grit in my mouth, the scent of my own sweat and his sharp in my nostrils.

William grunted, hesitated a moment, then twisted and began climbing down.

I watched the top of his head for a moment, strangely disappointed, then followed.

All of the other teams were finished. William collected all of the lists and sat down at his desk to begin comparing them to the master list. My stomach growled, and I realized I hadn't eaten anything since that morning. The inventory had taken up most of the day. It was almost dusk. But looking around at all of the exhausted faces of the workers from the Dredge, all beginning to take on the edges of strict rationing, I found I didn't mind. I'd gone days in the slums without eating, knew I would survive a little hunger now.

I turned back to William when he grunted. He leaned back from his lists, held them up to scan them again, then turned, surprised.

"Well?" I asked.

He shook his head in disbelief. "There's nothing missing. Everything that's supposed to be here . . . is here."

✝ Chapter 9

"Well, that's certainly not true at the rest of the warehouses." Avrell paced back and forth on the garden path as he fumed, his hands tucked in the sleeves of his dark blue robes, his head bowed forward.

I glanced toward Eryn, seated on the stone bench beside me. I'd never seen

Avrell so agitated, so angry; not even when he'd thought Eryn had tricked him somehow by smuggling in the Capthian wine without his knowledge. I seethed with anger myself, but unlike Avrell, I found myself retreating into myself, reverting to old habits: I'd become deceptively calm, my hand itching for my dagger. But Avrell and Eryn weren't the ones responsible for the missing food, and so I waited, the anger held tight and controlled inside me.

"How bad is it?" Eryn asked.

Avrell paused in his pacing, looked up at her, at me, then spat in irritation and waved the question toward me before continuing.

I straightened, thought about the reports from the individual warehouses that had come in throughout the evening and night yesterday, then began.

"It's bad," I said grimly. "The worst warehouse hit was the one on Havel Street, near the wharf. Twenty casks of wine and almost forty crates and barrels of assorted food—pickles, beans, and dried meats—were missing. The Priem warehouse had thirty barrels missing, including the salted fish we knew about earlier. Both warehouses on Lirion Street and Tempest Row were missing foodstocks as well. In fact, all of the warehouses established after the fire in the warehouse district have something missing, except the warehouse we set up on the Dredge."

Avrell snorted. "The one warehouse you would have thought would have been robbed blind by now."

I shot him a glare of mixed anger and irritation. He grimaced and had the grace to look embarrassed.

"That is rather curious," Eryn said.

I turned the glare on her.

She shrugged. "Why is it that the warehouse on the Dredge isn't missing anything? Whoever is taking the food is obviously not afraid, nor stupid. And they must be well organized. Look at how much has gone missing already, and we've just now noticed. Why is it that they've left the Dredge stores alone?"

"Probably because they would have been seen," I said bitterly.

Avrell frowned. "They should have been seen no matter what warehouse they chose. We have guardsmen posted at all of them. And Darryn is watching the warehouse on the Dredge with his militia."

Eryn shook her head. "But not all the time. And besides, guardsmen can be paid to look the other way, bribed with money or perhaps even some of the food that's being taken. The guardsmen aren't all reliable."

"I didn't mean they'd be seen by the guardsmen," I said, annoyed that they didn't understand. "I meant that nothing goes unnoticed in the slums. There's always someone watching, whether you can see them or not. The streets are never empty, even when Darryn and his militia aren't there. If someone had tried to take something from the warehouse, they wouldn't have lasted ten minutes. Someone else would have seen them and reported it, or killed them and run off with the food themselves. We'd have found bodies. And someone would have seen *that* as well. And eventually someone would have told Darryn." I shook my head. "No, whoever is taking the food knows that they'd never get away with stealing from the Dredge. They'd find themselves with their throat slit, their body dumped in a back alley somewhere, probably with Darryn's permission." I sighed. "Besides, the people of the slums have too much invested in that food. It's the only chance they have of surviving the winter. Most of them won't be willing to risk that, and they won't be willing to let anyone else steal it from them either. The warehouse on the Dredge is probably the safest warehouse in the city."

Avrell and Eryn mulled this over quietly. Finally, Avrell sighed and settled down beside Eryn on the stone bench. He picked at invisible dirt on his robe.

"So how are they getting the food out?" he asked. "It's not like they're lifting a few loaves of bread or an apple. They're taking entire crates. That requires wagons, and men to do the work."

"Some of the guardsmen must be involved," Eryn added. "More than a few, since more than one warehouse has been hit."

Avrell shifted in his seat. "We can't compare the lists of which guardsmen were working which warehouses, because we don't know when the food was taken. And at least one of each of the merchants' warehouses was hit, so we can't narrow it down that way. None of their personal estates reported anything missing either, probably because most of the merchants have manses behind enclosed walls."

I stared across the gardens, through the few denuded branches of the trees and shrubs, to where Keven stood watching us from a discreet distance. "Erick said I could trust Keven and the guardsmen he chose for my personal guard before he left," I said. "I'll ask them to question some of the other guardsmen quietly—both palace and city guardsmen—and see what they can find out. Maybe some of the other guardsmen have seen something suspicious."

Avrell nodded. "That may give us somewhere to start looking."

I felt my tightly controlled anger slip a little. "So who did it? I don't care how they did it, I just want to know who it was. And where the food is now. I want that food back."

Avrell looked up at the sharpness in my tone. "My guess would be one of the merchants. Regin, Yvan, Borund, and the lesser merchants all have unquestioned access to the warehouses. All they have to do is show up with a cart and tell the guardsmen they're there to move some of the food to a different warehouse. They could even have papers. It wouldn't matter. Most of the guardsmen can't read, and there's no reason for them to doubt the merchants in the first place. We've moved hundreds of supplies that way already, almost on a daily basis. So even if we find some guardsman who thinks he saw something suspicious, we can't prove anything."

"But she doesn't need to prove anything," Eryn said, one eyebrow rising slightly. "She's the Mistress."

I thought about that for a moment, then shook my head. "I'm not going to raid every merchant's estate looking for the missing food. Especially since we don't even know it was a merchant in the first place."

Eryn's eyes darkened. "You may have to," she said. "Not everything you'll be forced to do as Mistress will be fair, Varis."

I stiffened in defiance, then realized Eryn wasn't trying to force me to change my mind. She was simply offering advice.

And she was deadly serious.

I forced the tension in my shoulders to relax. "I'd rather have some type of reason before I act right now," I said. "But I will act when I have to." It wasn't a concession, but it let her know I'd heard what she meant.

Eryn held my gaze a moment more, then nodded.

All three of us lapsed into thoughtful silence, a cloud drifting over the sun high above.

Eryn's shoulders tightened. "What if you used the throne?"

I frowned. "What do you mean?"

She straightened up even more, her eyes alight. "I mean use the throne. It's connected to the city. You can use it to see individual streets, the people on those streets, get a feel for their emotions. Why not use it to search out each of the merchant's estates individually? They'd never know."

"Then what?" Avrell asked.

Eryn snorted as if the answer were obvious.

"You raid that merchant's estate," she said.

The anger I'd been holding in check leaped forward at the idea. I stood up abruptly, the weight of my dagger pressing into my back where it was tucked into my belt. Energy seemed to bleed off me, the same sensation I'd felt working in the warehouse the day before. I'd been trapped in the palace and in politics too long, inactive. I needed to move, to hunt, and here was my opportunity.

"Where are you going?" Avrell called from behind me. I was already halfway across the garden.

Without slowing, I said, "To the throne room."

The city's life pulsed around me and for a long moment I let myself simply float in it, the eddies and currents soothing. The black despair I'd felt in the slums immediately after assuming the role of Mistress had lifted with the stationing of a warehouse and kitchen in that area, with the creation of the Dredge militia, and with the work force that traveled daily from the slums to the burned-out warehouse district. Construction there had slowed since the readily available stone had run out, but now teams of carts and workers streamed from the city to the northern quarry and the Dredge, so the building continued. The roiling fear that had hovered over the city since the coming of the White Fire had abated.

I gathered myself and pushed higher above the city, turned south to where the flickering Fires that I'd placed inside Erick and Laurren could be seen. At this distance, they appeared as a single flame, with no way to distinguish between them. I thought about taking a moment to check up on the ship, but my anger over the missing stores pulled me back down to the city.

I wanted to know who had stolen that food.

I started with Borund's estates. Not because I didn't trust him—I didn't think he'd taken anything—but because I was more familiar with them. As his bodyguard, I'd escorted him everywhere, to all of his warehouses, all of his buildings in the city. He'd lost a significant portion of his warehouses near the wharf in the fire, but there were still a few left. I started with those.

Skimming over the wharf, over the flow of the people on the docks and working on the ships, I slid down and down and slowed until I'd settled into the currents on the main thoroughfare. Weaving in and out among the people, I came swiftly to the first warehouse, slipped through the half-open doorway and inside.

A few men and women were moving among the boxes and crates, but I soon decided they were doing nothing suspicious and so I drifted down among the stacks of supplies, the crates closing in overhead, muting the sounds of the other workers. After a few feet, weaving in and out amongst the crates, the stacks reaching almost to the ceiling, I felt totally isolated and a little claustrophobic. The scent of straw struck me, and I shuddered, felt sweat break out on my forehead and in my armpits. Unconsciously, I gripped my dagger tighter. Then I realized why.

I'd chased Cristoph into a warehouse exactly like this after his ambush had failed, had killed him among the warren of paths among the crates. In his attempt to stop me, he'd flung his oil lantern at me and started the fire that consumed over half of the warehouse district. All to keep me from killing his father, Alendor; and to avenge his friend, who I'd killed earlier on the wharf when Cristoph tried to rape me.

I halted in the middle of the crates at the memory, but shook myself and shoved the memory aside. It was useless to dwell on it. Alendor was gone, had fled the city according to Avrell's network of spies; and Cristoph was dead. Pushing forward, I continued my scouting of the warehouse, ignoring the pungent scent of straw and oil.

When I'd completed a circuit of the warehouse, I'd found nothing out of place.

I scanned it again once, watched the workers a moment more, then shrugged and pushed up out of the building and down the street to the next warehouse.

It was the same as the first. When I finished with Borund's warehouses near the wharf, I moved to his personal estate.

The manse was just as I remembered it. Gerrold manned the estate with the help of Lizbeth and Gart, the stableboy. I paused to watch Gerrold let Borund in at the gates, Borund dismounting and handing the reins of his horse off to Gart. Then I went inside, scanned the rooms downstairs, ducked into the kitchens and down the back staircase to the cellar where rough-woven sacks of the essentials—rice and barley—and strings of vegetables hung from the rafters. I scanned through all of the food stores, but found nothing that seemed out of the ordinary. No hidden crates of wine, no stacked barrels of salted fish.

I moved back upstairs, then to the second floor. I paused in my old room, stared at the bed, the dresser, the table and chair. Nothing much had changed. I found Lizbeth in Borund's room, fussing with the bedcovers, folding them over just so before moving on to pull the curtains back from the windows to let in the midmorning sunlight.

I stayed the longest in William's rooms. Lizbeth had already been there, the bed already made, the curtains pulled back so that sunlight lit the entire space. I edged up to the desk, stared down at the sheets of paper scattered over its surface. Lists of goods and prices, with sources written in tight, legible script in neat columns. I smiled as I remember Borund telling me how much William had hated keeping track of everything when he'd first arrived as the merchant's apprentice. Now, he kept everything more organized than Borund himself.

A piece of paper that seemed out of place caught my eye and I shifted to the back corner of the desk. It was a sketch of some sort, a drawing.

I frowned, leaned forward for a closer look—

Then jerked back with a gasp of surprise, my heart thudding in my chest.

It was a sketch of me, of my face.

Guilt surged through me, and I quickly scanned the room to see if anyone had noticed, unconsciously sinking into a defensive stance. But of course no one was there, and they couldn't have seen me even if they were. I wasn't actually in William's room, I was back in the palace, sitting on the throne, Avrell, Eryn, and Keven watching over me.

My heart settling a little, I turned back to the sketch, reached out to touch it, but then withdrew my hand.

I hadn't known William could draw, even after living in the same house with him for almost two years. All I'd ever seen him do was work on lists for Borund—inventories and sales records.

I looked more closely at the face. It was definitely me. Straight dark hair cropped about shoulder length on either side of a narrow face. A few tendrils fell over my eyes even though my bangs were trimmed short, and I felt an urge to reach forward and brush them out of the way, as Erick always did to me. My head was tilted a little to one side, my eyes questioning, a few creases between my eyebrows. I had the faintest hint of a smile, the entire expression on my face making it seem as if I was uncertain whether I was supposed to be laughing or not.

I leaned back. Was this what William saw when he looked at me? It wasn't what I expected. It wasn't hard, or cold, or angry. I didn't see the edges I saw in Erick's face, the edges I associated with being a Seeker. I didn't see the calculated deadliness of a Seeker either.

I withdrew from the manse, paused on the street outside, watched the people walking by without really seeing them.

Perhaps Marielle was right. Perhaps William didn't look at me and see a disgusting, cold-blooded killer, someone who'd hunted for marks as a Seeker on the Dredge, someone who'd killed on command for Borund and Avrell later on.

On the street, a man almost walked into me, but before I could react he stepped to one side for no apparent reason, the flows on the river forcing him around me. I watched him as he continued on, his sudden deviation not even registering on his face. But he'd interrupted my thoughts on William, and I suddenly remembered what I was here for.

Borund was cleared as far as I was concerned. Time to move on to the other merchants.

I spent the next few hours scouring warehouses and buildings that had been converted into warehouses after the fire, as well as the personal estates of each of the merchants. Most of the warehouses were uninteresting, workers shifting goods or handing them off to the kitchens. At one warehouse, goods were being loaded onto a cart. I waited until all of the sacks of grain were loaded, then followed the cart, hoping that it would lead me to the thief, but it halted at the mill, the grain they unloaded to be ground into flour for use at the communal ovens.

I sighed and continued searching.

The estates were more interesting, servants moving out and about at various tasks, the merchants in meetings. I saw stableboys snoring, shovels dropped forgotten at their feet; maids giggling as they worked, passing along gossip; cooks bellowing out orders in stifling kitchens. Once, I intruded on a guardsman and a maid in a tryst on the second floor of a manse, the guardsman hissing for quiet when the woman squealed and giggled in delight.

Toward dusk, the sun beginning to set on the mountains far to the east, exhaustion lying heavy on my shoulders, I slid down the back stairs of the last manse and pushed through the door at the bottom.

I blinked into the darkness of the cellar, noticed the sharp scent of freshly turned dirt before my eyes adjusted. As soon as I could see, I stepped into the earthen room, past a sack of walnuts, a bushel of dried apples, a string of garlic.

Nothing out of the ordinary. Except I could still smell the scent of fresh earth.

All of the other cellars had smelled of old earth, dry and packed down with use.

I scanned the room, breathing in deeply, then moved to the right, where the scent seemed strongest.

I halted before a stack of barrels and glanced down at the earthen floor.

The barrels had recently been shifted. There was a gouge in the floor, and a pile of loose dirt on the hard-packed earth of the cellar floor.

I stepped toward the barrels, slid along one side and behind—

And entered a narrow tunnel.

The scent of new earth was dense here, almost overpowering.

Crouching down instinctively, even though the roof was high enough for me to walk upright, I moved down the tunnel, emerging into another room after only ten paces.

A room packed with crates and sacks stacked to head-height in the narrow space.

The anger I'd felt since I'd learned that someone was stealing from the warehouses—an anger that had died down during the course of the day and the long hours of fruitless searching—resurfaced with a rush of heat to my chest. My jaw tightened; my nostrils flared.

Without thought, I pushed myself out of the manse, up above the city, and rushed back to the throne room. I had a moment to notice that Eryn had left, that only Avrell and Keven remained, and that someone had brought in a tray of food, and then I settled back into my body and pushed myself up off of the throne.

Both Avrell and Keven gave a start at the sudden movement, Keven reaching for his sword before settling back down. Avrell lurched up from his seat on the stone steps of the dais.

"What did you find? Do you know who's taken the food?"

I caught both his and Keven's gaze.

"It's Yvan," I said, and the contempt in my voice made Avrell step back a pace.

It took Baill almost a full day to organize enough men for the raid on Yvan's estates. When I'd told him, he'd seemed surprised, but then his face had gone blank, the same expressionless facade he'd worn when I'd first seen him as Borund's bodyguard and he had barred our entrance into the palace.

Except he still seemed exhausted.

Noticing the dark smudges around his eyes, I'd said, "You should get some rest. I can have Captain Catrell plan the raid."

"No!" he'd barked, his eyes glinting. As I raised my eyebrows at the harshness of his tone, he scrubbed at his face with both hands, then placed them flat on the desk before him. "I mean, no, Mistress. Captain Catrell is currently busy elsewhere. I'll have the men ready by this evening."

Now Avrell, Baill, myself, Keven, and an entourage of twenty palace guardsmen hid in an alley in the outer ward where most of the merchants lived. At the entrance to the alley, Baill peered around the corner, his hand resting lightly on the pommel of his sword, searching the darkness. The sky overhead was cloudless, the night lit by an almost full moon. Baill no longer acted exhausted, although the dark smudges remained.

I watched him quietly, already beneath the river, the currents surging around me. All of the men were tense, their emotions wild and erratic. Armor clinked and clothing rustled as they shifted nervously. We'd been waiting for over an hour as the rest of the guardsmen moved into place on the remaining sides of the wall that surrounded Yvan's manse. We already knew he was in residence; he'd been driven through the main gates in his carriage a few moments after we'd entered the alley, and the rest of the group broke off for their own positions.

Baill nodded at a signal from someone I couldn't see, then pulled back from the alley's entrance. The rest of the guardsmen edged closer to listen in.

"Everyone is in position," he said. "They've closed and locked the main gates, so we'll have to batter those down."

"Leave the gates to me," I said, voice hard. Without conscious thought, I'd slipped back into my role as a Seeker, a bodyguard.

Baill frowned and glanced down to where I idly swung my dagger through various moves with one hand. I hadn't even realized I'd drawn it. "Mistress?"

I caught and held his gaze. "I'll handle the gate," I repeated. "It won't be a problem as long as you put me in the lead."

He suddenly realized that I meant to be part of the party entering the walls, that I didn't intend to wait in the alley until everything was over. He shifted uncomfortably, seemed about to protest but sucked in a breath instead, trapped between my intense gaze and the fact that I was the Mistress, someone he should be protecting at all costs. He shot a hopeful glance at Keven, expecting him to intercede as my personal bodyguard, but Keven only shrugged.

Finally, Baill grunted in disgust and nodded toward Avrell. "And you?"

Avrell shook his head. "I'll come in after everything has settled down."

"Very well. I don't expect much resistance."

"He might have a few bodyguards," I said. "Most of the merchants had them by the time we ended Alendor's consortium. But that's all. They shouldn't be a problem."

"Very well," Baill said again, looking over the rest of the guardsmen, catching their eyes, making certain they were ready. He didn't glance at Keven or Avrell, his gaze ending on me. "After you."

I nodded in acknowledgment, then stepped out from the alley.

Yvan's manse stood at the end of the street, the main gates opening directly onto the cobblestone road. Stone walls ran parallel to the cross street in both directions from the large arch of the wooden doors of the entranceway. As I came out of the alley, dagger clutched in one hand, I paused, did a quick scan of the area using the river, but sensed no one other than the guardsmen in Baill's force. Satisfied, I started walking to the gate.

As I moved, I pulled the waters of the river tight before me, gathered it into a solid wall of power. I felt Keven immediately behind me to my right, his sword drawn. He smelled of earth and dew. Baill moved to the left, radiating calm intent. The rest of the guardsmen came up behind.

When we were ten paces from the closed wooden gates, I paused. Jaw clenching, all of the fury I felt toward Yvan pounding in my blood, I punched the gathered power of the river forward.

The gates exploded inward with a rending shriek of twisted metal and splintering wood. A sharp crack followed as the stone surrounding the hinges shattered, debris pattering to the cobbles of the street, the gates crashing to the ground in the garden beyond the wall. All of the guardsmen jumped—one cried out—but neither Keven nor Baill faltered.

Then we were through the gate, into the outer garden, picking our way over the broken debris, a loose stone path running from the street up to the front door of the manse. Candlelight burned in most of the downstairs windows. As soon as we entered the garden, Baill's men scattered to the left and right, streaking toward the other entrances, where the rest of the group were waiting for the doors to be unlatched. Only seven guardsmen remained with Baill, Keven, and me.

Shouts began to filter through the night, coming from the back of the manse, where the carriage house and stables would be.

"He'll try to make a break for it as soon as he realizes what's going on," Keven said.

I nodded. I didn't intend to give him the chance.

We reached the stone steps that led to the double doors of the manse. Someone—a servant—opened the front door and peered out into the darkness, lantern raised high. His eyes widened as he saw me, and he jerked back.

Before he could react, Baill's guardsmen leaped up the steps, shoved through the half-open door and dragged him out onto the porch. He cried out, dropped the lantern, which shattered on the ground and went out, and then one of the guardsmen thumped the struggling man over the head with the pommel of his sword.

Guardsmen held the doors open as Baill, Keven, and I entered, both escorting guardsmen on edge, swords drawn. The foyer opened onto two flights of stairs leading upward, and two doors to the left and right. A layout similar to Borund's manse, but larger. And filled with ostentatious and elegant furniture, rugs and tapestries and urns.

I frowned at the extravagant display of wealth.

"Where is he?" Baill asked.

I stood in the middle of the foyer, glanced up, to the left. With the power of the throne and the river, I could sense the fear of the servants as the guardsmen worked their way through the manse. The men in the stable and carriage house had already been taken, were being held outside behind the manse. The servants in the kitchen had been cornered as well. A few others were scattered throughout the house, mainly on the second floor, some still asleep.

But there was a small group of people off to the left.

"There are a few servants still left upstairs," I said. Three guardsmen broke off and headed up the stairs. "Yvan is down here."

I led the way, Keven and Baill a step behind. When we reached the closed door, I halted, let the guardsmen shift into position on either side, swords drawn.

The scent of sweat and fear lay thick on the river. I caught Baill's eye, then nodded.

He stepped back, kicked the door in with a grunt. It burst open with a sharp crack, the doorframe splintering. Inside, someone gasped, and something shattered. Someone swore, followed by a flurry of activity and the sound of swords being drawn.

Then everything went quiet.

Baill, Keven, and the remaining guardsmen slid into the room, stepping to either side of the open door.

Then I entered.

It was a dining room, the table almost fifteen feet in length, running from the door to the far side of the long room. It was lined with empty chairs and platter upon platter of food. Candles stood in candelabra on all sides and down the center of the table. At the far end of the room, Yvan sat at the head of the table, a cloth napkin tucked into the front of his shirt, stained with grease and sauce. He held the greasy leg of a chicken in his hands, staring down the table at Baill and the guardsmen in horrified shock. Two bodyguards, swords drawn, bodies tense, stood to either side of him, protecting his flanks. A servant trembled to one side, the remains of a broken platter of what looked like sauced strips of pork staining the rug at his feet.

Yvan recovered quickly. Tossing the chicken leg down on the heaping plate before him, he shifted forward, his face suffused with anger, grunting with effort as he tried to stand. The servant leaped forward to help, staggering under Yvan's weight.

Gasping, breath short, Yvan bellowed, "What is the meaning of this?"

I glared at him in disgust, felt my anger triple as I breathed in the heady scent of all of the food—more food than had been served in the palace in the last three days, more food than most of the people of Amenkor would see in a week. I felt myself trembling with rage.

"Take him," I said, surprised at how calm my voice sounded.

Baill's guardsmen moved down the length of the table. For a moment, Yvan's bodyguards hesitated, swords raised, and the river thickened with resistance. But the bodyguards knew me, knew Baill. Glowering, they relaxed, sheathed their swords and stepped aside, allowing the guardsmen to surround Yvan. His servant moved swiftly out of the way.

When the guardsmen attempted to grab Yvan's arms, he jerked out of their grip.

"How dare you touch me!" he shrieked.

"How dare you pretend you've done nothing when you're gorging yourself on enough food to feed half the barracks!" I barked, my restraint finally broken. I felt Avrell enter the room behind me, heard him gasp at the sight of the food on the table.

In a much deadlier tone, I asked, "Where did you get all of this?"

"It comes from my personal estate—"

"You stole it from the warehouses!" I shouted, cutting him off, taking a step forward, my hand slamming down on the table. "You stole it from Amenkor!"

Yvan spluttered, face shocked. "I did no such thing!"

I snorted in disgust and motioned to Baill, who stood to one side, his eye on the bodyguards. "Bring him with me."

I led the group down the hall into the kitchen, where even more food was being prepared. Behind, Baill and the guardsmen herded Yvan along as fast as his bulk would allow. Avrell and Keven kept up with me.

We descended into the cellars, Yvan's servants scurrying to find lanterns at Keven's direction.

"I don't see anything out of place here," Avrell said cautiously.

Keven sniffed the air. "What's that smell?"

"Freshly dug earth," I said. I headed straight for the barrels that covered the entrance to the second room.

With Keven's help, I shoved aside the barrels covering the tunnel.

One of the servants gasped. Keven ducked down into the tunnel, emerged a second later, his face grim.

Avrell frowned, then ducked into the tunnel as well.

Baill, Yvan being forced down the stair ahead of him at sword point, appeared in the cellar.

I glared at Yvan. "Now tell me you haven't robbed Amenkor blind," I growled.

Yvan straightened where he stood, his mouth clamped shut. But his eyes blazed raw hatred.

I shifted my gaze to Baill. "Take him back to the palace and hold him. I'll deal with him later."

Baill jerked Yvan back, and for the first time a flicker of fear appeared in Yvan's eyes. But before he could protest, Baill shoved him up the stairs.

I heaved a sigh of relief, felt pent-up anger and tension release from my shoulders in a wave. I let the river go.

Avrell reappeared, a worried frown creasing his forehead.

Before he could speak, I said, "Seize everything. And search the rest of his estate as well. I want to know everything that he's taken."

Avrell nodded, but the concern remained.

I caught Keven's gaze, exhaustion settling onto my shoulders like a blanket. I'd sustained myself by sheer rage for the last two hours. All I wanted to do was crawl into bed. "Let's head back to the palace."

Keven gathered a few of the other guardsmen as an escort, and we began to wind our way through the outer ward. The streets were quiet, only a few windows still lit with the faint glow of lanterns or candles. Most of the buildings were dark, hidden behind their own low walls, everyone asleep.

I moved slowly, too weary from the day's activities to pick up the pace. As we reached the gate to the middle ward and began the trudge up the hill toward the gates of the palace, I turned to stare at the inner walls, at the parts of the palace that could be seen beyond them.

The walls of the palace seemed to glow in the moonlight, the white stone almost silver. Large bowls of flaming oil were lit at intervals, and at various spots on the palace—along the promenade, on the tower—the fire flapped fitfully in the breeze coming off of the harbor.

A sudden sense of the surreal stole over me and I paused, the guardsmen drawing to a halt. Keven moved to my side, face creased with concern. "Mistress?"

I shook my head, gave him a withered smile. "It's nothing. I'm just tired."

"We could send for a horse, perhaps a carriage."

I shook my head. "No. I'm fine."

I took one last look at the palace, then continued on.

We passed through the inner gates into the courtyard, proceeded up the steps of the promenade and into the palace. Here there were more people, servants preparing for the coming day's activities, guardsmen on the walls, page boys and Servants moving about at odd tasks. We passed through the heavy set of double doors guarded by a phalanx of silent guardsmen into the Mistress' inner sanctum—doors that had once been the outer gates of the original gray stone palace—and turned toward my personal chambers.

As we passed by the throne room, I paused again, then bowed my head.

"What is it?" Keven asked.

"I haven't checked in on Erick since yesterday morning."

I hesitated, weariness dragging my shoulders down, but eventually I sighed. "Just a quick look, to make sure he's safe," I said.

The guardsmen drew back the double doors and I made my way down the aisle, past the stone columns, then up the steps to the throne where it twisted and warped itself on the dais. As I settled into it, I almost changed my mind, almost decided I was too tired. But then the throne settled down into the familiar curved shape, my hands coming to rest on the front of the arms, and I felt the power rush through me, the voices surrounding me, the sound now almost soothing.

I drew strength from them, then lifted myself up, searched out the White Fires far, far to the south, and leaped.

I skimmed over water, the waves undulating beneath me, almost totally black in the night, the moon like a cold silver coin on the darkness. I focused in on the two White Fires ahead of me—one scented with oranges, the other like lilies—both rushing toward me as I Reached, and then I saw a streaking flash of fire, real fire, saw the fleeting outline of three other ships . . . no four! . . . in the fiery afterglow of an explosion, felt a moment of confusion, of disorientation—

And then I dove into the orange-scented Fire.

I heard a scream, a bellow of rage, heard swords clash and then suddenly a man's body fell backward before me, blood flying up to spatter my face. I shoved the dead guardsman—one of Baill's men—aside with a grunt, raised my own sword, felt the descending blow shudder through my arm as I caught it and thrust it back with a heave, sending the attacker stumbling over another body, and then suddenly I was in the clear.

I gasped, wiped my face free of the blinding blood, and spun.

The entire ship was being overtaken. One of the attacking ships had come up alongside, had tethered itself to *The Maiden*, men pouring over the side.

But not ordinary men.

Within the Fire, I lurched back in shock, withdrew even further as I realized I was too entwined with Erick, with his emotions. Then I turned my attention back to the attack, fear shuddering through my body.

Someone stumbled into Erick from the side, grabbed his arm to steady himself. Erick jerked back, startled, raised his sword, then halted.

"In the Mistress' name," Mathew swore, voice thick with horror, "who are they?"

And deep inside, I heard one of the voices—one of the Seven, I thought, perhaps Cerrin—gasp, *Gods, not them.*

Erick drew in a deep breath, tried to steady the dread and adrenaline that coursed through him. He shook his head. "I don't know."

"They're sea-demons," one of the crew gasped behind them, blood running down his face from a cut in his scalp. His eyes were wide with terror. "Sea-demons, from the tales!"

Erick watched as more of them poured off the sleek ship tethered to *The Maiden.* They were short, dressed in loose clothing, almost like silk, in a riot of colors, with armor underneath. They screamed as they struck—high, piercing ululations, black hair flying as they jumped from one ship to the other, strangely curved swords glinting in the fires all along the deck. Most were covered with tattoos, along their arms, on their faces. A few wore necklaces of shells.

But the most telling feature, the thing that struck horror into Erick's gut, into *my* gut, was their skin. It was a pale, pale blue, like a winter sky.

Deep in the White Fire at Erick's core, one of the voices in the throne wailed in recognition, radiating shock and disbelief. *It can't be them.* A sob, almost a wail.

Who are they? I screamed at the voices, screamed at the Seven, choking on the scent of blood and fire.

But before anyone could answer, another ball of fire lanced out from the second ship, arced out over the water that separated the two, and crashed into the mast high above, flames shattering and raining down on the deck. Erick and Mathew ducked, lurched out of the way, moving swiftly up the foredeck.

"Where in hells is Laurren?" Erick hissed under his breath. He shot a glance out toward the half-seen ships that circled the trader ship. He thought there were three others, aside from the one tethered to the trader ship, but he couldn't be certain.

"I saw her on the aft deck," Mathew said, "but then I was cut off from her."

Erick grunted. "Head down the port side," he said, motioning with his hand. "Have everyone move in this direction. We can't defend ourselves if we're scattered all over the ship!"

Mathew nodded, broke away from Erick, clambering down the deck over dead bodies and broken shards of the rigging. Erick turned, caught another blade with his sword, then drove the dagger in his left hand up under the make-shift armor into the gut of the attacking blue-skinned man. The attacker gasped, blood pouring from the wound in his chest, and then Erick thrust him aside.

"At least they die like ordinary men," he muttered to himself.

Someone screamed, a bloodcurdling death cry, and he glanced down the deck. Part of the crew huddled together, swords and axes flailing, two guardsmen with them, but they were surrounded, backed up against the railing of the deck.

Erick leaped forward, body slipping into old rhythms. Within a heartbeat, three of the attackers had fallen. The rest turned to face him, two more dying as the guardsmen cut them down from behind, and then the group was free.

"To the foredeck!" Erick shouted, shoving them along toward the prow of the ship. They stumbled forward, eyes wide in shock.

Erick glanced toward the second ship, noticed another that circled farther out in the glow of the firelight on the ocean. He spat a curse.

On the second ship, a ball of fire flew up into the air. In the backwash of light, he saw a woman standing on the prow, her black hair flying wildly about her in the wind, her hands lifted before her. Her face was twisted with concentration, her eyes cold and deadly with intent. She wore loose clothing, like the warriors, but her ears were pierced with gold rings, three on each side.

Then, before the aft deck, the thrown fireball struck something in midair and exploded, fire raining down an invisible wall of force to the surging ocean below. In the fiery light, Erick saw Laurren, her face screwed up in a scowl of hatred. A sharp gust of air followed the explosion of the fireball, but before Erick could react, another ball of fire arched out from the ship circling farther out, striking the same invisible wall.

A bright ball of light exploded across the ocean, illuminating the other circling ships clearly, flashing hot on the surface of the ocean. In the near-blinding explosion, Erick saw two other women, one each on the other two ships, both dressed like the first, both with gold earrings.

Then he was hit by a concussive force of wind that shoved him back. Everyone on the ship staggered, some crying out in shock. The sheet of fire winked out.

The next ball of fire slid past Laurren's shield, shuddered into the side of the ship, exploded and rained down the side into the water, the pungent scent of smoke prickling in his nose. Erick heard wood creak with strain, felt the ship rock up on a swell and thud hard into the ship already tethered to the port side. As they separated, someone fell down between the two ships into the water with a scream.

On the aft deck, Laurren raised her hands, drew back, and flung her arms forward as if throwing a spear out into the darkness of the ocean.

Wood planking shattered on the nearest ship, chunks flying out from its side.

A weak shout of triumph went up from The Maiden's crew.

Erick pressed his lips together grimly.

Three against one. He didn't like Laurren's odds.

I didn't either.

Gathering myself, I leaped out of Erick, sped across the deck, fire dripping down from the burning sails, rigging collapsing to the body-strewn deck, and sank into the Fire at Laurren's core.

Laurren, I'm here.

"Mistress," Laurren gasped, her face already covered in sweat, her eyes wide, her heart thudding so hard it hurt. "They're so strong!" Her voice was nothing more than a whisper.

Another fireball struck her shield and I felt the force rippling as Laurren staggered backward, her hands raised before her. Gritting her teeth, she spat, "And there are so many of them."

Anger boiling up from inside me, I said, *Give the shield to me. Use your strength to strike back at them. Try to take out the women.*

Laurren nodded, flinched back as two fireballs struck almost simultaneously, the force shuddering through her arms, down into her chest. Jaw clenched, she released the flows of the river, the shield collapsing—

And at the same moment I reached forward—through the Fire, as Cerrin had reached through the Fire to help me guide the river so many times before— grabbed the disintegrating edges and pulled the shield tight.

Laurren cried out in relief and staggered forward, her hands coming up to her face, trembling with the effort.

Grappling with the shield, a fireball hitting it with a glancing blow and shuddering down its length to strike the ship, I spat, *Laurren! You have to fight back! I can't hold the shield and strike back at the same time!*

With an effort, Laurren drew herself upright, breath harsh, choking as smoke drifted across her face.

Then she gathered the river into a focused rod of power, like a spear, and with a grunt of effort and pure hatred, she hurled it toward the nearest ship.

It struck with a rending of wood and the bowsprit of the circling ship sheared off, splinters flying up into the face of the woman at the prow. She screamed in fury, arms flung up to protect her face, and then ducked out of sight.

Laurren chuckled, the sound somehow dead.

Don't stop. There are at least two others like her.

Laurren nodded, sucked in a deep breath, and began to send spear after spear out into the darkness, targeting the three circling ships. The first, naked with the lance of the bowsprit missing, turned back and the attacking Servant appeared again, fireballs shooting out from its side now. The first hit the mast, *The Maiden* shuddering as it exploded, fire raining down in tatters; the second caught my shield. More fire arched out of the darkness, pummeling the shield, the mast, and Laurren answered, each spear sent with a gut-wrenching growl.

Then the fireballs shifted. I saw three arch out of the night, had a moment to realize they weren't aimed at the ship itself, had time to say, *Laurren*—

But the warning came too late.

Even as I strengthened the shield before us, the first fireball hit, followed instantly by the second, the third a breath behind. Laurren cried out, flung her arms up to ward herself as each exploded, fire coruscating out from my shield in all directions, surrounding us in a wash of hellish light. I grunted, pulled the shield in tighter, sacrificing the protection of the ship in order to keep the fire at bay. Heat seared Laurren's upraised arms, scorched away her eyebrows, turned her skin waxy. I felt the shield shudder again, felt another barrage of fire strike it before the first had even faded, felt the heat intensify, felt Laurren's hair catch fire. Three different attacks, from three different directions, all with the same purpose.

It was too much. I couldn't hold the shield, could feel it shredding even as I gasped in a broken, ragged voice, *Laurren! I can't hold it! I can't*—

And then it collapsed.

Fire roared into the opening, enveloped Laurren in a seething mass of flames that flung her back. Fire raced up her arms—my arms—seared into flesh, crackling and spitting like a roast thrust onto a spit on the hearth. I screamed, Laurren's voice rending the night, shrieking, and flames scorched down into my lungs, burning inside and out, choking me, charring deeper into skin, into bone—

And then I flung myself out of Laurren's body, still screaming, in pain, in hatred, in denial, my gut clenching and twisting because I couldn't save her, because I hadn't been able to hold the shield.

Laurren staggered across the aft deck, her scream dying, her body a pillar of flame reaching high into the night, and then she came up against the wheel, hard, back twisted. She spun, arms trailing fire, gripped the wheel in desperation, as if trying to hold herself upright.

And then collapsed to the side and lay there, not moving, not even twitching.

A fireball arched past where I hovered on the river, my own scream dying as the sensation of being burned to death faded. I gasped, choked on smoke, on fire itself, felt as if I were weeping, sobs hitching in my throat even though my body was over a thousand miles distant.

The fireball struck the mast, and I suddenly heard the screams of the other men on the ship.

Thrusting Laurren's pain aside, I dove down into Erick again.

"Erick!"

Erick spun, saw Mathew and a group of men hacking their way down the starboard side. He leaped forward, joined the fray, sword used mainly to guard as his dagger slashed in and out. All horror vanished as calm settled over him, the skills he'd been drilled in as a Seeker coming to the fore, taking over.

One of the curved rapiers snicked in and sliced along his jaw, nothing but a nick, but the blue-skinned man fell back as Erick's dagger cut across his throat. Two more of the attackers took the man's place, black eyes seething with rage. They let out a piercing shriek, but Erick didn't flinch, cutting in sharply. A blade slashed along Erick's side, the pain like white-hot fire cutting across his ribs, and he hissed, punching his dagger hard through the leather armor into the man's heart, and then the entire ship lurched and everyone stumbled to the side, the remaining attacker falling away.

Erick suddenly found himself among Mathew's men. He gasped, slapped a hand tight across his side, felt blood—his own blood—coat his fingers.

"They've brought another ship up alongside," Mathew yelled over the fight. He grimaced as a blow landed hard on his shoulder, then brought his own blade down hard, slicing through the man's wrist. The blue-tinged man screamed. Blood fountained from the stump as he lurched away, splashing the man next to Mathew before the hand-less man fell to the deck and was trampled underfoot. "And we've lost Laurren."

Erick shot a glance toward the aft deck, saw the billowing flames where Laurren's body had fallen, and grimaced. His stomach twisted with regret, with actual pain. The cut along his side was worse than he'd thought. But there wasn't time to deal with it.

He drew breath to order everyone to the foredeck, but another ball of fire roared out of the night and landed squarely on the deck, at the base of the mast.

Erick expected it to explode into fragments, like the other ones. Instead, this one's flames spread outward like a pool of oil . . . and then began snaking along the deck, tendrils of fire shooting out toward the feet of the men all around it. I could see the forces at work on the river, could see it being guided. . . .

It caught one of the crew almost instantly.

Before Erick could yell out a warning, the man's clothes erupted like a torch, fire seething upward. The man screamed, the sound sending shivers down Erick's spine. Arms flailing, the man stumbled, hit the mast with his back, then staggered toward the side of the ship, hitting the railing with his hips, then rolling over the top.

He struck the side of the tethered ship once before vanishing from sight.

"Shit!" Mathew breathed. He wiped his mouth with the back of one hand as their gazes met, and in Mathew's eyes Erick saw hopelessness.

They weren't going to survive this battle.

Erick felt the realization settle over him with a strange sense of calm, interrupted only by the pain in his side.

"Get the men to the foredeck," he said, voice steady. "We'll take as many of the damn blue-skinned demons as we can with us."

Mathew hesitated. Then his face hardened, grew grim, and he nodded.

Turning, he bellowed out an order and shoved the men closest to him forward. On the deck, the eerie fire continued to spread, flames streaking out and engulfing men as they ran, swerving around the blue-skinned warriors as they drove Mathew, Erick, and the rest back. I tried to watch, tried to reach out with the river to disrupt the flows that controlled the fire, but Erick was moving too much, dodging and retreating, all in fluid motion, his side screaming at the abuse. Another fireball streaked out of the night and hit the mast, the entire ship shuddering, and then another. Erick fought back, dagger slicing in and out, sword cutting through skin, striking bone, getting tangled in the clothing the warriors wore. And still the men came, pouring in from the starboard side as grapples were thrown from the third ship and the two were tethered together on that side.

The Maiden's crew and the few remaining guardsmen, mostly those provided by Captain Catrell, were driven into the prow of the ship, the group tightening up, the guardsmen shoving the regular crew into the back to defend them as the spacing narrowed. Fire resumed arcing over from the outer ships, striking the deck, the mast, flames now roaring along the port railing, eating away at the aft deck. Most of the sails had been consumed; only tatters remained. Rigging dangled down from the crosspieces of the mast.

Then a ponderous groan shuddered through the ship.

Erick stepped back from the edge of the fighting, caught Mathew's gaze from across the group of crewmen.

The captain of *The Maiden* nodded toward the mast.

Another groan, and this time the majority of those still fighting paused and turned.

Erick heard wood beginning to splinter, a soft, insidious sound, then noticed that fire still roared at the base of the mast.

With a heartrending groan, the mast listed. Wood cracked, the retort hard and sharp and reverberating in Erick's chest, and with a slow, ponderous grace the mast began to fall, trailing fiery sails and rigging behind it.

It struck the aft deck of *The Maiden*, the decking splintering upward at the force, the shudder running through the ship and vibrating in Erick's teeth. He clenched his jaw tight, turned back to the surrounding blue-skinned men—

And then threw down his sword, wincing. It clattered on the deck, the sound small compared to the crash of the mast. His free hand went to the cut along his side. He pressed hard, trying to staunch the flow.

To either side, the guardsmen tossed their own weapons to the deck, their eyes hard and angry.

The tension on the ship didn't decrease. Instead, one of the blue-skinned men stepped forward from the crowd, pointed his curved sword at Erick.

He spat something in a language Erick didn't recognize, eyes blazing with anger. His face was covered with tattoos, swirled, like waves, and the lower half of one ear was sliced off.

The blue-skinned man eyed Erick, then snorted in contempt. His blade retreated.

Movement came from the back of the attackers, and then a woman stepped out from the crowd. Back straight, head held high, she advanced on Erick and the crew, and the blue-skinned men around her retreated, giving her a wide berth.

She was dressed in the strange silk-like cloth of all the others, but her dress had lengths of cloth attached at the waist and wrists, and her ears were pierced with more of the gold rings than the women on the other ships—seven on each side. Her long black hair was held back with a band of gold on her head. Her blue skin was flawless, her eyes black and hardened like stone.

She halted a few paces before Erick. The man who'd spoken to Erick drew back another step, but his eyes never left Erick's face.

The woman spoke, and again the voice in the throne responded—a roar of rage. But I couldn't distinguish who it was amid the chaos. I couldn't catch the scent.

Erick shook his head, frowning in confusion. The woman glared at him, then scanned the rest of the guardsmen, the crew, her eyes falling on Mathew before finally returning to Erick.

She waved her hand in dismissal, said something low, and the man who'd threatened Erick nodded, smiling tightly, a look of anticipation in his eyes. She began to turn away. The blue-skinned men around her stepped forward, swords raised.

I suddenly realized what she intended.

She meant to kill them all.

I leaped forward, horror causing the Fire around me to flare higher. Seizing control of Erick's body, I screamed, "No!" using his voice. I reached for the river using the Fire at Erick's core, wound it tight and flicked it outward like a lash.

It licked across the front rank of blue-skinned men and they shrieked, thrust backward by the force of the invisible blow, and then the whip slid across the woman.

And there it met a wall of force, as tightly woven and dense as anything I'd ever seen Eryn wield. The whip struck the wall and leaped back, recoiling, almost snapping into Erick and the rest of the crew before I brought it back under control.

The woman spun, eyes flashing, and then she moved, so fast I barely saw her, too fast for me to react.

The wall of force surged forward, shoved everyone back from Erick, and then snapped in hard around his throat, crushing into his neck like a hand and lifting him up. He choked, feet dangling off of the deck, pain screaming up from his side with its own white fire, and then the woman stepped forward, peered up into his eyes.

I felt more lines of force reaching out, probing. I withdrew behind the wall of Fire, let my control of Erick slip, suddenly afraid, cursing myself for losing control, for lashing out.

The woman frowned and I suddenly realized she sensed the Fire. She could taste it, as Eryn had tasted it when I'd tried to kill her in the throne room. She could sense it.

And she recognized it.

She frowned, the probing tendrils retreating. Erick continued to choke, his vision beginning to blur, to narrow, but then the invisible hand holding him relaxed, lowered him to the deck.

He gasped as it loosened enough for him to breathe. But it didn't release him. Instead, it pressed him farther downward, forced him to his knees.

The woman stared down at him, her eyes narrowed, her frown deepening.

Behind her, the man who'd threatened Erick earlier took a tentative step forward, said something.

The woman didn't answer at first. Then she motioned to the rest of the guardsmen and crew and repeated her earlier command.

Hatred seized me, and as the crew screamed, guardsmen cursing and diving for their dropped weapons, the blue-skinned men attacked. Blades fell, the night filled with the sounds of death.

I surged from the Fire again, reached for the river in desperation to stop the slaughter, to save Erick, to save someone—

But the grip on Erick tightened. With horror, I felt the river gather around the woman, felt it harden into blunt force.

Before I could react, before I could begin to form a wall to protect myself, to protect Erick, the woman struck.

I saw the hammer of force fall, felt it shudder through Erick's body, heard him scream as a horrifying pressure built up behind his eyes, throbbing with his heart. Blood fountained down onto his forehead, ran down into his eyes, filled his ears, his mouth, as he arched back at the pain, as the pressure inside his head increased, as it escalated, until it streamed from his body like sweat, soaked into his clothing like blood—

Then the world exploded.

And everything went dark.

⊹— Chapter 10

Varis.

I moaned, the pounding in my head somehow more intense than usual. I could feel it radiating outward, sending pain away in waves. I felt as if I were adrift, lost and directionless, tugged here and there by invisible currents, the sensation soothing, like sleep or the sigh of wind through the leaves of a tree.

Varis. You need to wake up.

I winced at the voice, tried to shove it away, tried to ignore it. But it was more than a voice, it was a presence, permeating me, surrounding me. It persisted, nudging me, prodding me, the movements becoming more desperate.

Varis. You're dying.

I woke with a gasp. But that wasn't correct. I became *aware* with a gasp, as if I'd struggled through water, almost out of air, lungs aching, and had finally reached the surface. I flailed around, felt the comforting eddies and currents of the river surrounding me, felt the presence of the voice—of many voices—hovering just out of reach, watching me carefully, subdued and sad and concerned. Not all of them. A few still wailed at the edge of the Fire, but the majority of the voices were quiet.

And then I calmed, abruptly, forced myself to remain still, to focus on my surroundings.

Ocean. Beneath where my consciousness drifted, I could see the slow undulation of waves, lit by fractured early morning sunlight, golden and soft. I could smell it, sharp with salt, damp and heavy, like syrup. It rolled silently below me, a breeze drifting out of the west.

Where am I? I asked.

The voices conferred, but it was the voice that had woken me that spoke. Cerrin's voice.

You've been adrift on the river, he said, his voice still tinged with his usual self-pitying sadness, but with a hint of energy now as well, of renewed purpose. It hurt when he spoke, my head throbbing with a steady pulse, in sync with my heartbeat. *The Ochean severed your link to Erick, and in the process knocked you unconscious. You've drifted wherever the currents of the river have taken you for the last eight hours.*

Erick! Everything that had happened on the ship came back with the blunt force of a hammer. I suddenly felt his searing pain, felt again the pressure building inside his head, felt the blood pouring down his face as he arched back, mouth open in a blood-chilling inhuman scream.

I lurched up on the river, sent myself high, began scanning the ocean in all directions. There was no land in sight, nothing but black water rising and falling, the sun a blazing gold on the horizon, the sky a pale cloudless blue above. I spun around again, grew more focused, more frantic, and then I spotted a cold flare of White Fire on the horizon, faint and far away.

I sped toward it, heart shuddering. Erick's pain lashed through me again, the river around me roiling at the memory.

I had to find Erick. I had to save him. He'd gone on the mission under my orders, had risked everything because of me, because of my plan, my idea.

The White Fire began to draw nearer, but slowly. To distract myself, I asked, *The Ochean? I've never heard that name before.*

Another whispered conference.

The blue-skinned woman on the ship who has the Sight, the one who attacked Erick, the one with seven gold earrings in each ear. She's the leader of those people. They call themselves the Chorl.

I frowned. I'd never heard of the Chorl, never heard of any blue-skinned people. The Zorelli who manned most of the trading ships were dark-skinned— a deep brown—but they came from the islands to the south. Everyone knew that. The rest of the people I'd seen in Amenkor or had ever heard of had pale skin, white that had been tanned to various shades of light brown. Aside from the Zorelli, everyone on the Frigean coast was pale.

No one could even remotely be called blue-skinned.

The memory of the warriors streaming up over the side of the ship, their cries piercing the night, sent shivers of horror and revulsion through my skin. Their tattoos, their clothes, their rounded, flattened faces—everything about them was too strange, too inhuman, almost unreal.

How do you know this? I asked harshly, the horror already edging into hatred. *How do you know who they are?*

I felt Cerrin's presence hesitate. Another voice, a woman's voice, Liviann's or perhaps Atreus', hissed at him sharply, and he grew grim.

Because we fought them once before when they came to the Frigean coast. We fought them. And when we defeated them, we banished them, sent them back to the ocean from which they came, sent them west. They decimated the coast for the span of five years. We thought we'd never see them again, thought perhaps that they'd died out, but we prepared nonetheless. That's one of the reasons we created the thrones: to protect the coast from attack.

Who is this "we"?

The Seven, Cerrin said, his voice sad again.

He fell silent, withdrew back into the maelstrom of the voices, back into a pain I didn't understand.

I felt a surge of anger, thought about demanding that he answer more questions, but beneath me the color of the ocean had changed, no longer a deep dense blue verging on black. It had lightened.

Ahead, the White Fire blazed. My heart raced, pulse quickening. Perhaps I wasn't too late. Perhaps I could still save Erick.

And then I saw the coastline, saw the rocky shore, saw the arms of land reaching out to embrace the harbor.

Amenkor.

The blaze of Fire wasn't Erick. It was the Fire inside me.

The revelation was staggering, and I shuddered to a halt outside the influence of the throne, outside the entrance to the harbor, waves crashing into the stone arms of land, spray sheeting up toward the two stone watchtowers at their ends. I spun, searched the horizon to the south and west, desperate. I soared higher, higher still, until the air began to feel thin, until the river itself felt thin, diluted, like the air, and still the horizon was empty.

Damn it! I screamed, frantic. *Help me!*

The voices remained silent, withdrew even further, unnaturally quiet. A somber quiet, filled with pain and loss and understanding. A quiet that somehow smothered those that still fought to escape their prison, to seize control. Because those that still fought to escape were so few.

But I barely noticed, pushed myself higher still. There was no Fire. No tag for me to follow. No way for me to link up with Erick. Which meant—

I halted, a cold certainty seeping down into my gut.

I drew in a harsh, trembling breath, held it.

I scanned the horizon one more time, knowing I would find nothing.

I felt a pain begin to build inside me, begin to sting at the corners of my eyes. A pain totally unlike that which had racked Erick's body, had seethed in his veins and shuddered in his heart, had built and built behind his skull. This pain started deep in my chest, swelled and seeped outward, a hot, visceral pain that felt fluid and sick and left me drained and weak and useless. This pain closed off my throat with a hard, nauseating lump. I tried desperately to hold the pain in, the stinging in my eyes increasing, tears beginning to stream down my face. I felt myself shudder with the effort—

Until I couldn't hold it in any longer.

I screamed. A raw scream of rage and pain and loss. Of guilt and regret and unfairness. And when that breath had died, strangled into nothingness, I gasped in another breath, the sound ragged and harsh and broken, and I screamed again, so hard it felt like my throat had torn.

The voices responded. The Seven—as well as those that were now calm, now quiet—shifted forward, reached out through the protective Fire under Cerrin's guidance, surrounding me, holding me, comforting me. I shut off all consciousness of the river, closed myself off from the world, and surrendered to the fluid pain, let it sear through me. I let the voices protect me as my screams descended into racking sobs and twisted guilt.

I curled in upon myself.

And I let myself drift again.

The pain receded like the slow ebb of the tide and my awareness of the river returned. First nothing more than a sound: ocean waves crashing up against a rocky shoreline. It took me a moment to recognize it, for it to seep through the numbness left behind by the pain. But once I did recognize it, my awareness spread, like a drop of oil on the surface of water, or blood seeping into cloth. I smelled the shore, sand and wind and stone. And seaweed drying in the sun.

I opened my eyes, breathed in deeply, and stared down the length of beach to a rocky crag jutting out into the ocean, the surf pounding into the stone with crashing spray and sparkling mist. I stared at the beach a long moment without thinking, barely aware of the afternoon sun against my face, until I noticed movement.

A crab scuttled across the sand, heading for the rocky plinth.

I glanced around, noticed the beach running up to a layer of rocks and driftwood, then a dune with wisps of grass that merged into a bank of pine trees. Behind me, another rocky crag cut off the view of the beach to the north.

It reminded me of the little cove near Colby, where Eryn had investigated the remains of the shipwreck.

I turned back to the water, looked out over the waves, to where the sea darkened into true ocean.

Erick.

The ache in my chest returned, but it was dull, nothing more than a throb of grief. I was too numbed, too exhausted.

I reached for the voices of the throne, felt their presences in the background behind the wall of Fire, but none of them came forward. They'd changed. For the first time, that realization sank in. They were no longer fighting among themselves, no longer bickering and biting and seething in a maelstrom of hatred. Instead, they were calm, intent, and focused.

Except for a few still screaming at the edges, they'd banded together, had united with a purpose. The Seven were keeping those that had not joined them under control themselves, and now they were simply waiting.

I should have been concerned, should have used the river to renew the net that protected me from them, should have thrown up a second net for additional safety. I shifted uneasily. . . .

And then I let the concern go. It didn't matter. Nothing mattered now.

Time passed, the sunlight overhead shifting. I did nothing, said nothing, felt nothing.

And then:

Varis.

It was the woman with straight black hair. Atreus. She stood with the rest of the Seven arrayed behind her, Cerrin in the back, his form shifting restlessly, his presence troubled.

Varis, we need to speak to you. About the Chorl. About the Ochean.

What? I said.

You have to understand how dangerous they are, Atreus said. *You have to warn Amenkor, warn the entire Frigean coast. If they have returned—*

Garus snorted. *They have returned! Open your damned eyes!*

Garus!

What!

I focused on the man who'd cut Garus short. He was younger than Garus, had no neatly trimmed beard, was thin where Garus was broad. And I recognized him. I'd witnessed the creation of the thrones through his eyes, felt his pain as the rest of the Seven fell around him, consumed by the raw energies they'd called into existence.

He leveled a stern gaze on Garus, and the older man backed down with a grumble.

Thank you, Seth, Atreus said.

But Garus is right, another woman said. She had straight black hair, just like Atreus, had the same facial features as well—thin face, high cheekbones, fine nose. An older version of Atreus, harsher, her mouth set into a perpetual frown. *The Chorl have returned, and you need to know how dangerous they can be. And Cerrin is going to show you.*

All of the voices in the throne turned to Cerrin. He glanced up. *Why me, Alleryn?*

Alleryn's frown deepened. *Because yours is the more powerful, more convincing story. And because your story was the beginning.*

Cerrin grimaced, then steeled himself. Without shifting forward, he said, *For Olivia, then, and my daughters.*

He reached through the Fire and grabbed me, and before I could draw breath, I was trapped.

Wind blew across the veranda, rustling in the long, thin leaves of the potted plants in urns on the edges of the stonework lining the edge of the patio. The air was raucous with the cries of seagulls and other birds. I moved to the edge of the balustrade, stared down over the cliff into the bay far below.

Venitte lay spread out before me, the wide bay filled with ships of all kinds, birds wheeling both above and beneath my position, horns and bells joining their cries occasionally. Sails bellied out in the wind, drawing the ships out to one or the other of the two channels that branched north and south around the island that protected the bay from the worst of the winds and the storms. Other boats streamed toward the main wharf farther inland and the domed buildings on the hills behind, or toward the hundreds of jetties and piers that lanced out into the water beneath the cliffs on either side of the bay. On the opposite cliff, white stone buildings with red clay-tiled roofs and lush inner gardens formed a bright mosaic in the sunlight.

"Do you have to go in to Council?"

I turned, smiling even before I saw Olivia, her skin dark and vibrant as she exited the shade of the house and came to my side. Behind her, Jaer and Pallin scampered out into the sunlight, laughing. Pallin, seven, reached out to grab her sister, but Jaer—two years younger and much smaller—eluded her, ducking and screaming with delight as Pallin gave chase.

"You know I do," I said, taking Olivia into my arms. I kissed the top of her head, breathed in the scent of her hair. "The Council has many important decisions to make."

"More important than me?" She said it lightly, mocking me.

"Hmm . . . you ask dangerous questions. More dangerous than the Council." She laughed.

Down on the water, there was a muffled sound, like an explosion, echoing against the cliffs.

"What was that?" Olivia said. Pulling free from my grasp, she moved closer to the stone balustrade, leaned on it.

Frowning, I joined her.

Another muffled *whumph,* and another, the sound distorted as it bounced against one of the stone walls of the channel.

Olivia shook her head. "I don't see anything."

"It's coming from the channel," I said. I glanced toward the wharf, toward the Council chambers, the largest stone building in Venitte, its spire reaching into the sky, then back toward my wife.

Olivia turned at the tone of my voice, her eyes flicking toward the children. "Should I . . . ?"

Before I could answer the unasked question, ships began pouring through the mouth of the channel. Black ships, their hulls glistening in the sunlight as they threw up spume before them. They lanced into the bay, sails all unfurled, bellied out with the wind, moving at a fast clip. First five appeared, then ten, then twenty, spreading out on the bay as they breached the channel. And still more came.

"Cerrin?" Voice taut, strained, worried. "Who are they?"

"I don't know."

The lead ships encountered the first Venittian, and fire leaped out, arched across the water in a sizzling ball and exploded in the Venittian's sails. Olivia gave a startled cry, the fear tight and hideous in her voice—

And then suddenly there was fire everywhere, arching up and out from every ship, searing through the sky trailing smoke, striking ship after ship as bells and horns began to blow, as birds scattered with harsh cries, fleeing, the ships in the harbor doing the same, turning ponderously and skimming back toward the inland wharf, toward the city, the Council and the walls that could protect them.

But the fire wasn't restricted to the ships. Great sheets of it flew high, bursting with deadly intent in the bright mosaic of houses on the cliffs on the far side of the bay.

"Cerrin!"

I spun, anger boiling like acid in the back of my throat, curling tight about my fear. "Get Jaer and Pallin. Now!"

Behind, I heard fire sizzling close, felt a wash of heat across my back and glanced up in time to see a huge fireball roaring overhead, heard it explode in a house higher up the cliff above us. Olivia cried out, her eyes wide with fear now, and Jaer screamed.

"Olivia!"

She turned from where smoke and fire leaped into the sky behind our house, and in her eyes I saw the fear drain away. "Pallin," she snapped. "Get your sister. We're leaving."

I turned back toward the bay, moved up to the stone railing as three more fireballs arched into the houses to either side. Screams came from the left, and a body fell from the cliff, trailing flames and smoke.

Real fear began to boil in my gut. The bay was choked with black ships.

I shoved away from the veranda, stalked across the patio to where Olivia waited with the girls inside the arched doorway. "Come on," I said. "We have to get to the Wall."

Behind, the veranda exploded into flame.

Ducking, Pallin trembling in my grip, we raced through the house. Olivia screamed at the servants as we ran, ordered them to get to the Wall. We spilled out onto the street, smoke blowing across the stone paving, people shrieking on all sides, a few stumbling with blood drenching their faces, others staggering, arms burned. A body lay in the gutter, facedown. The house two buildings down was a blazing inferno, flames leaping high into the air.

"Go!" I yelled through the roar when Olivia hesitated. "Go now! Head down—"

A fireball exploded in the street not ten paces away, the sound deafening, heat searing outward, a concussive wave that sucked my breath away, that knocked all of us flat, Olivia's form slamming into my stomach and chest, her arms still around Jaer. Pallin was wrenched out of my grasp and pain scorched its way up my arm. I heard a muffled scream, smelled the sickening stench of roasted flesh, felt the hair on my arms singe, my face turn waxy with heat, blister—

And then I crashed into the stone of the street, the rounded cobbles gouging into my back. A form landed on top of me, crushed the breath from my lungs, but I lay stunned, unable to breathe, unable to think. I stared up into a blue sky interrupted by trails of heavy, dense smoke, the world reduced to a muted roar, to the scent of burned cloth and hair.

My breath returned with a startled gasp, my throat tearing as I sucked in air, then coughed. I fought the urge to vomit, tasted the bile at the back of my throat but swallowed convulsively, then tried to shift.

The weight holding me down didn't move.

I glanced down, saw the blackened flesh of an arm clutched tight to a smaller body.

I screamed, lurched up onto my elbows, kicked out sharply, and then I saw the glint of gold on the child's arm.

The bracelet. The bracelet I'd given her for her fourth birthday.

My heart stopped, caught in my chest for a breath, for an eternity—

And when it resumed, it brought with it a devastating calm.

I sat upright, clutched the two bodies close, ignoring the crackle of charred skin, ignoring the pain from my own damaged arm, saw the third body crumpled on the cobbles beside me, twisted in upon itself. I held Olivia and Jaer close, tears coursing down my face as panicked citizens of Venitte swept past, screaming, as fire scorched the sky above, exploding on all sides.

Then, still unnaturally calm, I stood, carried the two bodies—so light, so fragile—back into the house, returning a moment later to retrieve Pallin's body. Calm, careful, my motions slow and methodical. I laid them in the cool shade of the inner sanctum, where the household fountain gurgled playfully, cooling the air. I arranged their arms across their chests as best I could, stroked the distorted metal of Jaer's bracelet, still weeping, the tears coming in a flood, burning in the heat blisters on my face, then I drifted back out to the veranda, where the fireball that had struck as we fled had left a scorch mark on the stone, had eaten away a chunk of the balustrade itself.

I stood at the edge of the cliff and watched the ships burn their way down the bay, listened to the shriek of voices on all sides, listened to the spitting hiss of fire.

I watched the city of Venitte go up in flames.

I sat on the ground and let the rhythmic sound of the waves wash over me, breathed in the heady scent of the beach and let it clear my lungs of char and smoke and death.

Those are the Chorl, Cerrin said, and I suddenly understood the melancholy that always surrounded him, understood the self-pity, the self-hatred that sometimes flared up as anger, the vacant desolation of his voice.

And that was only the first assault, Liviann said, her own voice full of righteous anger, *the first of the devastation. After the attack on Venitte, which we managed to halt at Deranian's Wall and then repulse after two months of siege, they began marauding the coast, attacking ports, villages, setting up camps in inlets and coves. And their Adepts—*

No, Garus barked. *They were not Adepts. They could not control all branches of magic.*

But they were *powerful,* Atreus intervened. *And there were many of them.*

So many it seemed we would never prevail. This from Silicia, a slight woman who usually remained quiet in the background. I remembered her death when the thrones were created, remembered the blood trailing from her mouth after she'd collapsed.

That is why we created the thrones, Cerrin said. *We managed to drive them away, mainly by focusing on their . . . on their Servants. We targeted them, because that was their edge in battle. We Seven could not protect the armies against so many, and so we began hunting them, assassinating the Chorl Servants in their own camps, killing them in their sleep, focusing on them in battle.*

Exterminating them, Garus said.

Silicia shuddered, her essence twisting with distaste. Atreus grew grim.

And it worked, Liviann said, her voice matter-of-fact. *When their Servants dwindled, when we began to turn back their armies with ease, both on land and sea, they withdrew, back to the ocean, back to its depths.*

But the coast was decimated. Cerrin shifted forward, his voice intent. *Amenkor, Venitte, all of the major cities had been hurt or destroyed. We might have pursued them, wiped them out completely if possible, but winter approached. Most of the cities retreated behind their walls, concentrated on survival.*

We sent out ships in the spring, Seth said, *tried to find the lands they originated from, but we found nothing.*

And we knew that there were no Adepts being born, that there was no one to replace us. Atreus again.

And so we created the thrones. Back to Cerrin. *To help those that did survive after us, those that had some of the Talent, if not all.*

We didn't realize the thrones would destroy us, Alleryn said, her mouth pressed into a thin line. *We underestimated the power that would be required in their creation.*

You have to warn Amenkor, Varis. You have to prepare. Determination had entered Cerrin's voice. *And we can help you. All of the voices of the throne can help you. We have them under control now.*

Let me think, I said, felt the majority of the Seven straining forward, ready to argue more. But Cerrin gave them all a stern look, ushered them back.

I sat on the beach, in the cove, and watched the sun descend toward the ocean. I thought of Erick, of Laurren, of Mathew and the entire crew of *The Maiden*. I thought of Cerrin's memory, of Olivia and Jaer and Pallin, of him clutching their charred bodies to his chest. I thought of Venitte, reduced to burning buildings, columns of black smoke billowing into the blue sky, and thought of the vision of Amenkor itself burning, fire orange and pulsing in the night.

And when the sun began to set, when the first stars began to appear on the horizon behind me, above the trees, I stirred.

I rose up above the seclusion of the cove and looked for the White Fire. It blazed to the south. Without rushing, I Reached for it, felt the world blur beneath me, felt it grow more dense as I entered the influence of the throne, felt the life of the city fall over me like a mantle as I settled into myself in the throne room. As I settled, I felt people in the throne room, most removed toward the far end near the doors, but two others stood closer: Eryn, pacing in front of the throne, and Marielle, seated on the steps of the dais.

I gasped in a deep breath of air, the sensation sharp and painful, as if my body had grown accustomed to not breathing, then choked on the air and bent over in a fit of coughing.

"Thank the heavens!" Eryn murmured. And then, in a louder voice, "She's back! Keven, send someone for Avrell. And get that healer back in here!"

The coughing fit ended.

I stood, stepped away from the throne, stumbled as tremors coursed through my body, worse than at any other time before, my legs so weak I could barely stand. I was suddenly surrounded—Eryn, Marielle, Keven—all talking at once, demanding explanations, demanding to know if I was all right, voices tinged with worry. Someone grabbed my arm, held me upright, helped me step down from the dais. Someone else tried to present me with a cup of tea, the scent of earth and leaves sharp, biting through the smell of the stone and tallow of the throne room, the bitter scent of fear beneath the stone, and suddenly it was all too much.

"Stop," I said, too weakly to be heard. I tried to shove the helping hands away, but when no one retreated, when someone pressed a damp cloth against my forehead, fury flared sharp and fast.

"Just stop!" I shouted, my voice cracking through the throne room, bringing everyone up short.

Into the new silence, Avrell and a man I didn't recognize hurried into the hall. Avrell, eyes wide, face as open and readable as I'd ever seen it, came to an abrupt halt as he saw me, the other man halting beside him. He stared at me, met my eyes, his own full of fear and worry, and then he bowed his head, murmured something I couldn't hear, a prayer of some sort, and then he signed himself with the Skewed Throne across his chest.

When he glanced back up, there were tears in his eyes. "Mistress," he began, but halted. He struggled to continue, but couldn't.

Instead, he straightened, cleared his throat uncomfortably, then motioned the man beside him toward me.

"This man is a healer," he said. Thin, with gray hair and kind eyes, the healer hurried forward.

"I'm fine," I said, the tremors still shuddering through my arms, through my legs. I realized Keven was the one keeping me upright, and I leaned into his solid weight.

The healer took my hand and placed two fingers on the inside of my wrist as he began to scan my face, his lips moving, as if he were counting beneath his breath.

"I said, I'm fine." I glared at him as I tried to pull my hand out of his, but I was too weak. He returned the glare and refused to let go, his count never faltering.

Avrell had moved forward and now stood directly behind him. In a calm but warning tone, he said, "Let him check you." He glanced toward the waiting guardsmen, who stood hovering at the edges of the throne room, toward Marielle, who stood to one side in obvious distress. Eryn and Keven were also concerned, although they hid it better.

I tensed, ready to argue, but then relented.

The healer felt my muscles relax and nodded. Satisfied with whatever he'd found with my wrist, he laid a hand on my forehead briefly, then began probing beneath my neck.

As I waited, I felt something on my upper lip. With my free hand, I reached up and rubbed it, my fingers coming away with flakes of dried blood.

I shot a questioning glance at Avrell, but it was Eryn who answered.

"That happened late last night, about an hour after you sat down on the throne." Her voice was grim. "That's when we first sent for the healer. But he couldn't help you, not while you were sitting on the throne. We couldn't let anyone get close, and we didn't dare take you off the throne. We didn't know what it would do to you."

I nodded.

The healer finished with my neck, then stepped back. "I don't see anything wrong with her aside from the obvious trembling and the bloody nose. And the nose stopped bleeding hours ago. Some rest should handle the trembling."

Everyone heaved a sigh of relief, the tense guardsmen in the background relaxing, Marielle signing herself with one hand.

"Satisfied?" I asked curtly.

Avrell frowned, assumed a more formal pose, then nodded. "Yes."

I grunted, straightened, feeling more steady on my feet, and pushed past him, moving toward the doors, Keven remaining at my side. I felt everyone hesitate behind me, the other guardsmen in the room coming to attention and forming up near the door. Eryn, Marielle, Avrell, and the healer remained in the throne room.

"Where are you going?" Avrell asked.

"To my chambers," I said, voice still harsh. "I need to rest."

"What about Erick and the ship?" Eryn called after.

I halted, felt a stab of pain deep inside, felt my anger flinch.

But then I hardened and continued toward the doors. "He's dead," I said. "They're all dead."

They left me alone for two days, under the careful watch of Keven and his guardsmen. I stayed in my chambers for the most part, pacing my bedroom, or staring out at the city from the balcony. I watched the progress in the warehouse district while sipping tea and nibbling food brought by Marielle, although I wasn't hungry. She'd enter, set the trays down on the various tables, her eyes lowered, her head bowed. But I could see her biting her lower lip with worry, could feel her wanting to reach out to talk to me, to comfort me, but not daring. Then she'd pick up the tray containing the used dishes and leftover food I couldn't eat from the meal she'd left before and leave, Keven closing the door behind her.

I had Keven escort me to the rooftop twice, where I stood at the stone half wall at the edge and stared out at the sea or frowned down at the entrance to the harbor. Keven stood a short distance away, ready to leap forward and grab me if I showed any inclination to jump. I could feel the tension radiating from him, could taste his worry and smell him berating himself for not knowing what to do or say to make me feel better, all mixed in with his own grief.

They all thought I was grieving. For those lost on the ship. For Laurren. For Erick. But I'd already done my grieving, on the river and in that cove. On the Dredge, there was no time for grief. Not if you wanted to survive. The palace was no different. But the seclusion it allowed me was necessary. I needed to think. And learn—about the Chorl, about the Ochean. And I needed to plan. With the help of all of the voices of the throne, but in particular, the Seven—Cerrin, Liviann, Atreus, Alleryn, Silicia, Seth, and Garus.

They *had* been waiting . . . for me to be ready to hear them, to *listen* to them.

When Avrell and Eryn finally did send someone to speak to me, it wasn't who I expected.

*   *   *

Keven knocked on the door, then looked in. "There's someone here to see you, Mistress."

I glanced up from the slate I held with a frown. If it had been Marielle, he would have simply let her in. I sighed and set the slate aside. "Send them in."

Keven hesitated. "Are you certain?"

"Yes."

He withdrew and a moment later William stepped through the door.

I rose with a start, thought immediately of the sketch I'd seen of myself on his desk, and felt myself blush. "William," I blurted, then caught myself. The blush grew hotter.

He halted inside the door, scanned the room with nervous curiosity as if he had wandered somewhere he didn't feel he should be, but then his gaze fell on me. He smiled awkwardly, still nervous—but not about being in the Mistress' chambers anymore—and asked, "Do you want me to leave?"

"No. I was expecting . . . someone else."

He nodded. "They almost sent Borund, but then Marielle convinced them to send me instead."

Marielle. My eyes narrowed as I remembered her comments at the warehouse.

The silence grew. My gaze flicked around the room and fell on the slate on the settee.

The blush faded. William wasn't here to see me. Not really. He'd been sent because Avrell and Eryn and the others wanted to know what had happened. They needed to know.

Because I couldn't do everything necessary myself.

I sighed. "They want me to come out and speak to them, don't they?"

I caught William's grimace. "Yes."

I nodded. He'd wanted this to be something more than just a summons from the First and the former Mistress. He'd wanted it to be about us. I could see it in his face. But something always seemed to come between us: the assassin after Borund, the ambush when William had been stabbed, my intent to kill Alendor. And now the threat of the Chorl and the Ochean.

I moved a few steps toward him, felt him tense, and stopped. I wasn't certain what I should do, and so I fell back on what I did know. "Tell them to get everyone together in the throne room in an hour. All of the merchants and their apprentices, the captains of the guard, and whoever else with the guard they feel should be brought along, plus Avrell, Eryn, Nathem, and the Servants."

William nodded solemnly, then turned to leave.

"And William."

He paused at the door.

"I'm glad you came."

His shoulders relaxed a little as he left.

I entered the throne room from one of the two side entrances near the dais and the throne itself, Keven and two other guardsmen entering a few steps ahead of me, the rest of my escort coming in behind. Conversation filled the room with a dull roar, the aisle before the throne and the spaces between the four massive columns on either side packed with guards in various forms of armor, Servants in white robes, Avrell and Nathem in dark blue, and a few multicolored, gold-embroidered merchant jackets and the plainly dressed apprentices. As soon as Keven appeared, his men fanning out along the dais of the throne, the conversation stilled, the room falling mostly silent. Only the faint sounds of rustling cloth and scuffing feet remained as people shifted nervously.

I mounted the three steps of the dais without looking out into the faces of those gathered, my palms sweaty, and not from the heat of all of the candles that had been lit or the bodies in the room. I'd worn my whitest shirt, my cleanest pair of breeches, and my newest pair of soft leather shoes. My dagger was tucked into my belt at my waist and I'd allowed Marielle to cut and comb my shoulder-length hair. I could feel everyone's eyes upon me, could sense their expectation, their curiosity, their fear. I'd never called them all into the throne room like this, never spoken to many of them directly at all. They didn't know what to expect.

I hesitated a moment before the throne, stared down at it as it shifted from one shape into the next: narrow and thin, rectangular then round; a simple slab of stone, then a gaudy ornamented chair. The first time I'd seen it, the motion— the very feel of it, prowling around the room like a wild cat—had made me nauseous and sent shudders down my back. But not anymore.

I reached out and touched it, felt it recognize me, felt the stone tremble beneath my fingers . . . and then the throne twisted one last time and settled into the shape I knew so well now: a simple curved seat with no back, the armrests curled under.

I turned and sat, and the entire room seemed to sigh.

I stared down at those assembled, noted Avrell, Eryn, Baill, Catrell, Westen, Borund, and Regin at the forefront, near the base of the dais. Darryn was with them, shifting uncomfortably. I wondered who'd thought to summon him, then saw Westen's casual nod. I caught each of their gazes, then scanned the rest of the men and women in the room, felt them fidget with nervousness, some glancing at their neighbors, others craning their necks to get a better view of me and the throne. The room was tense, as if everyone had held their breath.

I glanced down toward Avrell and Eryn and announced, "We have a new enemy. A people called the Chorl."

A moment of confused silence, people drawing back, brows creasing in confusion—

But not everyone. I saw Avrell cast a horrified glance toward Eryn, saw her own shocked look before she controlled herself, her eyes devoid of any emotion. Avrell took his cue from her, but I saw him shudder.

Everyone else began speaking at once.

I let them talk, knew that it would not last long. Aside from Avrell and Eryn, no one here knew anything about the Chorl, about who they were or where they came from, except perhaps a few of the ship captains, who might recognize the Chorl as the sea-demons from the tales they were raised on as children. But the tales did not mention the Chorl by name. It had been too long, the tales too distorted. The sea-demons had been reduced to creatures of the deep, not a race of blue-skinned men and women who bled as we did, who fought with swords and ships and magic.

The sense of confusion that permeated the room escalated as the crowd quieted, and then Avrell stepped forward, in the space just before the throne.

"And who are the Chorl?" he asked. Only I heard the tremor in his voice.

I stared down at him, saw that he'd asked the question purposefully, even though he already knew the answer, and smiled. It was not a nice smile. It was twisted with the pain of Erick's and Laurren's deaths and the lives of all of the rest of the crew of *The Maiden*. It caused Avrell to take an uncertain step backward.

"Let me show you," I said.

I reached out on the river, threw a net wide, so that it encompassed everyone in the room. A different net than the one that Eryn had shown me to keep the voices of the throne in check. This one I'd learned from Cerrin while secluded in my chambers. Even as I set it into place, I felt Cerrin's nod of approval. It bound everyone in the room to me temporarily and as it did so, I felt all of the Servants in the room gasp, heard Eryn suck in a sharp breath at the base of the throne. No one else felt anything, turned in consternation to frown at the Servants, some taking a tentative step away.

Before anyone could react further, I sank myself down into memory, placed myself back on the ship, inside of Erick . . . and then I pushed the memory out along the strands of the net and forced everyone to relive Erick's last moments on the ship.

Blood flew up into their faces and the entire room gasped, some hissing in shock, lurching back, hands raised. A few guardsmen started to draw their swords, but halted as Erick thrust aside the dead body of the guardsman, as he raised his sword to block the descending sword. The blade jarred into Erick's upraised sword, pain shivering down into his shoulder, and the room gasped again, but the initial shock and babble of voices subsided.

Then Erick spun, and those in the room got their first sight of the Chorl.

Someone screamed. A few others fainted dead away, their bodies hitting the floor with slithering thuds since no one moved to catch them, all still caught in the grip of the memory. Guardsmen cursed, merchants and Servants cringed, and somewhere in the back of the room someone was violently sick.

"Enough!" someone shouted, the sound intervening on the memory. I frowned, recognized the panicked voice as Regin's, but I didn't relent. Concentrating harder, I focused the net, made the memory more real, more visceral, until everyone in the room could smell the blood, could taste the fear as Erick surged forward to save the crew, as he began the retreat to the prow.

And then I shifted the memory, slid into Laurren's head. I heightened her fear, her desperation, her determination to inflict as much damage as possible on the Chorl Servants and their ships with her spears as I held the shield. I sent my horror through the net as my grasp of the shield failed, intensified the sensation of being burned alive, fire drawn down into my lungs, scorching my body, as Laurren writhed in agony.

And then I pulled back, returned to Erick as he dodged into the melee surrounding Mathew and retreated, horrified, from the fire as it snaked across the decking, engulfing man after man like human torches. The reactions in the room intensified, someone screaming continuously, unable to stop, more sounds of retching as guardsmen and Chorl died, bellies slit open, throats cut, and still I pushed harder. I wanted them to feel the pain of the crew, to live their sacrifice. I wanted them to understand what knowledge of the Chorl had cost.

Erick's death would mean something. Laurren's death would mean something. Not like the murder of the white-dusty man, killed by Bloodmark for no reason other than to hurt me.

Another horrified, awed gasp from those caught in the net as the mast groaned and cracked and shattered into the deck, seeming to shudder through the stone of the throne room beneath their feet. Utter silence—nothing but in-drawn, held breaths—as the fighting halted, as the man threatened Erick and the Ochean shifted through the blue-skinned warriors.

She ordered the deaths of *The Maiden*'s crew, turned back when I lashed out with the river . . . and then she killed Erick.

I held nothing back. I let everyone in the room feel his torment, forced everyone to shudder with his pain as the screams of the rest of the crew sounded all around him as they were butchered by the Chorl.

But I cut the memory short a moment before the pressure inside Erick—before the pain—knocked me unconscious.

When I let the net release and the memory faded, there were ten people in the room who had fainted, another twenty who had bent over or collapsed to the floor, moaning or vomiting in a corner. Everyone looked pale, eyes wide with shock, limbs weak and trembling. Avrell was holding Eryn by the arm to support her, her face utterly exposed, and I suddenly realized with regret that I'd forced her to witness—no, worse, I'd forced her to *live*—Laurren's death.

Even Baill and the guardsmen were shaken. The purple bruise on Baill's bald head from the rock thrown in the Dredge stood out, livid, against his pale skin.

I waited a moment to let everyone catch their breath, to let the scent of blood and smoke and ocean clear from their senses.

Then I said, "Those are the Chorl."

"What . . ." Avrell began, but his voice cracked. He licked his lips and cleared his throat, his gaze wandering about the room as if uncertain where to look, where to focus. "What . . . do you intend to do?"

I leaned forward, caught his wandering gaze, held it. "I intend to fight them."

A stunned silence, interrupted by a bark of laughter.

Everyone turned their eyes on Baill. "You expect to fight them?" His voice seethed with disdain. "How?"

"All work on the warehouse district will cease. Everyone will shift to fortifying the encircling juts of land that surround the harbor and rebuilding the two guard towers at their ends. There was once a wall there. We'll rebuild it. That will be the first line of defense, because when they come, they will come from the sea."

Baill seemed shocked that I had a ready answer.

Catrell stepped forward. "How do you know this? How do you know they will come here, to Amenkor?"

Because the Ochean recognized the Fire inside of Erick, I thought. Because she recognized the power there. She didn't know what it was, but she'd seen it before, tasted it before.

And she wanted it for her own.

But that was not what those in the hall would believe.

"Because I've seen it," I said instead. "The Skewed Throne has shown me."

I didn't want to show them the vision of the city burning, of the harbor filled with blood, didn't want to show them the destruction. It would be too disheartening, too horrifying.

I didn't have to. Eryn stepped forward, faced the throne room. "I saw it as well, before Varis replaced me as Mistress. They *will* come here. But we can prepare for them. We *will* prepare for them."

Murmurs filled the room, laced with fear. One of the fears found a voice.

"What about those fires? How can we defend against those?"

I couldn't see who'd spoken, but it didn't matter. "The fires were produced by women like the Servants of the Throne, women who have power. Since I ascended the throne, Eryn and I have been training the Servants of the palace. They will defend the city from the Chorl Servants."

"The Servant on the ship didn't last long," someone grumbled, loudly enough to be heard by everyone. Others nodded.

Eryn flinched, her eyes going tight with grief.

I felt a surge of anger. "Laurren was overwhelmed by three of those women! She sacrificed everything to protect that crew! It won't be one against three when the Chorl arrive."

No one responded. No one questioned how I knew this. Which was good because I had no idea how many of the Chorl had the Sight.

Westen stepped forward. "You said the watchtowers at the entrance to the harbor were the *first* line of defense. What else do you have planned?"

All eyes turned to me and I settled back into the throne. The despair I'd seen on the faces of those gathered after I'd shown them *The Maiden*'s death had faded, had begun to slip from shock into wary hope. All I had to do now was convince them that they had a chance. I had to convince them when I had not convinced myself yet.

"Here's what I intend to do. . . ." I began.

And everyone in the room shifted forward to hear.

It took three hours to discuss and argue the rest of my plans with those gathered in the throne room, and by the end, most of their faces were tense but filled with determination and hope.

As they began to file out of the room, I stood up from the throne, stepped partway down the steps of the dais. Keven shifted forward to stand beside me, and at the bottom of the dais, Avrell, Eryn, and, surprisingly, Captain Catrell stepped forward. Baill gave Catrell a sharp frown, but after a moment turned to push his way through the crowd of people at the door, guardsmen falling in around him.

No one said anything until the majority of the Servants, guardsmen, and merchants had left. Then Avrell turned toward me, his face grim. "Do you think it will work?"

I shrugged, exhausted, drained by the arguing, by the tension that still gripped my shoulders. "It has to. It's all that we've got."

He nodded.

"You already knew about the Chorl. I saw it on your face." I let anger touch my voice, directed it at both Avrell and Eryn, unconcerned that Catrell and Keven would overhear. "Why didn't you tell me about them?"

Eryn answered. "Because they never crossed my mind as a possibility."

"They haven't been seen on the Frigean coast in almost fifteen hundred years," Avrell said. "They're . . . a history lesson, something I read about as part of my duties as the First of the Mistress, nothing more."

Keven frowned. "They aren't history anymore. How long do we have to prepare?"

"According to the throne, they won't attack until the summer. That gives us a little less than four months." Even as I said it, I felt a twinge of uneasiness in my gut. My hand drifted to the hilt of my dagger for reassurance.

Keven grunted with satisfaction, eyes widening. "That should be plenty of time."

Eryn's lips were pursed, her brow creased. She looked as uneasy as I felt. "We should still move quickly. The more training the regular citizens that will form the militias have, the better. The Servants will need more extensive training. They've made significant progress so far, but nothing like what they'll need to defend against the Chorl. And the walls and towers won't go up overnight. There will be unforeseen problems."

Her words didn't seem to lessen Keven's optimism.

Out of the corner of my eye, I could see Captain Catrell shifting his weight as he waited, unwilling to interrupt. But before I could turn to him, Avrell said, "Then we should all get busy. There's plenty for all of us to do."

"No," I said, my eyes narrowing. "There's one more thing that needs to be handled before we direct our energies to the walls and preparing the citizens and Servants." In answer to their perplexed looks, I added, "Yvan."

Avrell straightened abruptly. "There's something you need to know about Yvan and the raid on his manse."

I didn't like the sudden formal tone. "What?"

He grimaced. "Yvan was indeed hoarding food. Everything in the second cellar you found had not been reported to the guild or to you at your request. However . . ."

I felt a spike of irritation at Avrell's hesitation. "However what?"

"Yvan isn't the one who took the food from the warehouses."

Dead silence. No one moved, all eyes on Avrell.

"What do you mean?" I asked finally, my voice sharper than intended. Avrell flinched.

"I compared the food we found in Yvan's cellar with the report of what was missing . . . and it doesn't match. There's not enough food in his cellar to account for all that's missing . . . not even after making allowances for what Yvan may have already eaten. And there are stores in his cellar that we aren't missing at all." He took a deep breath. "I think Yvan hid stores that he already owned when you demanded an inventory at the end of the fall. I don't think he's stolen anything from the warehouses at all. It's someone else."

"But who?" When Avrell shook his head, I turned to Keven. "What did you find out by questioning the guardsmen?"

Keven shrugged. "We stopped checking around once we caught Yvan, but before that, we had a few tentative leads. Some guardsmen had seen a group of other guardsmen leading some wagons near the stockyards, on the edge of the city, as if they were escorting cargo. Except it was late at night. They thought it was odd, but nothing in the city has been normal in the last few months. A few others have gotten sudden changes in orders at the last minute, mainly a change in what warehouse they were assigned to guard. Other than that, we hadn't found out much."

I frowned, irritation turning to anger. "So who is it? Who's been stealing from the warehouses if it isn't Yvan?"

At that, Captain Catrell stepped forward with a stiff, nervous bow. "It's Captain Baill. I know. I've seen him."

I was still fuming over what Captain Catrell had revealed when I met my escort at the palace gates. My anger was like lightning, white-hot and snapping out from me on the river in sharp jagged lines, making everyone around me jittery. But, for the moment, I was holding the anger in check. There was nothing that could be done about Catrell's suspicions, not at the moment anyway.

But there *was* still Yvan to deal with.

I reached the last steps of the promenade and checked on the covey of guards Keven had assembled and the entourage of people that were lined up to follow us down to the main market square. Avrell was there, of course, along with Eryn and Nathem, the two administrators dressed in their finest dark blue robes, Eryn in a brilliant white dress. Behind them were Masters Borund and Regin, both in their merchant robes and both with appropriately somber faces. They were mounted, their horses dancing impatiently at the wait, tossing their heads. William and Regin's apprentice rode behind them, backs stiff, mouths pressed tight.

Behind them was another group of guardsmen, leading a team of horses at the head of a cart. But this wasn't a normal cart. This had been modified into a rough metal cage on wheels, the vertical bars only four feet high, so that the prisoner inside had to stand hunched over or sit with his legs drawn up to his chin or dangling through the bars outside the cart. Yvan was fat enough he was forced to sit, his legs dangling. He still wore his merchant's coat, but the material was filthy, the usually immaculate cream-colored material now stained a dull brown-gray, the black embroidery almost impossible to see. As soon as he saw me his face twisted with hatred, and he seized the bars of the cage, screaming obscenities across the courtyard.

I watched him for a moment, saw Borund wince as he began to yell, Regin's

face tightening as if in pain. Then I turned away and approached Keven, who
held my mount.

Yvan's yelling escalated, then dropped away into heated murmuring as the
guardsmen surrounded the cart.

"Is everything in the market ready?" I asked. A sense of nervous tension
had slid into the anger and I felt the palms of my hands go sweaty.

Keven nodded sharply. "Yes, Mistress. Everything is set."

"Then open the gates."

Keven motioned toward the gates. As they began to creak open, I mounted,
Keven doing likewise beside me, and everyone in the entourage came to attention, straightening their clothing or calming their own mounts. My horse—a
relatively calm dusk-colored mare—shifted beneath me and I felt my stomach
twist. Yvan fell silent, but I could feel the anger radiating outward from him on
the river, like a slowly pulsing sun.

It wasn't until Keven, the escort, and I rode through the gates that I noticed
the crowd.

I shot a questioning glance toward Keven.

"I told the guardsmen to spread the word," he said. He caught my confused
frown. "The people of Amenkor need to know that the wealthy get punished as
swiftly and as harshly as the poor. They've come to expect it from you after you
had that man Hant whipped on the construction site. They'll want to see justice
done with Yvan as well, especially after what he's done. His crime hurt them as
much as it did the power of the Skewed Throne."

I didn't respond, wasn't certain I really understood. As we emerged out into
the street, the crowd of townspeople shifted out of our way, a murmur rippling
from the front ranks to the back as they saw me. But unlike that first time I'd
appeared outside the palace, when I'd forced Avrell to accompany me to the
stablehouse where we'd discovered the Capthian wine hidden away, this murmur was one of excited awe, not frowning curiosity. Women leaned their heads
together, pointed, eyes alight. Men craned their necks to see, and children el-
bowed their way to the front. A number of those gathered signed themselves
across the chest with the Skewed Throne symbol.

I looked toward Keven again, who held himself proud, back straight and
rigid, his attention on what lay ahead. His men fanned out around us without
any evident order given and kept the townspeople at bay, even though they
weren't being unruly. I saw a smile touch the corner of Keven's mouth, a
flicker of movement, there and then gone, the deadly serious expression returning.

Straightening, I turned my attention back to the street ahead, noticed that
people lined the entire route, blocking the cross streets and alleys, some hanging out of the windows of the second floor.

The farther we moved, the louder the murmur grew.

Then Yvan and the cage emerged. The awed murmur turned to a hiss, anger welling up like an ocean wave on the river, rippling out as word spread down the street faster than we were moving.

Keven picked up on the sudden change, his stolid poise slipping as he frowned. "We'd better move a little faster. I'm not sure the guardsmen will be able to hold the people back if we don't pick up the pace."

I nodded, feeling the rage swell, and then Keven motioned sharply to the guardsmen on either side. Our horses began to walk faster.

We passed through the middle ward gates into the outer ward, the crowd content to hiss, shifting in agitation as the cage drew up alongside them. Once it had passed, the men, women, and children fell in behind the entourage, until we trailed a large contingent of townspeople behind us. And the more people that joined the entourage, the more agitated the crowd became.

We passed out into the lower city, through the gates of the inner ward, and the temper of the crowd changed. In the upper city, it had been composed of businessmen, lesser merchants, guildsmen, the wealthier citizens and their families, but once we reached the lower city. . . . Dockworkers and sailors and servants to the wealthy mixed with those from the Dredge who had come to the warehouse district to help with the construction. Hawkers and farmers shouted out cruel obscenities alongside gutterscum and whores. The noise grew to a roar as we descended down through the streets, past alley and narrow, courtyard and tavern, escalating as the crowd behind Yvan's cage tripled.

As we entered the edge of the marketplace and began to shove our way through the hundreds gathered there toward the pillory at the center, Keven kneed his horse forward and leaned in close. "This is uglier than I thought it would be!" he shouted over the cacophony as those already in the marketplace caught sight of the cage. "We'd better get done with this quickly and get out, before it gets out of hand!"

Not able to answer, the guardsmen pressed in close, the crowd shoving in from all sides, I nodded. Keven's hand latched onto my arm as we were crushed together, then pulled apart, our horses snorting and tossing their heads, until we burst into the center of the marketplace where the guardsmen had cleared a wide area around the pillory itself.

I gasped, drew in a few steadying breaths as Avrell, Eryn, Nathem, and the merchants cleared the crowd. The cart carrying Yvan was having more trouble, the crowd closing in tightly, threatening to overwhelm the guardsmen set to protect it.

Dismounting, all of us watched, stunned, as it inched forward, until it finally reached the edge of the cleared area.

Keven heaved a sigh of relief. As we turned, I saw Baill approaching, his gaze sweeping the mob as he drew to a halt. "Do this quick," he growled, then caught my gaze.

I tried not to flinch, felt myself tense instead, felt my fury escalate, supported by the roiling hatred of the crowd.

He hesitated, as if he saw something in my eyes, in my stance, then he spun and bellowed out an order to pull the cart up onto the raised platform of the pillory. I watched him as he retreated, snorted in contempt.

"We'll deal with him later," Keven murmured, his voice unnaturally calm. He turned toward me, and I saw in his dark eyes the same hatred and sense of betrayal I felt deep down inside myself. There was a promise there—a promise he'd made to Erick, a promise he meant to keep.

I nodded, and set my feelings aside, focused on Yvan. The guardsmen had managed to haul the cage up onto the pillory's platform, were ready to pull him out and clamp him into the pillory.

But there was one last thing that needed to be done . . . and it needed to be done by me.

I walked up the ramp leading to the platform, my attention entirely on Yvan, not even noticing that Keven and a select group of guardsmen had followed me until I'd reached the edge of the pillory and halted before Yvan. Only then did I become aware of something else as well.

The entire market had gone silent.

The silence sent an itching sensation across my shoulders and down my back, but I didn't let the prickling touch my face. Eyes as hard as I could make them, anger as blatant in my frown as possible, I stared at Yvan.

He smelled. Of sweat and piss and grime. The smell of terror. All of the hatred, all of the vituperative obscenities he'd flung at me, all of the haughty arrogance of the wealthy merchant elite, was gone. He stood in front of the pillory, held by guardsmen, eyes wide, shaking.

I sighed, saw a faint flare of hope wash over him, then I reached for the river, cast out another net, also passed on to me by Cerrin, that encompassed the entire market square.

"You are guilty of hoarding food," I said in a quiet voice, but because of the net everyone in the market heard it clearly. There was a rustle of reaction from the crowd, but it subsided. "Do you deny it?"

Yvan flared with defiance, the scent sharp and bitter, like dandelion milk, but then his shoulders sagged and he hung his head. "No, I don't deny it."

A grumble rolled around the square, the crowd shifting, uncertain, their anger blunted.

Yvan lifted his head slightly, enough so he could see me, so that he could judge my reaction.

It was a look of sly cunning, of buried deceit.

It reminded me of Bloodmark.

Anger flared, sharp and acidic and I turned toward the crowd, drew my dagger, and held my arms up to the sky. Yvan jerked back from the movement, startled.

"People of Amenkor," I said, raising my voice even though I still held the net in place. "Merchant Yvan has declared his guilt. As Mistress of the Skewed Throne, I pronounce the following sentence."

A hush fell, and I turned back to Yvan.

"Yvan will be stripped of all of his possessions except for the clothing he currently wears. All of his estates, all of his goods, belong to the Skewed Throne. His license from the merchants' guild is revoked. All of the rights and protections, given to him as a citizen of Amenkor, are removed." I took a careful step forward, my grip tightening and loosening on my dagger. Yvan tried to pull away, but the guardsmen held him tight. "He is no longer under the protection of the Skewed Throne. He is a traitor and will be branded as one."

I didn't give him a chance to react. Without hesitation, with a smoothness and quickness that Erick would have been proud of, I raised the dagger, placed the tip on the side of Yvan's forehead, one hand behind his neck to hold him steady, and with three quick slashes I carved the Skewed Throne into his forehead.

Yvan screamed and jerked back, a short, high-pitched bark of sound that cut off and sank into panting whimpers as the guardsmen caught him and shoved him forward again. The sly look of cunning was gone, cut away. Blood welled in the three slashes, began to slide down between his brows, past his nose, and into his mouth.

I let the net go, leaned forward into his stench, caught his wild eyes and held them. "You're gutterscum now."

Then I stepped away, motioned with one hand to the pillory. The guardsmen shoved Yvan forward, thrust him down to his knees and over the open block of wood. He struggled, cried out, and kicked, but there were too many guardsmen. Three held his head in place, two each for each arm, and then the top of the pillory was slammed down over his neck and wrists and the lock slid into place.

The guardsmen stepped away as I reached the end of the ramp. Keven and my escort formed up around me, leading our horses, the rest of the entourage—Avrell, Eryn, Nathem, and the merchants—hastily mounting and filing in behind them.

The mob surged forward, streaming around us and our mounts as if we were boulders in a river. The first stone was thrown before we'd made it halfway to the edge of the market square. A small stone, nothing more than a pebble.

Yvan screamed like a stuck pig. The mob burst into vicious laughter. Someone started a chant, others applauded, more stones sailed through the air, no longer just pebbles.

"He won't last the night," Keven said, his voice grim. "They won't be satisfied with small stones for long."

My eyes narrowed. "We have more important things to worry about."

"Like Baill?"

I shook my head. "We'll get Baill eventually. I meant the Chorl."

⊢— Chapter 11

The wind gusted sharply on the top of the tower overlooking Amenkor, catching in the loose folds of my shirt and tugging at my hair. The banners attached to the outside of the tower walls snapped and whuffled. The wind brought with it the scent of the ocean and a hint of warmer weather. Winter was ending, spring officially only a few days away.

My stomach growled and I pressed a hand against it to quiet it. I wasn't the only one hungry. In the last three weeks, since Yvan had been stoned to death on the pillory, rations had been cut back severely. Winter might be ending, but we still needed enough supplies to last us another month, until the first spring harvest. Farmers were already out on the surrounding land plowing fields and planting in hopes that the weather would hold and an early harvest would be possible. But it wouldn't come soon enough. There were already deaths reported in the Dredge.

I sighed, drew the power of the throne in tight around me, and Reached for the Dredge, slipping into the flows, drifting on them, then directing them until I stood on the broken cobbles near Cobbler's Fountain, where once I'd gone to meet Erick, to tell him I'd found a mark . . . or killed one.

The memory, the sight of the dry, dead fountain, brought a sharp pain, one that I thought would have been blunted by now. I suppressed it as best I could, stared up into the cracked and pitted face of the woman who stood at the center of the fountain, as I'd once seen Erick do. He'd been searching for something in her face then, didn't know that I'd followed him, that I was watching. I hadn't completely trusted him yet.

But seeing the doubt in his face, the mute appeal for something I couldn't understand back then, had felt wrong, had made my stomach queasy. It had been too personal.

It was the last time I'd followed him.

The stone statue of the woman—one arm holding an urn on her shoulder that had once poured water into the fountain, the other on her hip, only a stump at her shoulder and a few fingers remaining—revealed nothing, so I turned away. There was a flash of bright sunlight, a faint echo of a giggling child splashing in the pool of water at its base, but these faded quickly. That part of my life was over. I'd survived it and moved on.

I turned to the warren of alleys and narrows beyond the Dredge instead, moved down the old familiar paths, into buildings where people huddled or slept, their faces gaunt, haggard, but still alive. I saw families, saw children roving in gangs, saw a cat that had managed to survive instead of being eaten, its ribs sticking out through its matted, mud-caked fur.

I moved deeper, not bothering to creep from shadow to shadow as I once would have done. I wasn't really here, was only observing. So I stalked down the middle of the alleys, ducked and slid through impossibly small holes into niches and alcoves, into secluded rooms, using the throne and the river to seek out those that still survived.

Until I found a woman and child tucked away in a crumbling courtyard. The woman, hair thin, face pale and sweaty in the sunlight seeping down from the opening above, gasped in short, irregular, phlegmy breaths where she lay on a twisted, tattered blanket on the ground. The skin around her eyes was blackened with sickness, her eyes staring off into nothing.

The child, a girl of no more than six, dressed in a makeshift dress, played with a doll with no arms or legs in the dirt of the courtyard to one side.

The woman coughed, the sound horrible, tearing at her throat, and the girl looked up. "Mommy?"

She stood, motions careful and ponderous, doll clutched tightly in one arm, and moved to her mother's side. The woman had rolled onto her side, and the girl halted a few small steps from her and stared down.

"Mommy?"

With a supreme effort, she rolled her head to one side, eyes finding her daughter. She couldn't move her arms. She was too weak. It was obvious any food she'd had had gone to her daughter.

"Ana," she gasped, voice nothing more than a whisper.

Ana crouched down on her knees and elbows in the dirt, doll still tucked tight to her chest, and leaned in close so she could hear.

The woman's eyes closed and her panting breath halted. For a horrified moment, I thought she'd died. But then she gasped, eyes flying wide. She focused again, licked cracked, dry lips.

"Ana, go to the kitchen. Go . . . to the guardsmen."

Ana frowned, eyes squinched tight. "Can't leave you, Mommy."

The woman snorted, the sound defeated, lost.

She knew she was dying.

"Just . . . go. Bring them back."

The words exhausted her. Her head rolled back into place, and her eyes closed. Her breaths panted, her form shaking with each one. Her skin took on a waxy, feverish quality.

Ana hesitated, stood and watched her mother's trembling form a long moment, one hand petting the top of her doll's head where it was clutched to her chest.

Then she turned and walked to the edge of the courtyard, mouth set in a pouty, uncertain frown. She paused once, turned back, then dashed out into the narrow.

I could sense her terror as she ran, followed it with one part of my mind as I turned back to the woman, as I knelt down beside her.

Her breathing was coming faster now, and on the river I could sense her fever, could sense the sickness in her, like a splotch of darkness in the sunlight.

I reached out to touch it, but her breath caught. Her eyes flew open again, latched onto mine.

"Oh," she breathed. A light suffused her face, a smile touched her lips. "It's you."

And then she died.

My hand fell to my side.

I stayed with her a moment, then followed Ana until she made it to the kitchens, until Darryn had been summoned. He'd take care of her.

Then I returned to the palace, to the tower, knowing that people like the woman were dying all over the Dredge, succumbing to sicknesses they would normally survive if they had enough food, some dying of exposure, or starvation. Mostly the old and the young, but a few like this woman, who'd sacrificed everything to save her daughter.

And there was nothing more I could do.

My stomach growled again, but I ignored it.

I heard Eryn approach from behind. She halted beside me, stared out over the harbor, face to the wind. Her white dress and long black hair hissed and flapped in the breeze, but she didn't seem to mind.

"Any word from Captain Catrell?" she asked. It had become a daily question, something I asked Keven every morning upon waking, to the point where all I needed to do was send him a questioning look.

I shook my head, lips pressed grimly together, Keven's usual response. "And no word from the guardsmen Keven has set to keep a lookout either."

Eryn bit her lower lip. "Baill is laying low. He managed to keep Catrell busy and distant until your summons to the throne room to tell us about the threat from the Chorl. He must have known Catrell was suspicious of something. But he couldn't order him to disobey a direct summons."

I nodded, but said nothing. There was nothing to say. Catrell had told us he'd seen Baill with a group of guardsmen escorting a cart away from the warehouse on Lirion Street almost a month before. He'd approached Baill without thought, had chatted with him—

Then noticed later, as he looked at the roster, that there had been no scheduled transport of goods from Lirion Street. That, in fact, the guardsmen that had formed the escort were supposed to be watching various other warehouses.

After checking the assignments and speaking to a few of the other guardsmen on duty that day, he'd discovered that Baill had ordered replacements for those in his escort at each of the warehouses and had reassigned them to Lirion.

It was within Baill's rights as captain of the guard to rearrange the guardsmen as he saw fit, but it had felt . . . wrong to Catrell.

He'd almost revealed what he'd seen at the meeting I'd called about forming a garrison for the ship. But as far as he could tell, nothing was wrong. He hadn't heard of the missing food until later, after Yvan had been caught and he thought the problem resolved. And before that, Baill had kept him busy, out of touch with what was happening in the palace.

As Catrell spoke to me, Avrell, Eryn, and Keven listening in, he'd cursed himself for being a fool, for not realizing that Baill was distracting him, keeping him away. His guilt and regret had flooded the river, tinged with outrage at the betrayal.

But in the end, it was only a suspicion. Catrell hadn't seen where Baill had taken the wagon and its supplies, and Keven hadn't been able to learn anything from discreet inquiries with the guardsmen involved. No one knew anything; no one had seen anything.

If Baill was stealing the supplies, he'd chosen his cohorts well.

In my gut, I knew Baill was guilty. I could see the same betrayal in everyone else's eyes as well, knew that they wanted him caught and punished as much as I did.

"You should just arrest him," Eryn said, as if she'd read my thoughts. Her voice was low, her eyes hooded, staring out at the two watchtowers and the newly rebuilt walls. "You should confront him in the throne room, force him to touch the throne. It would kill him, but you'd know for certain he was guilty."

A shudder of horror passed through me at the thought of forcing Baill to touch the throne. A reaction more from the horror that passed through the voices in the throne than from myself.

Some of them had used the throne in such a way, as a last resort. But the death of the person who touched the throne . . .

I repressed another shudder, forced the thought away.

But then I thought of the woman dying in the slums, of her daughter, Ana, and felt anger spark.

"But what if he's not guilty?" I asked.

Eryn snorted. "He's guilty. You know it, and I know it. That's why the Dredge warehouse didn't have any missing food. Baill never had control of the guardsmen there; he couldn't get past Darryn and the militia."

"Knowing it and proving it are two different things." I shook my head. "No. We'll do what we originally planned: wait until he tries to steal more, then catch him in the act, force him to tell us where he's taking it so we can get it back. We just have to be patient."

"It's been three weeks. I'm running out of patience. What if he doesn't try again? What if he decides he's taken enough, now that he thinks we know?"

Now my expression darkened. "He'll try again."

Eryn wasn't convinced, but she didn't argue further. Instead, she took another step closer to the edge of the tower, motioned out toward the watchtowers and the walls. "Those went up faster than I expected," she said.

I moved up beside her. "Avrell said that the masons were surprised by how well the old wall had held up. The watchtowers, too. It was only a matter of repairing a few sections that had crumbled, shoring up the supports inside the towers and finishing off the one side that had collapsed. They've turned their attention to the defenses inside the city now and left the watchtowers to the guardsmen." I'd ventured out along the juts of land on the wall myself once, gone to visit those keeping an eye on the ocean in the watchtowers and to see the massive signal fires that would be lit if they caught sight of the Chorl. But the wall and the towers were close enough to the edge of the throne's influence that it made me uncomfortable. Not sick, like the sensation of knives shifting around in my stomach I'd gotten when escorting Eryn's envoy to Colby, but queasy enough that I hadn't gone back.

I shifted my attention from the watchtowers to the wharf and the lower city. I could see carpenters and other workers crawling over the trading ships in the harbor, altering them so that they had at least minimal defenses. The palace's sleek patrol ships that had sealed the harbor while Eryn was the Mistress were circling the water near the entrance to the harbor. And deeper within the city, in the streets that led up to the wall surrounding the outer ward, others were working on barricades and other defenses, some suggested by the guardsmen, most by the voices in the throne—Mistresses who had been forced to defend the city in the past, both successfully and unsuccessfully. Voices that were cooperating with each other for the first time in decades.

If the Chorl got past the watchtowers, the ships, and the lower city, they'd hit the three walls that surrounded the palace, separating it from the middle ward, the outer ward, and the lower city itself. And all along the way they'd be fighting the guard and the militia, the citizens currently training in the courtyard below and the marketplaces in the city, the Servants who were training in the palace gardens even now. I could sense them plying the currents of the river behind me, Marielle leading the lesson today.

Amenkor would not fall lightly.

Eryn pressed her lips tightly together. "Is it enough?" she asked.

I didn't answer.

She turned toward me, caught my gaze. "Have you tried to use the throne to scry, as I did when I was Mistress? Have you tried to see the future?"

I hesitated, not certain she'd want to hear. But she'd been the Mistress once before. She deserved to know.

"I've tried. Twice. Both times it was the same as before: the city on fire, ships in the harbor burning, the water filled with bodies and red with blood."

Eryn growled, slapped her palm down flat on the stone of the tower's edge in frustration. "It should have changed!" she spat out over the wall, into the wind. "It should be different!"

My eyes narrowed. The vision had changed: the warehouse district was no longer completely rebuilt. Because we'd abandoned it to work on the watchtowers and the other defenses. And now the watchtowers were destroyed first, rather than after the city had mostly fallen.

But I saw no reason to tell Eryn. It didn't change the outcome of the vision at all. In fact, it verified that the vision wasn't of some long distant future attack, but of something imminent.

I felt Eryn's frustration as well, crawling across my skin. But we were doing everything we could think of to prepare. All that was left was to wait.

I felt someone enter the spiral stairwell to the roof, felt his tension, his excitement, his panic. The guards at the top of the tower straightened as they heard the boy's pounding footsteps echoing up from below—

Then he burst out onto the tower. I'd already turned, already taken a step forward in anticipation.

"Mistress!" the boy shouted, then gasped and pounded his chest, trying to catch his breath. His eyes were wide, his face flushed red with exertion. "Mistress! Captain Catrell says he's done it."

I felt a surge of satisfaction as Eryn asked, "Who's done what?"

The boy glanced at her. Still breathing hard, he grinned. "Baill's rearranged the guard on the warehouses."

I crouched down at the edge of an alley and glanced out into the night-darkened, cobbled street in both directions, listening to the rustle of Keven and his guardsmen settling into place in the alley's depths behind me. Armor clanked, someone splashed in an unseen puddle, and someone else cursed.

Then everyone fell silent.

Keven crouched down beside me. "Anything?"

I shook my head. "The street's empty."

We'd chosen to ambush Baill in a circular market with a fountain at its center where three major streets intersected. One street provided a direct route from the Tempest Row warehouse to the fountain square. Captain Catrell had insisted on covering that route. He was to wait until Baill had passed him, then close off that escape route. The street Keven and I covered was Baill's most likely choice once he reached the fountain—it led south, past the stockyards and out of Amenkor, meeting up with the southern trade route. Captain Westen covered the third street away from the fountain. He'd been as enraged as Catrell at Baill's betrayal, but—unlike Catrell—he hadn't voiced it. His stance had shifted, had become deadly, a motion that reminded me painfully of Erick.

He'd offered to send the Seekers after Baill, as they'd been sent after the murderers and rapists on the Dredge, but I'd said no.

We needed the food Baill had stolen—all of it. We needed to take him alive, so he could be questioned, so we could get that food back.

A muscle in my leg began to cramp, and I winced and shifted uncomfortably, then grimaced. I'd been Mistress too long. I'd never have cramped this early in a watch when I'd been on the Dredge. Not even after being a bodyguard for Borund.

I began massaging the muscle, caught Keven's eye. "Now we wait," I said.

He nodded, signaled his guardsmen, then leaned back against the wall and stared up at the stars overhead. The moon was already out, everything cast in a faint gray light.

I sighed and settled in as well.

Old habits asserted themselves. I checked out the rough stone of the alley, noted the deeper darknesses of alcoves and doorways and windows. All possible escape paths. But unlike the Dredge, these darknesses weren't wide open and crumbling, with empty rooms and corridors beyond. This was east of the city, Amenkor's River only a few streets north. This stone wasn't falling into ruin and slicked with sludge and ground-in mud.

And the people here weren't starving. Not like those on the Dredge, like Ana's mother.

Yet.

I sighed, saw Keven glance toward me out of the corner of my eye, then I slid beneath the river, pushed myself deep enough so I could feel the city of Amenkor pulsing around me. For a moment, I held myself in the alley with Keven and the guardsmen, felt their boredom mixed with tension, then I turned my attention out into the street. I could see it clearly now; no darknesses, no escapes. To the left a rat paused, beady eyes looking in my direction as if he sensed I was watching, then he skittered away.

My stomach growled. On the Dredge, he would have been dinner. On the Dredge, his fellows had already been dinner, Darryn sending out rat patrols like hunting parties on a regular basis now, hoping to bring back fresh meat.

I turned to the right, leaned out from the alley far enough I could see the water of the fountain dancing in the moonlight, then focused and *pushed* at the river, the same way I'd pushed to see the vision of the city burning. But this was limited to a small area—the fountain—and a short period of time.

I grunted, then pulled back into the alley. At Keven's questioning look, I said, "Baill will be here in an hour."

Keven frowned, then motioned to a page boy, who sped off deeper into the alley with the news. He'd inform Catrell and Westen.

The men shared a few glances, then shrugged.

A little less than an hour later, everyone just beginning to get restless, Keven's page boy returned.

"Baill passed Catrell's position a few moments ago," he reported breathlessly.

Everyone in the alley tensed. I drew my dagger, felt its handle slip into a familiar grip, and edged closer to the alley's entrance.

To the right I heard low voices, too distant to make out, and the creak of a wagon. But I still couldn't see anything.

Then Baill appeared. He glanced down the street and I pulled back out of view slowly. All of my instincts were screaming, but I forced myself to wait, to allow Catrell and Westen time to move into position. The sounds of the wagons grew louder, the voices clearer, cutting off the splashing sounds of water from the fountain—

And then, at a barked command from Baill, the wagons halted.

I froze, muscles tensing, shot a quick frown at Keven.

He shrugged, motioned that we should head out into the street, reveal ourselves.

I shook my head. Something was wrong.

And then I heard the sound of horses, of shod feet clopping onto cobblestones.

Coming from the left.

With horror, I realized that someone was coming to meet Baill.

I shoved Keven toward the darkness at the other end of the alley, his massive bulk resisting a moment, until he heard the horses. With a sharp gesture, he ordered the men back, everyone scrambling to move, fast, without making a sound. Armor scraped against stone, and boots dragged across the cobbles. Someone splashed through the puddle again. I followed, Keven a step in front of me.

And then suddenly Keven motioned everyone down, halting as the sounds of the horses drew even with the alley's entrance.

I spun, my butt on my heels, my back pressed flat against the wall, dagger tight to my side as sweat dripped down my back and between my breasts, and watched as a group of horses passed in front of the alley.

Thirty horses in all, each mounted by a man dressed in armor like the guardsmen. But they weren't guardsmen. These were gutterscum. Bodyguards. Mercenaries.

My heart sank. They were here to guard the food Baill had stolen, here to take control of it, to smuggle it out of the city and transport it somewhere else.

Which meant we'd never get back the food he'd already taken.

Despair seized me, but then, in the few moments it took the thirty mercenaries to pass by the alley door, it transformed into hard cold fury. Fury solid as a stone, sitting in the center of my chest.

Someone touched my shoulder and I spun, recognized Keven a moment before I would have struck with the dagger. He didn't flinch, his eyes boring into mine. "This is going to be harder than we anticipated," he said.

I heard what he hadn't said, what he hadn't asked. But I wasn't going to let Baill escape now. Not after this, and not with any more of Amenkor's food. Not after witnessing Ana's mother's death. Not after seeing how everyone else was suffering on the Dredge.

Keven must have seen the answer in my eyes, for he straightened where he crouched, then motioned toward his men, the gestures short and sharp.

The alley grew suddenly grim as men shifted, loosened clasps on swords, checked their armor. I crept to the end of the alley, scanned the dark street in both directions again.

The mercenaries had just made it to the end of the street, were entering the fountain's circle. One of them broke away, horse trotting forward to meet Baill, who stood before a cart loaded with crates and surrounded by palace guardsmen.

I almost darted across the street to the opposite side, crouched low and moving swiftly, as I would have done on the Dredge, but I caught myself. Straightening, I let the anger slide through me, drew it around me like a cloak, felt the guardsmen behind me respond with their own anger, their formation tightening, stances solidifying.

I stepped out of the alley, Keven at my side, his sword drawn, the rest of the guardsmen close behind. We walked to the mouth of the street where it emptied out onto the circular plaza and halted, Keven's men shifting to block off any escape.

Someone in Baill's group saw us, barked out a warning.

The guardsmen and mercenaries reacted instantly. With a sharp cry, the guardsmen abandoned the cart and food, scattering toward the other two entrances to the plaza. The mercenaries cursed, kicked their horses into a milling confusion of rattling metal and frightened animals.

I lost sight of Baill. The guardsmen at my back tensed but held firm.

Baill's guardsmen had almost escaped to Tempest Row when Catrell's party appeared. Shouts of despair filled the circle and Baill's guardsmen turned, ran blindly toward the last remaining escape. But Westen appeared before they'd made it halfway across the plaza.

Baill's men ground to a halt, wavered at the edge of the fountain. The stench of fear flooded the river, mixed with the smell of horse and dung.

Silence descended, interrupted only by the snort of a horse, the stamp of a hoof. The mercenaries had formed up in a wall around Baill and the man who'd gone to meet him.

I took a step forward. "It's over, Baill!" I said, loud enough so that everyone in the plaza could hear.

I watched the crowd of horses.

No one emerged.

I felt my anger spike. "Come out! All of your escape routes have been cut off!"

Silence. No one moved. I glared at the mercenaries, their faces tight, eyes dangerous, their unshaven jaws clenched tight. A few had drawn their swords and they watched me balefully from their saddles.

Then, with no warning at all, the mercenaries charged.

I slid into a defensive crouch without thinking, heard the guardsmen behind me gasp, then surge forward and tighten up, Keven bellowing orders. The mercenaries roared, an unintelligible battle cry of pure sound, the pounding of hooves on cobbles descending upon us like the crash of an ocean's wave. I breathed in the scent of desperation, almost overwhelmed by horse sweat, and then the first mercenary reached me.

I lashed out with the river, a solid punch of force that slammed into the massive chest of the horse bearing down on me. The animal screamed, tossed its head, tried to lurch backward, and ended up rearing high, hooves kicking down at me as the mercenary attempted to regain control. I punched out again, shoved the river forward hard in a solid wall as the horse twisted sideways and began to fall.

I grunted as animal and rider crashed into the shield, the mercenary screaming as his leg was crushed between his horse and the shield he couldn't see. Heart thundering, I shunted man and horse aside, stepping to the left as they came shuddering to the ground beside me. The man screamed again as the horse rolled onto his chest, and then the scream cut abruptly into a gurgle and died.

The scent of blood flooded the river.

The horse flailed, eyes wild, kicked out sharply, head twisted back by the reins in the dead man's hands. Its hooves connected with another horse, the rest of the mercenary's charge grinding to a halt as they hit Keven's guardsmen hard. The line gave, the horses parting around their fallen brother, then held, the entrance to the street collapsing into a melee of mercenaries, guardsmen, and horseflesh.

Gripping my dagger in one fist, I dove deep into the river, settled into its flows—

And then I slid into the melee.

My dagger slicked across flesh, cut into legs and hands and arms, anything that became exposed. I growled as I fought, felt blood spatter against my face, but continued on. I plunged my dagger into a thigh, heard the mercenary shriek even as I reached up and jerked him from the saddle to be trampled underfoot. Swords flailed and I ducked, tasting the metal as it snicked by my head, then dodged as the horse on my left staggered, almost crushing me into the one on my right. I stepped on something soft, felt it roll beneath my foot, and lurched forward, grabbing onto a saddle for support. A mercenary glared down at me, eyes like flint, raised his sword for a thrust, but another blade punched hard into his armpit and back out again through his shoulder and he screamed, his arm half-severed from his shoulder. Blood poured down on me, blinding me for a moment and then the horse surged forward, out of my grip, the man's scream fading.

I wiped the blood from my eyes with the back of my arm and found myself surrounded by Keven's guardsmen in a protective circle. He stepped back from the edge of the fighting, the last mercenary threatening us falling, and said, "The attack is faltering."

He pointed to the far side of the fountain, where Westen and Catrell's men had seized the wagons of food. As we watched, the last of the mercenaries that had attacked Westen and Catrell's men broke off, galloping toward the open street Westen had abandoned in order to protect the food.

"Shit!" I swore, seeing the open street. "Where's Baill?"

"I never saw him," Keven said.

"Shit, shit, shit!" I shouted. I began checking the faces of the bodies that surrounded us, turning those facedown over. A few groaned, but I left those for Keven, searching frantically.

I wanted Baill. I *needed* Baill. I could feel Ana's mother's eyes burning into me, could hear the awe and hope in her voice as she whispered, "*Oh, it's you,*" before dying.

Keven and his guardsmen began searching as well, stumbling among the dead horses and pools of blood in a widening circle.

I'd almost reached the street where the attack had started when one of the guardsmen cried out.

I spun, was halfway to the man before anyone else reacted. "Is it Baill? Is he alive?"

The man shook his head. "He's alive, but it's not Baill."

He kicked the body over. I heard the mercenary moan, had begun to turn away in disgust, when something clicked.

The man was familiar.

I crouched down next to the man's side, his breaths coming in short little gasps, stared intently into his face, looking beneath the black blood, the long, lanky hair, the mercenary's clothing. I looked close . . . and then I sat back on my heels and scowled.

"Hello, Alendor," I said, my voice cold and deadly, twisted with sarcasm. "Welcome back to Amenkor."

Then I reached down, grabbed the neck of his shirt, and hauled him up-right.

He screamed.

Avrell and Eryn were waiting on the steps of the promenade with torches flapping in the breeze when Keven and I emerged from the gates of the inner wall, my escort dragging the bound, gagged, and fuming Alendor behind us. Captains Catrell and Westen came in last, their guardsmen hauling the remaining mercenaries that hadn't died in the attack off to the cells.

I wanted to deal with Alendor now.

"Baill escaped," I said as I approached Avrell and Eryn. Avrell's face fell, Eryn's grew grim.

"But how?" Avrell asked. "He should never have had a chance in that plaza—"

"He wasn't just stealing food and storing it elsewhere in the city," I said, cutting Avrell off, my voice tight. "He was smuggling it *out* of the city. The men sent to meet him to take the food were there—mercenaries on horseback. Once they attacked, it was chaos. He slipped away during the fighting."

They considered the implications of that in silence. Eryn nodded toward the man Keven and his guardsmen were holding. "Then who is that?"

"That," I said, drawing in a deep breath to steady myself, "is Alendor."

"What!" Avrell blurted, his shock evident, but he quickly regained control. "How did he get back into the city? Why is he here?"

"I don't know," I said, turning to move up the steps to the palace. "But it's obvious he was working with Baill. I want to know why, and to what purpose."

"But how are you going to find out?" Avrell asked as he and Eryn fell into step behind me, Keven, Alendor, and the rest of the escort following.

I didn't answer, shot a glance toward Eryn. She'd already guessed how, and I saw her give an imperceptible nod of agreement. Her lips were pressed tightly together, her eyes, her stance, deadly serious.

Because if Alendor was involved, then the missing food took on a much greater import than some of Amenkor's citizens starving. It meant there was much more going on, something much bigger. Alendor didn't work for trivial ends. When I'd been hired to kill him before, he'd been trying to take over all trade within Amenkor itself by forming a consortium of merchants, killing those merchants that refused to join or that were in the way. With Baill's help, he would have had control over the palace guardsmen as well. He could have controlled all of Amenkor.

The implications of Alendor and Baill working together . . .

I felt an empty pit open in my stomach, making my mouth dry. Because something else was going on here, something I couldn't quite see. Something that threatened the entire city of Amenkor.

And I needed to know what, needed to know *now*.

We entered the palace, Eryn sending servants hurrying ahead of us to light sconces and candles. It was the dead of night, but the palace came suddenly alive with activity.

"Where are we going?" Avrell asked.

"The throne room."

We passed down the long corridor leading to the doors to the inner sanctum, the phalanx of guardsmen stepping to the side as we moved through what once had been gates in an outer wall but were now at the heart of the palace. Then we were outside the double doors of the throne room.

A couple of guardsmen moved forward and pulled the doors outward, and I entered, walking down the long aisle between the massive columns, my eyes on the throne as it twisted and warped from shape to shape. I felt its presence sifting through the entire room, draped that power around me as I mounted the dais, the others—Avrell, Eryn, Keven, the guardsmen—arraying themselves around the room. But I did not sit. At the top of the dais, standing to the left of the throne, I halted, turned around and stared down at Alendor. Keven had forced him to his knees at the bottom of the dais. The guardsman looked as if he wanted to slit Alendor's throat now, his face hard and angry. But he only held the ex-merchant in place, hands on his shoulders.

I could sense terror in Alendor, but his eyes smoldered with hatred. Not the petty hatred of Yvan. This went deeper, had burned longer. I studied his face. I remembered seeing him in Charls' manse, plotting with the other merchants to kill Borund. He'd had a mustache, gray-streaked hair pulled back in a ponytail. His face had been shaven, the mustache trimmed neatly.

Now, he had a bristly, gray-shot beard, and his mustache was ragged beneath his long nose. His skin was tanned and dry with the exposure to the elements, and still flecked with dried spots of blood from the attack in the circle. His mercenary armor and tattered, bloodstained clothing clashed with the mental image I held of his always pristine mustard-colored merchant's coat.

But the eyes were the same. Cold. Sharp. Calculating. Even here, bound and gagged before the Skewed Throne.

"Remove the gag," I said.

Keven jerked the knot in the back free, Alendor wincing, and when it fell to the floor, Keven stepped back a pace, drawing his sword. Alendor coughed, then worked his mouth as if he'd tasted bitter ash and spat onto the throne room floor. He stayed on his knees, but drew himself upright, back straight and defiant, stance as poised as possible. His jaw clenched as he glowered at me.

I'd hoped that the presence of the Skewed Throne stalking on the dais like a caged animal would cow him as it had me when I'd first entered the throne room, before I'd become the Mistress. But as a merchant of Amenkor, he'd been to the throne room before. He knew what the Skewed Throne felt like.

"Avrell told me you'd left Amenkor, gone to the southern cities," I said. "Why have you come back?"

Alendor's glower intensified, but he said nothing.

"Where are you taking the food? Who are you giving it to?"

"I'll tell you nothing, bitch."

Keven growled, and, with a move so swift I barely saw it, he backhanded Alendor so hard the ex-merchant toppled to the floor with a cut-off cry followed by a stifled groan. Two guardsmen rushed forward and jerked him upright again, Keven circling around behind him as Alendor used his tongue to probe his split lip. Blood dripped from the cut, on his chin, but he only sneered.

For a moment, I felt a stab of pity.

But then I remembered him leading me into an ambush, remembered the gutterscum he'd hired as bodyguards as they kicked and punched and beat me into a bloody pulp in a back alley of the warehouse district. He'd meant for them to kill me, meant for his son to eliminate me because I was in the way, screwing up his plans for the consortium by protecting Borund, keeping him alive. The only reason I'd survived was because Erick had intervened, had distracted them long enough for me to regroup.

The thought of Erick sent a spike through my anger. I'd come out of that with more than just a bloody lip. So had Erick.

And I thought of Ana, of her mother, of all the other people I'd seen that morning as I wandered the slums. I saw their gaunt faces, their ribs standing out, their sallow skin. And as each face flickered before me, I felt my anger surge higher, felt it spill over into rage.

"Where are you taking the food?" I shouted, voice echoing in the chamber, throbbing with the power of the throne behind it. I saw a few of the guardsmen flinch, saw both Avrell and Eryn stiffen in surprise.

Alendor spat blood. Then he smiled, his eyes smug. "You'll have to do better than roughing me up with your pet guardsmen," he hissed.

Keven stepped forward, hand raised again, and for all his bluster Alendor flinched back, but I halted Keven with a raised hand.

"Very well," I said.

Then I reached out with the river, with the power of the throne, and as the Ochean had done with Erick, I seized Alendor about the throat with an invisible hand, squeezed it tight as I jerked him upright, lifted him completely off of the floor, and threw him down onto the dais steps before the throne.

As soon as I let the hand of force go, Alendor heaved in a sucking breath, his legs kicking out as he tried to roll himself onto his back. His breath came in shortened, ragged gasps of terror as he managed to get himself onto his side, but before he could begin to roll off the dais steps, I punched him hard in the gut with the river.

His eyes flew wide, grew round as he tried to breathe but couldn't, and then something broke, and he coughed and contorted into a protective curl around his stomach, blood splattering onto the steps from his cut lip. He sucked in another breath, the sound torturous, as if his throat had been torn, and he coughed again.

I moved down the few steps to where he lay in a fetal position.

"Where are you taking the food?" I repeated, my voice calm once again.

He gasped, shifted enough that he could look up at me, his body angled across the steps of the dais, the throne behind him. Blood and snot covered the lower half of his face, and a bruise was beginning to form on his temple where he'd struck stone after I threw him.

But his eyes still blazed with hatred. "Fuck you."

I took a single step forward, and he kicked out, forced himself up another step, then another, trying to get away from me. He shoved himself up onto the top of the dais, the Skewed Throne directly behind him, the stone sliding smoothly from shape to shape.

"Fuck you, Varis," he repeated, my name twisted into a curse. He gasped with pain, but was still defiant enough to attempt a grin. "I'm not going to tell you anything."

Silence settled over the throne room. Behind me, I could feel Avrell and Eryn tensing. They knew what was coming, had seen it before, had suffered through it in Eryn's case. But the guardsmen were only confused, most a little afraid, uncertain what was happening.

"No," I said, and I could hear the sadness in my voice, heard the voices inside the throne grow quiet. I reached out, grasped the front of his mercenary's clothes with the river, and lifted him upright. "You're going to tell me *every-thing.*"

A look of confusion crossed Alendor's face, and then I shoved him onto the throne.

For a moment, nothing happened. The throne solidified, its constant motion shuddering to a halt halfway between transformations. A look of awe crossed Alendor's face.

Then, both he and I gasped, the sound sharp, reverberating through the room. I felt something stab deep down inside my gut, the sensation cold and visceral and twisting inside me. Alendor sucked in a hissing breath, teeth clenched tight against the sensation—

And suddenly I was looking out over the throne room through Alendor's eyes, could feel the ties binding his hands cutting into his flesh, could taste the sick slickness of blood on his lips. The knife in my gut—in Alendor's gut—sank deeper, grew colder, and I hissed again at the pain, and a moment before I closed my eyes, the pain escalating sharply, I saw my own body collapse to the throne room floor, saw Avrell and Eryn step forward, both their faces grim.

And then the frigid pain in Alendor's gut exploded outward and he screamed, a bloodcurdling masculine shriek that rose and rose as the knifing cold stabbed into his chest, into his lungs, seared down his arms and legs and sliced through every vein and nerve in his body.

When it reached his head, jabbing through his eyes, everything went mind-numbingly, blindingly white.

And the screaming stopped.

We have him.

I shuddered as Cerrin's voice intruded on the whiteness, then felt the voices of the throne surrounding me, the same maelstrom I'd felt before, when Eryn had forced me onto the throne. Except this time the voices weren't screaming at me, battering at my defenses in an attempt to seize control, shrieking with the winds of a hurricane and trying to tear me apart. This time the maelstrom was the roar of a thousand voices talking among themselves in a crowded marketplace. A few madmen were still shrieking at the edge of the plaza, but the other voices had surrounded them, were keeping them in check.

Cerrin's presence, smelling of the sharp scent of pine, shifted forward in the crowd, followed by Liviann, Atreus, and the rest of the Seven.

"We have him," Cerrin repeated.

"Where?"

Cerrin drifted away and I followed. We worked our way through the crowded marketplace, Liviann and the rest of the Seven trailing behind us. As before, when I'd thought of the throne as a crowd on the Dredge, the women

interspersed with a few men jostled into me, reached out and touched me. But
this time they weren't trying to overwhelm me, to crush me. This time, the
touches were reverent, supportive, most giving me a small nod, a quick smile,
before stepping aside to let me pass.

Cerrin led me to the center of the marketplace. When we emerged from the
bustling crowd, I halted.

In the center of the marketplace sat a pillory, Alendor already on his knees
and locked into place. He struggled, spitting curses, his neck and wrists bloody
where he'd already scraped them raw. He ceased as soon as I stepped forward
to where he could see me.

"You fucking bitch," he gasped, his face red with rage. "What have you
done?"

"I forced you to touch the throne."

He heaved, eyes squeezing shut as he strained to break free of the pillory,
hands flapping in their restraints.

Finally he stopped, breath heaving. "Release me!"

I shook my head. "I can't. You're already dead. You've become part of the
throne."

He stared at me in horror, refusing to understand even though deep down
inside he knew it was true.

I reached forward, felt him flinch as I touched his forehead and closed my
eyes. "Now, tell me where you were taking the food."

He tried to resist, flailed as I concentrated, but it was futile. This is what the
throne had been created for: storage of knowledge, of memory, so that the
Mistress could access it, use it, learn from it. It had just done a little bit more
than that as well, storing personalities, . . . and storing souls.

I felt a rush of wind against my face, tilted my head up and drew in the deep
scent of the ocean and sand, and then opened my eyes.

Alendor rode on the back of a horse, the animal walking slowly down a rocky
road toward an abandoned village. It was dusk, the light beginning to fade. I
heard the rumbling roar of ocean waves against a rocky beach through the
trees, heard the creak of wagons and the dull thuds of horses behind him.

He turned. Behind, a group of mercenaries surrounded two wagons loaded
down with sacks and crates. Amenkor's mark stood out clearly on the nearest
crates.

The food Baill had stolen.

I felt a flare of anger, but then we entered the village.

The buildings were nothing more than shacks, the wood bleached white by
the sun, most ready to collapse at the slightest touch. A few broken crab traps

lay about, some caught in torn netting. There were no doors, no windows, only gaping openings no longer even covered by cloth. Outside a few of the hovels were small boats with jagged holes punched into the bottoms.

Alendor led the mercenaries and the wagons down to the edge of the village, where the dunes rose above the high tide marked by heaps of driftwood and tufts of saw grass. The wind blew sharper once Alendor reached the top of the dunes, catching hold of the horse's mane and tugging at his ponytail.

Without a word, the mercenaries began pitching a camp, a few trotting off to gather wood, others breaking out tents and organizing a campfire, still others setting up a watch. As they worked, Alendor shaded his eyes against the setting sun and stared out at the ocean. As soon as the smoke of the cook fire drifted across his senses, he dismounted, one of the mercenaries taking the reins of his horse and leading it away.

The men settled in. Someone returned with a brace of hares, which were quickly skinned and set to roasting on the fire. Three men started a game involving thrown dice and runes, curses and laughter punctuating the darkness. Alendor kept to himself, a mercenary presenting him with one of the charred, roasted hares. A sense of quiet expectation fell over the group as the night progressed.

Then, as the moon rose over the treetops, one of the sentries cried out and everyone around the campfire looked out across the dune toward the cove.

Torches bobbed above the water.

Alendor stood, straightened his mercenary outfit with a frown, then motioned to the men.

The mercenaries jumped up and began hauling the sacks and crates down to the edge of the water. Alendor followed, a few of the huskier, deadlier-looking men at his side.

He halted and watched the torches on the cove move closer. When three boats rowed into view from the darkness, he muttered to the two men at his side, "Be careful. Don't antagonize them like last time. Let me do the talking."

The men grunted and shifted uncomfortably.

The boats ground into the sand and figures jumped out, most moving toward the pile of crates and sacks to one side, the mercenaries backing off as the others began to load them. Three of the figures moved toward Alendor.

As they came into view, their torches guttering in the wind from the ocean, I gasped.

The Chorl.

The leader, face set in a permanent scowl, spat something to his two escorts, then stepped forward, glaring at Alendor and then the two mercenaries. He was short, dressed in the same silky cloth as those who had attacked Mathew's ship. A series of dark blue tattoos lined both cheeks from ear to jaw, and one of his ears—

The lower half of one of his ears had been sliced off.

It was the same man who had attacked Mathew's ship, the same man who had held Erick at sword point, who had ordered the crew's death.

"You brought shipment," the blue-skinned man spat, the words sharp and halting and unfamiliar in his mouth.

Alendor nodded. "And I expect to be paid."

The blue-skinned Chorl watched him with cold, black beady eyes. Then he shrugged, pulled a sack that had been tied to his belt, and tossed it onto the sand. It clinked, but Alendor did not move to pick it up.

"Another shipment in one month?" Alendor asked instead, never taking his eyes off of the leader of the Chorl.

"No!"

Alendor froze, a frisson of fear trembling through his arms. He knew their agreement was tenuous, that at any moment the Chorl could turn on him. He was only useful as long as he could provide them with food.

"Attack move," the man said haltingly, sneering. "Now first day spring."

The two Chorl behind him chuckled, and the blue-skinned man grinned, then burst out laughing before turning and sauntering back toward the boats, now loaded. His strangely curved sword ran silver in the moonlight at his side. When he reached the boats, he turned back and spat into the sand in contempt.

A shiver shuddered through Alendor, then he cursed as he reached for the sack on the sand, the boats slipping back out into the cove, vanishing in the darkness.

"What was that all about?" one of the mercenaries asked as they headed back to the campsite.

"Amenkor," Alendor growled. "They're going to attack Amenkor the first day of spring."

I gasped, lurched upward before realizing I was lying on the floor of the throne room. The cold gray stone of the vaulted ceiling arched above me, interrupted a moment later by Avrell's concerned face.

He knelt at my side. "Alendor is dead."

"I know."

He nodded, and along with Keven, helped me to stand. I staggered slightly, felt myself trembling, couldn't seem to make it stop.

"What did you find out?" Eryn asked. Behind her, I could see Alendor's body draped across the stone steps of the dais, face down.

The raw rage that enveloped me almost made me gasp. "That he and Baill have betrayed us."

"To who?"

I caught Eryn's eye, then Avrell's, and finally Keven's. "To the Chorl. They're going to attack Amenkor the first day of spring.

"In two days."

✝— Chapter 12

I stared at the ceiling of my chambers in the darkness. The faint sheen of moonlight illuminated the open doorway to the balcony, the curtains billowing inward from the breeze.

I breathed in deeply, smelled ocean and salt and smoke from the hundreds of sconces that had been kept lit on the palace walls the last two nights, since I'd learned that the Chorl intended to attack the first day of spring.

Today.

I let the breath out in a long, heavy sigh, then sat up and shifted to the edge of the bed.

I wouldn't be able to sleep. I doubted if many would.

I pulled on my breeches, a white shirt, my boots, and tucked my dagger into the belt, then drifted out onto the balcony and stared down at the city.

Amenkor. Torches lined the three walls surrounding the palace, as well as the lengths of wall on the juts of land leading out to the two watchtowers. Sentries occasionally passed in front of the flames, silhouetted briefly before passing on. In the city below, the streets should have been quiet for the most part, the only movements bakers getting ready for the morning rush a few hours off or guardsmen meandering the streets. Instead, there were groups of men at critical cross streets, their torches marking key defensive points throughout the city. The wharf was crowded with boats, carpenters even now working on the trading ships, frantically trying to install some additional defenses. Most of the palace's patrol ships were already out in the harbor, dark shadows sliding through the moonlit waters.

Drawing in a deep breath, I closed my eyes and slid beneath the river, focusing on the city below, concentrating until I could pick out the flickering white flames of the people I'd tagged with the White Fire over the last few days. Catrell and Westen had volunteered, as well as a few other guardsmen and Seekers, and they were now stationed at various locations throughout the city. Westen and his Seekers had been split between the city and the palace, their skills better suited to attacks from cover and in narrow, confined spaces. Ca-trell, now captain of the palace guardsmen in Baill's stead, as well as captain of the regular guard, had sent the majority of his men into the city. The palace guardsmen had been left on the palace walls and the watchtowers, a few more on the boats.

Baill had taken at least twenty guards with him when he vanished, cutting the palace guardsmen down to just over a hundred men. Catrell had had an-other hundred and fifty city guardsmen under his control before Baill left. With the thirty Seekers . . .

It wasn't much of an army. But with the militia we'd been training, with the citizens who had taken up arms and joined them, with Darryn and the deni-zens of the Dredge . . .

Divided among them all were the Servants, most able to provide some pro-tection from the powers of the Ochean and her own Servants. As much as could be learned in such a short period of time anyway. Most of them, includ-ing Marielle, had volunteered to be tagged by the White Fire as well.

I could see those flames now, scattered throughout the city like stars.

I opened my eyes, let the river go.

Just before it slid away completely, I felt a surge, a ripple of power—

And one of the watchtowers exploded.

A fireball roared into the sky at the edge of the harbor, wood and stone and bodies arching up and out as a concussive crack of sound split the night. I jerked back from the edge of the balcony, gasped as debris began to rain down into the water of the harbor, boats silhouetted against the conflagration, and then the flames died back down.

A sudden, shocked silence fell. I could hear myself gasping, could feel my blood thudding in my veins.

Then a bell began to ring from the second watchtower, answered by others inside the city as the alarm began to spread. Activity along the walls doubled as men raced to positions. In the city, more torches were lit, bonfires raised along the lengths of barricades in the streets. The wharf erupted with frenzied activity, lines untied, trading ships casting off into the harbor. The patrol boats streaked toward the bay's entrance.

The door to my chambers crashed inward and I spun, Keven streaming into the room with twelve other guardsmen, a look of panic crossing his face as he saw the empty bed. But then he caught sight of me on the balcony.

"Mistress," he said, stepping quickly to my side.

"It's started," I said.

Keven stared out at the fiery ruins of the watchtower, his hand on the pom-mel of his sword. His eyes widened at the destruction, then his attention turned toward me. "We have to get you to the throne room."

I'd slid back beneath the river, could feel his tension, his fear. But even as it registered on my senses, the fear was suppressed and the tension slipped into controlled channels, harnessed and used. This is what he'd been trained to do.

I felt the next surge of power a moment before the second watchtower exploded, a pulse that shivered across the harbor like a ripple on water, its source somewhere beyond the influence of the throne. Keven didn't flinch as the fireball that had been the tower rose into the sky, didn't even turn in that direction, his eyes never leaving my face, his jaw clenched.

I met his gaze, the urge to draw my dagger and rush down to the city below almost overwhelming. My hand already gripped the handle of my dagger, anger making me tremble. Anger at this attack, at what they'd done to *The Maiden* and the other trading ships.

Anger over what they'd done to Laurren and Erick.

But I'd be more effective here at the palace.

I blew my breath out in exasperation, then nodded. "The throne room."

The palace was strangely empty, the hallways echoing as we made our way down the corridor to the main entrance to the throne room. Most of the Servants were already out in the city, along with the guardsmen. But Avrell and Eryn were waiting for me. Neither looked like they'd gotten any sleep.

"What's happened?" Eryn asked immediately as the guardsmen opened the double doors and began lighting torches and candelabra. Avrell, Eryn, and I moved down the walkway to the dais.

"The watchtowers have fallen," I said. "They'll be entering the harbor soon."

She nodded grimly. "The patrol ships and trading ships should halt them for a while. Did you see how many of them there were?"

"I didn't see them at all." I stepped up the dais and sat down in the throne, felt it settling into its usual shape beneath me. An echo of the city's emotions flooded through me—terror, resistance, fear, anger; a seething turmoil—but I held it back, looked down at Avrell and Eryn. "I won't let them take Amenkor."

Both nodded, signed the Skewed Throne symbol over their chests, the gesture startling coming from them. It sent a shiver down my back.

"Remember," Eryn warned, "Reaching drains your strength, makes you weak. Don't overextend yourself trying to help those in the city. They can take care of themselves. Save your strength for later, in case you need it."

I frowned in irritation, saw the answering stiff-lipped admonition in Eryn's eyes, and grudgingly nodded.

Then they were moving, both marked with the White Fire now, both heading to the outer walls and the city below with looks of determination, Avrell to the middle wall, Eryn to the inner.

Keven took their place, gazed up at me expectantly. "Keep me informed of what's happening."

I inclined my head, drew in a deep breath, closed my eyes. . . .

And plunged myself into the river, the force of the throne behind me.

The rage of emotions that represented the city crashed into me like a wave, threatening to drag me under in the riptides. I struggled, cried out involuntarily, flailed against the currents of hatred and fear. I could feel the city's attention drawn toward the burning watchtowers, could feel the shuddering apprehension as they watched the entrance to the harbor in the darkness, all of the bells in the city ringing, the patrol ships and trading ships that had managed to cast off the only counter to the heightening anxiety. The men and women in the ships sped toward the entrance with grim determination, and I latched onto this emotion and stabilized myself in the torrent of the river.

Settling myself in the currents, I streaked out over the black water of the bay, the flames of the watchtowers getting closer. As I approached, I could feel the disruption the destruction of the towers had caused on the river, a disruption brought on by a tremendous release of power. Whirlpools had formed, one each at the centers of the watchtowers. I skirted around the first whirlpool's edge, felt its energy tugging at me, trying to draw me into its mouth.

One of the voices within the throne shifted forward, not Cerrin or Liviann, but Garus. He smelled of ale and roasted meat. *It took more than one person to do that much damage that quickly.*

They'll have to recoup, Seth broke in. *Regain their strength. We'll have a little time.*

A multitude of other voices agreed, but the tone of the agreement was grim.

What's wrong? I asked, and felt Cerrin shift forward to respond.

When the Chorl were pushed back from the coast the last time, they had not progressed to the point where they could combine their powers in such a way. This much focused energy means they're working together, augmenting each other, as we combined our powers to form the thrones. It seems the Chorl have learned a few things since they were here last.

Why didn't you warn me they could do this when they attacked The Maiden?

Because they didn't combine their strength then. They simply turned their separate attacks on one person.

Laurren.

My stomach clenched, and I thought about the Servants scattered about the city below, waiting to deal with the Chorl and their powers. If the Chorl Servants attacked them with their combined strength . . .

But there was nothing that could be done about that now, so I forced the sickening sensation aside and focused back down on the harbor, on the black waters.

I noticed a flare of White Fire on one of the ships close to the harbor entrance and dove for it.

I found myself staring out through the eyes of one of Catrell's high-ranking guardsmen, the patrol boat rocking on the waves beneath him, the motion sharper and more violent than what I'd experienced through Erick on *The Maiden*. Swallowing hard, suddenly feeling nauseous, I realized it was because the boat was smaller than the trading ship.

And then something skimmed out of the darkness beyond the burning watchtowers, its edges limned with reflected firelight. The bow and spit pierced the cloaking darkness like a dagger, the sleek ship gliding almost silently on the water, painted black so that it melded with the night—

Then it was past the juts of land, within the harbor itself, moving fast and deadly, streaking straight for the wharf and the docks at the mouth of Amenkor's River, just like the ships that had entered the harbor of Venitte in Cerrin's memory. And behind it came more ships, as sleek and silent, like lances from the night, twice the size of Amenkor's patrol boats, all painted black, no light visible on the decks, even the sails black, the rigging, the masts. They were like shards of night, splintered off and sent hurtling toward the city.

The guardsman I inhabited jerked out of his shock and pointed, bellowed, "Ready! The ships have entered the harbor! The ships have entered the harbor!"

Cries rang out on all sides and the patrol boat suddenly listed, turning sharply to the left, directly toward the smooth lines of the first ship. The lead guardsman I inhabited clutched the railing before him to keep balance, shifted his weight, cursing silently. Fear slid down his arms like cold water, but he tightened his grip as he watched the ships knife into the harbor. Four of them . . . no, seven . . . no, twelve at least! And even as the patrol boat came up alongside the first enemy ship, he saw two more spits pierce the darkness beyond the harbor's entrance into the firelight from the burning towers.

But he had no time to watch and count the enemy ships. His patrol boat had drawn abreast of the first ship. He barked orders. Grapnels were heaved up onto the enemy deck even as it sped past, the length of rope attached to each grapnel tied down to the front of the patrol boat. Rope hissed, trailing into the darkness, then snapped taut.

The patrol boat lurched, guardsmen on the deck grunting as they lost their footing and crashed to the deck, the smaller patrol boat swinging around and crashing into the side of the larger enemy ship as it sped on. The captain of the patrol boat screamed at his men to get up as they were dragged alongside the ship deeper into the harbor, cursing as men regained their feet slowly, grasping a few by the scruff of the neck and hauling them upright, shoving them toward the side of the Chorl ship. A rope ladder with grapnels on the end was flung up the side of the enemy ship grinding at their side and men began to climb.

I felt fraying rope scrape into my palms as the captain of the guardsman seized the rope ladder nearest to him and began the climb up to the deck. Halfway up the ladder, a scream rang out, and as he glanced down the length of the patrol boat, he caught his first sight of the Chorl.

He gasped and froze. Leaning over the railing above, three blue-skinned warriors with black hair glared down at the patrol boat, then caught sight of the ladders and the grapnels holding the two ships together. Abruptly, two of the faces vanished, returning a moment later.

There was a flash off the head of an ax, followed by a solid thump of metal digging into wood.

Adrenaline flooded the captain's numbing arms with heat, overtaking the sizzling terror of the strange and horrifying faces of the Chorl. "Climb!" he bellowed, his voice tearing at his throat. "Climb, you bloody bastards! Before they cut us free!"

He lurched farther up the ladder, grasping the next rung even before the feet of the man above him had cleared it, pulling himself up with all his strength. His breath hissed between his gritted teeth. A few paces away, men screamed as the ladder they were climbing suddenly went slack and they fell back, hitting the deck of the patrol boat with a thudding crash followed by moans, but the captain didn't turn, didn't hesitate.

The man above him kicked out, almost catching him in the face as he dove over the railing of the enemy ship. The captain reached up over the railing next, pushed off with his feet as he pulled with his arms—

And then he was up and over, rolling onto the deck of the enemy ship, his back thudding up against a yielding body, his hand landing in blood.

He gasped, saw the dead, vacant eyes of the man who'd been climbing the ladder above him—

And then he rolled away. A curved blade swished out of the darkness and bit into the deck where he'd been, then he was up and balanced, sword drawn with a hissing snick of metal.

The blue-skinned Chorl spat what could only be a curse, face twisted in a grimace as he jerked his blade free from the deck and turned to confront the captain. Beyond the Chorl, beyond the stunted mast of the sleek ship, I could see the watchtowers retreating. The patrol boats hadn't even slowed the ships down. They were still streaking toward the wharf, toward the docks and the city.

I spat my own curse.

Where were the trading ships?

Then the Chorl struck, the guardsman parrying on instinct, my attention drawn back to the fighting that was spreading quickly across the Chorl's deck. More and more guardsmen had breached the railing, had pushed the Chorl back so that others could join the fight from the patrol boat below. I watched the interplay, settled into the flow, ready to intercede if the captain needed it. I could feel the instincts Erick and Westen had trained into me screaming to be let free, but I held back. The captain was competent, and Eryn's warning still rang in my head. I'd exhaust myself faster if I seized control of the captain's body.

The Chorl overextended himself, and the captain took advantage, his blade snaking in, punching through the Chorl's silky clothing and armor at the mid-section. The blue-skinned man gasped, red blood spurting from his mouth, his hand gripping the sword slid into his belly.

The captain withdrew the blade and the Chorl fell to the side with a low, gurgling growl.

As he turned, I caught sight of movement at the aft of the ship. A woman, dressed in filmy clothing, the glint of gold at her ear.

I also caught sight of another Amenkor guardsman from the patrol boat, fending off two Chorl not three paces away.

To hells with Eryn and her warning.

I claimed the captain, took two paces forward and with coldly calculated movements used his sword to kill the Chorl the other guardsman faced. I felt the captain's surprise as he lost control of his own body, but shrugged it aside.

Captain! I said. *Kill the woman! She's one of the Chorl Servants!*

"What?" he gasped. The guardsman he'd just saved clutched at a wound along his side, bewildered. "What are you talking about?"

This is the Mistress! I shouted, letting anger bite through his confusion. *Kill the woman! She's vulnerable right now, but I don't know how long she'll stay that way!*

Then I spun, the captain's sword flicking out, slicing through the neck of the Chorl that had been coming up from behind, blood flying in a wide arc.

The guardsman stared in shock, eyes widening as I turned back, letting the captain take control of his own body again, retreating back into the White Fire. He shuddered as he regained control, but then stiffened with resolve, shaking his head.

"Kill the woman!" he growled, motioning toward the Chorl Servant with his bloody sword. "Pass the word that we're to focus on getting to the woman! We'll try to flank her on both sides!"

The guardsman I'd saved hesitated, then nodded and moved to the left. The captain watched him go, then turned, saw another group of guardsmen fighting heatedly to the right, and charged into the fray.

I surged up out of the captain's body, up above the ship, its sails, rigging, and mast rushing past beneath me as I scanned the battle in the harbor. There were twenty-five of the Chorl vessels, seven of them crawling with Amenkor guardsmen, patrol boats latched onto their sides like leeches. In their wake, four other patrol boats had been crushed, guardsmen flailing in the waters of the harbor among the debris. A few other patrol boats were cutting through the waves, picking up the survivors. There was nothing else they could do. There was no chance the patrol boats could catch up to the Chorl ships already past them.

The Chorl hadn't even been slowed.

Then, as I watched, one of the Chorl ships began to swerve, cutting sharply to the right, the men on deck toppling over as the ship tilted. Amenkor guardsmen were at the helm, steering the ship hard and fast toward a second Chorl ship, one not yet boarded. The Chorl on the deck of that ship began shouting, pointing at the spit of the other ship as it bore down on them. The ship began to veer away, the Chorl shrieking—

But it was too late.

The two ships collided with a reverberating crunch, wood splintering as the spit punched through the side of the second Chorl ship, chunks of wood planks flying. A shudder passed through the river, a shock wave of force that pushed me back, and everyone on both ships crashed to the deck and rolled, men from Amenkor as well as the Chorl tipping over the rails to the ocean below. The second ship listed, its sails falling limp as part of the mainmast snapped, rigging falling down onto the deck, into the water. The two ships slowed, began drifting off to the right, into the path of a third Chorl vessel, but it had time to swerve, the movements of the Chorl on its deck frantic, laced with sweat and terror. It cut left, its deck tilting harshly, skimmed past the aft section of the two stricken ships, then began to veer back onto course—

And suddenly Amenkor's trading ships slid into the fray.

Lines of flaming arrows pierced the night, cutting up and out from the decks of the trading ships, then turning and plummeting down onto the Chorl ships' decks and sails. As they struck, pouches of pitch tied to the arrows burst and caught fire.

Within moments, three of the Chorl ships' sails were aflame and fires were spreading across many of their decks. The trading ships and the Chorl attackers met, the harbor degenerating into a flurry of sails, rigging, ships, and screams. The Chorl ships were sleeker, faster, easier to maneuver than the trading ships, but the trading ships could sustain more damage, could take a more direct hit.

In the chaos, twelve of the Chorl ships broke free, two still fighting fires in the rigging or on the decks. They headed directly toward the wharf.

I spat a curse, felt the river roiling around me as the battle continued, then noticed three more of the White Fire beacons in the battle below.

I dove down quickly, stayed long enough with each person to seize control and pass the word about targeting the Chorl Servants.

Then I sped back to the palace, drew in a gasping breath and focused on the people in the throne room.

"What's happened?" Keven asked. He was surrounded by other guardsmen.

They'd encircled the dais, were standing ready with swords drawn, facing outward. A page boy waited at Keven's side, eyes expectant, as if Keven had just been about to issue him an order.

"They're almost to the wharf," I said. "Twelve ships made it past the patrols and trading ships. The rest are battling it out in the harbor."

Keven nodded. "Based on the reports I've heard from the men watching on the walls, that's only half their fleet."

"I know," I said, frowning. "I expected more ships, expected more of a fight."

"Maybe this is all they have," Keven said, but I could tell he didn't believe that, even without the throne, without the voices of all of the previous Mistresses murmuring warily. I could hear it in his voice. "We'd only seen four of their ships before this, after all."

I shook my head. "No. They're planning something else." I stared down at the throne room floor a long moment, thinking, then glanced back up. "Keep watch on the harbor. I'm going to check out the wharf."

Keven nodded, then turned back to the page boy as I closed my eyes and sped up and out of the palace.

As I swooped over the walls surrounding the palace, I saw guardsmen lining the battlements, packed in tight, arms pointing toward the fiery conflagration on the waters of the harbor. Situated on the top of a low hill, the walls like tiers, they could see the battle as it progressed, could see the mass of ships as they wove in and out among each other, flaming arrows arching up into the night in all directions, a few ships dead in the water, listing as they burned, their masts black skeletons in the reaching flames. And they could see the sleek Chorl ships that had escaped the patrol boats and the trading ships and were racing toward the docks, their shapes silhouetted by the fires of the battle behind.

I skimmed over the rooftops of the city, the streets below packed with people, men and boys fighting through the crowds of women and children heading toward the outermost wall of the palace, guardsmen hurrying the people along. Terror drifted up from the streets like smoke, the guardsmen at the gates funneling the people through as quickly as possible, shouting and bellowing orders. The crowds thinned as I passed down into the lower city, the streets now filled with men manning the barricades we'd spent the last few days erecting, others streaming toward the wharf, where the first Chorl ships would land.

As I neared the docks, the black Chorl ships rushing in fast, I spotted a flare of White Fire behind a hastily constructed barricade, recognized Borund in the torchlight a moment before I slid into the Fire at the core of his soul.

"Here they come," Borund said, and his voice was steady even though his hands shook. He held a short sword awkwardly in one hand, the other on the edge of the barricade of crab traps, netting, empty crates, and furniture that had been hastily thrown together. He glared out over the top of the barricade, down the length of a dock.

Out on the water, the twelve Chorl ships had separated, each angling for a different point on the wharf, spread out like a fan.

One of the ships was heading directly for Borund's position.

He glanced to either side. I felt a frisson of fear as I realized William stood to his right, his hair more tousled than usual, his eyes widened in fright. To either side, a mix of sailors, guardsmen, and tradesmen watched the approaching ships, crouched behind the barrier. Most had a look of disbelief on their faces, as if this couldn't possibly be happening, as if they expected any moment to be woken from the dream.

"Ready!" someone shouted, and Borund flinched, swallowed hard, and turned toward the man standing on top of the barricade. A captain of the guard I didn't know, his face tight with hatred, with confidence. "I said, ready!"

A shout went up all along the barricade, swords raised, or daggers, a few knives and spears, even a fishhook.

The captain turned toward the advancing ships, and in a deep voice that carried all along the barricade, bellowed, "Amenkor!" dragging out the last syllable into a battle cry.

All along the wharf, men raised their weapons to the night and took up the cry, a roar of pure defiance.

On the river, the frayed tension I'd felt earlier, the terror, settled into a sense of purpose as the broken battle cry formed into a chant.

Borund stared around at the men in fear, his hands shaking even more. He licked his lips, tightened his grip on the unfamiliar short sword. His palms were sweaty.

I frowned. I could hear his heart thudding in his chest, could feel the tremors running down his arms, could taste the sourness in his mouth.

Borund was close to panic.

"They haven't slowed," William said abruptly.

Borund jumped, startled, his head snapping around to William. "What?"

William nodded toward the ships. The fear had left his face, had faded from his eyes, a consequence of the chanting; it seemed to have bolstered him. "They haven't slowed," he repeated. Then he swore. "They don't intend to slow," he said, and pushed back from his position at the barricade, began shouting toward the captain still standing on the barricade. "Get down! Get down! They aren't going to slow down! They're going to ram the docks!"

The battle chant faltered.

And then the first Chorl ship slammed into the docks, its bow plowing through the planking, wood splintering, cracking with sharp retorts and flying up into the air. Tremors shuddered through the wharf, juddering up through

Borund's legs and shivering in his teeth as he clenched them tight, ducking his head as shrapnel from the docks was flung up over the barricades. More ships plowed into the docks to either side, wood shrieking, the battle cry lost in the rending of wood against wood, in screams as flying debris cut into flesh, as terror overcame resolve and a few men began to flee. Borund gasped as something cut into his shoulder, the wound like fire, and then he slammed flat onto the wharf behind the barricade, reached up and grabbed the back of William's shirt and hauled him down to safety. The sound escalated, the Chorl ship grinding its way closer, and Borund squeezed his eyes shut, gasped as the sound intensified, as it crashed around him until it seemed to fill the world, reverberating in his chest, in his heart. He suddenly realized the Chorl ship wasn't going to stop, that it was going to crush him as it plowed through the dock and hit the wharf—

And then the roar of splintered wood retreated, dying down into the distance as the other Chorl ships ground to a halt.

Silence settled, broken only by moans and the clatter of the last of the debris as it fell from the sky. People began to pick themselves up, brushing splinters of wood from their hair, their shoulders, coughing at the dust. Someone close panted loudly and whimpered, the sound wet and painful.

Borund let out an explosive breath, his heart still racing at triple the speed. His shoulder burned.

"Holy shit!" William swore. Blood leaked from a small gash above his left eye.

Wood slapped onto wood, a sound Borund recognized instantly. "They've lowered planks!" he hissed, his voice no longer steady. "They're disembarking!"

And they both jerked as someone down the length of the barricade screamed, a bloodcurdling scream that sent cold shivers into Borund's blood.

"Amenkor!" the captain bellowed again, and Borund saw him standing up twenty paces away, dragging men up off of the wharf as he began making his way down the barricade. "Get up, you bloody bastards! For Amenkor! For the Mistress!"

At his side, William suddenly stilled. Borund saw something kindle deep inside William's eyes, something deep that burned through the last of his fear.

"For the Mistress," William said softly, almost to himself.

Then he leaped up, his own sword brandished high, and he screamed, "For the Mistress! For the Skewed Throne!"

And he began a charge over the barricade. Men on all sides who'd wavered, who'd acted as if they were stunned and shocked, suddenly gripped their swords tighter, roared with hatred and released terror and tension, and tore over the barricade after him.

Borund heaved in a deep breath in surprise, held it, then lurched to his feet with a shouted, "William!" He reached the barricade in time to see the rush of men led by William encounter the first of the blue-skinned Chorl. William's blade struck out, unwieldy and unfamiliar in his grip, but it sliced into the first startled Chorl's arm, cut through the cloth at the elbow, blood splattering—

And then the crowd of people overtook William and he was lost from Borund's sight.

Borund gasped as he saw the end of the dock—or what remained of the dock; the Chorl ship having smashed through its upper half—degenerating into a melee of swords and screams and blood.

"This can't be happening," Borund murmured. He took a step back from the barricade, scanned up and down the wharf, saw men fighting on the docks, on the wharf, on the barricade itself in the torchlight. He took another step back, shook his head. "This—"

Someone lurched up onto the barricade directly in front of him and Borund cried out, the sailor stumbling on the uneven footing. He was splattered with blood, his face strangely open with shock. In that frozen moment, Borund felt as if he could see into the young man's soul, as if the sailor's entire life had been exposed.

Then the sailor pitched forward. His foot caught in the barricade and he sprawled down over it, head hanging, arms limp, hands trailing on the ground.

A sword had cut open the man's back from shoulder to hip.

Borund gasped, jerked away, bile rising in the back of his throat. He stood there, trembling, his mouth working but no sound coming out. Sweat broke out over his entire body, and the pounding of his heart in his veins escalated, drowned out the sounds of battle, the screams and clash of swords. He felt suddenly cold.

He stood shaking for a long moment, the world reduced to nothing but the bloody gash on the sailor's back and the thunder of his heart.

Then he dropped his own sword as if it had caught fire . . . and he ran.

I felt a momentary flash of anger, almost reached out from the Fire and seized control of him, forced him to pick up the sword, to charge onto the dock as William had done.

But then the anger died.

I let Borund go, watched him flee into the streets behind the wharf in panic. I couldn't stay here and force him to fight; Amenkor needed me for other things. Fighting was Borund's choice.

I pulled back from the docks, scanned down the length of the wharf at the twelve Chorl ships and the pitched battles going on everywhere.

A horn sounded. A heavy, deep, sonorous note that held and held, then faded.

I glanced up and frowned at the horizon, where the sun was just beginning to rise.

None of our signals were horns.

Then I froze, my gut clenching. The stench of Borund's panic filled my nostrils as I sucked in a deep breath, but I fought the sensation back.

At the entrance to the harbor, where twin towers of smoke rose into the sky against the dawn from the smoldering watchtowers, more ships were gliding into the bay. A massive ship, half again as large as one of Borund's trading ships, led the group, other smaller ships fanning out behind it. These ships were not as sleek as the initial attack ships, but they were definitely Chorl. Hulls painted black, decks packed with blue-skinned warriors, the smaller ships began to edge out in front of the lead ship, sails billowing out in the breeze coming from the sea. The lead ship's sails were white, some type of spiny shell painted on the largest in yellows and golds.

A man dressed in yellow robes on the lead ship raised another shell to his mouth and the horn sounded again, echoing across the water, throbbing in my ears. A woman stood next to him, dressed in iridescent blues this time, her ears ringed with gold.

The Ochean.

Deep inside, I felt the Fire pulse, its warning flames licking upward. I shivered at their frigid touch.

On the dock below, the Chorl renewed their attack in a frenzy. Our lines were pushed back. Someone called for a retreat and the Amenkor men scrambled back behind the barricade and attempted to hold there.

I rose higher into the dawn, despair washing over me as I watched the Ochean's second wave of ships flooding into the harbor, spreading like oil on water. The battle between the trading ships and the first Chorl ships in the middle of the bay had thinned, at least half of the ships on both sides burning. Debris floated on the surface, bobbing in the waves. And bodies. Dozens of bodies. Some clinging to flotsam, others simply floating, empty faces turned to the lightening sky.

The Ochean's ship reached the remains of the ships and slowed, edging through the wreckage. The conch-shell horn continued to sound at steady intervals, like a death knell. Some of the survivors in the water shouted out to the passing ships, but they were ignored, Chorl and Amenkor alike. The fighting on the decks of the remaining ships paused as the fleet slid past, the faces of the men exhausted, hope dying in the Amenkor men's eyes as they were surrounded.

I sped back to the wharf, saw the men at the barricade falter as the new wave of ships came into view, hidden before by the smoke and fire and ships of the first wave and their battle. The Chorl pressed harder, broke through the barricade to the south, near the half completed warehouse district, blue-skinned men spilling through the gap and onto the wharf and the streets beyond like ink, Amenkor men racing toward the walls of the palace before them. And with that one break, the entire barricade began to crumble.

I watched as the new Chorl ships drew up to the remains of the docks and the wharf, watched as planks were lowered and more of the Chorl warriors disembarked, flooding the wharf with men. And with them came the Chorl Servants, dressed in pale greens, shell necklaces around their necks, gold ear-rings glinting in the early morning sunlight. The Ochean strode down onto the wharf surrounded by Servants and surveyed the barricade, still loosely held in a few locations.

She motioned to a few of the Servants, who broke off with warrior escorts of their own and spread out along the barricade and the pockets of resistance that remained.

Once in place, they raised their arms and I felt the river gathering, felt it being manipulated.

William, I thought with horror, my gut wrenching. I didn't know if he was still down there, or if he'd fled when the line began to break. I couldn't find him either. He hadn't been one of those tagged with the Fire.

I wanted to close my eyes as the pressure on the river built, wanted to lash out. But I knew it was useless. I couldn't stop all of the Servants, couldn't hope to hold them back. And there was no one close who'd been tagged with the White Fire in any case. I couldn't manipulate the river when Reaching unless I worked through the Fire.

Save your strength, the voices of the throne whispered.

I cried out when the Servants released the pressure—in despair, in frus-tration.

Amenkor was dying. I could see it. I could feel it.

Fire exploded from the hands of the Servants, rushing forward to slam into the barricades, enveloping Chorl warriors and Amenkor defenders alike. Fresh screams rose into the air with the scent of burned flesh and oily smoke.

"Fall back!" someone bellowed—the captain from the initial attack, still alive, blood covering one eye from a cut across his forehead. "Fall back to the second barricade!"

The Amenkor resistance held a moment more . . . and then lurched back, the men retreating slowly at first, then breaking into a run as the Servants re-leased more fire.

I shifted, glared down at the Ochean as she climbed over the remains of the barricade accompanied on the left by a man I didn't recognize dressed in yellow robes, holding some type of reed scepter, his face twisted into a scowl. They were surrounded completely by blue-skinned warriors.

I did recognize the warrior to the Ochean's right. Circular tattoos on his cheeks; a ragged half ear.

He was the one who'd led the attack on *The Maiden,* the one who'd met with Alendor in the cove and taken our food.

I spun, flashed past the Chorl as they entered the lower streets beyond the wharf, searched the lower city for flares of the White Fire, for a particular flame . . . and found it.

I dove down, seized control of Captain Westen's body where he watched the wharf from the rooftop of a building. A group of twelve Seekers, both young and old, surrounded him.

I turned to them, eyes flashing. "This is the Mistress. The Chorl have broken through the barricade on the wharf and entered the lower city. They have their Servants with them, dressed in green. They'll be heading this way. I want you to target the Servants. Take out as many as you can before they reach the market-place."

The Seekers nodded, faces settling into the same dark, dangerous look I'd seen on Erick's face so often beyond the Dredge. These men and women didn't radiate fear. They were strangely empty of emotion, all of it crushed.

Erick had never felt as depthless to me as most of the Seekers did now. But perhaps I had simply known him better, longer. Perhaps the emotions were there, just hidden deeper than usual.

The Seekers scattered, descending from the rooftop and spreading out in the streets below. I followed their movements for a moment through Captain Westen's eyes, then released him, lingering behind in the Fire.

Westen shuddered, closed his eyes and bowed his head, breathing in deeply.

When he'd recovered, his mouth twisted in a tiny smile. "Well," he murmured. "That was certainly strange."

Then he shifted, all thought centering on the hunt. He reached down into the shadows of the roofline at his feet and drew forth a crossbow and a pouch containing steel bolts. Slinging the pouch over one shoulder, so that the opening rested on his hip, within easy reach, he sprinted in a low crouch along the edge of the roof to a corner, scanned in the direction of the wharf, where thick columns of smoke now rose into the lightening sky from the burning barricade. Hooking the crossbow to his belt, he slid over the edge of the roof, holding onto the stone abutment, then climbed down the brick wall like a spider.

He jumped the last few feet, crouched down in the alley's entrance, then darted across the street, heading toward the wharf.

A moment later, he heard running footsteps and ducked into the shadows of a doorway, absolutely still as a group of Amenkor guardsmen tore by, mingled with a few random citizens, all bloody, some wounded. The sounds of the battle were growing nearer.

Once they'd passed, Westen took a quick look out into the street, then to the door at his back. He eyed it carefully, then stepped back a pace and kicked the door in.

He moved into the interior rooms as the piercing cries of the Chorl rose on the street behind him. Without turning, he strode into the back rooms, found the stairs to an upper floor and sprinted up those, noticing that the stairs continued to the roof before moving again to the front of the building.

Sidling up to a window, he glared down onto the street, watched ranks of Chorl move past, wincing at their harsh, barked commands. None entered any of the buildings, continuing on down the street, in pursuit of the fleeing guardsmen.

Westen grunted, settled down next to the window so that he'd be hidden in the shadow of the room, then reached out and swung the window outward.

The breeze brought with it smoke and blood as well as the taint of sea salt.

Westen ignored it all, pulled out his crossbow, and proceeded to load a bolt.

He scanned the room—a bed, two dressers, a wardrobe, a table with a jewelry box and a chair. Reaching out, he dragged the chair closer to the window and sat, angling the crossbow down to cover the street.

He began to wait.

His mind flickered through numerous images as he listened to the sounds coming from the street. Foremost was a woman, her hair a light brown and her eyes green, smiling as she held out a sheathed dagger. A child clutched her leg and she ruffled the boy's hair. Concern bled through Westen's cold Seeker reserve as he thought about them, and I suddenly realized it was his wife and child. I hadn't known he had a family, found it surprising that any of the Seekers had families.

More images of the two flashed by, mixed with worry that they'd made it to the palace in time. Then he shoved those thoughts aside and concentrated on the sounds in the street. They were getting closer. He could hear explosions in the distance, wondered how the other Seekers were faring.

Smoke drifted down the street and he tensed, leaned forward, and shifted the crossbow.

Shouts, in the strange language of the Chorl, and then the street was flooded with Chorl warriors, this batch moving slowly, swords drawn, escorting—

Westen didn't smile, didn't react in any way, but all thoughts of his family, of the other Seekers, of everything but the street below faded away. His vision seemed to narrow as he concentrated, as my vision narrowed on the river, but without the strange textures of the river that told me so much. He edged the crossbow to the left, then down, sighted on the flash of green among the blues and browns of the Chorl warriors. The Servant's face came into focus, the skin smooth, tinted the palest of blues, the lips a much darker blue. Her eyes flashed left and right as the group moved, her jaw set in a stern line. Three gold earrings glittered in each ear, and there was a trace of a tattoo at the edge of her throat, hidden beneath the iridescent green dress.

For a moment, Westen hesitated.

But the image of his wife and child resurfaced, followed by a flood of hatred for these invaders.

He pulled the crossbow's trigger.

He was moving before the bolt struck the Servant in the chest, flinging her backward, her arms flailing outward, her face startled. A roar erupted from the Chorl in the street. He heard them entering the building below, furniture crashing to the floor as it was thrust aside, and then he was at the stairs leading to the roof, sprinting up them two at a time. He burst out through the trapdoor to the rooftop, hauled himself up into a roll, then slammed the trapdoor back down into place and dashed across to the roof's edge.

In the street below, he caught a brief image of Chorl surrounding the fallen Servant in a rough circle, their faces enraged as they searched for the culprit. The Servant's face was slack, her green dress stained a dark, grisly black-red, the bolt sticking out just above her left breast, directly over her heart.

Then Westen leaped from the roof, thudding down hard onto the roof next door, rolling back up into a sprint.

Just before I withdrew from Westen, I felt a surge of satisfaction from him at the Servant's death.

I lifted up, surveyed the scene in the lower city, saw buildings on fire in three different locations, saw two other Seekers streaking across rooftops or edging through the back streets, all of them retreating slowly to the market-place and the second line of barricades as the Chorl advanced. But the Seekers were slowing the Chorl down. Their groups weren't running from street to street anymore, the Servants held back as the Chorl warriors sent out advance parties to flush out the Seekers before they struck. As I watched, one Seeker's bolt took a Servant in the shoulder, too high for a killing stroke, and the Servant lashed out, the flare of pain and fury as she unleashed the fireball like a slap in the face. The fireball exploded on the second floor of the house, heat searing upward, the blast so powerful the windows burst outward, glass shards flying down into the street. But the Seeker was already sprinting away through a back narrow, cursing himself under his breath.

Closer to Amenkor's River, the Chorl had almost made it to the second barricade.

I sped toward the marketplace, found Captain Catrell, slid into the Fire at his core.

They're almost here, I said.

He grunted in surprise at my voice, those men nearest him frowning. "Mistress?"

Westen and the Seekers have slowed them down, but they're going to reach the second barricade any moment. You won't be able to hold it long. The Ochean's Servants will break through it.

"Then we'd better prepare our own Servants for some defense," he said under his breath. He barked orders and three page boys took off at a run. One came back almost immediately, Marielle in tow, her white Servant robes discarded and replaced with ordinary breeches and a brown shirt. The white robes would have been too easy to target. I'd wanted my own Servants to meld into the fray.

To be gray.

The guardsmen surrounding Catrell parted as Marielle stepped forward. She was shaking, her face a mask of terror. I thought of Borund, my heart dropping.

"You'll be fine," Catrell said.

Marielle snorted, but I reached out on the river and touched her through the Fire, abandoning Catrell, saying, *Catrell is right, you'll be fine.*

Marielle relaxed instantly, keeping her voice low. "I didn't want to go on the ship."

I frowned. *What?*

"The ship. *The Maiden.* I thought, in your chambers when you were tagging Erick, I thought you were going to put me on the ship, too. I was terrified. But Laurren went instead, and I was so relieved." I felt her gut twist with pain and grief. "And look what happened to her! I should have gone instead! She should be here, defending the city, not me!"

But she isn't here, I said. *You are.*

"Here they come," Catrell said quietly, his voice grim, no sign that he thought Marielle conversing with herself was strange entering his voice. Then he bellowed out orders, men shifting up to the edge of the barricade on all sides.

Marielle's terror had returned, supplanting her grief.

You know what you have to do, I said.

She shuddered, then shook herself. Her shoulders straightened, and she glared out at the empty marketplace before the barricade.

Chorl began pouring from the streets into the square. Marielle closed her eyes, drew in a deep breath to steady herself—

And I felt the river shift, felt it gather in a wall before the barricade. An invisible shield centered at Catrell's position and extending in both directions for at least twenty feet.

I grunted.

"A Chorl Servant," Catrell said, motioning with his sword.

I glanced in that direction, frowned as the woman emerged from the side street, thankful there was only one. The Chorl warriors around her halted, leaving a wide open space between her and the barricade.

She raised her arms, the green of her sleeves flapping in the breeze. I felt the river gather, heard Marielle whimper.

And then fire exploded toward the barricade.

The men cried out, lurched back, and ducked behind the makeshift barrier, but Catrell held steady, his face grim, his jaw clenching.

The fire struck Marielle's wall, and she gasped, wincing. I resisted the urge to help her, bit back a sharp sickening memory of Laurren, of feeling her burn to death. But Marielle held the wall tight, shunting the fire upward as she'd been taught so that it shot harmlessly into the air over the heads of those behind the barricade, heat radiating downward in palpable waves.

Then the fire cut off. Sweat lined Marielle's face, but she straightened.

A cheer went up from the Amenkor guardsmen as they realized the barrier had held, and Marielle smiled.

In the marketplace, the Chorl Servant stepped forward, shoving warriors aside, her eyes enraged. She raised her hands to try again, and I felt Marielle brace for the impact, steadier this time, more confident.

"Take the Chorl Servant out as quickly as you can," Catrell said to the men at his side, issuing orders even as the second blast of fire struck Marielle's wall and I lifted free from the Fire at Marielle's center.

The second barricade seemed to be holding, the palace Servants holding off the Chorl's Servants all along its length. I slid from Fire to Fire inside Amenkor's Servants, helping some to tighten their shields or boost their confidence, others to push back and attack, but I never stayed long. The group of Chorl near the River had reached the barricade there, but had run into a different problem: Darryn and the denizens of the slums. The militia had come out in force, backed by hundreds of other residents who'd managed to survive the winter. They surged across the Dredge's bridge into the Chorl's flanks brandishing anything they could lay their hands on as weapons, Darryn at the forefront, screaming into the smoke and wind drifting inland from the ships burning in the harbor. What they lacked in organization, they made up for in numbers, the mob overwhelming the Chorl warriors, crushing them into the barricade where the Amenkor guardsmen were holding them off with little effort.

But the wharf and the lower city were both in shambles, entire streets on fire, smoke rising into the midmorning light in thick, black columns. The battle in the harbor was over, trading ships nothing but burning husks, a few of the sleek Chorl ships moving toward the wharf, battered but still whole.

Then I caught a flicker of Fire, nothing but a sputter, barely visible. It came from the Chorl ships already at the docks.

It came from the Ochean's ship.

I hesitated, ready to return to the throne room, ready to warn Avrell and Eryn and the others on the walls of the palace. I'd been out too long as it was, had been using the river, had been Reaching from person to person.

But the Fire flickered again, and so I dove for it, speeding through the columns of smoke, feeling the heat from the fires below as the city burned, intending to simply check out the Fire and then leave. No lingering as I'd done with the others.

I slid down into the Ochean's ship, slid into the Fire—

And almost screamed with the pain. An all-consuming pain, like white hot flame, seething in my arms, my legs, my back, my chest. It felt like a thousand needles being shoved into my skin simultaneously, digging deeper and deeper with each breath, piercing all the way down to the bone. Each breath, each pulse of blood, sent the pain shooting through my body again, and again, and again, until the pain began to grow numbing, until I felt my heart ready to burst.

Until I remembered that this wasn't my body.

With effort, I forced the excruciating pain to recede, to fade into the background. But I couldn't force it to stop. It throbbed with the beat of a heart, ever present, ceaseless and unending. But it receded enough that I could focus on the body I inhabited, enough that I could recognize the man writhing beneath the pain.

Erick.

I almost screamed again, almost unconsciously jerked Erick's body, a movement that might have killed him. Shock overcame me, utter and complete shock. Followed by a horrible, tortuous, unbelievable joy.

And then, instantly crushing the joy, a terrible, choking grief. That I'd thought he'd died, that unknowingly I'd left him, abandoned him . . . to *this*.

I wanted to sob, felt the pressure building up inside me, inside Erick, knew that if I let it out it could kill him. He was almost dead, his body tortured, bruised, and crushed. I tasted blood on his lips, felt hundreds of small cuts on his arms, on his legs, his back and shoulders and abdomen. Hundreds of pin-prick burn marks. Something inside was broken, a rib, each breath sending sheets of pain into his right side, and the cut he'd received during the battle on the ship hadn't completely healed yet, seethed with its own fire. His throat was raw and torn, to the point that I knew he couldn't scream even if he wanted to. And the muscles in his neck . . .

He must have screamed, I realized. Even when he could no longer make a sound. He must have screamed and screamed, for the muscles in his neck were strained to the breaking point.

Shifting carefully, I tried to open his eyes. Only one of them complied, the other swollen shut and caked with blood. Even that small movement increased the pace of his breath, to the point where he was panting, his breath hissing in and out through a clenched jaw, blood, spit, and snot blowing in strands from his lips.

He lay on the floor in the corner of a lavishly decorated room, bolts of blue-and-green cloth draped from the ceiling, covering the outlines of a bed, hiding the rough wood of the ceiling and the walls. They drifted as the boat rocked, undulating in the waves. Pillows littered the floor, strewn in all directions, most blue and green as well, but a few a vibrant yellow or red.

The pillows closest to Erick were splattered with blood.

I heard a footfall, saw two sandaled feet move into view, the edge of a yellow robe.

One of the Chorl crouched down next to Erick, his tattooed face impassive. "Awake?" he said, the word awkward in his mouth, harsh, with a strange clicking sound at the end. He grinned, the expression sending a shudder through me. "Amenkor burning."

Erick didn't react. He had retreated deep inside himself. I could sense him huddling in a far, far corner, locked away from the pain.

But rage flooded through me. I couldn't suppress it, could feel Erick's breath quicken, his heart beating faster.

The Chorl must have seen my rage in Erick's eyes, for he shifted closer, eyebrows raised. He grunted, the twisted grin returning.

With careful, practiced ease, I felt him reach out on the river, felt it . . . churn. I couldn't see what he was doing, could only sense it.

But I felt the consequences instantly. Every prickling needle on Erick's skin erupted in white-hot fire.

Erick screamed, back arching, his heart shuddering, faltering, dying—

And then the sensation ended. It had only held for a moment, a single breath.

But it had brought Erick to the brink of death. His heart thudded once, hard, then relaxed back into a faint weakened beat. Erick's body relaxed as well, slumping to the floor, trembling.

The Chorl leaned back, considered Erick for a long moment, then snorted in contempt and stood, moving out of view.

I wanted to lash out, to seize the river and hurt the Chorl bastard. Hurt him as the Ochean had hurt Erick, torture him so that he screamed with pain without me even touching him. I wanted to kill him.

But I couldn't. Erick's body couldn't take it.

So with utmost care, I slid free, felt him exhale softly, his eye closing. I watched his huddled, battered form for a moment more, wanting to touch him so badly I ached.

There was nothing more I could do here.

And I couldn't abandon the throne room, couldn't abandon Amenkor.

But I couldn't leave him here. Not with the Ochean. Not now.

Who else . . . ?

I pushed up and out of the Ochean's ship and scanned the lower city, found the Fire I was looking for and dove into Westen's body. He was close to the second barricade, hidden in an alley, attempting to get close enough to pick off a few more of the Chorl Servants from behind. But he was almost out of crossbow bolts.

Westen, I gasped, my voice sounding more frantic than I felt. *You have to get to the Ochean's ship at the docks!* I felt him frown in confusion. *Erick's alive! He's being held on the Ochean's ship, guarded by a Chorl dressed in yellow. Kill the guard if you have to, but get Erick out of there! You'll have to be careful. The guard can use the river. And Erick's hurt. You won't be able to move him far.*

I left Westen's body, felt his shock as my words sank in. Then he hardened, as he'd done before, grabbed his crossbow and pouch, and sprinted down the alley, back toward the wharf, without a word.

I hovered in the alley, fretting, hesitating between following Westen and heading back to the palace, but an explosion near the barricade, followed by a billowing black cloud of smoke, forced my decision.

I lurched above the buildings, saw an entire section of the marketplace barricade enveloped in flame, spent a moment worrying about Marielle, then fled toward the palace and the throne room.

"Keven!" I barked as soon as I'd settled into my body. Weakness rippled through my arms and I gasped, but it hadn't sunk in deep yet, only made my hands tremble a little. I gripped the edges of the throne hard to stop them. Guardsmen and page boys were running in and out of the chamber, lining up to give reports. The guard surrounding me had doubled.

Keven broke away from a breathless guardsman in mid-report and vaulted up the three stone steps to the dais. "Yes, Mistress." His face was lined with worry, with anger and frustration.

"The Chorl have breached the second barricade. They'll be at the outer gates in moments. Close them. Now. Close them all."

"There are still people trying to get within the safety of the walls," he said calmly.

I grimaced. "It's too late. Everyone will have to fend for themselves."

He nodded, as if he'd expected the response but felt obligated to report. He turned and barked a command, one of the guardsmen surrounding the throne rushing off to the tower to sound the appropriate warning bells.

Then he turned back to me expectantly. "The harbor? The lower city?"

I sighed. "The battle in the harbor is over. And the Chorl brought in another wave of ships in addition to the first. I didn't count them. There were too many. The Ochean came with them. They overran the barricade on the wharf in moments, with the help of her Servants. Westen and the other Seekers managed to slow their advance, and our own Servants halted them at the second barricade for a while, but as soon as they broke through that, I came here."

Keven's eyes emptied of all emotion, became stoic. It was obvious he'd heard some of this news before now, but not all.

I watched him, considered not telling him the other news, but then decided he—of anyone in this room or on the palace walls—deserved to know.

I leaned forward. "Keven."

He glanced toward me, his expression still blank.

"Erick's alive."

For a moment, the words didn't seem to register. But then something deep inside stirred. His shoulders straightened and he drew in a long, slow, full breath . . . and held it. "Erick's alive?"

I nodded. "He's being held on the Ochean's ship."

His jaw clenched, unclenched, then clenched again. The spark in his eye hardened, began to seethe with fury. His brow creased and in a rough voice, his eyes meeting mine with raw intensity, he said, "We have to save him."

I held his gaze, let him see my own rage. "I've already sent Westen to get him."

Keven drew in another breath, as if to protest, as if to say that wasn't enough. But then he nodded.

Satisfied, I leaned back, broke eye contact. I gazed down into the throne room, surveyed the long walkway between the four stone pillars on each side, the scattering of statues and tapestries and candelabra in the recessed areas behind the pillars. I scanned the guardsmen surrounding the throne, the page boys, some servants from the palace ready with paper and ink, or a few trays of food or drink.

I frowned.

"Keven."

He turned back.

"Keep everyone off the promenade," I said. "And keep everyone away from the central corridor in the palace to the throne room as well. Remove the guardsmen at the doors to the inner sanctum and leave those doors open. I want a clear passage from the inner gates, up the promenade, to the throne room."

When his eyes flared, I shook my head and smiled. "If the Ochean and the Chorl breach the inner gate, I want no resistance."

His brow creased with disagreement. "What about you? What about here, in the throne room?"

My smile faded, and I glared out at the open doors of the throne room, out into the corridor beyond, thought about Erick on the Ochean's ship, thought about the intensity in the Ochean's eyes when she'd recognized the Fire at Erick's core on *The Maiden*. There was no reason for her to have kept Erick alive. Unless . . .

"I don't think she's come for Amenkor," I said. "I think she's come for the Skewed Throne. Let her try to take it."

Keven hesitated, uncertain, ready to argue, but in the end he complied. Stepping down from the dais, he motioned a group of guardsmen near, began issuing orders, more forcefully, more vehemently, than necessary. But he issued the orders.

I drew myself away from the throne room, pushed myself up to the tower, concentrated on the three walls below me, on the gates. Fire flared at the inner gate and the middle gate—Eryn and Avrell, respectively.

I dove down to Avrell, and said, *They're coming*, then settled back to wait.

Like the others, he shuddered as I spoke, then regrouped and moved up to the edge of the wall above the gates, motioning to a captain of the guard beside him. "Get ready. The Mistress says they're coming."

The captain turned and passed the word down the wall. Avrell glanced toward the gate in the outer wall—closed, so that he couldn't see what was happening beyond. As he watched, the guardsmen on that wall suddenly broke into activity, archers leaning out through the crenellations, firing at the Chorl on the far side. Men began tipping boiling oil over the wall, or chucked stones onto the attackers below.

And then suddenly the gate exploded.

Chunks of wood and stone blasted into the air, arching up and over the outer ward, shattering into buildings, caving in rooftops.

"Mistress' tits!" the guardsman to Avrell's left whispered in shock.

Avrell shot him a disapproving glare, then turned back to the dust cloud caused by the explosion. The men on the wall were scrambling away from the gate entrance, fleeing along the parapet. Another explosion followed, more debris raining up and out through the air, landing with distance-muffled thuds. A building near the gate collapsed with a slow grinding crunch.

Then, through the dust and debris, Chorl poured into the streets.

Avrell straightened as everyone on the walls tensed.

"What in hells was that?" The captain of the guard had reappeared, his eyes wide.

"I don't know," Avrell said. "Are the gates sealed?"

"For all the good it's going to do us."

Avrell grunted.

The Chorl headed straight for the second gate, a massive wave of blues and reds and purples and browns, the greens of a few Servants scattered among them. Tension along the wall mounted as they approached, men shifting from foot to foot, armor scraping against stone.

"Ready!" the captain called when they were two blocks away, but still out of sight. Their piercing war cries could be heard, growing louder and louder, echoing off the buildings into the afternoon sky.

Shouts of "Ready!" echoed down the wall, men stepping forward, craning to see.

Then the Chorl appeared on the street below, a mob of blue skin and raised swords, the blades curved strangely, their war cries suddenly roaring. It crashed into the gates and wall like an ocean wave, increasing as more and more of the Chorl appeared, surging forward like a tide.

They struck the gates, then split and piled outward. The captain roared, "Now!" but his voice was drowned out in the cacophony of noise. His sword arm slashed downward and all along the wall Amenkor guardsmen responded, arrows flying, stone arching outward, falling indiscriminately among the screaming mass of blue-skinned men. To Avrell's left, two burly men hoisted a vat of bubbling oil up into the crenellation and tilted it over the edge. Fresh screams arose, the Chorl below retreating from the scalding oil. Someone else chucked a flaming brand down after the oil and fire seared the wall. Black smoke, reeking of charred flesh, billowed up into Avrell's face.

He pulled back from the wall coughing, face twisted in distaste.

Before he could recover completely, the roar of the Chorl died down abruptly.

Avrell staggered back to the wall, forearm lifted to cover his mouth and nose, still coughing. Through tear-blurred eyes, he glared down at the space below the gate.

Then his eyes widened.

The Chorl were falling back, leaving the square and street open. Guardsmen still heaved things over the walls to either side, but all fighting in the immediate area had halted, men crowding back to the edge of the wall, perplexed.

In the square below, the edge of the Chorl force parted and the Ochean stepped forward.

Tense mutters passed among the guardsmen as she moved forward, halting just out of reach of the archers. Her black hair shifted in the gusting breeze from the harbor, and the folds of her iridescent blue dress trailed on the ground behind her. Shell necklaces hung down from her neck, and strings of shells had been plaited through her hair.

She surveyed her forces, the gates, the walls, her face unreadable, her pale blue skin flawless.

Then her gaze fell on the top of the gates, on Avrell's position.

Her expression hardened, grew taut, and she raised her arms, blue cloth arching from her wrists to her waist as she held her hands outward, palms facing the wall.

I felt the force gathering on the river, reached out to Avrell to warn him, but he'd already seen the danger.

Eyes widening in fear, he lurched back and to one side and bellowed, "Run!"

He'd taken two steps, the guardsmen to either side turning to frown at him in confusion, when the pressure on the river released.

The gates exploded, the force shuddering through the stone wall beneath Avrell's feet. Then a concussive blast hit him from behind, flung him forward to the parapet, the skin of his hands scraped raw on the stone. He gasped, rolled to one side, and struck the stone of the crenellation with his back, grinding to a halt. Something soft landed on the parapet before him—a body, the guardsman already dead, eyes wide in shock—and then the body slid off the wall and Avrell could see wood and stone flying outward, away from the wall.

Avrell gasped again, realized he could barely hear his own breath, sounds muted, felt a trickle near his ear and reached up to his jaw. His shoulder screamed at the movement and his hand came away bloody.

Boots pounded past, their thuds like muffled cloth. Through the fog of dust from the gates, he could pick out shouts and screams, too soft and chaotic to make out words.

The stone beneath him rumbled, shuddered again, and he felt the wall shift, suddenly leaning inward.

He jerked himself up onto his elbow, ignored the sharp pain in his chest, and scrambled to his feet. His dark blue robes were covered with grit, his hands throbbing where they'd been skinned raw. He huddled against the canted wall, coughed as he tried to make out what was happening.

The gates had fallen. The stone above where the gates had stood had collapsed, and the walls to either side were threatening to give way as well.

He stood on the parapet, guardsmen running past, retreating from the walls, and stared. Chorl filled the street below, surging in all directions, their main force angling straight for the inner gates.

The wall trembled again, the motion piercing Avrell's numbness and shock, and he suddenly said, "Eryn."

He shook himself, pain shooting up from his elbow and shoulder where he'd hit the stone parapet. Clutching that arm to his chest with the other hand, he began to stagger back along the parapet, looking for a way down to the street.

I left him, pushed up through the middle ward, past the huge three-horse stone fountain in front of the merchant's guild, the plaza already swarming with Chorl, up through the streets to the inner wall, the inner gate, and settled inside Eryn.

She'd seen the middle gate fall, had seen the dust, debris, and smoke from the outer gate. Her jaw was set, her hands flat on the stone wall before her as she stared out into the street. "Avrell," she said to herself.

Then the Chorl flooded the street below, came screaming up to the wall, and the arrows began to fly.

Eryn didn't pay any attention, guardsmen bellowing orders all around her. Instead, she closed her eyes, concentrated inward.

I felt her heart slow, felt the faint tremors of concern and fear leave her, her arms steadying.

The river around her calmed, the turbulence caused by the guardsmen, by their raw terror, by the death, faded away, evened out.

Until, when the roars of the Chorl died down as they had at the middle gates, when the Chorl retreated and the guardsmen on the wall fell silent and Eryn opened her eyes, she stood in a pool of total serenity.

On the street below, the Chorl parted and the Ochean stepped forward. She surveyed the wall as she had before, and her arms lifted.

Eryn drew in a deep breath, her hands on the stone before her, and summoned the river.

It solidified fluidly, the wall of force she constructed flawless as far as I could see, stretching from the ground to the top of the parapet, completely covering the gate, and curved like a shield.

She finished it a moment before the Ochean released.

I saw the Ochean's power flash across the square, raw and blunt, channeled like a battering ram and aimed at the center of the gates.

When it hit Eryn's wall, it struck like a solid punch to the gut. Eryn gasped, her eyes flying wide, one arm leaving the wall and clutching her stomach. The shield she'd created flexed, wavered, the force of the Ochean's blow being shunted to the side as swiftly as possible. For a single moment, it seemed that Eryn would be overwhelmed. The wall stuttered, frayed at the edges—

But it held.

In the square below, the Ochean stepped forward, her eyes flashing with hatred. The Chorl began to mutter, shocked. Then she spun, clapped her hands and shouted an order.

Instantly, three of the Ochean's Servants stepped forward.

The Ochean swung back to the gates, arms outstretched, face livid. The three Servants fell into position around her, one each to either side and a step behind, the third directly behind her and two steps back, so that they formed a rough diamond.

The three Servants clasped their hands before them and bowed their heads. Lines of force wavered into being on the river, connecting them to the Ochean, solidifying into thick conduits.

The voices of the throne drew in a sharp breath.

Except that wasn't true. Most of the voices seemed merely confused, murmuring with worry, some stunned into silence by the previous explosions. Only the Seven had drawn breath.

They're Linking. They've advanced farther than I suspected, Cerrin said.

Then I have to help her.

I reached, even as Eryn steadied her shield, a thin pain shooting up from her stomach. Even though her shield had held, she'd still felt the force behind the Ochean's blow. I began to weave the river into a second shield behind Eryn's.

No, Liviann said, and I felt her step forward, felt Cerrin recede. *We can't teach you how to supplement Eryn's power as the Servants below are supplementing the Ochean's—there's no time—but we can show you how to effectively reinforce Eryn's shield.*

She reached through the Fire with Cerrin's help, the rest of the Seven stepping forward as well, all of them guiding the shield's lines that I'd already put in place, shifting them slightly so that my own shield wove into Eryn's, slipped along its edges, forming buttresses between Eryn's shield and the physical stone walls themselves.

As the last currents slid into place, Eryn straightening and murmuring a soft, grim, "Thank you, Varis," under her breath, the Ochean unleashed another hammer blow of power.

On the river, the hammer descended with horrifying strength, not just the power of the Ochean and three Servants, but more than ten times the power.

It struck, and a solid core of heat and pain exploded in Eryn's gut, like a sizzling ball of fire. Both Eryn and I gasped, Eryn's arms wrapping around her stomach as she staggered. The shield held, power dissipating outward, shuddering along its length, the buttresses bleeding the power down into the walls themselves until the stone began to shudder. More power slammed into the shield, pressure building, the tremors of the wall increasing, until a few of the guardsmen cried out. Eryn's shield began to collapse, crumbling in from the sides—

And then the Ochean's power halted.

At the same time, a horrendous crack reverberated through the inner ward as the stone of the wall split. Guardsmen leaped back from the sundered stone, shouts rang out, but the wall held.

Eryn gasped and collapsed forward, holding herself up on the edge of the parapet with one arm, knees weak. The captain of the guard shifted forward in concern, to where Eryn hunched forward, arm still clutching her stomach.

Eryn waved him off, forced herself to straighten and stand, her breath coming harsh and fast now, gasping. The white hot fire radiated up from her abdomen, seething, shooting flares of pain down her arms, into her heart. But she closed her eyes, reached out and steadied the wall of force before the gate yet again, sucked in another deep breath and held it as the Ochean gathered her power, and that of the Servants, for a third strike.

Eryn's shield never had a chance, even with my help, even with the guidance of the Seven. It held for one short breath, two—

Then it collapsed.

And the gates exploded.

Eryn sagged to the stone wall in front of her as it shuddered, groped blindly for the stone as debris flew outward behind her, dust enveloping her in a shroud. She coughed as she tried to breathe through the grit, raised an arm weakly to her mouth, covering it with the sleeve of her white dress. Grit settled into her eyes, too fast for her to blink it away, and she felt herself slipping down the stone of the crenellation, felt it shuddering beneath her hands, ready to crumble, to collapse.

Then someone gripped her beneath the arms, a guardsman, heaved her up as she coughed and hacked, and dragged her away, the fire in her gut exploding with the movement, tasting of acid and blood in the back of her throat.

She held on to consciousness a moment more, enough to see the captain whose name she did not know hauling her to safety.

And then everything went black.

I pulled away, stared down at the wreckage of the inner gates, watched as the parapet Eryn had just been pulled off of caved in, stone raining down onto the base of the promenade. I lifted up, shifted to the tower, and turned, staring down over the city, the taste of acid and blood moving with me, tainting the river. The harbor was filled with burning ships, the water crammed with bodies and debris, rising and falling with the waves stained red with blood. Smoke billowed through the afternoon skies, rising in thick columns from the city, from the harbor, from the watchtowers. Even as I watched, a building in the middle ward collapsed, dust rising in a thick cloud. And everywhere there was fire—on the wharf, in the warehouse district, in the inner city. Even in the slums.

It was the vision. Amenkor lay in ruins, the stench of smoke and blood and death clogging the air.

I turned from the image, sank down through the tower, down through the stone to the throne room, and settled into my body, breathing in with a hard, shuddering, painful gasp, tears at the corners of my eyes, weakness coursing through my arms, through my chest. And still the taste of acid and blood lingered.

Keven stood at the throne's side, guardsmen lining the walkway, stationed behind the pillars. I frowned in irritation, thought about ordering them all out of the room, but halted when I saw the set expression on Keven's face.

"They've broken through the gates," I said instead, my voice ragged, hoarse, my throat raw. "The Ochean is inside the palace."

⊹— The Throne Room —⊹

Keven shifted nervously, the throne room utterly silent. Outside in the corridor, through the open double doors, the palace felt deserted. No servants tread the halls, no guardsmen guarded the entrance to the inner sanctum, nor the entrance to the throne room. The only sign of life came from Keven and the score of guardsmen lined up in the spaces between the columns along the central aisle.

She'll come straight to the throne room, Cerrin said.

I tensed at his voice, then relaxed. The voices had remained quiet since helping Eryn at the gates, so quiet I'd barely noticed they were there. Now, I felt them all—all of the previous Mistresses, the Seven who had created the Skewed Throne, the men and women who had touched the throne at some point and died because of it, like Alendor. They were all quiet, even the madmen, the silence in my head, behind the protective wall of Fire that still encircled them, eerie.

I could feel Cerrin and Liviann at the forefront, hovering at the edge of the white flame, Liviann slightly behind Cerrin. I could feel Atreus and Alleryn, Seth and Garus and Silicia, could smell their individual scents, all mingling.

She'll try to seize control of the throne, Cerrin added, his melancholy voice intense. *You can't let her take it, no matter the cost. The Chorl are ruthless. They'll destroy everything.* I could hear the echoes of the pain over his wife's death in his voice. Of his daughters' deaths.

"I don't intend to let her take it," I said, and a few of the guardsmen jumped at the sound of my voice.

Then, out in the corridor, came the tramp of boots on stone.

Everyone tensed, Keven taking a step forward, his hand falling to the pommel of his sword.

"Leave them to me," I said sharply.

He frowned without turning, but he didn't draw his sword.

The sound of footsteps grew louder, closer.

Then a group of five Chorl warriors stepped into the doorway to the throne room and halted, curved swords drawn and at the ready, gazes darting around the room, taking in me, Keven, the guardsmen along the sides.

They hesitated, unsettled, obviously expecting more resistance.

Someone barked a command in the corridor, then stepped to the center of the group of warriors.

The Chorl captain. The man with the circular tattoos on his cheeks, his ear half cut off.

He surveyed the throne room, his face set in a dark frown as the men to either side of him relaxed, his eyes finally settling on me.

I could see his hatred, could sense his malevolence, could almost taste it, like smoke.

Inside my head, I felt the voices in the throne stir.

See, Cerrin whispered.

The other voices murmured agreement.

Still watching me, he motioned to the side, and more Chorl warriors flooded the corridor outside. But they left a narrow space between them.

When her escort was in position, the Ochean moved into view, followed by the Chorl man in yellow robes carrying the reed scepter, both stepping up to the Chorl captain as the others closed in behind them.

The Ochean hesitated at the edge of the throne room, then stepped inside, alone, walking down the aisle between the pillars imperiously, as if she'd already seized control, as if the throne—the entire city of Amenkor—was already hers. Her captain followed her, a pace behind, a few of the warriors behind him, fanning out to the sides, their stances wary, gazes locked solidly on the guardsmen at their flanks.

The Chorl in yellow robes remained behind, frowning.

My eyes narrowed with anger. When she'd made it halfway down the aisle, I stood abruptly, felt the weakness from Reaching shiver through my legs to the point I almost collapsed. But I steadied myself, shoved the weakness back.

The Ochean halted, lowered her head slightly as she considered me, jaw clenched.

Behind me, I felt the throne begin to twist, reshaping itself into another form. I felt its power reaching out, the voices stalking the room like a predator hunting its prey. I could feel their hatred, as harsh and malevolent as the expression on the Chorl captain's face . . . or on the Ochean's.

Her eyes widened in surprise as the throne twisted, as the power of the throne filled the room, but she crushed the reaction swiftly, her glare settling back on me. Behind her, the man in yellow didn't bother hiding his surprise.

I smiled. "Welcome to Amenkor."

I didn't know if she understood the words, but she heard the sarcasm, condescension, and hatred in my voice.

Her frown deepened, almost into a scowl.

Then she lashed out using the river, a whip crack of force that snapped across the shield I raised at the last moment. I felt the tip of the lash skid across the invisible barrier, sending ripples of force out into the river, but before they could dissipate, I flung a barrage of daggerlike shards across the throne room.

They hit her own shield like ice pellets, shattering into a thousand scintillate fragments of visible light. The guardsmen gasped. Keven lurched forward, suddenly aware that I'd already been attacked, but—my voice cracking through the room—I barked, "Stand back!" The Ochean spat something herself, her captain and warriors edging back toward the doorway.

Keven growled, and I flashed him an angry glare.

"Don't interfere," I snapped. "No matter what happens."

Sword half drawn, he stepped back behind the throne grudgingly, sheathing his blade.

I turned back to the Ochean. Her eyes flashed, her shield pulsing. A solid wall of force, like Eryn's, the weave tight, controlled.

She had more practice at using the river than I did, more experience. Perhaps even more experience than Eryn.

A shiver of doubt coursed through me.

But you have us, Cerrin said, and his voice was no longer sad, no longer weak. It was angry. All of the Seven radiated anger, had shifted forward, ready to help.

Drawing a steadying breath, my heart thundering in my ears, I stepped down the three steps of the dais to the main floor.

The Ochean watched me coldly.

I thought about the dagger at my waist, about the drills Eryn had put me through in the courtyard, about Erick and Westen and the hours of training with the Seekers.

And then I struck.

The blow fell on the Ochean's shield with blunt force, like a mace, and I heard her grunt. I smiled in satisfaction, but the emotion was fleeting. Her wrist flicked and a blade, curved like the Chorl warriors' blades, slashed into my own shield. I shunted the stroke aside, let the power bleed out into the river, struck back with the mace again, raining blows down left and right, dodging her sword slashes, shoving them aside when they struck, grunting with the effort. Sweat broke out on my forehead, began to trickle down my face, but I concentrated on her blade, watched the fluctuations in her shield as each of my blows landed, searching for a weak point.

We began circling each other, the Ochean edging left, me right. Her hands, fingers long and supple, flicked as she directed her sword. The shells in her necklace and laced through her hair clacked together, a strange counterpoint to the soundless and mostly invisible battle waged between us. Shards of light, in all colors, sparked from the shields occasionally, flaring and dying in a heartbeat, the guardsmen and Chorl warriors gasping at the more intense displays.

I could feel myself beginning to tire, to flag, drained by the Reachings I'd done to keep track of the battle in the city below, so I increased the intensity of the mace's blows, shifted them subtly so that they struck at odd angles, and still her shield held, shuddering under each blow, but steadying in a heartbeat, not weakening in the slightest.

My own shield began to fray at the edges. I pulled back some of the power from the mace, used it to fortify the shield, and just when I felt I'd have to break off my attack entirely, the Ochean withdrew, her sword rippling away on the river.

I gasped, noticed we were both heaving, sweat dripping down our faces, staining our clothes.

We'd circled enough that our backs were facing the pillars, the throne to my left, its shifting form at the edge of my vision. The guardsmen and Chorl warriors were utterly silent, waiting, no one daring to enter the walkway between us. Not when they couldn't see the weapons being wielded.

The Ochean said something, the words sharp, but edged with respect.

Then she sneered, emitted a short, piercing shriek, and her arm lashed out.

She'd changed tactics. Instead of a curved blade, she hit me with a barrage of fistlike punches, aimed at my midsection at first, then shifting the blows outward.

I hissed through my teeth, felt some of the force seeping through the shield, striking my body with light taps. But if the shield failed . . .

I cried out, poured all of my strength into the shield, not even attempting to counterstrike, and even that wasn't enough.

I needed more strength, more power.

The voices in the throne responded.

I felt the surge of their support, felt the shield around me sharpen as Alleryn and Atreus reached forward with subtle flows, felt additional strength pouring into my arms from Seth and Garus, Cerrin allowing the previous Mistresses to help through the Fire. The Ochean's eyes widened slightly, only for a moment, and then the pummeling redoubled, her eyes narrowing, the fists striking at random now, left, right, midsection, thigh, chest, one sharp jab to the head, to the throat, but the shield held.

I began to fight back, Liviann and Silicia taking over part of the shield. Using daggerlike thrusts, I slashed across the Ochean's shield, cut across her eyes, saw her flinch back, then recover. I used every technique Erick had taught me beyond the Dredge, everything Westen and the Seekers had taught me in the rooms deeper within the palace, everything to maim, to kill, to distract—

And then I realized that even with the throne behind me, even with the Seven and their knowledge, my strength was fading.

But how . . . ?

I suddenly recalled Eryn in the garden, beating at my shield, no longer attempting to pierce it, simply hitting me over and over with force, battering me heedlessly.

Because she was attacking me somewhere else, subtly, the blunt force merely a diversion.

I continued slashing with my dagger, but began searching the river, searching my shield—

And there, I saw the pinhole, saw the threadlike conduit snaking back toward the Ochean, saw my strength being leeched away and used to supplement the Ochean's, just as Eryn had done during training.

I felt a seething flash of rage envelop me, caught the Ochean's eye across the aisle between us, then withdrew the power I'd focused on the dagger slashes and with a speed Eryn had drilled into me in the gardens formed a needlelike dart of raw force—a second, a third—and fed them into the Ochean's conduit one after the other.

The Ochean screamed when the first dart struck, her attack faltering. The second slammed into her a heartbeat later, followed by the third, spinning her around, her hands clutching her side, the conduit between my shield and her snapping as she withdrew it with a jerk.

The pummeling fists dissipated. Her shield wavered, flickered, and began to fail as well, but even as I stepped forward, even as I seized part of the river to retaliate, it shuddered and held.

But her conduit had given me an idea.

Breath coming in hoarse gasps, the Ochean spun back, eyes flashing, straightened as much as she could, pain clear on her face, one hand still clamped to her side. She spat something vicious, her face twisted into a cruel scowl, contorting the subtle beauty of her features. With her free hand, still half-turned, she lashed out again with the sword, the stroke heavier, weighted with more force, more thrust, shuddering into my shield, forcing me down into a low crouch. I cried out as it struck again, and again, then retaliated with my own strokes, using the lash as she'd done earlier. But my cries were exaggerated, the cracks of the lash meant to distract, as she'd tried to distract me.

I began to form my own conduit. Not to siphon off strength, as the Ochean had done. No. This conduit was meant to work in reverse, to send something to the Ochean.

What are you doing? Liviann snapped. *She'll send something back, as you did! Something more lethal than darts!*

Let her work! Cerrin spat, cutting off any further remarks from the Seven.

I ignored them, formed the river into a small funnel on my side of the shield, let the tail of the funnel snake outward, toward the Ochean. It stretched, shuddered beneath the flows of the battle on the river above it, stretched and thinned—

Until its tail touched the Ochean's shield.

I felt her gasp, saw her begin searching the river for the conduit, her eyes flicking left and right. The sword strokes lessened, their strength reduced as she concentrated elsewhere.

What's she doing! Liviann snapped, screaming at the other voices in the throne, trying to gain the support of the other Seven. *Garus! Seth! She's going to get us all killed!*

Wait, Cerrin said. He'd seen. He understood. I could hear it in his voice.

Give her a chance, Liviann, Garus growled, although there was doubt in his voice.

I brought the mouth of the funnel close to the Fire at my core. White tendrils of flame began streaming down the tail, snaking as the conduit twisted and roiled in the currents, but moving steadily toward the Ochean.

The Ochean's sword strokes halted, her attention completely on the river, her head snapping to the side, frantic.

The Fire had covered half the distance between us . . . two thirds.

If I could tag her—as I'd tagged Erick, as I'd tagged Eryn and Avrell—if I could tag her . . .

I could use the Fire to seize control of her.

The Fire had almost reached her when the Ochean saw the conduit.

She lashed out instantly, a short, decisive gesture, like a cleaver being brought down on a block of wood.

The funnel I'd created snapped, its tail severed where it had been attached to the Ochean's shield, severed at the tip, so that none of the Fire reached her.

The funnel snapped back, the Fire, the river, lashing out, striking me hard, shattering my shield and throwing me back. I screamed, crashed into the pillar behind me, head cracking into stone, and crumpled to the granite floor, stunned.

I'd barely taken a breath when half the voices of the throne shouted *Varis!* in warning, the sound mingling with the Ochean's shriek of triumph.

I flung a shield up, half dazed, felt the Seven pouring their own strength into it, felt the river roil as the Ochean manipulated it, her sword falling fast and swift. Twisting where I lay, blows raining down on the shield, filtering through with bruising force, I gasped, tried to strengthen my defenses, felt the Ochean's sword change to fists, to thrown daggers, a lash. I heard the Ochean stalking across the floor, felt her presence as she stood above me, her hands stretched out, fingers spread, her face a hideous mask of scorn and hatred and cruelty. Her eyes blazed with determination, any pain I'd caused earlier with the darts masked, buried beneath her contempt.

And I saw my death. I felt drained, barely able to sustain the shield, even with the strength of the Seven, of the other voices of the throne, infusing me. I'd expended too much energy following the battle in the city below, used up my reserves. My muscles trembled with every blow, the seepage through the shield increasing, each stroke sinking deeper and deeper into my flesh.

I felt a shudder of regret pass through me, heard it break free in a sob of pain, of heartrending defeat. I thought of everything I'd worked for over the last winter: the reconstruction of the warehouses, the desperate search for food, the setup of the work force and the communal kitchens. I thought of everything that Amenkor had accomplished, all lost now, burning beneath the Ochean's fires, nothing but charred, smoking husks on the harbor and in the streets. I thought of Avrell and Borund, of Catrell and Westen, struggling to hold together the city as Eryn went insane, then struggling to recoup when I'd supplanted her as Mistress and the food supply ran short, unknowingly fighting against Alendor and his alliance with the Chorl.

And I thought of Erick, of his beaten, tortured body lying in the room of pillows, in the Ochean's personal chambers.

Tortured by the woman glaring down at me now, eyes flashing with malice. Erick.

She'd kept him alive, even when she knew she'd taken everything from him, when she'd learned everything she could about Amenkor and the throne.

Beneath the Ochean's assault, beneath the despair, I hesitated.

Why? Why had she kept him alive? There was no reason, no need. Not any longer, not once she'd decided to attack Amenkor first. But she'd kept him alive anyway, had brought him here to Amenkor to witness the attack. . . .

I felt the hesitation shift into certainty.

She'd kept him alive because she wanted him to see what she'd done to Amenkor when it was over.

I felt myself weakening, felt the shield I held faltering, edging closer and closer to my body, more and more of the force of her blows passing through to strike my body. My hands were raised now, as if to ward off the attack.

In another few heartbeats, my shield would fail.

But perhaps . . .

I cried out, harshly, and as if my strength had given out completely, I let the shield fall.

The voices of the throne gasped. Liviann leaped forward, tried to take over as she had once before and reestablish the shield, but I used the Fire to hold her back, heard her scream with frustration, flail against the restraint, felt the other Seven reach forward and haul her back, subduing her.

The Ochean hesitated as the shield failed, as if she thought it were some kind of ruse, but then a slow smile touched her dark blue lips, her almost black eyes. A malicious smile. A triumphant smile.

She drew in a deep breath . . .

Then struck me again, fists punching hard and sharp, once to my face and once to my stomach. My lip split, the pain like fire, and I gagged, curled up into a ball as I'd learned to do on the Dredge, knees tight to my chest, arms close, hands covering my face. But the fists didn't stop. They continued, struck my back, my butt, my forearms, my shoulders, the back of my head. The voices of the throne cried out in protest, tried to seize control, raise the shield again, more of them this time, not just Liviann, but I forced them all back, held them all in check, felt Cerrin block their access through the White Fire. I suffered through the Ochean's beating, felt my strength flagging, thought of Erick lying among the bloody pillows, thought of the denizens of the slums pouring out across the Dredge's bridge to attack the Chorl, thought of all the death and destruction in the city below. . . .

And finally the punches slowed . . . and stopped.

I lay on the throne room floor, trembling, barely able to breathe, my back, my shoulders, my arms and lower legs bruised by the force of the Ochean's hatred. My muscles screamed with pain. I shuddered, tasted blood from my split lip, but dared not move. I wasn't certain I could move.

Above me, I heard the Ochean gasping, her breaths thick with phlegm. I listened as she slowly calmed, heard her dress rustle as she lowered her arms.

When her breathing had almost returned to normal, she spat on me. I flinched, but didn't move, let the spittle trickle down my neck, beneath my chin, mixing with my blood. I kept my hands tight over my face, and waited— for ten heartbeats, for an eternity—

Then I heard her move away.

I drew in a shallow breath and held it, listening intently as her footsteps retreated. Carefully, I lowered one hand, peeked out through my spread fingers.

The Ochean had moved to the center of the aisle again, had turned to face the Skewed Throne, twisting and morphing on its dais. Keven had shifted forward, his face grim, hand on his sword.

I silently cursed him, willed him to stand aside.

The Ochean stepped forward, moving toward the throne.

Keven tensed, made to draw his blade—

With a careless motion, the Ochean used the river to fling him out of the way.

He struck the stone pillar to one side, grunted as he collapsed to the dais, and didn't move again. But I could still see him breathing.

I felt a renewed surge of hatred.

The Ochean stepped up to the dais, movements poised, casual, even though her blue dress was stained with sweat. She turned at the top, surveyed the throne room, expression triumphant, locking meaningfully on the Chorl captain's face, on the man in the yellow robes with the reed scepter. Something passed between them, something I didn't understand, but the Chorl captain's eyes blazed with hatred a moment before he gave her a grudging nod. The man in yellow merely frowned.

The Ochean's gaze fell on me. I saw a flicker of satisfaction when she saw me watching.

She wanted me to see, as she'd wanted Erick to see Amenkor's destruction.

Then she sank onto the throne.

I lifted my head, all pretension set aside. It hurt, more than I expected, and required almost all of my strength. But I wasn't as beaten and drained as I'd led her to believe.

On the dais, the throne shuddered and twisted. The Ochean sucked in a sharp breath of surprise. Her eyes widened and she suddenly stilled, muscles rigid, back stiff.

The voices of the throne paused. The predatory presence of the throne in the room hesitated.

Then the voices rose into a shriek . . . and pounced. As they'd pounced on me when I'd sat on the throne almost five months before. A maelstrom of screams, roaring for attention, howling their hatred, their fear, their disgust. A hurricane that leaped toward the blue-skinned woman who sat on the throne.

And they dragged me along with them.

I found myself back in the marketplace, trapped in a crowd, jostled and crushed as everyone tried to shove their way to the center of the plaza, everyone screaming, yelling to be heard over everyone else, the voices all melding into an indistinguishable roar. Fear lanced through me as I stumbled and almost fell, shorter than most of those around me. With sudden horror, I realized that here, if I fell, I'd be trampled to death.

But someone reached out and grabbed me by the arm, hauled me upright and pulled me close to them.

"Careful now!" Cerrin bellowed, smiling tentatively down at me.

"What's happening?" I asked, trying to be heard over the noise.

Cerrin's face grew stern. "The Ochean touched the throne. She's trying to seize control."

"We can't let her!"

"I know." He glanced around at the faces in the crowd, gripped me tighter as the mob suddenly surged left. Someone's elbow jabbed into my side, made me gasp. "They're fighting her," he said, nodding to indicate the people—all of the previous Mistresses, all of those that had touched the throne before this. "But she's strong."

I glanced around, noted the pure hatred of those in the crowd, saw the panic beneath the anger, the fear. I could smell it, a rank stench of sweat and blood. But the faces of all of the old Mistresses, of all of those that had touched the throne over the last fifteen hundred years, were determined.

I turned back to Cerrin. "Take me to her."

He stared down into my eyes, frowning, his own eyes filled with doubt.

But then he nodded.

We began working our way through the crowd, Cerrin shoving the terrified and frantic people aside, forcing a passage wide enough for me to squeeze through, then roughly following behind. A few people backed off when they saw it was me, a few spat in my face for betraying them.

I ignored them all, anger building as the crowd grew thicker, more desperate. I started using my elbows, my fingers, jabbing into tender muscles, punching soft flesh. I came up against a man—face unshaven, several teeth missing, hair patchy, thin, and wild—who leered down at me, reached forward to grab my breast. I kneed him in the groin and stepped on his back as I passed.

Then suddenly, I broke through an edge, stepped out into a small space barely three paces across, the Ochean before me, her back turned. She slashed at the crowd around her with a sword, curved like the Chorl warriors', the strokes smooth but with a hint of desperation. Bodies lay at her feet, most moaning, blood flowing from cuts to their faces, to their chests.

She seemed to sense someone behind her, spun.

Her eyes widened in shock and she jerked back.

I smiled, then reached out and touched her.

I stood on a porch built of thousands upon thousands of wooden poles, like reeds but thicker and segmented. Huge green leaves covered a latticework of more wooden poles overhead for shade, and lay in thick layers on the floor. I could feel more of the poles beneath the leaves through the soles of my bare feet.

I moved to the edge of the porch, out into the sunlight.

Below, the land sloped down to a pristine beach, the sand a blinding white, the cove beyond a myriad range of greens and blues. The porch was surrounded by more huge, flat leaves, by dense foliage and tall trees, the trunks bare until they branched out at the top into dozens of huge, serrated palms. Closer to the beach, I could see small houses made of the same poles as the porch, thatched in the palm fronds, sandy paths leading from house to house, down to the beach, where strange boats had been drawn up onto the sand. Long and narrow, they could fit barely two men side-by-side, and had no sails.

I stared down at the scene, hands crossed arrogantly over my chest, and watched the people moving among the huts, or down on the shore. Blue-skinned people.

My people.

Then, the ground shuddered.

I frowned, reached out to steady myself against the edge of the porch. But the trembling had already subsided.

Down on the beach, the people near the boats and in the shallows had halted their activities, were now staring inland, their hands raised to shade their eyes as they looked up.

I turned, shaded my own eyes against the glare of the sun, and stared up beyond my summer palace.

The land rose in a gentle slope beyond the palace, to the base of a huge peaked mountain, the sides of the mountain covered in dense jungle, the peak itself conical.

The mountain had been silent for almost fifty years, but now . . .

Now, a thin column of smoke rose from its crater.

Back in the marketplace, I frowned, then concentrated, shifted the focus of the throne, filtered through the Ochean's memories.

And found myself back in the summer palace, in one of the interior rooms, seated on a throne built of the thick reeds, draped with cloth in greens and golds and purples and skeins of shells. Chorl warriors stood to either side of the throne, wearing breeches of dark blue filmy cloth, their chests bare and covered with tattoos in circular patterns. A figure knelt before me, bowed down, head pressed into the floor. He was dressed in yellow breeches, the tattoos on his chest curved crescents, like sickles, and black instead of dark blue.

The kneeling man raised his head.

"Ochean, the prophecy says—"

I hissed, cut him off. "I don't care what the prophecy says, Haqtl!"

The Chorl warriors around me shifted uncomfortably, and I sensed their anger. This man was a priest, communed with the gods.

And the warriors were pledged to the gods, not to me.

I clenched my jaw, forced my irritation and impatience down.

In a grudging voice, laced with undertones of scorn, I said, "Continue."

Haqtl, his expression darkening, began again. "The prophecy says the mountain will destroy us. It was sung ages ago, and now the time has come."

I shoved myself up out of the throne, began pacing before it. "You know this for certain? The gods have spoken?"

"The gods have spoken. They forewarned us ages ago, and there have been signs. The land rumbles. Poison gases boil from the ocean, killing the fish. And then came the Fire of Heaven from the west."

I spat a curse, heard the warriors shift again. I stifled a growl, suppressed the urge to slap Haqtl, to beat him. I knew the gods had not spoken, that there were no gods, that the priests were opposing me to gain more power, as usual. They were seizing upon the now constant rumbling from the mountain and using it against me. And the sea always boiled before the mountain erupted. It had done so before.

But the Fire of Heaven . . .

I shuddered as I recalled it sweeping in from the ocean, falling on the islands of the Chorl. It had covered the evening harvest in a pall of fear, the weak-souled villagers in their ships screaming as it approached, trying to make it back to shore.

For all the good it did them. There had been no escape. The Fire had touched everyone.

And the power! The raw energy! I didn't know where the Fire had come from, but I wanted it, needed it if I was to continue to rule the Chorl.

I could not deny the priest the Fire of Heaven, no matter how much it galled me.

The anger seethed beneath my skin, forced my hands into balled fists. This should not be happening. Not during my reign, not now. I'd crushed the priests, had regained the power of my family, power that had been stolen from my father.

This should not be happening!

I spun toward the warriors, saw them frowning at me darkly, their expressions troubled, rebellious.

My gaze fell on the captain of the warriors, on Atlatik, on his half-missing ear and the tattoos that riddled his face.

The warriors would side with Haqtl, with the priests, with the gods. I could see it in Atlatik's eyes, in his stance. He would do anything to thwart me, no matter what he felt about the gods, about the priests and their manipulations.

I emitted a strangled sound of frustration, the urge to lash out, to wipe the doubting looks from his and the warriors' faces, almost overwhelming.

But I needed them. I couldn't control the islands without them.

I moved to stand before the priest, glared down at him imperiously, almost reached out to strangle him when he glanced up, his eyes victorious.

"What," I spat, then tempered my voice, gritting my teeth. "What is it that the *gods* expect us to do?"

Shifting position, Haqtl's expression became serious. "We must abandon the islands. We must take to the ocean and attack the lands to the east, as we did once before."

I recoiled from Haqtl in shock, fell back into the throne, the shells of my necklace and those on the throne clattering together.

Even the warriors seemed stunned.

"What do you mean?" I said, voice weak.

Haqtl stood slowly, gathered himself together, and said calmly, "I mean that the mountain will destroy the entire island when it erupts. If we stay, we will all die.

"We must find another place to live. And the only other place to live is the coastlands to the east."

I shuddered, drew back from the Ochean's memory, my stomach sick with anger, with hatred.

Then I shifted the focus again.

The ground jolted, seemed to fall away beneath my feet. I screamed in the darkness, warriors reaching out to catch me before I fell, and then we continued running, fleeing, following a line of torches through the trees to the port, men and women and children shrieking into the night as they picked themselves up off the ground where they had fallen.

Behind, hidden by the jungle, something hideous, something horrendous, roared. A bellowing sound, like a thousand claps of thunder, that slammed into the air around me, that drowned out the screams of all of the people running to the port. My heart pounded in my chest, thudded in my ears, and I gasped, felt my escort tearing down the path around me, heard them shouting commands, shoving stragglers aside.

The ground lurched again as we crested the rise and stumbled down the slope to the beachhead, following the torches to the docks on the bay where the ships waited. Men, women, and children crowded onto decks, others scrambling up the planks.

My ship was docked at the end of the pier.

The mountain roared again, the wood of the dock shuddering, then we reached the plank and sprinted up onto the deck. As soon as I was aboard, the ship cast off, edging out into the water.

I turned, chest heaving, arms trembling with terror that was slowly beginning to calm.

Behind, on the dock, people were screaming as they tried to find room on the ships. Some had already cast off, as we had, were pulling away from the island as quickly as possible, their decks packed with panicked men and women. As I watched, some tumbled overboard.

Then the air seemed to shudder, another booming thunderclap resounded, and I jerked my attention upward.

The mountain had exploded. Thick jets of magma leaped into the sky from the crater, throwing up spumes of ash and steam and gas in a thick roiling column as black as the night. Lava flows were already streaming down the mountain's sides, rushing to the ocean.

Another thunderclap. A shuddering of the air. And what seemed like the entire western side of the mountain trembled, then slid slowly, horrifyingly, into the water.

I stared at the destruction in shock, the tremors of panic fading as the ship drew farther away from the island. But they were replaced with tremors of fear, with a hollow feeling of hopelessness, of disbelief.

The priests had been right. The mountain was tearing the island apart. There were other islands in the chain, other places to flee to, but none large enough to support the Chorl for long. If the mountain continued to erupt, the Chorl would die.

The only option was the coastland to the east. We'd attacked them once before, been repelled after five vicious years of fighting. But we'd grown since then, learned much.

A cold sensation filled the hollowness. My brow creased in thought, with purpose. I could use this. I could use this against the priests, against Haqtl. I could turn his own gods against him.

A smile touched my lips.

Perhaps the gods were correct.

Perhaps it *was* time to cross the ocean.

I shivered at the cold calculation of the Ochean's mind, skimmed farther ahead in her memories, saw the Chorl fleet gather and head east under the Ochean's and the priests' direction, watched them attack a group of islands—the Boreaite Isles—and overrun the ports. They began raiding the trading lanes, seizing entire ships and taking them back to the isles, converting them into fighting ships to expand their fleet. I watched, sickened, as they slaughtered entire crews.

And then they'd attacked *The Maiden*.

"What do we do with him?" Atlatik asked, voice rough with contempt.

I glared down at the crumpled form of the guardsman on the deck of the ship we'd just conquered. All of the other crew had been killed, and Atlatik's warriors were tethering the ship to our own so it could be towed back to the isles, the fires being put out by the Chosen.

Before I could answer, my mind spinning—he had part of the Fire of Heaven inside him! I could taste it!—someone approached from behind, Atlatik stepping to one side.

Only one other person could force Atlatik to move.

"Haqtl," I said, trying to swallow the bitterness that flooded my mouth at his name.

"Another victory," he said. "We must thank the gods."

I almost snorted, but pursed my lips instead. "The gods have favored us today."

"In what way?" Suspicious, wary. As he should be.

I smiled.

"This man has the Fire of Heaven inside him. I can feel it."

Atlatik gasped, glanced down at the man who lay unconscious on the deck, his hand moving unconsciously to the tattoos on his neck, stroking them as he uttered an inaudible prayer. He'd almost killed the man, before I'd even gotten to the ship.

Haqtl knelt down next to the bloody body, spread one hand over the man's head and closed his eyes. I felt the Elements shudder as he probed, searching.

Then even Haqtl gasped, standing quickly, as if he'd been jerked upright. He turned to me, eyes blazing with fervor. "We have to heal him, find out where he came from, find out everything we can about him."

Interesting. I could see how I'd gain control of Atlatik and the warriors, could see how I could get even the priests to follow me. This man was the key. This man, and the piece of the Fire of Heaven he carried inside him. He could lead me to the Fire itself, Haqtl would drag the Chorl there even against my wishes. I could see the intent in his eyes, could feel his body trembling with it.

But of course I wanted the Fire as much as Haqtl, wanted it even more.

I broke Haqtl's gaze, glanced down at the warrior's body. Such strange pale brown skin. And no tattoos. It made me shudder.

"Oh, I intend to find out where he came from," I said. "And when we finally begin attacking the coastline in earnest, we'll attack there first."

Haqtl breathed a sigh of relief.

Neither Haqtl nor Atlatik saw the underlying twist in my smile.

I withdrew from the Ochean's memories, stared hard into her face as my hand dropped to my side. I'd relived her memories in a matter of heartbeats, her expression still locked in shock as she recognized me.

Then it twisted into bitter hatred.

She lashed out with her sword, but the blade passed through air as Cerrin yanked me back into the crowd. The mob closed in around us instantly.

"What did you find out?" Cerrin asked.

"Why they're here, why they attacked us. Why they returned." I caught his gaze. "They had to come. The island they were living on has been destroyed. They didn't have any other place to go to."

Cerrin grunted, then swore, glancing around at the turmoil of the throne.

"What?" I asked. I could sense a change in the mob, a subtle shift.

The voices were beginning to panic.

"She's beginning to win," Cerrin answered. Overhead, the sunlit sky above the marketplace began to darken, clouds roiling in. Cerrin glanced toward them, then back down at me. "I don't think we can defeat her."

His voice had changed. The melancholy air had returned. The hatred that had enlivened it had bled away, replaced with resignation.

Around us, the jostling had eased. There didn't seem to be as many people anymore.

"We can't let her have the throne," I said, and desperation tinged my voice.

"She's too powerful," Cerrin said, and now his voice seemed dead.

The clouds had completely blanketed the sky now. The crowd had thinned to half its original number, the people that remained milling about in uncertainty, most with expressions of defeat on their faces.

Liviann suddenly appeared at my side, trailing Atreus and Garus and the rest of the Seven. "Do something! You can't let her win! She'll destroy everything!"

"I tried!" I spat. "I thought the throne would destroy her, as it did Alendor, as it almost did me!"

Liviann scowled. She turned to Cerrin. "What else can we do?"

He shook his head. "Nothing."

"We can't let her take the throne," Liviann hissed. "We can't. Not the Chorl. We defeated them once already. We can't have them back. Remember what they did. Remember the death. Remember your wife, your children, for the gods' sakes!"

"I know!" Cerrin spat, his face strangely enraged and vulnerable at the same time. "I know! They killed them, slaughtered the people of Venitte, decimated the entire southern coastline! Do you think I don't remember?"

"Then do something!" Liviann screamed.

"What?" he spat. "What can we do?"

Liviann fell into bitter silence, glanced toward me.

"Can we destroy the throne?" I asked quietly. I was thinking of their attack on Venitte, of the fires, of Cerrin's daughters. Of Erick and Laurren's sacrifice. It would all have been for nothing if the Chorl claimed the throne.

Liviann harrumphed.

But Cerrin stilled.

"What?" Liviann asked.

He stared at her in silence for a long moment, then said quietly, "We can."

Liviann frowned.

Around us, the crowd had been reduced to no more than a hundred people.

Garus shoved himself forward. "You know we can, Liviann. And it might be the only way."

"Would you rather have the Chorl take control of the throne?" Alleryn spat. "I don't like it any better than you do, but considering the consequences. . . ."

The rest of the Seven nodded in agreement.

"We'll die," Liviann said, but her voice was quiet.

"We're already dead," Cerrin said. "We've been dead for far too long."

Liviann shot him a glare, then focused on me.

There were only fifty people left in the square now.

"Here," she said, taking Cerrin's hand, "we'll show you how."

When she touched my hand, I gasped.

The clouds over the marketplace had darkened, rushed past so close to the ground I thought I could reach up and touch them. The buildings at the edge of the marketplace were gone, had blackened and vanished. There was no one left on the plaza anymore, no more voices, no more bodies, except for me.

And the Ochean.

She stood ten paces away, her blue dress sweaty, torn in a few places. Her chest heaved as she breathed in deeply, almost panting, but her expression was hard, determined. She still held the curved sword in one hand.

Reaching down, I drew the dagger from my belt, the blade dull in the half-light of the plaza.

"I can't let you have the throne," I said.

The Ochean hesitated, then grinned.

She settled into an open stance, her sword steady.

I slid into a crouch, dagger held before me.

We held each other's gazes a long moment.

And then the Ochean lurched forward, brought the sword down in a diagonal strike.

I dodged, not even attempting to parry, knowing that my dagger wouldn't last long. This was a distraction, nothing more. A ruse. But I'd try to hurt her as much as I could nonetheless, using everything Westen and Erick had taught me. As I moved, I hissed, cut upward under her guard, but she was too quick, spinning back and out of reach as she brought the sword around, slashing across my midsection. I leaped back, felt the blade slice through my shirt, felt a stinging line of fire across my stomach, felt blood. But it was only a scratch.

I settled instantly into another crouch, the Ochean doing the same. I tried to ignore the cut, but I felt my shirt sticking to the wound.

In my peripheral vision, I noticed that the marketplace had shrunk. The clouds were lower still, the darkness on the sides pulling inward as the Ochean solidified her control of the throne.

The Ochean smirked as she saw the blood staining my shirt. Anger rose, but before I could use it or suppress it, she attacked.

Her blade flashed as she cut and I dodged, stroke, counterstroke. I ducked under her guard, nicked her on the arm, and she cursed, thrust out hard. Side-stepping, I tried for another mark, but she twisted, turned her own blade inward, the edge slicing down along my thigh. I screamed, backpedaling fast to get out of reach.

I glanced down at my leg, the scent of blood sharp. This cut was deeper and burned with a white-hot intensity. I sucked in a breath through clenched teeth, blew it out through my nose. Sweat dripped from my forehead, from my hair, from my chin.

I settled into a guarded position. The Ochean did the same.

She closed in again. But this time, I couldn't dodge as quickly, the slice along my thigh burning, seething in pain. I cried out, cut in hard, and twisted as she lunged, missed, brought my dagger back up and out, but her elbow crunched into my wrist. My hand went numb, and I dropped the dagger, even as she grabbed me hard about the waist and drew me in tight against her, my head against her shoulder.

Before I could react, she brought the sword up, placed its edge against my throat.

I gasped, tried to arch away, but she tightened her grip, pressed the blade even closer, enough that I felt it cut into flesh.

I grew still.

She chuckled, the sound reverberating through my skin, her breath against my cheek.

Then the muscles in her arm tensed as she readied to slit my throat.

I closed my eyes and dove, down and down, deep inside myself, deep below the plaza, deeper and deeper into the throne, into its essence, into its heart. I felt the others in the throne brushing past me, like spider's silk, their threads subdued and tangled in the Ochean's power. I felt their wrath at being overtaken, and it drove me onward.

Until suddenly the spider's silk of the others thinned, until only seven threads remained, converging and twining together the deeper I sank, throbbing with life, with power. I followed the threads, dove faster as I felt the Ochean's blade far above begin to cut deeper, felt skin parting, felt blood beginning to flow—

And then suddenly the threads ended, all seven coming together at the throne's heart: a blinding, pulsing, pure-white light.

I hesitated a moment, transfixed. The ends of the seven threads at the center of the light touched, were held together by the Seven who had created the throne, by the strength of the magic that had bound them, by the strength of the throne itself. The raw energy, the pureness of it, made me shudder in awe.

Then I reached out, and with a twist, broke the seven threads apart.

I gasped, breath entering my lungs with a shudder, and reached up for my throat. My arm screamed with pain, my hand touching blood, and my heart stopped, fear slashing through my heart—that I'd been too late, that the Ochean had cut my throat.

But then I heard someone else gasp, heard voices cry out in shock.

I opened my eyes and stared across the stone floor of the throne room. The blood came from my split lip, not a cut throat. The pain came from the bruises of the Ochean's rage.

The Ochean.

I lurched upright, almost passed out as every muscle in my body shrieked, but steadied myself with my hands.

The Ochean still sat on the Skewed Throne. Her face was intent, focused inward, but it was the throne that caught my attention.

It had settled into a shape: a granite seat, wide, with arms that flared slightly to the side; short, fat legs; a back rounded and scalloped like a seashell.

But something wasn't quite right. One of the arms of the throne hadn't changed to fit the new form. Its top was curled, the side shaped like an S.

Like the arm of my throne.

Something pulsed, as if a wave had swept over the room, a wave felt only in your skin. The air thickened, grew suddenly heavy, and began to tingle. The guardsmen to either side shifted back; the Chorl at the door backed out into the corridor. All except the Chorl captain Atlatik and the Chorl priest Haqtl.

The Ochean stiffened, cried out sharply, then arched back, the muscles in her neck standing out in a silent scream.

Beneath her, the throne began to twist, slowly at first, then the pace accelerated, faster and faster, shifting from throne to throne, passing through all of the previous forms, from ruler to ruler starting with my own and working backward. A grating sound filled the room, began to shudder through the stone of the floor, through the pillars, escalating to a piercing shriek.

And then suddenly the throne stopped. On a form I'd seen once before, when Eryn had first thrust me onto its seat: a rough granite block with a straight rectangular back.

Its original form, before it had become the Skewed Throne, before the Seven had lost their lives in its forging.

The grating sound peaked, steadied, began to tremble—

And then it snapped.

There was no sound, no light, no smell. There was nothing to feel, nothing to touch.

Except on the river.

On the river, something exploded.

I felt the force blow over me, a gale that thrust me back, that shoved me hard into the pillar behind me, that deafened me with its intensity. It washed over me for a heartbeat, two, three . . .

And then it faded.

The density on the air sank down to nothing.

I sat on the floor and breathed in deeply, blood coating my neck, my entire body throbbing, my lip pulsing with the beat of my heart . . .

And then realized something was missing.

I could no longer feel the city, could no longer feel its pulse, the throb of its life, of its people.

I felt strangely empty. Hollow.

On the throne, the Ochean's body suddenly slumped forward, then tilted and fell to the dais, her dress rustling. Behind her, the throne split, a jagged crack appearing in the granite down its back.

No one in the throne room moved.

I shifted, winced as I pulled my legs underneath me and forced myself to a crouch, then up, using the pillar for support, until I faced the Chorl captain, until I faced Atlatik.

Trying not to tremble, gathering what little strength I had left, I growled, "It's over."

I don't know if he understood me, but he glared at me. Behind him, his warriors suddenly stepped forward, surrounding him and Haqtl in a wall of men.

Instantly, the palace guardsmen under Keven's control leaped forward, swords snicking from sheaths. I had my own escort in no more than a breath.

Pushing myself away from the pillar at my back, I stepped forward, raised my hands as if I were going to use the river, as the Ochean would have done.

Haqtl barked a sharp order, and I felt the river ripple as he erected a defense around them both.

I hesitated. I couldn't sustain another pitched battle using the river.

Haqtl spat something else, his voice leaden with scorn. He motioned toward the Ochean's dead body, to the cracked throne on the dais, and spat on the ground. He would have felt the power of the throne being released, could sense that there was no power there now.

And he could sense that the throne had nothing to do with the White Fire, what the Chorl called the Fire of Heaven.

Behind me, I heard Keven stir where he'd collapsed, regaining consciousness.

Atlatik frowned as Haqtl spoke, seemed shocked when he spat in the direction of the Ochean. But he was listening, his eyes never leaving my face.

Keven stood and came to my side, one hand on the pommel of his sword.

"Go!" I shouted at the Chorl. And then I gathered as much of the river as I could, saw Haqtl's eyes go wide, saw him reach out and catch Atlatik's arm.

Atlatik broke. With a barked order, the Chorl on edge, they began a careful backward retreat to the door of the throne room.

The palace guardsmen shifted forward, following them.

As soon as they left the room, vanishing in a sudden dash down the outside corridor, I let the river go, sweat pouring down my face.

"Mistress?" Keven said, and I heard the request in his voice.

"Kill them," I said, voice wavering with exhaustion, thinking of Erick, of Laurren, of everyone who'd died in the city today. "Kill them all."

And then I collapsed.

✠— Epilogue —✠

I awoke in my chambers, the breeze from the ocean billowing in the curtains over the balcony. Keven was speaking quietly to Avrell and Eryn near the open doorway, half hidden by the curtains.

I tried to sit up, but moaned instead.

The conversation broke off, and all three rushed over to the bed, smiling. Eryn seemed on the verge of tears, and even Avrell's smile was strained, the skin around his eyes tight. His arm was in a sling and tied across his chest.

"Don't get up," Keven commanded. "The healer said you weren't to move."

I didn't tell him I couldn't move. Every part of my body protested when I breathed.

I caught Avrell's eyes, held them. "The Chorl?"

He straightened. "They retreated to their ships and left."

"Once the Ochean died," Keven added, "all of the fight seemed to leave them. We harried them to the wharf, slaughtered them as they boarded their ships."

I sighed in relief. Amenkor had been the Ochean's target, Haqtl's target, not Atlatik's. And they'd wanted the Fire of Heaven. Once Haqtl realized the Fire wasn't here, there was no reason to stay and fight. Not when they'd lost the Ochean.

"And the city?"

Avrell smiled thinly. "It will survive."

I snorted, but nodded, settling back into the pillows.

"Varis?" Eryn stepped forward, her face lined with concern. There were shadows under her eyes, and it looked as if she'd aged ten years. One arm lay over her stomach and I remembered the pain she'd felt as she'd resisted the Ochean's advance at the gates. "Varis, the throne—"

"I know," I said, cutting her off.

She didn't know what to say, her expression lost.

Then Keven cleared his throat and Eryn stepped back awkwardly. "There is one other thing," he said, then hesitated, as if uncertain he should tell me.

"What?"

He glanced toward Avrell and Eryn, then said, "Westen brought Erick back."

I sat up instantly, sucked in a sharp breath, and through gritted teeth said, "Take me to him."

All three seemed about to protest.

I let my expression darken.

"Take me to him *now*."

Westen had hidden Erick in a back room of a tavern near the wharf, afraid to move him any farther from the ships in the condition he was in.

The captain of the Seekers opened the door warily, the room beyond dark, so that I couldn't even see him through the crack. But a moment later, he opened the door completely and stepped aside, going to light a lantern.

I moved to the edge of the bed that had been shoved into the far corner and stared down at Erick. Avrell hovered at my side, ready to catch me if I fell. Keven stood on the other side.

Erick's eyes were closed, his face twisted up in pain. Sweat glistened on his forehead, and his skin was pale, the bones of his cheeks clear. His torso was covered in cuts and burns, the skin around most of the wounds red and swollen. Where the Ochean had not touched him, you could see the older scars, covering his chest, his arms; the scars of a Seeker.

"The healer said he should recover," Westen said from deeper in the room. His voice was muted.

I nodded. I couldn't speak. Something had forced itself up from my chest and lodged itself in my throat, something hot and solid. I swallowed, but it didn't seem to help.

I reached out a tentative hand and touched Erick lightly on the forehead.

For a moment, his pain seemed to ease, as if he sensed the touch, but as soon as I withdrew, his face contorted again.

I fought for control, and when I felt composed, turned to Westen.

The Seeker had seated himself in a chair against the wall, his arm resting on the table beside the lantern. Like Eryn, he also looked older, and I thought suddenly of his wife, of his son, wondered if they'd survived the battle.

But instead, I asked, "The priest? The man who guarded him on the ship?"

He shook his head. "He wasn't there." He sounded disappointed.

For some reason, I wasn't surprised.

I nodded, glanced back to Erick.

Avrell shifted awkwardly. "Do you think they'll be back?"

I thought about the Ochean, about Haqtl and the priests and the volcanic islands that had been their home, about the Chorl captain, Atlatik, then sighed.

"They'll be back," I said. "They have nowhere else to go."

The Vacant Throne

Part I: Amenkor

✛ Chapter 1

I stood in the middle of a field of wheat, the bristly heads of grain pattering against my outstretched hands. The breeze that rippled through the stalks tugged at my hair, at the folds of my sweat-stained shirt. In the moment before dawn, the world was quiet, expectant.

Then, far ahead over the fields, near the road that snaked down from the city of Venitte into the hills, a flare of light lit the darkness. Harsh and orange, the fire arched up into the sky, and I felt a tug of grief, a pain that bit deeper every time I felt it, still new and raw and fresh. It twisted in my chest, burned at the edges of my eyes, but I clenched my jaw as I watched the fire crest, begin a long descent, fall down and down—

And explode among the trunks of olive trees. In the burst of light when it struck, I saw an army marching through the fields. A moment later I heard screams, faint with distance.

The pain in my chest writhed.

I'd moved before I'd made a conscious decision to move, pushed through the wheat toward the road. As I plowed forward, grain rattling against my legs, catching, holding me back, more fire bloomed and I marked its source, marked my

targets. Then I reached the road, broke into a sprint, the screams from my fellow
Venittians among the olive trees growing louder. Heart thundering in my chest, I
stretched out with my mind, drew the Threads around me, wove them tight,
bound them, twisted them, prepared. Ahead, the screams intensified, grew heated,
broke into a rumbling roar of challenge and hatred and fear as the two armies
met. Sunlight touched the surrounding hills and fields with a patina of gold, although I didn't need the light. Through the Threads, I could see everything. The
Venittians charged through the low, flattened branches of the olives, fire lancing
out, roaring through their ranks, leaving behind charred bodies and burning trees,
and in the backwash of light . . .

The Chorl—skin tainted a faint blue, like winter sky, tattoos black in the
dawn, faces contorted with rage. The Chorl—curved steel swords raised to the sky
as they screamed in a harsh, ululating language.

The Chorl—who had killed my wife and two daughters.

Cold, hard-edged rage tingled through my skin, rippled out on the Threads I'd
bound around me, and I slowed as I came at the battle from the side. No need to
run. There were plenty of Chorl to kill. They'd invaded the Frigean coast two
weeks before, invaded the city of Venitte. They'd come from the western sea with
no warning, had attacked the port and overrun a significant portion of the city
before anyone had known what was happening.

But the Chorl themselves were not my targets. I would have attacked with the
rest of the Venittian army if they had been. No, the attack was a diversion, the
army bait. I wanted the Adepts, the ones wielding the Threads, the ones who'd
thrown the fire that had killed so many in that initial attack on the city.

The ones who had killed Olivia, who'd killed five-year-old Jaer and her older
sister Pallin.

I slid past the first of the Chorl, moving slowly, calmly, their piercing howls
surrounding me as they tried to surge forward to the front of the battle. They
broke around me as if I were a stone in their currents, not consciously realizing
what they were doing, the Threads shunting them to one side while concealing me
from their sight. I angled toward the back of their forces, focusing on the source of
the fire that still arched up out of their ranks. The Chorl thinned. The road ended,
and I was once again among wheat, the stalks trampled into the earth, broken
and shattered. Ahead, a Chorl woman in a mud-splattered dress wove the Sight
into a tight, blazing fireball and hurled it high into the air, her face strained with
effort, sweat streaming down her cheeks, down the cold blue skin of her throat,
where corded muscle stood out in stark relief. She was surrounded by ten Chorl
warriors and two Chorl priests. The warriors were dressed in a riot of colors—
blue, red, orange, green—over crude leather armor. Their eyes were locked on the
battle behind me, their bodies tense, hands on the hilts of their swords. The priests
were dressed in vibrant yellow-and-red robes and wore necklaces of shells. One

carried a scepter of some type of reed and feathers. All of the men were covered in tattoos; on their faces, their necks, their hands. The woman wore five earrings in each ear, the gold glinting occasionally through the long strands of her black hair. She had no visible tattoos whatsoever, her skin flawless.

I slipped through the ring of warriors without them noticing, one sidling away from me as I passed, and halted in front of the woman, looked up into her dark eyes, a surge of regret passing through me that there was only one Chorl Adept in this attack. This close, I could smell her sweat, could hear the priests chanting under their breath on either side of her, could feel the tension coursing around me on the Threads. It reeked of fear, of blood, of trampled wheat.

I glared up into the woman's face.

Someone like this had stood on the Chorl ships that had entered Venitte's harbor and attacked the fishing and trading ships, catching them unaware. Someone like this had flung fireball after fireball up onto the cliffs and houses that surrounded the harbor, had flung the fireball that had killed Olivia and Jaer and Pallin.

Jaer. I felt again her charred skin as I clutched her small body to my chest, felt it flaking off beneath my touch.

Only five years old.

The pain stabbed into my chest again, and tears seared the corners of my eyes. The queasy rush of emotion closed off my throat with the hot, sickening taste of phlegm, and I flung out my arms to both sides, gathering more Threads to me as bitter rage flooded my mouth, stained my tongue. I could kill them all with a touch of my hand, could stop their hearts in their chests. They'd drop to the ground, dead before they even knew what had happened. I could send invisible needles of pain into their skin and flay them where they stood. I could call down lightning from the clear morning sky, or open up the earth beneath them and bury them alive. I could kill them all in a hundred different ways, using any or all of the Five Magics.

I chose fire.

In the moment before I ignited the Threads I'd woven around them all—the priests, the warriors, the Adept—the Chorl woman tensed. Through the tears blurring my eyes, I saw her frown, a fireball half formed before her. She sensed something. A ripple on the Threads, a disturbance on the ether. Or perhaps she'd heard the sob that had escaped me.

It didn't matter. I didn't give her a chance to react.

I let the fire loose, roared as I ignited the Threads that bound the twelve Chorl men and the Adept together. A roar of grief, of pain that would never end, formless and harsh and guttural. Eyes clenched shut, I felt the shock of the priests and warriors and the woman in the single breath before the fire struck them, before it consumed them, flinging them back with its force, scorching through clothing,

*through flesh, through bone, as the fire that had charred the flesh from Olivia
and Jaer and Pallin had done. I poured all of my sorrow into it, all of my rage,
all of the feelings of uselessness and despair I'd felt in the last two weeks as the
peace of the Frigean coast collapsed under the Chorl onslaught. And when I felt
the last breath of life flee, when the thirteen charred bodies lay around me in a
grisly circle, I collapsed to my knees, panting, head bowed, tears still streaming
down my face, hands clenched in fists at my sides.*

*Because the pain still beat with my heart. It burned through my veins, prick-
led in my skin.*

I sobbed.

*I should have died with them. I should have died protecting Olivia, my body
shielding her from the fire, not the other way around.*

*I lifted my head, stared at the blackened bodies, felt the rage boil up again,
bitter as ash, then turned to gaze up into the lightening sky.*

It wasn't enough. It would never be enough.

*I stood slowly, rage settling around me. A calm rage filled with nothing but
grief. With nothing but visions of Olivia on the veranda, held in my arms. Of the
scent of her hair, the smoothness of her skin. Of the sounds of Jaer and Pallin
shrieking in delight as they played around us.*

*I turned, cloaked in memories, and waded into the Chorl forces from behind,
trailing fire and death behind me.*

I woke with a gasp and an ache in my chest like a hand gently crushing the life
from me. I tasted hot, fresh tears, realized that I'd been crying as I slept, my
muscles stiff with tension, my body drained, overwhelmed by grief.

But not my own grief. Someone else's. The man in the dream; a man I knew.
Cerrin.

I dove beneath the river, hope surging forward, the dark room before me
shifting subtly, becoming gray and partially visible with the Sight. I could see
the edges of the bed I slept in, could see the settee where the Servant Marielle
instructed me in writing and math, could see the tables and chairs and the
bowl that contained water so I could wash my face. A breeze blew the curtains
back from the doors leading out to the balcony, scented with ocean salt and
spring night. The balcony overlooked the city of Amenkor. My city, for I was
the Mistress.

And we'd survived the winter . . . and an attack by the Chorl.

But at a cost.

I closed my eyes, reached out on the river toward the Skewed Throne,
toward the symbol of Amenkor's power. Cerrin had been a part of the throne,
one of the personalities that had been trapped within it, one of the original

seven Adepts that had created the throne almost fifteen hundred years before, when the Chorl had first attacked. If I'd been dreaming of him, had lived out one of his memories, then perhaps . . .

The hope that quickened my heartbeat died.

The throne wasn't there. I couldn't touch it, couldn't feel it enfolding me with its power.

Because it was dead. Because I'd destroyed it in order to save Amenkor from the Chorl. From their leader, the Ochean.

I opened my eyes, pushed myself up and to the edge of the bed with a sigh. The tightness of grief in my chest had receded, but not much. I knew I wouldn't sleep anymore, so I rose and moved across the room to the curtains, stepped out onto the balcony.

As in the dream, the sky overhead was just beginning to lighten with dawn. If the balcony had faced east, I would have seen the eastern mountains lined with golden light.

Instead, I stared down into the husk of what once had been Amenkor, watched the details of the damage done by the Chorl attack emerge as the sun rose. The watchtowers at the ends of the juts of land that protected the harbor were nothing more than heaps of broken stone. The Chorl had destroyed them first, stone and debris arching up and out into the darkness: our first warning that the Chorl had arrived. I shivered at the memory, at the raw power it had taken to destroy them. So much power it had left vortices in the eddies of the river for days afterward.

Then the Chorl's black ships had knifed into the harbor, where they'd been met by the trading ships, and the real battle had begun. What ships remained from that attack were anchored off the shattered piers, both Amenkor and Chorl ships alike. In their haste to retreat, harried by Amenkor guardsmen and militia, the Chorl had left some of their own ships behind. Small boats ferried men to and fro between them even now. The wharf itself had been utterly destroyed when the Chorl drove their ships into the docks.

From there a clear path of destruction wound upward, from the wharf up through the lower city, through the twisting streets, through the marketplaces, to the gates of the outer wall of the palace. Buildings had been consumed by fire, stone walls collapsing under the heat. Hastily constructed barricades had been breached, the chairs and tables and crab traps used to make them tossed aside. The Chorl had destroyed everything as they came, might have razed the entire city in their fervor, but they'd been intent on reaching the palace, on reaching and seizing control of the throne.

They'd almost succeeded. The gates to the three walls that surrounded the palace had been breached in the span of an hour, the Ochean and the Chorl

Servants—the women like me that could wield the river; the women Cerrin had called Adepts in the dream—had blown the gates apart. Only Eryn, the previous Mistress, had been able to slow them, and only then with my help.

I stared down at the jagged holes in the three walls, tasted again Eryn's desperation to hold against the combined strength of the Ochean and her Servants. They'd linked their powers somehow, so that the Ochean's power had been augmented by her Servants.

We'd never had a chance.

But we'd prevailed in the end. After I'd killed the Ochean—and in the process destroyed the throne—Captain Catrell, Keven, and the rest of the guardsmen and militia had driven the Chorl back to their ships, had driven them back out to sea. The Chorl had retreated, and hadn't been seen since.

On the balcony, overlooking the blackened buildings and streets of Amenkor, I straightened, felt a tightness in my chest. We'd survived the winter, the late winter planting ready to be harvested in another few weeks, the early spring planting already in the ground. The shipment of grain from the northern city of Merrell—promised to us at the beginning of winter—had finally arrived over the treacherous northern road. The Dredge was intact, left untouched by the Chorl, as well as the eastern portions of the city.

We were wounded, but we'd survived.

I knew the Chorl would be back. They wouldn't stop attacking the coast, couldn't stop. Because they couldn't return to their homeland. I'd seen it destroyed through the Ochean's eyes when she'd attempted to seize control of the throne. The Chorl had simply retreated to the Boreaite Isles off the Frigean coast. To regroup, to plan. They couldn't stay on the Isles forever. There were too many Chorl for the islands to support.

But for now, the fact that we'd survived their initial attack was enough.

I took one last long look out over the charred city, plans already forming in my mind. We'd had two weeks to burn the dead, to grieve, to clean up and take stock, to begin drilling the citizens in their own defense in case the Chorl returned. It was time to start building again.

"No, no! Take the reusable stone over there. The rest pile up on the side street so that we can cart it off later." Avrell shook his head, one hand on his hip. The other arm was tied up in a sling across his chest, his shoulder hurt during the attack on the walls. The First of the Mistress, Avrell oversaw the administrative details of Amenkor, which included its rebuilding.

He turned as he heard my escort's approach, his posture stiffening, becoming more formal as he raised one eyebrow in question. He would have folded his hands inside the sleeves of his dark blue robes if he could have, but the sling wouldn't allow it. "Mistress? How may I help you?"

"Actually," I said, "I came to help you." I reached down and picked up a chunk of shattered stone, what had once been part of the outermost wall of the palace. We stood where the gates had held the Chorl at bay . . . for approximately ten minutes. Weighing the stone in one hand, I glanced around at the jagged edges of the wall to either side, at the debris that lay in a fan spread outward from where we stood into the outer ward. I could see how much force had been behind the explosion in the pattern of stone, could see where the stone arch over the gates had collapsed in upon itself once the wall had been breached. Buildings to either side of the wide street leading up to the palace had been shattered in the blast, walls caved in, windows and doors nothing but gaping, empty holes. One entire building had sagged inward, on the verge of imploding. It reminded me of the Dredge. Except this damage was new, fresh. The pall of dust still hung in the air, the broken stone sharp with edges. On the Dredge, everything would have been coated with the slick ruin of age, would have reeked of decay, would be worn smooth with defeat.

A narrow corridor had been cleared through the debris immediately after the attack, to allow access between the city and the palace, but other than that, everything lay where it had fallen.

I turned back to Avrell with a grunt. "And I brought helpers." I motioned to Keven, my personal escort, and the remaining guardsmen behind me. They shifted in surprise, until Keven gave them a harsh glare.

"You heard the Mistress," he barked. "Let's move some stone! Arcus, you take the left, I'll handle the right. Move, move!"

I grinned as Avrell's eyebrows rose in surprise, then reached down and picked up a few more chunks of stone, moving to toss them into the discard heap. All around us, the men and women of Avrell's work detail paused in surprise as well, then grinned as the guardsmen joined them. They'd gotten used to the guardsmen being in the city since the attack.

Avrell watched until he was satisfied the two groups were working well together, then turned back to me, taking up a position halfway between the pile of stone I was digging into and the heap that would be carted out into the city.

"You shouldn't be doing this," he said in disapproval.

"Why not?" I gasped, straining as I hauled a stone a little too heavy for me to the reusable heap.

"Because you're the Mistress."

I snorted. "And . . . ?"

Avrell pursed his lips but didn't answer.

I motioned to Avrell's work detail. It was composed of only fifteen men and women, all of them still lean from the harsh winter, most from the lower city— the portion above the wharf but below the walls. I knew there would be other work details like this one spread throughout the city. Catrell would be at the wharf, overseeing the cleanup there; Nathem—the Second—would be doing the same on the Dredge, which had been left mostly untouched, and in the lower city. Darryn was in the marketplace, training any citizens who would come in the basics of swordsmanship and self-defense. "You need the help, Avrell. And we don't have enough people to let anyone rest." I paused as the words sank in. "How bad is it? Do we have anything other than estimates yet?"

He frowned as he glanced around at those working. "Nothing precise. But at this point I don't think we'll ever have anything precise. We lost almost half of the militia in the attack, mostly men from the Dredge. Darryn's men."

I grimaced. Darryn had been a dispossessed mercenary, relegated to the Dredge when the White Fire had scoured its way across the city and sent the trade routes into a death spiral, cutting off his source of income as a guard-for-hire. I'd gone against Baill's and Catrell's wishes and put him in charge of the militia after he'd helped quell one riot and interceded in another to save Avrell's life. But Captain Baill had ended up betraying us to the Chorl, and Catrell had changed his mind after training with those from the Dredge for a few weeks.

And Darryn had done well, keeping those on the Dredge alive as best he could, protecting the warehouse and kitchen we'd set up there to feed them. During the Chorl attack, he'd led the Dredge in a raid on the Chorl's flanks, had kept the Chorl out of the slums altogether.

Since then, the people of Amenkor had been calling him Lord of the Dredge. Not the most gratifying title, but fitting. It was also the reason he'd been chosen to teach the citizens how to fight. They already trusted him, and he could relate to them better than Catrell.

"And what about the people? What about the guardsmen?" I asked.

"There were casualties among the people, but it's hard to judge how many. If we include the Dredge, we never had a viable count to start with. We lost some to starvation, others to disease, and then the Chorl arrived. . . ."

I stopped hauling stone, caught Avrell's gaze. "How many?"

"Three to four hundred. Maybe more."

I winced as if punched in the gut, the sensation similar to the pain that Cerrin had felt over the loss of his wife and daughters. Similar, but not the same. Not as visceral; not as deep.

"And the guard?"

"A third of the men died in the attack, about eighty overall."

I lowered my head a moment, closed my eyes, then straightened and returned to sorting stone. I'd known the losses had been bad. I'd watched the columns of oily black smoke rise from the stockyards to the east of the city, where the bodies had been taken to be burned to prevent the spread of disease. Some of those burned had been Chorl, but not all.

The smoke had marred the sky for four days.

"What else?" I asked, shrugging the grisly image aside.

"We've cleared the majority of the streets between here and the wharf as you directed. I have men inspecting the watchtowers now, to determine what's necessary to make repairs there. The engineers are already arguing about how to repair the three gates and the walls."

"Good," I said.

"May I ask why?"

I halted, wiped sweat that had mixed with grit and dust from the stone from my forehead. My shirt stuck to my back, my hair lying in sweaty tendrils across my forehead and neck. "What do you mean?"

"Why rebuild the watchtowers, the walls, when we know the Chorl can destroy them so easily?" he spat, his free hand motioning toward all the debris, his face twisted into a scowl. He shifted where he stood, unable to look at me. "Why waste the effort?"

The bitterness shocked me, and hidden behind that, the fear.

Then I remembered. He'd stood on one of these walls during the battle, had watched the Chorl approach, had felt the wall crumbling beneath him.

And he'd been helpless, unable to do anything but choke on the dust and escape before the shattered stone crushed him.

"Because," I started to say, then hesitated. Avrell needed more than a flippant answer.

I moved toward him, caught his gaze, held it, my expression stern, harsh. "Because the Chorl will come back, Avrell. And the Chorl—the warriors themselves—can be stopped by the walls, by the watchtowers and the gates. The Ochean and the Servants destroyed the walls last time, and the Ochean is dead."

"There will be another," he said hoarsely.

"But we'll be better prepared for her and the Chorl Servants next time. With Darryn's training, the citizens will be better able to defend against the Chorl warriors. I've learned a few things about the Chorl and their Servants since then. And I intend to learn even more."

He heard the emphasis I placed on the last sentence. His brow creased in confusion, then smoothed in comprehension.

We'd found more than the dead in the debris of Amenkor. But only a few knew about our captive—Keven, Eryn, Avrell, Catrell, and Westen, the captain of the Seekers; the Seekers and Servants who guarded her; and the guardsmen who had found her, of course.

Avrell's eyes searched mine, and then he nodded.

"What about the wharf?" I asked, brushing dust off of my clothes.

"The engineers and carpenters say it can be rebuilt easily, in comparison to the rest of what needs to be done."

"Good. Have them start on that as soon as they're ready."

"And where are you going?" he asked as I moved toward Keven.

"To visit Erick," I said, and then, my voice laced with hatred, "and after that, our . . . guests."

There were two guardsmen outside the door to the chambers I'd had Avrell set up for Erick, one of them a Seeker. He nodded as I approached, murmured, "Mistress."

"Tomus," I said. I knew all the Seekers by name; had trained with them under Westen's direction. "How is he?"

Tomus didn't need to answer, I saw it in his eyes and felt something grip my heart and squeeze.

I dropped my gaze, not willing to let Tomus see the pain, then straightened my shoulders with an effort and stepped past the two guards to the door. I heard Keven following, almost ordered him to wait outside . . . but Erick had chosen Keven to take his place as my personal guard after I'd sent him on the trading ship we'd used as a lure to draw the Chorl out of hiding. It had been a trap, one that those on the ship hadn't been expected to survive.

And only one of those on the ship had.

I stepped into a room harsh with sunlight, glanced sharply toward the servant inside, to the healer Isaiah who'd been assigned permanently to Erick's care, the same healer that Borund had found to help William when he'd been stabbed by Charls' men. Isaiah met my gaze without flinching, stood abruptly behind the desk where he'd been sitting, one hand keeping his place in the book he was reading. He was thin—we were all thin after the winter—but his was a natural thinness, not one brought on solely by starvation. A slim build, narrow face, sharp features. Lanky brown hair peppered with gray fell down over the narrow glasses he wore for reading. He was dressed like a merchant's apprentice: white shirt, brown-cloth breeches, shoes rather than boots. Except, unlike an apprentice, his breeches were tied off at the knees and beneath those, visible from shoe to knee—

I halted. "What are those?"

Isaiah frowned, caught off guard. "What are what, Mistress?"

"Those," I said, motioning toward his legs.

He glanced downward, still frowning. "Ah. You mean my stockings."

"Stockings?"

"Yes," he said, a little sarcastic. "Something to cover my legs when I wear shoes instead of boots. To keep warm."

"They look . . ." Stupid, I almost said, but caught myself, fumbling for something else instead.

Isaiah raised an eyebrow and waited, shifting where he stood.

I was saved by Erick, who sighed heavily and stirred.

Both Isaiah and I looked toward the bed, and both of us moved at the same moment, Isaiah unconsciously placing a small rectangular stone in the book to hold it open. We went to opposite sides of the bed, Isaiah leaning forward to scan Erick's face, reaching for his wrist to take his pulse. The servant assigned to assist Isaiah moved up beside him, a damp cloth in one hand; I felt Keven halt behind me.

I stared down into Erick's face and tensed.

Erick's gray-brown hair lay matted to his head with sweat, his skin held a sick pallor I'd seen on the Dredge a hundred times. Those who'd looked like this had been avoided by even the deepest denizens of the slums, the threat of disease on the Dredge a constant fear. He was covered in scars—on his face, on his chest and arms and shoulders—most of them old, achingly familiar to me after days upon days of training with him, but some were new, given to him by the Ochean, by Haqtl—the leader of the Chorl priests—and by the priests that had tortured him to find out about the Fire. A Fire I'd placed inside of Erick so that I could see who attacked the ship we'd sent as bait. In the process they'd learned of the Skewed Throne.

And that had led them to Amenkor.

My hand itched, fingers opening and closing into a fist. I wanted my dagger, wanted its weight in my hand, wanted the comforting feel of the handle pressing into my skin. I wanted to hunt, to kill, the instinct trained into me by Erick on the Dredge. But I choked the instinct down, tasted bitterness and blood as I did so, and swallowed hard.

"What's wrong with him?" I asked.

Isaiah shook his head. "I don't know. He should have healed completely by now, at least in body, if not in mind. He should have woken, should be conscious. His wounds have healed a little, but not as they normally would have, and the fever, the tremors . . . He should have healed. It's as if something is actively stopping him from healing."

The servant brushed Isaiah's arm, and he took the proffered cloth, wiping the sweat from Erick's brow. Erick moaned, the sound long and low and torn. Isaiah grimaced, then caught my eye.

"I'm not certain there's anything else I can do."

I heard the dry bitterness in his voice, saw the grudging defeat and despair in his eyes. He'd been dealing with Erick for the last two weeks, first down in the back room of a tavern on the wharf, where Westen had stowed Erick after retrieving him from the Chorl ship where he'd been held captive, then later when we'd moved him up to the palace. At first, Isaiah had been optimistic, claiming Erick would be awake and moving around within a week. But then, after a week had passed, after ten days . . .

Erick began trembling, shudders running up through his body, his arms flopping at his sides, dead white and lax. It hurt to watch, hurt even more when Isaiah and the servant reached out to control him and he cried out, face twisted with pain, tears squeezing from the corners of his eyes. I felt an invisible hand clench around my throat, felt my lungs burn as Erick's trembling intensified, his cry escalating into a scream—

And then the trembling stopped, Erick's body falling back to the bed, his scream cut short, breath escaping in a long, wheezing sigh.

Isaiah, hands on Erick's shoulders, weight leaned into Erick's chest, hesitated a moment, then drew back. "I just don't know what else to do except wait."

We stood a moment in silence.

Then I said, "Keven, catch me."

As I dove for the river, I heard Keven say, "What?" Then I Reached for the Fire inside of Erick. I hadn't tried to Reach inside anyone since destroying the throne—there'd been no need—but now I wanted . . . no, *needed* . . . to know whether Erick was suffering. And so I Reached for him.

Except it wasn't as easy without the power of the throne behind me.

I gasped as I hit a wall, as if something were trying to hold me back, to keep me from stretching outside my body. But I gathered all of my anger—all of the pain of watching Erick day after day in this state, all of the guilt I felt for sending him on a mission in which I knew he might be killed—I gathered all of that emotion into a sliver-thin blade and thrust it through the wall, pierced it with a sharp pain, and then I sped across the short distance to Erick, to the Fire that burned in his soul as behind I heard Keven curse and catch my body as it sagged and fell—

And then I was inside Erick, and the pain . . . the pain *burned*.

I writhed beneath it, drawing the Fire up higher around me, blocking the pain out, separating myself from Erick, until I huddled inside the Fire, completely free, gasping. The pain had been unexpected, because there was nothing, no wound, no visible reason why Erick should be in such pain.

But he obviously was. And perhaps from here, I could figure out why.

As the last of the burning sensation faded, I gathered myself, then Reached out and touched the Fire, let its protective flames relax, let what Erick felt seep inward so that I felt what he felt. But slowly.

I hissed when the pain first touched me, crawling across my skin like a thousand stinging ants. I held the pain constant, until I'd grown used to the sensation, and then I relaxed the Fire even more. The prickling of ants increased steadily, penetrated deeper, until it felt like a heavy blanket of needles, hot and piercing, just beneath the skin.

And then the pain leveled out. It still seethed against Erick's skin, but it no longer grew in intensity.

I drew in a ragged breath, held it a moment, then released it in a sigh. I felt Erick's chest rise and hold, heard him sigh through his own ears. His heart pulsed in his chest, strong and steady. Here and there, through the blanket of needles, I could feel smaller aches, recognized the places where he'd been cut while being tortured, where there were wounds that were not healing as fast as Isaiah expected. But these wounds were minor. His body was trying to fight the stinging needles, trying to heal that pain instead.

But it couldn't. There was nothing tangible for it to heal. It was pouring all of Erick's energy into a hopeless battle.

I turned my attention away from Erick's body, began searching for Erick himself.

I found him curled in upon himself in the deepest recesses of his mind. He lay huddled, trembling slightly, but not moving. This was how I'd found him on the Chorl ship, the pain inflicted upon him so great he'd retreated into himself, shut himself off from the world.

And his situation hadn't improved much since then. We thought we were healing him. And we had to some extent. His muscles no longer felt bruised, no longer hurt from kicks and blows. His chest and neck no longer ached from screaming. He'd healed a little.

But not enough. Because the pain hadn't stopped.

I drifted down beside him, reached out and brushed his forehead, a gesture he'd done to me a thousand times since he'd first found me on the Dredge, vomiting over the dead body of the second man I'd killed.

His body hitched at the touch and I leaned in closer.

Erick.

Another hitch. The trembling halted a moment, then resumed.

Erick, it's Varis.

Erick shuddered with a sob, his body pulling in tighter upon itself, his emotions twisting—regret, defeat, tenderness, and sorrow. Disappointment. But not with me. With himself.

He thought he'd failed me.

I felt my own heart clench, felt something hard and hot lodge in my throat. I stretched out, enfolded myself around him, pulled him in tight. And everywhere our essences touched I sent out comfort, sent out relief, sent out joy that he was alive. It pulsed through me, the same joy I'd felt when I'd first found him, only this time devoid of all the accompanying rage. I'd expelled that rage when I'd cracked the throne, when I'd released its power and destroyed the Ochean.

You haven't failed me, I whispered, sending the sentiment through the contact, pushing it forward. *You've never failed me . . . Father.*

Erick sobbed, something inside him releasing. I held on, letting the emotions flood through him, letting them flow outward and away.

A pang of guilt bled through me, and I felt tears burn my own eyes. I should have come sooner, should have checked on him sooner. I should have tried to reach him here, through the Fire.

No.

I stilled, pulled away from his essence. He still curled in upon himself, but the trembling had stopped and the sobbing had quieted. The tenderness and sorrow remained, but the regret, the defeat and disappointment, had been replaced by weariness.

His eyes were open, focused on me.

No. You came soon enough.

I shuddered, swallowed against the hardness lodged in my throat. I couldn't speak.

Varis. His voice caught, edged with pain. His eyes closed as he winced, then opened again, his essence hard and intense. A Seeker's essence. An assassin's essence. *Make it stop, Varis. Do whatever you have to do, but make it stop.*

Then his eyes closed and he retreated. Back into himself, back into the protective shell he'd hidden behind since the trading ship *The Maiden* had been captured and he'd fallen under the Ochean's and Haqtl's control.

But he no longer felt as tense.

I retreated back into the Fire, the sensation of the stinging needles fading, then pushed myself up and out, catching a flicker of my body slumped over into a chair hastily pushed up to Erick's bed before I fell back into myself.

I gasped, felt tremors sinking into my arms even as I drew in a breath, tasted the salt of my tears on my lips. "Gods!"

"Mistress," Keven said, stepping forward smartly, kneeling at my side. I tried to raise a hand to my face, to scrub away the last sensation of burning skin I'd pulled back with me from Erick, to wipe away the tears, but I couldn't lift my arm. "Mistress, are you all right?"

"Give me a moment," I said. Reaching for such a short distance, for such a short time, had never been this taxing.

I grimaced. Because of the throne. I'd used more of the throne's power as support than I'd imagined in the last few months. I'd come to rely on it. I'd have to be careful. I could overextend myself without thinking, counting on the throne to supplement me when the throne no longer existed.

"Here."

I glanced up, even the simple act of lifting my head difficult.

The servant held out a cup of tea, the scent from the steam intoxicating. I smiled, took a sip from the cup as she held it up to my lips, the tea sending warm tendrils of energy down through my limbs. The tremors in my arms quieted.

The servant nodded as I found the strength to take the cup from her. Behind her and Keven, Isaiah fidgeted, his thin features pinched with worry.

"What did you find out?" the healer asked, voice curt.

Keven glared at him, but he didn't seem to notice.

"He's in a lot of pain," I said.

Isaiah frowned, brushed past Keven to lean over Erick's body. "What kind of pain? Where's it coming from? I couldn't find anything broken internally, no shattered bones except the rib that I've already reset. Is it his liver? His spleen? Something bleeding internally? What about—"

"It's none of those things," I said weakly, and suddenly I remembered the Chorl ship, remembered finding Erick in excruciating pain, body crumpled on the floor of the Ochean's shipboard chambers, the room rocking gently with the waves. I remembered prying open one of his eyes, taking in the folds of silken cloth hanging from the walls, the pillows that covered the floor, all shades of blues and greens and gold.

And I remembered the Chorl priest who had guarded him. The man had goaded Erick, thinking it was Erick looking out through those eyes, not me. And when the priest had seen my rage over what they'd done, seen that rage reflected in Erick's eyes, he'd reached forward and done something on the river, something I couldn't see, something I could only sense.

The blanket of burning needles had covered Erick then, and with a touch by this priest, that blanket had erupted into molten agony—agony that had almost killed Erick. The priest had brought Erick to the edge of death . . . and then had backed off, had released whatever pressure he'd applied to the river, and the pain had subsided.

My eyes darkened, and I caught Isaiah's gaze. "It's the river," I said, and Isaiah's brow creased in confusion. "The Chorl did something on the river. That's what's keeping Erick from healing. They've cast some kind of spell over him."

"Can you break it?" From Keven and Isaiah both, short and sharp.

I stood, felt the others step back. All except Keven, who shifted forward to my side, in case I needed the support. But the weakness had passed. I set the cup of tea aside and moved toward the bed, sinking beneath the river as I went.

Carefully, I searched the river around Erick from head to toe, feeling his essence in the eddies and flows as I looked, breathing in the pungent scent of oranges that I associated with him, with safety. . . .

Then I shook my head.

"I can't even sense it, whatever it is."

"Which means what?" Isaiah this time.

I frowned. "I don't know." And then I thought of the guests currently residing in the palace's prison, of one guest in particular. "But I know someone who might."

As we left Erick's chambers, I told Keven where I intended to go. His brow creased with disapproval, but without a word he motioned one of the escorting guardsmen to gather a few extra guards to accompany us.

"You should also summon another Servant," he said, catching my eye briefly as we moved. "Just in case."

I shot him a dark look. "I can handle it."

He grunted. "She almost escaped the first time she woke. She laid out three guards before we even knew she'd regained consciousness. If Marielle hadn't been there . . ."

"I know," I said, thankful that Marielle had been there. I bit my lip, was about to concede to Keven's advice when Eryn, the previous Mistress, rounded a corner twenty steps away. She wore a simple white dress, embroidered at the cuffs and neck in blue and gold. Soot stains marred it from the knees down and the edges of the sleeves. One black handprint was clearly visible on the front, as if she'd clutched her left side. She halted when she saw us approaching and smiled.

"Good," she said, matching our stride and falling into step beside me. She smelled of ash and sea salt. "Exactly who I was looking for. I went down to the wharf with Catrell and his group and have news from the engineers looking at the damage." She paused and frowned when Keven and I turned right at the next corner and began descending to the lower levels of the palace. "Where are we going?"

"To visit our prisoner," Keven grumbled, although he'd relaxed somewhat now that Eryn had joined us.

"Which one?" When no one answered, Keven's expression only tightening, her lips compressed into a tight line. "Alone?"

"Not anymore," I said, suppressing an irritated sigh. "What about the wharf?"

Before she could answer, she broke into a violent fit of coughing, enough that she was forced to halt, one hand pressed up against the wall for support, the other clutched over her stomach. Keven and I traded a glance, but knew that Eryn would only wave us away if we tried to help her. Since the collapse of the innermost wall—the wall Eryn had held for a short while against the Ochean and her Servants with the help of myself and the throne—Eryn had felt shooting pains in her stomach, had had coughing fits like this one. The healers could find nothing wrong, but I'd been lurking inside Eryn during the battle, inside the Fire I'd placed inside her just like the one I'd placed inside Erick. I'd felt the damage when the Ochean had thrown her power against the invisible shield Eryn had erected to protect the wall. I'd felt the tearing pain, the taste of bile and blood at the back of my throat. And I'd choked on the dust as her shield failed and the wall began to crumble.

Something inside Eryn had been damaged in the process, something that didn't seem to be healing. But unlike Erick, this damage was internal, as if something inside had been bruised.

And it wasn't getting any better.

We gave Eryn a moment to collect herself as the hacking coughs ended, the silence awkward. She waved us forward again, her face twisted into an impatient grimace, as though she hated the fact that the coughing couldn't be controlled.

"The engineers say," she began again, her voice rough, "that the wharf is in better shape than it looks. The Chorl rammed the docks, but for the most part the damage was confined to the planking, not the pilings and supports. Catrell should be able to clear away the splintered planking and have it replaced within a few weeks. The wharf will be as good as new."

"And what about the ships?" We'd descended another level, the texture of the corridors changing. Above, in the palace proper, the walls were mostly white or an eggshell brown, like sand, except for the inner sanctum where the Mistress' chambers and the throne room were. There the walls were the gray stone used to build the original palace thousands of years before. It had grown as Amenkor grew, the original outer walls subsumed in the expansion.

Here, the eggshell walls had given way to gray stone again. We were within the confines of the original palace, but deeper. Much deeper than I'd ever been before, even deeper than when Westen, the captain of the Seekers, had led me down here to test me, and later train me.

"Regin says—"

"Regin?"

Eryn's eyes grew grim. "Yes, Regin."

"What about Borund?"

She sighed. "Borund hasn't come out of his manse since the Chorl's attack."

My eyes narrowed. I knew why. I'd watched as Borund fled the wharf, the Chorl overrunning the docks. But we needed every able-bodied man if we were going to recover fast enough to face the Chorl again with any chance of winning. "I'll deal with Borund. What did Regin say?"

"That the crews of the ships are working as fast as they can to repair the damage, and to upgrade the ships' defenses. They're also checking out the Chorl ships left behind, looking for weaknesses, for ways to defend against them if they attack again. He has three trading ships that are seaworthy already. He expects two more can be made seaworthy in the next week. The rest are going to require longer to repair."

We drew to a halt in front of an unobtrusive door. Unobtrusive except for the two guards that stood outside, both Seekers I knew. They nodded as we approached, stepped to either side of the door. They radiated a constant tension, their stances deceptively relaxed. I felt myself slipping into the same posture, my hand brushing against the handle of my dagger without thought. All of the guardsmen in Keven's escort had tensed; word of what the prisoner had done when she first woke had passed through the guards like wildfire.

They'd been caught off guard before; they didn't intend to have it happen again.

"What about the other prisoners? The thirteen Chorl warriors we captured as they retreated?" Eryn said abruptly. "Would you like to check on them?"

"No," I said. "Not now."

Eryn stiffened at the curtness of my tone, at the rage even I could hear at its edges.

"Should I remove the warding?" she asked. Her voice had dropped, become guarded, and as I slipped beneath the river, the world graying around me, I breathed in the sweat of fear, sensed her wariness and knew she had already raised a protective shield around herself, had readied it to extend to the guardsmen if necessary.

"I'm ready."

I saw the currents of the river roil as she reached forward toward where the protective warding that shielded the room had been tied off earlier and twisted the eddies, releasing the warding.

The reaction from inside the room was instantaneous, the door crashing inward on its hinges, wood cracking into stone, a blade-eddy—swift and deadly—slicing out from the interior darkness—

But it met the barrier I'd placed across the door, the blade-eddy shunted harmlessly to one side.

Someone inside the room shrieked in frustration, tried to slam the door shut, but I held it open with minimal effort and moved into the opening, Eryn a step behind.

Using the river, I could see the room, could see the corners, the rough stone of the walls, the straw pallet and chamber pot to one side. A wooden platter that had contained food—bread and cheese and water—sat beside the pallet, barely any crumbs remaining. The Chorl had been starving as well; no food had been wasted this past winter. And standing against the far wall, body tensed, one hand thrust forward, palm flat, chin lifted in arrogant rage—

A Chorl Servant.

The hatred I tasted was instantaneous and bitter, tightening inside my chest like bands of iron, making it hard to breathe.

Behind, I heard Keven order torches brought forward, the room flickering in the new light, revealing the Chorl Servant's long black hair, her stained green dress. Her posture didn't change, her nostrils flaring as her glance darted around the room, following the guardsmen as they positioned themselves behind Eryn and me. But she didn't attempt to use the river, or what Eryn called the Sight.

Her fear filled the room, reeking of piss and rotten fish. She'd been confined to this room for two weeks. The palace Servants brought her food, cleaned the chamber pot, changed the straw in her pallet. No one had attempted to speak to her after that first day.

We'd had other things to attend to.

Now, I glared at her across the expanse of the small room, thinking of the destruction in the city below, thinking of all of the men and women who had died, thinking of Erick. I clenched my jaw at the defiant look in her eyes, at the cold tension in her blue-tinged skin, and the iron bands around my chest tightened. The rings in her ears, four on each side, glinted in the torchlight.

"What have you done to Erick?" I asked, voice hard.

Confused shock radiated from Eryn, tightly controlled, an emotion I only sensed on the river. The other guardsmen shifted, edged forward as their own shock slid into anger.

The Chorl Servant sensed the change, her eyes darting once toward the guardsmen, then back to me. She didn't understand what I'd said, didn't understand the coastal language. But she could sense the rage.

Uncertain, the scent of her fear spiking, she lashed out with the river. I slapped the eddy aside, moved forward with two sharp steps, and wrapped my hand around her throat, shoving her back against the stone wall, my hand squeezing. Her skin felt smooth beneath my grip and I could feel her blood pulsing beneath my thumb, beneath my fingers. She cried out, swallowed against the pressure I'd put against her windpipe, gasped. Her hands clawed at my grip, and she choked something in her own tongue that sounded like a curse. Her black eyes blazed with hatred, but, aside from the hands clawing at my arm, she didn't struggle.

I could squeeze, cut off the flow of blood in her jugular until she passed out. Or I could shove my palm forward, crush her windpipe and kill her.

"What did you do to Erick?" I repeated.

"Varis," Eryn said behind me, her voice calm, reasonable, yet filled with disapproval. "Varis, she can't answer you. She doesn't know what you're saying."

I ignored her, focused completely on the Servant, on her blue-tinged skin. Skin that stoked the rage, fed it as images of the attack on the city flashed before my eyes, images of fire, of the watchtowers exploding, of ships and buildings burning, walls collapsing. Because of *these* people. Because of *her*.

My jaw clenched and I squeezed, cutting off her breath.

Her eyes flew wide. And for the first time I saw true fear beneath the arrogance, beneath the hatred.

And I saw something else as well.

She was younger than me. Fourteen perhaps, maybe younger.

The age I'd been when Erick had first found me on the Dredge.

My intense hatred stumbled, faltered. The muscles in my forearm relaxed imperceptibly. The urge to wring an answer from her surged forward, almost overwhelming—

But it halted at her fear. A familiar fear. An instinctual fear.

I relaxed my grip and she heaved in a strained breath, the hands that had tightened on my wrist loosening. Then I pulled back, let her go.

She slumped against the wall as I turned, gave me a hate-filled glare that I chose to ignore.

"You won't get anything from her by threatening her," Eryn said quietly but harshly as I approached the door.

"I agree," Keven said, motioning the rest of the guardsmen out into the corridor. "What do you want us to do with her?"

I halted, frowned as I turned to watch the Seekers close the door behind us, catching a glimpse of the Chorl Servant through the opening. She still huddled against the far wall, her shoulders now slumped, her hand massaging her throat. The arrogance lay over her like a cloak, like a shield, but the defiance . . .

I recognized the defiance.

I drew in a short breath, reset the warding over the door, then said, "Move her somewhere close to my chambers."

"What for?" Eryn asked.

I caught her gaze. "We need to teach her our language. I want to know what they did to Erick. And I want to know how to end it."

┼ Chapter 2

"Mistress' tits!" Eryn expelled a frustrated breath and opened her eyes. Her gaze immediately found mine. Sweat beaded her brow and tension etched the corners of her mouth and eyes, her lips pressed into a thin line. "I'm sorry, Varis. I can't find anything at all. I can *sense* something, but . . ."

My shoulders tightened, even though I'd been expecting the answer. "Show me."

She nodded, and then we both dove beneath the river. The world faded to gray, background noises softening, melding into a hushed wind, until the only thing in focus was Erick lying on the bed. I could feel Isaiah and his assistant in the background, blurs of gray on the general world of gray, could sense the guardsmen outside the opened doorway, but I pushed all of that to the side, concentrated on Eryn's presence as she manipulated the river over Erick's body. The eddies shifted beneath her touch, and I edged forward, following her movements.

"Whatever it is," Eryn said, her voice brittle beneath the river, distinct and sharp, "I can sense it best right here."

The eddies indicated a region just over Erick's heart, above a small puncture wound in his chest, its edges a purplish red. I grunted. "The Fire I placed inside Erick is there," I said. "Are you certain you aren't sensing that instead?"

Eryn's lips pursed. "I'm positive. I can sense the Fire as well, even though I can't see it. It has a different flavor, a different taste." She paused, her brow creasing in thought before she continued. "I'm not surprised the two are located in the same position, though. The heart is a focal point, a source of great energy. It would make sense to connect something of power—like the Fire, or this . . . this blanket of needles—to such a source."

I frowned, pushed forward on the river to where Eryn had indicated and tried to sense what Eryn sensed. "I don't feel anything."

Eryn leaned over Erick's body. "You're in the right area. You can't feel it? It's like . . . like a strand of spider's silk brushing against the back of your hand."

I closed my eyes, let myself sink into the sensations of the river where I hovered. The currents flowed around me, soft and soothing, pulsing with the beat of Erick's heart, flush with warmth. Beneath, I felt the steady heatless flame of the Fire I'd placed at his core. I could smell the lavender soap used to wash the sheets of his bed, could smell the musk of his sweat beneath that, along with the scent of oranges. I let the scents enfold me, comfort me for a moment, and then I opened myself to the river, relaxed into its flow, searching. . . .

Nothing but Erick's presence. Nothing but the stench of Eryn's increasing concern. No spider's silk brushing against skin. No tingling from some layer of the river I couldn't see. No taste. Nothing.

I rose with a sharp jerk. "I can't feel anything," I said, the words curt.

Eryn reached across Erick's body and touched my arm. My hands were gripping my upper arms tight across my chest, and with her touch I could feel how tense my shoulders had become. "We'll find some way to break this, Varis."

The words were meant to be reassuring, but Eryn hadn't felt Erick's pain, hadn't heard him plead for me to end it. I'd warned Isaiah to touch Erick only when necessary, since any prolonged contact made the pain worse. But he was still in pain. And Isaiah had no idea how long Erick could remain like this and survive. He thought having me come to visit, having me talk to Erick through the White Fire as I'd done before, would help, but . . .

I didn't know how to respond to Eryn's touch, so I shifted away slightly and gazed down into Erick's face. "What about the Chorl Servant?"

Eryn's hand dropped from my arm. "Keven says that she's finally stopped destroying everything in her new rooms. He thinks it's safe to see her."

I caught Eryn's gaze. "Then let's go."

As we left Erick's rooms, I sent one of the servants to the kitchen, then gathered my escort around me as we moved down the corridor. It had taken a full day to figure out how to rig the wards around the new room so that the Chorl Servant wouldn't be able to use the river to subdue the guards. Since she could use the river herself, the wards had to be set so that she could not unravel them from inside the room. A variation of what Eryn had used on the Dredge to keep the denizens of the slums away from the food she'd stored in the warehouse there had been used on her cell. However, these rooms were much larger, so the ward had been expanded and layered. It felt weaker than the previous ward, but so far it had held. As a precaution, we had the other true Servants in the palace standing watch along with the Seekers in shifts.

If the throne were intact, Cerrin could have shown me how to make the warding more stable. He could have shown me how to combine the Servants' powers as the Ochean had done during the attack on the palace, when she'd destroyed the walls. Or, more likely, I could have done the warding myself, with the power of the throne behind me.

But I'd destroyed the throne before he—or any of the Seven that had created it—had had the chance.

We halted outside of the Chorl Servant's new rooms, the guardsmen exchanging nods with the two Seekers on duty before fanning out to either side. The Servant on duty—a blonde-haired young girl named Trielle—stepped to the right side.

"We'll have to start working with the Servants to figure out how the Chorl combined their strength with the Ochean's to bring down the gates," I said as we waited. "We need to learn how to do that ourselves, and then figure out a way to protect against it."

Eryn nodded. "I have some ideas about that. We can start experimenting during the training sessions in the gardens. And perhaps, if you can get her to talk . . ." Eryn nodded toward the warded chambers.

Before I could answer, the servant reappeared carrying two oranges. I took them both, noting Eryn's raised eyebrows and questioning look, then said, "I want to go in alone. Stay here with Trielle, in case I need you. Set the wards up again after I'm inside."

"Very well."

I slid beneath the river, the scent of the two oranges sharpening. Eryn reached forward and loosened the warding and I stepped through to the door, the warding drawing closed behind me. Taking a deep breath to steady myself, to steady the hatred that rose instantly when I thought of the Chorl and of Erick, I pushed through into the inner room, expecting an instant show of force from the Chorl Servant—an attack, a shriek, something.

Instead, I found her standing at the far side of the room, back to a wall, still in the same sweaty green dress she'd worn during the attack, the stains of soot and ash and crumbled stone clear in the sunlight. The room lay in shambles, the bed canted to one side, one leg broken, the mattress torn, straw flung throughout the room. The two chairs had been reduced to flinders. Feathers from shredded pillows drifted about the room at the slightest draft. The curtains from the two windows hung listless, the material ripped and ragged at the edges, lying in rumpled heaps on the floor.

Anger rose, sharp and sour at the back of my throat, but I ignored it, didn't react at all, didn't *allow* myself to react.

On the far side of the room, I felt the Chorl Servant's smug satisfaction falter. Her back stiffened with the same arrogance she'd hidden behind before. Her head rose. I remembered that arrogance in the Ochean. Except, in the Ochean, it had been part of her personality. The Chorl Servant before me wore it like a shield, to hide what lay hidden beneath. I'd seen behind the shield for a brief moment before, when I'd held her in the choke hold. I'd seen that she was not so different from me . . . or at least what I had once been on the Dredge, before Erick found me.

"I see you've been busy," I said, my voice calm. I stepped into the room, closed the door behind me, felt the Chorl Servant tense, felt the river gathering around her defensively. I didn't react to this either.

I moved to one of the windows, looked out onto northeastern Amenkor, out over the three walls to the lower city, the River, and the Dredge, my back turned toward her. She hesitated, the river swirling around her uncertainly. Only a thin slice of the harbor could be seen from this vantage, part of the northern edge, where the land was too rocky and sheer for a wharf. I wanted her to see the portion of the city that had not been significantly damaged by the Chorl, wanted her to see that they hadn't harmed us as much as she might have thought.

I set one of the oranges down on the edge of the window opening, kept the other in one hand, then turned.

"My name is Varis," I said, watching the Chorl Servant closely. I didn't expect her to understand, and she didn't, her brow creasing in confusion. Or perhaps consternation at the tone of my voice. "I'm the Mistress of Amenkor." I motioned toward the window, toward the city beyond.

The Chorl Servant sniffed in disdain, but her eyes were uncertain. Dark eyes, almost black, like her hair. I drew in a deep breath and recalled something I'd learned a long time ago on the Dredge:

The eyes are everything.

A moment later, her gaze, holding mine with determination, flicked toward the orange I still held in my hand and the corners of my mouth twitched.

"Varis," I said again, then held the orange up with one hand. "And this is an orange."

She stared at the proffered orange, her chin tilting upward. Her nostrils flared, and after a moment I could see that she trembled. But not in rage.

With a quick gesture, I dug my thumb into the tough skin of the orange, the sharp tang flooding the river as sticky juice coated my fingers. I peeled the orange deftly, the scent strengthening as images of Erick surfaced in my mind, images I thought I'd forgotten: of him on the Dredge, handing me that first sack of food, his voice soft as he told me there was more where that came from if I helped him find marks in the slums; of him training me in the decrepit court-yards, barking orders or bursting out in laughter as I did something unex-pected, catching him off guard. Scents had been everything on the Dredge, and I'd associated oranges with Erick. A good scent; a safe scent. Strong and thick and sweet.

Orange peel fell to the floor, and when I finished peeling it, I jabbed my thumb into the orange's core and pulled the fruit apart, selected a piece and ate it, spitting the seeds out into my hand and setting them on the window's ledge.

Only then did I look up at the Chorl Servant again. She watched me closely, a frown touching her lips, her head still held high, bruised neck ex-posed. But she was breathing deeper now, her eyes latched onto the fruit. She'd been fed only bread, cheese, and a few portions of meat for two weeks. It was better fare than most of those on the Dredge had had all winter. Even if she didn't know what an orange was, I was betting that the scent of fruit would be familiar.

I'd learned more from Erick on the Dredge than simply how to use a dagger.

I broke another piece from the orange, the Chorl Servant's mouth twitch-ing, and ate it as I began to pace before the two windows. A slow pace, thought-ful and nonthreatening. "I know why the Chorl came to Amenkor," I said, talking slowly as I ate, even though I knew she wouldn't understand. I tried to keep the anger out of my voice, the hatred that rose so readily when I thought about the attack on Amenkor. It wasn't easy. "The Ochean wanted the throne . . . or rather, she wanted the Fire and thought it was contained in the throne. But the Fire didn't come from here. It came from the west." I paused, frowned out the window at the city. "Do you know where the Fire came from? Do you know what it was, what it was meant to do?"

I turned back, caught the Chorl Servant's expression, and sighed. "I suppose not. If the Ochean didn't know, why should you? But it's an interesting question. I haven't had much time to think about it. I didn't care much about it on the Dredge—there wasn't a reason to care, knowing where the Fire came from couldn't help me survive. And after I became the Mistress, there were more pressing matters. But now . . ."

I paused, took another bite of orange, then shrugged. "It doesn't matter."

I caught the Chorl Servant's eye, saw her stiffen at the look. I wasn't trying to hide the anger anymore. "You do know things I need to know, however. Such as how to combine the powers of the Servants, how to link them. And I'm betting you know something of what's been done to Erick. So . . ." I pulled another sliver of orange from what remained in my hand and held it out to her, forcing most of the anger out of my voice with effort. "Have a piece of orange."

She hesitated, her eyes narrowing in suspicion. But the scent of the orange was too strong. Edging forward, she raised one hand tentatively toward the fruit.

In one quick move, she snatched it from me and retreated, scowling. For a moment, I thought she wasn't going to eat it. She glared at me instead, defiant, the orange clutched protectively in one hand.

Then her stomach growled.

She dropped all pretense and stuffed the orange into her mouth, juice dribbling down her chin.

The sight sent a strange shocking ache through my chest. This is how I must have acted when Erick first brought me food. Starved, desperate, almost feral. I remembered how grateful I'd felt, and later, how ashamed, even though there had been nothing to be ashamed about.

My anger—at the Chorl, at the Ochean, at what they'd done to Erick and to the city—faltered, and I frowned. This woman wasn't responsible for those events. She'd been trapped by circumstance, just as I'd been trapped by circumstance on the Dredge. Until Erick found me.

I didn't move when she finished the slice of orange, then edged around behind me to take the one I'd left on the window's edge. Instead, as she began to peel the skin as I'd done, I moved toward the door.

When I reached to open it, she spoke.

"Ottul."

I halted, turned back.

The Chorl Servant stood between the two windows, back straight, the peeled orange held close in one hand. She held my gaze steadily for a moment, eyes blazing, and repeated, "Ottul."

Then she faltered, her gaze dropping in uncertainty.

I opened the door, saw Eryn, Trielle, and the guardsmen shift forward out of the corner of my eye, then turned and stepped through, Eryn releasing the warding long enough to let me pass.

"Well?" Eryn asked.

Still unsettled, no longer certain how I felt but unwilling to let the anger go, I said, "I think her name is Ottul."

I stepped into the hall of the merchant's guild, Keven and my escort of guardsmen at my back, and felt a shudder pass through me. The room was empty, weak sunlight slanting down through the narrow windows onto the marble floor, dust drifting in the beams. The entire building smelled of age, of dryness and death.

The merchant Alendor had decimated the guild in his attempt to take over trading with his consortium, an attempt I had helped to stop. But not before he and his allies had killed off a significant portion of the merchant class itself. Of the three remaining merchants of power, one had been discovered hoarding food during the past winter and had been stoned to death in the market square by the people of Amenkor after I'd passed judgment on him. The second, Regin, had unwillingly agreed to my seizure of all of the supplies in Amenkor in order to keep the citizens of the city from starvation. And the third . . .

I scanned the murky interior of the once thriving guildhall, found William seated at a table in the far corner. My heart clenched as it always did when I saw his tousled brown hair, his white apprentice's shirt vibrant in the beam of light that illuminated the scattered sheets of parchment he worked on. Since the battle, since I'd watched William charge into the midst of the attacking Chorl on the wharf, I'd seen William almost every day either at the palace giving a report on the cleanup in the city or the status of the dwindling supplies, or in the city at a work site, overseeing the clearing of the debris from the streets or the removal of the dead.

But I wasn't here for a report. At least, not a report about the city.

William didn't hear our approach until I'd halted before the table. Then he looked up with a start. He stood instantly, his chair juddering back as he lurched to his feet.

"Varis! I mean, Mistress," he added, his gaze darting toward the guards where they'd settled into position at a distance. "I didn't know you were coming."

"I didn't send word that I was coming."

"I see." His brow creased in confusion as he tried to decide whether this was a formal visit, or a friendly one. He opted for formal, his stance shifting slightly, his tone changing. "What can I do for you?"

I sighed. "I came to speak to you about Borund."

"Ah." His hands fell to the table and he dropped his gaze.

"William." When he didn't look up, I rounded the makeshift desk and caught William's shoulders, forced him to look at me. "William, I need to know what's happening with him."

"You know what happened with him," William said, shrugging out of my grip, his voice angry. "Everyone knows! He ran on the wharf. When the Chorl ships hit the docks and the rest of us charged into their ranks, he turned and fled. He left us there to die. He left *me* there to die!"

The bitterness of William's words, loud and harsh, echoed in the recesses of the room. He held my gaze a long moment, long enough so I could see the pain in his eyes, a pain he'd hidden the last few weeks, a pain he'd kept hidden even from me.

But then he spun, turned his back on me, and stalked away, toward an alcove containing a few chairs and a small table with a plant.

I hesitated, caught Keven's questioning look, but shook my head and headed after him.

"He never meant to run," I said to William's back, letting my own anger tinge my words.

"How do you know? You weren't there."

"Yes, I was."

William's shoulders tensed and he turned. "What do you mean?"

"I was there, inside the White Fire I placed inside of him. I was watching through his eyes when the Chorl ships hit the wharf. I watched as he dragged you down behind the barricade when they struck. I watched as the Chorl spilled down from the ships and swarmed the docks. I watched as you led the charge into their ranks, and I watched when Borund turned and fled. I saw it all. I *felt* everything that Borund felt."

His eyes widened. "You did? But then, why didn't he stay and fight? Why didn't you *make* him stay and fight?"

"Because . . ." I began, but then ground to a halt. Because I *could* have stayed and made Borund fight. I could have seized control of his body through the Fire, could have forced him into the Chorl's ranks. I'd wanted to, the sense of betrayal as Borund fled sharp. But I couldn't stay. I was needed in the palace, to fight the Ochean, to stop her, whatever the cost.

But William didn't want a rational reason. He wanted to know why Borund had betrayed him, had abandoned him.

I sighed, heavily, pushed my own anger at Borund back.

"He couldn't stay, William. He couldn't. His fear was too great. He tried. He honestly tried to stay and fight, but the fear overwhelmed him. I felt it overwhelm him."

William held my gaze a long moment, the hope that I'd give him a reason fading.

When I reached for him, to touch his arm as Eryn had touched mine earlier, standing over Erick, he flinched away as I had done. I let my hand drop.

He winced at the gesture. "I'm sorry, Varis, but . . ." He lowered his head, loosened the tenseness in his shoulder with visible effort, then caught my gaze. "How's Erick?"

I stilled, and he must have seen the answer in my eyes because he reached for me. And unlike before, with Eryn, I let him draw me in close, let him hold me. I breathed in the clean scent of his shirt, smelled the hint of fresh straw beneath on the river.

"He's not getting any better," I said, and was surprised at how rough my voice sounded, how thick. "And neither Eryn nor I can do anything for him."

"What about Isaiah?"

I shook my head, rested it against his shoulder for a moment, then drew back, even though his warmth was comforting. "Isaiah's done what he can, but he can't help with this. The Chorl did something to him using the river."

William's brow creased. "And you can't fix it?"

I gave a short, barking laugh. "I can't even sense it."

On the far side of the hall, a door opened and three other apprentices—two of Regin's and one who had worked under the hoarder Yvan—stepped into the room, their voices carrying in the dusty silence. William took a step back from me, separating us. The moment of closeness broke.

When the other apprentices moved on, William asked, "What are you going to do?"

"I don't know." I thought of Ottul, hesitated as I wondered whether I should tell him about her. But I'd moved her to the upper palace. Word would be spreading soon enough. "We captured a few of the Chorl in the attack, including one of the Chorl Servants. I'm hoping we can find out how to heal Erick from her."

William's eyes widened, but before he could begin questioning me about Ottul, I asked, "Where's Borund?"

William snorted, his anger returning in a heartbeat. "He hasn't left the manse since the attack, hasn't even left his study. He isn't working, isn't doing much of anything. All he does is drink. I've never seen him like this before."

I shuddered. Because I had. He'd done the same thing after William had been stabbed, when we weren't certain that William would survive. Locked himself in his study, drunk himself into a stupor.

Until I'd made the offer to kill Charls for him.

I winced.

"He needs something to do," I said. "He needs something that will give him purpose again."

"Like what?"

I shrugged, letting some of my own anger slip free again. "I don't know. Something that will make him active again. In the guild, in the city. We can't afford to have the guild brought to its knees simply because he's feeling sorry for himself. I need him. Amenkor needs him. He's one of the few remaining people of power left in the city. But if he's going to be of any help, I need him to be visible to the people, and I need him to be stable."

William glanced toward his table, toward the stacks of parchment he'd been working on. "What about ships?"

"What do you mean?"

"We lost most of our trading ships to the Chorl, when they were attacking them in the trade routes and later when they struck the city. All Regin has been complaining about lately is the fact that the guild can't operate effectively unless we have ships to trade with. We can't rely on the roads. Shipping overland isn't fast enough. Why not have Borund rebuild the ships we've lost? He can even help with the financing. I've seen his ledgers, I know how much he's worth. He can probably underwrite at least five ships, perhaps more, depending on what size and scale you're talking about. It will give him something to do other than drink. It will give him a chance to redeem himself."

I stared at William. Then, impulsively, I leaned forward and kissed him. A light kiss, startling me as much as him.

Before either of us could react, I spun away. "Come on."

With a start, he followed me back toward Keven, the remaining guardsmen straightening as I approached. "Where are we going?"

"To Borund's manse."

I felt William halt, felt the coldness radiating from him as I turned.

William shifted awkwardly under my gaze. "He ran, Varis. He left me there to die. I can't forgive him. Not yet. Not that easily."

I felt my jaw clench, but nodded.

Then I turned and left the merchants' guild, Keven and my escort in tow.

"Master Borund will see you now, Mistress."

Gerrold, Borund's manservant, spoke the words formally, but his eyes were alight, completely ignoring Keven and the escort of guardsmen that surrounded me. He motioned us into the main corridor, leading us down a familiar hall toward Borund's study.

I breathed in the scents of Borund's manse as I followed Gerrold—polished wood, the dust of parchment, the faint scent of bread baking. I didn't see Lizbeth or Gart, the two other servants Borund kept around the manse, but the rooms we passed and the halls themselves brought enough of their own internal ache from memory. I hadn't been physically in the manse for months, for what felt like a lifetime, but I had come here in spirit using the throne when searching for the stolen food. I'd had a purpose then, hadn't allowed myself to let the memories affect me.

But now they came unbidden. I wanted to be harsh, didn't want the edge I felt over Borund's cowardice to be blunted, didn't want his betrayal of William to be lessened, but I was suddenly assailed with the taste of butter, with images of Lizbeth dunking me beneath the water in my first real bath, of William laughing at something Borund had said and Borund grinning, casting me a furtive look to see if I was laughing as well.

And then Gerrold halted before Borund's study. Before opening the door and allowing me in, he said, "Please, Mistress. Do something to help him."

He stepped aside and walked away, not allowing me to respond and without announcing my arrival.

I stared through the open door, smelled the alcohol, the staleness of the room, and grimaced. It reminded me of the depths of the slums beyond the Dredge.

Without turning to Keven, I said, "Wait here." Then I entered, closing the door behind me.

The windows were closed, the shutters drawn, faint sunlight visible at the edges. In the shadows, I could see the large desk, ledgers scattered haphazardly to one side, sheets of parchment sticking out from the edges. Various shelves and tables held more ledgers, a few plants, and other simple artifacts from locations all along the Frigean coast—an intricately carved pipe from the southern islands, fossilized leaves and shells embedded in stone, a feather-and-bead headdress from Kandish across the eastern mountains, a vial containing the blue waters of the far northern Taniecian lands. A large rug covered the floor before the fireplace; a great sword hung above the mantel.

Among all the ledgers and artifacts were empty bottles of wine. A few were tipped to one side, others contained a few fingers' worth of liquid, but by the smell of the stagnant room, they had clearly turned.

Borund sat behind his desk, one hand clutching the stem of a glass. Another bottle sat close at hand, already half empty. He glared at me over the desk, brow furrowed, face flushed and angry. He hadn't shaved recently, and his eyes were bloodshot and puffy.

"What do you want?" The words were spoken in a gravelly, hoarse voice.

I squinted into the dimness of the room, crossed my arms over my chest, feet a shoulder's width apart. A soldier's stance.

"What do you want!" Borund barked, his free hand slapping down onto his desk with a hard crack as he surged to his feet, not quite stable.

I didn't flinch, didn't move. I met his eyes, met the rage there with a steady gaze, and said simply, "You ran."

He jerked back, face contorted with shock as if I'd reached out and slapped him, the reaction magnified by his unsteadiness.

I walked across the room, set my own hands down flat against his desk, felt the stickiness of spilled wine beneath my palms, and leaned forward, directly into Borund's face. His eyes widened, the rage gone. The reek of stale, used-up liquor came thick on his breath, had been ground into his skin. He looked ten years older than he was, his flesh hanging on his bones, the wire glasses askew on his nose.

"I was there," I spat, letting all the rage I'd felt in that moment come through in my voice. "I watched through your eyes as the Chorl ships rammed the docks, watched as William took up the battle cry and led the Amenkor men over the barricade to meet them. I watched as you stood there, staring, unable to move, and I felt your heart falter."

"And then I watched you run. I watched you abandon William to the Chorl."

Horror widened Borund's eyes further. His mouth opened, then closed. Opened again. "I—" he began. I could see his pulse throbbing at his throat, in a blood vessel on his forehead. Sweat coated his skin in a thin sheen. His gaze darted away, searched the room in a panic, and then settled back onto me. "Oh, gods," he whispered.

And then he collapsed back into his chair. Tears streaked down his face, and his body shook with silent sobbing. "I couldn't," he heaved, voice strangled, barely there. "I couldn't. I tried. I tried to turn back. But I just kept running. I didn't even know where I was going." His face contorted. "I'm sorry, Varis. So very sorry."

The emotion on his face was too raw, too visceral. I pushed back from the desk, an empty wine bottle on its side shifting position at the motion. I stared down at it a long moment, thought of William, of what Borund's cowardice had done to him. I glanced around at the rest of the bottles throughout the room, and then I moved to one of the shaded windows.

I stared at the material of the shade—deep red, suffused with sunlight from behind—and said, "Then do something about it."

Borund's sobbing caught. "I can't," he said viciously, the anger aimed at himself, his voice thick with phlegm. "The attack is over. There's nothing I can do to change it now."

"You can't change what happened," I said. I reached up and pulled the shade back, sunlight spilling into the room with a harsh glare. Borund sucked in a deep breath at the light, almost a hiss, but I ignored him, moved to the rest of the windows and jerked all of the shades aside, opening the windows, fresh air spilling in with the sunlight, sharp with spring and sea salt.

I turned to face Borund, hands on my hips. "But you can attempt to redeem yourself. For me. For Amenkor, which needs you now more than before Alendor and his consortium, more even than before the Chorl arrived. But especially for William."

Guilt flashed across Borund's face and he slumped even farther back in his seat. "William," he whispered.

I took a step forward, halted. I no longer felt the seething rage over his cowardice on the docks, but I was still angry. It would take more than a few words and some sobbing to change that. Like William, the forgiveness wouldn't come easily.

"You've lost him, Borund."

Borund stared at me from across the room, mouth open, one hand raised to shade his eyes against the sunlight, as the words sank in. "H-How?" he finally stammered. "How can I redeem myself? There's nothing—"

"You can build ships," I said, cutting him off. "Lots of ships."

"Now that the wharf is repaired, we can begin working in earnest on the repairs to the surviving ships," Regin said.

We stood at the edge of the wharf, people streaming around us, mostly workers hauling rope and carting wood out to the ships tied up at the docks to either side of us. But there were some fishermen, crab traps slung across their backs, their skin tanned into a thick hide, their hair bleached by the sun. There were also shopkeepers from the upper city; peddlers and hawkers; the dark-skinned Zorelli that made up the majority of the ships' crews; and one or two others from outside the main coastal regions. All these people had survived the winter in Amenkor and were trying to start anew. Sailors bellowed from the rigging, and crew called back and forth across the decks, the sounds accompanying the creak of the new planking beneath our feet and the slap of waves against the wharf's supports. Birds wheeled in the air—gulls and terns, one or two pelicans—their shrieks blending into the general noise. The scent of fish and brine clung to the air, the breeze coming in occasional gusts from the ocean. At least seven ships had been brought in to the docks, most still with damage to be repaired.

"When will the first ship be ready to send out?"

Regin snorted. "We could send out a few trading ships immediately, but none of them are equipped to defend themselves against the Chorl. Their captains aren't exactly leaping at the chance to leave the relative safety of the harbor."

"Not even to trade to the north?" So far, there had been no evidence that the Chorl were ranging farther north than Amenkor. All of the attacks on trading ships last summer had come to the south, between Amenkor and Venitte, along the main trading routes between the two sister cities.

Regin shook his head. "Not even to go north to Merrell. They're waiting for us to upgrade their ships, or to finish repairing the warships the Chorl left behind so that they have an escort ready to defend them."

I turned to look toward where three of the Chorl ships were also docked, their decks swarming with carpenters and engineers. Regin looked in the same direction.

"Our carpenters are drooling over them," he said. "I've already sent a few to check them out in detail. They seem to think they can adapt them somehow. Something to do with their construction." When I gave him a questioning look, he shook his head. "Don't ask. I'm a merchant, not a shipwright."

I wasn't either. In fact, I'd never even been on a ship. Gutterscum from the Dredge typically never made it down to the wharf. Most never made it across the River that separated the slums from the lower city.

That was changing though. There was less of a divide between the city and the slums now.

"How long before we can provide the trading ships with an escort?" I asked.

"By the end of the week. We should have three of the Chorl ships ready to go by then. If we send one with each trading ship, that should allow me to send two ships and Borund one."

At Borund's name, I tensed, frowned. Even though I'd spoken to him two weeks before, had practically ordered him out of his stupor, I still felt anger boiling beneath the surface. I'd seen him on the docks, had seen him in the warehouse district taking stock of his supplies. But I hadn't seen William and Borund together yet, had met with William repeatedly. I hadn't mentioned Borund, and William had carefully sidestepped the issue whenever it came up.

Borund hadn't proved himself yet. And I hadn't forgiven him.

"He was raised to be a merchant, not a warrior."

I turned to meet Regin's eyes, startled. He watched me with calculated intent. I suddenly wondered where Regin had been during the attack, wondered what he had done. He'd been assigned to one of the barricades in the lower city, but I'd lost track of him during the attack, too caught up in events to watch everyone.

But Regin had changed. Before the attack, he'd hated me, hated how I'd seized control of the food and supplies, how I'd set up the kitchens and warehouses. He'd helped me only grudgingly as I tried to feed the city.

"Borund should have stayed to fight on the docks," I said, my voice level. "He should have stayed with William."

Regin didn't waver. "Not everyone was made to fight. Not everyone was built for survival. Mistress."

Regin held my gaze a moment more, then looked away.

"In any case, William has handled all of Borund's affairs since the attack, while Borund was . . . otherwise occupied. And he's done a splendid job of it. Since Borund and I are the only surviving members of the merchants' guild of any consequence, I was thinking of making William a full merchant in his own right, perhaps a few of the other apprentices as well. The guild needs to begin recovering from Alendor and his consortium. What do you think?"

I thought of William charging into the advancing Chorl, sword raised awkwardly before him. I thought of my first excursion to the middle ward at William's side, saw his face as he gazed longingly at the merchant shops and manses that had lined the streets, and smiled. "I think he'd like that."

Regin grunted, a faint smile touching his own lips. "And I think he'd like you to come to the ceremony." At my frown, he gave me a knowing look. "And I need to go see to my own estates, which are still in total disarray after the past winter. I assume that now that winter is over, and the city has survived, all of the merchants have free access to do their usual business? No more joint warehouses? No more communal kitchens?"

"No. The merchants' guild is free of the palace. But I do intend to keep the warehouse and kitchen running on the Dredge. They need it."

Regin raised an eyebrow but said nothing except, "Mistress."

He gave a slight but respectful bow, then moved off, a few waiting apprentices and personal bodyguards closing in around him as he merged with the crowd on the docks. My own escort moved in closer, Keven coming up to my side.

"Good news?"

"More or less. Trading ships should be ready to leave by the end of the week."

"Then might I make a suggestion?"

I turned to him, somewhat surprised. "What?"

He motioned to the people milling around us. "We just barely survived a harsh winter, were attacked by an invading force, and we've done nothing since but clean up, repair, burn the dead, and drill the citizens in case of another attack. Can't you feel the tension?"

I frowned, and for the first time took note of the faces of everyone around us, of their haggard appearance, the set of their shoulders. As if at any moment they expected the facade of normality to cave in, revealing a horde of Chorl behind it.

And if I slid beneath the river, I could feel it as well, a trembling beneath the calmness of activity. The citizens of Amenkor were holding together through sheer movement, keeping themselves busy so that they didn't have to think, to feel.

"We need something to celebrate besides mere survival from the attack," Keven said.

"Such as?"

"A festival to celebrate the launch of the first trading ships, perhaps? It doesn't have to be a huge event, but . . ."

I gave him a narrowed look of doubt. "I suppose we could spare a little extra food for a festival."

Keven grinned. "I'll let Avrell know immediately."

Behind Keven, I saw the crowd part, Captain Catrell moving forward, trailing an escort of his own, including Darryn. Catrell was dressed in the full armor of the palace, having been promoted, taking the place of Baill as the head of the palace guardsmen. He was a short man, Darryn at least a foot taller, and carried himself with a sense of serious reserve.

Darryn was dressed like any other denizen of the Dredge, except that beneath his somewhat used and frayed clothing he wore leather armor and carried a sword. He'd been offered Catrell's old position as captain of the regular guard, but had turned it down and remained captain of the militia instead, insisting that he'd be more useful on the Dredge . . . and that full armor would only isolate him from the people. Since he was training them to defend themselves from another Chorl attack, no one had argued with him. He came forward a step behind Catrell, a smirk on his face.

"Mistress," he said, half mockingly, bending at the knee with an exaggerated bow.

Catrell gave him a sidelong frown, then nodded himself. "Mistress."

"Captain. Lord of the Dredge."

Darryn snorted. "At your service, of course."

I signaled Keven, the escort shifting position to open up a path through the crowd as I led Catrell and Darryn down the wharf toward the southern jut of land that protected the harbor. The two captains fell into step to either side, their own entourage melding with mine.

"I wanted to discuss Amenkor," I began, and both Darryn and Catrell became instantly intent. "In particular, what more we need to do to defend it against another attack. I know that you're training anyone with a will in the marketplace so that the citizens can defend themselves if necessary, Darryn, and that you're also training the more formalized militia, but there has to be something more substantial that can be done."

Catrell frowned. "You're certain that the Chorl will return?"

"They'll return. If not here at Amenkor, then somewhere else on the Frigean coast. Marlett, Temall, Venitte—any of the southern cities are under the Chorl threat. Merrell to the north as well, to a lesser extent. The Chorl will be desperate. Their homeland has been destroyed, and there are too many of them to remain on the Boreaite Isles for long."

"So what can we do?" Darryn asked.

We'd reached the end of the wharf, were passing now through the trailing edge of the warehouse district, coming up on the wall that branched out from the inner walls of the city and ran down the full length of the narrow strip of land that struck out into the water. The crowd had fallen behind, most of the city's activity centered on the wharf and the ships there. I stared up at the wall.

Here, it was barely twice my height, its main purpose to keep an eye on whatever ships might be approaching the city from the ocean on the far side.

"We need to warn the coast, the southern cities especially," Catrell said, angling along the wall to where a small gate allowed access to the heights.

I nodded. "Avrell has already sent dispatches overland, since no ships have ventured out of Amenkor since the attack."

"But it could take weeks for them to arrive," Darryn protested. "By then, the Chorl may have already struck somewhere else."

"I know. It's the best we can do at the moment."

Both Darryn and Catrell mulled this over as we climbed the stairs to the top of the wall, emerging into a stiff breeze from the ocean. Patrols ran in regular intervals along the wall, the guardsmen taking a moment to acknowledge our little group as we passed before turning back to their scrutiny of the ocean and the search for sails and the possibility of the Chorl's return. We were headed toward the remains of the watchtower at the end of the jut. I wanted to see the damage. Before the attack, I'd ventured out onto this wall only once. It had been at the limits of the throne's influence, and had been extremely uncomfortable, like knives digging into my gut, so I hadn't returned.

But now that the throne was dead . . .

I shoved the thought aside.

"What do you have in place right now?"

Catrell drew in a breath, then exhaled as he shook his head. "The losses from the attack, and those guardsmen that disappeared along with Baill, were significant. But I've set up watches along both walls in case the Chorl decide to return. Since the watchtowers were destroyed in the battle, I've set up warning bells down the lengths of both walls as well. If any foreign sails appear, they give warning to the city, with a second set of signals once the danger of the ship has been established. Darryn has been drilling the citizens on what each signal means, and what they should do in the event that a ship does approach. Most will head to the walls and the palace, although anyone with training or who can pick up a weapon is supposed to help defend the harbor."

"That covers the ocean approach," Darryn cut in abruptly. "What about to the east? An attack from land?"

Catrell grimaced. "That's harder to defend. Aside from the walls surrounding the palace, there are no defenses to the east. We haven't needed them. The eastern portion of the city—the stockyards, the tanneries—"

"The Dredge," Darryn added sharply.

Catrell nodded in agreement. "—they're all exposed. Along with all of the fields and farms, of course. I've set up scouting patrols along both the northern and southern roads, a few along the eastern route as well. The southern approach is the most easily defended, since the terrain is such that they'd have to climb a cliff to reach the edge of the palace in that direction. But the northern and eastern routes . . ." He shrugged.

"The good news is that most of the citizens of Amenkor have moved inside the walls of the palace or into the outskirts of the slums along the River," Darryn said into the silence. "With the lower city between the wharf and the palace mostly destroyed, they've had to find somewhere else to go. A significant portion of them should be protected by the walls if someone does attack by land, and with enough warning, those on the Dredge should be able to make it to the walls in time. There's not much we can do about the outlying farmland. All of that is at risk."

"Haven't the patrols here and on the roads stretched the guardsmen thin?" I asked.

"Yes. But since the battle we've had a significant surge in men and women interested in the militia."

Darryn nodded. "Many of those come from the Dredge. They may not be skilled with a sword, but they make up for it with nastiness and determination." A tight, proud smirk lit Darryn's face.

"Many of those who joined the militia before the attack have been shifted to the regular guard to fill the gaps, since they had some minimal training already. The rest have already started training under Darryn and his men." Catrell shrugged. "There's not much more that can be done."

We'd reached the end of the jut and halted, were now staring down at the remains of the watchtower. The wall, slightly shorter here than in the city, abruptly ended, stone jagged at the edge where it dropped down into a shallow hole. To the right, waves crashed onto the natural stone of the jut, slapping into rock with a hollow booming sound, spray hissing upward, errant wind blowing it into our faces occasionally, my hair flying about my face. I licked my lips, tasted salt and sand.

Three weeks before, there had been a tower here. A short tower, only two levels, but enough to give the guardsmen a greater view of the ocean.

Now, there was nothing but a crater littered with shattered stone and twisted wooden beams. One wall of the tower had slid to the side, a fan of stone tumbling down to the greedy ocean below.

I felt again the surge of power that had wrought such destruction. Felt it like a thud to my chest. Slipping beneath the river, I could still sense the disturbance in the eddies and flows around me.

Without releasing the river, I turned away from the debris, away from the ocean and the wide open threat that it represented, and looked to the city. I could see the masts of the ships at the docks, could make out movement along the wharf, even though we were too distant for me to pick out individual people. Skiffs darted back and forth across the bay, and other fishing boats bobbed

on the waves closer to the tower, men leaning over the edge to haul up traps
from the harbor's bottom. And beyond, rising up from the water's edge and
outward from the River's mouth, buildings and streets, a charred husk just
above the wharf where the Chorl had landed, the palace to the south, the
Dredge to the north.

I watched the activity near the wharf for a long moment, noted the empty
berths at the docks.

"No," I said finally. "There is something else that can be done."

Both Darryn and Catrell frowned.

"What?" Darryn asked.

I motioned to the harbor, to the city beyond. "We can build another wall."

"It will bankrupt us," Avrell said.

"What, the festival? It's a little too late for that. It's already started."

Avrell clenched his jaw and visibly controlled himself. "No, not the festival.
Building the wall."

I paused in my preparations to frown at him. We were waiting in the antechamber to my bedroom, Avrell seated while I tucked the folds of my shirt into
my breeches. Isaiah had removed the bandage keeping Avrell's arm immobile
a few days before, declaring his shoulder healed. "What do you mean? Just
build it. We have stone available in the quarry to the north, wood in the forests
to the east. We have plenty of laborers in the city; just recruit people from the
Dredge. The carpenters and engineers are practically begging to get started."

"Yes, but all of that requires money. Money that we don't currently have. Or
at least, don't have enough of. We used a significant portion to gather enough
food to get us through the winter. We have enough to continue paying the
wages of the servants and guardsmen and to keep the palace running at a nom-
inal level, but that's it. Spending our resources on the labor necessary to build
the wall is out of the question, unless you have a cache of buried gold hidden
somewhere in the slums that you haven't told me about."

I shot him a withering glare. "We need that wall. The Chorl attacked by sea
the last time, because that's what they were used to. According to Catrell and
Darryn, our most significant weakness at the moment is the unprotected parts
of the city to the east, including the stockyards and the Dredge. We need some
type of defense for that portion of the city. We can't rely on the Chorl giving us
enough of an advance warning to get all of the people in those areas into the
walls of the palace!"

"Then you'll have to figure out a way to fund their construction."

Before I could form a scathing reply, a knock came at the door, which
opened a moment later to reveal one of the Seekers set to guard my chambers.
"Marielle is here to help with your preparations, Mistress."

"I'm already done," I said.

Avrell's eyes shot wide open, and from behind the Seeker I heard Marielle say, "What?" She shoved past the bemused Seeker, who quietly shut the door behind her. Her gaze raked over my crisp white shirt and tan breeches, my boots, the dagger at my belt. She wore a pale green dress, tied at the waist with a swath of trailing blue cloth. "You can't possibly be thinking of wearing that to the festival."

I frowned in confusion. "This is what I always wear."

"Exactly."

Marielle stalked across the antechamber into the inner room, moving swiftly toward the wardrobe. "You must have something in here suitable to wear to this event."

I cast a surprised look at Avrell, whose face was now suspiciously neutral. "Like what?"

"Like a dress!"

A knot of horror clenched in my gut, all thought of the problem of the wall forgotten. I followed Marielle into my chambers, Avrell a step behind me. "I don't have a dress. I don't wear dresses. I don't *like* dresses."

Marielle pulled back out of the wardrobe, a thin sleeping shift held up before her. She tossed it to the floor in disgust, then saw Avrell. "Eryn," she said.

Avrell seemed to understand. With a quick nod, he vanished through the door. I heard the outer door open and close, followed by footsteps moving fast. Not at a run, but close.

I caught Marielle's gaze, held it, my face set in the sternest frown I could manage. "I don't wear dresses," I said, my voice hard, edged with the deadly intent most people identified with the Seekers. "I'm the Mistress."

Half an hour later, Eryn stepped back from straightening the folds of one of my sleeves and said, "There. What do you think?"

Marielle gave me a penetrating look. "It will have to do. We're already late. If we don't leave now, the ships will have to launch without us there to see them off or they'll miss the tide."

I stood stiffly, the dress feeling awkward against my skin. What skin it covered. Yellow, embroidered at the edges as almost all of Eryn's dresses were, it hung down to my ankles and was fitted at the waist, two servants having hastily measured, pinned, and stitched it to the right size. The sleeves were loose, the shoulders a little poofed, the neckline square. I could feel the air against my skin across my chest and shoulders. And my feet. Instead of boots or shoes, they'd forced me into some kind of sandal, but with many more straps.

The only concession they'd made was my dagger. Strapped to my forearm within easy reach, in a leather sheath Westen, captain of the Seekers, had given me, its weight was comforting.

I glared at the two through narrowed eyes and lowered my arms, breathing in the heady perfume they'd applied. "Are we finished?"

Eryn smiled, smoothing the creases of her own white dress. "I think so."

They herded me out into the antechamber, where Keven, Avrell, Nathem, and Westen waited. Catrell, Darryn, and Regin were already down at the wharf seeing to the last minute details of the three trading ships and their escorts.

Avrell drew in a sharp breath, began to say, "You look completely diff—" but then caught Eryn's eye and halted. Keven looked slightly stunned and confused, as if he didn't recognize me. Westen's only reaction was a raised eyebrow. They were all dressed formally—the guardsmen in maroon uniforms with glints of armor showing here and there; Avrell and Nathem in the deep-blue-and-gold robes of the palace.

"Let's go," I said curtly, not willing to acknowledge the nervous sweat that suddenly prickled the palms of my hands and back of my neck.

An escort of no less than twenty guards on horseback led the three carriages down through the cleared streets of Amenkor. It was the first time I'd ridden in a carriage, but the dress made it impossible to ride a horse as I usually did when moving through the city. I found it . . . bruising, the cobbles of the street rough, and remembered my first sight of a carriage, after killing Bloodmark and fleeing the slums, crossing the River to the lower city. I'd thought it strange, a room on wheels, so far removed from anything I'd experienced on the Dredge that I'd hidden deeper in the familiar territory of the alley until it had passed.

Now, I stared out of the small rectangular window and watched the alleys drift by. We passed through the wards, the broken walls, just now beginning to see signs of repair, glowing in the late afternoon sunlight. A few people still remained in the upper city, most obviously heading down toward the wharf and the festival. The windows and doorways of the buildings we passed were decorated with garlands of grass or boughs of pine and aspen from the forests, tied with ribbons that fluttered in the light wind. Banners hung from poles erected at the corners of the streets, or jutted out from above shopkeepers' doorways. The citizens of Amenkor had leaped at the news of the festival, decorations appearing within hours of the general announcement.

Then we passed into the lower city. I turned away from the heaps of rubble and charred buildings with a grimace.

"You saved the city."

I glanced up at Westen, seated across from me. He watched me intently, jostled by the rough ride. Keven and Marielle also rode with us, the others divided between the other two carriages. "Did I?"

He smiled. "Yes. Don't let anyone, including yourself, ever doubt that."

"But—"

"No," he said, cutting me off, shaking his head. "There is always a price—buildings, ships . . . lives. You can never escape that. You did what had to be done."

"But we lost the throne."

His smile faltered, grew grim. "Was there any other way?"

I turned back to the window, thought about those last few moments in the throne room, in the throne itself, as the Ochean attempted to seize control. "No."

"Then the throne was part of the price."

We'd passed through the worst of the damaged streets, were coming up on the wharf. People were already crowded on the docks, and the carriage was forced to slow. Men and women danced, tankards and cups raised to the sky, laughter and screams combining into a low roar of frenzied noise. Someone slapped the side of the carriage, bellowed something slurred and unintelligible but obviously ribald into the window, then spun away, lost almost instantly. Marielle blushed and laughed.

I turned toward her, caught her gaze, and grinned as well.

Then we were at the wharf, the carriage drawing to a halt as the guardsmen pushed the riotous crowd back and Westen opened the door and helped me down. A cheer broke over us in a wave as Westen escorted me to the open area that had been cordoned off on one of the docks. Chairs had been brought down from the palace, along with tables now lined with platters of food, all set up on a raised platform. Music from at least three different sources merged into a cacophony of sound almost subsumed by the crowd itself, and somewhere someone was roasting a pig, the scent of sizzling meat and smoke making my stomach growl.

Regin, a few of his apprentices, Borund, Catrell, and Darryn were waiting on the platform.

Along with William.

My stomach clenched and I tensed, suddenly conscious of my dress, enough that Westen glanced toward me out of the corner of his eye. William straightened where he stood at Regin's side, as far from Borund as possible. I could feel the tension on the river between the two, saw Borund cast William a glance, then turn his attention toward the docks, toward the crowd. William was dressed in the crisp white shirt of an apprentice, with breeches and a plain long brown jacket; Regin must not have told him he was to be made a full merchant yet. Regin wore his own merchant's jacket—dark blue, riddled with the gold embroidery that signified his power within the merchants' guild, the symbols indicating what resources he traded. Borund's jacket was blood-red.

I gave Borund and William both a sharp frown.

Regin stepped forward. "We'll have to launch immediately, if we're going to catch the tide," he said. Behind him, I could see the crew of the trading ship lined up at the dock already getting ready to depart, men scrambling in the rigging, others releasing the ties to the dock. The two other ships had already pulled away from the wharf to either side, the refurbished Chorl ships that were to be their escorts waiting out in the harbor. "You should make your speech now."

I froze. "Speech?"

"You have to say something to the crowd," Avrell said. The rest of the group had come up behind us. "They'll be expecting it."

I turned back to the wharf, saw the docks lined with people, packed into the small space so tightly the guardsmen were having a hard time keeping them away from the platform where we stood. The entire city must have come, including those from the Dredge. I felt a hand seize my heart, felt fresh sweat break out on my forehead.

Someone touched my arm, leaned in close to murmur, "Make it short. It doesn't have to be complicated. Remember, most of them are already half drunk."

Eryn.

I pressed my lips into a thin line, not amused. Reaching for the river, I threw a net out over the crowd, as far as I could spread it. Not as far as I'd been able to in the marketplace when I'd condemned Yvan as a traitor, when I'd had the power of the throne behind me, but that hardly mattered. Only those closest to the platform needed to hear.

I stepped forward, and with a low murmur, the crowd closest grew quiet. The festival continued farther out, raucous and loud, but here, on the edge of the dock, it was dead quiet.

Raising both arms, using the net to project my voice, I said, "To Amenkor's survival."

There was a pause.

And then the crowd erupted into a deafening roar. Bells and horns from all sides of the harbor joined the tumult. Through the crash of sound, I heard the captain of Regin's ship bellow a command, turned to see sails belling out with the wind, a familiar sense of excitement seeping through me at the sight. I watched as the trader began to pull away from the dock, echoing the movements of the other two on either side. The roar spread along the wharf in both directions, subsiding only when the ships had cleared the pier and pulled out into the center of the harbor, the sun behind them, setting the clouds afire. The musicians broke out into a dance and the wharf degenerated into a seething mass of people dancing, drinking, eating, and celebrating.

I wondered how many of those from the Dredge were picking pockets. It's what I would have done, if I'd even risked coming down from the Dredge at all.

I grinned, the energy of the festival infectious.

William cleared his throat beside me. I'd felt him approach. His presence made my skin tingle.

"Nice speech."

I snorted. "Avrell is going to kill me."

"I know."

I turned, caught William's malicious grin, and hit him on the shoulder. I saw Borund behind him, watching his back with a strange expression on his face—hope and sadness and regret all mixed together—as he spoke to Regin.

I glanced back toward William, who stood rubbing the spot where I'd struck him. "Borund's been busy."

William stilled, the grin vanishing from his face, his expression a wall. "Yes."

I thought William would say more, but he stood staring out at the crowd. Behind, some of those on the platform had begun to dance.

I sighed. "What do you expect him to do, William? He can't change the fact that he ran on the wharf. He can't change the fact that he left you."

"I know that." Tight. Angry.

"Then what more do you want?"

He held that anger in for a long moment, then heaved a sigh of exasperation. "I don't know. I don't know what I want."

"Have you spoken to him?"

"I've done what needed to be done for the guild. I've done what he's asked of me. But we haven't spoken about that."

I nodded. I'd seen the two on the wharf, in the palace, knew that they hadn't. "Maybe you should."

William didn't say anything. Far out in the harbor, the ships were passing through the protective arms of land that jutted into the water, slipping out into the ocean, two of the traders turning south toward Venitte, the other heading north.

As soon as the ships passed from view, Regin broke away from Borund, headed toward where William and I stood. I straightened, William doing the same as he saw Regin's approach.

"Are you ready?" I asked.

Regin nodded, his expression neutral. "Whenever you're ready."

"Give me a moment, and then you can begin."

Regin nodded and stepped away, motioning Borund forward. William shot me a confused glance that I ignored, turning instead to face the crowd, reaching out again with the net I'd used before, capturing as many of those that surrounded the platform as possible.

Then I nodded toward Regin.

"Citizens of Amenkor," he bellowed, and I could feel his voice reaching out over the noise of the crowd, reaching all of those touched by the net. Those nearest quieted, those farther out too caught up in the celebration to care. On the platform, the musicians brought their song to a close, and those dancing slowed.

Regin waited until he thought he had most of the people's attention, then continued. "We have all survived a rough winter, and the attack of the Chorl, as the Mistress said. And during these past long months we've suffered significant losses. Many of us are still grieving. But we have survived. The wharf has been rebuilt. The streets have been cleared. And we have just sent out the first ships from our harbor since the attack!" At this a cheer rose from the audience, a cheer that spread outward from the platform and beyond the net I'd placed over them. Regin nodded, raised his hand to calm the sudden enthusiasm.

"But," Regin continued, and the crowd quieted grudgingly. "There is one more thing we can do tonight, something that will rebuild Amenkor's strength in a way that no mere stone, nor wood, nor sailing ships ever will. With the Mistress' blessing, Master Borund and I would like you all to participate in something that has traditionally only been done within the hallowed halls of the merchants' guild, something that has never been witnessed by those outside its halls before." Here, Regin paused, and those closest to the platform whispered to each other, the hush in stark contrast to the distant sounds of revelry. Everyone had stilled, had pushed a little closer to the platform itself.

Regin turned from the crowd, toward where William stood at my side, a slight smile touching the seriousness of his face, of his voice. "William Hartleton, apprentice to Master Borund, please step forward."

Stunned, William hesitated, then moved stiffly up to Regin's side. Regin gave him a small nod, then turned to the other waiting apprentices on the platform. "Illum Forestead, Jack Trevain, and Walter Davvens, apprentices to Master Regin, please step forward."

All three of Regin's apprentices stepped forward as well, with a mixture of shock, elation, and confusion.

When all four were lined up before him, he said, now deadly serious, all traces of the smile gone, "As Masters of the merchants' guild, with all of the powers that the titles ensure, and with the approval of the Guild in its entirety, and that of the Mistress of Amenkor herself, I now rescind your status as apprentices of the guild . . . and declare you Masters of the guild in your own right, with all of the privileges and duties that the title entails."

Silence held for a long moment as the import of Regin's solemn words sank into the crowd . . . and then it erupted into cheers and thunderous applause. One of Regin's apprentices—Jack—seemed on the verge of fainting. As the applause continued, Regin motioned forward one of the servants from the palace.

She laid a heavy box at Regin's feet, and Borund stepped forward. I let the net go as Regin pulled a dark blue jacket from the box and handed it to Borund. A few silver-embroidered symbols stood out on the jacket. Regin pulled out another in a dark hunter's green with gold embroidery.

Borund stepped up to William, both standing straight, backs stiff, faces tight. Borund held out the jacket so that William could slip his arms through the sleeves, then met William's gaze.

I don't know what passed between them in that look, but I sucked in a sharp breath, held it. For a long moment, I didn't think that William would accept the jacket. His jaw tightened, his eyes on Borund's face, searching.

Then his gaze dropped and he turned, pulled off the plain brown jacket he'd worn to the festival, thrust his hands through the sleeves, shrugged the new jacket onto his shoulders, and turned back. Borund dusted off the shoulders, tugged the sleeves into the correct position, scrutinized the cut, the tailoring, the embroidery.

And then he glanced back up at William and I could see that he was on the verge of tears, that he barely held them in check.

He suddenly grabbed William and pulled him in tight, hugging him roughly. "I'm so sorry, William," he half sobbed, half choked into William's tense shoulder. "I'm so sorry I abandoned you at the wharf, and I know there's nothing I can do to change that, and I wish to all hells that there was. I wish that I could take it all back, relive the whole experience. I wish—" The rush of words caught in his throat and he pulled William in tighter, then released him, stepping back, scrubbing at the tears on his face with one hand, not able to meet William's eyes for a long moment.

But before William could say anything, before any of those on the platform could react, he caught William by the shoulders and looked him directly in the eyes. "You are the closest thing I have to a son, the closest I will ever have, and I am proud of that. I'm proud of you, William. And I will always be proud, even if you can't find it within yourself to forgive me."

Then he let William go, turned toward where Regin held out a second jacket—a bright yellow with dark red embroidery. He handed it to Borund, who moved to stand before Illum, while Regin presented Walter with his own black jacket with silver edging.

As soon as the last two shrugged into their jackets and Borund and Regin stepped back, the crowd erupted into fresh applause. When this died down, the musicians broke into a lively dance.

All six merchants shook hands, congratulating each other, and then they broke apart, most heading toward the platters of food that had been laid out. William moved toward me.

"Nice jacket," I said.

William laughed, then said accusingly, "You knew about this."

"I'm the Mistress," I said mockingly, mouth quirked. "I know everything."

He grinned, and it suffused his face, wrinkling the skin near his eyes. The wind tousled his hair, tugged at his jacket. A few months before, I'd thought he despised me, despised what I'd done as a bodyguard for Borund. A month ago, he would have flinched if I'd reminded him I was the Mistress.

The moment stretched. Around us, those on the platform had split up into pairs and returned to dancing. Torches were lit as the sun set completely.

"Would you care to dance?" William said suddenly.

I stilled, felt my carefree smile fade. "I don't know how."

"Oh." An awkward moment, and then, tentatively, "I can show you."

William held out his hand, his expression hopeful. To the side, I felt the other dancers swirling on the river, heard one of them cry out in delight as they were spun. The motion, the movement, drew me, even though fear roiled in the pit of my stomach.

I hesitated, trapped. But in the end, William's look won out.

He led me to the edge of the ring of dancers, pointed out steps, demonstrated the position of the feet and hands. I shivered when he placed his hands on my waist, showing me a lift, and then, all of his directions still a jumble in my head, mixed with the queasy warmth that had filled my gut at his touch, he took my trembling hands and began.

I stepped on his foot three times, tripped once. He caught me with a grin, and then I let myself relax, let myself forget that I'd never danced before, let myself sink into the river, into its flows, and suddenly it wasn't awkward anymore. It was like the Dredge, like slipping through the crowds of people without touching anyone, all about the eddies, the movements, the patterns. I slid along the currents of the other dancers, anticipated William's direction, let the rhythm of the dance take control.

Through the whirling motion, I caught Marielle's face, caught her significant look before she was spun away by Keven. Sometime later, Avrell and Eryn flashed by, Eryn laughing in delight.

Three dances later, William slowed to a halt as the music ended and the dancers broke out into applause. A gust brought another whiff of the roasting pork, and my stomach growled.

"I need a break," I said, gasping and sweaty. My heart pounded in my chest, as if I'd been practicing for hours with Westen, and yet I felt exhilarated, not exhausted.

"Very well," William said, face flushed, eyes bright.

We moved toward the food-laden tables. All along the wharf and on the remaining ships, lanterns and torches lit the night, the crowd spreading out into the lower city.

William handed me a glass of water, piled some forkfuls of shredded pork and some bread onto a platter, and led me off of the platform onto the dock, moving down its length. We settled onto some crates near its end and ate in silence, watching the distant movement on the wharf. Behind, I felt the presence of a few guardsmen—my ever-present escort—but I ignored them, didn't think William had noticed them at all.

"Catrell told me you intend to build another wall," William said when the platter held nothing but a few strands of meat and some crumbs, "one that surrounds the entire eastern part of the city."

"Yes." It came out brusque.

William hesitated. I felt his eyes on me. "What's wrong?"

For a moment, I considered shrugging it aside, not willing to let the palace intrude, but then I sighed. "Avrell says it's impossible. We don't have the money. Not after the past winter. Not after the Chorl attack."

"Ah." William lapsed into thoughtful silence, seemed almost to speak, reconsidered, then said quietly, "You have four new merchants now. Have you thought about asking them?"

I stilled in thought, but before I could answer, before I'd even had a chance to consider it, William continued.

"I know we haven't had a chance to set up our own houses yet, that we'll be starting out fresh. But typically our Masters, the merchant that we apprenticed under, will give us a gift, a portion of their own houses, something to get us started. It still won't amount to much, but at least it's something. Perhaps all of us together, all four of us, will have enough to help back the building of the wall."

I stared at William, at the mute appeal on his face, at the need in his eyes. He wanted to help, was desperate to help, but not because of the city, and not because of his new merchant house.

He wanted to help me.

"William," I said, then halted.

He shifted, set our empty plates set aside.

Then, I leaned forward and kissed him. A light kiss, but not the sudden, unexpected kiss I'd given him before, when he'd suggested Borund build the ships in the harbor. I felt his indrawn breath a moment before we touched, felt the trembling of his body, smelled his scent—straw dust from the warehouses, sea salt—strong and rich on the river.

Then I drew back, heard him sigh.

Before either of us could react, a harsh, urgent clanging of bells pierced the night, coming from the walls protecting the harbor. William turned toward the sound in consternation. I leaped to my feet, two guards appearing out of the darkness at my side.

"What is it?" I asked, tension coursing down my arms, even though I already knew.

"A warning," one of the guards answered roughly, already motioning to the other guardsman, who took off back toward the wharf at a run. "Unknown sails on the horizon."

┼— Chapter 3

Fear spiked on the wharf as word spread, the raucous celebration grinding to a halt. Masses of people broke away from the docks and headed up to the palace walls in a slow-moving but orderly tide as the warning bells fell silent. But just as many people scrambled to find weapons, joining the guardsmen on duty at the edge of the water, as they'd been drilled to do by Darryn. The river churned with mixed emotions—fear, despair, determination—and I felt myself harden under the tumult.

"Is it the Chorl? Did they attack our trading ships?" William asked, moving up beside me and the guardsman who'd remained behind to protect me. Tension ran off him in tendrils. Others approached as well, almost everyone who'd been on the platform, including Westen, Avrell, Marielle, and Eryn.

"I don't know," I said, but I pulled back the sleeve of my dress, ripping the fabric slightly as I exposed the sheath containing my dagger.

"All of the citizens have headed back to the palace," Avrell said. "For whatever good that will do. We still don't have gates."

"The guard is on the way," Westen added. "Catrell is organizing the men who remained and can fight on the docks."

We waited in silence, breath held, ears straining. The quiet was unnerving, the only light the torches and lanterns lining the docks and the bowls of flaming oil lighting the palace and the broken walls. Wind gusted from the ocean, tugging at my dress, my hair.

Then new bells broke the darkness and the guardsmen all around sighed in relief.

"Not the Chorl," Westen said. "A foreign trading ship." He frowned as the bells paused, new notes ringing out. "And it shows signs of damage."

I thought immediately of the ships we'd just sent out. Had they run into trouble already? But Westen had said the ship was foreign. And the incoming ship could have been damaged by many different things—a storm, pirates.

Yet, somehow, I didn't think so.

Had they encountered our own trading ships? Had they even seen them?

"It could be a while before the ship docks," Avrell said. "Should we head back to the palace?"

I hesitated. I wanted to know what had happened to the ship, and whether it threatened the trading ships that had left the port just over an hour before. But Avrell was right. It could be a full hour before the captain was ready to speak with me.

"Spread the word that it isn't another attack," I said, "but keep a contingent of guardsmen here at the dock, just in case." I caught Westen's eye. "I want to speak to the captain as soon as he's ready."

The captain of the Seekers nodded. "I'll escort him to the palace myself."

Almost two hours later, a page boy halted, breathless, in the open door of an audience chamber inside the palace.

"The captain of the *Reliant* is here to see you," he gasped a moment later.

At my nod, he darted away, leaving me alone with William, Avrell, Eryn, and Keven. Keven stood beside the section of floor where I'd paced the last hour, a solid beacon of calm. Not as soothing as Erick's presence would have been in the same place, but still calming. Avrell stood not far off, beside Eryn, who was seated to the side of the single table at the end of the room.

I'd asked William to stay, had seen Avrell frown in disapproval. But I'd ignored the First. With Erick barely alive, I found William's presence comforting.

"The *Reliant*?" Eryn asked.

Avrell frowned. "One of Lord March's ships, from Venitte, I believe. They must have left the city close to the first day of spring to have made it here this fast."

"Or been traveling with little cargo."

Avrell raised his eyebrows at that, and I felt a surge of irritation. I didn't understand what the comment might mean, but before I could ask, William said, "The trading ships can travel faster if they aren't loaded down with the weight of cargo."

I gave him a thankful glance, tried to ease the tension in my shoulders. Even with William and Keven in the room, I felt on edge.

Westen appeared in the doorway.

"May I present Captain Tristan of the Venittian ship *Reliant*, and Brandan Vard," Westen caught my eye, his face and voice impassive, his warning clear, "Servant of the Lord of Venitte."

Avrell and Eryn stiffened, Avrell's hand tightening on the back of Eryn's chair.

Then Captain Tristan stepped into the room. He wore the formal jacket of a captain, like the merchant jackets, but without the heavy embroidery to signify rank. A dark blue, like William's, it was banded with gold at the cuffs and neck, with gold buttons and red-and-gold-tasseled epaulettes on the shoulders. His mouth was pressed into a thin, grim line, the skin beneath his eyes dark with exhaustion.

Brandan Vard entered a step behind him, his face a schooled mask that did not successfully hide the last dregs of shock and horror beneath it. Slightly older than me, he wore a simple shirt and breeches, although the material was obviously of high quality. A large circular gold pendant hung from a chain around his neck, a domed and spired building emblazoned on the front. A familiar building. I frowned a moment, then remembered.

I'd seen the building from Cerrin's veranda, overlooking the harbor and channels of Venitte. Cerrin had looked toward the building when Venitte had been under attack by the Chorl the first time, had intended to go there to join the other six members of the Council, until his wife and children had died. It was the seat of power in Venitte.

My gaze shot toward Eryn and Avrell, but both were focused on Tristan, who'd moved to face Eryn. With a stiff but respectful bow, he said, "Mistress, I bring word of warning from Lord March and the city of Venitte. Although it would appear that it comes too late."

An awkward silence fell, broken only by a cough by one of the guardsmen who'd entered behind Tristan and Brandan. Tristan rose, brow knit in confusion.

I stepped forward. "I am the Mistress of Amenkor."

Comprehension dawned swiftly, no more than a flash across Tristan's eyes. He turned sharply and repeated his bow to me, more stiffly this time. "I deeply apologize, Mistress. We had not received word of your ascension in Venitte at the time that we sailed."

"When did you sail?" Avrell asked.

"Three weeks ago. We came directly here, without stopping."

Avrell glanced toward me. "I sent couriers to Venitte the moment you took the throne. They should have arrived well before the end of winter."

"By land or by sea?" Tristan asked.

"Both."

Eryn shifted in her seat. "None of the ships made it to Venitte, I assume?"

Tristan's expression tightened. "None."

"The only ship that returned after heading south was Mathew's ship," William said. "He didn't make it as far south as Venitte. He chose to stick close to the coastline, hitting numerous smaller ports, rather than going out into the main trade routes, those that the Chorl targeted."

Tristan grunted. "So you know of the Chorl?"

"We know of the Chorl," I answered, my voice dense with anger. Both Tristan and Brandan understood, however. They would have had to pass through the charred shell of the lower city to reach the palace. "They attacked Amenkor on the first day of spring."

"But you managed to drive them back." It was a statement, not a question. And it held an undertone of respect.

Avrell shifted forward. "What about the couriers I sent by land? None of them arrived either?"

"None. We've had no word from Amenkor—from any port north of Bosun's Bay—since autumn."

"What happened?" Westen broke in.

Before Tristan could answer, Brandan—silent until now—stepped forward. "The Chorl. They've seized control of Bosun's Bay and the surrounding area."

No one in the audience chamber moved. I'd known that the Chorl could not stay on the Boreaite Isles for long, but I hadn't expected the expansion to the coastline to be so swift. Not after the attack on Amenkor.

But then the full import of what had been said sank in. The Chorl must have seized control of Bosun's Bay before winter to have halted Avrell's couriers. They'd already begun the invasion of the coast before coming here, or at least seized enough land to live off of during the winter. I didn't remember Bosun's Bay being in the Ochean's plans when I'd filtered through her memories while she was on the throne. But then I wasn't focused on what she might have done elsewhere; I was focused on her and what she intended for Amenkor.

Amenkor had been a distraction, the promise of the Fire and the throne's power too much for her or Haqtl, the leader of the Chorl priests, to resist.

But now, Haqtl and Atlatik, the captain of the Chorl warriors, must have returned to their original plan.

"How far away is Bosun's Bay?" I said abruptly, breaking the silence.

"A map!" Avrell snapped to one of the guardsmen at the door, "Find Nathem and have him bring a map of the Frigean coast."

"And find Captain Catrell," Westen added.

One of the guardsmen nodded and left immediately. Everyone else shifted closer to the table, William moving to my side, close enough I could feel him. I glanced back at Keven, who shook his head grimly.

"How did you find out about Bosun's Bay?" Avrell asked.

Brandan glanced toward Tristan, who nodded for him to answer the question. He straightened, one hand holding the emblem around his neck. "Lord March noted that a significant portion of our ships were being lost over the course of last summer. He sent out search parties. They discovered the Chorl on the Boreaite Isles and in Bosun's Bay just before the ocean became too rough to navigate for the winter."

"And you didn't send word?" Westen remarked, although it was clear he already understood what had happened.

"Of course we sent word," Brandan snapped, then stopped himself. His hand had clenched on the disk about his neck, but he forced himself to relax, to breathe. "We sent warning by land. Obviously, the Chorl had infiltrated farther inland than we estimated. They must have stopped our couriers."

Westen nodded.

"Is that how your ship got damaged?" Eryn asked. "Were you attacked by the Chorl?"

"No," Tristan said. "The *Reliant* wasn't part of the search effort, and we knew enough to bypass Bosun's Bay on our way here. The trade routes were a little trickier to sail through without meeting up with the Chorl, but we managed."

"Then where did you get attacked?"

Tristan met Westen's eyes squarely. "Just south of Temall."

Avrell swore.

"Did you meet any other ships on your way here?" I asked. "We sent a few trading ships south, with an escort, a few hours before your ship was sighted."

Tristan shook his head. "No. We didn't see anyone. But we were staying close to shore because of the damage we sustained. If your ships headed out into the trading lanes, we wouldn't have met."

At that moment, Nathem entered, a bundle of rolled parchment in his arms, followed immediately by Captain Catrell.

"Nathem," Avrell spat, motioning his Second to his side, while at the same time Captain Catrell said, "What's going on?"

As Avrell and Nathem began sorting through the maps, William leaning forward to help, Westen answered. "The Chorl have apparently taken over Bosun's Bay, and Captain Tristan here says that he encountered the Chorl as close to Amenkor as Temall."

Catrell frowned.

And then Avrell cried, "Here," and slapped a map down on the table.

Everyone leaned forward, Nathem and William placing weights at the corners of the paper to hold it down, Avrell pointing with one hand to a location on the edge of the coast marked with a heavy black dot, script off to one side. "Here's Amenkor," he said, to orient everyone. His finger followed the edge of the curve of coastland marked out in black, blue shading to one side for the ocean, greens and yellow to the other. "Here's Temall, about five days' south of here by ship. Another three days beyond that is Bosun's Bay." Both Temall and Bosun's Bay were marked with smaller dots.

Avrell's finger halted, but my gaze continued down the coastline, until it came to rest on Venitte, almost the same distance from Bosun's Bay as Amenkor. And, like Amenkor, it was marked with a large black dot, the city's name scrawled across the parchment in curved letters. It lay in a jagged cut in the land, like a tear at the edge of the paper, a large island filling up the space left open by the tear. Two channels of water surrounded the island, then sliced inland toward Venitte itself.

I thought about standing on the cliffs above Venitte's harbor, watching as the Chorl first attacked fifteen hundred years ago, shivered as their ships slid into sight through the channels on both sides of the island. I felt Cerrin's initial confusion, followed swiftly by horror and rage as the first volleys of fire arched up from the Chorl ships and fell onto the Venittian ships in the harbor and the houses perched on the cliffs.

William brushed up against me. I caught his concerned look, frowned, and shook my head.

"We ran into the Chorl ship just past Temall," Tristan said, bringing my attention back to the map, pointing to the ocean just to the south of the town. "About here."

Catrell frowned. "Just one ship?"

Tristan nodded, a note of irritation creeping into his voice. "One was enough to almost take us. If Brandan hadn't been on the ship . . ." He trailed off, and Brandan straightened slightly.

"I had to use the Sight to force them off," Brandan explained.

The tension that had spiked and then faded when Brandan had been announced escalated once again. A wariness that I could feel in all of the guardsmen in the room . . . and surprisingly, from Tristan himself.

Tristan seemed to be of higher rank than Brandan, and yet he feared the Servant. A fear that wasn't evident on his face, but could be felt easily on the river.

"I'm surprised you escaped at all," Westen murmured. And in his voice I heard the echoes of what Mathew, Erick, Laurren, and the rest of the doomed crew of *The Maiden* had endured when they were attacked by the Chorl. I'd forced everyone to live through those events using the throne, forced everyone to feel their desperation, their pain, their deaths.

Tristan's irritation escalated at the suspicion hidden in Westen's voice, in Catrell's gaze. A suspicion I felt as well . . . until I realized why Tristan's ship had survived, why Brandan's presence had turned the Chorl away when Mathew and his crew had never had a chance.

"Did the Chorl ship have any Servants?"

"What do you mean?" Brandan interjected.

The tension between the two groups heightened.

Drawing in a steadying breath, I said, "We sent out a ship of our own to find out why the trading ships had vanished. It was destroyed, completely, because the Chorl ships it encountered had Servants aboard, women with the Sight who could control fire."

Tristan's eyes went wide, and he swore under his breath, his hand making a reverential motion across his chest that reminded me of the Skewed Throne gesture the people of Amenkor used when they saw me.

Brandan rolled his eyes. "No, they did not have any Servants on board."

"That we know of," Tristan added more seriously. I'd seen the same reaction at the mention of fire from almost every captain and sailor I'd met on the wharf.

Brandan shifted, his brow furrowed, eyes locked on the map.

I frowned.

"If they'd had Servants on board," Eryn said, her voice hard, "they would have used them."

"It must have been a scouting party," Catrell said, diverting everyone's attention back to the map. "They must be interested in Temall."

"With good reason." Avrell leaned back from the map, his hand splayed on the table for support. "Bosun's Bay and the surrounding area may have had enough resources to keep them through the winter, but not through that and the spring as well. It's not that large of a port. Even if they began farming," he pursed his lips at this thought, the idea obviously striking an unpleasant chord with everyone from Amenkor, "they'd still need more resources. Temall is the closest option."

"What do you mean, 'if they began farming,'" Brandan said sharply.

"The Chorl aren't here to raid," I said. "The islands where they come from were destroyed. They need land, a place to live. They're here to conquer."

"And it appears," Westen said quietly, gazing down on the map, at the town of Temall, "that they're heading north. To Amenkor."

North. To Amenkor.

Westen's words from the night before echoed in my head as I made my way to my chambers to wash after a morning dealing with the daily disputes brought before the Mistress as well as the dispatches Tristan had brought from Venitte, with another visit to Ottul, whose almost daily lessons in the common tongue of the Frigean coast—a task I'd assigned Marielle—were advancing, if at a slow pace, and with training sessions both with Westen and the Seekers as well as Eryn and the Servants. My muscles ached from all the practice, my body weary from the exertion.

And from lack of sleep.

I was still dreaming. Of Cerrin mostly, but occasionally of some of the others of the Seven who had created the Skewed Throne. Not every night, and most not as vivid as that first dream of Cerrin attacking the Chorl Servant outside Venitte in the olive groves and wheat fields. But all of them were emotionally draining. I'd woken numerous times with tears streaking my face, a hard knot of grief buried in the center of my chest. Other times I'd jerked out of sleep in rage, usually after dreaming of Liviann or Garus.

Except they weren't dreams, I thought as I entered my rooms, pulling off my sweat-dampened shirt, followed by my breeches, using the motions to stretch the tightness out of the muscles in my shoulders and lower back, wincing slightly. I poured water from the waiting pitcher into the basin on the table against one wall, soaked a cloth, and began to wipe the grit and grime from my face and body.

No, they weren't dreams. They were memories, with the same connection and intensity I'd felt when I'd been bound to the throne, the same realistic feel as—

I halted, washcloth held against my neck, staring off into the middle distance.

They *were* memories. Memories of the Seven and the Chorl attack on the Frigean coast almost fifteen hundred years before. Memories that, when I'd been connected to the throne, I would have been able to access if I'd wanted.

But the throne was dead. I shouldn't be able to access any memories now at all, except those that I'd relived while connected to the throne before the Chorl attack. These were new memories. They contained images and places and people and events I hadn't known about when the throne was destroyed.

But I knew them now.

I tossed the cloth aside, dressed in the breeches and white shirt that had been laid out for me on the bed, and jerked open the door to the outer corridor, startling the guardsmen waiting there.

"Mistress?"

"Come with me."

I halted before the throne room door, laid one hand on the polished wood between the heavy bands of iron. The room had been closed off since the Chorl attack. I'd come a few times in the days after, to check on the throne, to touch it, to search for the faintest flicker of life in hopes of filling the cavernous hole where the throne had been inside me.

But when there'd been no flicker, no tingling beneath my touch after a few days, I'd abandoned it and hadn't come back. There had been no reason to come.

I shoved, the heavy doors swinging open, and entered. The long room was dark, the light from the corridor touching the edges of the first set of columns that lined the sides of the walkway, but nothing farther. Guardsmen slid past me and began to light the torches to either side, the candelabra and bowls of oil scattered throughout the room. As flickering orange light suffused the room, I moved down the walkway, to the dais at the far end where the throne sat, a banner marked with the three slashes of the Skewed Throne on the wall above it. Ascending the three steps of the dais, I halted before the throne itself and shuddered.

The room felt . . . empty. The first time I'd entered, I'd been stalked. An energy, a presence, had filled the chamber, prickled against my skin, the voices of the throne manifest, whispering to me, rustling like autumn leaves against stone, unintelligible but there. And on the dais, the throne had shifted, warping from shape to shape, always changing as the multitude of personalities took control, the motion hurting the eyes. I'd hated it, hated the texture of the room, the *feel*.

But then I'd seized the throne myself, taken control of those voices, become part of that presence that had prickled my skin. Instead of itching, the presence had become a power, a living, pulsing connection that had extended throughout the city of Amenkor, a presence that throbbed in my blood, that I drew in with each breath.

Now, I reached out and touched the rough granite . . . and felt nothing. No whispering voices shivering through my skin. No thrumming of life, of the city, beating with my heart. The throne remained a single solid form: rough rock, a stone seat with a rectangular back, unadorned.

Except for a crack.

I reached out, traced the crack with one finger. As long as my forearm, from elbow to the tip of my finger, it cut through the back of the seat like a scar, starting at the top, on the left, and angling downward to its center.

The emptiness of the room hurt, a pain deep and hollow. A pain as deep as what I'd felt when I'd found the white-dusty man's body on the Dredge, along with his wife, killed by Bloodmark to spite me. The pain trembled, threatened to break free as I pressed my palm to the throne, felt the grit of the stone against my skin, the pocks in its surface. I willed the stone to shift, to shudder, to *change*—

I felt Eryn enter the room behind me, felt her approach the dais and halt at the bottom of the steps.

"Anything?" she asked, and I heard an echo of my pain in her voice. She'd been connected to the throne far longer than I had.

I let my hand drop, drew in a breath against the thickness in my chest. I shook my head. "Nothing."

She sighed. "There's nothing you can do, nothing any of us can do."

"But I'm dreaming," I said. When Eryn didn't respond, I turned, repeated, "I'm dreaming, Eryn. I'm reliving memories from the Seven—Cerrin, Liviann, Garus, Seth, all of them. Memories that, unless I'm still connected to the throne, I shouldn't have."

Eryn's brow creased and she came one step up onto the dais before halting again. "But you don't feel anything when you touch the throne?"

"No."

"What about the city? Do you feel anything from Amenkor, any connection—"

"Nothing," I said, cutting her off. "I didn't feel anything when I went out onto the jut to the watchtower either, and before, that was at the edge of my limits."

Eryn remained silent, but I could see her thinking, could see it in her eyes as she held my gaze.

"It doesn't make any sense," I said, breaking the heavy silence.

Eryn drew in a breath, glanced toward the immobile throne, then exhaled heavily. "Unless . . ."

"Unless what?" I said, too sharply.

"Varis," Eryn said, coming up another step on the dais, "the Seven created two thrones. You know this, you witnessed their creation. You were *there*. What if you aren't getting these memories from this throne, what if the two thrones were connected in some way and you're getting the memories—"

"From the other throne," I finished, the idea catching like fire in my mind. If we could find it, if we could use it to replace the Skewed Throne, if we could use it to defeat the Chorl again. . . . "But where is it? What happened to it once the Seven created it?"

I caught Eryn's gaze, saw her shake her head with regret. "I don't know."

I thought about everything I'd experienced while connected to the throne, every memory of the Seven I'd lived through then, or dreamed of since. "It was intended for Venitte," I said urgently. "It was intended to help protect them from the Chorl—from any attacking force—just as the Skewed Throne was intended to help protect Amenkor."

"Then why didn't Venitte use it?" Eryn asked.

I growled in frustration, feeling as if the answer were at the tips of my fingers, that the memories were hovering just out of reach. "I don't know! Everything I remember of the Seven came from before the thrones were created . . . or from what the Seven experienced through the Mistresses of the Skewed Throne after it came to Amenkor."

"Because the Seven sacrificed themselves to create the thrones in the first place," Eryn said, nodding in understanding. "There wouldn't be any memories in the Skewed Throne for the Seven after that. There would only be the memories of the Mistresses who took control of the throne itself."

I felt some of my initial excitement dying down, doused by the realization that what I knew of the Skewed Throne wouldn't help. "So how do we find out what happened to the other throne?"

Eryn sighed. "I don't know. But there must be some record of what happened to it somewhere. Have Avrell and Nathem start looking through the archives. Perhaps they can find some mention of it in there. And you can ask Captain Tristan or Brandan Vard. They're from Venitte. If the second throne was truly intended for Venitte, perhaps they will know what happened to it."

I turned back to the throne, ran my hand across its surface once again. "If the Chorl *are* returning to Amenkor," I said, and let the thought trail off. The Skewed Throne was the only reason we'd survived the first attack. If we could replace it, before the Chorl attacked again . . .

North. To Amenkor.

I shrugged the ominous words aside, stepped back from the cracked throne. I hesitated at the top of the dais, then turned my back on the hollow emptiness of the room, and moved down the dais, Eryn falling into step behind me.

"Where are you going?" she asked.

"To see Brandan Vard," I said. "I want to know what he knows about the thrones."

"And that should take care of the last of the petitions from Venitte's merchants' guild," Captain Tristan said. He took the sheaf of papers Avrell held out to him, checked the last few pages to verify that all of the marks and sigils were in place, and then tucked them into a large satchel. "I'm glad to see that the guild here in Amenkor is recuperating. Four new apprentices have been raised to merchants in the last few days, so I've heard."

I didn't like Tristan's tone, caught Avrell's hooded glance as he made his way back to his seat in the small audience chamber, then looked to Brandan. But the Venittian Servant's gaze was locked onto me, waiting for my answer, so I turned back to Tristan. "Alendor and his consortium were rather devastating to the merchants' guild here."

Tristan smiled, his lips thin. "Yes, so I hear from Regin. He's somewhat defensive about the matter, although I gather that you played a role in . . . eliminating the consortium."

I frowned as his eyes narrowed, felt a subtle shift on the river as his attention focused on me. "Yes. I killed Alendor when it was discovered he was stealing Amenkor's food and selling it to the Chorl."

"You've killed many people, so I've heard."

I bristled, felt myself shift in my chair into a more defensive position. "Yes."

Tristan's eyebrows rose. "I'm surprised you admit that so freely."

"I grew up in the slums of Amenkor," I said. "I killed to survive . . . and then to escape."

Brandan grunted, but Tristan didn't take his eyes off of me. "That explains . . . much." He reached to fill a glass from a decanter of wine. "Regin and Borund wouldn't say much about your past when I asked. Instead, they chose to defend your reign as Mistress. But the Lords and Ladies of Venitte, including Lord March, will be interested once they learn that there is a new Mistress in Amenkor—in you, in Amenkor's stability." He sipped from his glass and settled back. "They say in the streets that you are a Seeker."

Behind, I felt Avrell stiffen in outrage, but I leaned forward, met Tristan's gaze squarely. "I was trained by a Seeker on the Dredge. He taught me what I needed to know to survive. He taught me enough that I used it to escape to the upper city, to the wharf, where I became Borund's bodyguard. But I am not a Seeker."

Tristan said nothing, met my gaze without flinching. His brow creased as he considered what I had said, as he judged it, and in that moment I realized that he already knew everything I'd told him, that he already knew all about my past. He'd learned as much as he could in the past day, from Regin, from Borund, and from the people on the streets. And those people knew everything. I'd kept nothing from them.

Which meant he knew about the attack on the city as well, and the past winter.

"What about Venitte?" I asked, letting my irritation at being tested tinge my voice.

"What do you mean?"

"You know about the Chorl, have known for at least a month, since your ship left port to come here three weeks ago. What has Venitte done to prepare for the Chorl?"

Tristan hesitated, until Brandan cast him a sharp look. Setting his wine to one side, he rested his elbows on the edge of the table between us, fingers clasped beneath his chin. "Since the first ships disappeared, and we began to suspect that their losses were from something other than bad weather or pirates, we've set up patrols at the mouths of the two channels leading in to Venitte. We've also established outposts along the coast and farther inland to the north, since none of the trading ships to the south of Venitte have vanished. But at the time that the *Reliant* left the port, the Chorl had made no attempt to attack Venitte directly."

"They were focused on Amenkor," Avrell said.

"Apparently."

"And what about the throne?" I asked, slipping deeper beneath the river so I could judge Tristan's reaction.

He frowned, honestly confused. "What throne?"

My gaze shifted toward Brandan, who'd tensed. He was no longer watching me. His gaze had fallen to his hands, his face blank. "At the time that the thrones were created, there were two—one for Amenkor . . . and one for Venitte. They were created to protect the coast from attack, created specifically to defend against the Chorl. What happened to Venitte's throne?"

Tristan snorted. "The throne of Venitte—the Stone Throne I believe it was called—was lost nearly fifteen hundred years ago. We've never used it. We've never needed it."

I turned my attention fully on Brandan Vard. "Is that true? Do the Servants in Venitte not use the throne?"

The Venittian Servant took a moment to gather himself, then said, eyes on me, "The Stone Throne vanished within ten years of its creation. The Servants in Venitte have never used it in their training. No one knows where it is, although many have searched for it over the years."

I didn't answer, my frown deepening. Because Brandan was telling the truth . . . but not the complete truth. He knew something more about the throne, I just couldn't figure out what.

"What about the Chorl Servants?" I asked. "How do you expect to defend against them?"

I'd asked Brandan, but it was Tristan who answered. "I don't know yet. Lord March and the rest of the Council doesn't know about the Servants as far as I know. We haven't encountered them. But if what you say is true—and after seeing the city, after hearing what the people of Amenkor suffered during the attack, I have no reason to disbelieve you—then we'll have to plan a defense against them."

"We have our own Servants," Brandan interjected. "We've been trained to fight as part of the military's Protectorate."

I almost snorted, but caught myself. "Amenkor had Servants as well. We barely survived. The Chorl Servants have changed since the attack fifteen hundred years ago. They've learned to combine their powers, to such an extent that, in order to stop them, I had to destroy the Skewed Throne itself. Are the Servants in Venitte ready for that?"

Brandan's eyes flashed at the tone of my voice. "How dare you—" he spat, leaning forward, but Tristan placed a warning hand on his arm to cut him off. He turned on the captain, but Tristan glanced down toward the gold medallion that rested on Brandan's chest, and after a tense moment Brandan settled back into his seat.

"The Servants in Venitte will have to be ready," Tristan said, a hard edge to his voice. "Now, Mistress, if you'll excuse us, we have business to attend to with the new guild members."

"Of course," Avrell said, rising as both Tristan and Brandan stood. They nodded as they left, and Avrell closed the door to the audience chamber behind them, turning immediately to me.

"Brandan knows more about the throne than he's letting on," I said immediately.

Avrell nodded. "I agree. And Tristan is more than a simple captain from the merchants' guild. He must have a connection to one of the Lords or Ladies of the Council. We'll have to be careful around both of them."

I stood, moving toward the door. "I need to know more about the creation of the thrones, about what happened to the Stone Throne and the Skewed

Throne after they were created. With the Skewed Throne dead, the Stone Throne may be the only way to stop the Chorl when they next attack."

As Avrell opened the door and preceded me into the hallway, my escort of guardsmen waiting outside, he said, "I'll see what I can find in the archives. And I'll have Catrell keep a discreet eye on both Tristan and Brandan."

When Marielle first entered Ottul's room, a box of random objects in her arms, she found the Chorl Servant kneeling on a folded blanket in the middle of the room, body hunched down over her knees, hands cupped over her head. She rocked back and forth in the tucked position, a low, murmured chant barely breaking the silence of the room.

Inside the White Fire at Marielle's core, I watched through Marielle's eyes as she paused at the threshold, felt the warding being reset behind her.

Does she do this often? I asked through the Fire.

Marielle nodded, frowning. *Almost always. And always facing the same direction: west.*

What is she doing?

Marielle shrugged. *I don't know. And I haven't worked with her long enough to find out.*

I grunted.

Ottul suddenly stilled, her chanting cut off sharply. In a strangely fluid motion, her back curving upward, she lifted herself, sitting back onto her knees as she turned toward the doorway with narrowed eyes.

Her expression was fixed in anger, but tears streaked down her face.

When she saw Marielle, however, her anger faltered.

"Hello, Ottul." Marielle moved toward the table in the middle of the room, set the box down and began removing objects from it—a wooden bowl, a goblet, a scarf.

Ottul reached forward instantly for the scarf, but Marielle's hand closed over hers before she had a chance to draw away.

Both froze, Marielle catching Ottul's confused gaze. "What do you say?" she asked.

Ottul's brow wrinkled in angry annoyance, but then she sighed. In a tight growl, thick with accent, she said, "Hello, Mar-ell." Then, when Marielle didn't let go of her hand: "Pease?"

The plaintiveness of the tone twisted in my gut, touched something inside Marielle as well, for she loosened her grip on Ottul's hand, let her pick up the blue-green scarf. The material was fine, from the Kandish Empire across the mountains, and Ottul ran the scarf across her hands, her arms. She wore Amenkor clothing now, Marielle having persuaded her to give up the filthy green dress we'd found her in beneath the pile of collapsed stone.

But her dress was coarse, not as fine as the scarf, and tan in color, accentuating her blue-tinged skin. The neckline was low enough that the edge of a tattoo could be seen just beneath her collarbone. That had been a surprise. I hadn't realized the Chorl women had tattoos, although I vaguely remembered seeing one on the Ochean. The men wore their tattoos openly, on the arms and face. The women seemed to prefer their tattoos hidden.

When Ottul drew the cloth up to her face, rubbed it against her cheek, Marielle reached out, slowly, and touched the four gold rings in Ottul's ears.

Ottul jerked back, breath hissing out harshly through her teeth, a barrier slamming up sharply between her and Marielle on the river—

But when Marielle didn't react, she halted.

"What are they?" Marielle asked. "What do they stand for?"

Ottul frowned. The shield around her wavered, then dropped.

She stepped forward, one hand lifting to Marielle's ear. "You . . . no."

Marielle smiled. "No, I don't have any."

Ottul's frown deepened. Then she touched the first ring in her left ear. "Ona," she said, and began to draw the river close about her, not as a shield, and not in an attack. Instead, she seemed to be playing with the river at random, swirling its eddies, pushing it this way and that, creating whirls, tightening it and releasing it.

Manipulating it.

She pointed back to that first gold ring and said again, "Ona."

The first ring indicates she can use the river—the Sight, I said through the Fire. *That she's a Servant.*

Marielle slid into the river deeper, began to manipulate it, and at the same time said, "Ona."

Ottul smiled, but tightly. A layer of sadness tainted the river, a whiff of emotion, strong and sweet and potent, like an onion. "Ona." Her fingers touched the second ring. "Ket."

On the river, Ottul pulled the currents of the river into a shield, the threads woven tightly.

Marielle did the same. "Ket."

Ottul nodded, touched the third ring. "Tora."

Releasing the shield, she drew a small bundle of the river into an outstretched hand, into a configuration the Servants in the palace had never seen before.

But I had.

I sucked in a sharp breath a moment before Ottul ignited the threads. Fire burst forth in her hand, a few inches above her palm, contained there, held there—

But not controlled. Not like the fire that had snaked its way across the deck of *The Maiden* and killed so many of its crew. This was simple fire. Ottul could call it, could perhaps hurl it toward targets so that it retained its integrity, but she couldn't force it to obey her will. I could feel the strain of simply holding it in her hand already; sweat beaded her forehead, and her concentration remained on her hands, on the flames.

I can't make fire, Marielle said internally, a twinge of worry snaking through her.

You could, I answered, *if I showed you how, if we practiced. But for now—*

I slid through the Fire and seized control of the river through Marielle. Sensing my intent, she held out her hand, palm upward.

I drew the river close, spun the threads the same way Ottul had done, as I'd done through Cerrin's memories, only tighter, more controlled, and then I ignited them.

Marielle flinched when the fire sparked and bloomed in her hand. In a shaky voice, she said, "Tora."

I let the fire go, Ottul doing the same.

"And the last ring?" Marielle asked.

But Ottul turned away, moved toward the windows.

"What comes next, Ottul?" Marielle said. "Ona, ket, tora . . . ?"

Without turning back, Ottul said, "Qal." She hesitated, then said bitterly, "Ona, ket, tora, qal, etai, kona, u mer."

The words were angry, laced with hatred, with an undertone of fear and want I didn't understand. The scent of onion strengthened, until Ottul's shoulders slumped, the scarf still clutched in one hand forgotten.

Enough for now, I said to Marielle. *Work with her on other things. But keep working with her. I need to know if she can help with Erick.*

Marielle grimaced at Erick's name, then nodded, shifting forward to the box again, letting Ottul remain at the window.

I withdrew from the Fire, Reached back through the palace to the outer chamber of my rooms, slid into my own body with a heavy sigh. Exhaustion washed through me, arms tingling with sensation. I leaned my head against the back of the chair, eyes closed, waiting for the trembling to set in—

And noticed another presence in the room aside from the Servant set to watch over me while I Reached.

I lifted my head with effort, my strength drained, opened my eyes. "What is it, Keven?"

Face set in a serious expression, he said, "We have a problem."

"This is how we found them," Catrell said, his voice tight.

I stood in the doorway of the cell, one hand against the gritty granite of the wall to one side, still weak from the Reaching. The stench of death hung in the air, blood and piss and shit mixed with dampness and decay.

The Dredge. A rankness so familiar it barely turned my stomach.

But this wasn't the Dredge. This was a cell in the depths of the palace, where the thirteen Chorl warriors captured alive during the Chorl retreat had been kept.

Now, those thirteen Chorl lay slumped against the walls of the cell.

I stepped into the room, knelt down beside the nearest body.

The man's head rested against his chest at an awkward angle. I lifted it, felt the awful fluidity of the neck, the bones snapped, and set it back down gently. I glanced over the rest of the bodies, noted they still wore their Chorl clothing, the garish colors now blackened and stained with weeks of wear and use. They'd refused to accept the clothes we'd offered them.

Catrell moved into the room behind me, crossed to another body, the Chorl's shirt black with blood.

"Most of them have broken necks," Catrell said from where he'd knelt. "Four of them killed themselves with this." He pointed to a thin spine jutting out of the man's chest over his heart, no longer than a knife, with no handle. "It's some kind of shell or bone. And there are inscriptions etched into it."

"Where did they get it?"

Catrell shrugged. "I don't know. One of them must have had it on him and we didn't find it when we searched them, when we took their armor, their weapons. Perhaps it was in a shoe, the lining of their clothing. Something."

"Are you certain it didn't come from one of the guards?"

Catrell stilled, hesitated, as if the thought hadn't crossed his mind.

I stepped around the body, came to within a few inches of Catrell's face. "Are you certain this was suicide, and not some guardsman taking out his anger over the attack on the city?"

He nodded. "Yes, it was suicide. We wouldn't have snapped their necks, wouldn't have killed them so cleanly. They would have been bloody and bruised and beaten. And none of us would have used a shell's spine as a weapon."

I frowned, glanced back at the bodies. Because he was right. The deaths were too clean to be revenge. And I'd never seen a knife like the one used to kill the last four Chorl.

But I didn't understand it. Why would they kill themselves? They'd remained in the cells for over a month. Why now?

Catrell hesitated—I could taste it—then asked, "What should we do?"

I sighed. "Burn them. Like the others. Like all of the dead from the attack."

As Catrell motioned the waiting guardsmen into the room and issued commands, I thought of Ottul.

I wasn't certain how she'd react, but I'd have to tell her. She was our only connection to the Chorl now.

*   *   *

"*The left flank is beginning to fail!*" *Liviann screamed over the roar of a thousand clashing swords and bellowing men.*

I spun my horse from the back of the melee, my armor spattered with blood and gore, my sword held high. Liviann stood on top of a low rise, overseeing the battle on the outskirts of the town of Rymerun. She was surrounded by an escort of guardsmen, all watching the field intently, runners darting back and forth, flags being raised and lowered behind them. The huge banners of Venitte snapped in the wind coming from the west.

"*The left flank!*" *she screamed again, her voice amplified by the river so it could be heard, and then she pointed.*

I turned, felt the line behind me surge forward, then back, felt the entire battle like a living thing, pulsing in my blood—

And then I saw the breach, saw the line of Venittian guards failing, struggling to hold.

But they couldn't. Because the Chorl were attacking with the help of their Servants. Servants who weren't supposed to be here.

I growled, kneed the horse sharply, felt the animal's muscles tense and then surge forward and suddenly the wind was in my face, my eyes tearing, and I could feel the pound of the horse's hooves vibrating up into my torso, could feel the spike of adrenaline scorch through my chest.

"*Cerrin! Wait!*" *Liviann yelled, true panic in her voice. "*Gods curse you, wait!*"

I ignored her, thrust her words away with a disdainful shrug. I could see the shifting of the battle ahead, could feel the energy of the Threads wrapping around me as I charged, shivered beneath the White Fire as it scorched along my arms, could taste the Lifeblood on my tongue. I drew the Sight around me, pulled the Threads in tight, felt the Fire building inside me—

And then I plowed into the faltering line with a hoarse, guttural, elemental roar, sword held high as I forced a path through the Venittian lines with the Threads, then descending onto the Chorl when I broke through to their forces.

My first swing lopped the Chorl warrior's arm off at the elbow. He screamed, a harsh, ululating cry, and then he was trampled beneath my horse's hooves, the animal stamping down hard, snorting, eyes wild with the scent of blood. I swung again and again, felt the blade sink into flesh, blood arcing up and out from the edge of the blade with each swing, and with each connection of steel to flesh I grunted, lips drawn back from gritted teeth, putting all the pain, all the grief, into each thrust. Steel clashed, men bellowed.

Then I felt the Threads shift, felt the Sight gather and release.

Men screamed, fire flared, heat shimmered on the Threads and dissipated, and I spun left. Hate surged inside me, muting everything else.

I wanted the Servants. I wanted their blood.

In the moment of distraction, one of the Chorl cut down my horse.

The animal shrieked, the sound piercing the thundering roar of the battle, and suddenly I was falling sideways. I spat a curse, felt the beast slam into the mass of men on my right, felt them stagger and give way, and then I was kicking free of the stirrups, still falling.

We slammed into the ground, the impact jarring through my bones like a hammer, rattling in my teeth, two Chorl crushed beneath the writhing horse's side, my leg free. . . .

But not completely.

Pain shattered upward as it was caught beneath the horse and the ground, white hot and seething. I roared, leaned up onto my elbow and pushed hard against the horse as it shrieked again, struggling, its weight rocking away. I dragged myself out from beneath its death throes through squelching mud, the ground already soaked with blood, my leg a dead weight. I realized I was sobbing, teeth gritted against the pain, the battle still roaring around me.

A Chorl warrior staggered out of the general fray, blood streaming from a shoulder wound. He saw me and grinned wickedly.

He managed one step forward before I released the fire.

He burst into flame, stumbled backward, arms flailing, body twisting until he fell over the dead horse's body and lay still.

Using the sword for support, point dug into the ground, I pulled myself to my feet, leg dragging behind.

More fire gathered through the Threads, this time from three different directions.

And they were all targeted in my vicinity.

I pulled up a shield at the last moment, gasped as the three fires hit, clutched tight to the sword as fire boiled around me, heat seeping through the shield, fresh sweat drenching me beneath my armor. I could feel the Servants shifting position, could feel them approaching as they narrowed their focus, searching for me.

They only had an approximate location, but it wouldn't take them long to find me.

Gripping the hilt of the sword tight, I drew my weight fully onto my good leg, then jerked the sword free of the earth and thrust it into the ground a step away, hopping forward. My leg twisted at the movement, fresh pain shooting up my body, but I choked the pain down, shifted, lurched forward again.

Another pulse and my shield hissed, a glancing blow, but the second shot was dead on, fire roaring up and over my head. Men in the battle around me bellowed as they were caught in the blaze.

Then the fire cleared, the smoke blown away by the wind, and I found myself facing one of the Chorl Servants.

I held her black eyes, saw her own protective shield drawn tight around her, so flimsy, so easy to circumvent with one of the other four Elements. Because these women were not Adepts at all, seemed only to be able to control the Sight, some of the Threads, but nothing more.

The Chorl Servant smiled, and I spat on the ground before her in contempt.

Her smile turned to rage. She raised one hand, the Sight gathering into a tight knot before it, and then her gaze shifted and her smile returned.

Four other Servants stepped clear of the battle still raging on all sides, two with seven gold earrings in each ear, the others with no fewer than four.

I straightened. I'd assumed there were three of them. Three, I could handle, even with shields to protect them, even if they all wore seven rings.

But five . . . ?

I began pulling Threads to me, began strengthening my shield. My leg throbbed like a bitch, and I tasted death. Like blood and smoke mixed together on my lips.

Rymerun suddenly felt like a trap. The Servants had lured us here, the chance to take back the town too good for us to pass up, especially with the knowledge that there weren't any Servants here to protect the Chorl warriors.

But that wasn't true. They'd remained out of the battle, hidden, until they were ready to lure me away from my position, away from Liviann.

They'd changed their strategy; they were hunting us now, instead of the other way around.

All five raised their hands and I felt the gathering force. Grimly, I pulled my shield tight, began weaving Threads to circumvent some of their own shields. My shield wouldn't hold for long against the concerted effort of all five, but I could take a few of them with me.

They released and I cried out, stumbling down to my knee, weight full upon the sword. I felt my shield beginning to crumble, clenched my jaw, thought of Olivia, of Jaer and Pallin, and sent a sheet of fire out along the Threads.

The force raging against my shield faltered as two of the Servants screamed and their attacks cut off as they were incinerated, but the damage had been done. I couldn't sustain my shield, felt it crumbling around me, felt the heat of the remaining three Servants creeping in, edging closer, closer.

I bowed down over the sword planted in the ground, the thought of death . . . calming. As the Servants' fires began to lick my skin, I smiled.

And then suddenly the fire ended, the focus of the Servants shifting elsewhere. With barked commands, fire arched out from my position, angled toward the hill.

Toward Liviann.

I surged up onto my leg, saw Liviann leading a charge of reinforcements down the hill. She deflected one of the fireballs, threw a jagged lance of lightning that sizzled into one of the Servants, body juddering as it absorbed the current—

And then the remaining two Servants bolted, vanishing into the ranks of the Chorl like smoke, lost among the seething men.

The reinforcements hit the line of Chorl like a ram, thrusting them back, away from my position. Venittian men streamed around me, on foot and on horseback, and then Liviann stood before me, enraged.

"You fool!" she spat. "You bloody fool! What's wrong with you? What in hells did you think you were doing? You were almost killed. We can't afford to lose any of the Seven. Not now."

"It was a trap," I said, and then the weakness brought on by the pain, by the effort to defend myself from the Servants, hit hard and I collapsed.

Liviann caught me, spat a curse. "We should never have come here. We should have remained back in Venitte, defending its walls."

Rage filled me. "No!"

Liviann snorted, lowered me to the ground gently, eyes already scanning the leg. I could feel her reaching for the Rose, could feel its warmth enfold her, begin to enfold me as she directed its power.

"No!" I repeated, and grabbed her upper arm, pulled her in tight, until I was certain I had her attention. "We had to leave Venitte, Liviann. We can't cower behind its walls and expect the Chorl to just leave. We have to stop defending and attack. If we don't, they'll never leave."

Liviann met my intensity with a doubtful frown. "You may be right, Cerrin," *she said, voice hard. "But no one on the Frigean coast will survive without the help of the Seven. You're too reckless. Olivia and your daughters are dead. You can't throw your life away over them. Not when we need you."*

Then she turned her attention back to my leg and reached forward with the Rose and its warmth embraced me—

I woke in my chambers in the palace. My leg throbbed, as if it had been crushed beneath the weight of a horse. I shuddered at the memory, at the horror of the carnage on the battlefield. I stared up at the cloth draped from the tops of the four posts of my bed, hanging down in supple folds, and let the raw emotions wash away from me.

As they did so, Cerrin's words sank in.

"We can't stay in Amenkor," I said to the empty room, my voice quiet. "We have to attack."

⊬— Chapter 4

"I agree. We'll have to take the battle to the Chorl eventually. Otherwise, we're simply a target to them. A vulnerable target." Captain Catrell gazed down the table toward me. Between us, Avrell, Eryn, Westen, and Darryn shifted in their seats. Keven stood behind me. "I've been meaning to approach you about this," Catrell continued, "but we've been so focused on repairing the wharfs and the gates that there hasn't been much time, or manpower, for anything significant. We're barely manning the walls as it is."

"So you're saying we don't have enough guardsmen?" I asked.

Catrell pressed his lips tight, one hand on the table before him. His thumb circled the tip of his middle finger as he thought. "Not at the moment. Not for an all-out assault on the Chorl's position."

"Then what?" Avrell asked. "We just sit here and wait for them to attack again? We need to cut them off, establish a boundary, something."

Catrell nodded. "But we can't do that right now. Darryn and I are training men as fast as we can. Once the current group is finished, we'll have doubled our numbers. And we've just started a new group of militia in training. We should have a formidable force in another month, an army that I wouldn't feel guilty about sending into battle against the Chorl." He caught Avrell's eye, then mine, face stern. "Throwing these men against the Chorl right now would only get them killed. It would accomplish nothing."

Silence descended, Catrell and I squaring off. I wanted to meet the Chorl head on. I was tired of sitting in the dark, waiting for something to happen. I wanted to take the offensive. I felt frustrated, powerless—unable to help Erick, unable to have ships repaired instantly, or walls and gates built.

The fact that I trusted Catrell, knew that he was right, didn't help.

"However," Darryn said.

The word hung in the air, caught everyone's attention.

"What?" I asked.

"We don't have enough men to send out an army . . . but we could spare enough for a scouting party. If we do intend to meet the Chorl somewhere along the way, to make a stand, then we need to know where they are. We need information. Have they taken Temall yet? Where are their forces? Where is their supply train? How do they intend to approach us—by land or sea?"

Catrell was already nodding.

"We could send a ship southward," Westen said. "Land a party near Temall, see what the Chorl are up to. We know nothing about their forces—how many men, how many ships they have."

How many Servants, I thought grimly.

"Do it," I said. "Get a group together, as many as you can spare but not so large that the party will be easy to discover." Catrell and Darryn nodded. I could see Catrell already planning, his face set, brow slightly creased. "How long will it take?"

Catrell shrugged. "The men can be equipped and ready to go within a day. We can outfit one of the recovered Chorl ships in about the same time once the next one is ready to sail, probably another few days. But it will take about five days to reach Temall once they sail."

"Keven," I said, heard him step forward, "gather an escort. Coordinate it with Catrell and Darryn."

"What for?"

"Because, when the ship leaves for Temall, I want to be on it."

"Absolutely not!" Avrell barked, standing abruptly. Until now, he and Eryn had remained quiet. But now his face was suffused with a stubborn glare.

The others at the table shifted.

"What do you mean?"

Avrell must have heard the dangerous tone in my voice, but he ignored it.

"You can't go on this ship. The thought is ludicrous! Not so recently after an attack on the city. Not when the people of Amenkor are drawing all of their strength, all of their perseverance, from you. In their minds, *you* are the only reason we survived this past winter. *You* are the reason we survived the attack by the Chorl. If you leave now, with the city barely in the first stages of recovery, with the throne cracked and useless, it will strike everyone in Amenkor as abandonment, no matter what you tell them. No." He shook his head forcefully. "You can't leave. Not now, and especially not for something as simple as a scouting party."

I bristled, ready to argue with him, but glanced around at the other faces and realized that everyone at the table agreed with him.

But the need to *do* something, *anything,* burned in my arms and legs.

"Varis," Eryn said, and leaned forward, reached out to grip my forearm. "Avrell's correct. Even without the throne, you are Amenkor. You *became* Amenkor this past winter, in the minds of its people. And you can still keep track of the scouting party using the Fire if Catrell is there."

I frowned, my gaze skimming over all of them one last time, looking for support, for an ally.

I didn't find one.

Even without the throne, I was trapped in the city.

"Fine," I said, the word curt, and still dangerous.

Keven sidled back into position behind me. An awkward silence followed, Darryn fidgeting restlessly.

"Mistress," Westen said, leaning forward. "Regarding the ship . . ."

I shot him a baleful look. "What?"

Westen's lips twitched with a smile; he was impervious to all of my dagger-sharp looks, he'd seen them all during our practice sessions. "I believe that Catrell should stay here. He's needed to train the guardsmen. However, I can be spared."

I stared at Westen a long moment. Seekers would make much better scouts than guardsmen, and could be used for other purposes once they were there.

"Yes," I said, and something in the tone of my voice must have changed because everyone suddenly relaxed, tension bleeding out of the room. "How many Seekers can we spare?"

"Enough."

I nodded. "Catrell, work with Westen. Let me know as soon as the ship is ready to sail."

"So you want us—all four of us—to help you build a wall around the entire city, is that it?"

I felt my jaw clench at the thick derision in Illum Forestead's voice, but forced the anger down. I remembered him from the ceremony on the wharf, when he'd been raised to full Master, remembered Borund holding out the bright yellow jacket with dark red embroidery that he now wore.

But I didn't remember this blatant arrogance.

Settling back into my seat in the audience chamber, I suddenly wished I'd called all four of the new merchants into attendance in the throne room. Even cracked, the throne would have lent me more weight than simply having Avrell and Keven at my side. I could feel Avrell's anger at Illum's temerity, a throbbing pulse of darkness on the river. "That's exactly what I want."

Illum snorted. "And what do we get out of it?"

Jack Trevain almost gasped, his look of horror only slightly more open than Walter Davvens' and William's.

"Protection," I said, before anyone else could respond. "Your assets would be protected from any further attacks if we had a wall enclosing the city. The warehouses are already protected from a sea approach; however, they are out-side of the current walls. They're vulnerable to a land attack."

Illum frowned. "I can protect my resources myself, if necessary. What else can you give me?"

"Oh, stuff it, Illum," Walter suddenly spat. "In case you've forgotten, this is the Mistress of Amenkor! She drove the Chorl out of Amenkor. If not for her, you wouldn't even have any resources to protect. You wouldn't even be a merchant!"

"Most likely," Avrell added tightly, "you'd be dead."

Utter silence. But I could see that the thought wouldn't hold Illum for long. I could *feel* it.

"If you help fund the building of a wall—one that will enclose the eastern portions of the city as well as the Dredge—I will give you a portion of the land inside that wall."

All four of the merchants' interest piqued.

Avrell stepped forward and laid a sheaf of papers out onto the table of the audience chamber. "Our engineers have studied the surrounding land and have decided that the best place to build the wall is here, with three gates leading out of the city—one for the main road to the east obviously, and two others, here and here. The wall would connect to the existing walls of the palace here, above the southern cliff face and extend around to the wall along the southern jut of land leading out to the watchtower on the harbor."

"What about the River?" Jack Trevain said. He usually kept silent, letting the others speak for him, but once the plans had been produced, he'd leaned forward intently, brow creased in thought.

"Aside from the gates themselves, the River would be the most vulnerable part of the wall. We intend to build the wall over the River, with a metal gate that could be lowered into the River's bed in the event of an attack."

Jack nodded.

"What holdings would we get inside the wall?" Illum demanded.

Walter shot him a disgusted glance.

Avrell shoved the map of the wall's plans to one side, producing another map of the city as it stood after the attack. "A significant portion of the lower city was destroyed during the attack. We've divided up the worst sections into four parcels, all of which have a few buildings that remain intact."

All four merchants, including William, leaned forward over the new map, mumbling under their breath as they traced the allotments out. Avrell stepped back, arms crossed on his chest. Jack and Walter seemed impressed, their first low mutters escalating into excited whispers. William had already seen the map, had helped Avrell and me draw it up.

But Illum stood back after a long moment and said, "There's nothing in the middle ward here. It's all in the lower city."

Everyone in the room stilled. Jack and Walter kept their eyes on the table. Keven took a single, meaningful step forward.

I stood, let my irritation furrow my brow as my eyes narrowed. "Are you saying the terms are not acceptable?"

Illum hesitated, fear flashing briefly in his eyes. He brushed at his straw-colored hair, glanced once toward the other merchants, then straightened. His eyes hardened. "I'm saying that the addition of a building in the middle ward—a building to house our new operations—would *make* the terms acceptable."

No one moved. I could feel Avrell willing me to say no, could feel Keven's disapproval like a hand pressing into my back.

But I thought of what Catrell had said, that the army wasn't large enough for us to meet the Chorl outside the city and expect a good outcome, that it wouldn't be large enough for such an attack within the next few months. We needed this wall.

And according to William, I needed the resources of all four of the new merchants' in order to build it. If I couldn't get Illum to agree . . .

I let the tension in the room hold for a moment longer, then said in a dangerously flat voice, "Very well. Avrell will draw up the agreements and send them to the guild."

Illum nodded, a self-satisfied smirk flickering across his face as he turned toward the door. I felt the urge to draw my dagger, restrained myself with effort as Illum, Jack, and Walter filed out the door.

William lingered.

"You shouldn't have given in," Avrell said, moving to reassemble the pages scattered on the table.

"I had no choice," I said shortly.

"Next time, he'll want more."

"Next time," I growled, "I need to have more options."

Avrell didn't say anything, but he paused at the door. "I'll have Nathem start the work on the agreements right away."

When he left, I sank back down into my chair with a heavy sigh.

Silence reigned for a long moment, but then William stood. "Illum is an arrogant bastard."

I gave a short laugh, then caught William's gaze. "He reminds me of Bloodmark. Except he doesn't carry a knife."

William's expression sobered. Not many knew of Bloodmark, the first person I'd killed in the slums because I'd *wanted* him dead. Because he'd killed the white-dusty man and his wife, to hurt me. He hadn't been one of Erick's marks.

But he'd deserved to die.

William looked up. "How is Erick?"

I shook my head. "The same."

When William didn't respond, I stood. I could feel William's sympathy and grief, knew he could do nothing to soothe the same ache I felt inside myself. "In fact, I need to go see him now. Isaiah has me help feed him. I use the White

Fire to get him to eat, since he can't feed himself. And for a little while, I take away his pain."

As I moved toward the door, William said, "I'll come with you."

"No!"

Ottul stamped her foot where she stood looking out over the eastern portions of Amenkor, her arms folded obstinately across her chest, her back rigid, her face contorted into a fierce scowl.

I almost growled in frustration, shot a glance toward Marielle, who stood behind me near the doorway to Ottul's room.

Quietly, Marielle said, "It started a few days ago. She's refused to work with me since. All she says is 'No!' and then stands there rigidly, like now, or falls into that hunched over position, moaning and chanting. Praying. I don't know what to do."

I frowned, turned back to Ottul.

Four days ago, I'd informed her of the captured Chorl warriors' deaths. It had taken a while to get her to understand, but when I placed the spine the last few warriors had used to kill themselves onto the table, she'd gasped and reached out toward it, almost involuntarily—

Then halted. Withdrawing her hand, she'd stepped away, turned her back on the table, on me. She'd muttered a single word, "Antreul," and then fallen silent, staring out over the city, trembling.

On the river, her grief had been thick, but not enough to overwhelm her fear.

Even as I tried to sort out the emotions that lay beneath the fear, she'd stepped back from the window, had curled up into the same kneeling position I'd seen before, her face already wet with tears, and started to pray. Her voice choked with phlegm, face twisted into a tortured look—like grief but not completely grief—she'd covered her head with her arms and begun to rock.

It was a reaction I'd expected . . . and yet it wasn't. I didn't understand the emotions that lay beneath the grief. I didn't understand the guilt, the self-loathing. *Antreul.*

Now, I bit back the bitter, commanding words that leaped to my mouth, forced myself to relax, to think. She no longer cooperated with Marielle, and I needed her to cooperate. Erick needed her to cooperate. I needed to trust her enough to let her look at Erick, to see if she could help with the spell placed on him.

But at the moment, I wanted to throttle her. I suddenly wondered if Erick had ever felt this way during the training sessions with me in the slums.

The thought brought a faint grin to my lips.

A gust of wind blew through the open window and Ottul closed her eyes, leaned in toward it, her long black hair fanning out behind her. She sucked in a deep breath and held it, savoring the fresh air.

I turned suddenly, moved toward the door behind Marielle, sensing by the prickling in my neck that Ottul was watching me from behind. I opened the door to the hall and spoke a few moments with Keven and the Servant Trielle, who was guarding the wardings. Keven frowned in disapproval, but nodded. Two guardsmen were sent, and all of those that remained tensed, glances passing between them.

I turned back to the room, to Marielle.

Ottul watched with blatant distrust from the window. But the distrust was tinged with curiosity.

"Do you know what's wrong with her?" Marielle whispered.

I shook my head. "No."

Without closing the door, I moved back into the room, halting two steps before Ottul. She didn't draw back. But her eyes narrowed.

"Then what?" Marielle asked, frustration tainting her voice. "What are you doing?"

"We," I said, "are going to go on a little . . . excursion."

Ottul scowled as she tried to figure out the words.

I smiled, even though my shoulders had tightened. Behind, I heard the arrival of the additional guardsmen Keven had sent for, felt Trielle unravel the warding to let them into the room.

Ottul's eyes widened, her arms coming down into a defensive posture, the river roiling as she prepared to fight. She hissed, the sound harsh with warning, like a gutterscum cat cornered at the end of an alley.

I didn't react, didn't prepare a shield or shift my stance.

After a moment, the guardsmen staying near the door, Ottul faltered.

"Follow me," I said, turning my back to her as I moved to the door. At its entrance, I glanced back, motioned her forward. "Come here."

She knew those words. Uncertain, she straightened from her defensive stance and shifted forward, her gaze flickering between the guardsmen to either side, to Marielle in mute question, then back to the guardsmen. She halted when one of them coughed, glared at him, then continued until she stood at Marielle's side.

The guardsmen closed in around us, Trielle still outside, ready to pull the warding back into place if Ottul showed any sign of attacking. Another Servant—Heddan, a young girl from the north, her straw-colored hair vibrant compared to Trielle's darker tangles—had joined her. I gave them both a nod, saw Heddan bite her lip. Trielle was older, close to my age, her face grim, her eyes locked on Ottul's every move. They'd all heard how hard it had been to capture and hold Ottul initially.

Keven waited in the hall. "Are you certain this is a good idea?" he asked as we began moving down the hall, guardsmen on all sides, the two Servants behind. Ottul kept close to Marielle. She tried to see everything at once, her neck craning to peer through the guardsmen ahead and to the sides while at the same time trying to remain out of sight.

"I have no idea," I said. "But she's no longer cooperating, and I need to know what's happened to Erick. We've run out of things to do while she's trapped in that room."

"I suppose."

I shot Keven a dark look. "We're taking her to the gardens where the Servants are training. If she can escape from all of us there . . ." I let the thought trail off, heard Keven grunt in agreement.

When we reached the gardens, Eryn had the Servants paired off and scattered throughout the paths among the newly leafed trees and bushes and the spring flowers. She was moving among them, barking out orders or correcting flaws. She saw us pause at the garden's entrance, but didn't immediately head over.

As we waited, Keven motioned to the guardsmen, who spread out along the perimeter of the garden in both directions.

Ottul barely noticed. Her eyes had narrowed as soon as she saw the Servants, her back going rigid. She watched the practice session intently.

Breaking away from the last pair, Eryn came to my side. "Keven sent word that you were coming. I have them practicing shield placement and manipulation, something innocuous, since . . ." Her gaze flicked toward Ottul.

"Good."

"What do you want to do with her?"

I shrugged. "Let her watch. Keeping her in the room isn't working anymore. If we want her to cooperate, we're going to have to let her out sooner or later. Let's sit her down near the pool. Trielle and Heddan can watch her. I want to see what you've come up with regarding the linking of the Servants."

I caught Ottul's attention, led her to a small pool, a curved stone bench at its edge, and forced her to focus on my eyes. "Stay here."

When she gave a grudging nod of understanding, Eryn, Marielle, and I moved aside, leaving Trielle and Heddan behind to watch her.

"We haven't had much success with linking the Servants," Eryn said. "Basically, we're working off the idea that the link is forged like the strength-draining conduit I and the Ochean used against you while sparring or fighting, except in reverse. So far, I've managed to get a few of the Servants to connect using such conduits, and to transfer their strength back and forth."

"But?" I prompted.

Eryn shook her head. "But even though they're supporting each other, augmenting each other's power, it still isn't increasing their strengths to the level that the Ochean and the Chorl exhibited. I don't think this is what they're doing when they forge a link."

"Show me what you've done."

"Gwenn."

One of the Servants halted her construction of a merged shield with another Servant, letting the currents of the river flow back into their natural paths, and stepped forward.

"Yes, Mistress. Eryn," Gwenn said, and bowed her head, fidgeting nervously. She was young, no more than ten, and practically seething with energy.

"The Mistress wants to see you and Marielle attempt a linking. As you've done during practice."

Gwenn groaned, but Marielle grabbed her by the elbow and stepped to one side, kneeling before her and whispering to her, hands on her shoulders, but not loud enough for me to overhear. Gwenn shot a glance toward me, eyes wide and terrified in her rounded face, then to the ground. Her hands clasped before her, she stared at the ground hard, then closed her eyes and drew in a short breath.

Satisfied, Marielle stood and stepped away, closed her eyes as well.

On the river, the flows between them grew disturbed, as if someone had reached forward and swirled them with their hands. Then I felt tendrils reach out from Gwenn toward Marielle, snaking forward and intertwining until they formed a thin conduit. When the conduit reached Marielle, it attached itself to a place near Marielle's heart, where I could see the White Fire I'd placed inside Marielle before the Chorl attack burning.

Marielle smiled in satisfaction. "Now form a shield, Mistress."

"What for?" I asked, already forming the shield before me. I noted that Eryn had stepped away, had deferred to Marielle now that she and Gwenn were linked.

"So I can show you how it works," Marielle said with a twisted smile.

I waited, shield in place—

And suddenly felt Marielle pushing at the shield from the far side. It wasn't an attack, wasn't an edged blade or a punch of force, but instead a widespread gentle pressure that steadily increased, to the point where I felt myself unconsciously pushing back in order to keep the shield in place, a wall being held up by another wall.

"This is just me," Marielle said, her voice a little short with effort. "Now we'll add in Gwenn."

Before she'd finished, I felt energy pouring down through the conduit from Gwenn—

And I gasped, staggered as the pressure on my shield doubled, shoving me back.

"Enough," Eryn said.

Gwenn let the conduit go, and Marielle dropped the pressure against my shield. Both had satisfied expressions on their faces, although Gwenn's appeared more exultant than Marielle's. The older Servant reached out and ruffled the hair on Gwenn's head, an unconscious gesture that sent a pang through my heart. Erick had ruffled my hair the same way on the Dredge.

Behind us, I heard someone snort.

Frowning, I turned and caught Ottul watching, her face twisted into a sneer. As soon as she caught my gaze, the sneer vanished and she dropped her head, as if she were inspecting the reeds at the edge of the pool, or the little minnows in its depths.

"That felt fairly significant to me," I said, turning back. Gwenn looked crestfallen, her eyes on Ottul. "Why do you think the Chorl are using something different?"

"Because when we try to link more than two people together there isn't a subsequent doubling of the power for each person, as we saw from the Ochean and her links. When four of them were linked together—the Ochean and three of her Servants—the resultant force was around eight times the strength of just one. When we link four people together, we only get about four times the force."

"The difference is geometric, rather than arithmetic," Marielle broke in. "When we link, we're only *adding* individual strengths together. When the Chorl link, their strengths are being *multiplied* together."

It sounded suspiciously mathematical. "So they're using a different kind of link." I tried to think back to the attack on the outer walls, as seen through Eryn's eyes. That was the only time we'd witnessed the Chorl actually linking, so that they could destroy the inner gates. They'd linked to destroy the watchtowers over the bay, but no one had seen that attack, only the consequences. "Do you remember seeing how they linked to destroy the gates?" I asked Eryn.

"No." Her voice was laced with regret. "I was too distracted trying to defend the gates to pay that close attention."

"So was I. They used conduits somehow, though. I remember seeing the conduits form. But it happened too fast for me to see details."

We both looked toward Ottul.

"She knows how to do it," Eryn said, and Ottul turned, as if she sensed that we were talking about her. "That's obvious now."

"Yes. We just have to figure out how to get her to tell us."

"I see you have a Chorl prisoner," someone said as I left the gardens where the Servants continued to train, Ottul still sitting beside the pool, watched by Trielle and Heddan. "Is she one of the Chorl Servants you spoke of?"

I halted, blinked at the darkness of the palace corridor, my eyes still dazzled by the sunlight of the gardens.

Brandan Vard stood at one of the open arched windows that looked out onto the garden a few paces down the corridor, the sigil of Venitte catching the light as he turned toward me. Light brown hair, bleached almost blond by the sun; brown eyes; narrow face with high cheekbones and a thin nose. I hadn't seen him since I'd questioned him and Tristan about the throne, hadn't really looked at him even then, too focused on learning about Venitte, about their preparations for the Chorl. But now . . .

"So, is she?"

I started, frowned at myself, then straightened. "Is she what?"

Brandan smiled, dimples appearing in each cheek. He nodded out the window, leaning back against the sill. "Is she one of the Chorl Servants?"

"Yes."

"And you let her watch your training sessions?"

"Not normally. Today is an exception."

Brandan looked over his shoulder into the garden. "She seems more interested in the fish in the pond than in the training."

I hesitated, then moved up to Brandan's side, felt Keven and my escort of guardsmen shift around me without coming close. Brandan seemed . . . different. Relaxed.

I wondered if it was because Captain Tristan wasn't here watching over him. I suddenly wondered what I could learn from him when he wasn't under Tristan's supervision.

Out in the garden, Gwenn had knelt down beside the pond, was pointing to something in its depths, Ottul leaning forward from the bench, listening to the girl's excited chatter. She couldn't possibly understand Gwenn's explanation, but she seemed to be concentrating more on the words than when Marielle tried to explain things to her in her room.

"Maybe I should have taken her out of her rooms earlier," I said with a frown.

Brandan didn't respond, and when I shrugged and turned away from the scene in the gardens, I found him watching me, head tilted slightly. The intensity of his look sent a shiver through my shoulders, down into my gut. A pleasant shiver.

"I thought you would have left for Venitte already," I said, then cursed myself.

His eyebrows rose slightly, but he laughed. "Hardly. Tristan has business to attend to with the merchants' guild, especially now that there are four new merchants. He's kept busy the past few days, arranging shipments, learning what he can of the new Amenkor . . . and the new Mistress."

I frowned. "And what have you done?"

"Everything." He gave me a mischievous grin, then sighed heavily. He shook his head. "Nothing much, actually." I could sense the lie . . . but again it was tinged with truth. And on the river, he appeared both gray and red. "I was sent as a token of sincerity, a representative of Lord March and the power of Venitte, nothing more. Once Tristan delivered the message, my duties were done." A note of bitterness had crept into his voice. His hand drifted to the pendant hanging around his neck, tilted it this way and that in the sunlight. Then he shrugged, met my gaze squarely. "But it got me out of Venitte. Sometimes, with the constant training, both as a Servant and Protector, it feels like I'm trapped in the city, never free to do what I want."

My gut twisted. I tried not to think of Avrell telling me—no, *ordering* me—to stay in Amenkor. The throne had trapped me here before, and now that the throne was gone, now that I was free, I found myself trapped anyway. By my role as Mistress.

And Brandan had seen me wince.

"Have you seen the city?" I asked without thought, trying to distract him, to turn him away from whatever he may have seen.

"No."

"Perhaps," I began, then hesitated.

I drew in a sharp breath, suddenly suspicious. But there was no taint on the river, only the smell of sunlight, of the sea.

Brandan was looking at me uncertainly.

I shrugged the vague suspicion aside. "Perhaps I could show you? I need to check up on a few things anyway."

Straightening, Brandan grinned. "I'd love to." He bowed his head, glancing up through the locks of his hair. "Mistress."

That pleasant little shiver coursed through me again. A shiver I distrusted, even though it intrigued me.

I turned to Keven, caught his warning frown. "Ready some horses."

We rode down through the two wards, pausing to inspect the reconstruction going on at each gate, Brandan shocked by the devastation and skeptical at my claim that the gates had fallen within the space of an hour, that in fact the entire attack had lasted no more than a day. Nathem, the aged Second of the Mistress, was overseeing the progress there and reported that everything was proceeding smoothly. The walls to either side were covered with scaffolding crawling with workers and engineers, ropes and pulleys hauling huge stones off of carts that had brought the granite from the quarry to the north of the city. The stone portion of the inner gates was almost completed, a rough arch beginning to sprout from the edges of the two rebuilt walls. Blacksmiths were already forging the iron that would bind the wood for the doors themselves.

"And there was no way to stop them?" Brandan asked, disbelief still coloring his voice.

"The Servants were our only defense from the Ochean once she reached the walls. The army was useless. And Eryn and I didn't hold the wall for long."

Brandan shook his head, brow creased in thought.

From the walls, I turned left, heading away from the main road down to the wharf that passed through the worst of the devastated city and moving east along the River.

As we passed into the industrial quarter, where the stockyards, tannery, and most of the blacksmiths and other tradesmen worked, I said, "You mentioned training as a Protector. What's that?"

Brandan barked laughter. "It sounds more interesting than it actually is. Those of us with talent—like the Servants you have here—are raised in the city, although we aren't as constrained as it appears you are here. We don't have to remain in the palace. In fact, we can roam throughout the city, which is much larger than Amenkor, maybe twice as large."

"The Servants leave the palace," I said, although now that I thought about it I realized that they didn't leave very often. Everything was provided for them in the palace; there was no need for them to roam the city. They'd probably spent more time in the city this past winter organizing and running the kitchens associated to the warehouses than they had their entire time here.

And Venitte was larger than Amenkor? Twice as large?

I tried to imagine Amenkor spreading out along the River and up and down the coast, holding twice as many people . . . and couldn't.

"In any case," Brandan continued, "as Servants we, of course, have to train in the use of the Sight. We do that at the College, located in the heart of Venitte, inside Deranian's Wall. But all Servants are also required to take training as guardsmen as well. In fact, we train to be Protectors, guardsmen who have the honor and distinction of serving under Lord March's direct authority." He twisted the words *honor and distinction.*

"You don't make it sound as if it's much of an honor."

Brandan snorted. "It's not. At least not for the Servants. Most of the Protectors become Protectors by first training in the guard and then earning some type of distinction so that they are promoted to the Protectors. But for the Servants . . ."

"It's automatic," I finished.

Brandan nodded. "Most of the regular Protectors don't feel that we've earned our place. They think we should be part of the regular guard at first, and only made a Protector once we've proved our worth. As a consequence, the Servants tend to keep to themselves. Thankfully, the regular Protectors have a healthy respect for the Sight and aside from some rude comments and general ridicule they leave us alone."

I frowned. It sounded like living on the Dredge, where those that were alike banded together into gangs, keeping those that were weak or different apart, separated and ridiculed, until they formed a gang of their own.

Or until those that were different learned to survive on their own.

Or died.

"How many of the Servants are there in Venitte?" I asked.

Brandan didn't immediately respond, as if uncertain he should, or surprised that I didn't already know. "About sixty."

"All men?"

"Of course. Any women that we find in or close to Venitte that we think can use the Sight are sent up here to Amenkor to train, just as you send the men down to us."

I nodded. Something was niggling at the edges of my mind, as if there were something here I was supposed to see . . . something I should realize. I concentrated on it a moment, but it slipped away.

"What about here?" Brandan asked. "How many Servants do you have in Amenkor at the moment?"

"Twenty-nine. We lost three during the attack, killed by the Chorl."

I didn't tell him that seven had died last year, when Avrell and Nathem had been trying to replace Eryn as Mistress while she was still seated on the throne and going mad.

We'd reached the edge of the blacksmithing section and as I dismounted, Brandan following suit, Keven sent one of the escorting guardsmen into the long open building that roared with the sound of bellows and the steady clangor of hammers on steel and anvil. I'd been forced to raise my voice to answer Brandan as we approached and now didn't even attempt to talk. I stood outside one of the open arches into the interior of the building as heat rolled outward, blowing the hair back from my face and turning my skin taut and waxy with sweat, sucking the breath from my lungs and making it hard to breathe.

Inside, heat distorted the air, men and boys moving among the seething coals and embers, sparks flying from white-hot metal as it was shaped, steam rising as pieces were dunked into waiting pails of water. Finished pieces—armor, swords, pikes, halberds, and daggers—lined the nearest wall. A few other unidentifiable pieces lay among these, parts needed for the gates, the reconstruction of the ships, or any of the other hundred projects scattered throughout the city.

Brandan's eyebrows rose as he saw the stockpile of weapons, but he said nothing.

The guardsmen Keven had sent returned abruptly with one of the blacksmiths: Hugh, the man huge, at least twice as wide as me and half again as tall.

I watched him approach, feeling myself tense even though I was surrounded by Keven and the escort.

Which made it all the more disconcerting when the man suddenly dropped to his knee, sketched the sign of the Skewed Throne over his chest, and bowed his head down before me. "Mistress," Hugh murmured, his voice deep and pleasant, booming over the roar of the smithy, "it's an honor. You saved us all."

The noise of the smithy fell into a sudden lull.

Swallowing against the heat, conscious of all of those watching me, including Brandan, I reached forward and touched the blacksmith's head. "Thank you."

Hugh rose, and the clamor of work rose again. As he stood, I could see the pockmarks of scars up and down his arms from the sparks of the fires. An old but vicious burn ran the length of his upper arm, pink and rough compared to the smooth heat-tanned skin around it.

"An accident when I was an apprentice," Hugh said in answer to my unasked question. He grinned. "It's nothing. What can I do for you?"

Drawing my eyes away from the burn, I shouted, "I came to see how things were progressing."

Hugh nodded, face becoming serious. "We should have enough to outfit the entire group of men currently in training. We've already started on the armor for the next contingent." He led me a little deeper into the heat of the forge, pointing to the stacks of completed armor, then moved on. "Avrell and Catrell wanted us to start working on some shields as well. Then there's the chain." He halted before a heap of huge linked ovals, each link as tall as I was, and as thick as my waist.

My eyes widened. I didn't think I could lift one of the links by itself, let alone several of them together.

"What's the chain for?" I asked.

Hugh grinned. "For the entrance to the harbor. Avrell and Regin think we can stretch it across the opening, hung close to the bottom so that it won't interfere with the ships. They want the ends to be connected to some heavy-duty winches inside the new watchtowers. Then, when the Chorl return . . ." He mimed grappling with a winch, and in my mind's eye I could see the heavy chain, strung across the harbor, rising until it was high enough that it would impede incoming ships. "Like a gate for the harbor," Hugh finished.

"An ingenious idea," Brandan said, startling me. I hadn't realized he'd followed us into the ironworks.

Hugh nodded. "If we can get it to work."

It made me wonder what else Avrell and the others had been thinking up in the way of defenses.

"And what's all this," I said, nodding toward a heap of unfamiliar objects to one side.

"That is for Master Borund. For the new ships he's building."

Surprised, I waved Hugh back to work, the large blacksmith bowing before ambling off toward the fire, pulling on heavy work gloves as he went. I hadn't realized Borund had progressed so far. I knew he'd begun work on a portion of the wharf, redesigning it for his new ship-building operation, but other than that. . . .

I'd have to ask William about that.

Brandan and I carefully made our way back to the forge's entrance, mounted up, and headed back toward the center of the city. As soon as we were away from the tumult of the smithy, Brandan said, "Many of the people have made that sign on their chest as we passed them on the street." He mimicked the smith's gesture. "What is it?"

I shifted uncomfortably in my saddle, the horse snorting as it picked up on my discomfort. I hadn't noticed the people making the sign. "It's the sign of the Skewed Throne. Don't they have something similar in Venitte?"

"Nothing like that. The people of Amenkor revere you as more than a leader, almost like a religious figure."

I didn't answer. "Don't they treat Lord March the same way? Doesn't he have the Sight?"

Brandan gave me a strange look. "Lord March isn't one of the Servants. Servants serve as Protectors, and our Master, Sorrenti, serves on Lord March's Council as an adviser, but Lord March isn't one of us himself. The other Council members would never allow it. Someone with the Sight controlling the Council . . . it could never happen. They would have too much power. Even Lord Sorrenti's presence on the Council is barely tolerated."

I frowned. "I don't understand. Lord March doesn't rule the city?"

Brandan snorted. "The Council of Eight rules the city. Lord March is the head of the Council, and has enough power that he can generally do whatever he wants. But he has to get the Council to agree, since they control the key interests in the city—the trade, the lands, the guilds. For anything significant, Lord March has to have their approval."

"But if the Council members control the land and the guilds, where does Lord March's power come from?"

"The Protectorate," Brandan said. "Lord March controls the Protectorate and the general guard. He controls the army."

We continued down to the Dredge, crossing over the River so that I could check on the kitchen and warehouse I'd kept running using the palace's resources in the slums. While there, I noticed that those that worked in the kitchen—mostly women and children—all wore white dresses similar to the ones the palace servants wore, and all of them bowed or nodded their heads to me, signing across their chests.

And the Dredge itself had changed. Near the River, some of the buildings had been damaged in the attack, but for the most part the slums had remained untouched by the fighting. However, the streets and alleys, niches and narrows, were all . . . clean. No heaps of piled stone and debris, blurring the edges of the buildings and crevices. Cobblestones were still cracked underfoot, uneven and broken, but all the garbage and detritus I'd come to know while living in the slums had been removed. Part of it was because Avrell had used the old stone of the crumbling buildings in the slums as part of the reconstruction efforts in the warehouse district near the wharf, the stone cheaper and closer than stone taken from the quarry. But that couldn't account for all of it.

Then I noticed the militia, those men under Darryn's command who had taken it upon themselves to protect the kitchen and warehouse over the winter and who were now extending that protection to the rest of the slums. A rogue gutterscum thug—one not unlike what I'd once been—hovered near the entrance to an alley, watching those passing by on the street with sharp eyes. When he caught the militia man's eye, the soldier simply frowned, and without a word the thug vanished into the alley, moving on to better hunting grounds.

The two militia men moved farther down the Dredge. Before passing from sight, I noticed that the Skewed Throne symbol had been hand-stitched to the front of their shirts.

As we crossed the bridge back into the lower city of Amenkor and began to head toward the wharf, I thought about what Eryn had said. *Even without the throne, you are Amenkor. You* became *Amenkor this past winter, in the minds of its people.*

"You're quiet," Brandan said.

I glanced toward him, noticed he was watching me carefully, realized he had been watching me carefully since the tour had first begun. I gave him a hesitant smile. "It's . . . different. It's not the same as when I lived there. It's cleaner. Safer."

Brandan turned to look back toward the Dredge, brow furrowed in thought.

"What about you?" I asked.

"What do you mean?"

"Where were you before you were sent to become a Servant?"

Brandan fell silent, a troubled look crossing his face. For a long moment, I thought he wouldn't answer. But then he straightened in his saddle. "I was the fourth son of a shipwright in Venitte. My eldest brother was to take over my father's work when he died, and both of my other brothers were apprenticed to guilds as favors to my father. I was to be put to work as a regular hand on one of the ships as a favor to its captain." He looked down at his hands. "I would never have survived," he said, almost under his breath. "It would have killed me."

I'd seen the hands of those that worked on the ships, the harshness of their skin, sunburned into tanned leather, scarred and callused. Those men contained a roughness I associated with the denizens of the Dredge. Gutterscum, like me.

Brandan—with his pale skin, his fine features and thin build—would never have fit in.

When Brandan looked up, there was a twisted smile on his face, and for the first time since the tour began, his expression was completely open and honest. "But they discovered I had the Sight after the first few hellish voyages. Sailors are a suspicious lot. They wanted nothing to do with me after that. Neither did the rest of my family. So I was shipped off to the palace."

We continued down to the docks in an awkward silence, Brandan intently surveying the damage to the lower city caused by the Chorl, although he'd already seen it numerous times since his arrival. Once we reached the wharf, Keven and the guardsmen turned south.

"You captured a few of the Chorl ships," Brandan said as we progressed down the docks through the crowd of people, mostly dockworkers, Zorelli shiphands, and carpenters. Men swarmed the decks of the ships at dock, the pounding of hammers and the shouts of orders barked across the deck overriding almost all other sounds. Gulls and terns shrieked overhead, wheeling in the breeze, and water slapped against the ship's hulls.

He spoke as if he'd never mentioned his family, or how he'd become a Servant.

After a moment, I said, "Once I killed the Ochean, the leader of the Chorl warriors, Atlatik, ordered a retreat. We harried them all the way down to the harbor and in their haste they left a few ships behind."

"How many?"

"Five of the smaller attack ships, like those over there." I pointed to one of the sleek black ships still at dock. Two others were waiting for repairs, anchored in the harbor. "There were two others, but we sent them out as escorts for some of our trading ships."

Brandan nodded. "With the Chorl presence, we'll all have to have escorts for our trading ships. Either that or the ships will have to travel in convoys, to protect each other." He frowned. "That's going to affect trade pricing."

I was about to answer when someone ahead shouted.

"It's William," Keven said, sidling his horse closer.

And then William broke through the crowd on the dock and into sight. He was followed almost immediately by Borund and Captain Tristan, both locked in animated conversation.

"Varis!" William shouted again, one arm raised to catch my attention. "Varis!" He pushed forward, almost knocking people over in his haste, then suddenly seemed to notice the escort of guardsmen . . . and Brandan.

He drew up short, a dark frown passing over his face as his eyes flicked once toward me, then fixed on Brandan. "What are you doing?" he asked, the question directed toward me, his tone suspicious and strangely hostile.

"I'm giving Brandan Vard a tour of Amenkor."

"I see." On the river, I sensed William's hurt, as if I'd betrayed him somehow. As Borund and Tristan approached behind him, Borund nodding seriously at something Tristan said, William stepped toward me, positioning himself between Brandan and me. He raised a hand to steady my horse as it shied away, but his eyes never left Brandan.

"Mistress," Captain Tristan said, giving a short bow. "I hope that Brandan has not been monopolizing all of your time."

"I was giving him a tour," I said into the tension. "It was my idea."

"Ah, I see, very good." Tristan and Brandan shared a glance and Brandan shifted in his seat.

To one side, Keven coughed, his horse edging close enough it brushed up against me.

I didn't need the warning. All of the instincts I'd honed on the Dredge to warn me of danger had already begun to flare.

Borund cleared his throat. "Tristan and I were just discussing Amenkor's new fleet of trading ships. The one that I intend to build, anyway."

"The one you've already started building, you mean," Tristan said.

"Yes, well," Borund began, but William cut in.

"It will rival anything that Venitte has to offer," he said stiffly. "The ships will have a larger hold, so we can carry more cargo. And we'll be able to carry the cargo farther, without the need to stop into port as often."

Borund shot William an irritated glance. "We have to get the ships built first."

"You seem to have a decent start," Tristan said, his tone dry. "And now, if the tour is finished?"

Brandan glanced in my direction, his eyes unreadable, but with a tinge of disappointment about his lips. "Thank you, Mistress, for escorting me around Amenkor." Then he dismounted, handing the horse's leads off to one of the guardsmen. William stepped out of his way.

Tristan turned to Borund. "I'll have the papers drawn up for your mark. And I'll want to discuss the terms on the tea from Marland at some point. I'm sure we can come to some kind of agreement."

"Of course, of course."

"Mistress," Tristan said.

I nodded and watched the two head off down the wharf, Tristan taking hold of Brandan's upper arm tightly just before they vanished into the crowd.

William turned toward me, straightening, suddenly cold and formal. "I don't think he ran into you by accident."

My brow creased in irritation, but before I could answer, Keven added, "Neither do I."

I thought about Brandan waiting for me outside of the garden entrance. He could have seen me there in the yard, working with the Servants. He could have hung around, waiting for me to finish.

A page boy suddenly appeared at Keven's side. He leaned down to listen, then straightened.

"Catrell sends word that the scouting party to Temall will be ready to depart on the evening's tide."

I stood at the end of the dock, the sun beginning to set on the horizon, the Chorl ship tied to the berth already mostly loaded, the contingent of guards-men and Seekers that Westen and Catrell had worked out filing up onto the deck of the black ship. Westen stood beside me, Catrell on the other side, Keven and the rest of the guardsmen behind.

"How are your wife and son?" I asked.

Westen's eyebrows rose. "Not many know I have a wife and son," he said, clearly wanting to know how I knew.

I didn't answer.

He smiled. "They're fine. I said my good-byes earlier."

I nodded. Farther down the dock, the last of the guardsmen boarded. A bell clanged on the deck, orders issued, and dark-skinned Zorelli began untying the ship from the dock.

"You'd better board," Catrell said.

"I'll keep watch." I caught Westen's eye and he nodded, knowing that I meant I'd keep watch through the Fire I'd tagged him with before the Chorl attacked. I felt a twinge of worry, recalling how hard it had been to push myself into the Fire at Erick's core at first, about how it had drained me to watch Ottul through Marielle's eyes. I thought about mentioning it to Westen, but then thrust the concern aside. I needed to know what the Chorl were doing, how far they'd advanced toward Amenkor. This was the only way.

Westen must have seen some of the worry in my eyes, for he gave me a reassuring smile and said, "I'll return."

Then he moved down the dock and boarded the ship.

✛— Chapter 5

Westen jumped out of the unsteady boat and splashed onto shore, seawater spilling down into his boots. He grimaced in distaste, slogging up onto the sand as groups of his men disembarked from three other boats to either side in the faint light of the moon and a few torches, another group already waiting for him—a scouting party that had been sent ashore the previous night.

"Report," he said, coming to a halt before the Seeker who led the party already on the beach.

Watching through the Fire at Westen's core, having Reached from the throne room of Amenkor with Marielle's aid, I recognized Tomus, the Seeker who had been guarding Erick's chamber. His dirty-blond hair gleamed in the light of the torches carried by the scouting party.

"No sign of the Chorl. We went south as far as the outskirts of Temall, but saw nothing. I don't think they've taken Temall yet."

"Good. We'll set up a temporary camp here then, restock the ship with water, whatever food we can find. Then we'll head south."

Tomas nodded, turned to pass the orders on.

Westen remained on the beach, hands on his hips. He watched empty water casks being off-loaded and hauled inland to the stream that emptied into the cove where they'd decided to make landfall. Torchlight glared orange on the waves, leaving a trail of fire from the sand to the black ship hidden in the inlet. A sea breeze brought the scents of salt and seaweed, the trees behind rustling.

He grunted, satisfied, then found the nearest rock and took off his boots, pouring water from each before setting them aside to dry.

I pulled back from the Fire, feeling again that resistance I'd felt when I'd first attempted to Reach toward Erick. Piercing through the veil, drawing on some of the strength fed to me by Marielle, I rose high, sought out the Fire that burned inside me in Amenkor, and skimmed northward.

I gasped as I entered my own body again, felt the tremors beginning in my arms before I'd managed to draw my first true breath, and silently cursed, felt Marielle releasing the conduit she'd used to link to me.

"Mistress?" Marielle asked, leaning forward, although I could hear weakness in her own voice. She laid a hand over my hands where they rested in my lap.

"I'm—" I swallowed, my throat dry. "—fine."

Marielle shifted where she sat on the top of the dais of the throne room, reaching for the tray containing a pitcher of sun-steeped tea and two glasses. I leaned back against the cracked throne behind me, let the tremors wash through me in waves.

The first attempt to Reach for Westen had come the morning after his ship had left the harbor. Overnight, the *Prize* had managed to get significantly far down the coast, but then the winds had changed and their progress slowed.

That Reaching had been difficult. Far more difficult than any of the Reaching I'd done while using the Skewed Throne. It had drained me, to the point that it had taken almost an hour before I could stand and walk from the throne room. Eryn had pointed out that I didn't need to be sitting on the throne any longer, but I'd done almost all of my long distance Reaching before on the throne, because the throne had made it easier. Somehow, it felt wrong not to be in this room while Reaching outside the city, not to have its solid stone beneath me. Even if it was now dead.

I'd tried again the next day, the effects of the Reaching worse because Westen had managed to get farther down the coast. After that, I didn't think I'd be able to Reach again, that I'd have to wait for him to return to hear any news.

But Marielle had suggested she link to me using the conduits, so she could share her strength with me, as Gwenn had shared with her in the gardens.

The Reachings since had been much less draining.

I lifted my hand, watched it tremble with the effort, then let it flop back down into my lap.

"I'm not sure how much longer we'll be able to remain in contact with Westen," I said, voice weary.

"Why?" Marielle handed over a cup of tea, which I managed to sip from without spilling a drop.

"The effects of the Reaching are getting worse, even with your strength added to mine. If he travels too much farther south, we won't be able to reach him."

"We'll just have to add Trielle to the link."

Marielle seemed utterly confident this would work, but I was doubtful.

"There has to be a limit, Marielle. We can't link all twenty-nine Servants together just for a Reaching."

"Why not? We know it works for at least five Servants. Why not more?"

I shook my head. "I don't know. Aside from the fact that it's impractical, I'd think that after a point adding another Servant wouldn't increase the strength that much."

Marielle shrugged. "You might be right. We haven't tried linking more than five Servants at one time. And besides, we know there's a more efficient way to link, the one the Chorl use."

I pushed up off of the throne, letting Marielle help steady me as I stretched my legs, the muscles and tendons popping.

"I hate this throne," I said, casting a vicious glare at the static chunk of granite behind me. "I liked my own version of it better. It didn't have a back to it, but it had armrests."

Marielle didn't respond, gathering up the cups and pitcher of tea, placing everything back onto the tray before accompanying me down the length of the cavernous throne room, heading back to my chambers.

"So . . . Brandan Vard seems . . . nice."

I glanced toward Marielle with a frown, caught her smiling at me knowingly. "What do you mean?"

"I mean, he seems . . . nice. That light brown hair. And those eyes! All of the other Servants are talking about him. He's been wandering around the palace lately, watching us all as we train, sparring with the guardsmen in the yard. He's . . . well built."

"Hmm."

Marielle waited expectantly, eyes alight. "I heard there was an incident down at the docks," she finally prompted.

I scowled, thinking back to the tour of Amenkor, to running into William and Borund and Tristan. "Who told you about that?"

"Keven. It required a little . . . encouragement on Trielle's part to get him to talk."

I gave Marielle a look and she burst into laughter.

"So what happened? On the wharf."

We'd reached my chambers, passed through the antechamber into the inner rooms, and I slumped down into the settee, Marielle setting the tray aside. "Nothing. I'd run into Brandan in the hall outside the gardens and took him on a tour of Amenkor. We ran into William, Borund, and Tristan." It had been good to see William and Borund working with each other again. I could still sense some tension between them, and I didn't think their relationship would ever be the same as when I'd been Borund's bodyguard, but they'd reconciled to some extent.

I caught Marielle's expectant look, her eyebrows raised. "That was it."

Marielle snorted. "That's not what Keven said."

I narrowed my eyes. "What *did* Keven say?"

"He said that you were having a grand old time flirting with Brandan until you ran into William. And when William saw you with Brandan . . ." Marielle let the thought trail off.

"I was not flirting with Brandan," I said darkly. "I don't know how to flirt."

Marielle smirked. "I can help with that if you want. Keven also said that Tristan dragged Brandan off, and that he didn't think that you simply 'ran' into Brandan in the hall. He thinks Brandan was waiting for you, to find out more about you. And Amenkor."

I didn't say anything, thinking instead of William. He hadn't been to the palace as usual since the wharf, had avoided the palace altogether.

"I can understand why William would be flustered," Marielle went on. "You know he's interested in you. And then there was the festival, where you two danced with each other and then disappeared down to the end of the dock." The knowing voice had returned, smug now. "All kinds of rumors are going around about *that.*"

"Nothing happened," I said. "We talked, and then I—"

I cut off abruptly.

"You what?" Marielle leaned forward.

Disconcerted, I said, "I kissed him."

Marielle's mouth flew open. "Oh, gods, you didn't?" When I didn't answer, she leaped out of her seat and clapped her hands together, suddenly a bundle of energy, circling the settee. "No wonder William reacted like that on the wharf! He thinks you're interested in Brandan! He's jealous!"

I flushed. "It wasn't that kind of kiss," I protested, but even I heard the weak lie in my voice. Irritated, I spat, "And why can't I be interested in more than one person?"

Marielle plopped herself down on the end of the settee, her excitement undiminished. "What kind of kiss was it?"

Suddenly extremely uncomfortable, I said uncertainly, "A . . . friendly kiss?" On the Dredge, there were only two kinds of kisses: rough and deadly. The rough ones usually ended up in rape, the deadly ones in blood, for either the man or woman. Rape and death were indiscriminate on the Dredge.

But this hadn't been like that. This kiss—and even the light, quick kiss at the guildhall—had been different. Even thinking about it sent a warm shiver through my skin.

Marielle frowned in disappointment. "I don't think William took it that way. And besides, you've been spending a lot of time with William since the attack. Here in the palace, out in the city, at the guildhall. Everyone in town is talking about it."

"I still don't see why I can't be interested in more than one person," I growled, retreating toward anger. "What does William care if I talk to Brandan? I can speak to—and kiss—whoever I like."

Marielle shook her head. "I have a lot to teach you about men."

"I already know about men. I grew up in the slums."

"Oh, there's much more to it than *that.*"

Someone knocked on the door leading to the antechamber, a guardsman leaning in a moment later. "The First of the Mistress is here to see you," he reported.

"Let him in," I said, a little too quickly.

Avrell stepped into the room, "Did you reach Westen? Where is he? What's happening?"

As he took a seat, Marielle reached for the used tray, casting me one last decidedly meaningful look before departing.

Knowing that Marielle and the rest of the palace were talking about me and William was one thing. But learning that the whole city had noticed, that they were probably talking about me right now . . .

I sighed. "I reached Westen. He's set the *Prize*'s crew ashore north of Temall. It doesn't look like the Chorl have attacked Temall yet. He's going to begin moving south tomorrow."

"Good. Right now, Temall is our buffer zone to the south. The Chorl will have to take it before they can make an effective attack on Amenkor by land from that direction." He paused. "It took Westen a few more days to get down there than expected."

"He was being careful not to run into any of the Chorl ships," I said.

"True. But we need to know where the Chorl are and where they're headed. The sooner we know, the better."

I leaned back heavily into the settee and closed my eyes, feeling every ache and muscle in my body. "Was there something else, Avrell? It's late, and I'm exhausted."

Avrell hesitated. "You asked me to do some research in the archives . . . about the thrones."

I sat forward suddenly. "Do you know where the second throne is? What did you find?"

He grimaced. "Not much. Records were kept from far earlier than the introduction of the Skewed Throne to the city, but they aren't complete. Some have been lost due to fire or flood. Some have just disintegrated with age, even though we attempt to transcribe older documents when they begin to decay." He stood, began pacing before the settee, hands clasped behind his back. "The records that have survived from that time are, understandably, focused on the Skewed Throne itself, not its counterpart. But they do mention a second throne."

"Where?"

He paused, glanced toward me, brow furrowed. "It seems that the two thrones were created in Venitte by the Council of Seven."

I nodded. "Yes, the Seven Adepts. I was there when they forged the two thrones, in a manner of speaking. I was there when they died."

"And that's the problem," Avrell said. "They all died when they created the thrones, and they didn't leave very specific instructions on what to do with the thrones after they'd been created, or even how to use them."

"Because they didn't expect to be killed while creating them," I said sardonically.

"In any case, that left the decision about what to do with the thrones to those that found the Seven dead on the Council chamber floors. The intent of the Seven was clear: they'd created the thrones as a means to protect the coast from possible attacks by the Chorl, who'd been repelled at this point and had vanished into the western ocean, but who were expected to return. Here, I brought the journal of Patris Armanic, the Lord of Amenkor at that time."

"Lord of Amenkor?" I asked, as Avrell drew a heavy scroll from his pocket. He pulled the small table Marielle had set the tray of tea on earlier over to the settee. "Amenkor had a Lord?"

Avrell smiled. "This was before the Skewed Throne existed, remember. Amenkor had many Lords—and Ladies—before the throne arrived. In fact, we had a Council much like Venitte does now. But the arrival of the Skewed Throne changed all that. Not overnight, of course, but over the years the Mistress of the Skewed Throne came to be the single most revered power in Amenkor. The Lords and Ladies diminished, until there was only the First, and the leaders of the guilds, the most powerful being the merchants' guild. And all of that happened because one of the Mistresses—Torlette, I believe—managed to get the guard to back her and Lord Rathe when the other Lords and Ladies were weakened, effectively severing the last links of the council system."

He spread the scroll out on the table, handling the dry, yellowed parchment with the utmost care. Even so, flakes fell from the edges, the scent of dust drifting up.

Leaning over the sheet, Avrell squinted at the extremely fine print, then said, "Here."

I shifted forward. The scrawl of black lines on the page at first seemed illegible, nothing but curled scratches. But then I picked out a few letters, realized that they were elongated, as if they'd been stretched and thinned, and tilted to the right. Also a significant number of the words themselves had different spellings.

Struggling with the strange script, but becoming more excited the further I got, I read, "Returned from Venitte. After forty-seven days of heated argument, the August Representatives of the Frigean coast—including Lord Wence of Venitte, Lord Barton of Sedine, Lady Corring of Merrell, and Lord Iain of Langdon, among others—have concluded that the Council of Seven intended the Two Thrones for Amenkor and Venitte, being central to the Coast and the Heart of the Chorl Attack. Per this Agreement, Mistress Susquill and the Granite Throne have accompanied me upon my Return, the Stone Throne remaining in Venitte under Master Tyrrone's control. Mistress Susquill has been ensconced within the palace walls along with the Throne, and already her Presence, and the Throne's, is felt."

Avrell cleared his throat, cutting me off. "It goes on to describe how the

Council here in Amenkor reacted to Susquill's arrival. They did not welcome her. From Patris' account, she was a strong but bitter woman, with a tongue to match. In essence, Susquill was the first Mistress of Amenkor."

"What about Tyrrone and the Stone Throne?"

"Apparently, a huge political war broke out in Venitte, the lords and ladies vying for power in the vacuum created by the loss of the Council of Seven, all fighting for position, for control of the Stone Throne. Tyrrone was not a political man—few of the Servants were at the time, because the Council of Seven, the Adepts, effectively ruled the coast—and he was overwhelmed. In the midst of the upheaval, he and the Stone Throne . . . vanished."

"Vanished?" I said, incredulous. I thought about the Skewed Throne sitting in the throne room even now. "How could it possibly vanish?" I asked darkly. "It's made of stone, it would require ten men to lift it. And not everyone can touch it, only those with the Sight. How could it have been moved?"

Avrell began gingerly rolling the parchment back up. "I don't know, but they managed to get the Skewed Throne onto a ship and all the way to Amenkor, so . . ." He shrugged. "During the height of the political struggle in Venitte, the streets were no longer safe to travel at night due to the sudden rise in assassination attempts. The Stone Throne vanished from its place at the center of the Council of Seven's main chamber. And Tyrrone vanished with it. No one saw it being moved, and no one saw Tyrrone after that. The chamber itself was sealed by the Servants that remained."

"No one searched for it?"

Avrell snorted. "Everyone searched for it. It was the key to their safety from the Chorl! Or so they thought at the time. But remember, they'd just managed to repulse the Chorl attack, were in the midst of political upheaval unlike anything they'd experienced in decades, and winter was hard on their heels. They couldn't afford to spend too much energy searching for the throne when each lord and lady had their own estate—and people and power—to protect. The deaths of the Seven created a huge power vacuum, and Venitte fell into total chaos for a period of years before it finally stabilized with the introduction of the Council of Eight to replace the Adepts. Other cities, such as Amenkor, didn't suffer as much from the sudden absence of the Seven. We already had our own Councils, who reported to the Seven when anything of significance occurred that could affect the entire coast."

I slumped back into the settee. "So the other throne is lost. We can't use it to defend against the Chorl Servants. We can't use it to replace the Skewed Throne." The little flare of hope I'd held inside since Eryn had brought the possibility of the second throne up in the throne room guttered and died.

Avrell tucked the scroll back into his pocket, his motions thoughtful. "I didn't say that."

I glared at him. "You just said—"

"I said that the throne vanished. But I don't think it's lost. There are too many hints in the archives, too many vague suggestions and allusions to what might have happened to the throne for me to believe that it's completely gone."

Feeling the long day creeping up on me, I said impatiently, "Then where is it?"

Avrell drew in a deep breath, let it out in a sigh. "I have no real evidence to support this, but I think it's still in Venitte."

"That would make sense," Eryn said.

We stood in the middle of the throne room, both looking down the open walkway to the dais and the unnaturally static throne. I'd related what Avrell had told me a few days before of his search in the archives for the second throne.

"Why?"

"Because of what you said: the throne is heavy. It would require a massive effort and extreme planning in order to move it. Which means that more than likely it wasn't moved far. And a huge risk was taken to move it anywhere at all, because anyone who touched the throne—even then, when there would have been at most a dozen personalities stored within it, perhaps as few as eight—could have been overwhelmed by its power. The effort to move the Skewed Throne safely to Amenkor must have been immense. Keep in mind that the Seven were Adepts, the most powerful men and women of the time. No one could control and manipulate the Sight as well as they could. But there were others that could use the Sight, others like us. The non-Adepts, those that were even then called the Servants. They were the ones who inherited the thrones. Perhaps—"

But here something caught in Eryn's throat, and she began coughing. She reached out and clutched my shoulder, bending forward and hacking into her other hand, the sound torturous. I gripped her upper arm and shoulder, steadying her as it continued, until she heaved one final shallow breath and seemed to catch hold of herself.

She smiled as she straightened, her expression grim. "I thought it was getting better," she said, voice weak and hoarse. "I haven't had a fit like that in over a week."

"Maybe it is getting better, then."

"No." She shook her head. "Look."

She held out her hand, the one she'd used to cover her mouth. It was speckled with blood.

A strange numbing panic raced through me, tingling in my arms, my fingers, squeezing my heart hard.

"You have to go see Isaiah," I said. The words sounded distant, lost, as if the numbness had crept into my ears.

"No," Eryn said, that grim smile still on her lips. "There's nothing he can do. You know that, Varis. We've already tried."

She pushed away. I didn't want to let her go, my hand refusing to release her.

She held my gaze, her eyes calm, accepting. Accepting of what the blood on her hand meant.

I forced my hand to let go of her upper arm, stepped back. I suddenly felt cold.

"Now," Eryn said, voice cracking. "Let's check in on Westen."

I didn't move until Eryn made it halfway to the dais and the throne, my legs refusing to budge. And once I was in motion, it was slow, uncertain. The numbness remained, the sense of distance.

I sank onto the cracked throne. "Should you—"

"I'm fine, Varis." Stern, strong, commanding. The voice of the Mistress.

I should have been comforted. I wasn't.

"There's another reason to suspect that the throne is still in Venitte," she said.

It was said to distract me, to turn me away from the speckled blood on her hands.

Our eyes met. She knew I recognized the distraction, and written in the lines of her face I saw the plea to accept it and move on.

I drew in a short breath, not quite ready to give in . . . but then I sighed. "What?"

Eryn nodded. "Think about the two thrones, and about the agreement between Amenkor and Venitte. Since the thrones were created, the two cities have been tied together, certain agreements between us upheld even when the cities themselves have been at odds."

"What do you mean?"

"I mean that even when the two cities have been at war with each other—over trading rights, or land—we've always sent the female Servants to Amenkor to be trained, and the male ones to Venitte. Why? For that matter, why is there such a division between the sexes? Why do the females get sent here, and the males to Venitte?"

I frowned. "I don't know."

Eryn paced behind the throne. "I never thought about it before, but once you told me what Avrell had found in the archives, I began to wonder. We've never had a Master of Amenkor; it's always been a Mistress. Why? When any men touch the Skewed Throne, they die, whether they are Servants or not. I think the two thrones are split somehow, two halves of a single whole, one female and the other male. I think Amenkor ended up with the female version of the throne, and that's the reason the female Servants are sent here to train. The male throne remained in Venitte, so all the male Servants are trained there. Being close to the appropriate throne must somehow . . . accentuate the Servants' power."

"And the male Servants, like Brandan Vard, are still trained in Venitte," I said. "Which means the throne *is* still in Venitte."

Eryn nodded. "I find it hard to believe that the throne would simply vanish. It must still be in use, just not as openly as here in Amenkor. In fact, I wouldn't be surprised if Brandan Vard knows exactly where the second throne is even now."

I thought about Brandan's dark blond hair, of his eyes . . . and of the way he'd hesitated before answering my questions regarding the Servants of Venitte. I'd thought at the time that it was because he'd expected me to already know the answers.

But maybe it was because he had something to hide. It would explain why everything he said felt like a lie—or rather, a half-truth, as if he were holding something back.

And it would explain why he wanted to know about me, about Amenkor and how it had survived the Chorl attack.

Perhaps William and Keven were right. Perhaps the few meetings I'd had with Brandan since he'd arrived hadn't been by chance.

"Now," Eryn said, drawing me back to our reason for being in the throne room, "let's check in on Westen."

I dove into the river, barely concentrating on what I was doing, my thoughts scattered, jumping from Eryn, to the spots of blood on her hand and the pain she felt in her gut, to Brandan and the secrets he might hold, to my own churning unidentifiable emotions about William and the fact that it *hurt* that he hadn't come back to the palace to see me. But then I pushed up and out, barged through that thin veil that still tried to hold me back, and sped southward. Coastline surged by beneath me, a blur of motion, of half-glimpsed inlets and coves and rocky plinths reaching into the sea. Halfway to where I'd last contacted Westen, pinpricks of sensation coursed through my ethereal body as Eryn linked with me, flooding me with her strength—

And then I saw the Fire inside Westen, smelled his scent—honeysuckle and dew—and I let the Fire enfold me, let my concern over Eryn and Brandan and William fade into the background.

I took a moment to look around through Westen's eyes—a cook fire in a copse of trees, heavy with the scent of smoke and sizzling meat, hidden in a depression of land, evening sunlight streaming through the branches in thin bands—and then I said, *Report.*

Westen froze where he sat before the fire, the sudden lack of movement so subtle and fleeting that none of the surrounding guardsmen noticed. I felt him grin through the Fire, then he turned and reached for the skewered rabbit on a spit before him.

We've skirted Temall and are now to the south, on our way toward Bosun's Bay. It didn't appear that Temall had suffered any major attack by the Chorl, although they are aware that there's an enemy force out there. They seal up the walls of the city during the night and have guardsmen on duty at all times. The outer city is mostly abandoned at dusk, but people still come out during the day to work in the surrounding fields. He bit into the rabbit and I felt hot juice dribbling down his chin, the gamy flavor of the meat flooding my tongue. He wiped at the dribble with one hand, chewing slowly.

I've sent a few men in closer, and it seems that the surrounding towns and villages to the south have also been attacked by the Chorl, mainly raids for food and supplies. But here's the strange thing.

He paused to sip from a flask of water.

What? I said impatiently. I was suddenly hungry.

Westen smiled, and I realized he was teasing me with the food.

Not all of the Chorl raids have been successful, he said.

What do you mean?

Westen set the flask aside, the rabbit forgotten.

It seems that on a few of these raids, the Chorl have met with some unexpected resistance.

Men from Temall?

No. These men attack from the forest to the east, hitting the Chorl raiders hard, pushing them back until they retreat . . . and then the men vanish. I thought at first they were bandits, but according to what the scouts have heard, the group is too organized for regular banditry, and they only take a portion of what the Chorl would have made off with, almost as if they consider what they take as payment for their services. Most of those that they've aided were more than glad to give up those few supplies in return for their protection.

I pondered this for a moment, but didn't see how it changed anything. I turned my attention back to Temall, to the Chorl threat.

Temall doesn't seem to realize how dangerous the Chorl are. You need to warn them.

Agreed. But I'm not certain they'll be willing to listen.

Be convincing, I said, voice hard.

Westen was about to respond when a guardsman stumbled into the hollow.

Westen reacted instantly, crossing the copse before anyone else had even moved. "Report."

The guardsman straightened, one hand clutched to his side. "Temall," he gasped, then swallowed, wincing, "is under attack. By the Chorl."

Adrenaline surged through Westen's body even as he barked orders, motioning to the Seeker Tomus to join him. The fire was smothered, roasted rabbit removed from the skewers and stowed away with cold efficiency, the copse abandoned within ten minutes.

Moving swiftly, they pushed northward, angling to the west through the cuts and folds of the land, following the guardsman who'd brought the warning. Urgency bled through Westen, tingling in his blood as the group splashed through a stream, up over a ridge, the guardsmen behind grunting as the earth shifted out from beneath them—

And then the leading guardsman slowed.

Holding up a hand, Westen stopped. The group of forty guardsmen and Seekers ground to a halt behind him, most heaving at the sudden strain.

The guardsman they'd followed scrambled up another incline, then pointed.

On the far side of the low hill, the ground swept down to a scattering of fields, a few lines of trees used as windbreaks and dirt roads between them. Then the land rose again, cottages appearing among the fields, and suddenly there were stone walls, only half as high as Amenkor's walls. A dry ditch had been dug around the entire enclosure at least three feet deep, the dirt removed from the ditch piled up at its edge, away from the wall, creating an embankment. The dirt appeared fresh, the ditch recently dug. A thin strip of land gave access to the gates, and a group of people—women and children mostly—rushed through the opening, a harsh bell ringing, muted by distance.

I thought Temall was a port, I said.

Coming up along Westen's side, Tomus said, "Where's the port?"

"On the far side of the town," the guardsman answered. "The main portion of the town is encircled by the wall. There's an access road that leads down to the docks and harbor. There isn't much there—some warehouses, a few taverns, and brothels." He shrugged.

A blood-freezing scream sounded and everyone's attention turned toward the southern edge of the fields.

A group of men were struggling to hold the Chorl back. Only a few of the men wore armor and carried swords, the rest were in field worker's clothes, wielding hoes and shovels.

And they were outnumbered. There were nearly twice as many Chorl as Temall defenders. Even as we watched, the Temall line began to crumble, men shrieking as they fell, the Chorl's piercing battle cries a harsh counterpoint.

"Tomus."

Without another word, Tomus spun and descended from the hill, shouting out orders for the men to ready. Armor clattered and swords hissed from sheaths.

Through the Fire, I felt the tension on the river double.

Westen glanced toward the gates, toward the group of women and children still trying to reach safety. "They need to close the gates," he said. Images of his own wife and son flashed through his mind and his jaw clenched. He pushed the thoughts away, his hand gripping the hilt of the dagger at his waist.

To the south, the Temall line staggered, then completely crumbled. Chorl began pouring through the breaches, heading straight for the gates. Someone at the gates noticed, and cries of terror echoed across the fields, the women and children surging forward.

Westen spat a curse, spun, shouted, "Tomus!"

"Ready."

Even as the group charged over the ridge, down into the fields, I could feel Westen sinking into the calm center I'd felt once before, during the Chorl attack on Amenkor. The center all Seekers sought. Devoid of emotion, cold and calculating, he let it wash away all thoughts of his family, focusing solely on the battle scene ahead. His gaze flicked over the Chorl ranks, estimated the force at well over a hundred, noted the riot of color in the clothing that the warriors wore, vibrant in the evening sunlight, noted the glint of light from the raised, curved swords, the blue skin, the darker blue tattoos on the warriors' faces.

And then his gaze caught the unmistakable blaze of yellow and another swath of dark green.

The Chorl had one of the priests with them.

And a Servant.

With Westen's men halfway to Temall's gates, tearing through a field of half-grown corn onto a road, the Chorl fell on the back of the stragglers trying to push through the still open gates. Cries of terror erupted into screams of pain and anguish, growing louder and louder—

And then suddenly Westen was there.

But the Chorl had seen us coming.

Westen drew to an abrupt halt ten paces from the edge of the Chorl line that had turned to meet us. He'd outdistanced the rest of the men from Amenkor. The leading Chorl warrior in the front ranks—tattoos curling across his face, even along the ridge of his nose—smiled.

Deep inside Westen, straining to keep myself from surging forward and seizing control of his body, I felt the last subtle shift at Westen's core . . . and he became utterly calm.

He smiled in return.

The Chorl warrior roared, a cry picked up by all of the Chorl surrounding him. On the river, I felt the rest of the Amenkor men catch up, felt them sprinting past as the Chorl roar changed cadence and the blue-skinned men leaped forward.

The leader of the Chorl was the first to die. As he charged, spittle flying from his dark blue lips, Westen sidestepped, drawing his Seeker's dagger in one smooth motion and cutting it across the leader's exposed throat. Blood sprayed outward, but Westen had already shifted, the Amenkor and Chorl warriors clashing with a sound that reverberated on the river. The taint of blood flooded outward, tinged with sweat and freshly turned earth and desperation. I felt myself reaching forward through the Fire, my emotions tangling with Westen's, my heartbeat trembling, quickening, then meshing until his heart and mine pulsed as one. We melded, the hours of practice I'd endured under his training over the last several months allowing me to anticipate his movements. Joining with him, I used the river, nudged him this way and that without ever fully seizing control.

He punched his dagger forward, the blade piercing through the Chorl warrior's blue-and-purple silken clothing, through the leather armor beneath, and into his heart. The Chorl gasped, a bubble of blood flecking his lip, and then Westen used the man's momentum to shove him aside, the dagger pulling free with a jerk. Westen's hand shifted, altering the grip on the hilt, and he cut to either side, left and right, slicing open an arm, the man shrieking, then sliding the dagger into another man's side, the man's back arching as his body toppled, all while Westen waded deeper into the confusion. Blades rose and fell, men gasping, crying out, cursing. Screams were cut short and blood flew from sword edges, spattering clothing, armor, skin, drenching the ground, and still Westen waded forward, thrusting bodies aside, trampling those that had already fallen. Through the roar of the battle, muted at the edges by the river, I could feel Westen's intent, could see his focus.

The yellow robes of the priest. The green of the Servant.

I narrowed the river down further, as I'd done on the Dredge, pushed it, used it to shove a path forward. A blade descended toward Westen's flank, toward an opening in his defenses, but I shunted it aside with a hastily raised shield, felt the startlement of the Chorl warrior as his sword struck thin air and skittered away, but Westen pushed forward again, the press of bodies that surrounded him swallowing up the warrior before he could strike again. Westen's dagger fell again and again, glancing off armor, sinking into flesh, and then the bodies became too dense, too close together, and we ground to a halt, unable to slash at bodies that were pressed too tightly together.

"We can't get closer!" Tomus shouted at Westen's back. Two other Seekers had forged through the Chorl warriors with us, were guarding Westen's back. "They're packed in too close!"

Westen snarled into the face of the Chorl warrior before him, the warrior sneering back.

Then, I felt power building on the river.

The Servant! I yelled. *She's going to attack!*

Fear lanced through Westen, and he bellowed, "Fall back!"

The gathering force on the river released. Heat streaked by overhead, a fireball searing past, trailing flames—

And exploded.

A concussive wave surged through the battle, anguished screams piercing the clash of metal, warriors pushing away from where the fireball had landed. The packed bodies around Westen loosened, and with a satisfied grunt he reached forward. One hand caught the sneering Chorl warrior by the throat, high up, near the jaw, the other reached around to the back of his head, still holding his dagger, and then with a wrench—

The Chorl's neck snapped. I felt the bones break through Westen's fingers, a crunch like a snapping twig, tingling in his skin. Then he let go, the body slumping back but remaining erect.

Another fireball released. Fresh screams arose, another wave pulsing out on the river and through the crowded men. Black smoke, in two separate columns, began billowing into the sky.

"Fall back! Fall back!" Tomus roared.

Desperate, the other Seekers withdrew, hauling Tomus and Westen along with them. The Chorl surged after.

"We can't hold them," Tomus spat. "There aren't enough of us."

"What about the gates?" Westen growled, slicing across a Chorl warrior's face, the man lurching back.

"Still open!"

Westen cursed. He fought a moment longer, considering, then said, "Fall back. At least a few more made it inside—"

A horn broke through the roar of the battle.

"What in hells?" one of the Seekers said.

Westen turned in the direction of the horn, squinted against the smoke and fading sunlight . . . and saw a band of a hundred men pouring over the top of the nearest ridge, the twenty at the forefront on horseback, charging, carrying a tattered black flag with some type of red symbol on it.

The attention of the Chorl shifted, away from the gates and from Westen's group toward the new threat. And then the leading horsemen of the new group plowed into the Chorl ranks to one side.

The Chorl line crumbled, then gave way as the rest of the force struck behind the horsemen.

The Chorl were shoved forcibly back from the gates.

Power built on the river, the taste of rage behind the effort, but this time I was distant enough from the source that I could see the river being manipulated, could gauge the direction of attack.

Reaching forward through the Fire, I flung a shield up a moment before the fireball was released.

The fireball hit the shield and exploded in midair, tendrils of flame skating down the shield's edge into the Chorl ranks themselves. Shock coursed through the river, from the Chorl Servant, from the Chorl priest, tasting of fear. As the Chorl forces were pushed back even farther, attacked now on two sides, I felt the Chorl leaders hesitate. . . .

And then another horn blew, this sound familiar: the sound of a shell being winded. Everyone in Amenkor had heard it when the second wave of Chorl ships had entered Amenkor's harbor, the Ochean's ship among them. It had sounded over and over as the ships rammed into the docks.

But this time, it only sounded twice, the last note fading. For a moment, nothing changed. . . .

Then the Chorl forces began to withdraw. They left a third of their men behind, either dead or dying.

"Do we follow?" Tomus asked. His breath came in ragged heaves, his face drenched with sweat, his dagger coated with blood. All of those around him looked the same.

On the field, the men who came under the black flag were harrying the Chorl as they fled.

Westen shook his head. "No. We don't know how many more Chorl there may be beyond the hills."

"But the others—" someone began to protest, motioning toward the other group.

At the same time, the force beneath the black flag halted their pursuit, angling away, cutting across the fields in front of the walls, heading back where they'd come from.

The red symbol stitched onto the black flag snapped fully into view and everyone around Westen gasped.

Three slashes—one horizontal, two slanted vertically down and outward from that.

The Skewed Throne. The symbol of Amenkor.

Westen tensed, his gaze falling instantly to the figure on horseback in the lead.

The group was distant, but neither Westen nor I could mistake the man who led them.

"It can't be," Tomus said, his voice incredulous.

Westen grew grim. "It's Baill."

Inside the Fire, I felt rage envelop me.

Captain Baill, the man who had backed the consortium of merchants that had almost torn Amenkor apart, the traitor who had helped Alendor steal supplies from Amenkor during the past winter, handing the food over to the

Chorl. He'd escaped the circular plaza in the eastern part of the city, escaped the trap we'd set for him, and he hadn't been heard from since.

I almost reached forward, almost seized control of Westen and ran after him, ready to make him account for all of his actions, had already grasped the river, had begun to twist it, when Tomus said, "But that doesn't make any sense. Why is he attacking the Chorl? Why is he helping Temall?"

"And why is he doing it all under the name of the Skewed Throne?" Westen said. He turned to Tomus.

The blond Seeker, blood matting his hair, looked stunned.

Behind them, the last of Temall's people entered the gates and a force of armed guardsmen streamed out after them, the man on horseback at the forefront heading straight for the Amenkor party's position. Westen stepped forward, still reeling inside over Baill's sudden appearance. The rest of the group ranged themselves wearily behind him.

The men from Temall halted ten paces away, the man on horseback—graybrown hair and trimmed beard, brown eyes, and a stern expression on his face—eyeing Westen first, then the others.

"Who are you and where do you come from?" he asked, tone wary. His voice rumbled from his chest, grating like stone on stone.

"I'm Captain Karl Westen," Westen said, wincing slightly. The adrenaline was fading, the bruises he'd sustained during the fight beginning to throb. "We come from Amenkor, to warn you of the approaching Chorl."

The man snorted. "We know of the Chorl. Are you part of the Band?" He pointed with his chin toward where Baill and his group had vanished over the hillside.

Westen frowned. "No. We were sent by the Mistress. The Chorl have attacked Amenkor, and we believe the Chorl are on their way back. We have no idea who . . . or what . . . this Band is, even though they fly the Skewed Throne."

The man's eyes narrowed. For a long moment, silence reigned, broken only by the creak of armor and the clank of metal as the two forces fidgeted.

Then, the man raised his head, glancing over Westen's group.

"Well, Captain Karl Westen, I am Justaen Pyre, Lord of Temall. I thank you for your help with the Chorl attack, but your warning was unnecessary. We know of the Chorl, of their seizure of Bosun's Bay, and we've suffered under their raids for the last few months. But I can assure you that the Chorl have no interest in Amenkor." He paused, leaned forward in his saddle.

"They're heading south, toward Venitte."

✟— Chapter 6

"Venitte?" Darryn said. He thought about this for a moment, then turned to the rest of those seated around the council table. "Then I guess we don't have to worry. Amenkor should be safe."

Avrell snorted in derision, Darryn shooting him a dark glare, but it was Captain Catrell who spoke first.

"Safe for now. But for how long? The problem was never where the Chorl were headed, it's the Chorl themselves. We're in as much danger with them conquering Venitte as we are with them coming straight for Amenkor. In fact, we're in greater danger."

More than Catrell even knew. I exchanged a glance with Avrell and Eryn. Both of them had reacted the same way once I told them what Westen had learned from Lord Pyre of the Chorl's movements, but for different reasons. Because of the second throne. If it was in Venitte, and if the Chorl gained control of it with the Skewed Throne destroyed . . .

"What do you mean?" Darryn bristled. "Why should we help defend Venitte against the Chorl when we've barely survived an attack by them already? We're still recovering. We can't afford to help them."

Everyone at the table grew taut with affronted anger.

Everyone except me. I understood what Darryn was saying. We'd learned the same instinct in the slums: survive at all costs. Which meant preserve yourself, don't worry about those you've left behind. If the threat has focused its attention elsewhere, slink off to hide and nurse your own wounds, forget about the next victim, thank the Mistress that you'd survived, and focus on making yourself stronger for the next confrontation.

But even in the slums I'd never been able to do that. Not after meeting Erick.

Catrell glanced toward me, waited for a nod before continuing. Shifting forward in his seat, he said, "From a strategic standpoint, if the Chorl seize Venitte, they will have a base of operations that allows them access to virtually every resource they may need—food, lumber, stone—while at the same time putting them in easy reach of almost all of the sea trading routes. Right now, they have the Boreaite Isles and Bosun's Bay. The Isles allow them to raid the trading routes, but there's a wide swath of ocean between them and the mainland. They can't patrol that lane and expect to catch all of the trading vessels that sail through it."

"However, almost all trading routes pass through Venitte," Avrell interjected. "It's a major port, more so than Amenkor when it comes to the shipping lanes. Amenkor is significant as a port, yes, but mostly as a stopping point for those tradesmen heading farther north by both land and sea and as a crossroads, with the pass to the eastern Kandish Empire. Even if lately the Empire has fallen unsettlingly quiet."

"They could use Venitte as a launching point," Eryn added. "It would give them the ability to stage an attack anywhere along the Frigean coast. So even though they aren't attacking Amenkor directly now, they would be able to launch an attack from Venitte in the future . . . and from a much stronger position."

Darryn leaned back in his chair. "I see."

But it was a grudging acceptance. I could still see the urge to lick wounds and thank the gods in his eyes, leaving Venitte to fend for itself.

Eryn must have seen it as well. "There are other reasons why the Chorl turning their attentions to Venitte is a problem," she said.

Avrell nodded. "Amenkor has a treaty with Venitte, an agreement that both sides have honored for hundreds of years. We're allied, which means that in the event of war, Amenkor must come to Venitte's defense, and they will come to our defense in return. If we'd had forewarning of the Chorl's intent to attack Amenkor on the first day of spring, Venitte might have been able to help us defend the city."

"But Venitte and Amenkor have fought each other before," Darryn countered. "The Carter's War, and the Ten Year's War."

"Those disputes were between the two cities themselves," Avrell said. "This threat is from outside. It's not a trade dispute, or a misunderstanding between the Mistress and the Lord of Venitte. This is an assault by a force that's invading the coastal region, the same force that prompted the alliance between the two cities in the first place."

"And there's a more significant reason we can't ignore the Chorl attacking Venitte," I said.

All but Eryn turned toward me. I could feel their eyes on me. Everything that Catrell and Avrell had said—all the reasons they'd given for going to the defense of Venitte—they were all true. But there was only one reason to keep the Chorl out of Venitte. A reason impressed upon me by the Seven when the Chorl were attacking Amenkor.

The second throne.

"When the Skewed Throne was created, there was another throne made, one just like the Skewed Throne, called the Stone Throne. I think that throne is still in Venitte. I think that's one of the reasons the Chorl are concentrating their attention there, rather than here in Amenkor. I don't know how they came to know the second throne is there, but I do know they came to Amenkor to seize this throne, the Skewed Throne. They came here specifically because of that. And now that it's been destroyed . . ."

I let my gaze fall on Darryn and Catrell, watched them stir beneath it. I thought of the priest who had tortured Erick on the Ochean's ship, thought of Haqtl, the priest who seemed to lead the Chorl priests themselves. I recalled the fervor in Haqtl's eyes when he realized there was a piece of the Fire of Heaven inside of Erick on the deck of the doomed ship *The Maiden*. It had been that fervor the Ochean used to get the Chorl to attack Amenkor, that had led Haqtl to the Skewed Throne. He'd only ordered a retreat when the throne had cracked. If he'd somehow learned there was another throne, another source of power . . .

And if Eryn was right, and the second throne was a male version of the Skewed Throne . . .

The Chorl seemed to be divided into three segments: the Ochean and her Servants; Haqtl and the priests; and Atlatik and the Chorl warriors. The Ochean had been destroyed, her power structure lost. Which left only Haqtl and Atlatik. And from what I'd witnessed through the Ochean's eyes before she'd died, the Chorl warriors followed the priests' advice.

Haqtl's advice.

"We cannot let the Chorl take the second throne," I said. "We're going to Venitte."

Everyone remained silent for a moment, and then Catrell nodded. "We will need to begin planning."

"Draw up a list of what you will need," Avrell said. "Nathem and I will handle it." At Catrell's nod, both captains of the guard rising and filing out, the First turned toward me. "You will have to speak to Captain Tristan and Brandan Vard about this. As representatives of Venitte, they need to know of the Chorl's intent, and our . . . offer to aid them."

I frowned, hearing the warning in his voice.

"You are planning on sending a military force—an army—into a foreign port," Eryn said. "You can't do that unannounced unless you intend to attack them. You need to ask for Tristan's sanction. He needs to accept your offer of help on Lord March's behalf."

"You may have to convince him," Avrell added.

I stared at them both, then sighed and turned to Keven. "Send someone for Captain Tristan and Brandan Vard."

"You wished to speak with me, Mistress?"

I motioned Captain Tristan to one of the seats in the outer rooms of the Mistress' chambers. He frowned, glanced toward Avrell seated to one side, and then settled himself while Marielle poured him a glass of wine.

"Where is Brandan Vard?"

"Occupied at the moment."

I nodded. "I have news of the Chorl that concerns both of you."

Tristan stiffened. The slight smile that had touched his lips faded. "I will pass on whatever information you have to Brandan Vard as soon as possible. What have you heard?"

I thought about Tristan leading Brandan away at the docks and wondered if Tristan would inform Brandan, but pushed the concern to the side. "As you may have learned, Amenkor sent a scouting party to Temall to determine the extent of the Chorl forces, their location and resources. I've had word from the party. It seems they have not yet taken Temall, that in fact they haven't begun to march toward Amenkor. It seems they have a different goal.

"They intend to march on Venitte."

Tristan became absolutely still, face a rigid mask.

But beneath the river, the currents roiled.

Tristan's eyes locked with mine. "I haven't seen any ships return, haven't seen or heard of any group of guardsmen returning from the south. How have you learned this information?"

I'd drawn breath to tell him of the Fire within Westen, but Avrell leaned forward.

"You are speaking to the Mistress of Amenkor," the First of the Mistress said. "Suffice it to say that she is indeed in contact with the scouting party."

"Even with the Skewed Throne destroyed?" Tristan snapped.

"Even so," Avrell said coldly.

Tristan's gaze had never left mine, and in their depths I could see him reassessing me. The wrinkles at the corners of his eyes tightened, and his lips thinned. "Lord March must be warned. Immediately." He stood abruptly, bowed low. "Forgive me, Mistress. I must ready my ship for departure, leave on the next tide."

"Amenkor would like to extend an offer of help," I said. "Captain Catrell has already begun to assemble a force. We can escort you and your ship to Venitte."

"I'm . . . not certain that is necessary."

I shifted forward. "You are Lord March's representative. And it's my understanding that Amenkor and Venitte are allied, that Amenkor will come to Venitte's aid in case of an attack."

"But Venitte did not aid Amenkor this past winter when the Chorl attacked you."

"Because we had no advance warning," Avrell said. "If we'd known, we could have asked for aid. And, given our current relationship with Venitte, I'm certain that Lord March would have helped."

"We have experience with the Chorl, Captain Tristan. We've fought them once already, and won. It's in our own interests to keep them out of Venitte. Are you willing to turn down our aid?"

Tristan remained silent long enough I thought perhaps he would, but then he smiled tightly. "No. No, it would be foolhardy to refuse such a generous offer. On behalf of Lord March, the Council of Eight, and all of Venitte, I accept. Any aid you can offer would be greatly appreciated."

"Then I will have Captain Catrell coordinate our preparations with yours."

"Very well."

Bowing again, toward me and Avrell, he left the outer chambers, Keven closing the door behind him.

"He seemed somewhat reluctant," Keven said.

"No," I said, frowning. "He was hesitant. He wanted our help, he just isn't certain he can trust it."

"You are an unknown to him, Mistress. And he just agreed to allow Amenkor's forces inside of Venitte's walls."

I shook my head. "It's more than that. But I don't know what."

"Can you get all of that ready before the ships are set to sail?" I asked, handing over the list that Avrell had prepared.

"Of course," Regin said, glancing over it again with a frown. We were walking briskly down the wharf, gulls shrieking overhead, wheeling in the wind. "Trade caravans have started arriving from the north. Most of the supplies on the list we already have or can get from them. Which ships are you intending to take?"

I motioned out toward the harbor, where one of Borund's trading ships, the *Defiant,* was anchored, two of the smaller Chorl ships nearby. All three had been refurbished and repaired, were simply waiting to be stocked and given orders. "The *Defiant* will be the main ship, escorted by the *Spoils of War* and," I winced, "the *Booty*."

Regin laughed. "I see a trend in the naming of the captured Chorl ships. *Prize, Spoils of War, Booty . . .*"

"Avrell was horrified with the last one," I said. "He tried to get them to change it—the *Treasure* or even just *Salvage*—but it had already stuck. Someone even painted *Booty* on the hull overnight."

Regin glanced down the length of the docks, turning serious. "That doesn't leave Amenkor many ships."

We paused. Two other traders were tied to the wharf, along with Tristan's ship; the last two Chorl ships were swarming with repair crews, having just been pulled in to berth. In the other direction, three docks had been given over to Borund and the construction of the new ships. Some type of scaffolding had been erected, carpenters working in a frenzy of activity.

"Borund is working as fast as he can," I said.

"But what about the defense of Amenkor while you're gone? What if the Chorl do return?"

Eyebrows raised, somewhat surprised at the concern in Regin's voice, I said, "Ships didn't seem to slow the Chorl down much last time. And William and the other new merchants have begun work on a new outer wall."

"True. But having no ships doesn't make me—or any of the other guilds for that matter—feel any more confident. And the wall will not be built overnight; it will take years to complete. You and Avrell are taking a significant portion of the army with you. No ships, an army composed mostly of recently trained militia . . . no, Mistress—it doesn't make me or anyone else comfortable."

"You'll have Eryn. She's staying here, along with a few of the Servants."

"It wasn't Eryn who saved us from the Chorl," Regin countered, eyebrows raised.

I frowned. "I can't stay behind, Master Regin. I can't just sit here in Amenkor knowing that the Chorl are going to attack Venitte." The words came out more vehemently than I'd intended, and something hardened in my chest, beneath my breastbone. Something hot and visceral. I needed to be active, needed to move. I couldn't simply sit in Amenkor and pass judgments on petty disputes while the Chorl destroyed the coast.

"A few months ago, you wouldn't have had a choice," Regin said. "The Skewed Throne would have kept you here."

I turned toward him, eyes wide. Because that was exactly it. A few months ago, I'd felt trapped in Amenkor, imprisoned by the throne. I'd resented it, especially since I'd just come to realize that there was more to the world than the streets of Amenkor, had only been able to withstand it because of the desperation of the city and then the attack by the Chorl.

But now the throne was dead. I was free, could travel beyond Amenkor and its boundaries. And I *wanted* to, the urge to explore like an itch beneath the skin, one that until now I couldn't scratch. That's why I'd tried to leave on the scouting ship with Westen, why I'd resented everyone arguing that I had to remain behind.

This time, I didn't have to stay behind. In fact, Avrell was insisting that I go. No Mistress of Amenkor had traveled to Venitte, to any of the coastal cities, because of the throne. Diplomatically, he said I had to go, as a show of good faith, and to emphasize the seriousness of the Chorl threat and Amenkor's allegiance to the treaty. And with me being inexperienced in the ways of true diplomacy, he felt he had to accompany me, to explain the intricacies of the politics involved in Venitte, to guide me.

To make certain I didn't screw up, I thought wryly.

But I didn't care about any of that. I just wanted out of the city. I wanted to feel the deck of the trading ship rolling beneath my feet, wanted to feel the wind stinging against my face as we sailed, wanted to taste the salt of the spray kicked up from the bow of the ship cutting through the water. I'd dreamed about it since I'd first come down to the docks. An unidentifiable yearning at the time, because it had seemed impossible, but that had changed the longer I'd been around the wharf as Borund's bodyguard.

The yearning had grown, I just hadn't realized it until now.

"—just send these down to the warehouse, then," Regin was saying, and I returned to the conversation with a jerk.

"What?"

Regin grinned. "I said I'd take care of everything, have everything sent down to the warehouse for loading as soon as possible. And I think the merchants' guild needs to send William to Venitte, a representative to meet up with the guild members there, inform them of Alendor and his cohorts and what really happened with the consortium. And what's happening now with the Chorl of course. He needs to stretch his legs as a Master Merchant, needs to start making contacts. This is the perfect opportunity."

"I suppose so," I said. Me and William on a ship for two solid weeks, at the least. I could already feel myself tensing up. And not simply because we'd barely spoken to each other since the incident with Brandan on the wharf.

"Very good," Regin said. "Then if you'll excuse me." He bowed and headed off down the wharf, immediately calling over his apprentices as he moved, motioning toward the paper Avrell had prepared. Messengers had already been sent before he passed from sight.

"Where to now, Mistress?"

Keven had come up behind me. Feeling unsettled, I motioned toward the palace. "I want to go see Erick."

Keven's face grew grim. "Very well."

I pursed my lips as we headed away from the wharf, winding up through the streets of the lower city, past stalls and warehouses, taverns and shops. I'd checked up on Erick almost daily at first, had spent hours inside the Fire at his core consoling him, comforting him, speaking to him. I'd managed to pull him up out of his self-imposed stupor enough to eat on occasion, but he always retreated from the pain eventually.

A pain that neither I nor Eryn could lessen. We'd tried, repeatedly. Tried to dampen it, since we knew we couldn't deal with the spell directly. A few of our tricks worked, but only for a short time, the seething needles that pricked Erick's skin returning, sometimes worse than before.

But it hadn't all been worthless effort. His other wounds—the burns, the nicks and bruises from the fighting on *The Maiden* and the subsequent mundane torture by the Ochean and Haqtl and the others—had healed. All except one, the circular puncture wound in the middle of his chest that Eryn had identified as the location of the spell placed on him. That wound was still angry, still raw. The fact that everything else had healed had kept everyone's hopes up for a while, Keven's included.

Not any longer. Erick had been lost for almost three months now. Hope was fading. I'd heard it in Keven's voice, could see it in the healer Isaiah's bitter eyes every time I entered Erick's chambers.

Perhaps it was time to see if Ottul could help. I hadn't called on her before because I couldn't trust her—still didn't trust her—but I was becoming desperate.

As we entered the Great Hall of the palace, the long corridor with the vaulted ceilings that had awed me when I'd first come to the palace to kill the Mistress, I said, "You don't have to come with me, Keven. You can wait outside."

For a moment, it was as if a huge burden had lifted from Keven's shoulders. He straightened, shoulders back, and relief flickered through his eyes.

But then he sighed and shook his head, his jaw clenched. "No, Mistress. Erick and I trained in the barracks together. We've known each other far too long."

I nodded, and then a movement far down the corridor caught my eye.

I slowed, felt the escort slow around me. Keven's brow knit in consternation, then relaxed.

Down the length of hall, on the left, near one of the numerous open doors that led to the interior halls and rooms of the palace, Eryn and Avrell stood together, conversing softly. Even as we slowed, Eryn shook her head, and I saw tears on her face.

Avrell reached up and, with a care that sent a tingling sensation through my chest, cupped a hand to her jaw and brushed the wetness away with his thumb. Eryn smiled, the contrast of tears and happiness terrible and wonderful at the same time.

Avrell leaned forward and kissed her on the forehead. When she glanced up into his face, he kissed her on the lips.

I suddenly thought of both of them, here, in the palace, Eryn trapped by the throne. I thought of them talking animatedly this past winter as we searched for the supplies Eryn thought she had hidden throughout the city, discussing parties and people, scandal and gossip. And I suddenly remembered being with each of them as they stood on the walls of the palace, the Chorl surging through the newly breached gates, stone crumbling around them, both hurt, both wounded, the world seeming to collapse in on them.

They'd thought of each other then.

I hadn't seen it, hadn't even noticed.

But now a hundred little gestures—a comforting hand here, a slight nod or smile there—flickered through my mind. A hundred little gestures now seen with completely new meaning.

And now, Avrell was coming to Venitte with me, while Eryn stayed here.

Far down the hall, Eryn began to cough, the sound painful to hear. She raised a cloth to her lips, while Avrell gripped her shoulder, his expression tortured as the fit worsened, as she tried to control it.

And suddenly it was too personal a moment to be seen by me, by anyone.

"Keven," I said, turning, but he was already directing me toward one of the arched doorways that led off of the main corridor, had escorted me through and into the hall beyond, the guards following, before either Eryn or Avrell noticed us watching.

"How long?" I asked, when I'd regained my breath, when the harsh hot stone in my chest had receded.

Keven looked at me as we walked, face troubled. "Off and on for years."

I thought about how I'd suspected Avrell of wanting to assassinate Eryn in order to seize the throne, thought of what pain it must have caused him to watch her sink into madness, to come to the decision that the only way to help her was to kill her, and felt sick to my stomach.

"Here we are, Mistress."

I glanced up, saw that we'd made our way back to the main corridor near the inner doorway, had passed through and were now in front of the door to Erick's room.

I drew in a breath, was surprised to hear it catch. Then I entered, Keven following close behind.

The room reeked of old sweat and sickness, of a body that had remained stationary for too long. I went to order the windows open, then realized that they were already open, that the reek I smelled came from the river.

I'd smelled the scent before, on the Dredge, and I felt my gut twist. It was the reek of despondency, of hope lost.

Of death.

On the far side of the room, at his desk, Isaiah looked up, his expression bruised and weary. "Nothing's changed."

"I know," I said. I moved across the room, pulled a chair up close to Erick's bedside. Reaching out, I almost touched his hand, almost gripped it in my own, but then remembered the invisible needles that would prick his flesh at the touch.

Withdrawing, I leaned back, tried not to sigh, blinked back the tears that threatened inexplicably at the corners of my eyes.

"Keven." My voice came out rough and thick. "Get Marielle. Have her bring Ottul here, with Trielle's help."

I felt him hesitate, sensed Isaiah's disapproval.

"Are you certain?" Keven asked.

I nodded. "I don't know what else to do. And we've waited long enough."

Keven didn't reply, just moved toward the door and murmured something to the guardsmen outside, then returned. I felt him at my back, felt Isaiah moving away from the bed, back to his desk. Both of their presences were comforts.

But neither of them were the comfort I sought.

I wanted William. I wanted to feel his fingers twined in mine as I stood by Erick's bedside. I wanted his hands on my shoulders, as they had been the last time I withdrew from the Fire inside Erick, holding me, giving me strength. I wanted his touch.

Because the last three months had been hell. The last three months of staring at Erick's sickly pallor, at his sweat-drenched skin, at his flushed face. William had made it bearable.

And now William was gone. Over petty jealousy.

I hadn't realized I'd miss him this much.

Someone knocked on the door and Keven moved to answer it, opening it wide to allow Marielle, Trielle, and Ottul inside. The Chorl Servant moved uncertainly between the two Servants, stepping away from Keven, her gaze wary.

Then she caught sight of me and halted, anger flaring in her eyes.

Anger sparked deep down inside me as well. Narrowing my gaze, I said, "Come here."

Ottul hesitated, chin lifting in defiance—

But then something in that defiance crumbled. Grief flickered through her expression, and I thought of the hours Marielle said Ottul spent kneeling on the floor of her rooms, back hunched, rocking as tears streaked her face and she whispered guttural prayers. Grief that had started when she'd learned of the other Chorl captives' suicides.

With a glance toward Marielle, toward Trielle, Ottul stepped forward and bowed her head.

I drew in a deep, steadying breath, then said, "Look at him."

When Ottul didn't glance up, didn't move, I barked, "Look at him!"

Ottul started, her head snapping up, eyes flashing. Behind her, Marielle and Trielle flinched; Keven stiffened.

But Ottul looked where I pointed, looked at Erick. Her eyes flared again with heat, with hatred, but then her brow creased in confusion and she turned back to me.

"What did the Ochean do to him?" I asked. "Tell me what she did to him, and tell me how to stop it."

I could feel the tears burning at the edges of my eyes again. When Ottul didn't answer, I reached forward, grabbed her arm, and hauled her forward to the side of Erick's bed, felt her resist, her eyes wide. "Tell me what she did to him," I repeated, and then I tore open the shirt above Erick's chest, exposed the angry red mark above his heart.

Ottul gasped and jerked backward, one hand clutching at her chest, the other gesturing as words poured from her in a rush, short and sharp and clipped. My hand latched onto her upper arm again before she could flee and I dragged her to a halt. She fought me, tried to twist out of my grasp, fell to her knees, her voice cracking.

"What is it?" I spat. "What is it and how do I heal it? Help me!"

"No," Ottul whispered, then broke into her own language. Her eyes closed and she sank lower to the floor, collapsing forward, until I was forced to let her go or hold her upright. "No! Not help," she gasped, her terrified words degenerating into sobs. "Not help."

I stood back, all of the anger sapped from me, replaced by a dull sense of resignation. I watched as Ottul sank over her knees, her arms pulled in tight, hands clutched behind her neck. A protective curl, completely different from the kneeling position she used for prayer in her room.

She was frightened, had taken up a defensive posture, her shoulders trembling. I recognized it from the Dredge, arms and knees tight to protect the face and most vulnerable parts of the body from harm, that let the rest of the body absorb the blows.

Ottul expected to be beaten.

I felt Keven draw close behind me. "I don't think she's going to help."

"No. I don't think she *can* help. I don't think she knows how. But she's seen this before." My voice was lifeless. I drew in a deep breath, smelled Ottul's terror on the river, sharp with salt. "Take her back to her rooms."

I turned away as Marielle and Trielle moved forward, gathered Ottul up, and led her to the door. I listened as her sobs continued, interspersed with broken words, with gasps and moans. I could follow her movements, tremors reverberating on the river.

When the room had quieted, I sighed.

Then I dove deep into the river and pushed outward, toward Erick's Fire. *Hello, Varis.*

I settled into the Fire, the seething pain from the needles piercing Erick's flesh a nagging intrusion in the background. A familiar intrusion now. *Erick.*

I felt Erick's essence twist, felt him scrutinize me. *What's wrong?*

I'd thought I'd controlled myself before Reaching, but at Erick's words, layered with concern, with a vicious protectiveness that was meaningless where he now lay, trapped inside his own body, I broke.

The fear over Eryn's sickness, the despondency over Erick's condition, the fact that Ottul wouldn't be able to help, the turmoil over William and Brandan, the tender bitterness seen in the kiss Avrell had given Eryn—all of it welled up and surged forth in uncontrolled sobbing, all mixed together, all indistinguishable. A miasma of raw emotion that felt too large for me to hold.

Erick responded by drawing me in, uttering nonsense words to hush me, rocking me back and forth as he'd done before, when I'd killed the fat man who'd snuck up behind him while he was taking care of another mark. Back then, he'd bundled me up in a blanket that reeked of grease and sweat while I cried hysterically, and he'd taken me back to my niche.

I smelled the grease and sweat of that blanket now, felt it enfolding me, smothering me . . . and I fought it back, pushed up and out of its comfort. I wanted nothing more than to let Erick hold me, to let him take the pain away, but not this time. I hadn't come here to be comforted.

I can't, I sobbed, thrashing away, the ache and turmoil melding over into anger. *I can't help you, Erick. Eryn has tried, I've tried, and now even Ottul can't help you. I don't know how to help you, Erick! I don't know what to do!*

The admission tore something deep inside me, a pain that was visceral, almost real. A pain like that which had torn Eryn inside, that was tearing her up even now, that was killing her, visible only in the hacking coughs . . . and the speckled blood on her hands.

The pain sapped the last of my strength. I quit struggling out of Erick's comfort . . . and found that he was no longer offering it.

We sat in silence. I could hear my breath—his breath—echoing raggedly in his chest. As if we'd physically struggled, actually fought.

There was a distance between us, a gulf that felt as if it would never be breached.

Perhaps, Erick began, his voice strangely empty, lifeless. He hesitated a long moment, then continued. *Perhaps there's nothing you, or anyone else, can do.*

I didn't answer. Because I'd been thinking the same thing for the last month. Ottul had been my last hope. I just hadn't been willing to voice it.

And because I didn't know where that left him, where it left me. I was afraid of where it left us.

What . . . should I do?

I didn't like the tentativeness in my voice. I could hear an unspoken possibility hidden behind the words, a possibility that I couldn't voice, that I would never have brought up, had never intended to bring up.

A possibility that apparently Erick had also considered.

End it.

My breath halted.

My gut instinctively clenched, screamed no, but I'd distanced myself from the roil of emotions, had fought them back.

I can't stay like this forever, Varis, Erick said, and I felt his anger as he voiced the unspeakable. But not the unthinkable. *I can't live like this! You've tried everything you could think of, Eryn's tried, Isaiah's tried, there's nothing left to try!*

I thought of Ottul. Perhaps she'd misunderstood, perhaps she could help after all—

But I knew that wasn't true. I'd seen her reaction, had sensed her terror on the river. She couldn't fake that, couldn't hide it.

I could smell the death in the room.

Varis, listen to me. Erick reached out in the Fire. But not in comfort. He grabbed me, shook me, his anger palpable, his fury at what he had become bleeding into my essence like oil. *You don't know what it's like in here, Varis.* His voice was a vicious growl. *I'm trapped in here! I'm trapped in here with nothing but memories! Memories like* this!

And with a violent lurch, he dragged me in, dragged me into *himself,* past the barrier between us, the barrier that kept us separate from each other, that kept us distinct. I cried out, in denial, in shock—

And then I screamed. A hideous, roaring scream of pure and utter pain as white-hot fire touched skin. A scream that tore at my already raw throat, that went on and on as the iron spike pressed deeper in my thigh, searing flesh, muscle, tendon, the black stench of cooking meat filling the stone chamber.

When the iron spike was removed, the man who'd held my naked body upright during the torture, hand entwined in my hair, another around my neck, body tight against my back to keep me from writhing, thrust me to the side. I landed with a thump on the sand-covered floor, wrenched my shoulder, my legs—tied with thorny vines—twisting beneath me. I barked at the new pain, but the throb in my shoulder was nothing compared to the sizzling heat from my thigh.

Arms tied so tight behind my back that my chest muscles screamed at the tension, I rolled until my forehead rested against the sand. It felt cool against my sweat-drenched skin, and I sobbed, sand blowing away from my face.

A sandaled, blue-tinged foot fell in front of my face and I squeezed my eyes tight. Cloth rustled as the man knelt down beside me, a hand gripping my face, turning it harshly, squeezing until I snapped open my eyes, stared up at him through the blur of tears, of sweat, of blood.

Haqtl. The head priest. Black eyes. To complement the black tattoos that writhed on his face, stark against his yellow-and-red-banded shirt.

I sucked in a ragged breath, tasted blood on my lips, phlegm. Today would be a bad day.

Haqtl thrust my head back down into the sand, ground it in deep, grit getting into my eyes, sucked into my lungs as I tried to breathe, as he shoved harder, closing off the last tendrils of air. I struggled, began to kick and twist, thrashing my legs, the muscles in my chest reawakening with renewed pain, the white-hot patch on my thigh cracking open, blood trickling down my leg, but the struggles were weak . . . so weak. I'd been here for days, for weeks, each day the same, each torture unique.

But the worst days were with Haqtl.

I ceased struggling, and with a wrench, Haqtl lifted my head free, glared down at me as I spat blood and sand into his face. He didn't flinch, simply thrust me onto my back.

"Queotl," he barked, a phrase he'd repeated a thousand times during these sessions. He placed one foot on my chest, began exerting pressure. "Queotl!"

The pressure increased, pain beginning to shoot through my back, my arms caught beneath me. The thorns from the vines used to tie them began to dig into flesh, into scratches that had finally scabbed over that morning after days of abuse.

I began to roar, Haqtl pressing down harder, the thorns digging deeper, until the roar broke into wretched sobbing.

Haqtl's weight lifted. I rolled to the side instantly, released the tension in my arms, on the vines twisted around and around the muscles there.

"I don't understand you," I spat in anger, then rolled back again.

Haqtl glared down at me, face severe.

"I don't understand you!" I bellowed.

Without flinching, Haqtl stepped forward, barked something else, something I'd never heard him say before.

The Chorl behind him moved instantly, bringing forth a box. Carved of wood, riddled with curved icons like the tattoos on the Chorl men's faces, on Haqtl's face, the Chorl priest set the box down in the sand beside him and lifted off the lid.

From within, he withdrew a thin needle as long as his hand, the spine of some seashell or sea creature, and a clay bottle stoppered with wax. He pierced the wax with the spine, withdrew it slowly, then set the bottle back into the box.

I jerked back when he stepped forward, a drop of liquid falling from the tip of the needle onto my skin. Where it landed on my chest, my skin *burned,* an agonizing burn that spread into the surrounding muscle, deep, deeper, like a thousand needles, as if my skin had literally caught fire.

And he hadn't even touched me with the spine.

I writhed to one side, sand spraying outward as I kicked, and Haqtl barked another command, the two Chorl warriors stepping forward. One kicked me in the stomach, then fell to my side with one knee planted on my chest. The other grabbed my legs.

Immobilized, I could only watch as Haqtl came around to my head, knelt beside me and raised the spine over my chest, over my heart. He glared down into my face, mouth set . . . and then he closed his eyes.

A blanket fell over me, a pressure that smothered me from neck to toe.

Haqtl began to murmur something, a whisper, barely audible.

And the spine began to descend.

I tried to struggle, felt the muscles in my neck tense as I willed myself to jerk free of the Chorl warrior's hands, as I commanded my body to move!

But the blanket that smothered me didn't slacken.

A moment before the spine touched the skin over my heart, before it sank into flesh, pierced skin and dug deeper, and deeper still, Haqtl opened his eyes . . . and smiled, his whispered chant falling silent.

And then I screamed—

And Erick thrust me back, pushed me from the memory with a roaring cry of his own, our two howls melding until we both broke at the same time, gasping into the trembling silence.

Still heaving, Erick said, more calmly than I expected, voice hoarse, ragged, *That is what I'm living with. Those memories. That pain. That is what you're asking me to endure, over and over again.*

Varis, I can't remain in this body. I can't live with it anymore. You need to set me free, Varis. You need to end it.

You need to kill me.

And then he released me, withdrew, left me sobbing again, my essence twisting in upon itself, unable to reach out for comfort, unable to find comfort within. Is this what it had felt like for Avrell, when he'd tried to free Eryn from the throne and finally realized his only way to save her was to kill her? Had he suffered like this?

I didn't know. I'd dealt with him for less than a year on a regular basis. He'd shown none of this pain when he and Borund had ordered the Mistress' death. But if he had felt this way, if he had felt this vicious scintillant pain, as if someone had knifed him in the gut, someone close, someone trusted, how had he survived?

Varis . . . please.

And I fled, pushed up and out of the Fire, collapsed back into myself with a wrenching half gasp, half sob.

"Varis?"

A concerned hand fell onto my shoulder and I opened tear-blurred eyes. "He wants me to kill him, Keven. He wants me to end it."

Keven recoiled, hand jerking back from my shoulder, head snapping to look at Erick.

Erick's face was streaked with tears where he lay on the bed, but it was utterly calm. There was no emotion there. No tension around the eyes, no frown, no hint of a smile. Perfectly empty.

Except for the tears. Tears that I had most likely unconsciously forced him to shed as I shared his body, as I felt the pain inflicted upon him by Haqtl, by the Chorl.

When Keven turned back, I saw acceptance in his face. Understanding.

And with a strange horror I realized I understood as well, perhaps more so than Keven.

Because I couldn't even remain trapped in a city without rebelling, let alone remain trapped in my own body, trapped reliving those memories.

Death would be better.

And with that, the tears stopped. Suddenly, abruptly. Without even a hitch.

Keven stood, his eyes never leaving mine. "If you won't," he said, "if you *can't,* I will. For Erick."

"No," I said, rising slowly. I could feel the weight of my sheathed dagger pressing into my back. "No. I'll do it."

Drawing the blade, I felt Keven nod and step back, heard a rustle of cloth as someone else stepped forward.

I was so focused on Erick, on his face, so expressionless, so devoid of anything I thought of as truly Erick, that I didn't acknowledge Isaiah until he gripped the wrist of the hand holding the dagger with the force and strength of iron and said, "I can't let you do that."

His voice, usually bitter and resentful, now reverberated with pure and utter resistance.

"You would defy me?" I asked, anger bleeding through the words, laced with pain.

"Yes."

"But I'm the Mistress."

He nodded. "I would defy even the Mistress over this." His eyes never left my face; his hold on my wrist never wavered. I could break that grip with a sharp twist, could kill Isaiah and Erick both in the space of two breaths, the potential hanging in the air between me and the healer like a living thing. Isaiah knew it, recognized it . . . and still he held me.

"There's nothing left to try," I argued, trying to break him, heard the tremor in my voice and forced it down. "You don't know what he's living through. You don't know what it's like. This is what he wants!"

Isaiah's eyes narrowed. "Sometimes, the patient—and those that are closest to the patient—are too blind to see. He is alive *now,* which means there is still hope. Mistress."

We glared at each silently for the space of a breath, for two—

And then I felt an unidentifiable surge on the river and the door burst open.

"Mistress!" someone shouted in warning.

With one quick turn, I broke free of Isaiah's gaze, ripped my hand free of his hold, and stepped in front of Erick's bed, Keven at my side an instant later, both of us facing the intruder at the door.

Brandan Vard.

"Venitte!" he shouted, stepping forward once, twice, the palace guardsmen that had been set to guard the door stumbling into the room behind him, kept at bay by some invisible shield, by the Sight. "They intend to attack Venitte—and you didn't tell me!"

"Mistress!" one of the stumbling guards barked. "We tried to halt him at the door, but—"

"Enough," I spat, cutting the explanation short. I could feel the effects of the force Brandan used on the river, even if I couldn't see the manipulations myself. He truly was a Servant of Venitte. "What do you want, Brandan? This is not a good time."

Face twisted in rage, he growled, "You find out that the Chorl are going to attack Venitte and you don't warn me! I had to learn this from one of your servants? Amenkor and Venitte have an alliance!"

Trying to keep my voice level, I said, "We did warn you, as soon as we found out ourselves. We told Captain Tristan. He informed us that he would let you know immediately. Obviously, he didn't."

That brought Brandan up short. He spluttered for a moment, his anger spiking—

And then, abruptly, all of his anger settled into a tight coiled ball. His stance shifted, stiffened, grew formal.

"I apologize for this intrusion. I will speak to *Tristan*—" he spat the captain's name, "—and find out why he did not feel it important to inform me of—"

He cut off, his gaze falling on Erick's prone form. "What's this?" Sharp, commanding, but without any of the anger of his earlier words.

"This . . . is none of your business."

We locked eyes. "That man is under a spell."

"I know that," I began.

And then realized what Brandan was saying.

Stepping forward, fighting against the hope that surged forward with the force of an ocean's wave, I asked, "You can see it? You can see the spell?"

"Of course."

"Can you break it?" Keven said.

Brandan frowned, uncertain now, confused.

Drawing a deep breath to calm myself, feeling the wave rising inside me, surrounding me, I tried to explain. "This man's name is Erick. He's a guardsman here in the palace, a Seeker, and my personal bodyguard. He was captured by the Chorl, and then rescued during the attack on Amenkor. But when we brought him back, we found this spell on him, one that none of us can see and only a few of us can feel. If you can see it, if you can break it . . ."

Brandan hesitated, watching me intently, as if trying to decide whether I spoke the truth, if I was deceiving him, but then he nodded. "I can try."

Without waiting for permission from Keven or the guardsmen, he stepped up to Isaiah's side of the bed, Keven and I moving to the other, and leaned over Erick's body. Slipping beneath the river, where the hope I was trying to suppress grew almost overwhelming, I felt the river shift beneath his probing. I couldn't tell what he was doing, but I could see the occasional consequences of his actions, like ripples on water caused by a fish hidden beneath the surface.

"It's some kind of shield," he muttered after a long moment, "layered close to his body, like a second skin. And it's secured near his heart."

"Yes." I thought about the needle that had been pressed into Erick's skin by Haqtl, about the burning sensation of the poison that had coated the needle. "Can you remove it?"

Brandan glanced up. "No."

I almost staggered back, the wave of hope cresting, beginning to crash down, threatening to crush me.

But then Brandan added, nonchalantly, "But Zachari could."

"And where is Zachari?"

Brandan leaned back. "Venitte."

"We'll have to bring Zachari here," Keven said. "Quickly."

"There won't be enough time," Isaiah said, and his voice was calm, collected. The familiar resentful bitterness had returned. "Erick won't survive long enough for you to send word to Venitte, get Zachari on a ship, and get him back here. Erick's too close to death."

"Then what can we do?" Keven said in frustration.

I leaned over Erick's placid face. I reached out and brushed a stray lock of hair away from his closed eyes.

"We take him with us to Venitte," I said.

"Why couldn't we see it?" Eryn asked.

On the wharf, the four nearest docks were a torrent of activity, the two Chorl ships, Borund's trader, and Tristan's ship all being loaded at the same time, casks and crates winched up and overhead or hefted onto shoulders and hauled up planks. The lower city itself was a riotous mix of guardsmen, their families, hawkers, Servants, carts, horses, carriages, and sailors.

I couldn't help thinking it was a gutterscum's dream. Easy marks, easy pickings.

"Because we're women," I said, turning my attention from the ships and docks to Eryn. "Brandan said that the Sight, and another one of the Five Magics he calls the Threads, are split into two sources—male and female. Essentially, the Servants of both Amenkor and Venitte are using both the Sight and the Threads when we manipulate the river, even though we think of it as only one source of power. But for the most part, whether or not we can see what each of us has done depends on our skill with both magics . . . and whether we're male or female. He can't see what we're doing when we manipulate the river any more than we can see what he does. Some can feel the other side of the magic, like you could feel the spell on Erick, but no one he knows can see both sides.

"The spell put on Erick was placed there by Haqtl, not by the Ochean and the Servants. I know. I was there when Haqtl used the needle to pierce Erick above the heart and secured it. Erick showed me. That's why that wound won't heal when all of the others did. And since neither one of us can see the spell, we can't remove it."

"What if Brandan is lying? What if he's manipulating you for some unknown political reason? We know he and Tristan aren't exactly friends, we know that there's something else going on, and we have no idea what's at stake there. In fact, we have no idea what the political climate in Venitte is at the moment at all."

I thought about Brandan barging into Erick's chambers, about how confused he'd looked when he'd first spotted Erick. "I don't think he's lying about Erick. And I know he can see the spell. He described it and its effects too well."

"But he could still be lying about being able to remove it in Venitte."

I turned to Eryn. "I don't have much choice. Neither one of us can help, and with what he's told us, Ottul was never going to be of any use either."

Eryn shook her head. "I know. It's just . . ."

Farther down the wharf, a crate crashed to the planking and split open with a crunch, apples spilling out, the caged chickens nearby flapping in agitation, a goat bleating. The dockmaster bellowed in rage, dark-skinned Zorelli leaping to gather up the apples.

Avrell stood watching from the end of the dock, a dark frown on his face. Eryn's brow grew troubled and she coughed once, the sound halfhearted and empty, almost like a habit now.

I glanced out toward the waters of the harbor. "Avrell can stay here. I can survive Venitte without him."

I felt Eryn's eyes on me, felt her considering, but then she sighed. "No. You need him more than I do. We've been separated before, by duty, by choice. This is no different."

Except it was. The blood-speckled white cloth Eryn kept tucked in her sleeve spoke of that.

But I didn't say anything. Because I thought I *would* need Avrell in Venitte.

"The carriages have arrived," Eryn said.

I turned back toward the city, caught sight of the three carriages as they drew up alongside the end of the *Defiant's* dock, the crowd being pushed back by Catrell and a slew of guardsmen. Most of those on the wharf weren't interested in what was happening on the docks themselves, too busy hugging and sobbing and saying farewell to loved ones as guardsmen and sailors loaded themselves onto the four ships, but when the occupant of the first carriage emerged, a hush overtook those closest, and a dark surge of hatred and resentment and fear coursed through the river.

"I still think you should leave Ottul here," Eryn muttered.

I didn't answer.

The darkness on the river swelled as Ottul was escorted down the pier toward us by four Servants and ten guardsmen. She hadn't caused any serious problems since that first attempt to break free after we'd found her, but I wasn't taking any chances.

She sensed the hatred on the river as well. Her eyes darkened, and that defensive arrogance settled into the lines of her face. Tossing her long black hair, she straightened, proceeding down the dock at a swift pace, as if she were being presented with honor, not guarded as a prisoner.

"Mistress," Marielle said. She, Trielle, Heddan, and Gwenn were the four Servants keeping Ottul under guard, Gwenn chosen because Ottul had bonded to her in some way during her excursions to the training grounds.

"The room has been prepared and is ready," I said.

Marielle nodded, the others following suit, and then they swept past, heading for the *Defiant*. I'd already put Ottul out of my mind, stepped forward now to the end of the pier and the second carriage.

Catrell and three other guardsmen helped Isaiah down from the carriage, then reached in to begin pulling out the carrying board that Erick had been lashed to for transport. He'd been made as comfortable as possible with pillows and blankets, but I still winced as they tilted him out using the handles built into the sides.

The fiery pain of the needles caused by the lashing, by the jostling movements, would be excruciating.

"Get him onto the ship and settled as quickly as possible," I said to Isaiah.

"Of course, Mistress."

As they moved carefully by, I dove into the Fire at Erick's core, sent him a surge of hope, of sympathy, but retreated quickly.

The pain *was* excruciating.

The third carriage carried William and Borund, both dressed in their formal merchant jackets.

"—and remember to give Master Tanser the contract for the casks of salted fish. You'll want to keep on his good side; he runs half of the silk trade to the southeast."

William rolled his eyes. "I know, Master Borund, I've dealt with him before."

"But not as a Master yourself. Make him deal with you respectfully, or he'll take advantage of you. Keep in mind, you're a representative of Amenkor, of its merchants' guild. Make them all treat you with respect."

William suppressed a heavy sigh. His gaze swept the docks, locked onto me for a lingering moment before glancing away, a troubled frown crossing his face.

Borund noticed. He settled an arm over William's shoulder and led him forward, leaning in close to mutter something in his ear. William shot me another furtive glance, mouth pressed tight, and then Borund slapped him on the back. "Safe voyage. And beware of Master Handleford! He'll try to get you to wed one of his daughters!"

William ignored him, moving off down the dock without a backward glance to me or Borund, although I could see the tenseness in his shoulders.

Borund turned toward me. "And you," he said, voice dark.

"What?"

He placed his hands on my shoulders, his serious expression breaking into a soft grin. "Don't let his mood keep you away. He cares for you more than he's willing to admit."

When I frowned, he laughed and drew me in for a quick hug. I could feel him chuckling as he held me tight, then pushed me back. "I'll rebuild Amenkor's fleet, just you watch. It won't happen overnight, but I'll do the best I can."

We hadn't had much chance to talk since I'd stormed into his manse and commanded him to build Amenkor more ships, but I found I was no longer angry with him. Not over his inability to fight on the docks when the Chorl attacked, and not over what that had done to William.

And then orders were being bellowed all along the wharf, the four docks steadily emptying as the last of the crates were loaded, the last of the guardsmen extricating themselves from their wife's or children's clutches, picking up their bundled clothes and possessions, giving one last lingering kiss, and then hurrying down the dock and up the planks onto the ships.

"Well," I said, about to turn toward the *Defiant,* noticing that Catrell had sent one of the carriages away, had come up to my side, waiting patiently beside Keven. The other two carriages waited to take Eryn back to the palace and Borund to his manse. Catrell would be on the *Spoils of War,* Darryn taking his place as captain of the guard in Amenkor.

Before I could say good-bye to Eryn, someone shouted, "Wait! Mistress, wait!"

I frowned, everyone turning toward the distant shout. A woman, hair a light brown and eyes a startling green, waved from the edge of the cordon of guardsmen. She was vaguely familiar. A young boy was clutched to her side, his arms wrapped around her leg. The boy had the same hair as the mother—

But he had Westen's eyes.

"Let her through," I said, and when Eryn turned toward me in question, I shook my head.

The woman rushed forward as soon as the guards let her pass, the boy letting go of her leg and grabbing on to her hand. She knelt before me, head bowed, and I thought she would have sketched the Skewed Throne symbol across her chest if she hadn't held something tightly in the other hand.

"Mistress," she said breathlessly, but before she could continue, I touched her gently on the head and motioned her to rise. The boy latched back onto her leg.

"What do you need?" I asked.

"Could you give this to him?"

She held out the object in her hand—a braid of hair, twined with ribbon and a sprig of honeysuckle.

I shot her a sharp look, wondering how she knew of Westen's scent. I could see where she'd cut the locks of hair from her head.

"Of course," I said, taking the braid from her.

She smiled, her face radiant.

I glanced down at the boy, who tightened his grip on her leg and swung himself backward, hiding behind his mother's form. "And who's this?"

Westen's wife rustled the boy's hair. "We named him Ash," she said, and I winced. My name, the name I'd forsaken on the Dredge to become Varis. But she didn't seem to notice, continuing with, "And I'm Nadeen."

At my back, I felt Keven shift forward. "Mistress, the ships are ready."

I caught Nadeen's eyes, saw the muted question she couldn't bring herself to ask.

"He's fine," I said. "And I'll make certain he gets this. I'll give it to him myself."

She didn't seem to know what to say, the fear and worry she'd kept suppressed so far beginning to break free. Taking Ash by the hand, she finally said, "Keep him safe," and then she backed off, drew Ash up into her arms, and slid back into the crowd.

"I had no idea," Eryn said after a long moment.

"He's kept it hidden well."

"Mistress," Keven said again.

"I know," I said, somewhat curtly. All along the docks, ties were being undone, one of the Chorl ships already edging away from the wharf toward the open harbor. "Let's go."

Catrell barked an order, the last of the guardsmen splitting into two groups, Catrell heading toward the *Spoils of War*, Keven waiting impatiently at my back. Farther down, I saw Tristan motioning the last of his men onto the *Reliant*, Brandan at his side sending dark glares at Tristan's back.

"Safe journey," Eryn said, when I turned back.

And then Keven and the escort led me down the dock and on board the *Defiant*.

A half hour later, I sailed out between the watchtowers of the harbor.

And out of Amenkor.

Part II: At Sea

✠ Chapter 7

"It's becoming harder to target the Chorl's Servants," Liviann said. "They've altered their strategy, have begun actively attempting to kill our own Servants in the field, as well as us." Here, she threw a heated glance toward me, toward my leg, held stiff and straight out before me with splints, elevated onto a stool. It still throbbed fiercely, even weeks after having been crushed under my dying horse. Some days more painfully than others.

Like today.

We were seated in the wide round room known as the Council of Seven. Made entirely of black stone, the floor polished to a high obsidian gloss, the chamber stretched over fifty paces in diameter, seven pillars rising from the floor to the edges of the domed ceiling high above, rounded alcoves between the supports. Light glimmered in each of the alcoves—an ethereal light, pure white in nature, the work of Garus and Seth—and at the moment there appeared to be no entrance or exit from the room. It had been sealed off from the outside world.

In the center of the room, seven seats sat facing each other in a wide circle. Each seat was different, representing the personality of one of the Seven—a solid oak chair with arms for myself; a rounded cushioned ottoman, no arms, no back, for Silicia, so she could stretch out; a simple seat for Garus, no arms, but with a low back.

Liviann sat in a rigid chair made of ash, with a tall back and no arms. Almost like a throne. She'd arranged her dress so that the folds fell just so.

"Rymerun was a trap," I said. "An ambush. They caught us off guard. They won't do so again."

Liviann waved aside my comment angrily. "You should not have charged off on your own. The Seven are too important for the survival of the Frigean coast, especially now, with the Chorl."

"Enough," Garus spat. He rose from his own seat and began pacing behind it. "We've heard the argument a hundred times, Liviann, I don't care to hear it again."

"Yes," Alleryn interjected. "It's become tiresome."

"Tiresome!"

For a moment, it seemed that Liviann would launch into a tirade and I sighed, adjusting the position of my leg with a wince and a silent curse. But instead, Liviann abruptly calmed.

I frowned. She was more dangerous when she was calm.

"Do you deny that at the moment, with the threat of the Chorl hanging over the coast, that we—the Seven, and through us the Servants—are the only ones holding the Chorl back?"

"The armies of Venitte have been able to push the Chorl out of the city," Atreus said.

"But only because we and the Servants have been able to neutralize the Chorl Servants. Without their Servants, the Chorl are just men, just guardsmen. Every battle fought without us, without a Servant or Servants as part of our ranks to counter their Servants, has been lost."

Grudging silence.

Liviann leaned back into her seat. "At the moment, we walk a thin line. We've pushed the Chorl out of the city and the surrounding lands, and that took us over two years. With the help of Amenkor and Marlett, we've kept them out of all of the major cities, all of the major ports. But the Chorl have become entrenched now. We haven't gained any significant ground on them in months."

"Not for want of trying," Garus interjected with a low murmur.

Liviann ignored him. "The problem is the Servants, both theirs and ours."

"How so?"

Liviann turned toward Silicia, lips pursed. "We've come to an impasse. They know of us and we know of them, of their capabilities. We were only effective against each other when everyone was an unknown. Since then, we've decimated their ranks by targeting them in battle when they weren't expecting such magical resistance. Their advantage in numbers has been destroyed. But they've changed their tactics, and now we can't simply charge in—" another swift glance toward me; a slight hardening of her voice, "—without the threat of an ambush. They've begun to defend themselves and we've lost our advantage. While they can't defend against the power of the Council members in particular, there are only Seven of us, not enough to effectively counter all of the Chorl Servants that remain. And our own Servants are vulnerable because they don't have use of all of the Five Magics; in effect, our Servants and the Chorl's are evenly matched."

"What are you saying, Liviann?" I said, irritated, suddenly tired of the discussion. The throb in my leg had become a steady pulse, worse in the hip. I wanted out of this chamber, wanted to retire to my room so I could soak my leg in hot water.

Reaching down, I began massaging my hip.

"I'm saying that the Seven have become indispensable. Venitte—the entire Frigean coast—can't afford to lose any of us or the balance that we've sustained so far will crumble. At the same time, I think something needs to change. We need to do something to upset the balance in our favor."

"But what?" Garus growled.

"If we can't risk ourselves," Seth interjected, "then we'll have to rely on the other Servants."

Alleryn scowled. "Yes, but as you say, Liviann, our Servants are at most evenly matched with the Chorl Servants. We'd be risking them with no guarantee of the outcome shifting in our favor. Linking them decreases their ability to protect our own armies, because we then don't have enough Servants to spread out over all of the units."

"And our Servants are indispensable," Liviann added. "We've all commented on the fact that there seem to be fewer and fewer Servants discovered on the coast every year."

"And of those found," Silicia said, "they have less and less power. We have not found a true Adept since Atreus and myself, and that was almost a hundred years ago."

Garus halted his pacing, his face thoughtful as he rested his hands on the back of his chair and scanned the Seven. "We need something that will shift the balance of power into the Servants' hands, something that will strengthen them, give them an edge over the Chorl."

"Yes," Liviann said. "And more. We need a way to preserve the knowledge that we possess, in case one of us is lost. Something that will allow us to pass our knowledge on to future Servants and Adepts. Something that they can use to protect the city against the Chorl, against any invader that threatens the coast."

I felt the weight of Liviann's words press down on me and with a sinking sensation in my gut realized all of the other Seven had turned toward me.

"What do you want me to do?" I asked warily.

Liviann stood, stepped toward me, but halted a pace away. "You are the Builder here, Cerrin. And you are the one most balanced in all Five Magics. Build something that will give our Servants an edge in battle. Build something that will preserve our knowledge, that will preserve us."

I hesitated.

She must have seen the skepticism in my face, for she stepped forward, placed her hands on the arms of my chair, and leaned in so close our noses almost touched. I could smell the perfume she'd used to cloak her sweat: lavender and mint, so pungent it made my nose twitch.

In a voice pitched so softly that I doubted any of the other Seven heard, she said, "Build something that will destroy the Chorl. For Venitte. For the coast. And for your wife and daughters."

Something deep inside my chest hardened and for a moment the pain in my leg vanished, forgotten. I saw Olivia's face, her dark skin, her silky hair, smelled her vibrant scent—a sea scent, salty and sunny, overriding even Liviann's perfume—as I held her, rested my chin on the top of her head while she nestled back into my arms, feeling her warmth through my shirt. Like an echo, I heard Pallin's laughter, heard Jaer shriek with delight, and the bright, happy sounds twisted painfully in my chest.

Always the same memory: all of us on the veranda of the estate on the cliffs above the channel, a moment before the Chorl appeared, before they attacked.

The last memory of us all together.

I drew back, focused on Liviann's face, close enough I could feel her breath against my skin. She'd used my wife, my daughters, to manipulate me, and I felt an urge to deny her because of that.

But my mind had already begun to plan, to build.

And Liviann knew it. I didn't even need to answer her. A smile touched her lips, there and gone, and she pushed back from my chair.

"In the meantime," she said, moving toward her own seat, "I think we need to be a little more aggressive with the Servants themselves."

"How so?" Garus asked in a low rumble.

Liviann sat down in her chair—in her throne—and arranged the folds of her dress around her.

"We need to send them into the Chorl camps and attack the Chorl there, not just on the battlefield. We need to make them assassins."

I woke with a cry as the ship lurched and the hammock I slept in swung wildly. I flailed around, disoriented. The sensation of falling closed off my throat and sent waves of tingling panic through my arms and fingers.

Then someone grabbed me, hissed, "Mistress," and when I recognized Marielle's voice, I ceased struggling.

"What's happening?" I barked.

In the darkness of the cabin that had been given over to me, Marielle, and Trielle, I felt Marielle shift away. "I don't know. I sent Trielle up to the deck to find out. It started picking up about fifteen minutes ago."

Even as she spoke, the ship rolled beneath us. The hammock swung with the motion, and I gripped the edges as a wave of sea-sickness washed over me. I'd been violently ill the first few days after we'd sailed, but I thought I'd finally gotten my "sea legs," as the crew of the *Defiant* said, usually through grins. Swallowing against the taste of bile, I tried to right myself in the hammock, managing to slip from it gracelessly just as a flame sparked and light filled the cabin.

The ship lurched again, and I heard water slapping against wood, the boards beneath us creaking. Marielle frowned as she hung the lantern she'd lit on a hook beneath one of the massive squared timbers low overhead. So low that most of the guardsmen and Servants had to duck.

Marielle looked pale, almost gray.

Before I could offer any reassurances, Trielle returned.

"Captain Bullick says that we're skirting the edge of a storm," she said, succinct and businesslike, but with a trace of excitement. "He doesn't think it will get much worse than this. He thinks we'll outrun it."

"I'd like to go up on deck," I said, and I saw Trielle's eyes light up.

Marielle almost moaned.

A half hour later, hammock stowed away and dressed in my usual white shirt and brown breeches, I climbed up the ladder with Trielle onto the deck into post-dawn light, having left Marielle behind in the cabin. Salt spray struck my face and I grinned, suffused with a strange energy. I stood a moment on the heaving deck, felt its rocking motion beneath me, my legs now adjusting to compensate for the sudden shifts, and let the wind gust over me.

Ahead, at the railing, Captain Bullick saw me and motioned me over.

"Mistress," he said in greeting. He held a long tube up to his eye, but after a moment he dropped it to his side, the tube sliding together into a more compact form. He wore the standard captain's uniform, a colored jacket like the merchants used, embroidered at the edges, because the captains were so closely affiliated with the merchants' guild. Bullick's jacket was gray, with blue embroidery.

He stared at me with a slight frown. "I can't suggest you remain on deck, Mistress, not in such dangerous waters."

Not quite a command, I chose to ignore it.

"Trielle mentioned a storm."

Bullick grunted and motioned out across the water. "See for yourself."

On the horizon to the right—to starboard, I thought, chiding myself— black clouds billowed skyward, the ocean black beneath them, a roiling darkness illuminated only briefly by jagged blue lightning. I realized I could taste the lightning on the river, bitter and metallic. Putting a hand to the railing to steady myself, the wood shuddering beneath my fingers, I raised the other to shield my eyes from the wind.

"You can see where it's raining," Trielle said at my side.

"Where?"

Trielle pointed. "See where the lighter gray is slanting down near the cloud's edge? That's rain."

I nodded, picking out the diagonal cut across the darker gray of the clouds in the background.

For a moment, the crest of a wave blocked the view and I drew back, focusing on the ocean closer at hand. I gasped. "The waves!"

"Yes," Bullick said. "They're almost cresting higher than the deck. Which is why I suggest you stay below."

"But Trielle said you thought we'd skirt the storm."

"And so I still think, but that doesn't mean we won't see some rough seas. It's safer if you remain below, just in case."

As he spoke, the ship tilted up and over one wave and began to descend into the trough behind. I felt the motion in my stomach, the vile taste of vomit again at the back of my throat.

The *Defiant* slammed into the next wave, fine spray thrown up and over the prow, washing across the deck. Bullick didn't even turn to look, barely affected by the ship's motion at all, but deckhands were scrambling through the rigging, already adjusting the sails.

A small frisson of fear coursed through me, cold and electric. I remembered the storm Erick and *The Maiden* had been caught in, recalled the waves crashing over the deck. Men could be swept overboard.

And I couldn't swim.

"I think you're right," I said. "I'll wait out the storm below."

He nodded. "Very well."

His tone suggested the idea had been all mine, but it was satisfied.

"How much longer until we hook up with Westen and the *Prize*?" I asked.

"If the storm doesn't put us too far off course, we'll reach the port of Temall in another day."

Then he turned away.

As Trielle and I returned to the open hatchway and the ladder that led below, I caught a glimpse of the other three ships in our group—Tristan's *Reliant,* and the two Chorl ships. All three were off to the left, farther away from the storm, and all were beginning to turn toward the coast that could not be seen on the horizon.

"I wonder how they're faring," I said, thinking of Catrell. And of Brandan Vard and Tristan.

Trielle snorted. "Better than we are, I'm sure."

As I descended the ladder, I felt the *Defiant* change course, heading toward the other three ships.

*   *   *

The rough seas broke a little before dusk, and everyone spilled out from below onto the decks as soon as Bullick gave permission. The initial excitement tinged with fear had quickly worn into a sickening rhythmic monotony as the ship heaved, the single lantern allowed swinging back and forth in the cramped quarters. I'd spent the first few hours with Avrell and Keven, Marielle and Trielle in attendance, discussing the protocol and politics of Venitte, then escaped to Erick's room where I helped Isaiah try to ease Erick's pain using the White Fire. The sudden movements and hard rocking of the ship aggravated the prickling needles on Erick's skin, since he had to be tied down to keep from slipping from his cot. I'd been forced to seize control of Erick's sweat-soaked body in order to make him eat.

But as soon as the ship calmed, I left Isaiah and Erick and joined everyone else on deck. I sucked in the fresh air, stretched cramped muscles, and only then realized that the close quarters below deck, the tight niches and small boltholes, reminded me of the Dredge and the slums beyond.

"Bullick says we were pushed far enough off course that we won't reach Temall until late tomorrow," Avrell said. He and Keven had approached me almost as soon as I emerged from below. "But at least we didn't lose any of the other ships during the storm." He nodded to where the three ships surrounded us, one of the Chorl ships just ahead, the *Reliant* and the second Chorl ship behind. "Bullick seems to be a fair captain."

I shrugged. "He's too stiff and formal."

Avrell grinned. "You'll find most of the captains stiff and formal, then. Ships require strict discipline."

"Worse than the palace?"

"Worse than the palace."

"Hmm." I made a face that forced Keven to chuckle.

Leaning onto the rail, I stared out at the faint edge of land that could be seen off the port side, gliding by smoothly under the light breeze. Too distant to pick out any details, it appeared more as a gray-green haze trapped between the deep, deep blue of the ocean coursing by beneath us and the lighter blue of the cloudless sky above.

"Here," someone said, and I turned to find William holding out the strange compact tube that Bullick had used earlier, before the storm. In the cramped quarters of the ship, we'd been forced to see each other on a daily basis—while eating, taking breaks on deck—but William had been cold, had averted his gaze, had mumbled something too low to hear as we passed each other in the narrow corridors. He hadn't given me the chance to start a conversation with him, let alone try to explain that nothing had happened with Brandan. I'd found his entire attitude irritating and, after the first few days, had avoided him as much as possible.

But now he stood before me, Bullick's device held out in one hand, a strange pleading expression on his face.

Our eyes met, held for a moment. I realized he was trying to apologize.

And then he dropped his gaze and sighed.

"It's called a spyglass," he said. "You can get a better look at the coast from here. Like this."

He pulled the tube out to its fullest extent, and I could see how the cylinders collapsed into one another. Raising the smallest end to his eye, he peered through it, stepping up beside me at the railing. I felt his shirt brush my arm.

"Mistress," Avrell said, and with a start I realized he and Keven had stepped back. With a nod, Keven trying to withhold a knowing grin, they wandered away down the deck.

Behind them, I saw Marielle and Trielle watching closely, Marielle leaning in to whisper something in Trielle's ear. Trielle laughed, the sound light and mischievous, and I frowned, thinking about what Marielle had told me, about what we'd discussed since, about me and William and Brandan, about kissing, about sex.

"Would you like to try?"

I turned back to William, felt my skin burning on the back of my neck as I realized he meant the spyglass and not . . .

"What do I do?" I said, accepting the tube in one hand, my voice short. It was heavier than it looked, and I realized there were lenses at each end, like the lenses on Borund's glasses, but rounder and thicker.

He hesitated, uncertain. Then: "Hold the small end up to your eye and point it toward whatever you'd like to get a closer look at."

I did so, pointing the glass toward the land and closing my other eye as I'd seen him do. I frowned. "All I see is a blur of blue."

"You have to hold it steady. And I think you're still looking at the ocean. You don't have it high enough. Here, I'll help."

I jumped when he stepped up behind me, so close our bodies touched, and involuntarily pulled the spyglass away from my eye. The heat on my neck crept upward, but then his hands closed over mine, his arm reaching around me, and he pulled the glass higher.

"Ready?" he asked.

His head was next to mine, his mouth close to my ear. I could feel his breath against my neck.

I drew in a long breath. "I guess."

I didn't like how strained my voice sounded, but I swallowed and brought the end of the spyglass up to my eye, leaning back into William slightly as I squinted and closed the other eye.

"See anything?"

I couldn't breathe, let alone see anything. I felt my hands trembling, threw a curse at Marielle for putting vague, alluring thoughts into my head—

And then a swath of green and tan interrupted the blurred field of blue through the glass.

I gasped and my arms tensed as I tried to hold the spyglass steady, all thought of sex, of my annoyance at William's actions on the wharf, of his curtness on the ship, gone as the green and tan settled down into a length of rocky beach and a fringe of pine trees, appearing so close I almost reached out to try to touch them. The branches of the trees thrashed in the breeze, and waves rushed onto the rocks in a boiling froth of white foam, accompanied incongruously by the sounds of the ship—calls from the men in the rigging, conversations on the deck, the clang of a bell signaling the hour and the constant shush of the ocean sliding by.

The juxtaposition of the noise of the ship against the expected but nonexistent sound of waves crashing onto a beach and wind singing in the trees felt eerie. It sent a shiver down through my spine.

William's hands dropped away and he stepped back, leaning on the rail beside me. I lowered the spyglass.

"How does it work?"

"The lenses," he said, then shrugged. "All of the ship captains use them."

I didn't remember Mathew, the captain of *The Maiden,* having one, but I hadn't spent that much time on board his ship. And what time I had spent aboard his ship had been within the Fire at Erick's core.

I turned back to the shore, looked at the far shore through the spyglass again. "So what happened at the wharf?"

I felt William stiffen, his presence on the river prickling. "What do you mean?"

I snorted, turned toward him, let some of my anger and irritation seep into my voice. "After that little incident with Brandan, after the tour, you barely came to the palace. You avoided me when I was out in the city, barely acknowledged me on the docks before we left."

"I was busy. With guild matters."

"Like hell. What about here on the ship?"

He shifted uncomfortably and I turned away in disgust, brought the spyglass back to my eye, even though I wasn't focusing on anything, wasn't even trying.

William straightened, grew still. "It's Brandan Vard."

"What about him?"

A short silence. "I don't trust him. He's hiding something."

I almost sighed, disappointed. Because I was speaking to William the merchant now, not the William who had spent hours with me at Erick's bedside, not the William who had held me when Erick's condition had driven me to tears. "I know that, William. I just don't know what it is he's hiding. What it is that he's not telling me. Do you?"

"No."

When I held out the spyglass, he took it reluctantly, staring at it a moment before he met my gaze.

"I just don't trust him," he said forcefully, and I could see what he couldn't say in his expression. "You shouldn't be dealing with him. You shouldn't—"

But he cut off abruptly, looked away, frustration and anger tightening his face.

"I have to deal with him," I said, reaching out to grip his arm. "I'm the Mistress of Amenkor, and he's a Servant from Venitte, a representative of Lord March."

That William knew all of this was obvious, but it didn't help him relax. Because that wasn't the real issue.

The light began to fade, dusk approaching.

William closed the spyglass and slid it into his pocket, turned.

"Varis," he began, but then he halted, unable to continue.

Varis, not Mistress.

Before I could say anything, before I had even begun to think, he stepped in close and kissed me.

The touch of his lips shocked me, sent something both warm and cold down into my gut, something both soft and harsh that tingled through the hands I'd raised to his shoulders without thought, something that simultaneously made me want to lean forward, wanting more, while pushing away in uncertainty, because I was still angry with him. Because the kiss was rough and thick and tender at the same time. I could taste it on the river, could taste the frustration, the jealousy, the intensity, like butter and brine combined.

And then it was over, William pulling back. My hands fell to my sides.

Then he was gone, heading back down below deck to his quarters.

I stood in the darkness on the deck, shivering. But not from the chill that the fall of night had brought to the air. I could still smell him in the air—the usual sweat and straw dust, as if he'd just come from a warehouse, now mixed with the salt of the sea.

If I'd been uncertain of his feelings before, even after seeing the drawing he'd done of me in his rooms, after the kiss in the guildhall and the kiss on the dock, he'd made his intentions clear now. Because unlike the first two kisses, he'd initiated this one himself.

I hesitated on the deck of the ship, then descended to my own rooms.

Marielle and Trielle were waiting.

"So?" Marielle said as soon as I entered. "What happened?"

"Nothing."

Marielle's mouth pursed in disappointment. "Maybe you should speak to Brandan more once we reach land. He seems to be a little more focused than William, a little more direct with his interest."

I caught Trielle's eye. She watched me with a slightly raised eyebrow.

She didn't believe me. She knew something had happened, she just didn't know what.

"Help me with the hammocks," I said, ignoring them both.

I needn't have bothered. There are no secrets on a ship, a fact I realized the next day as soon as I came up on deck and saw Avrell glaring at me.

"You could have been a little more discreet," he said curtly. "At least on the dock at Amenkor it was dark and you were out of general view."

I bristled instantly. If it hadn't been Avrell, I would have drawn my dagger. "I didn't realize that was part of the First's duties."

Avrell stiffened. "Everything regarding the Mistress is part of the First's duties. Especially this!" He caught himself, forced himself to calm, turning out toward the ocean as it slid past, his jaw working. "You are the Mistress. Everything you do affects me, affects Amenkor. Every word spoken, every action taken . . . every kiss."

"You never seemed that concerned in the palace," I spat.

"We aren't in the palace anymore, Mistress," he answered coldly. "Everything you do is being watched and judged and commented upon now. Everything is being reported to people you haven't even met." He motioned toward the *Reliant,* sailing behind and to the right, close enough I could see the shapes of men on the deck, could pick out Tristan in his captain's jacket. A spyglass glinted in the sunlight as he lowered it, turning away.

I couldn't be certain, but I thought Brandan Vard stood at his side.

I thought suddenly of what William had said, that Brandan couldn't be trusted, and my gut twisted.

"What do they care who I kiss?" I demanded.

"They care because perhaps they can use it against you somehow. We're headed to Venitte, Mistress, where politics can be deadly. Much more so than in Amenkor. The death and deception begun by Alendor and the merchant's consortium is nothing compared to what the Lords and Ladies of the Venittian court practice at, what they *play* at." He shook his head. "I should have warned you earlier, as soon as the *Reliant* appeared in our harbor. But I forgot you weren't raised in the palace, forgot you aren't—"

"The true Mistress?" I finished scathingly.

"I forgot you aren't trained to *be* Mistress," he said sharply.

We both fell silent, Avrell struggling to control himself while I fumed inside.

Even without the throne, even outside of Amenkor, I was trapped.

"You must always think before you act," Avrell finally said, his voice calm again. "Out of all the protocols, all of the warnings I've given you about Venitte, that is the one lesson you must learn. Someone is always watching. Nothing you do will ever be a secret."

I didn't respond, and after a moment Avrell turned and walked away, leaving me alone.

No one else approached all day, Servants, guardsmen, and sailors all giving me a wide berth. At one point, William appeared, started to head across the deck to where I stood at the railing, but Keven intercepted him, escorted him off to one side for a lengthy discussion that was mostly one-sided, William frowning through all of it. It must have been a lecture much like the one Avrell had given me, for William glanced toward me, toward the surrounding sailors and shipmates, and finally toward the *Reliant*.

A few hours before dusk, Captain Bullick announced we would be reaching Temall within the hour. "We have not seen any Chorl ships, but I would still approach Temall cautiously," he added, and behind him, in the rigging, I could see sailors, unfurling sails. A young crewman flashed flag signals to the other three ships. The *Defiant* listed beneath my feet, angling to port, toward shore again. We'd sailed out of sight of it, even with a spyglass, the night before.

Within the hour, no Chorl ships in sight, we sailed into the port of Temall, almost everyone crowded into the prow of the ship, myself included, Keven and Avrell to either side, a cold formality creating a wall between me and the First.

I frowned as the *Defiant* rounded the break. "It's . . . small."

The port contained a single wharf with three docks stretching out from a rocky shore and only two other ships in evidence, a trader half the size of Bullick's at the dock and the *Prize* anchored in the bay. A few buildings—warehouses, a tavern or two, a scattering of small fishing houses not much more than huts—surrounded the wharf. A road led up a hill through a slightly denser clustering of houses, then to the gates of the outer wall.

I'd seen Temall once before, through Westen's eyes, had known that it was a small port, but seeing it in person . . .

"Amenkor is three times as large," I added.

Avrell nodded, his attention on the people gathered on the wharf. "But at the moment, Temall is much more significant. It's the buffer between us and the Chorl. Because of that, we cannot afford to alienate Lord Pyre. We need him as an ally." His eyes narrowed. "I believe there's someone here to meet us."

I scanned those on the pier as Bullick brought the ship slowly in to dock, saw Westen and a small group from the scouting party—

And with them, Lord Justaen Pyre, with a large entourage of guardsmen.

My hand fell to my dagger. Suddenly, having Avrell at my side felt reassuring, rather than constraining.

"What does that mean?" I asked.

Avrell leaned back from the railing, folding his rank as First around him like a cloak. "Probably nothing more than that he wanted to greet us. Westen did forewarn him of our arrival, and he's never seen a Mistress outside of Amenkor."

But there was a hint of uncertainty in Avrell's voice, a crease forming in his brow as he spoke.

It took another twenty minutes to dock, the sun now low on the horizon. At Avrell's suggestion, I'd gathered an escort around me, composed of Keven and his chosen guardsmen, Avrell, Heddan, and Gwenn. I'd sent Marielle and Trielle to guard Ottul, relieving the other two girls. Both fidgeted nervously until Avrell reprimanded them with a curt word. After that, they tried to remain poised and respectful; only Heddan, the older of the two, was somewhat successful.

Bullick descended the plank first, accompanied by William dressed in his merchant's jacket, both speaking to the harbormaster before bowing at the waist before Lord Justaen, the words spoken lost to distance and the gusts from the ocean.

Then the two of them stepped to one side and Avrell descended to the dock. Keven nudged me to follow, moving up close behind me.

I suddenly wanted the familiar confines of Amenkor, wanted the back streets and alleys of the lower city, the halls and corridors of the palace, the crumbling narrows of the Dredge and the fish-gut smell of the wharf. I'd even take the uncomfortable reverence of the people as they sketched the Skewed Throne symbol on their chests and bowed as I passed them in the streets.

"Lord Justaen Pyre of Temall," Avrell said as he halted before the Lord's entourage. He did not acknowledge Westen or any of the men from Amenkor. "May I present the Mistress of Amenkor."

Outwardly, Lord Justaen didn't react at all, merely shifting his stance so that he could nod his head slightly. But on the river—

On the river, he gave a start of surprise as I stepped forward, a twitch of the currents, nothing more. He smelled of worry, of fear and wariness, like the smell of the air before a storm, wet and dangerous, none of which showed in his bearded face.

But he was gray. Not a danger to me personally. Not a threat.

"Mistress, I welcome you to Temall," he said, in the same calm but grating voice I remembered hearing through Westen's ears. "You are . . . not what I expected."

I wondered what he had almost said, but nodded in return. "Thank you."

His eyebrows rose at that. "As soon as we are joined by Captain Tristan and his guests," he said, motioning to where the *Reliant* was already tying up at the wharf, "we can head up to the keep. I've had a meal prepared."

"During which we can discuss the Chorl," I said.

Avrell frowned, but Justaen only nodded as if that were obvious. As the First continued the introductions, I glanced toward Westen, saw him shake his head minutely. I didn't understand what the gesture meant, thought about Reaching to ask, but realized I couldn't. If I did, I'd collapse on the docks, which would draw more attention than I, or Avrell, wanted.

So I settled back to wait, trying not to fidget like Gwenn, trying not to look at William even though I felt his eyes on me more than once, wondering what Keven had told him. The two Chorl ships remained in the harbor, not drawing up to the dock, but a small boat was sent out and a few of the guardsmen ferried over to join us, including Captain Catrell.

And then Tristan arrived, Brandan Vard in tow, and I felt the tension on the river escalate. Brandan kept his attention focused on Justaen, not once looking toward me.

Tristan kept close to Brandan's side, as Avrell did to mine, his presence felt, watchful but silent, like a sentinel.

Lord Justaen led the group up through the gates of the outer wall and into the keep. Made of coarse granite, half again the size of the palace in Amenkor, it felt vaguely familiar until I realized why: this is what the palace in Amenkor had once been like. I'd felt this granite beneath my hand when I'd snuck into the walls and found the archer's niche that led to the inner chambers, had felt its grittiness as I scraped and squeezed my way through it to reach the throne room. This stone had been used on the original walls, walls that had been subsumed into the structure as the palace in Amenkor grew in size. In fact, all of the inner chambers had been constructed using the same stone—the Mistress' chambers, the throne room, the tower.

Temall's keep had the same general layout, but when we entered what I expected to be the throne room, I found instead a great hall lined with tables and benches for feasting, thick tapestries hung on all of the walls, banners hung from the pillars to either side. On the dais, instead of a throne, was a single large table, chairs on the side facing the room. Justaen led Avrell, Tristan, Brandan, Bullick, William, and me to the head table, the rest of the guardsmen and Servants taking seats on the benches throughout the room. Keven, Catrell, and Westen sat as close to my position as possible, Westen keeping watch over Heddan and Gwenn.

Seated between Justaen and Avrell, Tristan and Brandan on Justaen's far side, I felt lost, overwhelmed, and daunted. I'd never eaten in such a large room, among so many other people, and found my hand resting on my dagger for reassurance.

Avrell leaned over as soon as we were settled and said, "Eat first. Don't question him about the Chorl until afterward. Be careful with the wine. You aren't used to it. And try not to touch your dagger. It's not . . . polite."

Before I could respond, Justaen rang a large hand bell on the table before him and suddenly the room was full of servants carrying large platters of food and pitchers of water and ale and wine. A woman not much older than me with hair tied back behind her head set a trencher before me, the heavy scent of smoked meat and spices assaulting my nose. Loaded with bread and cheese, the meat in a thick sauce surrounded with roasted vegetables, my stomach growling after over a week of mostly dry biscuits on the ship, I reached for a slice of bread and the butter, but felt Avrell's hand on my arm.

"Wait," he said, and his gaze flicked toward Justaen.

The Lord of Temall had not touched any of his food. Neither had anyone else in the room. He waited until everyone had been served, drinks poured, then he raised his flagon of wine and said, "To the visitors from Venitte and Amenkor," taking a sip.

Everyone in the room raised their own cup and drank; a murmur that could have been agreement but sounded mostly like grunts ran through the room.

Then Justaen set down his glass. That seemed to be the signal to eat, for everyone dug in, the roar of conversation filling the hall, worse than a tavern.

"Eat," Justaen said, motioning toward my platter even as he reached for a strip of meat for himself. "We'll have much to discuss afterward, but for now, enjoy."

I slathered a chunk of warm bread with butter, Justaen grunting as I bit into it.

I almost spit it out, choking, but managed to chew and swallow, coughing slightly. "It's not butter. It tastes different."

"It's apple butter," Tristan said from Justaen's far side.

I frowned down at the bread, then tried another bite, this time actually tasting it. Justaen watched closely, a dribble of the meat sauce staining his beard. I hadn't realized there were different kinds of butter, but now I could taste the flavor of the apples, sweet and yet tart, the texture a little different as well, creamier.

"I like it," I said.

Justaen smiled. "I'll make certain you have some for your ship," he said, then he raised his cup, sipped, and turned toward Tristan.

I glanced toward Avrell, who gave me a reassuring nod.

The meat was spicy, the sauce too biting by itself. I had to cut the spice by eating it with bread, leaving most of the sauce on the platter. I took careful sips of the wine, more used to water and tea, but still felt its effects by the time the meal had wound down. Justaen talked with everyone at the table at some point, but about nothing important—the voyage down from Amenkor, the storm, the latest trends in Venitte.

By the time Justaen pushed his chair back, the room falling silent gradually around us, night had fallen and my patience had worn thin. I felt anxious, my legs twitching beneath the table, my hand falling unconsciously to the handle of my dagger again before I realized and jerked it away. Avrell had resorted to shooting me occasional warning glances, which I ignored.

"If you would care to accompany me," Justaen said.

I stood without responding, everyone else at the main table following suit. We were joined by Keven, Westen, and Catrell, and a few guardsmen from Venitte as we were led to an antechamber off of the main hall.

Without preamble, settling himself into a chair behind a large desk, Justaen said, "What is it that you want?"

I felt myself stiffen at his tone, felt a subtle shift in the room as the guardsmen from Amenkor tensed. Without looking, I knew that a frown touched Avrell's face.

There were no other chairs in the room, only small tables with books and papers, casements with statues, a glittering dagger, a large tapestry taking up an entire wall. Nothing rested on his desk but a quill and bottle of ink.

And a sword. Long and straight, sheathed and resting flat at the edge of the desk.

Aware that Tristan and Brandan were standing beside me, I felt myself loosen, my stance altering slightly into a position that I knew Westen would recognize. A guarded position, ready but wary, as if I faced an unknown foe. "I want to know your intentions regarding the Chorl."

"My intentions," Justaen rumbled.

I frowned. "They've invaded the coast, taken over Bosun's Bay, a few days travel from here. They've already attacked Amenkor, are now, according to you, heading toward Venitte. What do you intend to do about it?"

Justaen said nothing for a long moment, his eyes on me. I slid beneath the river, felt the surge of emotions on the currents, tasted intense interest from Tristan, turmoil from both Brandan and William, a measure of hatred as well. From Westen, I got a strong sense of warning, and from Justaen—

I drew in a sharp breath.

Anger and resentment, mixed with indecision, with doubt.

The roil lay heavy and thick, dense against my skin. I shifted beneath it, realized that he was now a mixed gray and red, where he'd been only gray before.

A possible danger. An undecided danger.

"Who are you to ask me?" he said.

"She's the Mistress of Amenkor," Avrell said in outrage.

"Is she?" Justaen spat, standing abruptly, one hand steepled on his desk. "The Mistress has always been the one who controlled the Skewed Throne, and from all accounts I've heard of what happened this past winter, the Skewed Throne has been destroyed. What is she the Mistress of now? What is it that she controls?"

Avrell stepped forward, but I halted him with a sharp, "No!"

Livid, Avrell backed down. I could feel the outrage from Keven and Catrell as well, even William. Only Westen seemed unaffected, as if he had expected this.

I settled a heated glare on Justaen, found my hand resting on the hilt of my dagger and left it there. "I *am* the Mistress of Amenkor."

Out of the corner of my eye, I saw Tristan nod, felt him straighten.

Lord Justaen of Temall did not flinch, did not react at all.

"So it was you who sent the Seekers into my lands without permission," he said, his voice as deadly and as plain as mine.

"I sent them because we thought the Chorl had already taken Temall. We thought the Chorl were heading back to Amenkor."

"And did you send the Band as well?"

"No."

"They fight under the banner of the Skewed Throne. They are led by men that your Seeker," he motioned toward Westen, "tells me were once guardsmen of Amenkor."

"Yes. The leader of the Band is named Baill. He was once captain of the palace guard in Amenkor."

"But no longer?"

"No." I shook my head. "He betrayed us to the Chorl."

Justaen's face was suffused with doubt. "Then why is he here now, fighting against them? Why does he use the Skewed Throne as his call to battle?"

I shook my head again. "I don't know."

His eyes narrowed. He wanted to believe me, wanted to trust me. . . .

"No," he finally said. "Take your Seekers and go."

"But the Chorl—" Avrell began.

Justaen cut him off. "Temall will handle the Chorl on our own. We've managed to defend against them so far."

"Because you haven't seen their main force," I said. "Because at the moment they are only interested in your food, your resources. If they come . . . No. *When* they come, you won't be able to stand against them. If they seize Venitte, there will be no stopping them."

Justaen didn't respond.

Tristan stepped forward into the silence. "You will not help us defend Venitte?"

Justaen hesitated at his formal tone. "My duty lies in protecting Temall."

Tristan nodded. Motioning to Brandan and his guardsmen, he moved toward the door.

Avrell stepped up behind me, his intention to leave obvious.

"You will not survive," I said.

Justaen merely frowned.

"Come," Avrell said quietly. "He's made his decision."

I held Justaen's gaze a moment longer, then spun, letting Keven, Catrell, and Westen lead me through the door into the hall beyond. William followed close behind.

"Don't you have guild business to conduct with Lord Justaen? With his merchants?" Avrell asked as we headed down the hall, toward the main gates and the port below.

"I have no business here," William said curtly, and I could hear the lie in his voice, realized he was cutting those ties because of Justaen's insult to me.

"I tried to warn you at the docks," Westen said. "But we were never given the chance to talk."

"It doesn't matter," I said, anger like heat inside my chest. "But I don't understand. Can't he see the threat the Chorl represent?"

Catrell shook his head. "He thinks that if he presents no threat to them himself, the Chorl will leave him alone."

"Then he's blind as well as stupid," I spat.

"I agree," Avrell said darkly, "but there's nothing more we can do about it now."

We collected the rest of the Amenkor and Venittian guardsmen in the main hall, along with Heddan and Gwenn, both Servants' eyes going wide as they picked up on the tension in the group on the river, both suddenly quiet and formal. Within twenty minutes we were outside the gates of Temall, the Venittian group distancing themselves from us.

At the docks, the two groups split up.

Before breaking away, Tristan caught my attention, his gaze black. At his side, Brandan looked angry and concerned.

"You've cost Venitte an ally," the captain of the *Reliant* said, and then he turned and headed toward his ship.

At my side, Avrell drew in a deep breath and let it out in a heavy sigh.

"That," he said, "was not an auspicious start."

Chapter 8

It's not an auspicious start, Eryn said, her voice grim through the White Fire at her core. *Not only have you lost the support of Temall against the Chorl, you've isolated Tristan. And I think it's obvious now that he's more than just captain of the* Reliant.

I felt a surge of resentment, tried to suppress it. *Perhaps you should have come instead of me.*

No, Eryn said quickly. *It had to be you. Temall may have accepted me more readily, and I may have been able to gain some type of concession from him, but those in Venitte would not.*

She seemed to sense that I was not consoled. *You did fine, Varis.*

I sent the Seekers along with the scouting party.

And everyone agreed with you. We thought the Chorl army had headed north. We thought Temall had already been taken. Perhaps we could have had Westen petition for permission, but that would have required exposing the ship to the port, and if the Chorl had already seized control . . .

I heard the truth of what Eryn said, but Justaen's dismissal still rankled.

What about the Band? What about Baill?

Eryn hesitated. As she thought, pain radiated upward from her stomach. Not a seething, prickling pain, like Erick's, but a slow, acidic heat. Occasionally, it would burn up into her throat, spilling over into her lungs, and the coughing fit that resulted would send daggers through her stomach muscles and her chest. I'd only been in contact with her during one such fit, and it had been enough to drive me behind the protective shield of the Fire.

I don't know what to think about Baill and his Band, she finally said, placing a hand against her side. She sat in an alcove outside the training gardens. Rain poured down outside the arched opening in a sheet, the breeze cool against her face. *Perhaps the Chorl betrayed him in return. But it doesn't matter. At least he isn't actively working against Amenkor.*

At the moment.

Eryn winced at my tone. *At the moment.*

What about Amenkor?

Eryn shrugged. *No sign of the Chorl. Darryn continues to train the militia and seems to have adjusted well to being captain of the entire guard, although he continues to emphasize that it's temporary. The gates are finished, and we've begun work on the watchtowers, including placing the winch and chain across the inlet. The blacksmith, Hugh, is overseeing that, along with Nathem. The newest merchants have already broken land for the wall they intend to build around the city, but no stone has yet been laid. And Borund is moving along faster than expected on the ships . . . with the help of the Servants.*

Here, an intense satisfaction coursed through her, overriding the momentary pain in her side.

What do you mean? I asked.

Eryn grinned. *I went to Borund to ask if there was something that could be done to speed the process along. He didn't see how, but when I pressed him, we figured out a way that the Servants can help treat the wood to make it stronger using the Sight. They can also help with the shaping of the wood, both for the frame and applying the strakes to the frame. It's cut that part of the construction phase down by half. And Borund thinks that because of the increase in the strength of the wood, he may eventually be able to build bigger ships, ones with larger holds so that they can carry more cargo.*

That's . . . good. I didn't understand half of what she'd said. Even after spending time on Bullick's ship, I didn't understand half of what the crew said either.

Eryn shook her head in amusement. *It is good. It means that we can produce ships faster than anyone on the coast. Borund has three ships already under construction. They should be finished by winter.*

I don't think the Chorl are going to give us that much time, I said.

Some of Eryn's satisfaction faded, and through that I could feel weariness. And pain.

I need to speak to Westen, I said, gathering myself for the Reach back to my own body.

Eryn heard the intent in my voice. She straightened slightly, her tone stern. *Listen to Avrell, Varis. He knows more about Venitte and their politics than I do. He's been there, seen it firsthand.*

I leaped out of the Fire, sending her a last surge of reassurance. Her shoulders sagged as I sped out up into the fury of the afternoon thunderstorm, the river in turmoil around me, but I could feel the pull of the Fire inside me, could feel the tethers that Marielle and Heddan had used to give me additional strength, and so I fought through the storm, passing out of the cold, dark clouds and veering southward over open ocean. Fire blazed white and frigid on the horizon ahead.

We'd departed Temall that night, once everyone had boarded or been ferried to their respective ships, including the *Prize*. There were now five ships in the group—three of the Chorl ships, the *Defiant*, and Tristan's *Reliant*. But we were entering the sea-lane between the Boreaite Isles and Bosun's Bay controlled by the Chorl. Bullick hoped that the number of ships in the group would discourage the Chorl from attacking, but at the same time it made us easier to spot and we were hoping to slip through unnoticed.

Catrell had suggested traveling only at night, hiding close to shore during the day, but Avrell said we needed to get to Venitte as fast as possible. The city needed to be warned, and the more time they had to prepare for the Chorl, the better.

After what they'd done to Amenkor, I'd agreed.

And then there was Erick and his condition to consider.

Before diving down into the Fire that blazed on the deck of the *Prize*, I did a quick scan of the ocean, saw nothing but the scattered formation of our own ships, the *Reliant* keeping close but with a visible separation between it and the *Defiant*. Then I settled into the Fire inside Westen.

What happened?

Westen didn't react at all. Not a muscle moved in his stance at the prow of the ship, the wind from the ship's passage full in his face. He held the lock of his wife's hair in one hand, the honeysuckle she'd twined with it now looking limp. I'd given it to him on the dock, before he boarded the *Prize*.

Nothing, he said. *Lord Pyre kept us confined to the keep after we helped defend the gate against the Chorl. Not prisoners, but our movements were restricted.* He smiled thinly. *Or as restricted as a Seeker's movements can be made. When you reported you were headed for Temall, I told him everything—the attack on Amenkor, our defenses, the destruction of the throne. I thought that once he knew, once he realized we were no threat, then he'd release us.*

Instead, he kept us under tighter control.

Did you find out anything more about Baill? About this Band?

Westen shook his head, frowning. *I saw them once more from the walls. They appeared out of the forest and took the road heading southward. It looked as if they were on the move. They had two wagons loaded down with supplies. A good-sized force. More than the hundred that joined the battle at the gates.*

Justaen says the force has been growing.

I grunted. The anger Baill's name brought forth was instant and harsh, but from all accounts he seemed to be helping Temall defend against the Chorl. Which didn't make any sense.

I don't trust him, I said.

Neither do I. The cold hardness that stilled Westen as he said this made me shudder. *But he's out of reach for now. And Justaen has made his choice. Focus on Venitte.*

I withdrew from Westen, surged across the sun-glittering ocean to the Fire inside myself, and heaved a heavy sigh, weariness falling over me like a blanket. The trembling in my arms started immediately, and I sank back into the wooden folding chair I'd been sitting in as Heddan withdrew her conduit. Marielle held hers a moment longer, passing along more of her strength, and I smiled thinly in appreciation before waving weakly for her to release it. She did so reluctantly, motioning Heddan toward the waiting pitcher of tea, sun-steeped earlier on the deck of the ship.

"Amenkor?" Marielle asked, holding the cup that Heddan handed her to my lips so I could drink.

"Fine."

"And Eryn?"

I turned to where Avrell stood anxiously in the doorway. I hadn't noticed him as I skimmed across the water and into the ship, and I should have.

"Also fine," I said.

He heard what I did not say: that she was no better. For a moment, he seemed lost, the focus in his eyes internal, and strangely exposed. As if the fa-cade had been lifted, what lay hidden behind revealed.

Then he returned, straightening where he stood. "Very well."

I drew breath as he turned to leave, not knowing what I could say, but he was already gone.

Marielle's expression as I settled back down was stretched tight with sad-ness. "We should get you up on deck," she said briskly, her tone a little forced.

"No," I protested.

"Don't," she warned with a glare, already bustling around, shoving items into Heddan's hands to carry up to the deck. "The sea air will work better than the tea at reviving you."

After a half hour on deck, Marielle planting the folding chair front and center on the foredeck so that I could see the whitecaps on the ocean waves ahead, the horizon bobbing and dipping with the motion of the ship, I grudg-ingly admitted that Marielle had been right. Mood lightened, I ordered Ottul brought up on deck. She'd been confined to her small room since we departed Amenkor. With a frown of disapproval, Marielle went below, returning with the Chorl Servant, Trielle and Gwenn in tow to watch over her.

Ottul moved to the railing almost instantly, so fast that for a moment I thought she meant to leap overboard into the black water. But she merely stared down into the waves and the white spray from the ship hungrily, her black hair streaming out to the side, gold earrings glinting in the sun. She wore shirt and breeches, like almost everyone on board, except the Servants and Avrell. Gwenn joined her, and not long afterward they were both shrieking in delight, pointing over the ship's rail.

"What are they looking at?" I said.

Marielle shrugged.

With Marielle's help, I moved to the edge of the ship.

As soon as we arrived, something erupted from the water, no bigger than my hand, followed almost instantly by two others. They sailed through the air in a low arc, then splashed back down, disappearing into the depths in a flash of silver. Gwenn shrieked and clapped, jumping up and down at the railing a few paces farther down; Marielle gasped.

"What are they?"

"Fish."

It took me a moment to realize that Ottul had answered. In the coastal tongue. When I turned, the blue-skinned Servant was struggling to continue, scowling in concentration. Her hands waved in the air, her thumbs hooked together.

"Like bird," she said, making the flapping hand gesture again. Her voice was soft, tentative, but intent as she tried to find the right word. "Fish."

As she spoke, five more of the fish burst from the water next to the ship one after the other, flying through the air alongside the hull before vanishing. I could see an entire school of them below the surface, bodies flashing as they came close and caught the sunlight.

"Flying!" Gwenn cried out suddenly. She said something short and harsh, something in the Chorl tongue, and Ottul nodded in relief. "She means flying fish," Gwenn said.

Ottul and I held each other's gazes a moment, her scowl of impatience gone. In its place, I saw not the arrogant mask she'd worn at first, not the obstinance that had followed, but a resigned gratitude, a tentative smile, touched heavily with sadness.

Then Gwenn grabbed her arm and pointed as two of the flying fish launched at the same time and she turned away.

"They follow the ships sometimes," Bullick said from the other side of Marielle. A bunch of the crew and a few guardsmen had come to the railing or climbed up into the near rigging to see what all the fuss was about. They had all steered well clear of Ottul. "Are you certain it's safe for her to be on deck?" Bullick added, nodding toward the Chorl Servant.

"No," I said honestly. "But I'm not sending her below just yet either."

He grunted. "Very well."

Then he drifted away, barking something to one of the crew as he went.

I tired of the flying fish and made it back to my chair under my own power, Trielle and Heddan joining me. Marielle remained at the railing, where Ottul seemed content pointing out things to Gwenn, the two switching from the coastal tongue to Chorl and back again. Ottul seemed extremely familiar with the ocean and the ship, and much more comfortable on deck than she had seemed in the corridors of the palace.

Avrell commented on that when he and Keven joined us an hour later, both bringing their own chairs.

Keven shrugged. "That's not much of a surprise. You said they lived on a group of islands. They'd have to be familiar with the ocean and ships."

"You're right," Avrell said. He gazed at Ottul intently, but I could tell he was thinking of something else.

"What, Avrell?"

He started. "Nothing. Just wondering what that means for the Chorl attacking by land. If they're used to ships, to attacks from the sea, they won't be prepared for all the . . . subtleties of a land attack. Things like terrain and such."

"Especially the terrain around Venitte," Keven said. "We'll have to bring that up with Catrell."

Avrell and Keven fell into a discussion about the Chorl and tactics, while Trielle and Heddan chatted about the ship and some of the more interesting crew, Heddan giggling occasionally. I sat in silence, listening. William appeared on deck, but saw Avrell and wandered toward the back of the ship, disappearing below again after a short time. Afternoon slipped to evening, the sun sinking toward the horizon, creating a harsh gold band on the water. Light clouds appeared, scudding across the darkening sky.

And then one of the lookouts above yelled, "Sails! Sails off the port bow!"

Avrell surged to his feet, shouted, "Ottul!" but Marielle and Trielle were already herding her back toward the ladder, Gwenn at her side, urging her to hurry. I hadn't even seen Trielle move. The Chorl Servant strained to see around them, eyes searching the water frantically, face intent, but she didn't resist the Servants either.

The crew reacted instantly, flying up into the rigging, ready for orders, while Bullick stalked toward the port side, his spyglass already out. He began scanning the horizon, face set into a frown, signals passing to the rest of the ships in the group. Sails were adjusted and the other ships began to draw closer, tightening the distance between us.

"I don't see anything," I said.

"On Bullick's left, about a handspan away," Keven said, his gaze fixed on the horizon. "It's almost lost in the sun."

I grunted as I spotted it, nothing more than a white speck. I wouldn't have noticed it if Keven hadn't pointed it out.

"The lookouts have sharp eyes," Avrell said.

Around us, Heddan had begun collapsing the chairs, readying to go below.

We all waited tensely as Bullick watched the far ship through his glass, two crewmen waiting at his elbow for orders. Finally, he lowered the instrument.

"It's one of ours," he said. A few of the crew around us exhaled held breaths. "A trader. They're moving away, heading north. They probably don't trust our colors, since three of our ships look to be Chorl."

He handed the spyglass to one of the waiting men, but did not move from his spot, his hands clasped behind his back.

The mood on the deck had been broken.

"Perhaps we should go below," Avrell said into the awkward silence, "and see what there is for dinner."

"Yes," I said. The tension hadn't yet unknotted itself from my shoulders. I could recall the attack on *The Maiden* too vividly—Laurren's death, the slaughter of the crew, Erick's capture—did not want to repeat that horror again.

We descended below deck, leaving Captain Bullick to keep watch at the rail.

The mood on the ship did not improve over the next week. Everyone moved about with tightened shoulders, coming up to the deck at random intervals to stretch their legs and taste the fresh air. But they spent most of their time watching the horizon, searching for the telltale speck of white that signaled a sail or an approaching ship. Few stayed on deck for long, descending below again, preferring the cramped quarters and the thick air flavored with the scent of straw and the stench of animal waste from the hold. Tempers grew short, flaring up over small things—a muttered, half-heard word or a look. I tried to soothe the tensions using the river, tried to smooth out the currents and eddies, but it seemed to have little effect.

Bullick preferred having fewer of his passengers on deck. He kept a constant vigil, making corrections in the route in an attempt to avoid the more well-traveled lanes of the ocean. Twice, he adjusted the course because of sails spotted on the horizon. Both times, the other ship seemed more inclined to keep its distance. One of them Bullick identified as a ship from Merrell, moving south like us. The other he simply shrugged about when asked, too distant to get a good look.

I assumed it was a Chorl ship.

On the evening of the eighth day out of Temall, I came to the deck with Trielle and Keven as escort to find William at the railing at the prow, staring out into the dusk, the sun already set, the sky darkening from deep blue to indigo. A few stars pricked the blackness to the east, the moon not yet risen.

I frowned as I caught sight of him. We hadn't spoken since the night he'd kissed me, both of us rarely on deck at the same time, and then usually with Avrell present.

But not now.

"Wait here," I said.

Keven started to protest, his brow creasing in disapproval, but Trielle placed a hand on his arm and led him away, toward the back of the ship. She cast a quick glance over her shoulder as she went, whether in encouragement or warning I couldn't tell.

I focused on William's back. Suddenly, Keven and Trielle no longer present, I found myself uncertain. He hadn't seen me yet. It would be so much easier to retreat back to my cabin.

Disgusted with myself at the thought, I stalked forward, slid into place at the railing beside him without looking at him.

"You've kept your distance," I said, glaring down at the luminescent white froth churned up by the ship as it slid through the water.

I could feel William staring at me. He'd pulled back slightly, but his hands still rested on the wooden rail.

"Keven made it clear that Avrell wanted me to stay away," he said finally.

"And you listened to him?"

"Avrell is the First of the Mistress."

"But he's not the Mistress, he's not me. You should have come to ask me what I wanted."

William was silent a long moment. "What do you want?"

I stilled, only then realizing that I'd been tapping the rail nervously, something with talons clutching my gut. I wanted to reach for my dagger for reassurance but thought William might take it the wrong way, so I slid beneath the river instead, let the familiar currents wash over me.

Forcing the queasiness in my stomach to relax, I said, "I don't know."

A twinge of anger and disgust from William. And hurt. "I see."

He began to turn away, to silently storm off, and I felt a surge of anger as well.

"Wait," I said, the anger coming through in my voice. I sighed in exasperation. "I grew up in the slums, on the Dredge. I don't know much about how to handle all of," I waved my hand vaguely, "this. All I know is that on the Dredge, there's only survival. There isn't time for anything else. Sex is usually harsh and rough and violent and often deadly. There is no love, no romance, no courtship. It's usually over in five minutes and if you aren't lying dead in the shit in the back corner of the alley, you pick yourself up and move on."

"I see." Still affronted, but with a tinge of humor. It didn't help relieve my anger at all, but it was better than the pissed-off dismissal he'd given me before. "Are you interested?"

"In what?"

He shifted forward, leaned on the railing and caught my eyes, his expression serious. "In me. In me courting you, no matter what Avrell says?"

I frowned, but couldn't look away from his gaze. "Avrell never said we couldn't see each other."

A vague answer, but William nodded. "And what about Brandan?"

"There's nothing between me and Brandan," I said coldly. "I took him on a tour of Amenkor, nothing more. There's nothing to be jealous of, nothing to be worried about."

William tensed, as if ready to argue, but then forced himself to relax. He gazed out over the water. More stars had appeared, the sky almost completely black now, only a thin band of blue on the western horizon to starboard.

He smiled suddenly.

"Then meet me here tomorrow, after dusk."

I glared at him skeptically. "Why?"

"You'll have to find out tomorrow."

I grunted, suspicious. I didn't like surprises. On the Dredge, surprises were never good. But a thrill of excitement coursed through me nevertheless, tingling in my fingers. "Very well."

I thought he'd leave then, but he didn't. We stayed at the railing as the quarter moon rose, lining the black waves with silver.

The next day seemed to last forever, and I didn't see William at all. Trielle had informed Marielle of the meeting the night before, and they spent most of the day gossiping about what William intended for that night, their suggestions growing wilder and wilder as the day progressed . . . and more and more ribald.

"We're on a ship, at sea," I said in disgust at one point. "He can't possibly come riding in on a horse. And why would he in the first place?"

Trielle rolled her eyes. "Hush, Mistress. We're only teasing."

They broke out in laughter.

As dusk fell, excitement slid over into apprehension.

"Stop pacing," Marielle said soothingly. Trielle had gone to watch over Ottul so that Heddan and Gwenn could sleep. "It's just William."

I shot her a glare, my hand kneading the hilt of my dagger. They'd tried to get me to remove it, just for tonight, but I'd refused.

Above, the bell that kept track of the time at sea clanged the hour. I halted, something hard shuddering at the base of my throat. I swallowed.

Marielle stood, drawing my attention. She gripped my shoulders and repeated, quietly, "It's just William," squeezing once before ushering me out of the cabin door.

I stood in the narrow hallway a moment, heard a bark of laughter from deeper in the ship, heard a low murmur of conversation from Erick's cabin and frowned, recognizing Isaiah's voice but not the other. But Isaiah had been acting as the ship's doctor since he came on board, so I shrugged aside the momentary concern and gathered myself together, heading toward the ladder and ascending to the deck above.

Bullick greeted me with a short nod as I made my way to the front of the ship, a few of the deckhands doing so as well. I could see William waiting there, a vague shadow in the darkness, outlined by the moonlit sea beyond.

He'd dressed in his formal merchant's jacket, the dark blue appearing black in the light, the silver embroidery leeched of all color, the white shirt beneath a vibrant gray. He turned as I approached.

"Varis," he said, bowing at the waist formally.

My brow creased. "What are you doing?"

"I'm courting you," he said, then motioned to where two blankets had been laid out on the deck, along with pillows, glasses, and a bottle of wine. "If you'd care to sit?"

I hesitated, caught off guard by the strange formality of the situation, although I couldn't have said what I'd expected. But I sat down on the blanket, cross-legged. William sat as well, picking up the bottle of wine, uncorking it with an assured twist—he must have opened it earlier—before pouring out a glass for each of us.

Handing over my glass, he said, "It's Capthian red."

I laughed, took a careful sip, watching William's grin over the lip of the glass. Capthian red had been the wine Eryn had hidden in the palace stable, covering the entrance to the tunnel beneath the walls that Avrell had used to get me into the palace unnoticed. I'd never had any until now. It was tart and dry, better than the wine Justaen had served in Temall.

Taking a swallow, William set his glass aside. "Now, lie down."

My eyebrows shot up and he grinned.

"Trust me. Use the pillows to get comfortable. Here, let me help."

I shifted around on the blanket under William's direction, placing the pillows beneath my head, adjusting them until my neck no longer felt crooked. I could feel the planking of the deck beneath the thin blanket, the motion of the ship more pronounced lying flat like this. William rustled around beside me, his elbow digging into my side once. He murmured an apology, shifted around some more—

And then we were lying side by side, staring up at the stars. A few ropes and blocks from the rigging blocked our view, but here at the prow they were minimal. If I moved my head slightly, I could see the top of the main mast, could see the moonlight on the bellied-out sails and the lookout's post.

"Do you know anything about the stars?" William asked, his voice rising into the night. The sky was clear, the pinpricks of the stars bright, glittering against the blackness.

"No."

"I didn't think so. That's how we know where the ship is, where we are in relation to the coast. We use the stars to figure out our position."

"How?"

"We use a compass and an instrument called a sextant. And a lot of mathematics."

"Never mind, then."

I heard him chuckle and I hit him on the thigh. He quieted instantly although, on the river, I could still feel him grinning.

"There's a simpler way. Less exact of course, but still worthwhile if you need a reading of position." He pointed up into the night. "See that star? The bright one just off to the left?"

"Yes."

His arm fell. "That's called the Northern Guide. Since from this perspective the Guide appears to the left, that means we're actually headed southwest, away from the mainland and out into deep ocean. We'll have to change course tonight."

I frowned, wiggling around to find a better position. "Why?"

"Because we're heading out of the sea-lane between the Boreaite Isles and Bosun's Bay. We passed through the most congested portion of it two days ago, but Bullick is playing it safe, taking us farther out to sea before turning back and heading to Venitte. If he doesn't turn back, we'll end up sailing into empty ocean."

I thought about this a moment, then said, "Except we know it's not empty."

"What do you mean?"

I rolled my head to the side so I could see William's profile in the darkness. "The Chorl. They came from islands somewhere out there. The White Fire came from the west as well, and it didn't come from the Chorl. So there must be something more out there, something even beyond the Chorl islands."

"If there is, it must be fairly distant. Ships have sailed to the west, but they've either returned to report nothing but ocean . . . or they never returned at all."

"The Seven searched as well," I said, thinking back to what I'd learned from Cerrin and the Seven while connected to the Skewed Throne, to what I'd dreamed of since. "After the first Chorl attack. They found nothing."

"But we have larger ships now. They can carry more cargo, sail farther without the crew starving. And if we can find the Chorl islands, or other islands like them, use them as a place to stop and restock . . ."

I thought about Borund telling Eryn he could build larger ships using whatever technique the Servants had come up with to strengthen and shape the wood. Perhaps, with the new ships, we would be able to find the Chorl's homeland . . . or what was left of it.

Perhaps we could find the source of the White Fire.

The thought sparked a desire to set sail immediately, a different kind of fire that burned deep in my gut, but I pushed the fire back. Nothing could be done about it at the moment.

But the fire didn't die. I could feel it seething deep inside me, throbbing with heat. Like the coals of a fire that had burned down, waiting for fresh fuel so it could reignite.

"What else can you tell me about the stars?" I asked.

William turned to look at me, brow creased, as if he thought I were simply humoring him. But then the creases smoothed out and he relaxed, settling back against his blanket. He pointed up into the night sky again. "Those three stars over there, the ones that form a triangle?"

"I see them."

"They're called Omarion's Tryst. . . ."

And with that all of the tension—over Avrell, over Brandan—drained out of the night.

The next day, I woke to find Marielle and Trielle hovering expectantly, eyes full of questions.

"Don't ask," I said, swinging out of the hammock. "I'm not going to say anything."

"But the crew of the *Reliant* won't say anything either," Marielle protested. "Captain Bullick warned them off, and they're all keeping quiet, even the Zorelli!"

"And they're the worst gossips of the bunch," Trielle threw in.

"Then you'll just have to live without knowing what happened."

"Ooo, she's evil," Trielle said mockingly. "How have you managed to put up with tutoring her for the past eight months?"

"It hasn't been easy," Marielle muttered darkly.

The good humor lasted until we reached the deck, where Avrell, Keven, Captain Bullick, and William all stood in a cluster staring out behind the ship, their faces serious. I could sense the tension on the river the moment we emerged into the sunlight, knew that Marielle and Trielle sensed it as well. Their laughter cut off abruptly.

I slid up to William's side, shaded my eyes against the sun's glare. "What is it?"

He glanced down briefly. "Two ships. They've been following us since dawn."

"They're Chorl," Bullick said, lowering his spyglass and handing it off to Avrell.

"But they haven't approached?"

Bullick shook his head. "They're probably keeping their distance because there are five of us."

"Can we outrun them?" Avrell asked. He'd taken the spyglass and now held it up to his eye.

"No. Not at our current weight and not with these winds. The three Chorl ships might be able to, but not the two traders."

I glanced up at the sails. I couldn't see any difference in the configuration between now and earlier, but it did feel as if the ship were moving at a slower pace.

"Perhaps we'll get a chance to test out those modifications to the ship after all," Keven said.

Bullick grunted, then bellowed a command, men to either side scurrying below decks.

"What modifications?" I asked.

"Since *The Maiden* and the attack at Amenkor, we've tried to add a few additional defenses to the trading ships," Keven explained.

"Even if they do attack," Bullick said, "it will be hours before they catch up to us. No need to continue watching from the deck."

It was a clear dismissal, but no one moved. Avrell passed the spyglass to Keven as the crewmen began to reappear on deck, carrying buckets, ropes, grapnels, and a few large trunks.

William turned to me with a grimace. "And we were almost out of the sealane."

I ordered Marielle and Trielle below and told them to keep Heddan and Gwenn there as well. Trying to keep out of the way, I watched as the buckets were lowered and filled with seawater, then set aside on deck in case of fire. More trunks appeared, revealing hatchets and axes, swords and daggers, crossbows. Bullick disappeared for fifteen minutes, returned dressed in a more formal captain's uniform, including a sheathed sword belted to his waist. Keven, William, Avrell, and the guardsmen armed themselves as well. Signals flew between the five ships, the grouping reorganized since the Chorl ships had been spotted so that the two traders sailed close together in the center, surrounded by the three smaller defensive ships. I could see individual people on the deck of the other ships now, although they weren't close enough for me to pick out faces.

At noon, Bullick reported, "They've started to gain on us. I estimate three hours before they catch us."

A grim tension settled over the ship.

I wandered below deck, found Marielle, Trielle, Heddan, and Gwenn huddled outside Ottul's room, Gwenn curled up close to Trielle. In Erick's room, Isaiah was gathering together equipment, his pace methodical, his expression severe. He glanced up when I entered.

"Captain Bullick requested that I set up in the crew quarters," he said. "He expects casualties."

"Of course." I stepped to Erick's side. Isaiah continued collecting supplies behind me.

Erick's face was drawn, the grayness more pronounced now than it had been a few weeks before. His eyes looked sunken, the skin around them bruised almost black, and his breath came in long, ragged gasps.

"He's declining faster than I expected," Isaiah said, abruptly at my side. I jumped. "The rigors of traveling at sea are taking a toll. We need to get him to Venitte."

"I'm trying," I said. But I wasn't certain we could make it in time anymore.

I stayed with Erick until Isaiah had finished setting up, but didn't dare Reach for him. Not if the Chorl attacked. I might need my strength. Then, setting one of the crew to watch over him, I returned to Ottul's room.

"Gwenn," I said, squatting down beside her on the deck. Her eyes were strained with the effort of keeping her fear at bay, Trielle holding her protectively. "Gwenn, I'm going to need Marielle, Trielle, and Heddan up above, in case the Chorl ships have Servants on board. I want you to stay here and guard Ottul. Can you do that?"

She considered this a moment, then nodded, pulling slightly out of Trielle's embrace. "I can do that, Mistress."

Her voice was surprisingly calm and serious.

"Good," I said, and stood. Marielle and Heddan stood as well, smoothing out the folds of their dresses. Gwenn pulled out of Trielle's arms completely, and Trielle ruffled her hair as she joined us.

On deck, the Chorl ships were shockingly close. So close I could see movement on their decks, although I couldn't pick out individual people.

But I did catch a flash of green.

"They have Servants," I said, and a sickening stone of heat and anxiety formed in my gut.

"At least two," Avrell said. We'd moved to join the cluster of guardsmen and crew at the aft deck. "They'll catch us within the hour."

I frowned. "They seem closer than that."

"They aren't traveling much faster than us. We're using the same winds."

Battles at sea involved a lot of waiting, I thought. On the Dredge, the fight would have been resolved hours ago, daggers drawn and blood spilled. I didn't remember the fight on *The Maiden* taking this long.

But then I'd come into that battle after it had already begun.

I'd just drawn breath to comment on this when a panicked voice yelled, "Ho! Sails off the starboard bow! Coming in fast!"

"What!" Bullick bellowed from midship.

"Starboard bow!" the lookout yelled again, and glancing up, shading my eyes against the glare of the midday sun, I could see him gesturing sharply to the right. "Ships to the starboard!"

Bullick swore, began booming orders at the top of his voice, crew leaping to the rigging, others scrambling for weapons. Everyone's attention in the aft deck turned from the two Chorl ships trailing us to the starboard bow—

And the four Chorl ships heading directly toward us, closing in fast.

"They drove us right into them," Keven said, respect mixed with grim horror in his voice. His hand rested on his sword hilt.

Sails snapped above, and the *Defiant* suddenly listed to port beneath us, all of the guardsmen on deck caught off guard, stumbling. To either side, all of the other ships in our group began turning as one.

"We aren't going to make it," Avrell said flatly.

And suddenly, power surged on the river, gathering quick and deadly, from the direction of the four new ships.

"Marielle!" I barked, but she and Trielle were already moving, already shaping the river into a tight shield, throwing it up and across the starboard side of the ship, covering the sails.

Fire arced out from the Chorl ships, shattered against the shield in a coruscating sheet of flame that rained down the barrier's length and fell harmlessly into the sea.

"Heddan," I said, "try to protect the *Prize*."

Heddan darted through the suddenly active deck to the prow, Westen's ship the closest of the defensive ships in front of us.

"Behind us," Keven said in warning.

I turned. The two Chorl ships had leaped forward, were almost within reach of Catrell's ship. The other two ships in our group—Tristan's *Reliant* and the *Booty*—were to port, away from the direct line of fire.

"They gained ground because we were forced to turn," Keven growled.

I stepped forward to the rail while sinking deep beneath the river. The world grayed around me, grew thick and dense, and I settled into the smooth, calm, focused power of a Seeker. Everything collapsed to a single goal, the details of the ships behind the *Spoils of War* bright, brittle, harsh in the sunlight, the crew on its decks—dressed in the garish, vibrant colors of the Chorl—visible now, the green dresses of the Chorl Servants clear, one per ship. I focused on them, on their long black hair, on their cold blue skin, on their almost black eyes, so arrogant with power. And then I stretched out beyond the *Spoils of War* on the river, not quite Reaching, not quite separating from my body—

And with a cold precision learned from Westen and Erick, with a heartlessness learned on the Dredge, I slashed across the first Servant's throat with a blade-eddy.

She hadn't raised a shield. Blood flew as she fell back onto the deck, arms rising in belated shock, the Chorl warriors around her stepping away, stunned. Then they roared in outrage, the ululating cries weak and distant from the deck of the *Defiant* but hideously raw on the river, shuddering on the edge of the Chorl ship's deck.

I'd already turned to the second Servant, already readied the blade-eddy for another cut. But the Servant had been forewarned. She held a shield around her, the barrier almost glittering beneath the Sight. Her face contorted with raw hatred. With an outstretched arm, she seized the river and flung fire toward the *Spoils of War*.

I spat a curse, erected a shield, but not quite fast enough. The fire exploded over its edge and spattered down onto Catrell's ship, the guardsmen and crew of the ship leaping to the buckets of seawater as fire scorched the deck, caught in one of the sails. All flames were quenched within moments, my shield preventing the Chorl Servant from guiding the fires as the Servants had done on *The Maiden,* keeping her from sending it trailing out, seeking victims. But her rage grew. She began flinging fireball after fireball at my shield.

"Keven," I said, and heard the strain in my voice already. I wasn't used to directing the river from such a distance. Every encounter on the Dredge had been up close and personal, every battle with the Chorl in Amenkor confined to the gates or a single room.

Not over such a distance. The effort to stretch as far as Catrell's ship *hurt.*

"Yes, Mistress."

"See if you can get Bullick to bring the ships in closer together. It will be easier to defend them from the Chorl Servants if he does. And see if you can pick off some of the Servants with crossbows!"

"I'll do it," William barked, and moved instantly toward Bullick.

Beneath my feet, I felt the *Defiant* shudder. I wondered how Marielle and Trielle were faring, but didn't dare look. I could feel the surges of power on the river behind me, could feel the heat as fire exploded on shield, knew that whatever Marielle and Trielle were doing, it was holding. Farther back, I could feel Heddan's shield holding steady as well.

Ahead, the second Chorl ship, the one I'd killed the Servant on, slid forward toward the *Spoils of War,* and I growled low in my throat. Keeping the shield steady from the Servant's relentless attack, I gathered the river into a spear and hurled it, following it with another, the effort causing sweat to break out across my forehead.

The first struck, wood splintering from the side of the ship, Chorl screaming as chunks flew up into their faces. The second tore a hole in the side of the ship, well above the waterline.

But the ship didn't falter. It began to draw up alongside the *Spoils of War* on the starboard side, the other ship coming up to the port. Chorl stood at the railing, ready with grapnels and rope to tether the two ships together, most with swords raised, screaming across the span of ocean between the two ships. Guardsmen on the *Spoils of War* roared back. A few crossbow bolts were unleashed, Chorl men falling back from the onslaught. I could see Catrell on the deck, talking to the pilot, gesturing frantically with his arms, strain written in the lines of his face—

And suddenly the wheel spun beneath the pilot's hands, the *Spoils of War* lurching to the left, away from the ship threatening to board.

Straight into the Chorl Servant's ship.

The two ships collided with a hideous crunch of cracking wood, men thrown to the decks on both ships with short cries. Groaning, the two ships ground against each other, the pilot fighting the wheel, and then they broke apart.

On the Chorl ship, the Servant stumbled, the barrage of fireballs faltering. I dove into the opening, sliced hard across her arm, heard a biting cry as I tasted blood, coppery and thick, struck again with deadly swiftness, but encountered a shield.

And then the *Defiant* truly shuddered. I heard a sigh, felt the ship slow with a sickening motion, and glanced upward.

The sails were falling limp, whuffling as they went slack, men scrambling in the rigging to draw them in tighter.

"The bloody bastards stole our wind," someone close murmured.

I looked toward the starboard side, toward the other four Chorl ships. Three had pressed the attack, coming in from the side, one nearing the *Prize*, almost ready to board, the other two running parallel to the *Defiant*.

The fourth had fallen slightly behind on purpose, had swung around windward, their sails cutting us off.

Stealing our wind.

I spun to port, saw Tristan's ship and the *Booty* banking hard to starboard, coming in tight near the *Prize* and the Chorl ships near the front of the ship to help Heddan. Without warning, a blaze of pure white lightning lashed out from the *Reliant*, sizzling as it skated across one of the Chorl's hulls, leaving a trail of charred wood behind. I hadn't seen it form on the river, hadn't even felt the force gathering.

Because it had been formed by Brandan. I could see him in the prow of the ship, hands raised, wind tearing at his clothing, his hair. Face shuttered, skin creased in concentration, he ducked his head, narrowed his eyes—

And another bolt seared across the ocean, glaring white on the black waves. But this time it skittered across a raised shield.

Fire exploded, jerking my attention away from Brandan and the *Reliant*. It washed up and over the rigging of the *Defiant*, heat pressing down through Marielle and Trielle's shield. I heard one of them cry out, realized they were holding off at least two Servants on their own. In the backwash of flame, I turned back toward the ships behind us.

And gasped.

We might have lost our wind, but the *Spoils of War* and the two Chorl ships hadn't.

And they were right on top of us.

"Keven!" I barked, and even as he spun, the Chorl ship carrying the Servant banked sharply left, pulling away from Catrell's ship. It skimmed the *Defiant's* port side, so close a few of the Chorl threw grapnels across the distance even though they were moving too fast to board, the metal hooks clanking on the deck, gouging the planks, guardsmen and sailors leaping out of their path before they caught the railing, ripping the sturdy wood from the ship. One hook caught in a sailor's calf, jerking him off his feet and dragging him across the deck screaming before it ripped free.

At the prow of the Chorl ship, the Servant had straightened, blood staining the left arm of her dress black and dripping from her fingers onto the deck. She glared across the distance as her ship slid past. Keven stepped up beside me, raised a crossbow and fired in one smooth motion, the recoil jerking his arm.

The bolt shattered against the Servant's shield, metal shards spraying outward around her, cutting into the Chorl at her side. The force of the impact thrust her back and I heard a gut-wrenching gasp of pain as she doubled over.

Keven spat a curse.

On the starboard side, Catrell's ship scraped the paint from the *Defiant's* hull, caught between Bullick's ship and the attacking Chorl on the far side, both ships squeezed between the *Defiant* and the other two Chorl ships. Amenkor guardsmen on Catrell's ship lined the railing, hacking at the first tethers thrown from the Chorl ship, Catrell standing calmly next to the panicked pilot, crossbow bolts flying between all of the ships.

And then all three ships were past—two to starboard, one to port—their sails momentarily slack as they slid into the path of the stolen wind, then filling again, the ships lighter, moving faster. The ship carrying the Chorl Servant had already begun to turn, readying for another pass.

Keven locked gazes with me.

"I didn't want them *that* close," I said.

Keven laughed, the sound strained.

"To the large crossbows!" Bullick suddenly bellowed, his voice breaking through the stunned moment. The crew on deck began running below, jumping down the ladders, Keven's guardsmen remaining above. He barked a command and two of the guardsmen hauled the still screaming sailor with the grapnel-sliced calf down to Isaiah, leaving a trail of slick blood behind. I heard the slap of wood against wood and leaped to the starboard side of the ship. Leaning over the rail, I could see six rectangular hatches being opened in the side of the ship, the doors clattering against the hull as a spiked steel point emerged through the opening. I frowned, recognizing the bolts from my visit to the blacksmith with Brandan.

Crossbows. Giant crossbows.

"The only problem with them," Keven said at my side, the smaller crossbow he'd used against the Servant still in one hand, "is that the other ship has to be close. You can't aim them worth shit."

I glanced up, saw the two Chorl ships bearing down on us from the front, Catrell's ship and the Chorl ship locked in battle with him blocking the view for a moment as they pulled ahead of us, then shoved myself back from the railing. Marielle and Trielle had held the Chorl Servants' attack at bay, but they couldn't do much about the ships themselves.

But perhaps I could. If the other Servants kept the Chorl occupied . . .

As one of the Chorl ships slowed and came abreast of the *Defiant,* I gathered the river before me into a spear, as before. But this time, my attention wasn't split between protecting a ship and forming the spear itself.

On the deck, I heard everyone's breath catch and hold. The tension hovered as the Chorl ships edged nearer. I could see the blue-skinned Chorl warriors as they shouted across the short span of water at us, a few grapnels thrown, but falling short. Marielle and Trielle's shield shimmered in the air between us, but it wasn't strong enough to push the ship back. The Chorl Servants on the two ships had halted their attack, the fire they threw threatening their own ship at this distance.

The air shivered with fear, with violence, tasting of blood, of smoke and fire, of sweat and sunlight and the sizzling crack of lightning from ahead. . . .

And then Bullick bellowed, "Release!"

In the bowels of the ship, six triggers were pulled, and six giant crossbows released gathered tension with a shudder, the mechanisms recoiling. Six bolts flew; at the same time, I released the pent-up energy of the river and flung my spear.

Two bolts struck wood and shattered, digging a deep groove in the hull. A third had been angled higher, punching through the railing of the ship, slicing through the Chorl on deck with vicious speed, cutting a path through the warriors like a knife, leaving blood, body parts, and screaming men behind. The three others pierced through the hull with a hollow crunch of wood, strakes snapping and splintering outwards, wood shards flying in a deadly hail.

I'd aimed my spear lower. It shattered the hull as well . . . but below the waterline. Through the river, I felt water pouring into the breach and smiled with grim satisfaction.

Then Keven dragged me back from the edge of the ship. Grapnels were thrown as the wounded ship tried to tether itself to the *Defiant.* With their strange ululating war cries, the Chorl leaped across the distance, a few grapnels catching, the ships edging closer together, hulls grinding, the Chorl now boiling over the edge into the guardsmen's swords and suddenly the river was thick with the reek of blood.

"They're taking on water!" I yelled over the cacophony of the battle.

"That will only make them more desperate," Keven replied. He and five others had formed a rough circle around me and Avrell, even though we weren't close to the actual fighting. "What happened to the other ships?"

I glanced ahead and to port. "Two of the Chorl are fighting with Westen and Catrell's ships, but they're drawing away. They still have wind. Heddan's protecting them with a shield, but Brandan's keeping the remaining Chorl Servant on those ships busy. The third Chorl ship, the one that came from behind that still has a Servant, is circling around. The one that stole our wind is still too distant to worry about."

"So we've only got these two to deal with."

Fire flared at the prow of the ship, but it came from Heddan. It arced out over the water and struck one of the Chorl ships attacking Westen, flaring up on the deck. Even as the first struck, Heddan sent another to the second ship. Lightning cracked across the air as Brandan pressed the attack.

And then I felt the shield around the *Defiant* falter. Eyes snapping back to the edge of the ship, I saw the guardsmen's defense around Trielle crumble, saw her fall back, disappearing in the jumble of men.

"Trielle!" I barked, and darted forward, my dagger drawn without thought. Marielle struggled as Trielle's portion of the shield released, seized its edges and brought it back up, but she wasn't strong enough to cover the entire ship—

Fire flared, the Chorl Servants on the two nearest ships seizing the opening. Before I'd taken two steps, flame exploded on the foredeck, another hitting the aft deck, screams of pain erupting on both sides, someone shrieking as they ran for the edge of the ship trailing fire before leaping over into the ocean. Triumphant Chorl spilled through the crumbling line onto the deck of the *Defiant*, and suddenly we were surrounded on all sides, blades slashing, the rest of the deck lost to sight.

I sank deeper into the river, drew my focus so tight I could see only those around me, Keven, Avrell, and the guardsmen at my back blurs of gray, the Chorl red. So deep I could taste the metal of the blades as they spun. So deep the sounds of the battle were muted, grunts and screams and hisses shoved into a background roar of wind. The White Fire inside me flared higher and I seized on it, used it to direct my hand as I cut with the dagger, all of the forms I'd learned from Erick slipping back into place as if I'd never left the Dredge, all of the tricks Westen had taught me since melding with them, the Fire warning me of threats. My dagger sliced through a Chorl's shoulder, cut across another's face, punched through leather armor and into a side, blood slicking my hand. I punched with my free hand, pinched exposed muscle, gouged at eyes. I wrapped the river and the Fire around me, flowed with it as Keven and the guardsmen wielded their swords at my back, protecting Avrell. One of the guardsmen fell, gurgling, his throat cut; another staggered back with a gasp as one of the curved Chorl swords opened a gaping wound in his thigh, but the rest closed the gaps as Avrell dragged the wounded guardsmen into the protective circle. Blood slicked the deck, making the footing slippery—

And then suddenly Keven spat, "Mistress' tits."

I spun, crouched low.

And saw Ottul scrambling out of the hatch leading down into the ship. I thought instantly of Gwenn, assuming Ottul had killed her in order to escape, felt hatred well up . . . then choke in my throat as Gwenn appeared next to Ottul.

Ottul stood up, looking odd dressed in Amenkor clothing when her own people were dressed in oranges, reds, greens, and blues all around her. She stared at the Chorl, a strange mixture of hope and fear clear in her eyes, on her face.

Her eyes locked on the figure of the Chorl Servant on the ship tethered to the *Defiant*.

The two stared at each other for one breath . . . two . . . Ottul's eyes pleading.

Then the Chorl Servant on the other ship gestured across her chest, the action strangely formal, her eyes narrowing with hatred. Ottul reeled back as if punched.

Raising her hand, the Chorl Servant sent a shimmering, deadly wave of fire at Ottul.

A shield flew up at the last instant, Gwenn stepping between Ottul and the other Servant with a defiant expression twisting her mouth into a scowl.

Ottul hesitated, tears coursing down her face, then reached for Gwenn on the river.

A conduit snapped into place. Not a conduit like the one Eryn and the Servants of Amenkor had devised.

A conduit like the one used by the Ochean.

Gwenn's shield surged with power. But Ottul seized some of that power and sent a hammer of force toward the Chorl Servant.

It caught the Servant by surprise. Even as her shield crumbled beneath the blow, Ottul sent a dagger of force into the Servant's heart.

The Chorl Servant dropped dead to the deck.

Resting a hand on Gwenn's head, Gwenn herself immobile with shock, Ottul scanned the deck. Her eyes caught mine for a moment, and in their shining depths I saw total devastation, complete loss.

Then she looked away, found Marielle, and reached for her with another conduit.

Marielle's shield exploded with energy, reaching out to encompass the entire ship.

At the same time, the sails above ruffled and snapped, filling with wind.

I shot a glance toward the third Chorl ship, the one that had stolen our wind. "It's withdrawing!" I shouted.

As the *Defiant* seized the wind—Bullick shouting orders, his captain's jacket dripping blood, William at his side—the tethers binding the *Defiant* to the Chorl ship snapped taut and the wood railings began to groan. The Chorl on the other two ships began to shout, those on the *Defiant* retreating toward their own ship, Keven and the guardsmen roaring forward, shoving them back. Wood began to splinter, and the Chorl broke, turning and leaping for the safety of their own wounded ship. With a final hideous crack, a chunk of the *Defiant's* railing and deck sheered away, plunging down to the ocean, still attached by the tethers to the Chorl ship. The *Defiant* shuddered as the wind caught fully, leaping forward, the Chorl ship falling behind as the water it had taken on through the hole in its hull dragged it down.

Cheers erupted on the deck of the ship, the last of the Chorl either leaping into the fast-moving water or being cut down by the guardsmen. Ahead, one of the Chorl ships blazed, Heddan's fire running out of control, and the second Chorl ship had banked away. The last ship—the one that had begun to turn, that carried the Servant I'd wounded—had turned and now fled into the open ocean.

"Should we pursue them?" Bullick asked, chest heaving, breath short. He wiped sweat and blood from his face, sword still drawn.

"No," I said.

He turned sharply at the sound of my voice, then spun to look in the direction of my gaze.

To where Heddan knelt weeping, Trielle's body clutched tight to her chest.

✛ Chapter 9

Thirteen bodies lined the deck. Each had been wrapped in cloth, the same cloth used for the hammocks, then sewn shut, lead weights added to the lining so that the bodies would sink. Seven of them had been sailors, their shrouds sewn by their shipmates. Five of them had been guardsmen.

The last a Servant.

I stared down at Trielle's shroud, resting on a board with one end on the deck, the other tilted up onto the railing as, beside me, Bullick spoke a few words, his voice loud, those gathered on the deck—almost everyone on board—silent. I didn't hear him, his voice nothing more than a murmur, the words meaningless. And yet every other sound on the ship rang clear, almost brittle in the quiet. The creak of wood. The rush of water past the hull. The thud of a wooden pulley against the mast. The flap of the flag above.

The ship rocked on the ocean swells, and the breeze tossed my hair into my face, but I didn't move to brush it away.

Gwenn had sewn Trielle's shroud, silently weeping the entire time. Her stitches were perfect, for her hands had remained steady, even as the tears dripped from her chin and stained the cloth with dampness. Marielle had wanted to help, and Heddan, but in the end they'd left it all to Gwenn, helping Keven, William, and the remaining guardsmen deal with the shrouds for the fallen guardsmen instead, everyone subdued, everyone morose.

I hadn't realized how the rest of Amenkor looked upon the Servants, hadn't realized that—since this past winter, since the general population had seen the Servants on a daily basis, working in the kitchens and handing out food—the Servants had become almost as honored and revered as the Mistress herself.

But I could see it in their faces now, could see it in their eyes, in the way they bowed their heads. I'd seen it the day before, when the realization that one of the Servants had fallen had cut the elation of the Chorl retreat short, as smoothly and cleanly as if it had been an ax severing a tether.

Trielle . . .

For a moment, I felt her on the river, manipulating it, assured and precise. I sensed the mocking quality in her voice as she teased me about William, about Brandan, saw her lift an eyebrow in appreciation as a man walked past on the streets of Amenkor . . . or on the deck of the *Defiant*.

I heard her laughing.

Then I realized that Bullick had stopped speaking, that he'd leaned toward me slightly.

"Did you wish to say anything?" he said, in a low voice.

I glanced out toward those gathered on the deck, the guardsmen and sailors lined up at the feet of the thirteen shrouded bodies—their shipmates, fellow guardsmen, and friends. Avrell stood beside me. Keven, William, Isaiah, Heddan, and Marielle surrounded me, a wall of support. Gwenn remained below, with Ottul.

All of those on deck watched me, expectant. And beyond them, on the other two ships that had suffered during the attack—the *Prize* and the *Spoils of War*—I could feel the crews standing before their own dead, waiting for the signal, for the first body to drop from the *Defiant* into the ocean, so that they could do the same for those they'd lost.

Normally, I hated speaking in front of a crowd. But not this time.

I drew in a deep breath, slid beneath the river and threw out a net, stretching it toward the other four ships, even Tristan's, so that all could hear, no matter how softly I spoke.

"I was told once that there is always a price," I said, my voice rough and cracked. I didn't care. I sensed the shock from the other ships as they heard me, heard the murmur on the *Defiant*, the sudden shifting of feet. "I know this. I grew up on the Dredge. But sometimes the price seems too high." I looked toward the bodies, forced myself to gaze upon all of their shrouds, and then I lifted my chin, jaw tight, eyed all of those on deck, stared into all of their faces, into their tear-swollen eyes or their solemn grief. "These men and women paid that price for the rest of us. They paid to give us all safe passage to Venitte. Remember that when we pull into port. Remember them."

Bullick stepped forward into the stark silence that followed, cleared his throat awkwardly. "With those words, we commit these bodies to the sea in the name of the Mistress. And for all of Amenkor."

A bell clanged, the sound harsh. A few of the guardsmen flinched; Marielle gasped; Heddan cried out, the sound short and sharp. Stepping forward to the first body—Trielle's—two sailors reached down, gripped the end of the plank her body rested on and lifted, raising the end to waist height, level with the railing, then shifting and tilting it higher.

The sound of her body sliding from the plank forced me to close my eyes, the scrape of cloth on wood digging deep into my gut.

A momentary breath of silence . . .

And a splash.

The back of my throat grew hot with tears. I swallowed, choked down the sound of her body hitting the ocean, tasted phlegm, but forced my eyes open, staring unseeing across the deck as the plank shifted, as the sailors moved to the next body, hefted it up onto the plank. Marielle sobbed to one side, but I refused to look at her, knew that if I did, the carefully controlled living thing in my gut, writhing like a snake, would escape. I listened to the clang of the bell, the scrape and splash of the next body, and the next, saw the flash of tan as a body fell from the edge of the *Prize* to one side, and then I dove beneath the river, deep, let the river's wind take the sounds, dampen them so that I would not hear, let the world gray so that I could not see. I let the river be my refuge.

When it was over, Avrell touched my arm. He asked a question with his eyes, but I shook my head, the motion curt.

The gathering broke. Sailors moved back to their posts on deck, guardsmen drifted to the railing to look down at the waves, to where the bodies had vanished beneath the black surface, their mood somber. Bullick nodded to me before turning away, his expression tight, his grief controlled, hands clasped behind his back as he stared out toward the horizon. Marielle took Heddan's arm and led her below, Keven and William trailing after, William catching my gaze, face tight.

I came last.

Marielle left Heddan at our cabin, to let her rest and grieve in isolation, but she did not stay herself. Instead, Heddan settled, she followed the rest of us as we proceeded down the narrow corridor.

To Ottul's cabin.

When I opened the door, I found Ottul sitting on her cot, Gwenn cross-legged at her feet on the floor. She looked up when the door opened, the hand that held the brush she used on Gwenn's hair halting, dropping to her side.

The other hand moved to rest on the top of Gwenn's head. A protective gesture.

Gwenn stood.

"We heard the bells," she said, her voice weak, but steady. "Is it over?"

"Yes." I wanted to say more, could see that Gwenn needed more, but no words came.

Then Gwenn took the two steps that separated us and hugged me tight, her arms encircling my waist.

I stiffened, surprised. No one had ever approached me for comfort; no one had ever thought to.

I reached down tentatively and laid my hand on her head, as Ottul had done, saw Ottul's mouth tighten, her brow crease slightly. I felt Gwenn trembling, but she didn't sob, didn't cry. Her arms tightened at my waist instead. I pulled her in close, stroked her hair, as Erick had once done for me, and simply held her.

Then I pushed her away, gently, knelt down beside her, looked her in the eye. "I need to speak with Ottul," I said. "You can stay if you want, or Marielle can take you back to my cabin." Which was what I had intended: for Gwenn to stay with Heddan. I hadn't intended to give her the choice.

Gwenn watched me closely a long moment. "It wasn't Ottul's fault," she finally said.

I frowned. "What do you mean?"

"It wasn't her fault. I heard the ship, heard the Chorl on deck. I thought I could help, but you told me to watch Ottul, so I brought her with me. . . ."

I glanced toward Ottul, her blue face impassive, her eyes on me, watching. No arrogance. No defiance. Something else lined her face, something I didn't recognize.

I turned back to Gwenn. "It's all right. I'm not going to hurt her. We're just going to talk."

Relief flooded her eyes. "Then I'll stay. I can help."

I hesitated, even then, stood. "Good," I said, and faced Ottul. Marielle gathered Gwenn to her, while Keven and Avrell, waiting stooped over out in the corridor, stepped into the room and to one side. The quarters were tight, almost too crowded with six people in them, but even as everyone shifted about, Ottul's eyes never wavered from mine. She didn't react at all, until everyone was settled.

Then, her eyes narrowed. In a voice hard as stone, weighted with importance, she asked, "You gave to sea?"

I frowned. I should have been the first to ask a question, not her.

But she was talking, in the coastal common tongue, if haltingly and with strange inflections.

Her time with Gwenn had been well spent.

"I don't understand," I said.

"Dead," she said, motioning with one hand toward the upper deck. She'd remained above in the aftermath of the battle, as the bodies were laid out, both Amenkor and Chorl alike, as the deck was cleaned.

She hadn't been there when the Chorl dead were unceremoniously heaved overboard.

"You gave dead to sea?" she asked again.

I nodded, uncertain. "Yes."

"Good." Ottul relaxed, muttered something under her breath, a prayer, and lifted her hands, palms up, to the ceiling, head back, eyes closed. I thought she might have collapsed into the hunched position she'd used so often in her room in Amenkor, but there wasn't enough room here. She hummed something, not quite a song, more like a deep-throated phrase repeated over and over, and then she halted, opening her eyes and dropping her gaze back to me, dropping her hands to her lap, the brush she'd used to comb Gwenn's hair still in one hand. There was something different about her posture, something new.

And then I realized that she was no longer tense, no longer rigid. She'd relaxed, as if she'd been freed . . . or as if she had nothing left to fear.

"All Chorl given to sea," she said, the harshness gone, but not the intensity. "All return to sea, or become . . ." she struggled a moment, then gave up, "become ankril. Cannot find Queotl."

"Ankril? Queotl?" I glanced toward Avrell and Keven, saw perplexed expressions on their faces.

"Lost," Gwenn said softly. "She's saying that you have to give the bodies to the sea, or the warriors become lost, that they can't find Queotl." She spoke to Ottul in the Chorl language a moment. "The ankril are those that are lost."

"And what is Queotl?"

Gwenn shook her head. "I don't know. 'Que' means fire. 'Otl' is like heaven. Fire-heaven?"

My eyes widened and I murmured, "The Fires of Heaven." I turned to Avrell and Keven grimly. "That's what the Ochean and the priest Haqtl called the White Fire."

"When they die, they must seek the Fires of Heaven," Avrell said. "From what she's saying, they can only find it if their bodies are 'given' to the sea."

"Where is Queotl?" I asked Ottul. "Where are the Fires of Heaven?"

Her brow knit in consternation, whether because she could not find the words or because the answer should have been obvious I couldn't tell. "Come from ocean. From west. Lives in east."

West. The direction the White Fire had come from. I tried not to show my frustration. Apparently the Chorl knew as little about where the White Fire came from as I did.

Except they thought it came from the ocean. Because they had seen it originating from the ocean, or because as far as they knew there was nothing to the west *except* ocean?

Thinking back to the rooftop on the Dredge, when the Fire had first appeared over the water on the horizon and scorched its way across Amenkor, I could understand how they could believe it had come from the ocean. But somehow, I couldn't bring myself to believe that the ocean was its source.

And they thought it lived in the east? Is that why they'd come to the coast? Or was it because their history told them that we were here?

I sighed. I hadn't come down here to find out about the Fire.

I waved toward the deck above, hardened my own voice. "What happened up there? Why did you kill the Chorl Servant? Why didn't you try to escape, to return to your own people?"

Ottul straightened. A hint of the old arrogance returned, but it did not hold, faltering and crumbling until she lowered her head, a few strands of her long black hair falling before her face.

"I . . . cannot."

The words were almost unintelligible, soft and hoarse, full of a deep despair.

And on the river I tasted sadness, the same pungent sweet onion I'd smelled before.

"What do you mean you can't?" Avrell asked.

Ottul jerked her head upright, her eyes red with withheld tears, but she could not meet any of our gazes, not even Gwenn's. "I am antreul," she said, no more than a husk of sound, her dark blue lips pressed together, trembling, shoulders slumped. "I am . . . Forgotten."

I leaned back, remembered the ritualistic gestures the other Chorl Servant had made, recalled the look of utter horror and despair on Ottul's face, the way she'd reeled back, as if she'd been physically struck.

"Why?" I said, although I thought I already knew.

Ottul met my gaze. If it had been any of the others who had asked, I wasn't certain she would have answered. "I am captured. I am . . . lost." She stumbled over the word, looked at Gwenn briefly.

The deaths of the other Chorl we'd captured in Amenkor after the attack suddenly made sense. They'd waited weeks to be freed, to be rescued, and then they'd killed themselves so that they would not be made antreul, Forgotten.

Or they'd killed themselves because they already were in their minds.

"And why did you kill the Chorl Servant?" Avrell interrupted. "Because you were Forgotten?"

Ottul didn't answer, not in words. But she winced, and her eyes flickered toward Gwenn, before sliding away, back down to the floor, her head bowing forward again.

For a moment, I considered dismissing Avrell and Keven, speaking to Ottul alone, certain that she'd reveal more if the two men were not listening.

But then Gwenn stepped forward, moved to stand before Ottul. "I know."

Everyone in the room stilled.

"What do you mean, Gwenn?" I asked.

She turned toward me, her face intent, serious for a moment. But then she bit her lip, as if uncertain.

Ottul said something, reached out a hand to touch Gwenn's shoulder before turning away.

Gwenn relaxed, drew in a deep breath. "It's because of me. I remind her of her sister, and her sister was killed by the Ochean, by the other Servants."

I frowned, shot a glance toward Ottul. "I don't understand."

Gwenn stepped forward, speaking fast, voice filled with fury. "She's been telling me what they have to do to earn the rings in their ears, what they have to go through. It's horrible! It's nothing like what we do to train. They're forced into the temple once they know that they can use the Sight, taken from their families and hidden. And in the temple they get tested. If they can't do something—raise a shield, create a warding—then they're beaten, and beaten again the next day, and the next, until they can. And sometimes the beating is so bad that the Servant doesn't recover.

"Ottul said she went to the temple first, that she barely managed to gain the fourth ring, that it took her years to get that far. When she had passed ket—the second ring—they brought her sister to the temple. She'd prayed that her sister wouldn't have the Sight, and she tried to protect her once she was in the temple, tried to help her—"

Gwenn broke off, reined in her escalating rage. "But she couldn't. One day, when her sister failed to reach ket, the other Servants beat her unconscious, left her on the sands. Ottul found her there—"

Gwenn broke off again, this time because she'd choked on her own tears. She tried to control them, almost succeeded. "She says that I remind her of her sister."

I turned to Ottul, her head bowed forward. "You were supposed to kill yourself like the other Chorl we captured, weren't you? Because you were Forgotten. Antreul."

Ottul flinched, but then straightened defiantly.

"She didn't because she hates them," Gwenn said. "Because they killed her sister."

But not completely, I thought. I'd seen the hope in her face when she'd come up on deck during the attack, the hope that perhaps the Chorl would take her back. Only after the other Chorl Servant had made that slicing gesture across her chest—and after they'd threatened Gwenn—had she retaliated.

I sighed. Suddenly the tension of the battle, the grief of its aftermath, the funeral on deck, were too much.

Turning to Marielle and Gwenn, I said, "Stay with her. See if you can find out anything more. Anything at all."

Marielle nodded, although I could see her own grief bruising the edges of her eyes. Exhaustion, and more.

Motioning to Avrell and Keven, I started toward my cabin but remembered Heddan, coming up short.

"Use mine," Keven said.

I nodded, turned sideways to slide past the steep ladder leading up to the deck, and pushed into Keven's cabin.

Even as Keven ducked through the door and closed it behind him, Avrell said, "She seems much more cooperative now."

"Something happened on the deck while the Chorl were attacking, when she came up from below with Gwenn. Did you see it?"

Avrell shook his head, but Keven grunted. "The other Chorl Servant did something, made some sort of gesture, as if she were drawing a blade across her chest."

"I think Ottul thought they might still take her back, but the other Servant cut her off. And then the other Servant tried to kill her."

Avrell's eyebrows rose. "So being Forgotten means death?"

"Apparently. That's why the Chorl warriors we captured killed themselves. And Ottul seemed willing to accept death at first."

"What do you mean? She retaliated. She killed the other Servant."

I shook my head. "No. She did nothing at first. She only intervened when Gwenn stepped between her and the other Servant, when Gwenn protected her, tried to save her. I think she killed the other Servant to save Gwenn. She's bonded with Gwenn, because she reminds her of her sister."

"So can we trust her?" Keven asked.

I shrugged. "I don't know. But she's cooperating because of Gwenn . . . and because she is Forgotten. There's no doubt for her now. Without Gwenn's intervention, I think she would have allowed the other Servant to kill her."

"But can we trust that? Is that enough?"

I shook my head. "No. Not yet."

Avrell straightened, grew more formal. "She could prove her loyalties, though."

"How?"

"She could allow you to put a portion of the Fire inside of her."

I stilled. "I could see what she was thinking, could seize control of her if necessary."

"Why can't you just put the Fire in her anyway?" Keven asked. "With or without her permission."

"Because she's a Servant. She can protect herself with a shield."

"And it would have more meaning if she gave her permission," Avrell added. "It would verify where her loyalties now lie."

"I'll have Gwenn explain it to her. See if Ottul would be willing. But not right now." I scrubbed at the tightness around my eyes, at the grief and pain and exhaustion.

"Do it before we reach Venitte, though. We need to be certain of her before we present her to the Council of Eight and Lord March." At my nod, Avrell sighed. "At least she might be willing to help with the conduits you and Eryn are trying to construct now."

"She's already been helpful. She used one to help bolster Gwenn during the fighting, used it again to steady Marielle and protect the *Defiant* from further attack while the Chorl were retreating. Even if she refuses to help after this, I learned enough from those two examples that I can probably figure out how to form the conduits on my own."

"Then something good has come of this."

I slumped down into a folding chair, the long night recovering from the attack and readying to bury the dead catching up to me. But the heated grief that I had locked so tightly away during the funeral still seethed inside my gut.

"There is one other thing," Avrell said.

I sighed heavily. "What, Avrell?"

"Ottul said that all of those that are not returned to the sea are Lost."

"Yes. They won't be able to find the Fires of Heaven."

He nodded, his face grim. "It seemed to be . . . significant. To her, and I assume to the Chorl in general. Look at how intent she was that we'd given the bodies on deck to the ocean, even our own. Look at her reaction when you told her we had."

"So?"

He took a careful step forward. "Before this is over, we will more than likely have to deal with the Chorl, come to some kind of truce, agree to the terms of a treaty of some kind. As you said, they have no home to return to. We can't drive them back into the sea as the Seven did before. We can't expect them to live off of their own ships. They'd turn to piracy. The safety of the coast would be in constant jeopardy. In the end, we'll have to work with them."

I frowned. I hadn't thought that far ahead, hadn't considered what might have to be done if we managed to keep the Chorl out of Venitte . . . and away from the second throne.

But Avrell was right. The only other option would be to kill them all.

And that, even after the attack on Amenkor, even after the attack on the ships, wasn't an option I was willing to accept.

I turned my attention back to Avrell. "And?" I said, already not liking where Avrell was leading me.

He hesitated, in full First mode, his hands tucked inside the sleeves of his shirt. "Think about what we did with the bodies of the Chorl after the attack in Amenkor, what we did with the thirteen Chorl warriors who killed themselves after their capture."

My frown deepened. "We burned them—"

I broke off, shot a horrified glance toward Keven.

"Exactly," Avrell said softly. "How would you react if you found out the people that you were dealing with, the people that you were trying to form a treaty with, had desecrated your dead, had in effect kept them from attaining the Fires of Heaven?"

"Is she ready?"

"I think so," Avrell said, turning toward the closed door of Ottul's chambers. "Gwenn explained everything. As far as she can tell, Ottul understands what we're asking her to do." He turned back, frowning. "Are you certain you want to go in alone?"

"You should at least take Gwenn with you," Keven interjected.

I shook my head. "No. This needs to be between just us."

Keven looked troubled, but both he and Avrell stepped aside.

"We'll wait out here," the First said.

I stepped forward, then opened the door.

Inside, Ottul and Gwenn looked up, the Chorl Servant seated, Gwenn standing before her. When Gwenn saw me, she turned to Ottul, hugged her, and murmured something to her in the Chorl language. Ottul smiled uncertainly.

And then Gwenn left, closing the door behind her.

As soon as the door slid shut, Ottul stood, stepped forward, and knelt before me. Bowing her head, she murmured, "Ochean."

I frowned, felt a shiver course through me. "I'm not the Ochean."

Ottul looked up. "You use Sight. You use Queotl . . . Fire. You rule ship, city, warriors. You Ochean."

I shifted uncomfortably. The thought that the Chorl would think of me as the Ochean, that they would associate me with the woman I'd killed in the throne room of Amenkor . . .

I shoved the thought aside. "I am the Mistress, not the Ochean. Are you certain you want to do this? You'll be betraying the Chorl, betraying your own people."

Ottul bowed her head again, her hair falling before her face, obscuring her. But I heard her voice, a low murmur, barely a whisper. But steady, not broken. Riddled with a pain I didn't understand, but certain. "I am Forgotten."

We stood in silence for a long moment.

Then I stepped forward, reached for the river, dove deep as I gathered it together, creating a hollow conduit that stretched out from the White Fire at my core toward Ottul. She remained kneeling, head bowed. She had not touched the river, hadn't raised a shield to protect herself. She was completely exposed.

The river smelled of fear, of tension, of sweat and the ocean. It tasted of anxiety, bitter and sharp on the tongue. But there was no deceit, no threat. Ottul was gray.

When the vortex I'd created touched her, Ottul gasped, but did not move. I forced the Fire down through the conduit. When a small portion had touched her, I severed the link with a blade-eddy.

Ottul gasped again, her head rising. She stared at me, tears at the corners of her wide, deep eyes. A profoundly reverential look, tinged with what she had lost. And I suddenly realized I had touched her with the Fire, with the Fires of Heaven. With Queotl.

"Mistress," she whispered.

I'd intended to reach for the Fire at her core, to feel what she felt, to learn the truth about whether we could trust her, but looking into her eyes, hearing that one single word, I realized that wasn't necessary.

The next few days on board the ship were somber and tense. Bullick had turned the group toward Venitte, expected to be at the port within the week, assuming the weather held. Everyone on deck kept a vigilant eye on the horizon, in a constant search for more Chorl ships. Even Tristan on the *Reliant* had turned his focus outward, no longer casting his spyglass toward the *Defiant* as often.

Bullick kept the crew occupied by having them build new railings, the ship's carpenter concentrating on the structural damage to the ship's hull below deck. We'd taken more damage than it had seemed when first the *Spoils of War* had scraped past and then the Chorl ship had tethered itself to the same side. Nothing that the carpenter couldn't fix. Some of the guardsmen helped out, while members of the crew had the guardsmen show them a few moves with the swords and axes. Where before the battle the crew and guardsmen had kept themselves apart, they were now mixing, talking, cooperating.

Three days out from Venitte, on the aft deck, leaning on the rail and only half watching the churning wake of the ship, I asked, "What do you believe in, Keven?"

My ever-present guardsmen shifted awkwardly. Behind us, on the deck, one of the sailors had brought forth a fiddle, had begun to play a few strains of music, lonely and forlorn. A couple of guardsmen paused to listen.

"I believe in what everyone in Amenkor believes in," Keven said, after a long moment of thought. "I believe in the Mistress."

I turned, expecting to find a mocking expression on Keven's face, a teasing glint in his eye.

But his eyes were steady, the lines around his mouth set and serious.

It brought me up short, made me shift stance, suddenly uncomfortable.

"You don't believe in the Skewed Throne?"

He shrugged. "The Mistress and the Skewed Throne are one and the same. The throne is simply a symbol of the Mistress' power."

"But the throne is dead."

"You aren't. And the general population of Amenkor never sees the throne. To them, it truly is a symbol, a gesture they make over their heart, a sign they see on a dead man's forehead after you've passed judgment and the Seekers have carried that judgment out. What *is* real to them, what they see practically every day, is you. You walk their streets, even going down to the Dredge, to the slums beyond. You stand on the wharf or in the market square and speak softly, yet allow everyone to hear, as you did on the ships here during the funeral. They see your power, have witnessed it with their own eyes. Don't think that word did not spread of the fight in the throne room between you and the Ochean. Guardsmen witnessed it. There are stories being told in the streets. To them, *you* are the power, and it's you that they—and I—believe in. Not a chunk of stone sitting in an empty room."

I turned back to the white foam of the wake of the ship, contemplated what Keven had said, the truth I heard in the simple statements, the conviction. And I thought about what I'd seen in Ottul's eyes as she stared up at me, the Fire now burning at her core.

It took a long moment before I could speak again, and even then my voice was raw and quiet. I couldn't bring myself to look at Keven's face, continued to stare down at the churning ocean, at the gentle swells.

"I didn't believe in the Mistress," I said. "Before. On the Dredge. I feared her. Or rather, I feared her guardsmen, her Seekers, because they were a danger to me, a threat. I had only contempt for her. She was . . . distant. She couldn't help me survive, couldn't provide me with food, with clothing, with warmth, so I despised her. But others on the Dredge did believe in her. They thought she watched over them, that she protected them. I'd find them in the alleys, whispering prayers to her, some even as they lay dying. But I had no time for her. I didn't understand the faith they put in her. I still don't understand it, even after becoming the Mistress myself, even after learning that in some strange way they were right. The Mistress does watch over them, just not as . . . personally as perhaps they thought. That's what the Seekers are for—to protect, to carry out justice."

I pulled out my dagger, stared down at its edge, hilt lying flat in one hand, the point resting against the tip of one finger of the other hand. A simple blade, no etching, no leather-wrapped grip. Just cold steel. I'd cleaned it thoroughly after the fight with the Chorl, as Erick had taught me, had washed the blood off as the sailors washed it off the deck.

"But even that small understanding didn't come until later. On the Dredge I didn't believe in anything. Not until I killed the man who tried to rape me. Not until Erick came. Then, I think I believed in this." I held up the dagger, grimly. A cloud scudded across the sun, casting the ship into shadow. Otherwise, the blade might have glinted in the light. Even in the shade it appeared deadly, smooth and sharp and full of strength. And strength had been what I needed back then.

"But?" Keven said.

I could hear understanding in Keven's voice, as if he knew my answer already, as if he'd found the answer himself at some point.

And perhaps he had. He carried a sword after all.

"But then I killed Bloodmark." I glanced toward Keven, then away. Because I wasn't being honest, and I could sense Keven's frown, even though his expression was blank. I grimaced, sighed. "No. It wasn't Bloodmark's death that changed me.

"It was Charls."

I thought Keven would condemn me, but he said nothing, merely nodded once.

An acceptance, almost an approval.

"After that, I don't know what I believed in," I continued. "I *relied* on the dagger, to protect Borund, to survive, but I didn't believe in it anymore. I didn't feel the need to believe in anything, but I felt there should be something more, something . . . better." I struggled a moment more to express it, then let my shoulders sag.

"But now we've met the Chorl, have been attacked by the Chorl, because of belief. From what Ottul has said over the last few days, and from what I found out from the Ochean before I killed her, the Chorl believe in the White Fire, truly *believe* that the Fire is what they seek after they die."

"And I can understand why," Keven said softly. And now he was the one staring out over the water, his hands gripping the rail tightly. "It . . . had a presence. When it passed through Amenkor six years ago, I was on the palace walls, on patrol. But when it burned across the water, when it descended and touched me, I felt it . . . inside. Deep inside. I felt it burning there, felt it . . . judge me."

I shuddered, remembering the first man I'd killed, remembered his hand pressing hard into my chest as he fumbled with his breeches, as he readied to rape me. But the Fire had intervened, had burned down inside of me, exposed me, judged me . . . and somehow it had given me the strength to kill the man who I'd known would kill me in the end.

Then the Fire had left a part of itself behind, inside me.

And I suddenly realized that no one spoke of the Fire, of what it had done to them. Not to each other, as Keven had just done. It was too personal, too private, something that could only be shared with yourself.

Or the person you worshiped. Like a confession.

"The Fire is what brought the Chorl to Amenkor," I said. "The priests believed they would find the Fire there, because they could feel it burning inside of Erick. They tortured him to find out where it had come from."

I shuddered at the memory, at the white-hot pain of it, the blood and sweat and sand.

And at the look on Haqtl's face, the intense hatred in his eyes as he drove the spine into Erick's chest.

Keven shifted. "They came east, to the coast, in search of Heaven," he said.

We thought about that in silence, the strains of the fiddle behind us shifting, the pace picking up, slipping from sadness to something a little more light-hearted, the music a strange juxtaposition to our conversation.

Turning away from the water, Keven asked, "And what do you believe in now, Mistress?"

I didn't know.

Before I admitted this, Gwenn emerged from below in a rush. Eyes locking on me, she ran toward me, gasped, "Mistress! Isaiah says to come down now. Something's wrong with Erick!"

I found myself at the door to Erick's cabin without remembering how I got there. Inside, Isaiah and two sailors were struggling to hold Erick's convulsing body down onto the cot, Isaiah barking orders, both men crying out as Erick kicked and flailed, his arms and legs moving without real purpose.

The sight sent a cold hard weakness into my legs.

"Gods," I murmured, "what's happening?"

Isaiah shot a black look toward the door.

"Help us!" he spat, and I surged forward, felt Keven at the door behind me.

Then we were both pushing between the other two desperate sailors, a bruise already swelling up on one man's cheek. Both were panicked, one trying to hold down Erick's arms, the other his legs, Isaiah in the middle over his chest. As Keven and I slid into place, Isaiah retreated.

"Hold him so that he doesn't hurt himself!" he barked. "I need to find something for his mouth!"

Gasping, I snatched one of Erick's arms, but not before it struck the side of the cabin wall with a hideous, meaty smack. He'd been bedridden, had weakened recovering from his weeks of torture even though his muscles had been exercised by servants, his legs and arms bent and stretched on a regular basis, but still his spasms almost ripped the captured arm free from my grip. I spat a curse that made the nearest sailor's eyes widen, heard Keven cursing under his breath at the other end of the cot, and then I shoved Erick's unruly arm down to his chest, leaned over it to keep it down, the sailor doing the same.

This close, I could smell oranges, could feel Erick's sweat-soaked shirt beneath my arms and chest, could hear his heaving, rasping breath, could feel it against my neck.

And then his back arched.

"Keven!" I cried as my grip began to loosen, to slide. Erick's legs were still free and he was using them to push upward.

"I'm trying," Keven growled. I shot a glance toward Erick's legs, saw Gwenn cowering in the door to the cabin over the sailor's back, hands covering her face, eyes wide and filled with terrified tears—

And then Isaiah returned and I spun back, his sharp face locked in a grim expression. "Hold him!" he barked, and Keven grunted, the sailor beside him at his feet doing the same. "I said hold him!"

"Put in the gods-damned stick!" Keven spat back.

Isaiah ignored him. Kneeling down beside Erick's head, he began to pry open Erick's mouth, Erick's jaw locked shut, the muscles in Erick's neck standing out in strained cords as he convulsed, arching back farther.

He began to tilt, rocking off the cot.

Everyone cried out, and then Gwenn shoved in beside me, arms extended, pushing Erick back, holding him in place.

"I can't—" Isaiah began.

And then all of the tension snapped out of Erick's body.

He collapsed back to the cot, everyone falling on top of him, but the seizure hadn't ended. His arm still continued to spasm beneath my grip. His breath still hissed in and out, far too fast. I could feel his heart shuddering, the beats irregular, and his body felt hot to the touch.

"Got it," Isaiah said, and I turned to see the stick he'd held slip between Erick's teeth.

A moment before another spasm hit. Erick bit down, hard, teeth sinking half an inch into the soft wood, almost snapping it in two.

Isaiah caught my eye. "More than one doctor's lost a finger that way," he said in a bland voice. Then his focus shifted, his frown deepening. "We have to get the seizures to stop. He'll kill himself."

"What can you do?"

His brows drew together in thought. Then: "Hold on."

I rolled my eyes, but tightened my grip on Erick's arm.

He turned to his small desk, rooted through a satchel, vials clinking together.

A moment later, he withdrew a thin glass tube filled with a clear liquid that looked like water.

Kneeling again, he pulled the cork free from the tube with his teeth, spat it aside, and said, "Hold him still."

All of us leaned our weight onto Erick's chest and legs, pressing him down to the cot. As we did, I wondered if this is what it had been like for Erick when he'd carried me back from the warehouse district, fire blazing behind him, the tremors from my overuse of the river coursing through me. Had he felt this terror, this pain?

Then Isaiah poured the vial into Erick's mouth around the stick.

It may have looked like water, but it reeked of the deepest depths of the slums.

Erick immediately choked, spit half the fluid back up through his clenched teeth, splattering me and Isaiah, but Isaiah didn't flinch, his hand massaging Erick's throat, forcing him to swallow.

And then Erick stopped breathing.

My heart skipped in my chest, halted.

And so did Erick's.

"Let him go!" Isaiah growled, leaping to his feet. "Let him go, let him go!"

I didn't react fast enough, too shocked to move, Erick's chest so still beneath my hands, so lifeless, I *couldn't* move. Isaiah gripped me by the shoulder and, with a strength I wouldn't have known his thin body possessed, pulled me up and away. The others jumped back from Erick's still muscle-seized, still breathless, body. Isaiah stood over him, his face intent, doing nothing, for one breath, two, so long I wanted to scream at him.

Then he raised his arm, hand clenched into a fist, and brought it down sharply onto Erick's chest, right above his heart.

The force of the blow, the viciousness of it, halted me where I stood, halted everyone, Keven sucking in a sharp, shocked breath. I could feel his shock slipping over into appalled anger.

He reached for his blade when Isaiah struck Erick again.

"What in bloody hells—" Keven began, his sword beginning to snick from its sheath—

And then Erick gasped. A harsh, tortured, indrawn breath that seemed ripped from the air.

Isaiah had raised his fist for another blow—oblivious of Keven standing behind him, hand gripping a hilt with white knuckles, two inches of steel bared—but now he paused. They both paused.

Erick heaved in another breath. Another . . .

Then he collapsed back onto the cot, no longer flailing, no longer convulsing.

Silence held. No one spoke, breaths loud and ragged, chests heaving. One of the sailors coughed, raised a hand to wipe at his mouth, wincing as he touched the darkening bruise on his cheek.

After a long, tense moment, Isaiah lowered his arm. "I think it's over."

A strained tension bled out of the room with an almost audible sigh. Keven's blade slid back into place with a click, and Isaiah turned, as if he had just become aware of it. He cast Keven a derisive glare.

Keven did not seem contrite, anger still clear in his gaze. And his hand didn't leave the hilt.

"What happened?" I asked.

"He seized."

I drew in a breath, the fear of a moment before sliding into an anger similar to Keven's, but I held it in, forced myself to calm. "Why?"

"He's dying," he said bluntly. "He's been inactive for months. He's been tortured, is still being tortured according to you, and his body is giving up. If he isn't freed from this spell within the next few days, he won't survive, no matter what we do."

I held Isaiah's eyes, searched their depths, even touched the river.

What I saw there made me straighten, my jaw clenched.

Then I spun on my heel, moved down the corridor and up the ladder to the deck into early evening sunlight. I searched the crew, found Captain Bullick near the prow.

"Venitte," I said, without preamble, cutting off whatever Bullick had been saying to one of his sailors.

"Yes, Mistress?" he said, stiffening slightly in disapproval.

Only then did I realize my hand rested on my dagger.

"How long until we reach Venitte?"

"Three days."

I shook my head. "Erick doesn't have three days."

"But the Chorl—"

"I don't care," I said, my voice deadly. I could hear it, could hear the gutter-scum in it, the street rat bleeding through. I could feel power building on the river, the currents riled. "Get us to Venitte in two days, no more."

He straightened even further, nodded formally. "Yes, Mistress."

I turned, headed back to the hatch, to my rooms. Behind, I heard Bullick exhale sharply, then bark orders.

*   *   *

Two days later, the *Defiant* approached the docks of Venitte in the dead of night, the ancient city that I'd seen only through dreams, through the memories of others, a blaze of light spread across the port mouth and distant hills, nothing truly visible. We'd entered the northern channel that led to the port an hour before, had watched the flames of torches from the manses and estates that lined the cliff heights to either side slide past in the darkness, had glided past lantern-lit ships on the black water, answering only those hails that were necessary. The Venittians had patrol ships out, guarding the entrance to the channel, and we were held up an interminable amount of time at first, the Venittian patrols unwilling to allow the three escorting Chorl ships through, even though it was obvious there were no blue-skinned Chorl on board, only Amenkor guardsmen. But finally Tristan intervened, using whatever influence he held in Venitte to get all five ships past the blockade and on their way.

I paced the deck, everyone—crew and guardsmen alike—staying well clear. I barely saw the lights that enthralled everybody else on the ship, merely glared up at the cliffs, the anger fueled by fear still seething inside me. I willed the ship to move faster as we emerged from the northern channel and headed directly for the port. I ground my teeth as the ship slowed to come in to dock, the crew leaping prematurely from the deck to tie the ship down in haste. Bullick had ridden them hard, still rode them as they lashed it into place, barking orders like a whip, the crew leaping to action almost before he spoke.

Then, suddenly, Bullick appeared at my side, dressed in his formal captain's jacket. "Wait here while I speak with the harbormaster and get permission to come ashore."

He turned without waiting for a response and stood at the edge of the deck until a plank was lowered and he could disembark.

I glared at his back until he vanished, then found Isaiah. He stood over Erick, who was tied to the plank we'd used to bring him aboard. The plank reminded me viscerally of the one used to slide the shrouded bodies of the dead into the sea, but I fought the image down. Marielle, Heddan, Gwenn, William, and an escort of guardsmen surrounded Erick, ready to leave as soon as Bullick gave his permission. The Servants stood guard over Ottul, even though I could sense the White Fire inside her.

"How is he?" I asked.

Isaiah shook his head. "He's had two minor seizures in the last four hours."

I grimaced, shot a glance toward where Bullick had vanished, then out toward the other ships, fixing on the *Reliant*, pulling in to dock beside us. I narrowed my eyes. "Then he needs to be healed now," I said.

As soon as Bullick returned, nodding from the top of the plank, we disembarked and headed directly for Tristan's ship.

Tristan was speaking to the harbormaster when I approached. I didn't allow him to finish.

"I don't care what it takes," I said, my voice slicing through their conversation like a dagger, "but you *will* take me to see Zachari. Now."

Both Tristan and the harbormaster frowned. Tristan's gaze cut toward Avrell, expressionless at my side, toward Keven and the other two guardsmen standing behind me, their faces locked into dangerous lines, then toward the others, standing around Erick's prone form in a group at the end of the dock.

Then it shifted farther down the wharf, where a large contingent of guardsmen approached in formal lines, at least fifty men in all, banners flapping in the torchlight that blazed all along the pier.

"The Protectorate," someone whispered, and I turned to find Brandan standing behind Tristan.

Tristan relaxed, the release of tension subtle.

"That would be *Lord* Zachari Sorrenti," he said.

As he spoke, the Protectorate reached the end of the dock, broke into two groups. One surrounded the Amenkor contingent surrounding Erick. The other continued down the pier toward us. They were heavily armored, steel reflecting the fire of the torches, flickering red and orange and yellow, carrying shields, swords cinched at their sides, helmets with stunted flaring wings on the heads of those in front. The surplices the leaders wore and the front of the shields contained a sheaf of wheat in gold on a blood-red background. The same symbol adorned the long thin banners.

The sigil of the Lord of Venitte, of Lord March.

"I believe that General Daeriun is here to escort you and your party to your official estates," Tristan continued, "where you will stay until Lord March summons you."

I stiffened, felt the muscles at the base of my jaw tighten as I clenched my teeth. General Daeriun's men encircled us, the general himself—broad of shoulder, nose broken at least twice, with a respectable beard trimmed neatly, dark hair, and eyes cold and severe—stepping forward.

"He's dying," I said flatly, but Tristan ignored me, turning toward the general and bowing. Behind him, I caught Brandan's sympathetic look, but the Venittian Servant, the gold medallion around his neck glinting, didn't intervene.

"General Daeriun," Tristan said, before rising.

"Captain Tristan." The general's voice was deceptively soft, almost melifluous. "I hope the voyage was uneventful."

Tristan grimaced. "Not quite. I must report immediately to Lord March."

"Of course. A carriage is already waiting." He gestured, and two of the Protectorate stepped forward crisply. "These men will escort you."

"Very well." Tristan glanced toward me. "May I introduce the Mistress of Amenkor."

The general's brow lifted in respectful surprise. He bowed, as crisp and formal as the actions of all of the men in the Protectorate. "I'm honored," he said, rising. He was half again as tall as I was, at least twice my age. "Lord March sends his regrets that he could not be here personally to greet you. He asked that I escort you to your residence, and that he will see you as soon as possible."

"I need to speak with Zachari—"

Avrell cleared his throat quietly.

I frowned. "—Lord Sorrenti. Tonight."

General Daeriun's gaze flicked toward Tristan, his lips tightening, but he said, "I will send word to Lord Sorrenti. But it is late. I am not certain he will answer immediately."

I wanted to scream, to throttle Tristan and Brandan both, to draw my dagger and force them all to *move*, but I could feel Avrell's presence beside me, could feel him willing me to cooperate.

I drew a short breath, exhaled slowly through my nostrils, none of the tension in my shoulders easing. "Very well."

Daeriun nodded. "If you will follow me?" He motioned with one hand down the dock.

I hesitated, the urge to argue, to fight, almost overwhelming, then stalked down the dock, Avrell, Keven, and the guardsmen following.

"What's happening?" Marielle whispered as we joined the group on the wharf, the Protectorate merging fluidly and then striking off down the wharf, leading us deeper into Venitte.

"They're taking us to an estate," I said, clipped and harsh.

"But Erick!"

I shook my head, didn't answer, couldn't bring myself to speak. Not to her, nor Isaiah.

Instead, I focused on Avrell, thought of what Eryn had said, that I should trust him, that he'd been to Venitte before, that he'd dealt with them.

"What should I do?"

He pressed his lips tightly together, his gaze focused on the general, on the Protectorate that surrounded us. "Nothing for now. They've made their wishes clear." Then he turned toward me. "This is not the reception I was expecting."

"Maybe I can do something."

Both of us turned toward William, dressed in his merchant's jacket.

"I'm a merchant, part of the guild," he said, straightening under our gaze, one hand smoothing the front of his jacket. A gesture I associated with Borund. "They have to respect the rights of the guild members. They've left Bullick and his crew at the docks; only you and the guardsmen are being escorted to the estate. Which means I should be free as well, as a guild member. To conduct business."

I turned a skeptical eye on Avrell, who shrugged. "It couldn't hurt to try."

I glanced down at Erick, at his wan face, his bloodless lips.

"Go."

William broke away from the group, spoke a few words with the Protectorate escorting us, then slid through the opening they made and vanished.

I felt a pang as he left.

"Look," Keven said.

I turned, saw another large contingent of the Protectorate ahead. They were escorting the Amenkor guardsmen from the Chorl ships. I caught Catrell's eye, saw his dark frown, and motioned to him to cooperate.

He nodded, the frown not lessening, and passed the order to Westen and the rest of the Amenkor ranks.

"At least they aren't separating us," Avrell said.

I almost growled but controlled myself. I bit my lip as worry seeped into the anger.

"He will not survive the night," Isaiah said.

He did not need to say who. I shot him a hate-filled glance, one that the healer did not deserve, but he didn't react.

The Protectorate led us up through the streets of Venitte, over cobbles and flagstones, through wide open intersections with fountains or statues at their center. The water glinted in the faint light, barely visible, mostly sound, the stone figures of men and women, of horses and lions and other creatures at its center, etched in harsh, flickering shadow as we passed. Most of the streets were empty, too late for most of the citizens of Venitte to be out. Those few that were stepped out of the way as we approached, watching the procession with curious frowns. Most were men, dressed in shirts and breeches but with more buckles than there would have been in Amenkor. Many of their breeches ended at the knee, with stockings below, like those that Isaiah wore. The few women seen were dressed in loose clothing, the fabric hanging in subtle folds from their shoulders, tied at the waist, with long skirts and sandals, the look similar to that worn in Amenkor, but slightly off, the cut of the cloth different. They pulled their hair back and tied it or pinned it up using what looked like thin sticks.

The buildings were different as well, made of a gray-white stone rather than the gray granite, eggshell stone, or mud-brick of Amenkor, with more columns and detailed architecture on the outside, roofs peaked but low, the buildings themselves wide and short rather than narrow and tall. Windows were tall and thin, and arched at the top and bottom. Doorways were wide and arched only at the top. Most of the buildings had stone steps rising to the width of the building's front, many had rounded windows tucked into the peaks of the roofs.

They reminded me of the buildings in the second ward of Amenkor, like the merchants' guild. Except here they seemed to be everywhere. And they were larger, squatting in their plazas and at the edges of the wide roads with the discernible weight of time over them. They'd been built ages before we arrived, and expected to remain ages after we departed.

I shuddered.

The Protectorate halted in front of a wall at least twice my height, before an iron-barred gate, the detail of the ironwork exquisite, curled into a pattern of vines. Through the bars, I could see another of the white-stone buildings sprawling around a small courtyard.

As someone moved to open the gates, General Daeriun approached. "These will be your formal estates while you remain in Venitte. Household servants have been provided. The barracks for your men are to the left, behind the main house, next to a small practice yard and the stables. If you need anything, please inform the Steward."

I placed one hand on Erick's arm. "And Lord Sorrenti?"

Daeriun's gaze dropped to Erick's pale face. "I'll inform him of your request, with Lord March's permission."

Then he spun, the men of the Protectorate parting before the open gates.

With tight-lipped anger, I led the Amenkor entourage into the estate, moving swiftly across the circle of white stone between the gates and the stairs of the main building, noting the grass and night-shadowed gardens to either side, another path leading around the manse to the left. I could see a small group waiting at the top of the steps.

I halted before a thin man in tan robes and sandals, my hand on my dagger, my anger a shield before me. He wore a blank expression, his features dark, slightly exotic and sharp, with a narrow beard along his jaw and his hair cropped short, almost to his scalp.

He bowed. His gaze flicked once toward Ottul, then back to me. "I am Alonse, head of the household servants. For the duration of your stay in Venitte, I will serve you as your Steward in all things. Lord March has declared this manse Amenkor territory and has given it over to your use, Mistress."

"And can we leave?"

He straightened and gave a thin, pained smile. "Not as yet, Mistress. Lord March requests that you wait until he has had the time to formally welcome you."

It did not sound like a request.

I felt someone lean in close from behind, saw Alonse's gaze shift toward my shoulder.

"The Protectorate has left a . . . guard at the gates," Keven murmured.

"An honor guard, Mistress," Alonse responded.

I narrowed my eyes. Keven had spoken softly enough that Alonse should not have overheard.

"We need a room," I said. "One of our number is . . . wounded."

Alonse bowed, short and succinct. "Of course. Follow me."

He gave some unseen command to the rest of the staff behind him and they moved, some vanishing on unknown errands through the main door, others descending the steps to lead the rest of the guardsmen to the barracks. I saw Westen approaching.

"Captain Catrell is going to see that everything is in order in the barracks," he said, "then he'll join us in the manse."

"Good."

"He's not happy."

"I saw that on the docks."

Nothing more was said as Alonse led the entire group into the manse. The first room, a huge, circular foyer with marbled flooring, contained three doors and two curved flights of stairs to a second floor. Alonse ascended the stairs to the left into a wide hall branching left and right with small tables, potted palms, and huge urns set against the walls. The first door to the left opened into a room with a four-posted bed draped in filmy cloth, a cushioned bench at its foot, a settee, a few chairs, a table with fruit and a pitcher, and wardrobes against the walls.

"Will this suffice?" Alonse asked.

"Yes."

The four guardsmen carrying Erick's pallet moved to the bed, Isaiah and Marielle hustling to help.

"Can you send word to Lord Sorrenti?" Alonse's lips thinned and he drew breath to speak, but I cut him off in irritation. "Never mind. 'Lord March requests,' I'm certain."

Alonse frowned, the first true expression he'd shown since we'd met him in front of the manse. "Was there anything else?"

"Not right now."

"I could show you to your own rooms—"

He cut off as I turned.

"Leave."

He bowed and left, the doors remaining open behind him. Keven immediately stationed the guardsmen that had remained with us around the door and in the corridor beyond. As he did so, Catrell arrived.

Avrell, Westen, Catrell, and Keven converged on me. Heddan and Gwenn had moved to Erick's side with Ottul, helping Isaiah get him situated.

"This is not . . . encouraging," Westen said.

Catrell practically shook with fury. "We are an official envoy from Amenkor, with the Mistress in our company and an escort from Venitte itself. We should not have been greeted in such a manner. And now we are essentially locked within the walls of this manse, prisoners of Venitte!"

Westen shared a glance with me. Both of us knew that any of the Seekers could escape the walls undetected if necessary. But Catrell was correct regarding the rest of the guardsmen.

"I'm not concerned about that at the moment," I said. "We'll deal with it later. Right now, we need to figure out some way to get word to Lord Sorrenti. Brandan Vard said he was the only one in Venitte who could break the spell on Erick. And Isaiah says Erick won't survive the night."

"That only leaves us a few hours," Westen muttered, his voice calm although his brows creased in concern. "Should I . . . ?"

He trailed off. I knew what he was asking, thought about it a long moment.

But before I could come to a decision, Avrell said sharply, "No. You cannot allow the Seekers out of the manse. Look at what happened when you sent Seekers into Temall. Do you think Lord March will react any differently if he finds out that you allowed Seekers to roam the streets of Venitte without his knowledge? The repercussions to Amenkor would be devastating. Tristan has probably already informed him that you've brought them with you, and if not him, then General Daeriun. That in and of itself will not go over well."

"He would never know that we'd left the grounds," Westen said.

"No! No, I forbid it!"

I raised one eyebrow.

Avrell spluttered a moment, then added, "Mistress."

But Avrell was right. Lord Pyre's summary dismissal still stung. And I still didn't understand his decision. I couldn't afford to make the same mistake with Lord March.

"The Seekers will remain here," I said regretfully. "Would you even know where to look for help, Westen?"

He shook his head.

"I didn't think so. We'll have to rely on General Daeriun or William."

"Or Tristan," Avrell said.

I didn't answer, breaking away and moving to Erick's side. I reached out and gripped his hand. His skin was soft and cold and dry, his pulse thready. His breath came in long, drawn-out wheezes.

Marielle touched my arm in comfort, then stepped away, taking the other two Servants with her, leaving me with Isaiah.

I sat down on the edge of the bed and began to wait.

Time passed slowly, night bleeding toward dawn. No one spoke, the room filled with Erick's breathing, with the creak of a chair as someone shifted, the rustle of sheets as I moved from the bed to pace. The room had a window overlooking the front courtyard, the iron-vined gates. I watched the Protectorate guards in the torchlight at the gates until I couldn't stand it anymore and moved back to the bed. I ignored the glances that passed between Westen and Avrell, between Avrell and Isaiah, ignored the downturned mouths, the lowered heads of the Servants, Heddan's quiet sobbing.

And then, suddenly, William appeared at the door to the room.

Catrell leaped to his feet, hand on his sword. Avrell and Westen merely stood.

"He was the only one I could think of to turn to," William gasped, his breath short, as if he'd sprinted, the words half an apology, half a grimace. "But it worked."

Behind him stood Brandan Vard.

And Lord Zachari Sorrenti.

Part III: Venitte

⊢— Chapter 10

"Lord Sorrenti?"

He nodded, his eyes falling on me. Blue eyes, not the usual dark browns, hazels, or greens of the coast. And he had the same slightly exotic look of Alonse, the Steward, his black eyebrows narrowing to points, the same thin beard, but his hair was not shorn close to his head. Instead, it fell in waves down to his shoulders. He wore a pale blue shirt with light brown breeches and a dark gray sash. I could see glints of gold on his fingers and around his neck.

"Mistress. I was informed that you had a problem only I could address," he said, his voice smooth, no hint of anger in it or his expression.

But I could feel the anger on the river, and as I slid deeper, I straightened. Because I could feel his power, as weighted and predatory as the throne had first felt to me, but contained, controlled.

And because Lord Sorrenti was red.

His eyes narrowed as my stance shifted.

"Brandan has explained the situation. May I see the guardsman?" he asked.

I suddenly wasn't so certain, struck by the fact that Sorrenti was a Lord of Venitte, Avrell's warning that politics in Venitte were so much more deadly than in Amenkor. But there was no other choice.

I nodded.

Lord Sorrenti approached the bed. As he moved, I motioned quietly to Westen, felt the Seeker stand and shift into a position behind Sorrenti as the Lord leaned over Erick's prone form, as Sorrenti reached out and placed a hand over Erick's chest and closed his eyes. Catrell caught the movement, the warning, and he shifted as well, to stand near Brandan, who'd moved to Sorrenti's side.

Keven, William, and I joined Isaiah on the other side of the bed.

"The threads are secured near his heart," Brandan said.

"I see them," Sorrenti said, without opening his eyes.

"And can you sever them?" I asked. Beneath the river, I could sense his presence on the river, could see the currents shifting as he manipulated them.

He did not answer, frowning instead, his brow creasing, the anger I'd felt from him when he'd first arrived blunted, overtaken by curiosity. Everyone fidgeted as they waited except for Ottul, Marielle moving to touch Heddan's shoulder.

Then, abruptly, Sorrenti's eyes opened and he straightened, looked directly at me across the bed.

"The Chorl did this?" He did not turn, but I could feel his awareness of Ottul.

I nodded. "One of their priests. Their head priest, Haqtl."

He grunted, gazed down at Erick, then back. "I can break it, but it will be costly. In strength, in power. Is this guardsman's life worth that much to you?"

In Sorrenti's eyes, in Avrell's resultant frown, I saw that it would be costly in more ways than strength or power, but I did not hesitate. "Yes."

He lowered his head slightly. "Very well."

Then he placed his hand over Erick's heart again, closed his eyes. Beneath the river, I could feel energy build, could feel that heavy, feral power shift, the river shuddering beneath its force as it gathered. Sorrenti's face tightened, jaw clenching, lines of concentration appearing at the corners of his eyes, and still the power built, escalating, drawing tighter and tighter as he focused it. . . .

And then, it released.

I expected a shudder, a wave of reaction from the river that pulsed outward. But instead, I felt a narrow blade slice through the unseen threads of whatever spell had been placed over Erick, energy pouring through the blade as the incision was made, the river rippling, but nothing more.

Sorrenti hesitated a moment, the gathered energy releasing, flowing back into its usual currents.

Then he pulled back.

"It's done."

His voice trembled, and his hands shook. He folded them carefully before him, so that no one else would see.

On the bed, Erick's ragged breathing softened. Tension released, muscles that had been held rigid against the pain relaxing. Subtle changes, but visible.

Tears stung my eyes, and I found myself trembling. But, like Sorrenti, I hid behind a calm mask, my hands resting on the edge of the bed to keep them stilled.

"Thank you," I said, my own voice rough.

His eyebrow rose. "You've come at a dangerous time, Mistress. Proceed carefully."

Then he turned and left, the Amenkor guardsmen at the door parting before him. Brandan nodded toward me with an apologetic grimace, toward William, the motion a little perfunctory, then trailed behind the Lord.

As soon as they left, I turned to Isaiah, who'd already leaned over Erick, had already begun to examine him.

"How is he?"

Isaiah's bitter frown sharpened in irritation and I clamped my mouth shut, let him work.

When he stood back, he heaved a thin sigh. "He's better. His pulse is not as weak, and his breathing has improved." He caught my gaze and grimaced. "We'll know for certain within a day or two. He'll either wake up . . . or he won't."

I nodded.

"What about Sorrenti?" Avrell said.

"I don't know. He was angry about something, and he was red." I caught Avrell's eyes, saw understanding there.

His lips pursed and he looked toward the door. "You owe him now."

"I know," I said. "But he came, he helped."

Avrell said nothing.

Erick woke two days later.

I stood in his room looking out over the city of Venitte, over the gray-white buildings that seemed to stretch forever, smoke rising from the nearest streets that wound upwards to the summit of the hill, where the domed citadel that served as the heart of the city's government stood, where the Seven had held their meetings when they had ruled, replaced now by the Lords and Ladies. And Lord March. But the citadel could not be seen from Erick's windows. His view opened onto the south, onto the stretch of buildings and streets that led to the southern cliff edges of the port and the manses there. Mixed in with the buildings were occasional splashes of green—gardens and orchards and olive groves. Every courtyard, including ours, contained an arched trellis, grapes and wisteria and other climbing plants hanging down into the pathway that it covered. I could also see part of the harbor, the water a lighter blue than that of Amenkor, and ships. Many, many ships, of all sizes, with differing numbers of masts and sails, triangular and square, all skimming across the water in the breeze.

The city was at least twice the size of Amenkor, the buildings grander, the harbor more active. Because while Amenkor was a crossroads, a meeting place for those crossing the mountains to or from Kandish through the pass, and a stopover for those on the roads running north and south along the coast, Venitte was the hub of the sea trade. The true merchants' guild resided here, controlling all of the trade to the southern islands, and all trade north, including the icy reaches of Taniece.

I glared out at it, at the "honor" guard of Protectors that surrounded the estate, allowing Alonse and his servants from inside the manse through the gates, at their winged helms and tabards with the golden wheat on a blood-red field. They no longer allowed William outside of the walls either, after he'd brought Lord Sorrenti that first night.

"Their houses are designated using birds," Avrell said behind me, continuing a lesson that I'd already heard on the ship on the way here. "All except Lord March, of course. The Sorrenti crest is the heron, the Boradarn's the crane. The Casari use the egret—"

"Why hasn't he come?" I interrupted.

A momentary hesitation, then a sigh. "I don't know."

I turned from the window, from the warm breeze coming from the harbor. "We've been imprisoned in this manse for two days, without a word from Lord March. Or anyone else for that matter. Catrell is venting his frustration on the men, training them in the practice yard almost nonstop. Westen is doing the same with his Seekers, in a less conspicuous location. We're all restless.

"So where is Lord March?"

Avrell shifted in his chair, but before he could answer, Erick gasped.

Isaiah leaped up from the desk he'd had moved into the room, reaching Erick a moment before I did. William was a step behind me.

The first thing I saw was that his eyes were open.

"Varis," he rasped, his voice nothing more than a whisper, his eyes—those cold, calculating Seeker's eyes—searching and fixing on me.

Relief crashed down with the weight of the ocean, the wave overwhelming, crushing me, so sudden and unexpected I had no time to prepare. Tears scorched my eyes, burned as they washed down my face, and as I reached for Erick's hand, needing to touch him, I realized that I was sobbing harshly, my breath catching in my throat, hitching in and out even as I tried to control it. I tasted phlegm, wiped snot from my nose and tears from my eyes. But the months of worry, the weeks of dread, could not be controlled, and for a long moment there was nothing but Erick, his eyes, the scars on his face, his tremulous smile, and I was fourteen again, trapped on the Dredge, gutterscum, no longer the Mistress, and the fact that I was crying didn't matter. I felt Avrell and Isaiah withdraw slightly, respectfully if grudgingly, felt William lean forward, touch my shoulder in comfort.

Slowly, the crushing wave receded, and the painful hitching in my chest withdrew, leaving behind an ache that hurt worse than anything I'd ever experienced before.

Holding Erick's hand tight, I said, "I almost killed you." The admission brought a fresh surge of tears, the ache in my chest doubling. But I held it in, held it tight, grateful for its warmth. Grateful to William, who'd shifted up to my side.

"Hush, Varis. I know." He coughed, the sound painful to hear, but he smiled thinly. "I told you to, remember?"

I laughed, the sound half choked.

Isaiah now moved forward and coughed. "That's enough exertion for now, I believe." His tone was stern with disapproval.

I would have given Isaiah my darkest glare, threatened him with my dagger, but I could see the exhaustion in Erick's eyes, could see him struggling to stay awake, struggling to smile.

I made to rise, but Erick gripped my hand, harder than I thought possible. I leaned in close.

"Thank you," Erick whispered.

And then his eyes closed and his grip relaxed.

I waited a moment, stared down at Erick's face. His skin was still pale and drawn at the edges, but his lips were no longer bloodless and there was no longer a sheen of sweat on his forehead.

And he smelled of oranges, the scent tart and vibrant.

I smiled, then stood. I felt William behind me, felt his hand find my own, squeezing tightly.

When I turned, I saw Avrell at the main door to the rooms, speaking to a messenger. His eyes caught mine and he straightened, suddenly formal, the First of the Mistress.

"Mistress," he said, "Lord March and the Lords and Ladies of Venitte are ready to greet you, if you desire."

Carriages were waiting in the courtyard of the estate, enough so that I could bring an entourage. I left the majority of the choices up to Avrell, but gathered Marielle, Heddan, and Gwenn to escort Ottul, and William to escort me. Keven and a few handpicked guards accompanied us, all in their finest armor. The Servants wore dresses in various shades of yellow, green, and red.

I wore a crisp white shirt and breeches. And my dagger.

The carriages wound their way up the slope of the hill toward the council chambers. I could see the domed building through the window, the sun bright on the white stone, birds wheeling in the air above it, but then my attention was drawn downward, to the city, to the people.

Unlike the night when we'd arrived and been led to our estates, the streets were now crowded, the plazas thronged with women and children, the merchants' shops open. Bells clanged and voices rose in conversation, punctuated by laughter, and cries of greeting. Hands were shaken, hugs given, and everywhere, everyone was dressed in fine clothing, no wear, no frayed edges or oily stains. Pouches and bundles were worn openly, not clutched protectively or hidden from prying eyes, from nimble fingers.

Not like the Dredge. More like the upper city of Amenkor, within the wards.

I shifted my attention, noted the guardsmen interspersed among the crowd. Not armored and stiff, like the Protectors. These were the general guardsmen of Venitte, with leather armor, the sigil of Lord March on their chest, carrying swords and watching the crowds with a sharp eye.

But there were no gutterscum, no pickpockets, no street rats.

"Where are the slums?" I asked.

"What?"

I turned from the window, faced Avrell. "Where are the slums in Venitte?"

"On the far side of the hill, to the south. It's called the Gutter. Why?"

"Because I don't see any gutterscum on the streets. No beggars, no street-talkers."

"This is the Merchant Quarter," William said.

"Where the richest and most powerful live and work," Avrell added. "I'm not surprised there are no gutterscum."

"Then why are there so many guardsmen?"

Avrell shifted to the window, gazed out on the passing markets, at the guards. Keven and William did the same on their side of the carriage. But no one answered, and Avrell looked troubled.

I slid beneath the river, tasted the air. "They're on edge. Wary."

"About what?" Keven rumbled.

I shook my head. "They're searching for something."

"The Chorl," Avrell said. "Venitte already knows they are out there. Lord March must have increased the guard's presence in the city."

And then the carriages passed through a high arched gate in an immense wall, thicker than the walls in Amenkor, higher. Marielle gasped, craning her neck to see the myriad multicolored banners that snapped in the wind at its height as we passed beneath the arch, heavy wooden doors to either side, the points of a metal gate hidden in the shadows above.

"Deranian's Wall," Avrell said.

The wall where the Seven and the citizens of Venitte had halted the Chorl the first time they'd attacked Venitte. I gazed out the window, following the curving line of the wall with my eye until it vanished over the edge of the hill to the south.

Men had died on this wall. Thousands upon thousands, both Chorl and Venittians alike.

It seemed too white in the sunlight. Too clean.

Twenty minutes later, the carriages ground to a halt at the base of the wide stairs leading up to the domed Council building, long banners attached to the building and streaming down the walls ruffling in the breeze. An escort of the

Protectorate stood in the plaza before the stairs, waiting. As soon as everyone had assembled, Keven positioning Ottul and the Servants in the center of the group, we ascended the steps, passed through another plaza surrounded by high columns, a rectangular pool of water at its center, and then through two massive open doors. The boots of the guardsmen echoed on the marble floor as we crossed the foyer into another room, the people on all sides inside the building pausing in their activities to watch as we were led across this second chamber, lined with huge urns and potted plants, to another set of doors surrounded by more of the Protectorate.

Words were exchanged, and one of the Protectors slid through the doors.

And then we waited.

I exchanged an annoyed glance with Avrell, gazed out into the room, sank beneath the river and watched the flow of the people, the hurried pace of the young messengers, the more sedate walk of men and women conducting business. Two men were having a heated argument in the far corner, and all of the guardsmen radiated tension.

Then the doors opened again and another man, dressed in robes not unlike those worn by Avrell but burgundy and gold rather than the First's deep blue, approached.

"Lord March and the Council of Eight are ready to receive you now," the man said, and he motioned toward the open doorway.

Sudden fear gripped my stomach, and the palms of my hands grew sweaty. My hand drifted toward my dagger, but I snatched it away, drew my shoulders back, and nodded to the man in burgundy.

He led us into the Council chambers.

Lord March sat in a high-backed chair at the center of a group of tables set up in a U-shape that opened toward the door, the eight members of the Council split into two groups of four, seated to either side, all of them facing the center of the room. Behind each seat were more chairs, where pages and clerks sat, dressed in various forms of burgundy, awaiting the orders of their Lord or Lady. Above each seat hung a banner with the symbol of the house represented on it, all of them except Lord March's some type of bird, most with elongated legs, thin necks, feathered crests, and long, piercing beaks. The marble floor was patterned, the outside black, pierced by a circle of white rays, all of which sprouted from the curved wall behind Lord March. The curved portion of the wall was made of black stone, the surrounding walls gray-white granite, and with a start I realized I recognized what lay beyond the curved wall.

The obsidian chamber that Cerrin had called the Council of Seven, where the Seven members had met, had argued and planned.

And where they'd died creating the two thrones.

A shudder ran through me, a visceral ache as I recalled the Seven writhing beneath the throne's power, as I felt each of them die. It left the taste of ash in my mouth.

"Lord March," our escort said, bowing, "Lords and Ladies of the Council, may I introduce the Mistress of Amenkor."

I dragged my eyes away from the Council of Seven's chambers, away from the black walls and the taste of blood in my mouth, and focused on Lord March.

He wore a black-and-burgundy cape lined with gold thread that rustled as he stood, his piercing brown eyes settling on me, holding me, capturing me. His brown hair was streaked with gray and hung down to his shoulders, but his trimmed beard—a fashion that seemed common in Venitte—was almost completely gray, making his eyes appear darker than they were. His face was lined with age, but like Eryn, it made him more powerful rather than feeble. And he radiated that power, his confidence in his position permeating the chamber, as thick in the air as the throne's power had been when I'd first stepped into the throne room.

Beneath his gaze—both intelligent and dangerous, almost a Seeker's gaze, but without the Seeker's fine edge—beneath his presence, I shifted, aware that I was being judged, that an opinion was being formed . . . and that the opinion would decide everything.

The gutterscum came forward inside me, stiffened my shoulders, tightened my jaw. The same defiance I'd felt on the Dredge, when some carter had spat at me or tried to kick me; the same defiance that I'd felt when I'd first met the merchants of Amenkor as Mistress.

Lord March, like the carter, like the merchants, had no right to judge me.

His head lowered at the subtle change. His eyes glinted.

But on the river, unlike most of the other Lords and Ladies, he was a mix of red and gray. He could be a danger to me, or not.

He hadn't decided yet.

"Welcome to Venitte, Mistress." His voice filled the hall, although he did not speak loudly and I could not sense any use of the river to augment it. "May I present the Council of Eight. Lords Sorrenti, Boradarn, Aurowan, and Lady Casari." He motioned to his right. Lord Sorrenti nodded more deeply than the others, but only by a fraction. His eyes revealed nothing, and he made no gesture indicating that we'd already met. Lady Casari smiled, the expression tight-lipped, almost bitter. They all rose as they were introduced. "And on my left, Lords Demasque and Dussain, and Ladies Tormaul and Parmati." Demasque frowned as he nodded, his eyes never leaving my face. Dussain was younger than all of the others by at least ten years, smiling as he stood and nodded. Both of the ladies' expressions were blank, although Lady Tormaul held my gaze as she nodded, before looking down at the table before her.

As soon as everyone had been introduced, the Council of Eight sank back into their seats. A few pages were immediately called forward with a curt whisper or sharp gesture and sent running.

Lord March's attention never left me.

"Captain Tristan has informed me and the Council of what transpired in Amenkor—of the Chorl attack on the city, of the damage you suffered, not only to the city, but to the throne." At this, the low murmur that had built as he spoke quieted, everyone watching my reaction. "From what he said, the damage to the port was extensive, and the fact that you are here—when no Mistress has ever been able to leave the city before—tells us how extensive the damage was to the throne."

I felt my jaw clench, thought of Lord Pyre's accusations in Temall, that perhaps I was not the true Mistress, that perhaps the power of Amenkor was dead. There was a hint of this accusation in Lord March's voice.

"I'm certain that Captain Tristan's report was accurate," I said, "but Amenkor survives. The inner walls have already been rebuilt, as well as the wharf."

"And the throne?"

I turned to face Lord Demasque, felt a flicker of irritation from Lord March at Demasque's interruption.

I gathered the power of the river around me, felt Lord Sorrenti stiffen, lean forward in sudden alarm, but I did nothing but make the river heavier around all of the Lords and Ladies, let them feel its pressure, like a weight upon their shoulders. Darkening my voice in warning, I said, "Amenkor is alive and well. Enough that when we learned that the Chorl were not advancing on us, but on Venitte, we traveled here to offer you our assistance."

All of the Council of Eight straightened in their seats, the clerks and pages behind them shifting uncomfortably. I let them squirm beneath the river's weight a moment longer, kept my attention on Lord Demasque, then let the river subside and turned back to Lord March.

"The Chorl cannot be ignored. They almost destroyed Amenkor. In a day. They've seized the Boreaite Isles, have seized Bosun's Bay, and when we left Temall, Lord Pyre said they were marching on Venitte."

Lord March's frown had deepened. "Captain Tristan informed me of what happened in Temall as well. He claims that your actions have cost us Lord Pyre's support."

The rebuke stung and my nostrils flared in defiance, aware that Avrell had shifted in warning at my side. But before he could caution me, I caught myself. Taking a deep breath, I nodded.

"Yes. I thought that the Chorl had already claimed Temall, had already begun an advance on Amenkor, so I sent in Seekers as scouts without first seeking Lord Pyre's permission. He took offense.

"He also does not feel the Chorl are a threat. He is wrong."

Lord March considered the words a long moment in silence, as if trying to make a decision, his frown never wavering. But finally he nodded and leaned forward. "There are those on this Council," he said, "who believe that the Chorl don't exist, that they are simply a more organized band of pirates, that these pirates are using the old stories of blue-skinned sea demons to spread fear, to make their raids more successful." A note of derision had crept into his voice, and I sensed Lord Boradarn shifting in his seat, saw Lady Parmati frown out of the corner of my eye.

Lord March's focus shifted from me, toward Ottul. "But I see that you've brought proof that the Chorl are real."

Lady Parmati snorted. "She could be painted blue, made to look like one of the sea demons from legend."

"And risk us inspecting her? Here, in the middle of the Council of Eight?" Lord March was no longer hiding his derision. "This is not one of your staged stories, Lady Parmati. These are not actors spouting words for you and your guests' entertainment. Are you going to publicly claim that the Mistress of Amenkor is lying? Do you doubt the word of Captain Tristan, of his entire crew? They fought the Chorl, on the trip to Amenkor and again on their way back. Their stories have already begun to spread through Venitte. And those stories are being verified by other captains, other merchants."

Lady Parmati tilted her chin up at Lord March's tone, at his almost visible anger, and her mouth clamped shut. A faint blush had crept up the pale skin of her neck, reaching the base of her curled black hair, piled high and kept in place with two pins. Her dangling gold earrings glinted in the light as she trembled in rage, her eyes narrowing.

But she did not respond.

Lord March's gaze raked the rest of the Lords and Ladies present. "Does anyone else wish to question the Mistress' intentions?"

Silence. Not even a whisper of cloth from the pages or clerks.

But on the river, I could feel the hostility. From Demasque and Parmati, their figures washed in red. Hostility toward me . . .

And toward Lord March.

Lord March nodded at the silence, leaned back as he turned to me. "Amenkor has always been an ally. Always, even if we have had our disagreements at times. But in this matter, I do not believe we disagree. From what you have told me, from what Captain Tristan has seen and experienced firsthand, I believe the Chorl *are* a threat. And if they are marching on Venitte, then we must prepare. I only regret that we could not come to your aid when the Chorl attacked Amenkor."

As he spoke, the hostility on the river grew . . . but not from all quarters.

Lord Sorrenti—a mixed red and gray—shifted entirely to gray, as did Lady Casari and Lords Boradarn and Dussain.

Lord March himself became almost entirely gray, with only a faint sheen of red remaining.

"There was no forewarning," I said. "There was no chance for Venitte to help us."

"As you say. But we *have* been forewarned about the attack on Venitte, and for that—now that the contention that the Chorl are nothing but bandits has finally been laid to rest—we are grateful. If you will excuse us, we must begin our preparations."

I frowned at the dismissal, almost turned and retreated, felt Avrell willing me to do so.

But I halted, Lord March noting the hesitation even as his attention began to shift.

He raised an eyebrow in question.

Allowing my annoyance to color my voice, I asked, "Are we still restricted to our . . . estates?"

Some of the Council stilled, breath caught at the tone of my voice.

But, for the first time since we'd arrived, Lord March smiled. "Of course not, Mistress. All of Venitte is at your disposal."

I nodded, then turned, passing through my entourage as they parted before me and out through the door.

I didn't begin trembling until the carriage had made it halfway back to the Amenkor estates, and as I let out my pent-up breath in a long sigh, Avrell leaned forward.

"That," he said, "went better than I expected."

"In what way?" I asked snidely.

A smile touched his lips. "You have your own style, Mistress. You're direct, and you don't hide your emotions well. In Amenkor, as Mistress, there's no one to question you, to censure you."

"You question me all the time."

"True. But you rarely listen."

I couldn't respond to that, noticed that Marielle, William, and Keven were studiously watching the passing city outside the windows.

"But here in Venitte," he continued, "you aren't the only power. You saw the Council today. I expected your style and Venitte's to clash."

"They did clash."

Avrell shook his head. "Not as badly as you think. Lord March did more than simply welcome you to Venitte. He announced to everyone on the Council that he recognizes you as the Mistress of Amenkor, with or without the throne. He announced that, whatever dissension there may have been in the Council before this regarding the Chorl, the dissension is now over."

"And he's announced war," Keven said.

Avrell frowned, but not in disagreement. "Yes, he has."

"Why the frown?" William asked. "Wasn't that our intent in coming down here? To warn Venitte? To prepare them for the Chorl?"

"He's frowning," I said in answer, "because not everyone on the Council of Eight is in agreement with Lord March."

Avrell stared at me a moment. "You've never been to Venitte, never seen the Councillors. What did you see in the Council chamber today?"

I thought back to the room, sifted through all of the emotions I'd felt on the river. Not as the Mistress of Amenkor, but as gutterscum from the Dredge.

"Lord Demasque and Lady Parmati," I said.

Avrell nodded. "Artren Demasque has always been a thorn in Lord March's side. He'd like more control of the trade routes to the southern isles. He'd like control of them all. And Vaiana Parmati wants control of Venitte itself, something her family has not had for generations. Once, her family ruled Venitte as the head of the Council, the position that Lord March holds now. She wants to reclaim that title. Who else?"

I shrugged. "Lords Sorrenti, Boradarn, and Dussain—and Lady Casari—were gray by the end of the meeting. The rest were mixed."

"Which means?" Keven said.

"Those that are gray are Lord March's supporters," Avrell said, "and no threat to Varis."

"The others are unknown. They may be a threat, or not, depending on what happens. It usually means that they haven't decided whether I'm a danger to them or not."

"Which means we need to be wary of them," Keven said.

"And we should have Lord Demasque and Lady Parmati watched." Avrell caught my gaze. "Lord March has given everyone from Amenkor leave to see the city. Including the Seekers."

I glanced out the windows of the carriage, saw that we had arrived back at the estates. "Westen will be thrilled."

"No!" Ottul stamped her foot on the grass of the gardens within the walls of the Amenkor estate in Venitte. "No, no, no!"

Before her, standing facing each other, Marielle and Heddan let the shields and the threads of the river around them relax, turning toward the Chorl Servant. "What?" Marielle said in exasperation. "We're doing exactly what you said!"

Ottul muttered something in the Chorl language, and Gwenn, sitting cross-legged beside me in the grass at the edge of the garden, laughed.

"What did she say?" I asked.

Gwenn giggled. "She said none of us would have survived in the Teotohuaca—the Servant temple in the Chorl Isles. She said we would have been killed for incompetence before we even achieved ket—the second gold ring."

I grunted. "Like Ottul's sister was killed?"

The smile fell from Gwenn's face. "Yes."

I reached forward and tousled Gwenn's hair. She ducked her head, grinning tentatively again. "Then I'm glad we aren't at this temple."

On the grass, Ottul had moved up to Marielle's side, her expression stern. "Like so," she said, and then she reached out on the river, pulling threads into focus as I'd seen her do on the *Defiant* during the battle. She made an impatient gesture at Heddan. The other Servant gave a start, then pulled a shield into place before her.

Once Heddan was ready, Ottul carefully began to weave the threads she'd gathered, muttering, "So, and so, and *so!*" while Marielle squinted in concentration. I'd seen Ottul do the same thing on the ship, and had thought I could mimic it without her help, but the first few sessions in the garden had taught me it wasn't as simple as it looked. It was a variation on the conduit that Eryn had designed in Amenkor, but the manipulation of the river was more complex. The threads had to be placed perfectly for the conduit to work.

Conduit ready, Ottul attached it to Heddan's shield. The younger Servant gasped as the additional strength augmented her shield.

Then Ottul severed the conduit and stepped back. "Try!" Except it wasn't a request. Ottul made the single word a command, without any allowance for failure.

Marielle shot her a dark look, which was ignored, then pulled the river to her.

I watched Ottul for a moment, her arms crossed, back rigid, face set in a partial scowl. "She reminds me of Laurren," I said, under my breath.

Behind me, Keven heard. "Yes, she's a lot like Laurren."

I turned, caught Keven's gaze. For a moment, I could see a reflection of Laurren's fiery death on *The Maiden* in his eyes, could sense the grief I felt mirrored there.

Then Ottul barked again, something in her own language, and Marielle threw up her hands in frustration.

Before it could degenerate any further, a rumble of noise came from outside the manse. Keven immediately stepped forward, close to my back. All of the Servants turned in the direction of the entrance to the manse, hidden behind the corner of the building.

"What's that?" Gwenn asked, rising slowly.

"Men," Keven said. "Armored men. Marching."

I frowned and stood, motioned for Marielle to watch over Ottul, then headed toward the front of the manse. Keven and Gwenn followed.

When we turned the corner of the building, the group of Venittian guardsmen had reached the front gates, were passing by in line after line, sunlight glinting off of the winged helms of those in the forefront, off of the shields and armor of all of those behind. The sheaf of wheat on a blood-red field on their surplices and shields, on the banners that flapped in the breeze from the harbor, created a blur of vibrant color against the white-and-gray stone of the buildings, walls, and streets. As we moved to the gates, the Amenkor guardsmen that surrounded it watching the force as it passed outside, the noise of thousands of feet pounding the flagstones in step grew. Rank after rank of men, an entire phalanx.

And then they were gone, the backs of the rear guard trailing into the distance. Dust rose in their wake, settling slowly.

"It would appear that Lord March meant what he said." I turned to Keven as the guardsmen at the gate relaxed. "Venitte is preparing for war."

"Hold this, Ilya."

The Servant before me held out her hand dubiously, and I dropped the circular stone into it.

She gasped, her eyes widening.

"What do you feel?" I asked.

Trembling, Ilya said, "I feel . . . power, Master Cerrin. As if I were linked to the other Servants, but without any conduits."

I smiled. "Good. Now, keep hold of the stone for a moment."

Ilya nodded.

I reached out with the Sight, felt the stone like a presence, somehow more dense than the surrounding objects, more real. And it drew me, pulled at me, like a whirlpool in water, tugging at me, drawing me forward.

Closing my eyes, I let myself be drawn into the vortex, let myself fall into it.

The sensation was strange, as if for a moment I stood on a precipice, looking out over a vast open landscape. Something held me back, a thin veil that was easy to pierce, nothing more than an irritating nuisance, like spider's silk. I brushed it aside . . . and then I leaped from the precipice.

Then I was inside the stone, the texture and smell of rock—gritty and rough— surrounding me. I could feel it pulsing, then realized that it wasn't the stone pulsing, but Ilya's blood pounding through her body, a hot, visceral thrum that reverberated in the stone she held. And more. I could sense her, could feel her, as if the stone—as if what I'd done to the stone—had created a field around it, one that could sense the Servant.

I frowned in thought, tentatively explored the field, reaching out from the heart of the stone, aware that the Servant's pulse was increasing. I could feel the sweat as it slicked her palm, could feel her heart throbbing in her chest.

And then I slid into her mind.

Through her eyes, I saw myself slumped back into my chair behind my note- and object-littered desk, my head sagging backward, my arms hanging over the wooden arms, as if I'd been knocked senseless and tossed into the chair. I could taste Ilya's fear, bitter, like ash in my mouth, could sense her indecision. She wanted to rush forward, to see what had happened, but her awe held her back. I was a Master, one of the Seven. She didn't dare approach me. Not that close, not that personally.

But I was slumped there, the posture not quite natural.

I frowned, took a step forward, leaned in closer. I didn't think I was breathing.

With a lurch, I drew back, realized that for a moment, somehow my own personality and Ilya's had meshed. I'd started to confuse myself with her, had actually started to become her, had stepped forward using her body, her flesh, her senses.

I shuddered, and at the same time, Ilya retreated, confusion flushing her face. Her gaze darted around the room uncertainly. She hadn't intended to take that step forward, didn't remember taking the step forward. Her grip on the stone increased, her heart rate jumping. She was on the verge of fleeing, to find help, to escape—

Don't. Everything's fine, Ilya.

She screamed and dropped the stone, my connection to her severed as sharply as if she'd cut me free with a knife. But it wasn't a clean cut. A few tenuous threads connected the stone to her as she fled. Through them, I could feel her panic, could feel the adrenaline racing through her body, could hear her heightened breath.

I studied the threads for a moment, thought about leaving them connected. She'd obviously heard me through the stone somehow. Perhaps she didn't need to be touching it. Perhaps she'd been bound to the stone somehow, was still connected, and I could still reach her.

I hesitated a moment, then sighed and severed the threads, letting her go.

But she didn't vanish as I'd expected. Not completely. Something remained behind, trapped in the stone. A taste of her, of her essence. Nothing more than a hint of what she'd been, what she'd thought and experienced. A memory of her.

I pondered this for a moment, noticed that there was still a field of awareness around the stone, nothing more than a few feet. I wondered if I could increase that area. Perhaps if the stone were larger? Or perhaps if more people were involved in the stone's creation . . . ?

Still thinking, I attempted to pull myself out of the stone, reach back toward my own body. For a moment, the draw of the stone, that inexplicable whirlpool, kept me in place. I frowned, exerted more energy, more focus—

And managed to escape, falling into my own body with a gasp, lurching forward from where my body had sprawled, smacking my knees into the bottom of the desk.

I spat a curse, felt my heart thud once, twice, hard in my chest . . . and then I ex-
haled sharply, leaning forward to massage my throbbing knees.

Laying my head down on top of my desk, I took a moment to simply breathe
as exhaustion washed over me. I smelled the scent of dried flowers, of dust and
stone, the pungent odor of oil from the lantern and the mustiness of old books and
dried ink. But the scents were sharper, clearer, each one distinct, even though I
was not using the Sight. In fact, everything had altered slightly. I could feel the
stone floor beneath my feet, almost like a living thing, could sense the wood be-
neath my forehead, my skin prickling with the sensation. As if somehow it had all
become an extension of my body.

The stone.

I jerked upright, pushed away from the desk, and began searching for the
stone Ilya had dropped. I'd heard it bounce and rattle across the floor.

I didn't immediately see it.

I slid into the Sight, felt that same density, felt it drawing me forward, pulling
me into its heart. But not as strongly as before.

I grunted, stepped up to the cabinet and bookcases against one wall and knelt.
Reaching into the space beneath, I retrieved the stone . . . along with a few cob-
webs and a lot of dust. I didn't allow the servants to clean the study.

"Master Cerrin!" One of my servants charged into the room, eyes wild. His
gaze landed on the seat behind the desk first, saw it empty, and his eyes grew
wider still, his mouth opening in shock. Then I stood, and he lurched back, hand
moving to ward off evil before he recognized me and darted forward. "Master
Cerrin, are you all right?"

I waved him back. "I'm fine. Something neither Ilya nor I expected to happen
happened, that's all."

He stepped to one side, hands wringing before him, clearly uncertain about
what he should do. I ignored him.

The stone felt warm in my hands, but even as I gripped it tight I felt that
warmth fading. Felt its strange pull fading as well, as if some shift in the Threads
had upset the whirlpool and disrupted it.

And the stone . . . I would have sworn that the stone had been shaped differ-
ently when I handed it to Ilya.

"Cerrin?"

I glanced up, saw Garus dismiss the servant with a gesture. "What?"

"Nothing. Your servants seemed somewhat . . . concerned, that's all."

I sighed. "I frightened one of the true Servants. Ilya. She ran out of here in a
panic."

Garus raised an eyebrow. "Does that mean you've made progress?"

I motioned Garus to a chair, settled back behind my own desk, and set the
stone before Garus. He frowned down at it.

"What's this?"

I smiled. "Progress."

He picked it up, as dubious as Ilya, hefted it once or twice, then set it back down. "I don't get it. Are we going to chuck it at the Chorl? We already have catapults, and they use much bigger stones."

"No. We're going to give them to the Servants. They augment their powers, so that they'll be able to overpower the Chorl Servants in battle without the use of conduits . . . or the presence of another Servant for that matter."

Garus grunted. "Which means we won't have to group the Servants together so that they can Link to overpower the Chorl Servants. We can spread them out more, cover more area, protect more of the army at one time." He nodded, brow creasing in thought. Garus had always been the most militant mind of the Seven—the Strategist, while I was the Builder.

He stared down at the stone a long moment, then turned toward me. "That might be enough to break the current stalemate." But his eyes narrowed with suspicion. "What's the problem?"

I didn't answer at first, thinking about the vortex the crafting of the stone had created, about how much effort it had taken me to break free . . . but then shook my head. "The problem is that the effects seem to be temporary. It doesn't last. And there may be some side effects I didn't intend."

"Such as?"

"Some kind of bond is formed between the stone and the Servant. I'm not sure why."

"Is it dangerous?"

I shrugged my shoulders. "It doesn't seem to be. And it may present a solution to Liviann's other demand . . . that we somehow preserve our knowledge."

Garus grunted again. "Then I don't see a problem."

I narrowed my eyes.

For Garus, preservation of knowledge was secondary to defeating the Chorl.

Garus hesitated, then leaned forward, his gaze catching mine, his voice taking on a darker tone, a grim tone. "We need something to upset the balance, Cerrin. We've held it for two years, kept the Chorl at bay, relegated to a few coastal areas, a few cities. But I've just learned that they've taken Bottan. It's the reason I came down to see you. They've interrupted our supply routes south. If we don't regain those routes before winter . . ."

He trailed off. He didn't need to continue. I knew how low our supplies were, knew that we could not survive the coming winter without new supplies reaching the city.

He must have seen the understanding in my eyes, for he nodded, looked back down at the stone. "Can you make more of these?"

"Yes."

"How soon? And can you make the effect permanent?"

"I can have a dozen ready by the end of the week, another three dozen next week. But I don't know if I can make the effect permanent. I'll have to work on it."

He grunted. "Good enough." Setting the stone down in the center of my desk, he stood. "I'll inform Liviann."

I frowned at his retreating back.

Liviann.

It felt as if she'd seized control of the entire Council of Seven. Everyone reported to her. Everyone sought her approval.

Then, my gaze fell on the stone. Reaching forward, I picked it up.

How could I make the effect permanent?

It would require something more from me, something significant.

I closed my hand over the stone, held it to my chest as I leaned back into my chair. I sighed, closed my eyes as weariness coursed through me, and immediately the vision of Olivia enfolded me. The veranda, the smell of her hair, the heavy weight of the sunlight, my daughters' laughter.

My fist tightened on the stone.

Perhaps it would require something drastic.

Perhaps, to make the effects permanent, it would require something . . . truly permanent.

✝ Chapter 11

The dagger blade slashed across my field of vision, coming within a hair's breadth of nicking the bridge of my nose.

I grunted, kicked out hard toward Westen's chest with one foot, the river pulsing around me, the White Fire inside me leaping up in warning at the Seeker's slightest move. Sweat flew from my hair as I spun, my foot connecting with nothing but air. I used the momentum to carry me up and around, one hand raised to block Westen's downward thrust, catching his forearm and halting it, the tip of his blade hovering a handspan above my shoulder. The force of his blow knocked me down to one knee before him, and I hissed as my kneecap ground into the flagstone floor.

Here, in a secluded room in the bottom of the manse that Lord March had given us, the stone was older, grittier. I could feel its texture through my breeches as Westen put his full strength into lowering his dagger even further. Sweat dripped from his nose, his chin, his hair already matted to his head, his shirt sticking to his own skin.

But his face was calm. No strain showed there.

"Report," I gasped.

His dagger lowered an inch. Another. His arm began to tremble.

But he smiled.

"The Seekers have found nothing so far."

I frowned, almost absently gathered a portion of the river before me, and punched it into Westen's chest.

He barked at the blow, leaping back, one hand raised to halt the sparring match. I stood slowly, one brow arched in question as I wiped the sweat away from my face. We'd only been working for an hour. Westen usually worked me harder than that.

But now he shook his head, his expression serious. "We've been watching Lord Demasque and Lady Parmati for a week now. The Seekers should have seen something."

"What have the two been doing?"

"They spend most of the time either inside their own estates, or within the Council chambers. Lord Demasque has a preference for a particular . . . establishment situated near the docks. He usually stops on his way to his own estates on the northern cliff face of the channel."

"Conducting business?"

"Not that kind of business."

I nodded.

"And Lady Parmati?"

"She spends most of her time in the Merchant Quarter when not in the Council chamber itself, although she also has an estate on the northern cliff face, closer to the city than Demasque's. She's been to two of the other Lords' estates—Dussain and Aurowan—as well as to a meeting with Lady Casari."

"What are the meetings about?"

"The Seekers can't get close enough to find out. Or at least, I haven't ordered them to get that close yet. It would require . . . skill. And involves risk I did not think you were willing to take yet." He hesitated, then added, "The meetings are held at the heart of their estates. If Lord March—or any of the Council of Eight for that matter—discovered one of Amenkor's Seekers that deep inside one of the Council member's personal estates—"

I cut him off with a gesture and he subsided. "What about Lord Sorrenti?"

"Lord Sorrenti has done nothing unusual. But he is . . . more difficult to watch. He's a Servant. The Seekers are wary about getting too close. We know very little about him, only what Avrell was able to tell us from the few times he's been to Venitte. And the last time he came was almost ten years ago." Westen hesitated. "Are you certain he's who we should be following?"

I thought back to Sorrenti's arrival at the Amenkor estate, thought back to his presence as he stood over Erick and removed the spell. Since then Erick had improved, to the extent that he currently sparred with the other Seekers. He hadn't returned to his self-appointed guardianship of me, leaving that to Keven still, but it wouldn't be long before he did.

"Yes. Lord Sorrenti knows where the other throne is. I could feel it the moment he stepped into Erick's room behind Brandan Vard. I could feel it in the Council chamber. He carried the weight of the throne around with him. He's the Master of the Stone Throne, and if he's here, in Venitte, then so is the throne."

For a moment, I considered telling him about the dreams—no, the *memories,* of Cerrin. Of the others as well, but it was Cerrin's memories that seemed the strongest. They'd become more visceral, more real. And somehow they were building, reaching out, drawing me in. Like the subtle pull of the stone that Cerrin had felt, luring him toward that vortex, that whirlpool of power.

But instead, I said, "I asked a few discreet questions, had Avrell and William question a few of their associates here in the city. Lord Sorrenti hasn't left the city in the last twenty-five years."

Westen grunted, and we shared a significant look.

"As for Lord Demasque and Lady Parmati," I said, motioning Westen toward the doorway and stairs that led to the upper reaches of the manse, "perhaps the Seekers aren't watching the right people. The next time either one of them meets with someone—merchant, clerk, whore, anyone—have the person they meet with followed."

Westen nodded. "There is one other thing."

"What?"

"Word of the Chorl has spread throughout the city. It started at the wharf, because of the attacks on the ships, but the rumors have spread all the way to the slums. They're talking about the attack on Tristan's ships, on the arrival of our troops, of you. And have you noticed the sudden increase in Protectorate and general guard throughout the city?"

I nodded, thinking back to the training session with Ottul and the other Servants a few days before, of the phalanx of guards that had moved through the Merchant Quarter to the north. "I've seen it."

"The tension within the city has increased dramatically. The fear."

I heard the question Westen had not asked in his voice. "I haven't heard from Lord March or any of the Council since that first meeting. I don't know what they have planned, or if we're part of that plan."

Westen said nothing.

When we emerged at the top of the steps into the main part of the manse, the Steward Alonse was waiting with a tight, irritated frown. He, along with all of the other servants that had been provided with the manse, had been forbid-

den to enter the section of the lower rooms that I'd given over to Westen and
the Seekers.

"Mistress," Alonse said. "You have received a request. Lady Casari asks that,
if you are free, you join her on a cruise of the harbor."

"What do you think she wants?" I asked as the carriage that Alonse had arranged jounced over a rough spot in the road on its way down to the docks.

Avrell reached out to steady himself, grimacing. He was dressed in the
First's formal robes, dark blue with the eight-rayed gold sunburst around the
neck. "I have no idea. But the fact that she requested a meeting when we haven't
heard anything from Lord March or any of the other council members for the
last week is encouraging. Especially since you said she supports Lord March."

I grunted, thought back to the meeting of the Council of Eight. Lady Casari
had been short, barely taller than me, her skin a darker shade, almost olive in
color, her hair and eyes dark, her smile bitter. She'd worn white, fringed with gray
and a few startling patches of yellow. Her banner had been an egret in flight.

"She didn't say much at the first meeting."

Avrell snorted. "None of them did. They didn't know what to expect, from
you or from Lord March. And they've had their own troubles."

"Such as?"

Avrell shifted uncomfortably, but when I drew breath to press him, he
sighed and said, "They suffered a harsh winter as well. Not as bad as Amenkor,
since they are the central port on the coast and they have substantial arable
land under their control—olive groves, wheat fields, and vineyards cover the
hills surrounding the city on all sides—but the lack of goods was felt."

I glanced out the window of the carriage, toward the large buildings sweeping by in the sunlight. "It doesn't look like it."

"That's because we've kept to the Merchant Quarter." Avrell hesitated, then
grimaced. "This section of the city did not feel the brunt of the winter. However, the Venittian equivalent of the Dredge did."

I turned from the window, and Avrell met my eyes without flinching. "They
let the gutterscum starve?"

"They did not initiate any communal kitchens or warehouses, as you did,
no. Riots broke out in almost every quarter of the city except the Merchant
Quarter. The mobs were brought back to order by the Protectorate and the
general guard combined. Harshly, and with force. There were . . . significant
deaths in the Gutter, followed by disease."

In a much quieter voice, he added, "If you had not been the Mistress, the
same would have happened in Amenkor. It's happened before."

I turned away from him, felt anger simmering inside me, even though it
was now too late to do anything about it. The dead were dead. But I knew Avrell

was right. If I hadn't forced the merchants to combine resources, hadn't threatened them with starvation themselves, hadn't made examples of a few of the hoarders with raids . . .

The carriage reached the wharf, skirting down the ends of the docks. I picked out the *Defiant,* one of the refitted Chorl ships tied next to it. The other two Chorl ships were anchored farther out in the harbor.

As we passed, I saw Captain Bullick standing on the deck, overseeing the repairs to the rigging, masts, and railings that had suffered damage during the Chorl attack. Half a dozen men were seated on planks that had been lowered over the side and were slapping fresh paint onto the hull.

Keven, seated beside me and utterly silent up till now, leaned forward. "He gave them shore leave as soon as Lord March let us enter the city. Looks like that's ended. William's been busy with his own affairs, but he's managed to get Captain Bullick everything he needed to make the repairs."

I nodded. I hadn't seen much of William since the meeting with the Council. He'd been busy with merchant business, establishing his own contacts in the city for the future, distinct from Borund's. And Westen had kept me busy with training, when I wasn't working with Marielle, Heddan, Gwenn, and now Ottul. The Chorl Servant had managed to get Marielle and the others to link and share strength as the Chorl did, and now worked with them on how to call fire. But she couldn't show them how to control it as the Chorl had on *The Maiden.* She hadn't earned her fifth gold ring yet, didn't know how to direct fire herself, only call it.

The carriage slowed, and I scanned the dock ahead. A ship was tied to the dock, a little smaller than the main Chorl fighting ships, with a single mast and sail, obviously meant for use only in the harbor itself. The Casari colors—white and gray-blue with a splash of yellow—flew at the top of the mast, the sail not yet raised. Men, no more than a dozen, all dressed in breeches and white shirts with the winged egret stitched over the heart, were preparing to depart.

Lady Casari was waiting on the dock already, accompanied by a covey of ten guardsmen.

And Lord Sorrenti.

I tensed, felt Keven stiffen as well. We traded a glance.

"Looks like we'll have company," he said. "I'm glad I brought a few extra guardsmen."

Avrell leaned forward to peer out the window as the carriage drew to a halt, the crease in his brow deepening as he saw Sorrenti. "This is not going to be a simple tour of the harbor."

We stepped down from the carriage into afternoon sunlight, the guardsmen Keven had chosen who had followed us in a second carriage falling into place around us. Sorrenti was speaking to Lady Casari as we approached, a frown etched in the lines of her face. But as soon as we came within earshot, Sorrenti quieted, and Casari's frown vanished, replaced with a thin smile.

"Mistress," she said. "I'm glad you could join us. Lord Sorrenti and I felt that your welcome in Venitte was lacking and we thought we'd try to make amends."

"We aren't used to having the Mistress of Amenkor visit," Sorrenti added. I thought for a moment the comment was a subtle threat, but Sorrenti's smile was genuine. "Tell me, how is your guardsman faring?"

Lady Casari shot him a penetrating look, her lips tightening into a frown, but Sorrenti ignored her, kept his gaze on me.

"He's doing well," I said carefully. "I think he'll be fully recovered within the week. At least physically."

"Good."

He left it at that, and after an awkward pause, Lady Casari said, "Since this is your first visit to the city, we thought we'd show you the harbor sights." She motioned toward the ship as she spoke, and the entire group began moving toward the waiting plank. "I hear you arrived at night, and were rushed rather unceremoniously to your manse."

"Yes."

"Then you haven't had the pleasure of seeing the city from the water. It's really the best view." She flashed the same tight smile and I suddenly realized that was the only smile she ever gave—stiff and formal, as if smiling were unnatural to her.

"I beg to differ," Sorrenti said. "The best view is from the cliffs of the Isle."

Lady Casari's eyes darkened in irritation, but she didn't respond.

As we followed them onto the deck of the ship, Avrell leaned in close and murmured, "Sorrenti hasn't told her about his visit the night we arrived."

"No. And they certainly aren't friends."

"None of the Council members are friends." Avrell frowned, watching the two Council members as they led us to the side of the ship, where chairs had been arranged, along with a folding table set with a wide, flat-based ship's decanter, glasses, a tray of assorted breads and cheeses, and a clutch of grapes. "It's all a pretense," he added, turning to look out at the wharf. "For whomever may be watching."

I scanned the docks as well, knowing that somewhere out there, one of the Seekers—Tomus perhaps—was watching us. But the Seeker, whoever it was, wouldn't be able to follow Sorrenti into the harbor. . . .

And that was the point, I thought suddenly. No one could follow us. No one would overhear us except the guardsmen and the crew. This was a meeting, one made as private as possible, as secure as possible, nothing more.

Some of the tension in my shoulders bled away.

Neither Lady Casari nor Lord Sorrenti settled into the chairs, moving instead to the railing. The guardsmen dropped back, Keven and the Amenkor guardsmen following suit, leaving Avrell and me to join the Council members. Around us, the crew began raising the sail and untying the ship, the sail's material flapping fitfully in the breeze. The ship began moving away from the dock, joining the dozens of ships—large and small—already on the water.

"How do they keep from running into each other?" I asked, watching a trader bearing down on a small skiff. I felt certain the two would collide, but the skiff skimmed out of the trader's way at the last moment.

"Sometimes they do collide," Sorrenti said, "but for the most part it's survival of the fittest. The harbormaster has established a few designated lanes for shipping, but if a captain can't keep his ship out of trouble, he won't be captain for long."

As the captain of Lady Casari's ship maneuvered through the congested area near the docks, bells clanging from all sides, shouts passing from ship to ship, Lady Casari pointed toward the main city, as if this were an actual tour.

"You can see the domed Council chambers from here, of course," she said. "The chambers can be seen from any point in the city or along the harbor. The long, rectangular building with all the columns along its front is the College, where Lord Sorrenti and the other Servants study their . . . arts. The building on the other side of the chambers is the official merchants' guild. Behind the chambers—you can see the shallow peaked roof from here, but nothing else— is Lord March's estates, which also contains an adjoining building for the Protectorate's use, mainly a barracks and training yard. And then there's Deranian's Wall." Her arm followed the undulating length of the wall as it separated the upper city from the lower, a clear demarcation of status.

"The Wall was the first line of defense when the Chorl attacked almost fifteen hundred years ago," Sorrenti added.

"I know," I said, and caught Sorrenti's eye. "I was there . . . in a manner of speaking."

He nodded in acknowledgment. "It was the only reason Venitte survived the attack. It was so unexpected—no warning, no hint that the Chorl even existed before their arrival—that the wharf, the lower city, the Merchant Quarter, everything between the water and the Wall fell within a matter of hours. It took that long for Lord Wence—the ruling Lord at the time, beneath the Seven, of course—to organize the army into a defending force and get the gates to the Wall closed. There were only three of the Seven inside the Wall at the time, the rest were outside in the city, or elsewhere on the coast. It's our greatest defense. Some say that if it falls, all of Venitte will fall with it."

"It's a wall," I said, thinking of the three walls that surrounded Amenkor's inner city and palace, of the additional wall that the four newest merchants had begun to build. "During the attack on Amenkor, all of our walls fell, and we still survived."

"But at what cost?" Lady Casari interjected, bitter and condescending. "Your seat of power?"

"At whatever cost was necessary," I said, harsh with warning.

"But this time," Avrell intervened smoothly, "you have been forewarned. What have Lord March and the Council done to prepare so far?"

Sorrenti answered, Lady Casari still bristling. "Since the meeting where Lord March laid to rest any last argument over the threat of the Chorl, he and General Daeriun have mobilized the Protectorate as well as the general guard. The force on the Wall itself has been doubled. A significant portion of the army has been deployed to the northern reaches of the city. There are outposts farther out as well, now manned with horses for runners to give us advance warning of the Chorl's approach. All of the tower outposts along the two channels, on the Isle, and along the coast have been manned."

"And the Servants? The Protectorate and the general army will be able to defend against the Chorl warriors, but not the Chorl Servants or their priests, although so far we have not seen the priests actively participating in the fighting."

Sorrenti grimaced. "The general forces are too spread out for the Servants to fully cover them. Some of the Venittian Servants have been sent along with the main contingents to the north. Most of them have remained here, in the city, either on the Wall or with the units arrayed around the perimeter. But even so, it's going to be difficult to protect Venitte."

"Why?"

"Because the city has spread beyond the boundaries of the walls. There haven't been any serious threats from the surrounding lands for a long time. There's been no need to remain behind the walls, within their protection."

Catrell and Darryn had said the same thing about Amenkor.

Lady Casari stirred. "Lord March has asked us to formally request the use of your own guardsmen."

I nodded. "I'll have Captain Catrell report to General Daeriun as soon as we return."

"General Daeriun is eager to speak to him," Sorrenti said. "Your forces have fought the Chorl before. He wants to know what your captain has learned— about how the Chorl fight, about how best to defend against them."

"They will attack without warning," I said, my voice dark, echoing all of the emotions I'd felt as I'd stood on the tower in Amenkor and seen the watchtowers destroyed, as I'd watched the Chorl ships pour into the harbor and begin their devastating rampage through the city. "They will attack with force. And they will destroy everything in their path until they reach their goal."

"And what is their goal here in Venitte?" Sorrenti asked.

Lady Casari snorted. "They want control of the port, of course."

I caught Sorrenti's gaze, locked onto it and held it for a long moment, my lips pressed tight. For a moment, he simply stared at me, nothing touching his face. And then understanding dawned, his eyes widening slightly, then narrowing as his body stiffened, as his mouth tightened.

The silence that had followed Lady Casari's statement suddenly registered and she frowned. "Why else would they come here, if not to seize the port, to control the trade routes of the coast?" she asked. When Sorrenti ignored her, she added, "Lord Sorrenti?"

His gaze still focused exclusively on me, Sorrenti said quietly, "It's not general knowledge. No one outside of Lord March and the highest ranking Servants know of it."

"Are you certain?" I said. "I believe the Chorl know of it. It's why they've come. It's why *I've* come."

Sorrenti seemed about to defend himself, but then the instant denial in his face faltered, grew troubled.

"Lord Sorrenti," Lady Casari said, voice heavy. "What are you speaking of?"

"Nothing of your concern."

"I'm a member of the Council of Eight! Everything in Venitte is of my concern! How dare you presume to keep—"

"Elina!"

Lady Casari broke off, her eyes hard, the muscles in her jaw clenching.

I stilled. On the river, beneath the surface tension between the two, I sensed something else. They knew each other, knew each other intimately. Enough for Sorrenti to use Lady Casari's first name, enough for them to understand each other without words. And while it was obvious that they were no longer friends, at some point in the past they had been. Had been something more meaningful as well.

"I will inform Lord March," Sorrenti said, voice calm but thick with warning. "If he feels the Council members should be informed of the situation, then I will come speak to you immediately, but not before."

Elina Casari remained rigid for a long moment, then visibly forced herself to relax. "Very well," she murmured, and turned away.

The rest of the meeting was stiff and formal, Sorrenti pointing out different estates among the mosaic of red-tiled roofs on the cliffs as we passed, Lady Casari standing to one side. As we reached the mouth of the northern channel, the ship turned, circling back and running along the base of the southern cliffs after passing the point of the Isle, the huge island that separated the two channels. A large tower soared upward from the summit of the Isle's point, made of gray granite.

When we reached the docks, Lady Casari was the first one off the ship, immediately stepping into a carriage with her escort and heading off toward the upper city.

"She's not happy," Avrell said dryly.

Sorrenti shook his head. "She'll petition Lord March immediately. She likes to know everything that happens within Venitte. She doesn't like secrets." He turned to me. "And the existence of the throne is a carefully guarded secret. That's why I was so angry on the night you arrived. Brandan told me you had asked him about the throne in Amenkor. I thought you were here to expose it, for whatever reasons." He paused, then asked bluntly, "How did you know about the throne, Mistress?"

"I didn't." When I saw his expression darken, I said, "Not for certain. But ever since the Skewed Throne was destroyed, I've been having dreams, memories of the Seven that I did not access while they were part of the throne, memories that I should not have. Eryn, the previous Mistress, and I thought that I might somehow be connected to the Stone Throne, that perhaps it wasn't lost after all.

"I had no idea that the Stone Throne was still being used until I felt you using it to heal Erick."

Sorrenti's lips thinned, but he nodded. "That . . . would explain a lot. Ever since you entered the city, the Seven have been . . . agitated. The throne senses you, is aware of you, but nothing like that has ever happened before, because no Mistress has ever been able to come to Venitte. The connection isn't strong enough to locate you, but it's strong enough to be *felt*." He paused, stared out over the water of the harbor for a long moment, then turned back.

"The Seven believe I should trust you. I know the two thrones were connected. I felt the loss of the Skewed Throne, even here in Venitte, felt the pain when it was destroyed. If what you say about the Chorl is true, if what Tristan and Brandan report about the battle in Amenkor and on the ocean on the way here is true, then the Servants of this city will be crucial in its defense. I'd like you to help us prepare. Your captain can help General Daeriun and his men. I'd like you to help me with the Servants."

I straightened, stared directly into his blue eyes. "Of course, Lord Sorrenti."

With that, he nodded and gathered his own escort about him, vanishing into the crowds on the wharf.

On the dock, Keven, Avrell, and I watched him go.

"At least we now know for certain that Lord March and the others are taking the Chorl threat seriously and are preparing for it," Keven said. Then his gaze shifted. "It looks like someone's been waiting for our return."

I glanced in the direction of his gaze and saw William standing at the end of the dock, frowning.

"Let's see what he wants," I said.

*   *   *

"Captain Bullick noticed it first a few days ago and brought it to my attention," William explained as we walked down the wharf toward the dock that had been given over to Bullick and the rest of Amenkor's ships. The throngs of people were thick enough we'd elected not to use the carriages. "Since then, he's been keeping careful track of the trader's activities."

"And what has he seen?" Avrell asked.

"A pattern that doesn't make any sense." At Avrell's irritated look, he added, "I'll let Bullick explain."

We'd reached the end of the Amenkor pier. Catrell had left a contingent of guardsmen there to control access to the *Defiant* and the refitted Chorl ships, but we passed through the line unhindered, the captain of the force nodding and gesturing the Skewed Throne symbol over his chest as we passed, closing the line behind us.

We found Bullick in his cabin, a sparsely decorated room, not much larger than the cabin Marielle, Trielle, and I had shared on the journey down here. Bullick sat behind a desk that could be folded up into the wall—nothing more than a board and supporting leg that fit into two notches in the floor—with a logbook before him, quill and wide-bottomed ink bottle to one side, the bottle set in a depression in the desk's surface so it would not shift around at sea. When a sailor announced our arrival, he folded up the logbook and set it in a waiting trunk.

As soon as he saw William, he said to the sailor, "Bring the Mistress and her guests some folding chairs, Byron."

"Yes, sir."

As we waited, he said, "I assume this is about Lord Demasque's trading ships?"

William nodded grimly. "And what I've found at the merchants' guild."

Byron reappeared suddenly with another crewman and they set up the chairs, Bullick retrieving a ship's decanter and glasses from a cupboard and pouring us all a finger's portion. It smelled like rum, something I'd only tasted once, on the trip to Venitte, and hadn't liked.

Handing the glasses around, Bullick took a seat. "I don't know if this will amount to anything at all, but since we were forced to remain aboard ship when we first arrived, there wasn't much to do except watch the coming and going of the ships."

"And what did you see?" I asked.

Bullick hesitated, as if still not certain he should say anything at all. But then he took a swig of the rum and leaned forward, his face intent. "Every port has a flow to it, a rhythm, ships coming in, unloading their cargo, loading fresh cargo, departing, all in steady patterns. There are fluctuations in the pattern—

ships that arrive late because of storms, things like that—but in general it's always the same pattern: arrive, unload, load, depart.

"But a few days ago, one of the crew—one of the lookouts actually—noticed that one of the trading ships didn't fit the pattern. He came to see me about it. He said that about a week before, he'd noticed one of the traders pulling into berth, sitting high in the water, which means that they didn't have any cargo. That's unusual. Traders always have cargo. Captains don't remain in business long unless they're getting paid somehow. Their crews would mutiny. But this ship had no cargo. The lookout watched the ship for the next few days and nothing was unloaded during the day, and after questioning the other lookouts, nothing was unloaded at night either. However, on the last day, supplies were loaded aboard, and the next day the ship was gone. It had left during the night."

Bullick took another drink of the rum, set the glass aside. "My lookout shrugged it aside—this isn't Amenkor after all; Venittian captains can ruin themselves as fast as they like as far as the crew is concerned, it improves our own business—but a few days later the same ship, the *Squall*, which flies the Stilt—"

"Lord Demasque's flag," William interjected.

Bullick nodded but didn't break his story. "—eased into its berth again . . . and did not unload any cargo. This is when the lookout pointed the ship out to me. We've watched the ship for the last few days."

"Let me guess," I said. "It loaded supplies and left the same night."

Bullick nodded. "That's when I contacted William. I didn't want to come to you until I had something more concrete to report. After all, it's Lord Demasque's business. If he wishes to lose money by running empty ships, that's his affair. But I thought it wise to have William look into it. And once we were allowed to roam the wharf, I had a few of my more trusted and discreet crew ask around."

"What did they find?"

"That the *Squall* has been doing such runs since the beginning of spring, only once or twice a month at first, but in the last month the activity has picked up. Sometimes they're gone for a few days, sometimes for a whole week or more. . . . And no one knows what they're up to. Their crew doesn't talk about it. In fact, their crew almost never leaves the ship when they're in Venitte. I've only seen the captain off the dock where they berth, and I've only seen the first mate go farther than the deck to speak to the harbormaster. It's damn strange . . . and suspicious."

Bullick shook his head and his gaze shifted to William, who sat forward in his seat and set his glass on Bullick's table.

"At Bullick's request, I went to the merchants' guild and looked into the ledgers. The *Squall* is indeed one of Lord Demasque's ships. In fact, it's owned

by Lord Demasque, not by its captain, unlike most of the merchant ships in the
harbor. Every shipment that comes in to Venitte, or leaves, must register a
manifest with the guild, and that manifest is available to guild members. I
looked up the *Squall*'s manifests for the last few months."

"And . . . ?" Avrell prompted.

William shook his head. "Aside from the supplies that are loaded before
each departure, the *Squall* isn't carrying any cargo. As far as the guild is concerned, and from all appearances on the docks, Lord Demasque is trading in
nothing."

Avrell snorted. "He's doing something. We just haven't found out what yet."

I turned to Bullick. "Can we follow the *Squall* somehow without being seen?"

Bullick frowned. "No. Any attempt to follow in a ship would be obvious,
especially on the ocean. Especially if we're using Amenkor ships. We're the only
crews from Amenkor here at the moment."

"And we aren't here to trade," Avrell said. "Everyone on the docks on the
night of our arrival saw us off-load guardsmen, not cargo. If we leave, Demasque will take note."

"Then we need someone else's ship, someone from Venitte."

I glanced toward William, who grimaced.

"The *Reliant*," he said. "Captain Tristan's ship."

I frowned. "I need to speak with Lord March."

"You have some time," Bullick said. "The *Squall* left for its current run two
days ago. If they follow their most recent pattern, they won't return for at least
two days, perhaps more."

"What is it you wish to speak about?" Lord March asked.

Avrell, William, and I had just been admitted into his personal study, a
much smaller room than the Council chambers, but still twice as large as my
own audience chambers in Amenkor. Inside the same building that housed the
Council chambers, its floor was a mottled gray-blue marble, partial columns
rounding out the corners, the ceiling covered in wide tiles that gave the illusion
of sunlight breaking over the far horizon. Banners covered the walls to either
side, bookcases and shelves against the wall behind our seats, which faced an
immense oak desk, a large map spread out over the surface near me, the edges
and far side covered with stacks of papers, quills, ink bottles, and wax for seals,
all neatly organized.

As Lord March motioned us to take seats in the array of chairs before him,
a page boy stepped up to his side and handed him a sheet, distracting him. At
least three others were waiting with their own missives, two others sitting to
one side, waiting for directions. Clerks seated at their own smaller desks were
working to either side of the room beneath the banners.

Lord Sorrenti and General Daeriun leaned over the map, arguing about something in a low murmur.

"I'm sorry," Lord March said, the page boy darting off to one side, toward one of the waiting clerks, paper in hand. The next started to step forward, but Lord March halted him with a gesture. "As you can imagine, it's been rather busy in the last few weeks."

I nodded. "Lord Sorrenti told me. I hope Captain Catrell and his men will be useful."

"Oh, they will be," General Daeriun said, breaking off his discussion with Sorrenti. "Although at this point, aside from the Servant you brought with you, we have seen no sign of the Chorl at all near Venitte."

"Daeriun."

The general did not turn toward Lord March, but kept his eyes on me, waiting for my reaction.

I frowned. "They're coming, General."

He lifted his chin, not quite in contempt, but said nothing.

I dismissed him, shifting my gaze toward Lord March. I didn't need to impress Daeriun. I only needed to convince Lord March.

"Forgive my general," Lord March said, standing and moving from behind his desk. "He's a skeptical man. We have enough evidence to suggest there's some type of threat out there—ships lost, the report from Captain Tristan of the attacks at sea, other traders verifying sightings of strange ships. However, Daeriun won't believe it until the Chorl attack and he can sink his blade into them." Daeriun grunted. "Now, what did you need?"

"I need a ship."

Lord March's eyebrows rose in surprise. A ship was clearly not what he had expected.

From Lord Sorrenti's frown, neither had he.

"You have ships here in Venitte," Lord March said. "Why would you need one of mine?"

I shifted uncomfortably. My gaze flickered toward Sorrenti. "Because we've noticed something strange regarding one of the traders in the harbor. I'd like to find out what, but if I use one of Amenkor's ships, it will be obvious what I'm doing. I need to be more circumspect than that."

"Why?"

Meeting his gaze squarely, I said, "Because it involves one of your Council members."

He frowned. "I see."

For a long moment, he stared at me, considering. Then, he straightened. "Daeriun, have the guards clear the room, please."

Daeriun shot him a mute glare, then motioned to the few guardsmen stationed around the room. They began herding everyone out of the room, the clerks protesting a moment as they tried to cap ink bottles or gather papers to take with them.

Within minutes, the room was empty except for William, Avrell, Sorrenti, Daeriun, Lord March, and myself.

Lord March drew in a steadying breath, then asked, "Which one?" His voice was heavy with command, with expectation. He thought he already knew the answer. When I hesitated, he added, "I trust Lord Sorrenti and General Daeriun with my life, Mistress. As you no doubt trust your First and Master William with yours."

I nodded. "Lord Demasque."

March and Sorrenti exchanged a glance. Daeriun stiffened.

"Tell her," Sorrenti said. "It's obvious she has nothing to do with the current state of the Council of Eight. Why would she come here otherwise?"

"Do you trust her?"

Sorrenti's gaze fell on me, his mouth pressed tight. "I trust her, yes. And more importantly, the Seven trust her."

Lord March grunted. "Very well."

Daeriun said nothing as the other two spoke, although it was clear by his frown that he did not approve.

Lord March turned back to me. "The threat of the Chorl could not have come at a worse time. For the past seven years, since just before the Fire passed through our city as well as yours, the Council of Eight and the entire region has been slowly destabilizing. I noticed it almost immediately, was forewarned that such might happen by Lord Sorrenti, who said that it happened the last time the Fire passed over the coast."

Sorrenti nodded grimly. "The last time, famine and disease spread all along the coast. At least half of the population succumbed to the Black Death in Venitte alone, perhaps more. There was drought all along the coast. Many starved. The Council at the time grew desperate as everyone tried to protect their own estates, as they tried to protect their own families."

"At least half of the Council was killed," Lord March said, "either by assassination or during the riots in the city. The disease in the northern quarter, the deaths, became so prevalent that at one point Lord Haggen—the ruling Lord at the time—set fire to the district in an attempt to contain the plague. The fire raged out of control, burning nearly half the city to the ground. All of this happened over the course of eleven years, finally escalating to the fire. A kind of madness."

"And we're seeing signs of the same madness again."

"What do you mean?" I knew of the madness of the first coming of the Fire, had witnessed some of it through the throne, through the eyes of the Mistresses of the time. I'd lived through that previous Mistress' rape and death at the hands of her own personal guard, her body left battered and bleeding on the steps of the palace promenade.

"Haven't you felt it in Amenkor?" Daeriun asked, almost growling. "This past winter we had the largest shortages we've had in decades. Disease ran rampant in the Gutter. The citizens rioted, had to be quelled by the Protectorate. They came close to overrunning the Merchant Quarter, almost set fire to the wharf."

"And the Council has begun to break down." Lord March's voice overrode Daeriun's smoothly, the general settling back grudgingly. "Did you notice Lord Dussain? Richar Dussain?"

I frowned, thought back to my presentation before the Council. "The youngest Lord."

"He's the youngest for a reason. This past winter, his father was killed during one of the riots."

"An accident?" Avrell asked.

Both Lords turned toward the First.

"So it seemed," Lord Sorrenti said. "I do not believe so. The circumstances were suspicious, but nothing could be proven."

"In any case," Lord March continued, "since Lord Dussain's death—before that—Venitte has been unsettled. And it's only become worse. I can feel the tension myself, can sense it, even without Lord Sorrenti's advice." Here, he shared a hooded glance with me. He meant the throne, Sorrenti's connection to the city, the same connection I'd felt after I'd touched the Skewed Throne in Amenkor. As if the city itself were a part of me, part of the pulse of my blood, the beating of my heart.

"And now there's the Chorl," I said.

"And now the Chorl," Lord March repeated. "If they are out there, if they do intend to attack, I'm not certain the Council will be strong enough to stop them. Not in the current state of unrest. The Eight have already resisted helping Daeriun with the placement of units throughout the city, have already resisted providing the necessary supplies. They're afraid—of what happened to Lord Dussain, of what the winter might presage. They're gathering their resources, attempting to protect themselves. And one of the most obstinate of the Council, the least cooperative so far, is Lord Demasque. Which brings us back to your request."

He shifted forward slightly. "Anything regarding any of the Council of Eight should be approached with great caution. I rule here in Venitte, but only by the Council's agreement, and the threat I bring by controlling the Protectorate and the guard. I warn you to tread lightly, because I may not be able to protect you if you step on the wrong feet." He paused, to let his words sink in, then asked, "What do you think Demasque is doing?"

"I don't know. But my instincts tell me whatever it is can't be ignored. And I didn't survive as long as I did in the slums of Amenkor without trusting my instincts."

Daeriun snorted, but not in derision or contempt.

"I already know what Sorrenti thinks. What do you think Daeriun?"

Daeriun's eyes narrowed. "I think . . . that you should always trust your instincts."

Lord March nodded. "So, Mistress . . . what is it, exactly, that you need?"

"There she goes."

I turned to Brandan Vard in the darkness of the deck of the *Reliant,* Captain Tristan on Brandan's far side. Brandan looked out over the water, lit only by the lanterns of ships and the torches burning along the docks, but he wasn't squinting.

He didn't need to squint. He was a Servant; he could see the ship as clearly as I could beneath the river.

Captain Tristan could not. He lowered his spyglass, a frown touching his face. "And you were right. The *Squall's* captain loaded supplies for a short voyage, perhaps enough for a week, but nothing more." He turned toward me. If not for the river, his face would be nothing but a pale shadow in the night. "Now to see where he's off to with so little cargo."

With that, he stepped away, already ordering his crew to make ready. They moved about the deck and rigging in relative silence. But they'd been expecting this since midafternoon, when the *Squall* had begun lifting barrels and crates into her hold.

As the ship began to drift out into the harbor, the *Squall* just within sight ahead, I leaned forward on the railing, intensely aware of Brandan at my side. I hadn't seen him since the night he and William had brought Lord Sorrenti to Erick's room, but his presence still prickled my skin. I felt the urge to shift closer to him, could picture his light brown hair in the sunlight of the dock in Amenkor after our tour of the city, could see his smile before William and Tristan had arrived.

"I never thanked you," I said, trying to shrug the thoughts aside.

"For what?"

"For bringing Sorrenti to see Erick."

"Oh." He glanced toward me once, then away, back toward the night, toward the lights of the harbor slipping past in the darkness. "It was nothing."

I heard the lie in his voice. "Sorrenti wasn't pleased. He told me he wasn't happy with the fact that I knew about the throne here in Venitte. And William told me you risked a lot to get him to come."

Brandan shifted. "It was nothing."

I didn't answer.

Brandan turned to stare at me for a long moment. "What did William have to say about me coming on this little trip?"

I shrugged. "He wasn't happy. But he was there when Lord Sorrenti insisted."

"And what about you?"

I turned to face him. "It doesn't bother me that you're here."

He frowned. "I see."

It wasn't the answer he'd been hoping for.

I tensed, forced myself to stay at the railing and not walk away. "Brandan, why do you think Sorrenti sent you?"

He didn't answer, a crease forming between his eyebrows.

I sighed. "You told Sorrenti everything—about me, about Amenkor. In particular, you told him I'd asked about the throne. I knew you knew more about the throne here in Venitte than you told me in Amenkor. I could sense it. You knew about the throne and were trying to keep it a secret."

"Yes."

"And when we were forming the crew for this outing, Sorrenti insisted that you come along. He insisted that you be sent to Amenkor in the first place."

"Yes."

I grunted. "You're not just a Servant from Venitte, are you? At least, not as lowly a Servant as you made yourself out to be in Amenkor."

I could feel Brandan's smile on the river, would be able to see it in the darkness if I turned slightly. "No. Sorrenti is the throne's Master, but there are a few Servants beneath him who are aware of the throne, of its existence. I'm one of those few. I was sent to Amenkor to find out what had happened to the Skewed Throne. Sorrenti knew something had happened; he felt it. But he didn't know what. None of the voices in the throne here knew, because it had never happened before."

"And why are you here on this ship? Why did he insist you be sent?"

Brandan turned directly toward me, his attitude shifting subtly, making him more confident. He didn't seem as young as in Amenkor, as naive. "I'm here as Sorrenti's representative, nothing more. Anyone on the Council will be suspicious of the activities of this ship if it doesn't have another council member's presence on it. And I'm here as additional protection from the Chorl, in case we run into more of their Servants."

The shift in his attitude was a little disconcerting. "And what about Tristan?"

"What about him?"

I frowned. "In Amenkor, he seemed to be in charge. He seemed to lead you around."

Brandan smiled, and I could see a little bit of the naïveté return. Perhaps it wasn't all a facade. "In Amenkor, he *was* in charge. He is Lord March's official representative. He's beholden to him." He shrugged. "I didn't lie to you. I never lied to you, about anything. I was sent . . . to give his credentials a little more weight."

I considered this in silence for a long time. Then: "Lord Sorrenti seems to know a lot about the time surrounding the first Fire."

"He's been studying it since the second Fire passed through the city. All of the Servants in the College have."

"And what have you found out?"

He shrugged. "Nothing much. Nothing that isn't somehow brought out by the tales the street-talkers tell."

"Anything to indicate where the Fire came from?"

Brandan shook his head. "No. Except from the west of course."

I thought about Lord Sorrenti, about his eyes as he told me of the devastation brought on by the plague and the famine after the Fire had passed Venitte the first time. "What about its source? What its purpose was?"

"Nothing that we've found."

I didn't respond. Because I thought Lord Sorrenti had some idea of what the Fire meant. Maybe not precisely, but he'd known something more . . . Or suspected it.

The *Reliant* passed through the northern channel, the Isle and the torches at the height of its granite tower slipping by to the left, waves slapping against the rocky base of the cliffs. The ship began to shudder in the riptides, but continued steadily forward, the *Squall* ahead.

Then both ships passed out through the channel's mouth, past the line of Venittian patrol ships guarding the entrance, into the open ocean.

"Now we see where she heads," Tristan said. He'd rejoined us at the railing, along with Keven. A contingent of Amenkor guardsmen had joined the crew and were now scattered about the deck, mingling with a light force of Protectorate that Lord March had ordered to join us.

We waited expectantly, eyes on the lights of Lord Demasque's ship, just visible in the darkness ahead.

They continued straight ahead for a long moment, then began to turn north.

"Shouldn't we turn to follow them?" Keven asked, when Tristan didn't move.

"No. We'll let them think we're heading farther out to sea, for the longer trade routes, the ones that reach farther up the coast. Then we'll douse our lanterns and keep them in sight from the west. At least at night. Once it gets closer to dawn, we'll head back out to sea and try to pick them back up once night falls again."

Keven grunted in understanding.

Brandan and I kept watch on the deck for another hour, but then the initial tension bled away. I retired to my cabin, leaving Brandan on deck.

The next day the *Reliant* sailed farther out to sea, and we lost sight of the *Squall*. Everyone on board grew grim as the sunlight shifted overhead.

"We're passing into the inner trading routes," Tristan said, "where the Chorl are."

He doubled the watch.

Night fell, and the *Reliant* turned toward the west, angling toward the coast. Everyone not resting below or working in the rigging drifted toward the edge of the deck, eyes on the darkening horizon, searching for the *Squall*. An hour passed, darkness falling heavy and thick as clouds drifted by overhead, obscuring the thin moon, the stars. Tristan began pacing the deck, the corners of his eyes and mouth tight. The entire crew grew edgy, the tension prickling in the air.

And then Brandan whispered, "There."

At almost the same moment, one of the lookouts above shouted down, "Lanterns to starboard!" and was immediately hushed by practically everyone on board. Tristan stepped up to the rail, spyglass out, as the crew scrambled to attention around him.

"I believe it's the *Squall*," the captain said, lowering the glass.

A sigh of relief whispered around the deck, but the tension didn't slacken.

We followed the ship through the night. Keven repeatedly suggested I get some sleep, but I ignored him, until he finally quieted. No one else seemed inclined to rest either. According to the records kept at the merchants' guild that William had found, the *Squall* typically stayed out to sea for a week, which meant that they traveled at most three days up the coast before turning back.

Which put them a little over halfway to Bosun's Bay.

An hour before dawn, Captain Tristan approached me. "We'll have to turn back to sea, or they'll spot us. And if they make landfall during the day . . ."

"We won't know where," I finished.

I turned to stare out at the faint lights, clearer on the river than with regular eyesight. Tristan had been careful to keep his distance.

I sighed. "Do it."

He pressed his lips tight, turned to give the order, but one of the sailors at the railing suddenly gasped. "She's turning!"

Tristan's spyglass was out instantly. "Riley, hard to starboard. We have to get close to the coast before dawn."

"Aye, sir!"

"Won't they see us once the sun rises?" I asked.

Tristan grimaced. "That's a chance we'll have to take. The cloud cover will help."

I glanced toward the east, toward where the clouds were beginning to lighten.

Tristan began to pace, taking out his spyglass to check on the ship ahead, snapping it closed to pace again.

Keven joined us, and Brandan, both with dark circles under their eyes.

The sky lightened, the gray clouds rushing by overhead, low, threatening rain, turning the sea the color of slate below. The coast came into view, a dark band on the horizon, and the *Reliant* began a slow turn northward again.

Ahead, the lanterns on the *Squall* went out.

Keven muttered a black curse.

"Did they see us?" I asked sharply, stepping up to Tristan's side, the urge to rip the spyglass out of his hands and look for myself almost too great to suppress.

"Hard to tell," he said. "It could just be light enough they aren't necessary anymore." He sucked in a sharp breath.

"What?" I gripped the handle of my dagger hard, knuckles white. "What is it?"

He lowered the spyglass, turned toward me. "They've turned inland. They're headed toward an inlet."

"Is there anything there? A town? A village?"

He shook his head. "Nothing on the map."

I scanned the distance, where Lord Demasque's ship couldn't be seen in the grayness, not by the naked eye, not without lanterns, and not using the river.

I growled. "I need to get closer."

Tristan's lips pressed together so tight they turned white, but all he said was, "The boats."

An hour later, Keven, Tristan, Brandan, and I, along with an escort of ten guardsmen from both Amenkor and Venitte, sloshed through the surf onto the sandy beach, two crew from the *Reliant* pulling the boats we'd used onto shore behind us, the *Reliant* anchored within sight.

"The inlet shouldn't be more than half an hour north," Tristan said.

I nodded, motioned the guardsmen, Tristan, and Brandan forward.

We ran up over the edge of the dunes, sand flying, and plowed through the grass and into the trees, turning northward.

Twenty minutes after that, sweat slathering our backs, rain hissing down in a heavy drizzle, we topped a low rise and stared down into the inlet.

Through the windblown downpour, the *Squall* lay anchored, sails tied down. Men swarmed along the beach, three boats already grounded, two more in the water, one heading toward land, empty, the other heading toward the ship, fully loaded.

Brandan gasped. Keven swore, colorful and harsh.

Tristan turned toward me, his face utterly expressionless. "Heavens help us. They're working with the Chorl."

✛— Chapter 12

Behind his desk, Lord March stilled, his face utterly expressionless.

But his voice was not. It held a rumble, faint, as of distant thunder. Muted, but threatening.

"What did you say?"

Tristan shifted. "Lord Demasque appears to be working with the Chorl."

Silence, during which Lord March did not move, barely seemed to breathe.

I glanced toward Avrell, the First's lips pressed into a grim line, toward Brandan, who stood behind Lord Sorrenti. None of us were seated. We'd been ushered into the room as soon as we arrived, everyone else escorted out.

"If I didn't know you, Tristan," Lord March finally muttered, "I would call you a liar."

Tristan bowed his head. "I was there, Lord March. I saw them."

"What, exactly, did you see?"

"Lord Demasque's ship, the *Squall,* sailed north from the channel. They followed the coast for a day and half, along the standard inner coastal shipping lanes. We trailed them at night, headed for deeper waters during the day, and picked them back up the next night. Just before dawn, they turned into a well-known inlet, south of Bosun's Bay, near Fairview.

"We could not follow them into the inlet without being seen, so we anchored south of the inlet and put to shore using the long-boats. The Mistress, Brandan, and I, along with an escort of guardsmen, hiked to the ridge south of the inlet."

Tristan took a deep breath, loath to continue, but the pause was not long.

"The *Squall* had anchored in the water. Its crew was using boats to carry supplies from the shore to its hold. The Chorl lined the beach, to keep watch, and helped Lord Demasque's crew load the boats. Then, when all of the supplies on the beach had been loaded, they began carrying the Chorl to the ship itself."

As Tristan spoke, Lord March's eyes darkened. Now, the anger in his voice no longer distant, the threat no longer subtle, he asked, "How many Chorl?"

I shifted forward. "My personal guardsman counted at least a hundred and fifty. Along with three of the Chorl Servants and two priests."

Tristan nodded confirmation. "That agrees with the Protectorate's count as well. However, we did not remain long enough to see the ship sail. There may have been more."

"They must have been stacked on top of each other on that ship."

"Yes."

Lord March leaned forward, hands pressed flat onto his desk for support. "There's more, or you would not look so grim, Tristan. Continue."

"We sprinted back to the *Reliant* and followed the *Squall* as closely as possible. They left the inlet near to dusk and we were able to follow them most of the return trip. We didn't want to lose them, didn't want to miss where they put the Chorl ashore."

"And where did they put their . . . cargo to shore?"

Tristan tensed, then answered in a thin voice. "They didn't."

"What do you mean? They must have put the Chorl ashore, they returned to the docks with nothing in the hold."

Tristan swallowed. "I mean, they didn't put the Chorl ashore before entering the channel. They passed through the patrols at the channel's mouth—they're one of the Council's ships, carried Lord Demasque's crest, so they were not searched—and the last we saw of them they were at anchor in the channel."

"Where?"

"Beneath part of Lord Demasque's outlying estates. On the northern cliff face."

Lord March remained quiet a long moment, his nostrils flaring as his jaw clenched.

Finally, his breathing slowed, he met Tristan's steady gaze and said, "The caves."

Tristan nodded. "I believe so, yes."

"What caves?" I asked.

March's eyes flicked toward me. Then he thrust himself back from the desk, began pacing behind its length. "The channels—both the north and the south—are riddled with caves at their bases. Mostly, those caves are useless. The tide and the currents within the channels themselves make any attempt to sail into them treacherous at best. But that doesn't mean that desperate men—smugglers, pirates, merchants who wish to get goods into the city without paying the taxes—won't make the attempt. A significant portion have been successful.

"Lord Demasque must be using the caves to get the Chorl onto his estate without being noticed."

"They seem to have the passage timed so that they enter the channel at night," Tristan said. "They unload the Chorl and the supplies before dawn. Then the *Squall* sails into the harbor—empty—and no one's the wiser. No one has thought to ask the patrols when the *Squall* arrives, and as far as the patrol is concerned, the *Squall* is where it should be."

March grunted as he paced, head lowered, one hand stroking his trimmed beard, the other supporting his elbow. No one spoke.

Until he halted, abruptly, and looked at Tristan.

"This is a member of the Council of Eight. I cannot accuse him of treason. Not without proof. And the Council will not accept your word, Tristan. Or yours, Mistress." Here, he nodded toward me, his mouth twisted with regret, with anger. "The Council is too fragile at the moment. Such an accusation would rip it apart."

"I understand," Tristan said.

I felt a surge of anger, my hand dropping to my dagger. "But this means that the Chorl are already within your city."

Lord March nodded. "Yes. Hundreds of them. Perhaps thousands, if every voyage of the *Squall* has indeed carried Chorl within its hold."

"You cannot simply let this go," I spat.

Lord March's eyes narrowed. "This is not your city, Mistress." His voice was dangerous, almost a warning.

"No, it is not," I said, and met his gaze squarely. "But if the Chorl seize Venitte, it is not just your city that will be affected. The entire Frigean coast will suffer. Every city, every village, every inlet. Including Amenkor." I felt Avrell still beside me, felt his approval. But for the moment, there was no one else in the room except me and Lord March, nothing but his cold, dark eyes. Tristan, Brandan, Sorrenti, and Avrell had faded into the background, become gray. "Don't pretend that I'm not part of this fight, Lord March. There is more at stake here than the Council of Eight, more than even the loss of Venitte."

Lord March frowned at the harshness of my tone. "What do you suggest?"

I turned toward Sorrenti, who straightened. "You can find the Chorl. You can verify that they are at that estate."

He held my gaze a long moment, knew what I was asking. He had access to the Stone Throne, could use it to see the city, as I'd used the Skewed Throne to search for the person responsible for stealing food from the warehouses this past winter.

But Tristan was in the room, had already frowned, brow furrowed. Not everyone in the room knew of the throne, knew that Sorrenti controlled it.

Sorrenti bowed his head slightly, chose his words carefully, his voice laced with warning. "I'm sorry to say that my . . . influence does not extend that far, Mistress. Venitte is a much larger city than Amenkor. My reach is limited."

"I see."

I hesitated, then turned toward Lord March. "Then raid Lord Demasque's estate over the channel. Find the Chorl. Drag them before the Council of Eight and make your accusation then."

Lord March considered this in silence for a long moment, then laughed, the sound short and sharp, the grin that followed twisted. "I can't, Mistress."

"Why not?"

"This isn't Amenkor. Unlike you, I am not the absolute power here. I can't order the Protectorate to raid a Council member's estate without at least a majority of the Council's approval."

"Then get it."

"Getting such approval isn't easy," Lord March said, voice rising. "I barely got them to agree to the existence of the Chorl, to allow the use of the Protectorate and the general guard to defend against them."

"Do it without their approval."

"I can't!"

"You are the Lord of this city," I insisted. "You need to do something to stop this!"

Lord March's palm slammed down onto his desk, ink bottles and ledgers rattling at the force of this blow. "This is not Amenkor! I don't have that power!"

Everyone in the room grew still. In the silence following Lord March's declaration, everyone looked anywhere but at him, at me.

Jaw clenched, the muscles in his neck tensed, Lord March took a moment to collect himself. In a tightly controlled voice, he said, "I cannot use the Protectorate in such a fashion. Not against one of the Council members. It would destroy me."

And then Avrell, silent until now, stepped forward. "Then don't use the Protectorate."

Both Lord March and I frowned.

"What do you mean?" Lord March asked.

"Don't use the Protectorate—or the general guard—for the raid. You have Amenkor guardsmen at your disposal. We aren't under the Council of Eight's authority. We can raid Lord Demasque's estates without the Council's approval."

I nodded, my hand wrapping around the hilt of my dagger.

Lord March's frown deepened. "The Council would never allow it. They would never *believe* it. They would claim that you brought the Chorl with you, as you did with Ottul, your Chorl Servant, that you placed them on Demasque's estates to implicate him."

"Not," Lord Sorrenti said, taking a single step forward, "if there were representatives of the Council there to witness the raid. Brandan could represent my interests."

March shook his head, but the tension had drained from his stance. "The Council is aware of our ties, Lord Sorrenti. We would need someone else from the Council, someone not so closely allied to me."

Sorrenti nodded, hand raised to stroke his beard as he thought. "What about Lady Casari and Lord Boradarn? Their word would carry weight with the other Lords and Ladies of the Council. And everyone knows that Lady Casari and I . . . have had our differences."

Lord March grunted, shoved away from the desk. He strode back and forth, considering.

After a long pause, he turned back. "Very well. But General Daeriun will have to approve of it, and will very likely wish to send his own observer. When do you plan on attempting this raid?"

"It will have to be soon," Tristan said. "We don't want to give Lord Demasque a chance to learn of the raid, nor the chance to bring in more Chorl. And we should do it before the influx of people for the Fete begins in earnest."

"What Fete?" I asked.

Everyone halted in consternation. Sorrenti broke the silence. "It's a five-day carnival. It culminates in a Masquerade in the Stone Garden, Venitte's central square, on midsummer's night. People from all along the coast come to celebrate it. They will begin arriving in caravans and on ships from regions all along the coast in another week. I'm surprised you haven't heard of it."

I shook my head. "I grew up on the Dredge."

Avrell sighed. "I'm afraid that in our haste to depart, we did not come prepared for the Fete."

"I'll have Brandan put together what's necessary for your group."

"In the meantime," Lord March said, and all eyes turned toward him, "coordinate the raid with Daeriun."

"The formations look good, General Daeriun."

Daeriun turned from his position at the top of the wooden tower overlooking the training fields of the Protectorate inside Deranian's Wall to see who had spoken. Distracted, his brow creased in concentration, he acknowledged Lord Sorrenti with a nod before turning toward me. Surrounded by guardsmen in the blood-red-and -gold regalia of the Protectorate, he grunted and motioned one of the runners closer. "Tell Captain Farel that his flank is falling behind. They need to move into position faster." As soon as the boy took off, he barked to the rest of the men on the platform, "Signal a reset. I want these men to *move!*"

Flags were raised, guardsmen waving them steadily back and forth, and on the field below—where at least four units were spread out between the barracks on one side and Lord March's personal estate on the other, including a group from Amenkor led by Captain Catrell—men broke and began marching back into their initial positions, dust from the trampled field rising into the air. General Daeriun motioned for Lord Sorrenti and me to join him at the railing of the tower.

"It's going better than expected," Daeriun said, almost grudgingly. "Captain Catrell has been helpful. He's explained the tactics used by the Chorl in the attack on Amenkor, in particular how they used their Servants to push through the armies to the city walls. And the Chorl Servant you captured has been invaluable."

On the field below, I saw Catrell pull the Amenkor guardsmen back, noticed that Marielle, Gwenn, Heddan, and Ottul were among the ranks.

"You're using the Servants in the training."

Daeriun looked toward me, then back to the field. "It was Catrell's idea. And Lord Sorrenti's." He motioned to the field. "At the moment, the Amenkor unit is acting as the Chorl attackers. Your Servants are using their Sight to aid in the Chorl's advance, as they did in the attack on Amenkor, or so I'm told." He nodded toward the Venittian men. "I've incorporated some of the Venittian Servants into our own units in an attempt to counter the attack."

"While you were on the *Reliant,* chasing after the *Squall,*" Sorrenti added, "I had your Servants meet with those here in Venitte, to explain how the Chorl Servants operate. It was . . . informative."

"What about Ottul?" I asked, watching her closely on the field below. It was easy to pick out her blue skin and black hair among all of the rest of the Amenkor guardsmen. "Has she cooperated?"

"More than I expected. More than your other Servants expected as well. But they say that since the last few days on the *Defiant,* Ottul's attitude has completely changed."

Since I placed the White Fire inside her. Queotl.

I saw again the reverent expression on her face—the sheer awe—and frowned.

"In our first few trials," Sorrenti continued, his mouth twisting into a self-derogatory grin, "she laughed at our attempts to mimic the Chorl. Apparently, we weren't being vicious enough."

"No," Daeriun said. "It isn't viciousness. It's directness. According to what Catrell has told me—and your Chorl Servant has verified—the Chorl move directly toward their objective. There is no strategy involved. No attempts to outmaneuver the opposing forces, no subterfuge at all. They have a goal, and they move directly on that goal, using whatever advantage they have available."

On the training field, all of the units were once again in place. A horn blew, and everyone on the tower platform tensed, moved to the railing to watch, their muted conversations cut off. The first horn fell silent. Orders were barked on the field below, banners raised, men fidgeting. Marielle and Gwenn stood near the front of their ranks, near Catrell, with Ottul and Heddan farther out on either side. After a moment, I could pick out Sorrenti's Servants mixed among the Venittian ranks. Their uniforms were slightly different, the surplices longer, and they seemed to wear less armor. They also kept close to the front.

And then a second horn blew, a longer note this time, and Catrell's force surged forward, the men screaming. I gave a start, then realized they were mimicking the battle cries of the Chorl, their strange high-pitched ululations, and I smiled. I could see Catrell's sword raised as he charged, saw Marielle moving alongside him.

On the far side of the field, the Protectorate closed in, the central unit moving forward, the two to either side holding back slightly. They didn't charge, didn't break their ranks, the men moving in tight formation. Those in the forefront held their shields at the ready.

Catrell's advance was chaotic in comparison.

A moment before the two forces met, Marielle and Gwenn unleashed a rain of fire toward the central Venittian unit. I felt the gathered force release, fire arcing up over the battlefield, and felt a visceral twist in my gut as the attack on Amenkor flashed before my eyes, as I tasted the bitter moment when the first tower exploded, followed closely by the second. My hand fell to my dagger as the fire began to descend onto the Venittian ranks, as it dropped from the heights—

And then, to my side, I heard Sorrenti grunt.

The fire struck a shield, one that I had not felt form, but whose edges became apparent as the fire was shunted off to the side, out of harm's way. But the Venittian ranks beneath the shield faltered as the flames crackled above them, some men continuing the organized march forward, but many hesitating. A few raised their own shields up over their heads to keep the fire away, or to block off the heat that radiated down through the invisible shield the Venittian Servants had formed to protect them. Enough of them that the forward momentum of the Venittian army halted.

I could taste the army's fear, like blood in my mouth.

On one side, Daeriun spat curses as the Venittian force halted, its initial precision crumbling.

The left and right flanks began to close in as Catrell's men hit the forefront of the Venittian's central unit. The front ranks collapsed, and Marielle and Gwenn shifted the focus of the fire toward the incoming support, joined by Ottul and Heddan on either side.

Daeriun bit off another curse, motioned harshly toward the other captains on the tower, and another horn blew, calling the battle off.

"Fools!" Daeriun spat, leaning heavily onto the railing as the battle scene below ground to a halt. "They know that the fires will be shielded by the Servants, and yet they still cower in fear!"

"Not all of them," I said.

Daeriun turned to me with a dark look. "Enough to destroy the order of the unit."

I thought about what Brandan had told me in Amenkor, about how the Servants in Venitte were ostracized by the rest of the Protectorate. "It's because the regular Venittian guardsmen don't trust them."

"The Servants have never been integrated into the fighting force," Sorrenti added. "Not like this. They've always been kept . . . distant, sent to the College for research, left to train amongst themselves. You can't expect the army to welcome them with open arms when you yourself, and the captains of the Protectorate, isolated them."

Daeriun's eyes darkened, but he didn't answer, turning his black gaze out onto the field. The river roiled, the silence on the tower suddenly cold. "What is it that you want?"

I looked toward Lord Sorrenti, who shifted forward. Ignoring the tension, voice carefully neutral, he said, "Lord March would like your approval of a raid on Lord Demasque's northern estates. A raid to be conducted by the Amenkor forces, with a few representatives from the Council as witnesses."

Daeriun caught Sorrenti's gaze, straightened, giving him his full attention. "Why?"

"Because Demasque is working with the Chorl," Sorrenti said. "He has them hidden on his estate, and Lord March cannot risk sending the Protectorate onto a council member's personal estates."

"So he's sending Amenkor instead." Daeriun's gaze settled on me and I felt myself stiffen. "You realize the risk he's taking by sending you? If the Chorl are not there, if this is a mistake, he will not be able to support you. He will lose some of his support and control in the Council."

"I know."

Daeriun snorted, as if he didn't believe me. But he turned back to Sorrenti. "When do you plan on sending this raid to the estate?"

"Tomorrow night. Lady Casari, Lord Boradarn, and I will send representatives with the Mistress. Would you like to send your own representative?"

Turning his back to both of us in dismissal, gazing down on the training field, Daeriun said, "Oh, no. I'll be coming along myself."

"There it is."

I looked to where General Daeriun pointed, across a moonlit stretch of wheat fields, the stalks waving in a faint breeze, silver and gray. A road cut up through the field toward a low wall, an arched gate, three buildings behind—a small manse, a stable, and a larger storage building. The wall cut off a small section of land near the cliff face, ending abruptly at the edge.

There were lanterns lit within the manse in at least two windows. As we watched, someone carrying a torch moved from the manse to the stable. A servant.

I frowned. There should be more light, more activity. The manse was too quiet.

Daeriun turned toward the group of guardsmen coming up behind us, led by Westen and Catrell. All of them came from Amenkor except for five— Daeriun, Brandan, Tristan, a man named Thad representing Lady Casari, and a woman, Sarra, from Lord Boradarn. The last two wore frowns.

"Are you certain this is the estate?" Thad muttered.

My hand kneaded the hilt of my dagger. His voice had a faint whine, and he hadn't shut up since we'd left Venitte.

"Yes," I said, tightly.

"It doesn't look like anyone's here except servants," Sarra said. Her tone was clipped, as if she hated being here, had been ordered here against her wishes.

I cast Westen and Catrell a worried, irritated look. Westen shrugged. Catrell didn't respond at all.

I turned to look at the expectant guardsmen behind me, at their pale faces, nothing more than blurs in the moonlight, at the Skewed Throne symbol stitched onto their chests—red for the Seekers, gold for the regular guard— then back to the manse.

A prickling sensation coursed up my arms.

"Something's not right," I said.

"What do you mean?" Thad said sharply.

I shook my head.

"Then perhaps we shouldn't enter the estates," Thad said, even though I hadn't responded. "Perhaps we should return to the Merchant Quarter. This entire enterprise is a mistake."

My hand tightened on my dagger, and I turned to Thad, feeling a twinge of satisfaction when he stepped back a pace. "You're here to represent Lady Casari, at Lord March's request, not as a commentator. I'd advise you to shut up."

Thad snorted, but didn't answer, grumbling something inaudible under his breath, his eyes cold with anger.

Sarra frowned, but relaxed slightly when General Daeriun said, "Let's get on with this."

I met his gaze in the moonlight, saw the challenge there, could feel it pulsing on the river. He didn't trust us, didn't trust me. But he'd come himself, because he wanted to see Catrell and Amenkor's men in action, wanted to see how they fought, how they worked as a group, in real battle, not on the training fields. And he wanted to watch me. Lord March had accepted me as Mistress; Daeriun had not. He'd reserved judgment.

And he wanted to see the Chorl for himself.

"Very well." I motioned to Westen and Catrell, both of them stepping forward sharply. They'd seen General Daeriun watching as well.

"Mistress," Catrell said. Westen simply nodded.

"Westen, you and the Seekers go in first. Subdue the servants if you can. If there's any sign of the Chorl Servants or priests, come back immediately. Brandan and I will have to be at the forefront if they have Servants with them. Otherwise, we'll give you twenty minutes, then I'll send in Catrell and the rest."

Westen motioned to the other three Seekers and within moments they were gone, lost among the shadows in the wheat fields.

General Daeriun's frown deepened as he tried to pick them out in the darkness. He stepped up to take Westen's place, Brandan and the other two observers hanging back.

"There will be at least twelve servants in an estate of this size. Are four Seekers enough to subdue them all in such a short amount of time?"

"Yes."

Daeriun glanced down at me, at the utter conviction in my voice. I didn't look away from the fields, from Westen and the other Seekers' progress.

"They've reached the wall."

"How can you tell?" Daeriun asked.

"Because I can see them."

Daeriun grunted.

I caught Brandan's gaze in the darkness, saw him smile slightly and nod.

Ahead, the torch that lit the shuttered windows of the stable flickered and suddenly went out. For a brief moment, no more than a breath, a shadow appeared near one of the manse's windows and then it was gone.

Daeriun's breath stilled, held—

And then the light in the main manse died as well.

I heard Sarra mutter a mild curse, heard Thad whisper harshly to her, "And we let these men walk free in Venitte?"

I smiled. "Catrell?"

"It hasn't been twenty minutes yet."

I turned and he nodded, trying hard not to smile as well.

"I'll send them in now," he said.

I'd made my point to Daeriun, to Thad and Sarra as well. Let them report back to their respective Lords and Lady.

The guardsmen formed up around us, Catrell calling out orders as armor creaked, as swords were drawn, the rustle of over a hundred and fifty men getting ready for battle. Sinking deeper beneath the river, I felt their tension, their fear being channeled into heat, into sweat and readiness. Their breath caught on the air, someone coughing, another spitting to one side, but their faces were calm, almost anxious to begin.

Thad edged closer to Daeriun, eyeing the men with suspicion. Sarra cast him a sidelong look of disdain.

"Stay to the road," Catrell said.

And then they were moving, not running, but jogging down the road in the moonlight, a black shadow slicing through the silver of the wheat, heading straight for the gates of the manse.

As the last of the men passed, Daeriun muttered grudgingly, "Impressive."

I said nothing, focused on the estate below.

The force hit the gate and split, half surging forward toward the manse, the other half heading toward the storage building. A smaller force broke off and headed toward the stable.

The door to the manse was breached, men rushing inside. The stable door gave with no resistance, guardsmen charging into the room beyond.

On the rise, the entire raid happened in eerie silence.

Too much silence. I frowned.

"I don't see any Chorl," Thad said smugly.

I shot him a dark glare, but then men emerged from the manse. Catrell and Westen. I could tell by their stance.

"I think we can join them now," I said, and started downslope without waiting for the others, staying close to the road, paved in the manner almost all roads in Venitte were paved, with wide flat stones. I felt General Daeriun follow, Tristan, Brandan, Sarra, and Thad not far behind, but I ignored them.

"What happened?" I said the instant I passed through the gates of the manse.

Westen and Catrell turned. The rest of the guardsmen were milling about in the open courtyard between the buildings.

"There's no one here, no Chorl, no supplies, and barely any servants," Catrell reported, his voice without inflection, although he was clearly troubled. "We're searching the grounds now."

"I told you this was a mistake," Thad muttered.

I glanced toward Westen. "Did you find anything?"

"The storage building has been used recently. There are heavy gouges in the floor, obvious markings in the straw and dust that something had been stored there and moved within the last few days. Markings on the grounds indicate it was loaded into carts, but once the carts reached the road . . ."

He trailed off and I grimaced. There would be no markings on the road.

"What else?"

He frowned. "In the stables." Motioning us forward, he pulled open the stable doors, the musk of horses, straw, and dung wafting outward. Thad wrinkled his nose in disgust, raised one hand to his mouth, but when the rest of us entered without hesitating, he followed suit. A horse snorted and shook its head as we passed, coming to the edge of its stall, watching us with large dark eyes, but Westen headed to the back of the stable.

To an open trapdoor in the floor.

I moved up to its edge, stared down into its dark depth. I could see stairs leading downward, felt a breeze brush against my face.

A dank breeze, heavy with salt and the taste of the sea.

My nostrils flared. "Where does it go?"

"The Seekers followed it to the caves beneath the cliffs, all the way down to the channel. There's a dock down there, recently built, at least three boats tied there. And they found this."

Westen held out his fist, opened it to reveal a thin black cord, or rather, three cords twined together. Tied to the cords at intervals were shells of various sizes and colors, most smooth and mottled, a few spiny and sharp.

The necklace sent a visceral shiver of hatred through me.

I drew back, caught Westen's gaze, Catrell's, both of whom looked grim.

Anyone who had survived the attack on Amenkor knew what these were. The Chorl had worn them, on their wrists, around their necks, braided in their hair. Like jewelry.

And the men who had tortured Erick had worn them.

Sarra, Thad, and Daeriun leaned forward.

"What is it?" Daeriun asked.

"A necklace," Tristan said shortly. "Worn by the Chorl."

Thad snorted. "And how do you know?"

Tristan met Thad's gaze. "Because I saw the Chorl wearing them when they attacked my ship."

"But there are no Chorl here," Sarra said skeptically, turning toward me. "How do we know your Seekers didn't plant this here?"

"You don't," I said flatly. "But we certainly didn't build the dock in the cave below."

Sarra grunted in agreement. She still radiated doubt, but there was a sheen of belief to that doubt as well.

"What about the servants?" Daeriun asked suddenly. He'd leaned back from the shell necklace, turned now to Westen and Catrell. "Has anyone questioned the servants?"

Westen nodded. "I did. They know nothing. In fact, all of them were sent to the estate yesterday morning. They said there was no one here when they arrived."

"And you believe them?"

"Yes."

Daeriun nodded his head.

"Then we have nothing," Thad said shortly. "You've wasted our time and insulted Lord Demasque as well."

Then he turned and stormed out. Sarra hesitated, frowned down at the wide trapdoor, large enough to allow two men to climb up at once, large enough to heave a crate through, or a barrel, but then she left as well.

Brandan and Tristan stepped forward and watched them go.

"This is not going to go over well in the Council," Brandan said grimly.

"No, it's not," Tristan agreed.

I snorted. I could already feel the pit of my stomach churning with nausea. In rage, that somehow Lord Demasque had known we were coming, had moved the Chorl to another location. And in the thought that I'd have to face Lord March and the Council members with nothing to show for it except a braided necklace.

"But there is one thing."

Everyone turned toward the low, rumbling voice, toward General Daeriun, who faced me.

"You've convinced me."

"It will require all of us, working together, to do what you want, Liviann."

The Council of Seven stood in the center of the obsidian chamber, clustered around two granite thrones. Liviann stood immediately before the two stone structures, a small smile touching her lips, a strange light in her eyes. Alleryn reached forward, tentatively, and touched the stone, her hand brushing down the rough granite. She frowned, trading a glance with her sister Atreus. A meaningful glance, although I couldn't tell what it meant.

"Why are the seats so blocky, so rough?" she asked.

"I wasn't trying for aesthetics," I said. "And you've seen the stones the Servants have been using to focus their powers. The stones change shape. The effect is relatively minor in the stone they use, but if we do this, if we actually attempt to create these two thrones, I think the effect will be much more . . . severe."

"Meaning?"

"I don't think they'll remain this shape for long."

Alleryn's frown deepened.

Liviann turned toward me. "When can we start?"

"Wait," Seth said. "We, as a council, haven't even decided whether we want to do this, Liviann. From what Cerrin says, this . . . procedure sounds dangerous. It doesn't even sound as if the thrones will be stable."

"And do we really need them now?" Atreus added. "With the stones that Cerrin created, the Servants have been able to upset the balance. We've spread the

Servants out through the armies, managed to drive the Chorl out of all of our supply lines, pushed them back to a few of the coastal cities. Their own Servants are falling on all sides, to the point where they rarely risk them in battle anymore."

Liviann snorted. "But the Chorl aren't gone, Atreus. They've been pushed to the edge of the coast, yes, and we have Garus to thank for that. And Cerrin, of course. But that hasn't resolved the real problem—the Chorl themselves. They're hanging on to the coast—"

"We'll have them uprooted before winter sets in," Garus interrupted, cutting Liviann short.

"But will they be gone?" Liviann snapped. "No! They'll retreat. Back out into the ocean, back to wherever they came from. But they'll know that we're here, that we're vulnerable. They'll rebuild their forces, train new Servants, and they'll be back." She took a step toward Atreus, the youngest of the Council straightening, her chin up, nostrils flaring, not retreating beneath Liviann's menacing step as the older Council member came a little too close. "That's why we need the thrones. Because this threat won't be ended when the Chorl retreat. It will remain. The Chorl will figure out a way to counter the effect of the stones and they'll be back."

Liviann withdrew slightly, ran her hand over the arm of one of the thrones, almost a caress. "This tipping of the balance in our favor is only temporary," she said, her voice more calm. The smile had returned to her lips, but now it hardened. "We have to protect the Frigean coast at all costs."

Seth looked as if he would continue to protest, his eyes black. He'd taken a step toward Alleryn and Atreus, created a subtle division between the members of the Council, Liviann, Garus, and Silicia on one side. I stood trapped in the middle.

Garus had seen the division as well. He watched Seth with a slight frown. They'd been partners for over forty years, had their arguments, their disagreements.

But never over something as incendiary as this. On the Council, they almost always agreed, as Atreus and Alleryn almost always agreed.

"We need the thrones," Garus said, to the whole Council, but he kept his focus on Seth, and there was an admonition in his voice, almost a warning. "The Frigean coast needs the thrones."

Seth stiffened. "We've survived without them. The Chorl will retreat. And they've managed to disrupt our supplies enough that the coming winter won't be easy. We should conserve our energy for surviving that. The Chorl won't be returning in force any time soon. We have time."

Garus drew in a deep breath, ready to argue, the intention clear—

But Liviann intervened. "Enough. I call for a formal vote."

Garus stilled, jaw clenching. "Very well. I think my choice is clear."

"And mine," Seth said.

*Alleryn and Atreus shared another look. Atreus nodded, and Alleryn said,
"The two of us oppose the creation of the thrones."*

Liviann frowned, turned to Silicia. "And you?"

*"I don't see where creating them now or later makes much of a difference. I
vote to create them."*

"As do I," Liviann said.

Everyone's gaze fell on me. All except Garus.

"It appears that it's up to you, Cerrin."

*I stared into Liviann's eyes, saw the hunger there. She wanted the thrones, not
to protect the coast, but because they would represent power. For the Council, of
course, and she would die with the Council's name on her lips. But she wanted the
thrones for herself. She wanted to rule the Council.*

*I knew I should oppose her, knew I should never have built the thrones, never
have brought them before the Council, before her. The stones I'd created for the
Servants were nothing compared to the thrones. The stones were temporary, could
be wielded in the battlefield until their power was drained and then discarded.
The thrones . . .*

*But I was tired. Tired of the Chorl, tired of the Council, tired of living with the
harsh, ever-present ache in my chest. An ache that could never be filled, could
never be alleviated, could never be broken.*

Except by death.

*The creation of the thrones would require a sacrifice, would require a death.
Without it, the effects—like the stones the Servants now used—would only be
temporary. Even with all of the Council combined, the thrones would not last
beyond a year without a death to solidify the Threads, to hold them. And Liviann
wanted the thrones to survive beyond that, wanted them to survive all of the
Council member's deaths.*

One sacrifice. One death.

*I closed my eyes, felt the ache . . . there . . . beneath my breastbone. A pulsing
ache, throbbing with every beat of my heart. An ache that felt warm with sunlight,
that reeked of the flowers on the veranda above the sea, that grated with the
sound of children's laughter.*

I'm so very tired, Olivia.

*I sighed, the sound heavy and long, and opened my eyes, felt the faint sting of
tears in the back of my throat.*

Drawing a slow breath, I said, "I am the Builder."

And what does Lord March say? Eryn asked, and even though she sat alone in
the garden outside her own rooms, surrounded by sunlight, by large white-
flowered vines and large-leafed shrubs, the sky above blue and cloudless, the
air clear, she broke into hacking coughs.

Through the White Fire, I could feel the spasms as they shook her. Eryn's stomach tensed as the pain seared through her abdomen and into her chest, into her legs. A liquid pain that seemed to burn her very bones. I could feel her weariness through the pain, could feel her stubborn refusal to give in to it.

When she finally quieted, the cloth she had held to her mouth was stained bright red with blood. Not dotted with tiny flecks, or even small spots.

The cloth was saturated.

Eryn tried to hide it, barely even glanced toward her hand before she closed the cloth into a tight fist.

But I hovered inside her, had released myself enough from the Fire that I felt her wince, felt her jaw clench in mute acceptance and denial, hiding the cloth even as she straightened her shoulders, swallowed the taste of blood, of sickness. I heard her breath through her own ears, heard the harshness of it, the throaty, fluid denseness of it.

Well? she said, her inner voice harsh, layered with warning. She reached for her tea, sun-steeped, tried to smother the copper taste on her tongue, in her throat, with its bitterness.

Lord March has said nothing. I haven't spoken to him since we agreed to raid Lord Demasque's estate. I've asked for an audience, but have heard nothing. Not from him, not from Lord Sorrenti, Tristan, nor Brandan.

Because it's a political disaster, Eryn said, slamming her glass down and fighting back another coughing attack. *Not only did you find nothing, but you entered one of the Council member's estates with your own forces.*

I had an escort, I said sharply. *Members of the Council of Eight knew what we intended, what we expected to find.*

And now they're all scrambling to lay blame, and you're their scapegoat. They'll be trying to convince the other Council members that it was you who convinced them that Lord Demasque had hidden Chorl on his estate, that you tricked them into joining the raid, that they never believed he would do such a thing. Half of them are probably telling him they sent a representative because they knew it couldn't be true, that they were there to protect Lord Demasque's interests, not their own.

Lord Demasque won't believe them.

Eryn snorted. *He won't. But he'll pretend that he does. And since you know the Chorl were there, since everyone on Tristan's ship knows it, he'll use their scramble to get into his good graces to discredit you even more.*

But General Daeriun believes the Chorl were there. He must have some influence on the Council.

Not when it comes to the Council of Eight. Eryn frowned. *But he does have influence over Lord March. And if everything you tell me is true, Lord March believes you as well.*

It was meant to be soothing, because even though I was only present in her mind, in the White Fire at her core, Eryn knew I was nervous. I kept running through the raid over and over in my head, picturing the silvered wheat, the manse, seeing the empty storage building with the traces of straw and dust where crates had obviously rested days, perhaps hours, before the raid.

And the tunnel. The tunnel to the caves, to the small dock, the water lapping up against the stone, the boats bumping against each other where they were tied. They'd even rigged a hoist, to get the heavier crates and barrels through the steepest parts of the tunnel and into the stable.

How long has it been since you slept? Eryn asked, the question casual, cutting into my silence.

I almost didn't answer. Then, grudgingly: *I haven't slept well since the raid.*

Because of the raid? Because of Lord March?

That, and because of the dreams.

Dreams of the throne?

Yes. I hesitated. *They're stronger than before, deeper, more intense. It's harder to withdraw from them afterward.*

Because you're close to the second throne. Because you're under its influence there in Venitte. Sorrenti has already admitted that it's still there, that it's still in use.

I didn't answer.

Are they the same kinds of dreams as you were having here?

Yes. Cerrin's dreams mostly, about the previous attack on the coast by the Chorl. He's the one who designed the thrones. He's the one who sacrificed himself to create them.

Eryn grimaced. *They all sacrificed themselves to create the thrones.*

Yes, but that wasn't the intent. It should have only taken one sacrifice, according to Cerrin. He meant to kill himself, to escape his wife and daughters' deaths, to escape that pain.

Eryn stilled, suddenly thoughtful. *But something went wrong?*

I don't know. He thought that he'd die and that the others would continue ruling the coast without him. I don't think any of the others knew what he intended. I don't think he told them. They were already split about whether to create the thrones in the first place.

Eryn considered this for a long moment, lost within herself, then seemed to return.

You should return to Venitte, she said. *Lord March will summon you shortly, I'm certain.*

There was an undertone to her voice, something she wanted to keep hidden, something new that I could not quite sense, not without taking control of her through the Fire. Something to do with the Skewed Throne.

I thought about doing just that, taking control, just enough to find out what she'd been thinking . . . but then I relented. Because whatever it was also had something to do with her sickness, and that was a private pain, one that I already knew I could not help her with, even through the Fire. We'd already tried.

And so I retreated, pushed myself up and out of the Fire, up and out over Amenkor, the sight of the city—the walls, the outer city, the wharf with three ships at dock and five more under construction, the encircling arms of the harbor and the newly broken ground where the wall would be built—somehow calming. Then I sped south, along the coast, toward the pinprick of fire in the city of Venitte, where Gwenn and Heddan had linked themselves to me so that I could Reach this far.

As I sped over land, Venitte almost within sight on the horizon, I caught movement, caught the last vestiges of power as someone used the river. I slowed, glanced down at the ground speeding past beneath me—

And saw the Chorl, saw rank after rank of them, marching down a road, through rolling hills, spilling out onto the surrounding grassland, dotted with little copses of trees, the darker green paths of creeks. A huge line of supply wagons followed the army itself, stretching back into the distance. At the head of the army, riding on horseback, sat Atlatik, his face set, expressionless, the lower half of his left ear sliced off. The tattoos on his face stood out in the sunlight, and his eyes were fixed on the horizon.

On Venitte.

He was surrounded by other Chorl warriors on horseback, all of them uncomfortable astride their mounts, their faces set in scowls or grimaces. Four of these carried huge banners on poles, all four banners carrying the spined seashell that had been emblazoned on the Ochean's sails as she entered Amenkor's harbor. The banners were a variety of colors—green, gold, blue, and purple.

Behind this group were Chorl Servants, some trudging along the road in their sandals, most seated or curled up on pillows and blankets in carts and wagons. Mixed in among the Servants were priests dressed in yellow shirts and brown breeches, carrying scepters of reed with brightly colored feathers and shells tied to them.

I didn't see Haqtl.

And behind them: Chorl warriors. Hundreds of them. Thousands. Their multicolored tunics vibrant in the sunlight, their dark blue tattoos harsh and clear against their lighter skin.

I gasped, felt my heart falter.

Then I spun and fled toward Venitte, toward the city that waited on the coast only three days distant, toward the Fire that burned in its Merchant Quarter inside of my own body.

I fell into that body, felt myself shudder, felt Gwenn and Heddan pull back their conduits as I heaved in a gasping breath, lurched forward, then fumbled as I tried to catch myself and my arms refused to move, tingling as if the blood had drained from them, already beginning to tremble with the use of the river.

I heard Gwenn gasp, felt her reach forward—

But it was Erick who caught me.

"The Chorl," I gasped, my voice hoarse, weak with disuse.

"What about the Chorl," Erick said.

And then I realized it was Erick who had caught me.

Erick, not Keven.

I stared into his face, at his slightly grayer hair, shocked, afraid to touch him, even though he already held my arms, too afraid to move for fear that he'd step back and leave me again.

And he grinned.

"Erick," I said, and then I was sobbing into his chest, trying to control it, but trembling from weakness, from the exertion of sustaining the river for so long, for so far. I breathed in the scent of his sweat, tasted oranges, acrid and sharp, on my tongue, smelled for a brief, bitter moment the warmth of fresh bread, flour, and yeast . . . and everything felt right, everything felt normal again.

Erick held me close, rocked slightly back and forth. I could feel his pulse through his shirt, could sense a lingering weakness there, the last traces of his illness, of his torture, knew that there would still be a harsh red scar on his chest above his heart, one that might never fade. But he was healing, had healed, would continue to heal.

And he was here. Awake. After all the long months.

Finally, after I'd calmed, I pushed away, my arms no longer weak, no longer trembling. It should have taken me longer to recover, even with Gwenn and Heddan there to help me; I'd been gone much longer than expected, had spoken to Eryn longer than I intended. But I shoved the niggling concern aside and focused on Erick. I looked him in the eyes, held them, searched them as I asked, "Are you back?"

He smiled, but it carried with it a layer of blackness, a bleakness that I didn't think would ever go away. Not after what Haqtl had done to him, not after what he'd endured at the hands of the Chorl. "Yes. Westen is satisfied with my recovery. And Isaiah has finally given me leave to return to duty."

"What about Keven?"

Erick's face went blank. "Would you rather have him as your personal guard?"

I gave Erick my harshest glare and his blank expression cracked, just a little. A flicker of mirth, that was quickly smothered and put back under control.

In a dead serious voice, he said, "Keven and I have agreed that you are far too dangerous a person to be allowed to run free, and so we've decided that we will both be required to guard you."

I punched him in the stomach and he doubled over, gasping, faking extreme pain. I knew he was faking because I'd barely touched him. Westen and the rest of the Seekers had taken him almost instantly after he'd been freed from the blanket of needles, had brought him back from his deathbed fast. He'd seen the attack coming, had already shifted out of the direct line of the punch.

When he saw me smile, he straightened. "Now," he said, truly serious this time, all humor gone from his voice, "what about the Chorl?"

"I saw them, on my way back from speaking to Eryn in Amenkor. They're just north of the city."

"How many?"

I sat back into my chair. "Thousands of them."

Erick's jaw set. "We knew they were coming. It was only a matter of time."

Behind him, Gwenn and Heddan exchanged a look.

And then Avrell stepped into the door to my rooms, William a step behind, Alonse shadowing them both.

"Mistress," the First said, his voice anxious, "Lord March and the Council of Eight has sent a summons."

"What can I expect?" I asked Avrell as the carriage trundled through the streets of Venitte toward Deranian's Wall and the council chambers.

The First shook his head. "I have no idea. Lord March could side with you, or not. The other Lords and Ladies may side with you, or not." He sighed, grimaced. "At the very least, you can expect Lord Demasque to attack you, your credibility. And you can't use your dagger to defend yourself."

I turned away from him, the occupants of the carriage—Avrell, Erick, William, a few other guardsmen—falling silent. Avrell glanced toward Erick, who shrugged, but I ignored them, stared out at the city as it passed, my stomach churning. With anger, with anxiety, with fear.

After a long moment, I felt someone's hand enfold mine. I clutched at it desperately with both hands, breathed in William's scent on the river, drew in the comfort he offered. I turned toward him, caught his smile as he squeezed my hand, saw Erick's accompanying frown and quick questioning look toward Avrell beyond him, then turned back toward the window.

Outside, I could see the first signs of the upcoming Fete. Merchants had placed sheaves of grain above their doorways, tied ribbons to their signs or hung wreaths on their doors or in their windows. The hawkers and peddlers in the streets had shifted their wares toward the summer harvest, the first few squash appearing, bright yellow and deep orange, a few mottled with green spots. Tomatoes and cucumbers filled one cart. A woman stood at a street corner, a long thin basket tied to her back, the giant heads of vivid sunflowers sprouting from the top, their centers black.

Reaching for the river, I could feel the mounting excitement in the air. Like that in Amenkor before the festival I'd thrown to celebrate surviving the Chorl. But it was tainted, and I thought about what Tristan had said. That the rumors of the Chorl had penetrated the depths of the city of Venitte, that stories were being told of the attack on Amenkor, of the attack on the ships sailing out of the harbor, of the loss of Bosun's Bay and the Boreaite Isles. I could feel the uncertainty those rumors caused on the river, could taste the sourness beneath the anticipation of the Fete. It gave my nausea over the upcoming Council meeting a dagger's edge, and I swallowed its bitterness down as I settled back into my seat.

Then we passed into the shadow of the Wall.

The carriage pulled up to the same wide steps that led to the rectangular pool of water in the plaza surrounded by columns outside the Council building. There, a group of Protectorate greeted us, the commander of the unit bowing crisply.

"General Daeriun sends his regrets," the commander said, straightening as Erick, Avrell, William, and the other guardsmen stepped out of the carriage onto the stone of the roadway. He caught and held my eyes. "He told me to tell you that Lord March sends his regrets as well."

I frowned, but before I could ask anything, the commander turned and barked an order, the Protectors on all sides re-forming around us as he led the way up the steps.

"What was that about?" Erick asked, stepping in close so that only Avrell, William, and I could hear him.

"It was about the Council meeting," Avrell answered, his voice tight. "It's a warning."

"Lord March and General Daeriun aren't going to support us," William added.

I nodded.

And then we were inside the Hall itself, passing into the shadow of the foyer and through into its outer room. Erick's eyebrows rose as he took in the size of the room, the ornate marble flooring, the massive banners and detailed carving of the support columns, but he said nothing, his eyes falling to the people, to the clerks and pages, merchants and guardsmen that dotted the outer room. But none of these people were important, so in the end his eyes turned toward the two massive doors that led into the Council chamber, toward where the commander of the escorting Protectorate had paused, had turned to await our approach.

"The Council of Eight is already waiting," he said.

And then the doors opened and we were led inside.

I slid beneath the river as I passed through the doors. I thought I had prepared myself for what I would find there, but it still made me hiss. A sound so low that only Erick and Avrell heard it, and both of them knew instantly what it meant.

I felt each of them tense, felt Erick bristle and turn, his back slightly to me, facing outward, protecting me, his hands falling lightly to his side. A casual pose, but one deceptively calm. Avrell stepped forward, his chin high, shoulders back, meeting the hostile stares of the Council of Eight directly, protecting me as well, but in a different way, defiant and challenging. William stepped into his place at my side, his hand also falling to the sword at his side.

The Amenkor guardsmen that accompanied us reacted to Erick's, William's, and Avrell's stance, stepping up sharply on all sides, hands on hilts, creating a half circle with Erick and William on its inner edge, Avrell ahead, leaving just enough room for me to pass through its center.

I lifted my head, nostrils flaring for a moment, letting the river course around me. All of the council members were in attendance, watching me. Lord Demasque stood to the left, one hand reaching down toward the table, fingers resting there lightly. His jaw was set in indignant rage. Lord Sorrenti sat to the right, his face impassive. Lady Casari and Lord Boradarn both frowned, and Lady Parmati smiled. A spiteful smile, full of malice and triumph. Lord Aurowan and Lady Tormaul were quiet, and Lord Dussain seemed slightly confused, almost apologetic.

I ignored them all, let their emotions wash over me on the river as I stepped forward, through the opening between Erick and William, until I stood near Avrell's side but slightly ahead of him. I faced Lord March, noted Captain Tristan off to one side.

"Lord March," I said, without nodding. "The Council of Eight . . . requested my presence."

To one side, I heard Lord Demasque snort in disgust.

Lord March did not react at all. "We summoned you, yes. Lord Demasque has a grievance he wishes to make public and clear, against my recommendation." A few of the Council stirred at this, but Lord March ignored them all, turning toward Lord Demasque instead. "You may proceed, Artren."

Lord Demasque nodded sharply. "Thank you." He seemed oblivious to the warning in Lord March's voice. His entire attention was on me. Drawing a deep breath, gathering his rage around him, he began, "Three days ago, you and your guardsmen raided one of my holdings, an estate on the cliffs over the channel."

"Yes," I said.

It interrupted his flow. The muscles in his jaw flexed as he clenched his teeth. "Why?"

"I believe you know why."

"I want to hear you say it."

I shrugged. "Because you are working with the Chorl."

"No!" he spat, slapping a hand down on the table. "I am not dealing with the Chorl, as your *raid* clearly indicated. You found no Chorl on my estate, you found no smuggled goods, no blue-skinned demons, nothing! And yet you persist in maligning my name by suggesting that I am working with the Chorl!"

I waited until he'd calmed slightly. "We found a recently built dock, boats to transport cargo. And we found this."

From inside the sleeve of my shirt, I withdrew the braided strand of sea-shells. They clattered together as the braid unfolded, like beads.

Never taking my eyes off Lord Demasque, I said, "There *were* Chorl on your estate, Lord Demasque. Someone informed them of the raid, and they left before we arrived."

"Nonsense," Lord Demasque spat. "You have one of the Chorl in your party. She could have made that trinket so that you could plant it on my estate."

"And the dock?" Lord March asked. "The boats?"

Demasque spluttered for a moment, then muttered, "They were installed for my own pleasure, so that I could gain access to my manse without the need to come all the way in to port."

"I see."

Demasque stiffened at Lord March's tone, but gathered himself together. "All of that is beside the point. You were *summoned*," he said, spitting out the word, "here, Mistress, before Lord March and the Council of Eight, because during the course of your *raid* you not only maligned my name before the Council, spreading vicious rumors about me that you cannot prove, but you also damaged my property severely. My crops were destroyed, my servants were terrorized to the extent that they will no longer work for me, and the buildings on the property were damaged by your guardsmen.

"You overstepped your bounds, Mistress, if indeed you can be called such with the Skewed Throne destroyed by your own hands. This is Venitte, not Amenkor. You have no rights here. You are here at our mercy, at our whim. I request reparations for the damage that you have done, and a reprimand, if not formal expulsion from the city."

My jaw clenched and I felt rage boil up inside me, the urge to reach for my dagger so strong the muscles in my arm tensed with the effort to keep still, to not move. Not because he questioned my rule as Mistress, but because Lord Demasque lied. The servants had been taken before the guardsmen even entered the estate, the buildings had been left untouched. And only a small portion of the crops had been trampled when Catrell and the guardsmen descended upon the gates.

My gaze flicked toward Lady Casari, toward Lord Boradarn. Boradarn met my gaze steadily, his lips pressed thin, but Lady Casari stared down at the desk before her, brow creased, troubled.

I caught Lord Sorrenti's eye. He shook his head slightly, mouth grim.

And suddenly I thought of what Eryn had said, that they would scramble to lay blame.

And I was their scapegoat.

Feeling the rage burning deeper, settling into my bones, I turned back to Lord Demasque. My hand clenched on open air, the need to feel the hilt of my dagger stronger than before, but I flexed it, drew the hand into a fist, knuckles cracking at the tension, and forced the fist down to my side.

Dipping my head, narrowing my eyes, letting Lord Demasque see the anger in them, I said in a tight voice, "I . . . apologize. For the raid, and for any . . . damage my men may have caused to your lands."

Lord Demasque stood silent, his own eyes narrowing, then said, "That's not enough. You're a danger to Venitte's people, to the safety of its port. I want you out of the city."

"That's enough," Lord March said, his voice echoing in the chamber. "You overstep *your* bounds now, Lord Demasque."

Demasque glared at me, eyes black with intent . . . and tinted with smugness. He knew he'd won.

For a blinding moment, I was reminded of Bloodmark, of the gutterscum's viciousness, of his hatred.

Gutterscum always recognizes gutterscum.

I straightened, knew then that Demasque was a mark. It didn't matter that this wasn't Amenkor, that here in Venitte I wasn't Mistress.

I let my hand slide onto the hilt of my dagger, saw Demasque's gaze flicker, saw the skin around his eyes pinch, saw the smugness falter.

And then Lord March said, "Mistress."

I turned, dismissing Demasque with the gesture. But the anger and intent still burned inside me. "Lord." Terse and clipped, on the verge of being disrespectful.

Lord March frowned. I had not removed my hand from my dagger. "The Council will decide upon a sum for the reparations, which will be sent to you for your approval."

"And should I load my ships—my men and my Servants—and depart for Amenkor?"

He stilled, and on the river I felt his own anger, his own rage, not directed toward me but toward the Council, toward Demasque and Parmati.

Keeping his voice neutral, he said, "You may do as you wish."

I snorted, cast one last scathing glance around at the Lords and Ladies, saw

Lady Casari flinch, saw young Dussain's bewilderment, then I spun toward Avrell, William, Erick, and the rest of my escort.

"We're leaving the Council hall. *Now.*"

Erick barked an order, completely unnecessary. The guards were already forming up, closing in around me protectively as I stalked out of the hall, their eyes flashing hatred and derision to either side, making it clear that anyone taking a step toward me would regret it.

We passed through the outer room, clerks and merchants falling abruptly silent to either side, and then we reached the open air, sun glittering down on the water in the rectangular pool, banners snapping in the wind to either side.

Ahead, General Daeriun waited by the side of the water.

I slowed a moment, let my rage boil to the surface, then sped up. "You know Demasque lies," I hissed. "You were there."

"I know," Daeriun said, resting his hand on the pommel of his sword.

"Then where were you? You could have confronted him in the Council."

Daeriun's eyes flashed. "Lord March ordered me to stay away, and before you condemn Lord Sorrenti, Captain Tristan, and Brandan Vard, you should know he ordered them to remain silent as well."

"Why?"

"Because Demasque already has the majority of the Council on his side. Lord March can't do anything until we can prove that Demasque is indeed in league with the Chorl, and right now we have nothing but a string of shells and belief! We need something more!"

I clamped my mouth shut, stared up into Daeriun's rigid face, realized that he was furious as well, that the hand that rested on the pommel of his sword had clenched.

I reined my rage in with effort, and stepped back a pace.

"We don't have much time to find it," I said tightly. "The Chorl are already north of the city."

⊢— Chapter 13

"What do you mean they're north of the city?"

Daeriun had gone completely still.

"I saw them," I said. "I saw them marching south."

Daeriun glanced around, and for the first time I noted the Protectors who stood off to one side, obviously accompanying Daeriun. But there were merchants and pages and clerks running to and fro as well, the pool a blur of activity.

"Come on," Daeriun said abruptly, motioning toward his own men. "I'll accompany you back to your estate."

We descended to the carriages, Daeriun opening the door and ushering Erick, Avrell, William, and me inside, then glancing around the steps before climbing in himself.

He waited until the carriage was in motion before speaking, his voice deadly serious, his eyes locked on mine.

"What do you mean you saw them? How could you have seen them?"

"I used the river."

Daeriun frowned in confusion, but then Avrell said, "What she means is that she used the Sight, the power that rules the thrones, that makes her a Servant."

Daeriun nodded, the frown fading. But not far, and I recalled what Brandan had said on the ship, that the Servants of Venitte were Protectors, but that they were merely tolerated, not accepted.

Daeriun might be the leader of the Protectors, might even be using the Servants of Venitte in his own units, but he wasn't comfortable with the Servants in general.

Shifting in his seat, Daeriun asked, "What did you see?"

For a moment, I considered not telling him, the anger over Demasque and the Council still burning deep inside me. But I shook that anger aside. I didn't have many allies in Venitte. Daeriun might be a grudging ally, even an uneasy one, but he was still an ally.

"I saw Atlatik—"

"The Chorl general," Erick put in.

I nodded. "He's the head of their army, the leader of the Chorl warriors. He was leading a march south toward the city. The army was being followed by a wagon train of supplies. He also had a group of Chorl Servants and priests with him."

"How far north were they? When will they reach the city?"

I shrugged. "I don't know. A few days, at a guess."

"Probably a little longer," William said. And then, when I looked toward him with a frown, he added, "The movement of the armies is controlled by their supply wagons. Atlatik can only move as fast as his food."

Daeriun swore. "That's still within our outer outposts. We've heard nothing from them."

"Perhaps they haven't reached the outposts yet," Avrell said.

Daeriun shook his head. "We expected a runner from the outermost outpost last evening, and he never arrived. That's not unusual, so we hadn't grown concerned yet. But with this news . . ."

He trailed off into thought, the carriage jouncing and rumbling around us.

Then he glanced sharply toward me.

"Can you find them again?"

I nodded. "It requires a lot of power without the throne, though. I'd have to have help from the other Servants with me. And even then I can't sustain it for long." Not without a Fire to anchor me, like the one I'd placed within Eryn, and not for such a distance.

"Good." The carriage began to slow and he glanced out of the window, grimaced. "I need to recall as many of the Protectorate as possible from the outposts. Now, while there's still time to get them back to the city before the Chorl arrive. In the meantime, Lord March suggests that you and your men," he glanced significantly at Erick, indicating the Seekers, "remain on the grounds. Lord Demasque will be looking for any excuse to push his request that you leave the city. Don't give him one."

When the carriage stopped, Daeriun opened the door and left, stepping quickly across the open courtyard toward the gates, vanishing into the city streets beyond.

"He's kind of brusque," Erick said, stepping out of the carriage behind me.

I snorted.

"Are you going to listen to Lord March's suggestion?" Avrell asked.

I turned a blistering glare on him, but he did not flinch. "Find Westen and Catrell," I said.

"What for?" Avrell asked.

"I want to speak to Ottul. We need to find out what the Chorl are doing, and she may be able to help."

"I don't know," Ottul said, the shape of the coastal words somehow wrong coming from her mouth, clipped and harsh, with strange inflections.

I almost growled in frustration, glanced toward Catrell, who sat beside me in the chambers given over to the Servants and Ottul, toward Erick, William, and Avrell who stood behind us, then turned back to Ottul, Gwenn standing to one side. Marielle and Heddan were seated farther back. Westen had not been found yet, still on the streets of Venitte somewhere, watching Demasque.

"Perhaps she truly doesn't know," Catrell said. "She was captured in Amenkor, before the Ochean was killed."

"We aren't asking the right questions," Avrell said. "She won't know what the Chorl are doing now, but she might be able to tell us enough about the Chorl themselves so we can figure that out for ourselves."

"Like what?" I asked, impatience cutting the words short.

Avrell frowned, thought about it for a moment, his hands tucked into the sleeves of his official First's robes, then said, "We need to know how they'd react to the Ochean's death. We already know that there are three components to the power structure of their society—the Ochean and her Servants, Haqtl and the male Servants, and Atlatik and the warriors. We know that those three were in relative balance with the Ochean alive. What would happen once the Ochean was killed? How would the balance of power shift?"

Ottul had listened intently to Avrell as he spoke, but her brow was now creased in complete confusion. She looked toward me, bewildered.

"Gwenn, can you help?"

Gwenn sighed. "I can try."

She turned toward Ottul, screwed her face up in concentration for a moment, her expression so serious it brought a faint smile to Catrell's lips, and then she began speaking to Ottul in the Chorl language.

Everyone in the room shifted forward, almost unconsciously. Everyone except Erick. I could feel his anguish, knew that he trembled with it. Because of what Haqtl had done to him, what the Chorl had done to him. Since his return, Ottul had been kept in her rooms or at work with the male Servants and Protectors in Venitte. He'd only seen her at a distance. But now, up close, with her sitting in the same room . . .

He wanted to kill her. I could feel him fighting the urge, could feel him trembling with it. He'd barely controlled himself when he'd entered and seen her, didn't think he could control himself if he came any closer. I could feel the tension roiling on the river. He didn't want to trust her, a viscerally emotional reaction, and the only thing that kept him from following that urge was the knowledge that I'd placed the White Fire inside of her, that if necessary I could claim control of her.

I'd never seen him this close to losing control.

Ottul asked something, Gwenn answered, and then Ottul spoke at length, watching both me and Catrell, her gaze shifting back and forth, but staying mainly on me.

When she finally finished, Gwenn turned toward me. "She says that with the Ochean dead, the power would shift to Haqtl."

"Not Atlatik?" Catrell said sharply. "Not to the Chorl warriors?"

Gwenn shook her head. "No. Haqtl would take over, because she says the Chorl warriors believe in the gods, that they believe in the Fire of Heaven. She says that Atlatik will be forced to follow Haqtl because otherwise the Chorl warriors will rebel against him. They'll kill him and replace him."

"What about the female Servants? Won't a new Ochean be chosen?"

"Not right away. Ottul says there would be a battle." Here Gwenn frowned. "A *ginset,* where the most powerful of the remaining Servants who have gained the seven rings fight to see who will be the new Ochean."

"I doubt Haqtl would allow a new Ochean to be chosen given these circumstances," Avrell said.

"No," I agreed, thinking back to the memories I'd shared with the Ochean before her death. "The Ochean and Haqtl were struggling for power even before their homeland destroyed itself."

"So Haqtl is in control," Catrell said, then caught my gaze. "If that's true, then why wasn't he with Atlatik and the Chorl forces moving south?"

"Because," I answered, "he's already here, in Venitte. He must have been part of the forces Demasque brought into the city."

"But where are they?" Avrell said in frustration. "If they aren't on Demasque's northern estates, then where did they go?"

I suddenly thought of Sorrenti. "I don't know. But they have moved. Perhaps Sorrenti will be able to find them now with the Stone Throne. If they've moved farther into the city, if they've entered its influence . . ." I trailed off, then turned toward William, who straightened. He'd been silent through most of the discussion. "Perhaps you can find them, through the guild. If Demasque is hiding a force here, maybe there's some trace of it in the guild's records."

William nodded. "I can also look into what property he owns in the city, find out where he might be hiding Haqtl and a Chorl force of significant size."

Catrell shifted, catching everyone's attention. "You realize that if Haqtl is in the city, with a Chorl force to support him, that it represents a fundamental change in the Chorl's tactics. They're no longer being as direct as they were at Amenkor."

"What does that mean?" Avrell asked.

"It means we won't be able to predict their strategy as easily," Erick answered tightly.

The room fell silent, the tension breaking a moment later when Steward Alonse knocked on the door and entered. His gaze flickered over everyone in the room before settling on me. "Mistress, Brandan Vard has arrived with a trunk from Lord Sorrenti. Should I allow him in?"

William stiffened, but I ignored him and nodded to Alonse.

Brandan entered a moment later, followed by two Venittian men carrying a large, heavy trunk made of a pale wood banded with metal. He paused a moment, nodded toward Avrell and Catrell, then motioned for the men to set the trunk down.

"Mistress," he said. "I hope I'm not interrupting?"

"We were just finishing, Brandan."

"I see. Well, Lord Sorrenti asked that I deliver this." He reached down to open the trunk as he spoke. "It contains the costumes you'll need for the Fete." Pulling out some of the contents, he added, "Here's your mask. And here's your costume."

He held up a blue dress—deep blue, like the ocean—and a white mask fringed with white feathers on top, glittering waves of blue spreading from the corner of the eyes to the edge of the mask.

I frowned, then stood and took the mask in hand and turned it over, noted the cord used to tie it in place around my head, then shoved it back into Brandan's hand.

"I don't wear dresses," I said flatly.

"What's wrong?" Brandan muttered, mortified. "Is it the color?"

Avrell sighed and shook his head. "It's nothing personal, Brandan."

Heddan and Gwenn had both risen and moved toward the trunk. They started rummaging through the contents. Even Marielle's interest had been piqued. Gwenn squealed with delight, sliding a beaked black mask over her head. A ruff of feather floated in the air as Heddan tied the mask in back. Her face was completely covered, nothing but her eyes visible, and even those were mostly in shadow.

With the black costume on that went with the mask, you'd never know it was Gwenn.

I frowned, watching Gwenn, thinking about the Chorl, about masks, about Haqtl and blue skin, then turned back to Erick, to Catrell, William, and Avrell, catching their gazes.

"I know when the Chorl are going to attack," I said grimly.

"During the Fete," Lord March said, his voice flat.

"Actually," Avrell responded, glancing toward General Daeriun and Lord Sorrenti, standing to either side of Lord March on the stone balcony inside March's estate, "during the Masquerade on the last day of the Fete."

From this vantage, I could see the back of the domed building where the Council of Eight met, the College where the Servants of Venitte studied barely visible to one side.

"It's perfect," Sorrenti said after a moment. "They're wearing costumes and masks to cover their skin, to hide the fact that they're Chorl. Which means they can move about the city freely, without attracting attention, because everyone else in the city will be in costume, most of them wearing masks. Even if the mask slips and someone catches a glimpse underneath, sees blue skin—"

"They'll assume the person is wearing face paint," General Daeriun growled. "Catrell is right. The Chorl have changed their strategy."

"Demasque's influence, no doubt," Lord March said.

"And Lady Parmati's." When I turned a questioning look on Sorrenti, he shrugged. "The masks, the costumes—that came from Parmati. She's always loved the theater."

"So what can we do to stop them?" Lord March asked.

"Cancel the Fete," I said.

General Daeriun snorted, then fell silent when he realized I was serious. Sorrenti's face was utterly blank, but I could sense his amusement on the river. He leaned back and stared out toward the Council chambers, squinting at the harsh glare of the sunlight on its white-gray stone.

Lord March turned away from the view, toward me. "That's impossible."

I bristled at his tone, but caught myself, forced myself to relax. I was still upset over being left to defend myself at the Council meeting in front of Demasque, of being abandoned. "Why?"

March almost sighed. "Because the Fete isn't something I can control. It's tradition. There are too many people involved. Even if I attempted to call it off, to cancel it, it wouldn't be effective. The people of this city would rebel, they'd hold the carnival anyway, in defiance if nothing else."

"And it's not just restricted to the city," Sorrenti added. "The Fete is coastal. People travel from all reaches of the coast to come to it. Merchants come from Marlett, from Kent and Merrell, from Warawi in the southern isles, and the coastal cities beyond. Some of them rely on the Fete as their main source of income. If we cancel it—if that were even possible—they'd lose everything."

"But we have to do something," I said, and heard the frustration in my voice. I didn't try to hide it. "What about banning the masks? We'd at least have the chance to see their faces. The Chorl warriors all have tattoos. They won't be able to hide those without the masks."

March frowned. "We can try. But the people of this city spend months planning their costumes, in particular their masks. Even if we explain why we're banning the masks, that may not stop them."

"We can also use the returning patrols from the outposts to set up a perimeter around the city. They can search any carts traveling into the city. The patrols at the mouths of the two channels leading into the city have already started searching every ship that enters the harbor, whether they're owned by Council members or not." Daeriun grimaced. "But if Haqtl and his force is already inside the city . . ."

"And they are." Short. Clipped. I turned to Sorrenti. "Have you used the throne to search for them since the raid on Demasque's estates?"

Sorrenti nodded. "As soon as I realized they'd moved. I tried to find any sign of their passage, searched every building within the throne's limits. I've even followed Demasque. Nothing."

"Keep looking," Lord March said. "The Fete begins in a few days. We don't have much time."

"It's Demasque's whore," Westen said as soon as he entered the outer room of my chambers in the estate.

Heddan glanced up from where she sat working on embroidery, made to set the material and stitching aside so that we could have privacy, but I waved her back to work.

"What do you mean? And where were you?" I said from the window, where I could see the streets of Venitte crowded with revelers. The Fete had started. Raucous music erupted from the city at random intervals, faint this far from the main streets, punctuated by shouts, screams of laughter, bursts of ribald song. The people I could see from the window passing by the estate's gates were dressed in vivid colors, lengths of cloth streaming out behind them, some dressed in feathers. Their faces were painted to look like animals—mostly birds, the symbols of the Lords and Ladies of the Council, a few with long piercing beaks tied to their faces like a mask, but some looked like cats or dogs or some animal I didn't recognize. A few wore actual masks, feathered and strangely expressionless, even though Lord March had banned them. Most were decorated with swirls and random symbols.

The face paints looked like tattoos. And the garish costumes reminded me of the Chorl warriors' clothing.

I turned away from the window with a shudder, heard Erick shifting closer so that he could listen.

Westen took a seat close to mine. "I was following Demasque's whore. That's how Demasque has been sending orders throughout the city, controlling the movements of the Chorl and the *Squall* and all of the rest of it. She's the one who contacts the captain of the *Squall* when the ship is in the harbor. The captain met with her last night, on the edge of the Gutter. Tomus was following the captain."

"What did they discuss?"

"Neither Tomus nor I could get that close, not with the Fete starting. But the *Squall* has remained in the harbor since the raid on Demasque's estate. This morning, they loaded up with cargo and departed. According to William, who checked the lists in the merchants' guild, the ship is headed south, to trade with the Warawi in the southern isles. They aren't expected back for months."

Alonse suddenly appeared at the door to the chambers carrying a tray with glasses and tea.

We waited in silence until he'd set the tea service out on the low table before us and departed.

"What about the Chorl? Have you found them yet?"

Westen, still frowning in the direction of the door, where Alonse had vanished, said, "No."

I swore. "They have to be in the city somewhere."

"They are," Westen said, turning back to me. "We just haven't found them yet. Demasque hasn't gone to meet with them, and neither have any of his contacts, including the whore."

"Then either he's waiting for the attention you've brought on him to die down," Erick muttered, "or whatever they have planned is already in place."

I glanced toward him. "I don't think he'd wait to let things die down. He's too arrogant for that."

Neither of the Seekers said anything.

"Mistress."

All of us turned toward the door, and Alonse bowed his head.

"Lord Sorrenti is here," the Steward said. "He wishes to speak with you."

"Let him in."

Sorrenti halted in the door, looked at Erick, at Westen, then came forward. "What does the Council of Eight want from me now?" I asked coldly.

Sorrenti stiffened. "Nothing, Mistress. They are even now arguing with your First on the reparations."

"And you aren't there?"

"No. I excused myself. I needed to speak with you." He hesitated, glanced toward Erick and Westen, toward Heddan, then said, "About the thrones."

The room was quiet for a long moment, and I narrowed my eyes. "What about the thrones?"

Sorrenti remained silent, body tensed, then sighed. "Daeriun claims that you saw the Chorl army, that you told him they were marching southward, were perhaps no more than a few days away. How? How could you possibly see them?"

"I was speaking to Eryn in Amenkor."

"How?" A note of frustration had crept into his voice, as if he thought I were lying.

"I Reached for her, for the Fire I placed inside her."

Sorrenti stilled. "I don't understand," he said. But it was clear that he suspected.

"When the White Fire passed through Amenkor seven years ago," I said, speaking quietly, slowly, "it left part of itself behind. In me. Since then, I've placed a small piece of that Fire into a few people, used it as an anchor for when I Reach."

"So you can Reach all the way to Amenkor. From Venitte."

"Not without consequences," Erick interjected, a warning in his voice.

I nodded. "And using the Fire I can speak to whoever it is I've tagged with the Fire."

He was silent a moment. "But there's more to it than that, isn't there? More than just speech?"

I nodded, thinking of what I'd experienced when Laurren burned to death on *The Maiden,* of Erick's torture at Haqtl's hands, of the cough that consumed Eryn even now. "Yes. Much more."

"You have multiple Talents—the Sight and the Fire and the Threads," Sorrenti said. Not a question. "What of the other two? Do you sense the Rose? Have you been touched by the Lifeblood?"

I shook my head with a grimace. "I'm not an Adept, Lord Sorrenti."

"It would have been nice," he said. And then he smiled. "I suspected you had access to the Fire based on Tristan's report, but it wasn't until Daeriun said you were in contact with Amenkor that I—and the Seven—were certain."

"And what do you know of the Fire?" I asked. "What do the Seven tell you of it?"

He shrugged. "From my studies, from the voices of those who have touched the throne here in Venitte, and from the Seven, I know that the Fire is one of the five Magics, that at the time of the creation of the throne, the members of the Council of Seven could use it, because they were the last of the Adepts. Since then, there has been no Adept on the coast . . . and no one that we know of who could use the Fire, who could even sense it."

"Why? And if no one can use the Fire, where did the White Fires that passed through our cities come from?"

Sorrenti was silent for a long moment, then he shook his head. "No one knows. No one in the throne, anyway, not even the Seven."

But there was a hesitance to his voice.

I leaned forward. "What do they think?"

His expression hardened, then relaxed. "The voices—and those Servants here in Venitte that have been studying the records from the first Fire and before—believe that at one point there were many people on the coast who could use the Fire. Before it first passed over the city, there are even accounts of Servants who could use it, like yourself.

"But then the first Fire came.

"When it had passed, and when the madness that gripped the city in its wake had passed, those that survived found that they could no longer touch the Fire's flames. As if somehow the passage of the Fire through the city had quenched the source.

"For the next thousand years or so, no one on the coast has ever reported being able to use the Fire, to touch it, to manipulate it."

I stilled. "But now, since the second Fire . . ."

Sorrenti nodded. "Now, you can use the Fire. You are the first in over a thousand years."

"There must be others," Erick said.

Sorrenti glanced toward him, not quite frowning. "I'm certain there are, but they haven't discovered how to use it yet. Not like Varis." He turned back to me. "I think that the first Fire somehow sealed access to the Fire away, dampened it to the point that it was almost extinguished—"

"And the second Fire released it," I finished for him, when he ground to an uncertain halt. "But who sealed it away? Who released it?"

Sorrenti shook his head again, his smile twisting. "Someone from the west. Our oldest maps, those from before the first Fire, from before even the Council of Seven, show lands to the west. Not just islands, but an entire continent. As large as our own, perhaps larger. There must be people there. They must have done it, for whatever reason." Then, in a softer voice, "But if they did seal it away and release it, they must be powerful indeed. A working powerful enough to send a wall of Fire all the way across an ocean that we cannot cross. . . ."

He trailed into silence.

I sank back into my seat, thought about standing at the railing of the *Defiant* as we sailed southward to Venitte, staring out across the black waves of the ocean, out toward the Chorl islands, toward what lay beyond. And I thought about the ships Borund was building in Amenkor's harbor. Stronger ships. Larger ships.

An ocean that we cannot cross . . . yet.

"Are we ready?" Garus turned to me, his expression tense, his mouth pressed into a stern frown. Behind him, Seth wore the same expression. They'd been bickering when they entered the room, still arguing over whether or not the thrones should be created. "Are you ready, Cerrin? You're the one orchestrating this."

"I still think that this is unnecessary," Alleryn muttered. "The Chorl have retreated, returned to the depths of the ocean."

"And you've turned half of the Servants to your side," Liviann spat, "even though we agreed that this was not to be discussed among them. There was no reason to get them involved, not until after the thrones were created."

Alleryn bristled. "I felt otherwise. So did Seth and Atreus."

"So you went against the Council of Seven's wishes," Liviann said in a harsh, mocking tone.

"No. I went against your wishes. You are not the entire Council, Liviann."

Liviann flushed with rage, one hand coming up. I didn't know what she intended, but I could feel her power building.

But before the argument—a tired argument, old and useless—escalated, Garus bellowed, "Enough!"

Atreus and I winced; Silicia cringed. The word echoed through the Council chambers, had enough power behind it that the cold white light of the fires Garus and Seth had set to illuminate the room flickered.

Liviann stilled. She kept her arm outstretched, and I saw it trembling, saw the struggle in her face as she tried to control herself. Her power throbbed around her, ready to be unleashed. Alleryn stood, back stiff, hands tucked into the sleeves of her dress. She had not brought her own power to bear, but I could feel its potential, hovering just within her reach.

The moment held, suspended, no one daring to breathe. . . .

But then Liviann's arm dropped.

I shot a glance toward Garus, toward Seth. We'd discussed Liviann's growing arrogance, her slow seizure of the Council. But Garus kept his eyes on Liviann, and Seth remained focused on Garus.

"Now," Garus said, even though the tension in the room had not faded, "are we going to remain civil and do this, or not?"

"Yes," Liviann said immediately, although her eyes narrowed.

Alleryn snorted in contempt, then looked toward me, her head rising slightly. "Yes."

"Good," Garus growled, the warning in his voice clear. He turned toward me. All of them did. "What do you need us to do, Cerrin?"

I straightened, a momentary trickle of doubt seeping through me. But it didn't last, smothered by the grief I'd carried for years, crushed under its weight.

Yet, a surge of excitement did survive.

I was the Builder, and I—we—were about to create something new, something powerful, whether it would be used against the Chorl or not.

Drawing in a deep breath, my gaze settling onto the thrones that sat in the center of the obsidian chamber, I said, "We need to space ourselves out around the thrones."

Garus nodded. The rest of the Seven stepped back, spreading out, Liviann and Alleryn separating with a glare. I'd had the seven seats of the Council pushed back to the edges of the room by the Servants, so that only the two thrones remained in the center of the chamber. Two thrones, each made of granite, the workmanship harsh, blunt, utilitarian. There was no finesse in the stonework, no smoothed surfaces. Such niceties were worthless. They added nothing to the construct itself, no power.

And in the end, it wouldn't matter. The thrones would take whatever shape they wanted.

Whatever shape I wanted.

In the middle of the obsidian chamber, I reached forward, ran my hand over the rough granite.

"You'd better make this quick," Garus said under his breath at my side. "I'm not certain how long those two will remain in agreement."

"It won't take long at all," I said, withdrawing my hand.

Garus didn't hear the finality in my voice. Or perhaps he did hear it and chose to ignore it, as all of the Seven had ignored it for the last few months.

He stepped away, moved into position across from me, next to Seth, his partner. They did not speak, did not even acknowledge one another.

For a moment, I stood in the center of the chamber, the others arrayed around me. I met each of their gazes, nodded to Atreus, who smiled back tentatively. Silicia seemed bored. Alleryn barely met my glance, but Liviann smiled, head lowered.

I frowned at the look in her eyes. At its fervor, at its greed. Her need for the thrones, for their power, raised the hairs at the back of my neck and sent a shiver through my shoulders.

I almost ended the preparations.

But then I sighed, turned, and moved into position, Alleryn to my left, Silicia to my right. Closing my eyes, I reached out with the Sight, found the Threads of all of the others waiting. I drew them in, felt the Lifeblood coursing through them, felt it throbbing in myself, heated and liquid and vibrant. It suffused me, shuddering in my veins as I linked to the others, as I drew them close, felt their own blood rushing through their bodies, their power connecting with mine, doubling it, tripling it—

And then, their power coursing around me, I reached out, opened up conduits to the thrones, felt their solidness, felt their weight.

Throughout the chamber, the white lights that illuminated the alcoves dimmed. The entranceway that sealed us and the working from the outside world wavered, then held and solidified. I heard one of the others gasp.

"Are you certain this will work?" Liviann suddenly snapped.

"No," I said, but before she could respond, I let the power that I'd built—let the Threads that connected us all, the Lifeblood that coursed through the construct, the Sight that I'd gathered and the Fire that I'd pulled from inside me, from inside all of the Seven—release.

Instantly, the power doubled. The Threads snapped taut, threatened to break, and I heard Garus curse, heard the growl in his voice as he strengthened those Threads that connected to him. A backlash of power shuddered through the floor, trembling in my feet, but I held the complex construct tight, felt sweat bead on my forehead, felt the muscles in my body tense against the pressure. The floor shuddered again, and still I let the power build. If this was going to work, the power had to reach a threshold, had to peak at a certain level, had to be maintained—

I gasped as the Threads beneath my grip thrashed, rippled, and snapped as if alive. Pain shot down through my side, sharp and insidious. Reaching out, I gathered more of the Threads to me, tried to splice them, combine them. Atreus cried out, Silicia began to gasp at my side.

And still the power mounted. Sweat ran down my face. My breath grew harsh, ragged with effort.

But we were close.

A pain began to grow in the center of my forehead. A stabbing pain, white-hot with intensity. A pain that was shared through the links, that intensified as each of the Seven experienced it, as we were each melded together through the construct.

"Cerrin!" Liviann barked. "Stop this!"

"Yes," Alleryn shouted, panic tearing at her voice, shredding it. "Cerrin, halt it!"

Another stab of agony, this one deeper, cutting into my core, into my gut, searing through flesh, through bone. My teeth snapped shut, bit into my tongue, and the coppery taste of blood filled my mouth. I staggered, fell to one knee, the smooth obsidian floor sending a sheet of white-hot pain up through my thigh and into my spine.

And with that pain came a moment of clarity.

I can stop it, I thought, through gritted teeth, through the copper taste of blood. I could feel the vortex of power I'd built surrounding me, surrounding us all. I could sense every individual thread of force, could feel that force escalating toward an event horizon, a cusp that, once reached, I could not return from.

But we hadn't reached that cusp yet.

I can stop it right now. I can let the Threads go, release them all.

But then the grief would not end.

Olivia. Pallin.

Jaer.

Then Silicia cried out.

And at the same time, the monumental power that coursed around us, fluid and electric, reached its cusp . . . and slid over.

I gasped, my eyes snapping toward Silicia just in time to see her crumple to the floor, the Threads around her writhing, crackling with her power. Blood snaked from her mouth.

"No," I whispered. "It was supposed to be me."

And then the entire chamber shuddered. With Silicia's death, the power surged higher, grew suddenly oppressive and dark, almost black.

And with Silicia's death, every one of the remaining Seven focused their power on the thrones. It was too wild to release now. It would have to be contained in the thrones. It was the only way to stop it.

Fighting back the pain in my leg, in my knee, I staggered upright. Reaching forward, I forced the collected power into the channels I'd created, felt the others doing the same, all of them suddenly intent with purpose. The thrones throbbed beneath the concentrated channels. The Threads seethed, whipped back and forth, lashed and crackled with hideous abandon. Thunder rumbled through the room, followed almost instantly by another cry, the deep sound cut short.

Across the chamber, I saw Garus stumble, his face a rictus of pain.

And then he collapsed, face forward, hitting the floor with a sickening, meaty thud.

No, I thought, despair washing over me, draining away the strength in my arms, piercing my heart.

Seth bellowed, a sound of horror, of denial and disbelief.

"The construct is too intense!" I shouted. "We have to control it! We have to contain it or it will kill us all!"

But before anyone could react, something slipped. The power rose higher.

And the funnels opened wide.

I gasped, the sudden draw of power intense, sucking the breath from me. I struggled against its pull—the same pull I'd felt from the stones after I'd created them for the Servants to use against the Chorl, a vortex that drew me in, except this was a thousand times stronger. I fought it, felt the others fighting it as well, Atreus with a wild desperation, Liviann with arrogant strength.

But it was too late.

The vortex split, one snaking down and down to the first throne, touching the stone with a sizzling snap of energy I felt crackle through my skin. The second vortex touched, and suddenly it was as if my body had caught fire.

My back arched as the energy of all of the Seven coalesced and flowed through me, my mouth open to the ceiling in a silent howl of anguish, of raw, hideous torture. Seth fell, seizures racking his body, his silk shirt soaked in blood, his heels juddering into the floor as his own scream roared through the chamber and bled into my own. Atreus crumbled without a sound, succumbing to the ferocious pull almost gracefully, the only sign of her struggle a spot of blood leaking from her nose, staining her too pale face.

Alleryn and Liviann held out the longest, both contorted in pain where they stood, both with grim faces, each intent on surviving longer than the other. Alleryn's dress grew spotted with darkness as she began to sweat blood. Liviann's hands were clasped in front of her, her fingernails piercing her skin, clenched so tight her skin was white, the veins standing out like purple bruises. They glared at each other across the room, the thrones between them, power pouring down between them, sucked into the thrones, saturating them, crackling and potent.

And then Alleryn fell.

Liviann collapsed a heartbeat later.

And then there was nothing but the thrones. Nothing but the grief, now a thousandfold worse than before. Nothing but the tears coursing down my face.

Held in a vortex, the Threads that bound it together, the Fire that burned at its core, I had a moment to think, Olivia, what have I done.

And then the thrones swallowed me.

I woke with tears streaming down my face and my body tingling as if with residual energy. Cerrin's horror, his grief, washed over me, choked me, and I rolled to the side, reaching for the dagger beneath my pillow for comfort. My hand closed about its handle—

And then I froze.

Through the doors of my chamber, I could hear voices arguing, too muted to pick out any actual words.

I slid from the bed, dagger in hand, and shifted into the night shadows of the room, edging toward the door, back pressed against the wall. As I passed the window, someone screamed and my flesh prickled.

But the scream degenerated into laughter, faded.

I cursed softly to myself. It was the third day of the Fete, and even in the dead of night the citizens of Venitte celebrated.

And there was still no sign of Haqtl or the Chorl.

Edging forward, I slid through the open entrance to the outer receiving room, wound my way past the tables and chairs, and came up to the outer doors. Breath held, I crouched, listened.

Keven. Arguing with Alonse.

Sighing, I stood and wrenched the door open.

Neither man jumped, but both of them spun, their hissed conversation cutting off sharply, already well on its way to hushed shouting. Keven's hand rested on his sword, his grip white. Two other guardsmen stood to either side of the door.

Blinking into the harsh candlelight of the hall, sensing Keven's disgust, Alonse's agitation, I said, "What is it?"

Alonse flinched at my tone, then bowed. "Mistress, the Protectorate—"

He cut off, and I narrowed my eyes. I'd never seen Alonse so upset. He'd always been perfectly calm, if disapproving.

"What is it, Alonse?"

He straightened, and with a supreme effort, calmed himself. When he spoke, though, his voice still shook. "General Daeriun requests your presence immediately. The Protectors have found something."

"I didn't want to wake you," Keven said, "but he became insistent."

I nodded, noting the lines of tension in Alonse's face. His entire body seemed to be vibrating. "It's all right, Keven. Gather an escort." When Alonse sighed, tension draining from him, his head bowed as he murmured a prayer I couldn't hear, I added, "Quickly."

Alonse glanced up, his eyes dark, intent. "I've already summoned a carriage."

Ten minutes later, I emerged from the estate, dressed in my usual white shirt, brown breeches, dagger within easy reach.

"I tried to get him to stay," Keven said as he held the door to the carriage open before me.

I frowned, stepped up onto the carriage's outer step, ready to ask who, then paused.

Alonse sat in the carriage seat, his eyes wide but his face set, jaw tight. "I have to come with you," he said in a commanding tone. Then he seemed to remember his station as Steward. "Please, you have to let me come with you."

A sudden disquiet settled into my stomach. Somewhere, one of the Fete revelers cried out, the shriek—not quite laughter, not quite terror—smothered by a sudden burst of music.

"Very well," I said, then climbed into the seat next to him.

Keven traded a glance with me as he followed. Two more Amenkor guardsmen joined us.

And then the carriage moved, trundled out through the gates and into Venitte's streets. We passed a drunken group of men, staggering through the dark, bottles in hand. A lone reveler turned his head as the carriage sped by, the piercing beak of his mask startling, feathers sprouting from the mask above his eyes in a tuft of plumage.

"Do you know what this is about?" Keven asked Alonse. His tone was neutral, but Alonse stiffened.

"No," he said, but I could hear the lie in his voice. "Only that they found a body."

"Where?" I asked.

"In the Gutter," he answered grimly, voice thick with a sick dread.

I turned away.

The carriage ascended toward the council chambers, passed through Deranian's Wall, the celebrants crowding together in the Merchant Quarter, then dropping away as we entered the heart of the city. But we didn't halt at the Council chambers, the carriage slipping past the huge domed building, revealing the smaller palace behind, where Lord March resided, and then from there the carriage descended again, down toward where the Wall curved around the inner city, separating it from the slums.

We paused as the gates on this side were opened, then slid through into the Gutter.

I leaned forward, toward the window, breathed in the air that came into the carriage. It smelled of piss and refuse, of decay and sickness, the scent becoming heavier as the carriage meandered down through the streets, farther from the Wall and deeper into the Gutter. The street was still paved with stone, but here it was dirty, the buildings to either side also stone, slicked with grime. I caught sight of a few of the people that lived here, a furtive glance from a huddled figure crouched at the base of an alley, a flash of movement in the gaping emptiness of a window, the shifty movements raising the hackles on the back of my neck . . . and touching off the Fire at my core, the white flames flickering to life, edged with warning.

It was the Dredge, only different. There was no crumbling mud-brick, only well-worn granite from buildings that had once been part of the heart of the city. And unlike the Dredge, there was no transition from the inner city to the slums, no slow descent into shit and degradation. The Wall sliced through the two sections of the city like a dagger, cleanly separating Lord March and the members of the Council of Eight from the gutterscum.

Settling back into the hard surface of the carriage's seat, the ride suddenly rougher as the vehicle ground over the broken surface of the street, I noticed Alonse's grimace of distaste and smiled tightly.

Turning to Keven, I said blandly, "It reminds me of home," knowing that Keven would understand I meant the Dredge.

The Amenkor guardsman grunted. Alonse looked horrified.

Then the carriage slowed with a jerk, halted abruptly.

We stepped out into the shadowed darkness of a slum street in the dead of night. There were no candles here edging windows with warm light, no lanterns hung on street corners. Everything was black and gray, and I slid beneath the river without a second thought, breathed in the familiar stenches, felt the familiar presence of people hunkered in corners and bolt-holes, watching us.

And I felt the particular disturbance that told me where Daeriun and the other Protectors waited.

I moved before all of the guardsmen had stepped down from the carriage, heard Keven curse beneath his breath. Alonse followed at my heels, practically tripping over me. I shot him a glare that he couldn't see, noted his widened eyes, his quickened breath.

I startled the Protectors, stepping out of the shadows at their backs without a sound. One of them barked an order, hand flying toward his sword, the others reacting instantly, clustering around Daeriun at the end of the jagged alley. Daeriun didn't even flinch, his gaze locking onto mine.

It was not friendly.

"You wanted to see me," I said, as Keven and the Amenkor guardsmen filtered out of the narrow at my back to either side. Alonse remained close, peering over my shoulder.

"Yes," he said. "I wanted you to see this. I want you to explain it."

He motioned toward the other end of the alley.

I stepped forward, my shoulders tensing as I edged around the Protectors, their gazes hard, dangerous. The Fire licked upward, and beneath the river I could feel their own tension, their distrust. If I'd been the gutterscum I once was, I would have been contemptuous, but I wasn't, no matter how comfortable the Gutter felt to me, how familiar.

Slipping past them, their presence behind me prickling my skin, I moved toward where Daeriun had indicated, saw a body crumpled to the ground. The man lay on his side, knees tucked in slightly, back toward me. Even without the river I would have known he was dead. Had been dead for at least a day by the smell.

Frowning, I knelt down by his side, glanced toward Daeriun, toward the general's harsh face, stiff frown.

"Do you know him?" he asked.

Turning back, I reached out, touched the man's shoulder, and rolled him toward me.

My eyes settled on the wounds first. He'd been stabbed in the chest, twice, the bloodstains on the clothing still damp. Ship's clothing. A white shirt, a fitted jacket, the embroidery hard to distinguish beneath the blood. My eyes darted up to the man's face, expecting to see Bullick, or one of the *Defiant*'s crew—

I heard Keven suck in a sharp breath, heard Alonse gasp.

But it wasn't the man's face that caught my attention, that forced me to jerk back.

It was the deep cuts in the man's forehead.

Cuts in the shape of the Skewed Throne.

✝ Chapter 14

I stood abruptly, turned on Daeriun.

"The Seekers didn't do this."

"Who else could it have been?" he asked, almost snarling, his anger palpable, leaden on the river.

I stepped toward him, let him feel my own anger, my outrage, the Amenkor guardsmen and the Protectors both bristling at the sudden movement. Daeriun didn't stir.

"I haven't sent the Seekers out to hunt," I growled.

"This is the second body we've found with the Skewed Throne carved into the forehead tonight. Do you expect me to believe that?"

"Yes," I hissed, my voice heavy. "I haven't sent the Seekers out to hunt, Daeriun."

He drew a sharp breath in through his nose, held it, his eyes searching my face. I could see he wanted to believe me, that he needed to believe me. That's why he'd brought me here rather than simply had me arrested, so I could defend myself before word spread. But the body and its discovery was still too close, the smell of death still in the air. He hadn't decided whether he would believe me yet.

"Do you know who he is?" he asked.

I didn't need to look toward the mangled flesh of the man's face again. "No."

With a sneer of disbelief, he said, "It's the captain of the *Squall*."

I started with surprise, glanced down toward the man's face. But I'd never seen him up close, had only watched the men on the *Squall* from a distance. "That's not possible. Westen said the *Squall* left port a few days ago, with the captain on board, headed south, toward the Warawi islands."

Daeriun grunted in contempt. "I don't think he's going to make it."

I spun back, eyes narrowed, tried not to the draw the dagger that my hand now gripped with white knuckles. I felt as if I were under attack, but there was no one here to fight. "Who was the other man?"

Something in Daeriun's eyes flickered, a flash of doubt. He shook his head, but when he spoke there was still a hint of sarcasm. "It wasn't a man. She was a whore on the wharf."

A sudden pit opened up in my stomach, full of bile, and I settled back onto my heels, hadn't even realized I'd shifted my weight to the balls of my feet.

Demasque's whore, the *Squall* captain . . .

Demasque was cleaning house.

And he was throwing the bloody bodies at my feet.

Daeriun must have seen the shocked recognition in my eyes. He hardened, that moment of doubt fading. "Who was she, Mistress?" he asked, breaking through my shock. "Why did you have her killed?"

"It wasn't me!" I spat, and even I heard the hint of desperation in my voice. I forced it down with a dry swallow, feeling the trap closing around me, the alley suddenly more narrow, more enclosed than before, the body of the captain a heavy weight at my back.

Taking a deep breath, I tried for a calm, reasonable voice. "Demasque killed her. My Seekers were following her, were following the *Squall*'s captain as well. That was how Demasque passed information to the ship, by visiting his whore on the wharf and then having her take his messages to the captain."

Daeriun hesitated. The muscles in his jaw clenched. His eyes flicked toward the dead body and his brow creased.

Gathering myself, I stepped forward, so close he was forced to look down at me. In a low, tight voice, I said, "I'm not stupid, General. If I'd wanted them dead, I wouldn't have announced the kills to the Protectorate or the Council by marking them with the Skewed Throne. You would never have found the bodies. And I wouldn't have gone after Demasque's minions. I would have gone after Demasque himself."

Daeriun struggled a moment longer, then exhaled sharply, the breath coming out in a half-formed curse. He paced the end of the alley a moment, halted standing over the figure of the captain, the dead man's eyes staring up into empty space.

I hesitated, then moved to his side.

"He's cleaning up his mess," Daeriun said, tight but thoughtful. Angry.

"Yes. And he's doing it in such a way as to hurt me as much as possible."

"If I didn't know what he said in the Council, if I hadn't been told of his lies . . ."

I didn't respond, my lips tightening. The bastard was clever. He'd done everything he possibly could to damage my credibility, with the help of some of the other Council members.

"I'll want to see the whore's body," I said.

Daeriun grunted. Then he turned away from the captain's corpse, his face grim. "You know what this means."

I nodded. "Demasque doesn't need his network anymore. Whatever it is that he has planned, it's already been set in motion."

Before either of us could comment further, Alonse said, "His name was Bernard."

Both of us turned toward the Steward. He was trembling, and he couldn't take his eyes off of Bernard's body, off of the blood on the captain's chest and the gashes in his forehead.

Whoever had killed him hadn't been practiced making the mark. None of the Seekers would have left such ragged cuts.

Alonse sucked in a choked breath. "And the whore's name was Yvonne."

I narrowed my gaze, saw Keven shift slightly behind the servant, a few of the other guardsmen following suit. "How do you know?"

He must have heard the danger in my voice. With an effort, he dragged his gaze away from Bernard, toward me. "Because I knew her." He swallowed, wincing as if in pain. "Because I reported to her," he said in a dismayed voice. "She was one of my contacts."

I felt myself stiffen, watched as Keven's face grew rigid, the Amenkor guardsmen shifting forward. Alonse seemed unaware of them, his entire attention on me. He stepped forward, hands coming up in supplication, but Keven's hand clamped tight onto his shoulder, held him back. His grip must have been painful, but Alonse didn't react.

"You have to protect me, Mistress," the Steward pleaded. "He'll kill me!"

"Who?" Daeriun barked. "Demasque?"

Alonse shook his head. "No. Haqtl."

I felt the name like a physical blow to my stomach, stepped forward almost without thought and grabbed Alonse by the throat. He jerked back from my rage, but Keven held him, and beneath my hand I felt him shudder, felt his blood pounding through his veins, felt his throat click as he fought down an outcry.

"What did you tell him?" I growled. When the Steward didn't immediately respond, I shook him, spat again, "What did you tell him!"

"Everything," Alonse rasped. "Everything I overheard at the estate."

"Did you warn Demasque of the raid?" Daeriun asked from behind me.

Alonse nodded, and I involuntarily tightened my grip. The servant began to choke, his hands rising to grapple with my wrist.

"Did you tell him about the throne?" I asked, in a voice soft enough so only Keven and Alonse would hear.

Alonse couldn't speak, but through his increasingly desperate struggle for breath, I saw the answer in his eyes.

I released him, thrust him back toward Keven. But as soon as I let go, he collapsed to his hands and knees in the slick grime of the alley's center, coughing hoarsely, barely enough strength in his arms to keep himself upright.

I began to pace, thinking back to Haqtl standing in the throne room in Amenkor, seeing his placid face as he watched me kill the Ochean, recalling the hunger in his eyes when he'd seen the throne. And I remembered his cold fascination with the Fire inside of Erick after his capture on *The Maiden,* the visceral enjoyment he got out of torturing Erick afterward, his slow, twisted smile as he drove the poisoned spine into Erick's chest.

I caught Daeriun's gaze. "He's here, in the city. We have to find him."

"We've already tried!"

"I know!"

I spat a frustrated curse, thought of Sorrenti, of the throne, but he'd already tried to find them as well, thought of the Seekers, but they'd been searching since the moment Lord March had released them from the prison of the estate. And now the Seekers wouldn't have anyone to track. Not with Demasque killing off his network of spies.

Except he hadn't killed off everyone yet.

I stilled, my eyes settling on Alonse.

He'd recovered enough to sit back on his heels, hands raised to massage his throat. He flinched when he caught my gaze.

"Where's Haqtl hiding?" I asked.

Alonse shook his head. "I don't know. I only met with Yvonne."

I narrowed my eyes. Beneath the river, I could tell he wasn't lying. He was surrounded in total defeat, the river shimmering with fear, with weakness, with regret.

"And where did you meet with Yvonne?"

"Near the wharf, the northern side. A tavern in the back streets."

I reached down, grabbed Alonse by the arm and jerked him into a standing position. He didn't resist, although anger flashed through his eyes, there and then gone.

"Take us there," I commanded.

The carriage pulled up to the edge of a flagstone-paved street not far from the wharf. A light rain had begun to fall, casting halos around the few lanterns still lit for the Fete hanging on posts on the street corners.

"That's it," Alonse said, motioning toward a sign hanging above the tavern's door. A marshland bird was painted on the sign, a fish caught in its elongated beak. "The Wishful Catch."

After Keven had shoved him into the carriage, he'd managed to gather himself together, regaining some of the arrogance he'd exhibited since the first time I'd met him on the steps of the estates that had become our prison. The returning arrogance had faltered only once, when we'd halted to examine Yvonne's body. Keven had made him come with us, had forced him to look at the body. She'd been left in an alley, just like the *Squall*'s captain, blood staining her bodice, the material ripped at the seams, her breasts exposed. Her head lay twisted at an odd angle. As we'd stood over her body, the Protectors who'd been left to guard her waiting silently on one side, it had started to rain, the blood that congealed on her forehead where the Skewed Throne had been cut starting to trickle down into her hair.

Alonse hadn't been able to watch, had turned away, hands gripped tightly before him.

With a glance, I'd sent Keven back to the carriage with Alonse. I remained a moment longer.

Daeriun had looked at me strangely, but I'd ignored him. Yvonne had had something I needed.

Now, in the carriage outside the tavern, I stared at Alonse, at the harsh facade he'd pulled over the terror I could feel churning inside him. He'd made no move to escape on the way over here, had said nothing, responding mostly with grunts.

But when he sat back in his seat and caught my gaze, he flinched.

"When did you last meet with Yvonne?" I asked.

He swallowed. "Yesterday."

I turned to Keven. "Hand him over to the Protectorate. We're done with him."

He nodded, and when I reached for the door to the carriage and stepped out into the rain, I found Daeriun waiting.

"Where's Alonse?"

"We won't need him," I said.

Daeriun's brow creased. "But I thought he was going to lead us."

I turned away. I'd already submerged myself beneath the river, had already scented the surrounding area. The rain tasted like iron, the sharpest scent, but beneath it I could sense the rest of the street. The grit on the stone, the smoke from the lanterns, the sweat from a hundred people. Old sweat and new. And the deeper I dove, the more the scents unfolded.

I turned away from Daeriun, from his confusion.

I was no longer connected to the Skewed Throne, no longer had its power behind me, its force. But I'd learned how to track someone using their scent alone while still on the Dredge, had used it to track Garrell Cart, and later, Alendor's son, Cristoph.

And then I'd killed them.

But Garrell and Cristoph had been alive when I'd tracked them, their scents strong. I wasn't certain I'd be able to find someone who was already dead. I wasn't certain how long the scent would linger on the river.

I dove beneath the rain, beneath the smoke. I could feel the river flowing around me, could sense the entire street, the layers of scent like cloth, the oldest smells lingering but fading. I drew the oldest scents close. Normally, I couldn't distinguish between the scents, didn't even bother to try, all of them merging into a flat stench, a miasma of everyone who had passed by recently, but I wasn't searching at random. I needed Yvonne's scent, a scent that I'd found kneeling over her body. Diluted by death, but still there, faint.

Lilac and incense. Heady but still sharp.

If you knew to look for it.

I sucked in a breath through my nostrils, closed my eyes as I filtered through the rain, through the smoke . . . and caught it.

Opening my eyes, I pointed. "There."

Daeriun frowned heavily. "How do you know?"

"Because I can smell her."

Daeriun snorted, as if he thought I were joking, but he suddenly stilled at my expression.

"She entered the tavern from that direction," I said, pointing down the street, "and when she came out, she headed south, toward the wharf."

"How can you tell?"

"Because her scent is stronger to the south. Newer. To the north, it's fading." I hesitated a moment, then added with emphasis. "Fast."

He straightened, shoulders back. The longer he stared at my face, the more nervous his own scent grew. But he took the hint and, still uncertain, barked orders to the Protectors who had emerged from his own carriage.

Half of them swarmed the tavern. Daeriun, with the other half, turned toward me.

"Lead the way, Mistress."

I ran, heard a few of the Protectors curse behind me as they tried to keep up, but I ignored them, focused on the scent, on the thread of lilac and incense, followed it down the street into the depths of the northern wharf, the buildings here closer together, the streets narrowing, beginning a gradual climb up the slope of the surrounding hills to the tops of the cliffs of the northern channel.

When the scent turned abruptly toward the cliffs, I halted, hesitated.

"What's wrong?" Daeriun asked. His breath came in short gasps, but unlike some of the Protectors he was barely winded.

"I expected the scent to lead back to the brothel," I said, glancing at the cross street where we'd stopped. One stretch led down to the wharf, the other up a steep slope. "But she came from the cliffs."

"Maybe she went to see Demasque. That's where his estate is."

I shook my head. "Westen said she never went to his estate, at least not while the Seekers were following her."

"Shouldn't he have seen her get killed? Weren't they following her?"

I shrugged, brow creasing in irritation at his gruff tone. "I haven't spoken to him since she died. But the Seekers haven't been following her all the time. And they certainly weren't following the *Squall*'s captain. We thought he'd left. Recently, I've had them looking for the Chorl directly, searching buildings. Discreetly."

I turned toward the slope, began trudging uphill.

Yvonne's scent didn't move in a straight line, zigzagging back and forth across the street, as if she were dodging people in the crowds. The pattern was strangely familiar, until I suddenly realized she'd been hunting marks as she moved, picking pockets or stealing from carts or unguarded bundles. But she never paused for long, her scent pooling the longest at the mouth of an alley. I could feel her watching the people, as I'd done a thousand times from an alley's mouth on the Dredge, searching for opportunity.

I smiled. Yvonne had been a thief. Gutterscum, just like me.

But the smile faded as I recalled her mutilated face, her twisted neck, and broken body left in a back alley, hair matted with blood.

As we moved farther up the hill, the buildings changed, shifted from the tightly packed, smaller taverns and warehouses along the wharf to wider streets with walled in courtyards and gated entrances. Small at first, nothing more than a patch of land between a wooden or metal gate and the main house. But the higher we ascended the wider the courtyards became, some open enough to contain gardens. The roofs shifted from wood shingles to red clay, patchy at first, some of the tiles missing. The grounds became better kept. The higher we went, the less Yvonne's path meandered. There wouldn't have been enough people for her to hunt effectively. The crowds would have been too thin, the few people traveling mainly servants on foot, with nothing worth stealing, or the rich speeding past in carriages or on carts.

And then, the scent of lilac, of burned incense, began to tatter.

I picked up speed, felt Daeriun note the change and grow tense beside me, the rest of the Protectors following suit. But no one spoke.

I followed the scent as the thread thinned, dove deeper beneath the river until it grew stronger, tasted bile at the back of my throat, a sensation I hadn't felt since I'd overextended myself using the throne with Eryn, since destroying the throne to kill the Ochean. But I shoved myself deeper, nausea digging into my stomach. The scent strengthened and I pushed on, my arms beginning to tremble with weakness, my legs with the strain of running so long, so hard—

And then the scent—even submerged so far beneath the river it felt as if it would smother me—died.

I looked up, the last faint wisps of lilac trembling and dissolving away. . . .

And stared at a gate. A side entrance to a walled estate.

Letting the river go, choking down the sick taste of bile, I reached for the gate's handle and felt Daeriun's hand drop onto my shoulder, halting me.

"What?" I snapped, spinning toward him. "She came from here, from within these walls."

"We can't go in there," he said, his face a rigid mask. A general's mask. But beneath the mask I could see anger, carefully controlled.

"Why not?"

The muscles in his jaw worked as he drew in a deep breath. To calm himself, to steady himself.

Behind him, the other Protectors stood warily as well, not quite looking at me.

Meeting my gaze, his words heavy with meaning, Daeriun said, "Because that's Lady Vaiana Parmati's estate."

"We knew Vaiana supported Lord Demasque," Sorrenti said calmly. He stood at the window of my personal chambers, looked out at the rain that had become a downpour, the clouds thick enough that it looked like it was night outside, not midday on the fourth day of the Fete.

Sorrenti turned from the window with a frown. "Are you certain that the Chorl are hidden there?"

"No, I'm not certain," I said irritably. I rubbed at my eyes, leaned my head back against the chair. Weariness enveloped me. I'd spent almost all of last night dealing with Daeriun and the bodies, then tracking Yvonne.

Sorrenti didn't take offense at the curt tone. Instead, he sighed, glanced toward Daeriun standing opposite me, toward William seated in the chair beside me and Erick standing near the door. Erick had replaced Keven as my personal guard when we'd returned to the estate. "Then let me see if I can verify that."

He moved to a vacant seat, sat down and closed his eyes.

Within the space of a breath, his body grew rigid, back straightening, hands resting on the arms of the chair tightening on the wood. His face settled into a frown of concentration and his breathing slowed, as if he'd fallen asleep . . . but then it slowed further, to the point where he almost didn't seem to be breathing at all.

A silence settled over the room, no one daring to move. But when it became obvious that Sorrenti wouldn't be returning anytime soon, Daeriun shuddered, looked toward me.

"What's he doing?"

I caught his eyes, saw the wariness there, the suspicion and how uncomfortable that suspicion made him feel.

"He's using the throne," I said. "The Stone Throne here in Venitte. He's using the throne to see beyond Lady Parmati's walls."

The general spat a curse, paced away from all of us, toward the window, spun back. "If so few people know of the throne," he said, "how did Haqtl find out about it?"

I almost shrugged, but William suddenly shifted forward in his seat. "I can answer that. I'd been wondering how Haqtl—how any of the Chorl—managed to get in touch with Demasque or Parmati or any of the Council members here in Venitte. But then yesterday, while conducting business with Bullick and a few other merchants on the wharf, searching for anything that might lead me to where Haqtl is hiding, I saw Tarrence."

He turned to me significantly. I frowned, the name somewhat familiar.

And then I froze, felt fury seething upward inside me. I shifted forward on my seat. "Merchant Tarrence, from Marlett."

William nodded grimly. "He'd changed his appearance somewhat—shorn his hair short, wears a beard now, trimmed close. I almost didn't recognize him."

I swore. "It always seems to come back to Alendor and the damn consortium."

"Even after his death," Erick said from the door. I shot him a glance, but Daeriun had stepped forward.

"Who is Tarrence? And who is Alendor?"

"You don't know?" William asked, confused, but then he sighed. "Of course you don't know. None of the messengers we sent after Varis seized the throne made it to Venitte. And we've been concentrating on the Chorl threat since the moment we arrived."

I grimaced. "Which means that the merchant guild hasn't been actively searching out the merchants that formed the consortium all this time, as we assumed."

"What," General Daeriun said, voice tight, his patience worn thin, "consortium?"

I stared at him a moment, uncertain where to begin. "Before I claimed the throne, Alendor, one of the merchants in Amenkor, began forming a consortium, using a few merchants from Amenkor and others scattered up and down the coast. Tarrence was the consortium's connection in Marlett. They were attempting to take over all the trade in Amenkor, perhaps attempting to gain control of the Skewed Throne itself, but I . . . interfered."

"She kept them from eliminating the remaining merchants in Amenkor," Erick said, in a low rumble. There was pride in his voice, even though he spoke quietly. "And then she mastered of the throne itself, so that they could not use the ruling Mistress and her insanity as a mask for their own actions."

"But," Daeriun said pointedly.

I forced myself to look away from Erick.

"But," I said, "by the time I'd taken the throne, Alendor and his consortium had fled Amenkor. We sent out warnings through the merchant guild, and I was assured by the merchants in Amenkor that if Alendor or any of his cohorts were found, they'd be punished.

"It wasn't until later that we learned Alendor had run to the Chorl. He, with the help of Baill, the captain of the palace guard in Amenkor, stole supplies from Amenkor during the winter and handed them over to the Chorl."

Daeriun watched me intently, brow furrowed in thought. Then he turned to William. "And you think that not only Alendor but his entire consortium turned to the Chorl, helped them."

William nodded. "If Tarrence is here, then he—or someone else in the consortium—probably initiated the contact between the Chorl and Demasque. Demasque controls the most significant trading fleet in Venitte. And he, like Vaiana Parmati has . . . ambitions."

"He's greedy," Daeriun said shortly, vehemently. "He's been a thorn in Lord March's side since Olivan Demasque—Artren's father—died and Artren took over the business." He looked at me. "That still doesn't explain how Haqtl knew of the Stone Throne." He glanced toward Sorrenti, still seated rigidly in the center of the room, barely breathing.

"If Alendor's consortium brought Haqtl into Venitte for a meeting—with Demasque or any of the Council—I think Haqtl would have felt the throne. He would have known it was here." I paused a moment, then added, "I did."

Daeriun's eyebrows rose. "Would all of the Chorl Servants know? Would the Chorl priests?"

I shrugged. "I don't know, but I doubt it. If anyone with any amount of power could feel the throne, then it wouldn't have remained such a well-kept secret for so long. I felt its presence through Sorrenti . . . and I think I only felt it then because I'd touched the Skewed Throne. I'm connected to both of the thrones somehow." I paused, thinking back to the last time I'd Reached for Amenkor. When I'd returned, I'd recovered far too quickly, even taking into account the help of Marielle and the others using the links.

Perhaps I was more connected to the Stone Throne than I thought.

I shrugged the thought aside, turned back to Daeriun. "Haqtl has felt the power of the Skewed Throne as well. He was there when I defeated the Ochean, when I destroyed the throne to save Amenkor. He may have recognized the power behind the Stone Throne, where the other Servants—both Chorl, Amenkor, and those here in Venitte—would not. Marielle hasn't mentioned sensing anything unusual. Nor Ottul. If any of the Servants from Amenkor or of the Chorl could have sensed it, it would have been them."

Daeriun's thin frown twisted. "But would Ottul have told you if she did?"

I thought of Ottul sending out a killing blow on the *Defiant,* of her in her cabin afterward and since, of her face when I placed part of the Fire inside of her. "Yes, I believe she would have."

The general seemed surprised at how quickly I answered.

"But it doesn't matter whether Haqtl knew back then or not," I said. "He knows now. Alonse overheard us discussing the throne and reported it to Demasque."

Daeriun snorted. "But does he know where it's hidden?" He took a step forward. "Do *you* know where it's hidden?"

I stilled, my face expressionless. I couldn't honestly say I knew exactly where the Stone Throne was hidden—

But at the same time, I *knew*. I'd felt it, on more than one occasion. Its power was unmistakable. It permeated the area around it, made the river heavy with its presence.

I was saved from answering by Sorrenti. He gasped, sucking in a large gasp of air, noisily, as if he'd been holding his breath far too long underwater and had just surfaced. Everyone in the room turned, but only William jumped, startled. Erick and I had been expecting it; Daeriun was too much a soldier to be surprised by something so trivial.

After the first deep breath, Sorrenti broke into a coughing fit, wheezing as he leaned forward, eyes watering.

Everyone waited silently, William moving to pour a glass of wine, setting it down by Sorrenti's side.

As soon as Sorrenti regained marginal control, Daeriun asked, "What did you find?"

Sorrenti took a sip from the glass. Eyes still red, he said weakly, "There's definitely something hidden on Vaiana Parmati's estate. I can't see into an entire wing of the manse, nor the level below the main house. There's some kind of warding in place."

I stood abruptly. "We have to attack them. Now. Before whatever it is they've started by killing off their network of spies becomes an all-out attack."

"No."

The single word settled into the room like stone.

I turned to Daeriun, tried to smother the instant irritation from my voice with little success. "But you know they've already started moving."

Daeriun faced me, a solid wall, arms crossed over his chest, a pose that reminded me forcibly of Erick. "I know. But after what happened at Demasque's manse, Lord March will *not* allow the Protectors to search Parmati's estate, nor will he grant you permission to raid with the Amenkor guardsmen. He can't risk that again."

"But he's searching the Council members' ships!"

"That's different. He's searching all of the ships that enter the harbor, including those owned and operated by Council members. If he raids one of the Council members' estates, he's singling them out. Unless you have evidence that warrants the raid, of course. And smells and the Sight are not going to be enough to sway the Council."

I glared at Daeriun a long moment, but he didn't waver. Finally, I let the tension in my shoulders relax. "What about the Seekers?"

Daeriun didn't move. "What about them?"

"I've had them following Demasque and Parmati before this, but they've never risked entering their estates. We didn't want to push what grudging concessions Lord March and the Council had given us. But I can send them inside. They can find out what's behind the wardings, without being seen. I doubt the wardings have been set to keep people out, only to keep Servants from seeing in."

I glanced questioningly toward Sorrenti, who nodded in agreement.

Daeriun considered, taking enough time that I began to wonder if he would answer at all.

Sorrenti must have thought the same thing, for he suddenly said, casually, as if we were discussing the weather, "They could go in just to see if military action is warranted, perhaps bring us evidence, something more solid than a scent or the Sight."

Daeriun remained silent a few more moments, then exhaled slowly. "Any . . . action on your part cannot be approved by Lord March. And *if* the Chorl are hidden there, and *if* Lord March approves a raid based on what the Seekers see . . ." He trailed off into silence.

Erick stirred. "No matter what happens, nothing can be done about it today."

"Why not?" I said, already planning to send Westen and Tomus to Parmati's estate. I'd have done it even if Daeriun had not agreed. Because I *knew* that's where they must be hidden. Nowhere else made sense. And I was tired of Lord March and Venitte and all of its political maneuvering.

Erick nodded toward the window, toward the gray-black darkness outside, the rain that now came down so hard I could hear it roaring against the walls, against the roof above. A torrential downpour. Nothing could be done in such weather. Even with the river, I would barely be able to see three feet in front of my face.

"And tomorrow it's going to be next to impossible to get anything done," Sorrenti said, rising from his seat.

"Why?"

"Because it's the last day of the Fete," Daeriun growled. "Everyone anywhere near Venitte will be here, even with the warnings we've posted and the ban on masks and the searches at the outskirts of the city. And with the weather as it is now, everyone's remained inside, expecting it to break so they can enjoy the Fete tomorrow. The streets are going to be impossible to pass through. You won't be able to go anywhere in a hurry, and forget using a carriage."

"Besides," Sorrenti said with a tight smile, "as a visiting dignitary, you'll be expected to attend the Masquerade in the Stone Garden. All of the members of the Council of Eight will be attending, as well as Lord March." His smile widened as I frowned. "I'll send Brandan Vard as an escort. He can accompany you."

Out of the corner of my eye, I saw William frown as well.

The moment the rain broke, halfway through the night, Keven woke me and I sent Westen and Tomus out to Vaiana Parmati's estate.

I couldn't return to sleep after that. For a while, I Reached and tagged along with Westen, then withdrew when I realized it was tiring me too much. And I wasn't willing to call on Marielle or any of the Servants to support me, not for something so trivial. If I was connected to the Stone Throne, the connection wasn't strong enough to support such intensive use.

So I waited.

Not long after first light, the early signs of the revelers sounded from outside the estate's gates. Within an hour, the streets became crowded with people, all dressed in vivid costumes, almost everyone with a mask, but those few without one had faces painted garishly. More so than any of the previous days of the Fete, as if everyone had saved their most outlandish outfits for this last day.

For the Masquerade.

I snorted. So much for the ban on the masks. Or the warnings about the Chorl.

The rest of my retinue gathered in my rooms, Marielle, Heddan, and Gwenn, Ottul trailing behind them. Heddan and Gwenn fidgeted with nervous excitement, both of them slipping quietly to the window after a few moments, pointing out particularly wild outfits as they passed on the street outside the gates. Erick came to replace Keven, arriving with Avrell and William in tow.

And still no Westen.

All of them tried to start conversations, but they ground down into nothing, the tension in the room too high.

Then Brandan arrived, servants bringing in the trunk with the costumes.

"We won't be needing those," I said sharply.

"Some of you will have to wear them," Brandan said. He glanced significantly at Ottul. "With all of the warnings we've circulated through the city, she can't be seen in public. She'll need a mask. And I'd suggest that at least a few others wear masks or costumes so that she blends in more."

I hesitated, caught Gwenn's pleading look, Heddan's carefully neutral one, then nodded.

Both Heddan and Gwenn shot toward the trunk, Ottul following more slowly.

And then Westen arrived, Tomus a pace behind him. Both looked wet, clothes smudged with mud and dirt, a few strands of grass.

"Report," I said, although I could see that Westen's lips were pressed tight together with concern.

"We infiltrated the estate," he said quietly, stepping close. Both Erick and Avrell moved forward so they could hear. "There wasn't anyone there."

"What do you mean?" I said. "They have to be there. There's nowhere else in Venitte they could be."

"They *were* there," Tomus interjected.

"How do you know?"

"Someone was housed there," Westen said, shooting a glare at Tomus. "The entire wing was set up to house an army. Its rooms were lined with cots, recently used. It looked like a barracks, complete with a kitchen and dining hall. She could have housed over a thousand troops in there, and they'd never have to leave that wing. But they're all gone. I'd say they left an hour or so before we got there, probably while it was still raining."

"What about below the ground floor?"

Westen shrugged. "Supplies and numerous empty crates."

Erick swore and shook his head. "Whatever the Chorl needed for whatever it is they have planned."

"We know what they have planned," I said. "They want to conquer Venitte. They want the throne. We even know that they intend to attack today. We just don't know how they intend to do it."

"And we know that they intend to hide in the crowd using the masks," Erick said. "We'll have to alert Daeriun that they're already on the move, that they're already mixed in with the crowds."

"Get Catrell," I said sharply, turning to Westen. "Get all of the guardsmen here in the estate ready and send them into the streets in groups. Have them work their way up to the Stone Garden."

"Should they search for the Chorl as they move?"

I considered for a long moment, but I'd already made too many mistakes dealing with Lord March and the Council members.

"No. Forcing people to take off their masks would stir up too much trouble, and there are too many people on the streets. Just get them up to the garden as fast as you can."

"And what about you?"

"I'm going to the Stone Garden. Daeriun is most likely going to be there. And if he's not, then either Lord March or Sorrenti will be."

He nodded, motioned to Tomus, and then they both left.

Erick sidled closer. "What about the others?"

"Tell William, Marielle, and Brandan as soon as you get the chance. But not the others."

"Not Ottul?"

I watched the Chorl Servant for a moment as Gwenn forced her to try on the blue-white mask that Brandan had offered to me. She stiffened at first, then relented.

As the mask fell down to hide her face, I saw a tentative smile.

I tried to recall if I'd ever seen Ottul smile before, but couldn't. It softened her. I said, "Tell her. I trust her."

Thirty minutes later, we were all in the courtyard, the sun blazing down, the street outside a cacophony of noise as partyers yelled and screamed, horns and whistles blowing, tambourines rattling, the mass of people flowing upward, toward the central marketplace called the Stone Garden, a riot of color.

Daeriun had been right. There would have been no way to get a carriage out into the flow. Not without killing someone.

I watched as the gates were opened and a contingent of Amenkor guardsmen forced their way into the mass of people, their mostly brown uniforms marring the bright costumes like an ugly stain. Westen watched them go as the next group formed up, then saw me and moved to my side.

"I sent a group down to the docks to warn Bullick," he said, "but it's going to take forever for any of us to get anywhere."

"And what about you?"

"I'm coming with you."

I started to protest, but halted when I saw his expression. I'd seen it a hundred times during the grueling training sessions with him, in Amenkor and here in Venitte.

He wasn't going to back down.

"Where's Catrell?" I asked instead.

"He left with the first group. He thinks he knows where Daeriun is. The general has the Protectorate scattered in large groups throughout the city, but with the Chorl force marching down from the north, he's likely going to be in the northern part of the city. That's where he's focused the majority of his defensive preparations."

I grunted. "Then let's go."

Erick barked an order and a group of Amenkor guardsmen formed up around us, hemming us in tightly. Westen, Erick, and Avrell stayed close to me; none of us wore masks. The rest came up behind, their masks making them seem out of place.

The gates were opened, and then we became part of the crowd.

Every instinct I'd learned and honed on the Dredge came instantly into play. I slid beneath the river as the entire group was absorbed and subsumed, Erick's careful arrangement of guardsmen broken effortlessly as they were shoved and shifted out of position. Beneath the river, I heard Erick curse, heard him barking orders to get everyone back into place, the scent of oranges strong. But it was useless. The stream of people couldn't be avoided.

And so I let myself merge with the eddies and currents around me, used the river to begin to nudge that person wearing a sun mask to one side, edged that group of drunken men dressed like dogs to the other. Sinking deeper, I concentrated on the street ahead and behind, began drawing the guardsmen that were already straggling, already being separated from the group, back in.

A moment later, I felt someone else enter the flow, and another. Marielle and—

And Ottul.

I cast a quick glance backward.

The blue-white mask turned toward me, nodded slightly, then returned its attention to the crowd.

I shuddered. I didn't like the masks, didn't like the denseness of the river, the thickness caused by too many people in such a tight area.

But we were moving toward the Stone Garden.

I settled back, began working with Marielle and Ottul to move us along faster, keeping everyone together, while at the same time keeping an eye out for any sign of the Chorl. Erick continued to bark orders, swearing occasionally under his breath, although he'd relaxed a little as well. We wound our way up through the streets, Brandan occasionally breaking in with directions, pointing out a route or a side street. The crowds thickened, then spread out as the streets widened, grew dense again as everyone converged on the central marketplace.

A man blew a horn to one side. A woman shrieked, with raucous laughter. Another man—dressed like an ibis with a narrow beak and feathers tied to his arms in the shape of wings—towered over the crowd on long, thin stilts like legs, sauntering past.

And still no sign of the Chorl. No sign of the Protectorate or guardsmen or any of the Council members either.

We were three cross streets away from the Stone Garden when the White Fire inside me sparked into sudden life. Ahead, I could see the first of the hundred stone statues that had given the plaza its name—a huge hawk, wings spread up and out high over the crowd beneath it, talons poised, already extending to grasp its prey. Behind, I glimpsed a few of the other statues—the raised head of a phoenix engulfed in flames, the smooth curve of a dolphin in mid leap—

Then the Fire inside me flared in warning.

Without thought, I brought a shield up around myself so fast it felt as if I'd ripped it from the very essence of the river itself. It had barely formed—

And then something punched hard into my chest, a punch softened by the shield but still with enough force to fling me back into Erick, who grunted as he caught my weight. My vision wavered, my grasp on the river shuddering, beginning to loosen, to break apart, and I found myself struggling to take a breath.

Everything around me blurred. I heard Erick bellow an order, felt something soaking into my shirt on my chest, and still I couldn't breathe, couldn't force my lungs to work. The world began to blacken, shadow encroaching on the dazzling sunlight before me, on the faces suddenly leaning down over me, too bleary to recognize. The blue sky above began to burn with the sunlight, engulfed by whiteness, and I felt myself beginning to fall into it, to be consumed by it—

And then something in my chest *tore,* a wrenching pain that seemed to split my chest in two.

I arched backward, heard someone—Gwenn?—scream, rolled to the side and dry heaved onto the slate paving of the roadway, coughing and choking and retching all at once.

"Back off!" Erick shouted, and I heard a sword being drawn, heard fresh screams, this time from the crowd.

Taking their cue from Erick, the rest of the Amenkor guardsmen drew weapons as well.

The screams from the surrounding crowd tripled.

"Varis! Varis, are you all right!"

The retching ceased. Still coughing, I rolled onto my back again, blinked up into the sunlight, into the blue sky, into William's terrified face, Avrell's right behind, Marielle and Gwenn on the other side, tears streaking down Gwenn's cheeks as she sobbed, her hands reaching forward but afraid to touch. Brandan moved in next to Avrell, his expression horrified. They'd all removed their masks, William's shoved up onto his head.

All except Ottul.

The expressionless blue-white mask stared down at me as well, above all of the others.

"Shit, she's bleeding," William muttered.

I glanced down, pain seething in my chest at the movement, and noticed the blood on my shirt. And something else.

I reached up and drew a splintered length of wood as long as my hand from a rent in my shirt. It snagged in the cloth, but I jerked it free.

The end of the wood was fletched with gray feathers.

An arrow.

The breath caught in my throat.

Someone had tried to kill me. Someone had tried to *assassinate* me.

Rage filled me, and I began to choke.

William snatched the remains of the arrow out of my hand, handed it off to Westen as he leaned in close.

The Seeker took one look at it, his body going still. He stood quietly a moment, then turned and scanned the crowd.

His eyes settled on something. His face darkened . . . and then went utterly calm.

Then he was gone.

William began picking more splinters out of my shirt, his hands coming away stained with blood.

But not coated with blood. Not saturated with blood.

"I need some cloth, some water," William said. Too calm. He swallowed, his face pale, his eyes too wide. Then suddenly: "Water! Can someone get me some damn water!"

"I'm fine," I whispered, voice hoarse. It hurt to breathe, my entire chest throbbing, but I reached up and grabbed William's hands, forced them to halt, forced him to look me in the eye. "I'm fine, William. I used the river to stop the arrow. It must have splintered. The bleeding's already stopped."

I felt William trembling, saw the panic in his eyes, panic barely held in check.

But then, abruptly, it receded.

He sat back on his heels. "I thought—"

I squeezed his hands, halted the words. "I know." Still hoarse, still raw with pain. I coughed again, weakly, tried a grin.

William smiled back. A smile touched with fear and worry, but a smile. A

smile I remembered from the deck of the *Defiant*, in the darkness, when he'd
pointed out the stars.

"Help me up," I said.

"I'm not certain that's a good idea," Avrell said. "The assassin . . ."

"Westen's handling it," I said, wincing as William helped me lean forward.
I paused, knees drawn in tight, head forward, until the throbbing in my chest
lessened.

All of them helped me stand.

I surveyed the street, saw it cleared of pedestrians for at least a hundred feet
in all directions, the flagstone paving littered with broken horns, streamers,
discarded masks, tufts of feathers.

But the panic hadn't spread far. Ahead, the crowd still packed the plaza of
the Stone Garden.

I glared in that direction, the anger over the attack reasserting itself, my
heart thudding in my bruised chest. I narrowed my eyes, stretched outward on
the river, sensed the Fire inside Westen off to one side, moving away, fast and
furious—

And felt another disturbance a moment before the screams started. Distant.
Somewhere inside the plaza itself.

"What in hells?" Erick muttered.

The guardsmen on all sides shifted nervously.

Erick glanced toward me, but I shook my head. "I don't know. But let's
find out."

He nodded grimly. I caught Avrell's eye and the First of the Mistress took
Gwenn by the hand and pushed her behind him. Marielle stepped forward to
my side, Erick on the other. William, Brandan, Ottul, and Heddan formed up
behind Avrell and Gwenn, William borrowing a dagger from one of the guardsmen, Brandan doing the same, even though he could use the Sight to defend
himself if necessary.

The rest of the guardsmen on either side, we stalked forward and forced our
way out into the crowd thronging the plaza.

Beneath the river, I could sense the people's confusion, spikes of fear rising
in those closest as they saw the drawn swords of the guardsmen, as they met
the cold anger on the guards' faces. Unlike the mob in the streets, they gave
way, allowed us to forge ahead. Unable to see over the heads of so many people
crowded so close together, I extended myself forward using the Sight and felt
Marielle doing the same.

Almost immediately, I found a center of disturbance, drew breath to point
Erick in that direction, but halted when I felt another, farther away to the left,
and another, on the outskirts of the plaza.

I hesitated only a moment. "Over there!" I shouted above the noise of the throng.

Erick glanced in that direction, brow creased in concentration as he searched. Then he nodded, bellowed an order to clear the way as he struck out, the rest of us tight behind him. We passed a statue of a naked woman with long hair standing in a pool of glittering water, at least three times my height; a snarling wolf, the detail of the bristling hair so fine I could feel the animal's hatred; a man, a crown upon his head, his hand reaching forward as if to grasp something from the air. . . .

And then we broke through the crowd into a cleared circle, Venittian guardsmen at its edge holding the people back.

In the center of the circle, Sorrenti sat beside Lady Casari's body, her head held in his hands in his lap, a look of utter horror on his face.

He glanced up as we entered the area and in a choked voice asked sharply, "Can you help her?"

I stalked forward, knelt at her side. Brandan followed, standing over Lord Sorrenti's shoulder.

An arrow protruded from Lady Casari's chest, the end fletched with gray feathers. Blood had soaked into her yellow dress, a thick, viscous red, so dark it was almost black. It pooled on the gray flagstone beneath her, had begun to spread to one side. Blood flecked her lips, speckled her too pale skin, dripped from one corner of her mouth.

I shared a look with Sorrenti, a look he couldn't hold. Sucking in a harsh breath, he glanced away.

"Mistress," Lady Casari muttered, her voice nothing more than a breath, trapped between panting, liquid gasps. Her hand reached out blindly, and I caught it, felt the chill that had settled there.

"Lady Casari."

Her head turned toward my voice, but her eyes were blank, staring out into nothing.

But when she felt my touch, her breathing abruptly quieted.

"I . . . should have . . . trusted you. . . . I should have . . . supported you. . . . In the Council." The words were painful, her face contorted with the effort, tears squeezing from the corners of her eyes. She began to heave. "I'm . . . sorry."

And then her body slumped, chest collapsing without taking another breath, her head slipping to one side.

I held her hand a moment longer, then placed it lightly on her chest.

Sorrenti grew still, shoulders tensed. I thought for a moment he would break down and weep—

But when he looked up, it wasn't grief in his eyes. It was rage.

We held each other's gazes for a moment, and then his eyes shifted down to the rents in my shirt, the bloodstains there.

"They tried to get you as well?" he asked.

For the first time, I noticed the blood staining the sleeve of his shirt, the ragged hole that had been torn there.

Sorrenti noticed the glance and his eyes darkened. "They missed. The blood is Elina's."

"I was forewarned by the Fire," I said.

He nodded.

"What happened?" I asked. When fresh screams broke out from a new direction, I added, "And what's happening now?"

"Someone—"

"The Chorl," Brandan interrupted. Sorrenti glanced up toward him, his face stricken.

"They're here," I said, "in the marketplace, wearing masks. They'd already left Parmati's estate when my Seekers arrived. I sent a warning to Daeriun, to the Protectorate, but I'm not certain they received it in time."

Sorrenti paused to assimilate this. "They must be trying to assassinate all of the Council members—at least those that aren't allied with them." He looked down at Lady Casari's body, shifted, and laid her head gently down onto the pavement. "And for some they succeeded."

"It's more than that," Erick said.

Both Sorrenti and I looked up to where Erick stood over us. He nodded toward the north, mouth pressed into a grim line. "Look."

We rose, turned northward, where the plaza looked out over the city, out toward the northern trading roads, Deranian's Wall curving off to the east.

On the northern road, a mass of armored men poured down from the top of the hill into the city. Blue-skinned men, the banners of the Chorl flying high at the head of the army.

And then, much closer, at the massive gates of Deranian's Wall, I felt a pulse of power, heard Sorrenti and Brandan gasp, Sorrenti taking a step forward—

And the gates exploded.

✝ Chapter 15

"Lords preserve us!"

I glanced toward the Venittian Protector on the edge of the crowd who'd gasped, noticed that all of the Protectorate surrounding Sorrenti, Brandan, and Lady Casari's body had gone rigid with shock. Even the crowd had quieted, all eyes turned toward Deranian's Wall, toward the chunks of wood and stone that were flying through the air, dust rising in an off-white cloud, wind taking it northeast of us.

The only people not affected by the explosion were the guardsmen from Amenkor.

Before the dust could completely clear, Sorrenti sucked in another breath, and this time even I felt the disturbance on the river before the pulse was released, even though I knew that those attacking the walls were not Chorl Servants, but Haqtl and his priests.

The second explosion thudded across the distance, a huge block of stone hurtling skyward. But still the Wall didn't crumble. It was thicker than the walls in Amenkor, had withstood thousands of attacks before this.

But it wouldn't last against the Chorl. Not this time. Because the Chorl had learned how to link.

Confusion rippled through the crowd, through the stunned silence. People began to shift nervously, agitated. A thread of fear slid into the confusion, dark and insidious, tasting of metal.

"Look!" the man on stilts and dressed as an ibis yelled. One feathered, winged arm pointed to the north, beyond the wall. "Someone's attacking the city!"

Sorrenti shot the birdman a vicious look, turned to me to say something—

And that's when the Chorl, an entire phalanx of blue-skinned warriors shrouded in the garb of the Fete, tore their masks free, garish robes flung aside to reveal slightly curved sheathed swords. They filled the center of the Stone Garden, over a hundred of them.

When the leader drew his sword, the crowd broke.

In the space of a breath, the entire plaza exploded into motion. The man on stilts gave a sharp outcry as the people around his feet lurched away from the Chorl. Arms flailing, he toppled, vanishing from sight, trailing loose feathers. Through the sudden piercing screams of the Venittian people, I heard Erick bellow an order, felt the river surge with panic—an overwhelming blanket of raw emotion—felt Sorrenti take a single step toward me, Brandan on his heels—

And then the Amenkor guardsmen surrounded me, Erick and the others on the outside, a moment before the panicked crowd broke through Sorrenti's guardsmen and surged over us.

They struck with enough force to shove my guardsmen back, one of the men's elbows striking hard into my cheek. I hissed at the pain, felt an echoing pain from my chest where the assassin's arrow had struck, and then I was jostled into the guardsmen behind me, our bodies so close I couldn't move to draw my dagger, my arms crushed as the crowd shoved us this way and that, the close bodies stifling and hot, rank with sweat. One of the guards barked a warning, and I realized their swords were already drawn, the blades bare, but no one in the crowd listened. The people's faces were white, wide-eyed with fear, with tension, with unreason.

Within moments, I tasted blood on the river, close, felt something soft roll beneath my feet as I was pushed to the side, heard a guardsman curse. I glanced down and through the crush of arms and armor I caught a glimpse of a woman's face—long dark hair, skin pale with death, cat's mask cracked and askew, covering half her face—

And then someone shoved hard from the left, thrust me to one side. I lost my footing, began to slide down between the bodies of the guardsmen, down to the stone pavement where I'd be trampled like the cat-mask girl—

Someone grabbed my arm, hauled me upright. "I don't think so," Erick said.

His face was suffused with rage, turned outward, toward the Chorl, toward the insanity of the crowd, the raw fear breaking loose into chaos.

I felt my own anger surge forward in response.

"We have to get to the gates!" I yelled.

He shook his head, a sharp, hard movement. "We'll never make it! The streets are packed, the crowd's too panicked."

I cursed, took another elbow to the side with a wince, thinking frantically.

Fresh screams from the direction of the Chorl split the air. Hideous screams. I heard the slickness of blades falling, felt the shiver as metal passed through air, struck flesh. More blood tainted the river, the scent of copper suddenly so thick I gagged.

The Chorl were slaughtering the people in the plaza.

"Where's Sorrenti? Where are the others? Avrell? Marielle?" Stupid questions. I could sense both through the Fire at their cores. Could feel them off to my right, closer to the Chorl than I was.

"Sorrenti's surrounded by his own guardsmen and Brandan. The others—"

Before Erick could continue, I felt another hideous surge of strength on the river near the Wall, felt the pulse of power before the grinding thud reverberated through the plaza.

And I felt the Wall give through the soles of my feet, felt the ground trembling as it fell.

Erick shot me a grim look.

"They've breached the gate," I said in response. "They're heading toward the Council chambers."

"How do you know?"

"Because that's where the Stone Throne is."

He caught my eyes, nodded. "What do you want to do?"

"We have to get to Sorrenti," I said. "We have to get to the throne before Haqtl touches it." His brow creased in confusion and I suddenly remembered he hadn't been in the throne room when the Ochean touched the Skewed Throne, hadn't been there when we'd fought, when I'd collapsed and been forced to destroy it in order to survive.

But that didn't matter to Erick. He didn't need to know, not when the order came from me. The momentary confusion cleared, replaced by intent.

We began to shove back at the crowd, began to forge toward Sorrenti's position. We made slow progress. There were too many people in the plaza. No one was moving far at all.

Then I caught a glimpse of Sorrenti, of his dark hair, neat beard, his sharp eyes squinted in anger and desperation.

Reaching forward with the river, I shoved the few people between us and his guardsmen aside, clearing a path. Brandan turned defensively as the Venittian guardsmen cried out, hands raised. I couldn't see what he'd done on the river, but I could feel the prickling sensation of power against my skin, making the hairs on my arms and neck stand on end.

As soon as he saw me, recognized me, his hands lowered and he barked an order, catching Sorrenti's attention.

The two sets of guardsmen merged. Our forces doubled, they pushed back against the crowd, formed a rough circle of space to give us breathing room.

"We have to get to the gates," Sorrenti said immediately.

"We'll never make it. The crowd between here and there is too thick. Unless you know a different route."

Sorrenti scanned the plaza, swore softly beneath his breath.

"Where is Lord March?" I asked. "Daeriun?"

He caught my gaze, concern flickering there for a moment. "Assuming he wasn't assassinated like Lady Casari, you mean?" he asked, but he shook his head. "I don't know. Lord March doesn't usually arrive at the Fete until later, so he may still be inside the Wall. Daeriun would have been in the city somewhere."

"Would he—" I began, but then another thud rippled through the river, somehow more hollow, more distant.

I turned toward the sound with a frown, felt Sorrenti, Brandan, and Erick do the same as, belatedly, a whooshing roar echoed up from the harbor. Followed by another. And another.

Familiar roars. Ones I'd heard before . . .

"That's not coming from the Wall. Nor the northern part of the city," Erick said.

"It's coming from the channel," Sorrenti said. "From the northern channel."

And then I recognized the sounds. Not ones *I'd* heard before.

But ones *Cerrin* had heard, fifteen hundred years before, when the Chorl had first attacked Venitte. The sounds of the Chorl Servants' fireballs echoing within the walls of the channel as they destroyed the houses and estates on the cliffs.

I felt my chest tighten at Cerrin's remembered pain and loss, felt his sickening hollow grief clutch at my stomach, and I clenched my jaw tight against it, fought it back.

"The Chorl are attacking from the sea," I said. "They're coming up through the channel. And if they get through, they'll hit the port." I turned toward Erick. "The Chorl learn fast. They failed in Amenkor because they didn't seize control of the throne. They relied on a single assault from the sea."

"And they did not expect much resistance," Erick added. "They didn't expect you to be prepared."

I turned to Sorrenti, the tightness in my chest increasing with urgency, with the tingling need to *move,* to do something. "They're attacking on three fronts. They're trying to keep you occupied with the forces to the north and the ships coming in from the west, while the real threat—Haqtl and the priests—attempt to take the throne."

As the realization sank in, Sorrenti's face grew taut. His lips pressed together into a thin line and his shoulders settled.

"We can't do anything for the port," he said. "We have ships guarding the channels. They'll have to hold them off. And we can't help at the gates to the Wall or to the north. We'd never make it there in time. We'll have to leave that to Daeriun and Lord March, if they're still alive." He looked toward Erick. "But we can do something here."

Erick nodded.

"We have to get to the Council chambers," I said forcefully. "Haqtl will head straight for the throne. If he reaches it, if he touches it . . ."

Sorrenti frowned. "We'll never get a chance unless we can escape the plaza. And that won't happen unless we can clear out the Chorl and get the citizens of Venitte out of our way." When I didn't immediately agree, he added, "There are protections in place around the throne. It will take him time to get through those. Haqtl won't be able to simply walk in and find it."

I glared at him a moment in frustration. "Very well. But if Haqtl does reach the throne before we do, if he does touch it, you have to fight him, Sorrenti. Fight him as long as you can. And if you have to—"

He cut me off with a sharp gesture, a slash of his hand. "I know. The Seven have already informed me."

Then he turned toward his guardsmen, stepped over to the commander of the Protectorate, and began giving orders.

"We don't have enough men to defeat the Chorl here," Erick said quietly. "There were over a hundred."

"But there weren't any Servants or priests that I saw," I said. "And we have Marielle, Heddan, Gwenn, and me. And Brandan Vard. And perhaps Ottul."

He snorted, shaking his head. But he didn't say anything.

I bristled, but reined in my irritation. He hadn't seen the Servants fight in Amenkor, hadn't seen firsthand what they could do. And he hadn't seen Brandan fighting the Chorl ships when they attacked at sea.

Then we were moving, pushing forward through the seething mass of the crowd as people tried to flee the death the Chorl wielded behind them. The guardsmen formed up into a tight wedge, Sorrenti, Brandan, Erick, and I at its base, as we cut through the press of bodies, toward the center of the plaza. As we moved, I pulled my dagger free, sank deeper into the river, Reached forward—

And felt an eddy lash out, far to the right.

From Marielle's direction.

"Marielle and the others are already fighting the Chorl!" I shouted to Erick, motioning to the right, trying to be heard over the increasing screams as we drew closer to the slaughter. Erick nodded, the crowd pushing hard into the wedge, the guardsmen shoving back with enough force to topple a few of the people, their faces panicking as they slid underfoot. For a brief moment, the density of the crowd doubled, the scent of sweat and blood sharp.

And then the wedge broke through into the Chorl ranks.

The reaction was instantaneous. A ululating shriek pierced the air, shivered down my spine even though I'd heard it uttered a hundred times on *The Maiden* and in the streets of Amenkor. For a single moment, I saw Erick hesitate, draw back from the noise with a wince and a look of horror, of remembered torture—

But then his face slid into the cold, calculating mask of a Seeker.

The mixed group of Amenkor guardsmen and Venittian Protectors lurched forward with a wordless battle cry, swords raised, and hit the blue-skinned Chorl with a force that I felt on the river, a strength that tingled through my skin, through my bones.

I sank into the sensation, wrapped its warmth around me, and stepped forward.

A Chorl warrior lashed out with his sword. I forged a shield using the river, thrust the strike aside and plunged the dagger into his chest, above the edge of his armor, in and out, the motion sharp and smooth. Moving past his startled, tattooed face, his body falling to the side, I slashed through the next man's arm, felt the blue-purple cloth of his shirt tear, felt the dagger bite and score the hardened leather armor beneath. He shrugged the cut aside, grinning maniacally, thrust forward toward my exposed stomach.

But I'd already stepped aside, angled toward him, into the space alongside his sword.

His grin faltered a moment before my dagger took him in the stomach.

He slumped into me, shocked, and I caught him, spun him slightly before jerking my dagger free and letting him fall.

Behind me, I saw Sorrenti, his sword bare and bloodied. I saw the shock in his eyes, saw the momentary flicker of respect, of newfound wariness—

And then he turned, sword rising to meet another Chorl's attack. He caught the warrior's sword, metal ringing against metal, then thrust the man back.

I spun, dove back into the fight, thrusting forward, spinning back, slicing across arms, across thighs, across faces, feeling the Amenkor guardsmen and Venittian Protectorate roaring and cursing and dying on all sides. But the Chorl were dying as well, bodies making the footing treacherous, blood making it slick. I felt power gather and release on the river to the right, tasted Marielle's touch, Heddan's, even Gwenn's. Felt a wall of force being erected, but at our backs, and realized they were keeping the Chorl from attacking the remnants of the crowd, protecting the people as they tried to flee.

But there were too many Chorl. Over a hundred against perhaps a third of that. The Protectorate in the plaza had been scattered. We weren't a cohesive force.

Behind the front line, the Chorl rallied, fell back to regroup from the sudden attack, and then they pushed forward in a concerted effort.

They shoved our defensive line back almost a full ten feet when they struck.

The guardsman beside me cried out as he took a wicked cut to his arm. Gasping, he clutched the wound with one hand, staggered to the side. The Chorl moved in, grinning.

I sliced across the face of the warrior before me, forcing him to halt, and on the return slash I plunged the dagger into the other Chorl warrior's back as he bent over the injured guardsman. Wrenching the dagger free, I whirled, kicked outward with my other leg, and caught the Chorl I'd slashed across the face in the stomach and dropped him to the ground.

Sliding back into position, I felt a different surge on the river, saw blazing fire arc up and out, and felt something cold grip my throat, cutting off my breath.

The fire came down, trailing smoke—

And exploded in the center of the Chorl warriors.

Screams erupted, followed instantly by the acrid scent of burning flesh.

I grinned.

Ottul.

The Chorl's sudden press forward faltered. Into the hesitation, I felt the crackling release of raw power and lightning forked down from the sunlit sky, blindingly bright, edges tinged with purple, followed almost immediately by a tremendous crack of thunder that reverberated through the ground, through the air, pressing against the skin of my face. The lightning struck the Chorl line, danced down its length, men juddering as it touched them. An acrid bitter scent permeated the river, tasting of metal and rain, followed almost instantly by the black smell of burned flesh. Out of the corner of my eye, I saw Brandan smile, a vicious smile of triumph, before his expression slid back into cold calculation.

The Chorl advance halted completely, and the guardsmen around us grabbed the advantage.

I pushed forward with them, dagger rising and falling, blood slicking my hands, my face, mingling with the sweat. Smoke burned in my nostrils as more fireballs arched out over the field, and lightning continued to sizzle down from the empty sky, its metallic flavor mingling with that of ash and char. I sank into the flow of the fight, into the eddies of the river, felt answering pulses from Marielle, Heddan, and Gwenn as the two forces drew closer together. Time slipped as I became lost in the rhythm—

Until someone touched my shoulder and I spun without thinking, dagger cutting in hard and sharp—

I scented Sorrenti at the last moment—the dry dust of ancient paper— nostrils flaring even as I readied for a killing blow.

I stilled, the effort to halt my motion sending a twinge through my gut, through my shoulder and upper arm. The dagger stopped a finger's breath from his neck and he froze, head tilted away.

"It's me, Varis," he said. He had one hand outstretched, the one he'd used to touch me, but he withdrew it slowly. "It's over."

I glanced around, saw the guardsmen and Protectorate gathering close, some clutching wounds, others holding a fellow guardsman upright, all of them weary. Brandan held a hand across a nick on his forearm. Marielle led the rest of my entourage closer from the opposite edge of the plaza, Avrell and William at her back, the others behind, her face set, her clothes stained with blood and sweat. The sun stood almost directly overhead, and the plaza itself was empty of revelers.

Or almost empty. A few of the men who staggered or limped toward our position through the bodies of the dead weren't guardsmen. Some of the Venittians had thrown their masks aside and joined in the fighting.

I turned back to Sorrenti, pulling my dagger away carefully.

Sorrenti sighed and straightened, one hand rising to rub the skin of his neck where my dagger would have fallen. He left a smear of blood behind. Someone else's blood.

Behind him, Erick grinned.

Before Sorrenti could speak, a loud boom rose from the harbor.

Everyone turned.

There, in the deep blue water that flashed in the sunlight, shrouded by plumes of smoke, ships battled. At least two ships were burning, sails nothing more than sheets of flame. Even as we watched, fire arched up and out from a Chorl ship, shattering in the mast of one of Venitte's traders. A man fell from the rigging, clothes burning.

"Is that the *Defiant*?" Erick asked, coming up beside me. Any trace of satisfaction was gone from his voice, and I could feel the guardsmen and Venittian citizens gathering behind us, a row of grim faces.

I nodded. "And the three refitted Chorl ships that we brought with us."

"I think I see the *Reliant* as well. I can't imagine Tristan missing out on a sea battle."

I glanced toward Sorrenti. "The throne."

Sorrenti met my eyes, then turned toward the Wall, toward the gates.

Smoke rose from the northern city in thick clouds. Even as those on the plaza shifted to look, Avrell, Marielle, and the others from Amenkor joining me, a building collapsed, embers and cinders rising in a furious cloud, like crazed red gnats.

Closer, the Wall itself had been broken. Jagged white stone glared in the sunlight where the gates had once stood. I could see men on what remained, still fighting, throwing stones and cauldrons of oil and fire down onto those below, could hear the echoes of battle, faint but unmistakable, filtering through the streets and rising to the plaza. But the Wall had been breached.

The sight sent a ripple of despair through all of the Venittians on the plaza, a shudder I felt on the river. Shoulders slumped, and faces grew pinched and tight. Swords lowered, grips loosening.

For a moment, the plaza was still, silent. A breeze gusted from the harbor, carrying with it the stench of smoke.

Then, from the distance, a horn rose, a long clear note that reverberated in the air.

Before me, Sorrenti's shoulders tightened and he straightened, listening.

The first horn faded, but it was answered by another, and another, coming from two different sections of the city.

Sorrenti spun toward me, and hope softened the harshness of his face. "Lord March, Daeriun, and Lady Tormaul. They're outside the Wall. Daeriun is headed toward the gates. Lord March and Lady Tormaul are headed toward the northern precincts."

"What about the gates?"

"Hard to tell," Erick muttered. "From here, it looks like they've already been taken, that there's only a token Venittian force trying to hold them back."

"But Daeriun will have some of the Venittian Servants with his forces, as will Lord March. If he reaches the gates . . ."

I glanced at the men around us, then swore beneath my breath. We had barely fifty men, counting Marielle's force and the citizens who'd joined us. And a significant number of those men were wounded. Catrell and the other Amenkor forces would be with Daeriun or Lord March, would rally to the horns. And Captain Bullick and his crew were occupied in the harbor.

"We know Lady Casari is dead," I said. "What about the other Council members?"

One of the guardsmen stirred. "Lord Aurowan is dead. I was part of his entourage. We stayed with his body until we heard the fighting."

"Lord Boradarn as well," someone else said. "He was killed as we reached the plaza."

"That's three of the Council members lost so far," Sorrenti said grimly. "Perhaps more. I haven't heard any horns sounding for any of the others."

"I saw Lord Dussain being dragged by his men into the safety of one of the buildings," said one of the revelers who'd grabbed a sword and joined us. "He was wounded, but still alive."

Sorrenti nodded. I could see the tension in his face, the indecision.

Taking a small step forward, I said, "The throne."

He met my gaze with a glare. "The Chorl already control the gates of the Wall. How do you propose we break through with less than fifty men?"

I narrowed my eyes at the scathing tone in his voice, but said quietly. "I don't intend to storm the main gates. Let Daeriun retake the main gates. We only need to get to the Council chambers, to the throne itself."

Sorrenti's brow creased in confusion.

"The Wall has more than one gate," I added.

Sorrenti's eyes widened in sudden understanding.

"The Gutter's gate."

Sorrenti gathered all of the guardsmen and Protectorate together, passing quickly through the ranks, inspecting all of those with wounds, ordering some to stay behind to protect those too badly wounded to go with us. All the while, horns sounded to the north, distorted by the gusting wind, mingled with the hollow fwumps of fireballs from the harbor to the west. At one point, both Sorrenti and Brandan stiffened, heads turning toward the north, eyes distant. After the space of a breath, they traded a glance, Sorrenti returning to the organization of his men. Brandan caught my gaze, answered my unasked question tersely, "The Venittian Servants have joined the attack."

Before I could answer, jagged lightning flashed down from the sky into the buildings to the north, followed by ragged booms of thunder. At this distance, the lightning was almost beautiful, without the crackling intensity and prickling sensation against the skin, without the metallic scent that made me want to sneeze.

"The main gates of the Wall are still silent," Brandan noted. "Daeriun must not have reached them yet."

I nodded toward Brandan in acknowledgment. Then the group was ready.

"We have to move quickly," Sorrenti announced to the small group that intended to go, no more than thirty altogether. "Don't stray from the group. We're entering the Gutter, and if you get separated, if you get lost. . . ."

He trailed off, and those from Venitte stirred restlessly. The fear on the river smelled rank, and I shot a glance toward Erick, saw him raise an eyebrow, knew that he could sense the sudden tension as well. I'd grown up in the Dredge, had survived there, knew it to be dangerous. The Gutter had not seemed any different when Daeriun had taken me there to see the *Squall* captain's and Yvonne's bodies.

But before either of us could comment, the group was in motion.

Sorrenti and a few of the Protectorate led the way, moving out through the detritus of the Fete—dropped masks, crushed paper horns, trampled streams of coiled paper and confetti—the bodies of the dead from the battle, and the watching faces of the Stone Garden. We left the wounded behind, at the base of a winged woman, her head bowed, eyes closed, her hands clasped before her, her wings shadowing those below.

We passed from the plaza into the streets to the south and east. Streets that were not as rich and well-appointed as those in the Merchant Quarter where the estate that I'd been given stood. These buildings were of a coarser stone, the architecture different, older, the style the same but with sharper angles, steeper inclines. We passed through a section where solitary columns dotted the streets and corners, supporting nothing—

And then the streets grew darker, the stone facades dirtier.

I could feel the transition in my blood, could sense it on the river. The streets were mostly empty, those that had been at the Fete and scattered by the Chorl hidden, leaving nothing behind but a few discarded relics, gaudy pieces of clothing or a shattered mug. The trampled bodies and slaughtered dead had been left behind at the plaza. But once beyond the street of columns, the texture of the emptiness changed. People no longer huddled behind closed doors and shuttered windows. Instead, they waited in shadows, in alleys and niches all along the streets. I could feel their eyes watching, could taste their discontent, their malice, like soured wine, vinegary and tart.

The others could sense it as well, for the guardsmen tightened ranks, the Protectorate sharing glances. Sorrenti looked back, to make certain we still followed, his eyes flicking over Marielle and the other Servants, over Brandan and William, Avrell and Erick, then back to the street.

The street darkened further, the buildings closing in, making everything dense, everything black, even though the sun could be seen above, the sky blue and nearly cloudless.

Then we turned a corner, passed from one side street into a much wider avenue—

And there stood the Wall, the Gutter's gate, the huge wooden doors banded in metal, arching up to a point at least four times my height.

Here, in daylight, without a light rain pouring down, the gate seemed much more formidable and . . . solid than it had the night Daeriun had brought me to the Gutter.

The group halted, gathering in a cluster in the middle of the flagstone street.

"What's wrong?" I asked, joining Sorrenti and noting his frown.

He didn't turn to look, his eyes scanning the top of the Wall. "There are no guards. Someone should have hailed us by now."

"Do you often get people approaching from the Gutter's gate?"

"No. It's the least used gate in the entire Wall. But there is always a patrol here."

"Then they've either been drawn away to the battle—" Erick said from behind us.

"—Or they've already been taken by the Chorl," Sorrenti finished. "In either case," and here he did turn, "we can't get through this gate."

I straightened, thought about Amenkor, about the attack by the Ochean and the attack here in Venitte by Haqtl.

"Yes, we can," I said, not even bothering to turn to Marielle, Heddan, and Gwenn to see if they were willing. I could feel them already moving forward.

"What—" Sorrenti began, but then he saw the other Amenkor Servants gathering behind me. His eyes narrowed and he swallowed his question. "We can't defeat the Chorl with less than thirty men!"

"Why not? What did you think we'd find here? An army?"

"I expected to get reinforcements here," he growled. "Men from the walls, enough to at least double our forces."

"There is no one here," I countered. "So we attack with what we've got."

Sorrenti snorted. "And get slaughtered! We'd never make it to within a hundred yards of the Council chamber."

"Then perhaps we could help."

Everyone in the party spun at the new voice, the Protectorate and the Amenkor guardsmen instantly circling us, creating a wall against the three men who stood in the street of the Gutter behind us. They were dressed in armor, but it was worn, used, sunlight catching in nicks and dents. Their surcoats were coated with dust and dirt from the road, stained with sweat and blood. Two of the men wore their hair pulled back in a tight braid, tied and bound with twine. The third man, the leader, was bald.

The words had been uttered calmly, almost casually, the voice gravelly, like stone grating against stone. A familiar voice.

"Who are you?" Sorrenti demanded.

Then I saw the banner one of the men held, the pole tall, fabric tied to a crosspiece, hanging down and secured near the man's hands where he held it upright. And painted across the folds of black fabric in bright red—

The Skewed Throne.

My gaze flicked back toward the bald man, toward his face, partially shadowed by the banner. My nostrils flared, and in the depths of the river, I smelled him, recognized the presence, the flows that surrounded him, and I tasted the bitterness of betrayal.

The anger rose so fast and so sharp it felt as if it cut me from stomach to throat. With every ounce of that anger clear in my voice, I said, *"Baill."*

Baill—former captain of the Amenkor palace guard—shifted slightly, his face now visible in sunlight. His jaw was set, not in anger, but in regret, in respect.

He closed his eyes, bowed his head. "Mistress."

I moved before I thought, dagger out, my body in liquid motion, slipping through the wall of guardsmen meant to protect me. But before I could pass beyond them completely, a hand clamped onto my arm, so hard I knew it would leave bruises, and brought me up short.

I spun to face Erick, barked, "Let go!"

"No," Erick said, short and simple. If it had been anyone else—Sorrenti, Marielle, perhaps even William—I would have cut them, forced them to let go by drawing blood.

But it was Erick.

He caught my gaze, held it. I could hear myself breathing, the air huffing through my nostrils, my jaw clamped down tight, mouth closed. I narrowed my gaze, the rage seething inside me, hot and visceral, tingling in my arms, in my blood. I could feel it on the river, radiating from all of those from Amenkor, from Marielle and Avrell, William and Erick himself. "He sold us to the Chorl," I hissed. "He stole our food, sold it to them. *He betrayed us.*"

Before Erick could answer, Baill said loudly, "I didn't betray Amenkor. Not to the Chorl."

Avrell snorted with contempt. "You sold our food—food we'd hoarded so that we could survive the winter!"

Baill shook his head, his eyes going hard. He stepped forward. "Yes! But I sold it to Alendor. *He* sold it to the Chorl, a fact I didn't learn until after you attacked us at the fountain during our meeting and captured him. *He* betrayed us to the Chorl. Not me."

"And we should forgive you because of that!" Avrell demanded contemptuously, on the verge of attacking Baill himself.

"No," Baill said. But unlike Avrell, his voice had grown quieter. "No. Because I did betray Amenkor to Alendor. And I betrayed you, Mistress. I did not think you could rule. You were gutterscum. I thought you would fail."

I shifted, felt Erick's hand tighten on my arm, his fingers digging in deeper in warning, but I ignored him. "You thought you could hand Amenkor over to Alendor, and when he seized power—as he tried to do with the consortium— you would gain control of the palace through him."

Baill straightened, back stiff, shoulders pushed back in defiance—

But then he sighed, drawn breath exhaled loudly. "Yes."

The admission blunted my anger. Erick must have felt it, for his hand relaxed its grip.

But he didn't let go. He knew me too well.

"I've hunted the Chorl since I found out what Alendor did," Baill said, voice hard, harsh with hatred. "I gathered together what forces I could—those guardsmen who helped me steal the food from the warehouses and were forced to come with me when I fled, some of Alendor's men, some of his mercenaries. I used them to hunt the Chorl in Temall, and then when their armies headed south I hounded them down the entire coast, all the way here, to Venitte. I hunted them in the name of the Skewed Throne, in the name of the Mistress. In the name of Amenkor."

No one said anything, their anger still simmering on the eddies and currents. But now it was tinged with a thread of doubt. Grudging doubt, but doubt nonetheless.

Because Baill's words resonated with truth. A truth I could sense on the river, could *feel*, even though every part of me screamed not to trust him.

I had never seen Baill working directly with the Chorl. Only with Alendor.

And I *had* seen him fighting the Chorl in Temall, had watched him through Westen's eyes as he helped turn back the Chorl attack on the walls, using the Skewed Throne banner as his sigil.

Before I could respond to the silence, Sorrenti broke it himself. "You offer to help. But three more men will not change the situation."

Baill smiled. He motioned to the man on his left, the one not holding the Skewed Throne banner, and that man whistled, the sound piercing.

From the alleys and narrows behind them, from the empty windows and cavernous sockets of the doorways, men stepped forth. Not the gutterscum I'd assumed the watchers were when I'd sensed them on the river, but men in armor. Makeshift armor, as dented and nicked and dirty as Baill himself, the men with grizzled beards, hair tied or braided, eyes sharp, cold, and calculating. They formed up behind Baill and his two cohorts, shifting into neat ranks and files, no one speaking, only the rattle of armor and swords, the tread of heavy booted feet on flagstone, interrupting the silence. Over a hundred men emerged from the shadows, a few spitting to the side casually before taking their places, all of their faces pinched and drawn from the march down the coast, from the skirmishes they must have fought. And all of their gazes fixed on me. A few bowed their heads in short nods. Over half of them signed themselves across the chest with the Skewed Throne symbol.

And I suddenly remembered seeing Baill's forces leaving Temall, heading southward. Over a hundred men.

These hundred men. This Band.

Chasing after the Chorl.

"We are more than three," Baill said. He spoke to Sorrenti, but his eyes never left me.

I held his gaze, felt the guardsmen that protected us close in tighter as I hesitated.

I needed these men.

But the taste of Baill's betrayal lay like acid in my mouth. I couldn't trust him, couldn't trust his men, not after what he'd done, no matter what the river said.

I straightened where I stood, and felt Erick's hand fall from my arm, knew that he had reached for his sword. Out of the corner of my eye, I could see Sorrenti watching me, uncertain. He didn't understand the situation, didn't know who these men were, didn't understand the extent of the betrayal. But he'd picked up on the tension, on the anger and hatred.

I drew breath to turn Baill away—

And Sorrenti gasped. A horrified, choked gasp. One hand reached up to his chest, fingers digging into the flesh above his heart. The other reached out toward me.

"The throne," he wheezed, eyes stunned, bewildered.

Then he collapsed. It was completely graceless. All animation, all tension in his muscles, simply ceased.

His body hit the grit-blackened stone of the Gutter with a heavy thud, his scabbard grating against granite, his arms flopping to either side.

A moment of silence followed—

And then his guardsmen cried out, their commander lurching forward and kneeling at his side with a curse.

But Brandan and I had moved faster. Brandan knelt next to his Lord on one side. I knelt on the other, grabbed Sorrenti by the chin, jerked his head so I could see his eyes—

Wide open. Staring into nothing, into everything.

"What happened?" Brandan asked.

Sorrenti's commander replied, "He's barely breathing!"

I shot a glance at Erick as I sat back onto my heels, saw the same confusion in his eyes. He hadn't been in the throne room when the Ochean came, hadn't witnessed any of those events, hadn't seen my own collapse when the Ochean had touched the Skewed Throne.

"The Chorl have reached the Stone Throne," I said, and even I heard the deadness in my voice.

Erick's face hardened, the Seeker beneath slipping forward. He straightened where he knelt. "Then we have no choice. We have to take the risk."

Fresh anger spilled into the river. "I won't. We can't trust him. We can't trust his men."

"We have no choice!" Erick repeated, the teacher now, the man who had trained me on the Dredge. Curt, decisive, his tone suggesting there was no argument.

I frowned, felt the argument forming anyway.

And then Sorrenti's commander interrupted.

"You mean those men," he said, his voice tight, filled with derision. "They're nothing but mercenaries! They haven't even given us a price!"

I caught his eyes, saw him flinch back. "Oh, they've asked for a price," I growled, turned meaningfully to Brandan. "A hefty price." My gaze flicked toward Baill. "They've asked for my forgiveness."

And I didn't want to give it. Even with every eddy of the river telling me that Baill was sincere. I didn't want to give it because Baill had betrayed *me*, had hurt *me*. And I didn't want to deal with him anymore.

Baill hadn't moved. None of his men—his Band—had. They watched in silence, but I could feel their hope on the river, their fear that I would refuse them, would turn them away.

They wanted redemption.

I rose, felt Avrell step up to my side, felt his presence like a wall beside me.

"Mistress," he said, then hesitated, began again, in a softer voice. "Varis. Think of the throne, of the coast, of the Chorl."

I turned toward him with a twinge of surprise. I'd thought he'd tell me what to do, that he'd order me to do it, as he'd ordered me to stay in Amenkor instead of going on the scouting mission, as he'd ordered me to come to Venitte.

Instead, he simply nodded. "It's your decision."

Then he stepped back.

I looked at Baill, at his men, felt Brandan kneeling beside Lord Sorrenti beside me. In the distance, I heard a reverberating thud, an explosion, whether from the water of the port or the northern quarters I couldn't tell. It didn't matter.

I moved, stopped a half pace before Baill, a little too close. The two cohorts to either side shifted, restless, but Baill didn't react, simply stared down at me.

And then, before I could speak, he knelt.

With a rustle of armor and cloth, every member of the Band knelt as well, most crossing themselves with the Skewed Throne, a few murmuring prayers, too softly for me to hear the words.

I stared out over their hunched bodies, their bowed heads, the black-and-red banner flapping fitfully once.

And then I said, "We don't have time for this. Erick! Work with Baill to organize the men. You!" Sorrenti's commander started as I pointed to him. "Gather up Sorrenti's body and bring it with us. Carefully!"

The commander looked toward Brandan, who nodded curtly as he stood.

"And what do you intend to do?" Avrell asked as the group kneeling behind me suddenly lurched into motion, Erick's and Baill's orders shattering the silence, Sorrenti's men joining them, four squatting down by Sorrenti's inert body. Two of them threw his arms over their shoulders and lifted, his feet dragging on the ground beneath them.

"I intend to take care of the gate," I said, walking forward until I stood ten paces from the iron-bound doors themselves, the Wall looming above me, stone stretching out to either side. Staring up at its height, I barked, "Marielle, Heddan, Gwenn!"

When I turned, I found them already behind me, Erick ordering the rest of the men back. I frowned. Gwenn and Heddan stood to either side of me and slightly behind. Marielle stood two paces farther back midway between them, centered, directly behind my position. An array I recognized—the diamond pattern the Ochean had used with her Servants when she'd attacked Amenkor, when she'd shattered the gate in the last wall.

They'd already submerged themselves in the river. I could feel their power pulsing, felt a shiver as conduits slid into place.

Behind them, Baill's forces and those guardsmen that had survived the Chorl at the Stone Garden stood ready, William, Ottul, Avrell, and Brandan Vard among them. I caught Erick's gaze, Baill's, and said, "This is going to have to be quick."

"Then it will be bloody as well," Baill said in answer.

I nodded gravely in acknowledgment, then spun, flung my arms out wide to either side as the matrix of conduits that Marielle, Heddan, and Gwenn had formed snapped into place around me, touched me, and poured power into my body. An electric power, the force sizzling against my skin, wild and raw and ferocious, like the lightning that Brandan commanded, like the power Cerrin had called that had burned through him while creating the thrones. It surged up through my chest, up through my arms, pulsing with the beat of my heart, with all of our hearts as I forged it into a hammer, into a ram to beat down the gates. More energy then I'd ever handled without the throne to support me, more power than one person should wield alone. It tingled in my fingers, arced out from my hands in invisible sheets, flared higher and higher as it built, a coruscating field of light that I knew could only be seen by the Servants, smell-ing sharp and bitter, tasting of acrid smoke and the dry husks of dead pine needles, of sap and bark.

And when it felt as if I could no longer contain it, when it felt as if my body would explode with the contained power, I released it toward the gates, toward the Wall, with a wordless roar.

✝— Chapter 16

The hammer fell with ponderous and invisible weight, and the gates shattered. Wood beams as thick as a man cracked with a dry snap, like tinder. Metal shrieked as it twisted, wrenched from stone, the torturous sound piercing the shocked cries of the men behind me, blending with my own roar of frustration, of sheer anger.

But the Wall—Deranian's Wall—the stone that had stood for thousands of years . . .

The Wall itself resisted.

I had enough time to sever the conduits that fed the hammer, enough time to draw in a sharp breath, eyes widening in shock—

And then the backlash of power from the Wall, a shudder that rippled away from the gates in a wave, struck.

I flinched, flung my hands up before me, expecting the wave to hurl me backward into the mass of waiting guardsmen, expecting it to suck the breath from my lungs, to hit me with killing force because I hadn't had time to erect a shield to shunt it to the side. I heard Gwenn shriek, heard Heddan gasp in dismay, felt a dagger of guilt sink deep inside me for acting so rashly, for care-lessly wielding a power I'd never controlled before—

But with cold smoothness a shield appeared, stretching from building to building across the Gutter's street, the river solidifying in the space of a breath. I felt the wave ripple up the shield's length, wash past overhead, its horrible, angry weight pressing down on me like heavy cloth, smothering me, crushing me. I heard the horrifying rumble of stone as the buildings to either side took the brunt of the recoil of power and shattered beneath it, splinters of stone hurtling down into the street. I felt a sliver of pain as one nicked my neck, heard screams and groans from behind, tasted blood on the river. Dust filled the air, the grit cloying, and without thought I sucked it into my lungs, instantly began coughing, shielding my eyes against it. . . .

And saw Ottul, one hand raised, her eyes closed, their corners pinched against the strain of holding the shield as the wave of power washed overhead.

When the rumble of settling stone faded, she opened her eyes and her gaze fell on me. Lowering her hand, she bowed her head. The gold rings in her ears glinted with the diffuse sunlight. "Ochean."

I didn't respond.

To one side, dust beginning to settle, someone gasped, "Mistress' tits."

I shot the man a glare, then turned.

The gates stood open. One side hung by a twisted hinge, skewed inward, its center cracked and indented as if it had been struck with a battering ram the size of a wagon. The other door had been completely ripped free from the stone.

The Wall itself seemed whole. Only a few cracks had appeared in the outer edges of the arc, a chunk no larger than my head ripped free in one spot. The most serious damage had occurred where the iron of the hinges had been embedded in the wall.

And to the Gutter's buildings on either side. The backlash had collapsed the building on the right, and only two walls remained of the one on the left. They'd been reduced to heaps of rock.

"What happened?" Erick demanded, moving up to my side with Brandan.

"There's more to Deranian's Wall than just stone," I said flatly. "It protected itself."

"I wonder if the Chorl encountered the same thing at the main gates," Brandan said.

Erick's eyes narrowed as he took in the damage, then fixed on something on the far side. "There are bodies."

Something twisted in my gut, but before I could react, Erick had motioned the men forward. They surged over the strewn rubble, over the blocks of stone that had skittered out into the street, over the dust and shards of wood at the gate. After a quick glance to make certain that my Servants had survived—my gaze flickering over their somber faces—I followed, close on Erick's heels.

The guardsmen fanned out on the far side. In the near distance, horns sounded. I could see the Council chambers, Lord March's smaller palace behind, the barracks for the Protectorate. Men battled near the main gates, jagged lightning occasionally punctuating the sky. Daeriun's forces must have hit the gates while we were entering the Gutter. Smoke and dust rose into the air from that direction, and farther away, beyond the Wall to the north, where Lord March battled Atlatik.

But here, at the Gutter's gate, everything was quiet.

Because everyone that had been stationed at the gate was dead.

"They were killed hours ago," the commander of Sorrenti's guard said from where he knelt beside one man's body. The neatly trimmed beard of the dead man was matted with dried blood, the stain a flaky brown. He'd been stabbed in the neck.

Sorrenti's commander leaned back, his eyes flicking over the debris inside the Wall, over the bodies.

There were at least twenty within sight.

"I'd say they were killed when the battle first started, when the Chorl made their appearance in the Stone Garden," he said. Then he caught my gaze, Brandan's. "The assassinations of the Council members, the appearance in the Stone Garden, the elimination of the guards here—it must have been a coordinated attack."

"By who?" Erick asked. "Who killed these men if the Chorl were in the Garden or at the main gates?"

Standing beside Erick, Baill shrugged. "Does it matter? Someone with forces inside the Wall."

"Demasque," I said, with certainty, with fury, even though I had no reason to believe it. "And Lady Parmati."

No one answered. But when a thundering roar echoed from the main gates, followed by battle cries, all of the guardsmen tensed.

"Where do we go from here?" Brandan asked.

I straightened. "The Council chambers."

All eyes turned toward the immense building, toward the battle raging in its courtyard, a seething mass of men, indistinguishable from one another at this distance.

"Then let's get moving," Baill said, and I could hear the grim determination in his words, could feel his anticipation of the coming fight on the river. It smelled of old blood, of sweat, and strangely, of fresh earth and loam.

Erick barked orders—the orders repeated by Baill's lieutenants at Baill's nod.

And then we ran.

No one spoke, everyone's eyes fixed on the battle in front of the Council chambers. There was no need to speak. Everyone could see that the plaza in front of the building contained Venittian guardsmen, the Protectorate mixed with one of the Lord's or Lady's personal men. I couldn't tell which Lord or Lady, and it didn't matter. All that mattered was that the doors to the Council chamber were being defended by the Chorl, the area in front clogged with their brightly colored clothing, their fierce faces, the tattoos bold in the sunlight, their blue skin striking. They fought with a raw intensity, with no mercy, and unlike their attack on Amenkor, they fought in relative silence—no battle cries, no ululations. Because they didn't want to draw attention to *this* fight, to *this* battle. The real battle. Atlatik and the forces outside the Wall—the forces attacking to the north and in the harbor—they were the diversion.

Haqtl was the true threat.

If he took the throne, he would take the city.

And as we drew closer, as the screams and grunts of the men grew louder, clearer, as the clash of swords and armor became sharp and piercing, as the pool in the center of the plaza came into view and I saw it stained with blood and clogged with broken bodies, I realized it was going to be harder to get into the Council chambers than I'd thought.

Because on the river, power gathered, and fire bloomed, men shrieking as they fell back from the door, those closest to the building twisting as they were engulfed by flames.

I spat a curse, picked up speed, felt Erick and Baill, my shadows to either side, adjust to the new pace without thought.

"What?" Erick gasped. He wasn't winded, but his voice was tight and clipped with effort.

I shook my head. "Haqtl has Servants."

"Of course he does," Baill responded, his voice laced with condescension. "They helped take down the gates."

I nodded, would have cursed my own stupidity if I hadn't been focusing on the doorway, on the Chorl, on the ebb and flow of the battle.

We were almost upon the rear of the Venittian forces. Bodies littered the street, the trampled gardens and grounds to either side.

Our forces pulled in tight.

"Straight to the doors," I said, narrowing my eyes. "Whatever the cost."

I sensed both Erick's and Baill's acceptance, didn't turn to catch their nods. Reaching for the river, gathering it before me in a wedge shape, I thought of what Baill had said at the Gutter's gate.

This was going to be bloody.

And then we reached the fringe of the fighting force, a battle cry rising from the men on all sides, a warning to the Venittians already fighting, most at the rear clutching wounds, faces haggard with shock.

I didn't wait for them to get out of the way. I pushed the wedge on the river forward, thrust the Venittian men to either side, heard them cry out as the wall of force I'd created hit them from behind and *shoved*.

My forces plowed into the opening, the Venittians stumbling away to either side, or flung there.

In the space of one heartbeat, two, I found myself facing one of the blue-skinned Chorl warriors.

I'd already drawn my dagger, couldn't remember when. Without stopping, without even slowing my forward momentum, I slashed the dagger across his eyes, felt the blade connect with skin, grate against bone, heard the warrior scream as my other hand connected with his chest, grabbed the colored, silky cloth—purple and gold—and wrenched him out of my path, still alive but blinded. I had no time to think about him, the Chorl crushing forward. I took the next man in the gut, the dagger punching in and out in a single, sharp motion as my hand found the back of his head, pulled his body down and into the thrust and then shoving him down farther, to the flagstone underneath already littered with bodies, the white stone stained black-red. I heard Erick grunt to my left, tasted his blade on the river as it cut, as it slashed, felt myself sinking deeper and deeper into the ebb and flow as my dagger sank into a neck, slipped free smoothly, grated past ribs, pierced armor and cut sinew and muscle on arms, shoulders, faces. To the right, Baill bellowed, his roar filling the plaza, echoing against the walls. An answering roar came from behind, from the Band, from the Venittian guardsmen and the Protectorate, men surging forward. Lightning bit into the Chorl forces, plied by Brandan. I felt it on the river, had sunk so deep the entire plaza had coalesced into a single moving force with its own currents, its own tides. Like the ocean.

And like the ocean, I felt the Venittian forces behind beginning to swell, to build as they rallied and pushed forward against the Chorl.

The Chorl began to solidify in reaction. The Chorl Servants began to link, the conduits snapping into place with a visceral shudder.

Ottul barked out a warning, her voice behind, distant. Marielle shouted, "Mistress!"

I grunted as I shoved my dagger up into a Chorl warrior's arm-pit, his sword arm dropping limp to his side as he howled into my face, splattering me with blood and snot. Jerking the dagger free, I stepped back, let him fall, felt Erick take my place without pause, without direction, the motion smooth, practiced.

Marielle reached for me on the river, Heddan stretching out from the opposite side. All of the sessions in the palace garden at Amenkor slid into place as we linked.

Gwenn began to join the link, from farther back, near where Ottul's voice had come from, but I shook my head, even though she couldn't see, blocked her efforts using the river. I smelled her confusion, her disappointment, bitter, like smoke and ash.

"The Servants!" I shouted, not certain she could hear over the battle, over the screams and the clash of weapons. But her confusion faded.

Then there was no time. The Chorl Servants' power escalated . . .

And released.

Fire blasted upward, no longer targeted toward a single location. This fire spread out from the Chorl center in a wave, rising high over the Chorl warriors' heads, arching outward, cresting as the flames reached their peak and began to boil downward.

Down toward the Venittian forces, toward the Band.

I gazed up at the falling flames. Not a ball of fire like on *The Maiden*. A sheet of fire, falling like rain.

Men to either side screamed as they saw it, began to break the lines, to retreat.

Brow creasing, I drew from Marielle and Heddan and threw up a shield.

The fire struck; I gasped as it bore down, sank down to one knee, and gritted my teeth beneath its weight, hands flying up over my head, palms flat, as if I were pushing against the fire myself. It sizzled as it met the shield, hissed in fury as it boiled up its length as the Servants that controlled it sought the shield's edges, until the entire front ranks of Venittians and the Band were covered in a seething, roaring blanket of fire. Men cried out, first in fear as they had on the practice fields, then in shock and wonder. Heat seeped downward, turned my face waxy, sweat dripping from my chin in a stream. The ranks that had a moment before been on the verge of collapse hesitated.

And into the hesitation I felt the river form into a scintillant sliver of power, felt the dagger of force release.

Gwenn.

A scream erupted from the Chorl forces as the dagger struck. A scream of rage, of pain, and the power that fed the fire overhead jerked as one of the conduits was severed.

Before anyone could react, two more daggers flew into the Chorl forces— from both Gwenn and Ottul—followed by two more cries of pain.

The Chorl Servants couldn't defend themselves. They'd poured all of their strength into the fire.

The force behind the fire weakened. One Servant dropped out, her conduit cut, the energy shunted into a shield. Another held her conduit tight, in desperation, but another of Gwenn's daggers took her in the throat.

The awful weight of the fire overhead lifted. The flames shuddered as the power that fed them began to retreat, to pull back and regroup.

But they didn't retreat fast enough.

Lurching to my feet, I shoved my own shield upward and forward with a growl, tilting it—

And sent the retreating fire—its strength drained, the power that had controlled it dissipating—cascading down onto the Chorl warriors.

Screams pierced the plaza, instant and fierce, as fire rained down from above. Half of the Chorl forces were engulfed, the quarters too close and too packed for the warriors to retreat, to flee. They were trapped between the building and the Venittian forces.

The black smell of burning flesh, of charred, crackling skin, slammed into the river, drove me back a step as the backwash of wind from the feeding fire pushed against my face. Oily smoke rose, and the leading edge of Chorl broke.

The Venittians and the Band hesitated a heartbeat, two . . . and then surged into the disintegrating line.

"The doors!" Erick barked.

I spun, immediately spotting the Council chamber's open doorway and the relatively clear path the fire had purged to it.

"Baill!" I barked, but he'd already seen it. With chilling precision, he stabbed the Chorl warrior he fought through the heart, shoved the body off of his blade, and barked, "Warren! Patch!" and nodded toward the door.

The two men he'd singled out whistled sharply, and suddenly Erick and I were surrounded by twenty bloody, sweating men, all from the Band, all with swords drawn, a few with obvious nicks or wounds, none of them serious.

"Mistress," Baill said, gruffly.

"Go."

The men surged through the break. Erick and I followed, stepping over charred bodies, some still on fire, past the last desperate struggles between the Venittians and the Chorl, past the fallen corpses of two of the Chorl Servants, their green dresses stained black with blood from Gwenn's daggers.

We entered the grand foyer and huge inner chamber, Chorl wounded and dead lining the walls. Without asking, moving swiftly, Baill and the members of his Band cut the throats of those still alive, a few struggling to raise their swords, their wounds too grievous for anything but a token defense.

"Where to?" Baill asked as he cleaned his blade using one of the dead Chorl's brightly colored shirts.

I nodded to the inner doors. They'd been closed, but I could feel the power of the throne already, could feel its presence, could hear the faintest of whispers, a hissing of agitated voices, like the skitter of dead leaves across cobblestones.

I shuddered.

The Band formed up to either side of the doors. Erick stayed at my side, his jaw clenched, his hand clutching his Seeker's dagger, the knuckles white. I tried to catch his gaze, but he was too focused on the doors, on the inner chamber.

At Baill's nod, Warren shoved against the doors, hard, the cords in his neck standing out with the effort.

Finally, he gasped and drew back, shaking his head. "It's barricaded on the inside."

Erick's brow furrowed, but before he could respond, before Baill could even turn, I said, "Allow me."

I gathered the river, saw the comprehension on the Band's faces a moment before they leaped back from the doorway.

The doors exploded, the tables and chairs that had been stacked against it on the far side splintering as they were flung backward, Lord March's desk scraping across the marble floor. Men shouted warnings, blue-skinned Chorl rushing forward toward the breach, but Baill and the Band raced into the new opening and met them.

Swords clashed, but I didn't watch the fight, barely noticed it on the river as the last of the Chorl's minimal force were killed, as the Band formed up on either side of the door.

Because the Council chamber beyond, where the Council of Eight ruled, had changed, had been transformed.

The banners of the Lords and Ladies still hung on the walls, but the tables and chairs the Council had used to preside over Venitte's affairs had been turned into a barricade at the door and were now scattered and broken around the room, Lord March's immense desk now shoved to one side by the blast, scarred and cracked. Where it had stood, where the far black wall curved outward into the room, the patterned marble floor radiating outward from the wall in triangular rays like a sun, now stood a pointed, open arch, a doorway that led—

I felt the visceral pain of death, of memory, slide through me, bitterly cold and torturously sharp.

Cerrin, I thought.

And felt an answering whisper from the throne, a momentary rise in the whisper of voices, like a gust of wind.

"What is it?"

Erick's voice slid through the memories that cut me, through the barely audible voices that froze me in place.

I turned my head, caught his gaze, saw the raw urgency there, saw the hatred. A deep, burning hatred that halted my breath.

And then I remembered, then I understood: Haqtl waited on the far side of the room.

Haqtl—the man who had placed the blanket of pain over Erick, had tortured him at the Ochean's command, had driven the spine into his chest.

I drew in a short breath, forced the anger that rose from Erick's pain to one side.

"It's the entrance to the true Council chambers," I said, and even I heard the rawness in my voice, rough, like stone grating against stone. "The Council chambers the Seven ruled from." I turned back to the opening and in a much softer voice, I added, "That's where they all died."

The archway that now stood behind Lord March's position, where he had presided over the Council of Eight, was filled with a white light that obscured what lay within. A light as bright as the White Fire that had engulfed the coast seven years before. I'd seen the doorway many times from the far side, through Cerrin's memories, but never from the outside. Yet even here, I could feel the throne, its force so much more intense than it had been outside. It filled the room, heavy and dense. I breathed it in with every breath, felt it touching me, the fine hairs on my arms prickling beneath it. I heard it circling, tasted it against my tongue. Raw and powerful and angry.

And waiting.

No one moved. The Band shifted restlessly. I sensed their hesitation, their fear, knew that they could feel the throne as well, even if they couldn't identify it.

Drawing in a steadying breath, I stepped forward, through the debris, across the chamber where I'd faced Lord March and the Council of Eight, where I'd faced Lord Demasque. Splinters and stone grit ground beneath my feet, cracking and popping as I moved.

I paused before the doorway, before the white light, raised a hand before me, felt its soft glow without touching it, recognized its frigid taste.

The Fire inside me pulsed with the same heartbeat.

Then I stepped into it.

The Fire slid through me, entered inside of me, the flames licking down deep, deeper, as deep as they had when the wall of White Fire blazed through Amenkor, when I was eleven and trapped beneath the hand of the ex-guardsman I'd killed moments after the Fire had passed. I shuddered as the memory rose to the surface, as real and visceral as if it had just happened, as clear and penetrating as it had felt then. I trembled beneath the pain, beneath the terror, realized that I had trembled then, dazed, back grinding into the stone roof where I'd been thrown beneath the chill night air, beneath the stars as the man's hand pressed hard into my chest, forcing the air from my lungs, his hands fumbling with the drawstrings of his breeches, his voice hoarse, ragged with anticipation. I saw his rough, unshaven jaw, his feral eyes with grit at their corners, his dirty, splotchy skin, his matted chunks of hair. I smelled his rank breath, his musty clothing. And I tasted the cold steel of his knife, his dagger, forgotten in his haste, in his excitement.

Forgotten by him, but not by me. I reached for it—

And walked through the Fire into the chamber beyond, out of memory and into the Council of Seven. For a moment that felt like eternity I tasted that night, tasted that pain, that horror. . . .

And then the memory faded, and the Council chamber asserted itself.

It appeared exactly as I remembered it: obsidian walls, obsidian marble floor, domed ceiling as black as night. Ambient white light emanated from the surrounding walls as it had over fifteen hundred years before. Except this light seemed pallid, less vibrant. Aged. Seven seats filled the chamber, circling the outer edges, each one different, each one . . . personal; the seats of the Seven who had ruled from here, the last of the Adepts—Cerrin, Liviann, Garus, Seth, Atreus, Silicia, and Alleryn.

In the center of the room sat the throne. The Stone Throne, hidden for fifteen hundred years.

It had never been moved, had never left Venitte. It had been hidden in plain sight.

And seated in the throne, surrounded by a covey of Chorl warriors and priests, sat Haqtl.

The warriors hadn't seen me enter. Their attention was fixed on Haqtl, on the strange, intent expression on his face, the tension there. The Chorl priest—the man who had tortured Erick, who had held him prisoner and kept him in constant pain even after we had rescued him—sat perfectly rigid, back straight, hands on the arms of the granite throne. His brow was creased, his hands clenched. Sweat stood out on his forehead.

Because the throne fought him. Because Sorrenti fought him.

I felt the energy in the room shift, felt Erick pass through the White Fire behind me, followed by Baill, Warren, Patch, the others from the Band. I turned as they entered, saw some of them grimace in distaste or shudder convulsively, wondered briefly what memories the Fire called up for them, but then shrugged the thoughts aside. They didn't matter. Nothing mattered except Haqtl and the throne.

And Erick.

As they fell into place behind me, I turned toward the throne and stepped forward.

The motion caught one of the Chorl warriors' attention. He barked a curt warning.

With a flurry of commands and the clatter of armor, the group of men encircled the throne, swords drawn. But they stayed back from the throne itself, keeping a distance of at least three paces.

And then I noticed the bodies. Two of them, both Chorl, one a warrior, the other a priest. They lay against the marble two paces from Haqtl and the throne, their pale blue faces stark against the obsidian floor, their dark eyes wide with shock.

There wasn't a mark on them. No wounds, no blood. Nothing.

I narrowed my eyes, shifted my gaze to the leader of the men.

No one moved.

Not letting my gaze waver from the Chorl captain, I said, "You're outnumbered."

He didn't understand the words, but he understood the intent. His gaze flickered over Baill and the Band, settled the longest on Erick, then came back to me. He said nothing.

"Baill."

The ex-guardsman of Amenkor nodded at the command in my voice. Face locked into familiar stony creases, he ordered the Band forward.

"Don't get too close to the throne," I warned as the Chorl tensed, those behind the leader readying for a fight. One of the Chorl priests waved his hand, sent something I couldn't see flying toward Baill, but I deflected it with a shield, Baill never flinching. The priest frowned, but at a look from the leader, he halted another gesture in mid-motion.

Keeping his eyes on me, the leader straightened, then lowered his sword. Moving carefully, he and the rest of the Chorl stepped to one side, keeping their backs to the wall of the obsidian chamber, their swords toward us.

I turned my attention back to Haqtl, to the throne. Granite, like the Skewed Throne in Amenkor, and at the moment shaped like a simple chair. Fine lines, elegant, with subtle curves to the legs, to the arms and back. No ostentatious details, no real markings of any kind.

I could see Sorrenti sitting in such a throne.

"Are we in time?" Erick asked, and once again I remembered that he hadn't been in the throne room when the Ochean arrived, hadn't witnessed those events.

"Sorrenti is still in control," I said.

"How do you know?" His voice was rough, threaded with hatred, with a raw need, with remembered pain.

"Because that's Sorrenti's throne," I said softly, trying to calm him, to ease the tension I felt bleeding from him. And it *was* like blood, from a wound that had not healed, that perhaps would never heal. "If the throne starts to change shape, then we'll know Haqtl has begun to win."

He nodded. The hand gripping his dagger flexed as his attention shifted from Haqtl's face to the throne itself. "Then we need to kill him before that happens."

He started forward.

I sensed a sudden surge of anticipation from the Chorl, and my hand snapped out, latched onto Erick's arm. "Wait."

He halted. "What is it?" he asked, no anger, no doubt in his voice. But his attention never wavered from the throne, from Haqtl, and I could sense his frustration.

He wanted Haqtl dead, *needed* to see him dead.

I glanced toward the Chorl leader, saw his eyes narrow. Then I stepped in front of Erick, forced him to meet my gaze.

It was harder than I thought. And when he finally did look at me, I flinched back from the horror of memory I saw reflected there. I wanted to remove that pain, the terror that had bruised him, that I had sent him into by placing him on *The Maiden,* by putting him at risk.

But I couldn't. Instead, I swallowed, something hard clicking in my throat, and said in as calm a voice as possible, "There's something surrounding the throne, a barrier of some kind. I can't see it, but it's there. I think it killed those two Chorl, the warrior and the priest lying dead on the floor."

"It did," Baill said, his voice too loud, echoing in the chamber. "No one approached the Skewed Throne in Amenkor when someone was seated on it because they knew it would be their death. No one can get close. It's how the throne protects itself, protects the person currently in control." He glanced toward Haqtl. "Or trying to claim control. Otherwise, the person on the throne would be vulnerable."

Erick grunted, the skin around his eyes tightening. "Then how are we going to kill him?"

I thought about the Skewed Throne, about Sorrenti, about Cerrin and the rest of the Seven. I thought about the memories from fifteen hundred years before, of the death of Cerrin's wife and children, of the battles the Seven had fought against the Chorl and of their deaths here, in this room, as they created the thrones, as they *forged* them.

Memories I could not possibly have. Not with the Skewed Throne destroyed.

But memories I'd relived nonetheless. Because of the Stone Throne, this throne. Because somehow I was connected to it, bound to it, as I'd been bound to the Skewed Throne. Bound to it *by* the Skewed Throne. Sorrenti had felt that connection. The Seven had felt it, even though they hadn't understood it. And I'd felt it, when I'd returned from speaking with Eryn, from Reaching, and had recovered far too fast from the effects of that Reaching.

I turned away from Erick, stepped forward, and this time Erick reached out to halt me.

"What are you doing?" he asked, his voice hard, like stone. Stern, but with a slight catch. Not the voice of a teacher, of a trainer.

The voice of a father.

"I'm the only one who can do this," I said. "I'm the only one who can get close enough. I think the throne will recognize me. I think it will let me pass the barrier."

His brow furrowed, his eyes darkening as they gazed down at me. He wanted to refuse me, didn't want me to take the risk.

"I can feel it, Erick," I added. "I can *hear* it."

His hand tightened a moment, the muscles of his jaw clenching, but then he relaxed, his hand dropping from my arm.

He said nothing. He didn't need to say anything.

I turned back, moved to within two paces of the throne, to where the bodies of the two Chorl had fallen, and then hesitated. This close, I could feel the barrier, like a thousand needles pricking the skin of my face, my hands, my arms and torso, a sensation not unlike the blanket of needles that Haqtl had placed over Erick and used to torture him. And I could feel the presence of the throne, throbbing, pulsing with my own heartbeat beneath that prickling sensation, could hear the whisper of the throne itself, calling me.

Dry leaves scraping against cobblestones.

I raised my hands toward the barrier, drew in a slow breath—

And then stepped forward.

Pain lanced down my side and I cried out, heard at a distance Erick cry out as well. Daggers sliced down the lengths of my arms, down my shoulders, down my chest, blades cutting into flesh, flaying the skin from me. I heard a howling whirlwind of voices, the dry whispers I'd heard before escalating into a screaming frenzy, a cacophony of glee and rage and torment, of pain and suffering. The daggers dug deeper, sank into muscle, edges dragging through sinew as the tips of metal neared bone, as the voices grew louder, as a single voice began to roar above all of the others—

And then abruptly the pain cut off. The daggers withdrew and, as I collapsed to my knees on the floor, panting, hands cupped over my head protectively, the single voice bellowing above all of the others slowly began to drown them all out. A voice I recognized. A voice I knew.

Cerrin.

When all of the voices of the throne had quieted, lost beneath his roar, he broke the battle cry off, let everything fall into silence.

I heard a struggle, raised my head far enough through the last vestiges of the pain the barrier had inflicted to see Baill and Patch restraining Erick at the edge of the barrier itself.

When Erick saw me move, his struggling ceased. But Baill and Patch didn't back away, didn't even relax. "Varis?"

Varis? Cerrin echoed.

I sat up, slid into a low crouch. A familiar crouch, one I'd used a thousand times on the Dredge. "I'm fine, Erick. It . . . took a moment for the throne to recognize me."

Sorrenti can't hold out much longer, Varis. You haven't got much time. Haqtl's almost seized control.

Help him, I growled. *Stop Haqtl.*

Do you think we haven't tried? Liviann demanded.

We've done all that we can, Cerrin interceded, a note of warning in his voice, directed toward Liviann. *Haqtl is more powerful than Sorrenti.* He paused a moment, then added, *Haqtl can control the Fire.*

Like me, I thought.

I rose from my crouch, shifted my grip on my dagger, took the single step to the throne and stood before Haqtl, before the Chorl priest who had brought the Chorl armies here, to Venitte, before the man who had driven the poisoned spine into Erick's chest with a slow, twisted smile and laid the blanket of needles over Erick's body.

My heart hardened.

Kill him, Cerrin said. *But don't touch the throne. You were protected from the barrier because you were part of the Skewed Throne, but nothing can protect you from the Stone Throne itself, from direct contact with it.*

I frowned. The throne had a back, protecting Haqtl from my blade. I couldn't cut him from behind, couldn't slit his throat. I couldn't stab him low in the back so that he'd die slowly, as I'd killed men before. And I wanted him to die slowly. I wanted him to suffer, as much as he'd made Erick suffer.

But my choices were limited.

I slid closer, leaned in toward Haqtl's strained face, toward his blue skin, his black tattoos, until I could smell him. Sea salt. Seaweed. The stench of rotting fish.

I wrinkled my nose in disgust.

And then Cerrin shouted, *Varis!* and I felt the shudder as the throne began to change, the feet of the throne rippling, the stone morphing into the shape of reeds. The other voices of the throne cried out in dismay.

And the intensity in Haqtl's face relaxed, that slow smile touching his lips. The same smile he'd used while torturing Erick.

I plunged the dagger into his stomach with a harsh, vicious grunt.

When his eyes flew open, shocked, I said, too softly for anyone else except Haqtl and the voices in the throne to hear, "For Erick, you bastard."

Then I wrenched the dagger to the side, twisted it, felt it cut free, and stepped back, blood dripping from my hand, from the tip of the dagger where it hung slack at my side.

Haqtl gasped. His hands flew to his gut as he hunched over, blood splashing, staining his breeches, his yellow shirt, pouring over his hands until they were black with it, until his blue skin and tattoos could no longer be seen. He sucked in a single, horrible breath, his lean becoming a tilt, the momentum carrying him forward. He bent over his own lap, blood beginning to slide down the legs of the stone throne, beginning to drip from the seat where it pooled beneath him. He tipped his head to one side, arms clutching his stomach now, his face contorted with pain.

But then it transformed, the pain sliding into hatred, into rage, his jaw clenching, protruding forward slightly. It made him look cruel, barbaric. His eyes flashed, and the intensity there, the raw emotion, reminded me of his eyes as he'd stood over Erick and tortured him.

"*You . . .*" he spat. Blood speckled his lips, drooled from the corner of his mouth.

And with that one word, filled with all of his hatred, all of his derision and anger, he died.

His body toppled forward, sliding from the throne in a bundle, his face hitting the obsidian floor first with a dull thud, then shifting forward as the weight of his hunched body pushed him downward.

He came to rest, arms still folded across his stomach but loosely, body slightly curved. Blood began to pool beneath him.

I turned, sought out Erick. I needed to see his face.

He stood, Baill and Patch beside him and slightly behind. He stared at Haqtl's body, his eyes impassive, empty. Lost.

To one side, the remaining Chorl tensed, raised their swords. I thought about those we'd held captive after Amenkor, about their suicides, about what Ottul had told us of the Chorl themselves, and knew that these would not surrender.

"Baill," I said. "Try to keep as many of them alive as possible."

He understood immediately. Shoving Patch away from Erick, who didn't move at all, he barked an order to the rest of the Band. They closed in on the Chorl. I heard the Chorl battle cry, the strange ululations, piercing and sharp, heard the subsequent clash of swords, but I didn't take my eyes from Erick.

I moved to stand before him, noted that the shield that had protected the throne while Haqtl sat on it was gone.

"Erick."

When he didn't respond, I reached forward and caught his arm with my free hand.

He flinched, his gaze dropping to meet mine.

He looked . . . haunted.

"Erick," I said, squeezing his arm. "This isn't over. We still need to stop the fighting in the city, the battle in the harbor."

For a moment, his gaze held, the haunted, empty look remaining, as if he hadn't heard me. But then he shuddered, the tremor running through his body. He closed his eyes.

And when he opened them again, the emptiness had been shoved into the background, replaced by the coldness of a Seeker.

"How do you intend to stop it?" he asked.

I looked to where the fighting between the Band and the Chorl had ended— none of the Chorl had survived—and caught Baill's look.

"We'll need Haqtl's body."

We emerged from the Council building to find the Venittian and Amenkor forces searching through the bodies that littered the stone steps and the rectangular pool of water for survivors, slitting the throats of the Chorl and hauling the Venittians and those from the Band that had been wounded to one side, where Avrell and Brandan had organized a makeshift hospital. As soon as we exited into the early evening sunlight, Haqtl's body in tow, a cheer roared through the plaza.

Followed immediately by the dull thud of an explosion from outside the Wall, and a sizzling crack of thunder.

Avrell moved immediately to my side, William, Brandan, Marielle, and Ottul behind him. A gash ran across William's cheek, deep enough that it would leave a scar. Marielle and Ottul looked haggard and drained, but unharmed.

All of them looked weary.

"Where's Sorrenti?" I asked Brandan, before any of them could speak.

"Recovering," Brandan said, his tone grim. He pointed to where Sorrenti sat with his back against one of the stone columns surrounding the body-clogged and bloody pool. "He woke a few moments ago, but he's exhausted."

I remembered my own battle with the Ochean, remembered the sheer weariness I'd felt immediately afterward, and nodded. "What about Heddan and Gwenn?"

"They're helping with the wounded," Marielle said.

"We started triage as soon as the last of the Chorl were killed," Avrell added.

"Good." I scanned the people of Venitte, saw one of the Protectorate approaching, stepping carefully through the dead. "Baill, get the Band ready. We're heading toward the northern part of the city."

Baill moved away instantly, Warren and Patch following. Their piercing whistles broke through the moans of the wounded and the silence of the dead, the Band converging on the still standing black-and-red Skewed Throne banner.

When the captain of the Protectorate drew close enough, I said, "The Chorl within the Council chambers are dead."

He nodded grimly, his eyes falling on Haqtl's body, which the members of the Band that Baill had left behind had dropped unceremoniously to the ground. "Daeriun sends word that the Chorl at the gates have also been halted. Their priests and Servants caused massive damage in the first strike at the Wall, but he's managed to overwhelm them with the Venittian Servants." He shot a respectful glance toward Brandan, then continued his report to me. "He's finishing off the last of the Chorl resistance there now, but there is still fighting to the north and in the harbor."

"My men are forming up to head to the north. We'll join up with Daeriun at the Wall."

Before he could answer, someone said, "Ethan."

Everyone turned. I frowned at Sorrenti where he stood behind Avrell and

Marielle and Ottul. His face was tinged an unhealthy gray, but I saw no sign of tremors.

"Ready the men," Sorrenti said. "We'll be joining the Mistress."

The captain of the Protectorate nodded sharply, turned, then shouted an order across the plaza, men picking through the bodies glancing up.

I caught Sorrenti's gaze, but before I could speak, he bowed low and said, "Thank you. Haqtl had almost won. If you hadn't intervened . . ."

"I know." At his frown, I added, "The throne had begun to change shape."

He nodded. "But you were right. In the moments before he began taking control, I touched Haqtl through the throne. Demasque and Parmati were working with him. He'd promised Demasque control of the merchants' guild, not only here in the city, but for the entire coast. He'd promised Parmati rule of the city." He grimaced. "He never intended to keep those promises. He wanted the coast for himself, and he thought the throne—and the Fire—would give it to him."

"Is that enough to convince Lord March and the Council?"

His frown deepened. "Half of the Council is dead. But even then . . ."

I shook my head, turned away. I was tired of Venitte, of their Council. "Never mind. We need to take care of Atlatik now."

Within moments, the Band and the Protectorate had formed two groups at the edge of the plaza, the Protectorate under Sorrenti's command.

"What about the harbor?" Erick asked as I began to make my way through the plaza, my entourage following, the escort from the Band carrying Haqtl's body.

"I don't know. Let's see what happens to the north first."

He grunted.

As soon as I joined Baill, we headed out, Sorrenti and the Protectorate falling in behind us. We marched down through the streets and open gardens to the shattered gates of the Wall, gates that had suffered far more damage than we'd done to the Gutter's gate to the south. Here, the arch of stone above the gate itself had crumbled and lay in ruins across the threshold, bodies crushed beneath the massive stone blocks, dust, and debris. A phalanx of Protectorate held the entrance, but parted as we approached, revealing General Daeriun, surrounded by a core of captains and male Servants.

Daeriun turned. "Mistress. Lord Sorrenti." Blood dripped from a wound in his scalp, and his uniform of blood-red and gold was stained with sweat and blood and dirt. He didn't bother to wipe away the trail of blood on his face, his gaze falling onto Haqtl's body instead. He frowned.

"The threat in the Council chambers is gone," Lord Sorrenti said, "thanks to the Mistress and the Band."

Daeriun grunted, taking in the black-and-red Skewed Throne banners behind me. He raised his eyebrows, but didn't comment. "We've secured the gates here."

"You should also send a force to the Gutter's gate," Sorrenti said. "That's how we got to the Council chambers. But we had to breach the gate as the Chorl did here."

Daeriun turned immediately, motioned to one of his captains without a word. A phalanx of men broke off from his forces and headed to the gate. "Anything else?"

Sorrenti shook his head. "Nothing but Atlatik and the force in the harbor."

"Good. Let's get moving."

Daeriun joined us, his captains returning to the army behind. We began to wind our way north through the Merchant Quarter, through streets littered with the detritus of the Masquerade, with bodies of guardsmen and citizens and Chorl. Furtive glances greeted us from the cracks in window shutters, a glimpse of a pale face that retreated quickly, nothing more. On the river, I could feel the citizens huddled within the buildings, could sense their fear.

Then the sounds of battle grew clearer, sharper. Baill and Erick exchanged glances, and the escort at my sides drew close, a ripple of warning passing back through the ranks. Daeriun's men tightened their formation as well, without a word from him, and Sorrenti's stance shifted.

I sensed a gathering of power ahead of us, felt it being released, heard the explosion of fire and the resultant reverberations on the river. I breathed in the bitter scent of the Venittian Servants' lightning, glanced skyward to see columns of smoke rising into the air—

And then we rounded a corner and the sounds of battle were suddenly too close, screams echoing off of the surrounding buildings, fire blazing from the cavities of doorways and windows, glass shattering in an explosion. Even as we halted, Erick and Baill pausing a pace in front of me, protectively, horns sounded and Lord March appeared on horseback, galloping straight for the Chorl, the Venittian army—mixed with the Amenkor guardsmen led by Captain Catrell—charging beside him. The Chorl answered with their ululating battle cry.

The two met with a thundering crush of bodies and the clash of metal on metal. The disturbance on the river sent a wave scudding past me with a gust of wind. At the same moment, lightning forked into the Chorl forces from behind, some of it deflected by Chorl shields, the bolts striking the stone of the buildings nearby, rock splintering and melting. Fire arched up and over into the Venittian forces, the screams of the dying piercing through the sound of thunder, the explosions, and the clash of steel.

I felt more than saw Daeriun and Sorrenti halt beside me.

"How are we going to stop this?" Sorrenti said.

I shook my head, frowning, then turned toward them both. "We need to show Atlatik, the Chorl captain, that Haqtl is dead. This entire battle—both here and in the harbor—wasn't the main thrust of the attack. If he knows that Haqtl has failed . . ."

Sorrenti nodded once, the gesture sharp and succinct. His color had improved during the march. "Then we need to catch his attention. His and Lord March's."

Before I could ask how, he closed his eyes, drew a deep breath—

And in the sudden stillness that enveloped us, the battle ahead somehow removed, I felt a gathering of power, an echo of a much greater force that tasted of the Stone Throne.

A rumble began to fill the air, a sound that shivered up from the ground, into my feet, vibrating in my bones. It increased, the rumble escalating into a low growl, the stone beneath my feet beginning to tremble, then deepening and growing further, until the ground shook.

Ahead, the two armies—Chorl and coastal—paused, men stepping back, glancing around at the shuddering earth, at the increasing roar—

And then, with a dry, hideous crack, the earth split.

Shards of stone flew skyward as the street where the two armies clashed suddenly lurched and splintered open, a jagged fissure—no more than a handspan across—ripping through the cobbles and buildings to either side. Men cried out, stumbled back from the opening, those closest to the crack thrown off their feet. All of the fighting ceased, both sides stunned.

As the stone shards began raining down on the men nearest the fissure, dust starting to rise, Sorrenti sagged to the ground.

I shoved Baill and Sorrenti's guardsmen aside, knelt down beside him. Daeriun joined me.

Sorrenti tried to lift his head, failed, and gave me a weak grin. "I think," he gasped, coughing slightly, "you have their attention."

I stood, slowly, heard Sorrenti sigh before he lost consciousness, then turned toward the street ahead.

Men were picking themselves up from the ground, scrambling back to their own lines. All of them were looking to the south. Toward us.

Toward me and Daeriun, who stood at my side. Daeriun looked shaken.

"Sorrenti did this?" he asked, too low for anyone but me to hear.

I nodded, then raised my head. "Erick, Baill," I said, and only then realized how quiet it had become, my voice overly loud. "Bring Haqtl's body."

I moved forward, not glancing back to see who followed, aware that Erick and Daeriun stayed with me, that Baill and part of the Band hastily grabbed Haqtl's body and closed in behind.

I headed toward the banners marking Lord March's position, noted that

Atlatik's own banners waited on the far side of the fissure opposite him. The Venittian men parted before us, the Amenkor guardsmen among them nodding as we passed, some signing themselves with the Skewed Throne, a few kneeling. They closed in behind us as we came upon Lord March and his own entourage, his men waiting, swords raised. He dismounted, his face bloody, beard matted with sweat and gore, his eyes black with anger.

"What," he demanded harshly, as I halted before him, "have you done?"

I didn't answer, bowing my head instead. "Lord March."

"She's helped secure the Council chambers and the Wall," Daeriun said into the silence. "And now," he continued, when Lord March's anger faltered, "she intends to stop the fighting here."

His gaze fell on me, his breath coming out in short gasps through his nose. His hand clenched on the hilt of his drawn sword, his armor creaking. The horse behind him snorted and stamped a foot impatiently. He looked over his own men, over the winged helmets of the Protectorate, toward Catrell and his nearest captain, then came back to me. "You can truly end this?"

"I can try, Lord March." When still he hesitated, I added, "Haqtl is dead."

He grunted. "Then try."

I tasted his doubt on the river, heard it clearly in his voice. But I turned toward the Chorl, toward the banners that marked Atlatik's location, and without another word walked past Lord March and his retinue. I crossed the emptied area between the two forces, feet crunching against flagstones, paused at the fissure Sorrenti had created, stared down at its ragged edge a moment, then stepped across it and slowed as I approached the Chorl line. No one but Erick and Baill followed me.

I halted ten paces from the Chorl, glared at their front ranks, at their blue-skinned faces, at their dark blue tattoos, at the vibrant clothes they wore over their armor, now dulled and sullied with dust and blood and sweat. They watched me uncertainly, their dark eyes seething with hatred . . . and a little fear.

And I suddenly realized they thought I'd created the fissure, that I'd made the earth quake. And they knew what that force could do. They'd seen their homeland destroyed by something similar, seen their island slide into the sea beneath its force.

I'd seen it, through the Ochean's eyes in the moments before I destroyed the throne.

I let them relive that memory for a moment, then drew in a deep breath and shouted, "Atlatik!"

The Chorl forces tensed. I'd just drawn breath to shout again, when the group before me grew restless, men shifting out of the way as someone moved forward.

Atlatik stepped through the front line, his bloodied sword held at the ready. I glared into his eyes, remembered staring into them after I'd defeated the Ochean in Amenkor. He'd wanted to attack then, hadn't wanted to back down. But Haqtl had convinced him to retreat. I'd seen him a few times before, through memory—Erick's on *The Maiden,* and Alendor's on a deserted beach— recalled the tattoos that swirled across his face, more dense than those on the other men. The bottom of one ear had been cut off, and his nose had been broken, making his already flat face appear flatter.

He moved forward, came within five paces of me, two other Chorl flanking him.

Erick tensed to my right, and Baill stepped forward on my left, both with hands on swords.

I tasted the tension in the air, bitter, like sap.

"What you want?" Atlatik growled, in broken coastal.

"It's over," I said.

Atlatik snorted, scowled, and spat to one side.

I smiled, then motioned the Band forward.

The men carrying Haqtl's body shuffled forward and dumped the corpse on the ground between us. Both of Atlatik's guardsmen stepped forward threateningly, but they halted once the corpse came to rest, head rolling to one side, his wound obvious.

Someone among the Chorl gasped, said something filled with dismay, with horror, a concerned buzz spreading outward from the voice, carrying back through the ranks.

Until Atlatik barked a command and everyone fell silent.

He looked at me, looked into my eyes, and I saw him standing in front of the reed throne the Ochean had used in their homeland. She'd known then that the warriors would follow the priests, had known that the warriors believed in them, in Haqtl, in what he said. In order to control them, the Ochean had worked through the priests, had manipulated Haqtl to get what she'd wanted.

Seeing their head priest dead had already sent a wave of fear through the Chorl forces, a ripple effect that Atlatik couldn't hope to control. I could sense the unease of the warriors.

And Atlatik knew it. I could see it in his eyes, in the clenching of his jaw.

"It's over," I said again, more forcefully.

His eyes narrowed. His gaze flicked away from me, scanned Lord March's army arrayed behind me. Far in the distance, the battle in the harbor continued, its echoes dulled almost to nothing here in the streets of the northern quarter.

He had enough forces to defeat Lord March here. He might even be able to take the harbor.

But with Haqtl dead, he couldn't take the throne. Which meant he couldn't take the city, couldn't expect to hold it.

He turned back to me, and for a single moment, I thought he'd continue. Better to die fighting than to retreat; better to die than to concede defeat; better to die than be captured.

A sneer crossed his face. "If leave, you follow. You kill us."

I shook my head. "No. We'll let you leave, without fear of attack." Then I stiffened, let the river gather around me, let its menace enter my voice. "But you'll have to retreat to Bosun's Bay. And you'll have to stay there. Or we will attack you, we will destroy you."

His nostrils flared, his sword shifting in his grip. The men behind him grew restless.

In the end, he lowered his head. "We will . . . leave."

His voice was harsh. Grudging. Filled with contempt, with hatred.

I nodded. "Then leave."

He waited a moment, the muscles of his jaw twitching—

Then he turned, motioned with one hand, and shouted something.

A horn was blown—not the brass notes from one of Lord March's horns, but the deeper, throbbing notes from one of the Chorl shells. An answering horn sounded from the direction of the harbor.

The Chorl forces began to regroup, slowly, the Chorl warriors moving as grudgingly as Atlatik.

Atlatik turned his head, stared down at Haqtl's body, his own still rigid with contempt.

Then he spat to one side, sneering, and snapped an order in the Chorl language.

A covey of Chorl warriors ran forward and collected the Chorl priest's body, lifted it quickly, but with reverence, and walked it back toward the Chorl line.

Atlatik paused, gave me one last, long, unreadable look—

Then turned and vanished into his own ranks.

"That was . . . interesting," Erick murmured.

I shuddered, a tension I didn't realize I'd felt releasing in my shoulders. My hand fell away from the handle of my dagger. I hadn't even noticed it had been resting there.

"Come on," I said, heading back toward Lord March and his retinue, toward General Daeriun and the Protectorate. I halted before Lord March, felt the men around him shifting restlessly.

"The Chorl forces are retreating," I said. "They've agreed to go if you allow them to leave without being harried. They'll return to Bosun's Bay. You can try to slaughter them if you want, but they have more men than you, and they have their priests and their Servants—more Servants than you. Personally, I'd let them go."

Lord March sucked in a deep breath . . . then let it out in a heavy sigh. "They've taken the Boreaite Isles, Bosun's Bay and the surrounding area. They have a foothold on the coast."

"Yes. And at the moment they've lost two thirds of their leaders. They've lost their homeland. They've lost a good portion of their men, first in Amenkor, and now here in Venitte."

"We'll have to deal with them eventually," Lord March muttered.

I thought about what Avrell had said on the *Defiant* on the trip to Venitte. The Chorl would have to be dealt with, eventually. We'd have to form a treaty with them, come to some type of agreement about land, about the trade routes between the coast and the Boreaite Isles.

"But not at this moment," I said to Lord March.

Lord March glanced toward the Chorl forces, a frown touching his face.

"If you attack them," I said into his silence, "you'll have to kill them all. Every last one of them—men, women, and children. They came to the coast to find a home, because they have no home left to return to. They're going to stay on the coast. You won't be able to drive them away."

Then, more forcefully, because he still hesitated, "You'll have to kill them *all.*"

And with that, I turned away—

To find Westen waiting.

I took one look at his eyes and knew.

My would-be assassin was dead.

And then I saw the blood on Westen's shirt, the slashes in the cloth, and realized it was his own blood.

I raised my eyebrows and he frowned.

"It appears that the Chorl have their own Seekers," he said.

I stilled, thought of the assassinations attempted in the Stone Garden, thought of those that had succeeded, and sighed.

I began moving through Lord March's forces, leaving General Daeriun and Lord Sorrenti behind. Within moments, my entourage was joined by Captain Catrell.

"Mistress," he said, the question clear in his voice.

"We're leaving," I said, voice tight. "For Amenkor. As soon as possible.

"I want to go home."

✠ Epilogue ✠

Demasque and Parmati "survived" the Chorl's assassinations, I said.

Through the Fire, I felt Eryn's contempt. *What did they say? Where were they during the battles in the city and harbor?*

I snorted. *They claim that after the attempt was made on their lives, they were forced to retreat to safety, that they never had a chance to help defend the city after that. There was too much chaos, too much confusion.*

And yet Lady Tormaul managed to join Lord March in the north. And Lord Dussain ordered his forces to engage the Chorl as well, even though he was wounded and could not join them himself.

I didn't answer. There was no need.

But my silence was noted. Eryn's attention shifted more closely toward me. *What have you done?*

I pulled back from the Fire, drew myself in so tightly that nothing was exposed.

Eryn sensed the change.

What have you done, Varis?

I stiffened, frowned. *What I've always done. What* needed *to be done.*

Eryn sucked in a sharp breath, her body tensed with a reprimand, with a warning—

But the breath set off a coughing fit instead. Spasms racked her body, her entire chest aching, a sharper pain lancing up from her gut into her lungs, a piercing agony, as if someone were slicing her open from the inside. I reached out through the Fire, absorbed some of that pain into myself, tried to calm the spasms that set off the coughing. I tasted blood in my mouth as I became entwined with Eryn, as I merged with her, the blood thick, rolling over my tongue. I spit the taste of it—cold iron and bitter salt—into cloth, spit again, and again.

Until finally the fit subsided.

I slumped back into the chair, exhausted, my arms weak, my breath ragged, but short. I winced as I shifted, the pain in my chest lessening. Tears streamed from my eyes—tears of exertion, of resignation.

I lifted the rag clutched in my hand, opened it.

Blood. More blood than it seemed possible to cough up; not a mere speckling. And dark blood. Heart blood.

Eryn's blood.

I withdrew from Eryn's body, sank back into the Fire, and as Eryn took back control she let the hand with the bloodstained cloth fall to the arm of the chair.

Thank you, she said. *For trying.*

I didn't respond, didn't know how to respond. Because the fire in her stomach had not subsided, because the pain—that dagger slicing her open from the inside out—hadn't diminished even after the coughing faded.

We sat in silence, Eryn staring across her own chambers, across a room that felt empty even though a Servant waited to take care of any possible need. I should have left her, should have preserved some of the strength I was no doubt draining from Marielle, from Heddan.

But I couldn't. I couldn't leave Eryn alone. Not after what she'd done for Amenkor, what she'd done for me.

And eventually, she stirred, drew herself up straighter in her chair, became aware that I was still hovering within the Fire inside her.

When will you return to Amenkor?

Bullick finished the repairs to the Defiant *after the battle in the harbor yesterday. He's loaded the ships with cargo—William's cargo—and we intend to head out today. Assuming there will be no interference from the Chorl on the trip north, we should reach Amenkor in roughly three weeks.*

Eryn was silent for a long time.

Then: *I'll inform Nathem and Darryn.*

I frowned at the gentle dismissal, thought about remaining. . . .

But there was nothing I could do.

So I drew myself out of the Fire, pulled myself free, and found the glint of white burning to the south. With a last glance over Amenkor, over the city I hadn't seen in over four months, that I wouldn't see again for another three weeks, I sped toward that glint of light.

I gasped as I entered my own body, felt Marielle and Heddan withdraw their conduits, felt Erick's presence behind me, the scent of oranges strong, felt Westen's presence as well, and opened my eyes—

To find Sorrenti seated in the chair opposite me, waiting.

I straightened in my seat, but did not nod in acknowledgment.

"Lord Sorrenti. You look . . . well."

He smiled tightly. "It's been a week since the attack, since the retreat. I've had some time to recuperate. The use of the throne was . . . draining."

I felt the ground shuddering beneath my feet again, felt the tremors in my legs, recalled the crack the stone had made as the earth split. "I can only imagine."

"The current story in the marketplace and on the wharf is that you caused the earth to shudder," he said.

"We both know that's not what happened."

"Yes, but I'd like to let the lie continue. No one saw the Stone Throne except for you and your men. No one heard us discuss the throne except your men and the few Venittian guardsmen and Protectorate who accompanied us to the

Gutter's gate. The Stone Throne has been kept hidden for hundreds of years. I'd like it to remain hidden. I can keep the Venittian guardsmen silent. I assume you can do the same with your own men."

"Yes."

"Then let the rumors continue."

"Very well."

Sorrenti nodded, then stood. I rose as well.

"I wanted to thank you before you left. On behalf of Venitte, of course, but also on behalf of the Seven. If the throne had fallen into the Chorl's hands . . ."

"And is that a direct thank you?" I said, smiling tightly.

He grinned. "Yes. All of the previous Masters of the Stone Throne thank you, but, in particular, Cerrin does. He can still sense you, especially now that you've been close, within the Council of Seven's inner chamber itself."

But Sorrenti halted, his smile fading. He caught my gaze, held it, his expression intent, mouth pressed into a thin line that was not quite a frown.

"Have you heard?" he asked.

I tensed, felt Westen and Erick shift stances behind me.

"Heard what?"

"Lord Demasque and Lady Parmati," he said. "They were found dead, in their own bedrooms, on their own estates, their throats slit."

I didn't react, didn't flinch, didn't waver. My eyes never left his.

When it became apparent I wasn't going to answer, Sorrenti frowned. He looked toward Erick and Westen, lingering on the captain of the Seekers a long moment, then returned his attention to me.

"Lord March is waiting at the wharf for your departure, for a more formal thank you, and a more formal send-off. Along with General Daeriun and the two other surviving Council members—Lady Tormaul and Lord Dussain." He nodded his head. "Have a safe journey, Mistress."

As soon as he left, Erick and Westen stepped forward, Marielle and Heddan rising as well.

"It's time to go," I said. "I'm tired of Venitte."

The breeze from the channel cooled the sweat on my brow as I stood on the veranda. Sunlight glinted off the waves of the harbor far below, ships gliding back and forth in relative silence. A few bells clanged, an occasional shout could be heard; but otherwise it was quiet but for the wind.

And a sudden shriek from Jaer behind me.

I turned, leaned back against the stone balustrade of the veranda as five-year-old Jaer came tearing out onto the wide patio, dodging around the chairs and table already set with a decanter of wine, a pitcher of water, glasses, and a tray of bread and fruit. Pallin—two years Jaer's elder—raced after her sister, her face screwed up in wrath.

Jaer flew behind one of the potted trees that shaded the veranda, the urn used as its base as large as she was. Pallin swore. "You little . . . When I catch you!" She darted left, and Jaer shrieked again, skipping around the urn, just out of reach. Pallin growled in frustration, faked a move right, but backtracked as Jaer fell for it and snagged her by the arm.

"Pallin!" Olivia barked, coming out onto the veranda carrying another tray of food—a haunch of mutton, already sliced. "Leave your sister alone."

"But, Mother, she singed off a chunk of my hair!"

I almost snorted in laughter, but managed to keep quiet.

"I don't care. We'll get one of the servants to trim it back later. For now, let your sister go."

Pallin considered, until Olivia gave her the look, lips set into a thin line, eyes slightly widened. In disgust, she pushed her sister away from her, Jaer collapsing to the ground a little too melodramatically. Pallin ignored her, stalking around to the far side of the table, as far from everyone as possible, so she could stare out across the channel and sulk.

Olivia set the tray of meat on the table, then wandered toward me. Her black hair glistened in the sunlight, and I reached up to caress the olive skin of her cheek. She smiled.

"Do you have to go in to see the Council?"

"You know I do," I said, reflexively. A sudden sickening sensation coursed through my stomach, a thread of dread, of warning.

I frowned, my hand halting. Taking Olivia into my arms, I kissed the top of her head, breathed in the scent of her hair.

She looked up into my eyes, pressing in close. "You should eat before you go. Stay with Jaer and Pallin for a while."

"I can't. The Council has important decisions to make."

"More important than me, than your children?" She said it lightly, mocking me.

"Hmm . . . you ask dangerous questions. More dangerous than the Council."

She laughed, but that sensation of dread, that acidic burn in the center of my gut, flared higher, and I frowned. I turned, looked out over the harbor, out into the channels, listening intently, expectantly.

Olivia's brow creased, her smile faltering. "What's wrong?"

"I don't know. It feels like something's supposed to happen. I keep expecting to hear—"

Explosions. The muffled sound of explosions against the cliffs. I expected to see fire arching up into the sky, shattering against the tiled roofs of the estates that lined the channels. I expected to smell smoke, taste ash, breathe in the reek of burning flesh.

Because this is what happened when the Chorl attacked. This was the day— that last day—that I'd spent with Olivia, with Jaer and Pallin, before the Chorl destroyed the peace of the coast.

Olivia felt my body tense beneath her hands. I knew because the smile faded completely, and she turned to face the channels, to face the harbor, one hand shifting to the center of my chest, resting there in concern.

We stood there in silence, Jaer and Pallin behind us, both at the table now, picking at the food, the fight over the singed hair forgotten. The wind rustled in the long, thin leaves of the potted plants. Somewhere, a seagull shrieked.

But nothing happened. There were no explosions, no fires, no deaths. Business continued as usual in the harbor below.

"Cerrin, what is it?" Olivia asked again, and I hated the concern that laced her voice, hated the fear.

Where are the Chorl? Where are the Servants, the priests, the warriors?

I glanced down, Olivia turning her head to see me, so I could see her face, her eyes, could smell the slight citrus scent of her perfume.

And then I realized, then I remembered.

This was the throne. This was the haven I'd created for myself. Not the haven I'd expected, and not built at the cost I'd expected, but a haven nonetheless. A retreat from the pain of this loss, this grief.

I relaxed, tension draining from me like water, sliding free. I reached up and brushed Olivia's hair away from where the breeze had pushed tendrils in front of her eyes, then cupped the back of her head.

"It's nothing," I said, and then I leaned forward and kissed the worry from her mouth, the wrinkles from her brow.

"So will you eat?" she asked as I let her go.

I laughed. "Yes, I'll eat. I'll stay here—with you, with Pallin and Jaer—all afternoon."

"But what of the Council? What of the Seven?"

I slid my hand into hers and pulled her to the table. "The Council can wait."

"Amenkor, dead ahead!"

Everyone on board the *Defiant* crowded to the edge of the deck at the cry, necks craning to be the first to see the escarpment and wall of the city, or the tower of the palace. When the vague shape of the land gave way to the jutting arms that enclosed the harbor, a cheer broke out, the voices of guardsmen and crew mingling. Someone started a jig, another brought forth a fiddle and began playing madly.

When the watchtowers came into view, I smiled, felt something tighten in my chest, sting my eyes.

Someone laid their hand on my shoulder, their arm across my back.

Erick.

We watched as the walls drew closer, and then he frowned. "Those are new watchtowers."

I laughed. "Yes, they are. A lot in Amenkor will seem different."

He grunted.

William came up on my other side and Erick's hand dropped from my shoulder. He gave me a meaningful look, then wandered away as William leaned on the railing.

"Mistress."

"Master William."

We caught each other's eyes, and I grinned and butted him with my shoulder.

And then we passed through the narrow inlet between the watchtowers. A tingling sensation coursed through me, and I sucked in a sharp breath.

Varis.

William straightened at my side, frowned. "What is it?"

I shuddered, shook myself. "I don't know. For a moment, I thought . . ."

"Thought what?"

I looked William in the eye, saw the concern there, the frown that barely touched his mouth. "I thought I heard a voice. Eryn's voice."

William's frown deepened, but ahead, a clanging of bells began to ring out, spreading from the watchtowers up through the city. As the *Defiant* slid into the dock, the escorting captured Chorl ships waiting out in the bay, the noise grew. People lined the wharf, waving and yelling in welcome. I watched as a covey of guardsmen pushed through the crowd and onto the dock, led by Darryn and Nathem.

I frowned, my stomach clenching.

William gasped, and I turned.

"Look!" he said, and pointed toward one of the other docks.

A ship was berthed there, but it was unlike any ship I'd seen. Larger, its hull rising at least another man's height over Bullick's ship, and wider as well. And it carried more sails.

On the far side sat another, and in the docks beyond, even more. Only the two closest to the *Defiant* appeared finished, though. The rest were still being built.

"They're Borund's ships," I said, and smiled tightly. Because that sickening clench in my stomach had not receded. I tasted bile at the back of my throat, swallowed the bitterness, then steadied myself and turned back to the dock.

Captain Darryn and the Second, Nathem, were waiting, their escort of guardsmen behind them.

I pushed back from the railing, felt William hesitate, then follow.

We met Avrell, Erick, Marielle, and Westen at the head of the plank.

Avrell looked grim.

I paused, almost reached out to touch him, but turned as the plank slapped down onto the dock, crewmen tying the ship down in a frenzy of activity. The crowd continued to roar, but the sound had dulled, had faded into the background. I'd latched onto Darryn's face, saw the control there, the tightness.

Bullick descended the plank, greeted Darryn, Nathem, listened a single moment, then shot a look back up toward me before stepping aside.

I descended the plank slowly, the sounds of the crowd receding even further, all activity on the wharf withdrawing, a numbness filling me, tingling in my arms, in my fingers, in my legs. A familiar numbness. A familiar pain.

As soon as I stepped from the plank onto the dock, I asked, "Where's Eryn?"

Darryn's jaw clenched, and I saw the answer in his eyes.

He didn't say a word.

"Take me to her."

He nodded, motioned toward the waiting carriages.

Nathem had laid her body out in the throne room, before the throne, surrounded by candlelight. A white shroud covered her, draped down the edges of the table, the shroud itself stitched in gold with the Skewed Throne symbol. Beneath the cloth, her hands had been placed one over the other on her chest. Her eyes were closed, her skin pale and smooth. Her black hair pooled around her head like spilled ink.

"We found her here," Nathem said, his aged voice cracking with emotion. "At the base of the throne."

I stared down at her face, at the wrinkles that even death could not smooth, at the paleness of the skin, the lines of her throat, the chain of gold that someone had placed around it, at the gold-embroidered fringe of the white dress just visible at the edges of the shroud itself. I felt Nathem shift uncomfortably to my right, sensed Avrell to my left. No one else had accompanied us into the chamber except Erick and Westen, and they remained at the entrance, withdrawn, respectful.

I wanted to reach out and touch her, but couldn't. I didn't want to feel the coldness of her skin beneath my fingers, didn't want to feel the death there.

Instead, I lifted my gaze to the throne, felt the heat of the candles against my face, smelled the bitterness of their smoke.

And then I stilled.

Because the throne was no longer cracked.

Even as I watched, it began to twist, the rough granite seat morphing into a chair with a short, straight back, no arms.

Garus' seat, from the Council of Seven.

I gasped, looked down at Eryn's face again.

"What did you do?" I whispered.

The throne shifted again, settled into a large round ottoman. Silicia's ottoman.

I stepped away from Eryn's body, circled the shrouded table, and mounted the three stone steps of the dais to stand before the throne.

I reached out to touch it, but hesitated.

Because I could feel it now, a presence, hovering in the room. Not as weighted as before, not as smothering, but it was there.

And yet, I couldn't feel it. Not as I had before.

Because it wasn't part of me. Because I wasn't part of it. Because this throne was vacant. No one controlled it. No one had claimed it. Yet.

I stilled, stared down at the stone as it began to warp yet again, becoming a river rock, worn smooth with water and age.

"She healed it," Nathem said behind me, voice quiet. "She said that she was dying, that there was nothing that could be done to save her, and so she wanted to try to fix the throne, to repair it. She said that you'd given her the idea, that you'd told her its creation required a life, a sacrifice. So she decided to sacrifice herself to heal it."

I let my hand drop to my side, turned to face out into the throne room, into the mostly empty chamber. I met Erick's gaze, Westen's. Their faces remained blank, their backs straight, hands resting lightly on the hilts of their daggers.

I shifted my gaze to Nathem, to Avrell. Nathem bowed his head. But Avrell met my gaze, his face wet with tears, mouth tight with grief.

"You are the Mistress," he said, his voice raw and thick. "You *are* Amenkor."

I stared into his eyes, into the sorrow there, into the pain.

And into the hope.

I turned back to the throne, reached out, hesitated again, for a single breath, for two—

And then . . . I touched it.

you throughout life, especially those that encourage your dreams. These people not only made this a better book, they made me a better person.

For *The Cracked Throne*:
    The Usual Suspects:
    Ariel Guzman, a good friend, who is my first reader and who always manages to keep things real, even in a fantasy.
    Patricia Bray and Jennifer Dunne, two fellow writers. We all get together once a week to talk shop . . . and end up drinking, gaming, and being thankful there isn't a fan web-cam watching us. That we know of.
    Steve Stone, the artist who has brought all of my novels to life with such great covers. The Ochean is perfect!
    The Family: my brothers, Jason and Jacob; my sisters-in-law, Janet and Chrissie; and my mother. Without their support, I wouldn't remain sane long enough to get anything written.
    And finally, the most important person in my life, George. For all the little things, especially the understanding that I have to write, even if he doesn't understand what I write or why.

For *The Vacant Throne*:
    First and foremost, I want to thank all of the readers out there who took a risk and picked up *The Skewed Throne*, the first book by a new author. I hope you've enjoyed Varis and her companions throughout their journeys in the *Throne* books, and I hope that you continue to take risks on new authors in the future.
    There are certain friends that not only suffer through my first (and second and third and . . .) drafts, but also manage to somehow find it in their hearts after that to hang around and support me in my personal life. Or at least entertain me. *grin* They are Ariel Guzman, Jennifer Dunne, and Patricia Bray. Thanks for being there. And for bringing me chocolate. (Yes, they are my dealers. No, go find your own dealers.)
    My editor and agent, Sheila Gilbert and Amy Stout, are responsible for bringing you these books. They saw the potential . . . and then beat it out of me. After that, Debra Euler, Marsha Jones, and all of the others at DAW that work behind the scenes took care of the packaging. This is as much a labor of love for them as it is for me, and for that they have my thanks.
    And lastly, my partner, George. He's now seen me struggle through two books, with all the stresses and joys that such a struggle encompasses. Here's to all the future struggles to come.
    If you'd like to find out more about the *Throne* books, and other projects, check out my webpage at www.joshuapalmatier.com or my LiveJournal at jpsorrow.livejournal.com.

Acknowledgments

For *The Skewed Throne*:

First and foremost, I want to thank my editor Sheila Gilbert and my agent Amy Stout, for taking a chance on a new author and for not only believing in the story, but for helping to make it that much better. Baked goods will be had by all! Thanks as well to Steve Stone, the artist who captured the essence of the entire book in the cover art. I'm still stunned. Getting a first novel published is exciting enough; working with Amy, Sheila, Steve, and everyone else at DAW to get the story into book form and on the shelf is truly exhilarating.

Thanks also to everyone who read this novel in any or all of its various forms: two great friends and fellow writers, Patricia Bray and Jennifer Dunne; the best cycling partner in the world, Cheryl Losinger; the person who kept me sane while writing *and* teaching, Jean Brewster; the Vicious Circle—Carol Bartholomew, J. Michael Blumer, Kishma Danielle, Laurie Davis, Bonnie Freeman, Dorian Gray, Penelope Hardy, Heidi Kneale, Robert Sinclair, Larry West—an experimental critiquing group at the Online Writing Workshop that experienced greater success than I expected; and everyone else at the OWW who at some point critiqued one of my many novels and short stories posted there. All of them offered invaluable insight into this book.

I must acknowledge one first reader in particular: Ariel Guzman, a true best friend and critique partner, who was there from the very beginning, when I first set words down on paper in the eighth grade and announced I wanted to be a writer. He's suffered through everything I've ever written, and that first novel attempt was truly horrid. I still shudder. Without his encouragement along the way, I would never have made it to this point.

I must also thank Alis Rasmussen, for offering to read my first real (and as yet unpublished) novel and for offering two particularly relevant pieces of advice: "patience and persistence" and "cut at least half of the words out." She guided me through the rough terrain between the plateau of simply writing, and the heights of actually being published. She also introduced me to my first con . . . and everyone has regretted it ever since.

And last, but certainly never least, my family: my mother, who showed me that strength comes from the inside; my brothers, Jason and Jacob, who are the only other people more excited about this book than I am; and George, who has taught me more about myself than I thought anyone possibly could.

Nothing is more important than the people that support you and encourage